BEYOND THE POINT

BEYOND
THE POINT

A Novel

Claire Gibson

WILLIAM MORROW
An Imprint of HarperCollins*Publishers*

P.S.™ is a trademark of HarperCollins Publishers.

Designed by Diahann Sturge

Title page art © Lauren Ledbetter

ISBN 978-1-64385-271-3

To women on every battlefield, in every uniform.
You are not alone.

When the angel of the Lord appeared to Gideon,
he said, "The Lord is with you, mighty warrior."
"Pardon me, my lord," Gideon replied,
"but if the Lord is with us, why has all this happened to us?"

Judges 6:12–13

BEYOND THE POINT

PROLOGUE

November 10, 2006 // Tarin Kot, Afghanistan

Assuming her gear scared him, Hannah Nesmith took off her helmet and sunglasses and placed them on the ground.

"Da sta lapaara day," she said. *This is for you.*

The boy couldn't have been much older than seven. He wore navy blue pants and a threadbare shirt, both at least two sizes too big. Dirty toenails peeked out of his sandals, and his heels threatened to strike the rocky ground. Every student at the school was dressed this way. Nothing fit. Everything was covered in sand. His arms and neck and face were tanned and smooth. Any other day, in any other country, Hannah would have been tempted to reach out and stroke his head. He was just a child.

A U-shaped concrete building stood behind them, seemingly in the middle of nowhere, surrounded by large rocks the color of the desert. There were no roads. The infrastructure for education had crumbled under Taliban rule, which had turned this area of Afghanistan into a haven for opium production and sharia law.

Hannah wondered how far these children had to walk to school, what their parents did all day, and whether or not there was even food at home when they returned at night. In Afghanistan, the average life expectancy was only fifty years. Nearly half of the population was younger than fourteen. And these children were caught in the crossfire.

The battalion commander, Lieutenant Colonel Markham, sent Hannah's platoon on humanitarian missions like this specifically because she was a woman. He said her presence would put the children and teachers at ease. But these students would think she was a Transformer robot before they believed she was a female. She wore an ID patch on the bicep of her uniform and an M16 slung over her shoulder. A Kevlar vest flattened her chest, and before she'd taken it off, her helmet had hidden a bun at the nape of her neck. But surely this boy could overlook her dirty-blond hair and blue eyes for the sake of a free, fully inflated soccer ball, Hannah thought. When their convoy had pulled up an hour earlier, the children were using a ball of trash tied together with string.

She gripped the soccer ball in her hands and raised it a few inches higher. The boy took two steps backward, his mouth closed tight, like he was trying to swallow something bitter.

"For you," she repeated in English, wishing once again that she'd listened to Dani.

Sophomore year at West Point, her closest friend had tried to persuade her to take Arabic instead of Spanish. Of course, Afghan people spoke Pashto, something Hannah hadn't known until she arrived in March. But she wished she had familiarity with the tones and rhythms of Middle Eastern languages, and would have, had she listened to Dani. But the add-drop period for classes had ended in August—two weeks before the towers came down. The Arabic department at West Point was inundated after that. But the truth was, even if she'd known the future, she probably would have stuck with Spanish. West Point was hard enough without adding another challenge to her schedule. Plus, even if they could speak the same language, the boy wasn't listening.

Hannah wiped a stream of sweat from her forehead. Heat dragged its fingers up the sleeves of her uniform, down her back, against her neck. It was hard to breathe here. Hard to think. She recalled watching heat waves rise from the ground on her grandfather's ranch every summer of her childhood, distorting her vision, like transparent oil in the air. But this—one hundred and twenty degrees—was a formidable home-field advantage.

The heat made the days run together. Hannah had arrived in Afghanistan eight months earlier, in March. She'd taken two weeks of rest and recuperation in the summer with Tim, and now was staring down the barrel of seven more months in the Middle East. She closed her eyes and imagined her husband out kayaking on the water.

Husband. That word sounded as foreign in her mouth as any word of Pashto. The time they'd spent together on Jekyll Island during her R & R was a memory Hannah could hold on to until they were together again. She could still feel the grit of sand in his hair, taste the salt of his skin. She'd never seen him so tan.

People constantly asked her how they did it. By "it" she assumed they meant the deployment, the Army, or long-distance marriage. But to Hannah, it was just part of the package. She wouldn't have wanted to be married to anyone else. So if this was what it took to be Mrs. Timothy Nesmith, then so be it. No part of her felt resentful of the path they'd chosen. Somehow, it felt right for them—even if it was hard. Maybe specifically because it was. Their time apart intensified their time together, making every moment that much more romantic, that much more precious. They were like a magnet and steel: they felt the pull when they were apart, and when they were together, they couldn't be separated. The sacrifice was part of the sacrament.

She had a canned response ready to dismiss people's concerns. "We just try not to think about it," she'd say with a shrug.

But the truth was, she thought about the calendar all of the time. She counted down the days, the months. June 2007 lingered in the future as though it were their wedding date—even though they'd already had one of those. In less than a year, they'd be back together again. It wasn't that long, really. Not when you compared it to forever. If they could just endure, all would be well in the end. And as the days ticked off of her deployment, moving her closer to home, Hannah had never been more confident that the waiting would be worth it.

The little boy had started to cry. He looked back over his shoulder at his classmates, who were busy running after Private Murphy and Sergeant Willis. Willis and Murphy were terrible at soccer, bobbling around with the ball, holding their M16s to the side so they wouldn't swing around their backs. The children were laughing. It had turned into a game of chase.

"Look," Hannah continued. "See?"

When he turned back to look at her, the little boy's eyes narrowed with hate. Before she could move out of his way, a loogie of spit flew out of his mouth and landed on the shoulder of her uniform. Then he wiped his mouth, ran across the schoolyard to his classmates, and put his hands in the air. The boy was yelling. He pointed back toward Hannah, then at the soldiers, at the sky. Everyone froze, watching the veins in the boy's neck pulse. Wetness spread across his cheeks as deep guttural screams flooded out of his throat.

Slowly rising from the ground, Hannah put her helmet back on her head and had a dismal thought.

How were they supposed to win the war if they couldn't even give away a gift?

INBOX (7)

From: Avery Adams <averyadams13@yahoo.com>
Date: November 16, 2006 5:36 PM EST
To: Dani McNalley <danimcnalley@yahoo.com>
Subject: hi

I just heard. call me.

From: Wendy Bennett <wendy.l.bennett@hotmail.com>
Date: November 16, 2006 6:24 PM EST
To: Dani McNalley <danimcnalley@yahoo.com>
Subject: Hannah

D, we just heard. Please let us know when the funeral is set. We will be there.

We love you.

From: Locke Coleman <lockestockand@hotmail.com>
Date: November 16, 2006 02:59 AM EST
To: Dani McNalley <danimcnalley@yahoo.com>
Subject: r u ok

this is so fucked up. r u ok?

From: Eric Jenkins <ericbjenkins144@aol.com>
Date: November 16, 2006 5:58 PM EST
To: Dani McNalley <danimcnalley@yahoo.com>
Subject: My deepest sympathy

Dani,

I'm not sure if you remember me, but I was Class of '03 at West Point, and Tim and I were both on the parachuting team. I'm stationed at Fort Bragg and my wife and I live right down the street from them. I got your e-mail address from Avery Adams.

We've decided to stay here through Thanksgiving. I just wanted to let you know that everyone here is in shock. They were an incredible couple. Again, I am so sorry for your loss. It's a loss for all of us.

Eric B. Jenkins
Captain, US Army
82nd Airborne Division

From: Sarah Goodrich <goodrichs129@hotmail.com>

Date: November 17, 2006 1:26 AM HST

To: Dani McNalley <danimcnalley@yahoo.com>, Avery Adams
 <averyadams13@yahoo.com>

Subject::-(

I can't believe this is happening. Has anyone heard from Hannah's family?

From: Avery Adams <averyadams13@yahoo.com>

Date: November 17, 2006 4:37 AM EST

To: Dani McNalley <danimcnalley@yahoo.com>

Subject: re: re: re: **hi

I have a key to the house. Tim gave it to me before he deployed.

From: Laura Klein <laura.klein@egcorporation.com>

Date: November 20, 2006 05:59 AM GMT

To: Dani McNalley <danielle.mcnalley@egcorporation.com>

Subject: Bereavement Leave

Technically, you only get two weeks of bereavement leave. But that's only for immediately family members. You should check with HR.

Can you resend me your latest draft of the insights deck? I can't find it in my inbox.

Also, for future reference, if you need to leave a meeting, please say so. We have processes in place for emergencies.

I'm sorry to hear about your friend.

                                                              LK

BEFORE

Senior Year of High School

Winter 2000

1

Winter 2000 // Columbus, Ohio

From the beginning, Dani McNalley wanted to be known for more than basketball.

Her father had introduced her to the sport in the driveway when she was three years old, teaching her the mechanics of dribbling and switching hands and dodging defenders. She'd grown used to the feeling of thirty thousand little bumps under her fingertips and the hollow sound of the ball hitting pavement. Over the years, she'd advanced from the driveway to club teams, from club teams to a travel squad, and from the travel squad to the roster of the top point guards in America. College scouts had written Dani McNalley's name on their recruiting lists as early as her thirteenth birthday. That she would play NCAA Division I ball was a foregone conclusion—everyone said it was her destiny. What they didn't know was that while athletics was a big part of her life, it certainly wasn't her whole life.

That's why, on a cold February morning of her senior year in high school, Dani didn't feel nervous at all. What was there to be nervous about? She'd get up, go to school, go to practice, and then come home. Sure, there would be news crews, photographers, and a dotted line to sign. But once she announced what she'd decided, the story wasn't going to be about basketball. Not anymore.

Her small-minded suburban town of Columbus, Ohio, had tried to put her into a box. After she'd earned a near-perfect score on the PSAT, a reporter from the *Columbus Dispatch* named Mikey Termini had arrived at her house with a camera and a recording device. He'd only asked her about basketball, and the photo that ran in the cover story was of her shooting baskets in her driveway. He'd buried the fact that she was a National Merit Scholarship finalist below a list of her basketball accolades, and when she'd tried to take him inside to talk, he'd stopped her and said, "I can't take a picture of you doing calculus. People want to see you play."

It was the same story everywhere she went. But Dani worked too hard to believe in foregone conclusions. Anything was possible. Even now, she knew she could surprise herself and change her mind at the last minute. But she wouldn't. Whether she wanted to admit it or not, deep in her psyche, there was something about this day that felt as though it had already happened. Like she could remember it if she closed her eyes and imagined herself from the future.

Grabbing a Pop-Tart from the counter, Dani stuffed her AP Physics homework in her backpack and took the keys to the family sedan from the hook by the door.

"I'm going!" she yelled to no one.

At that moment, her mother, Harper McNalley, shuffled into the kitchen and looked her daughter up and down with the warm disdain of a woman who thought she'd raised her child better. Five foot nothing, Dani's mother had metal-rimmed glasses and facial expressions that spoke louder than words. Her eyes grew large as she scanned Dani's choice of wardrobe: sneakers, jeans, and a loose-fitting Nike T-shirt.

"What?" said Dani, sticking her hip out.

Harper reached for the coffee carafe and filled her travel mug. "Why don't you do something with your hair?" She swirled the carafe through the air, indicating her daughter's head. "Fix that situation."

Ever since she was young, Dani had worn her hair in a spiky ponytail. The edges near her forehead were frayed and broken, but athletic pre-wrap headbands did a decent job of keeping the wild parts off her face. She knew her mother was annoyed she hadn't made an appointment to get her hair relaxed at the salon. But there was no time for that nonsense. Dani didn't have the patience to sit in a chair and have her head doused with chemicals. There were better things to do with her time. Plus, if they were going to put her picture in the paper, it might as well look like her. Afro and all.

"Go on," her mother said, pressing her. "Comb it. They should at least know you're a girl."

Begrudgingly, Dani ran back upstairs to the hall bathroom, dropped her backpack by the door, and stared at the light-skinned black girl in the mirror. A constellation of freckles graced her face, as if God had decided at the last minute to splatter dark paint against a light brown canvas. Eighteen, with the attitude and swagger to go with it, Dani pulled a brush through her tangled hair and smothered the ends with oil.

They should at least know you're a girl. Of course they knew she was a girl! She had boobs, for God's sake. She played women's basketball. Just because she didn't wear makeup or wear skirts didn't make her less of a woman. Her mother of all people should have known that. Harper McNalley was a chemical engineer—a black woman at the height of a white man's profession. At times, Dani thought her mom was the wisest, most progressive person in the world. Then she'd go and say a thing like that.

A heavy fist pounded against the bathroom door three times in a row. *Bang, bang, bang.*

"Just a minute!" Dani shouted.

"Dani, I've got to go!"

High-pitched and incessant, her little brother's voice had yet to change. She could imagine Dominic standing outside the door with his little Steve Urkel glasses, holding his crotch and crossing his ankles. Dominic was a confident little boy, always reading some book too advanced for his age. A few nights earlier, he'd recited a Shakespearean soliloquy for the family at dinner. She loved him for how fiercely he chose to be himself. Of course, their father would have liked it better if their talents had been switched at birth, Dani knew. Tom McNalley had hoped to have an athletic son and an artistic daughter. But realizing there was no changing his children, he'd enrolled Dominic in every music lesson, acting class, and audiovisual club the greater Columbus area had to offer. And when Dani showed promise on the driveway basket-ball court, he'd signed her up for club teams, private coaches, and ultimately, the AAU team that had shaped Dani into the point guard she was today. All opportunities available to white chil-dren were equally available to the McNalleys: Tom and Harper had worked hard for that to be so.

Dani knew the stories. Her parents had both grown up in the South—her mother was among some of the first children to inte-grate her white North Carolina elementary school. After meeting at Howard University in the late 1970s, Tom and Harper uprooted and replanted in Ohio, hoping to chart a new future for their family. They lived in a gated community, the children attended great public schools, and they had two cars in the driveway. By every measure, they had "made it"—whatever that meant. Dani still wondered sometimes if they'd swung the pendulum a bit too far. They were the only black family within a twenty-mile radius, and though it didn't bother Dani to be different, she wondered if there was something she was missing, some experience that she'd lost, in the shelter of their suburban zip code.

"Dani, I must say, I've never seen a black person with freckles," her friend's mother had said once, as if Dani were a new species at the local zoo. "Where does that come from? You know, in your gene pool?"

At the time, Dani just shrugged it off and said she wasn't sure. But if she were asked that same question today, she would say, "Mrs. Littleton, no offense, but I would never ask about your gene pool." Or, more likely: "That's easy. One of your ancestors prob-ably raped one of mine."

Smiling, Dani would of course add that she was joking. But every joke comes with a dose of truth, and sure enough, when Dani's aunt had dug into the family history several years earlier, it turned out their great-great-grandmother, Scarlet McNalley, had birthed eight children with her slave owner's son. That was why light skin ran in the family genes.

Most people in the community had pigeonholed Dani as a superstar athlete. She couldn't really blame them, since her most public achievements took place on the court. But when she earned a near-perfect score on the PSAT, suddenly, Dani was being recruited by the Ivy League for her brain even as state schools chased her for her brawn. People kept assuming that Dani was going to UConn or Tennessee. But that's what made today so exciting. Because while everyone in the community thought they knew where this shooting star was headed, they were wrong.

Bang! Bang! Bang!

"Open up, D!" her brother shouted. "I'm going to wet myself!" Opening the door, Dani stared straight ahead at her little brother, dressed in long khaki pants and a maroon shirt, the uniform for the arts school he attended. He pushed his glasses up his nose. "I don't really have to go. Mom just said to—let me see if I can do this right." Twisting his face and sticking out his hip, Dominic pointed a finger toward his sister and turned his voice into his mother's. "Get your ass out the door or you're going to be late!"

Wrapping her little brother's head under her arm, Dani rubbed his cranium with her knuckles until his glasses nearly fell off. "Well why didn't you say that, bro?"

THE COURSE OF her fate had changed last fall, when a thin brunette woman arrived at the Lincoln High School gymnasium. Though she hid in the shadows, the woman's tall and thin silhouette was the picture of pure authority. Her dark hair was sliced with streaks of silver and cut short for easy maintenance. Close-set blue eyes with raised eyebrows made her look strangely alert. Her nose was small and upturned, softened by rosy lips and a quick smile. The femininity of her facial features was offset by the rest of her body: ungraceful and bony arms and legs mimicked the sharpness in her fingers. She was a beautiful woman, but intense, for sure. A hunter.

Unlike other university recruiters who'd leave halfway through practice, Catherine Jankovich stayed to the very end, through conditioning. When she stepped out of the shadows and introduced herself as the head women's basketball coach at West Point, Dani was impressed by her stature.

West Point. Standing in front of the coach, Dani racked her brain to remember how she'd heard of it before. Eventually, a picture from her AP history textbook surfaced in her mind. Thomas Jefferson and George Washington had chosen West Point as a strategic position during the Revolutionary War. A hillside overlook onto a narrow hairpin turn in the Hudson River, West Point was the perfect position from which to capsize British ships as they tried to navigate north from New York City. Against her better judgment, she was intrigued.

"West Point?" repeated Dani. "Is that a high school?"

"No. It's a college," the coach said.

"They have a women's basketball team?"

"Would I be here if we didn't?" the coach said, setting her jaw slightly. "I know you've got a lot of other colleges trying to get you to pay attention to their programs, Dani. And that's great. You deserve those choices. You've earned them. But I happen to think you need to go to a school that will serve you athletically, academically, and personally. West Point is not exactly a normal school. But I have a feeling that you're not necessarily a normal girl."

That in itself might have been enough to convince Dani to pack her bags and buy a pair of combat boots. But when the coach explained how West Point operated, Dani felt transfixed. An interested applicant couldn't just apply—she first had to interview with her congressman or senator to receive a nomination. With that nomination in hand, an applicant could send on essays and transcripts and SAT scores to West Point's admissions office. But even then, only 10 percent of applicants were accepted. Of those, less than 15 percent were female. As a university, West Point had a reputation for excellence, and its students went on to leadership in business, military, and government sectors. It wasn't a normal school. It was better.

Coach Jankovich had insisted on flying her in for an official visit, and three weeks later, when she stepped on campus, her decision was made.

That day, the Hudson River was like a long glittering road, reflecting mountains on the east and granite on the west. Gray stone buildings towered over a green parade field, oozing with history and dignity. The campus teemed with handsome, athletic students in gray uniforms walking to class with full backpacks and square jaws. There were kids of every race, and girls like

Dani, who didn't seem to mind that they were wearing the same uniform as the guys.

Dani's mother had never been the type to cut out newspaper articles about Dani's successes. Her ribbons and trophies had been lost or thrown away, not displayed around the house. "Let someone else praise you, and not your own mouth," was Harper's favorite proverb, a biblical reminder to her precocious daughter not to become a braggart. But walking around campus at West Point, Dani met the gaze of every cadet that passed her by, and saw in their eyes a familiar self-assuredness, like she was looking in a mirror. Here, confidence wasn't a quality to hide; it was essential to survival.

For twenty-four hours, a sophomore on the basketball team named Sarah Goodrich showed Dani around, answering her questions and introducing her to everyone they passed.

"What's it like playing for Coach Jankovich?" Dani asked, right when they started walking to class.

"I don't know. I haven't played for her yet," explained Sarah. "You know, this is her first year. You're her star recruit."

With dark black hair, fair skin, and striking green eyes, Sarah looked like Snow White in a military uniform. Over lunch, she told Dani that she was one of five siblings who had all attended West Point, and that even though she'd been recruited by a different head coach, she would have played for anyone, just to say she played at Army. A psychology major, she planned to be an intelligence officer in the Army after graduation.

"But that's still two years away," Sarah said knowingly. "A lot can change in two years."

At other colleges, kids wore pajamas to class. Here, they wore "as for class"—a uniform of dark wool pants, a white collared shirt, and a flat wool cap with a shiny black bill.

"Then there's gym alpha," Sarah had continued, counting off the uniforms on her fingers. "Gray T-shirt, black shorts, ugly crew socks. Most of the time, I'm wearing gym-A. BDUs—that's 'battle dress uniform,' and they're the most comfortable. Then you've got full dress gray, which is the whole shebang, brass buttons, maroon sash, big feather on the hat. Sorry, am I going too fast?"

"Nope," said Dani.

"Some girls take their uniforms home to get them tailored, but I don't care that much. You get over it pretty fast. Looking like a dude."

Dani laughed at the casualness of Sarah's confidence. Her face shined with the kind of dewy skin normally seen in celebrity magazines, and when Sarah talked about West Point, it was like she was in some kind of secret club where everything had a code name. There were so many inside jokes and terms, Dani wondered if she would ever learn them all.

After shadowing her classes, Dani followed Sarah back to her dorm room, which was about as barebones as any Dani had ever seen. Two single beds sat on opposite sides of the room, wrapped tightly in white sheets and green wool blankets. Sarah explained that she rarely slept under the covers, since it took so long to make up her bed to regulation standards. Instead, she and her roommate both slept on top of the sheets with blankets they kept stowed in their trunks.

Two desks held identical government-issued desktop computers, part of every cadet's incoming equipment. Sarah and her roommate both had wardrobes that housed their uniforms, hung in perfect order, the hangers evenly spaced two inches apart. Everywhere they went, doors opened and people shouted Sarah's name—like she was famous.

"Is there anyone here you don't know?" Dani asked. They were on their way to dinner in the mess hall, guided toward a pair of arched wooden doors by a row of lights and a stream of students. The autumn air felt just cold enough for a jacket, but Dani's whole body felt warm and alive.

"That's just how it is here. Four thousand students isn't really all that many. You'll see," Sarah answered, reaching for the iron door handle. She paused and gave Dani a mischievous look. "You ready to see something crazy?"

Dani nodded and Sarah pulled the door open, revealing an expansive room of wood and stone. Inside, the mess hall walls stretched thirty feet high and were covered with golden lamps, state and Revolutionary War flags, oil paintings of epic battle scenes, and towering stained glass windows. The hall spanned the length of two football fields and it overflowed with the raucous, jovial sound of four thousand people breaking bread all at once. Cadets were seated ten to a table and there were 465 tables in perfect rows across six wings, likely in the same place they'd been for centuries. Each wing bustled with clinking plates, glasses, and silverware. Steaming dishes passed from one hand to the next, family style. One homemade pie rested in the center of every table, waiting for a knife.

"Come with me," Sarah said in Dani's ear. "We've got to get all the way to the back."

In the back wing of the mess hall, the noise increased by a few decibels. On the far left, Dani identified the football team: hefty boys nearly busted out of their uniforms and chairs, shoveling food into open mouths. The men's and women's lacrosse teams sat on the right, the boys leaning back in their chairs, roaring at some joke, the girls leaning forward, rolling their eyes. Sarah guided Dani toward a sundry crowd of girls—some tall, some muscular, some white, some black—that filled three tables in the center of the wing.

"Save yourself!" someone shouted from another table. "You'll hate it here!"

"Ignore them," Sarah said. "Of course everyone hates it here. But we love it too. It's hard to explain."

When Sarah introduced Dani to the team, they quickly pulled out a chair for her to join them.

That's all it took. An invitation and an empty chair. In that moment, Dani watched her future unfold before her. Wearing a uniform, joining the military? All that was secondary to the things she saw in the eyes of her soon-to-be teammates. They were like her. From that point forward, imagining a typical college, with its redbrick buildings and kids wearing hoodies and jeans, seemed lackluster. Boring, even.

And so, when she returned to Columbus two days later, Dani canceled every other college visit she'd scheduled. Her parents tried to encourage her to keep her options open, but there was no need to look anywhere else. She'd found her path. Her future existed in the Corps Squad wing of Washington Hall.

It was just like Coach Jankovich had said. At West Point, Dani could be all of herself. Not just a part.

DANI SAT AT the center of a table in the Lincoln High School gymnasium, staring at a gathered crowd of parents, students, and reporters. Two football players sat on her right side, hefty and smiling, while two cross-country runners sat on her left, emaciated and frail. Each of the five athletes had a contract and a ballpoint pen waiting in front of them. Dani read the page for what felt like the millionth time.

I certify that I have read all terms and conditions included in this document . . .

When she looked up, she saw Mikey Termini, the short, balding reporter, in the front row rubbing the lens of his camera with a cloth. He'd written more stories about Dani's basketball achievements over the years than she could count, and seeing her smile, he snapped a photo of her, checking the light in the room.

"So where's it going to be, Dani?" he asked. "UConn? Georgia?"

"Ah, come on, Mike. You know I can't tell you that for another . . ." Dani checked the clock on the gym wall. "Thirty seconds."

The crowd laughed. Dani's parents stood near the back of the gym, their smiles only dimly hiding what Dani knew was a growing sense of dread. They were nervous, understandably. Dominic was seated behind them, his legs crossed in a pretzel shape underneath him, reading a book, as if all this fanfare was beneath him. In the moments that remained between her past and her future, Dani replayed all the reasons she'd made this decision, and all she felt was confidence.

"Athletes, it's time."

The boys on either side of Dani quickly picked up their pens and scribbled on the page, exactly what everyone already knew they would write. Dan Williams had committed to play football at Auburn. His tie was blue and orange. Tyler Hillenbrand had signed to play for Miami of Ohio—though Dani wondered if he'd ever see the inside of a classroom. The other two, both runners, had pledged to go the distance at Ohio State. Dani waited for the hubbub with the boys to pass. Then she leaned over, pen in hand, and carefully filled in the blank.

She paused before the waiting crowd. Mikey Termini snapped a photo, sending a flash of light throughout the quiet gymnasium. Then Dani picked up the contract and read the final line.

"'This is to certify my decision to enroll at the United States Military Academy at West Point.'"

A gasp emanated from the crowd, followed by a roar of applause and a whistle from her father—the tallest man in the room, forefinger and thumb in the shape of a circle under his black mustache. Dani smiled, the freckles on her face nearly jumping with excitement. Classmates shook her hand. A line of adults formed around her to ask questions and offer hugs and well wishes. While the boys still had nine months before they headed to college, Dani had to report to West Point for Reception Day on June 29. As she scanned the room from right to left, she tried to etch the scene into her mind, so she could remember it forever.

If this was her destiny—if this was her fate—then so be it.

2

Winter 2000 // Pittsburgh, Pennsylvania

Snow fell from a charcoal sky, sticking to the ground and melting on the surface of a hot tub full of teenagers. Underneath the surface, legs and arms tangled, while above it, Avery Adams closed her eyes and swayed to the sounds of Third Eye Blind coming over the radio.

Wisps of platinum-blond hair curled at her neck, which was encircled by the black strings of her bikini top. The warmth of alcohol inched toward her cheeks and the smell of chlorine seeped into her skin, while inside Kevin's house, the party grew louder. Though she could have stayed here forever, eyes closed, muscles relaxing in the Jacuzzi, Avery knew she needed to get out before the steam and alcohol went from her cheeks to her head. She was an experienced enough drinker to know when she'd hit her limit.

As she stood, Avery's body emerged from the heat into the cold, drawing the eyes of every high school boy at the party. Toned shoulders, slender stomach, muscular legs—she had the body of an athlete, hewn from years sprinting up and down basketball courts, encouraged by the voice of her coach on the sidelines, shouting: "Faster, Avery! GO!"

She shivered, quickly realizing the difference in temperature between water and air.

"Hey, hand me one of those," she ordered.

A football player named Marcus Jones reached over the side of the hot tub and grabbed a folded towel from a plastic chair. "Where do you think you're going?" he asked as he passed it over.

"Inside," Avery explained, then shook her cup. "Time for a refill."

"Here," he said, reaching for her cup. "I'll get it for you. Stay."

"I can take care of myself." Avery stepped over the edge of the hot tub. Her mother always told her never to take a drink that someone else poured; it was one of the few rules Avery actually followed. "Plus, I wouldn't want your pruney hands all over my cup, anyway."

"These?" he said, raising his palms out of the water—they were large, wide-receiver hands, dark on top and pink on the undersides. "You and I both know what these hands can do."

The rest of the guys in the hot tub laughed, while the girls seemed to share a collective sigh of relief that Avery was leaving. Her presence attracted attention from the boys that they hated to share, Avery knew. But she was used to both responses—the attraction and the jealousy. She wavered, sometimes relishing her role as queen bee, and sometimes trying to shrug it off her shoulders, a weight she'd never intended to carry in the first place.

Ignoring Marcus, Avery wrapped herself in the towel and weaved her way through the warm house, between people dancing. A crowd encircled the dining room table, watching a group of guys who were in the middle of a game of flip-cup.

"Go! Go! Chug!"

Avery rolled her eyes. She was so ready for high school to be over. Senioritis felt like sitting in a brand-new car with no gas: all of the promise, none of the horsepower. Kids from her high school talked a big game about going to college out of state, but in the end, they'd all end up at the University of Pittsburgh. The boys would play the same drinking games in college until they were fat and bald. The girls would join sororities and attend themed parties until they gained communications degrees or engagement rings or fetuses—whichever came first. It was sad, Avery thought. So predictable. So convenient. So *not* her future, if she had anything to say about it.

She'd seen what the American dream achieved—and it wasn't happiness. Her mother and father coexisted in their house. Other than attending Avery's basketball games as a pair, they might as well have been strangers.

Avery's relationship to her parents was like that of a business owner to a bank. At the beginning, they were happy to finance her way to big dreams. Hank and Lonnie Adams justified the money they spent on private coaches and summer basketball camps with the assumption that Avery's future would be financed by her skill in basketball. But the more time passed, the more the pressure built for Avery to perform, and the more uncomfortable they looked writing the checks. Every day, her mother asked whether or not any college coaches had called, and while she waited for an answer, Avery could see her mother doing math behind her eyes. *Have you been worth it?*

Walking toward the kitchen, Avery held up the towel around her body and filled her empty cup with water, guzzling it quickly to counteract the anonymous pink punch she'd imbibed earlier. A cooler of beer sat on the counter and the smell of weed wafted in from outside, pungent and earthy. She wasn't much of a smoker, especially not during the basketball season—it took away her edge—but the smell sent her shoulders rolling down her spine. Maybe she would stay a little while longer. After all, what good was having an edge if she was just going to end up in the same place as everyone else?

"Yo, Avery!"

Turning, Avery spotted Kevin Walters across the kitchen, holding a corded telephone in his hand. The plastic spiral dangled from the phone to the floor and back to the wall, where it was plugged into the base. Rotund and jovial, with bright red cheeks and dark brown hair, Kevin had avoided years of bullying by making fun of himself before anyone else could, gathering friends by the dozen. It also helped that his parents were frequently out of town and chose to ignore the signs that he held ragers in their absence.

"Phone's for you," he said. He held a puffy hand over the receiver and extended it toward her.

Avery's thin, tweezed eyebrows immediately crunched together in confusion. Who in the world would be calling her here?

Swallowing hard, she walked across the kitchen, still barefoot, aware of the sticky layer of smut she was accumulating on the pads of her feet.

It couldn't be her parents.

Definitely not. In four years of high school, they hadn't once asked where she was going. They never waited up on the couch when she didn't come home by curfew. She wasn't even sure she had a curfew. If she did, her parents had never enforced it. Maybe that was because they'd assumed Avery would be like her older brother, Blake—bookish and square. At sixteen, her younger brother, Caleb, had only had his driver's license for a month. Plus, it wasn't like he had anywhere to go. Caleb was a sophomore with nerdy friends that were always watching sci-fi movies or playing board games, the names of which Avery couldn't pronounce. Settlers of Catan. Dungeons and Dragons.

But as lame as Caleb Adams might have been, at least he could keep a secret. Any time Avery arrived home from a party in the single-digit hours of the morning, smelling of guilt, her little brother would pretend not to notice. Bleary-eyed and drunk, Avery would place a single finger over her mouth in the universal symbol for "shhh," and then tiptoe up the stairs to her room. It was their secret. Don't ask; definitely don't tell. And Caleb never told.

She took the phone from Kevin.

"Hello?" Avery plugged her other ear with a finger, trying to block out the sound of Dave Matthews in the background.

"Avery?"

The voice on the other end of the line was quiet, shaking—and unmistakable.

"Caleb? Are you okay? What's going on?"

"I need you—" her little brother said, hiccupping like he'd been crying for hours. "I need you to come get me."

"Okay," she said, quickly trying to assess whether or not she was sober enough to drive. "I'm on my way. Where are you?"

"The Riverview police station—"

"The what?"

"—on the parkway. Hurry, Avery. They say they're going to call Dad."

SEVERAL HOURS LATER, Avery's little brother sat in the passenger seat of her beat-up Honda Civic, his Kurt Cobain hair hanging like a sheet in front of his eyes.

A six-inch piece of duct tape held a rip in the back seat together and the left rear window hadn't rolled down in more than a year, but there was no money to get this piece-of-shit car fixed.

"It has four wheels and an engine," her father had said. "Be grateful."

For her eighteenth birthday, Avery's mother had given her one of those cassette tapes with a cord that attached to her portable Discman, so at least she could play her CDs. That fact alone had bought the car another few years of life. Plus, she wasn't about to ask her parents for anything else. Not before, and definitely not now. Sitting in the driveway looking at the split-level house in front of them, she realized that this night would destroy any chance she'd ever had at getting a new car.

"Shit, Caleb," Avery said. "Do you even realize how much a lawyer costs?"

"I'm going to be sick," he said.

"Oh God. Not in the car. Open the door!"

And he did, spilling the contents of his stomach onto the concrete in the driveway.

Avery's jeans and black T-shirt were wet from the bathing suit she still wore underneath, and she shifted uncomfortably in her seat. Her brother sat up again, wiping his mouth with the back of his hand.

"Dad's going to kill me." A moment passed, and then he leaned forward, his head in his hands. "How could I have been so stupid?"

"If you'd just set the beer down, they probably would have let you go with a warning," Avery said. "Why did you run to the car? Why'd you take the keys?"

Caleb turned his gray-blue eyes on his sister, looking like a hurt puppy. Saliva gathered at the corners of his mouth. "How was I supposed to know, Avery? I've never even been to a party!"

"Shhh, shhh. Calm down." She worried his shouts might wake the neighbors. She looked at their house—every light was on. "It's going to be okay. Just . . . when we get inside, go to your room. I'll deal with Mom and Dad."

"He's going to kill me, Avery."

"He's not going to kill you. It's going to be okay."

She wasn't certain it would be. But, assuaged by her promise, Caleb walked up to the house, through the front door, and disappeared down the back hall. The bathroom door slammed hard behind him, followed by the sound of a loud retch. Liquid splattered against porcelain, then she heard the toilet flush.

At that moment, Avery's mother, Lonnie, appeared in the hallway, her shining face and worried eyes showing all that Avery needed to know. Her mother tightened the red terry-cloth robe around her waist.

"How did this happen?" her mother snapped. Her voice was as thin and cold as the snowflakes still falling outside. "Were you with him?"

"No . . . he called me from the station. Seriously, Mom. Everything's fine."

Moving past her daughter, Lonnie hustled down the hall toward the bathroom and began to bang on the door. "Caleb! Caleb! Open up. Now!"

From the front door, Avery could see into the kitchen, where her father, Hank, paced back and forth across the linoleum floor, holding the cordless phone to his ear. Lean and imposing, Hank Adams had dark features and a permanent five o'clock shadow that looked as though he'd spent his life in a coal mine, which, to be fair, he would have, if he'd been born a quarter century earlier. He was fit, though, with muscles that hadn't diminished over the years since he'd played football at Notre Dame. And despite the fact that he spent his life above ground, selling coal, there was always dirt under his fingernails, always a rasp in his voice, like he carried an aluminum pail to work every day. Avery felt the same grit in her blood, just underneath the surface, trying to break free. Coal was stubborn that way. It stayed in your veins.

"Sure," Hank was saying. "Can we do it in installments? Oh. Okay. Understood. Well, then, we'll get the retainer to you tomorrow. All right, Dan. We'll see you Monday."

Slamming the phone on the base, Hank turned to look at Avery, who put her chin up, pretending to be calmer than she felt. She'd never seen her father's eyes look so intense, his pupils so small. The dark hair on his forearms seemed to stand on end.

"Two thousand dollars, just to take on the case," her father told her.

A silence filled the room, so thick Avery struggled to breathe.

"Dad . . . I—"

"He watches you, you know," her father said. His lower lip quivered. "You go out. Drink. Carry on. And what happens? You get voted homecoming queen. He does the same thing, and his life is fucking ruined."

"Dad." Avery nearly felt like crying. "His life isn't—"

"What exactly do you think you know about life, Avery? Huh? I'm sorry to break it to you, but beauty doesn't exactly pay the bills. And you have the audacity to tell me about life? That's rich."

He paused his rant, rubbed his temple.

"All I know is, you better be on your knees thanking God that this wasn't you. Because you and I both know, it could have been."

He pushed past her and down the hall. "*Caleb!* Open the damn door!"

ON MONDAY, HER parents took her little brother, dressed in an oversized suit and tie, for their first meeting with the lawyer. Avery drove herself to school and pretended to pay attention in class, when in reality, all she could think about was the disappointment painted all over her father's face as he'd yelled at her Saturday night, and as he'd ignored her the next morning. For years, Avery had lived her life without fear of any consequences. But watching her brother suffer because of her bad example, she suddenly felt like she'd swallowed a toxic cocktail of anger and shame. Anger that her father would accuse her of causing Caleb's mess; shame that he was probably right.

ON FRIDAY EVENING, the gymnasium doors opened at five o'clock, sending a flood of light and a pack of girls into the darkened parking lot. They walked slowly under the weight of their backpacks, chatting idly while parents pulled up to pick up the freshmen. Soaked in sweat that defied the near-freezing temperature outside, steam rose off of Avery's bare limbs into the cold.

"Great job at practice today, Mandy," Avery said to one of the more promising freshmen. "I liked that little behind-the-back pass you did."

Mandy quickened her pace to catch up to Avery's side. "Thanks. Hey . . . I was going to ask, are you going to Kevin's tomorrow night?"

Avery walked with her chin up, blond hair glistening with sweat. She knew instinctively that Mandy Hightower wasn't looking for information; she was looking for an invitation.

"Doubt it," Avery replied flippantly.

She reached for the keys in her backpack before remembering with a surge of anger that they weren't there, and wouldn't be for another week. In a rare feat of parenting, her father had grounded Avery from driving—for what she wasn't quite certain. It wasn't like *she* was the one who'd been arrested. As she made her way across the parking lot, Mandy followed, hoping, Avery assumed, for the invitation that wasn't going to come.

"I've got a shit-ton of homework this weekend, Mandy," she said by way of explanation, "and nothing good happens at those—" She was going to say *parties,* but at that same moment, she noticed a dark and hulking figure standing in the middle of the parking lot. So instead she said, "Shit."

Following Avery's gaze, Mandy's eyes filled with concern. Standing on the passenger side of Avery's black Honda Civic, a short and stocky man waited with his arms crossed over his chest.

"Who's that?" Mandy asked. "He's hot."

With a sigh, Avery shifted the backpack on her shoulder and started walking faster toward her car. "That's my dad."

"Oh. Well, call me. Maybe we could go to Kevin's together on Saturday!"

When she reached her car, Avery rolled her eyes.

"You don't have to make such a scene, Dad."

Avoiding her father's gaze, she threw her backpack in the backseat and reached for the handle of the passenger-side door.

"Ah, ah, ah!" he said. "We had a deal."

Next to each other, Hank and Avery looked nothing alike. Avery was ethereal and glowing, her father earthen and rugged. But they shared a competitive spirit, or a persistent stubbornness. And any time Avery reached a goal Hank set for her, he raised the bar higher.

"*We* never had a deal," she said. "*You* had a deal."

Starting Avery's freshman year, Hank had driven up to the school like all the other parents, pretending to pick his daughter up from basketball practice. But instead, he'd instruct her to throw her backpack in the back of his car, start a timer, and send her on the three-mile run home. Each day she tried to beat the previous day's time. He'd presented it as a game—a way for Avery to work on her endurance.

Within a few months of starting high school, Avery could run a six-minute mile without breaking much of a sweat. Her father's mantra rang through her head as she ran: *The only way to run faster is to run faster.* In four years, Avery had learned that she could outrun just about anything. She could outrun her teammates. She could outrun the competition from other schools. She could even run the insecurities right out of her head, if she was willing to go hard enough. It was easy to be confident when you were faster than the boys.

The game had ended last year, when she'd started driving herself to school. But now, here he was, looking at the watch on his wrist. "You better get going. Clock's started."

"Dad," Avery said, her voice sounding desperate. "Coach made us do thirteen suicides at the end of practice. I can't."

Hank laughed out loud. "This from the girl who applied to West Point? It's hard enough to imagine you with a gun, Ave. But you gonna say 'I can't' when they hand you a fifty-pound rucksack and say *go*?" His tone turned dark. "You've gotta get serious."

Staring at his dark features, Avery knew suddenly why he was here. This wasn't about her future in Division I basketball, or even the long-shot application she'd mailed to West Point six months earlier, which he was now apparently using against her. This was about Caleb.

The parking lot cleared of cars, leaving rectangular imprints outlined with dirty snow. Avery stood in silence until she realized her father wasn't going to back down.

"I'll be in counseling someday talking about how you made me run three miles home every day like a maniac."

"Nah." He waved a hand through the air. "You love it." He unlocked the door of his daughter's car and jumped inside, immediately starting the engine and the heat. His hands slapped together, rubbing out the cold. "Better get moving."

"Hold your horses!" She pulled off her sweaty jersey, grabbed a dirty long-sleeved fleece from the backseat of her car, and yanked it over her head with force. Then, shooting her father a murderous look and a middle finger, she took off running.

Fury drove her legs over and over again against the cold. Tucking her fingers into the sleeves of her shirt, Avery pushed the pace. From her high school to their home was exactly 3.4 miles. She'd measured it at least ten times with her car odometer, hoping it would get shorter, which it never did. Wind whipped over her ears and eyes, giving her a slight headache. *Note to self,* Avery thought as she hit her stride, *tomorrow, pack a hat.*

Once her breathing steadied, she settled into a rhythm. That was the sole benefit of these long runs: they provided time alone, time to clear out the clutter in her mind.

First and foremost—she hated the fact that her father was using West Point against her. Back in the fall, her AP history teacher, Ms. Williams, had forced her classes to fill out West Point's initial screening form online. In the library computer lab, Avery typed out her GPA, SAT scores, list of extracurriculars, without thinking twice. But that night, the phone rang, and suddenly there was a deep-voiced man on the other end of the line, asking Avery a series of questions with military precision. When she'd placed the phone back on the stand, Avery stared at it for a long time before her mother's quiet voice broke through the silence.

"Well?" Lonnie Adams had asked. "What was that all about?"

Avery's parents were sitting still at the kitchen table, their forks suspended in midair. Oblivious to the phone call that had just taken place, Caleb shoveled a bite of spaghetti into his mouth.

"That was an admissions officer from West Point," Avery had said. "They want me to apply."

"You?" her father had grunted. He shook his head and went back to eating. "Will they let you wear your tiara while you shoot your gun?"

"West Point?" her mother repeated. "Do they even admit girls?"

The disbelief in their eyes was all it took for Avery to decide to apply. In the weeks after that phone call, Ms. Williams had helped Avery navigate the application. She explained that the U.S. Military Academy wasn't just an athletic and academic powerhouse of a school—it was also *free*. Free. As in zero dollars. That fit into Avery's framework. She didn't want to owe her parents anything anymore. And she was smart enough to know that they didn't have savings just lounging around in some bank account.

After some research, Avery learned that in exchange for that free education, West Point graduates committed to serve for five years as officers in the U.S. Army. But that didn't sound like that bad of a deal. She had a cousin who'd joined the military and got stationed overseas in Italy. So, a free education *and* a guaranteed job after college, possibly in an exotic location? To Avery, that seemed like the deal of the century.

Almost too good to be true.

After Avery passed the Candidate Fitness Assessment—the push-ups, sit-ups, and shuttle run came easy—Ms. Williams told Avery that she needed a nomination from a congressman, a senator, or the vice president.

"Uh," Avery had said with a laugh, "my family doesn't know anyone in politics."

In response, Ms. Williams set up an interview for Avery with the famed Pennsylvania senator Arlen Specter. When his nomination came in the mail, Avery started to think that she might just have a chance. On her own, she'd reached out to the women's basketball coach, a woman named Catherine Jankovich, whose e-mail address had been listed on West Point's athletic website. She'd mailed the coach videotape of games and practices, as requested. The coach had offered Avery a position on the team if West Point offered her admission, but Avery noticed she'd placed particular emphasis on the word *if*.

"Unfortunately, there's really nothing I can do to stamp your application through," Coach Jankovich had said over the phone. "It's quite competitive. We'd love to have you, of course, but I can't make any promises."

It was just the kind of challenge that Avery lived to overcome. *You say I'm not strong enough? Watch me flex. You say it's competitive? Watch me compete.*

And yet, February had nearly come and gone. A cloud formed in her chest, which distracted Avery from the tears in her eyes. Why hadn't she heard anything from West Point?

They probably don't want you, Avery told herself, in a voice too brutal to be her own. The voice was right, though. West Point was a *reach.* A long shot. Who was she to think she was special? Who was she to think she could get out of Pittsburgh? She was going to have to tell everyone that she'd been rejected, and everyone would secretly laugh, knowing she'd never had a chance all along.

She tried to ignore the voice in her head by moving faster. The harder she pushed, the more pain she felt, which released her emotions through sweat, rather than tears. It was simple math. By wrecking her body, she didn't have to face her wrecked soul.

But her father's words cut through the ache in her muscles, whispering like wind into her ears. *He watches you.* Was he right? Had Avery ruined her little brother's life, simply by setting a bad example?

She wanted Caleb to see her do something good. Something responsible. Something important. But time was running out. And she couldn't slow down. Not now.

Not ever.

Streetlights drew Avery westward, spilling an orange haze on bare tree limbs. She pushed to the top of the hill with long, purposeful strides, listening to her own breath: in through her nose, out through her mouth. The cold dried the sweat on her face and her slender legs flew past fences, children in white yards, and half-melted snowmen. The smell of wood-burning fireplaces filled her head as she sucked air and heaved toward the finish. She leaned forward as she passed the mailbox in front of the home at the end of the cul-de-sac. Her father was standing on the stoop, holding his stopwatch.

"Twenty-five thirty-two. So much for that six-minute mile pace."

"I'll get it back, Dad," she yelled, placing her hands on her head. "I'll get it back."

"That's my girl," he said, leaving her out in the cold.

Exhausted and sweating, Avery walked toward the mailbox, just in case. Inside, there was a stack of mail: a circular of flimsy coupons, a pink envelope with the words *Final Notice* printed on top, a *People* magazine, and a large manila envelope with West Point's gold crest glittering in the top left corner.

"Dad!" she shouted, ripping through the paper. "*Dad!*"

Her father stepped back onto the porch. The rest of the mail fell to the ground. Avery held her breath, frantically opening the leather-bound announcement.

"I got in," she mumbled to herself. Then, raising her eyes to her father, she screamed, "I got in!"

3

Summer 2000 // Austin, Texas

After dinner, they sat on the back porch and waited for pie. There was always pie.

Hannah Speer leaned her head back and breathed in the smells of the night. This was her very last dinner at her grandparents' ranch and she wanted to take it all in. Barbecue ribs, smoked on her grandfather's grill, had left a sticky brown residue under her nails. A light lemon-garlic dressing had been slicked across baby spinach and chard, the bowl dusted with Parmesan cheese. Soft salted butter had been spread on crusty homemade baguettes. Hannah had eaten three slices before her grandmother warned her to save room. It was a perfect meal, washed down with sweet tea, served on toile china. Every bite closer to her last.

Tomorrow, an airplane would transport her family from Texas to New York and time would speed up, racing toward West Point's Reception Day for the incoming class of 2004. Her duffel bag waited on her bedroom floor, stuffed tightly with the things she'd been instructed to pack: underwear, socks, an assortment of first aid gear, a pair of brand-new leather combat boots. Her grandfather had explained how to mold them to her feet: *Lace them up, wear them in the shower, and don't take them off until they're bone dry,* he'd told her. Hannah had spent the day walking around her house in a pink robe and combat boots. She hated to imagine having blisters all summer, just because she didn't break the boots in correctly.

Blisters and combat boots were still two days away. At the moment, the fertile smell of cow manure wafted in from the fields. Above her, the porch's tin roof reflected a string of twinkle lights, and just beyond the roof, a dark sky hovered over the pasture. The stars looked like the scene at a jewelry shop: tiny diamonds strewn across black velvet. Staring at this view, Hannah couldn't help but imagine a Creator who'd spread this tableau of jewels just for her. She gripped the cross pendant on her neck and slid it back and forth along its chain, her own secret signal, a prayer of thanks. Life was so beautiful, so vast.

Lowering her eyes from the sky, Hannah watched her grandfather walk up from the yard. Gates Speer was a young-looking sixty-seven, with a full head of white hair and tan skin that had held up to age. He pinched a piece of grass between his fingers, then let it fall to the ground.

Though he'd lived on the ranch full-time for the last five years, he still carried himself like he was walking through the halls of the Pentagon. Shoulders back, chin up. Hannah wondered if U.S. Army generals ever lost their military bearing. She imagined that even when they buried her grandfather someday, his muscles would be clenched. But underneath that rigid exterior, General Speer had a softness that few outside of his family had ever seen. Hannah knew she was one of the lucky ones.

He took a seat on the porch swing next to her, slid his arm around her shoulders. His scent was a mix of Old Spice and fresh-cut grass, the way a man was supposed to smell. But her grandfather wasn't a cowboy. He didn't have dirt under his nails or an unkempt shirt. "I judge a man by three things," General Speer often said. "His clothes, his posture, and his handshake."

If she wanted to see someone lackadaisical about his appearance, Hannah only needed to look a few inches over, to her father, Bill. He sat in a rocking chair and alternated between picking his teeth, scratching at his mustache, and adjusting the ball cap on his head. That's why Hannah had never understood the phrase "The apple doesn't fall far from the tree." It was a terrible analogy. Couldn't people see that a tree and an apple are nothing alike? Of course one came from the other, but one was round and sweet, and the other was tall and stoic. She tried to imagine the tree and the apple having a conversation. It would probably go about the same way as tonight's chat between General Speer and his son.

"Goats would do it," her father was saying. "Six or seven. You wouldn't have to mow ever again."

"Well, I like mowing," her grandfather replied. "I like making all those straight lines. Plus, if I had goats then I'd have to take care of the goats. There are no shortcuts. You're gonna work hard, one way or another."

Hannah's sister, Emily, snorted a laugh. She was swaying on a swing on the opposite side of the porch next to their mother, Lynn.

When they stood side by side, the three Speer women looked like triplets. Lynn appeared only slightly older than her daughters, a few wrinkles at her eyes. Emily's hair was lighter than Hannah's dirty blond. They all had sky-blue eyes, dimples, and sharp chins.

"I bet if Grandpa had goats, he'd end up chloroforming them all," Emily said, her voice flat.

The whole family broke into laughter, including the general.

At that moment, Hannah's grandmother emerged from the kitchen holding a pie plate and a ceramic pitcher.

"Oh Lord, not that story again."

Nearly as tall as her husband, Barbara Speer was a formidable woman. Hannah had always thought she looked a bit like Geena Davis in *A League of Their Own:* glamorous with gusto. Had she been born in a later generation, Barbara might have become the CEO of a major international company, but instead, she'd raised five children and successfully negotiated life as a general's wife. Entertaining heads of state had become second nature: she could hold her own with First Ladies, UN ambassadors, and senators. She read three newspapers every morning and could speak as many languages. To Hannah, her grandmother was like royalty, but to the rest of the world, she was simply a retired general's wife.

It was Barbara who had convinced her husband to transform their hundred acres into an organic cattle ranch. Now that he was retired from the Army, her grandfather had finally agreed, and the business was growing faster than anyone had predicted— anyone except Barbara.

"This pie is going to get cold if he starts telling stories," Barbara said.

"I'll do it," said Emily. Then, channeling her inner Jimmy Stewart, Hannah's sister began telling the tale, speaking as if she were holding a cigar in her mouth. "Now, *you see,* those Navy midshipmen had us beat down. Mentally. Physically. Spiritually. Emotionally! We were done for. Kaput! If West Point had a fighting chance, we had to do something. Something big."

They were laughing too hard for Emily to continue, but of course she didn't have to. They all knew the story by heart. In 1954, Gates Speer was a Firstie at the U.S. Military Academy at West Point—a senior. It was his last year at the academy, and he couldn't bear to watch the football team lose to Navy one more time. So in a moment of desperation, he and a group of friends decided it was up to them to turn the tide: they were going to steal Navy's mascot, a hundred-and-fifty-pound goat with massive curved horns that spanned more than five feet across. To successfully kidnap the mascot and transport him back to West Point, her grandfather hatched a plan that included a rag, a can of chloroform, and his roommate's convertible drop-top. They'd snatched the goat, heaved his passed-out body into the backseat of the convertible, and then put the roof up, speeding away from Annapolis in the dead of night.

"Damn if that goat didn't wake up," her grandfather said, picking up the story. "We stop at a gas station to fill up. And suddenly, Bill the Goat is ripping through the convertible top with his horns, trying to break loose. I jump on top of him and have to wrestle him all the way back to West Point. Scariest day of my life."

Of course, they all knew that it wasn't the scariest day of the general's life. Her grandfather had fought in the Korean War as a second lieutenant. He'd spent four years in Vietnam, too. A lieu-tenant colonel then, he'd been in charge of a large regiment of officers and soldiers and had probably seen a lot of terrible things happen, Hannah assumed—things she couldn't even imagine. But then again, she wasn't certain. He never told those stories.

"Of course, West Point isn't all just stealing goats," he said, clearing his throat. Suddenly, she felt her grandfather's arm stiffen. His teeth clenched behind his cheeks and he shook his head, like he was trying to shake a memory.

"Let's not get into all that," her grandmother said gently. "We've got pie!"

Barbara Speer placed the pie dish on the table and opened her hands over it as if to say, *Ta-da!* The sweet aroma of fruit and butter mingled with the tension in the air.

"Strawberry rhubarb," she announced. "Who wants more tea? Hannah, have I told you how much I love this pitcher? I get compliments on it all the time."

Hannah smiled humbly. The pitcher was a product of the one elective class she'd taken during her last semester of high school. The body of the pitcher was tall and slender, with a perfect triangle spout and a curved handle. As much as her grandmother entertained, Hannah had known it would get good use.

"It looks great, Barb," said Lynn. Hannah watched her mother stand up from the swing, raise her eyebrows, and make strong eye contact with the rest of the family.

"I'll grab the plates," her dad said, straightening his ball cap. "Emily, why don't you get the ice cream?"

Suddenly, the porch cleared, leaving Hannah and her grandfather alone on the swing. The exit had clearly been planned, because at the last minute, Emily turned back to Hannah and mouthed, "*Sorry.*"

So that's what this is, Hannah realized. *An ambush.* She felt the muscles in her throat tighten. She didn't like to be taken by surprise.

"Two days, huh?" her grandfather said solemnly.

"Yes, sir," she started. "But you don't need to worry. I broke my boots in just like you told me."

It was impossible to reassure a man who needed no reassurance. Arms crossed over his chest, he turned to her with his blue eyes, looking down at her the way she expected he'd looked down on so many of his subordinates over the years.

"It's not too late you know," he said. "Your dad knows the coach at UT. There are opportunities all over the place. Not just there."

Hannah bit the insides of her cheeks hard. Her grandfather had never encouraged his grandchildren to join the service. On the contrary, he'd almost downplayed the significance of his contributions to America. Hannah had to beg her father to tell her the truth: How, when he was a lieutenant, her grandfather had single-handedly saved his platoon from capture in North Korea. How he served as an Army liaison for the space program. How without him, Neil Armstrong might not have walked on the moon. He had medals that he wouldn't pin to his uniform, even though he'd earned them. To Gates Speer, wearing all the pins you'd earned was the antithesis of humility, and if he was anything, he was humble. That was the Speer way. Stay modest. Never claim credit. Avoid talk about politics and religion. Always smile demurely, even when inside, you're beaming with pride. Stay married for the long haul. Make pies. But couldn't her grandfather see?

As the second child, she'd spent her childhood watching Emily get into trouble for talking back, sneaking out, and getting bad grades. That was why Hannah had been so compliant: she'd learned early that it was easier to follow the rules than to break them. And the rules worked. If she studied hard, she aced the tests. If she went to bed on time, she felt refreshed in the morning, just like her parents promised. There was no need to rebel when following the rules worked in your favor every time. West Point's offer of admission was the direct result of all the success Hannah had accumulated by following the rules. Hannah was confident that she was making the right choice, and of all the people in her family, she'd assumed her grandfather would understand her decision. She'd expected him to look at her with joy and pride and respect. Instead, the worry in his eyes stretched across the swing, cutting Hannah like a knife.

"You don't think I can do it," she said, more of a statement than a question.

Her grandfather reached over and grabbed Hannah's hand. For the first time in her life, she realized that his skin was *old*— paper-thin, with veins pulsing purple below the surface. But his grip hadn't lost its strength: his long fingers wrapped around her palm and squeezed warmly.

"It's not a matter of capability. I know you *can* do it. I just don't think you should *have* to."

The cross on her necklace slid up and down its chain as Hannah prayed for the right words to land on her tongue. How could she make him understand?

When Hannah was in sixth grade, her grandparents had taken her to West Point for her grandfather's fortieth class reunion. They took a tour of campus, ate dinner in the mess hall, cruised the Hudson River on a party boat. Hannah watched white-haired men shake hands and retell old stories while their wives stood behind them, smiling with patience. Watching, Hannah decided she never wanted to stand on the sidelines as her husband told his stories. She wanted stories of her own. She loved her grandmother, but she didn't want to spend her life serving pies; she wanted to serve *people.*

Soon after that trip to New York, a neighbor in Austin had invited Hannah to church, and the preacher spoke at length about being "on mission" for God, helping the poor and defending the defenseless and living up to the call God had placed on your life. While he preached, Hannah felt a burning in her heart and remembered experiencing that same thrill at West Point. She took that sermon, that feeling, as a sign, and hid it away in her heart.

Though Hannah was new to faith, she knew that people who believed in the eternal could be unattached to outcomes in a way that perplexed people who didn't. The more you believed, the more you were willing to sacrifice. It was how someone like Mother Teresa could spend her life among lepers. It was how someone like Martin Luther King could risk his life marching for a dream. It's how Hannah could sense the concern in her grandfather's eyes and decide, in a moment, that she was okay if he never understood.

The general stood up from the swing and rubbed Hannah's

shoulder. "If you want to go to West Point, there's probably nothing I can say to stop you. But there are things I've endured that no woman should have to endure."

And then he rubbed his hands together, in anticipation of pie, as if he'd just had a conversation about the weather.

THE NIGHT BEFORE Reception Day, most incoming cadet candidates booked cheap hotel rooms for their families outside West Point's gates. But a member of the women's basketball team, Sarah Goodrich, had connected Hannah's family with a free place to stay on campus. Apparently, one of Sarah's professors, Colonel Mark Bennett, and his wife, Wendy, often hosted families for R-Day.

"The Bennetts live just a few hundred yards from the stadium," Sarah had told Hannah over the phone. "Wendy is amazing. You'll see. She's just like Martha Stewart. They're excited to have you."

As active-duty members of the military, West Point's faculty lived on campus in houses maintained by the Army. Quarters on other Army posts looked like prefabricated boxes, Hannah knew, because she'd visited her grandparents at Fort Leavenworth and Fort Knox, when he was still a lieutenant colonel. But West Point's housing matched its historic greatness.

At the center of campus, just in front of the granite barracks, stood a statue of George Washington, looking out over a green parade field known as the Plain. On the north side of the Plain, the superintendent's whitewashed mansion sat next to the commandant's home, a Tudor. Next to that was the massive redbrick mansion of the academic dean. Hovering behind the barracks, up a hill, was the towering Cadet Chapel, a reminder to Hannah that God was above it all. In another area of campus, there were tightly packed neighborhoods for junior faculty members, apartments for bachelor professors and TACs, short for "tactical officers." Within West Point's stone gates, a mini self-sufficient community existed solely to serve cadets.

The Bennetts lived in Lusk Area, a wooded neighborhood of high-ranking professors, comprising two-story redbrick homes, situated behind Lusk Reservoir and Michie Stadium. To Hannah, the homes looked like a string of paper dolls—each one a mirror image of the one that came before. American flags flew from each front stoop. Doorsteps displayed black and white placards indicating the name of the family who lived inside. *COL. Carter's Clan. Team Turner. The Bostwick Brood.* Hannah's parents sat in the front of the rental car, while she and Emily sat in the back, and when they pulled up to the right address, Hannah noticed the straightforward placard waiting in front of them. It simply read, *The Bennetts.*

Before they could unload their luggage from the car, the front door opened, and a petite woman with short brunette hair stepped outside. She wore dark jeans and a casual white button-up shirt with the sleeves rolled up, like she'd been washing dishes just before they'd arrived. As for makeup, Wendy Bennett didn't seem to wear much—mascara laced her lashes; a natural shade of mauve lipstick graced her lips. She smiled and waved.

"Come on in!" Wendy shouted. Her voice carried a slight Southern accent, the likes of which Hannah hadn't expected to hear this far north of the Mason-Dixon Line. "Y'all must be exhausted."

Wendy looked nothing like Martha Stewart, Hannah decided, but was a dead ringer for Sally Field, with the same bright eyes, high cheekbones, and easy smile that had made her America's sweetheart. But as soon as Hannah crossed the threshold, she realized why Sarah had made the comparison.

The Bennetts' house oozed comfort and gentility. Antiques graced every room, complemented by inviting upholstery. The house smelled like a cake was finishing in the oven, all sugar and butter and vanilla. Hannah caught herself breathing in the scent and feeling surprisingly at ease in this stranger's house.

In a flash of hospitality, Wendy took drink orders, showed Hannah's parents to a guest room, directed Hannah and Emily to another spare bedroom, and arranged three different kinds of cheese on a platter. Later, even Hannah's father, Bill, seemed relaxed, sipping a beer and helping Colonel Bennett tend the grill. Breathing in the scent of charcoal and grass in the Bennetts' well-manicured backyard, Hannah tried not to let her nerves about the following morning spoil her last night of summer. But every ten minutes, a wave of nausea crashed on her stomach, reminding her that the time was ticking away, bringing her closer to the end of one life and the beginning of another.

"How are you doing?" Wendy asked as Hannah refilled a glass of water at the sink. The cake was iced now, waiting to be cut. "Are you nervous?"

Hannah considered lying. She imagined shrugging her shoulders and pretending that everything was fine. But seeing the look of honest concern in Wendy's eyes, she exhaled instead.

"Completely," admitted Hannah. "I doubt I'll sleep at all tonight."

Wendy nodded, pursed her lips in a way that communicated deep understanding, then reached out and touched Hannah's arm, as if they'd known each another for much longer than a few hours.

"I want you to know that if you need *anything*—and I mean *anything*—all you have to do is ask," Wendy said. She grabbed a scrap piece of paper and wrote her phone number on it. "I know we just met. But I mean it."

"Okay," Hannah replied, receiving the paper from Wendy's hand. She folded it, tucked it in her pocket. "Thanks."

"Now," Wendy said, clapping her hands together. "How about cake?"

WHEN THEY LEFT the Bennetts' house the following morning, bellies full of homemade cinnamon rolls and strong coffee, the Speers walked across a stone bridge that traversed Lusk Reservoir and ended right at the entrance to Michie Stadium. Hannah shifted her black duffel bag on her shoulder, feeling the weight of everything she'd packed. It struck Hannah then that aside from bras and underwear, she hadn't brought any clothes. Unlike other college students who arrived to school with bedding and lamps and decor to "liven up" a dorm room, candidates for West Point showed up with nothing but the clothes on their back and faith that all of their needs would be met.

Ignoring the sound of yelling already coming from the other side, Hannah led her family beyond the stadium's stone facade, though its iron gates, and toward the beginning of the rest of her life.

4

Summer 2000 // West Point, New York

Dani lay prostrate on the ground, her finger wrapped around the trigger of an M16.

Movies make this look easy, she thought, feeling frustration crawl up her spine. Her elbows dug into the soft ground, along with a vertical pistol grip, creating a tripod for the weapon. She had to keep her knees, hips, and abs engaged to hold her body straight, low to the ground, and yet upright enough to see the target and shoot with accuracy. It was far harder than she'd anticipated. Any time she pulled the trigger, the kickback pummeled into her shoulder. She had bruises.

"*Miss,*" a voice said above her as the bullet whizzed past the target, wide by several inches. "It might help if you open your eyes, McNalley."

"And it might help if you shut your mouth, Nesmith," Dani replied.

She wiped her dirty hands against the legs of her green and brown combat uniform and let her platoon mate help her up. Eighteen, with dark hair buzzed completely to the scalp, Tim Nesmith had quickly become Dani's favorite person in their platoon, and one of the few reasons she hadn't quit. Had she been attracted to the all-American look, Dani might have had a crush on him. But she'd seen him pee in the woods more times than she could count, which meant that Tim had moved firmly into the friend zone. During breaks, Tim would lounge against the trunk of a tree, in the shade. He spent half the time sleeping; during the other half, he and Dani drilled one another on the inane definitions they'd been told to memorize out of a book called *Bugle Notes*.

"Definition of leather."

Tim would pause before saying, "'If the fresh skin of an animal, cleaned and'... oh God..."

"'Divested...,'" Dani would hint.

"'... divested of all hair, fat, and other ... uh ... extraneous matter ... be immersed ...'" Tim would groan, rolling over onto his stomach and pummeling the ground with his fist.

But if Tim was horrible at memorizing useless trivia, he more than made up for it with the kind of outdoorsy knowledge that was completely foreign to Dani. When orienteering, Tim naturally knew which direction was north. A week earlier, when their platoon had prepared to walk through a concrete bunker called the *House of Tears*, Tim had shown Dani how to tighten her gas mask.

"Don't worry," he'd whispered, ensuring that their platoon leader didn't hear him talking. "It's just tear gas."

Just tear gas? Dani had looked at him like he had three heads. That was like saying the flu was *just* a virus.

Every person in the platoon had lined up with their hand on the shoulder of the person in front of them, like elephants linking trunks to tails. When Tim placed his hand on Dani's shoulder, he'd squeezed it twice, as if to say, *You've got this.*

As soon as they were inside and told to remove their masks, a stinging sensation exploded into Dani's nose and mouth and eyes, clawing at her insides. Water, mucus, and sweat poured out of every orifice imaginable, like the tear gas was somehow melting her face. Not a second too soon, a door at the front of the room had opened, and the platoon had filed out quickly into the fresh air, all hacking and coughing and spitting into the grass.

"Wave your—*cough*—arms!" Tim had shouted at Dani, windmilling his arms through the air. She'd followed his instruction, mostly because she didn't know what else to do, and soon, it seemed the motion had circulated fresh oxygen over her body. Snot covered her upper lip and tears ran down her cheeks, but surprisingly, she was laughing. They all were. This, she was learning, was what West Pointers called "type two" fun. It wasn't fun while you were having it; it was fun later, when you could look back on it.

After they'd recovered, Dani asked Tim how he knew to circle his arms through the air. He'd just shrugged.

"Seemed like the right thing to do," he'd said.

That was the way it was with Tim. Everything came naturally to him. He never seemed flustered with the training, and not once had Dani seen him lose his cool or bite the insides of his cheeks to keep from showing emotion. The insides of her cheeks, however, were a disintegrating mess of flesh. She'd chewed them so hard in the last three weeks, trying to hold her tongue, that she was afraid she'd have a hole in her cheek by the time Beast Barracks was over.

They switched positions, Dani holding the clipboard while Tim took the prone on the ground. He shot three times in quick succession and hit the target in a perfect isosceles triangle, right in the center.

"Show-off." Dani took the weapon from him and went back to the ground, ignoring the growing pain in her lower back. It felt like her hip might snap out of its socket. But she knew better than to complain. Last week, the only other girl in Alpha Company had fallen out of a two-mile run with what she'd said was a sprained ankle. Soft in the face and around her middle, the girl looked genuinely in pain to Dani, but she'd watched as the men in her platoon rolled their eyes and groaned, as if she were faking the injury to slow them all down. The girl had quit three days later, packing up her gear and heading back to Arizona. Dani didn't blame the girl for quitting any more than she'd blamed the guys for rolling their eyes. If you wanted to be comfortable, you shouldn't have come to West Point. But now, the lone female in their platoon of twenty, Dani was highly aware that she was being watched. Any misstep, any wince, would confirm her status as the weak link.

The morning she'd reported to West Point, Dani's body felt perfectly ready for any challenge, bolstered by a rush of adrenaline. Through the night, Dominic had punched her in the side, annoyed by her relentless tossing and turning. But Dani didn't care. Dominic would be able to go back to sleep this afternoon. She, on the other hand, wouldn't get much sleep for the next six weeks.

The McNalleys had left the hotel an hour later, Dani carrying a black duffel bag over her shoulder, stuffed with everything that had been on the short packing list. Sarah Goodrich had told her to pack extra bandages, blister pads, moleskin, anti-friction gel, and foot powder, saying they might come in handy. Dani had shivered imagining how her feet might look at the end of Cadet Basic Training, torn up, blistered, and bloodied. But thankfully, the moment she shivered with fear, a fresh rush of energy soared through her veins. She could feel the thrill in her neck, her fingers, her toes. Her abs tightened. It was amazing how the body could sense impending danger and release a chemical to help carry you through the fear. At times, the body was smarter than the mind.

Her hair slicked back into a dark bun, black Nike sneakers looking sharp against her mocha legs, Dani walked through the gates to the stadium.

As they found their way to an area overlooking the fifty-yard line, the McNalleys joined other white families, black families, an Asian family, and even a few families that weren't speaking English. Most boys had preemptively shaved their heads, but several had grown their hair out long and bushy, knowing that at some point in the next few hours a barber would shear it off. Once they found their seats along the aluminum bleachers, Dani leaned forward and pressed her elbows into her knees. Everything in her body was on extreme alert—like she was about to run a marathon. Instead, she had to sit still and wait. On . . . *what*? An announcement? Someone to start yelling at her to do push-ups?

Just before the welcoming ceremony began, a tall blond woman had appeared beside Dani's mother. She was beautiful, with a sharp chin, brilliant blue eyes, and a Southern accent as smooth as Dani had ever heard. Behind her, there were two blond girls that looked like twins and an older man with a graying mustache, wearing a burnt-orange University of Texas ball cap. The woman pointed at the aluminum bleachers and smiled.

"Can we slide in?"

"Of course!" Dani's mother said. "Scoot down, Dani."

"It's so quiet," the woman said to Dani's mother as her family slid onto the row. "You'd think we're at a funeral."

Harper McNalley laughed out loud. "*My* funeral. Still can't believe my baby is going to college. *This* college."

"Is she your youngest?" the woman asked.

"No." Dani's mother pointed down the line to Dominic, who pushed his glasses up his nose. "Dominic will be a sophomore in high school this fall. Dani's our oldest."

"Oh, well then, you'll still have one at home," the woman said. "I'm about to have an empty nest."

Soon, Harper and this woman were chatting like old friends. Dani sometimes hated the fact that her mother had never met a stranger. They could be standing in line at the grocery store, and before they'd checked out, Harper would have a list of prayer requests from the person in front of her and the one behind her. Dani, on the other hand, would have been content to stay quiet, waiting. It wasn't like she would ever see these people again. Then again, she thought, there weren't going to be that many other girls in the class of 2004.

Dani locked eyes with her new classmate, and together they rolled their eyes at their respective mothers. A beat passed as the two memorized each other's faces. Without a doubt, she was a natural beauty: tall, with dirty-blond hair and dark blue eyes. Her face carried a carefree expression that would have filled the room with warmth, if they weren't sitting outside. And most notably, she looked comfortable in her own skin, which seemed like a commendable feat of bravery to Dani, considering the faint sound of yelling coming from the other side of the stadium.

"We're from Austin," the girls' mother said, answering Harper's latest question. "I'm Lynn Speer. And that's my husband down there with the mustache. Bill. Our daughter Emily, she goes to the University of Texas. And this is our daughter Hannah."

The beautiful girl extended a long hand toward Dani. They shook and shared a sigh of anxiety.

"Do you play a sport?" Hannah's mother asked. "Hannah's here to play basketball."

Dani's eyebrows crunched together in shock. "Really? Me too." *What are the odds?* She shifted forward excitedly on the bench. "What's your position?"

"Post," Hannah offered with a chuckle. "I actually thought I recognized you. Coach Jankovich sent me a newspaper article when you signed. You're from Ohio, right?"

In the quiet moment that passed, all the plays they could run together moved through Dani's mind. Hannah was so tall and

Dani so short; there were a lot of ways they could maneuver around another team's defense. They were going to be unstoppable! Dani was surprised to find that that little connection—that tiny, imperceptible moment of contact—had calmed her nerves. Though it was unspoken, Dani knew that she'd just made her first friend. It didn't matter that she didn't know much about this girl. They were going to be on the same basketball team, and that was enough.

"I need to get your phone number," Harper McNalley said to Lynn Speer. "I have a feeling you and I might need a support group."

She reached in her purse for a piece of paper and a pen, but before they could exchange information, a lone snare drum began to beat.

"Here we go," said Dominic, pushing his glasses up his nose again. "The show begins."

As a group of five cadets in uniform marched through a stadium tunnel and into the stands, the entire crowd went silent, listening to the sharp *tap, tap, tap* of their feet against the aluminum bleachers. All five cadets looked identical, stiff from the top of their hats to the bottom of their shoes. They wore starched white pants and crisp white overcoats, cinched at the waist by white belts with gold buckles. Suddenly, everyone in the stands seemed shabbily dressed by comparison. An officer in a navy uniform stepped forward to a microphone.

"Ladies and gentlemen . . . friends and family. Welcome to the U.S. Military Academy at West Point."

A collective sigh released from the crowd into the air as his voice echoed across the stadium, toward the reservoir. Then they all held their breath again.

"Today, you embark on the six-week journey known as Cadet Basic Training. CBT is rigorous and it is demanding. It will require every bit of personal fortitude, discipline, and determination you can muster. The people next to you—your family and friends—have helped you to get this far. But in just a few moments, you will say goodbye, and you will be going on alone."

Someone sniffled. In her periphery, Dani saw Hannah's father wipe his eyes. West Point's first captain, a senior who held the highest rank in the Corps of Cadets, introduced the rest of the CBT leadership, called Cadre. There were a few more speeches. And then, the officer who had started it all walked back to the microphone.

"Parents, family, and friends, please prepare your final good-byes. Candidates, you will be moving out in ninety seconds."

The shock of that statement seemed to hit everyone in the audience at once. A beat passed and they stood up to exchange hugs and tears and goodbyes, grasping for the seconds even as they disappeared into the past.

Dani felt the pressure of her mother's arms around her body, the softness of her father's lips against her cheek, the punch of her brother's fist against her shoulder.

"Go get 'em, D," Dominic said.

And then, with no opportunity to look back, she'd followed Hannah and several hundred other eighteen-year-olds down the stairs and onto the football field. They proceeded to the fifty-yard line and waited for their first instruction, their parents standing behind them watching in silence. In that moment, Dani's back stiffened, and her neck grew tall and straight. A cloud hovered above, threatening to pour rain on their heads.

"Cadet candidates," a cadre shouted from beside her. "Move your bags to your left hand. And move."

IN THE HOURS, days, and weeks after that moment, so much had happened, Dani could barely remember it all. In the first hour, they'd issued uniforms, inspected everyone's body for tattoos, and led every candidate through a barbershop, where the boys had their heads sheared like sheep. Hair covered the floor like in an image Dani had seen at the Holocaust Memorial Museum, and she'd fought the urge to gag. By the afternoon, they'd taught her to salute, to stand at attention, to march. By the time the sun had set, Dani didn't know if it had been six hours or six days since she'd said goodbye. The mediocre sleep she got every night felt like naps in one never-ending day. Cadre quickly started calling Dani "Headlights," simply because her eyes were permanently stretched wide, always on high alert. And her eyes weren't the only thing that had changed. Within the first week, she was speaking an entirely new language.

CBT stood for "Cadet Basic Training." If someone "smoked you," it meant he beat you in some kind of competition. "Racking" was sleeping. To "police" your area meant to clean up. But all that language was for the future, because as a plebe, Dani was only allowed to speak one of four responses:

Yes, sir.

No, sir.

No excuse, sir.

Sir, I do not understand.

The boys looked infantile, their heads shaved to the skull. The girls were scattered among the boys, hard to pick out since they were so few. The teammate she'd met on R-Day, Hannah Speer, had been assigned to a different company, and even though Dani kept her eyes peeled—*Headlights!*—she hadn't seen Hannah once. Dani wondered if the girl from Texas had already quit, but hoped she hadn't. When Dani felt the urge to give up, when she felt pain growing in her body, she imagined Hannah out there facing these same obstacles and tried her best to be strong.

"YOU'VE GOT TO breathe, McNalley," Tim Nesmith instructed her. He bent down in a low squat and repositioned the rifle to better aim it at the target. "Breathe in. And when you breathe out, right at the end of your breath—when you have nothing left— that's when you pull. Keep your eyes open. Trust yourself. You can do this."

As she found her position, Dani realized that his instructions— Breathe. Give it all you've got. Trust.—were basically what she'd been doing her whole life. But if that was the case, why couldn't she hit this stupid target?

Back on the ground, Dani inhaled, feeling her chest expand. The air smelled of spent ammunition, a combination of tin, mud, and grass. She exhaled, kept her eyes open, squeezed the trigger, and watched a rip the size of a quarter open in the outer ring of the target.

"I hit it!" she yelled, standing up, exultant.

Tim offered her a high five, and they laughed together until they saw their platoon leader, Mike Wilkerson, approaching them from down the field. Wilkerson was a Cow—West Point speak for a junior. A former football player who'd quit after his first season, he had a thick neck, big ears, and hair cut so short, he looked bald. For the last three weeks, he'd been staring over Dani's shoulder, constantly hazing her and refusing her any moment of rest. Before Wilkerson spoke, Dani already knew that he was coming for her. Her head, neck, and shoulders ached from the strain of feigning confidence.

"New Cadet McNalley," Wilkerson said as he stopped in front of them. "Recite 'Duty, Honor, Country.'"

Dani swallowed. Tim had worked hard on this one. And listening to him repeat it over and over again, she was confident she'd memorized it, too.

"'Duty, honor, country,'" she began. "'These three—'"

"Incorrect," the cadre spat. "Not *these three*. *Those* three. Attention to detail, New Cadet McNalley. Twenty push-ups, and then start again."

Dani went to the ground, performed the push-ups with ease, then stood, breathless, and began again.

"'Duty, honor, country. *Those* three . . . uh—'"

"I don't recall General Douglas MacArthur stuttering," Wilkerson spat. "Forty this time. Then start again."

Beads of sweat gathered along the top of Dani's cotton under-wear after she completed the push-ups. There was nothing she could do except try again until either she got it right or Wilkerson had mercy. He seemed to be enjoying her discomfort, even as he looked impressed by her ability to complete forty push-ups without pause. Closing her eyes for a moment, Dani tried to apply Tim's instructions for hitting the target. She inhaled, exhaled, and started again.

"'Duty, honor, country. Those three hallowed words reverently dictate what you ought to be, what you can be, and what you *will* be.'" She paused, then stared Wilkerson in the eyes. "'They are your rallying points: to build courage when courage seems to fail; to regain faith when there seems to be little cause for faith; to create hope when hope becomes forlorn.'"

When she finished, Dani held her breath. Wilkerson stood in front of her with a look of shock and admiration on his face. He raised his eyebrows.

"Wow," he said. "Nice job, McNalley. Not to sound racist, but normally black kids can't memorize shit."

Dani bit her cheeks harder than she ever had before, the tinny taste of blood spreading across her tongue. Later, she would cycle through all the things she wished she'd said to him—*What, so you've met* all *black kids?* or better, *And what about you, Wilkerson, how'd you do with plebe knowledge?*

But plebes were only allowed to speak one of four responses. So Dani lifted her chin, set her jaw, and chose the only one that applied.

"Sir, I do not understand."

Wilkerson offered her a half smile. "You did good. I'm giving you a compliment."

Dani's body went hot with rage. Most often, racism was expressed in small, imperceptible movements of distrust: in glances, in grabbing purses tighter, in moving to the other side of the street. Rarely was she confronted with a blatant admission that someone assumed she would be less capable, simply because of the color of her skin. She seethed. But thankfully, before she could react, the upperclassman moved on.

"I can't believe he said that," Tim said. "Are you okay?"

"Yeah," Dani answered firmly. "I'm fine."

Once again, she knew she couldn't complain. Not about her pain. Not about what Wilkerson had said. The look on Tim's face was one of compassion and sadness. He obviously understood that there was a lot she wasn't saying. But there was no use in dwelling on Wilkerson's ignorance. She remembered the words her mother had spoken once when she was younger: *They're ignorant, Dani. So they think you're different? They're right! You are different. You're better.*

"I think I'm ready to shoot again," she said with confidence.

"I should say so." Tim handed her back the weapon. "Let's go, soldier."

Dani found her spot on the ground and shot the target straight in the center three times in a row. This time, with her eyes wide open.

5

Fall 2000 // West Point, New York

Twelve thirty on a misty afternoon in early September, four thousand cadets gathered in the mess hall, eating pierogies and passing plates of lemon-pepper chicken counterclockwise around the tables. Avery Adams rolled her head from side to side, trying to work out the tension that had appeared overnight. Plebes weren't allowed to speak at meals, and since they only had fifteen minutes to jam food into their mouths before jetting off to classes, everyone kept their head down, stuffing their face as quickly as possible. It was disgusting. Like they were a bunch of farm animals at a trough.

In August, all of the new cadets that had survived basic training had put on their as-for-class uniforms and joined the Corps of Cadets for the regular academic year. Training would commence again next summer, but until then, they were students. Writing assignments replaced weaponry. Homework took over hazing as the heaviest burden, and every weekend, the campus came alive with school spirit for the Army football team, which still hadn't won a game. Avery dreaded the uphill walk to Michie Stadium, where she was forced to stand and freeze while the quarterback threw interceptions for two hours straight. Games were mandatory fun, and she hated every second.

Avery caught herself staring at the bespectacled cadet seated in front of her, whose face was as pale as the white uniform shirt he was wearing. He ate so fast, it was a wonder he had time to breathe. Shaking her head in disgust, she looked back down at her plate and sighed.

Six months ago, she'd screamed and celebrated, having received her acceptance letter. The summer had introduced her to camouflage, ruck marching, orienteering through the woods, and the joys of memorizing useless trivia. Thanks to all the running her father had forced her to do leading up to R-Day, she'd quickly risen to the top of her platoon, scoring the highest possible marks on the Army Physical Fitness Test. In separate two-minute drills she could complete seventy-five push-ups and a hundred sit-ups. And when they sent her off for the two-mile run, Avery always returned within thirteen minutes flat. She hadn't just met West Point's standards; she'd exceeded them.

The guys in her platoon had wavered between seeming annoyed that a girl had outperformed them and grateful to have her strength among their ranks. Avery had seen some of the other girls in other platoons. There were the butch ones, who'd cut their hair into pixie-like styles before R-Day to prove that they were serious. Then there were the unathletic ones, who failed to keep up with the guys and so immediately lost their respect. Girls who were pretty *and* athletic were the fewest and farthest between. For that reason, Avery knew that her stock was high, and the attention gave her a rush. Every sideways glance, every prohibited flirtation, helped her breathe just a little bit easier. She was wanted, and that made her feel powerful.

Of course, she couldn't fully savor the extra attention. West Point followed a strict "ninety-degree" rule—if two people of the opposite sex were in a room together, the door had to be open at a ninety-degree angle. It was so antiquated, so ridiculous, and yet, everyone seemed to follow the rule with religious precision. If a male and female cadet were found together with the door closed, it could mean long hours of walking back and forth along cadet area in full regalia. Marching tours were West Point's favorite mode of punishment. Her TAC had explained that the rules existed to keep them focused on their academic and military instruction. To Avery, it all felt like a waste of her college experience.

But sure enough, once the academic year began, her schedule grew so hectic, she didn't have time to worry about West Point's outdated rules of decorum and chastity. The Corps of Cadets reported every morning at 0630 for formation, standing at attention in silence, watching their breath enter the freezing morning air, four thousand miniature clouds. West Point required plebes to take at least twenty-two hours of classes, meaning that Avery had eight courses to keep up with, including chemistry, Spanish, calculus, and a class in the Department of Military Instruction. Plebes weren't allowed to talk as they crossed campus between classes, and she had to address every upperclassman she passed with the proper rank and greeting. Her head moved on a constant swivel.

"Beat Rutgers, ma'am," Avery said to a Firstie who passed her way, naming Army's next opponent, as required.

An upperclassman who happened to be in her company, G-4, whose mascot was a gator, walked by her, and she quickly stammered, "Go gators, Sergeant." She moved past him in case she'd used the wrong rank. Was he a sergeant? Or a sir?

In high school, Avery had regularly worn blush and foundation, but West Point prohibited her from hiding her flaws, even the ones on the surface. Female plebes could wear light tinted moisturizer, but the standard for what constituted too much makeup was subjective and judged mainly by men. She'd risked concealing the pimples on her chin and the dark circles under her eyes only once. On that same day, she'd watched an upperclassman force a plebe who'd denied having makeup on her face to wipe her eyes on a towel. Smudges of beige and black streaked across the white fibers, and the upperclassman shook his head three times. Rumor had it, he'd reported the girl to the Honor Committee for lying. Avery had immediately rushed to the nearest bathroom and washed her face with harsh hand soap, wiping her eyes with a rough paper towel. If she was going to leave West Point, it was going to be on her own terms. Not because she'd used a little Maybelline.

That afternoon, Avery's turn had come up to be the "minute caller"—a job she'd been dreading since her first day at West Point. Ten minutes before lunch formation, she'd taken her place alone in the hallway announcing a list of memorized information, speaking loudly, slowly, and in a low monotone, like a man, so every cadet on the hall could hear her. Any slip-up or stumble would draw unwanted attention, and so Avery had studied the script for nearly an hour before stepping into the hallway and beginning.

"Attention all cadets . . . there are . . . *five minutes* . . . until assembly . . . for lunch formation."

"Don't mess up, Adams," an upperclassman had taunted, prowling around her like a predator.

"The uniform is . . . *as for class* . . ."

"Oh. I see you smiling. Don't slip up. I'll make you start over."

"For lunch we are having . . . lemon pepper chicken . . . pierogies . . . and Gatorade . . . I repeat . . . *Five minutes remaining* . . ."

Cadets underwent daily inspections for shined shoes and polished brass buckles. Upperclassmen could stop and check that her uniform was properly "dressed off," meaning tucked into her wool pants at a perfect forty-five-degree angle. At random intervals during the week, plebes were required to sort, fold, and deliver laundry to the upperclassmen in their company. In addition to all of her coursework, Avery had to memorize the names and room numbers of more than one hundred people, in order to properly deliver laundry and avoid hours of unnecessary hazing.

"Do I LOOK like a *female*, Cadet Darby?" she'd heard a Cow shouting at a plebe last night. He'd held up a gray skirt. "This isn't even my SIZE!"

To complete all of her military duties and not neglect her homework, Avery had taken to staying up far past taps. When her roommate, a girl from California named Nadine, complained that the light was going to get them in trouble, Avery had started using a small flashlight instead.

Streaming through the darkness, the small spotlight shined on chemistry equations while Nadine snored on top of her cot. Avery's notebooks filled with little lists, outlining her days in fifteen-minute increments, as if, by scheduling each minute, all the tasks she'd been assigned could possibly be completed. Meanwhile, she found herself daydreaming about her friends back home, friends who were probably sleeping late, skipping class, and attending parties on the weekends just because they *could*.

When Avery considered adding practices, games, and a hectic basketball travel schedule to her already-packed daily itinerary, it made her want to be sick. Last week, the team's captain, Sarah Goodrich, had sent out an e-mail inviting all the new recruits to an "optional" practice that clearly wasn't optional, since she'd couched *optional* in quotation marks. And when Avery wrote the practice on her calendar, she realized that something was going to have to give. What, she hadn't decided. Perhaps she'd have to stop sleeping altogether.

Her decision to come to West Point was beginning to feel like an exercise in pride that had bitten her harshly in the ass. Who *chooses* to enroll in a prison? It was a cruel bait and switch, to tell prospective students West Point was prestigious, only to treat them like shit once they got there.

The mess hall filled with a cacophony of sliding chairs, stacked plates, heavy feet leaving for class. Avery looked at her plate, still full of food. How had fifteen minutes already passed?

"That's it, plebes," her table leader, John Collins, said. He checked his watch, then put his fork down on his plate and gave Avery a wink. "Time to get your ass to class."

LATER THAT AFTERNOON, Avery made her way to the Holleder Center, a large complex that housed coaches' offices and a basketball arena for the men's and women's teams. She arrived twenty minutes early, hoping to shoot a few baskets before the rest of the team showed up. She'd expected the locker room to be empty, but when she turned the corner, Avery found herself face-to-face with a girl who was standing in front of a locker, completely naked.

"Oh God." Avery averted her eyes. "I'm so sorry."

"It's all good," the girl answered. If Avery wasn't mistaken, the girl chuckled, apparently amused by Avery's blushing cheeks.

Dropping her hand from her eyes, Avery tried to act cool, but it was hard to ignore how stunning this girl was. She had smooth brown skin and dark freckles across her face that looked like a map of the constellations. With a small waist and muscle definition, she looked like she could be on the cover of *Sports Illustrated*. Avery felt suddenly mediocre by comparison.

"You should see your face right now," the girl laughed as she put deodorant under her armpits.

"No. It's no big deal." Avery found her way to an open locker. "I just wasn't expecting anyone to be here."

The girl smiled wide. "I'm Dani."

"Avery," she replied. "So you're here to play basketball?"

"Oh, because I'm black?"

"No . . . ," Avery said slowly. She laughed. "I assumed you're playing basketball because you're in the women's locker room before basketball practice."

Dani smiled like Avery had just passed a test she hadn't signed up to take. "That's good detective work. Good *attention to detail*."

"I guess that means you're a plebe too."

"I consider slitting my wrists most nights, so yes."

They laughed, then dressed in silence for a while. But soon, Avery could no longer handle the quiet. It was hard to admit, but she knew it was true. After nearly ten weeks at West Point, Avery was desperate for a friend.

"So what position do you play?"

"Point guard. You?"

In that moment, it felt as though a hot knife had sliced through Avery's gut. She busied herself fixing her ponytail, hoping that Dani wouldn't notice her disappointment.

"What?" Dani asked.

But Avery didn't answer, because right at that moment, another group of women flooded through the doors, and Avery took that opportunity to exit into the gymnasium.

It's all right, Avery thought, trying to coach herself as she walked out onto the court and started to stretch. *So what? So Coach Jankovich recruited two point guards. Who's to say she's any good?*

THREE MINUTES INTO their "optional" practice, Dani had made it abundantly clear to everyone in the gymnasium that the team was only going to need one point guard. Time and time again, when they went after the same ball, Avery ended up on the floor, while Dani sprinted upcourt for an easy layup. The girl was fast and nimble. She dribbled the ball like it was tied to the center of her palm with an invisible string. Dani couldn't have been taller than five foot four, but somehow, even her petite frame worked to her advantage. She kept her center of gravity low, fooling even the most seasoned defenders. Worst of all, the girl was obnoxiously confident, quickly aligning herself with Sarah Goodrich and the other Firsties, throwing high fives and patting butts, as if they'd all known each other for years.

"What's her deal?" Avery said breathlessly to a new teammate, Hannah, when they'd both taken a moment to get water. Hannah Speer was also a plebe, and impossibly tall. When she looked at Avery like she didn't know what she meant, Avery jutted her chin out in Dani's general direction. "McNalley. She's been showing off this whole time."

Hannah just shrugged. "Everyone wants to make a good first impression. Can't blame her for that."

Avery found herself retreating to the bench for water more often than normal, simply to gather the emotional wherewithal to continue. There's nothing worse than believing you're talented, only to encounter a greater talent. And as the practice went on, Avery grew more and more despondent. Her performance went from lackluster to awkward, from awkward to embarrassing. And just when she thought things couldn't get worse, she looked up into the stands to see a thin woman sitting in the shadows.

Even from so far away, Avery could see the whites of the coach's eyes, trained on the court. Her long and slender fingers, wrapped around a pencil, were writing on a page on her clipboard.

The NCAA had strict rules about preseason practices—coaches weren't supposed to be at practices until the regular season started. That's why Sarah Goodrich had organized the practice instead of the coaches, and why she'd strategically added the word *optional* in the e-mail. But staring up at the coach in the stands, Avery's ears turned red with frustration. So it was an ambush. This "optional" practice was, in fact, an exhibition.

AFTER PRACTICE, THE locker room filled with steam. The black and gold striped carpet hid years of sweat and smelled dank with age. Maybe the girls were tired, or, Avery thought, maybe they'd noticed Coach Jankovich in the stands, too, because other than the sound of water spraying out of the showerheads, it was quiet. Surely the coach would take into account the fact they'd been at Basic Training all summer—naturally, they were all a little rusty. Avery had nearly convinced herself that everything would be okay—that she would have another chance to prove her skill—when the locker room door creaked open.

Coach Jankovich walked in, wearing a navy pantsuit and black high heels. A rush of cold air entered the locker room with her. Without speaking a word, she taped two white pieces of paper to the cinder-block wall by the door, and then left the way she came—in silence.

THE GIRLS STOOD like statues, each afraid to be the first to speak.

"Well I'll look," said Avery. Ignoring the growing dread in her stomach, she walked to the wall as if she didn't give a damn and stared at the papers, covered in Coach Jankovich's barely legible handwriting. "You've got to be kidding me."

"What?" asked Hannah.

At that moment, Dani walked out of the shower wrapped in a towel, surrounded by a cloud of steam. She wiped the inside of her ear with her pointer finger. "What's going on?" she asked.

"They're . . ." Hannah had walked up behind Avery and was staring at the pages, her voice full of shock. ". . . rosters."

Avery laughed sardonically, turned to grab her gym bag, and shook her head at Dani, who stood stunned in the middle of the room.

"Glad to know I survived Beast for *this shit*."

The two pages fluttered as Avery blew past them and out the door. The first page had "JV" written at the top, and below it, a long column of names. The other page said "Varsity" and listed only one.

BY EARLY OCTOBER, the trees on campus had turned from green to orange, like the whole place had been lit up in flames. At breakfast, Avery took her seat at her table and stabbed at her eggs with murderous rage.

"Someone piss in your pancakes, princess?"

The upperclassman at the head of the table, John Collins, offered her a wide smile. A Spanish major with green eyes and wavy black hair, Collins was handsome, funny, and extremely bored it seemed, since he was surrounded by a table of plebes who weren't allowed to talk.

"No excuse, sir." Avery faked a smile, took an oversized bite of eggs.

But she did have an excuse. She had a million excuses.

After the first few varsity basketball games, Dani McNalley had become something of a celebrity on campus. Avery didn't need a crystal ball to predict how her career as an NCAA athlete was going to unfold. Dani was going to secure every possible minute of playing time for the season—maybe even all four years. Avery would ride the bench.

She felt trapped, like Coach Jankovich had promised her a place on the team, only to abandon her to the sidelines. In light of her rejection, everything about West Point chafed against her. She had to check the hall for upperclassmen before darting from her dorm room. Plebes were forced to walk like Pac-Man, in straight lines, only taking right-angled turns. You could spot plebes at West Point, walking along the perimeter of the hallways, squaring off with their eyes straight ahead, trying not to be noticed. By contrast, upperclassmen walked wherever they wanted and spoke freely among themselves. It was enough to drive Avery crazy, watching them flaunt their freedom. Every time someone yelled at her, the voice inside Avery's head repeated their instructions with an added layer of sarcasm.

"Adams, move to the wall!"

You move to the wall, she would rant in her inner dialogue.

"New Cadet, stop right there and recite the 'Alma Mater.'"

You recite the fucking alma mater!

Instead, she'd bite her tongue and do as she was told, allowing the anger to boil inside of her, unsure of when it might explode.

Avery placed her fork on her plate.

"Okay," Collins announced suddenly, breaking the silence.

"New rules. As long as you use your radio, you can talk. New Cadet Willis," Collins said, addressing the plebe who sat across from Avery midbite. "Your call sign is Trojan, because you'll never need one."

Avery fought back a laugh. He went down the table, assigning nicknames. When he got to Avery, he stopped, looked her up and down. "Adams. Your name is About-Face, because all you ever do is sulk, and if it's the last thing I do, I'm going to get you to smile."

"*Chhhhhh*—ah, Eagle for About-Face. Come in, About-Face," he started, pretending to hold a radio in his hand. "What's your twenty?"

Avery rolled her eyes.

"*Chhhh*—sorry, About-Face, I'm not getting that. Check your radio."

With her hand curled around an imaginary radio, Avery decided to play along.

"*Chhhh*—roger that, Eagle, I'm downwind of Trojan. Smells like he's looking for a place to defecate, sir. Over and out."

The table erupted in laughter, Trojan included. Satisfied, Avery offered a flirtatious wink to Collins, then picked up her fork and kept eating.

MIDTERMS SWALLOWED WHOLE weeks of October. Cadets attended nonstop review sessions and banged out sixteen-page research papers, and a chemistry exam nearly flattened Avery with its intensity. When she wasn't at basketball practice with the JV team, Avery was buried beneath her books, trying desperately to stay afloat. Her GPA was a sorry 3.2, and with that, Avery was happy. Then all the leaves detached from their branches, glittering through the air like falling gold. They'd gathered in rotting piles on the ground before Avery could appreciate the beauty of their death.

After that, campus went gray. People had warned her about this: during the winter, West Point was a depressing palette of black and white. Charcoal river, stone buildings and roads, slate uniforms, cloudy skies. Barren and lifeless, the whole place felt like Siberia, and the thin wool coat Avery had been issued over the summer suddenly didn't stand a chance against the wind chill.

"Attention all cadets . . . there are *four minutes* . . ."

"Today's uniform . . . is *battle dress uniform* . . ."

As the weeks passed, Avery's life fell into a rhythm that, if not enjoyable, was at least predictable. At practice, Dani McNalley barely spoke to Avery. Instead, that girl spoke exclusively to upperclassmen—as though if she separated herself from the plebes, she would no longer be one. Sarah Goodrich and her friends adopted Dani into their fold, and had even invited Dani to some *Bible study* they attended, an invitation Avery would never receive, but would have liked to turn down.

She tried her best to ignore her growing jealousy by taking long runs around campus whenever she had a spare thirty minutes. The only reprieve from the madness had become her twice-daily meals with Collins and his imaginary radio. West Point explicitly prohibited plebes from dating upperclassmen, but somehow, the fact that he was off-limits made Collins that much more attractive. By mid-November, she'd moved to the seat directly next to his, letting her leg brush up against his under the table. That went on for a few days, until he responded, clutching his hand around her upper thigh. She felt her eyes roll back in her head at the warmth of his touch.

It was innocent, she told herself. A game she knew she could win.

ON THE SECOND Tuesday in November, the day before they left for Thanksgiving break, Avery sat on a cold metal chair outside of Coach Jankovich's office, waiting her turn. The coach had scheduled one-on-one meetings with her players, called "MSTEs," short for "midseason team evaluations," which made Avery roll her eyes so hard, she thought they might disconnect from her brain. It was clear that Jankovich had worked hard to create an acronym of her own, as if West Point hadn't already filled their lives with an alphabet soup of abbreviations.

Fifteen minutes after Avery's scheduled MSTE, Coach Jankovich's office door opened, and out came Dani McNalley, holding a folded piece of paper. She made eye contact with Avery, her eyes full and intense—like two headlights on the front of a car, barreling through the night. Avery couldn't quite decipher whether Dani was angry or sad. It didn't matter.

"Adams," Coach Jankovich barked from inside her office. "You're up."

Inside, the office felt cold and lifeless. Empty plastic water bottles and stacks of paperwork covered her desk, unattended and unorganized. *No way this place would pass inspection,* Avery thought. It was a wonder Coach Jankovich still had a job at a place like West Point. Her players had to keep their beds made with hospital corners, their mirrors devoid of a single speck of dust, and yet, her office looked like a tornado had just passed through.

"Take a seat," the coach said. Her dark brown hair, streaked with white, gave her the appearance of a skunk, and for some reason, Avery suddenly felt on edge, like Coach Jankovich had caught her doing something illegal and couldn't wait to show off all of her evidence. Shifting in her seat, Avery opened her mouth, but was cut off before she could say a word.

"This is your midseason report. You can see here, you're fifty-two percent at the line. Not great. You've outpaced Hannah Speer and Lisa Johnson with your defensive rebounds, which isn't bad. But I think we both know you're not where you need to be. You had great stats in high school, but here, you've haven't exactly reached the right level of play."

Avery's body filled with heat, and she struggled to breathe, like a heavy cloud had formed in her chest.

"When I compare your stats with varsity, I mean . . . it's just impossible to compare." Coach Jankovich focused on the page in front of her, avoiding the eyes of her player. "For example, Dani McNalley hit seventy percent of her free throws."

Avery cleared her throat, trying to regain her confidence. "That's actually what I wanted to ask you about. Dani. I'd like a chance to play against her. I mean, she's great. I know that. But I've improved a lot since September. And I think if you gave me a shot, you'd be—"

"We don't reward players for being the most improved," Coach Jankovich replied. "We reward players for being the best."

"Okay," Avery said, swallowing the hurt. She'd never not been the best. The words that came next sounded foreign coming out of her mouth. "So what do I need to do?"

"Well, Avery, you just don't have the edge. And unfortunately, that's not something I can teach."

The hair on the back of her neck stood on end. Staring at this woman—this person who had convinced her that West Point was *the best option available*—Avery felt something deflate inside of her. "So that's it?"

Avery couldn't fight the tears any longer. "I'm sorry, but, if you're not going to give me a chance to play, why am I even here?"

Coach Jankovich crossed her arms over her chest and sighed. "To be frank, Avery, we assumed one of you would quit during basic training." She held out a tissue box, but Avery refused to take it from her. "I'm just being honest with you. With McNalley here I doubt you'll see much of the court. That's just the way it is. So you can come, participate in practice, and be part of the JV team. Or you can quit now, take a red shirt, and transfer to some other school, where you can play in a year or two. It's your choice."

The coach handed Avery the paper printout, then turned to look at her computer.

"Send in whoever's next."

AVERY EXPLODED OUT of the Holleder Center into the wintry air, breathless and angry. *We assumed one of you would quit.* Was that what she was to them? A backup plan? Not worth coaching? *You just don't have the edge.* What did that even mean?

Avery had ignored Hannah on the way out of the Holleder Center and ran back to cadet area, letting the wind freeze the tears on her cheeks. *It's just not enough.* That's what Coach J had said. And she was right. As fast as Avery was, there would always be someone faster. As pretty as she was, there would always be someone like Hannah, who was downright *angelic*. What was the point of trying to be good? She'd tried. And she was tired of trying.

When she found her way back to the barracks, Avery knew exactly what she was doing. It didn't matter that she was covered in sweat and tears and that she hadn't showered. His room was two floors above hers, she knew because she'd delivered his laundry just last week. If she was lucky, he would be there when she arrived, rules be damned.

She stood in the hallway outside of his door, her heart racing in her chest, looking to her left and to her right before she raised a fist to knock. If his roommate answered, she would be ruined. She had no way to explain why she, a plebe, needed to see Collins, a Cow, at ten thirty on a Tuesday night. But thankfully, when the door opened, the green eyes and half smile of her table leader were there, accompanied by a half-hearted laugh.

"About-Face?" he said, shocked. "What are you . . ."

Avery peered behind him, saw that his roommate was not there, and then stepped into his room, closed the door, and turned the lock. Breathless, she pulled her shirt off over her head, and savored the look on his face as his eyes dropped in awe.

"Get undressed, Collins," she ordered.

And he obeyed.

6

Spring 2001 // West Point, New York

I assume you're all ready for today's discussion?"

There was a quiet murmur of assent from all of the cadets in the room.

Hannah sat front and center, wearing BDUs and lining up her pens in a perfect row like soldiers. Red for the most important notes. A highlighter for text in the book. Black gel for transcribing portions of Colonel Bennett's lecture. There was little about West Point that Hannah could control, but at least in the classroom, she knew how to excel. The spiral notebook in front of her was full of notes from the semester, with dates written in perfect cursive handwriting at the top right of each page.

"Good, good." The professor dropped a copy of Plato's *The Republic* on his podium and smiled. "Before we cut into this juicy piece of philosophical goodness, let me check with our section marcher. Mr. Arant?"

While the cadet in charge looked around the room to take roll, Hannah looked at Colonel Bennett. He wore a green uniform with an eagle emblem on the lapel, showing his rank. He was in his midfifties, with peppery brown hair and the clean-shaven face of a man who'd been in the military for most of his life. At the beginning of the semester, when Hannah had walked into his classroom, she'd immediately recognized him. Colonel Bennett and his wife, Wendy, the couple that had hosted her family the night before R-Day, also had season tickets to all of West Point's home basketball games. During the varsity games, the JV players sat in the bleachers in the row just in front of the Bennetts.

"You doing okay?" Wendy would always ask Hannah at some point during each varsity game.

"Yes, ma'am," Hannah would assure her, even if it was a lie. "I'm doing good."

The piece of paper with Wendy's phone number on it was stuffed in the back of her desk somewhere. Hannah had never used it. More than once, Hannah had promised to try to attend the Bible study Wendy hosted at her house, but every Wednesday night, she'd find herself buried under a pile of homework, simply trying to keep up.

"You coming?" Sarah Goodrich had asked the previous Wednesday, popping her head into Hannah's barracks.

"I can't," Hannah had said, gripping the silver cross necklace in her hand and surveying the pile of textbooks and assignments in front of her. "Sorry . . . I just . . ."

"Books don't love you back, you know."

Guilt had washed over Hannah in that moment, and she'd groaned, putting her head on her desk. Against her better judgment, she let Sarah drag her out of the barracks and up a steep, snow-covered staircase to Lusk Area, where she'd defrosted in front of the Bennetts' fireplace, eating homemade chili followed by brownies and ice cream. It had been a moment of calm in a world of constant discomfort.

Now, waiting on Cadet Arant to finish taking attendance, Hannah flipped through the first few pages of the book, frantically trying to remember anything she'd read the night before. Passages were underlined and highlighted, but the words meant nothing to her. She wondered if overexercising could cause temporary amnesia.

After losing three games in a row, Coach Jankovich had transformed her practices from predictably horrible to outright sadistic. At the previous night's practice, it had been easier to name the girls who *didn't* throw up than those who did, and sadly, Hannah was among the latter.

"Do you *want* to lose?" Coach Jankovich had shouted after the varsity team lost on the road at Rutgers. She'd lined them all up on the baseline of the opponent's gymnasium, long after the stands had cleared of fans. Hannah saw the Rutgers janitor standing at the door, waiting to wax the floor. But Coach Jankovich didn't seem to notice him, or if she did, she didn't mind making him wait. She blew her whistle ferociously, sending them sprinting across the court, watching the Rutgers logo pass beneath their feet. Hannah and Avery hadn't even been a part of the varsity squad that had lost the game, and yet, they sprinted. Jankovich's shrill whistle pierced Hannah's ears. It echoed through her dreams.

"This can't be normal," Avery had whispered under her breath to Hannah on the flight back from Colorado last week, after they'd watched the varsity team lose to the Air Force Academy. In the last seconds of the game, Coach Jankovich had lost her cool, screaming maniacally at a referee. As punishment for the loss, the players were told to spend the flight back in silence.

"What if we all just quit?" Avery continued. "If we all quit at the same time, they'd *have* to fire her."

Hannah just shook her head and went back to doing her calculus practice problems, hunched over her tiny airplane tray table.

The truth was, there was nothing normal about Coach Jankovich. Hannah had spent the season trying to understand the woman's tactics, and the best she could come up with was that Coach Jankovich was simply scared of losing her job. As the first woman to ever hold the position of head women's basketball coach at West Point, she had a lot on the line, Hannah knew. Coach Jankovich hadn't shown her players a single moment of vulnerability—hadn't once provided an inspirational quote or a pat on the back. Instead, it seemed that the only way Coach Jankovich maintained her confidence was by belittling her players and reminding them of her authority. She was paranoid, Hannah thought, the kind of coach who believed she could shame her players into greatness, as if having all of their flaws exposed would suddenly make the players feel motivated to improve.

Hannah wondered if Coach Jankovich had always been this way, or if she'd adopted some twisted militant coaching philosophy when she'd arrived at West Point, imagining that her boss, a three-star Army general, would expect her to be tough. But the hazing Hannah endured in the barracks felt more productive than what Coach Jankovich put them through. At least the upper-classmen acknowledged Hannah's effort. At least they all laughed from time to time. Yes, the cadre in her company had broken her down, but were just as intent on building her up.

The only player who didn't put her head in a trash can at last night's practice was Avery, the second-string point guard from Pittsburgh. Early in the season, Avery had mentioned that she felt Coach Jankovich wouldn't care if she quit. Hannah didn't see that. Sure, Coach J was hard on them, and yes, splitting them into two teams was unexpected. But what else could they do? At least they got to play—even if it was just JV games.

But by the second semester of their plebe year, halfway through the basketball season, Hannah had started to notice that the harder Avery worked on the court, the harder Coach J worked to ignore her. Once, Hannah had literally watched the coach turn her back when Avery sank a three-point shot. Another time, when Avery recovered an impossible rebound in midair and threw it back into play before touching her feet out of bounds, Coach said *nothing*. It was strange. Neurotic, even.

Coach's willful disdain for Avery and some of the other play-ers had started to bother Hannah, if she was honest. She found herself worrying about Avery off the court too, the way a mother might worry over her rebellious daughter. Cadets savored stories like sweet and satisfying grapes plucked off of the vine of campus gossip. And with Avery, it seemed the harvest was plentiful.

"I heard she's slept with ten guys. All upperclassmen."

"I heard it was twelve."

"No, it's just one guy, but twelve times."

"I heard they did it on the roof of the library."

Hannah wasn't one to indulge in gossip, but there were too many stories being passed around for all of them to be false. Clearly *something* had happened with *someone,* because when Lisa Johnson had confronted Avery about it in the locker room, she'd just grinned and put a single finger over her lips, and said, "Don't ask, because I won't tell."

The whole exchange had made Hannah supremely uncomfortable. Did Avery *really* think that sleeping with some guy in the first few months of college was a good idea? Plus, if Avery was sneaking into an upperclassman's dorm room at night, as the rumors alleged, she was putting her entire future at West Point in jeopardy, let alone her reputation. Last semester, a couple in Hannah's company had been found making out behind closed doors, and they'd both been given a hundred hours of walking tours. For the next ten Saturdays, Hannah had watched them both walking back and forth along the concrete of cadet area, wearing full dress gray uniform, carrying their rifles against their shoulders—rain or shine. It was medieval punishment, all that walking. But it was better than the alternative, which was to be kicked out of the academy. It wasn't that Hannah was a prude, but she worried that Avery wasn't thinking clearly. Sooner or later, all those bad decisions would catch up to her. To Hannah, nothing was worth the risk of losing her Saturdays. After all, without her Saturdays, when would she get all of her homework done?

Cadet Arant had just read out the name *Nesmith,* bringing Hannah out of her thoughts—but as usual, there was no response. The professor paused. "Anyone seen Tim?"

The classroom door opened, and a tall, olive-skinned cadet hustled through, checking the clock to ensure he'd beat the buzzer, which he had, by mere seconds. Hannah sat up a little taller in her seat. Tim smiled, flashing a perfect row of white teeth to the class. He had one dimple in his right cheek.

"Sorry," the cadet said. "No excuse, sir."

"Isn't that what you said yesterday, Nesmith?" a classmate called out.

"Take your seat," Colonel Bennett said. "You're playing with fire."

Hannah watched Tim unpack his backpack and ask his neighbor for a pencil. Then, nonchalantly, he pointed at the book on Colonel Bennett's podium and turned his lips into a frown, like he was surprised to find that they'd moved on to another book. Hannah looked at the notebook in front of her, full of quotations that she'd jotted down while completing the assigned reading, and shook her head. She couldn't fathom being nearly late and so unprepared for class so many days in a row. But this kid? This Tim character? Nothing seemed to faze him.

She'd watched him out of the corner of her eye for weeks now, studying him as closely as she'd studied Plato. He was muscular but not bulky, tall but not gangly, with a stately jaw and that one dimple that indented his cheek every time he smiled. When he walked into the room, the energy shifted toward him, like he was the sun and they were all those jungle plants that grow at odd angles simply to catch a ray. Tim's humble charisma had even charmed their professor into letting his near-tardiness slide.

Hannah knew she shouldn't be attracted to him—he was a mess. Yesterday, he'd come in with toothpaste caked in the corner of his mouth, and she'd noticed the small black outline of a tattoo peeking out from under his short uniform sleeve more than once. She'd *never* been attracted to a guy with a tattoo. How could someone mark something so permanent on their body? Didn't he worry he'd regret it someday? And yet, there was something about Tim's smile that made her constantly look at him. He was interesting. Like a puzzle she wanted to solve.

Colonel Bennett wrote a question across the whiteboard with a red dry-erase marker.

"The rest of the semester, we will tackle this book, and its central question." The teacher pointed at the board.

WHAT IS JUSTICE?

The room was silent while Colonel Bennett walked through a comprehensive timeline of Greek philosophy. Hannah looked down at her notes and stared at the question, which she'd written at the top of a fresh page in her spiral notebook. *Justice.* She thought of *Law and Order* on television, bad guys getting what they deserve. She thought of a gavel slamming against wood and a widow receiving help from her neighbors. She thought of D-day and American soldiers liberating France from German occupation during World War II. These were examples of justice, weren't they? But she was pretty certain that wasn't what

Colonel Bennett wanted to hear. He wanted a definition. And all Hannah could think was that justice came from God. She wouldn't dare say that aloud.

The officer began pacing the room, shiny black shoes carrying him back and forth. He pointed at the board.

"So. What is it?"

A cadet to Hannah's left lifted his pencil. "Justice is doing the right thing, even when no one is looking, sir."

"Okay. Good. That's a fine place to start." The professor added *Righteousness* to the board. "Anyone else?" he asked.

Tim Nesmith cleared his throat and raised his hand. The professor pointed at him, giving him the floor.

"With respect to my classmate," Tim began, "all people have different definitions of what they see as *right*. For example, for some people, doing the right thing means following the law. But if there's an unjust law on the books—think Jim Crow South— wouldn't the right thing be to ignore that law? So, in my opinion, justice can't be defined as doing what's *right*. Because who defines *rightness*?"

The class grew quiet again. Hannah fought the urge for her jaw to drop, amazed at his confidence. Who was this kid?

"And if I may be so bold," he continued, "Army soldiers and officers are given permission to do something that in all other circumstances is considered morally *wrong*. Was it right in World War II to kill Nazis? Yes. But I'm certain the Nazis told their soldiers the same thing about killing the Allied forces."

"Mr. Nesmith makes an excellent point," the professor said. "Socrates points out that laws, even laws that we create for ourselves, can be unjust, with or without our knowledge." Colonel Bennett took a meaningful pause and then continued. "What are you going to do if the government you've taken an oath to serve asks you to do something that isn't just?"

"Civil disobedience," someone said.

"Conscientious objection," added another.

"Resistance," said Tim.

A slick of sweat took up residence on Hannah's palms as she considered whether or not to raise her hand. She hated speaking in class and rarely took the risk. It was an easy equation: if she never spoke, she'd never say something stupid.

But Tim had touched a nerve. Of *course* it was right to kill Nazis. Just because someone *claimed* that they were right didn't *make* them right. In Hannah's heart, she knew that justice existed far above any human opinion. But rather than bring her faith into the conversation, Hannah looked through her notes from the night before, searching for something to say. At West Point, she'd learned, you couldn't get by with simply nodding along. A good portion of her grade was participation, and with only twelve students in the classroom, there was nowhere to hide. Timidly, she put her hand in the air. Colonel Bennett looked her way.

"Miss Speer."

"On page one ninety-seven, Socrates says that stealing a weapon from a madman is actually the right thing to do. So— stealing might be wrong in most contexts, but stealing a weapon from someone threatening to harm himself or others is the *right* thing to do. I guess what I'm trying to say is that I . . . I think we're all born with a sense of right and wrong. We know what's right, deep down. And just because two people—or two countries—claim to be right, doesn't mean they're both right. There is such a thing as *right*, objectively."

Tim Nesmith shook his head. "But who gets to determine who's *actually* right?" he said. "You can't define a feeling."

Hannah felt her face flush red. Shut down, defeated, she sank back into her seat, desperately trying to disappear into the linoleum floor. Did this guy really believe that there was no truth at all?

"Fair enough, Mr. Nesmith," Colonel Bennett said, "but Miss Speer brought up a good point. And at least we know she completed the reading."

The class laughed in unison, and this time, it was Tim's cheeks that turned pink. But then he shrugged, laughing at himself. Moving back to his podium, Colonel Bennett picked up *The Republic* and held it in his hand.

"For students at other colleges, philosophy may seem theoretical and arbitrary. But the way that you answer this question will impact your life in real and tangible ways." He paused, put the book down, and then continued. "In just a few short years, you're going to be officers in the U.S. Army. Unlike those kids at other schools, you're going to be leading soldiers and making decisions that could have life-or-death consequences. As leaders of the U.S. Army, we must believe that justice is a concrete, definable concept, and we must always be striving to live our lives in line with that ideal. At the end of the day, we must be able to say with certainty that the Nazis *were* wrong. And although they might have made the same truth *claims,* in the end, it was the right thing to do to defeat them. Yes, Miss Speer?"

Hannah had lifted her hand again, which seemed to shock everyone in the room, especially herself.

"Sorry, I had one more thought."

"Never apologize for thinking."

"You asked us what we would do if our sense of justice conflicted with our sense of duty. What I was trying to say earlier was that if you believe in justice, you have to risk being wrong for the sake of what's right. You have to choose."

Nodding, the professor turned the back of his green Army uniform to the class. On the board, he wrote *CHOICE*. On another part of the board, he wrote *RISK*.

"Very good, Miss Speer," he said respectfully. Moving back to his podium, he picked up *The Republic* and continued lecturing, as his pupils scribbled frantically in their notebooks, trying to keep up. Asking more questions, prodding them further, the professor walked them through the rest of the reading, until the clock ran out on class.

"The next reading assignment is listed in the syllabus," he said. "And your first reflection paper is due next week, too. Don't forget. Class dismissed."

Chairs squealed against the floor and all the cadets stood up and adjusted their uniforms. Hannah packed her backpack quickly, hoping to reach Tim before he jetted out the door. Taking a risk had worked during class, and she was hoping it would work with him, too. Across the room, he slid his backpack over his shoulders, revealing the lean muscles in his arms and releasing a fleet of butterflies into Hannah's stomach. She was two steps behind him, about to reach out and touch his shoulder—to say what, she hadn't decided—when she heard her name.

"Hannah," the professor said, calling her back toward his desk.

All the courage she'd mustered fell apart as her arm lowered. Another opportunity, missed. She turned back and smiled at Colonel Bennett, trying to hide her disappointment.

"I just wanted to check on you," he said. "My wife and I were at that last game. I was sorry to see that you didn't get a chance to play."

"Oh, that's all right," Hannah said. "The older girls really are good. For some reason it's just not clicking yet. Actually, I have to get going." She pointed at the door. "Coach J makes us run if we're late to practice."

"Well, I don't want to hold you up, but I did want to say that we're here for you. Keep it up. I know it's hard to believe, but plebe year is almost over."

"Thanks, Colonel Bennett," said Hannah sincerely.

"And great job today," he said as she headed out the door. "Someone's got to keep that Nesmith on his toes."

RUNNING BACK TO the barracks, Hannah dropped off her schoolwork and picked up her basketball bag, certain she would be late to practice. As she sprinted uphill toward the Holleder Center, where the men's and women's basketball teams practiced, the first hints of spring called for her attention. Small packs of daffodils popped through the grass like little trumpets, heralding the end of winter. Buds on the trees outlined every limb with a hint of green. The brutal winter temperatures were finally breaking, and even though she was late, she loved the sensation of the first hints of warmth on her skin. The season always reminded her that no matter what, change would eventually come. Things could look absolutely dead—completely hopeless—and yet, the future always held the promise of new life.

Fearing Coach J's fury, Hannah picked up her pace and tried not to be distracted by the flowers in bloom. As she entered the gym and jogged down the hall, she quickly tucked her silver cross necklace into her T-shirt and checked her watch, which told her she was three minutes late. The next thing she knew, Hannah looked up, expecting to push through the door to the women's locker room, but instead crashed into a guy standing in the doorway.

"Whoa, whoa," he said to her, putting up a hand between them. "Slow down, plebe."

The cadet wore black gym shorts and West Point's typical gray T-shirt with his last name blazoned above the school crest. Hannah read it quickly, the way you'd read the license plate of a car in the midst of a hit-and-run. *COLLINS*. It sounded familiar, but Hannah couldn't exactly pinpoint where she'd heard the name before. The cadet had sharp green eyes, wavy black hair, and a smile that made Hannah feel unsettled. He was standing too close to her.

"Sorry," Hannah said, though she wasn't sure why she was apologizing—*he* was the one standing in her way.

"No problem," he said with confidence. "I was just checking on your TP supply. Someone said you guys were running low."

Something about his story didn't exactly add up. Hannah had never heard of a cadet working at the Holleder Center—and didn't they have janitors to resupply toilet paper? Perhaps he'd been in trouble with his company or sports team. Could he be cleaning as punishment? If she'd had more time, she would have asked him. But she was already late.

"Oh, okay. Thanks," she said, stepping around him to push through the locker room door. "See ya."

"Yep," he said. "See ya."

In the empty locker room, Hannah dropped her bag, changed clothes, and quickly forgot about Collins. It didn't matter why he was snooping around the Holleder Center. She needed to get out onto the court, and fast, before Coach J had her running suicides until she puked. Again. On a normal day, being this late would have put her in a panic. But Hannah couldn't help but smile, thinking about Colonel Bennett's last words before she'd left his classroom.

"Someone's got to keep that Nesmith on his toes."

He was right. And something inside Hannah's heart told her she just might be the perfect girl for the job.

7

Summer 2001 // West Point, New York

Here's your bay number, Cadet McNalley. Grab your rucksack from the truck. Cross over the gravel road. Bay number eight is a half mile up the hill to the left. Next."

Camp Buckner, part of West Point's military training ground, was located five miles from campus in the middle of the woods. It looked like the set of *Dirty Dancing,* only Patrick Swayze had been replaced by countless other shirtless boys, pretending to be on a mission. A group of guys commanded the volleyball court, already midgame. Another group carried kayaks out onto the lake. Cicadas, mosquitoes, and gnats buzzed around her, adding to the hum of the afternoon. *Now, this is college,* Dani thought to herself as she received her packet of information from the cadet behind the table and then moved back outside into the mid-July heat. A closed-lipped smile spread across her face.

Of course, all the fun happening today would end abruptly tomorrow when training began.

IN ONE YEAR at West Point, Dani had already learned that friendships born in comfortable circumstances rarely last when times get tough. Her friends from high school just didn't understand. There was something about being dirty, wet, and exhausted that forced two people to look one another in the eye and burst out laughing. When you get to the end of your rope, and the person next to you is at the end of theirs, it's possible to find a secret joy that you're simply surviving together. It was how she and Tim had become such great friends last summer, and how the entire varsity basketball team had bonded, over their shared hatred of Coach Jankovich.

People assumed they would have better friends if they hosted better parties. But the opposite was true. Shared suffering led to unshakeable connections. Pain wanted you to stop. Give up. Quit. But the truth was, you could go so much further than your body said you could, because when the body quit, the heart took over, and the heart was far more powerful than any muscle in the body. It had led women to lift cars off children. It had led men to sacrifice their own lives for their friends—even some for their enemies.

You couldn't teach that kind of strength. You had to live it. You had to believe what others who had been to that dark place told you. In whispers. In silence. "Trust me. There's joy down there."

You could believe them, but you still had to live it.

For the next eight weeks, the entire class of 2004 would live it. Together, they would learn to fire cannons, care for the wounded, shoot live rounds, complete urban missions, overcome a water obstacle course, and navigate through the woods with nothing but a gun, a compass, and a map. The entire place was like a little boy's dream camp, filled with real tanks, helicopters, and even a handful of enemy combatants—enlisted soldiers from nearby Fort Drum who would dress up like rebel fighters. Buckner would be far better than last year's Basic Training because she could talk, and because she no longer walked around with eyes permanently bulging. All of the upperclassmen had promised this would be the best summer of her life. And even though their words were drenched with sarcasm, Dani knew they were right.

A year ago, her idea of a dream camp had included a basketball, a hoop, and maybe a few good-looking coaches thrown in. But the Army? Field training? *When did I become so gung-ho?* Dani wondered. But she didn't have enough time to consider what a difference a year makes, because at that moment, an Army Humvee arrived, stuffed to the brim with rucksacks—one of which was hers. She needed to find it and go claim a bunk bed before the only one left was above a girl who snored.

AS SHE APPROACHED the truck, three boys opened the hatch and climbed up to start unloading. The tallest of the group was an African-American kid Dani hadn't seen before. He wore his camouflage pants high on his waist, with a belt cinched tight around his hips. There was something otherworldly about him;

his dark hair had been shaved close to his head, and he maneuvered the heavy luggage with ease. The more he worked, the silkier his dark brown skin looked in the sun, and Dani felt suddenly embarrassed. She wasn't normally one to gawk—but, *Lord,* she thought, *he is not normal.*

"Hey!" she shouted toward the shirtless marvel. Up close, he looked like an action figure. "You see McNalley up there?"

Turning, he wiped his forehead and shouted back, "You seen some patience?"

"Nope. Not lately," replied Dani.

"Why don't you come up and look for it," he said, offering her his hand. She took it, and in one motion, he hoisted her up onto the back of the truck, like she weighed nothing at all. For a moment, they were inches apart, Dani staring into his deep brown eyes, shocked by his disarming smile, punctuated by a gap between his front two teeth.

"Locke Coleman," the guy said, then opened up his hands as if to tell Dani that the truck was hers to explore. "You might as well look for mine while you're at it."

"Your patience or your bag?"

"I've seen you before," he said simply. "Aren't you that point guard?"

"That's right," said Dani, flattered that he'd seen her play.

"Sucks to lose, don't it?" he said jokingly. "Y'all had a rough season."

"Thanks for the pep talk."

"No disrespect! I play football. I'm familiar with the losing feeling."

"We're going to change that this year, Coleman," another cadet on the truck shouted. "Fuck Navy. Hey, what'd you say your name was?"

"McNalley," Dani answered.

A rucksack flew through the air and she caught it against her chest.

"Thanks, guys. See you around."

She and Locke Coleman exchanged one long moment of eye contact before she jumped off the truck and quickly walked off across the gravel road toward the bunkhouses. The pressure of his palm against hers had sent an electric shock up her spine. She didn't want to forget that feeling anytime soon, and yet, she didn't want to read too much into their interaction, either. Guys always loved to hang out with her, but they rarely saw her as *girlfriend material*." It was her constant relationship kryptonite. She was one of the boys.

BUNKHOUSE NUMBER EIGHT smelled like summer camp: a hopeful combination of sweat, sunscreen, and plastic mattresses, worn out by years of use. Down the narrow hallway, girls were hugging, laughing, and unpacking unnecessary toiletries. Boys roamed the hall half-dressed, checking out who would be living in close proximity for the next eight weeks. Dani shook her head, surprised by the insanity of the premise: West Point put a thousand nineteen-year-olds in the woods for a summer, crossed their fingers, and hoped for the best. It was like a social experiment, created to determine how much sexual frustration you could stuff into one square mile.

Suddenly, a girl with dirty-blond hair dressed in black shorts and a gray T-shirt stepped into the hallway. Dani immediately recognized Hannah Speer and felt a surge of gratitude fill her chest. Straightforward and honest, Hannah had spent last year working hard on the JV basketball team, never once complaining or holding a grudge against Dani for her success on varsity. Minutes earlier, Dani had had no idea who she'd be forced to live with, but now, seeing Hannah's bright blue eyes and easy smile, she knew she'd have at least one friend this summer.

"McNalley!" Hannah shouted. "Get down here!"

Trotting quickly, Dani arrived in the doorway and peeked inside. Five bunk beds lined the walls, leaving a square space on the floor. Smiling, Dani surveyed the girls in the room and realized she recognized every single face—the entire sophomore class of female basketball recruits. Lisa Johnson and Megan O'Leary had claimed the bunk by the back wall. Kate Shoemaker's rucksack waited on the bottom bunk near the door, and above that, Dani spotted a bright-blond ponytail hanging down from the top bunk, as if Rapunzel were letting down her hair. The girl turned over and looked down, her eyes assessing Dani with sharp disdain.

Avery Adams let out a loud sigh, then rolled back over. "Oh great. Gang's all here."

Dani looked to Hannah, who quickly waved Avery off with a gesture that said, *Ignore her.* But the moment was hard to disregard. If she was going to live in this tiny room, crammed with ten girls for the entire summer, Dani at least wanted to feel welcome.

"Is there a problem, Adams?" she said. "Because we can address it right now, if you'd like. Unless you'd rather go across the hall and sleep with the offensive line?"

"Excuse me?" Avery snapped, closing the magazine. "They don't have enough room over there for you? Your *ego* take up too much space?"

"Hey, hey, hey," Hannah interjected, putting her hands up. "Just everybody chill out, okay? Geez. We just got here."

Avery looked down at Hannah, who offered the same wave of the hand that minutes before she'd given Dani. Though she could have been pissed, the whole interaction made Dani laugh. Hannah was clearly the mother of the crew—already fulfilling her role perfectly.

Though Dani had never noticed it before, Avery and Hannah looked like they could be sisters. Avery's hair was lighter and Hannah was taller, but side by side, they looked like opposing reflections in a mirror. It was fascinating to Dani that two people who looked so alike on the surface could be so different beneath it. Avery cussed quickly and often, while Hannah's favorite curse word was *shenanigans*. Avery held her body like she knew how to use it, while Hannah bumped into things clumsily, like a little girl who still wasn't used to having an adult body. Appearances could be so very deceiving.

For the time being, Dani decided to follow Hannah's advice and ignore Avery's rude behavior. To room with the girls' basketball team all summer was far better than getting stuck with a bunch of random girls she didn't know. But West Point wasn't keen on giving out pleasant surprises. There had to be a catch.

"So is this a mistake?" Dani asked rhetorically. "Would they really put us all in the same room?"

"I unpacked as fast as I could," laughed Hannah. "Before they realize what they've done."

"No one's asking any fucking questions," Avery said, her eyes buried again in the *People* magazine photo spread of Brad Pitt and Jennifer Aniston.

"If it was a mistake, it's a good one," said Lisa, from the other side of the room. Taller than any girl on the team, Lisa Johnson had a head full of cornrows and long fingers that she presently used to point in all their faces. "I'm with Avery. No one talks."

"So what does this mean?" Dani asked, taking a seat next to Hannah on the bottom bunk. "Are we in the same company too?"

"Charlie," Hannah answered in the affirmative.

"The guys too," Lisa said, pointing across the hall toward the room of football players. "All Charlie Company."

Dani quickly realized her luck: if all the football players were in Charlie Company, that meant Locke Coleman—the guy she'd met just a few minutes ago out among the rucksacks—was going to be near her all summer.

"Oh snap!" Dani shouted excitedly. "If we're in the same company as those guys, then no one else stands a chance! We're the most athletic girls in our class, by far. And they're some of the most athletic guys. Our company is going to crush this!"

"Ooh," Avery cooed from the top bunk, raising an eyebrow. "Aren't we cocky?"

"I'm cocky because I know how awesome we all are," Dani replied. "And that includes you, Adams. You're fast as hell."

That seemed to soften her, because in that moment, Avery turned her gaze from the magazine and looked at Dani straight in the eyes, as if to determine whether or not the compliment was genuine.

"That's not what Coach Jankovich thinks."

"Yeah, well, screw Coach J."

"Can we *not* talk about her this summer please?" said Lisa from her bunk. "Thanks."

"I thought you two were like, best friends," Avery added to Dani.

"Are you kidding? That woman is the most racist person I've ever met."

"Here, here," added Lisa from her bunk.

"I'm beginning to doubt if she ever even *played* basketball, let alone if she can *coach it*," Dani said. "She is so horrible. You know she's as bad to us as she is to you guys on JV. Maybe worse."

"*See,*" Hannah said to Avery, as if she'd been trying to convince her of the truth before Dani had arrived. "I told you."

IN DARKNESS, DANI heard whispers.

"Shh!"

"Dani," Avery whispered into the top bunk. "Get up. Get your shoes."

Stumbling out of the bed, Dani rubbed her eyes until they adjusted. Avery and Hannah stood in the doorway, lit by the moonlight and waving her into the hall.

"What's happening?" asked Dani, her voice as quiet as she could muster.

Shaking her head, as if to say they couldn't talk, Avery tiptoed down the hall and carefully pushed the screen door at the end of the bunkhouse. It screeched open, threatening to wake everyone and blow their cover, but closed without a sound.

"We're meeting the guys," Avery said once they were outside, her eyes focused directly on the lake in front of them.

Hannah crossed her arms over her chest and kept looking back at bay number eight, where they were supposed to be sleeping. "We could get in trouble, Avery. It's the first night."

"Exactly," she said. "They won't expect us to sneak out on the very first night. That's why it's perfect."

At that moment, Dani heard a branch snap in the woods. She imagined an officer walking out of his bunkhouse and catching them in the act, and so grabbed Avery and Hannah's arms, pulling them to hide behind bay number six.

"Shh!" she said. "I heard something."

And at that moment, six guys emerged from the woods. Locke Coleman stood at the very center of the group, his gap-toothed smile shining through the darkness.

"We can see you," Locke said, and the girls stepped out from behind the shelter.

Without warning, Avery took off jogging toward the water's edge, followed by several of Locke's teammates. Clothes littered the sand under a grove of trees, and Dani tried to keep her composure as she watched Locke Coleman drop his shorts and tiptoe toward the water, wearing only boxer-briefs. He offered Dani a smile, then raised his eyebrows at Avery's pale body in the middle of the lake, as if to say, *Your friend's got balls.* Dani shook her head and shrugged, as if to say, *I'm not sure she's my friend.*

"I'm not getting *naked* in front of those guys," Hannah said under her breath. "We're going to get caught!"

"Come on," Dani said without breaking a sweat. "It'll be so fast. They're not even looking."

"Oh lord," Hannah groaned. "You two better not get me kicked out of this place. My grandfather would never recover."

OVER THE NEXT few weeks, it seemed that Avery warmed up to Dani a little bit more every day. Once, she'd even laughed out loud at one of Dani's jokes. It was small, but to Dani it felt like progress.

Baby steps.

During the day, their company soared to the top of the pack, always crushing the other companies in physical fitness tests. Soon it was clear that Avery had made a full 180-degree turn. When Dani and Hannah struggled to learn how to disassemble and reassemble their M16s, Avery came to the rescue, teaching them every step their platoon leader had glossed over.

"Do you think it's true?" Hannah had whispered to Dani once Avery had stepped away, leaving them with their weapons. "All those things people said last year?"

Turning her lips into a frown, Dani shook her head and shrugged her shoulders. "Does it matter?"

"I guess not," Hannah answered. "I'm not judging her. I'm just worried about her."

Dani worried about Avery too, but not for the reasons Hannah did. Hannah worried about the consequences—that Avery's reputation would be sullied, or that she'd get kicked out of the academy. Dani worried about the feelings Avery hid beneath the surface. Avery rebraided her hair every few hours. She applied concealer to the minuscule imperfections on her face before they left the bunkhouse every morning. And Dani observed these little tics, gathering them up as evidence of the truth. For all the defiant confidence Avery wore on her face, she was supressing a whole lot of self-doubt, just beneath the surface.

As the days passed on, their company passed first aid training with flying colors, and with any moment of free time, Dani and Locke held their positions as reigning beach-volleyball champions. The only son of a single mother, Locke was from Brooklyn, and had an encyclopedic knowledge of soul music. He'd taken it upon himself to educate Dani at night, starting with James Brown's *Live at the Apollo* spinning in his portable CD player. She relished the moments together, lying on his bunk side by side, with one earbud in his left ear, and the other in Dani's right. His finger tapped the beat out on her thigh.

"See? That riff? That's what I'm talking about."

The only possible threat to Dani's summer was the growing discomfort in her right hip. It wasn't something she wanted to complain about, but at times the dull ache would give way to a sharp, slicing pain in her back that stole her breath. The only person who had noticed a grimace on her face was Hannah, but Dani told her not to worry. As long as she popped a few preemptive Advil every morning, she could endure. She had to endure. She'd never quit a single thing in her entire life, and she wasn't about to start now.

THE MORNING OF the final field exercise, water poured out of the spout of an Army-green water buffalo into Dani's canteen. The four-hundred gallon tank on wheels had been marked on the map she carried in her hands. They'd been in the woods for two days straight. She was dirty, tired, and thirsty, and even in the shade of the trees, sweat poured from her forehead, smearing the camouflage paint on her face, stinging her eyes.

"Too bad you can't camouflage your blond-ass hair, Adams," Locke said jokingly to Avery, who was waiting for Dani to finish at the spigot.

"*Shut up, Coleman,*" said Avery, stepping to fill her canteen. "Dani, can you get your boyfriend to leave me alone? I can't get rid of him."

"You know Navy's not doing this shit," Locke said, changing the subject. "They send us out to the woods with nothing but a compass and a map. Haven't they heard of a GPS? Meanwhile, those Navy guys . . . they're cozied up with some private chef bulking for the season. I'd put money on it. No wonder we can't beat them. Have I told you? I've already lost—"

"Fifteen pounds. Yeah, you've told us, Coleman," said Avery. "Do you think there's a correlation between the amount of weight you lose and the age you act? Because . . . honestly . . . there's an uncanny . . ."

"Oh?" Locke raised his eyebrows. "D, your friend's a comedian!"

"Hush, you two," Dani said. She fiddled with the radio in her hand until she heard static. "Get your water. We've got to get back."

Together, the three of them tromped through the woods in a row, holding their M16s at the ready like they'd been taught. The entire day had gone by without a hitch, which worried Dani more than she wanted to admit. In the morning, before the sun came up, they'd met their company commander at a small outpost near the woods and outfitted all of their M16s with laser attachments. He'd passed out a bunch of folded "injury" cards, which they were supposed to unfold if the laser sensor on their chest was hit. Then he pointed into a glorified sandbox where a scene of wooden figurines illustrated the area they were meant to protect. An outhouse stood on the south side next to a general purpose medium tent, stretched out for shade where they'd been told to convene for lunch. The water buffalo station was a half mile to the north. A safe zone existed in the eastern section, up a tall hill, near a make-believe Red Cross station. They had from dawn until dusk to maintain the area while keeping a lookout for the OPFOR—a fake opposition force made up of soldiers from Fort Drum. They all knew the ambush was coming, but so far, there was no sign of them. Dani knew they needed to get back to the rest of their platoon, and fast. Out here alone like this—she felt suddenly like they were being watched.

Dried leaves crunched under their feet. Branches snapped, far louder than they should have.

"Shhh, Coleman," Dani whispered. "Walk lightly, dude."

Perhaps they should have returned to the rest of the platoon by a different route than the way they'd come, Dani thought to herself. If anyone had seen their tracks, walking toward the water buffalo, they could have staked them out, easily. As soon as Dani had considered that possibility, Locke stopped in his tracks. Silent, Dani gripped her rifle even tighter. She knew it was all in fun—just practice—but her heart was still pounding in her chest. She checked the laser attachment on the end of her gun, to make sure it was ready to fire.

"Do you hear that?" Avery asked, her voice a whisper. She stood right behind Dani, breathing like she'd just run a 5K. In the distance, a faint echo of loud voices rose into the trees.

"Turn up the radio, D," whispered Locke to Dani.

Dani turned the volume up slightly, just as she saw a man dressed in black behind a tree. He raised his rifle and aimed it directly at them.

"GET DOWN!" shouted Dani.

Pow! Pow! Pow!

"MAYDAY! MAYDAY! MAYDAY!" yelled Dani into the receiver of the radio. "*COME IN, SPEER! WE NEED BACKUP!*"

"Oh shit!" yelled Locke, seeing a whole new crew of men dressed in black moving their way. "Run!"

Avery took off sprinting through the woods, separating from Locke and Dani just enough to provide them cover from behind a rock. Out of the corner of her eye, Dani spotted another man in black, and she shot—hitting him square in the chest. *Take that!* Dani thought. *I'm a sniper!* At that moment, another enemy combatant emerged from behind a tree and took aim at Locke's back.

"Coleman! Get down!" Dani called out, then she fired her gun. The enemy fell to the ground, his laser attachment lit up in red.

Dani smiled. But turning back to look at Locke, she realized her shot had come a moment too late.

"He's hit! I've got your cover, Dani!" shouted Avery from across the woods. "Go! Go! Go!"

Her legs flew across the expanse of leaves and shadows. When she arrived at Locke's side, he held up the white injury card in his hand. "Head wound," he said. "Traumatic brain injury."

"Okay," panted Dani, trying not to panic. She tried to remember the first aid training she'd been given the week before. "We've got to keep your neck stabilized and get you to the safe zone."

The reality that he was nearly twice her weight suddenly struck Dani in the gut. How was she going to get him through a half mile of woods without getting shot? And how was she going to do it with this pulsating pain flaring up in her back? She looked around her and realized there was only one option. Dani struggled, shifting his weight from the ground to her back. Once she had him on her back, she began walking, one hobbling step at a time. Her hip screamed out in pain, like all the cartilage in her joints had disappeared. Bone rubbed against bone.

"I need cover!" Dani shouted to Avery.

"Go!" shouted Avery. "I've got your cover! Go!"

"Oh my God, Locke. Why do you have to be so huge?" she said. "I thought you said you'd *lost* weight."

"You got this, McNalley."

"Shut up. You're dying. Save your energy." She felt him laugh.

When they finally reached the hill, Dani watched the rest of her female company mates zigzag across the valley, providing cover fire and dragging the rest of the guys in their platoon, with their various feigned injuries, up to the safe zone. Apparently the ambush had been swift and fierce. Bodies were strewn everywhere. The girls had all survived, while the boys in their platoon had all been taken out of the game. Apparently the boys had been a bit overly aggressive; the girls had the presence of mind to assess the threat before taking action. Clearly, that was why they were the ones who had survived.

"GO, DANI! GO!" Hannah shouted when she saw Dani approaching the bottom of the hill. The final few OPFOR combatants exchanged fire with Hannah as Dani heaved as fast as she could up the hill with a two-hundred-pound football player on her back. When her legs gave out, she put Locke on the ground and pulled him up the hill by his foot, sliding him into the safe zone like a sack of heavy potatoes.

"I'm going to go out on a limb and say we failed this mission," Locke commented. "I had a head injury and you pulled me up the hill upside down, McNalley. I'm pretty sure I bled out."

Breathless, Dani tried to stand up, hoping to go rescue another fallen comrade. But the pain in her hip suddenly exploded into her back and skull. The woods went white in her eyes, and she cried out before hitting the ground. With her eyes closed, all Dani could hear were voices in the dark.

"We're in the safe zone, D," someone shouted. "You don't have to pretend to be injured."

"What's going on?"

"Hey, I think she's hurt."

"What's her card say?"

"No, dumbass!" Someone shouted back. "She's *actually* injured! Hey, someone call a medic!"

The next thing Dani heard was the loud peal of a siren over her head.

Eyes open, trying to focus through the pain, all she could see was blurry faces surrounding her in a small white room. Or was this a vehicle? Her body felt as though someone had taken a hammer to her lower back, crushing every bone into a million pieces. How would they ever put her back together again? The thought forced her to close her eyes and bite her cheeks. She tasted iron and smelled the scent of hospital bandages. They were driving fast. It was definitely a vehicle. An ambulance.

Faintly, she recognized the sound of Avery's voice.

"It's going to be okay, D."

A warm hand squeezed her upper arm, and opening her eyes, Dani saw a blond angel looking down at her. *Avery.*

"I'm here with you. I'm not going anywhere."

"Call Wendy," Dani said through clenched teeth.

"Who?"

"Wendy Bennett."

"I'm putting in an IV," someone else said. "Quick pinch. There you go. We're going to get you hydrated and figure out what's going on. A little ibuprofen in there to help with the pain."

Relief suddenly spread through her veins. Her body relaxed; it stopped fighting. And her mind wandered into a blackness that felt like bliss.

8

Fall 2001 // West Point, New York

On a clear Tuesday morning in September, every blade of grass at West Point looked like a tiny saber, reaching for the sky. The color turquoise stretched overhead without a single cloud to interrupt its hue, and as Avery moved toward Thayer Hall, her dark gray uniform shirt tucked into wool pants, all she could think about was how quickly life can change. All it took was an instant.

She'd seen it with her brother, Caleb. In one moment, he was an innocent sophomore on the way to acing Algebra I; the next, he was wearing an orange vest, picking up trash on the side of the highway for community service. She'd seen it this summer with Dani, too. With one misplaced step, she'd morphed from point guard to patient, undergoing emergency surgery to repair what the doctors had determined was a torn ligament. It was awful; Avery had never seen someone's face so contorted in pain.

That day, the EMTs had loaded Dani's body into an ambulance and drove her from Camp Buckner to Keller Army Hospital, which looked more like a Gothic castle than an infirmary. Without asking permission, Avery had hopped in the back of the ambulance and refused to leave Dani's side until the nurses wheeled her back for surgery. For hours, Avery sat in the hospital's cold waiting room alone, until the woman Dani had told her to call, Wendy Bennett, had arrived. She'd only met the woman a handful of times, at basketball games, but her presence somehow forced a crack in the dam Avery had constructed to keep her emotion in check. Still dressed in BDUs, her face painted green and black and brown, Avery had fallen into Wendy's motherly embrace, smearing camouflage face paint against the woman's white shirt.

"It's okay," Wendy had said. "It's going to be okay."

"I was horrible to her last year . . . I—"

"Stop that. People remember who showed up for the crappy moments far more than they remember who showed up for the party. And you're here, aren't you? You're *here*."

If she was honest, Avery still felt ashamed of how she'd acted toward Dani last year. Bitter and resentful, she'd isolated herself, choosing to believe that she had enemies rather than risk being rejected by new friends. But the summer had proven her wrong. Eight weeks had multiplied—breaking into tiny fragments, like the loaves and fishes from that old Bible story—until they'd spread into a million moments, some bitter, some savory, and some sweet. Time was malleable that way. Weeks could feel like years, if you filled them to the brim. A day could manufacture memories to last a lifetime.

During a late-night game of Never Have I Ever, Avery had even admitted to Dani and Hannah that she'd slept with John Collins last year. While Hannah winced, as if Avery's fornication had caused her physical pain, Dani didn't seem shocked or appalled; she just laughed and shook her head, which helped Avery feel at ease for once. They'd never spoken of it explicitly—Dani had never asked for an outright apology—but somehow, over the course of the summer, her fiercest competition had become one of her closest friends.

After the surgery, the commandant of cadets had agreed to let Dani move into a spare bedroom at the Bennetts' house while she recovered. Wendy's daughters were all in college, leaving three empty bedrooms and three empty seats at the dinner table, where Avery and Hannah would often join Dani, savoring Wendy's cooking. Vegetable lasagna. Roasted chicken with tabbouleh. Grilled salmon with mango slaw. There was always a gallon of cookie dough ice cream in the freezer, and Wendy would present it nightly with a pile of spoons, as if bowls were an unnecessary step between their stomachs and delight.

If Avery had ever felt embarrassed by Dani's nudity, all that dissipated as she and Hannah took turns helping Dani into the Bennetts' guest bathroom shower. Tears came often for Dani in those days, and not just from the physical pain. It was hard, Avery knew, for this former powerhouse of a woman to be so powerless. Everyone wants to be the friend who helps. No one wants to be the friend who needs the help.

"Shit, Dani, do you have to be as thick as a horse?" Avery had said once as she lifted Dani off her wheelchair and into the shower. Dani had clung to Avery's shoulder, and in the end, they both ended up drenched in soap and water.

"This is what I like to refer to as karma," Dani had replied.

Spending time at the Bennetts' was just one of many new privileges they had, now that they were sophomores, also known at West Point as "Yuks." The academic calendar boasted six B-weekends, when upperclassmen could leave campus in civilian clothes and pretend to be free for a while. And while Yuks still were low on the totem pole, they had far more freedom than they'd had the year before, and Avery relished every opportunity she had to leer at new plebes whenever they called minutes in the hallway.

"Attention all cadets . . . there are . . . *three minutes remaining* . . . until breakfast formation . . ."

At West Point, you couldn't escape the constant reminder that time was moving forward, counting down, drawing to a close. Urgency was the only operating mode because time was Avery's only resource and her greatest enemy. West Point operated on a true meritocracy. A cadet's academic and physical performance, measured by GPA, PT scores, and other evaluations, converted to class rank, which would eventually dictate her future.

A year earlier, Avery had watched from the wings as Sarah Goodrich leveraged her high class rank to receive an assignment to her desired Army branch, Military Intelligence, and to select the most coveted Army post: Oahu, Hawaii. Rain had poured over the class of 2001 at their graduation ceremony, their white hats soaring into the gray downpour. And though legend had it that any class that graduated in the rain would go to war, Avery would have done anything to trade places with Sarah. In a feat of personal achievement, she'd transformed her time at West Point into a one-way ticket to paradise.

As the days ticked by, Avery grew more uncertain that Dani could recover in time for the basketball season. Large inflamed patches appeared under Dani's arms where crutches had worn her skin raw. The four-inch incision across her right hip remained red and irritated, like an angry half-moon. Even when she'd moved back into the barracks, daily physical therapy sessions seemed ineffective in rebuilding strength in Dani's hip and back. Everywhere they went, she limped, crutched, and smiled. And Avery had never felt worse. A year earlier, she would have given anything to be on the varsity women's basketball team. But now, the inevitability felt suffocating. Like her envy had willed Dani's injury into existence.

Three days earlier, at the team's annual "optional" season-opening practice, Coach Jankovich had written Avery's name at the top of the varsity roster, relegating another plebe recruiting class to JV. Guilt, shame, and excitement had appeared in equal force as she read her name on that piece of paper. Her dreams for the basketball season only existed because Dani's had been torn apart—ripped to pieces like the ligament in her hip.

It was a cruel twist of fate. Loaves and fishes, in reverse.

One dream broken, so another could survive.

WALKING INTO THAYER Hall, yellow spots appeared before Avery's eyes as she adjusted from the brightness outside to the academic building's dim corridor. Normally, the hallway was abuzz with cadets rushing to class, hanging their hats on the hooks outside the doors, chatting before they shuffled through into the classrooms and into their seats. But today, the hallway was empty and silent.

Her freshly shined black shoes clicked against the linoleum floors for twenty paces, until she reached the door to the lecture hall. She'd expected her Physics professor to be standing at the front, handing out the midterm packets, while cadets frantically used the last minutes they had to finish studying. But instead, every person inside the classroom was statuesque, staring at a television screen that had been rolled to the front of the room.

Life could change so quickly. All it took was an instant.

Turning to look at what held their attention, Avery's stomach lurched, like she'd just stepped off the edge of a cliff. On the screen, two silver buildings glittered against a blue sky. The same blue sky she'd just been admiring outside. But something wasn't right. The buildings were on fire, gashes cut into their sides, flames spilling out. Black smoke pooled above the towers, reaching higher than the tallest buildings in the world. Smoke signals.

"Two planes. Back to back. Flew right into the buildings," the cadet standing next to her said.

"On purpose?" Avery asked, incredulous.

He nodded.

"Did they . . ." Avery stuttered. "Did they get everyone out?"

The cadet didn't answer, but simply turned to look back at the screen.

The news flickered between images of the World Trade Center and a confused anchor, frantically trying to assess what had happened in the world around him. When the room let out a gasp, Avery closed her eyes and tried to pretend that the *slam* she heard through the television speakers was something else. Anything else.

Only one thought went through her mind, circling and circling, like a plane waiting to land. Like the dress of the woman who'd just jumped.

Oh my God. Oh my God. Oh my God.

This changes everything.

"THIS IS WAR," Avery said, breaking the silence. "That's what I keep thinking. It's . . . just . . . I can't believe it."

The entire women's basketball team had gathered in Wendy Bennett's living room. Paper bowls of half-eaten chicken pot pie littered the floor, and were stacked on the coffee table. The team huddled under blankets, interlocking arms and passing around a tissue box. All twelve pairs of eyes were puffy and red. Women at West Point learned quickly to hold their emotion in check— never to shed a tear. But that unspoken rule had shattered to the ground, falling with the towers.

All day, people had speculated about what might happen next. Would they cancel school and send them all immediately to the Middle East? Avery heard more than one person say they wanted to go down to the city to help search for survivors. And though she didn't say it out loud, she wanted to remind them that two 110-story buildings had collapsed. From what they were showing on television, it looked like a nuclear bomb had gone off in the middle of the city. There weren't going to be any survivors.

"I just don't understand," said Hannah, wiping tears from her cheeks. "Why would anyone do something like this?"

"They're saying it's al-Qaeda," Dani explained. "Terrorists."

"But what do they want?" said Lisa Johnson. "What does killing thousands of innocent people accomplish?"

Avery had chosen a spot on the couch between Dani and Hannah, while the rest of the girls spread out throughout the room—some seated by the fireplace, others on the floor. Five plebes—girls who'd graduated high school a mere four months ago—sat in the corner, white faced. *Time to grow up*, Avery thought to herself. They would no longer get the liberty of treating their training like a joke. And Avery wished, suddenly, that she hadn't either.

At the beginning, she'd wanted to come to West Point to prove something: maybe to her father, maybe to herself. But the sound of that body hitting the ground had knocked her motivations completely off balance. Could it be possible that *this* was the reason she was here? That the universe had conspired to get her to this house, in this moment, with these people?

She shuddered, afraid of what that might mean. Dani was a natural leader. And Hannah was selfless, to a fault.

But what about me? Avery wondered. *Am I really cut out for war*?

Do I even have a choice?

Wendy sat on an ottoman with her hands resting in her lap. The television was still on, flashing scenes that made Avery cringe. People had walked out of lower Manhattan covered in white dust, their cheeks tear stained, their bodies hunched over in defeat. It was hard to watch. And yet, she couldn't turn her eyes away from their faces.

Wendy sighed deeply and looked around the room, as if she was trying to imprint the moment into her memory. Then she grabbed the television remote and pressed a button. The screen snapped to black.

"What does Mark think?" Dani asked suddenly.

Wendy's husband wasn't home tonight. Tonight, he'd gone to meet with the men's basketball team, who were likewise in shock. Avery felt oddly jealous of the familiar way Dani had called Colonel Bennett by his first name. She knew the Bennetts had a special bond with Dani after she'd lived here, recovering from surgery. But as Wendy stared across the room, eyes trained to the freckles on Dani's face, Avery felt a deep pang of sadness that she didn't have that kind of close-knit relationship anywhere, with anyone. Wendy, with her pearl stud earrings and tattered Bible, had probably heard the gossip. *She probably thinks I'm a lost cause.*

"He's in shock. Just like the rest of us," answered Wendy.

"Does he think we'll declare war?" Lisa asked timidly.

"I don't know."

Wendy paused, her chin quivering. "You know, a lot of people may not understand how people of faith—people like Mark and me—could choose to be in the Army. But what those men did today is evil. It's pure evil—killing innocent people. And I know that Mark feels honored to be part of a team that wants to rid the world of that kind of evil. It's an honorable path you girls have chosen. But it won't be easy." She dabbed a tissue under her eyes, then cleared her throat. "I've been thinking about you girls all day, and how scary this must feel. It's scary for everyone—it's scary for me too. But for you—this day will change the course of your lives forever. Maybe in ways we can't even predict."

Avery knew that was true. Already, she'd run through the memory of the morning countless times, and when she closed her eyes, the images wouldn't stop assaulting her brain. She'd never forget the color of the sky—an aggressive blue. The smell of fresh-cut grass in the air. The eerie quiet in the hallways before she turned and saw both buildings collapse, right there on television. Maybe that's what made a memory powerful. Not that it happened once, but that it happened over and over again on the screen of your mind.

They sat in silence for a long time before Wendy offered to pray. Around the room, all of her teammates had their eyes closed and they were nodding along, wiping their tears and noses.

What did they think all this prayer would change? Avery wondered. *Did they actually think someone was listening?*

"For some reason, I keep coming back to this story," Wendy said, once she'd finished her prayer. The pages of her Bible flipped back and forth, thin and worn, like she'd done this a lot. Her finger landed in the middle of a page.

"I'll paraphrase," she said, slipping on round tortoiseshell reading glasses. "Jesus was with his disciples and he got word from Mary and Martha that one of his best friends, Lazarus, was sick. And this is what blows my mind. It says, *'Now Jesus loved Mary and Martha. So, when he heard Lazarus was sick, he stayed where he was two more days.'*"

Wendy put her glasses down. "Doesn't that seem strange? He loved them, *so* he waited? When I think about love, I think of someone jumping on the first plane to come see me when I'm in trouble. But by the time Jesus arrives, Lazarus has already been dead for four days. *Four days!* He's already in a tomb; Jesus missed the funeral." She paused, letting that information sink in.

"And when Jesus finally arrives, Martha doesn't say, 'I'm so sorry you missed the funeral.' *No.* She says, *'If only you had been here, none of this would have happened.'* She's basically saying, 'You could have prevented this, but you didn't.' It's faith mixed with total confusion. 'I believe, but I have no idea what you're doing.'"

The silence was almost too much to bear. Avery wanted to jump out of her chair and scream: *EXACTLY!* If God had been there, all those people in those buildings and planes wouldn't have died. But God wasn't there, because there was no such thing as God. Tragedies happened *every single day.* To believe that God could prevent those tragedies but didn't? That wasn't confusing. It was offensive. That meant God wasn't loving—it proved He was cruel.

"I'm sorry," Avery snapped. "But I don't see what this has to do with anything."

Wendy closed her Bible. "Martha's prayer is one of the most honest, raw prayers I've ever read in the Bible. *'Lord, if you had been here, none of this would have happened.'* It's her cry from the trenches. And Jesus doesn't get angry with her. He doesn't walk away. He cries with her."

And suddenly, much to Avery's amazement, the girls were talking. Sharing. Dani said that she'd constantly felt that way about her injuries—that she wanted to believe there was a reason, but she couldn't understand what God was doing in her life. Lisa Johnson brought up Coach Jankovich. The woman grew worse and more vindictive with every passing day, and Lisa wondered how much more she could stand. Avery pressed her fingers into her eyes and felt wetness. She hated to cry. But somehow, she couldn't make the tears stop. She wanted to feel angry at God. But you can't be angry at a God you don't believe in.

"Let me get this straight. These assholes fly planes into buildings full of people," Avery cried. "And what? We're just supposed to trust that God has some bigger plan for all this? What's the point?"

Wendy took her glasses off. "That's a really important question, Avery. Keep going."

"Keep going?" Avery cried. "What else is there to say? It's bullshit."

Dani squeezed Avery's arm tight, and when Avery turned to look at Dani's face, there were tears streaking down her freckled cheeks, in heavy lines.

Wendy didn't respond immediately. Instead, she simply nodded her head, letting the sound of Avery's harried breathing fill the room.

"Yeah. It is," Wendy said finally. "It is bullshit. And I think that's why I love this prayer from Martha so much. She's saying, 'Where the hell were you, Jesus?'

"It's dirty. It's ugly. But it's faith, just the same."

9

Spring 2002 // West Point, New York

I have nothing to wear."

"That's not true," said Avery. "Here, try this." She threw Hannah a black dress.

Pulling it over her body, Hannah stared at herself in the mirror hung on the back of one of the wardrobe doors. The dress hugged her in all the wrong places.

"Um, no." She pulled it off her head. "That looks like I'm going to a funeral."

Her small dorm room was littered with clothes. Sequined skirts, spaghetti-strap shirts, Daisy Dukes, and dresses fit for nights of dancing were scattered across the floor. Since they were only allowed to have a few select civilian clothes in the barracks, Avery kept her stash in a trunk in the basketball locker room, where she would not get caught. For this occasion, she'd carted the trunk back down to the barracks. A pile of rejects draped the back of Hannah's desk chair.

They were allowed to wear civilian clothes only on the rarest of occasions: on infrequent Thursday night spirit dinners, B-weekends as they traveled home or to the city, and select events on campus. Thick with muscle, her thighs looked larger than she remembered, and her arms, though toned, looked strange against the pastel colors of Avery's clothes. To Hannah, dressing like a girl felt pointless, and suddenly, she understood why no guys at West Point had dared to ask her out. Who needed a ninety-degree rule when you had a wardrobe full of high-waisted wool trousers?

Propelled by a surge of anxiety, Hannah fell face-first onto her bed, wishing that she'd never agreed to let Avery Adams play stylist. How did Avery fit into these clothes anyway?

In high school, Hannah always got asked to dances. The student body had voted her homecoming queen, and the quarterback of the football team was her boyfriend for two solid years—that is, until they'd disagreed about sex. He'd wanted it; she'd wanted to wait. The relationship had ended abruptly and without much fanfare. And though she'd never been afraid of being alone in the past, with Avery around, Hannah couldn't escape the daily reminders that she was desperately, permanently single.

"You seen Avery?" a guy from the lacrosse team had asked last week, popping his head into her room.

"Nope, not here."

"Adams around?" ventured a dark-haired Latino cadet Hannah had never seen before.

"Sorry."

"Where's Avery?" John Collins would demand, for what felt like the millionth time. He was the only one Hannah knew for certain Avery was trying to avoid. Apparently, she'd broken off their fling, and the green-eyed Collins had gone green all over.

"Beats me, Collins. You might try *her room*," Hannah had said.

The last time he'd come around, Collins had thrown his fist into the cinder-block wall and Hannah thought she'd heard his knuckle crack.

"You should talk to him," Hannah had suggested a few days later in the women's locker room. She and Avery were both cleaning out their lockers after the season ended. "It seems like he might need some closure."

"Closure?" Avery said. "How much more closure can you get? I told him it's over."

As one of her closest friends, Hannah had a front-row seat to Avery's pattern of ups and downs, which started with Avery's pronouncement that she'd found *the one* and ended with her sobbing in the fetal position, because the guy had decided to date a cheerleader—better known as a Rabble Rouser—instead. The drama had grown predictable, and Hannah worried constantly that Avery would get caught behind closed doors, putting her entire future at West Point in jeopardy.

"Don't worry," Avery had said that night as they'd walked back to the barracks. "I'll take care of Collins. He won't bother you anymore."

IN THE SEMESTER that had passed since September 11, everything had changed at West Point.

As soon as the towers came down, West Point had increased security, outfitting every campus entrance with bomb-sniffing dogs and military police, fully armed with automatic rifles. Where once there had been open roads, spike strips now controlled the flow of traffic. Visitors used to be able to walk through the gates simply by showing their ID. Now they had to submit to background checks.

Conversation had changed too. Once a far-off land few could pinpoint on a map, Afghanistan had become the center of most discussions on campus. The name Osama bin Laden could be heard in the mess hall and between classes. At Grant Hall, cadets shared slices of pizza and opinions about military strategy. You couldn't turn on the news without seeing grainy images of the world's most wanted criminal: a thin, gray-bearded man seated in a cave. Whenever she saw Bin Laden's face, Hannah shuddered. But her unease was always short-lived. Perhaps because she imagined men like her grandfather at the Pentagon planning the response, she felt confident that the U.S.-led retaliation would be over quickly. After all, America's army was the strongest in the world. Its most recent military conflict, Desert Storm, had only lasted six months.

How long could it take to find and kill one lone terrorist?

But while headlines raged, the daily proceedings of college life had moved forward as usual. Professors went on teaching. Sports teams went right on practicing. Leaves fell into piles of gold on the ground, and soon, the sky turned the color of wool. With Dani still recovering from her surgery and the loss of last year's class of seniors, Coach Jankovich promoted Hannah to the varsity team, along with Avery and Lisa Johnson. During a basketball game over the Thanksgiving holiday against Cornell University, Hannah scored twenty points, and Avery hit a half-court three-point shot in the last second to win the game. The entire arena had erupted in chaos. Hannah had never seen Avery's face so lit up with joy. Even the Cornell fans celebrated, as if West Point's ability to win a women's basketball game somehow correlated with their future ability to take out terrorists.

When they weren't on the road, they were in the gym, listening to the shrill sound of Coach Jankovich's whistle reverberate across the court. Last year's losing season meant this year, her antics had risen to a fever pitch. She was extremely hard on the plebes, Hannah thought, and had replaced her hatred for Avery with ceaseless criticism of Lisa Johnson.

"LISA!" she'd screamed a few weeks earlier, throwing her clipboard to the ground. "THOSE CORNROWS TOO TIGHT? Maybe if you'd loosen them, you could actually *think!*"

The more Jankovich yelled at Lisa, the more Dani crutched to the sidelines to give her teammate quiet pep talks. Hannah marveled at Dani's ability to motivate her teammates, despite her injuries. She called out ideas for plays during time-outs, whispered tips to Hannah during games. And rather than see her as an asset, Coach Jankovich often sent Dani out of practice for speaking out of turn.

It didn't make sense to Hannah. The fact that the players had respect for Dani didn't mean they had less for their coach. Respect wasn't pie. But Coach Jankovich's unrelenting paranoia had turned into a self-fulfilling prophecy. Team morale had never been lower.

Even Hannah, who hated conflict, had ventured to ask for a change. Practices ran late every single day, leaving the girls little time to rush back to their dorm rooms before dinner. In January, when Hannah had asked Coach Jankovich to consider ending practice promptly at six o'clock, like other coaches, she'd offered only a thin-lipped smile in return.

"So you can spend more time *IM-ing* your boyfriend?" the coach had snapped.

Hannah didn't have the heart to tell her coach that she didn't have a boyfriend, and—as long as she was at West Point— probably never would.

It seemed ridiculous that while the world was on the brink of war, Hannah's thoughts veered so often to *guys,* but she couldn't help herself. Rooming with Avery during the spring semester had put a magnifying glass on Hannah's chief worry: not a single guy had expressed an ounce of interest in her since she'd stepped foot on campus at West Point. Least of all, the one she wanted.

Ever since Colonel Bennett's philosophy class, Tim Nesmith had been like the wind—blowing past, never knowing that he'd touched her. She'd see him in the library, poring over an Arabic textbook, refusing to look up from the page. In the fall, at home football games, cadets in the stands would point up at the sky while Tim parachuted with the rest of the skydiving team into the stadium. During Christmas dinner, held every year the week before cadets went home on break, a crew of cadets in Santa out-fits had picked up a table off the floor, as five others holding ever-green branches climbed up and built a human Christmas tree on top. Sure enough, when Hannah turned to watch the spectacle, it was Tim, dressed as an angel, who crowned the tree. From that perch, he'd led the corps in a rousing rendition of "The Twelve Days of Christmas," moving his arms like a conductor.

She couldn't escape him, and yet he still hadn't noticed her.

By April of her Yuk year, Hannah had given up all hope of having a date during the entirety of her college career. Basketball season had ended and Hannah had nothing to fill her newfound free time. A week earlier, in a striking role reversal, it had been Hannah on the bed in the fetal position.

Dani had just taken a seat in Hannah's desk chair, snacking from a box of Cheez-Its, when Avery walked in from class.

"What's with her?" she'd asked Dani, pointing at Hannah and dropping her backpack.

"Nervous breakdown number six of the semester," Dani had said casually. "Standard issue."

"I've told you a million times, Hannah, no one is ever going to ask about your GPA once we're out of here."

Hannah had rolled over and narrowed her eyes.

"It's not about grades, Avery. It's about . . ." She'd paused, then groaned. "Ugh. It's about the two of you."

Dani had laughed, pointing at herself as though she were completely innocent. "What did I do?"

"You're always off with Locke," Hannah had said, then pointed at Avery. "And *you*! There's practically a line of guys outside your door every day, there to pay homage. Seriously. Have you checked lately? Someone's probably out there right now."

Avery had laughed, while Hannah pulled herself dramatically off the bed and stuck her head into the hallway. Dani chuckled and dug her hand back into the bag of Cheez-Its.

"She's losing it," Dani had said.

"Come on, Hannah. It's not that bad."

"Yes it is! This place is swarming with guys. I'll never have odds like this again! And still . . . I haven't been *touched* by a guy in two years. TWO YEARS! What is wrong with me?"

Avery raised an eyebrow. "Nothing is wrong with you. Maybe something's wrong with *them*."

In a flash, Hannah had crossed the room, lifted the window, and stuck her head into the balmy April air, looking down to the darkness of cadet area below. Around the concrete courtyard, the barracks squared off, every window lit up with golden lamplight.

"WHY WON'T ANYBODY DATE ME?" she'd screamed, her voice echoing off stone.

Someone walking across cadet area whistled up toward her.

"HELLO!" Hannah had shouted. "Hey! You! WILL YOU GO ON A DATE WITH ME?"

Soon, all three girls were in hysterics on the floor, laughing.

When they'd wiped the tears from their eyes, Avery said, "Hannah, we can get you a guy, if it's a guy you want."

"She doesn't want *any* guy," Dani had said knowingly. "That's the problem. It's a specific guy."

With a deep sigh, Hannah had nodded, dropping her head into her hands.

"So what's his name?" Dani had prodded.

"I just have this feeling."

Avery had let out an impatient groan. "Okay, okay. What's his name?!"

"Tim Nesmith." Hannah had fallen again on her bed, cradling her pillow against her face.

"The guy on the parachute team?" Avery had asked, scrunching her eyebrows together in surprise.

Wrangling the bag of Cheez-Its back into its box, Dani had wiped her hands against her black shorts and then slapped them together. "Hannah. Why didn't you say something sooner? Tim was in my Beast squad. We're like this." She crossed her fingers tight.

Against her better judgment, Hannah had permitted a bubble of hope to rise in her chest and dropped the pillow from her face. "Really?"

"Yes." Dani limped over to Hannah's computer, and spoke with full confidence. "You and I both know I can make this happen."

West Point's event calendar populated the screen, teeming with possibilities—concerts at Eisenhower Hall, half-price tickets to Broadway shows in the city. But apparently, as Dani scanned the options, her eyes landed on a recurring meeting in Cullum Hall, scheduled by the Cadet Hostess.

While social etiquette was dying everywhere else in America, West Point had to ensure the nation's future leaders didn't embarrass themselves at a dinner with a VIP guest, or at a ball with a foreign dignitary. That's why West Point kept their very own Emily Post on the payroll, also known as the Cadet Hostess. The hostess's office offered frequent classes throughout the year, in table manners, chivalry, and decorum. On the docket for April were six weeks of ballroom dancing lessons—free for any cadet who wanted to participate.

Convinced that it was the perfect cover, Dani had sent a series of instant messages to Tim that night, each message fired off faster than the one before. Hannah had watched over Dani's shoulder in horror.

BBALL4EVA: Tim.

TIMNESMITH66: Hey Dani. what's up. long time no see.

BBALL4EVA: Hey—Locke and I are doing ballroom dancing lessons this semester—and I need one more guy to join our crew. You interested?

TIMNESMITH66: ballroom dancing?:-/

BBALL4EVA: tuesday nights in Cullum Hall. Six weeks.

TIMNESMITH66: six weeks?! wtf. i don't know mcnalley . . . I'm not the greatest on a dance floor.

BBALL4EVA: even more reason to come.

BBALL4EVA: and before you go giving me some crap excuse, might I remind you that without me, you never would have made it through Beast.

TIMNESMITH66: that's not exactly how I remember it.

TIMNESMITH66: who else is going?

BBALL4EVA: just us and my friend Hannah.

BBALL4EVA: She's awesome. You'll like her.

TIMNESMITH66: the tall girl you're always with?

BBALL4EVA: possibly. I travel with a lot of tall girls. comes with the territory.

TIMNESMITH66: six weeks, huh?

BBALL4EVA: what else are you going to do on a Tuesday
  night??? Plus. You know Locke and I will make it a blast.

TIMNESMITH66: all right. I'll do it.

BBALL4EVA: I'll e-mail you the details. No backing out.

TIMNESMITH66: why do I get the feeling I'm going to regret
  this?

BBALL4EVA: NONSENSE. I've got you. It's going to be great.

"I'm not going," Hannah said now, her voice muffled by the pillow.

She had nothing to wear, let alone the confidence to make it through the night without puking. Dani, dressed in a V-neck T-shirt that exposed just the right amount of cleavage, dug through Avery's trunk, pulling out more slinky dresses and tank tops.

"What about this?" she said, holding up a miniskirt.

"Oh my gosh, not that skirt," Avery said, pulling it back. "Bad high school memories."

Dragging herself back to the mirror, Hannah tried another dress and held her hair off her shoulders to see if that helped at all. It was a bright red number that clung to her hips and waist obscenely. "Nope." She dropped her hair. "Not gonna work. Plus," she said, pointing at Dani, "why does *she* get to wear jeans?"

Dani opened her mouth to speak, but Avery held up a hand to stop her.

"Dani doesn't think dancing with Locke is a date. And she's *barely* off her crutches, so let's give her a break, shall we?" She plunged her head deep into her trunk. "There are very few chances to look like a real girl around here, Hannah, and I'll be damned if I'm going to let you walk out of here looking less than perfect."

Hannah groaned. "I'm so screwed."

"One can only hope," Avery laughed.

Standing up, she pulled a cotton dress that tied at the waist from her trunk. Hannah assessed its maroon color, knee-length hem, and perfect cut—and gasped.

"Wow," she said. "Give me that."

DANI HAD ARRANGED to meet the boys on the flat stone walkway called the Apron, near General George S. Patton's statue overlooking the Plain. The sky turned red, the final light of the day dying in a flash of beauty. Locke looked like he always did: shoulders broad, muscles bulging. The gap between his two front teeth conspired to make his hulking figure far less intimidating, Hannah thought. Next to him, Tim stood with his back turned to them, his hands stuffed in the pockets of a camel-colored jacket. He wore a white collared shirt and dark jeans paired with leather loafers. He looked like a Ralph Lauren model—casual and handsome. Locke pointed over Tim's shoulder, and he turned, his face breaking into a sincere smile. Nearing the boys, Hannah inhaled the spicy scent of Tim's after-shave and felt her stomach drop. *Why does he have to smell so good?*

"It's about time!" Locke said to Dani. He checked his watch. "We're going to be late."

"Calm down," Dani shouted back. Just as they began walking

toward Cullum Hall, the streetlights flickered on, and Hannah looked up, grateful for the distraction from Tim's gaze. Locke and Dani were already several paces ahead of them before Tim cleared his throat and stroked his chin.

"So, how'd she rope you into this?" he said. "Blackmail?"

"Oh yeah," Hannah laughed. "You should see the dirt she has on me."

"Well, I hope you're ready to lead. I don't know the first thing about dancing."

"Where I come from, leading is the guy's job."

"Where are you from? Mayberry?"

"Austin."

"Close enough." He smiled.

She wanted to die. He'd just put his hand on her back, guiding her up the steps toward Cullum Hall. In response, all the blood in her body had rushed to that very spot. He dropped his coat on a hook outside the ballroom door.

"What about you? Where are you from?" Hannah asked, even though she already knew the answer. Dani had told her Tim had grown up on a farm in Maryland.

"California," he said.

"Dani said you were from Maryland."

"Then why'd you ask?" he said with a grin.

Hannah blushed.

"I was born in California, so I like to claim it," added Tim. The dimple in his right cheek appeared as he smiled.

"So when did you move to Maryland?" asked Hannah.

Tim raised an eyebrow, as if to do the math. "When I was . . . let's see . . . ten days old? My parents had to get special permission for me to fly on the plane because I was so little." A moment passed, and then he explained, "I was adopted."

At that moment, Hannah suddenly knew exactly why she'd been attracted to Tim in the first place. He had a certain confidence in the way he walked and talked that she wasn't used to seeing in the South. And yet, since he'd been raised on a farm in Maryland, he had all the qualities that Hannah had grown to respect in a man, thanks to her father's and grandfather's examples. Hard work. Intensity. Determination. He was the perfect combination of the familiar and the mysterious, the relatable and the unknown. She wanted to step closer to him, and yet felt an equal desire to step away, for fear that he might sweep her up in a wave she couldn't control. She tried to imagine what his birth mother must have felt, handing her child over to a stranger. And yet, she was grateful. Because of that brave woman, he was here. Loved by his adoptive parents into the kind of man that would attend West Point, even if he bucked the system every now and then. It all made sense. He made sense.

"You're quiet," he said.

"Sorry," she answered. "I was just wondering. Do you think you'll try and find your birth parents someday?"

He shrugged. "I doubt it. I had a great family growing up. If I wonder about anything, it's what it would have been like to grow up on the West Coast. I feel like there's this surfer in me just dying to break out. But that's enough about me. What about you?"

"Hm." Hannah thought. Compared to his story, nothing about her seemed all that interesting. "I grew up in Texas. My grandfather went to West Point."

"Is that why you came?"

"No. Actually he didn't want me to come."

"But you came anyway."

Hannah smiled. "I came anyway."

"Good for you," he said, then asked with excitement, "Hey, what did you get for the summer?"

West Point had just handed out summer assignments. Hannah would only get one week at home, before reporting for Airborne School at Fort Benning, Georgia. After that, she'd return to West Point and lead plebes through basic training.

"I've got Airborne School. Then Beast Two. I get to walk plebes through the House of Tears."

"You ever jumped out of a plane?"

"Not yet," Hannah admitted. "But I've seen you do it. At the football games."

He smiled broadly. "You're going to love it. It's terrifying. But the rush you get is incredible. Like you're flying."

"Are you ever afraid?"

Someone inside the ballroom clapped their hands loudly, so rather than answer her question, Tim offered her the crook of his arm.

"Believe it or not, I'm more afraid of what we're about to do in there."

She'd never been drunk before, but Hannah was certain this must be what it felt like. Warmth passed from his body to hers and she tried not to think too much about it. If she did, her hands might start sweating.

Cullum Hall boasted cherry floors and warm wooden beams that rose all the way to the ceiling. The ballroom looked almost candlelit, with sconces glowing against the wood and portraits of famous generals spaced evenly along the walls, like they were spying on the future. The parquet dance floor filled with cadets—upperclassmen laughed and whispered at the back of the hall—while Yuks like Tim and Hannah ventured toward the front. The instructor, a short, burly-looking man with a singsongy voice, clapped his hands, gathering the attention of the room.

"Okay, people!" he shouted over the din of voices. "Who's ready?"

There was a lackluster hoot from around the hall.

"All right, fine! Act cool now. I'll have you spinning like teacups at Disneyland before the end of the night."

The instructor pointed toward the back, where a woman wearing loud pink lipstick turned a dial. Suddenly the room filled with the sounds of classical instruments. The instructor looked annoyed, then pumped his thumb in a downward motion, telling the woman to decrease the volume, which she promptly did.

"The waltz . . . ," bellowed the instructor as he pranced through the room, making eye contact with each pair of dancers, "is about forbidden romance."

The students giggled.

"Laugh all you want, but it's true. If you're uninterested in seducing your dance partner, I'd suggest you leave. Perhaps there are shoes that need shining back in the barracks."

More laughter. But at this point, Hannah knew, he'd gained the respect of the room.

"That's what I thought." The instructor bellowed over the soft hum of violins. "The waltz was the predecessor of rock and roll, if you will. Just imagine!" he gasped dramatically. "Men and women twirling on the dance floor so close together and so fast! How vulgar! How positively sinful! In those days, men and women weren't even allowed in the same room together unchaperoned—"

"Sounds familiar!" a male voice behind Hannah shouted. It was Locke. Dani smacked him with her hand. The laughter in the room sounded like the ocean, coming in regular waves.

"Well then, I guess you don't have to imagine." The instructor grinned. "For the Austrians, the waltz was this sensual break from oppressive aristocratic rules . . . in three-quarter time. Now, each pair find a square!"

Tim and Hannah realized they were standing on top of a white square, which had been taped to the floor before their arrival. The instructor stopped just in front of them.

"Now, men, wrap your right arm around your partner's back and give her a nice squeeze."

Tim slipped his right hand between Hannah's hip and arm, and pulled her in tight. Their bodies were so close, she could feel him breathing. His breath smelled minty, but as she'd expected, the rest of his body smelled like spice and cologne.

"Now, turn your faces to the left, and stand cheek to cheek."

For a moment, Hannah felt a magnetism pull her closer and she thought she might collapse into him if she didn't concentrate on holding herself upright. When the instructor glided away from them, they both broke the pose. Around the room, laughter spread until most couples had stepped away from each other.

"Not easy, is it?" the instructor said. "I've always said if we could harness sexual tension at the United States Military Academy we could power New York City for a century. Am I right?"

"This guy," Locke whispered, rolling his eyes. He and Dani had sidled up to them, looking confident with their arms wrapped around each other. "And you said this is six weeks?"

"Yes, and you're going to love it," Dani ordered.

"Is she always this bossy?" Tim asked Hannah.

"Sometimes worse," Hannah whispered in his ear.

"Let's start with a basic box step," the instructor announced. "Gentlemen, face your ladies. It's just three steps. That's it. Toes pointed toward toes, please!"

Hannah and Tim both looked down at their toes at the same time, and their heads crashed together.

"Sorry!" said Tim, rubbing his head.

"First, gentlemen, we're going to start with our feet together. Forward with your left foot, to the side with your right foot, and then close your feet together. Left, side, close. Got it? Then you do the same thing with your right foot. Right, side, close. Right now, just focus on moving forward! Ladies, same thing, only you're going backward, and mirroring the gentleman's moves. Now give it a shot!"

Tim and Hannah took the first steps together perfectly. Soon, all around the classroom, couples were waltz-stepping like pros.

"Good. One, two, three! One, two, three!" the instructor shouted. "Keep moving!"

"Wait," Tim said, looking down at their mismatched feet, "I think I—"

"This way," Hannah laughed, pulling him back.

"And that is the waltz!" The instructor smiled, looking at all his progeny. "Wonderful, just wonderful! Linda! The music!"

The song started with long slow notes, filling the ballroom with orchestral formality. Meanwhile, the instructor moved from couple to couple, eyeing them with disdain and pride, depending on their performance.

"No, no, no! *Stop*," the instructor barked once he'd reached Hannah and Tim.

He grabbed Tim by the hips and Tim's eyes bulged. Moving them like a unit, the instructor pushed and pulled Tim's hips until they'd completed one perfect waltz step. All the while, Hannah tried hard not to break into hysterics. As soon as the instructor moved away, Tim's foot landed hard on top of Hannah's.

"Oh—God. Are you okay?" He winced, as if it were his foot that had been crunched.

"I'm okay," Hannah said, rubbing her foot. "I think he meant your other left."

Looking over Tim's shoulder, Hannah watched Dani and Locke, already twirling and box-stepping around the room like pros. Tim looked at her with big, puppy-dog eyes, then looked toward the exit door.

"I guess I suck at this, huh?"

They didn't move for a while, just stood there, looking at each other. His eyes were a hazel color, Hannah realized. Brown with flecks of gold scattered throughout.

"You know," he said, "I keep looking at you and wondering how I didn't notice you last year. How is that possible? Dani said we were in a class together . . . but for the life of me . . ."

"I didn't talk much in class," Hannah said. "You, on the other hand . . ."

"Yeah, I've never been one to shut up." He laughed. "Well. It's possible I'm sucking so bad because I'm so distracted. I wish we'd met a long time ago."

The compliment came out of nowhere. Equally genuine and playful, it sent blood rushing to Hannah's cheeks.

"It's hard to focus on my feet, when I'd rather look at this beautiful girl I just met."

"No, no, no," Hannah said with a smile, feeling her insides ache with joy. "You're not getting off that easy. We've got six weeks of this, mister, and flirting won't get you out of it."

"Oh, you thought I was talking about you?" he said. "I was talking about Linda."

They both turned to look at the pink-lipped woman in the back of the room, who was bobbing her head along with the music. They broke into laugher, then spent the rest of the class stepping on each other's feet and smiling uncontrollably. Hannah loved the pressure of his hand on her back, the brightness of his smile, the jokes he kept throwing out to distract her from how bad he was at dancing. She felt the muscles underneath his shirt flex and move with the music. Then she felt the pang of something else— something invisible taking root in her heart.

Love starts in the body. It starts with the tingling of toes and the rushing of blood and the lightness in the head. It feels a lot like pain, Hannah would realize later that week, as she and Tim shared slices of pizza in Grant Hall, and three weeks later, when they took a five-mile run together up Bear Mountain. There are convulsions, nausea, heartburn, and breathlessness. There is a physical ache you feel when you're falling in love. It's your heart making room for someone else, like a gardener is there, digging out a hole for a new plant. There is pain, and there is fear. The fear that the hole might stay forever.

Spring 2002 // West Point, New York

Fourteen days, D. Fourteen days and we're out of here."

A barbell loaded with two fifty-pound plates dropped from Locke Coleman's hands to the gymnasium floor with a loud crash. In the mirror, Dani watched him slide the large weights off and move two forty-five-pound plates onto the sides.

"Here," he said. "I think you're ready for one thirty-five. Do a clean."

For the last few months, Locke had made it his personal mission to help Dani fully recover from her injuries. He told her what to eat, how fast to run, how much to bench-press. And now he was monitoring how much weight she could lift from the ground to her shoulders. With a heave, she completed the move, in one snap of the wrists and hips.

She hadn't told him that the old familiar twinge was back again—that ache in her right hip. But it was possible that the discomfort was just residual scar tissue from last fall's surgery, or a by-product of doing cleans with the wrong form. Plus, if she ignored the static in her joints, she could lift nearly as much weight as she had this time last year, and that was something.

Three months earlier, at the last practice of the season, the entire women's basketball team had written the name of the player they wanted to serve as captain next year. Coach Janko-vich read the votes out loud with growing disdain.

"Dani McNalley . . . Dani McNalley . . . another for McNalley . . ."

Normally, the team chose a rising Firstie to be captain. And since Dani had truly only had *one* season on the court, this vote felt particularly kind. So she *had* to be better by next season—there were no excuses.

Releasing the bar, Dani looked at herself in the mirror. Her muscles had returned, arms sculpted, quads toned and strong. The scar on her hip had faded from red to dark brown, just a few shades darker than her skin. She finally looked like an athlete again, and not a moment too soon. This summer—in fourteen days, in fact—she and Hannah were headed to Airborne School. At times, the image of her body falling out of a plane with nothing but a parachute made her shiver with nerves. According to Tim, the biggest obstacle to overcome wasn't getting used to the height, or the equipment, or the risk. It was getting used to the fear.

"Everyone's scared," he'd explained a few nights earlier, while cooking a pot of spaghetti for Hannah on a hot plate in her room. "Everything in your body screams at you to step back from the edge—your palms sweat and your heart rate goes up, and everything in your head shouts that this is suicide. But once you're actually in the air—once you've jumped—all that fear goes away and you just fly. It's crazy. Most people never step over the boundary of fear."

Dani liked having Tim Nesmith around. Ever since ballroom dancing, he and Hannah had been inseparable. West Point's newest poster couple were nothing alike, of course. Tim was loud, opinionated, and spontaneous; Hannah was quiet, reserved, and thoughtful. But somehow, together, they were like opposite sides of a magnet that refused to separate.

"They're so attractive, it's annoying," Avery had whispered to Dani a few days earlier when they were passing between classes. Tim and Hannah were ahead of them, allowing the backs of their hands to touch every few steps. Academy rules prohibited holding hands.

"It's like, I can't decide who to look at," Dani said. "Him or her? They're both so beautiful."

They'd cracked up, mostly because it was true. The lovebirds looked like a Hollywood couple that had accidentally put on uniforms, and while Dani could admire their newfound love without growing a root of jealousy, she was pretty certain that it was becoming a difficult feat for Avery. It seemed hard for Avery to be content when faced with evidence that Hannah was happier with Tim than Avery had ever been with her fleet of boyfriends. Three weeks earlier, disregarding Hannah's new relationship status, Avery had planned a girls-only trip to New York City.

"We deserve this," Avery had said. And knowing it was their last B-weekend of the year, Hannah and Dani had complied.

Wendy Bennett had dropped them at the Garrison train station, and they'd taken the commuter train into Grand Central Terminal, stepping off the train and into the dirt, grime, and electricity of the world's most beautiful city.

"Soho," Avery had said decisively while they were on the train, pointing to the southwest corner of Manhattan on her map. "Then Greenwich Village or midtown. There are supposed to be some great clubs around there."

"The clubs all ID," Dani had said.

In response, Avery displayed a collection of freshly laminated driver's licenses like playing cards. "Here you go, Agatha. And you." She passed one to Hannah. "Juliette Ramsey."

"I don't know about this," Hannah had said. She turned her head to the side to inspect her alias.

"We won't use them unless we have to," Dani had said to Hannah, warding off Avery's annoyance. "And if we get some better clothes in Soho, I'm guessing we won't have any trouble getting into the clubs."

After a hearty brunch of French toast and coffee at a bakery on Bleecker Street, they'd meandered in and out of the stores in Soho, purchasing clothes that they'd later change into in the bathroom of a Starbucks in the Flatiron District. At Express, Avery had chosen a slinky black dress. Dani replaced her jeans with a tight miniskirt, to show off her newly sculpted legs. A fire-engine-red dress had called Hannah's name, and even though she'd cringed at the amount of skin it exposed, the girls had forced her to carry it to the checkout line.

They spent the night dancing, and when a limousine of FDNY

firefighters pulled up next to the club they were trying to get into, Avery had talked her way into their party, securing their entry into every club for the rest of the night. Because of their heroic efforts after the attacks on September 11th, the city still treated firefighters like celebrities, keeping their drinks full and their tabs on the house. At two A.M., Hannah had started to grow weary, rubbing her heels and staring at Dani pleadingly.

"Let's leave," she'd shouted over the music. "I'm ready to go back to the hotel."

"No, no, no," Avery had interjected. "Rally! Come on. This is our one chance to be in the city."

Hannah asked for a bottle of water from the bartender, who rolled his eyes as he delivered it to her hand. "Tim's going to love hearing that I partied 'til dawn with a bunch of bachelor fire fighters."

"Well—with all due respect—Tim can suck it," Avery had shouted back over the din of the music. "You're not doing any-thing wrong. And we've earned a little fun."

"She's kind of right," Dani had said, pinching Hannah's elbow. "Be a college kid for once. You can go back to being responsible tomorrow."

Hannah shook her head and chugged her water. Then she said, "It already is tomorrow."

"He's going to hold her back," Avery told Dani once they'd re-turned to life in uniform the following week. "They're both so serious."

"They're seriously in *love*," Dani had replied. But the explana-tion fell on deaf ears.

Lately, Avery had been sneaking around with God knew who at God knew what hour of the night, as if by the sheer volume of people she dated, she could find what she was looking for. Dani had started to wonder what had happened in Avery's past to make her so ravenous for attention. She was like a diabetic, only instead of sugar, she couldn't absorb love. Or, maybe, she absorbed it too quickly, and constantly felt the need for more. Whatever the problem, Dani wondered how long Avery could go on like this. Rather than dealing with her deficiency, Avery kept running, working hard to prove her worth and amass awards and achievements and admirers. But to Dani, all that effort seemed exhausting. She wondered if Avery would ever stop running. She wondered if she'd ever have the courage to stand still.

If she needed any advice, Dani knew where she could turn— after all, she was becoming an expert at being single.

"That looked good," Locke said, bringing Dani out of her thoughts. "Go again."

She picked up the bar, completed another perfect clean, and let the bar drop to the floor.

AFTER DINNER, THEY went back to Locke's dorm room to study for West Point's Term End Exams, known as TEEs. *The Miseducation of Lauryn Hill* played from Locke's computer speakers, mingling rhymes of revolution with Dani's pack of physics problems. While she measured velocity and torque, she grew distracted by other sounds coming from Locke's computer. A door creaking open or slamming shut. The sound of a loud *cha-*

ching, indicating that someone special had come online. The constant *ba-da-bing* of an incoming AOL instant message.

"You're popular tonight," Dani said, putting her pencil down on the paper in front of her. "What's happening up there?"

In truth, she worried Locke might be chatting online with some other girl, even while Dani sat comfortably on his floor. In the last six months, he'd had countless opportunities to make a move. Throughout the ballroom dancing lessons, they'd moved across the dance floor with more chemistry and ease than anyone in the room. She'd grown tired of feeling his hands spotting her in the gym, rather than reaching for her to pull her in for a kiss.

A few weeks earlier, Dani had been sitting in Wendy Bennett's kitchen, talking about this very thing, when Wendy had firmly set her coffee cup on the counter and sighed.

"You're going to drive yourself crazy waiting around for him to make a move."

Tears had welled in Dani's eyes, as if the truth had unlocked some inner door, letting the emotion free. A tissue box appeared on the kitchen table, but swallowing hard, Dani forced the tears back to where they came from.

"That's not true," she'd insisted. "Locke and I *are* friends. I don't want to lose that."

"You're going to lose him one way or another. One of you will start dating someone else. Someday you'll both be married. It won't be like this forever."

"So what? Stop being friends now because maybe someday we'll marry other people?"

"No. I'm saying you should tell him how you feel."

"It's not that easy."

"Of course not," Wendy had said. "Doing the right thing never is. That's how you know it's the right thing."

Locke's broad shoulders hunched over his keyboard, his eyes trained on the computer screen. And suddenly, the thought of spending two more years in relationship purgatory overwhelmed Dani with frustration. Wendy was right. She deserved an answer, but she would never get it waiting around on Locke's dorm room floor.

"Hey, Locke," Dani started. "I think we need to—"

"Oh man," said Locke, interrupting her. "D, you've got to come see this."

The somber tone of his voice and the shock on his face sent Dani's eyes directly to his computer screen. There, a collage of images assaulted her—pale white limbs, curves, pink nipples. Dani pushed Locke out of the way. She scrolled quickly, her eyes reflecting the bright light of the computer screen, the images of one naked female body, over and over again. Locke stood behind her, biting his lower lip.

"Where did these come from?" Dani snapped. She looked back at Locke, who raised his hands in the air—*Don't shoot*.

"Someone on the football team just forwarded them to me. It was a zip file. I didn't know . . . I . . . What are you doing?"

Clicking maniacally, Dani toggled through the photos, pressing *Print* on each one. She snatched the photos off Locke's printer. The pages felt warm in her hand.

"What are you going to do?" he repeated. "Where are you going with those?"

Without answering him, Dani limped out the door. As she made her way down the stairs and outside, Dani couldn't stop thinking about Lisa Johnson. Three weeks earlier, she'd found Dani in the library and tearfully admitted that in the fall, she was transferring to Tulane.

"I can't do it," Lisa had said. "I can't go to war, D. And even if that wasn't happening . . . Coach Jankovich. She . . . she's ruined this place for me."

For her part, Coach Jankovich had acted as if it was a personal victory. "*It was only a matter of time,*" she'd said in response to the news, as if Lisa had finally been outed as a weakling, rather than acknowledging her role in breaking her down so far that Lisa no longer saw a future for herself at West Point. Dani had spent hours trying to convince Lisa to stay, to no avail. It felt like a personal failure, losing a teammate. Her first failure as the next team captain.

And she wasn't about to let these photos be her second.

IN THE HOLLEDER Center, most offices were reserved for football coaches. Since spring football practice was in session at Michie Stadium, and the rest of West Point's coaches were on recruiting trips, the entire place was empty and quiet. Unfortunately, it was harder than ever to recruit competitive players, now that the U.S. was engaged in an all-out war on terrorism—*whatever that meant*. Dani still didn't understand the long-term strategy of a war against a network of people that had no flag, no country, no identifying characteristics other than hate.

How do you defeat fear? How do you defeat evil? It seemed like a never-ending task that could lead to never-ending conflict. *How would they ever know that they'd won?*

But the war was only one reason that recruiting had become so difficult. Fluorescent lights lit the corridor outside of Coach Jankovich's office, and one flickered, like a fly had been caught in its electrical circuit. It couldn't hurt to change a lightbulb or put a little effort into updating the facilities, Dani thought. But West Point wasn't like other colleges; they practically needed congressional approval to turn up the air-conditioning. And if recruiting had been difficult for Coach Jankovich before, it was about to get much harder. No one wanted to send their daughter to a place where she'd be treated like a piece of meat.

Taking a deep breath, Dani knocked on the coach's office door.

MINUTES LATER, THE printed photos were spread out over Jankovich's already-crowded desk, an array of identical bodies, like images from a crime scene.

"How did you get ahold of these?" the coach asked.

Each photo showed the same person from a different angle, decapitated by the top edge of a camera lens: light skin, thin waist, round breasts, hairless between her legs. A headless body—bare for the entire corps to devour.

"My friend received them in a forwarded e-mail."

"How do you know this is our locker room?" she asked, lifting one photo in her hand.

"The carpet, see?" Dani pointed to the distinguishing black and gold lines. "And the . . . well. I know it's ours, because I know who that is."

Blood rushed to Dani's extremities as she watched the coach inspect the photos, turning them from side to side. *What is she looking for?* Letting out a massive sigh, Coach Jankovich ran a hand through her short hair, and it stood askew, pointing in different directions. She suddenly looked Dani directly in the face, her steel-blue eyes narrowing.

Silence spread between them, leaving the room devoid of oxygen. Dani coughed, took a breath, and tried again.

"I think we should report this. Someone hid a camera in our locker room and is now—"

"The damage is already done, wouldn't you say?"

"Coach, I—"

"Doing that is going to cause a huge scandal. There will be news crews. A massive witch hunt. We have a hard enough time recruiting girls without something like this. Every one of our recruits will renege on their commitment, Dani. Is that what you want?"

"No. But this isn't about basketball—"

"Of course it's about basketball! So someone snapped a few nudie photos in the locker rooms. Big deal. It's not exactly rape we're dealing with here."

"Does it have to be, for it to be wrong?"

The coach steeled her gaze.

"Whoever did this used a digital camera," Dani continued pleadingly. "The angle is bad. That's why you can't see the face.

They were taken from above—like someone stashed a camera above our lockers or something. And they're not photos. You see the time stamp here? They're *still shots*. Whoever did this has *video footage*. The camera could still be there."

"Well, then, we will remove it."

"We can't just do that, Coach . . . if it's there, it's evidence." Dani hated how exasperated she sounded. She wanted to reach across the desk and shake her coach into caring. Into understanding.

"Jesus, Dani. You sound like you think you're on some crime show or something. We'll deal with it internally and move on."

There was a long pause, and in it, Dani knew she had to make a decision. She could walk away, or she could push back against what was an obvious attempt to brush this under the rug. Without a doubt, if she made any demands, her relationship with Coach Jankovich would never be the same.

After taking a deep breath, Dani decided to push forward.

"As the team captain, I felt it was my duty to bring this to your attention before I take it up the chain of command," Dani said with authority.

"Oh my *God*! You people!" Coach Jankovich laughed derisively. A square smile appeared on her face that looked forced and awkward. She stood from her chair, narrowed her eyes until they were dark slits. "I don't know what you're playing at here, but I can guarantee one thing. If you think you can come in here and make *threats*, you can think again. What did you do? Did you tell them all to write your name down, so you could lead your little revolution?"

"What?"

"You and your little *cult.* I bet you did this. Put the camera there. Sent the e-mail yourself."

"Coach, you and I both know that that's ridiculous."

"The only thing that's ridiculous is the fact that all of my work is going to go down the drain because of this trash." Picking up the photos off her desk, she gripped them tight, crushing the pages.

Dani bit the insides of her cheeks, hard. *How could someone be this paranoid? This blind?*

"What makes you so scared of the truth?" Dani asked boldly. "That's one of your *players.* And when she finds out what's happened, she's going to be *crushed.* Don't you care? Aren't you concerned about her at all?"

"I'm concerned about the big picture," the coach said.

"You're concerned about yourself."

They stood, facing once another across her desk, refusing to blink.

"You're dismissed."

Dani turned to leave. She took a halting step, feeling a surge of pain.

"And you can forget about being captain," the coach said, then lifted her chin toward Dani's hip. "That is, if you can even play anymore."

LATE THAT EVENING, Dani sat next to Hannah on her bed, the two of them poring over the photos. By this point, every male on campus had received the zip file, of that much Dani was certain. It was only a matter of time before the women on campus started to get wind of the fact that naked photos of a female cadet were being passed around like common pornography.

"We have to tell her," Dani said to Hannah. "Before we do anything else. We have to tell her."

Hannah shook her head and groaned. "This isn't going to go well at all."

"Where is she?" asked Dani.

"I don't know. I never know."

"Well then, let's go to her room. We'll wait."

WEST POINT ALMA MATER

*

Hail Alma Mater dear, to us be ever near
Help us thy honor bear, through all the years.
Let duty be well performed
Honor be e'er untarned
Country be ever armed,
West Point, by thee.
Guide us, they sons aright, teach us by day by night,
To keep thine honor bright, for thee to fight.
When we depart from thee,
Serving on land or sea,
May we still loyal be,
West Point, to thee.
And when our work is done, our course on earth is run
May it be said, "Well Done, Be Thou at Peace."
E'er may that line of gray
Increase from day to day
Live, serve and die we pray,
West Point, for thee.

BETWEEN

Three Months After Graduation

Fall 2004

11

Summer 2004 // Fort Bragg, North Carolina

A very woke up naked in bed with a twenty-six-year-old enlisted soldier named Josh Ramirez. Pushing a white-blond hair off her face, she stared at the Tilt-A-Whirl ceiling, wondering how much she'd had to drink the night before. She'd lost count somewhere around her seventh gin and tonic. A heavy arm fell across her stomach and a face covered in day-old stubble nuzzled her neck. Avery sighed loudly. It was time for Josh to leave.

"What's your exit strategy?" she asked.

The man kissed her neck and traced his fingers across her hip. "I was hoping for seconds," he mumbled into her ear.

Avery wrapped the scratchy comforter she'd bought at Target over her chest. "Well, that's too bad," she said. "Because I was hoping for breakfast."

She kissed him on the cheek, then turned to put her feet on the floor. The air mattress had partially deflated overnight, making it awkward for her to stand. Fighting the headache already building behind her eyes, Avery slipped into a robe and then walked out the door into the hallway, where she let out a silent scream and stamped her feet.

She couldn't believe Josh was still in her bed! It was Sunday, for Christ's sake. At the beginning of their relationship—if you could even call it a relationship—they'd agreed to one rule. *One rule!* No one stays over; no one gets caught. How hard was that for him to understand?

When she'd moved into her Army quarters four weeks ago, she hadn't considered that living across the street from another second lieutenant could make life so painfully awkward. Living on post meant that she was close to work, and could wake up at 0550 and still be at PT by 0600 every morning. But now, Avery deeply regretted her choice to live among her coworkers. As a part of the Signal Corps, she planned wartime communication strategies with her neighbor Lieutenant Erik Jenkins during the day, and waved to his twenty-three-year-old wife from the opposite kitchen window at night. There was no way Josh would leave undetected. Did he realize that her reputation was on the line? If someone saw her, an officer, with him, a first sergeant, it could mean the end of her career.

People get court-martialed for this shit, Avery thought. But did they? Really? With all that was going on in the world, would the Army really prosecute her for a little fraternization? Surely not. Avery felt painfully stupid, but not just because her head was pounding. Two days ago, she'd been sitting across from a female soldier having a conversation about this exact same subject.

On Friday afternoon, a girl with dark brown hair had appeared in Avery's office, having just arrived at Fort Bragg from Advanced Individual Training. The girl wore tight jeans and an even tighter white T-shirt. Thick eyeliner encircled her blue eyes; a slick of gloss accentuated her lips. With curves and a slight tan, this new private had all the flair you're supposed to have when you've just graduated from high school: dewy skin, bright teeth. She looked nothing like a soldier. Sitting in front of a woman in civilian clothes, Avery couldn't help but think how unfeminine and ridiculous she must have looked in her Army combat uniform. Loose at the thighs and tapered at the ankles, her ACUs looked like a better fit for MC Hammer, and the jacket was a size too big, with a black nameplate on her right breast pocket. Instinctively, Avery had touched the patch of acne that had appeared on her jawline. Wasn't she too old for zits?

"Welcome to Fort Bragg, Private Bradley," Avery had said, replacing the beginnings of jealousy with the voice of authority. "I'll be your direct superior from this point forward. If you need anything at all, if you have any questions, you can bring them to me."

"Yes, sir." The girl blushed. "Ma'am. Sorry."

As Avery thumbed through the girl's file, the new soldier chewed her fingernails. Eyes wide and anxious, she appeared dazed and jittery, just like Avery had been back at West Point on those first days. Cleavage threatened to spill out of the private's shirt, like she'd dressed for a job interview at a strip club, not the

U.S. Army. Had this kid looked in the mirror before walking in here?

"How old are you, Private Bradley?" asked Avery.

"Eighteen. Nineteen next month."

Eighteen. The number flashed before Avery's eyes. When Avery was eighteen, her civilian life had ended, too. Four years had passed since then, but somehow, seated at her own desk with West Point behind her, twenty-two felt ancient. In minutes, this new recruit would head back to the barracks, where an onslaught of twenty-something males would see her as their newest opportunity for conquest. Unfortunately, it was Avery's job to keep that kind of drama to a minimum. Her boss had sent out a memo the week before, reminding his lieutenants that certain STDs disqualified soldiers from readiness for deployment. Apparently chlamydia was making a comeback.

The girl had been sitting on her hands. Something about her oozing sexuality and ignorance had felt deeply embarrassing to Avery, like interacting with her former self. She refused to make eye contact, but instead kept looking at the items on Avery's desk: a half-eaten paper pint of oatmeal, a green juice in a clear plastic container, a framed photo of three girls standing in the middle of New York City. Watching the private's eyes widen with anxiety, Avery felt a sudden wave of compassion—a desire to keep this girl from making all the mistakes she'd made at eighteen, nineteen, and twenty. She wanted to tell her that even the nicest, most innocent-looking men could stab you in the back. In the heart.

"You just finished high school?"

"Yes, ma'am. Last spring."

"First time away from Mom and Dad?"

The girl nodded, smiled.

"There's no easy way for me to say this." She tapped the papers together into a stack, trying a firm and strict tone on for size. "It's very important that you carry yourself *professionally* here. I can't have you getting involved with anything that might distract you or your fellow soldiers from training. Because, to be completely honest, that training could save your life one day."

The girl sat up straight. Her eyes had a vacant and subtly terrified expression, like a deer on the verge of being flattened by an SUV.

"I'm just saying, be on your guard," Avery continued, trying a softer approach. "As far as any of these men are concerned, there's only one woman in uniform . . . and it's you."

"I'm not sure what you mean," she'd said.

"What you do reflects on all of us, Private Bradley."

Avery had known, seated there on Friday afternoon, that she was engaging in a losing battle. But she had to try.

DOWNSTAIRS IN THE kitchen, Avery pulled a carton of eggs from the refrigerator and a skillet from the cabinet. As a single second lieutenant, she had plenty of storage space that she didn't need and didn't use. Most of the cabinets were hollow and empty. She hadn't had the luxury of registering for everyday china after graduation like Hannah and Tim. Shouldn't girls have an *I'm single but I still want to cook registry*? Or an *I may never get married so someone buy me sheets shower*? Avery thought so.

And yet, all the Pottery Barn linens that Hannah and Tim had received as wedding presents were still in boxes. Avery knew, because she was the one tasked with collecting any delivered packages while Hannah was at Sapper School in Missouri and Tim was at Ranger School in Georgia. Three sets of perfectly good five-hundred-thread-count sheets sat in boxes in the Nesmiths' house, while Avery suffered under itchy cotton bedding that deserved to be in a Motel 6 Dumpster. It would have been easy to steal—no, borrow—the newlyweds' new goose-down comforter, but Avery hadn't resorted to theft. At least not yet.

She still couldn't believe one of her friends was *married*. Even the word sounded odd when it came out of her mouth. *Marriage.* Total commitment to one person, for the rest of your life, until you died or they did—whichever came sooner. It seemed like the worst possible contract you could ever sign. And Avery still couldn't believe that Hannah and Tim had decided to do it. They were only twenty-two years old, and both facing long-term deployments. Avery couldn't understand the rush.

But then again, Avery didn't understand any of their relationship. The summer after their sophomore year of college, while Hannah and Dani attended Airborne School, Avery had stayed at West Point to complete Air Assault training. She'd been grateful to learn that Tim Nesmith was in her company, but for some reason, he'd avoided her all summer. And when she heard that he'd kissed another girl in their training class, Avery went ballistic.

"Is it true?" she'd snapped at him one night, pushing him hard with both of her hands. She had tracked him down in a small tunnel that ran underneath Washington Road. The Beat Navy tunnel featured placards from the years Army had defeated Navy in football, and was echoey, a place where people shouted and cheered for their team. It was odd to stand in that tunnel and remain so silent. Tim stepped away from her, and though she didn't want to see his emotion, it was plastered all over his face: shame, fear, regret. The rims of his eyes turned red.

"It was a huge mistake," he'd said. "I'm going to tell her, Avery. Please. Just let me tell her first."

Avery had spent the better part of junior year telling Hannah not to take Tim back. Not after what he'd done. Not even after his apology. By the time they were Firsties, Dani had to stage an intervention of her own.

"You realize he's going to propose, don't you?" she'd said to Avery one night their senior year. It was after Tim's accident. After his radical conversion and Hannah's unconvincing speech to Avery that he'd *changed*. "You've got to forgive him, Avery," Dani had told her. "He's one of us now. He's in the cult."

After that, Avery had tried her best to swallow her pride. She'd even helped Dani coordinate Tim's ridiculous proposal—Avery was the one who'd scattered rose petals across the floor of Cullum Hall. She'd lit the candles. She'd sketched the ring: a full-carat diamond, princess cut, perched on a delicate gold band—the style Hannah had let drop to her friends in casual conversation, knowing Tim would ask for their input.

In June, three hundred guests had gathered at Hannah's grandfather's ranch in Austin, Texas, under Chinese lanterns hanging from trees, cows lowing in the distance. A dance floor and a ten-piece band set up outside, under the stars, and played loud into the night for Hannah, Tim, and all of their friends. Instead of cake, they'd served ten different types of pie—Hannah's grandmother had baked them all from scratch. Hannah wore a lace dress and her mother's old veil, and when she'd walked down the grassy aisle between the guests, Tim had cried. Hell, everyone had cried. It was all so soul-crushingly *meaningful*.

"I don't know if it'll ever happen for me," Avery had said to Dani, seated on the Speer's porch swing.

"Of course it will."

"Not like that," Avery had retorted, pointing her beer toward the outdoor dance floor. Hannah and Tim were swaying in each other's arms.

"Well of course not like that."

"There won't be pies," said Avery.

"Tequila shots, maybe."

"Yes." Avery had pointed her beer at Dani. "Tequila shots and maybe a man dressed in an Elvis costume, officiating. And my mother, sobbing in the corner because she finally has proof that I'm not Catholic."

"Just don't make me wear yellow," Dani had demanded. "On second thought, I'll do the Elvis thing."

They'd laughed their way back to the dance floor, arms wrapped around one another's backs.

While the memory simmered in Avery's mind, two eggs sizzled in a lightweight pan, whites oozing around the edges like spilled paint. As breakfast cooked, high-quality coffee beans filled Avery's kitchen with the bittersweet smell of oak and butter. If she was honest, it was kind of nice to have a man upstairs, waiting on breakfast. It felt good to have a chance to share her house with someone other than the cast of *Grey's Anatomy* on Thursday nights. She could get used to this new arrangement.

Just then, the dark-haired man from her bed snuck up behind her and cupped his hands over her hips. Turning, Avery admired Josh's eyes, deep brown, like the earth. And his hands, so warm against her skin.

"I should go," he said.

"What do you mean? I'm making breakfast." She pointed at the eggs with her spatula.

He yawned and raised his arms up over his head, revealing a thick torso rippled with muscles.

"Stay," Avery ordered, reaching for his pants seductively. "And that's an order."

The heel of his hand rubbed against one eye, as if he had a migraine. "Avery, I don't get you. It's yes, it's no. It's 'Don't drive to my house,' then 'Who cares about the neighbors.' I never know which version of you I'm going to wake up with."

He stared into Avery's eyes so unflinchingly that she burst into a nervous laugh. "Come on, Josh," she said. "You know we have to be careful. That's not fair."

"Yeah? Well, now you know how I feel."

"So go," she snapped. "Leave then."

"I can't."

Avery stared at him and he stared back in silence. The eggs hissed and whined in the pan, turning brown and then black at the edges.

"I need a ride back to my car," he finally explained. "You drove last night, remember?"

In one motion, Avery grabbed the skillet handle and slammed the eggs into the sink. As she climbed the stairs to change and get her keys, yellow trails of yolk inched toward the drain.

THE DRIVE BACK to the bar where they'd met up the night before only took them a few miles off post. They didn't speak, and soon Fort Bragg's gate filled the rearview mirror. The silence was a horrible sound. Avery knew that if Dani were here, she'd know exactly what to say—a joke to throw out and defuse the ticking time bomb. But anger had momentarily paralyzed Avery's vocal cords.

When she pulled her car into the bar's gravel parking lot, Josh coughed, as if he too needed to shake an emotion out of his throat.

Avery fully expected him to apologize for staying so late and violating the one boundary they'd established for their pseudo-relationship. She thought he'd kiss her and get out of the car, and they'd be back to their odd version of normal. Instead, he turned toward her and took in a breath.

"Can I say something?" he asked.

"I think you have that ability, yes."

"What is this?"

"This is me, dropping you at your car."

"No. I mean, *this*." Josh swung his hand back and forth between them. "Us."

Avery rolled her eyes. "You can't be serious."

"I want to hear you say it."

She tugged on her blond ponytail. "What? We're screwing around. Being kids. Is that what you want me to say?"

Josh shook his head. His voice barely exceeded a whisper. "You're incredible. Really, fucking incredible. You do whatever the hell you want, whenever you want. No matter who gets hurt—"

"Hurt?" Avery reared her head back in anger. Her voice was low and mean.

"I should have known—"

"I put my entire career on the line—"

"*Your* career?" he laughed. "You truly think you're the only one in this equation, don't you? It's the *Avery Adams Show*, twenty-four-fucking-seven."

"Get out of my car."

"Gladly." Josh opened his door and climbed out, then looked back at her again. "Do yourself a favor, Avery. Stop fucking around with people that love you."

With that, he slammed the door and walked toward his truck, a silver Toyota Tacoma—the only vehicle left in the parking lot. Avery stepped on the gas, spewing rocks and dust into the air behind her.

LOVE, AVERY THOUGHT with a laugh as she pulled back into her driveway. That was a joke. They'd only known each other a few months. When they'd met, she was recovering from a year of involuntary chastity at West Point, and Josh had the body of an English soccer player. The sex was good. Hell, at times it was great. But if this guy thought he was in love, well then Avery had fooled him. And she didn't feel bad about it either. If she felt bad about anything at all, it was being a hypocrite. She'd told Private

Bradley to be careful on Friday, just to return to her own reckless life on Saturday.

Avery was glad Josh had ended it. As with so many other relationships, she was convinced that this one should have never even started.

ON MONDAY, AVERY arrived at work before the sun came up and completed a freezing-cold PT run with her platoon, finishing the two-mile course in 12:07. Not her best time by any means, but she crossed the finish line a full minute before anyone else. She'd seen it time and time again: once her soldiers tasted her dust on a PT run, their skepticism softened into respect. She would have hated their conditional admiration if she didn't savor it so much. But she often wondered if without her physical edge, she would have remained invisible. What if she was slower? Would such weakness merit scorn? These were the questions that rolled in her mind while she savored her post run endorphins.

After a shower and a microwaved bowl of oatmeal at her desk, Avery noticed an e-mail in her inbox from her boss's boss, Major Philip Gaines.

"LT Adams, please report to my office this morning. I need to see you as soon as possible."

Avery's blue eyes scanned the screen again, while her heart raced in her chest. It was unusual for someone to jump the chain of command—up or down—but even more disconcerting, Gaines had carbon-copied her direct superior, Captain Morris. The subtext screamed that something was wrong. He'd sent the e-mail Sunday afternoon, meaning he'd heard something during off hours that he wanted to discuss. Did he know about Josh? Had someone, somehow, turned her in?

Erik fucking Jenkins, Avery swore internally. She closed her eyes and tried to remember her neighbor's porch, Sunday morning when she and Josh had rushed out in anger. Erik's wife—Melinda? Melissa?—whatever her name was, Avery distinctly recalled her red hair piled in a messy bun as she stared out the window onto the street, a hand resting on her hip. *Shit,* Avery thought. *We should have been more careful.*

The Army, at times, infuriated Avery. All of its rules. Its demands. Its ladders of authority. The Army was a lot like her dad, actually—constantly providing new bars to reach, moving each bar higher every time Avery got close. It wasn't that she needed to be coddled, but to hear that she was doing a good job every once in a while wouldn't have hurt. She could handle being read the riot act for leaving a job unfinished or not meeting the standards. But was she really about to be counseled about who she *dated* on the weekends?

She always chose the wrong people to date on the weekends.

As Avery took a deep breath, her eyes veered to the framed photo on her desk, and she felt longing mixed with regret. It wasn't like she wanted to go back to her dysfunctional family in Pittsburgh, or to West Point—her friends had left that place behind, too. And yet she couldn't shake the feeling that she wanted to go home. But where would that be?

How could she be homesick for a place that didn't exist?

In the photo, she and Dani stood on either side of Hannah, their smiling faces surrounded by the madness of Times Square.

The photo sent a kaleidoscope of memories spinning through Avery's mind. Hannah's short red dress, stretching as she pulled it down her thighs in the firefighters' limousine. Dani's commanding moves, dominating dance floors. The limousine's tinted windows, distorting city lights into a blur. A firefighter's callused hands rubbing Avery's lower back. Avery had been so committed to staying out all night—so convinced that it was their only chance to be young and free.

In some ways she was right. Only a few weeks later, she'd been blindsided. Knocked out cold. Avery would never forget walking into her dorm room and seeing photos of her own nakedness splayed out in Dani's shaking hands. Nausea had swelled into her throat, like the earth was falling out from beneath her. She'd collapsed into Hannah's arms, overcome with anger, sadness, and shame.

Wiping her eyes, Avery forced the memory back into the recesses of her heart where it belonged, like a collection of junk stuffed into a dark basement. There was no reason to unpack that box. It was in the past. Dealt with. Over. And reliving that time—that trauma—wouldn't help her now.

Steeling herself, Avery breathed in deeply, rolled her shoulders back, and stood from her desk. There was nothing to feel ashamed of. She hadn't done anything to deserve what Collins had done to her, and she definitely didn't deserve to lose her career over a momentary misstep—a relationship with Josh that no longer existed. She imagined facing Major Gaines and denying everything. After all, the Army took everything she had during the day. Couldn't they leave her nights alone?

"YOU WANTED TO see me, sir?"

Major Gaines was in his early thirties with thinning hair and a large, mostly bald head. Turning from his computer, he gathered a few papers off his desk and tapped them into a neat stack, without looking Avery in the eye.

"Yes, take a seat. I've got a few things to finish up, then we can chat."

Typing at his keyboard, he composed an e-mail, added an event to his calendar, then closed down all the tabs on his desktop. He worked quickly, Avery noticed, like a squirrel gathering nuts in the last few days before winter.

"All right," he sighed, finally turning to look at her. "Thanks for coming to see me."

"Of course." Sweat seeped out of the pores in her hands, her armpits, her neck. "How can I help, sir?" She forced a smile.

"I have a job that I need to assign. It starts in a few months. It's a big job, actually, and it's going to require someone that can remain focused and work really fast."

All of her pent-up anxiety deflated like a balloon. So he *didn't* know about Josh. *Thank God.* She shifted in her seat, listening closely.

"One of the new Special Forces facilities needs wiring. Phones, Internet. The works. It all needs to be wired and encrypted. Captain Morris says you're one of his best lieutenants. We'd like you to lead the job."

Avery nodded with confidence, though she simply felt relieved that this meeting had nothing to do with her romantic indiscretions.

"Wow, sir. Thank you. I'd be honored to do it."

"Those SF guys are always in and out, so the important thing is that you don't get in their way. You'll need a team of ten or twelve I'd say, and the same rules apply to everyone." He stared at her intently. "You don't talk. You don't ask questions. You don't make friends. You get in, keep your heads down, and get out. Understood?"

"Yes, sir. I'm honored that you'd choose me to lead the job."

"Is there a reason I shouldn't?"

A beat passed before Avery answered, "Absolutely not, sir."

"Good. Let's put a few more meetings on the books. You've got a few months to get all of your ducks in a row, choose your team, order all your equipment. And let's keep Captain Morris carbon-copied on all our communication on this. Keep him in the loop."

"Yes, sir," Avery said. It was rare for a second lieutenant to be given such a huge responsibility. *Special Forces. Just wait until the Nesmiths hear about my job.* Tim was hoping to join the Army's most elite unit as soon as he got the chance. He'd be green with envy.

From: Avery Adams <averyadams13@yahoo.com>

Subject: Re: Re: Re: **Update

Date: August 27, 2004 12:03:15 PM GMT +01:00

To: Dani McNalley <danimcnalley@yahoo.com>, Hannah Nesmith <hannah_nesmith@yahoo.com>

HEY HEY HEY.

How is everyone?! Dani . . . any news on the job front? Hannah—how is Sapper School treating you? I'm dying to hear an update from the cult.

Things here are fine—nothing major to report. Although, Hannah, you've received about 6.5 million presents in the last few weeks. I'm probably going to start opening them and picking out the things I want to take for my cut. It's only fair that your favorite bridesmaid get a little slush on the side.

In other news . . . I got a really crazy assignment today from my boss's boss. It's going to start in the spring, and I can't really e-mail about it because it's classified (what?! Who am I??)—but the good news is, it's here in Fort Bragg, so I'm still not going overseas for a while.

What about you, Hannah? Have you heard anything about deployment dates for your unit?

ALL HAIL THE CULT,
Avery

12

Summer 2004 // Fort Leonard Wood, Missouri

A fist slammed into Hannah's face, hard. An African-American soldier named Private Daniel Stanton stood in front of her, his red boxing gloves drooping at his sides. Her vision blurred and suddenly, all of the sounds in the gymnasium were submerged in water. She swayed.

The next thing Hannah knew, she awoke on the ground, staring at a ceiling of fluorescent light. The scent of old wrestling mats and sweat assaulted her nose, and she tasted metal in her mouth. When she touched her fingers to her nostril they were covered in blood.

Things were not going as planned.

When she'd arrived at Fort Leonard Wood for Sapper School, Hannah knew the odds would be stacked against her. In the history of the Army, only twenty-three females had ever attempted the highest training school available for combat engineers—and of those, only nine had graduated. Hannah wanted desperately to be number ten. In the past eight weeks, she'd built helipads, jumped from a moving helicopter into open water, and, just the day before, scored full points rappelling from a cliff with a 220-pound soldier strapped to her back. All of it without a single complaint. Not even a groan.

There was only one test left. If Hannah could just wrap Private Stanton's hands behind his back—if she could just achieve the clinch—she would graduate, the tenth female Sapper in history. All she had to do was step to her six-foot-three attacker, drive her head into his neck, push his arms out to the sides, and pin his arms around his back. But so far, every time Hannah stepped closer to him, all she got was Stanton's fists in the face.

"All right, boys, I think I found our weakest link." A shadowy figure leaned over Hannah's body until his face was just inches from hers. The barrel-chested NCO, Master Sergeant Moretti, had yellow teeth and breath that smelled of weak coffee. He flapped his clipboard over Hannah's face. "Come on, get up, Nesmith."

Stilted laughter pounded against Hannah's ears as Moretti offered her his hand.

"I'm all right," she said, forcing herself to stand without his help.

Moretti rolled his eyes and inspected her face. "It's broken."

"I've had a broken nose before," Hannah said. When she was six years old, her sister, Emily, had accidentally thrown an elbow in her face while they were playing freeze tag. "I'll be fine."

"Stanton, hold her head still," Moretti yelled to Hannah's opponent.

Stanton's palms pressed against her sweaty hair while Moretti placed both of his hands on either side of the bridge of her nose, like he was praying. He paused. "This is going to hurt."

"Just get it over with," Hannah muttered. She closed her eyes and braced for the pain.

With one swift motion, Sergeant Moretti slammed his fingers against the right side of her nose, snapping it back into alignment. A shock of blue light flashed through Hannah's brain. An involuntary shout emerged from her lungs. Hannah chewed on her lips to keep from crying, then walked a few paces to regain her breath.

"None of us enjoy watching you get the shit beat out of you," Moretti said. He'd followed her to the side of the gymnasium and placed a hand on her shoulder. "I'm thinking it may be time to call it quits. Come back next cycle. Try again."

Hannah forced herself to breathe. She didn't want his sympathy. She hadn't stumbled into Sapper School by mistake. Couldn't he check his clipboard? Wasn't it just that morning that she'd smoked them all on the six-mile run? But there was no way around the fact that Stanton's fists flew faster and harder than she'd expected. He was denser than she could ever be. And the way he looked at her, with some kind of perverse hunger, it was like he wanted to break not just her nose but something deeper. Hannah had been one of the highest-ranking cadets at West Point—guy or girl. Now her ovaries were a flashing neon sign to everyone in the room that she couldn't keep up. All around, men crossed their arms over their chests, waiting. Some looked bored. Some looked concerned. Most looked amazed that Hannah was still standing.

With a fresh wave of nausea, an echo of words swirled in Hannah's mind, a phrase she hadn't considered in some time. *It's not a matter of capability.*

What if her grandfather had been wrong? What if she really couldn't keep up? What if he'd been right, that she shouldn't be here?

Tim had warned her of this. That summer, after graduation and their wedding, Hannah, Tim, and a dozen other class of '04 grads had flown to Rome and boarded a cruise ship that had transported them between six different Mediterranean cities. While their friends drank themselves silly, Tim and Hannah had secluded themselves as much as possible, knowing it was the closest thing they'd get to a honeymoon. They were lounging on the deck of a ship, a few hours before it docked in Florence, when Hannah told Tim that she'd been given a slot at Sapper School, starting in the middle of August. He'd raised his aviator sunglasses and his eyebrows.

"Sapper School?" he'd said. "Really?"

"I think I can do it," replied Hannah.

"I *know* you can do it," he'd said. "I just don't see why you'd want to. Those guys will hurt you on purpose, just to prove a point."

"No they won't. And even if they did, should that stop me from trying? Why do you want to get a Ranger tab?" Hannah had added defiantly. "It's the same thing."

Tim leaned back in his chair, sighed, and put his glasses back on his face. Ranger School was the Army's most intense, brutal training. It was a rite of passage, a symbol of capability, an immediate indicator that an officer could be trusted, and the most direct path to the Special Forces, which had been Tim's dream since childhood. Sapper School wasn't nearly that extreme, but it held a similar cachet, and when Hannah arrived in Fort Bragg to lead her first platoon, she wanted her soldiers to know that she was a serious leader, serious about the Army. If anyone could understand that, she knew Tim would.

"Well then I guess we have to get you ready, Rocky," Tim had said, looking around the deck of the ship. "They got any stairs we can run around here?"

True to form, they'd spent their last few weeks together preparing. They went on long, fast runs through the hills of Santorini. He held her feet while she did sit-ups in the ship's fitness center. At night, they'd drink an entire bottle of Italian wine before walking back to their room, where Tim would undress his wife slowly and lay her down against the bed. He'd made her work hard, but he'd rewarded her for it, too.

In the three years since they'd gone dancing at Cullum Hall, Tim Nesmith had completely transformed her life, and she his. The entire corps of cadets was shocked to learn that they'd paired off—Tim was known for his wild escapades on the skydiving team, while Hannah's nickname was *Miss Congeniality*. At school, she and Tim would stay up late, having long conversations about religion and God and family. They'd dream about their future.

"Is that what you want?" he'd asked early on in their dating relationship, after Hannah had described her grandparents. "To grow up and be like Barbara? House. Kids. Ranch."

"I don't know," Hannah had said. "It's not a bad life."

"But what about a career? Do you want to work or stay at home?"

"Do I have to have an answer right this second?"

"No, of course not. You can change your mind a million times. I just wonder what you picture. That's all."

At the time, Hannah didn't exactly have a vision of what she wanted. She imagined getting married. Having children. But she'd been successful at West Point, far more successful than she'd even expected. At the time, her junior year, she'd ranked in the top one hundred of their class, even higher than Tim. Uncertain, she'd shrugged. "What do you picture?"

"My parents have such a traditional marriage," Tim had said. "Mom stayed home. Dad worked. She packs his lunch, even to this day. And at night, she fixes his dinner plate, like he's a child. I don't think I could do that. I don't want some wife that just sees herself as my servant or something. I want an equal. A teammate."

From that point forward, that's how they'd built their relationship. As a team. They always supported one another, always encouraged one another. In the summer, when West Point offered them different assignments or schools, they went, without talking about the distance. It wasn't always easy. They'd broken up for an entire semester junior year, after Tim had admitted to kissing another girl while he was at Air Assault School. That all felt so silly now. So long ago. His accident had brought them back together, and now, Hannah couldn't imagine a life without him.

A lesser man might have told Hannah to slow down—to choose a low-key Army career that could more easily follow his path. But Tim told her to live out loud. To take on the challenge of Sapper School. To chase greatness while they still had the chance.

"We're going to be married for our entire lives," he'd said to her when they parted ways after the cruise. He kissed her forehead. "These few months apart are nothing in the scheme of things. I know it's going to be hard. I know this isn't normal. But we're stronger together. And I'd rather have you and be apart than not get to call you my wife."

Just before Grad Week at West Point, Dani had jotted down the dates like a mathematician on a scrap piece of paper. Two weeks on the cruise. Then Hannah would spend a month at Sapper School, while Tim went to Ranger School. Three months at Officer Basic Courses in different states—Hannah to become an engineer, Tim to join the infantry. After that, they'd take turns at the National Training Center with their units. Then back-to-back deployments, twelve months if they were lucky, fifteen months if they were like everyone else. Staring at the list, Hannah had felt the onset of vertigo.

"Hannah," Dani had said. "Do you realize that you guys will have, like, five weekends together . . . in the next two years? No." She'd tapped on the paper quickly, as though arriving at the correct answer to some equation. "Four. Four weekends!"

Hannah knew. Tim knew, too. But as if ignoring the calendar would make the days pass more swiftly, they'd never spoken of it. So far, any time Hannah had ever taken a step of faith, God had provided her the strength to get through it. Fingering the cross necklace she wore, Hannah said a prayer and shook off all the uncertainty she'd felt moments ago, when Moretti adjusted her nose.

She could do this. If she could survive four years at West

Point—if she and Tim were going to survive the next two years apart—then she could survive a little hand-to-hand combat.

At least she hoped she could.

"I'LL GIVE YOU one more go. But after that, we've got to call it. Understood?"

"Yes, sir," she said to Moretti. "Just give me a second."

Stepping outside, Hannah placed one finger against her right nostril and blew air through the left. A rocket of blood and mucus flew to the ground. She did the same for the other nostril, and then wiped the rest of the blood on her shirttail, exposing a strong, toned stomach. It wasn't very ladylike, but at this point, Hannah didn't care. She didn't care whether or not these men thought she should be here. She just wanted to achieve the clinch with Private Stanton and get the hell out of this place.

"All right then." Moretti turned to the men waiting in the gymnasium once Hannah had returned. "Set it up, Stanton. She's coming back for more. Don't let him make you his bitch, Nesmith. Get in low and punch up."

Hannah knew what she had to do. This was her last chance to prove she was worth the investment the Army had already made. That four years at West Point were not in vain. That everything she'd already survived wasn't a fluke, and everything she was about to face she was capable of overcoming. That Tim wouldn't have to worry about her in Afghanistan, and that nothing could hold her back from coming home to him. Stanton's face blurred into nothingness. The walls of the gymnasium fell away and she focused on his chest. Then Hannah lurched forward, one last time.

THREE DAYS LATER, Hannah sat among three rows of men, all of whom were wearing desert-colored fatigues. A general delivered a speech. Someone projected a video onto a large screen with clips from their weeks of training overdubbed by heavy metal music. The video elicited plenty of oohs and ahhs from family and friends who'd made the trek to Missouri for the ceremony. But when Hannah's parents, Bill and Lynn Speer, had asked if she wanted them to fly up for the graduation, Hannah had insisted they save their time and money. In the Army, goodbyes were far more important than congratulations.

These days, when Hannah mentioned going to the field or breaking her nose in hand-to-hand combat, her mother barely flinched. Injuries, deployment, weaponry—it was as if she were talking about what she was making for dinner. Hannah looked around the room and had a depressing thought. All these parents would have to say goodbye soon enough. Then they'd know what all this was really about.

"Second Lieutenant Hannah Nesmith!"

Master Sergeant Moretti called her to the podium, where he reached out, shook her hand, and then saluted her.

The Army was organized into two distinct hierarchies. Officers, like Hannah, held college degrees, and could climb in the ranks from second lieutenant all the way to general. Soldiers, like most of Hannah's cohort at Sapper School, could enlist right out of high school and hoped to advance from the Army's lowest rank, private, to sergeant, first sergeant, or, like Moretti, master sergeant status. Because Moretti was a noncommissioned officer, it didn't matter that he had been in the Army for nearly as long as Hannah had been alive. Simply because she held a college degree—simply because she was an officer—she outranked him. For the weeks of Sapper School, Moretti had been her instructor, but now that was over, and protocol pushed Hannah immediately back into her rightful position as his superior. After his salute, she returned the gesture.

The small green patch in his hand looked like something her mother could have sewn onto her Girl Scout uniform when she was a kid, only this one was lined with rough Velcro. Hannah turned to the side and stood at attention.

"Sappers lead the way," Moretti said proudly. He attached the tab to the fuzzy patch on Hannah's left uniform sleeve. Then he saluted her again. Hannah saluted back.

"Sappers lead the way."

WHEN THE CEREMONY ended, Hannah lingered by the table of refreshments and twirled her wedding ring around her finger. She smiled and shook hands as people passed and introduced themselves, but on the inside, she felt like she'd swallowed poison. She tried to tell herself she shouldn't feel depressed. She'd just accomplished something incredible! Only nine other women in the history of the universe had graduated from Sapper School! Certainly they hadn't felt this crummy afterward. Hannah shook her head and took a swig of weak lemonade. Was it that she was alone? Or was it that having the patch didn't make her feel any more ready for what was ahead?

"You know, the Army doesn't love you back," Wendy Bennett had said to Hannah one night at her house.

It must have been Firstie year—around the time that Hannah was trying to decide which branch of the Army to choose. She'd been on a run around campus when she found herself surrounded by the trees and redbrick homes in Lusk Area. The Bennett's house was lit up, and despite her sweaty appearance, she decided to drop in to say hello. Maybe deep down, she'd known she needed a cup of coffee and some advice more than she'd needed the run.

"You and Tim are both really ambitious," Wendy had said knowingly. "But the Army will take everything you have to give. Uncle Sam rarely says thanks."

Just then, Hannah felt a tap on her shoulder. When she turned around, it took her a moment to place Private Stanton. He smiled so wide and so kindly that he hardly looked like the same menacing force that just three days ago had broken her nose. He stood next to a stout woman with dark braided hair and a large bosom.

"Ma," Private Stanton said, "this is the one I told you about. Lieutenant Nesmith."

Hannah smiled. The woman opened her arms wide, then squeezed Hannah in a tight embrace against her ample chest. Hannah couldn't help but feel relieved to have the human contact. Stanton's mother smelled earthy and fresh, and Hannah breathed her in greedily. The scent of cocoa butter reminded her of Dani, and made her suddenly homesick, not for a place, but for her people.

"Daniel tells me you're goin' to Fort Bragg, too," the woman said. She gripped a silver cross in her well-manicured hand—much larger and more intricate than the one hidden beneath

Hannah's uniform collar. "I just thank God someone's gonna be lookin' after my son."

Hannah stared at Stanton with wide eyes. Even though Hannah was combat trained, the Army had regulations against women leading combat platoons. Hannah would *not* be looking after him at Fort Bragg. She was headed to a headquarters unit, tasked with building combat outposts, not living or fighting in them.

"Please tell me your mother doesn't think I'm your platoon leader?"

"That's exactly what she thinks because that's exactly what he told me." Stanton's mother reared her head back. "You wanna explain, Dan?"

Private Stanton passed his mother a cup of lemonade. "No, Ma. I said I *wished* she was my platoon leader. You ought to get your ears checked."

Hannah was shocked. The fact that Private Stanton wanted her as his platoon leader spoke volumes about his respect for her—but then she laughed. "He's only saying that because he feels bad for breaking my nose. Let me guess. He didn't tell you that either."

"No, he told me that." The woman nodded, eyebrows raised. "I hear he messed you up good."

AS SHE WALKED out of the Army building, past a flapping American flag and into the dusk, Hannah pulled her cell phone out of her pocket. Indulging her sadness, she dialed Tim's number, knowing that because he was still at Ranger School, he wouldn't answer. But the sound of his voice on his outgoing voicemail message would be enough to soothe her loneliness. The phone rang once. Twice. And then she heard his voice.

"Hannah?"

"Wait." Hannah stopped in the middle of the parking lot, stunned that he'd answered. "Tim?!"

"Yes!" he laughed. "It's me! How are you? God, I miss you."

"I miss you too!"

"Am I talking to a Sapper?"

"*You are!* I'm literally walking out of the graduation ceremony right now. I did it!"

"I knew you would," he said with pride. "You deserve it."

"But I didn't expect for you to answer," she said. "What's going on? Did you finish?"

A sigh resounded across the miles, touching them both with its audible breeze.

"I recycled," Tim admitted. He'd been cut from the training, offered a chance to try again.

Hannah's eyes closed; she felt the pain in his voice. "Oh, babe, I'm so sorry."

"I'll start again in a week."

Hannah felt her heart sink. More time apart.

"I only have one more phase to pass," he continued. "The mountain phase. I think I can do it. I was just so sleep deprived and hungry, I just lost my cool. You should see me. I look like a skeleton."

"I wish I were there to nurse you back to health."

"Soon enough."

"I don't want to hang up," Hannah said as she approached her rental car. It was stuffed with her gear, ready for her drive to the airport.

"Then don't," Tim said.

With that, Hannah pulled out of the parking lot with a smile on her face, a phone on her ear, and the assurance that everything would be okay. Every risk had its reward, and hers was Tim's deep, smooth voice over the phone. Sure, their marriage wasn't traditional, but they were a team. Stronger together, even if they were apart.

"Tell me everything," he said. "You kicked ass, I assume."

"Well, I'll start with this. A private broke my nose."

From: Hannah Nesmith <hannah_nesmith@yahoo.com>
Subject: Update from Sapper School
Date: August 30, 2004 12:03:15 PM GMT +01:00
To: Dani McNalley <danimcnalley@yahoo.com>, Avery
    Adams <averyadams13@yahoo.com>

Check out this picture, ladies. You're looking at America's tenth-EVER female Sapper. Not bad for a day's work. (Actually more like a month, but who's counting?)

Tim is still at Fort Benning at Ranger School. We're hoping he'll finish up before too long, so we can finally have a minute together. Looks like Christmas will be our best bet. Seriously, our life gives new meaning to "ships passing in the night." To be honest, this is far harder than I ever expected. When I get back to Bragg, I'm going to need some serious hang time with my people.

Dani, can you come to Bragg to see us? Avery—hope your new job won't keep you too busy to hang when I get back!!

Can't wait to be home.

Hannah

13

Summer 2004 // New York, New York

Don't forget your swag bag!"

A man standing at the ballroom entrance offered a neon green tote to the woman standing in front of him. The banner above the door read, *Service Academy Career Conference,* and his name tag said, *Hello. My name is BRAD!* in dark marker.

"There's a lot of great stuff in there," he said, tipping a shock of white hair toward the ballroom of potential employers. He extended the bag a few inches closer.

Dani took the bag reluctantly. The truth was, she didn't want any "swag." The thought of being at a career fair had humiliated her enough before *BRAD!* had entered the picture. Since graduating in June, she'd collected three flimsy bags from three separate career fairs, sixteen brand-emblazoned pens, several empty promises, and not a single paycheck. Every swag bag was a rude reminder that she was broke, living with her parents, and on the verge of coaching middle school basketball, just to get health insurance. Couldn't *BRAD!* see that?

People back in Ohio kept saying inane things to try to draw a silver lining around her disappointment. "Everything happens for a reason," they promised her.

"When God closes a door, he opens a window!"

But that line of thinking wasn't logical, let alone biblical. Who was to say the room only had one door? And how did you know it was even a room? What if the room you were supposedly stuck in was really just a prison of your own making? Dani wasn't about to sit around waiting for some theoretical window to open in her life. She was going to pick up a hammer and make her own way out.

"What company?" *BRAD!* asked.

"E & G," answered Dani. "I'm supposed to meet Jim Webb."

He laughed. "No, I mean at West Point. What company were you in at West Point?"

"Oh, right," Dani said, trying to hide her surprise. Over the summer, she'd grown her hair into a short and twisted Afro, a modern version of what her mother's had been like in the 1970s. No one in the civilian world would ever have guessed that six months ago she'd been on track to be an officer in the U.S. Army. The way Dani dressed, with her new leather jacket and big hoop earrings, made most people assume she was an artist or a poet, and she didn't mind the mistake. She was impressed that Brad could cut through her appearance that quickly and see the truth. People saw what they wanted to see. She'd half-expected him to ask if she'd wandered into the service academy career fair by mistake.

"H-4," Dani answered.

"I was class of '66." He looked away for a moment, then looked back. "I should probably keep my mouth shut. But I'll say this. Perseverance. This whole transition thing can be a long road. Just keep on moving. Persevere."

A sudden rush of emotion swelled in Dani's throat. The constant pain in her pelvis, unaffected by the Advil she popped every few hours, didn't help. Hot tears filled her eyes and she fought valiantly to keep them from falling on her cheeks. Her lack of emotional vulnerability had made her successful at West Point and it was going to help her to succeed in the business world, too. But somehow, this man, with a class ring that matched her own, had spoken to a part of her heart that needed to be touched.

Persevere. She knew he was right, but she didn't want this to be a long road. She wanted a job. She wanted to feel that, like her friends' lives, her life was actually going somewhere.

"Thank you," she said, clearing her throat. "I appreciate that."

After shaking his hand, Dani limped past the entrance and into the hotel ballroom. But before she was out of his line of sight, two other veterans approached Brad and received swag bags. One had a prosthetic right arm, while the other looked completely normal—uninjured, unmarred by the journey he had taken to get here. Compared to the amputee, who'd clearly given a limb for his country, Dani's "disability" was a joke. The naked eye couldn't see why the Army had given her a medical release, setting her free from the five-year service commitment cadets had to complete after West Point. The men at this career fair couldn't understand how weird it felt to be here, in this ballroom, instead of preparing for war. Then again, Dani didn't know why the man standing next to the amputee had gotten out of the Army either.

Some wounds are invisible. It doesn't mean they're not real.

The room was larger than she'd expected, with several dozen rows of six-foot tables. Music thumped from speakers in the front. A host of young veterans in brand-new suits wandered through the room like lost, overdressed children. An NBC news crew held court in the center of the room, where a blond reporter interviewed men about their service. She kept asking banal questions that showed just how little she understood about the military: *What kind of job are you looking for today? Oh, and what exactly is civil engineering?*

When Dani had learned she wasn't going to receive a commission from the Army, Colonel Bennett had made several phone calls on her behalf, trying to help her scrounge together gainful employment. Surprisingly, his Rolodex didn't only include other Army colonels. He'd called several business owners in New York, three congressmen, and even one Supreme Court justice. All of those leads had turned into dead ends. Jim Webb was her last shot.

Dani rarely felt this nervous. If Avery were here, she'd march up to every table with a smile and her natural sex appeal and have three job offers before noon, Dani knew. But thanks to an undisciplined summer, Dani had gained more than a few pounds, thickening her middle, where her six-pack abs used to be. Even if the Nordstrom employee had been right—even if her black pants and brown leather jacket produced a natural slimming effect—sex appeal wasn't her strongest weapon anymore. And if her relationship with Locke was any indication, it probably never had been.

On the cruise they'd all taken through the Mediterranean that summer, Dani was convinced their relationship would finally cross into new territory. Tim and Hannah couldn't keep their hands off of each other. Avery was constantly flirting with the waitstaff, in particular a Syrian bartender named Ludo. Meanwhile, Dani and Locke continued their practiced dance, constantly stepping closer and stepping back. Days upon days of spreading suntan lotion over each other's bodies had driven Dani nearly mad. And just when she thought that it was all in her head, the ship had docked in Florence and Locke had disappeared with his football buddies for a few hours, only to reappear holding a brown package wrapped in twine.

"Open it," he'd said, with his signature gap-toothed grin.

Unwrapping the package, Dani found a saddle-colored leather jacket, supple and worn, just her size. She'd taken one look at the price tag and told him there was no way she could accept it, but he'd ignored her protests and placed it around her shoulders.

"Your new uniform," he'd said. "Trust me. It's perfect."

That night, he'd found his way to her room, into her bed, next to her body. They'd interlocked fingers and fallen asleep. That was it. Four years. One leather jacket. And then, nothing.

"Not even a kiss?" Avery had asked at breakfast the next day.

Dani shook her head. "Nada."

"Do you think he's gay?" she'd whispered.

Dani had rolled her eyes in response, as if that were the dumbest question she'd ever heard—though the possibility had crossed her mind, too. In the years since she'd arrived at West Point, her little brother, Dominic, had come out of the closet—and Locke knew that she'd supported him. If Locke was gay, she was certain he would have told her by now. As it was, Avery couldn't understand how two people could *not* fornicate when left alone.

"He's not gay," Dani had answered finally.

Her friend raised an eyebrow and took a bite of eggs. It was unspoken but understood that Avery should drop the subject, and she did. Over the years, Dani and Locke had had plenty of deep conversations—much deeper than the conversations Avery had probably had with her latest fling. Dani still held out hope that Locke would eventually realize the truth: they were best friends. And what else did you need in a soul mate than for them to be your best friend?

Standing to the side of the ballroom, she pulled a brand-new Motorola cell phone out of her purse and flipped it open. Her fingers flew fast across the Razr's thin keypad, toggling through each number to get to the right letters. Phones needed to be equipped with keyboards, she thought. It would save so much time.

Made it to NYC, she wrote in a text to Locke. *I'm the best dressed in this place. San Lorenzo 4 tha win!*

Atta girl, he sent back in a flash. *Tell New York hello for me. Just don't go getting lost with the FDNY this time, K?*

Dani chuckled, then replied: *No promises.*

PULLING A MAP from her neon sack, Dani quickly decoded the madness around her. E & G, the company she'd come to meet, was tucked between FedEx and a cable company on the opposite side of the ballroom. Google had a table on the far north side, Microsoft had set up to the south, and a host of Fortune 500 companies floated in between. There weren't any creative companies here, Dani noted. No television studios or music labels. As if America's veterans didn't have stories to tell. Shaking off that thought, she stepped into the maze, walking between booths like she was avoiding dirty carnies.

"Good morning!" chirped a woman with slightly bouffant hair. "Enter our raffle for a Bluetooth?" She pointed to a roachlike clip on her ear. "They're the next big thing."

Dani respectfully declined, turned a corner, and spotted a booth filled with two leather couches facing one another on a Persian rug. All the other booths looked sterile and boring, but the scene ahead looked like it had been ripped from one of Hannah's home decor magazines. An older man sat on the left couch, one leg crossed over the other. He wore round tortoiseshell glasses and a black half-zip sweater. A blue collar peeked out from beneath the sweater and his salt-and-pepper hair was trimmed close on the sides—handsome, Dani thought. Lean, like he woke up every morning to run. Like a West Pointer. Dani wasn't one to bet. But she would have put her life savings on the fact that this was the man she was supposed to meet. This was Jim Webb.

Suddenly, he stood from the couch and smiled in her direction. Dani limped forward and her heart began to pound.

"Now, I'll be damned if you're not Dani McNalley," he said. He had a Southern accent and a warm handshake, broken only by the cold platinum mass of his West Point class ring.

"Damnation avoided, sir," Dani said.

Jim Webb laughed out loud.

"Here, Dani," Jim said, "there's someone I want you to meet. Laura Klein, this is the kid I was telling you about. Dani McNalley."

Suddenly, a woman with short blond hair and a tight black dress appeared in front of her, fingering a pearl necklace and smiling, like she'd just been told some hilarious joke. Wrinkles fanned out from the sides of her eyes like spiderwebs. Red polish shined brightly on her fingernails.

"Oh, *you're* Dani," Laura said with an air of laughter. Her words were elevated by an aristocratic British accent. "I was expecting a man! You know. *D-a-n-n-y*," she spelled. "No offense, but you don't exactly look like you went to West Point."

"I don't usually bring my guns to interviews," Dani said. Laura Klein stared back blankly—apparently the British didn't follow American sarcasm. "I'm kidding. They took the guns away."

"What'd I tell you?" Jim said, addressing his colleague. "She's quick."

With a confused chuckle, Laura took a seat on one of the sofas.

"When did they start letting in your kind, Dani?" Jim asked.

Dani clenched her teeth to keep her jaw from dropping open. *Her kind?* "West Point admitted females in 1976, sir," she replied evenly. "Its first African-American in 1870."

"Well aren't you the double threat?" Laura remarked, taking a sip from her Evian water bottle.

"Triple," Dani said. "I'm also handicapped."

Jim laughed again. "Mark said I'd like you. Here, take a seat!"

Dani smiled and tried to hit her internal reset button. Jim Webb had made some strange comments—so had Laura—but Dani had heard worse. One awkward moment shouldn't ruin her chances at a great job opportunity.

"About that handicap. Now that you've brought it up," Jim continued, "I can legally ask. You just graduated this spring, right?"

"Yes, sir."

"So why aren't you out there fighting the Taliban?"

He said it like a Southerner—*Tally-ban*. As if they were an Afghan tribe that prohibited taking a count of anything. But it was a valid question. One that divided people into two clear groups: the people who genuinely cared about Dani's condition, and the people who secretly thought she'd invented an ailment to avoid the war. She couldn't tell which camp Jim fell into, but if nothing else, she appreciated his candor.

For a moment, she wondered how much of the story she should tell. Should she start at Beast, when she felt a twinge in her hip while trying to qualify with her rifle? Or fast-forward to Buckner, when her hip had snapped brutally while she carried Locke uphill? Should she recount the surgery? Or the moment the doctor had presented an X-ray showing the ligaments in her pelvis frayed like rope, white and fuzzy against the light? She could tell him she'd led the women's basketball team to a winning season her junior year—scoring more points than any female player in academy history. But that was a rabbit trail. Most important was the crack she'd heard while leading plebes on the thirteen-mile ruck march back to campus from basic training, when she was a Firstie. Once again, the X-ray blurred white, telling her everything she needed to know. Another surgery. Another round of rehab. Wendy sat next to Dani in April of her senior year, eight weeks before graduation, when a look of dismay appeared on her doctor's face. He shook his head, presented Dani with a form. *Medical Release.*

It was the longest story she'd ever lived, but the shortest way to tell it was to speak the truth.

"I'd always had aches and pains while at West Point. But, as you can imagine, I thought that came with the territory. I was running sprints and lifting weights with the basketball team. I did all the rucks. All the training. I had a few back spasms, here and there. But my health devolved.

"The doctors kept thinking I was tearing ligaments. There were surgeries. Two actually, one my sophomore year, and one my senior year. I thought I'd recover in time for graduation, but after that second surgery, I ended up getting a second opinion, and the civilian doctor said I shouldn't have had the surgeries in the first place. It was never a torn ligament—it was chronic arthritis."

"Arthritis? Isn't that something grannies have?" Laura Klein asked.

"Grannies and me," Dani said with more kindness than this Klein lady deserved. "The long and short of it is, I probably should never have been admitted to West Point. After that, my fate was sealed. I appealed it. But there was no way I was going to receive a commission. I was medically discharged the day after graduation."

"Well." Jim sighed. "That's quite a story. Although, you may have dodged a bullet. I'm not sure women should really be on the front lines anyway."

"Unfortunately, I'm not sure there are 'front lines' anymore, sir," said Dani.

"True enough. The good news is, in the corporate world, women have been my best assets. In my experience, women have more integrity. They're better listeners. Better multitaskers. Women don't let their ego drive decisions. Do you know what I mean?"

"Yes, sir, I think I do," said Dani.

Laura smiled, looking content with Jim's shower of compliments on their gender.

"A man earns a little money," Jim continued, "he makes a few good decisions, and he kicks back, thinks he's infallible. Like it's going to come easy. When a woman gets some success, it's never enough. She's already looking for the next challenge. All I'm saying is if I see two equally qualified people, I'd choose the woman every time."

Dani nodded. In some ways she agreed with him. She'd seen more than enough male ego at West Point to last her a lifetime. And sure enough, she was hungry for the next challenge. If her time at West Point had taught her anything, it was that she wanted to do something with her life that *mattered*.

"Your credentials are quite impressive," Laura said, picking up where Jim had left off. She looked down her narrow nose at a piece of paper Dani assumed was her résumé. "NCAA athlete, ranked in the top fifteen percent of your class. Somehow, you maintained high physical performance scores despite your condition, so I know you have a high pain tolerance. That counts in this profession, believe it or not. You have to have thick skin."

Laura paused, and in that moment, Dani assessed that everything she said seemed rehearsed, like she was playing a part for Jim's benefit. The smart, authoritative businesswoman. Dani wanted to reach over and tell her it was okay to take off the mask. To relax and be herself. Instead, she just listened to Laura's tight intonation and overconfident up-speak.

"I just want to make sure you have the math brain for what we'll be asking you to do here," Laura continued. "It's research. Statistics, data mining. Dry stuff."

The news stories Dani had scanned the night before had informed her that E & G was trying to land a five-hundred-million-dollar client, a men's product line based in France called Gelhomme. She'd already read the job description online, and every line she'd checked off in her mind—she had exactly what they needed.

"Behavioral psychology isn't dry to me. And, at the risk of sounding overconfident, I'm light-years ahead of any other applicant in terms of understanding the male psyche, simply because of my time at West Point. Honestly, if you want to get Gelhomme's business, you're going to need me."

After a long pause, Jim said, "You understand it will require you to watch men shower?"

"Well, they'll have on trousers," Laura said, to clarify. "Swim trousers."

"Of course," Dani added. "That doesn't bother me. The trousers or the showers." Just wait until Avery heard her job description. The research would have its perks.

Jim grabbed his chin and looked her straight in the eye. "You'll be based out of Boston," he said, suddenly shifting the tone of his voice. "It's going to require sixty, maybe seventy hours a week. And travel—a hundred global interviews in the first ninety days."

"I understand," Dani explained. "I'm not afraid of hard work."

"All right," he said. "Well in that case, welcome to the team."

WITHIN THE NEXT half hour, Dani had signed a contract. There was a hefty signing bonus, and somehow, the sight of those zeroes helped Dani breathe a little easier. Earlier in the day, she'd refused to hail a taxi, simply to save a few bucks. But now, exiting the hotel lobby onto the muggy streets of Manhattan, Dani smiled broadly, stepped to the curb, and raised her arm into the air.

"Taxi!"

From: Dani McNalley <danimcnalley@yahoo.com>

Subject: Re: Update

Date: September 1, 2004 17:56:41 PM GMT +01:00

To: Avery Adams <averyadams13@yahoo.com>, Hannah Nesmith <hannah_nesmith@yahoo.com>

GUESS WHAT?!

I got a JOB!!! Finally. Everyone exhale!

Now get this. I'm moving to Boston. Who's coming to visit? We can go to Martha's Vineyard, or whatever yuppie people do around here. I'm so stoked.

PRAISE JESUS, I'm not homeless anymore!

Now . . . you girls give me an update! Are you both feeling settled at Fort Bragg? Still don't know how you managed to get stationed at the same Army post. I'd be happy for you two if I weren't so jealous.

Much Love to the Cult:)

Dani

14

Spring 2005 // Fort Bragg, North Carolina

A wire snapped, shooting sparks into the air.

"Shit!" Avery spat. She sucked her finger for a moment, then shook the pain out of her hand. A soldier cutting a large hole in the wall lifted his safety goggles.

"You all right, Adams?" he asked, but replaced his glasses and revved the saw before she could answer.

Looking at the mess of wires in front of her, Avery knew she had to start over. *At least with that one,* she thought, tracing the cable back to the wall.

"Do we have another five-gauge?" Avery yelled over the noise. No one answered. The team was dispersed around the room, focused fully on their own tasks—breaking through walls, running wires, testing circuits. White dust filled the room like puffs of baby powder.

If Avery had known that joining the Signal Corps would mean managing an electrical construction team, she would have branched engineering, like Hannah. As it was, she could barely program her own television remote, let alone rewire and encrypt an entire building's communications system. But who wouldn't jump at the chance to work with the most elite unit in the entire Armed Forces?

"As in black ops, D," Avery had told Dani over the phone several months earlier. "Special Forces."

"Aren't they out somewhere hunting Bin Laden?" Dani had asked.

"Yeah, well, I guess the hunt's on hold," Avery replied, spooning cereal into her mouth. "They're home and I'm the cable guy."

Dani had burst into laughter and Avery had followed suit. It was completely absurd. But Avery lived for the kind of life-changing events that morphed into great stories. Plus, she had a simple philosophy on life: Say yes. Figure the rest out later.

When Avery stepped outside, she took a deep breath of fresh air. New York's false springs were really just extended winters—snow rarely melted at West Point until mid-April. But spring in North Carolina was proving to be a different experience altogether. The sun warmed her skin. Fresh grass, verdant green, emerged all over post. A cool breeze wafted across her face surprising her with its kindness. *Soon, everyone will be discussing their summer plans*, Avery thought before she realized that wasn't true anymore. All of her friends were professionals now. There was no such thing as summer break anymore.

In that way, Major Gaines's top-secret project had come at the exact right time. She needed a distraction from normalcy because normal—in the real world—sucked. Josh hadn't called. He hadn't written. Not even an e-mail. Not even a text message. But for months, she'd checked the mailbox extra carefully, imagining he might drop a love note in the mail in some grand romantic gesture to win her back. As if guys did shit like that anymore.

Every time, the stack of mail looked exactly the same— coupons, advertisements, *People* magazine. Her life had become like that pile of junk mail. Perfectly, absolutely unremarkable. It made her itch. And it made her run.

In addition to the PT workouts she did with her soldiers on post, Avery had taken up running again, nearly as intensely as she'd trained in high school. She logged fifteen, twenty, sometimes thirty miles a week, at night and on the weekends. She needed to sign up for a race, because at least then she could justify the amount of time she was spending in her running shoes. It was better to have a goal than to run with no destination. And that's how it had felt to Avery lately—like she was running fast with nowhere to go.

IN THEIR LAST meeting, Major Gaines had looked over Avery's final binder of plans with a surprised nod of approval and handed it back to her.

"The fact that I'm entrusting this to someone so junior should feel really good, Lieutenant Adams," he'd said. "This could be big for your career."

She knew he was probably full of shit—just trying to psych her up for a job that was going to dominate her life. But she'd taken his words to heart. Achievement in the Army was about all she could take home to impress her parents at the moment. When she'd explained how she'd be spending the New Year at Christmas, her father had grunted.

"As long as you're not deploying for Bush's ridiculous personal vendetta in Iraq," he'd said. "Fine by me."

"It's not a vendetta, Dad," Avery had said, surprised that she was taking up for a president who'd never earned her vote. "Saddam Hussein is a horrible guy."

"The world is full of horrible guys, Avery," her father had replied.

She hated to admit it, but every day, as men came home from deployments with combat patches stuck to their uniforms, Avery had started to worry that her empty sleeve looked weak in the hallways of their offices. More than a year had passed since she'd graduated from West Point, and most of her classmates had deployed to Iraq or Afghanistan, or, like Hannah and Tim, at least had a date on the calendar. With every passing month, the fuzzy square on Avery's uniform sleeve felt more and more like a barren garden plot: no fruit to show for her labor.

Shaking that thought from her mind, Avery marched diagonally across a field of grass, toward the tool shed.

"One, two, three, *one!*"

"One, two, three, *two!*"

Her eyes roamed from the ground in front of her to the bearded men finishing a training workout to her right. Eight men in a semicircle had dropped to the ground to complete a round of push-ups.

Gaines had been pretty clear with his instructions: get in, get out, and don't let anyone know you were there. It had taken Avery about 3.4 seconds to break those rules.

The lean, blond-haired man leading the workout wasn't tall— five foot nine at best. But he was barrel chested, with a gold beard and calf muscles that looked like steaks. Sweat glistened on his bare shoulders as he pressed into the ground, like someone had oiled him up for a photo shoot. He had a sleeve of tattoos on his right arm that spilled onto his chest. His face attracted the sun and shadows in a way that accentuated his beard, his straight nose, his gray eyes. Avery felt her insides go weak as he stood, hands on hips, and locked his eyes on hers.

They'd been doing this every day now for a week.

Avery quickly ducked into the tool shed, closed the door behind her, and tried to catch her breath. *Holy shit,* she laughed to herself. She stared at a wall of wrenches, wires, and cables. *What was it she needed, again?*

The one thing she *didn't* need was another failed attraction. Heartbreak always pushed Avery into a cave of isolation, and after the whole debacle with Josh had imploded, she'd vowed to be single forever. Relationships didn't work for her the way they did for everyone else. She was either too trusting and got burned, or too suspicious and exhausted the guy's patience. She either acted too serious and scared the guy away, or acted too cool, leaving the guy confused about her commitment.

At times, the psychologist in Avery wondered if her issues

stemmed back to high school. She'd been just fourteen years old when Matt Maloney, a senior, had spotted her in the high school cafeteria. After a few weeks of flirtation, he'd invited her to his house, where he'd carefully and patiently taught her how their bodies were designed to fit together. And then, two months later, Avery had crawled broken into her bed, the physical pain of his betrayal and disregard too heavy for her to stand up straight. Days later, her mother sat on the edge of her bed, stroking her daughter's cheek until she'd finally stopped crying.

"Don't you ever let a little shit do that to you again," her mother had said.

It was the most profound profanity her mother had ever spoken. And it was what Avery had repeated to Hannah when Tim cheated—only Hannah ended up marrying the little shit. Hannah may have forgiven Tim for his unfaithfulness, but Avery never would.

They were all little shits, really. Her high school boyfriend. The one at West Point, *he-who-would-not-be-named*. She knew it wasn't healthy, thinking about John Collins. But for some reason, lately, she couldn't get his green eyes out of her mind. Her memory played tricks on her, reminding her of all the mistakes she'd made—showing up to his room, breaking it off so abruptly. She wanted to find a wrinkle in time, a place to jump back and do something different that would change what he'd done.

Avery remembered walking into her dorm room at the end of their sophomore year, clueless that e-mails were transporting images of her naked body around campus.

"What's going on?" Avery had asked. Dani and Hannah were there, waiting for her, their eyes puffy from crying. Dani held a stack of papers in her hands.

And then her world had fallen apart.

"He won't stop unless he's caught," Dani had said after showing Avery the photos.

Avery didn't cry. She simply stared at the white cinder-block wall, feeling cold and numb. "Everyone will know that I slept with him. They'll know I ratted him out."

"He didn't just do it to you," Hannah had said. "He did it to all of us."

The world seemed to conspire to teach her the same lesson over and over again. You couldn't trust anyone.

In the tool shed, wire-cutters, stacks of batteries, and cables littered the walls, sorted on shelves and hanging from hooks. Avery's eyes scanned the equipment until they landed on the wire she needed, and she reached for it, feeling its weight in the palm of her hand. *If only there were tools like this to rewire her heart,* she thought.

Avery took a moment to remind herself of the facts. There were rules to follow. And this one, this gold-bearded, perfect-bodied Special Ops little shit, was extra shitty because he *lied for a living*! No matter how perfect he might have looked from the outside, he spent his entire Army career paid—no, trained—to manipulate other people for information. Road. Closed.

A sigh of relief exited her lungs. The responsible part of her brain had won the argument. She prayed that when she stepped back outside, he would be gone. She didn't want to see his face because ultimately, she didn't trust herself to walk through the mental gymnastics of "no" again.

Before she could leave, Avery heard the door behind her open and close. She turned, and there he was, standing between her and the door.

"Excuse me," Avery said, lowering her eyes and trying to walk around him.

He placed a single hand on her shoulder, stopping her from moving any farther. He'd put on a beige Army undershirt, but the tattoos on his right arm were visible from under the sleeve—a bird? A skull?—the colors were vivid, black and blue. His beard was tidy and combed. He stood several inches taller than she'd originally assumed. Avery lifted her chin and looked him right in the eye.

"Please move," she said.

"Are you married?" he asked.

Avery cocked her head to the side. "Excuse me?"

"I said, are you married." His voice didn't waver. His eyes were pale gray, two round clouds, about to storm.

"No," she huffed, while simultaneously eyeing his unadorned left hand. "Now, if you don't mind . . ." She tried to push around him, but this time, he grabbed her wrist. A folded note pressed into the palm of her hand under the weight of his thumb. And then he left.

Once the door closed, Avery found herself quickly unfolding the yellow Post-it note in trembling hands. Her whole body shook with desire and confusion.

8 PM *Friday. I'll pick you up. —Noah*

So that was his name. Noah. Staring up at the single hanging bulb in the tool shed, Avery shook her head and groaned. How arrogant was this guy to think she didn't have any plans Friday night? And how would he know where to pick her up? She found herself staring at his dark handwriting—a message written in the tiniest letters. She studied his name.

Was he the kind of man that would build a vessel to bring her to a new world? Or the kind of man that would shut her out and let her drown?

"JUST TELL HIM you're sick," Hannah said a few days later.

She sat cross-legged on Avery's bed, holding a cell phone between her hands. She was waiting for a call from Tim, who was finishing his Infantry Basic Officer Leader Course.

"How would I do that?" Avery replied, stepping out from her bathroom. "I don't even have his phone number. And what—like they're going to kick me out of the Army for having dinner with the guy?"

She wore nothing but black underwear and a matching bra, her hair held up in hot rollers.

Things had progressed so quickly in that tool shed, she'd completely forgotten that she and Hannah had made plans to hang out tonight. But it wasn't like they had tickets to a concert or reservations at a restaurant. When Hannah had arrived a half hour earlier, holding a pint of Ben & Jerry's Phish Food and a rented DVD of *Pride & Prejudice*, Avery had thrown her head back and slapped her forehead. Hannah's face had fallen in disappointment.

"I promise I'll make it up to you." Avery said, stepping out from the bathroom.

"It's fine. I'll watch Keira Knightley fall in love by myself. In my sad, empty house, by myself. Eating ice cream. *By myself.*"

Avery walked over and sat on the side of the bed. "You hate me."

"I don't hate you. I'm just annoyed."

"You'll understand when you see him."

"Isn't it weird that the very first question he asked was whether or not you were married?"

"So the guy doesn't want to get involved with someone else's wife," Avery scoffed, then stood and walked to her dresser. "I thought you'd like that."

"Just don't disappear, okay?"

"What, like he's going to kidnap me?"

"No," Hannah chuckled.

Avery began letting down her hair from the hot rollers at her dresser and turned to look at Hannah, who shrugged.

"I leave in March," Hannah said.

"That's still like, a year away."

"Eight months," Hannah said, correcting her. "It'll go faster than you think."

She sighed and placed her phone down on the bedside table.

"Just don't go fall in love with this guy and then vanish from my life."

In the silence that followed, anger and shame welled in Avery's chest in equal measure. The two emotions always seemed to travel as a pair. How could Hannah say something like that? It was Hannah who had gone off and gotten married. She was the one who had gone to Sapper School. *She* was the one who'd barely kept in touch. Avery didn't want to be ugly, but for some reason, she wanted to scream at her friend for not being more support-ive. Couldn't Hannah just be happy for her, for once? Instead, she had to infuse the entire conversation with worry and judgment, like Avery was about to do something unethical. But there wasn't anything *wrong* with going on a date! And what would Hannah know about dating in the real world, anyway? She and Tim had coupled off so fast, she never had a chance to experience single life. She would never understand.

"There's plenty of time," Avery said finally. "Don't worry so much."

Hannah sighed. "You're right. I'm sorry. It's just starting to feel real."

Now it was Avery who exhaled. "I really do feel bad about bailing tonight."

"Don't," Hannah said, heading back toward Avery's closet to peruse her clothes. "What are you going to wear?"

At that moment, they both heard the low grumbling sound of an engine coming to a stop right outside Avery's window.

Hannah peeked out the curtain. "I think it's him," she said.

"Oh shit!" Avery went into hyperdrive.

"He's on a motorcycle," Hannah narrated. "He's taking off his helmet. Oh my gosh. You weren't kidding. He's . . ."

A black silk camisole with lace trim slipped over Avery's shoulders. She wore black jeans, and for a layer of warmth, she chose a gray cashmere sweater that hung open in the front and draped toward her knees. Her blond hair curled in big, loose waves to her collarbones, offset by a rose shade of lipstick. As Avery slipped on a pair of black high heels, Hannah shook her head.

"Wear the sneakers," she instructed. Avery quickly switched to a black pair of high-tops.

"Oh my god, I'm so nervous." She stood, opened her arms. "How do I look?"

"Amazing," Hannah affirmed. "Text me if he's a psycho and you need me to come get you."

Smiling, Avery gave her friend a hug and grabbed her purse.

"Just lock the door behind you when you go," Avery said. "See you later?"

Hannah nodded.

"Thank you, Hannah. And I promise I'll make it up to you."

Avery stepped outside and closed the door behind her.

"YOU READY?"

Noah stood on the sidewalk, dressed in dark blue jeans, a gray T-shirt, and a black leather jacket. If it was humanly possible, Noah looked even better fully clothed than he had shirtless. As Avery approached him, he held out a shiny black helmet for her to put on.

"Where are we going?" she asked, taking the helmet in two hands.

"You're going to have to trust me."

"I just met you," she replied. "Of course I don't trust you."

He reached over and helped secure the helmet, and the warmth of his fingers under her chin sent shivers down Avery's spine.

"And how do you know where I live anyway?" she asked.

"I'd be a pretty bad Special Forces officer if I couldn't figure out where someone lives," he answered. "Ever ridden on one of these?"

"Yes," she lied.

"Good," he said, and then placed two hands on either side of Avery's helmet. With a smile that broke Avery's resolve, Noah winked.

He got on the bike, looked at her, and shrugged. "So are you coming or what?"

From: Hannah Nesmith <hannah_nesmith@yahoo.com>
Subject: urrg.
Date: April 12, 2005 17:29:15 PM EST +01:00
To: Dani McNalley <danimcnalley@yahoo.com>

She did it again. We'd planned to do dinner and a movie for weeks, but when I showed up she said she'd forgotten. And had some date with a dude she met on her assignment.

At what point do I just give up trying?

From: Dani McNalley <danimcnalley@yahoo.com>
Subject: Re: re: urrg.
Date: April 12, 2005 17:31:20 PM GMT +01:00
To: Hannah Nesmith <hannah_nesmith@yahoo.com>

Don't give up. We just need a chance to all be together. I'm working on a plan. What are you doing for Thanksgiving?

From: Avery Adams <averyadams13@yahoo.com>
Subject: Re: Hey Hey
Date: June 15, 2005 09:03:15 AM EST +01:00
To: Dani McNalley <danimcnalley@yahoo.com>

WHOA.

Can't believe that it's been a month since you sent your last e-mail, D. My apologies. As Hannah can probably attest, the Army is a real bitch and I'm barely keeping my head above water. But I do have some good news.:-)

I met a guy.

I KNOW, I KNOW. SHOCKER.

But seriously, this guy is the real deal.

His name's Noah Candross. He's thirty, so a little older than us, which you know I love. You know that Special Ops job I told you about a few months back? Well, it's a long story, but he basically cornered me in a tool shed and told me that he was taking me on a date. How's that for assertive, right? (I'm begging him to give Locke some lessons in that whole making-a-move thing . . . but alas.)

Anyway, for our first date, he picked me up on his motorcycle and we took a long drive through the hills during the sunset. We stopped and had wine at this little café far outside of town, talked for hours. You know. The basics. I attached a picture of us, so you can see that he's gorgeous. It's insanity.

He's taking me to Napa Valley next weekend. NAPA VALLEY.

I'm smitten. EEEEK!!!:-):-):-):-)

How's Boston treating you? And work? Sometimes I feel like keeping up with you is like a game of Where in the World is Carmen Sandiego. Hannah said something about you going to Paris soon? You're so badass.

Any guys up there I should know about?:-)

LOVE YOU. (Duh.)

Avery

Summer 2005 // *Fort Bragg, North Carolina*

I t would just be three days, Tim," Hannah said into her cell phone. "Fly up Wednesday, fly back Friday. Dani said she'd pay for our tickets and we can stay at her place. It's totally free."

Hannah felt anxiety crawl up the back of her neck. Logistics were the last thing she wanted to talk about in the few short minutes they had to speak. And yet, when else were they going to figure out their plans? Thanksgiving was just a few months away. Christmas would be here before they knew it. And then it would be 2006, the year they were both scheduled to deploy.

Her unit had already begun the predeployment protocol— cleaning equipment, writing supply packing lists, setting up home-front meetings for the wives her soldiers would leave behind. Training had ramped up. They'd received orders to pack their trunks. In less than two months, everything Hannah needed for a year would be put on the back of a cargo ship and sent to the

Middle East. At the moment, she was standing in a bare building in a far corner of Fort Bragg, waiting her turn to start Soldier Readiness Processing. March still felt so far away, but every day, it sped closer.

"I think my parents really wanted to spend Thanksgiving with us since I'll be gone next Thanksgiving," Tim replied. He sounded tired, like he was rubbing his eyes. "But we can figure it out. I know you want to see Dani before you go."

A week ago, they were supposed to have two overlapping days at home in Fort Bragg—the first time they'd been in their house together since they'd exchanged vows more than a year earlier. After a cycle in the laundry room, all of their uniforms exploded into the bedroom until it looked like the inside of an Army surplus store, the items mixed up and unidentifiable. They shared the same nameplate and rank, and they'd spent an hour sorting through their items, ensuring they ended up with the right things in their separate trunks. *So all that laundry duty plebe year really did have a purpose,* Hannah had thought dismally as she held up each T-shirt, inspecting it for size. She was a small. He was a medium.

Their first night at home, Hannah had burned a chicken. Saving the evening, Tim defrosted and seared two filets mignons in butter, roasted a head of broccoli, and opened a bottle of wine at their dining room table, an oval-shaped hand-me-down that Tim's parents had forced them to take after the wedding. It felt strange to eat at a table so big, Hannah thought, just the two of them. But they'd relished the chance to play house and had spent the evening talking about their favorite childhood television shows, the books they were reading, the vacations they wanted to take after their deployments were over. They'd grown expert at avoiding the massive gray animal that had taken up residence in every room—an elephant named *March*.

And then his phone rang, cutting the dinner short.

Hurricane Katrina had made landfall in New Orleans, displacing millions of people in its path. A storm of that strength hadn't hit the U.S. since Hugo, and the Army's swiftest infantry unit, the Eighty-Second Airborne Division, had been called to help in search and rescue efforts. Tim had only been home for twenty-four hours when he walked back out the door in uniform.

Now, listening to his voice over the line, Hannah remembered watching the news. Last night, video footage had shown a helicopter hovering over a house in New Orleans's Ninth Ward. A soldier descended on a ladder, then reached out his hand to save a family stranded on a roof. The camera angle was too far away. But Hannah had sat on her sofa, alone, wondering if the man in uniform might be Tim.

"We don't have to decide about Thanksgiving right now," Hannah said. "We'll figure it out."

"When?"

"Later."

He sighed.

"You sound tired," said Hannah. "How are you, really?"

"Well, I'm standing downwind of the rankest floodwaters you can imagine, and thousands of people still need to be evacuated from the city. So, you know. Basically the definition of awesome."

Hannah laughed. "Basically."

"I miss you," he said. "It's hot here. But at least we're doing something real, you know? Something that matters."

A woman at the desk waved at Hannah to come forward. She'd grown to hate goodbyes. Especially abrupt ones. "Hey, Tim, I have to go. I'm sorry."

"It's okay," Tim said. "I love you. And hey, happy birthday."

"Thanks. I love you too," Hannah said, feeling the tears well in her eyes. "Bye."

"NAME?"

"Lieutenant Hannah Nesmith."

"Date of birth?"

"Eight, thirty, eighty-two."

"Hey," the woman said. "That's today."

"Sure is."

"Any current medication?"

"No," Hannah said, then lowered her voice. "Actually, I'm on birth control. I don't know the name . . ."

"Sexually active?"

"Somewhat," Hannah joked, but the nurse stopped pumping the blood pressure monitor she'd wrapped around Hannah's arm and waited for a direct answer. "Yes," Hannah clarified. "I'm married."

The nurse raised her eyebrows. "Honey, that don't mean the answer is yes." She released the pressure that had built and made a mark on a clipboard. "Any sexually transmitted diseases?"

"No."

"Date of your last period?"

Hannah tried to remember. "Uh . . . I think about three weeks ago?"

The nurse handed Hannah an empty plastic cup. "We need a sample. Pregnancy screening." She pointed to a partition behind her. "You can go behind the curtain."

"Oh, I'm not pregnant."

"Let's just be sure. You'd be surprised how many women get knocked up so they don't have to ship out. We can't send a fetus to Fallujah, now, can we?"

The audacity with which the nurse spoke made Hannah's neck grow hot with anger. Not once had Hannah heard of a woman intentionally getting pregnant to avoid deployment, and yet, it was a trope that constantly passed through the ranks, as if it were a mark of weakness to conceive a child.

"Afghanistan," Hannah said, correcting her, now taking on the same short and snippy tone that the nurse had used. "I'm not going to Iraq. I'm going to Afghanistan."

"Same rules apply," the woman said, though her tight expression had softened ever so slightly. She pulled back a curtain and pointed for Hannah to go behind a three-paneled screen situated in a half-moon in front of the cinder-block wall. Squatting, Hannah held the cup between her legs and sighed as it filled with warm urine. There was nothing like the Army to humiliate you before sending you to war.

Next, a nurse checked Hannah's hearing and lung capacity. She moved down the hall for an eye exam. Then a male nurse wearing blue scrubs ordered her into a room, where she sat on a cold medical cot and lifted the sleeve of her gray PT shirt.

"Hepatitis A," he announced as he jammed the first needle into the fleshy part of her upper arm. He reloaded. "Polio." Hannah winced. "And, last but not least . . ." The needle looked like a small saber. Hannah closed her eyes.

"Typhoid."

The small tube of toxins released into her upper arm. The only way to fight a contaminated world was to contaminate yourself, too, Hannah thought dismally. He rubbed a cotton swab over the area he'd attacked and then taped a cotton ball over the wound.

"Drink plenty of water. And don't worry about your arm. It'll only be sore for a few days."

IN A SMALL office on the other side of post, an elderly man wearing a black cardigan sweater and a "Vietnam Vet" hat welcomed Hannah inside. She could tell, walking into his office, that this man wasn't in any hurry. With a single outstretched hand, he directed her to take a seat in front of his desk, and the calm with which he ambled to his own chair forced Hannah to take a deep breath. He pulled a large folder from beneath the desk and set it before them carefully.

"All right, Lieutenant Nesmith," he said, rubbing his hands together. "Now for the important stuff. This here is called a D—D—nine—three." He spoke slowly, as if Hannah needed to absorb each letter and digit individually. "Are you married?"

"Yes."

"Any children?"

Hannah shook her head. "No."

"Okay." He paused. "Sometime in the next few weeks, you'll need to fill out the name and address of your spouse . . . skip this line for dependents, and then down below, list your parents and any other family members that you would like to be notified in the event that you become a casualty."

He took his glasses off his face and watched her look over the blank form. Hannah swallowed and nodded.

"You'll need to keep a copy of this form in your possession. So pack one in your trunk and give a copy to someone at home—preferably a spouse or relative." He paused again, looking to Hannah for some kind of recognition or understanding. "Am I going too fast?"

"Nope," Hannah said. She felt herself detaching from the room. Detaching from the possibilities. The sooner he could breeze through the paperwork, the better.

"Good. Last few forms here and we'll get you on your way. This here is your S—G—L—V form eight—two—eight—six. Life insurance. You'll need to list your assets. Anything of value or debt. Your car, mortgage, any outstanding loans. That kind of thing. And this here? This is a power of attorney. You'll need to have this one notarized."

Hannah listened dutifully as he flipped through the rest of the paperwork, but her mind wandered. In contrast to the chaos of her life, the SRP documents all seemed so organized. As if paperwork had power over tragedy. As if all this preparation would help if the worst really happened.

She wasn't exactly sure what she'd expected life to feel like as an adult, but she hadn't expected this. She was married but hadn't seen her husband in months. She had friends, but they were spread out all over the country, or worse, they lived down the street but might as well have been light-years away. Avery had disappeared—again—like she always did when she started dating someone new. It would have been annoying if it weren't entirely predictable.

Hannah had assumed that after the trial, Avery would change the way she related to men. Of course, she'd never blamed Avery for what John Collins had done. He deserved what he'd received, and then some. But he was one in a long line of Avery's poor dating decisions, and Hannah worried that the streak wasn't over.

Instead of changing her patterns with men, Avery's relationship roller coaster had only grown more extreme. The highs got higher. The lows got lower. She and this new guy—Noah Candross—had only known each other for a few short months, and already, he'd basically moved into Avery's house. Hannah grew annoyed when her text messages to Avery went unanswered, even though she could see Noah's motorcycle parked outside of her house at night. And despite the fact that he seemed to always be around, Hannah had only met him once. They'd met at Noah's favorite vegetarian restaurant, because apparently he didn't eat meat—and though the things he said were nice enough, he kept looking around the restaurant, as if someone more interesting were going to arrive any minute. Meanwhile, Avery had never looked more in love, gripping his arm. Hannah had smiled and tried to act happy for her friend, but she couldn't shake the feeling that something about that guy was off. Hannah wanted to like him—after all, she remembered all too well how it felt when your best friend hated your boyfriend.

Ever since the summer after their sophomore year at West Point, Avery had held Tim at arm's length.

Tim had mailed Hannah a handwritten letter explaining the whole thing: How he'd made a mistake, allowing a flirtation to build with another girl. They'd kissed, he admitted. But as soon as it was over, he'd regretted every second. The letter was full of remorse and shame and scattered with round blots where his tears had fallen on the page. Hannah had read it in her bunk at Airborne School and cried, wondering what to do. She still loved him so much.

"You *cannot* take him back," Avery had insisted after they'd returned to school that fall. She'd read the note, and Hannah had to pull it out of her hands, for fear that Avery might rip it apart. "If he loved you as much as he's claiming, he never would have done this. It has to be over. You can't let people mess with you, Hannah."

Those months of junior year watching Tim from afar were some of the worst of Hannah's life. And while grudges seemed to give Avery something powerful to hold on to, they only weighed Hannah down.

Now, staring at all the forms assembled in front of her, Hannah wondered if their friendship would survive this deployment. They were so different. And if they couldn't make it work living on the same street, how would they do it living on separate continents?

"So that's that," the man in front of her said. He tapped all of the papers into a neat stack and slid them into a black folder with her name on it. "Do you have any questions? I've got all the time in the world."

From the look of the wrinkles on his face, the nearly imperceptible shake in his hands, Hannah wasn't sure that was true.

"I don't think so," she replied. "Seems pretty straightforward."

"Nothing is straightforward about war," he said, though not condescendingly. "Oh!" He snapped his fingers. "Last thing. Do you need assistance writing a legal will?"

"Actually, no," Hannah said. She remembered writing a will as a Firstie at West Point. A strange final assignment that she'd updated after the wedding. "I already have one."

"Then you, my dear, are all through." He stood and shook her hand firmly, passing her the black folder. "By the way. I noticed your necklace."

Hannah reached for the silver cross and wrapped her palm around it tight. It felt smaller, somehow, under the gaze of his eyes. "Yes, sir."

"You're lucky to have it," he said sagely. "Not the necklace. The faith." He smiled, took his seat, and put his glasses back on his face.

PULLING INTO HER driveway that evening, Hannah grabbed all of her gear out of her car and hauled it toward the front door—purse, PT bag, two empty plastic water bottles, accumulated over the last few days. It was always sad to come home to an empty house, lights off and eerily quiet. She'd started turning on the television as soon as she got home, just to have the sound of other people's voices to keep her company. But tonight felt particularly lonely. Last year, she'd been at Sapper School on her birthday, and Sergeant Moretti had led the entire mess hall in singing. He'd even procured a grocery store cupcake that he'd marked with a sloppy 22, in blue icing.

Tonight, Hannah's plans included eating the rubbery leftover salmon that she'd overcooked the night before, drinking a glass of wine, and tucking in early. After all, she had to be back at work at 0600 for PT in the morning. Her sister, Emily, had sent a bouquet of tulips to work. A card from Wendy Bennett had arrived in the mail the day before, stuffed with a $50 gift card to J.Crew—and her parents had sent exactly what she'd asked for: a small digital camera that she could take with her to Afghanistan. Other than Tim's phone call from New Orleans, she hadn't received anything from him in the mail. But that was okay. She couldn't expect him to send her a present for her birthday when he was busy saving lives.

Opening the door, she shuffled into the dark and put her bags on the ground. Flipping the light switch Hannah looked up toward the kitchen and gasped. A mass of people, standing beneath a silver banner, shouted, "*Surprise!*"

The crowd of familiar faces made Hannah laugh, even though they'd scared her half to death. Avery stood front and center, holding a cake. There were a few couples from church, all hooting and clapping. One of Tim's friends from West Point, Erik Jenkins, stood on the stairs with his pregnant wife, Michelle, who was holding a laptop computer face-out toward Hannah. On the screen, she saw Tim, alight with glee. The picture blurred as he laughed, leaning back in a chair.

"What in the world!" Hannah said. "You scared the crap out of me!"

"Are you surprised?" Avery asked.

"I nearly peed my pants! Was this your idea?"

Avery shook her head and pointed toward the computer screen.

"Happy birthday, babe," Tim said. The image was grainy and imperfect, his voice choppy from a bad connection, but she could still see the deep dimple imprinted in his right cheek. "I love you so much. We all do."

From: Dani McNalley <danimcnalley@yahoo.com>
Subject: Re: Re: Re: Update
Date: September 2, 2005 06:32:15 PM GMT +01:00
To: Avery Adams <averyadams13@yahoo.com>

(1) How was Napa? Tell me everything.

(2) We really need to see each other.

I've been trying to figure out a way to get us all together. Would you want to come up to Boston for Thanksgiving? I have a bunch of frequent flyer miles, so I'm flying my mom, dad, and brother up here. I asked Hannah and Tim, too. And Locke, of course.

I'll have a big turkey and some desserts. It will be amazing. I feel like we need a reunion so bad!! Apparently Thanksgiving up here is a big deal, too. If we want, we can drive up to Plymouth Rock or something equally American. Or we can all just stay here and eat until we're sick. Which is also American.

I really want you to come. Like I said, flight's on me. Will you think about it??

Also, I just talked to Sarah Goodrich. She's deploying to Iraq tomorrow. Thought you'd want to know.

Love you,

D

From: Avery Adams <averyadams13@yahoo.com>
Subject: Re: Re: Re: **Update
Date: September 3, 2005 13:27 PM EST +01:00
To: Dani McNalley <danimcnalley@yahoo.com>

FINALLY! A cult reunion! It's about time.

I'm totally in. And . . . feel free to say no . . . but would it be okay if I invited Noah?

A

16

Fall 2005 // Jamaica Plain, Boston, Massachusetts

A man stood under the drizzle of a warm shower in his apartment, wearing a pair of navy swim trunks. Coarse hair formed the shape of a heart on his chest and narrowed into a thin trail down his stomach. With broad shoulders and large arms, he was bulky and strong, Dani assessed, with hair cut short and an accent that proved he was definitely a local. *Boston* became *Bwaston*. *Coffee* became *cwahfee*. Shampoo bubbled around the edges of his temple, threatening to spill over the edge of his raised eyebrow.

"Am I doing okay?" he asked.

"Just pretend I'm not here," Dani instructed. She pulled the shower curtain open a little more.

The guy laughed. "You going to take me out to dinner, at least?"

"If you play your cards right."

"Well at least tell me something about you, so I don't feel so . . . exposed."

"Unfortunately that's not how this works. I get to ask the questions, and right now I don't have any. So just . . . keep on showering."

Since she'd been hired at E & G, Dani McNalley had completed sixty consumer interviews like this in twenty U.S. cities; she'd logged thirty-five interviews in Europe. The research was fascinating. Men would complete their morning routines and, without even knowing it, provide Dani with little nuggets of insight to take back to the office. Most men kept their shampoo bottles upside down in the shower, to more efficiently squeeze a dollop into their hand. In Europe, men still used a soft-bristled brush to apply shaving cream. In America, men slapped it on with their bare hands, and if they used after shave, they put it on like Macaulay Culkin in *Home Alone*. While washing their bodies, two-thirds of men faced the showerhead; the other third faced away. She hadn't figured out why that was significant, but it felt meaningful. Perhaps the ones facing away from the water had some psychological reason to avoid the heat.

There were other interesting trends too. She'd learned that most men hadn't seen the back of their heads in years. While women had mastered the physics of double mirrors to check that their hair looked perfect, men never took the time. They simply combed their hair until they liked the view from the front, then went on with their morning routine. Once, Dani's subject had noticed her playing back video footage. He grabbed her camera and pulled it in close to stare at his own bald spot.

"Wait, is that me?" he'd asked, touching the back of his head, as if to confirm the truth.

"Aw," Dani had said, patting his shoulder. "Maybe it's time to get into hats."

Dani had gotten pretty good at consoling men about hair loss. She'd gotten pretty good at a lot of things actually. Packing a carry-on bag that could pass through security with ease. Walking through airport terminals with a BlackBerry in one hand and a latte in the other, without losing the dexterity to push her four-wheeled suitcase in front of her. She'd grown used to ignoring the stares of men who found the presence of a young black woman in first class so disconcerting. With the amount of miles she'd racked up, she'd earned her position at the front of the cabin.

Sadly, the list of cities she'd traveled to in the last year didn't include the two places she'd hoped to visit: Fort Bragg, to see Hannah and Avery, and Fort Hood, to see Locke. Apparently E & G didn't believe it was necessary to interview America's military population, which made little sense to Dani, since men in the military were *required* to shave. It was just another way that her life felt separate from that of her college friends.

Dani had assumed that after college, her bonds of friendship would remain the same. But things were shifting. She could feel the seismic waves, like emotional plate tectonics. It had been weeks since any of them had replied to their dwindling e-mail chain, and a few months earlier, when Dani had made a conscious effort to call Hannah on her birthday, the conversation centered on the one thing that they couldn't seem to avoid. Schedules.

"Well, I was supposed to be with Tim this weekend," Hannah had said. "But you've seen the news."

"Sure," Dani had replied, though she wasn't sure what Hurricane Katrina had to do with Hannah's weekend plans. "It's awful."

"They sent Tim's unit," Hannah had explained. "He's literally there, fishing people out of their houses."

"Like a true disciple," Dani had said, trying to crack a joke. "A fisher of men."

Hannah had laughed, but had chased that with a sigh. Dani couldn't imagine surviving a long-distance relationship, let alone a long-distance marriage, but Hannah had a way of smiling through pain that put even Dani's endurance to shame. Of course, most of Dani's pain was physical. Maybe it was easier to tolerate pain if it only existed in your heart.

"It wouldn't matter that much if I had any friends around here," Hannah had said.

"What about Avery?"

"What about her? We had a plan to meet up for lunch last week and I sat there for an hour waiting."

"She never showed up?" Dani had asked, incredulous. "Did you call her?"

"I texted. She never texted me back. I have a weird feeling about this new guy she's dating."

"Something must be going on," Dani had said, trying to knock some sense into Hannah. "That's not normal."

"Ha! Normal? What's that word mean again?"

Dani had felt utterly helpless over the line. At one time, she was the glue that held their group together, but they were loosening and she had no control over it. In a way, that fact made Dani more uncomfortable than the arthritis in her hips. In college, they'd tackled countless challenges together. But with all this distance between them, nothing felt right.

Things with Locke had changed, too. They still talked on the phone every few weeks, exchanging stories about their jobs, laughing about old times, and swapping workout regimens, which Dani couldn't bring herself to admit she wasn't actually completing. As she walked around the streets of Boston, her limp only slightly hidden, Dani thought of Locke. If he ever came to visit, he'd like the open-mic poetry night she'd found in the Back Bay. And she'd take him to Copp's Hill Burying Ground, where they would plant their feet on soil where more than a thousand slaves were buried, discussing the confusing history of this misguided, imperfect nation that they both loved and he still served.

But those dreams had died when Locke let it slip that he'd taken a local girl out on a date.

"*Amanda*," Dani had reported to Wendy Bennett over the phone. Lately, it seemed Wendy was the only person who reliably called her back. "Apparently she's a kindergarten teacher."

"Oh, Dani," Wendy had said. "I'm so sorry."

"It's fine. I doubt it's anything serious. Just took me by surprise, is all."

"Life has a way of doing that, doesn't it?"

AS DANI TOOK notes on her clipboard, she noticed the date and felt accosted by shock. For her entire life, the rhythms of the academic year had marked the passing of time, like posts upon which you could hang the fabric of life. October used to come with football games and full notebooks and midterms. Breaking time into manageable academic chunks must have slowed it down, Dani thought, because out of college, the calendar had become a ruthless conveyor belt ushering her onward, crushing months like cans. In the real world, fall was no longer a beginning. It was just the middle, like everything else.

The pen in Dani's hand suddenly ran out of ink. She scratched invisible lines on the page, frantically trying to get it to come back to life.

"Damn it," Dani whispered under her breath.

"You okay?" her subject, James O'Leary, asked. He'd turned off the water and was toweling off outside the shower.

Digging a new pen out of her overstuffed purse, Dani stopped her stopwatch and jotted down the time. *7 min. 32 secs.* It was a relatively long shower. Most guys limited their showers to five minutes, tops. Ignoring the inquisitive smile on his face, she started in on her list of questions.

"So, James, when you're in the shower, what do you think about?" she asked. "What's going on in your brain?"

"I'd say I'm mostly going through my schedule. Or thinking about what I'm going to eat next. Don't write that down. That was a joke."

Dani wrote it down, mostly because she knew it was true.

The clipboard in her hands listed his name and demographic stats, and though she'd already read it over a half dozen times, she found herself studying his details again.

JAMES O'LEARY. White 28-yr-old male, $38K. Educator/coach.

It seemed impossible for someone to live on that kind of salary in a city like Boston. Sure, he lived in Jamaica Plain, and his apartment was nothing like the four-bedroom, three-bathroom pent-house with a view of the Charles River Dani had secured. But how did James O'Leary buy groceries on $38,000? No wonder he worried about what he was going to eat next.

Her yellow legal pad had filled with notes about everything from the type of shampoo he used to the order in which he washed his body. Observation was the only way to find insight— and that's what Dani needed to find. A lightbulb. A general psy-chological truth, baked into an aha moment, that E & G could use to inspire Gelhomme's next commercial campaign.

"What are you doing now?" she asked as he approached the sink.

"Now, I shave," he said, opening his arms to present the long counter in front of him. "If you must know."

"I must. It's why I'm here."

He spread a smear of shaving cream across his jawline—a square and impressive jawline, Dani noted. He rinsed his hands, then reached for a silver razor on the counter. Running it under warm water, James slid it down his face, cheek to chin, cheek to chin, in perfect vertical lines.

"Do you enjoy shaving?" asked Dani.

"Of course not. It's a chore. Does anyone like chores?"

"So why do you do it?"

He rinsed the blade under the faucet. Little black hairs had gathered like confetti along the counter.

"What do you mean, why do I do it?" he said. "I have to."

"Says who?"

He splashed his face with warm water and retrieved a hand

towel from the floor. Dingy and damp, it looked like it hadn't seen the inside of a washing machine in weeks. Dani made a note of the moldy smell in the bathroom and the water splotches on the mirror.

"I guess there's something to be said for a good habit," he said. "Like making your bed every day. There's a ritual to it. You may not love doing it, but it gives you something in return."

"What does it give you?"

He sighed, placing the razor back in a dirty cup on the counter.

"Control, I guess. Maybe that's all we want anyway."

Without waiting to see if his interviewer was satisfied with that answer, James disappeared into his bedroom.

"I'm just changing," he said through the crack in the closet door. "Help yourself to coffee in the kitchen. I'll be out in a sec."

TAKING HER SUBJECT up on his offer of coffee, Dani held a steaming cup in one hand and flipped through the set of notes she'd taken that morning, leaning over the island in his kitchen. Something about his answers had struck her as meaningful. Perhaps even essential. *Control. Ritual.*

There was something to what he'd said, but she couldn't put her finger on it at the moment, so instead packed away her notepad in her bag and prepared to leave.

Her subject emerged from his bedroom dressed in khaki pants and a slim fit collared shirt, in what Dani assessed must be his school's colors—burgundy and white. He picked up the remote control and pointed to the television screen, swapping the *Today* show for ESPN.

"You a Red Sox fan?" asked Dani, lifting her mug, which had the team's classic logo on the side.

"Unfortunately yes. Last year was incredible. But I doubt they'll win a World Series again in our lifetime."

"How can you say that? That's the beauty of sports—every new season is a fresh slate."

"Nothing's a fresh slate."

"Ah, so you're a pessimist."

"Sure, the Red Sox won a World Series. But that cursed mentality still persists. You got guys with those old mind-sets, old habits. Old injuries. You're always fighting the past. And the Red Sox. They've got a hell of a past. And I'm a realist, not pessimist."

He paused, then pointed his thumb back toward the bathroom.

"It's not like if I shave *really really* well one day, the hair won't grow back. No matter how good a job I do today, I know I'll look in the mirror tomorrow and have to shave again. Coaching is like that. It's just grooming. Every day I show up, and I have to remove the bad little insecurities and old habits that have cropped back up overnight in my boys. I can't change who they are or what they bring with them every day. Best I can do is groom it."

"That's actually quite poetic," Dani said, wishing she still had her pen and paper to write it down. She lifted her bag to her shoulder and started toward the door. "You know, I used to want to be a coach."

"Used to?" The guy laughed. "You don't look old enough to have a dream that died. How old are you, anyway?"

"Twenty-three."

"Ah, a geezer," he said. "So why aren't you coaching?"

Dani remembered the salary that had been listed under his name. "I don't really know," she said. "For one, my basketball career didn't really go as planned."

"Well, that's a dumb reason not to do what you love. Nothing *ever* goes as planned."

They stood there looking at one another for a moment before Dani shrugged and headed toward the door. "It's been good talking," she said, reaching her hand out to shake his. "Thanks for the interview."

"Hey, before you go, can I ask you something?"

"Shoot."

"Are you single?" he ventured, putting his hands on his hips. "I don't mean to pry, but I was thinking I could set you up. There's this girl—my sister actually. She's a few years older than you. But smart. Quick-witted. I think you two would really hit it off."

"Oh," Dani said. "I'm not . . . I'm straight."

"Oh shit. Well now I really feel like an asshole. I just thought . . . the short hair . . . the . . . Right? God. My bad. Forget it. Forget I said anything."

"Don't worry about it. Honest mistake. And hey, thanks again. You gave me a lot of good stuff to work with here. They'll send you a check in a few weeks for your time."

ONCE SHE'D MADE it into the back of a cab, Dani leaned her head against the window and groaned deeply. Shaking her head, she reached for the bottle of Advil in her purse, swallowed three pills dry, and carefully pulled the emotional dagger out of her chest.

At every turn, people got it wrong. Black people thought she acted too white; white people saw her as black. People knew she was an athlete, but any time she tried to succeed, they thought she was cocky. For years, she'd fallen more and more in love with Locke, but he simply saw her as a friend. And now, James O'Leary had tried to set her up with *his sister*. Clearly, the energy she was putting off was completely different than the energy she *wanted* to put into the world.

Was she too masculine? Too intense?

What was it going to take for someone to finally see her for who she really was? And like what they saw?

In her reflection in the window, wet tears glittered on Dani's cheeks, mingling with her freckles. Wiping the wetness with the palm of her hand, Dani blew air out of her lips and pulled herself together. There was no use in getting upset.

"Where to?" the cab driver asked.

She wasn't expected back at the office for a few more hours. And while there was plenty of work to do unpacking this interview with James, both professionally and personally, Dani knew she couldn't do it yet. Not when her frustration was this raw. In just a few weeks, everyone she loved would arrive for Thanksgiving. Her parents were driving from Ohio; her brother, Dominic, and his partner, Charles, were flying in from Chicago. And despite their crazy schedules, Locke, Avery, and Hannah had all found a way to travel to Boston, too—significant others in tow.

She'd be the only person at the table alone. The odd one out, who'd invited everyone in.

She thought about the fresh money in her bank account and the winter displays that had appeared in the windows of her favorite boutiques downtown. The idea of brand-new clothes with fresh tags, perfectly folded in a thick shopping bag, soothed her, and she hadn't even spent a dollar yet. Retail therapy. It was cheaper than real therapy, she told herself.

"Back Bay," she answered. "Anywhere on Newbury Street."

A FEW WEEKS later, the office buzzed with the chaos of a deadline. Phones rang loudly. The graphic design team moved their mouses briskly over multiple screens, deftly adding color and pizzazz to the research Dani had painstakingly compiled in the past year, hoping the numbers would tell a story. The first *deliverable*—another stupid marketing term that Dani loved to hate—was due to Gelhomme, and unfortunately, the French didn't celebrate Thanksgiving. No one was going home until the report was complete.

"Pete," said Dani, rolling her chair out of her cubicle to peer into his. The lead graphic designer was an overweight thirty-two-year-old with a muss of brown hair and a patchy beard. He wore a black hoodie to work every day and was so good at his job, no one even mentioned the fact that he smelled of cottage cheese. "For the final slide, we need *length of shave time, number of shaves a week,* and *number of razor brands purchased* in a year—all averages. Got it?"

"On it," he said, without lifting his eyes from the screen.

Dani nodded, closed a few windows on her browser, and breathed. *Wait 'til Gelhomme sees this,* she thought brightly.

She'd never been so proud of a project in her life. A year had passed since she'd joined E & G's research team, and she relished sifting through all those dry figures spread out across Excel spreadsheets. Survey answers coded and entered as numbers, each in its perfect little cell. Human motivations measured and analyzed. She could get lost in the matrix for hours, like a pirate searching for treasure. It didn't even bother her that this report would go up the chain of E & G without her name on it. In her view, excellence was far more important than ownership.

While Pete finished the presentation, Dani took a moment to walk to the office kitchen and refill her coffee mug, ignoring the ache in her hips. The pain had increased rapidly in the last few weeks, as she'd spent more time in her office chair, staring at a computer screen. Her general practice doctor had referred her to an allergist—apparently changes in her diet might help with the pain—but the allergist didn't have a free appointment until after the holidays. Her GP had prescribed a narcotic to help with the pain, but Dani hadn't filled the prescription. She'd heard how addictive those pills could be and didn't need to add that to her list of problems. Pain was nothing new. The only new thing was the word *chronic*.

Thankfully, there were more important things for Dani to focus on than her body. Though her town house in Boston's North End had been in various states of disarray since she'd moved in last fall, she'd used her incoming houseguests as an excuse to finish decorating. In a rush of hard work and expense, an interior designer had arrived with a team of handymen that helped finish positioning the furniture, hanging the art, mounting the television, and styling the tables. Yolanda, her cleaning lady, would do a deep clean Wednesday morning, and a local chef she'd found on Craigslist would come that afternoon to get a head start on the feast. The chef would arrive again Thursday promptly at six A.M. to finish off the preparations, filling her kitchen with aromas of thyme, sage, and cinnamon. It would be worth the cost.

Dani wanted this Thanksgiving to be perfect, but preparing the house hadn't done a single thing to prepare her heart for her guests—Locke in particular. *I'm thinking I might invite Amanda to come to Boston,* he'd written. *What do you think?* While changing the sheets on the guest beds, Dani couldn't stop thinking about what he would look like with a different girl standing beside him. The thought made her sick. But how could she say no? As soon as he arrived and saw her house, he would know that there *was* plenty of space at the table.

Tightening the sheets on the guest bed, Dani had tried not to think about who would soon be sleeping side by side on the mattress. She was going to have to meet Amanda. Worse, she was going to have to pretend to like her.

Dani sipped her coffee and stared out the office kitchen windows at the brilliant city below. The Charles River, a choppy dark navy, split the city into two sections: Cambridge to the left and North Boston to the right. If she squinted, she could nearly see her apartment, tucked near the harbor, surrounded in orange foliage. If they were lucky, the weather would stay like this all week: brisk but golden.

"Boston's skyline," said a familiar voice behind her, "compared to New York City. It's just so . . . quaint."

Turning from the windows, Dani found Jim Webb standing behind her. He wore a navy suit with a gray and burgundy striped tie, as dapper as the day they'd met. Dani suddenly felt like a foreign dignitary had come to visit.

"Surprised?" he said.

"Completely! What brings you here?"

"My wife's family does Thanksgiving in Nantucket. Thought I'd pop in. I had a few things I wanted to run past you about Gelhomme anyway. You have a minute?"

"Yep. Actually, Pete's about to finish up the report." Dani started toward Pete's desk. "Let me show you."

They walked through the numbers and figures, Dani pointing to each perfectly designed chart and graph, as Pete sat with his arms crossed, listening to the vice president of the company interrogate Dani about the work. From the questions Webb asked and the smile on his face—Dani could tell that their boss was impressed.

"You did this?" he asked the graphic designer once they'd finished.

"Yes, sir," said Pete, wiping a bead of sweat from his brow. It wasn't every day that someone as senior as Jim Webb showed up to your cube. "Dani's been feeding me the numbers. But I did the design work."

"Not bad," Jim said. "Not bad at all. Has Laura Klein seen this?"

Laura Klein, the woman who had helped Webb interview Dani last year, led E & G's London office. It was Laura's team that would create a commercial campaign informed by the insights Dani and the other junior research fellows had compiled into this report. Dani secretly wished she could follow the report through to completion—help with the creative side. But her job was nearly finished. Soon, Jim Webb would assign her a new research project for the next E & G client and the process would start over again.

"Not yet," answered Dani. "We're going to send it to her as soon as Pete finishes the design."

"Incredible. She'll be thrilled." Jim Webb straightened his tie. "Hey, let's step into your cube for a moment, Dani. I wanted to have a little chat."

Seated in Dani's nook, Webb looked like a giant—long legs crossed, mind deep in thought. Her desk was orderly, bare except for a coffee mug and a silver framed photo next to her keyboard. In the photo, she, Avery, and Hannah stood in the middle of Times Square, laughing. To this day, the thought of that crazy twenty-four-hour trip made Dani smile. Twenty years old, alone in the city. Dani was between injuries. Avery's world had yet to be rocked by scandal. And Hannah had just fallen in love with the man of her dreams. The shine on their faces said it all. They were unencumbered. They were free. It was hard to imagine that at the time their biggest grievance was Coach Jankovich. Now that woman was long gone from West Point. But then again, so were they.

"I'm thinking you should let the other researchers take the reins this next go-round," Mr. Webb finally said. "No need to waste your talent on the grunt work."

"I like the grunt work," Dani said. "I like the research."

"Well, unfortunately, I don't see you here much longer."

Dani furrowed her brow in an expression of utter confusion. What did he mean, he didn't see her here much longer? And why in the world was he smiling if he was about to fire her?

"Let me be straight with you, Dani," he said, then paused. "I'm here to offer you a promotion. How would you feel about moving to London?"

Dani stared at him and then laughed, thinking this surely was some kind of mistake. Twenty minutes ago, she was staring at Boston, excited about her Thanksgiving plans. And now Jim Webb was sending her to live in a different country?

"You want me to work on Laura Klein's team?" Dani asked. Her memory was fuzzy. She remembered the woman's British accent. The posh black dress. At that career fair, Laura had made some joke about expecting Dani to be a man. The few e-mails they'd exchanged in the last year had all been short. Terse, even. "Wait. Does she know about this?"

"It's less about what she wants, and more about what the company needs. We need someone like you on the creative side. Someone who can bring all that"—he pointed toward Pete's desk, indicating the research—"to the actual creative product. I think someone who knows the target consumer as intimately as you do needs to be on the marketing team."

Dani's mind raced. When she considered all the logistics of an overseas move—the housing and the packing and living so far away from family—it seemed like such a hassle. She'd only just finished decorating her apartment here! And she'd be even farther removed from her friends. But then again, Hannah was deploying to Afghanistan and Avery lived in North Carolina, which required a plane trip anyway. Why limit herself to the States?

"When?" Dani asked.

"January. That gives you a couple of months to move and get situated. Oh, and I forgot the most important part," Webb added. "It's a change in salary, too."

He wrote a number on a piece of paper and pushed it toward her. Despite the shock she felt at seeing the number, she kept her face neutral. She'd learned at West Point, the first rule of negotiation was to never to show your cards too quickly.

"That's great, but you and I both know the cost of moving will be steep. The cost of living in London, I imagine, is pretty different than Boston," said Dani.

"We can include a corporate travel account with Delta, so you won't have to pay for your flights to and from the U.S. And you'll be eligible for bonuses at this level. So that will sweeten the deal a good bit. You're good at your job, McNalley. You deserve this."

On the outside, Dani nodded and acted as though she were considering it all very soberly. On the inside, her mind was racing. To turn down this job would be stupid. So what if she was only selling razors? Razors made people's lives better. This was a blessing, Dani decided. A gift. Staring at the number on the page in front of her, she wondered what she would even do with that kind of money.

"Okay," Dani said, nodding as if she were trying to convince herself that this conversation was real. "Okay."

Fall 2005 // Boston, Massachusetts

C link, clink, clink!

"A toast."

Dani's brother, Dominic, stood at the center of the table, holding a glass of champagne. He looked almost exactly like Dani, Avery thought, only tall and bald, with thick Buddy Holly–style glasses and the same glowing McNalley aura. Dominic's partner, Charles, a Canadian-born physics professor, sat beside him, surreptitiously feeding their pug, Daisy, scraps of food under the table.

A half-carved turkey rested in front of Avery, surrounded by empty dishes, where an hour earlier had been the most beautiful assortment of delicacies: sweet potatoes, roasted corn, fresh broccoli, creamed spinach, acorn squash stuffed with mushrooms and rice. Tim stretched his arm over the back of Hannah's chair. Locke Coleman cut his girlfriend, Amanda, another slice of pumpkin pie. Dani's parents had retired to the living room to watch football, leaving two empty chairs beside Dani, who sat at the head of the table, rolling her eyes at her brother's theatrical toast. Noah's hand warmly massaged the back of Avery's neck, and a thimbleful of red wine sat in her glass. She was surprised to see the glass so empty. It had been full at least twice during dinner.

Everyone was leaning back in their seats, bellies full, smiles wide, though in all honesty, Avery was still hungry. Noah had convinced her of the benefits of vegetarianism, but staring at that leftover turkey on the table, Avery's mouth watered with desire. She'd never *not* eaten turkey at Thanksgiving. She found herself growing jealous of Dominic's pug.

"I drink to the general joy of the whole table," Dominic began, raising his glass.

"That's Shakespeare," interjected Charles. "How about something original, Dom?"

"Pipe down, Charles. I'm talking."

Noah reached for the open bottle of wine and refilled Avery's glass.

"Like I said," Dani's little brother continued, "I drink to your joy. But most of all, I drink to my sister, whose greatest joy in life is to share it with others."

"Here, here," said Locke.

"Here, here," said Hannah.

The table clinked glasses.

Avery took a big swallow of wine. Dominic was right: Dani did love to share her joy with others. And her wealth, too, now that she had it to share. Dani had purchased plane tickets for Avery and Hannah with her frequent-flier miles. She'd even offered to put Avery and Noah up in a hotel nearby, but Noah didn't feel comfortable accepting that much charity, so instead of staying at the Hilton with Hannah and Tim, they were stuck at a Holiday Inn.

It was strange to think that this soon after college, the world had already pushed Dani into such a different tax bracket. In the Army, everyone of the same rank made exactly the same amount of money—Avery could look at Hannah, Locke, and Tim, and know exactly what their bank accounts likely said. You had to hand it to communism. At least with forced equality, you didn't have to deal with your feelings of inferiority.

Avery hated that she felt—what was it? Envious of? *Surprised by?*—her friend's success, but it was hard not to. When Avery and Noah had arrived in Dani's cobblestoned North End neighborhood earlier that morning, they'd speculated how much rent she must have been paying to have such a stunning view of the river. The historic three-story town house must have been at least three thousand square feet. Her fully renovated chef's kitchen had black onyx countertops, a shiny marble backsplash, and stainless steel appliances. A man dressed in white was busy chopping onions on a butcher block—he turned out to be a private chef Dani had hired for the occasion. As if she couldn't be bothered with stuffing a stick of butter in the ass of a turkey. As if, all of a sudden, that was below her.

Across the room, an industrial dining table had been set for a crowd, with silver place settings and crystal water goblets next to delicate wine glasses, like in a restaurant. A brown leather sofa in the living room was flanked on either side by low-slung modern chairs. And Dani's apartment walls weren't bare, like Avery's quarters. Colorful African art had been hung professionally in every corner, like Dani had hired an interior designer. And the final touch was Tim and Hannah—Tim with his high and tight haircut and classic blue collared shirt, standing next to Hannah, whose long dirty blond hair fell in loose waves down her shoulders. When Avery and Noah had arrived, the Nesmiths had stood in Dani's kitchen sipping a beer, like the entire scene had been staged for an open house. Avery's mouth had hung open, in awe.

"Insane, right?" Tim had said, noticing Avery's surprise. "Not exactly Fort Bragg. But it'll do."

Hannah had given Avery a stiff hug and mentioned how ironic it was that Noah and Tim would meet for the first time in Boston, rather than at Fort Bragg, where they all lived.

"Where have you been, stranger?" said Hannah.

Avery had tried not to take that dig personally, but there was an edge in Hannah's voice that was hard to ignore.

Just after three o'clock, Locke Coleman had arrived, walking through the door with his arms up over his head, like a heavyweight wrestler who had just won a match. He looked exactly as he had in college: shining face, gap-toothed grin. Hugs abounded. And Dani looked the same as she always had whenever Locke was around: dazzled. But before Avery could leave the kitchen to welcome Locke, a petite girl with rich brunette hair came up the stairs behind him, holding a pie. For the second time in one day, Avery's jaw had dropped.

"I'm fine," Dani had said later, when she, Avery, and Hannah were alone together in the kitchen. "Why wouldn't I be? Locke and I are just friends. We were always just friends."

Avery and Hannah had exchanged a look, their agreement over Dani's denial momentarily bridging the distance that existed between them. They stood in silence until Dani poured herself a generous glass of wine and took a long guzzle.

"Let's talk about something else," Dani had said, changing the subject. "Tell me about tool shed guy."

Avery started with the long rides on his motorcycle that he'd taken her on throughout the spring, rides that ended in lakeside picnics or hikes to waterfalls. She'd described his vintage two-door BMW—*so sleek*—and the trip they'd taken to California that summer, which he'd paid for entirely. She'd complained about his schedule: Noah constantly left on deployments that were sporadic and unpredictable in their length and location. And since his work was classified, she'd had to learn to be comfortable not knowing where he was going or when he might return. She told her friends what she and Noah shared in common—a love of fitness, good wine, and music—and avoided any subjects that might raise their concern. As it turned out, Noah wasn't thirty, like he'd originally said. He was actually thirty-six, a fact Avery only discovered when she'd asked to look at the picture on his driver's license and noticed the year he was born. He said he'd never lied—he promised that on their first date, he'd told her he was in his *thirties,* but Avery remembered it differently. Not that it mattered. It was only a thirteen-year difference.

She knew his age would matter to her friends, though. So she avoided admitting the truth about his age, because she didn't want to spend Thanksgiving justifying their relationship. Instead, she was going to spend it feeling his warm hand against her neck.

As Dominic took his seat, the table quieted and candlelight flickered across all of their faces. In particular, Avery focused on Tim and Hannah, who were seated across from her. All night, they'd been leaning into one another. Touching. Kissing. Nothing inappropriate, of course—it was Hannah after all—but even from the outside, you could sense an urgency in their faces. Time was running out before they deployed. And while Avery still wasn't a huge fan of Tim, she appreciated how quickly he'd welcomed Noah into their fold, offering him a beer and talking to him about the Army all afternoon.

Avery tapped her spoon against her glass. "Okay, my turn." She stood, straightened her black silk top, and tucked her hair behind her ears. She was horrible at improvising, especially when she was a little bit drunk. But if she couldn't get sentimental *now*, then when?

"To West Point. The place that brought us all together," Avery said. "West Point took a lot from us, but it gave us each other. And for that, I'm grateful."

"Here, here!" Dani said, looking shocked by the softness of Avery's toast.

Locke picked up where Avery had left off: "And to all the eighteen-year-old assholes who are finishing their applications and have no idea what they're signing up for."

"Here, here!" said Tim, raising his glass.

The toast ended and Dominic sighed heavily. "Well, I'm stuffed," he said.

"Amanda, your pie was incredible," offered Hannah. "I wish I could make pie from scratch. Believe me, I've tried."

"I can show you how to do it," said Amanda. "It's actually pretty simple. Nothing compared to all this. I still can't get over the meal, Dani. The sweet potatoes! That acorn squash was divine. What was that cream sauce on top? Did you make that?"

"Didn't you see the guy in there earlier?" said Locke. "Dani hired a chef."

Dani laughed. "Life's too short to chop onions."

"Locke has told me so many stories from West Point," Amanda continued, looking up and down the table. "You guys are in all of them. Especially you, Dani."

Avery fought the urge to cringe. *This chick is so completely oblivious.*

"He told me one recently. What was it, Locke? Something about New York City and a tongue ring?"

Locke pointed his fork in Hannah's direction. "Didn't Coach Jankovich make you rip it out when you got back?"

"She did," affirmed Dani. "It bled all over the court at practice."

Tim leaned forward to look at Hannah, whose face was nearly as red as the wine in Avery's glass. "Wait a second," he said. "How do I not know this story? My wife had a tongue ring and I didn't know it?"

Hannah shook her head in embarrassment. "It was when we were on our little *break*," she explained. "Junior year. Locke and some of the other football guys went with us to the city for a twenty-four-hour pass. And you kept telling people . . . what was it?"

"That I was—" Locke started.

"That he'd just been recruited by the *Ravens*," finished Dani.

"The Ravens!" exclaimed Avery, bubbling over with laughter. "All the other guys with us were acting like Locke's bodyguards. Which was annoying, because no guys would come near us."

Dani picked up where Avery had left off. "So, everywhere we go, doors are opening. Drinks are flowing. And suddenly, we look around and Avery and Hannah are gone—"

"We were there to meet men, not to be protected from them," added Avery.

Dani continued. "—and no one can find them. And when we finally get back to Grand Central to catch the last train back to West Point, there they are—"

"—and Hannah is holding an ice pack to her mouth," Avery squeaked, barely able to contain her laughter. "You were, like, drooling and couldn't speak in full sentences, because your tongue was so swollen."

"You sanctioned this piercing, Adams?" said Tim, looking at Avery.

"Of course I did!" Avery said, holding up her hands. "I was try-ing to help her get over *you*! I guess I failed at that job. She needed help. Before that, she was begging to go to the *Today* show, all right? I wanted her to live a little."

Hannah's mouth opened, like she'd just been stabbed in the back. She pointed across the table at Avery. "You know Katie Couric is my idol!"

They were all laughing hysterically now. But when Avery turned to look at Noah, to ensure that he was having as much fun as the rest of them, he'd vanished from the table.

"HEY, WHY'D YOU leave?"

She found Noah on the balcony outside, talking on his cell phone and smoking a cigarette. The river was black, like the sky. Once she stepped outside to join him, he quickly ended the call with a brief, "*Yep, love you too.*" Stuffing his cell phone in his pocket with one hand, Noah put out his cigarette on the railing with the other, then pulled Avery in for a kiss.

"You know I hate it when you do that," she said.

Smoking was a disgusting, carcinogenic habit. But then again, his bad-boy persona was part of the ethos that had suckered her in. "Who were you talking to?" she asked, trying to sound nonchalant.

"My mom," he said. "I was wishing her a happy Thanksgiving."

Avery checked her watch. "Aren't they still on a plane?"

Noah nodded, looked down at his feet, and rubbed out an imaginary cigarette on the ground with his toe. "Yeah, it was delayed."

"Oh. That sucks. I bet your brother's pissed."

"Yeah. They'll be all right." Noah reached for her waist and pulled her close to his body. "You ready to head out of here?"

"It's only eight o'clock. Dani has a whole game night planned or something."

Noah rolled his eyes. "Game night? What are we, five?"

"Come on," Avery said, cajoling him. "It'll be fun."

While he nibbled on the edge of her ear, Avery looked over his shoulder through the window at Dani, Hannah, and Amanda, who were busy cleaning the kitchen.

"I should go help them," Avery said.

"Okay," he said. "I gotta make one more call. I'll be right in."

Avery paused and looked at him quizzically. Who else would he need to call on Thanksgiving?

"It's a work thing," he said. "It'll be quick."

AVERY LEFT THE balcony and walked around a corner toward the kitchen. But when she heard her friends talking in hushed voices, she paused, standing behind a column.

"He's been on his phone the whole night," Hannah said.

"Avery seems happy," added Dani. Avery felt a sudden surge of gratitude. At least *someone* was taking up for her. "But I keep wondering how old he is. He seems older, right?"

"Here's what I don't understand," Amanda said. Locke's girl-friend wore a black crewneck sweater with a white Peter Pan collar. Avery could see her from around the corner, with her little ballet flats and little ballet voice. Who did she think *she* was to weigh in on Avery's relationship? She didn't even belong here! "He doesn't eat meat, but he *does* smoke cigarettes? In what world does that make sense?"

Clearing her throat, Avery stepped into the kitchen. They all froze.

"You know, you guys can say these things to my face," Avery said.

The silence persisted until Dani cleared her throat. "We're just curious, Ave," she said. "That's all."

"About what?" Avery was suddenly overcome with a readiness to defend herself. Like she'd stepped into battle. "Speak now, or forever hold your peace."

"Okay," said Hannah. "So, nicotine aside . . . you like him? He's treating you okay?"

Avery groaned and poured herself another glass of red wine. "He came all the way up here." She paused, taking in the sight of Hannah's concerned eyes and Dani, who was staring straight at her, wiping her hands on a kitchen towel. "Yes, he *treats me okay.* He treats me great. What is the problem?"

Hannah looked at Dani pleadingly, which sent heat rushing to Avery's face. "Stop," she said, no longer trying to keep her voice down. "Stop silently communicating with each other right in front of my face. Just say it. You don't like him."

"I didn't say that," Hannah said.

Amanda stepped gingerly off the step stool she'd been using to put away dishes in cabinets she couldn't reach. "I'm going to . . . let you ladies talk." She tiptoed out of the room.

"He's been looking at his phone all night," said Dani. "It just seems odd, that's all. We just want to make sure we're seeing it clearly. Maybe there's something we don't know."

"There's a lot you don't know," said Avery. "He's been on his phone because his parents have been stuck in an airport all day, trying to get to see his brother in Kansas City. He's been trying to rebook their flights. I promise you guys, once you get to know him, he's great."

At this they seemed to soften, and Avery felt a mix of relief and shame—relief that she'd won them over, and shame that she'd had to try so hard. She didn't know for certain that he'd been trying to rebook their flights. But that helped his case, so the white lie felt justified.

"So how serious is it?" Dani asked.

Avery shrugged. "I don't know. Noah . . . he's different. He seems committed to things. To us."

"Good," Hannah said. Stepping forward, she placed her hands on Avery's shoulders. "He's extremely lucky. Do you know that? You deserve for someone to completely cherish you. That's what we want."

For some reason, Avery cringed at Hannah's shower of compliments, her touch. Was it because she'd questioned Noah behind her back? Or because Avery didn't believe the things Hannah had said were actually true? Ever since Noah had shown up in that tool shed, it was Avery who had felt like the lucky one.

"And you," said Avery, stepping out of Hannah's embrace, toward Dani at the sink. She picked up a dry dish towel and snapped it against Dani's leg. "You did so much to make this happen today. I don't think I've had a chance to say thank you."

To Avery's surprise, thick tears formed in Dani's eyes. She turned off the water and turned to look at Avery and Hannah.

"What's wrong?" said Hannah.

"I have to tell you guys something," Dani said. "Don't worry. It's good news."

"Then why are you crying?" Avery asked, then whispered, "Did you poison Amanda's drink?"

Dani coughed a laugh. "No. I got a promotion. At work."

"That's great!" Hannah sang.

"Yeah." Dani scrunched her nose. "There's just one catch."

THE REST OF Dani's guests hurried into the kitchen when they heard Hannah scream.

"Dani's moving to London!" Hannah announced.

"London?" Locke repeated. "Like, England? Dude, I'm coming to visit."

Amanda looked at him as if this international visit was news to her but smiled and grabbed his hand, as if to say she was fine with it.

"That's crazy!" Tim said. "I'm not surprised. You were always the smartest one of all of us. Way to go, D."

Dominic started laughing. "You're gonna do it, right? You've got to do it. Charles, tell her she has to do it."

While Dani rapidly described all of her moving plans, Avery tried not to let her jealousy show on her face. She wanted to be happy for Dani—she really did. But how could you celebrate someone else's successes when your life felt completely stalled? In just a few short months, Hannah would be in Afghanistan, Dani would be in London, and Avery would still be stuck in Fort fucking Bragg. Her friends were moving on to bigger and better things: marriage, deployments, promotions. And she was . . . what? Here? In love? She looked outside at Noah, who had finished his second cigarette but was still on the phone.

"You all better come visit," said Dani. "Oh, Avery, why are you crying?"

"I don't know," she lied. The truth was, she felt like she was being left behind. And unfortunately, all the questions they'd brought up about Noah hadn't rolled off her shoulders like she'd hoped, but were sinking into the pit of her stomach. Everything suddenly felt very out of control. She had no idea how to express any of that except to say, "I'm going to miss you guys. That's all."

Hands damp from washing dishes, they stood in the kitchen in a small semicircle with their arms wrapped around each other's backs. If time could stop, Avery would have pressed pause right then and there. Before Hannah packed her trunk and put it on the back of a cargo ship headed to the Middle East. Before the movers arrived in Boston to pull down all the art from Dani's walls and wrap it in paper. Before Avery put her purse over her shoulder, said goodbye to her friends, and walked out the door under Noah's heavy arm, smelling the stale odor of cigarette smoke, masked by mint gum.

They say hindsight is twenty-twenty. But what good is hindsight when all you want to do is look through the glass and shout at your old self to not take one more step?

"Stop that," said Dani. "We'll be together again before you know it."

18

March 2006 // Camp Buehring, Kuwait

Prayer flags waved at the front of the bus, flapping against the air-conditioning vents. The driver, a bearded man wearing a tunic, turned up the volume on a recorded track of Arabic prayers, loud enough to drown out the sound of the engine. To Hannah, who sat in the third row behind the driver, staring out the window to the right, the prayers sounded ghostly, more like chants than prayers. Tim was the one who'd taken Arabic at West Point. When they'd said goodbye a few weeks earlier, he'd given her a phrasebook that he'd marked up and tagged, sticking little pink Post-it notes on the pages he thought would be most helpful. Now, staring out the window at an entirely new world, Hannah wished she'd memorized some of the phrases. At least then, the prayers coming from the speakers wouldn't sound so foreign. She imagined that Muslims asked God for the same things she wanted: Help. Protection. Peace. They said there was nothing more genuine than the prayer of a man in a foxhole. And this whole country was one big foxhole.

Hannah's parents and her sister, Emily, all understood that this deployment wasn't a disruption to her life. It wasn't something that scared her or made her feel anxious. The night before she left Fort Bragg for the airport, Hannah didn't worry any more than a child frets knowing they're leaving in the morning for Disney World. To say she was excited would be wrong—because this was a war zone—but she felt ready. After years of anticipation, Hannah wanted to get started and get it over with. She kept a pocket calendar and had already marked off two days. Four hundred and forty-eight to go.

The bus barreled down an unpaved road toward the entrance to Camp Buehring, where her unit would spend two weeks acclimating to the heat and recovering from jet lag, before their final flight into Afghanistan. Her silver cross rested between Hannah's thumb and forefinger and she slid the charm right and left on the delicate chain, before hiding it away again under her uniform. The air inside the bus smelled stale and brimmed with the quiet tension of fifty soldiers on board, each one staring out their own window at the same merciless view. Sand stretched for miles in every direction. A woman in a long black cloak with only slits for eyes—a burqa—walked along the road in the dust. Where she was going, Hannah had no idea. And for the first time, she felt a jolt of fear. From this point forward, it was going to be nearly impossible to tell friend from enemy.

Soon, the line of buses reached a security checkpoint and

a crew of Army soldiers dressed in desert fatigues checked the buses for explosives, then waved them through.

That was all it took to get to war. Five years of training and a wave.

OVER THE NEXT few weeks, Hannah's unit conducted a series of training events. They were instructed to drink a gallon of water a day to hydrate, and at night, Hannah fought to stay awake until it was time to go to sleep in Kuwaiti time. Each morning, she woke up before the sun, not because she was forced to, but because her mind hadn't caught up to her body's geography. Despite her surroundings, everything in her heart and mind believed she was still in North Carolina. One morning, she woke up in the darkness of her tent completely confused about where she was and why the air smelled like burning trash.

She adjusted soon enough. They completed medical simulations and vehicle rollover simulations, and for two consecutive days near the end of their time in Kuwait, her unit practiced counter-IED training, to help them detect and disable roadside bombs. Every time Hannah stepped outside, sand whipped up from the ground, into her ears, eyes, and mouth, as if it were trying to bury her alive. And everyone had the same complaint: it was so *hot*. In an e-mail to Dani, she'd tried her best to explain how it felt: like someone was blowing a hair dryer in your face. Temperatures stayed in the hundreds and regularly hit 125 by the afternoon. Breath stifled, pores full of dirt, Hannah learned to drink water before she was thirsty, to walk in the shade, and to stay inside between the hours of twelve and three P.M. The climate was as much of an enemy as the Taliban.

By the time her unit reached Forward Operating Base Sharana in southeastern Afghanistan, thirty kilometers from the border of Pakistan, Hannah had marked thick black Xs through seventeen days on her pocket calendar.

She carved out a routine, which Sarah Goodrich, who'd completed her first deployment, had promised would help pass the time. An alarm went off every day at 0530. She ran around the perimeter of the forward operating base, showered, and read a few pages in her Bible. Then she'd make it to the cafeteria for breakfast, before heading to the tactical operations center to meet with her superior officers and discuss tasks for the day.

At times, it was easy to forget she was even in Afghanistan— that is, until she would walk outside, feel the dry heat attack her sinuses, and see dusty mountains in every direction. Afghanistan had a barren beauty that Hannah grew to appreciate and even admire. At night, the sky was so lit up with stars, it looked like a laser-light show and far outperformed the view from her grandfather's porch. There, she could see constellations. Here, she saw galaxies.

In an area this remote, snail mail was still the most reliable and consistent form of communication. Tim's handwriting—dark, all-caps—became the thing Hannah most longed to see on the outside of a white envelope. They wrote often, filling the pages with minutiae like what they'd eaten the day before or their most recent workout. But every now and then, Tim would surprise

Hannah by sending a poem or a long passage from a book he'd been reading, if he felt it applied to their situation.

She kept his letters in her pillowcase until the stack became too thick. By the time her unit took their first convoy away from FOB Sharana to build an outpost for a crew of NATO troops, the collection was three inches tall. She wrapped the letters with a spare shoestring and locked it in the trunk at the foot of her cot. When they returned a week later, she riffled through them again, laughing at the little drawings he'd put in the margins. The most recent one featured a sketch of Hannah and Tim on opposite sides of the world, arms wrapping around the globe like Stretch Armstrong, reaching across the oceans. He'd never been much of an artist.

It's only 15 months, she told herself. *That's nothing.*

Once at West Point, Hannah's computer had crashed, destroying a sixteen-page term paper in the process. Tim had shown up at her room with a carafe of coffee and a calculator.

"Look," he'd said, crunching the numbers of her GPA. "You can literally turn in nothing, and you'll be okay." She was crying. The numbers hadn't convinced her that the world wasn't ending. He'd put his hands around her face, wiped her tears with his thumbs, and then kissed her softly on the mouth.

"I dare you to believe me."

After that, Hannah had spent the entire night drinking coffee and listening to Tim tell stories instead of rewriting her paper. It was a risk, and not once during the night had she felt comfortable taking it. But in the end, he'd been right. She'd turned in five pages of nonsense—something she'd written quickly the following morning. And even though she received an F, the world didn't end. Her GPA only changed by a tenth of a point. She believed he was right about this deployment, too, that spending all this time apart would be worth it in the end. Like one failed paper didn't impact her GPA, one year apart wouldn't change the totality of their relationship together.

It was just fifteen months. Basically, a year.

A year is nothing in light of a life.

"HE SAYS A U.S. mortar round landed on his land, killing his prized cow."

An interpreter spoke quickly in Pashto to a dark-skinned Afghan man, the plaintiff, who spat back something angry and defiant, pointing once again at the photo on the table in front of them.

Three months into her deployment, Hannah had been called into a JAG meeting. The translator, Amjad Ebrahim, was something of a minor celebrity around FOB Sharana. When their unit had first arrived, the translator had collected a few dollars from every officer and showed up the next day with a freshly slain lamb. Skinned, bled, and roasted over a fire, the lamb accompanied an assortment of sauces, spices, tandoori bread, yogurt sauce, chopped mint, preserved lemon, falafel, rice, and steamed greens. It was still the best meal Hannah had ever had—and that included all the meals Wendy Bennett had made at her home at West Point.

Twenty-seven, with a wife and three children at home, Ebrahim had long hair that curled slightly under his ears, dark eyebrows, and a ready smile that defied his circumstances. Every day, he wore a uniform that matched Hannah's, only his had a patch on the left that read "U.S. Interpreter" where hers said "U.S. Army."

But today, Ebrahim's face was all business. The man across from him wore a white shalwar kameez, frayed and dirtied on the edges from his long trek into the Army compound.

"Does he have documentation?" the JAG officer asked. "A receipt? Any kind of evidence?"

The interpreter repeated the question in Pashto, and the offended Afghan man answered vehemently in the affirmative, pushing his photo and a piece of paper across the table. The paper was covered in writing, but Hannah couldn't help but think the ink looked fresh. She'd only been asked to attend this meeting because the finance officer attached to their unit was down with some kind of stomach bug, but she suddenly felt way out of her league. The room felt tense, like the man was about to explode with rage.

"He says it's a receipt," said Ebrahim.

"What does it say?" the JAG officer asked. "Is it a receipt?"

Shrugging his shoulders, Ebrahim continued, "It says he purchased the cow this year for two hundred U.S. dollars."

Without thinking, Hannah laughed out loud, forcing the JAG officer to scowl. She felt mortified at her accidental lapse in decorum, but there was no way this man had paid that much money for a cow. For many Afghans, two hundred U.S. dollars was enough to feed a family for a year! She looked at Ebrahim for some sign of recognition. Some mutual understanding that they were being swindled.

"Pay him," the JAG officer instructed Hannah after looking over the paper. Then, looking at Ebrahim, he said, "Thank him for coming. Tell him we hope this makes up for his loss."

A bead of sweat ran down Hannah's temple as she passed an orange envelope of cash to the man across from her. He accepted the envelope haltingly, as if a woman's hands had soiled the funds. When he pulled the cash from the envelope, he began to argue with the translator again. Ebrahim shouted in return, his face reddening, as if he were scolding a child. Hannah noticed he pointed toward the door, but the Afghan man refused to leave.

"What's he saying?" Hannah asked.

"He says without the cow, they've missed out on income," Ebrahim answered, exasperated. "He demands another two hundred dollars."

Wide-eyed, Hannah turned to the JAG officer, stunned. Surely the U.S. Army wouldn't be extorted by a petty thief. He probably didn't even own a cow in the first place! And even if he had, $400 amounted to a half year's salary in Afghanistan. Would the JAG officer really enable this man to quit his day job? Military Intelligence was clear on what unemployed men spent their days doing—and it wasn't milking cows. It was fighting alongside the Taliban.

"Do it," the JAG officer ordered.

And Hannah followed orders, sliding another $200 across the table. But this time she didn't laugh.

"BAD DAY?"

Hannah looked up from her plate of gray meatloaf topped with red sauce to see Private Murphy staring at her. He kept shoveling food into his mouth, but she knew from the tone of his voice that he actually cared. He tapped his fork on the table and went back to his plate, stacked high with mystery meat.

"Suit yourself. But it's got to go somewhere, ma'am."

Pushing her food around her plate, she realized her eyes must have looked as heavy on the outside as they felt in her head.

"We paid a local guy four hundred dollars today for a cow that probably never existed."

Private Murphy grunted.

"I feel like I'm just wasting my time here," Hannah said.

"You could always come to the clinic," he said. "We could use an extra set of hands."

The week before, at the exact same table, Private Murphy had told Hannah about the medical center outside of FOB Sharana. The battalion that had lived at the FOB the year before had set up an old containerized housing unit, or CHU, a few hundred yards beyond the base to act as an emergency room for locals. Afghans traveled, sometimes for days, to get there. The rectangular clinic was outfitted with medical equipment—old stretchers, IVs, first aid gauze, and a dwindling stash of Medihoney, a medical-grade honey product for the management of wounds and burns. They weren't doctors, but with the training they'd received in the military, they knew more than most. The battalion commander, Colonel Markham, allowed them to go out on Saturdays between building assignments.

"So you treat mostly burns?" Hannah said.

"Yeah. I guess it's common here for parents to burn their children as a punishment," Private Murphy said with cold indifference. "Last week, a father brought in his seven-year-old son. He'd disobeyed somehow, and as punishment, he'd dipped his son's arm in kerosene and then lit a match."

"Oh my God."

"It's pretty messed up. But they won't take the children to an Afghan hospital."

"Why not?"

"Well, for one, the closest hospital is in Kabul. It would take about a week to get there. Plus, Afghan doctors would amputate. We're not equipped to do all that. So we do the best we can. Try to save the limbs. The parents like that."

"I want to go," Hannah said.

"No you don't. It ain't pretty."

Hannah stared him down until he relented.

"Don't say I didn't warn you."

THE FOLLOWING SATURDAY, Hannah woke at 0530, slung her weapon over her shoulder, and slipped out of her room into the rising sun. Colonel Markham, Private Murphy, and three other soldiers waited at the FOB gate, and once Hannah had joined them, Markham waved to the soldier on guard. A heavy concrete door clicked loudly and swung open, then closed behind them.

The scene from beyond the wall unfolded before Hannah, shocking her with its beauty. The rising sun cast an eerie red light across the desert. Heat waves swirled through the air like the ones she used to stare at when her father grilled steaks on the back deck, only this was natural heat—terrifying, since it was still so early in the morning. She could hear the short, fast *pop-pop-pop* of magazine fire in the distance, and as they crested a small sand hill, the makeshift CHU she'd been told about came into view, next to an open-air wooden structure, built as a waiting room for patients. Under the structure, a crowd of families waited in utter silence as the medical team arrived.

Mothers wearing hijabs fanned their children, who'd been carried on quilts or doors. Red and burgundy burns slashed and splotched the children's faces, arms, and legs. Some of the burns oozed, others bled. Dark skin flapped in charred masses and fresh white splotches of exposed epidermis screamed with pain, though the children refused to cry. Fathers stood, stoic and dark eyed, watching as Colonel Markham passed the patients, evaluating each case by sight. He didn't waste any time choosing the most severe cases. *It's triage,* Hannah realized. Worst cases first.

"One," Markham said, and pointed to a child stretched out on a quilt. "Two." He pointed to another child, on the opposite side of the shelter. "Three . . ."

Hannah, breathless and sick to her stomach, waited for him to finish creating an impromptu appointment list.

"Just like every other day, don't go crowding the gate," he said. "We will get to everyone eventually."

Once they were inside the CHU, Markham closed the door behind them. The structure was long and thin, with three stretchers for patients lined up diagonally down the middle of the trailer. Shelves on every wall held equipment: thermometers, Medihoney, steroids, bandages. Two rotary fans and a small AC unit churned stale air. A radio filled the room with the sounds of old Beatles songs. As Hannah moved about the room, trying to find the right place to stand, Private Murphy and the rest of the soldiers took off their uniform overcoats.

"Lieutenant Nesmith," Murphy said, "time to scrub in."

Hannah mimicked Murphy's every move: she secured her M16 in a locker, removed her helmet and Kevlar, hung up her jacket, rolled up the sleeves of her tan T-shirt. Standing next to Murphy at the center of the CHU, they both snapped a pair of purple rubber gloves over their hands.

"This is the real fight. A chance to show mercy," Markham said as he propped the door open with a rock. "Number one!"

Two soldiers at the entrance waved metal detector wands over the patient, who was covered by a white blanket, then checked the patient's parents as well. And before Hannah could prepare, Markham had directed the patient's parents to stand in the back corner and began to slowly lift the quilt off the small body underneath.

A young girl lay naked, shaking, watching as her skin peeled back off her arms, stomach, legs, and feet, still attached to the blanket. Without thinking, Hannah squatted down beside the patient, stroking her dark black hair. The child opened and closed her eyes with pain, the sounds of her small cries drowned out by the music coming from the radio.

"Shh . . . shh . . . ," Hannah said, holding all of her emotion in her belly. "It's okay. It's going to be okay."

The girls' father looked on, blank and expressionless, as his daughter's skin peeled off like brown paper, attached to the fibers of the blanket. Hannah found herself praying. *Please, God, save this child.*

Private Murphy started in, cutting dead skin away from the girl's body with a pair of sterilized scissors.

"If you leave it, infections will set in," he said. "She needs an IV. Morphine. Nesmith. Can you do it?"

Hannah suddenly remembered the training she'd done at Buckner, when she'd shoved a needle into Avery's arm.

"It's been a long time," she answered.

"It's okay. Just do what I say."

Following his instructions, Hannah placed a long needle through a vein in the young girl's forearm, trying carefully not to cause more pain. And as she did, Hannah did everything she could to keep herself from crying.

LATER THAT EVENING, as the sun was setting, Hannah sat in her room stewing. She had propped her bed on stilts in order to fit a trunk underneath, and had built a set of bookshelves so she could have a place for books—most of which had been chosen by Tim. As little as he'd liked to complete assigned reading in college, he was a voracious reader now. He said books tasted better when you were hungry for them. At the moment, she was one hundred pages into *East of Eden*. And he was right. She couldn't get enough of Steinbeck's words. The more she consumed, the more she desired.

On her desk, a stack of supply requisition forms waited for her signature, necessary for the upcoming site build her platoon was scheduled to complete. But she didn't feel like reading or doing paperwork. She didn't feel like doing anything.

She was still trying to understand what she'd witnessed that morning at the burn unit. It seemed utterly evil, what those parents had done to their children, but culturally speaking, it was completely acceptable—around here, it was discipline. Sitting in her CHU, Hannah remembered Colonel Bennett's philosophy class her plebe year, and the conversation he'd led about justice. Was it injustice, what these people were doing? Or was it cultural difference? Was it up for debate, or was there truth, with a capital T? Did God care about those children? Did he see?

Shaking the thought from her mind, she changed into a pair of black shorts and a gray T-shirt, and pulled her hair into a ponytail. Being in an engineering platoon had its perks—one of which was that they could build just about anything if they had the right materials.

A week earlier, she'd joined a group of soldiers in building a makeshift basketball court on the tarmac. Since then, they had an unspoken standing pickup game every night at seven P.M. Even the translator, Ebrahim, had started playing, though admittedly, he wasn't very good. Hannah always picked him for her team, just as a show of good faith.

When she arrived at the court, the interpreter was already there, stretching. He wore a pair of white Air Jordans that Private Murphy had given him.

"Hydration is the key to longevity," he said philosophically. He offered Hannah a plastic water bottle and she took it.

"I swear, Ebrahim, your English is better than mine," Hannah said, taking a sip of the cold water.

In the months since she'd arrived at FOB Sharana, he'd become the closest thing Hannah had to a friend. His English was impeccable, his sense of humor approachable, and his addiction to outdated American romantic comedies common knowledge. He'd told Hannah that he'd learned most of his English by watching Julia Roberts in *My Best Friend's Wedding*. He would often stop and shout "Kimmi!" for no reason, as though he had Tourette's syndrome. It always made Hannah laugh.

"Hey, can I ask you something?" she said.

He nodded. "Shoot." He put his hands up. "Don't shoot!" They laughed at his silly joke, and then he said, "Of course. Ask me anything."

"The other day. That guy with the cow. What are the chances he was telling the truth?"

After a pause, Ebrahim shrugged. "Who's to say?"

Shaking her head, Hannah sat on the tarmac to tighten her shoelaces. "How can you be so calm about it?" she asked. "Doesn't that kind of thing keep you up at night?"

"I don't lose sleep over things I can't control."

Hannah focused on the sky while her mind reeled. Her interpreter worked with her nearly every day, having conversations, not offended that her hair was uncovered or that she spoke to him without first being addressed. But she was well aware that his wife at home wasn't allowed to speak out of turn, or leave the house without his permission.

"For the life of me I don't understand," Hannah said, finally letting her arms drop to her sides.

"Don't understand what?"

"With any other woman, you wouldn't dare sit and have a conversation like this. Out in the open."

"No."

"So what's the difference?"

"You're American."

Hannah sighed. "But what about your wife? Your daughter? Don't you want them to have an education? Don't you want them to have opportunities?"

"And what has your education gotten you? A trip to a war zone?" Ebrahim laughed, still trying to keep the tone light. "I imagine your father wishes you were at home."

Hannah raised her eyebrows. He had a point.

"Sometimes I just wonder if being here is really going to make any difference," she said. "It just seems impossible."

Ebrahim let Hannah's question linger between them. Then he cleared his throat.

"When I was a boy, my father would get up every morning and call around to his brothers, to see who was still alive after the bombing through the night.

"The bombing was constant. After the Russians left, this area was controlled by warlords that constantly fought for territory. Then the Taliban came in and kicked out all of the warlords. And the rules they put in place—they were crazy, sure. It seemed a small price to pay for safety. To sleep and know that you would wake up in the morning.

"I was fifteen when things changed. First, they said that women couldn't go to school, which wasn't hard because my family was too poor to send my sisters to school anyway. Then they destroyed the cinemas. We couldn't listen to music. There was no art. No industry. No festivals or feasts, like there had been when I was a boy. My wedding day was one of the bitterest days of my life. I went to pick up my wife from the salon—there were salons then, if you can imagine that. We drove together to my parents' home for the celebration. But on the way, they stopped us. Pulled me out of the car. Beat me. Cut my hair. They said I shouldn't have been with her, like that, alone, because we were unmarried.

"And things just kept getting worse. They killed people and hung them from streetlights. They'd leave the bodies there for weeks, until they rotted and fell to the ground for the dogs to eat."

He paused, although Hannah couldn't be sure if it was to collect his thoughts or contain his emotion.

"We can never go back to that. Never," he said, looking straight at her. "We were dead under the Taliban. There was no life. No reason to live. No traditions. No beauty.

"But now, we feel again. We hope again. I can listen to music and dance." He snapped his fingers, wiggled his hips. "I'm here, playing basketball with my American friends. That's something. Right? That's a . . . what did you say? Lasting change? Yes."

He unscrewed the cap of his water bottle, took a long sip, then twisted the cap back in place and wiped his mouth.

"Maybe hope is the only lasting change one human can give to another. And for the first time in my life, I have hope. You gave that to me."

Spring 2006 // London, England

D ani!"

Laura Klein had the annoying, completely unnecessary habit of shouting across the office to get Dani's attention, when, in reality, all she had to do was stand up and look outside her office door and kindly say, at a normal decibel level, that she needed something.

That woman always needed something. But at the moment, Dani didn't want to move. She'd just read an e-mail that had stunned her into paralysis.

From: Locke Coleman <lockestockand@hotmail.com>
Subject: booked!
Date: April 6, 2006 9:13:15 AM CST +01:00
To: Dani McNalley <danimcnalley@yahoo.com>

Booked my ticket! Coming to London May 14–21. Call me and let's start to make some plans.

—Locke

"Dani!"

Pushing away from her desk, Dani limped from her chair to her boss's door frame. The London office was aesthetically disappointing—dark carpet, clusters of cubicles, a tiny kitchen with a refrigerator full of other people's forgotten lunches, stinking and spoiled. Laura Klein, it turned out, was as short and brittle as a boss as she'd been in that first interview a few years earlier. She had platinum blond hair, and wore the same dark maroon lipstick and black three-quarter-length dress, as if it were easier to wear the same thing every day than to make fashion decisions. In nearly every conversation, she found a way to mention her current separation from her husband of twenty-two years, and Dani wondered if he'd grown bored with her clothes or simply annoyed by the sound of her nagging voice. Either way, she couldn't really blame the guy.

Dani poked her head into Laura's office. "Yes?"

"What's this I hear from Webb about new slides?"

"I cc'd you on that."

"Cc," she repeated, lowering her glasses down her nose.

"Carbon copy."

"Right. Well I didn't see that. And I need to see them before my presentation."

Dani wondered if she'd heard Laura correctly—if her boss had actually put emphasis on the word *my*. As if Dani would forget who was giving the most important presentation in E & G history. After more than a year and a half of global research, they were finally presenting their research findings and marketing recommendations to Gelhomme. Dani had been assigned the task of building the PowerPoint deck that Laura would use to deliver the presentation, which meant that nearly every other moment, the woman was calling Dani to her side.

"I'll send them again," Dani promised. "But the gist of it is that I think we should add digital advertising to our recommendations."

"Digital," Laura repeated, as if it were a foreign word. "As in..."

"As in the Internet."

Her boss laughed. "You must be joking. Everyone knows banner ads are a colossal waste. Gelhomme doesn't need that. They have a thirteen-million-dollar budget, Dani."

"I'm just saying that it may be worth using some of that budget to start playing online."

"Our clients don't want to *play*. They want to make a *profit*."

"Sure. But you should take a look at the numbers. There's this new website called the Facebook that's really taking off with college kids—"

"What is it, porn?" Laura laughed at her own joke and went back to work at her computer.

"It's a place you can chat with your friends, see what they're up to. Share pictures. There are like, thirteen thousand new users every day and—"

"We are not advising our biggest client to throw money away at some online fad. They'll laugh us out of the room. They hired us to create TV commercials. Not reinvent the wheel."

"The wheel is about to be made obsolete," Dani said with conviction.

Laura stared up at Dani, her fingers perched on the keyboard of her computer.

"I don't think you appreciate the opportunity you've been given here," Laura said, putting her glasses on her desk. "When I got my start in this industry, women were seen as secretaries, not future executives. I had to keep my head down. Learn the rules. Play the game. I suggest you do the same." Laura picked her glasses up again and said under her breath, "Of course, you wouldn't understand."

Dani stared at the side of Laura's face, which was now trained on the computer screen. "I'm sorry. Why wouldn't I understand?"

"Well, you know. There's such a push for diversity these days. It's easier for you. Things didn't get handed to us, back in the day."

Dani's head reared back, as if Laura's words had hit her in the face with force.

"Easier," Dani repeated. "You think it's easier. For *me*?"

She wanted to show Laura pictures of her grandmother, picking cotton as a sharecropper on a white man's land in North Carolina. She wanted to recite the statistics: How unemployment among black women was nearly twice as high as among white women. How even though white women earned eighty cents for every dollar white men earned, women of color earned just sixty-three cents. Dani wanted to take Laura back and show her how hard she'd worked at West Point, earning the respect of her peers and professors, only to get tossed to the curb when her body couldn't keep up with her mind.

Easy? she wanted to say, and show her the pharmacy of medication in her purse. *Nothing about this is easy.*

"You know what I mean," said Laura, with an added layer of kindness. To Dani, it seemed like her boss was trying to say something sincere, but it was coming across so desperately insulting. "You're good at your job, and it looks good for the company to have you at the table. It's a win-win. Comparatively, I just look like the old hag that refuses to retire. That's all I'm saying."

Dani sighed and chose to push forward with the marketing, rather than the debate over who had it easier in the workplace. "Let me just tell you a few more things about this online strategy."

Laura leaned back and nodded.

"With TV ads, you can get certain data from a consumer: age, zip code, gender, race," Dani conceded. "But with the Internet, we can drill down to the minutiae—what kind of music they listen to. How they lean politically. Where they spend their time online. It's data on a whole different level."

"I hear you. But unfortunately, we don't have the benefit of time," Laura replied. "The presentation is next week. It's too late. What we have will do."

Laura looked Dani up and down, taking in the sight of her black trousers and blue button-up shirt.

"Oh, and Dani, don't take this the wrong way, but you'll need to wear a dress and heels to the presentation," she added. "It's Paris, after all."

THE MORNING OF the Gelhomme presentation, Dani showered in an expansive hotel suite in the Seventh Arrondissement of Paris, then toweled off while taking in the view of the Eiffel Tower. The rain outside her window tempted her to get back in bed, but thankfully, a shot of pre-presentation adrenaline pumped through her veins, which acted like speed to get her moving.

The last weeks had been moving at a breakneck pace, as E & G prepared to present its final recommendations to Gelhomme's CEO, Paul Duval. The London team had fleshed out six different marketing campaigns, which, thanks to a focus group of consumers, had been narrowed down to the final one. Somehow, through it all, Dani's concept had survived. She had a football coach in Jamaica Plain to thank for that.

When the pressures of work mounted, Dani found herself staying up late at night to either revise Laura's PowerPoint presentation, plan the itinerary for Locke's upcoming trip, or shop online. The clothes and shoes she purchased only made her happy for a few days before they found their way to the bottom of her closet, a pile of unfulfilled promises. But she had no time to travel. And her doctor had put her on an extremely restrictive diet, hoping it would help with the arthritis pain. So she couldn't eat out at fancy restaurants or drink alcohol. So what if clothes had become her guilty pleasure? What else was she supposed to do with all that money?

Wrapped in a Burberry trench coat and lavender cashmere scarf, Dani stopped to check her reflection. It had been nearly impossible to find a barber in her Notting Hill neighborhood who could do black hair—but she'd finally found someone, and he'd relaxed her hair and added a weave. It was straight and silky, parted on the side, with extensions that reached her collarbone. But no matter how she styled it, she still didn't feel like herself when she looked in the mirror. Even her freckles seemed to have faded in England's rainy climate. Her skin glowed thanks to the high-end products she could afford with her new salary. She looked expensive. But she felt cheap.

Yesterday, she'd received an e-mail from Hannah detailing life in Afghanistan. In the photos her friend had attached to her e-mail, Hannah stood in the midst of a desertscape, wearing ACUs and her Kevlar vest, smiling widely. Her platoon had convoyed out to a remote location, where they were building an outpost for incoming NATO troops. The photo looked like the set of *M*A*S*H*. There were six GP medium tents, Army green against sand. In another photo, Hannah posed outside of a wide aluminum shipping container with three young girls whose hands were wrapped in white bandages. The burn unit Hannah had described in the e-mail sent chills down Dani's spine. In the photo, Dani saw dark shadows under Hannah's eyes, pain hidden within her smile. By comparison, Dani's life was completely self-serving—a picture of comfort and luxury. How could she complain to her friends about the existence of Laura Klein, or the loss of a man she'd never had, when by comparison, their chief complaint was the existence of Afghanistan?

WHEN SHE ARRIVED at Gelhomme's Paris office, Dani made her way directly to the conference room to set up the audiovisual equipment. A simple spread of pastries, fruit, and coffee waited at the center of the table. The rest of the room looked like it had been prepped for a visit from the queen: wood floors waxed, windows washed, oriental carpet steamed, table shined, all twelve leather chairs placed in a perfect oval around the table. The buttery scent of croissants tempted Dani, teasing her senses with the memory of bread, but she refrained. The allergist's proposed diet—no dairy, gluten, sugar, or inflammatory vegetables—had decreased her pain significantly. Hanging her jacket on a hook outside the door, Dani felt immediately powerful in the dress she'd chosen to fulfill Laura's demand. White, with cap sleeves and a conservative neckline, the dress fit tight around her curves and stopped just below her knees. "Showstopper," was the word the shopkeep had used when Dani had walked out of the dressing room. When he rang it up at the register, Dani hadn't even listened when he said the total cost. She'd just handed over her credit card.

Jim Webb had flown in from New York, with three other E & G executives. They lingered outside of the conference room, in crisp suits of different shades of gray. The tension in the atrium became palpable as the minutes drew closer to nine o'clock. Hundreds of thousands of dollars spent—on the building, the research, the insights, the art, the preparation—and if the deal happened, another few million dollars would change hands in an instant. All of this just to sell disposable razors, Dani mused, eyeing her superiors' glittering watches and shined shoes. Four little blades on a plastic stick.

Just then, Laura Klein came through the door, a flurry of energy and anxiety. She wore the exact same black dress she wore every other day, only this time, the blond-haired woman had chosen a pair of red high heels and red-rimmed glasses to match. Giving Dani a once-over, her boss winked, the closest thing to approval Dani had received from her to date.

"Is it ready?" Laura asked.

"Yep." Dani picked up the remote from the table and clicked through a few slides, then back to the beginning. "It's all ready to go."

"Audio, too," said her colleague Philip, who was standing behind the computer, testing the speakers.

"Good," Laura breathed. "No surprises. This has to be perfect."

"You'll do great," Dani said, hoping to sound encouraging. But from the look on Laura's face, Dani knew it came across as condescending.

As the crowd of white men migrated into the conference room, Dani stood back in wonder. It felt like a dream, really, to be this female, this black, in this room. Jim Webb made the introductions, taking time to properly flatter the man of the hour, Gelhomme's CEO, Paul Duval. Dressed in a three-piece suit, with a swooping hairstyle, Duval held the seat at the head of the table, looking unimpressed. He checked his watch.

"Over the last year and a half or so, our researchers have conducted nearly one thousand in-home interviews in more than one hundred target countries," Jim Webb began. "This is the largest consumer study E & G has conducted for a single client."

"I can assure you," Laura said, interrupting Webb, "we've watched more men shower in the last six months than you'd care to know."

The CEO didn't laugh.

"Laura, why don't you go ahead and share what we've come up with for Gelhomme's new razor launch," Jim said.

Laura smoothed her black dress. She stood, took her place at the end of the table, and switched the computer screen to the presentation Dani had painstakingly written and designed for this very moment.

"As you well know, Gelhomme is the standard bearer for men's products," Laura said. "In interview after interview, we found that subjects mentioned Gelhomme with reverence, by name. You have a brand that is trusted and respected, Mr. Duval. That is no small feat.

"But . . ." Laura pressed a button, but the slide didn't change. She shook the remote, pressed the button again. "Well. Sorry. This was supposed to go to the next slide."

Philip quickly moved to the computer and tried to manually move the presentation forward. Nothing. You could feel the energy in the room shift, and Dani exchanged a worried glance with Jim Webb across the table. It was doubtful Laura had the order of the presentation memorized, Dani knew. She and Philip were the ones who'd written it and rewritten it time and time again. When they'd run through it last night, Laura had stumbled over the taglines—to get it right, Dani had noticed her boss had to read them off the screen.

"Sorry," Philip said. "I think we're frozen for a moment. I have to restart the computer."

"That's fine," said Duval from the head of the table. "Just continue. It'll eventually catch up."

"Certainly, certainly," said Laura, but by this point, she was visibly flustered. She cleared her throat, shuffled some papers in front of her, and adjusted her glasses. Buying time. "Well, as I was saying . . . uh . . . Gelhomme is a household name. A trusted brand. But. Er . . . There's no denying that the market is changing."

Quietness fell on the room. The CEO of their biggest client checked his watch again and looked at the door. Dani felt her stomach twist. Laura was fumbling. *She was ruining all the work they'd done for nearly two years.* Jim Webb shot Dani a look of desperation. He lifted his chin, as if to say . . . *You. Now. Take it away.*

"Laura's right," said Dani, still seated at the table. Paul Duval turned to look at her. "The women's beauty market is a massive thirty-billion-dollar industry. By contrast, the male beauty market figures in the single-digit millions. Minuscule in comparison. Obviously, the two pies will never be the same size. We won't argue that point. Women are too vain to let men look better than they do."

The CEO grinned. Laura adjusted her weight on her high heels and smiled, as if this were all part of the plan.

"But clearly, there's an opportunity up for grabs in the male sector," Dani continued. "Our research shows that in the next ten years, men's grooming will grow from a ten-billion-dollar industry to something closer to twenty billion. Unfortunately, if you continue with the messaging of yesterday, Gelhomme won't capitalize on that growth."

"Go on," Duval said, spinning his chair toward Dani.

"For decades, your brand has dominated the market by making one promise: your razors provide the closest shave. Period. It was a functional claim, and that worked for a while. But what happens when every razor gives a close shave? What happens when your consumer stands in front of the mirror, day after day, knowing that no matter how close the shave is today, he'll be back again tomorrow doing it all over again?"

Laura leaned her hands against the table, and Dani felt the energy in the room shift in her direction. She wasn't bold enough to stand up, but she sat up straight and began using her hands demonstratively, the way she'd been taught in her West Point public speaking classes.

The computer finally came back to life, and Philip quickly advanced the slides until the photo on the screen showed an image of John F. Kennedy, Marilyn Monroe, and his wife, Jackie Onassis.

"What happens is, he cheats on you. He shops around. Tries different products. And why wouldn't he?! If every razor does the same thing, with the same results, why not try a different model?"

The men chuckled and leaned back in their seats.

"You are not in a monogamous relationship with your customers," Dani said. "If you want them back, you have to win them back. You have to make them love you again."

She paused, thankful that the joke had worked. Jim Webb looked relieved, Laura Klein looked furious, but all that mattered was that Paul Duval was still listening.

"I met a guy six months ago named James O'Leary," she continued, the screen showing a silent video of their morning in Boston. He leaned toward the mirror, making one long strip with his razor from cheek to chin.

"He's a football coach. An all-American, middle-class guy, smack-dab in the center of your target market. You wouldn't think he's a sensitive guy. But he is. He cares about the athletes he coaches. He cares about the kind of men they become. For him, shaving is just another ritual. Like running. Like lifting weights. You don't do it once. You do it day in, day out, to fight off decay. You do it to prove to the world that you're still in the fight.

"Rituals give us a routine. They give us a grounding. Rituals give us hope.

"It's our belief that male consumers are ready to be engaged on a level beyond function," Dani said. "It's not about how close the razor shaves, but about how that ritual prepares them for the day ahead. About how that ritual makes them *feel*. Not here." She touched her cheek. "But here." She pointed to her heart.

Images played on the screen in front of them, flashing everyday scenes: A man burning a piece of toast while his child screams in a high chair. A man stuck in traffic. A football coach on a green field, helping a player up off the ground. A soldier in BDUs, staring in a mirror, his face covered in shaving cream. Then the words they'd worked on for months came up on the screen—white letters against a field of black. Dani read the words aloud.

"Gelhomme Quattro. Your first weapon in the fight."

THREE HOURS AFTER the presentation, Laura Klein, Jim Webb, and Dani were still seated at the conference table.

"Calm down, Laura," Jim was saying, pressing his hands down on the table in front of him. His voice was quiet but insistent. "Dani was just trying to redeem the presentation."

"It didn't need saving," Laura said, her voice several octaves higher than normal. Someone had shut the door. "My authority was completely undermined. As far as Paul Duval knows, I didn't even touch that presentation."

You didn't, Dani wanted to say. But she knew better than to open her mouth; she'd already done enough of that today.

"They seemed pleased," Webb said. "That's all that matters. We're moving forward."

Laura grabbed her things and left in a hurry. Jim put his hands on his temples and shook his head.

"She didn't know the slides," Dani said, by way of explanation. "The way you looked at me, I thought you wanted—"

"You overstepped, Dani. It makes us all look like a bunch of bumbling idiots to Gelhomme. You don't think they know you're Laura Klein's junior? You gambled with nearly thirty million dollars, Dani. Our biggest client. For most people, a move like that would get them fired. Of all people, I thought you would understand respecting the hierarchy."

They sat in silence. Webb stared at the conference table, while Dani stared straight ahead, holding her emotions in check.

"Laura is going to expect an apology from you tomorrow. And it needs to be a good one," he said, gathering his things. "You took a big gamble today, Dani. And you better hope it worked."

IN THE MIDDLE of May, three weeks after the Gelhomme presentation, Locke Coleman emerged from the international terminal at Heathrow Airport, followed in close succession by two friends who had decided to join him on his trip to London.

"Holy shit, McNalley!" Locke yelled. "Since when do you drive a Land Rover?"

They filled the SUV with their suitcases, then pulled out of the airport parking lot, with Dani perched in the right-side driver's seat. Locke sat beside her, running his hands across the beige leather interior.

"I got us tickets to *Wicked* for tonight," Dani said. "It just debuted in the West End, so people are going crazy for it. And tomorrow, Portobello Road Market sets up right outside my house."

"I'm just glad to be out of Fort Hood," one of Locke's friends said from the back seat. Will Chapman had strawberry-blond hair, strawberry-blond eyebrows, and a reddish face, trained toward the Thames River out the window to his left. Locke's other friend, Joel Truman, had light brown skin and deep brown eyes that kept closing, pulled down by jet lag. Will punched Joel in the arm.

"Dude, don't give in. You've got to push through."

After dropping their bags at Dani's flat, Will and Joel took off for Buckingham Palace, while Locke and Dani walked to the pub next door for lunch. Locke ordered a pint of beer and a basket of fish and chips, while Dani ordered her usual, an undressed Caesar salad with chicken. Her doctor would have been proud.

Sitting across from him, Dani couldn't help but notice how little he'd changed in the two years since they'd left West Point. He'd lost the football weight, so his body looked thinner, but his smile was still just as mischievous.

In the weeks since the Gelhomme presentation, life at work

had become even more unbearable for Dani. This visit was the only thing that had pulled her through the rainy days of spring, days in which Laura Klein had continued to act cold and distant, sending most of her communication via e-mail, even though Dani's desk was mere feet from her own. Luckily, Paul Duval hadn't just bought E & G's commercial campaign recommendations—he'd decided to expand the advertising budget by 10 percent. Laura Klein had accepted Dani's apology, but they both knew she had no choice.

In preparation for Locke's arrival, Dani had outfitted the guest bedroom in her apartment with a king mattress positioned to best appreciate the impressive view of Notting Hill's pastel row houses. His friends were a surprise, but Locke had promised Dani that Will and Joel would be happy crashing on air mattresses. Taking a personal day, Dani had spent the morning cleaning and blowing up two twin air mattresses in the home office. At half past ten, she'd jumped in her SUV and headed to the airport.

Scarfing down the fried fish, Locke told stories about Fort Hood, his soldiers, his unit, his family. She noticed that he hadn't mentioned Amanda—and wondered then if they were even together anymore. Locke paused and washed down the food with half his beer.

"What?" he said. "Do I have something in my teeth?"

In truth, Dani was enjoying the feeling of sitting across from someone that she knew so well. She hadn't realized how lonely she'd been in London until Locke was seated across from her, picking his teeth with a toothpick.

"Just thinking," she said finally. "Do you ever wonder how your life would have gone if you'd done something different?"

Locke focused his brown eyes on Dani's, and after a pause, said, "Different than the Army?"

"Yeah. Like, what if you'd played football for USC instead of West Point. Or . . ."

"Of course. Sometimes I wonder if I would have made it to the NFL or something. But you can't think that way."

"Why not?"

"It's easy to imagine an alternate reality better than the one you're in. No one ever imagines an alternate reality that's worse. I can't question all the decisions I've made. I'd drive myself nuts. Where's this coming from?"

Dani put her fork down. "Sometimes I wonder why I even went to West Point. I look at all of you, going off to war, and I think, what was all that for? Why did I go through all that pain, just to abandon ship?"

"You didn't abandon ship."

"Well, I didn't get on it."

"That's not your fault," he said. "Let me ask you this. If you could go back, what would you do differently?"

At this, Dani grew quiet. The truth was, when it came to choosing where to go to college, she wouldn't have done anything differently. She'd been so confident in her decision, so convinced that West Point was her destiny. Only now, her destiny was beginning to feel like a dead end. Locke's skin shined under the dim pub lights. The clear whites of his eyes glimmered around his brown pupils as he waited for her answer. The only thing that she would change was sitting right in front of her.

"Do you ever wonder what would have happened if we . . . ," she started.

He looked down, picked up his fork, and took a bite of fried fish.

"If we'd what?" he said, his mouth full.

"If we'd given it a shot. You and me."

The silence stretched on for what felt like an eternity. Locke sighed and finished off his beer.

She'd splurged on a shiny manicure the day before, and it reflected the pub's sconces as her fingers danced around the edge of her water glass. She wanted to tell him that it was all for him. The hair, the nails, the new outfit she'd bought to wear when she picked him up from the airport. She wanted to tell him that she'd been dreaming of his visit for months, and wanted every day to be perfect so he'd come back again and again and again until he never left. Instead, she just shrugged. He reached for her hand and squeezed it on top of the table warmly.

"D," he said. "I have something to tell you."

20

Spring 2006 // Pittsburgh, Pennsylvania

Y ou know, it'll be the *whole* family," Avery stated over the sound of the Foo Fighters on the radio. Her manicured toes tapped the beat on the dashboard of Noah's 1986 BMW. A black M3 coupe, it had charm, dignity, and a plug-in air freshener to mask the scent of his cigarette smoke.

"You mentioned that," Noah said between drags.

She smacked his arm. Like usual, Noah looked calm, confident, and unfazed by the fact that his car was barreling down the highway toward certain disaster. And yet, Avery felt extremely concerned. She knew how critical her father could be. And worst of all, her brothers would be home. That, in and of itself, would prove to be a challenge. But Noah had promised he'd rather be celebrating Avery's father's sixtieth birthday than be at Fort Bragg alone. No amount of warning had deterred him.

She had to admit, she was grateful that he'd come. These days, his socks intermingled with hers in the laundry. Little golden hairs from his beard trimmings were scattered across her bathroom counter. Their lives were intertwined, and since Avery was no longer working on the Special Forces compound, they didn't even have to keep their relationship much of a secret. She still hadn't met any of his friends—simply a matter of bad timing, Noah had assured her. In truth, the fact that he'd had a chance to meet Dani and Hannah last Thanksgiving was a miracle, considering that Avery's closest friends were both now out of the country. And plus, she didn't care that much about meeting his friends. When Noah was home, she wanted him all to herself.

He flicked the lit cigarette through his window onto the road, then rolled the window up, sealing the car from the sounds of the highway. "Don't worry. I'm good with parents." He paused and looked her in the eye. "They're going to love me. Because you love me."

Avery shifted in her seat. "Is that some kind of Special Ops trick?" she said. "Force me to confirm or deny?"

"Well you do, don't you?" He smiled, took her hand.

Staring at his profile—sharp jawline, eyes gray like stone—she wondered what he'd seen in the last three years of his life. She imagined him in a war zone, under the cover of night, jumping from a helicopter into unknown territory. Busting down doors. Waving his weapon in the faces of terrified women. He'd said terrorists always sent their wives out first. Using women as a shield gave the men time to escape.

"I do love you," she said. "I do."

Noah looked back at the road as if what she'd just said wasn't the biggest deal in the entire world. A determined black column of asphalt rushed underneath them at eighty miles per hour. Avery's mind raced just as fast. Was that all? He was going to make her say it, and then not say it in return?

"Every time we're apart, I think about you constantly. God. I wish . . . I wish so many things," he said, breaking the silence. He stared at her evenly, his eyes heavy.

"What do you wish?"

"I wish I wasn't gone so much, for one," he said. "And I wish . . . I wish you weren't so damn young. You were not in my plans, Avery. But here you are. And yeah. I love you, too."

He spoke as if all of his feelings of love existed against his better judgment. But Avery chose not to hear the sadness in his voice. She refused to see the clouds in his eyes, any more than she paid attention to the storm brewing outside. Instead, she began imagining their wedding. They'd have to wait until Hannah got back from Afghanistan, of course. The bridesmaids would wear blue, or maybe hunter green. Green looked good on everyone, Avery thought, and Dani would just have to get over the fact that she was going to have to wear a dress . . .

"Oh shit," Avery said, suddenly throwing her hand to her forehead.

"Not exactly the response I thought I'd get, but I can take it."

"No, yesterday was Dani's birthday. I just remembered."

"Dani?"

"Dani McNalley. We stayed with her in Boston," Avery said, annoyed that Noah had forgotten her friend. Her cell phone was lodged in the bottom of her purse, uncharged. "Great. My phone's dead. Can I use yours?"

In a snap movement, he quickly put his hand over his phone, like a protective shield. She furrowed her brow in his direction— what was that about?

"Of course," he said, releasing the phone into her hand. "But we just had a moment. I thought we could, you know. Enjoy it."

Avery sighed. Noah was right. Dani would understand. Plus, it was the middle of the night in London. What was one more day?

While they'd been talking, thick clouds had rolled in, filling the sky with a dark gray blanket. A crack of lightning followed a low rumble of thunder, and soon, thick drops of rain gathered on Noah's windshield. The wipers turned on, swishing water out of the way, so Noah could see the road ahead. It was all red lights.

"There must have been an accident," he said. "Everyone's slowing down."

Avery put her head on his shoulder, closed her eyes, and believed the future was opening up before them like an empty four-lane highway. They were in love and they were happy.

That's how it's done. You can deceive yourself into believing almost anything, if you want it badly enough.

"TOOK YOU LONG enough."

Hank Adams came down the stairs, staring at the watch on his wrist, as if he'd been timing his daughter since she'd left North Carolina that morning.

The Adamses' home hadn't changed one bit. Beige carpet, dusty oversized light fixtures, a dining room painted red. The phone with its accordion-style stretchy cord was still attached to the wall next to the fridge, right where it had been for more than twenty years. The place looked like it had frozen in time, and it immediately transported Avery back to her childhood. For some reason, she felt like she needed a shower.

"You stop to pee every two hours?" Hank wrapped his arms around his daughter tight, then pulled back to stare at her. "You nearly missed dinner."

Ignoring his comments, Avery leaned into Noah's side and wrapped her arm around his waist.

"Dad, this is Noah," she said, looking between the man that raised her and the man she loved. They couldn't have looked more different. Noah's muscles were bulging under the sleeves of his light gray T-shirt, and as he reached his arm out, she watched her father's eyebrows lift at the sight of so much black ink.

"Thanks for having me, sir." Noah shook Hank's hand firmly.

"Well, she refused to come if we didn't invite you, so we really didn't have a choice," Hank said jokingly. "Can I get you a beer? We've got Yuengling."

They moved into the kitchen, where Avery introduced Noah to her brothers. Caleb, now twenty-one years old, had the same sheet of blond hair covering his eyes that he'd had since he was sixteen. The tongue of his Rolling Stones T-shirt looked as if it was trying to lick Avery's chest as Caleb reached out to hug his big sister, who now was several inches shorter than him. No longer in his awkward phase, he'd stretched nearly six feet tall and was considering applying for film school in California.

Blake looked exactly as he always had—thick brown hair,

with a square jaw and clean-shaven face. He'd just finished his residency and had moved back to Pittsburgh to practice family medicine. The most boring kind of doctor, in Avery's opinion: he'd be treating colds and hemorrhoids the rest of his life.

"Hey." Avery's older brother shook her boyfriend's hand. "Heard a lot about you, man. This is my wife, Carolyn."

"Carolyn." Avery smiled, reaching to hug her sister-in-law. "How are you?"

From the looks of it, Carolyn had either gained thirty pounds or was three months pregnant—Avery couldn't be sure and wasn't about to ask. They hadn't spoken since Christmas, when Carolyn had given Avery an extremely ugly sweater from Ann Taylor Loft that still hadn't come out of the box.

"I'm good," she said, reaching for a Yuengling from the counter. *Not pregnant, then*, Avery assessed. Carolyn lifted her beer toward her husband. "Blake's been forcing me to go to the gym with him. Me! In the gym! Can you imagine it?"

No, Avery wanted to say. *I'd rather not.*

"Where's Mom?" Avery asked Caleb.

"In the back. Sweet sleeve," Caleb said, noticing Noah's arm of tattoos. "How long did that take?"

While Noah showed off his body art, Avery walked toward her parents' bedroom, where she could hear the low hum of her mother's hair dryer.

It was strange to watch your parents age, Avery realized, inspecting her mother's reflection in the master bathroom mirror. She finished drying her hair, then applied lotion to the sagging skin on her neck. In your twenties, time was measured in milestones: marriages, new jobs, promotions. But later, time marked itself with wrinkles, like scars. Her mother looked great for her age—her skin glowed and her hair was an enviable shade of gold—but something in her eyes betrayed a quiet sadness. Like she was embarrassed by what she saw in the mirror.

"Mom."

"Oh, Avery!" Lonnie jumped. "You scared me!"

They embraced tightly, rocking back and forth, before Lonnie pulled back and got a bright glint in her eye. "Is he here?"

"Yes," Avery answered, rolling her eyes. "Don't make a big deal out of it, okay?" No questions about her job. Not even a question about the drive. Her mother had jumped straight to the one thing she cared about: Avery's relationship status. "We're taking it slow," Avery added.

"Well, it *is* a big deal." Her mother fished a pair of pearl earrings from a jewelry dish on the bathroom counter and slipped them into her sagging lobes. "Meeting the family."

"Just be cool."

"I'm cool!" Lonnie said. "Oh, before I forget, something came in the mail for you."

Her mother led the way across the hall to Avery's childhood bedroom, which Avery expected to have remained untouched, like the rest of the house. But when the door opened, rather than her pink-painted walls and queen-sized bed, she saw the room had been transformed into a home office, complete with a large desktop computer and a rolling ergonomic chair. Gone were her AAU basketball trophies and the bouquets of dried flowers, hung upside down on the wall like trophies of their own—artifacts of relationships long past.

Avery's mind tried to quickly catch up to what her eyes were seeing. Everything of hers had been removed. A stack of cardboard boxes waited in the corner, with her name written on them in Sharpie marker.

"What happened to my room?"

Her mother looked amused by Avery's surprise. "You've been gone for six years, Ave. I needed an office."

"For what?" Avery said cruelly. Her mother didn't work. "And what about Blake's room?"

Her mother's face stiffened. "Blake still comes home, believe it or not." She walked to the desk, picked up a white envelope, and handed it to Avery. "It's from West Point. I didn't know if it was important. You'd think they'd have your current address."

Lonnie walked out the door toward the kitchen, muttering something about checking on the pot roast. When they entered the kitchen, Avery mindlessly ran a finger under the envelope's sealed flap. While Noah traded workouts with Blake, a single sheet of paper unfolded in Avery's hands.

Our records show that you were listed as a plaintiff in the Department of Defense Case #03–2754, Department of the Army vs. Jonathan T. Collins.

Avery closed the letter quickly. The warmth disappeared from her face.

"What was it?" her mother asked from the other side of the kitchen.

"They're just, uh, asking for an alumni donation."

"God. As if you haven't given that place enough already." She pulled the pot roast out of the oven, its juices oozing into the bottom of the pan. "Who's ready for dinner?"

"Oh, we're . . ." Noah looked to Avery. "You didn't tell her?"

After slipping the envelope in her purse, Avery furrowed her brow, unsure of what Noah meant, until she realized the hunk of meat steaming in the dish didn't fall within Noah's restrictive vegetarian standards. "Right. Sorry, Mom. He's . . . Actually, we're both vegetarians."

Avery faked a smile to Noah, ignored the silent derision in her father's eyes, and then helped set the table. But as a bowl of salad passed from one set of hands to the next, Avery filled her plate, without a second glance toward the main dish. Somehow the news delivered in that thin envelope had ruined her appetite.

THAT NIGHT, IN Blake's childhood bedroom, Avery couldn't sleep. Noah was in the living room, on the pullout couch. She'd tried to convince him that her parents wouldn't notice if he slipped into her bed after they'd all gone to sleep, but he'd refused.

"It's one night," he'd said. "I'll see you in the morning." Then he'd pointed her down the hall.

Flipping on a light, Avery reached for her purse, dug out the envelope, then buried herself under the covers, holding it between her hands. Back then, Dani had been so certain that going to the authorities was the right thing to do. But she didn't know what it was going to cost.

None of them did.

They'd traversed campus in silence, until they stood inside the Criminal Investigation Command office, staring at a man behind a reception desk, whose eyes bulged when they explained why they were there. He'd moved them to a windowless office, offered water. The investigator, a short woman in her midforties, had thanked them for coming forward and had started with simple questions. Dani had turned over the photos. Hannah had made a statement about what she'd seen the year before: Collins, coming out of the girls' locker room, with a thin excuse and a guilty look in his eyes. After Avery admitted that it was her body in the photos, she'd answered the investigator's questions honestly and directly, encouraged by the presence of Dani on her left and Hannah on her right.

"We're going to need more evidence to pursue charges. We'll use your statements to get a warrant to search his room."

Avery had turned her eyes pleadingly to Hannah. The truth was, if John Collins was arrested out of the blue, people would want to know who'd turned him in. Locke was trustworthy enough, but Avery knew how rumors at West Point worked.

"Is there any way to do this without relying on our statements?" Hannah had asked. "At least for now?"

The female detective had exhaled heavily. "It's hard to protect victims and witnesses on college campuses," she said. "Rumors spread so fast. A story like this is hard to contain."

"His computer," Dani announced suddenly. "Cadet computers are government property, right? And the academy does sweeps every six months or so to check for viruses and porn and whatever. Can't you do a sweep? I mean, get the warrant. But search everyone. That way, it can seem random."

The detective had exchanged a glance with her colleague, who looked simultaneously annoyed and impressed by Dani's suggestion.

"It's not a bad idea."

The detective had nodded, then looked back at Avery.

"This kid. This . . . Collins. It seems like the risk of getting caught was part of the thrill for him. We can charge him with criminal trespassing. Criminal video voyeurism. Distribution of pornography. Misuse of government property. Maybe more. He could go away for a long time. But, Miss Adams, since the majority of these photos are of you, you'll still have to be the one to press charges in the end."

She'd paused, rubbed her forehead.

"It'll take at least twenty-four hours to do the sweep. And for this to work, the three of you have to stay silent. You can't tell anyone that you came here tonight."

Avery breathed a sigh of relief and looked to Hannah and Dani as if to check that this was the right plan. Dani nodded.

"So that's a yes?" the detective asked. "As you can imagine, I haven't had great success with nineteen-year-olds keeping secrets."

Dani spoke with certainty. "We're not your normal nineteen-year-olds, ma'am. We're like a cult. You can be certain, nothing will leave this room."

Now, staring at the letter in her hands, Avery's eyes began to water. So much time had passed since that moment, and yet, she still felt the same sickness in her stomach that she'd had forty-eight hours later, when military police had escorted John Collins out of the barracks in handcuffs. The Corps of Cadets had turned into a cacophony of gossip as the students guessed at the cause of his arrest. No one understood why someone so close to graduation would be taken away. They'd grasped at straws, wondering who had turned him in—was it a member of the football team who'd seen the photos, or the girl—*who was that girl?*—on display in them?

Putting those memories out of her mind, Avery unfolded the letter and read it quickly, as if the faster she read, the sooner it could all be behind her again.

March 15, 2006

Dear Ms. Adams,

Our records show that you were listed as a plaintiff in the Department of Defense Case #03–2754, Department of the Army vs. Jonathan T. Collins.

On behalf of the Department of Defense and the Criminal In-vestigation Command of West Point, it is our responsibility to inform you that the defendant in this case is to be released on parole on March 17, 2006. A restraining order remains in place and the defendant will be listed on the National Sex Offender Public Registry for the remainder of his probationary period, which ends on 05–13–2015.

*We have included in this letter a one-page copy of the sum-
mary case record. We apologize for any disturbance this may
cause and are available to address any concerns you may have
about your case.*

Respectfully,
Capt. Peter Irving
Judge Advocate General Corps
Criminal Investigation Command, West Point, New York

On Sunday, Avery pretended to sleep as Noah navigated south.
He'd won over Avery's parents and brothers far more quickly
than she'd anticipated. He'd complimented her mother's cooking, helped with the dishes, and even put the foldout couch
back together before they'd left that morning.

"I think this one might be a keeper," her mother had said before
they'd hit the road that morning. Avery wanted to believe that was
true. But something about receiving notice that John Collins
was out in the world again, free to live and do as he pleased, had
set Avery's instincts on high alert. Suddenly, all of the old red flags
she'd ignored were flapping wildly again.

"What?" Noah said. Avery had pulled her head off the pillow
against the passenger window to look at him.

"Can I ask you something?" she asked.

"Shoot."

"Why were you so weird about your phone the other day?"

He reached for his pack of cigarettes. "What are you talking about?"

Wrapping the pillow in her arms, Avery looked to the side
mirror, where she saw her reflection. Her blond hair had grown

long, past her shoulders. Eating like Noah, as a vegetarian, meant she'd resorted to eating a lot of pasta, which had made her face puffy and bloated. She didn't feel like herself. But she couldn't blame her irritability on her diet or the man sitting next to her.

"I feel like something has been up with you this whole weekend," Noah said, deftly turning the conversation back to Avery. She didn't force him to answer the question he'd avoided. Instead, she sighed.

"You know that letter I got from West Point?"

He nodded.

"It wasn't about making a donation."

"What was it?" he asked.

And then she told him everything. When she was finished, she held her breath, waiting for Noah to say something to soothe the gaping emotional wound she'd just undressed before his eyes. Vulnerability can bring two people closer together, or it can expose a distance that can't be overcome. Avery closed her eyes and waited for him to speak.

"Well," Noah said with a smirk. "Can I see the pictures?"

Avery felt herself shrink, like she was Alice in Wonderland. Falling down that rabbit hole. Swallowing that pill. Suddenly, she was three inches tall.

He reached for her hand. She pulled it away.

"Oh come on. I'm only kidding," he said. "What do you want me to say?"

"I don't know," Avery replied. "But not that."

21

Summer 2006 // Jekyll Island, Georgia

In the middle of her war, Hannah flew home for two weeks of paid leave. It was strange really, the thought that she could fly out of the Middle East, while her men and her mission stayed put. Rest and recuperation, better known as R & R, was a benefit that every soldier and officer received when they were deployed. Two weeks to regroup and be with your family, followed by several more months overseas, finishing the deployment. It was an odd pause. A whiplash of change, from one part of the world to another. From fear to safety and back again.

It was the middle of August. And thankfully, this year, there were no hurricanes on the horizon. After picking Hannah up from the airport in Savannah, Georgia, Tim drove her to Jekyll Island, where he'd rented a place for them to pass the time.

The cottage smelled as though salt water had seeped into the clapboard siding, giving the entire place the odd feeling that it had been built by the tides themselves. Canopied by gnarled oak trees, the white bungalow was perched at the tip of a peninsula, where a creek ended and the ocean began. A dock jutted into the creek, outfitted with kayaks, fishing rods, and a hammock. There was another hammock on the front porch, and a third out by the wooden steps that led to the beach. Humidity wafted through the air and snuck through the cracks in the old windows, but they hadn't let the heat defeat their plans. Summer in south Georgia had nothing on Afghanistan. Here, even 100 percent humidity felt like a reprieve to Hannah. They had two weeks alone together, with no plans, nowhere to be—just the two of them and the ocean.

It felt like a dream world. Every morning when they woke up, Hannah would hold his face in her hands and say, "Can you believe it? We don't have to say goodbye!"

They'd start the day with coffee, watching the sun rise over the ocean, and end the day with wine, watching it set into the marsh.

On their seventh morning together, Hannah lay in bed beside her husband, in no rush to start the day. When they'd first arrived at the house, she'd felt nervous to undress, aware that he hadn't seen her naked in months. Would he still like what he saw? But that initial hesitation was immediately replaced by an overwhelming sense of urgency and desire. They only had fourteen days. There was no time for modesty.

The clock on the bedside table read 4:58 A.M., but Hannah knew she wouldn't be able to go back to sleep. Instead, she admired Tim's chest, rising and falling with each breath. His hair had grown back since Ranger School and was dark on the white pillow. The tattoo of an Irish cross on the inside of his left bicep had faded slightly, as tattoos do. Hannah wanted to wake him—to shake him until he opened those bright hazel eyes and looked at her with that same sense of childish adventure she'd grown to love. But he looked too peaceful to disturb.

Hannah ran a finger along the jagged scar on his right shoulder. Unlike the tattoo, it hadn't yet faded.

The accident had happened about this time, four years ago. During the season-opening football game their junior year, Hannah had stood in the stands with the rest of the Corps of Cadets staring at the sky. The crowd had erupted in shouts as six tiny black specks emerged into view, and all of a sudden, all six parachutes spread out like small yellow blooms over their heads. Hannah scanned the sky for Tim. After what he'd done that summer during Air Assault training, they weren't speaking. But she still loved to watch him fly. She saw the red and white stripes of the American flag waving behind him and breathed a sigh of relief.

What happened next would forever remain in Hannah's memory. A strap snapped off his shoulder, sending the yellow parachute vertical. He spun out of control, falling like a bird shot out of the sky. The entire crowd gasped and Hannah went silent, covering her mouth with her hands.

When she'd arrived at the hospital, Hannah immediately knew that she was no longer angry. Tim had been propped up in a bed, his right arm and shoulder stabilized in a metal contraption that looked like a vise. When he noticed her in the doorway,

Tim shook his head, his chin quivering and face reddening with emotion.

"I didn't think you'd come," he said. "I'm so sorry . . . I—"

"Shh." Hannah had placed a hand on his uninjured arm, squeezing it tight. "I forgive you."

He'd started laughing through his tears. "When I was hanging in that tree, all I could think of was how mad I would have been if I had died and we hadn't made up. We have to make up. I still love you."

Hannah had laughed through her tears, too. Six months later, they were engaged.

Tim's accident hadn't just resurrected their relationship. It also resurrected his belief in God. Even the doctors couldn't understand how he hadn't died, simply from the height of the fall. Had he not been scarred, Hannah wondered if she would even be sitting here, in his bed, married. So she loved his scar. It symbolized everything that had brought them back together. And even though Tim wasn't perfect—he was flawed and cocky and at times a bit too charming for his own good—Hannah knew he was perfect for her.

Slipping from the sheets, Hannah grabbed her copy of *East of Eden* from the bedside table and stepped outside onto the porch, where she could watch the sun rise over the Atlantic. Two months earlier, on Hannah and Tim's second wedding anniversary, Dani had sent her a sweet e-mail, full of memories and photos of their wedding day. Even her sister, Emily, remembered the anniversary—sending Hannah a bouquet of flowers all the way to FOB Sharana in Afghanistan. But not Avery. That girl had fallen off the face of the planet.

Hannah only heard from her in group e-mails that Dani addressed to all of them, and even then, Avery's responses were shallow and short. Hannah couldn't understand how you could be so close with someone for so long only to let the friendship fade. After everything they'd been through, Hannah had been certain that Dani and Avery would be her best friends until they were old and gray. But things had changed. She was married now. Maybe her best friend wasn't supposed to be a girl from her college basketball team—maybe her best friend was supposed to be the man still sleeping in the other room.

Just then, Tim emerged onto the porch with two steaming mugs of coffee. Passing one to Hannah, he stretched and yawned.

"How many people our age do you think wake up this early?" he asked.

Tim took a seat in the rocking chair next to hers and began rubbing her neck slowly with his warm hand. Hannah involuntarily closed her eyes. His touch was like a drug.

"I guess we get more out of life than they do," he said.

"Maybe. But they get more sleep than we do."

Tim sipped coffee, then said, "Eh. Sleep's overrated. I'll sleep when I die."

Hannah bristled. She didn't like hearing that word. Not when they were counting down the days. Her flight back to Afghanistan left in less than a week. Tim left for Iraq a few weeks after that. It would be late 2007 before they were together again.

"What?" Tim asked, feeling her tense up. "Die?"

"Yes. Don't say it."

Tim laughed. "Okay," he said. "I won't roll the die, or discuss your hair dye, or remember Princess Di. There are so many conversations we'll miss out on now. But whatever you need."

Hannah punched him in the arm. "Don't be an ass," she laughed.

"But I'm so good at it." Tim looked up at the sky. "I think it's supposed to storm today," he said.

Indeed, the sun hadn't yet come up, or if it had, it was covered by a mass of dark gray clouds. In the distance, a roll of thunder pealed loudly. Hannah's sister used to tell her during intense thunderstorms that it was just God bowling. Thunder was the roll of the ball, the lightning a signal that he'd hit a strike. Apparently, God always hit a strike.

"Oh, that's too bad," Hannah said ironically. "What in the world will we do all day?"

HOURS LATER, THEIR bodies feeling light and connected by invisible strands of energy, Hannah shook her head and slid the cross charm on her necklace from side to side. They dressed, ate lunch, and then watched a cheesy movie on the Hallmark Channel before scrounging through the kitchen to put together dinner.

Tim had found an old game of Scrabble in a closet, and opening a bottle of wine, they sat near the windows overlooking the rain and the ocean, smiling at each other and placing individual letters in a row.

"No." Hannah pointed at the word Tim had just played on the board. "*Quid* is not a word." Taking a sip of wine from her glass, she remarked, "*Squid*, maybe. Not *quid*."

"It's a word," argued Tim. "I'm telling you."

"Use it in a sentence."

"Easy . . ." Tim squinted his eyes and a little wrinkle appeared between his eyebrows, like it always did when he was thinking hard. "I bet you a hundred quid that *quid* is a word."

"Look it up," said Hannah. "You think you're so smart."

And he did, running a finger down the page of the dictionary they'd found on the shelf next to a stack of John Grisham books. Tim sat back, smiling, as he read out the definition.

"It says here, 'Quid: One pound sterling. Or, a lump of tobacco for chewing.'" He replaced the tiles where they were meant to go. "Triple word score. That's forty-two points."

"This is the worst game ever invented," Hannah said. "You're destroying me."

"You're not too far behind," he lied. "Just, a couple . . . hundred points."

Hannah set down her glass and looked out the window. "I wish it weren't raining. I feel like we deserve perfect weather, every single day we get together. Don't you think?"

Tim inspected her face, put his glass down on the table, and then stood up and took his shirt off.

"What are you doing?" laughed Hannah. "You're not done beating me."

"Come with me," he said, offering her his hand.

"Out there? It's pouring!"

"We can do this the hard way or the easy way," said Tim as the dimple appeared in his right cheek.

Hannah crossed her arms over her chest and shook her head. Her husband—it still felt so funny to say that, to think it!—her *husband* was crazy. And accordingly, he grabbed her waist, hoisted her over his shoulder, and carried her out the door into the rain.

"*Tim!* Put me down!"

He did, and in moments, they were both soaked through, the water piling up on their eyelashes. He grabbed her hand, and together they ran down to the shoreline.

"Take off your clothes!" Tim shouted as he pulled off his own.

"*Tim!*" Hannah instinctively looked around, even though she knew for a fact there was no one else on this beach. "We're going to get struck by lightning!"

"Don't be scared!" he shouted, running toward the water. She could see his outline through the rain—round shoulders, thin waist, and white butt—all in perfect contrast to the gray water and sky. As she hesitated, the rain began to slow, and the sun's heavy rays began peering through the clouds from behind the house.

"I married an idiot," Hannah said to herself and the rain. But as she was saying it, she was pulling off her clothes, tentatively at first, and then quickly.

"Come on!" shouted Tim from the choppy surf.

And soon, she reached him, their bodies touching under the surface, their mouths touching above. All she tasted was salt.

SIX DAYS LATER, they stood outside of the security line at Jacksonville International Airport, trying to say goodbye. Like he'd done so many times before, Tim held Hannah's face in his hands and wiped the tears from her cheeks with his thumbs. He was wearing board shorts, flip-flops, and a gray T-shirt, while Hannah, on the first leg of her flight back to war, was wearing her full combat uniform. Her hair twisted in a bun, rucksack full and snug on her shoulders, she felt encumbered by the weight of it all. Of this moment. Of the future. For once, Tim didn't try to put it in perspective.

He pulled her into his chest. "I'll leave you a perfectly clean house. When you get home, it'll be spic-and-span."

"Leave Avery a key," said Hannah, angry that she was using their last few moments together to discuss logistics. "Just in case."

"Okay." He squeezed tighter. "I love you."

"I love you, too," Hannah said, her voice small and choked.

"I'll see you soon," Tim offered. "Write me. Call me. We'll figure it out."

"Okay."

And with that, Hannah forced herself to step away.

Sometimes the greatest wars we fight are in our own minds. And for the next three days, Hannah battled hard. She tried to remember why they said this would all be worth it. She prayed for strength, and whether God provided it or not, she wasn't certain, but she arrived back at FOB Sharana, back at her CHU. Back to Ebrahim and her soldiers and the heat. This time, it took longer for her heart to catch up to her body. Without a doubt, she'd left half of it behind.

From: Hannah Nesmith <hannah_nesmith@yahoo.com>
Subject: made it back
Date: September 2, 2006 03:19:02 PM GMT +01:00
To: Dani McNalley <danimcnalley@yahoo.com>

Hi:)

I'm sorry I missed your Skype call. Internet here is spotty at best, but I have a little time now and the signal seems good so I figured I'd send you an update.

The last two weeks with Tim were . . . perfect. There's really no other way to say it. We literally put Nicholas Sparks to shame. Every day I woke up and had to remind myself that I wasn't dreaming. The weather sucked the last half of the trip, but we watched movies and cooked meals together and drank tons of wine. I just can't believe how much time is going to pass before we can be together again. If I think about it, I get overwhelmed with sadness so I'm just trying not to count the days.

How did Locke's visit go? I think of you often and hope that you're finding friends there in London. Have you met anyone?

Much love to you, Dani. Miss you.

H

Fall 2006 // London, England

Dressed in jeans, wellies, and her slick new Barbour rain-coat, Dani grabbed a large black umbrella from beside the door and walked down the steps of her flat and into the gray. Despite the impending rain, Portobello Road Market had assembled itself into a beautiful stretch of life. Clanging garage doors opened to reveal storefronts. Colorful tents popped up for miles. The voices of people haggling filled the air, while the rain sprinkled the pavement. Customers shielded under umbrellas inspected tables full of antiques and curios. They perused stalls of hot bread, sniffed at fresh-cut cheese, watched as young women spilled batter in large circles at the creperies. Three German tourists loitered outside Dani's apartment entrance, wrapped in scarves and holding a map. Humidity increased the pain in her joints, but she couldn't stay inside. Out here, she could be anonymous. Part of the scene, not the leading actress. She could roam for miles, looking. Thinking. Hidden by the crowd.

In the last three weeks, so much had changed.

The Gelhomme advertisements had hit the airwaves and though it was too early to measure, preliminary benchmarks indicated that the campaign would increase sales by more than 12 percent. Though she still acted suspicious of Dani's instincts, Laura Klein had grown to rely on them more than ever. Every additional assignment found its way to Dani's desk, and one draft was never enough. Laura required four, sometimes five drafts of the same presentation. And worst of all, in their most recent meeting with Paul Duval, Laura had presented a groundbreaking new strategy: digital marketing on the Internet, with a keen eye on a new social media platform called the Facebook.

Dani had sat at the table, dumbfounded that Laura had so blatantly stolen her idea and claimed it as her own. But aware of Jim Webb's eyes on her every action, Dani had stayed silent. After all, what would she do? Stamp her foot and say, *That was my idea*? She was proud, but she wasn't an idiot.

The next day, Laura had called her into her office.

"I saw your surprise yesterday," her boss had said in an uncharacteristically kind tone. "When I gave them your idea for the digital push."

"I wasn't surprised you presented the idea. I was surprised you said it was yours."

Laura had paused, then sighed and put her reading glasses down on her desk. "The divorce was finalized last week."

"I'm sorry to hear that," said Dani.

"I shouldn't have done that. I shouldn't have presented your idea as my own. I think I've just been realizing how high the stakes are for me. For ten years, I've enjoyed this job, but now I *need* it. To support myself. My children. I think I acted out of fear. I hope you'll forgive me."

Dani had nodded, shocked by her boss's candor. It didn't justify her actions—but at least it provided context.

Work wasn't the only place her life felt unmoored. Hannah was back in Afghanistan after her two weeks of R & R, and soon, Tim would follow his wife overseas for his own fifteen-month deployment to Iraq.

We put Nicholas Sparks to shame, Hannah had written in her latest e-mail. Dani didn't know if it was a blessing or a curse that Tim and Hannah would be deployed at the same time. On one hand, they would complete all their time apart faster that way. On the other, Dani couldn't imagine knowing that you *and* the person you love were in constant danger. Hannah had more faith than any person she'd ever met.

But the hardest change of all?

That was the news Locke Coleman had dropped when he'd come to visit in the spring, and the trip to South Carolina that awaited Dani at the end of the week.

Choking on her Caesar salad in the pub that day, Dani didn't have to feign surprise, but she'd had to strain to hide her emotion. She didn't sob. She didn't wail. That came later, once he and his friends had left the continent and Dani had found herself alone in her apartment shower, where the heat and the water washed away her internal pain. But at the table, she simply coughed and wiped her mouth with a napkin. Locke had gazed at her with sympathy in his eyes, as if he'd known all along how much the news would hurt.

"I didn't know how to tell you," he'd said. "I thought in person would be best."

"You could have just called."

The rest of his trip had passed in awkwardness, until Dani had hugged him at the airport, promising that she'd do what he'd asked and book her ticket.

"I wouldn't miss it," she'd said, aching. "I'm happy for you guys."

Now, walking among the chaos of the market, Dani allowed herself to feel everything she'd been avoiding. Sadness and anger, of course. But the emotion that seemed to rise without warning was an all-pervasive fear—that somehow, somewhere, she'd made a terribly wrong turn.

THE WEEKEND OF Locke and Amanda's wedding, a United Airlines flight attendant brought Dani an extra hot towel to her seat in first class. The flight from London passed in a haze of mediocre movies and fitful sleep. In Atlanta, she burned a two-hour layover with a venti Starbucks vanilla latte that tasted like heaven but made her body feel like hell. During the final flight to Charleston, pain crept from her hip into her back. It was her own fault, she knew. Airplane seats offered little relief for her joints, and if she veered from doctor's orders and drank caffeine and dairy, all bets were off.

At first, things weren't as hard as she'd anticipated. Locke had been kind enough to include her in all the wedding week-end activities: a brunch on Friday morning, the rehearsal Friday night. They'd even asked her to read scripture at the wedding.

"What passage?" Dani had asked when the happy couple had cornered her at the brunch. Amanda looked positively radiant, dressed in a baby-blue strapless dress.

"Surprise us," Amanda had answered.

Late Friday night, alone in her hotel room, Dani picked up her cell phone and tried Avery. After Locke's visit to London, they'd been playing a never-ending game of phone tag. The time differ-ence had made catching up nearly impossible, and so Dani had finally decided to drop the bomb in a two-word text message. *Locke's engaged.* Avery had called her back immediately. But that was weeks ago. Since then, they'd gone back to their normal rou-tine of missed calls and unreturned messages, and all of Dani's attempts to add a stop at Fort Bragg to her itinerary had come up empty. The phone rang three times, and then Dani heard Avery's serious outgoing voicemail message.

"This is First Lieutenant Avery Adams. Please leave a message. If this is an emergency, please call the Fort Bragg . . ."

This is *an emergency,* Dani seethed as she ended the call. Staring at the BlackBerry in her hand, she dialed a different number— one of the few she remembered by heart.

"Bennett residence," said a familiar voice, "Wendy speaking."

"Wendy. It's Dani."

"Dani! How are you?" she said. "What time is it there?"

"Well, I'm actually not in London. I'm in South Carolina."

"South Carolina? Why?"

"It's kind of a long story," said Dani. "Do you have a minute? And a Bible? I think I might need some help."

THE NEXT DAY, the wedding quartet began with Vivaldi at six P.M. sharp. Dani had slept in that morning, then walked the streets of Charleston alone. A technician filed and painted her nails in the afternoon, and once the sun had set into the Atlantic, she emerged from the hotel dressed in a black silk gown that draped gracefully across one shoulder, ready to join a group of guests in a shuttle to the chapel. Dani was grateful that she'd splurged on the thousand-dollar dress, with its modest slit up the left side. There was no price too high for feeling beautiful at the wedding of someone you loved, especially when that person was marrying someone else. A thousand wasn't too much, Dani decided, especially because she'd saved on the shoes—a pair of simple snakeskin flats with pointed toes. Amanda's father was a retired army colonel who now served as athletic director at the Citadel, and the crowd of guests looked fit for a royal ball— ladies shimmered in long jewel-lustered gowns; men tugged on their ties, tuxes, and tails. When she crossed the church to ascend the podium for the reading, Dani hoped no one could tell she was wearing flats underneath the designer dress. With her hip in this much pain, she couldn't have risked wearing heels.

"A reading from the Old Testament."

The congregation of more than three hundred sat in their seats, silent, a diverse crowd of black and white, military and civilian.

They stared up at Dani with expectation as Locke and Amanda stood hand in hand at the altar, waiting. Wendy had helped Dani pick out her selections, the first for fun, the second for sentiment.

"Deuteronomy chapter twenty-four, verse five," Dani began slowly. "'If a man has recently married, he must not be sent to war or have any other duty laid on him. For one year he is to be free to stay at home and bring happiness to the wife he has married.'"

When she looked up from the Bible with a smirk, Locke's groomsmen, many of whom were his football teammates from West Point, began laughing and clapping. One of them shouted *hooah*. Amanda laughed and shook her head, looking supremely happy that she'd chosen Dani for this job. All of the gathered guests snickered as they realized what she'd read was a joke.

"Now, seriously," Dani said. "A reading from the New Testament." She flipped the pages toward the back half of the Bible. "A reading from First John. *Dear friends, let us love one another, because love is from God . . . The one who does not love does not know God, because God is love. . . .*

"'Love consists in this: not that we loved God, but that He loved us and sent His Son to be the atoning sacrifice for our sins. Dear friends'—Locke and Amanda—'if God loved you in this way, you also must love one another . . . There is no fear in love; instead, perfect love drives out fear. . . .

"'*We love because He first loved us.*'"

She paused and looked at Locke, whose face was still and serious. In his dress blues, dark jacket and blue pants with gold stripes on the side, Locke looked devastatingly handsome, just as he had the day she'd met him, on the back of that truck at Camp Buckner. So handsome, in fact, Dani found it difficult to look him in the eye. But she did anyway, wiping a tear from her cheek, knowing that this was the most loving thing she could do for a friend.

At the reception, Locke's saber sliced through the first layer of a three-tiered cake. Twinkle lights hung around the white reception tent, millions of little gold orbs. And while Amanda swayed with her ring bearer on the dance floor, Locke pulled Dani in for a hug near the open bar. For a moment, Dani thought he might ask her to waltz, like they'd learned to do so many years ago. But then, in a pang of deep sadness, she realized those days were over.

"You got a little emotional up there, McNalley," he said, pinching her elbow.

Dani took a breath and held it, wondering if it was too late. What would it matter now if she told the truth? What would it change?

"Of course I did," she said, turning her eyes to meet his.

They stared at one another, and in that moment, Dani saw recognition. A slight nod of his head. A longing in his eyes and hers that spoke clearly, even as they said nothing at all. *I thought it would be you,* her eyes told him. And he squeezed her hand. *I did too,* he didn't say. Dani looked down, satisfied that it was over.

She sighed. "You better get out there." Amanda was waving him toward the dance floor as the band struck up the next song.

Later, Dani stood underneath that white reception tent, among the twinkle lights and candles, watching. With every turn of Amanda's gown, the life Dani had written for herself unraveled. The person she thought she would marry had married someone else. The friendships she thought would survive anything now felt as thin as smoke. The future, once a destination, had become a cloud of confusion. Nothing was clear. Nothing was certain. And yet, she'd still put on that dress. That was something. And when the song changed and Amanda reached her open arms toward Dani, she still found the power within her to dance.

"DO YOU HAVE anything a bit more feminine?"

A week after Locke's wedding, Dani stood in the dressing room at her favorite store in London, inspecting her reflection in the mirror. The retail associate waiting outside the velvet dressing room curtain was a slender brunette with blunt bangs and thick-rimmed glasses. She looked young, Dani thought—younger than Dani, which felt strange, since she still felt like she'd only just graduated from college. Could there actually be people working in the world that had graduated from college after her? Nonsense.

"Have you seen the new gray lot we got in?" the girl asked, her accent posh and British. "It just arrived this week. I'll grab one. You're a U.K. size twelve, right?"

Dani hated to think she shopped here so often that this woman knew her size.

"Right. Bring a ten too, just in case." That was the other resolution Dani had made, after eating a Nutella crepe that morning at the market. She needed to get back to clean eating like the doctors told her to, to keep her arthritis from flaring. And she needed to join a gym. It was time to revive the athlete inside. It was a thin plan, full of vanity, she knew. But sometimes, when the future looks foggy, you have to draw your own map.

An hour later, Dani left AllSaints with a slate-colored leather jacket that draped open in the front. No zippers. No buckles. Just the perfect cut in the perfect color, with all the promise she'd desired. As she made her way back to her apartment, the sun teased London, dropping little specks of gold onto the ground. It was the perfect temperature for an afternoon coffee—decaf, of course. After the wedding, she'd been following doctor's orders—but before she could duck into the coffee shop on the corner, Dani heard a familiar sound.

They say sound and smell are the senses that connect most to our memory. The hollow bounce was like a laugh, a clarion call from the past. So full of meaning and regret and nostalgia and promise. She felt transported in her spirit to her driveway as a kid, then to the gym at West Point. The game she'd so wanted to leave behind, she couldn't fully abandon. It was knitted into her skin, into her senses. The sound made her heart beat faster.

A chain-link fence encircled a court to her right. The five-on-five pickup game looked like it had been raging for quite a while, based on the amount of sweat that had gathered on the boys' faces. They looked to be teenagers—thirteen or fourteen, Dani guessed. There was one black kid among the white boys, all equally lost in the game. They shouted and shuffled, playing shirts against skins, as the boy with the curly hair dribbled, shoulder down, and pushed into his defender. The defender fell and the game stopped. No ref blew a whistle. No one yelled or started cursing. The offending player offered his hand, and the defender stood up and took the ball to start the game again.

Mesmerized by their ungraceful steps, botched passes, and poor shots, Dani had to keep herself from laughing out loud. They were terrible. But they didn't care. They kept right on playing. Dani wondered if they were even keeping score. She wondered if the score even mattered.

Her senior year, after the second surgery, Dani had planted herself on the sidelines, leaning on her crutches, forced into silence. Two plebes had quit midseason, and after they lost four games in a row, West Point's athletic director had called Coach Jankovich into his office. Avery reported that she'd seen the coach walking in, wringing her hands. But when the season ended and Jankovich still hadn't been fired, Dani, Hannah, and Avery had started scheming. They couldn't leave West Point without telling someone the truth.

"You gotta pump a fake!" Dani shouted instinctively after one of the kids on the skins team threw up another blocked shot.

The game stopped. All ten kids turned to look at the woman behind the gate. The black kid put his hands on his hips and laughed, lighting up the court with his smile. He reminded Dani of Locke, all confidence and swagger.

"Oh yeah?" the kid shouted, his smart British accent calling out across the court. "Care to demonstrate?"

The boys all groaned, using the spontaneous break to grab water and wipe their faces on their oversized shirts. Taking the dare, Dani walked around the chain-link fence and dropped her shopping bag by the entrance.

"Oh rubbish!" one boy shouted, shocked. "She's going to play!"

"What?" Dani laughed. "You don't think I can hack it?"

"American! Go figure. Cheeky bastards," someone shouted.

"Here." The boy passed her the ball. "Let's see what you've got."

Dani bounced the ball a few times, just to appreciate the sensation. It had been nearly two years since she'd touched the leathery plastic of a basketball. The tiny bumps massaged her hand as it fell to the court and bounced back to her palm. Knowing she was showing off, but without a care, Dani picked up the ball and spun it on one finger.

"Okay, okay," the kid answered. "But can you shoot?"

With that, Dani took off, dribbling first to the left and then to the right, unaware of the pain in her hip. Her opponent matched her steps, lifting his arms up and mimicking her every move. Dani took a step back to the three-point line and pretended to shoot. In that moment, the boy lurched up and toward her with one hand high in the sky, and as he landed on the ground, Dani took her shot, the ball soaring from her fingertips straight through the net.

Swoosh.

"OHHIIHHH!"

"DAMN! SHE SCHOOLED YOU!"

Dani spent the next hour teaching them things she'd nearly forgotten she knew. A set of streetlights went on. The sun fell, spilling cans of purple and red paint across the sky. She lost all sense of time, just like a little kid. On the court, something changed in her, like a key had been placed into a lock. The boys looked at her to learn. There was no ego. No disdain that they were hearing from a woman. Just the honest hope that they would improve their game. Respect and gratitude appeared in their eyes. And it didn't matter that Dani's body ached.

Her soul soared.

23

Fall 2006 // Fort Bragg, North Carolina

T he first Sunday in November, Noah left for a monthlong deployment to an unknown destination. Saturday, he'd packed his rucksack, thrown the rest of his gear into his car, and told Avery not to worry. Like usual, he'd kissed her goodbye in the middle of the night, and then he was gone.

In the morning, she found an empty water glass, an open jar of peanut butter, and a plate full of crumbs on the kitchen counter—remnants of Noah's midnight snack. She put the peanut butter jar away, wiped the counters of the trail of ants that had invaded, and then stared out the kitchen window onto the street outside. Throughout the neighborhood, fathers with military haircuts were mowing their grass. Pairs of mothers pushed strollers down the road and waved with gloved hands. Yellow ribbons wrapped around trees where wives sat alone inside, wrangling children without the aid of their husbands. The Nesmiths' house was all dark, with two blue-star flags hung side by side in the front window. At the beginning of October, Tim had arrived at Avery's door with a spare key to their house and a zip-lock bag full of morning glory muffins.

"Since when did you become Betty Crocker?" Avery had said, receiving the bag from his hand.

"Just cleaning out the freezer," he'd said. "Thought you might enjoy a snack. Microwave them in the morning, thirty seconds."

"You all packed up?"

"Yep," he'd said, rocking back on his heels. "Tomorrow."

"You ready?"

"As I'll ever be."

A moment passed between them, and Avery considered inviting him inside, but before she could, Tim clapped his hands together and smiled. "Guess that's it."

Avery reached for him and hugged him hard, if not for herself, then for Hannah.

"Geez, Adams," Tim had said with a laugh. "It's not like I have cancer."

"Just be safe," she'd replied.

"Will do." He'd offered a small salute. "Hey. When Hannah gets back—watch out for her, all right? I think when she gets home, it'll be harder than when she's over there."

"I will." Even as she made the promise, Avery wondered if she could keep it, or if Hannah would care.

Then he'd walked back to his house, three doors down.

OPENING THE GATE to her neighbor's backyard across the street, Avery found the dog leash underneath the grill. She and Eric Jenkins had struck a deal—Avery would take his dog, Bosco, on long runs, and in exchange, he shoveled her driveway in the winter and mowed her lawn during the summer. It was a good deal because Bosco helped Avery feel safe when she ran alone in the woods. But unfortunately, Eric's wife had a permanent scowl on her face every time she saw Avery leashing up their dog in the backyard, as if Avery were purposefully trying to point out that she was out of shape. Michelle *was* out of shape. But Avery wasn't trying to rub it in.

Seeing her, in the kitchen window, Avery gave a little wave and a false smile.

Bitch.

The word came into Avery's head before she could stop it. When had she become so hard? Had she always been that bitter? Who cared if Michelle stared at her and Noah, judging them, when he left in the mornings? Who cared if she hadn't *once* invited Avery to any of their barbecues that they had in their backyard? She still shouldn't call the woman a bitch.

At that moment, Michelle opened the back door and smiled at Avery.

"You sure you want to take him?" she asked kindly, bobbing a baby on her hip. *When did she have that baby?* "I know he's a lot to handle."

Just then, a black Labrador came barreling out of the house. He darted around Michelle's legs, through the yard, and jumped straight at Avery's knees.

"Whoa, Bosco! You want to go running?" Avery looked back at Michelle. "No, it's fine. Really."

"Eric and I are heading to Oklahoma next week for Thanksgiving," Michelle said happily. "We leave Tuesday."

"Oh great," Avery said. "To see your family?"

Michelle gave a slight shake of the head. "Eric's." She stepped outside and looked at the sky, as if to assess the day's temperate weather for the first time. "I wish I liked running. I've never understood it. It's like . . . what are you running from?"

"Yeah," Avery said. She felt so tired of holding up the neighborly charade. "Well, I'll bring him back soon. Maybe in an hour?"

Michelle raised her eyebrows like she'd never heard something so insane. "Knock yourself out," she said with a laugh, then looked at the baby. "We'll be here."

The dog panted, stretched, and flipped his black tail back and forth with force. Avery felt a surge of gratitude toward the dog—*At least you want to hang out with me,* she thought, staring at his happy brown eyes. *There it was again.* That little, bitter voice. The only thing she could do to shut it up was to run. And so, turning out their gate, she ran.

THE TRAIL WAS eight miles long, hidden by the woods. The entrance, an inconspicuous path marked only by a small wooden post, was Avery's confidential cardio treasure. It weaved an oblong loop and passed over a creek twice, ascending and descending gradually across varied terrain. There were roots to dodge, rocks to kick, and spiderwebs to pull off her face along the way.

Avery pushed herself faster than she'd ever run before. Off his leash, Bosco sniffed grass, marked his territory, and trotted far ahead, a black spot among the rotting brown leaves on the ground. Avery breathed in perfect rhythm—inhale, four steps; exhale, four steps. Her hair collected sweat and her legs turned over, warm on the inside even as a cold breeze passed over her thighs. This was perfect running weather—cool enough to keep her going for hours. And at least when she was running, she was supposed to be alone.

As she ran, she did the math. She and Noah had been together more than a year now—several months longer than Avery's longest relationship, and that was back in high school. But the truth was, Noah had become like a ghost, coming in and out of her life as he wanted, never giving much explanation for where he was going, how long he'd be gone, or why he couldn't answer his phone. When his job took him away, it was like he didn't even exist. Avery didn't want to be demanding—she couldn't imagine stooping to the level of a girl who stamped her foot and asked for a ring. But some kind of assurance that their relationship was moving *forward* would have been nice. It didn't even have to be moving forward! Just moving . . . somewhere.

Instead, Noah left her alone in her kitchen to watch her neighbor's children grow up before her eyes. Dani was living in London and gallivanting all around Europe on the weekends. While Avery was sure deployment sucked at times, at least Hannah had a chance to put her training to work. And what about Avery? She had a shadow boyfriend, a messy house, and not much to show for her two years out of college, other than a few pieces of furniture she'd bought at IKEA.

Then there was the letter. Ever since she'd received notice from West Point that John Collins had been paroled, nothing had felt right. The first thing she should have done was call Dani and Hannah. But that night, sitting on the guest bed in her parents' house, she couldn't bring herself to pick up the phone. It was the middle of the night in London, and Hannah was tucked away in some far corner of Afghanistan, unreachable. It had been a year since they'd been together at Dani's apartment in Boston for Thanksgiving, and even then, they'd seemed so suspicious of her new boyfriend. She couldn't call them with the news about John Collins or her worries about Noah. She didn't want to hear *I told you so.*

As she ran, Avery tried to untangle the web of her own shame. Who was she to feel bad about her life, when Dani had just watched the person she loved most tie the knot with someone else? And Hannah—she wouldn't see Tim for another *year.* Compared to them, Avery had no right to feel anything but fine.

At that moment and without warning, Bosco halted in the middle of the trail. Stumbling over his body, an eighty-pound obstacle, Avery caught herself, her hands planted in a puddle of fresh mud.

"Bosco!" she cried. "What the . . ."

Standing up, Avery brushed her soiled hands across her pants, leaving trails of dirt behind. The dog crept into the woods next to the trail, sniffing at something in earnest. Stepping closer, Avery caught her breath and peered into the pile of leaves. A small rabbit lay on its side, its brown pelt punctured in two places at the neck. A small trickle of red blood seeped from its mouth. Bosco pushed it with one careless paw.

"Hey, leave it," she ordered. Bosco whined, then stepped away.

The rabbit's mouth opened and closed once.

Avery crouched closer. It was still alive—barely. Its eyes were open wide, as though it was experiencing terror in its last moments. The woods were very quiet now, her loud thoughts halted by death. And for a moment, Avery felt scared and alone.

"Leave it, Bosco," she said. "Let's go."

The dog bolted up the trail. Then, with a sigh, she started running again.

LATER THAT NIGHT, a pot of water boiled on her kitchen stove, jumping in eager anticipation for the box of fettuccine sitting on her counter. She'd recorded Thursday's *Grey's Anatomy*, and the episode opened with Derek and Meredith making out in a bathtub, which, Avery knew, was one of the most uncomfortable things a couple could do. She and Noah had tried once, with some success, but at times, she wished television shows would include the *actual* awkward moments in a relationship: the moment you realize you can't step *out* of the tub without his seeing you from all the wrong angles; the strange, uncomfortable clean-up that happens after the main event. Sex wasn't nearly as seamless as television led everyone to believe. But with Noah, it came close.

Whenever he arrived at her house, he could barely drop his

bags by the door before filling his hands with her breasts, her hips. He looked at her like he wanted to devour her—and his hunger made Avery feel sexy and powerful and in control, even as the voice in the recesses of her spirit warned that he was taking rather than giving. Whenever he prepared to leave again, he'd grow agitated and uncomfortable, like he was sitting on pins. He blamed his anxiety on the impending deployment—and Avery would try to rub his shoulders, but eventually he'd push her off. After his last trip, Avery had found a pile of Pakistani rupees on the nightstand next to a receipt for two foot-long Subway sandwiches that he'd purchased at Fort Bragg. Looking at the date on the receipt, Avery's eyes had narrowed. October 12. How could he have purchased two turkey club sandwiches at the Fort Bragg post exchange if he was supposedly in Pakistan? And why did he need two? Avery had willed her eyes away from the receipt, refusing to follow those questions to the root. Surely there was an explanation.

But now, as the pasta water began to boil over, Avery reached to turn down the heat and began wondering again about that little piece of paper. Perhaps there was an error in the computer system that had misprinted the date. Or maybe she was forgetting what dates he'd been gone in the first place. Maybe she was going crazy. Or maybe she was just too paranoid for her own good, always looking for evidence that he was like every other guy she'd ever dated. She didn't want to be distrusting. But then again, some quiet voice in the back of her head that sounded a lot like Hannah wouldn't shut up about that stupid receipt.

Avery took a seat on her couch, placing her cell phone on the coffee table and holding the bowl of pasta in her hands. For a moment, her body looked at the noodles, covered in butter, and craved meat—it had been nearly a year since she'd eaten beef, simply because Noah had convinced her to be a vegetarian. Now she remembered the look on Dani's face when Avery had passed on the turkey last Thanksgiving. It wasn't a look of disapproval. It was a look of confusion.

"*Is he treating you well?*" Hannah had asked.

In a flash of certainty, Avery set her dinner down and grabbed her cell phone. The phone would likely go straight to Noah's voicemail like it always did when he was gone. But she couldn't stand it. She had to ask him. About the receipt. About those fucking foot-long sub sandwiches. Turning the television on mute, she waited, listening to the sound of three distinct rings.

"Hello?"

Avery pulled the phone away from her ear. The voice on the other end of the line wasn't Noah. It was a woman. Something in the woman's voice had trembled. Or maybe the cell service had cut out. Avery wasn't sure. She stared at the phone, verifying that it was Noah's name on her screen, then placed it back to her ear. Her hands began to sweat.

"Hello?" the woman repeated. "Avery? I know you're there."

So this woman knew her name. A long pause passed, while on the silent television screen in the living room, a doctor lifted her bloodied gloves in the air.

"I'm sorry, who is this?" Avery said, her voice angry and defiant.

The woman on the other end of the line sighed. "This is Noah's fiancée."

24

November 12, 2006 // Tarin Kot, Afghanistan

Hannah's platoon swung their arms up and down like they were playing timpani in slow motion, hammering raw wood boards together to create a platform for the GP medium tent that would house the TOC, or tactical operations center. The crevice between Hannah's thumb and forefinger was red and bleeding. She sucked it, then shook her hand. Sweat spilled over Hannah's eyebrows and into her eyes. She breathed, tilting her head toward the sky, letting the salt water roll into the hair above her ears.

Had she known what the day would entail, would she have smiled at the sun? Had she known, would she have laughed?

In the eight months since they'd arrived in Afghanistan, Hannah's platoon had built six infantry outposts like this for incoming troops. From their headquarters in Sharana—where Ebrahim's family lived—her platoon would convoy out far into the desert into hotly contested areas and get to work building, so that a surge of troops could arrive and retake the territory from the Taliban. Everything they built was temporary. An infantry team would secure the area while Hannah's platoon built tents, dug trenches, and assembled plumbing for a future bathroom trailer. It took two days to get the first tents erected, so her engineers would have a place to sleep. Then they built a simple sand wall for defense, which took about four days. Then they'd move on to digging trenches for bathroom facilities.

They'd arrived in mid-October. By the time they left a month later, the outpost would be ready to house NATO troops for a short-term deployment, fighting in the hills no more than five minutes from where they stood. Hannah's soldiers worked round the clock in 120-degree heat, always aware that they were sitting ducks. After three weeks in this remote location, her hands were showing evidence of all her hard work, and her body ached. Dirt caked under her fingernails; calluses formed on her palms. And every morning, she found handfuls of her hair on her pillow—it had started to fall out because of the stress.

Two days ago, her platoon had returned from dropping supplies and soccer balls at a nearby school. Since then, the little boy's angry face had haunted Hannah's dreams. But the physical exhaustion helped her sleep at night, even when she knew that Tim had arrived in Kuwait, hundreds of miles away, and was preparing to fight his own war. If she'd been at home, Hannah was certain she wouldn't have been able to function knowing he was in harm's way. But if Tim was going to be deployed, at least she was here, distracted by her own mission. It felt good to do work that mattered. And the harder she worked, the faster the time seemed to pass.

It hadn't crossed Hannah's mind that she might want time to slow down.

ONCE THE TARIN Kot tactical operations center was up and running, Hannah had spent several hours connecting a secure cable to the post's sole computer. Technically, the line was only supposed to be used for military communications and since there were so many people around, there wasn't much privacy. But with the few spare moments Hannah had alone with the only secure Internet connection, she decided to take a risk.

iCasualties.org, a rudely named website, logged all military casualties in both Iraq and Afghanistan since 2001. Hannah checked it at least once a week when she was at FOB Sharana. It wasn't a fancy website. No graphics. No photos. Just a crude table of data. Each row described a tragedy. Every column defined the details. Date, name, rank. Age, cause of death, place of death. Military branch, hometown, unit. The final column listed the soldier or officer's current duty station. Most newspapers could, from one line of text, write an entire obituary.

Hannah scanned the most recent additions. She looked at the dates first—in October, 107 U.S. soldiers had been killed in Iraq. Thirty-four more had been added to the list since the first of November. After scanning the dates, Hannah skimmed the names for any she recognized. It was a morbid ritual—a sacrament

Hannah knew every soldier and officer and wife and mother had completed more than once over the last four years. But by reading the list, searching for names she knew, Hannah inadvertently honored the names she didn't.

Martinez, Misael, a staff sergeant from North Carolina.

Powell, Kyle W., twenty-one years old.

Hannah had read the names so many times that she'd learned to do it unemotionally. But every now and then, a name would stop her from scrolling, and the weight of anonymous loss would hit her all at once.

Seymour, David S. "Scotty." Specialist. 24. Hostile—hostile fire—small-arms fire.

Hannah wondered who'd given him the nickname and whether he liked it or hated it, smiled or sulked when guys called him "Scotty." He and Hannah were the same age. Twenty-four. This year, her birthday had passed without much fanfare. Tim had mailed her a care package, but as of last week, it still hadn't arrived.

After she scanned iCasualties.org, she opened an e-mail that had arrived from Tim. Two sentences, short and to the point, like all his e-mails. But for some reason, this one left Hannah with a heavy feeling in her chest, like her lungs were filling with water.

Heading out for a ten-day mission. I'll be in touch when we get back. RILY.

RILY had become their secret code. Their shorthand for all the emotions wrapped up in these months apart. *Remember I love you.* She remembered. It was forgetting so she could focus on anything other than her fear that was the hard part.

"LIEUTENANT NESMITH!"

Private Murphy called to her from across the build site, holding a two-way radio in his hands. An eighteen-year-old kid from Arkansas with a girlfriend at home and an unhealthy obsession with NASCAR racing, Murphy was a great soldier. Tough as nails, and always the last one to put away his tools. Hannah had grown to respect him.

"Yeah, Murph," she yelled. "What's up?"

"They're saying we've got a big one coming. Twenty miles out."

"Shit," Hannah cursed, shocked at the profanity that came out of her own mouth. But there honestly couldn't have been any worse news. It was sandstorm season in Afghanistan, and though they'd prepared for this possibility, Hannah had never expected it would come so soon. Twenty minutes wasn't long enough. But it was all she had left.

Looking at the nearly finished construction site, Hannah put her forefinger and thumb in her mouth and whistled hard and loud, gathering the rest of the platoon together.

"Listen," she ordered, commanding their attention. "We can't afford to waste a single second. Murph, you and Willis join me and finish platform one. Johnson, Kiggler—stop digging the trench and help finish the plumbing so that's not ruined by the sand. And then the rest of you, get moving securing the anchors and any other equipment. We've got less than half an hour. Any questions?"

Without hesitation, her platoon moved into overdrive. For the next fifteen minutes, Hannah forgot that she was thirsty and hot and tired. She simply pushed through the pain until her heart took over and the sky turned dark. Soon, they were all sitting in the shade of the tent, drenched in sweat, laughing at the feat it had required to finish the work in such a short amount of time. As they chugged water and tried to regain their breath, Hannah spied the rumbling darkness in the distance and felt her eyes narrow.

An ocean wave would terrify an ant. That's how Hannah felt, standing several thousand yards away from the edge of a sandstorm. Every second the wall grew, massive and brown, with arms and fingers rolling more dust into its belly, stretching wider and higher into the sky. The majesty of it struck Hannah so immediately, she didn't even have time to register that it was coming right toward them.

Where did it get the energy to move?

Was God himself in the storm?

Tiny particles of sand flew into her hair, her neck, her cheeks, like a thousand shards of glass.

"Get inside," she ordered. "Everyone get inside."

The platoon moved underneath the cover of the canvas, zipped closed the door, and checked that all the window panels were securely attached—so they could watch it go by, without the sand destroying every weapon and tool in the tent. If you think you're important, if you feel that your life matters, all you need to do is spend some time in nature, Hannah thought. Stand before an ocean. Climb a mountain. Stare out over a canyon. Creation— wild and untamed—reminded her of her size in this universe. But feeling small did not send her into despair. She was like a child, trusting her Father when he said the storm would pass.

As the storm rolled over their heads, Private Murphy held a camera up to one of the clear plastic tent windows, recording video. "Holy shit. It's a fucking monster . . ."

The entire world turned from day to night as the cloud passed over, pummeling the tent with twenty-five-mile-per-hour winds.

"Looks like we might be in Tarin Kot a little bit longer than we thought, Lieutenant Nesmith," Murphy said.

"It'll pass," Hannah answered. "It may take some time. But it'll pass."

THE STORM DIDN'T pass.

For twenty-four hours, they were stuck inside that tent, smelling of sweat and dirt. They ate MREs, read books, and slept. They only ventured outside to relieve themselves, and even then, came back in the tent coughing, and covered in dust. Hannah filled her time with paperwork, and stopped every so often to listen to the sound of the wind. The Taliban were unlikely to fire rockets or mortar in the midst of a storm—their equipment was just as susceptible to sand as the U.S. Army's—but Hannah still felt on edge. She'd rather have heard the constant, sporadic accompaniment of gunshots outside the camp than the sound of the wind swirling around her. Rapid fire, popping in the distance, reassured her. It meant the enemy was being defeated. But in silence like this—quiet like this—there was a real temptation to forget she was in danger. Hannah found herself straining to listen so she wouldn't be caught off guard if an explosion disrupted her imagined peace. To die in the midst of a firefight or while on convoy was one thing. But what Hannah feared most was death arriving, when it was completely unexpected.

ONCE THE SANDSTORM passed, Hannah's platoon finished construction. On Wednesday, they began the long, winding convoy back to FOB Sharana, stopping overnight in Kandahar. On Thursday, their six-vehicle convoy bumped along the unpaved roads, churning up dust under their tires. Buckled into the front passenger seat of the second Humvee, Hannah watched the walls of the FOB come into view and breathed a sigh of relief. Their work was done, and the storm had done limited damage. As they passed through the gates, she made a mental list of the things she wanted: a shower and a chance to check her e-mail. She needed to see if she'd received an update from Tim.

Murphy put the Humvee in park. Hannah stepped out.

But as soon as Hannah closed the vehicle's door, she knew something was wrong. The unit's commanding officer, Lieutenant Colonel Markham, stood a few feet away from the vehicle, looking directly at her, as if he'd been waiting for her to arrive. His eyes spoke of sadness. His shoulders slumped under an invisible weight.

Before he even said a word, Hannah knew what he was going to say. Her jaw went numb. The sky above and the views around her blurred as her eyes focused on only his face.

"Hannah," he said, using her name and not her rank. "I need you to come with me."

In his office, he told her to sit, but Hannah refused. It was the first time she'd ever disobeyed a direct order. A blue tissue box sat on the colonel's desk. The Army chaplain sat in a chair, leaning forward with his hands intertwined. Hannah couldn't breathe. She couldn't remember if it was night or day or if it mattered.

For years, she would replay this moment in her mind, wishing to erase it from her life. It was a doorway. And as soon as she walked through it, the door behind her would shut and disappear, closing her off from everything before. Including the girl who could look up at an Afghanistan sky and smile.

Bracing for impact didn't help at all. Even if every muscle in her body had tightened, there were no muscles strong enough to protect a heart from breaking.

"No," she said. "Please."

"I'm so sorry, Hannah," the colonel said. "I'm so very sorry."

THE CORPS

The Corps bareheaded, salute it, with eyes up thanking our God
That we of the Corps are treading,
where they of the Corps have trod
They are here in ghostly assemblage
The men of the Corps long dead
And our hearts are standing attention
While we wait for their passing tread
We sons of today, we salute you, you sons of an earlier day
We follow close order behind you, where you have pointed the way
The long gray line of us stretches
Through the years of a century told
And the last man feels to his marrow
The grip of your far-off hold
Grip hands with us now, though we see not
Grip hands with us strengthen our hearts
As the long line stiffens and straightens
With the thrill that your presence imparts
Grip hands, though it be from the shadows
While we swear as you did of yore
Or living or dying to honor
The Corps, and the Corps, and the Corps

BEYOND

November 2006

25

November 16, 2006 // London, England

The limp was worse than it had ever been.

With every step, a searing knife shot through Dani Mc-Nalley's right side, forcing her to put more weight on her left leg while dragging her right. And yet she moved forward, her feet bobbling over the cobblestones. She had to get back to her apartment, and then she had to go home.

The pregnant sky released its first few drops of rain onto her head. Dani watched them fall and die on the sidewalk. In her haste to leave work, she'd forgotten her umbrella on the hook by her office door. Paralyzed with indecision, she couldn't decide whether to go back to the office for the umbrella or keep walking forward toward Notting Hill. People maneuvered around her with their chins down, hands stuffed deep into their pockets, like Dani was a lamppost or trash can—simply an obstacle to avoid. Life was moving on as if nothing had happened. Cars and taxis barreled down the road, kicking up water under their tires. The tube underground rumbled, moving people from one stop to the next. It was hard to believe all this activity. All this life. A couple of toddlers on the other side of the road dressed in yellow raincoats had the audacity to laugh, turning their faces toward the sky to catch the rain on their cheeks.

Dani felt her chest tighten and for a moment, she thought she might lose control right in the middle of the street. Gripping her BlackBerry tight in her hand, Dani looked up to the sky and blinked back the tears in her eyes, swallowing the emotion. She'd done it plenty of times before. At some point, she would need to let her tears flow freely. But now was not the time.

An hour ago, she'd been sitting in a meeting with Laura Klein and the rest of the E & G marketing team discussing their next round of commercial shoots when her phone buzzed on the table. Laura's eyes had bored into the side of Dani's face as she reached for the phone. She hadn't planned on answering it. She thought she would look at the caller ID and send the call straight to voicemail. But the name on the caller ID sent ice into Dani's veins.

Bill Speer.

Hannah's father. She imagined him on the other end of the line somewhere in Texas, waiting for Dani to answer. And without thinking—without explanation—she took the phone in her hand and walked out of the meeting.

"Mr. Speer?" Dani had said, her voice already shaking. "Is everything okay?"

She heard him clear his throat.

"Dani, I'm sorry," he'd said. "I have some very bad news."

Dani sat down in the office kitchen, a windowless room with bright fluorescent light. Her breath went shallow and she clenched her eyes shut. Bill's voice was steady as it traversed an ocean to speak the truth.

"Tim was killed in Iraq, Dani. I'm so sorry."

Since then, the BlackBerry in her hand hadn't stopped buzzing. Messages arrived often. E-mails, texts, and phone calls, all of which went unanswered.

From Sarah Goodrich: *I just heard that Tim Nesmith was KIA. Tell me that's not true?*

She knew she wouldn't sleep tonight. Most people didn't even know that she was living in London—a full six hours ahead of Eastern Time. The phone would ring, buzz, and beep through all hours of the night, with messages from people who had questions—the same ones she'd asked Hannah's father.

Have you talked to her? How is she? I can't believe this. How did it happen? When is the funeral? What can we do?

She had no answers. Neither had Bill Speer. A sandstorm had rolled into the southeastern region of Afghanistan, stalling all transportation and communication. Hannah was stuck waiting for the air to clear so she could go home. But Dani had no such obstacles. She'd grabbed her purse and computer from her cubicle and left the office, without telling Laura a single thing. She was getting on the first plane to North Carolina. And until her feet were on American soil—until she saw Hannah face-to-face—everything else could wait.

A stream of tourists emerged from the train station and walked east along the sidewalk, smiling and chatting under their hats and umbrellas, anticipating the pleasures that awaited them down the road. Dani moved between them, parting them as if they were the Red Sea. As she stuffed the phone back into her pocket, she descended into the bowels of the tube. And somewhere along the way, without even noticing it, she forgot about the pain in her hip.

THAT NIGHT, AS Dani packed a bag and searched for flights online, she tried to call Avery, without success. She would keep trying. But in the meantime, she needed to pack a bag—if nothing else, just to have something to do.

Her suitcase opened up like a black mouth on her bed, while the heavy square phone vibrated against her nightstand. The name *Wendy Bennett* flashed at the center of the screen. Dani could picture her in the living room of their home at West Point, waiting for Dani to answer. At the thought of hearing Wendy's voice, Dani's eyes flooded. She pressed the green button and answered.

"Hi, Wendy." Dani moved slowly to the side of her bedroom, leaned her back against a wall, and sank into the floor, listening to Wendy's sobs on the other end of the line. After some time had passed, Wendy finally spoke.

"Has anyone heard from her?" Wendy asked, her words interrupted with a hiccupping cry. "At all?"

"I don't know," Dani said, wiping her eyes. "I haven't. She won't answer her phone."

"What are you doing right now?"

"Packing," Dani said, though the word felt weak as it came out of her mouth. "I don't know what else to do. I found a flight that leaves tomorrow, first thing. I haven't bought it yet." She sighed. "I just have to get there."

"I understand," Wendy said. "Did you tell your boss you're leaving?"

"No," Dani replied. "It doesn't matter." And it didn't. Laura Klein would be angry that Dani had walked out of the meeting without an explanation. But there was no way she was going to stay at the office waiting for her boss's permission to leave. Laura could get over it, or she could fire her. It didn't matter anymore.

"Have you talked to Avery?" Wendy asked.

"No," Dani said finally, her voice cracking with emotion. "I . . . I'm sorry, Wendy . . . I need to go."

"Okay. I love you. I'm praying. I'm praying so hard."

If only I'd kept my nose out of Hannah's business, maybe Hannah and Tim would never have dated in the first place, Dani thought. *Maybe then things would be different. If only I'd been commissioned into the Army. Then I would understand. If I'd lived through the war, maybe I would be less shocked.*

In the place of combat boots, Dani's bedroom floor was covered in designer shoes and limited-edition sneakers. A cream-colored cashmere scarf hung from the hook on the door, and her latest extravagance, a Cartier watch, mocked her with every click of the second hand. She ripped it off and threw it against the wall, then screamed, her face buried in the carpet on the floor.

Eventually, Dani moved to her bed and tried to close her eyes. Perhaps a few short minutes of sleep would help her to breathe easier. To calm down. As much as her soul ached, it soothed her to lie in one place and cry.

With her eyes closed, a memory appeared bright and clear in her mind. A crowd of children playing soccer in a schoolyard. They were laughing, all chasing around the ball. Rather than fight the memory, she let it come back to her. She focused on the little black girl sprinting down a green field, her braids flopping in the air as she ran. She was always so happy when she ran.

Back then, she had no limp. No pain. For this invitational soccer tournament, the coach had decided to move Dani, just twelve years old, up to the team of fourteen-year-olds. Her team wore bright yellow jerseys, and Dani stood a head shorter than the rest. She'd been so excited to play that day, Dani remembered. Eager to prove that she deserved the spot she'd been given.

The little brown-skinned girl tore up and down the field, sweating under the heat of the sun. Smiling. Her freckles jumping like little flecks of dark chocolate as she cut left and right, dribbling the ball deftly between defenders. She kicked a ball as hard as she could and it soared past the goalie into the top right corner of the net. Her teammates ran toward her, wrapping their arms around her in excitement. It was her first moment of athletic success. Her first taste of glory.

But as she'd walked off the field, a sound carried over the wind. The adults behind the opponent's bench were laughing. A tan man with a swoop of brown hair had wrapped his hands around his mouth, shouting in Dani's direction. She remembered looking at him, wondering if he was yelling at her or the referee.

"Bahh!" he'd shouted, his voice shaking like a sheep's. "Bahhh!" he'd yelled, letting his arms drop to his sides. The other parents, dressed in red, all joined in laughing and bleating, some loudly, and some out of the corners of their mouths. They were bleating at her, the black sheep.

That night, still dressed in her yellow uniform, Dani had cried, sitting on the closed toilet in the bathroom. Her mother wiped her tears.

"Those people are ignorant," Harper McNalley had said.

"They said I was a black sheep," Dani cried. "Like I didn't belong out there."

"So what?" her mother had snapped defiantly. "So they say you're different? Guess what. They're *right*. You *are* different. You're better."

Dani couldn't remember how many soccer games she'd played after that. Five? Ten? The following year, she'd told her parents she didn't want to play soccer anymore. She'd explained she wanted to try basketball instead.

The ceiling of Dani's apartment in Notting Hill blurred, distorted by the hot tears in her eyes. At first, she didn't know why that memory had come to her mind. But now, she knew.

Had those parents not singled her out—had they not shouted their hate—she would never have played basketball. And if she hadn't played basketball, she would never have attended West Point.

The dominoes that put her on her back, grieving for Tim and for Hannah, had been put into play far before she'd ever signed some document for Coach Jankovich. For some people, that lack of control might have made them angry with God. But for Dani, she finally felt like she saw her life with clarity for the very first time.

What if the only reason she'd attended West Point was to be available for Hannah, when she needed a friend like Dani most? What if it took all the injuries and the pain and the sacrifices they'd made simply to forge a friendship that could withstand even this?

Dani had earned more frequent-flier miles in the last two years than she would ever know what to do with. But now, without thinking, Dani pulled up an airline website on her computer and cashed several thousand in.

She was going home.

November 16, 2006 // Fort Bragg, North Carolina

A week after she spoke to Noah's fiancée, Avery still hadn't gotten out of bed. A stomach bug was going around the unit, which had made it easier to call in sick, stay in bed, and throw up occasionally. It wasn't a total lie; Noah was a virus and she had to get him out of her system.

Her room was a disaster area, covered in tissues and water glasses filled to varying levels—most of the contents dusty and undrinkable from sitting on the nightstand for three days' time. Her cell phone sat in the corner, turned off, so she wouldn't be tempted to call him. Laundry grew in piles around the room, stinking with dried sweat from the punishing ruck march she'd made her platoon complete for no other reason than she could. She had no energy left for running. No desire to take Bosco on a backwoods trail. All she could bring herself to do was sleep, wake up, remember that she'd wasted more than a year of her life on a liar, and then turn over and go back to sleep.

The puzzle pieces fell into place in Avery's mind, each one a crude reminder that she was an idiot, unfit for love. Red flag number one: the first question out of his mouth had been whether or not she was married. Red flag number two: he rarely explained where he was going, or for how long, or why. Red flag number three: she'd never been to his apartment, never met his parents. Red flag number four: at Thanksgiving, she'd known he was lying about talking to his mother, and had looked up their flight online and seen it was not, in fact, delayed. Red flag number five: Did she need five red flags? Really?

If she was honest with herself, really honest—if she listened to her *actual* heart and not the heart that she *wished* existed—if she got in touch at *that* level, then she'd known all along he was lying, or at least that something was wrong. But even now, she preferred to live in a world where he *wasn't* lying and did love her. That was her first question. *Did he ever really love her?*

Maybe he did. It was possible to love two people at the same time, Avery knew. But from the beginning, he had kept a part of himself hidden from her. For that reason, they'd never had a real chance. And the worst part about it, the part that made Avery pull the sheets up over her head and cry so hard she thought her eyes might fall out, was that he hadn't really wanted them to have a chance. He'd just wanted . . . what?

That was her second question. *How did he think it was going to end?*

Noah's fiancée hadn't sounded angry or bitter on the phone. She hadn't cussed or threatened. She'd just stated the facts.

"I know about you and Noah," she'd said. "And it needs to stop."

"I didn't know," Avery had said, her voice trembling. "I truly— truly—didn't know."

Avery wondered how Noah's fiancée had found out. Was it the receipt for their hotel room in Napa last summer? Or the smell of her perfume on his clothes? The calmness of her voice, the reservation, had set Avery on edge. Had Noah done this be- fore? Was this the cyclical pattern of their relationship—their *engagement*—with him constantly running, and her constantly bringing him home?

She got up from her bed and went to the toilet to throw up once more. *Why did this keep happening to her?* That was her third and final question.

Avery became her own judge and jury, and the conviction came swift. All the things John Collins's lawyer had said during the court-martial came back to her mind. She'd worn her dress gray uniform for her testimony, as she'd been told to do, and tried to keep her eyes away from John Collins's expressionless face as he sat next to his team of lawyers—four in total. His hair was cut short and tidy. And his eyes, bright green, followed the lead defense lawyer as he paced in front of the witness stand.

"Ms. Adams, you had a consensual sexual relationship with my client, isn't that correct?" the lawyer began.

"Yes."

"And you enjoyed these sexual liaisons?"

Avery felt her throat constrict, but she refused to be unsettled. "To be honest, the sex was mediocre, at best."

The judge cleared his throat. "Get to your point, counsel."

"Isn't it true that you initiated these sexual encounters, arriving of your own volition to Mr. Collins's dorm room repeatedly throughout the 2000–2001 school year?"

"I . . ." Avery looked to the prosecutor's table, and the lawyer there nodded. "Yes. But we both—"

"And he asked you to keep the relationship a secret, isn't that right?"

"Yes. We both chose to—"

"He was ashamed of you. Wanted to hide you away from his friends. That must have been hard to hear."

"No . . . like I said—"

"It must have hurt to think he didn't want his friends to know about you."

Avery steeled her jaw. She knew where Collins's lawyer was going with this, and she wasn't going to let him get away with it.

"What hurt was knowing that he violated an entire group of women by filming us in the privacy of our locker room and then distributing those images across campus."

"You've already testified that the images that were distributed were of you. And only you. Isn't it possible that you were angry that he'd cut off the relationship? And, feeling rejected, sent pictures of yourself to him to try and seduce him? Just like you'd done the first time?"

"No," Avery said. Hot tears had gathered in her eyes. "I . . . that's not—"

"No further questions, Your Honor," he'd said. Then he sat back down next to his client, whose green eyes twinkled in smug satisfaction.

Avery wondered now how she'd been so blind. Steadying herself against the bathroom sink—another disaster area, covered with jewelry, toothpaste splatter, and a mildewing hand towel—she stared at herself in the mirror and read the verdict aloud. *It's your fault,* she said to herself in the mirror. *This is what you keep getting, because it's what you deserve.*

Turning on the shower, she twisted the knob until the hot water covered the mirror with steam. The pressure pounded her naked body, turning the front of her stomach, arms, and legs red. As soap crossed over her body, she realized that she'd never get clean enough. Something was wrong with a person who only chose men who abused her, or abused the men that she chose.

AN HOUR LATER, Avery made her way downstairs, dressed in sweatpants and an oversized T-shirt. The window over the kitchen sink framed the Jenkins house, across the street. She filled a glass of water, and at that moment, Eric and Michelle Jenkins walked out of their front door. They were supposed to be gone by now, Avery thought—hadn't Michelle said they were visiting Eric's family for Thanksgiving?

But the couple both looked pale, like they'd caught that stomach bug everyone kept complaining about. Eric slid his hand back and forth across the top of his head and wiped his nose. Michelle's eyes were bright red, like she'd been crying. It seemed odd that they would come outside looking so disheveled, odder still that they were crossing the street toward Avery's house. *Did something happen to Bosco?* she wondered. *Or the baby?*

Avery left the kitchen to meet them at the front door. She opened it before they could even knock. They were standing on her stoop, shivering, both of them with their arms crossed over their chests.

"We came over as soon as we heard," Michelle said.

Avery felt her heart drop several inches in her chest as she stared at them with confusion all over her face. "Heard what?"

Eric and his wife exchanged a worried glance.

"We thought you knew," Eric said. "Y'all were so close."

Avery couldn't breathe. She wanted to reach out and strangle them until whatever they were talking about came exploding out of their mouths. "Who? What's going on?"

"Avery," Eric said, looking her straight in the eye. "Tim Nesmith was killed in Iraq three days ago. I'm so sorry. We thought you knew."

SEVERAL HOURS LATER, Avery had no tears left. She'd turned on her phone and it had blown up with messages—from their classmates, and from Dani, who'd left several voicemails. She was now midair, on a flight to Fayetteville.

"I don't know what's going on with you, Avery. But I'm going to need you to pull yourself out of whatever hole you're in and come get me at the airport," Dani had said in her last voicemail message. "I land tomorrow at three."

Michelle had sent Eric home and stayed with Avery for a long time, sitting next to her while she sobbed on her bed. For two years, they'd stared at one another from across the street. Avery had always assumed that Michelle hated her, but now, everything she'd ever believed was being called into question. While Avery returned phone calls and e-mails, Michelle had pulled her red hair into a bun on top of her head and busied herself picking up dirty clothes in Avery's room. She started a load of laundry, filled the sink with dirty dishes, wiped the counters, swept the floors. Emptied of all emotion, Avery didn't even have the energy to tell Michelle to stop. By the time her neighbor finally left, it was well past ten P.M., and the house was cleaner than it had been since Avery moved in two years earlier.

Michelle's kindness reminded Avery of something Wendy Bennett had said a long time ago, while they sat in that hospital waiting room. *People remember who showed up for the shitty moments far more than they remember who showed up for the party.* And for some inexplicable reason, Michelle Jenkins had shown up.

In light of everything, it became painfully clear to Avery that she'd *not* been that kind of friend. Not in years. She'd grown envious of Dani's travels and her wealth. She'd grown cold toward Hannah, too. God—she'd treated Hannah horribly. Her friend had been deployed for more than a year and Avery had done little more than send her an e-mail on her birthday. Kind, loyal, dependable Hannah. For years, Avery had taken advantage of her loyalty. She'd taken her for granted.

The clearest sign of her failure was that somehow, Dani had become the point person for every friend, acquaintance, and distant relative who wanted to express their condolences and find out how they could help. Avery lived down the street from the Nesmiths, and still, a girl who lived five time zones away had become the hub of all communication. It hurt to know that in the years since they'd graduated from West Point, she'd let her relationship with Hannah deteriorate that much. But the more Avery asked Dani what she could do, the less it seemed her friend had any answers. *Just pray,* Dani had typed in her last e-mail, sent from thirty thousand feet above the Atlantic.

Pray. For what? To whom?

Avery crawled into her freshly made bed with her cell phone and laptop, and tried to stop shivering. It was too horrible to imagine. From what Eric had heard through the Eighty-Second Airborne Division newswire, Tim was killed by small-arms fire in a skirmish in Samarra. Two of his soldiers had been shot, and running to their aid, Tim found himself in the midst of the cross-fire. The soldiers both survived. Tim bled out before the medical evacuation team could arrive.

Clenching her eyes closed, she tried to put those images out of her mind. The Tim she wanted to remember was the one at Thanksgiving—sitting at the table, rubbing his wife's neck. Laughing. Clinking his glass against hers. Or the one senior year, getting on one knee in front of Hannah, surrounded by rose petals and candlelight. Or the one four weeks ago, who'd dropped a key in her hand and smiled, giving her one final salute. She couldn't just sit here, thinking about him and worrying about Hannah. And so, in a rush of movement, Avery flipped open her laptop and began clicking quickly.

Flights from Austin, Texas, to Fayetteville, North Carolina, weren't cheap at the last minute. Avery clicked through a list of options on several different screens. Hannah's family would need to be here when Hannah finally got home. Then, scrolling through her phone contacts, Avery landed on Hannah's sister's name. *Emily Speer Daniels.*

Married with a two-year-old son named Jack, Emily was living in Austin with her husband. Avery had met them several times over the years: a few times at West Point, most recently at Hannah's wedding. She didn't know Emily all that well and it was possible that she was overstepping. But Avery couldn't spend another moment without doing something for her friend.

Holding the phone up to her ear, Avery heard a few voices in the background before Emily answered.

"Avery. I'm so glad you called."

"I just heard," Avery said weakly. She paused, aware that the conversation might need to move slowly.

"Yeah." Emily sighed heavily. "We're all still in shock."

"Have any of you heard from Hannah?"

"She's still in Afghanistan. They still haven't found a way to get her out of the FOB. Apparently, a sandstorm has shut everything down."

"Have you guys decided when you might come to Fort Bragg?"

"No," Emily replied. "We thought we'd wait to hear from Hannah. See when she wants us to come."

Avery knew she needed to tread lightly here. It wasn't her place to make plans for anyone else, but then again, she knew the Army well enough to know that it could be several more days before Hannah's plans were finalized.

"I've been thinking," Avery said. "I really think you need to be here as soon as possible. Things with the Army can move slow. And I don't know when Hannah will get home, but I do know she'll want you to be here when she does. I'm just a few streets down, and I've got a spare key. I'm not sure how Tim left things. So we can go get the house ready for her."

Emily was silent for a while, considering what Avery had said.

"I took the liberty of looking up some flights," Avery said. "I hope that's okay."

Emily gave a light laugh. "You're amazing, Avery. Really."

"It looks like there's one leaving Austin on Sunday morning. I've shopped a bit, and it looks like a pretty good deal." It was silent on the line, then Avery sat up in bed. The words that followed bubbled up from a place within her that she didn't know existed. "Emily, I know this may sound crazy, but I want to pay for your flights. For you, your husband, and Jack. And for your parents, too."

Avery tried to ignore the dollar signs adding up in her mind. She wasn't even sure she had that much in her savings account.

"Oh, Avery," Emily said, voice trembling. "You don't have—"

"It's not about the money. I want to."

"We couldn't possibly—"

"Please let me. I just need to do something. I'm sitting here going crazy by myself and it's the least I can do."

"Gosh," Emily said. "I don't know . . ."

"You don't even have to tell your parents. Just tell them the Army paid for it," Avery said, then chuckled. "It's not a total lie. And it's one less thing you have to do right now. Check it off your list."

Avery waited a moment while Emily blew her nose.

"Ugh, I'm such a mess," Emily said. "Okay. I think Sunday sounds good. Let's do Sunday. But that's *five* plane tickets. Are you sure?"

"I've never been more sure of anything in my life." Avery clicked "purchase" on the computer screen, then pinched the cell phone between her ear and shoulder to type with both hands. "Okay, tell me your full name..."

27

November 19, 2006 // Camp Buehring, Kuwait

No one ever tells you that when someone you love dies, you still have to eat.

You still have to brush your teeth and pack a bag and look at the clock and watch it ticking. No one tells you that grief feels like fear—it amps you up, making you want to run for your life, even though there's nowhere to go, no place where death will be unreal. Grief chokes you and paralyzes you, making the most menial decisions feel impossibly huge.

"Who do you want to call?" the chaplain had asked.

She'd stared at him in utter confusion. Tim. *She wanted to call Tim.*

Who do you call when your husband dies and you're twenty-four years old, alone in Afghanistan?

Who do you call when the only voice you want to hear no longer exists?

AS IF IT had chased Hannah all the way across Afghanistan, a sandstorm had arrived at FOB Sharana, hours after LTC Markham broke the news. Once again, everyone was shut up in their rooms, unable to move or operate. Trucks were halted. Helicopters grounded. Alone with her grief, Hannah waited. Two days later, the storm lifted. The chaplain told her to pack, which she'd already done, and a convoy transported Hannah eight hours from FOB Sharana to Bagram Airfield. From there, a helicopter flew her to Camp Buehring, Kuwait, where a silver-haired transportation officer told her to find a bunk in any female tent—that they'd get her on the first flight out with an available seat. Forty women slept in each tent, and for all those women knew, Hannah was going home on R & R, just like the rest of them. For all they knew, she just stayed in bed because she was lazy.

The next morning was a Sunday—the only reason Hannah knew this was because as she walked across Camp Buehring to the Mess Hall, she heard hymns coming from a tent nearby. Strong and harmonious, the voices sang a familiar song, but she didn't let them draw her in. Instead, Hannah forced herself to eat a full breakfast—though now, stretched out on a bottom cot near the door of the bunkhouse, she couldn't remember what she'd put on her plate. Everything tasted bitter. Everything tasted like nothing at all.

The mess hall tent had been decorated with orange accordion-style pumpkins and brown streamers. Fake ivy hung from the rafters and twisted down tent poles. She hadn't tasted a single thing as the meal slid down her throat. *Is food really the only thing that keeps us alive?* Hannah asked herself. If that was true, why couldn't they revive Tim with a piece of bread and a cup of wine?

She couldn't understand how a person could just end. The more her mind circled around that drain, the more she felt the beginning of a battle she would someday have to fight with God. But for now, she couldn't sleep unless she held on to her cross necklace and prayed—begged—for a moment of rest, for a moment to forget. She took Tylenol PM in the highest possible dose. When it finally came, sleep was relief, but when she woke up, the nightmare began all over again.

Hannah cried through much of the second night at Camp Buehring, grateful for the girl in the bunk above her, whose snores muffled her sobs. She envied army wives who got to hear the worst news of their lives in the comfort of their own homes. There were three parts of her heart: One that wanted to get on a plane and run away from this place. Another part that wanted to dig a hole in the ground, get inside, and never get out. And the third, loudest part of her heart wanted a bomb to drop right on top of her—because that was the only thing that made sense. If he was gone, she wanted to be gone too.

IN THE MORNING, her cell phone rang.

Hannah stared at it for a long time, reading her sister's name on the caller ID. If she didn't answer, she could go on pretending for a few minutes that Tim was still alive, that there had been a mistake, that some other young soldier with the same name had been killed. That some other girl was about to hear news that would shatter her life. That Hannah could piece hers together again.

But the phone kept ringing.

She'd ignored every single call that she possibly could. She'd spoken to Tim's parents from the satellite phone on FOB Sharana, and the ache in Margaret Nesmith's voice sank Hannah's heart so deeply, she already feared seeing them once she made it back to the States. Hannah was completely submerged in the grief of losing a husband; she couldn't carry the weight of their loss, too. Tim was a husband. A son. A friend. He was a different person to everyone he knew—filling a thousand different roles. But Hannah could only grieve one Tim at a time.

Text messages from Dani and others kept pouring in, but Hannah couldn't respond. She didn't know what she would possibly say. But Emily had called three times in a row now. So finally, with a heavy arm, Hannah reached for the phone and spent the energy it took to open it and place it on her ear.

"Hey." Her sister's voice was so slow and soft. So unlike her normal voice. "Did you make it to Kuwait?"

"Yes."

"What are you doing now?"

"Sitting on my bunk."

"Have you opened the letter?"

Hannah peered at the stack of books at the foot of her bunk. A Bible. *East of Eden,* with the corner of page three hundred dog-eared to hold her spot. Neither of which she had opened. In the middle of the Bible she could see the small white edge of a letter, acting like a bookmark. The chaplain had handed Hannah the letter just before she'd boarded the helicopter at Bagram Airfield. Covered in Tim's signature all-caps handwriting, it was postmarked November 12. The day he'd left on a ten-day mission into Samarra. One day before insurgents opened fire, sending three bullets into the chest of a soldier in Tim's platoon. Before her husband ran to stop the bleeding and sixteen shots ripped through his chest, ending his life. The day before her husband died, he'd written her a letter.

Every moment, it felt like an elephant was stepping on her chest. She couldn't breathe. *This isn't your life,* she told herself as she stared at the edge of the letter. *This can't be happening.* She hadn't had a moment alone since the chaplain had handed her the letter and she didn't want to open it until she could scream and wail as loud as she wanted.

"Hannah?"

"No. I haven't."

"Okay."

Hannah placed the phone beside her head and listened to her sister breathing. Hot tears created a warm wet circle where her cheek met the pillow.

After some time had passed, Emily said, "Any update on when you'll be back?"

The words made whatever was in Hannah's stomach start to swirl. Like something was in the back of her throat, pushing on all sides of her esophagus. "No," she said.

Silence.

"Okay. Well we're trying to decide if we should stay at the house with you or get a hotel. Either way. Whatever you want."

"It doesn't matter," Hannah said. But even as the words came out of her mouth, she knew it did. She had an opinion. She just didn't know what it was. She couldn't find it in her head. But it was there.

"Okay. We'll be here waiting for you when you get home."

LIKE EVERY OTHER building, the transportation office was a series of small offices, all inside a large tent. Fans whirred and buzzed in every corner, and men passed Hannah in beige camouflage uniforms, unconcerned about her presence. They didn't know what she was doing or why she was here, which made no sense. She felt like a part of her body had been ripped off. The fact that everyone didn't stare seemed absolutely impossible. How could a loss that big be that invisible?

By the afternoon, no one had come to retrieve Hannah and send her home. She wondered if they'd forgotten about her, the war widow, in the back of the bunkhouse. Days could pass before they remembered. Weeks.

So pulling herself up, Hannah had walked across Camp Buehring, to the office of the man in charge of outgoing flight manifestos. After she'd waited for more than an hour outside of his office, Lieutenant Colonel Williams stepped out of his door and waved her inside.

"Sorry about the wait, Lieutenant Nesmith," he said. "What can I do for you?"

The colonel leaned forward in his desk chair, brown eyes full of a sickeningly sweet emotion that Hannah realized she'd have to get used to: pity. He had three combat patches on his uniform, dark eyebrows, and steely eyes that seemed to look both at Hannah and beyond her.

"I understand you're trying to get home," he said. "Emergency leave."

"Yes, sir. I don't mean to bother you. I just want to know if there are any updates. I heard there's a flight leaving tomorrow."

"Unfortunately, there's not an open seat." He spoke so quickly, it felt like he'd slapped her across the face. "The R & R schedule has been set for months. You understand. These soldiers have plans with their families. I can't schedule your flight without bumping someone else."

Hannah felt her throat tighten, like she was being strangled by an invisible hand.

"But, sir, I really . . . I need to go home. Doesn't emergency leave give me any precedence?"

Cruelty was staring grief in the face and pointing to a spreadsheet.

Hannah didn't try to stop herself from crying. She let the tears fall onto her uniform, right in front of him. He could say no. But she couldn't shield him from the pain of that denial. She was done following the rules. She wondered why she'd ever followed them in the first place.

"Please don't make me beg for this. I've done everything you've asked of me. I voluntarily put my life on hold. I left my family and friends behind. I dug the trenches and built the tents and led my soldiers. I haven't complained. Not once. But now? Now that I actually have to grieve the war you asked me to wage? You say I have to wait? How can America ask me to sacrifice everything I have to give . . . *everything* . . ." Her voice broke. "And now to deny my request when I'm begging, begging to go home? Sir. It's been a week. Please let me go home."

"I wish there were something I could do," he said, his eyes softening.

"There is, sir," Hannah said. "You can put me on that plane."

He sighed, looked at his computer, and began rubbing his temples.

"All right," he said finally. "Let me see what I can do."

28

Dani had arrived at Fayetteville Regional Airport late in the afternoon on Friday, feeling jet-lagged and exhausted. Inside the terminal, countless men in uniform had moved in and out with purpose—though it had been hard for Dani to tell who was coming and who was going. The men leaving held their wives close while their children cried. The men arriving did the same thing.

Avery had pulled up to the arrivals pickup lane in her rusty old Honda Civic, dressed in jeans and a gray hoodie. It had been more than a year since they'd seen one another, but Avery's massive CD case of angry alternative nineties music still rested on the passenger seat. The sight of it had given Dani a sense of nostalgia and comfort. Cheekbones high, ankles exposed, Avery looked thinner than Dani had ever seen her, with her bright blond hair piled on top of her head. But even if their bodies had changed,

Dani hoped their hearts would be found in the same place. It was time for the cult to make good on its promises.

"Thank God you're here," Avery had said, wrapping her arms around Dani's neck. They didn't cry—it was too surreal for that. Instead, they'd loaded Dani's luggage in the trunk and drove down the highway in silence.

AN HOUR LATER, they'd sat staring at the Nesmiths' front door, arguing about what to do. Two blue-star flags hung side by side in the window. The shrubs were slightly overgrown, the yard full of leaves. Inside, not a single light was on. It looked like it had been abandoned. Which, in a way, it had.

"I can't do this," Avery had said.

"We have to," Dani replied. "She can't go into the house with it like that. We have to turn on some lights. Turn on the heat."

"He was the last person in there." Avery held the key that Tim had given her in the palm of her hand. It was the color of her hair, Dani had noticed. Bright gold.

"He gave it to you in case something like this happened. Man up. We can do this. We don't have a choice."

With that, they'd walked to the front door. Avery carefully turned the key in the dead bolt, and then the door had opened, spilling sunlight all over the scene. Knowing that Hannah would come home from Afghanistan before he returned from Iraq, Tim had strung a banner across the stairwell with the words *WELCOME HOME* painted in big gold letters. There were multi-colored balloons all over the floor.

"Oh God." Avery had put her hands to her face.

Dani had exhaled loudly and kicked a blue balloon out of her way. She hadn't expected this. Clearly, from the pained look on Avery's face, neither had she. Together, they had slumped onto the bottom stair and kicked the balloons in silence. Avery had been wearing a pair of brown leather boots, Dani a brand-new pair of hot pink sneakers.

It didn't seem fair that they were there, in Hannah's house, while she was still stuck in the Middle East, alone with her grief. At the time, Dani wasn't sure it was the right thing to do. But sometimes, when tragedy strikes, you just have to act. And if Dani were in Hannah's shoes, she wouldn't want to crush the last of her husband's breath out of the universe. There are some things a person just shouldn't have to do.

"What are you doing?" Avery had shouted when Dani jumped up and started stomping on the balloons with her foot. "Stop! Shouldn't we leave it?"

"I'm not leaving it like this." Dani had spat back. "She shouldn't"—*pop!*—"have to"—*pop!*—"do it." *Pop! Pop!*

Haltingly, Avery had stood from the stairs and joined her. Together, they'd slammed their heels into rubber, sending the sound of gunshots throughout the house.

ON SUNDAY, HANNAH'S family had arrived in a rental van from the airport, looking like the flight had gone through severe turbulence, although Hannah's sister, Emily, promised Dani the flight was fine. Dani knew that Hannah hated when people said she looked just like her mother, but the resemblance was striking. Lynn Speer had always looked young for her age, but as she'd approached the house, carrying her luggage, that no longer seemed true. The weight of grief had transformed her face. The skin underneath her eyes was thin and blue, like translucent paper. She had two deep wrinkles between her eyebrows. She looked like she hadn't slept in days. The sight of Lynn, like an aged version of Hannah, had made tears come to Dani's eyes. They'd held each other on the sidewalk for a very long time, neither of them daring to say a word.

She'd received a long, warm hug from each member of Hannah's family, ending with Hannah's father, Bill. He'd looked just as he had a few years earlier, when she'd seen him at West Point's graduation: tall, with a thick gray mustache and his signature University of Texas ballcap. He'd wrapped an arm around Dani's shoulders and kissed her cheek. And though his body had felt sturdy, his voice had wavered.

"It's going to be all right," he'd said, sounding unconvinced. "It's all going to be all right."

But nothing was right. Hannah still had not boarded a flight out of Kuwait. Dani left London in such a hurry, and now, all she could do was sit around in silence, aching for the fact that the one person who needed to be in the comfort of her own home wasn't.

Hannah's family moved their luggage into the house, but tried not to touch or disturb a single thing. Tim had left Post-it notes everywhere, little surprises for his wife to find when she returned from her deployment. His handwriting hovered around every corner. *You grow more beautiful every day*—stuck to the mirror in the hall bathroom. *RILY*—waiting on Hannah's bedside table. *I like the way you smell after PT*—a joke left on her sneakers in the closet. No one had dared move a single one, but Dani had begun to feel like she was avoiding a ghost.

That night, she'd slept at Avery's house, only to wake up and walk down the street to Hannah and Tim's, where everyone was keeping vigil, waiting in pained silence. Emily and her husband, Mark, were in the backyard chasing Jack, who didn't realize that this was not a time to be rambunctious. Inside, Bill Speer had claimed a seat in front of the TV, while Lynn sat at the dining room table, where she drank from a seemingly bottomless mug of coffee. Dani had joined Lynn at the table when Tim's parents finally arrived, their presence bringing with it an even heavier darkness. And even quieter silence.

It had struck Dani on her flight across the Atlantic that in losing their only son, Margaret and Charlie Nesmith had lost their entire family. Hannah had told Dani that after several miscarriages and years of waiting, they'd decided to put their savings into adoption, which brought Tim into their lives. For that reason, they'd put immeasurable pressure on themselves to be perfect parents. Where Tim was strong and vivacious, the Nesmiths were short, round about the middle, and awkward in large social settings. While Tim jumped out of airplanes and lived without fear, his parents seemed to be the worrying type, even before he'd left for war. And though the Nesmiths looked and acted nothing like their son, Dani remembered the thick laughter that came from their bellies at Hannah and Tim's wedding—the joy they found in their son's happiness. That much was never in question. They loved him unconditionally. And now they would grieve him unconditionally, too.

When Margaret and Charlie arrived at the house, there was

nothing to do except welcome the awkwardness with open arms. Dani stood in the kitchen while Margaret Nesmith spread her son's SRP paperwork out on the dining room table. All four adults sat down, staring at the papers, knowing there was nothing to decide. Two still had their child. Two had had theirs ripped away. There were moments you couldn't put into words, and seeing the Nesmiths stare at those papers was enough to send Dani back to bed in the middle of the day. Without making any announcement, she slipped out the front door and walked back to Avery's house.

THAT MORNING, AVERY had left a note for Dani on the kitchen counter.

Headed to work. I'll be done around 6:30 tonight. Text me and let me know how things are going. Tell Wendy I can't wait to see her. —A

Dani tried to answer a few work e-mails from Avery's living room couch, but the thought of discussing Gelhomme's latest commercials made her head spin. Her e-mails sounded garbled and confusing. She couldn't seem to focus or communicate with any clarity. And so, after an hour of effort with little to show for it, she shut her computer.

The clock seemed to move at a snail's pace. Outside, a breeze blew leaves up off the ground and back down again. Over the weekend, Eric Jenkins had raked and bagged all the leaves in the Nesmiths' yard, and Avery's as well. Seated at a round table in the kitchen, looking at the empty street outside Avery's window, Dani tried to think.

With their bullets, insurgents in Iraq hadn't just killed Tim. They'd sent aftershocks to Afghanistan, London, Texas, Maryland, Ohio, North Carolina . . . the list went on and on. One of their classmates stationed in Korea had just sent Dani an e-mail, asking where he could send flowers. People all over the world were dealing with the fact that enough evil existed on the planet to end the life of someone so young, with so much promise. That was the real cost of war, Dani thought. The aftermath.

It was difficult to grieve for Tim, because all Dani could do was think about Hannah. She'd tried to imagine her friend, alone in the desert, hearing the news. Convoying for eight hours with practical strangers. Knowing that somewhere in the world, her husband's body was broken in pieces. In every memory Dani could conjure of Tim, he was running, laughing, moving, sweating, or soaring through the air. How can someone that alive all of a sudden not be alive at all?

And what for?

Dani shut that line of thinking down quickly in her mind. She couldn't let politics cloud what needed to happen first, which was for Hannah to get home and be surrounded by the people who loved her most.

AT ONE O'CLOCK, a white Chrysler minivan pulled into Avery's driveway, saving Dani from her thoughts. Walking out into the cold, Dani waved at the driver and waited for her to unbuckle her seat belt and get out of the van.

Wendy didn't even shut the door behind her. Arms open wide, she fell into Dani's embrace, her body shaking from dry sobs. It was odd to Dani, to feel like the strong one. Wendy had always been the supporter, the cook, the listening ear, the shoulder to cry on. And now, it was Dani who held her up, keeping her from falling to the ground. After wiping her eyes, Wendy and Dani climbed back in her van.

On military installations, the commissary looked exactly like a civilian grocery store, but the products were tax free. That's why you had to have a military ID to get inside, and why Dani was so grateful that Wendy had arrived. Grabbing a grocery cart, Wendy showed her military ID to a security guard at the door and explained that Dani was her guest.

"What should we make?" Wendy asked, when they'd walked inside.

The plan was to stock Hannah's freezer with meals. Crowd pleasers. Things that their families could eat for days or weeks, if need be. They decided not to cook a traditional Thanksgiving, even though the day was fast approaching. Instead, Dani tried to remember which of Wendy's meals Hannah had loved the most.

When they were at West Point, every time they'd gone to the Bennetts' house—whether it was to simply have a break from the barracks or to have a full-on breakdown—Wendy had always had something delicious waiting on the kitchen counter. Lasagnas, spaghetti, fried chicken. Brownies, pies, and apple fritters. That woman only lived in New York because the Army had stationed her there, so even if there was snow outside, there was always warm Southern hospitality inside. "Oh, this old thing?" Wendy would always say when someone complimented her cooking.

She'd follow up with her favorite line from the movie *Steel Magnolias*: "'It's in the "freezes beautifully" section of my cookbook.'"

The memory made Dani smile.

If Dani wanted to cook, she had to grocery-shop from a handwritten list, but Wendy had so much experience in the kitchen, she knew what they needed by heart. Ingredients for lasagna and chili filled Wendy's cart, as they roamed the aisles mindlessly. As they walked side by side, Dani wondered how grief would affect Hannah's appetite. And not just for food. She wondered if Hannah would ever again have an appetite for life.

"So, what's it been like at the house?" Wendy asked. She pulled four cans of diced tomatoes off a shelf and put them in the cart.

Dani sighed. "Really quiet. Tim's parents got here this morning. But there's just nothing to do until Hannah gets back. So it's just . . ."

"Hurry up and wait," Wendy said, finishing Dani's sentence.

Dani nodded. "I can't stop thinking about her. Over there, still waiting. It's got to be excruciating."

"It's hard now. But she's still in shock. The hardest parts will come later. Six weeks from now. Six years."

"I just don't understand how this could happen," Dani said. "It still feels so surreal. It feels like a mistake. Like he's still out there."

"Mark said when Tim was in his class, he was late every single day. That he never completed the reading."

"I could see that," Dani said, and then smiled. She remembered sitting against the trees during Beast, helping him memorize passages from the plebe handbook. "He was so fun. I think that's what I'm worried about. Hannah can be so serious. Tim . . . he always made sure she had fun."

Wendy stopped, looked at her cart. "Oh shoot," she said. "What am I doing? I forgot the stuff for the soup."

"I've been doing that too!" Dani said. "I can't think straight. I feel like I'm walking through a cloud."

"I guess, in a way, you are," Wendy said.

And then they turned the cart around and walked back to the beginning.

A FEW HOURS later, Dani and Wendy unpacked the ingredients they'd purchased at the grocery store and got to work making lasagna in Avery's kitchen. Tomato sauce and cheese were off-limits for Dani's anti-inflammatory diet, but suddenly all those dietary rules didn't seem to matter anymore. They needed to eat. And if she had pain, she had pain. At least she was alive to feel it.

Her knife sliced through a raw onion, pulling sharp tears from her eyes. Meanwhile, Wendy smashed garlic cloves to release them from their paper skins. Dani cut fast and hard, letting the anger and her sadness come through the blade. Soon, the kitchen filled with the savory aroma of minced garlic and onions simmering in oil. Wendy stirred them together with a wooden spoon.

"You know," she said, looking at the little white pieces caramelizing in the heat, "when the girls were little, I used to hate it if Mark got home from work and I hadn't started on dinner. So I would just chop some onion and garlic real quick and sauté it in a pan. That way, when he got home, the house would smell like I was cooking, even if I had no idea what I was going to make yet."

"Nice trick," Dani said.

"I've always found it interesting that when you cook, everything has to be sliced, peeled, or smashed in order to be used. The best flavors come out when the ingredients are broken and exposed to heat."

Dani nodded.

"I think that's true for us, too. Faith isn't really faith until it's beat up and put through a fire. When you're crushed, you feel like you're dying. But you're actually coming to life. When you're broken, that's when the best of you comes out."

As good as that sounded—as true as it felt—it didn't make the sting of the onion in Dani's eyes any less painful.

Later, when the lasagna was baking in the oven, Wendy stood at the sink cleaning dishes.

"What ever happened to that guy Avery was dating?" Wendy asked. "The one that came to Boston?"

"Noah," Dani said. "To be honest, she hasn't said anything about him since I've been here. I don't know."

"And you?" Wendy didn't look up from her work. "Any guys in London I should know about?"

Dani shook her head.

"Well then. When are you going to tell me about the wedding?"

Dani sighed, handed Wendy the dirty cheese grater, and then sat down at Avery's kitchen table. "How much time do you have?"

29

November 23, 2006 // Fort Bragg, North Carolina

On Thanksgiving morning, Avery woke up fully clothed, sleeping next to Dani. It was still dark. The only light in the room came from an orange floodlight outside, cutting through the blinds. After two years of five A.M. wakeup calls for her job with the Army, Avery no longer had the ability to sleep in. She envied Dani's even breathing, the sure sign that she was deep in a REM cycle, and wondered how late she'd stayed up talking with Wendy Bennett, who'd driven down from West Point a few days earlier.

Wendy had rented a hotel room nearby, for her and Mark, who would fly in for the funeral and drive back with his wife. As time went on, more and more family and friends would arrive, Avery knew, filling hotel rooms and the Nesmiths' house. Avery worried that Hannah would feel overwhelmed by the sheer number of people. She worried too that Hannah wouldn't even want to see Avery. It was possible Avery had damaged their relationship beyond repair.

Fearing she might wake Dani with her tossing and turning, Avery rubbed her eyes and slipped out of the room without making a sound.

When the coffee finished brewing, Avery poured herself a cup and went to the living room, where she turned on the television, making sure to keep the volume on low. The *Today* show news team reported from the Upper West Side of New York City, waiting for the start of the Thanksgiving Day Parade. Avery's cell phone rested on the coffee table, conspicuously silent. It had been two weeks since Noah's fiancée had answered his phone. Since then, Avery had cradled her phone in her hands almost constantly, willing herself not to contact him, while simultaneously hoping he'd text or call. If they spoke again, would he try to justify what he'd done? Would he pretend it had never happened? Or would he simply disappear, free to proceed with his life, his marriage, his future, without feeling the consequences?

Over the last few days, as Avery had spent time in Hannah's house, it was impossible not to see the differences between her relationship to Noah and that between Hannah and Tim. Tim had left handwritten notes to Hannah all over their house. Everywhere Avery turned, there were photos of them together— including one on Hannah's bedside table of the couple in Rome. In it, Tim was smiling so wide. He held Hannah up off the ground, like a husband would carry his wife over the threshold of a new house. Avery had taken that picture. And even then, she remembered looking through the lens and feeling a sort of reverent melancholy. Not once had a guy looked at Avery the way Tim looked at Hannah: He was only smiles. Only pride. Only encouragement. And Noah? What was he?

Only absent. Only mystery. Only smoke.

No matter what people said, Avery knew they were wrong about the truth. The truth didn't set you free; it chased you down. It came at you from behind, gained speed, and then eventually overtook you until you could no longer deny its power. Lies might have been fast, but truth had endurance. And it would always outlast the competition.

Avery pulled her knees into her chest and let the tears fall on her cheeks. She held her phone in her hands and opened it and closed it, over and over again, wishing for a call to come through.

She hadn't told Dani about Noah, nor had she told her about the letter she'd received about John Collins's parole. With the money and resources in Collins's family, he would probably have a job on Wall Street in no time at all. It seemed completely unfair to Avery. Why did these men get to get away with their violence? Why did they get to move on from their crimes, while she felt so trapped by them?

"What time is it?"

Dani's groggy voice suddenly broke through Avery's thoughts. Avery turned and saw Dani standing in the dark hallway, rubbing her eyes.

"Six thirty," Avery said.

"My body is so confused. I never wake up this early. But it's like, noon in London."

"I made coffee," Avery said, lifting her mug. "Oh wait. You don't do caffeine anymore. I forgot."

Dani waved off Avery's concern, padded into the kitchen, and returned with a hot mug of her own. She sank into the other side of Avery's couch, under a thick blanket. "I'm not supposed to drink the stuff," she said, taking a long sip. "But I need it right now."

"Did you sleep okay?"

Dani shook her head. "I just keep thinking about her stuck over there."

"They can't keep her there forever." Avery shook her head as tears welled in her eyes. "I doubt she'll even want to see me when she gets back."

"That's not true."

"I flaked on her so many times last year. And for . . . such stupid reasons."

"Hindsight is an unfair standard to use against yourself," Dani replied.

Avery took a deep breath and another sip of coffee. It felt strange to be sitting so close to Dani and yet to feel so far away. A huge wall existed between them, built with bricks of time and distance and things left unsaid. But if Tim's death had taught her anything, it was that you couldn't waste a single moment with the people you love. As much as it was going to hurt, she had to muster the energy and scale that wall.

"I got a letter," Avery said finally, dispassionately. "I got it this summer, actually. I guess I just was trying to pretend it didn't matter."

Dani's eyes grew a few sizes larger. She put her coffee mug down and looked at Avery with concern.

"John Collins got paroled."

"Oh, Avery."

"I sure know how to pick 'em, don't I?" she continued, surprised by the sarcasm in her voice. "Every guy I've ever dated has ended up screwing me over. Or maybe I'm the one screwing myself over. God. Listen to me. Complaining about my life when Hannah—"

"Don't do that," Dani said, this time with force. "Do you hear yourself? Do you ever give yourself a break? A second to breathe? To feel what you're actually feeling before judging yourself so harshly?"

"That's the problem. I don't *feel* anything. I'm completely numb."

Avery felt hot tears form in the backs of her eyes, and soon, they were falling. How did Dani do it? She could always cut straight through the crap and directly to the heart of the matter.

"I don't feel like I deserve to feel upset about my life," Avery admitted. "I should be fine."

"You should *be* what you *are*," said Dani. "Sure. Your husband didn't just get killed. But your *friend* did. And all of this other stuff? The letter? That matters too. You don't have to be so strong all the time."

They sat in silence, letting their coffees go cold.

"You said every guy you've ever dated screwed you over," Dani said, disturbing the quiet. She let the statement linger in the air, without turning it into a question. But the subtext was clear.

Avery chewed on her cheeks. It was so complicated. Ever since she was a little girl, she'd learned that the only way to survive life was to suck it up. Hold it together. Get the grades. Earn the stripes. Go faster than anyone else, and never let them see you cry. She'd trained herself to be harder than she really was and couldn't fathom opening the box in which she'd carefully packed away her grief. Her weakness. If she opened it, she was pretty sure it would swallow her whole.

"He's engaged."

"You're joking."

"You and Hannah, last Thanksgiving . . . you tried to tell me. And I wouldn't listen. I didn't want to see what was right in front of me."

"We thought he was *aloof*," said Dani. "We didn't think he was *engaged*."

"He never took me to his place. Never introduced me to any of his friends. I was so blind." Avery shook her head and wiped her eyes with the sides of her forefingers. "And you know the worst part about it? That girl is going to *marry him*. I'm sure he's just groveling at her feet, telling her it was all some huge mistake. As if I was some seductress that pulled him into my web. But we were together for *a year*. He talked about buying us a *house*, Dani."

"He met your family!"

"He met my family!" Avery repeated, groaning at the thought of having to tell her mother.

"How did you find out?" asked Dani.

"I called him and his fiancée answered his phone," said Avery. "I think she found a way to unlock his phone. She said she'd read all of our texts. I haven't heard from him since." She laid her head in Dani's lap and let her friend stroke her hair. On the television, all the Macy's Thanksgiving Day Parade balloons floated above brownstones, ready for their march down Sixth Avenue.

"You know, you're not the only one that's made mistakes," Dani said after some time had passed. "I was so afraid of losing Locke as a friend, I never took the risk to tell him how I really felt, until it was too late."

"The wedding," Avery said, feeling herself cringe. She sat up and put her face in her hands. "Oh, Dani, I didn't even ask how it went."

"It's okay. It was hard, you know? Seeing him with her. And she's so nice," Dani said with a roll of her eyes. "Her dad works at the Citadel, so it was this whole big Southern wedding, which was just weird, seeing him marry someone so white, and all the things that come with that. I read scripture at the ceremony."

"No you didn't."

"I did," said Dani. "In a gorgeous gown, of course. I looked great. But I felt terrible. I just wished I could go back and do it all over again."

"What would you do differently?"

"I wouldn't be so afraid." Dani paused. "As a woman, you don't want to be the one that makes the first move. But now I realize if I had, I could have gotten it over with a long time ago. I could have saved myself a lot of pain."

"Is that the point?" Avery said. "Saving ourselves from pain?"

"I guess not."

"You did the best you could. Maybe deep down, you knew he wasn't the right one. And so you just let it play out. You can't fault yourself for that."

"And you can't fault yourself for believing Noah."

"Yes I can," Avery said. "I mean, thanks. But I'm realizing now, I can't keep blaming everyone else, like I'm some kind of victim. With Noah, I knew there were red flags; I just pretended they weren't there. I *wanted* to believe him. That was my choice. And I have to own that, or else I'm going to keep doing the same thing over and over again. I deserve better than to dupe myself into a relationship simply because I don't want to be alone."

Dani raised her eyebrows and nodded slowly, as if she was impressed.

"Dang, Avery," she said. "Did you just have a breakthough?"

"Yeah. Maybe I did."

"You know we can't talk about this stuff with Hannah," Dani added. "When she gets home."

"Oh my God, of course not," said Avery.

"We have to just put all this aside and focus on caring for her. She's going to be inundated with people. But you and me, we can be her buffer."

Avery sighed, picking up her coffee mug and feeling the cold porcelain in her hand. She needed a refill.

"I just can't believe she's still not home."

30

November 27, 2006 // Fayetteville Regional Airport

Twelve days after learning that Tim had been killed, Hannah felt the lurch of the airplane as its wheels touched down in Fayetteville. After begging him for mercy, LTC Williams had finally put her on a flight from Kuwait to Germany. Then she'd taken three commercial flights—Germany to New York, New York to Atlanta, Atlanta to Fayetteville.

While the final plane taxied up to the gate, a stewardess reminded the passengers that the seat belt sign was still on and not to move from their seats. The man seated next to Hannah pulled out his cell phone and turned it on. A woman a few rows ahead reapplied her lipstick, blood red. The cabin grew hot and stuffy as passengers donned their jackets and scarves, preparing to battle the cold outside. Tim would never get another winter, Hannah realized. He wouldn't be there to celebrate another Christmas or his birthday or even go on that trip to Hawaii they'd planned to take when their deployments were over. Every realization was a new death. He died a million times a day in her mind.

Pulling her camouflage rucksack down from the overhead compartment, Hannah found her tiny flip phone inside, powered off. Normally, after a long flight, she would have immediately shot off a few text messages to tell her family that she'd arrived. But she had no desire to turn it on. It only brought bad news, thin apologies, and people's *thoughts and prayers,* which, to Hannah, felt like a really poor response to someone's life ending. She was grateful in some ways that people cared enough to reach out. But she couldn't text back, *I don't want your prayers. I want Tim back.* So she'd stopped looking at her phone altogether.

Finally, when the flight attendant at the front of the cabin opened the airplane door, the passengers filled the aisle, trapped in a long line of anticipation, eager to get off the plane and back to the people they loved. The cabin was airless and all the energy pushed forward, though people weren't moving at all. Hannah's body surrendered to a cold sweat.

"Thank you for your service," said the woman with red lips. "I'm sure you're glad to be home."

Hannah stared at the woman with grotesque horror and felt a surge of bile in her throat. She fought the urge to scream. The woman's words were like sandpaper over an open wound. Hannah's neck turned red, and she touched her forehead with her hand. It was clammy. She saw the people at the front of the plane shuffling out, but she still couldn't move.

She didn't know it was going to feel like this. Like every moment that passed was a step deeper into grief. She wanted to be walking straight. Instead, every step forward felt like a step down.

Eventually, the plane cleared and Hannah made her way through the terminal. It had been ten days of this. Ten days of moving, waiting, and remembering, with nowhere to go where Tim wasn't dead. *Dead.* The word had no meaning anymore; she'd thought it too many times.

Her soldiers had convoyed to the next building site in Afghanistan without her. She didn't care. Grief had filled her with a kind of numbness she'd never experienced before. She felt either far too much and wanted to hold back, or far too little and wondered why she couldn't muster any emotion. Most of all, she was tired and hungry and angry at herself for being tired and hungry. How could she eat when Tim would never get to taste ice cream or bite into a peach ever again? How could she sleep when Tim's eyes had been shut forever? She didn't want to live in a world he wasn't in. She didn't want to go to sleep and add another day to the days he'd been gone. Someday, Hannah thought, she would have more days without him than the days she'd had with him.

And just like that, he died again.

EVENTUALLY, SHE FOUND herself at the top of an escalator, with the sign for baggage claim pointing down. She took a deep breath, adjusted her backpack, and stepped on the moving staircase.

They waited at the bottom of the escalator. Her mother, wearing a gray turtleneck. Her father, standing tall with his silver mustache, wearing a black half-zip sweater. Emily and Mark, holding a squirming Jack in their arms. Dani and Avery, one in a leather jacket, the other in uniform. Hannah buried her face in her father's shoulder.

"You're home, sweetie," said Bill. "You're home."

They hugged quietly for a long time.

31

November 28, 2006 // Fort Bragg, North Carolina

The house was quiet early the next morning, when Dani heard the doorbell ring. She pulled on a pair of black sweatpants and stepped into the hallway, carefully tiptoeing around Hannah's father, who'd slept on a pile of blankets right outside Hannah's door. Hannah's neighbor, Michelle Jenkins, had brought over a spare air mattress, and Dani and Avery had blown it up in the upstairs office, sleeping next to unpacked boxes of books. Avery had already left for work, and even though it was ten A.M., no one had made the coffee. No one had dared wake Hannah up.

Dani was certain she would never forget the way Hannah had looked when she'd moved slowly down that escalator at the airport. Her face appeared ghost white. Her eyes bulged, her skin pulled taut with fear. Grief had aged her, and she looked sixty years old—even her hair looked tinged with gray. When they'd arrived back at the house, Hannah had walked straight to their bedroom, their closet, where she'd pulled a pile of his clothes to her face. Dani and Avery had waited outside the door, sitting in the hall. After hours of crying, Hannah had crawled into the bed, laid her head on his shirts, and finally fell asleep.

Downstairs, Dani opened Hannah's front door, just as a man in uniform reached to ring the doorbell again.

"Mrs. Nesmith?" the man asked. The man had brown eyes, dark brown hair, and a slightly Hispanic accent. He wore an Army combat uniform and held a stack of binders under his arm.

"She's upstairs," Dani explained. "Can I help you?"

"I'm Captain Huerta," he said, offering his hand to shake Dani's. "Mrs. Nesmith's casualty assistance officer." He checked his watch. "We had an appointment at ten. Do you mind if I come in?"

Ten minutes later, having rustled Hannah out of her bed, Dani sat next to her at the dining room table. Margaret Nesmith had arrived just after Captain Huerta, and seeing one another for the first time, she and Hannah embraced while the rest of them looked on in silence, willing themselves invisible. Dani knew she wasn't family—in some ways she didn't have a right to sit at this table. But Hannah had asked Dani to stay by her side, and now she was grateful she'd agreed. Seated on the same side of the table as Captain Huerta, Margaret Nesmith wore her dark hair in a low ponytail. Like Hannah's, her face and lips were the color of the third casket Captain Huerta had offered as an option: eggshell white.

Hannah held the binder full of pictures of caskets in her hands. One page displayed a cherrywood box, and the next page, black onyx. She flipped through the pages blankly, like she couldn't see anything at all.

Dani stared from the binder up to the face of Captain Huerta seated across from them. She was grateful that he hadn't tried to hurry Hannah along, although Dani could tell from the other binders in his bag that there were many other decisions to be made. Decisions no twenty-four-year-old should ever have to make. Choosing the coffin. Choosing the flowers. A location for the burial. Hannah looked at Dani, her eyes pleading for help.

"I think this one is beautiful," Dani said, pointing to an all-wood casket near the front.

Tim's mother lifted her chin to see. Dani turned the binder so she could see it more directly. "I like that," Margaret said. "It's classic. Like Tim."

Dani watched Hannah tense up at that statement, and knew exactly why. Tim wasn't *classic*. In Hannah's eyes, he was wild and willing to break the rules and so different from the parents who'd raised him. But Dani could see that all the fight had gone out of her.

"Okay." Hannah pushed the binder back to Captain Huerta. "We'll go with that one."

Dani watched her take a sip of water and place the glass back on the coaster. Every motion slow, purposeful, and pained.

"Can I ask a question?" Margaret Nesmith began, her voice a respectful whisper. Her eyes filled with tears and she wiped a tissue under her nose. "Where is he? Where have they taken him?"

The question hung in the air for several moments, awkward

and cumbersome, like a piece of furniture too large to fit through a door. Dani saw Hannah clench her jaw.

"Your son's remains are at the mortuary," Captain Huerta explained. "His remains are viewable for identification purposes only. That's something we'll need to schedule for you, Hannah. But more importantly, right now, we need to choose a date for the funeral. Do you have a day in mind?"

"December fifth." Hannah and her mother-in-law said it at the same time. He nodded at both of them, then wrote down the date.

"And location?"

"Springfield," Tim's mother answered. "Maryland. Our hometown."

A moment of silence passed, full of awkwardness and tension as thick as fog. Dani turned to Hannah. It was time for her friend to break this next piece of news. Last night, Hannah had told Dani that she didn't want Tim to be buried in Maryland. The only thing she'd decided about the funeral—the only thing Hannah seemed to care about at all—was that it took place where Tim would have wanted it to be.

"Actually, Margaret, we're waiting to hear back from Arlington National Cemetery," Dani explained, speaking on Hannah's behalf.

The elder Mrs. Nesmith looked confused and sad, her blue eyes swimming. "Hannah, we have a family plot in Maryland. We've already made arrangements."

Captain Huerta closed his binder. "Perhaps that's enough decision making for one day."

SEVERAL HOURS LATER, Dani sat in the living room, quietly listening to the terse conversation happening in the kitchen. She'd texted Wendy earlier that it wasn't a good time to come over, but that if she and Mark had any connections at Arlington National Cemetery, they'd appreciate their making some calls. Dani had asked Emily to write Tim's obituary and had called Eric to see if he could help make a list of the forms that Hannah would have to fill out for Tim's life insurance to kick in. The amount of bureaucracy that came after a death was enough to make your head spin. Dani wanted to shield Hannah from as much of that as possible.

"Maybe this isn't the best time to have this conversation," Hannah's mother was saying in the kitchen.

Tim's mother tried to whisper, but her voice came out louder than she'd likely intended. "Well, when *is* the best time? He's been gone for two weeks and I think—"

"Well, Margaret, Hannah . . . she just got home," said Lynn, trying to tread lightly.

When Dani opened her eyes, Avery had walked into the room, holding her keys. She'd taken the second half of the day off and had arrived back from work.

"I'm thinking we should take Hannah on a drive," Avery said quietly.

"I couldn't agree more," Dani replied. And with that, the two of them called Hannah out of the kitchen, and led her out the door, the banner still hanging from the ceiling behind them. *Welcome Home.*

THE WEATHER WAS unseasonably warm for late November. As they drove off post, the road shrank to two lanes and the scenery morphed from strip malls to cotton fields. The plants had dried into dark brown stalks, and some of them still held bright white bulbs of cotton, the ones the harvesting machines had missed. Dani looked out the passenger-side window. Every few minutes she heard Hannah sigh, as if she had to remember to keep breathing.

It should have been me. I want it to be me. Those were the words that Hannah had sobbed into her pillow the night before. And she was being serious. Dani had never sat with someone in so much pain for so many hours. And while she sat there, listening to her friend cry, all she could do was listen. Tim's life wasn't the only one that had ended. The life Hannah was going to have, the children she was going to raise—all of that had ended, too. Like they'd come to a fork in the road with God in the center. He'd pointed Tim and Hannah in separate directions, their momentary love lost forever.

Avery pulled the car off to the side of the road, under a canopy of large oak trees.

"Let's just stop here," Avery said, putting the Honda Civic in park. "I have no idea where I'm going anyway."

They all opened their doors and started walking along a gravel road, surrounded on both sides by fields of cotton. Hannah was wearing one of Tim's old sweatshirts. She looked so young, Dani thought. Her hair was bleached nearly as blond as Avery's from all the days she'd spent under the desert sun. Somewhere buried below the sadness, Dani knew, the old Hannah was still there.

Despite the sorrow, there was still a clearness in her eyes. Dani looked around and started to chuckle.

"What?" Avery said, turning to look at her.

"This is where you take me?" Dani laughed. Looking at Hannah, Dani whispered dramatically, "Did she bring me out here on purpose?"

Avery looked at Hannah with furrowed eyebrows. "What?" she asked. "What did I do?"

"You take us out of the house to cheer us up, and *this* is where you take me?" Dani said, putting a hand on her chest in disbelief. "Taking me on a walk through a cotton field? All you white people! Should have known all along."

Avery started laughing and so did Hannah. Dani, feeling the momentum of their release, frolicked through the cotton field, bending over and inspecting each plant for blooms. She stuck her butt up high into the air.

"Do you want me to start picking? Is that what you guys brought me out here to do?"

Deep in the brush of one plant, she found a white puff, covered over with leaves. She held it up in the air and then threw it at Avery, who ducked, unnecessarily. The cotton flew only a few inches from Dani's body. The laughter was real and deep, and seeing Hannah smile for the first time since she'd arrived back home touched a place inside Dani's heart that hadn't moved in a long time.

"Ahhhh, my gosh," Avery sighed, grabbing her cheeks. "I've missed you girls."

"Bringing me out here to pick cotton. As if that's gonna cheer me up," Dani said, but her words were cut short when the phone in Hannah's jean pocket started to ring.

Hannah held it in her hand as though she were trying to compute a difficult math problem. She walked over and handed it to Dani. It had been this way ever since Hannah had arrived home a few days earlier. She couldn't deal with people calling to offer their sympathy. She didn't know what to tell them when they asked how they could help. So, she either ignored the calls or passed the phone to someone else to answer.

Dani couldn't blame her. In the week since she'd left London, she'd received more than fifty work e-mails, none of which she'd had time or energy to answer. What did it matter now if Gel-homme sold thirty million or forty million razors? If life was this short, Dani wasn't sure that she could spend hers in an office with Laura Klein. How could she go back to London and care about a commercial or a digital banner ad ever again? How could she go back to making money but no impact in the world?

Standing in a field of cotton, thinking about how her ancestors had fought to free her from this place, she realized that she couldn't repay their sacrifices with a purposeless life. It was clear to Dani that God had sent her to West Point so that she could know these women. So she would be right here, right now. Beyond that, nothing was certain.

Dani took the phone from Hannah's hands and answered the call.

"Hello? Yes. . . . Okay. . . . Yes, sir. Thank you, sir."

After the call ended, Dani held the phone in her hand like she'd just spoken to a ghost.

"That was Arlington," she choked out. "They only have one opening in the next six months."

The whites of Hannah's eyes were whiter than the cotton in the field, her irises bluer than the sky. Dani couldn't bear to see her friend bracing for disappointment, but there, in that moment, she saw Hannah's shoulders fall.

Avery stepped closer and put her hand on Hannah's shoulder. "Oh, Hannah, I'm so sorry."

"No. The opening . . . ," Dani replied, her eyes welling with tears. "The opening they have is December fifth. He said we could have it."

32

The Saturday before the funeral, Avery walked down to Hannah's house at noon with her fingers wrapped in the sleeves of the same sweater she'd worn the night Noah picked her up for their very first date. Could you call it a date if the person picking you up was engaged to someone else? Could you grieve a relationship that should never have even happened?

Her sadness about Noah paled in comparison to what Hannah was experiencing. And for that reason, Avery was grateful for her proximity to Hannah's sorrow. The sheer size of the mountain Hannah had to climb overshadowed the hills of Avery's life. When you allowed yourself to enter someone else's trauma, there were so many benefits: a righted perspective, a deeper sense of friendship, a holy devotion to the sacredness of now. Avery hadn't gone running once since Hannah had returned home. At the moment, nothing seemed more important than being present and available for her friend.

The temperature had fallen overnight to below freezing but was supposed to climb into the high forties by midday. Tree branches, bare and gray, sliced through the sky like witches' fingers. She shivered. Emily had agreed to go to the mall with Dani to find Hannah something to wear to the funeral, which left Avery to volunteer for a much different job. She didn't feel ready.

Hannah placed herself heavily in the passenger seat of Avery's beat-up Honda Civic. Tim's parents sat in the back, and the four of them drove across Fort Bragg to a redbrick building near the hospital. When they'd walked through that cotton field a few days ago, Hannah's face had momentarily regained its color— red cheeks, dimpled like God had touched her when her skin was soft as dough. But as they drove, Avery could tell that a tsunami of grief had wiped her out again. Margaret reached her hand around the headrest to rub Hannah's shoulder, but she pinched her shoulders up by her ears, refusing to accept the touch.

"Are you sure you want to do this, Hannah?" Margaret asked once they'd parked.

"I don't have a choice," she said dismally. "I have to see him. Otherwise . . . I—I just have to."

"I'm going to go in with Hannah first," Avery said, hoping she wasn't overstepping. But Hannah looked back at her with gratitude, like she'd just saved her life. "Captain Huerta said there's a waiting room. I'll send him to get you after."

"I hope it will give you some closure," Tim's father said. "Even just a little."

The night before, Avery and Dani had slept on the floor next to Hannah's bed. Every few hours, they would wake up and find Hannah in the bathroom, or on the floor, or in the closet. She kept saying the same thing over and over again, every time they helped her back into bed: "*If he's really gone, wouldn't I feel it? Why don't I feel it?*"

Avery felt her breath catch as they stared at the front doors of the mortuary. She couldn't imagine what Hannah was feeling, knowing that in just a few moments, she would walk inside that building and see the lifeless body of her husband.

Avery reached for Hannah's hand.

"Are you ready?" Avery said. Hannah's eyes welled with tears and she nodded, thankful and brave. In that moment, Avery was certain she'd never seen a more beautiful woman. Magazines airbrushed celebrities. Television romanticized relationships. They showed sex and flirtation and forbidden moments of passion. But they never showed this. This love without makeup and without pretense. This love that forgives. This broken gray bravery in the face of loss. And that was part of love too. To be willing to see it die.

Tim's parents found the waiting room, while Avery and Hannah walked down a hallway lit by fluorescent lights. With each step, Hannah's breathing grew more irregular, her grip on the silver cross around her neck more intense. At the front desk, a woman asked Hannah and Avery to show their military IDs, then pointed them to the elevator.

A momentary loss of gravity filled Avery's stomach as the elevator ascended. When the elevator doors opened, they walked down another hallway, to Captain Huerta's office. He navigated them through a maze of hallways to a heavy door that required his fingerprint to open. And then, he unlocked a smaller door with a key. Inside that room was a closed casket made of dark stained wood. *Classic.* Just like Hannah.

"Take your time," said Captain Huerta, closing the door behind them.

Now it was Avery's breathing that grew fast and shallow. Hannah took three steps forward. Several hot tears streamed down her cheeks, one after another, and her cries sounded like whimpers, caught far in the back of her throat. As Hannah lifted the casket lid, Avery tilted her chin down, wishing she could melt into the walls and disappear. But when Hannah collapsed on the side of the casket, sobbing loudly at her husband's side, Avery rushed over to hold her steady.

"It's okay," Avery said, though she wasn't sure she believed that was true.

Holding Hannah's broad shoulders, Avery let her eyes wander to the open casket. She held her breath, hoping to see what she'd always seen in the movies. A perfect Tim, quiet and at peace.

But the man in the casket was a shadow of the Tim she'd once known. His hair was the same dark brown; his nose held the same straight line. But his lips were a stiff shade of blue. His face was ashen, misshapen. The right ear seemed larger than it ought to be. And his eyes were closed and sewn shut—so shut, it almost seemed as if he were clenching his eyes closed. She found herself willing him to wake up, to shake and bring the color back to his face. But he stayed perfectly, tragically still. Avery fought her own breakdown so she could keep holding Hannah up. The green service uniform had his *NESMITH* nameplate above the right pocket, but aside from that, there was nothing left of the man she'd known. His spirit was gone. Only his body had been left behind.

Breathless, Avery walked Hannah toward the door, where there were two chairs waiting for them to sit.

"It's okay," Avery said, stroking Hannah's back. "It's over. You did it."

"It's not him," Hannah cried. "Tell me it's not him."

33

December 5, 2006 // Arlington National Cemetery,
Arlington, Virginia

Eight officers stepped up to a black hearse in two rows. They wore dress blue uniforms: dark jackets, light blue pants with a golden stripe down the side. The bills of their caps and the shine of their shoes reflected a gray sky. A carriage waited just ahead of the hearse, with seven dark horses standing perfectly still. This, Hannah knew, would go slowly.

And that was what she wanted. That was what Tim deserved. To have the slowest funeral procession ever recorded. For years to pass and the grieving to never end.

On the opposite side of the road, a full military band raised their instruments and seven riflemen raised their guns. The band began to play a hymn as one of the eight officers walked between the two rows toward the back of the hearse. Hannah looked through them, beyond them, feeling a cold gust of wind cross her cheek. She wore a brand-new dress—something Dani and Emily had picked out at a department store—but because the weather was threatening snow, she'd had to put on her down jacket and a scarf. She'd refused to wear sunglasses and hadn't put on mascara either. Her eyes were unadorned and looked tired, but at least they were still open.

Grief unimaginable coursed through her veins with every slow, painful step. They removed Tim's casket from the vehicle with exacting precision, as though they wanted to give his widow time to process each moment of the end. In unison, all eight officers stepped away from the hearse. They took another step away. Then another. And soon, the casket had turned several degrees, until it pointed toward the band. The American flag of the color guard waved in the breeze just behind the instruments.

There were no tears in Hannah's eyes, but she held a handkerchief in her hand just the same. Wendy Bennett had sewn a band of lace around a square of delicate white fabric and had given it to Hannah a few days ago, when she stopped by the house to see her for the first time. Knowing Hannah had been inundated with decisions and visitors, Wendy had waited in the wings, finishing the cooking that she and Dani had started, picking up people from the airport, and probably praying. It was an unselfish person that could arrive at a funeral and serve without expecting a single thing from the grieving widow. It was strange to see Wendy, just as it had been strange to see every other extended family member and old friend arrive in Virginia. Hannah still couldn't wrap her mind around the fact that they were really here for her—they were here because Tim had really died. But at least nothing hurtful had come out of Wendy's mouth. Hannah's grandparents and cousins felt they needed to comfort her with thin platitudes: *Everything happens for a reason; You're so brave; God has a plan.* Their words grated on Hannah. She was grateful they'd come but wished they would leave her alone. For some reason, it was different with Wendy. Wendy's service, with no strings attached, felt like real comfort. The dichotomy of her emotions was something she'd have to dissect another time. For now, she gripped the handkerchief, thankful for its presence in her hand.

The sound of the officers' shoes hitting pavement filled the air. When they reached the horse-drawn carriage, the men lifted the casket, then slowly moved it from their hands to the platform on four spoked wheels. With the casket secured, the horses began their steady, melodic walk to the grave, as if coaxed by the wind.

Hannah followed twenty-one paces behind the carriage, taking in the sights and the smells of the cemetery. She kept reminding herself that this wasn't a dream. That her husband was in that casket, being carried by those horses, to a grave that would bear his name. Hannah couldn't take it all in. The beauty of this place. The deliberate honor the officers were showing her family. The police escort that had shut down the Beltway for their procession to Arlington National Cemetery. The hundreds of souls that followed her up this hill. Mark and Wendy Bennett. Locke's new wife. Every basketball teammate she'd ever had—including Sarah Goodrich, who'd flown in all the way from Hawaii. There were old professors, Tim's parachuting team, and hundreds of others she hadn't had time to see or greet. Every step they took was sacred. *Tim would have wanted it this way,* she knew. *He deserved it this way.*

When they reached the graveside, Hannah lowered herself into a foldout chair, trembling. If it hadn't been for the birds, the hushed sniffles, and the phantom breeze, it would have been completely silent.

Seated in the cold, the image of that stretched, strange face in the casket resurfaced in Hannah's mind, and she clenched her eyes closed. She didn't want to remember Tim that way. Recalling a different memory, her mind expelled the image of Tim in the casket and replaced it with his smile as he stood at the center of Cullum Hall.

That night, their senior year at West Point, the doors had been propped open by two large lanterns, flickering against the darkness. When Hannah passed through the entrance, a glowing line of candles had directed her path through the darkened building to a wooden door. The ballroom was behind that door—the place where she and Tim had first danced, awkward, bumbling, and happy. Nervous, her hands shaking, Hannah had reached for the metal handle, pulled the door open, then burst into tears.

Tim stood at the center of the room, dressed in jeans and a white polo shirt, surrounded by hundreds of candles, dancing their golden light against the walls. Yellow rose petals had been strewn across the floor, lining a curved path between them. She walked across the petals slowly, her hands clasped over her mouth, in shock. She knew what this meant, and yet, she couldn't believe it was true. He wanted her. *Forever.*

He'd had tears in his eyes when she reached him. "Hannah," he said calmly. "You are beautiful, inside and out. You are smart and courageous and strong. You are forgiving and kind. And patient—Lord knows you're patient. You love your friends so deeply and I've been the grateful recipient of that love, even when I didn't deserve it. I've loved you for the last three years, but if you'll let me, I want to love you for the rest of my life."

He'd lowered down to one knee, pulled out a small box, and before he could even ask the question, Hannah was laughing and trembling, down on her knees right next to him.

"Yes," Hannah had said, wrapping her hands around his face. "Yes!"

He'd opened the box, slipped the platinum ring around her finger, just as the door to the ballroom opened again. Before she could turn to see what was happening, Dani and Avery had run up to scream and jump and hug her, as if they'd been listening with their ears pressed against the door. Then Hannah's family walked in—her parents, Emily and her husband, her grandparents. Mark and Wendy. All of Tim's friends from the parachuting team. Everyone filed in, and without hesitation, they all were dancing and hugging and celebrating. Unselfishly, Tim had known that she would want to share that moment with everyone she loved most. Turning back to look at him, she'd seen joy in his eyes, as he watched her relish her moment as the center of attention.

Now all those people were gathered here again, for such a different purpose. The memory ended and she stared ahead at the gray sky, surrounded by darkness, listening to the sound of her own breathing. He was gone. There was nothing she could do to undo what had been done. There was no rewind button, no do-overs. Overwhelmed and letting the tears fall quietly, she tried to picture his face as she'd dreamed it: lit by candles, full of joy. Instead of how she'd seen it in the morgue. It was a battle she knew she'd have to fight for the rest of her life.

Around her, hundreds of white tombstones snaked through the grass, rows and rows of lost sons and daughters. It struck her then that as soon as she walked away, Tim's tombstone would become anonymous to the visitors who walked these grounds every day. Her husband. Her philosopher. Her lover. Her friend. A striking visual. Another tomb of another unknown soldier.

A line of seven soldiers shattered the noiselessness, cocking their rifles. All seven pointed their guns at an angle, then fired, sending a violent burst of gunpowder and smoke into the sky.

A second round of shots was fired.

Then a third.

All three volleys from all seven guns emitted a sour, metallic odor. Then the smoke wafted away.

A lone officer under a canopy of red leaves raised his trumpet. He played taps. The song of a long, hard day of work, and a well-earned night of rest. Two sluggish and lonely stanzas, ending in one echoing note of finality. Then everything was quiet again.

She wanted to stop time and hold on to all of the memories, because the greatest injustice was that those memories would fade into sepia tones. Her brain wouldn't remember what her heart had seen. Not perfectly. Not in full color. He was gone, and soon time would rob her of what little she had left.

The men raised the American flag that had been draped over the casket, then began a choreographed and unhurried dance, passing hand over gloved hand, end over end, folding the flag thirteen times until it became a triangle of stars. Then the eight honor guards moved the triangle slowly through the air down the middle of the casket—it floated—until it was pressed firmly into the hands of an officer at the head of the grave.

Turning, he took four deliberate steps and bowed before Hannah with one knee on the grass. He raised the folded flag up, offering it to her as a gift.

How many days earlier had she been kneeling in the dirt, offering a soccer ball to a young boy, hoping he would believe the words that were coming out of her mouth? A year? A decade? The boy had spit on her shoulder. He didn't have the strength to accept a gift, knowing that gift had been tainted. Hannah looked at the flag and had the same dismal thought. She didn't want the flag. She wanted Tim.

"On behalf of the president of the United States, the United States Army, and a grateful nation, please accept this flag as a symbol of our appreciation for your loved one's honorable and faithful service," he said.

Placing one trembling hand on top of the flag and another on the bottom, Hannah received it from this man who wanted nothing more than to soothe her pain. Did he know he was making it worse?

Hannah didn't yell, holding her hands up to the sky, screaming at this injustice. She held the flag in her lap and did her duty to hold her emotions in check. Just a little bit longer. A single tear fell from her cheek as they lowered his casket into the ground.

He would never come back to her. And though she was surrounded by more than five hundred people who loved her, Hannah knew the truth.

She was alone.

December 5, 2006 // Arlington, Virginia

An hour after the reception started, the line to speak with Hannah hadn't shrunk at all. Dani went to the table of refreshments, picked up three water bottles, and walked them over to Hannah and Tim's parents, who accepted them with gratitude.

"The first time I met Tim . . ."

"God has a plan for all of this . . ."

"You're so strong . . ."

Hannah nodded, smiled when she could, and continually said the same words over and over again. "*Thank you. Thank you for coming.*"

Eventually, Dani made her way to a round table toward the middle of the reception hall. All of the tables were covered with white tablecloths and had a small flower arrangement at the center. Lilies and eucalyptus. One of the many choices Dani had made out of Captain Huerta's binders, when Hannah had lost the ability to make any more decisions. In the foyer, Dani could see Avery collecting coats from guests filing through the entrance. Dressed in a black coat and gray dress, Amanda Coleman had just arrived. It surprised Dani to see her; Locke had told her in an e-mail that he wasn't going to be able to make it to the funeral, because his unit was leaving for a two-week training in the field that he couldn't miss.

Spotting Dani across the room, Amanda waved. After handing her coat to Avery, she found her way to Dani's side. Her dark brunette hair fell in a single braid down her shoulder, and she hugged Dani tight.

"I only met him that one time, at your house," she said. "But still. I . . . I just can't believe it. You're such a good friend. To come here, all the way from England."

"What else was I going to do?" Dani said.

Amanda pursed her lips together and nodded in understanding.

For a moment, the two women stood in awkward silence. Then they sat down at the table beside them.

"Locke said they had a great time over there, last spring," she said. "That you have a great flat. Notting Hill, right?"

Dani nodded, feeling no desire for small talk.

Amanda looked around the room, then sighed, her eyes falling on Hannah. "How is she doing?"

Dani shook her head, angry that Amanda would ask such an obvious question. *How did Amanda think she was doing?* "She's devastated."

Amanda seemed to let Dani's harsh response sink in before gathering the courage to try again.

"I don't keep up with any of my friends from college anymore," she said. "When I see the way y'all are with each other, it makes me wonder if I had friendships or just . . . proximity."

Dani looked at her, surprised by the insight in her comment.

"I don't know," she said, shaking her head. She chuckled. "Push-ups aren't exactly my forte. But seeing you guys together makes me wonder if I could have done something like West Point. It kind of makes me wish I'd tried." She took a sip of water. "Locke tells so many stories about you. 'Did I tell you about that time Dani and I did this? Or the time that Dani did that?' If I'm honest, sometimes I'm jealous of all those memories you guys have together. I feel like I'll never catch up."

Dani felt a sudden surge of compassion. She'd never considered how it must feel to Amanda to constantly be on the outside. "You will. It'll take time, but you will."

"I guess I should get in line," Amanda said, looking over her shoulder at the long queue of people, waiting to speak to Hannah. She looked back at Dani and squeezed her hand again. "Hannah is really lucky to have a friend like you. So is Locke. And so am I."

AFTER AMANDA LEFT, Dani pulled the BlackBerry out of her pocket and clicked on the small envelope icon. It felt rude, but with the spare moment she had alone, she scanned through the subject lines of 112 unread e-mails. Most of them were junk, but several dozen were work-related. All had gone unread. Unanswered. Near the top of her most recent e-mails, a message from Laura Klein had been marked *urgent* by its sender. It had a little exclamation point at the end of the subject line. She opened it.

From: Laura Klein <laura.klein@egcorporation.com>
Date: December 5, 2006 06:39 AM GMT
To: Dani McNalley <danielle.mcnalley@egcorporation.com>
CC: jim.webb@egcorporation.com, sandra.myers@
egcorporation.com, legal@egcorporation.com
Subject: Re: *URGENT:* Bereavement Leave (!)

Ms. McNalley,

I've been in touch with Jim Webb, Sandra in HR, as well as our team of E & G lawyers, all cc'd here.

At this time you have overspent your allotted leave by six days. You no longer have any sick days, personal days, or bereavement leave available. However, as stated in my previous e-mail dated November 21, and confirmed by an e-mail sent to you from Sandra dated November 26, bereavement leave is a benefit to be reserved for immediate family only, with the presentation of a death certificate, for which, per your e-mail November 20, this current trip does not qualify. Your salary has been reduced for the missed workdays. Someone from Accounting will be in touch with the details.

Please respond immediately with your explanation of this extended absence, and your intended date of return. Please keep all parties above included on the correspondence.

Respectfully,

Laura Klein

Dani felt sick to her stomach. Of all people, Jim Webb would understand why she'd missed so much work. It would take one e-mail to explain to him why she'd left London in such a hurry and why she hadn't been in a rush to get back. Laura's e-mail was a thinly veiled threat and cc'ing Jim was only going to backfire on Laura—not Dani. Plus, in the days since she'd arrived at Fort Bragg, Dani had realized that all that pressure she'd put on herself with work was an illusion. Nothing was that urgent. Most things in life could get postponed, delayed, pushed back.

They were selling razors, for God's sake.

She put the phone on the table in front of her and rubbed her eyes. The thought of getting on a plane to go back to London, only to ride the train to the office every day while Hannah stayed at Fort Bragg, made Dani want to hit her phone with a sledge-hammer.

"Can we join you?"

Dani looked up to see Wendy Bennett standing next to her, followed by her husband, dressed in a gray suit. That was all it took for the tears to start flowing. The welcome scent of Wendy's perfume. The embrace of her arms around Dani's neck. Wendy wore a classic black crepe dress with white pearl earrings. After they'd all hugged and sat down, Wendy looked at the receiving line and shook her head.

"I've never seen so many people," she said. "This is going to go for a while."

Dani nodded, and watched as Wendy's eyes landed on Locke's new wife, who'd joined the end of the line.

"I just met Amanda," Wendy said, looking back on the little sandwiches on her plate. "She seems nice."

"Yep," Dani said. "She is."

"Hannah is going through something unimaginable," Wendy explained, "but that doesn't mean you can't grieve the ways your dreams have shattered, too."

It was difficult to swallow those words. *Your dreams.* What dreams did she even have anymore?

"I know your life hasn't exactly gone the way you'd expected," Wendy continued. "But Hannah is going to be experiencing a lot of loneliness now. A lot of loss. And you understand that pain, more than most people in this room. You know what it feels like for the future to implode. You know what it means to start over."

"That's true," Dani said, wiping her eyes. "I just . . . I don't know how to help her. She's so strong, Wendy. And I . . . I don't know. Everything just feels wrong."

"Of course it feels wrong. That's called life."

"I'm earning all this money. And what for? I'm making all these connections, in a field I never wanted to be in in the first place."

"Your job in London afforded you the chance to be here now, for Hannah. Who else could drop everything for two weeks and set up camp for a friend? And you have to remember. God hasn't forgotten you. He hasn't forgotten Hannah, either. None of this makes sense. But the story isn't over."

A deep sigh came from the depths of Dani's lungs. Tim had touched so many people in his short twenty-four years. It was painfully clear to Dani now that if she died, far fewer people than this would attend her funeral. You only get one chance at life. And Dani was certain now that she couldn't live it behind a computer screen. Not anymore.

"You know what surprises me?" Wendy asked. She looked around the room, then back at Dani. "I don't see *her* here."

"Who?"

"Her," Wendy said, raising an eyebrow.

"Oh," Dani said, then sighed. "It doesn't surprise me at all. She never really knew us."

"I should have done more. I think about it so often. I should have tried to have her fired. But I thought if she found out that I was trying to get her fired she wouldn't let you girls come to our house anymore. I just . . . I didn't want to make things worse than they already were."

"You did plenty," Dani assured her.

After a pause, Wendy leaned across the table. "What happened? I mean, *really?*"

Dani took a sip of her water and smirked. She knew what Wendy was talking about, even if she hadn't said it outright. In the summer of 2004, just a few months after their graduation ceremony, West Point's athletic director had asked for Coach Jankovich's resignation. It made national news. But true to form, Coach Jankovich played it off like she'd received another coaching job and had chosen to leave. West Point didn't correct the error, but Wendy knew better.

"The cult happened," said Dani.

In April 2004, two months before their graduation, Avery, Hannah, and Dani were eating sub sandwiches in Grant Hall when their coach walked through the room, holding her head high like a crane. She'd passed them without saying a single word. Not a hello, not a goodbye. And after she'd gone, the girls had groaned and recounted all the ways she'd failed them over the years.

"Like I said," Avery had said, "if we'd all quit, they would have fired her. A player strike would have made a statement."

"Too bad it's too late for that," Hannah had added.

Dani had set her sandwich down. "What if it's not?"

That night, they'd gone back to Dani's room and written three separate letters, outlining every NCAA infraction, racial slur, personal attack, and poor coaching decision that woman had made. Dani had e-mailed upperclassmen who'd already graduated, requesting that they do the same, and by midnight, she'd received six more letters. It was disloyal, for sure. It even amounted to mutiny—but even Hannah had agreed to participate. They couldn't leave that woman behind to ruin the experience of any more athletes. Female cadets at West Point had it hard enough.

That night, Dani had slipped all nine letters into the mailbox of the commandant's house. Then she'd walked away.

"We didn't know what he'd do with the letters," said Dani, after recounting the tale to Wendy. "But when we heard they fired her over the summer, we knew that he'd listened. She'd always accused me of leading a cult to get her fired. And it turned out, I did."

Wendy sat, mouth agape, taking in the story.

"I think that's the best thing I've heard . . . maybe ever," she said, with a reverent shake of the head. "You girls. You know, it's not the same at West Point without you there. Mark's going to have to retire from the Army eventually. Maybe you can help him with his resume. Is E & G hiring?"

Dani laughed. Imagining Wendy's husband with his military-grade haircut discussing commercials seemed odd in Dani's mind. "I don't think he'd like the culture there all that much."

"Fair enough." Wendy took a sip of water. "You know, while we were talking to Amanda, she mentioned her father works at the Citadel."

"Yeah. I met her dad at their wedding. Nice guy."

"She also mentioned the Citadel is hiring."

"Oh, yeah? Think you guys would like Charleston?"

"Not for us, Dani," Wendy said slyly. She leaned forward and touched Dani's hand. "I hear they're looking for an assistant basketball coach."

35

December 5, 2006 // Arlington, Virginia

Avery stood at the front of the reception hall, smiling somberly at guests as they arrived to pay their respects. She and Emily had been standing in the foyer for an hour, taking people's coats, directing them toward the back of the reception line, which still stretched around three walls of the room. The closet had filled with peacoats, rain slickers, long down jackets, and even a few furs. Every time the door opened, a gust of cold air reminded Avery of the freezing temperature outside. But inside, she could barely breathe, the air was so thick with warmth.

She'd shed silent tears through the entire funeral. Arlington cemetery was a national monument, and watching the honor guard fulfill their duty with such painstaking precision felt like watching a movie of someone else's life. Throughout the procession, the burial, the twenty-one-gun salute, Hannah's face had remained serene. Avery didn't understand it. How could you stay so still in the middle of a hurricane?

While Emily took a few more coats into the closet, Avery turned to see a projector inside showing images of Tim's life. First came a photo of Tim, his cheeks flapping in the wind, mid-free-fall during a skydiving jump. He was giving the camera a big thumbs-up with both rows of teeth fully exposed. That photo faded out while the next faded in: Tim in a hospital bed, his right arm propped up by a sling, the same thumb still pointed in the air. There was a murmur of laughter from the people in the room. That was Tim—happy and fearless, whether flying through the sky or bound to a hospital bed. Over the loudspeaker, a song played that Avery didn't recognize, but she opened herself to absorb the music, though she couldn't make out the words.

Soon, the photo of Tim in the hospital dissolved and was replaced on the screen by a picture from Thanksgiving last year. The photo was crowded with people: Dani's family, Locke and Amanda, Hannah and Tim. Noah and Avery smiled from their position at the center of the photo. He had his arms around her waist. Like a fool, she stood there smiling, unaware of the future. Noah's steel gray eyes cut through the photo and stared straight at Avery across the room.

The sight of Noah sent Avery straight toward the coat closet. A cry came out of her throat, raw and guttural—a wail. Avery stumbled through the closet door, slammed it behind her, and then sobbed, loud and deep, like something in her gut was trying to crawl out of her throat and could only do so if she opened her mouth wide enough. Everyone out there could probably hear her, and so she shoved a row of beautiful coats off the rack and onto the floor, where she fell into the cloth and fur and wool, which muffled her cries. She couldn't begin to feel embarrassed when there was so much else to feel. Decorum didn't matter when compared to despair.

For the first time in many years, Avery thought about Wendy Bennett and a conversation they'd had in her living room. Something about Lazarus. And a prayer. What was it?

The words came to her as if from outside of herself. As if someone else had whispered them into her ear from the past. *Lord, if you had been here, none of this would have happened.* Suddenly, that felt like the most honest, heartfelt prayer she could possibly muster. She repeated those words over and over again until it became the cry of her heart. Where was God when she'd arrived at West Point, only to sit at John Collins's table? Where was God when he broke into their locker room and hid his camera? Where was God when she sat on the witness stand, being berated and called a liar? Where was he then?

And where the hell was he now?

Suddenly, the closet door opened, revealing a petite silhouette, a strand of pearls. Wendy must have seen Avery escape into the closet, because her hands were full of clean tissues that she handed to Avery after closing the door behind her. She was the last person Avery wanted to see, and yet, as Wendy took a seat on the floor beside Avery, she realized she didn't have the energy to pretend anymore.

"I don't really need a sermon right now," Avery said, letting her bitterness hit Wendy hard. She'd expected it to send Wendy out the door as quickly as she'd come in. But to her surprise, Wendy didn't budge.

"Keep screaming," Wendy coached. "You've got to let it out."

"I guess everyone heard me," Avery said, using the tissues Wendy had offered to wipe her eyes. The white fibers went black with smudged mascara.

"You're feeling what everyone is feeling. You're just brave enough to express it."

"How can Hannah be so calm? I just want to hit something. To tear something apart. I'm so angry."

"Hannah will get there. It might just take some time."

"I found out a few weeks ago that John Collins was paroled," Avery admitted. "And then, after that, I found out the guy that I'd been dating for a year was engaged to someone else the whole time.

"And, meanwhile, everyone keeps saying these are supposed to be the best years of our lives. College. Our twenties. But that can't be true! It just can't. And do you want to know the worst part?"

"Tell me the worst part," said Wendy.

"Hannah . . . Hannah has to stand out there smiling at her husband's funeral! And this whole time, I've been coming back into this closet and checking my phone because even though I know he's a liar and horrible, I miss Noah so much. And I just want him to call and tell me that he still loves me, even though I know that's never going to happen. What's wrong with me?"

She looked up at Wendy, waiting for her to give her some Bible lesson, some thinly veiled offer to pray. Avery wished that someone else had come into the closet, because Wendy's green eyes were just too intense. She wanted Wendy to say that *nothing* was wrong, and that it was all Noah's fault, and that Avery deserved better. Instead, Wendy sighed and clasped her hands together on her lap.

"You know, we're not all that different, you and me."

Avery laughed, looking at Wendy's short haircut and patent-leather shoes. "I don't mean to laugh, Wendy, but I highly doubt that."

Wendy raised an eyebrow. "You'd be surprised. I wasn't always married with kids."

Avery paused to consider that. It was odd to try to picture Wendy at twenty-four, but of course, at some point, she had been.

"When I was twenty-six, Mark and I—we were both really struggling. Our marriage was falling apart because I'd realized that he was never going to be enough for me. But I knew that if we got a divorce, I was going to be just as lonely—I'd been with enough men to know that the other guys didn't have what I wanted either."

"And what was it you wanted?"

"That's easy," said Wendy. "I wanted everything. I wanted great sex and movie-grade romance and love and electric connection, twenty-four/seven. I wanted perfection. But it turns out, here on earth, we don't get perfection; we get people."

"And people suck."

"And even the ones that don't suck let us down," said Wendy, her voice softening. "I know Noah hurt you. But you have to know that even the best relationship isn't going to fully give you what you're looking for. Look at Hannah. She had it. And now it's gone. The point of life isn't to quench our thirst, it's to realize we're thirsty for something that we can't find here."

Avery allowed her breathing to slow down. She imagined Hannah standing out there, still smiling, still forced to shake hands with every person who had ever known Tim. Hannah was so gracious and so beautiful in the midst of her pain. And here she was, throwing a tantrum. Like a child.

"How do I go back out there?" Avery said finally.

"With your chin up. You're the bravest one in this room, Avery, because you're actually being honest about how messed up things are. But you can't stay in here forever."

"I can't?" Avery laughed through tears.

"Don't think so."

There was no voice. No angel coming down on the clouds. But in that moment, a quiet peace washed over Avery's body. If Wendy was here, still loving her after that display of insanity, then maybe there really was hope. For the first time in two years, the knot in her stomach unraveled. The tears in her eyes dried up. And suddenly, she found she had the strength to grab Wendy's hand and stand up off the floor. The coats she'd pulled off their hangers were in a pile at their feet. Now she looked at them and laughed.

"Don't worry," Wendy said, pointing to the other side of the closet. "Mine's over there. You didn't ruin it."

One by one, she and Wendy put the coats on hangers and back on the rack.

Maybe this is faith, Avery decided as they worked in silence.

Maybe faith was having the humility to scream at God and the audacity to get up off the floor.

36

December 6, 2006 // Interstate 95

They'd been on the highway for several hours now, riding in silence. Hannah hadn't slept at all the night before. The funeral had completely exhausted her, but when she closed her eyes, all she could see was some imaginary slum in Samarra, Tim's body falling on the body of his soldier, and bullets ripping his insides apart. When Hannah was alone, the gagging set in. She forgot to swallow, and when she did swallow, even the saliva threatened to come back up. There was no place she could get comfortable. Not on the bed. Not on the floor. Not on the balcony overlooking Washington, DC. She'd imagined Lincoln's statue, staring over the reflecting pool, with his words from the Gettysburg Address engraved around him.

We here highly resolve that these dead shall not have died in vain.

What did that even mean?

And who got to decide?

"Do you want to listen to any music?" Avery asked, breaking through Hannah's thoughts. "My CDs are down there on the floor."

Hannah turned to look at Avery, whose voice sounded so distant, it was hard to believe they were in the same car. Avery was in the driver's seat, her hair loose and wavy, like she'd slept on it wet. She offered Hannah a closed-lipped smile. Adrenaline had pumped through Hannah's veins yesterday, enabling her to survive the three-hour receiving line. But now, she had no energy for false smiles. Somewhere in the recesses of her mind, she knew she was grateful for all that Avery had done—paying for her family's flights to Fayetteville, offering to drive to Virginia, taking off work. But those acts of service didn't make up for the ways she'd been a disappointing friend in the last few years. Hannah hated that she was angry, but she didn't have any other emotions to spare. So she looked back out the window.

"Avery, please tell me you've heard of an iPod," Dani said from the back seat. "Get with the times."

"It's not the same," Avery replied. "There's something therapeutic about looking through those CDs. It's the soundtrack to my life."

Mindlessly pulling the heavy leather CD case to her lap, Hannah began to flip through the sleeves, each one holding four CDs to a page. Foo Fighters, *The Colour and the Shape*. Dave Matthews, *Live at Luther College*. Alanis Morissette's *Jagged Little Pill*. Third Eye Blind. Avery had always been a nineties alternative junkie, Hannah knew. Tim loved hip-hop and country. The two most polar-opposite music styles, which he claimed weren't opposites at all. "Rap and country artists sing about life how it is, not how they wish it would be," Tim had said once. "Pop music is shiny. Rap and country are real."

Her mind flashed back suddenly to his dorm room at West Point, when they'd pulled an all-nighter studying. At West Point finals were called "TEEs," short for "term end exams." He'd forced her to listen to the four-CD set of Garth Brooks's greatest hits and pulled her away from her computer to dance—terribly—to "Two of a Kind, Workin' on a Full House." Hannah stopped paging through the binder and put her head between her knees.

As she stared at the dirty floor of Avery's car, Hannah noticed the edge of a letter sticking out of the purse resting next to her feet. She knew she couldn't read it yet. Not in this car, with this little air to breathe. The phone at the bottom of her purse lit up. Someone was calling. She fought the urge to chuck it out the window and watch it get smashed by the tires of the car behind them.

"Sixty more miles," Avery said, placing her hand on Hannah's back. "It's okay. We're almost there."

THE REST OF the afternoon went by in slow motion. Her parents, sister, and nephew went back to a hotel. Hannah's brother-in-law said goodbye after the funeral and headed back to Texas, so he could return to work. Avery and Dani went to the kitchen to pull out another of Wendy's meals from the freezer to defrost. Exhausted from the drive, Hannah told them she needed some time to herself and retreated to her bedroom. *Her* bedroom. The pronouns of her life had changed. She was no longer a we. *Theirs* was now *hers*. *His* was now nothing at all.

After taking a shower, Hannah wrapped herself in a robe and got back in bed, holding Tim's clothes against her body and his letter in her hands. His scent was fading from the fibers of his shirts, she knew, and that made her angry. His words, tucked under the seal of the letter, called to her. Even clean, she felt tainted. Even warm, her body shivered. Even embracing the letter in her hands, her soul resisted.

Before the funeral, she'd walked through the house collecting every Post-it note Tim had left behind. Those he'd written months ago. But the letter he'd written days, maybe even hours before he'd died. It wasn't thick. But it was the last thing she had. For some reason, she felt empty and achy, holding it in her hands. Like if she read it, then he would be really, finally gone. If she left it unopened—even just for a few more minutes, a few more seconds—there would still be more that Tim could say.

She was crying when she slid the pocketknife Tim had left in his bedside table underneath the envelope flap. She didn't want to risk ripping what was inside. The paper unfolded in her hands, light and ethereal, and the date written in the corner crossed her eyes. November 12, 2006. And then she read slowly, trying to take each word in and make it last.

Dear Hannah,

We're leaving tomorrow for what they say will be a ten-day mission, so I'm sitting down to write you this letter, to assure you that I love you. I miss you. And we will speak again soon.

I'm not naive. I believe fully in the training I've done and in my ability to do this job well, but I also know that what we are doing is dangerous and uncertain. But that's just life. There's no guarantee that anyone gets to see tomorrow, and I am no different. My only prayer is that I do well with the days God gives me. I pray the same for you.

If catastrophe strikes here, I will still feel so blessed because I have lived the equivalent of four men's lives in my short twenty-four years on this planet. I owe it all to God, who met me in that tree the day my parachute failed. And to you, Hannah, my best friend, who had patience with me as I learned to love you with everything I had, and not just a part.

I don't pretend to know what the future holds. I imagine us bringing children into the world, sipping wine, breaking bread, and growing old together, using our bodies up until they are sore and bruised and wrinkled and aching. But our joy does not depend on that dream coming true. No matter what happens, we of all people can afford to live fully unafraid because we know these breakable bodies house unbreakable souls.

I know our love can withstand everything that this year will bring. I know we can endure it. Here's a poem for you (I wrote it, don't laugh):

We are an oak tree, planted deep in the soil of love.

The heat comes to batter our branches,

The winter brings its icy burden,

But the oak will never fall.

Though it dies, it will rise to new life when the spring comes
  again.

Remember I love you.

Tim

37

December 9, 2006 // Fort Bragg, North Carolina

Y ou've got to get her out of the house."

Emily stood in front of Dani, bobbing a screaming Jack on her hip. Outside, snow fell and stuck to the ground in thick flakes, adding to the sense that they were trapped. A red bird flew across the yard and landed on a bare tree branch. Dani watched it sit there, undisturbed by the cold.

"To do what?" Dani asked.

"Anything." Clipping Jack into his high chair, Emily placed a bowl of oatmeal on the tray and tested its temperature with her forefinger. "She's got to start experiencing the outside world. You've got to take control, D. Start calling some shots."

"What about a movie?" Avery suggested. She was standing at the stove trying and failing to make eggs over-easy. The yolks both broke.

"I think she'd feel claustrophobic in a movie," said Emily. "Maybe you should just ask her. See what she's up for."

Holding the plate of scrambled eggs, Avery walked upstairs, with Dani close behind. A large box fan whirred on the second-floor landing, which made enough noise so everyone could sleep at night—even if Hannah couldn't. A comforter was still crumpled on the floor beside Hannah's bed, where they'd taken turns sleeping night after night. Dani had finally purchased a one-way ticket back to London, scheduled to leave tomorrow. She hated to think of facing Laura Klein—but life was too precious to waste today worrying about tomorrow. And Emily was right. If this was Dani's last day with Hannah, she needed to make it count.

Stopping at Hannah's door, Dani placed her ear to it carefully. Hearing nothing, she turned the knob and went in. In the soft winter light coming through the window, Hannah looked angelic. She tossed a handful of used tissues into the air, and they fell on the bed like snot-laden snowflakes.

"Look at me," she said. "What a mess."

Dani smiled as she walked into the room. "Yep. You look like hell."

"Let's get you out of the house today," Avery said, handing over the badly prepared eggs. "Get some fresh air. Change of scenery."

Hannah blew her nose, loudly. "To do what?" she said through the tissue.

"One thing at a time," Dani said. "First, shower. I'll pick your outfit."

Dani pulled the covers off Hannah's legs and clapped her hands. "Rise and shine, soldier. We're burning daylight."

While Hannah trudged to the shower, Dani scanned Hannah's closet. Everything carried a memory. Nothing was void of emotion. Choose the wrong outfit, and the whole mission could be thwarted. She considered each piece carefully, then realized they hadn't even decided where they were going.

Ice cream? She considered. *No. It's too cold for that.*

Shopping? No. Too many choices. Too many screaming kids.

Then she thought of it. Grabbing Hannah a pair of stretchy jeans and a black T-shirt, Dani folded them perfectly and topped the stack with a bra and clean underwear.

Whether Hannah liked it or not, they were going to the spa.

HALF AN HOUR later, they arrived at a small strip mall outside of Fort Bragg, where an Asian woman invited them to come in from the cold. The walls inside were white and powder blue and somewhere an electronic fountain trickled water through stones. Dani could see several women with their hands lit by table lamps, getting manicures. All along the right wall, mirrors reflected women getting haircuts. And from the looks of the menu, there were waxing rooms, massage rooms, and a staff of hairdressers on site to cut, color, and style hair. In the back, a row of white chairs sat enthroned behind a row of water basins, where women could get pedicures. Dani pointed in that direction.

"Pedicures," she said to the woman at the front of the spa. "And can we sit together?"

"Sure. Pick color," the woman said, pointing toward a wall of nail polish.

As Avery walked toward the rainbow assortment of colors, Dani noticed Hannah's face contort with emotion.

"No, no, no . . . ," Dani said, grabbing Hannah's shoulders tenderly. "It's okay."

Without a response, Hannah pushed through the salon door, back out into the cold. A bell rang as she exited. Dani motioned to the staff to give them just one minute. Then she and Avery followed Hannah outside.

Dani shivered against the cold. Hannah unwrapped the scarf from her neck, as though it were suffocating her.

"Why did you bring me here?" she said, her eyes wet with tears.

"Maybe it will make you feel better, even just for a few minutes," said Avery.

"Feel better? Feel better?! Avery! I'm never going to feel *better*. TIM DIED. HE DIED."

Hannah collapsed onto a bench and put her head in her hands.

They sat next to her for a long time, watching their breath. Dani knew better than to touch Hannah or to respond too quickly. Sometimes you just needed the truth to linger between you, even if it felt awkward. Even if there were no silver linings.

Hannah finally looked up and locked her blue eyes on Dani's face. "Who do I have to look beautiful for?"

Dani sighed and Avery scooted closer.

"You're so young, Hannah, you have so much life ahead of you," Avery said.

"Oh my God, would you stop?" Hannah shouted, then shook

her head. "Don't talk to me about *my life*. You have no idea. You *weren't there*," she said, turning to Avery. "You were never there when I needed you. Tim was gone all last year, and you left me over and over again. And now what? You just want to pretend like nothing's changed? You know nothing about my life."

Dani was shocked at the anger in Hannah's voice, but in a way, she was also grateful. At least now she could speak her mind without having to tiptoe around everyone, being polite and charming. Death would do that, Dani realized. It would make you speak the truth, even if it was ugly.

Avery's face, rather than looking hurt and defensive, fell in shame and sorrow.

"You're right. Hannah, I'm so sorry. I fucked up. I really did. I let you down. I know that now." Avery turned to look at Dani, as though Hannah's anger confirmed her fear that their relationship was beyond repair. "I love you, Hannah. You know I love you."

"What are you feeling?" Dani said, putting a hand on Hannah's shoulder to calm her. "Explain it to us."

Hannah grabbed her cross necklace, pulled at it, digging a line in her skin that turned red, as if she wanted to rip it off.

"This wasn't how it was supposed to be," she said. "We did everything right. We . . . we did everything we were supposed to do. We waited to have sex until we were married. We went to church. And read the Bible and prayed together. We trusted . . . that . . . God would take care of us. And now . . . what was that even worth?" Looking up to Dani, Hannah's eyes were full of tears. "Take me home. Please. I don't want to do this. I don't have a reason to be beautiful anymore."

"Then do it for *you*," said Avery. Crouching down in front of Hannah, she put both hands on Hannah's knees. "Be beautiful just for you."

"You have millions of guys lining up for you all the time. I had *one. One.* And I lost him."

"You think that's it?" Avery sighed. "I just want to come here to look beautiful for all my thousands of boyfriends?"

"Millions," Dani corrected.

"Hannah." Avery sat down again on the bench. "I haven't told you this because I didn't think it was the right time. But Noah and I broke up. It turns out he was engaged."

That seemed to shock Hannah into sitting up straight. She wiped her nose with her gloved hand. "What? You're kidding. He met your parents!"

"I have never been in love like you and Tim. After everything that happened—I wanted to hate him, but the longer you two were together, the more I realized that I didn't hate him, I hated that I couldn't find what you had. You don't think that makes me want to crawl in a hole and never come out? What y'all had . . . it was . . ."

"Once in a lifetime," Dani said.

They sat outside for a few moments in silence. Hannah shivered and put her scarf back on.

"I'll wax my eyebrows off, okay?" Avery suggested. "Or . . . I'll shave my head. Do you want me to? You know I'll do it."

Hannah rolled her eyes.

"I'd pay to see that," Dani offered, digging in her purse for cash. "Here's a twenty for Avery going all GI Jane."

"Tell me what I can do. It won't make you feel better," Avery said to Hannah. "But maybe it will make you smile. Name it. I'll do it."

"You know she will," Dani said, laughing.

Hannah sat up straight. "Dye your hair."

"You want me to dye my hair?" Avery repeated.

Hannah nodded. "We should all do it."

"All right. You heard the girl," Dani said. Her voice was full of competitive excitement. "Let's move before she changes her mind. Hair dye it is."

DANI SWIVELED BACK and forth in a chair, wearing a black cape snapped around her neck. All three girls faced away from the mirror: Hannah and Avery's heads had been painted in wet, colored goop. Dani's head was covered in aluminum foil. Underneath the wrap, the dye had grown warm and itchy on her scalp. The hairdresser promised it wouldn't do too much permanent damage to Dani's already bone-dry hair, but she honestly didn't care. Hannah was smiling—she'd chosen the colors, keeping her choices a secret from Avery and Dani.

"Just tell me," Avery begged Hannah. "What color did you choose? Please say it's red. I've always wanted to be a redhead."

Hannah smirked, then nodded to the stylists standing in front of them. For the first time since Tim had died, Dani thought she saw a faint glimpse of something like joy in Hannah's eyes. She knew they were all at the end of their ropes, but at least they were hanging on together.

After washing and styling their hair, the stylists waited for their cue from Hannah.

"All right, turn us around," Hannah said. "On the count of three."

"Oh great," Avery moaned. "Here we go."

"One . . . two . . . three!"

HANNAH WALKED OUT of the salon with voluminous hair the color of roasted chestnuts. Dani followed with hair cropped short and bleached platinum. Trailing them, Avery hid behind black sunglasses and a mop of raven-black hair. She looked like a celebrity after a particularly rough night at the club, pulling a hoodie up over her head.

"My head is a white Brillo pad," Dani joked.

"At least you don't look like a witch," Avery shouted. "Sorry, Hannah. You know it's true. You screwed me on purpose."

When they reached Avery's car, Hannah turned around and looked at her friends.

"You guys look ridiculous." As her chin began to quiver, she laughed. "And I absolutely love you for it."

BEGIN AGAIN

One Month Later

January 2007

38

Winter 2007 // Fort Bragg, North Carolina

Avery Adams was pretty sure that yoga was bullshit. But then again, if she'd learned anything in the last year of her life, it's that you can't judge a book by its cover—or by willowy women who stand in a doorway and welcome you with their soft voices, braided hair, and lavender scent.

After spending fifteen minutes on the floor of a closet with Wendy Bennett, Avery had decided that she couldn't simply go on with her life as if nothing had happened. As if Tim hadn't died and Noah hadn't cheated. Michelle Jenkins recommended Mona Anderson, a counselor who lived in Fayetteville and practiced out of her home—just a couch and a chair and several built-in bookcases, full of titles like *Inside Out, Shattered Dreams,* and *On the Road to Recovery.* The first time she'd walked in, claustrophobia had overtaken Avery, and it took everything inside her to stop herself from turning around and leaving. Mona had white hair cropped short, and was so petite, Avery thought she might crush the woman just by speaking. She'd tried to shock Mona, telling her every sexual escapade she'd had since age fourteen. But when she'd finished, Mona hadn't flinched. She'd simply looked at Avery and said, "That's all very interesting. But I'd rather start at the beginning. Tell me about your parents."

"My parents?" Avery had said, incredulous. "What do they have to do with this?"

"I'm not sure yet," Mona said. "But I'd like to find out."

With Mona's guidance, Avery realized that from a young age, her parents had taught her to run—both literally and figuratively. Her father, unable to connect with his sons, had begun to resent his daughter's success. Her mother, unable to receive the intimacy she'd needed from her husband, had detached, leaving Avery with a void that she'd filled with anything she could. She'd run to win everyone's approval. She'd run to find a place in the center of their eyes. But you can't outrun yourself. The emotions you've got, you've got. And ignoring her problems had only led to greater problems. Yoga had been Mona's idea, too—because it was a "*practice*," not a sport.

"Practice for what?" Avery had asked at her most recent session.

"Practice at being with yourself," Mona had answered. "Practice for standing still."

Though she was resistant to the idea, Avery prided herself on being the kind of person that would try just about anything once. What was the worst that could happen?

THE MORNING OF Avery's first yoga class, she stopped at the post exchange for a smoothie. Dani had mailed her a new iPod for her birthday, and she wanted to buy an adapter for her new car. The shiny black crossover SUV was the largest purchase she'd ever made, and she'd driven off the lot in tears. She hated saying goodbye to her rusty old Honda Civic but loved that she'd followed Mona's advice.

"You don't need permission to be an adult," Mona had said earlier that morning. "If you need a new car, you can buy yourself a car."

When Avery complained that she didn't have enough money, Mona waved her off.

"You have a stable job. You can finance the car and make payments, just like the rest of us." Mona had paused, seeing the look of surprise on Avery's face. "You can go today."

The post exchange, or PX, was like a military minimall, complete with name-brand clothing, a Clinique makeup counter, and an electronics section full of the latest gadgets, all tax-free, of course. Avery picked up the adapter, went through the checkout line, and was waiting at Smoothie King for her drink when the sliding glass doors of the PX entrance opened and Noah walked inside.

Avery's stomach sank. Her hands grew sweaty, her breath shallow. Had he seen her? Did she want him to?

He'd shaved his beard, but other than that, Noah Candross looked as he always had. He was dressed in a form-fitting gray T-shirt and jeans, since it was Saturday afternoon. He removed his sunglasses and looked right at her. She didn't have time to decide whether to run toward him or away, because as soon as he saw her, he began moving toward her.

Avery took her drink from the teenager behind the counter and tried to open a straw. The first buckled against the counter, breaking as it released from its paper skin. She grabbed another but fumbled again. Why was she shaking? How did his presence have such power over her body? Noah was standing there, beside her, but she didn't want to look at him. He reached for her trembling arm.

"Don't," Avery said, her voice even and sure. Her arm moved out from under his hand. "I don't have anything to say to you." Even as the words came out of her mouth, she knew they were a lie. She had so *many* things to say to him.

"Avery . . . ," he began, looking back at the interested teen behind the Smoothie King counter. "Lower your voice—"

"Does your fiancée know that we went to California? Does she know you met my friends? My *family?*"

"It's not what you—"

"It's not what I think? What is it then?"

Silence. Noah lowered his chin and shook his head—it was the first time she'd ever seen remorse on his face. "I told you, you weren't in the plans."

"Oh my God, you and your plans," Avery said, letting the tears come to her eyes. "You made me into a cheater. And a fool. But you know what? Those days are over. So thank you. Thank you for opening my eyes. I just pray that your fiancée sees the light before she marries you."

Noah held his hands up to his temples. "If you would just listen to me," he said, his voice suddenly loud and defiant. "I need . . . I need my uniforms back, okay? I think I left two of them at your house."

Avery blinked twice, and then started laughing the way you laugh when it's two in the morning and you're so ridiculously tired that everything sounds like the funniest thing you've ever heard. "No," said Avery. "You need help, okay? I don't have anything for you. Go home to your fiancée, Noah. And please don't talk to me again. If you see me, just keep walking."

With that, she turned to the teenager and pointed her Styrofoam cup toward Noah's shocked face. "He's gonna pay for this one."

SHE ARRIVED AT her yoga class fifteen minutes later, her limbs still shaking with adrenaline. A stream of lithe women walked through the door with rolled-up mats tucked under their arms. Avery watched from her car, slurping the cold smoothie into her mouth, shivering. Finally, she turned off the engine and walked inside. The instructor, a woman half Avery's height with a long brunette braid running down her back, pointed Avery to the center of the room.

"So you can see me," the teacher said.

And so I can fall flat on my face in front of everyone, Avery wanted to reply. But instead, she smiled, sat down with her legs crossed in front of her, and tried to breathe.

Much to her surprise, she felt an immediate resistance to the simple task of sitting. Her legs wanted to move. She wanted to bolt out the door and call Hannah and rehash everything she'd just said to Noah and the shocked expression she'd left on his face. She wanted to leave this place and go back to her office to accomplish the hundreds of tasks that she'd left undone over the holidays. Her unit had started SRP paperwork, in preparation for their upcoming deployment. Before Tim had died, Avery couldn't wait to get her turn overseas. But now, the prospect of getting on a C-130 for Iraq terrified her more than she wanted to admit. Noah's face interrupted her thoughts about work. She pushed that away, only to immediately feel overwhelmed by a deluge of things she needed to get done before her trip with Dani and Hannah. They'd decided to spend a week together in February, a last hurrah, before they all parted ways again. She'd thought about the trip, then realized all this yoga wasn't going to help her get the beach body she wanted.

"Breathe in, and breathe out," the instructor said. "Keep your eyes closed."

Avery opened one eye and peered around at the rest of the class. Most of her classmates were older women, sitting with their eyes closed, breathing, looking perfectly at peace. She had no idea how they were doing it. Maybe they were faking. Maybe inside their minds, they were fighting battles, too. After all, you don't have to be in the Army to be in the middle of a war. She had no combat patch to show for it, but she'd fought tooth and nail in the last few months to reclaim her life. Her sanity. Her dignity.

"The voice in your head will try and defeat you, before you've even started," the yoga instructor said. "If you feel an itch, instead of scratching it, try and welcome it and let it be there with you. It's just your body after all. The itch will eventually go away."

Avery took a breath and closed her eyes.

"In the same way, if you have a thought—even a negative thought—just let it come," the instructor continued. "Your work. Your relationships. All those demands you've put on yourself? Let those come to your mind. Welcome them, don't resist them. We spend so much of our lives in a state of *resistance*. Why don't you release your grip? Welcome the discomfort. Welcome the distraction. Thank it for reminding you that you are *alive*. And then let it go."

Avery tried welcoming the part of her body that wanted to run. The part of her that was hurting, and the part that was healing. The part that still wanted Noah to love her, and the part that had told him never to speak to her again. Both were real. Both mattered. The first was a girl with desires, the second was a girl content, even if those desires went unfulfilled.

This was the work her counselor wanted her to do. To stop running.

To breathe. Forgive. And live.

39

Winter 2007 // London, England

I don't understand."

Laura Klein sat behind her desk in the same black dress she'd worn every day since Dani had started working in her office. A clump of eyeliner had gathered in the corner of each of her eyes, making her look tired and unkempt. And for the first time since she'd made the decision to have this conversation, Dani felt guilty.

They'd never spoken about Dani's extended absence. But as soon as Dani had returned, Laura had come to rely on her more and more to carry her professional weight whenever an unforeseen personal obstacle arose. In the divorce, Laura had received full custody of her children, and a week earlier, her older son had come down with the flu. The week before that, she'd had parent-teacher conferences. Dani didn't mind holding down the fort in Laura's absence—she certainly didn't send any e-mails to HR about it. But now, the shock and awe on Laura's face betrayed an insecurity that Dani had always assumed was there but never expected to see this clearly.

"You take two weeks off for your friend's . . ."

"Funeral," Dani reminded her.

"Funeral. And Webb *still* gave you another two weeks off for Christmas." Laura Klein laughed nervously. "I mean really. What else do you want? If this is about the whole Gelhomme bonus . . . I don't know what—"

"What bonus?"

"That's not what this was about?" Laura continued. "I assumed Webb told you, seeing as you two are so . . . chummy."

"Told me what?"

"The online Gelhomme ads worked so well, they increased their digital advertising budget by ten percent. So there was a bonus. A commission. I'll split it with you, if that's what this is about."

"That's not what this is about," Dani said. In all honesty, she didn't care. Money didn't change the facts.

"Truly, I don't understand," her boss said again. She was beginning to sound like a plebe at West Point. "The sky is the limit for you here. You make more money than anyone at your level. We both know Webb is priming you to replace me someday. And you're . . . you're really good at your job. I don't understand why you would walk away from all of that."

It had been a long time since she'd heard Laura Klein's voice fill with such sincerity. It was a nice sound, but it wasn't going to change her mind.

"There are more important things than money. I might be good at advertising, but I could be good at a lot of things. I think I was made for this."

Laura looked over Dani's resignation letter, a single page that rested in front of her. "And you think you were *made* to be a . . . college basketball coach?"

"I don't know for sure," Dani answered honestly. "But I'm certain that if I never try, I'll always wonder. And that's enough for me."

Laura shook her head and laughed. "Are you sure that hair dye didn't go to your head?"

Dani touched her short hair, offering Laura a small grin. She liked her hair, just like she liked what she saw in her future.

"And, if you don't mind me asking," Laura continued, "what are you wearing?"

Dani looked down. She wore a tight athletic shirt, sweatpants, and Air Jordans on her feet. She hadn't felt this comfortable in years.

"I've got a game in an hour. Which is why I can't stay here and keep explaining my decision," Dani said. "I just wanted you to hear it straight from me."

"You know, we're going to be sunk without you."

"You'll be all right," Dani said as they shook hands. "You've got Pete and the crew. They're all great."

"Sometimes I think they hate me." Laura sighed.

"Give them a break every now and then," Dani said kindly. "We're all just doing the best we can."

With that, she turned and limped out the door, carrying a box of her belongings with her.

"*Dani!*" Laura shouted, one last time.

When Dani looked back, she noticed Laura's eyes had softened. Even the wrinkles on her face seemed to smooth out as she offered a nod of respect and mutual understanding.

"Good luck," Laura said. "And for what it's worth, I believe you'll be a very good coach."

WHEN DANI GOT home, she walked to the basketball court in Notting Hill where she'd spent the last three weeks coaching the boys and reveling in the sound she loved most. She still felt discomfort in her joints. They groaned more than ever, really.

But pain comes for you, body and soul, whether you're ready or not, Dani thought as she jogged onto the court. For some people, pain arrives in a phone call that shatters the once-perfect window through which you'd seen the world. For others, pain grows into a poisonous plant, buried so deep, the only way to uproot it is to dig it out slowly. For others—for people like Dani—pain was a constant companion, nagging and persistent. You could numb the pain. Bury it again. Ignore it forever. But you couldn't get rid of it. That was a war that would never be won.

A basketball flew through the air from a child to Dani and back again. She smiled, taking her first step toward the basket. It hurt. But she chose to enjoy the ache.

40

Winter 2007 // Aliʻi Beach Park, Oahu, Hawaii

Hannah lounged in a beach chair, reading the final few pages of *East of Eden*. In the book, the main character, Adam, was nearing his end while his son Caleb stood at his deathbed, begging for forgiveness.

Picking her eyes up from the page, Hannah looked out at the water, breathing in the scent of coconut and salt. The sun hovered above the horizon, casting long golden rays across the sand. The water looked like bright blue Kool-Aid, rolling and crashing with waves. Nature, again, reminded her of her size in the universe. But if humans were so small, why did they want life to matter so much?

Sarah Goodrich had e-mailed Hannah after the funeral with an offer. Their old basketball teammate was deployed to Afghanistan—her second deployment since graduating from West Point in 2001. But because she was deployed, her beachfront home on the North Shore of Oahu was currently un-occupied. In that e-mail, Sarah told Hannah the house's lockbox code and said that she could go any time she wanted, no questions asked. And so, at the urging of Dani and Avery, the three of them had booked round-trip tickets using the last of Dani's frequent-flier miles. There were perks to having a network as wide as the Army and a friend as wealthy as Dani. And if she was going to wake up at four in the morning anyway, she might as well wake up in Hawaii.

The grief counselor said that sleeplessness was a common symptom of grief—that it might take more than a year before she could sleep normally again. But Hannah didn't want to be normal. If not sleeping was how she could keep Tim's memory alive, then she hoped she'd never sleep a full night again. That was why she was out there, alone. Digging her feet into the warm sand. Watching the surf come in. She wanted to remember him.

Out in the distance, three tanned surfers sat on boards, bobbing up and down in the water, waiting for the right wave to ride. Hannah caught herself watching them, wondering if they were teenagers, or if they were older. It was hard to tell. Soon, one paddled hard in front of a growing swell. He stood on his board and glided seamlessly across the water until he crashed. When he emerged from the surf, he shook his long dark hair and gave his friends a wave of his pinky and thumb, the shaka. A girl throwing a Frisbee for her dog along the water's edge noticed Hannah and smiled, as if to say, *Isn't this morning amazing?*

It was amazing. And that was what made it so difficult. Tim had never been to Hawaii, and now he never would. Would every amazing moment she experienced now also feel like a loss? The grief counselor had said she would have to learn to hold grief and joy at the same time without minimizing either emotion. She wondered if she'd ever grow tired from the weight.

Tim would never learn to surf, although she could imagine his young body adapting to the waves with ease. And that was part of the sorrow, too: Tim would only ever have a young body. There would be no old Tim. No Tim the dad or Tim the grumpy Old Grad, visiting West Point for a class reunion, like her grandfather did when Hannah was young. Was her future already decided, even then? Would Tim the grandfather have told his granddaughter to choose a different school, just as Hannah's grandfather had tried to do? She wasn't sure. But despite it all, Hannah was still grateful she hadn't listened to her grandfather all those years ago. She just wished the story had a different ending.

In light of a life, four years together was far too few. Soon, the time she'd spent with Tim would pale in comparison to her time without him. Inevitably, her memories would fade. She feared the day she wouldn't be able to conjure his face in her mind. A flat, two-dimensional picture would never capture the sound of his laugh or the little wrinkle between his eyebrows when he was concentrating. Everything she had to remember him by was a shadow of the real thing. More than once, she'd let herself call his cell phone, just to hear the prerecorded voicemail message. At some point, that phone plan would be canceled. His voice would be deleted. It was more than she could handle.

She'd attended West Point, despite her grandfather's fears, because she felt God telling her it was the right move. She'd met and married Tim for the same reason. Every leap of faith had been worth the risk. Until now.

She looked down at the page in front of her. Caleb begged his father, Adam, for a blessing. Hannah had never had to beg for anything in her life. But she knew that if she didn't beg, her faith would grow cold and brittle, until it crumbled into dust.

Standing up from her chair, Hannah walked down the beach, letting the emotion well up inside her. For so many years, she'd followed a prescription that she'd trusted would result in a beautiful life. Girls don't fight back. They don't get angry. They don't demand things—especially not from men. They are loyal and faithful and quiet and trusting. But slowly, surely, all of those rules had unraveled. It was time to release. To let go. This was why she'd come here. To let the sound of the ocean drown out the sound of her cries.

Soon, the water lapped up against her bare ankles. She remembered the salty taste of Tim's mouth and the feel of his body next to hers in the water last summer. And then she screamed.

She screamed that it wasn't worth it.

That she hated God.

That she didn't trust him.

That if *this* was what having faith meant, then she wasn't sure she wanted it anymore.

She screamed of the betrayal and the fear and the loss. She screamed the same three words, over and over again, until her scream became a whisper.

"How could you?"

The wild waves pulled away from her feet and soon, quietness filled the space of her screaming. She left her shorts on the sand and dove under the water, feeling its cool, salty relief on her skin. When she emerged from under the water, the little cross necklace felt warm and wet in her hand.

EVENTUALLY, HANNAH CAME out of the water and walked back to her chair, dragging her feet through the sand. When she returned, Dani and Avery were sitting there, beside her things, holding an extra cup of coffee.

"You okay?" Avery asked.

"No," Hannah said. "But I'm still here."

"Good," Dani said. She patted a place on the towel next to her, and Hannah lay down, putting her head on Dani's lap. The sand was warm beneath her body.

THAT EVENING, BACK at Sarah's bungalow, Hannah sat under the twinkle lights on the lanai, sipping something fruity. Sarah had styled every corner of the patio as though someone from *HGTV* were arriving any moment with a camera crew. The guest room had a plush queen-sized bed, which, despite her sadness, Hannah had still managed to make like the Army would require, hospital corners and everything, every morning of their vacation. Some habits were hard to break.

On the floor next to the bed, Hannah's uniform sat pressed and ready. Her rucksack was fully packed with the same gear she'd brought home from Afghanistan two months earlier. It was time to go back.

Hannah was proud that Dani had decided to take the coaching job at the Citadel. The salary would force her to take a big step down in lifestyle, Hannah knew, but if anyone could adjust, Dani could. That girl was unstoppable, no matter where you put her. She wasn't a shooting star; she was a solar panel, always absorbing energy and putting it back out into the world again. And Avery had changed, too. They'd been talking daily since Hannah had returned from Afghanistan. She was softer, kinder—and for the first time since Hannah had known her, Avery didn't have a boyfriend. Baby steps. That was what had changed, Hannah realized. Avery had slowed down.

Tim's death had spurred on those changes. That much was obvious. But Hannah found herself constantly wondering how it would change her. Would it make her bitter? Would it make her angry? Would she lose her faith in God or gain more? She was afraid of the person she might become in a world without Tim.

And what about her war? Colonel Markham had given her permission to take on a rear-detachment job at Fort Bragg for the remainder of the deployment. She didn't have to go back. But she couldn't imagine working at a desk while Private Murphy and the rest of the guys sweltered in Afghanistan without her. What kind of message would that send? It was important to show her soldiers and her friends, and, to be honest, *herself,* that life could continue. That she could still have a role and a purpose. That her breakable body housed an unbreakable soul.

She looked down at the tattoo on her wrist—an oak tree, deep roots and high branches, with two dates scribbled into its limbs: 6.19.04., the date of their wedding, and 11.13.06., the date of Tim's death. The beginning and the end. Or the other way around, depending on how you looked at it. The tattoo was Avery's idea. A breaking from the Hannah of before. A new Hannah had been born.

"Dinner's ready."

Avery came out to the patio holding a bowl of ahi tuna poke that she'd purchased from a shop on the way home from the beach. She placed it at the center of the patio table. Dani emerged from the kitchen, her hair back to a large, natural Afro. She added a bowl of mango, corn tortillas, and her famous avocado salsa to the assortment. With her strange restrictive diet, Dani had become quite the chef. Avery put a pitcher of margaritas on the table, and suddenly, a memory came to Hannah's mind.

She'd made a pitcher for her grandmother back in high school, during an elective ceramics class. The first two pitchers she'd tried to make had fallen apart in the kiln. Both times, she hadn't scored the handle deep enough for it to attach to the body of the vase. But her third attempt came out just as she'd imagined. Staring at her friends at this table, she realized that their lives were like that pitcher. They all had rough edges, but those places were necessary to forge deep connections. All the things they'd survived. All the ways they'd laughed and limped and cried together. It was like a knife had cut into them so they could latch together and never break apart, even when they were put through the fire. She'd wanted to bond that way to Tim, but looking up at her friends' faces under the glow of the twinkle lights, Hannah knew she was equally lucky to be connected to them. Some people spent their whole lives avoiding pain. But by avoiding it, they avoided *this* too.

They'd all taken their seats when Dani placed her hands palms-up on the table, ready to pray. "Shall we?"

But just as they'd gripped hands and bowed their heads, Hannah's phone began to vibrate on the table. The phone number was long and unrecognizable, like a military call coming from overseas.

"Sorry," Hannah said, trying to turn it off. "It's not important..."

"No, get it," Avery replied. "We can wait."

Hannah looked at her phone. That little piece of metal that connected her to the world. She'd been so scared to answer it. She'd ignored it and turned it off, and at one point considered throwing it out the window of a moving car. The ringer sounded like a wind chime blowing in the breeze. She couldn't avoid it forever. She couldn't escape beauty or the passage of time, any more than she could escape breathing. Whoever was calling needed her. And it was a good thing to be needed.

She could do this. She wouldn't do it well. She wouldn't do it perfectly. There would be more tears, she was certain. There would be more death and more life. There would be more screaming at the sky and wondering if Someone was listening. But whatever came her way, she knew she was still of use in the world—not because of her own ability, but because like a pitcher, scored and scarred, put through the fire, she was ready to be poured out.

Hannah took a deep breath. She picked up the phone, flipped it open, and pressed it against her ear.

She said hello.

It was a small act, to answer that call. But it wasn't small to Hannah. In taking that breath—in saying hello—she told the world that she was still here. That she was still breathing. And in that way, it felt like a beginning.

ACKNOWLEDGMENTS

The great thing about being a writer is that I'll never have a band threaten to play me off stage when I'm trying to say thanks.

First and foremost, this book would not exist if it weren't for my friend, mentor and creative consultant, Dionna McPhatter, who originally envisioned telling a story about the experiences of women at West Point, and entrusted me to do the job. From the beginning to end, she offered belief, encouragement, financial support, creative solutions, and a listening ear, and never failed to provide a hearty kick in the butt when I needed it. You inspire me in every way and I'm grateful God put you in my living room twenty years ago. The best is yet to come.

To my agent, Alison Fargis: I am forever grateful that you own a piece of real estate across the Hudson River from West Point. Thank you for pushing me to revise this manuscript into the novel it is today. Thanks also to Maria Ribas, who saw promise in my writing and introduced me to Stonesong.

I owe many thanks to my editor, Lucia Macro—your suggestions for this book helped tie up so many of my loose ends. And to the entire William Morrow team at HarperCollins—thank you for your kindness, enthusiasm, and prompt attention.

I am indebted to a long list of women who candidly shared their memories, feelings and experiences with me, without reservation. Jen Wardynski, Jackie Asis, Charlsey Mahle, Mandy Psiaki, Katie del Castillo Vail, Haley Dennison Uthlaut, Tiffany Allen Archuletta, Abby Moore, Mallory Fritz Wampler, Jenny Jo Hartney, Ariel Gibson, Kristin Gatti, Caroline "Annie" Pestel, Mary Tobin, Jenn Menn, Sarah Travaglio. Thank you for your vulnerability, courage, and patience as I asked so many invasive questions.

West Point is a small community with roots that extend deep and wide. Thank you to the many cadets and families who made an impact on my life during my most formative childhood years—especially Laura Walker (Class of '03), Tim Cunningham (Class of '06), Emily Perez (Class of '05), and John Ryan Dennison (Class of '04)—strong men and women of character who were killed in the wars in Iraq and Afghanistan.

To my parents, Bee and Laura. Mom, your wise counsel helped guide me during the years it took to write this book. Thank you for being one of my most early trusted readers, and for inspiring what I believe is the character at the heart of this book. Dad, your brilliance in engineering is the reason we lived at West Point in the first place. Thank you for your reflections on 9/11, for your selfless service to our country, and for always reminding me to "chip away at it."

To the community of writers, artists and encouragers in Nashville and beyond. Thanks to Lauren Ledbetter whose hand-drawn illustration resides in the first few pages of this book. To Russ Ramsey, I finally did what you told me to do; now go write your memoir. Katherine Carpenter, you read the first words of this thing, and managed not to laugh—bless you. And many more thanks are due to Holly Sharp, Sarah and Andrew Trammell, Shelley Ellis, Amelia Cornish, Jamie Lidell, Joe Johnson, Lisa Burzynski, Kim Green, and Susannah Felts. And a huge thanks to the ragtag community of homeless creatives that find shelter (and caffeine) at Ugly Mugs in East Nashville.

And finally, my deepest gratitude is and always will be reserved for my husband, Patrick, whose long-suffering patience, love, and kindness have sustained me in every way. Thank you for loving a broken vessel like me. RILY.

The Late, Lamented Molly Marx

The Late, Lamented Molly Marx

A NOVEL

Sally Koslow

BALLANTINE BOOKS / NEW YORK

Copyright © 2009 by Sally Koslow

Published in the United States by Ballantine Books, an imprint of The Random House Publishing Group, a division of Random House, Inc., New York.

BALLANTINE and colophon are registered trademarks of Random House, Inc.

ISBN 978-0-345-50620-7

Printed in the United States of America on acid-free paper

www.ballantinebooks.com

1 3 5 7 9 8 6 4 2

First Edition

Book design by Susan Turner

To Rob, Jed, and Rory

The true mystery of the world is the visible, not the invisible.

—OSCAR WILDE

The Late, Lamented Molly Marx

One

KILL ME NOW

When I imagined my funeral, this wasn't what I had in mind. First of all, I hoped I would be old, a stately ninetysomething who'd earned the right to be called elegant; a woman with an intimate circle of loved ones fanned out in front of her, their tender sorrow connecting them like lace.

I definitely hoped to be in a far more beautiful place—a stone chapel by the sea, perhaps, with pounding purple-gray waves drowning out mourners' sobs. For no apparent reason—I'm not even Scottish—there would be wailing bagpipes, men in Campbell tartan, and charmingly reserved grandchildren, or even great-grandchildren, coaxed into reciting their own sweet poetry. I don't know where the children's red curls come from, since my hair is chemically enhanced blond and straight as a ruler. The bereaved—incredibly, those weepy old souls are my own kids—dab away tears with linen handkerchiefs, though on every other occasion they have used only tissues. The service takes place shortly before sunset in air fragrant with lilacs. Spring. At least where I grew up, in the Chicago suburbs, that's what lilacs signify: the end of a long winter, life beginning anew.

I didn't expect to be here, in a cavernous, dimly lit Manhattan syn-

agogue. I didn't expect to be surrounded by at least four hundred people, a good three hundred of whom I don't recall talking to even once. Most of all, I didn't expect to be young. Well, maybe some people don't think thirty-five is young, but I do. It's far too young to die, because while my story isn't quite at the beginning, it isn't at the end, either. Except that it is.

She's dead, all those bodies in the pews must be thinking. *Depressing.* On that last count, they would be wrong. In fact, if the congregation knew my whole story—and I hope they will, eventually, because I need people on my side, not on his, and especially not on *hers*—it would be clear that I, Molly Divine Marx, have not lost my joie de vivre. On that point, I speak the truth.

"She would be here if she could," he says. "She would be here if she could." That's Rabbi Strauss Sherman, pontificating over to my right. I wish he were the twinkly junior rabbi whose adult ed classes I kept telling myself I should take, not that I am—*was*—keen on the music of Jews in Uganda. But the speaker is the senior rabbi, the one who says everything twice, like an echo, though it stopped short of being profound the first time. I suppose I should get off on the fact that he's the big-shot rabbi invited to homes of people who contribute gigabucks and, thus, rate succulent, white-meat honors on holidays. I wonder if Barry, my husband, made sure Rabbi S.S. spoke today just to stick it to me, since whenever he gave a sermon I'd squirm and mutter, "Kill me now." I'd hate to think God decided on payback.

I realize I am not being kind about either Rabbi S.S. or the heartsick husband. Barry's sizable schnozz is chapped from crying, and I caught more than a few people noticing as he discreetly swiped his nose on the sleeve of his black suit, soft worsted in a fine cut. *Armani?* they're wondering. Not a chance. It is a close facsimile purchased at an outlet center near Milan, but if they took it for Armani, Barry would be glad. That was the general idea.

Perhaps some women in the pews wonder what I'm dressed in. The casket is closed—talk about a bad hair day—but I am being buried in a red dress. Okay, it's more of a burgundy, but one thing that's putting a smile on my face (only metaphorically, unfortunately) is that for all eternity I will get to wear this dress, which cost way too much, even 40 percent off at Barneys, where I rarely shop because it's generally a

rip-off. I'm sure if it had been up to my mother-in-law, the enchanting Kitty Katz, today I would have been stuffed into a button-down shirt and pleated pants that made me look like a sumo wrestler, but my sister, Lucy, intervened. Lucy and I have had our moments, but she would understand how psyched I was to be wearing the dress to a Valentine's party this coming Saturday.

Wherever it is I'm off to, I hope they notice the shoes—black satin, terrifyingly high slingbacks, with excellent toe cleavage. I only wore them once, those shoes, and that night Barry and I barely left the dance floor. When we shimmied and whirled, it was almost like sex: we became the couple people thought we were. The Dr. and Mrs. Marx I, at least, wanted us to be. I loved watching Barry move his runner's body in that subtle but provocative way of his, and how he nestled his hand on the small of my back, then cupped my butt for the whole world to see. It's a pity we couldn't have merengued through life as if it were one endless Fred and Ginger movie.

Will there be dancing where I'm headed? I digress. I do that. Drove Barry nuts.

"Our dear Molly Marx, she would be here if she could," Rabbi S.S. is saying. That makes three. "The circumstances of her death may be mysterious, but it is not for us to judge. It is not for us to judge."

As soon as someone tells you not to judge, you do. Everyone in this chilly sanctuary is judging—both Barry and me. I can hear it all, what's in people's heads as well as on their lips.

"Foul play."

"Killed herself."

"Jealous boyfriend."

"*She* had a boyfriend? That mouse?"

"You have it all wrong. *He* had a girlfriend."

"If it's suicide, then why the ginormous funeral?"

I hear a smug tone. "For Jews, with a suicide it's the burial place that gets questioned, not the funeral."

"He won't be single for six months."

"Especially with the little girl."

Yes, there is a child. Annabel Divine Marx, almost four, black velvet dress, patent leather Mary Janes. My Annie-belle is clutching Alfred the bunny, and the look on her face could make Hitler weep. Right

now, I will not allow myself the luxury of thinking about my baby, who wonders where her mommy is and when this nasty dream will end. If I could be alive for five more minutes, they would be spent memorizing Annabel's heartbeat and synchronizing it with my own, tracing the bones in her birdlike shoulders, stroking the creamy softness of her skin. *I will always be Annabel's mother.* My mantra.

People can call me anything, but in the mommy department, there was never a moment when I wasn't trying to do the right thing. I attempted to live for my child—not through her, for her. I tried. I really did. I never would have abandoned Annabel. Nothing ever mattered more to me than my unconditional love for her, a long, unbroken line that continues even now. The best compliment I ever got was from Barry when he said simply, a few weeks after Annabel was born, "Molly, you get motherhood. You really do."

"Our dear Molly, our lovely Molly," the rabbi is saying. "She was so many things. To our grieving Barry—a trustee of this very institution—she was a beloved wife of almost seven years, a woman with her whole life ahead of her. To Annabel, she was Mommy, tender, devoted. To her parents, Claire and Daniel Divine, she was a cherished daughter, and to Lucy Divine, she was an adored twin sister, absolutely adored. To her colleagues, she was a . . ." Rabbi S.S. refers to his notes. "A decorating editor at a magazine."

Wrong. I stopped being a decorating editor when Annabel was born. Lately, I was a freelance stylist—the person who brings in the tall white orchids and fluffs a room so when it's photographed for a magazine it shames most of the readers, since there's no way their homes are ever going to look like that. Then they blink and smugly wonder if people actually live in that picture with not one family snapshot in a teddy bear frame sold at a Hallmark store. Who actually buys white couches and scratchy sisal rugs? How do you clean them? They turn the page.

I wasn't brokering peace in the Middle East, or even teaching nursery school like my twin sister. But I loved my work, and in my sliver of a world, I was a giant. What I could do with a mantel was almost art. People must have hated inviting me to their homes, for fear that I'd rearrange their bookshelves and suggest that they sell half of their tchotchkes on eBay.

"Molly was a loyal friend, an accomplished biker, a graduate of Northwestern University with a major in art history."

Is the rabbi going to recite my entire résumé? Disclose that I was rejected from Brown and never made it off the Wesleyan wait-list? Share that I took a junior semester in Florence and skipped every class—did I even buy textbooks?—while Emilio fra Diavolo taught me Italian of the nonverbal variety? Mention the two jobs from which I was fired and the fourteen-month gap between them? Point out that Barry and I were seeing a marriage counselor?

There's Dr. Stafford right there. Goodness, she looks quite moved. I always imagined that when Barry and I were carrying on at her sessions she was thinking, *How did I get stuck with these two completely shallow, nonintrospective, loser brats? Oh, I have three private school tuitions to pay. That's why.* But I see tears and I can tell they are real.

The Lord giveth and the Lord taketh away, and when he takes away big-time, I have discovered he compensates you with a finely tuned bullshit detector. It is a minor consolation, but I think I am going to like it.

"And now we will hear from Molly's husband," the rabbi says. "Barry. Dr. Barry Marx."

Barry kisses Annabel on the head and untangles his hand from hers. She takes a look at Kitty—who forbids the word *grandma*—and considers whether to move closer to her. "Kitty smells funny," she used to say. "It's just her cigarettes, honey," I would respond. "Don't smoke when you grow up or you'll smell funny, too." I hope Annabel remembers that. If she becomes a nose-ringed, tattooed fourteen-year-old hanging out in the East Village with a cigarette dangling from her lips . . . there won't be a damn thing I can do about it.

Kitty is wearing a severe black suit—either Gucci or Valentino. She'd be horrified to know I can't tell or appreciate the difference, though I admit it looks stunningly appropriate. The tailoring shows off her yoga-buffed sixty-four-year-old body, which, in clothes, we both privately acknowledge looks a good bit better than mine. Today she seems to have hijacked the first floor of Tiffany's. With Kitty, more is more. She is wearing diamond studs the size of knuckles, a sapphire-and-emerald brooch dribbling over her breast like Niagara Falls with a

bracelet to match, and a black lizard handbag that, no doubt, contains her smokes.

I hope Annabel eventually inherits some of Kitty's baubles. I'm not saying Kitty's glad I'm dead, but at least she has a good excuse now for not willing me any jewelry.

When Barry arrives at the front of the synagogue and bounds up the six steps, he clears his throat and takes some notes from his jacket. He tears them in half with a flourish. I knew he would do that! We saw the same stunt at my aunt Julie's funeral last year. Does he think my family won't notice he stole it? Ah, but he doesn't really care about them, does he? And what makes it worse is that except for the Divines, everyone in the congregation is buying into his heart-wrenching grief. From every corner, I hear sniffles and snorts and see tiny tributaries of tears.

"I fell in love with Molly when I was a senior at college," he begins.

I was a sophomore. He was the pre-med guy who finally had room in his schedule for a class on twentieth-century art and took a seat next to me in a darkened auditorium. Barry wanted to become a collector, he said, and I remember thinking the remark pretentious; no one I knew aspired to own anything more than an Alex Katz dog litho or a student's work snagged at a silent auction on open-studio night. But Barry dreamed on a grand scale. When five years later I found out that he'd become a plastic surgery resident at Mount Sinai in Manhattan, I wasn't surprised. If ever a doctor were born to woo women into rhino-plasty, it was Barry Marx, who managed to incorporate his own nose into his well-delivered pitch.

At least forty of his patients must be here today. All those weepers with the delicate, symmetrical noses aren't my mommy-buddies, magazine pals, book club friends, or cycling partners. Do Barry's patients have a phone tree, like the one at Annabel's school in case of inclement weather? Did someone start making calls at 5:30 A.M.? "Sorry to wake you, but I thought you'd want to know Barry Marx is single. The funeral's at ten. Pass it on."

"There are four things you should know about my wife, Molly," Barry begins. "First, she had the most musical laugh in the whole world. Many of you know that laugh. I married her for that laugh. I cannot believe I will never hear it again."

So far, okay. To be fair, there was a lot of laughing, and no one thinks Barry married me for my breasts, which most wives of plastic surgeons would have had enlarged from nectarines to melons.

"Second, Molly was the most brutally honest person I know. You couldn't get much past her. She was honest about her shortcomings—"

He's going to discuss my *shortcomings*?

"—and mine."

Would that include flirting with more than half of my friends?

"Third, I have never known anyone who loved life more than Molly. She should have lived to be a hundred."

No argument there.

"And one more thing . . ." Barry falters. "One more thing . . ." He bows his head slightly. I don't need a bullshit detector to realize he must truly be bereft, because his yarmulke drops, which allows the whole congregation to see his baby bald spot. Barry doesn't rush to return the yarmulke to his head. Rabbi Sherman comes over and cradles him with his arm. Barry walks to the casket, kisses his fingers—on one he's wearing his wedding band, which he usually keeps in a drawer—and presses them to the mahogany. Then he returns to his seat and pulls Annabel onto his lap.

I guess I'll never learn what the other thing is.

"Molly's closest friend, Sabrina Lawson, wishes to speak now," the rabbi says. "Sabrina Lawson."

I am glad Brie has volunteered for this eulogy, because I can safely say that Brie, who has recently decided she is a lesbian, is one friend who hasn't succumbed to Barry's charms. She definitely wasn't gay when we were roommates, but last year she met Isadora, the gorgeous Chilean architect who wound up moving into the loft she designed for Brie. Isadora tenderly kisses Brie on the lips before Brie walks to the front.

I have always been proud to be Brie's friend. We were quite a pair. She is almost six feet tall—a model before she became a lawyer—and I topped out at five-three. Today her glossy brown hair is braided down her back and she is wearing a flawless charcoal trouser suit over a crisp white blouse. Everything about Brie is hard edges except her heart.

Brie takes no small measure of pride in being the first of our friends to try girl-on-girl sex. I'm glad she's found Isadora, but I

wouldn't bet my life, if I still had one, that Brie won't switch back to Team Hetero. I can't believe that anyone who liked men as much as Brie did will give them up. In a voice that sounds ready to break, she begins.

There's something quieter than sleep
Within this inner room!
It wears a sprig upon its breast—
And will not tell its name.

Some touch it, and some kiss it—
Some chafe its idle hand—
It has a simple gravity
I do not understand!

My poetry appreciation stalled at e. e. cummings, but Brie kept Emily Dickinson by her bed. When she gets to the last stanza, she sobs and bites her lips.

While simple-hearted neighbors
Chat of the "Early dead"—
We—prone to periphrasis,
Remark that Birds have fled!

After a moment, Brie goes on. "Molly sometimes forgot to eat, yet she had more energy than anyone I know. She was always begging me to go on long bike rides. Just last Saturday, she picked me up with Annabel in her bike seat and insisted we pedal over the Brooklyn Bridge to go to this diner. . . ." Another memory is of us getting lost on a mountain trail in Aspen. I wonder if people aren't now thinking of me as an extremely dumb jock.

"We have one last speaker," Rabbi S.S. says. "Representing the Divine family . . . Lucy?"

No one ever took the two of us for sisters. We were fraternal twins, though I wondered why there wasn't a more apt term. At our bat mitzvah, Lucy towered over me by eight inches and outweighed me by forty pounds. Everyone clucked about how awful it must be that I hadn't gone through puberty yet, when Lucy had bazooms. But I know she

hated looking at me in my mini, and I just thought she was fat. Envy spiced our relationship like a red hot chili pepper, and most of it came from Luce. I got married, while every relationship she's had has ended—often with a guy moving to another continent with no forwarding address. I had a child. She wants one, desperately. People misunderstand Lucy. She wasn't an easy sister, but I adored her.

"When Molly and I were five," she says, "she convinced me that broccoli was an animal, and that my real name was Moosey. We were Molly and Moosey."

Her timing is good. The congregation laughs. I am sorry I saddled her with that name, which stuck until she left for college—*she* got into Brown—and probably cost my parents twenty thousand dollars in therapy bills. Lucy rambles and shares too many anecdotes from seventh grade. Mourners check BlackBerrys. "I will tell you one thing," she concludes. "We will find out who did this to my sister, Molly. If you are out there, the Divine family will hunt you down." My sister sounds as if she is giving a speech on the eve of a doomed election.

People snap back to attention. The rabbi does not like Lucy's tone any more than the buzz of conversation that has trashed the decorum of his service. He rushes over to Lucy, who shoots him the fierce look that scared away her last five boyfriends. She stares down Barry. He won't meet her eye.

"Interment will be private," the rabbi says quickly, "but shiva will begin tonight at the Marx home." He announces our address and then, suddenly, a stranger with an unmistakable Barry-crafted nose breaks out in song. Accompanied by the synagogue's turbo organ, her volume crescendos. "I could fly higher than an eagle," she sings, knowing that the Upper West Side is the closest she will get to Broadway, "for you are the wind beneath my wings."

I am mortified. Thank God I am in a box. Every one of my true friends—there have got be at least sixty in the room—as well as my parents, sister, and aunts and uncles are embarrassed by this ignominious display. Is this song Barry's idea of a joke? Or Kitty's?

Kill me. Kill me now.

Two

JUST. LIKE. THAT.

I don't know if I am dead or alive. I remember little. The spires of Riverside Church. Pain everywhere. A long, bottomless blackness.

This wasn't the way I'd planned it. My bike? Where did it go?

I hear the river, steady, like a pulse. Instinctively, I count the waves, which match my weakly pounding heart. One, two, three . . . forty-eight, forty-nine . . . one hundred one, one hundred two.

Cold.

Cold.

Cold.

Snow falls. Flakes cover my face.

So.

Damn.

Cold.

I am still wearing one biking glove, shredded and streaked with blood, which exposes my frostbitten fingers.

Never.

Been.

This.

Cold.

Nev—

With the wisp of a shallow exhale, I am gone. A leaf blowing away, an ash falling off a cigarette, a dewdrop evaporating on a flower petal.

Just.

Like.

That.

No.

Big.

Deal.

I have watched too many bad movies. There is no traveling down a tunnel with an eerie white light, harps and—on the other side— clouds like Provence crème. I have crossed over, but there is just darkness and the *whoosh-whoosh-whoosh* of traffic on the Henry Hudson Parkway.

Dawn arrives. Not ten feet from where I lie, under the tangle of bushes between the rock-bordered Hudson and the bike path, I begin to hear runners. This time of year, at this hour, they pass infrequently and keep their gazes straight ahead, because this is not Central Park, a social watering hole. The path is lonely and narrow. "Only an idiot would jog here," Barry said once to a friend who boasted about the purity of running by the river. "I don't know why you ride your bike there, either," he added, turning to me.

It was one of my favorite short trips, up to the George Washington Bridge, where a little red lighthouse still keeps guard on a tiny spit of land in its vast shadow—for me, a small, private holy place. I loved reading the little red lighthouse book to Annabel, just as I loved when my mother had read it to Lucy and me.

The runners continue, and then I hear her voice. "Oh my God," she says, barely audible, and then she yells the same words. Her footsteps grow closer. Above my legs stands a woman in tight black running pants and a loose parka. She removes an iPod earbud. "Are you alive?" she shouts to me. "Are you alive?" She tries, unsuccessfully, to push away brambles that cover the upper half of my body as she bleats those words again and again.

Her voice is trapped in her throat, as if she were screaming in a dream. She takes out a cell phone, pulls off her gloves, and punches in 911.

"I'm in Riverside Park," she says between heaving breaths. "There's a woman here—and I'm not sure if she's . . . alive."

I learn that my angel's name is actually Angela, a grad student in philosophy at Columbia. I am sorry because I know that for the rest of her life she will carry the hideous image of how I looked in death.

When the police and paramedics arrive, they determine that I have been dead for several hours. There is no record, they say later, that I was reported missing.

Three

A GATED COMMUNITY

I admit it. I am being buried in New Jersey, land of big-box discount stores, earsplitting accents, and oil refineries. The *garden* state? C'mon.

My parents wanted me flown back to Chicago to rest happily ever after next to Nana Phyllis and Papa Louie. Kitty was fine with the idea of shipping me off like a camp trunk. At the end of the day, so to speak, she probably wants a berth by her only son—the next best thing to a double bed. But Barry vetoed Chicago. "Molly's a Marx," he declared. "She belongs in the family plot."

There was, however, a glitch: only one more Marx could squeeze into the real estate in Beth David Cemetery, within earshot of the Belmont Park racetrack, where Barry's father and grandparents were laid to rest. So, faster than he chose his last laptop, Barry bought into a truly gated community, my new home away from home, Serenity Haven. I will, forever, be only six exits away from Ikea. A shame I don't need any furniture, because I have plenty of time to decipher the directions.

Outside the synagogue, a cold rain starts to fall. Most of the mourners scatter back into their lives: jobs, lunch dates, toddlers to collect after nursery school. Three limousines gridlock in front of the

building's entrance. Barry, Annabel, and Kitty pile into one. My parents and Lucy fill the next. Second-tier Marxes and Divines crowd the third. Isadora and Brie streak away in a blur of British racing green Jaguar, while at least twenty less-distinguished cars packed with friends, neighbors, cousins, and colleagues follow the hearse.

Though it is only eleven-thirty, headlights glow through the drizzle. I feel like a drum majorette from the Chippewa Valley High School marching band, which we watched at the Thanksgiving Day parade a little over two months ago surrounded by a large, loud group in our own living room, with its Central Park West view. On account of Barry's vodka-heavy Bloody Marys—not, I suspect, Big Bird—few guests ever refused our annual invitation.

A familiar khaki-colored Jeep joins the halting procession of cars but abruptly exits the Henry Hudson Parkway at 125th Street. Did the driver simply lose his nerve or did he suddenly get the yen to shop at Fairway? If that's the case, I hope he's buying the makings for a nourishing soup thick with root vegetables. I believe he's in need of comfort.

It might have seemed odd if Luke had stuck with the entourage, odd to everyone but me. I would have liked him there, with his black overcoat flapping against his long legs, the pale blue cashmere scarf I gave him for his birthday tied around his neck, mirroring the color of his eyes and still smelling faintly of my perfume. Would he have cried? Cursed in silence? Introduced himself to my parents? Barry? Pulled Annabel to his chest and wept? How would he have explained himself? Too many questions.

Perhaps it's just as well he's not here, because we have arrived at the cemetery. The graveside service is abbreviated yet unbearable. Annabel hides her face against Barry's hip. My parents—suddenly looking ten years older than the sixty-two they turned last year—lean on each other and Lucy like fragile plants whose roots have grown together for support. The gravediggers struggle as they center my casket. I am having trouble centering as well. I focus on the grimy granite bench nearby and wonder if Barry and Annabel will ever return to sit on it and talk to me. Or will Barry come alone? Will he apologize—or find a reason to complain?

There are prayers in both Hebrew and English. Then I hear it, the

thud. Like a bomb, a shovelful of dirt wallops the top of the casket. Barry, the envy of every thirty-eight-year-old at the gym, pitches the earth with athletic zeal. My parents go next. At intervals of about a half minute, I feel tremors. Lucy brings Annabel to the grave and, with my daughter's tiny, purple-mittened hands atop hers, which are bare and raw, they sprinkle a handful of gravelly Jersey mud that lands above my left shoulder, the one that didn't break. Brie and Isadora approach the casket and hold each other around their narrow waists as they do the same. Kitty stands back, her head tilted down. At the end of the line, some of the others walk tentatively to the casket and dump in a shovelful. Unfamiliar with my religion's ritual, they look shocked when, as if on cue, every member of the tribe suddenly chokes up ten seconds into the Kaddish, the prayer for the dead. *Yeetgadal v'yeetkadash sh'mey rabbah . . .* The foreign yet familiar words of finality pierce my flesh. This spiritual punctuation is for me, Molly Divine Marx.

Aleynu v'al kohl yisrael v'eemru. The Kaddish is over. *Amein.* Barry bellies back up to the grave and with the help of the Serenity Haven hunks blankets my casket with dirt until it is fully covered. Never again will I complain about lack of privacy.

"I'm starving," I hear someone say. In the English translation, I believe this is the last line of the Kaddish.

"There'll be a spread at Molly and Barry's." A voice repeats our address.

"From Zabar's?"

"Barney Greengrass."

"Even better. See you there?"

The mourners disperse, leaving me behind. I wonder how many will do a little shopping on Route 4 on their way back to Manhattan.

Four

SWIMMING WITH THE NOVA

*B*arry and I moved into our apartment four years ago, when I was seven months pregnant with Annabel. Until then, we rented the dollhouse sized one-bedroom on Jane Street that I'd found the year before we got engaged. In the back of a brownstone, the apartment overlooked the owner's garden, and from our kitchen you could see a crab apple tree blooming in May and in the winter squirrels gathering black walnuts. Usually I was behind schedule—organization never being my strong suit—but once in a while, before I left for work, I made time for a scone with bitter orange marmalade washed down with Earl Grey and let myself imagine I lived in London.

I would have been content to stay in this cozy nook and keep our baby in a cradle next to the bed. But Kitty insisted that it would be "disadvantageous" for Barry's practice if potential patients thought we couldn't afford a larger place. Word would get around—plastic surgery candidates research. Neither Barry nor I was drawn to the suburbs, and bigger apartments were hard to come by in the Village. Despite the fact that few of my magazine friends lived above Fourteenth Street, Kitty—who was lending us two-thirds of the down payment—declared SoHo and Tribeca to be Sodom and Gomorrah, the East Village Siberia, and

the complete borough of Brooklyn junkie heaven, even though real estate prices were through the roof. Which is how we landed uptown. Barry wanted the East Side, to be near girls' schools, he said, though I suspected his mother on Park and Seventy-sixth was the real draw. Rather irritably, I told him I'd never be old enough for that neighborhood, although I loved gawking at Madison Avenue's windows as much as the next woman. If we were to live uptown, I saw myself on Riverside Drive, which to me is—next to the Village—as British as Manhattan comes.

We settled on Central Park West, an East Side–style street that leapfrogged west of the park, in the kind of building where on Wednesday every owner receives the *New York Review of Books.* I tried to talk Barry into letting me create a neo-Victorian fantasy. I fell in love with a paint shade called Grape Thistle, wallpaper that mimicked damask, and a stuffed peacock perched inside an iron aviary six feet tall. In our classic six—two big bedrooms with a Lilliputian room off the kitchen where Delfina, our nanny, slept—I wanted worn, Turkish rugs, leatherbound Jane Austens, and tattered footstools. Maybe an English spaniel I'd name Camilla. I longed to walk through my front door and shake off the twenty-first century. I shared my vision with Barry.

"Where will I put a plasma TV?" he asked. "Molly, are you nuts? I'll never be old enough for an apartment that looks like what you're describing. I can practically feel my asthma kicking in from the dust." With a look you'd offer a closely related lunatic, he pulled me toward him. "Must be the pregnancy hormones. It's okay, honey."

I pushed him away and ran out of the room, slamming a door behind me, my fantasy shattered like bone china hurled down a staircase. I could be dramatic.

Again, we negotiated, which in decorating is no different than it is in anything else—nobody gets what he or she wants. Our capacious kitchen looks as if it belongs in New Canaan, Connecticut, with glassfronted, white-lacquered, nickel-latched cabinets, the home for an undistinguished collection of blue-and-white transferware bowls and platters. The countertops are creamy marble, which immediately became stained by red wine. To Kitty's horror, I painted the old wood floor shiny cobalt, like the ocean in *The Little Mermaid.* When she saw it she said, "Why don't you work with my decorator?" using a tone that

demonstrated, for her, considerable restraint. "My treat, darling," she added, which translated to "No taste, moron."

"Because I'm a decorating editor, Kitty," I reminded her. This never impressed my mother-in-law.

Except for Barry's dumbbells, which I invariably tripped over on the way to the bathroom at night, I rather like our bedroom; it has a spindly-legged secretary desk and no fewer than five different muted flowered prints, all from vintage fabric I found while on a photo shoot in a Portobello Road shop. Annabel's bedroom is baby-chick yellow, with a green velvet upholstered rocking chair in the corner next to a bookshelf whose marquee items include *Eloise,* my mother's copy of *The Secret Garden,* and every other book a small girl might have read before *Dora the Explorer.* But the rest of the place is spare and bare. Modern or soulless, take your pick.

Barry got his monster television, which rules the room where I would have liked a mellow, scratched dining table with leaves meant for many large dinner parties. Instead, the table, which seats only six, is glass and steel, and in front of the TV is a pair of recliners. The leather couches are butch enough for a buckaroo. I will say I love the fact that a few moody black-and-white photographs hang on the walls and there are several examples of art pottery, although I can't tell Weller from Roseville to save my life, an expression I just realized I'd best retire.

I'm being snide about the apartment, which is a lot more luxurious than most city dwellers'. I wish I could say I wasn't occasionally petty, but if I can't be honest now, then when? I had flaws. I liked to gossip. I didn't always rejoice at others' successes. I occasionally forgot birthdays and relied too much on takeout food. I IM'd at Mommy and Me classes. I never voted in primaries and ate dark chocolate every day far in excess of the 6.3 grams that might have lowered my blood pressure. I don't even know how much 6.3 grams are. And I should have lost five pounds. Okay, eight. I let the *New York Times* accumulate unread, especially the Science section, and I never opened Circuits, not once. I failed to polish my shoes, which I allowed to run down at the heels. I didn't wash my hairbrushes and sometimes went to bed without removing my makeup. E-mail chain letters terminated on my watch, and

I never looked at friends' Internet photo galleries. I subscribed to two cheesy celebrity magazines. Unless my parents were visiting, on Friday nights I preferred to go to the movies and gorge on a tub of popcorn for dinner instead of making a proper Shabbat meal with a roast chicken and challah. I could never complete a crossword puzzle (not even the easy one on Monday), play Internet Scrabble, or understand football. My abs were going to hell because I did crunches only sporadically. I hated opera and spin classes. In whodunit movies, I could never follow the plot, even when someone explained it to me afterward as if I were in third grade.

I could have been a better wife. The problems in our marriage were as much my fault as Barry's. To piss him off, I have been known to force myself not to laugh at his jokes, which were frequently the pee-in-your-pants kind our friends quoted for years. I used too much witless detail when I told him a story. I only gave my husband a blow job every few months.

I could go on recounting my negatives, and probably will. One thing I did right, though, was to hire Delfina Adams and pay her a living wage.

Today Delfina has recruited her friend Narcissa and a few other stray Jamaican dynamos and the apartment looks as buffed as it ever has. Dull black synthetic fabric, supplied by a funeral home, drapes the enormous mirror in the foyer, and around the living room, following Jewish custom, squat cardboard boxes—where the immediate family will sit—have popped up like online ads.

On the piano, next to a bouquet of lush white roses—which Delfina must have bought, because Jews aren't big on flowers during mourning—at least ten framed photos have been gathered and stand in a conga line that represents the life of Molly Marx: Lucy and me as newborns; me dressed as Malibu Barbie for Halloween; my high school graduation picture, proving definitively that short brown Audrey Hepburn hair is not my look; Brie and me burdened with backpacks during our postcollege Roman holiday; my wedding portrait in the strapless gown now carefully preserved for Annabel; big fat me, hugely preg-

nant; beach-bunny me, and damn, I didn't look as bad in my bikini as I thought, which makes me wish I'd had dessert every night, as kitchen magnets suggest.

"She was cute," a brunette in skintight black suede pants observes, "in a midwestern way." Who is this stranger who feels comfortable enough to critique my appearance on the first afternoon of a weeklong shiva? She must be a friend of the funeral's soloist because together they march over to Barry and give lingering hugs.

"I am so sorry for your loss, Dr. Marx," Black Pants says as she leaves her hand on Barry's arm. "I'm Jennifer, Adrienne's sister. I wanted to pay my respects."

To his credit, Barry doesn't extend the conversation, although—I can't be positive—he may have rested his hand on Adrienne's perky behind for one short beat, which is one beat too long. I do notice that he is wearing a small black ribbon with a tear in it on his lapel. If he were really traditional, he would have cut his funeral suit, which would have been a shame. It was expensive, even if it's faux.

"What a waste," I hear Lucy say. I'm not sure if she is referring to my life, my death, or the food. I think it is the last of these, since the delicacies Kitty has ordered, augmented by the crowd's offerings, cover every inch of the dining table: a sea of Nova Scotia smoked salmon and sable sprinkled with capers, pickled herring, sturgeon, whitefish salad, cream cheese with and without pale shoots of green chives, bialys, bagels, and babka, both chocolate and cinnamon. Much babka. All washed down with cup after cup of high-octane coffee. Kitty must have rented dishes for the occasion, because my Tiffany china— service for ten, a blue and white chickadee pattern—is nowhere in sight. Shiny silver bowls heaped with cashews, chocolate truffles, and other delicacies line the side tables. Kitty obviously made sure that Delfina and her crew got out the polish. I was lax in that department. Flaw number fifty-one.

By four o'clock, the crowd swells to more than a hundred. Guests leave their coats downstairs on a rack off the lobby. At our front door Delfina's sister, in a dignified black dress instead of her usual sequined jeans, gracefully accepts bakery boxes tied with red string. End to end, there is enough rugelach to pave a road to Scarsdale. Inside the kitchen, platters of sandwiches and mountains of fruit—fresh and

dried—artfully arranged under colored plastic wrap arrive by messenger at the apartment's back service entrance. Manhattan Fruitier should write me a thank-you note, although I'm not sure why people think the bereaved have a sudden yen for unripe papayas. I predict that my practical mother and sister will eventually check out whether City Harvest accepts donations.

"Molly would have loved this party," Brie says as she divides a white-chocolate-covered pretzel and feeds half to Isadora. Indeed, a party is what it seems to have become. Guests drift away by five-thirty but come back in triple the force by eight, when Rabbi S.S. holds a short service.

After the prayers, Annabel's meltdown begins. My parents put her to bed, Alfred the bunny at her side and her thumb in her mouth, although she hasn't sucked it for over a year. Her serious blue eyes close in less than a minute.

My spirit settles in beside her, arms around my tiny, motherless child. I try with all my strange might to will her to dream of us together, so she can feel how much I love her. I conjure up her third birthday, where every guest brought her favorite doll and we had a real tea party. "Mommy, can we do this every year?" Annabel had asked. "Of course, Annie-belle. It'll be our tradition." I had already started planning her fourth-birthday party, for which I'd wanted to order a real tea set. The catalog sits by my bed, with a stickie on page thirty-two. Now what? Will Barry take her to McDonald's instead, hire a juggler, and give her a video game?

I want that tea party dream as much for me as for Annabel, but she is too tired to dream. She sighs deeply and curls into a fetal position, a tiny comma whose blond curls barely peek above the soft white blanket. I breathe in Annabel's powdery innocence and count her sweet breaths, wishing my chest could move along with hers. And then I force myself to return to the living room, vibrating with nearly 150 visitors. Which is why, at first, I don't see him. Luke arrives with Simon, his business partner, and brings paperwhites in a white china pot. I am sure anyone who notices Luke and Simon assumes they are a couple: matching handsome men wearing kindness and Italian loafers of fine, thin leather.

Simon walks toward people he knows. Luke searches the room.

"You must be Mrs. Katz," he says, approaching my mother-in-law, who appears surprised and flattered by the attention of this black-haired stranger.

"And you would be . . . ?"

"Luke Delaney," he says. "A friend of Molly's." No reaction from Kitty. "From work."

"Luc?" she says. "Like Jean-Luc Godard?"

I hear him think, *Cool Hand Luke,* what I called him. "Like Luke Skywalker."

The reference is lost on Kitty. "Where did you say you and Molly worked?" she asks.

A small smile begins to light up Luke's face, crinkling his eyes. "I'm a photographer," he says. "We met on a shoot in London."

Kitty says nothing.

"Molly was very talented," he adds.

"I see," Kitty says. "Do you know my son?"

"No," Luke says. "But of course Molly talked about him all the time." Guilty as charged.

Kitty looks around the room. Luke thinks she is trying to find Barry, but I know she is simply pretending to do that because she has no interest in Luke, which is fine, because Luke does not want to meet Barry. Not tonight, of all nights. Kitty excuses herself. Luke walks over to the photograph display.

The picture he stares at is of me cuddling Annabel when she is a month old. I hear him think, *You're beautiful, both of you,* even though I am without makeup and my hair can benefit from not just a cut but a shampoo. When he senses no one is looking, he touches my lips gently, as if he can feel them. He moves his finger back and forth.

I swear that I can feel the warmth of his fingertips.

Five

I, GOOGLER

keep thinking there's something I could have done."

"You weren't even in this hemisphere," Brie's lover, Isadora, murmurs. She tenderly kneads almond oil into Brie's long back, starting at her square, slim shoulders and ending where smooth olive skin meets the top of her heart-shaped tush. I look away, and not just because I always thought Brie's butt was better than mine, which was shaped like a bustle no matter how skinny I got, or because girl sex has never been my thing. To exercise my gift now feels like a grievous violation of intent. I'm sure my ability wasn't given to me so I could visually Google a friend.

"But there had to be a clue," Brie says as she sits up on the tautly made white bed. Her dark brown hair, unfurled from its braid, spreads across a crisply starched pillow sham. The design of the loft shows well-muscled discipline. Every surface is black or white-white, the floors are a deep walnut, and each piece of metal—down to the hinges— is matte stainless steel that shows not one fingerprint. Books and magazines sit in neat piles, as if the owners go on a daily rampage with a T square. The furniture is the direct offspring of esteemed midcentury designers—Knoll and Saarinen and names lost on me. It's so pure here

I always wanted to show up wearing rock-and-roll drag, carrying carnations dyed electric blue.

To live as Isadora thought they should, Brie jettisoned three-fourths of her possessions. It may still be unknown to Isadora that the stuff wasn't sold on Craigslist, as Brie led her to believe, but landed in a Bronx mini-storage bin. At least Brie listened to me on that one. I'll bet right now she wishes she were wrapped in an old granny quilt, rocking in the rickety blue chair we scored at a barn sale in Bucks County.

"A clue?" Isadora says. "Like a mysterious phone call?"

Color rises in Brie's face.

"Kidding," Isadora says in her seductive Spanish purr.

"I was hoping," Brie says, "a postcard, at least, with a word on it."

"Well, the New York mail may be bad, *mi amor,*" Isadora says, "but it's been over a week." She reaches for Brie's hands, but Brie slips on her robe—whipped-cream white, matching Isadora's—walks to the window, and stares toward the street below. "I'm sorry," Brie's lover says. "I know you're hurting. I wish there was something I could do."

Isadora leaves the room—she realizes nothing she can do or say right now will be a comfort or received well. Brie continues to look into the beating rain. "I can feel you, Molly," she whispers. "I know you're here, close by. I can't explain it. I swear I can smell your perfume." Every duty-free shop called my name; I'd worn Eternity each day of my life for the last five years. Half a bottle of the eau du toilette spray still sits on my bathroom counter.

"Yes, I'm here," I say. "I'm here. Turn around." Brie was as true a friend as any woman could want. There was nothing syrupy about her, yet she always let me know she wanted only good things on my behalf. Brie brought out my best self. In her presence, even if it were only over the phone, I wanted to rise to the occasion and try to be more—funnier, happier, sharper. I wish she knew I was with her now. "I'm here," I say.

Brie looks out the window, seeing nothing. "Molly, send me a sign," she says.

Six

THE DURATION

I'm Bob," he says as he shakes my hand. "I've been assigned to be your guide."

"Are you an angel?" Have I read one too many of the *Guideposts* Delfina has left behind?

He is well pressed, dark-haired, square-jawed, as snappy as the young priest the Vatican puts on television. "Are *you*?" Bob asks seriously.

Am I?

Bob clears his throat and laughs. "Yes, Molly, that was humor. We try not to use loaded words like *angel*. A little woo-woo for us. Think of me as a personal trainer, a seeing-eye dog, a big brother."

"I never had a brother."

"We know," Bob answers. "That's one reason I was assigned to your case. I'd have introduced myself sooner, but you seem to be figuring out the rules on your own."

Is this a compliment?

"Yes," Bob says. "You can take it as a compliment."

"Thank you," I say.

"Frankly, over the last few days, I've been dealing with my needier cases. You know the type. Can't tell an insight from an isosceles triangle."

I try to remember what one of those looked like, or if I ever knew.

"Molly, don't worry," Bob says. "Taxes? Spreadsheets? Unless you do logarithms to amuse yourself, math is entirely optional here."

Perhaps I will like wherever it is I am.

Bob takes out a clipboard. "We should, however, review some basics. Let's start with just now, when you were hoping to reach Brie in her bedroom."

"Yes?"

"Everyone tries that at least once." He tsks. "You remember that phrase your mother always used, 'Like talking to a wall'?"

My mom said that to Lucy and me at least four hundred times. "Bedtime, girls." We'd tune her out, glued to *Love Boat*. "Molly! Lucy!" No answer. "Like talking to a wall," she'd mutter.

I get it.

"I knew you would," Bob says, and winks. "You'll only upset yourself trying to communicate that way." He refers to his notes, then sinks into a loveseat upholstered in suede as soft as kitten fur and pats the spot next to him. I sit.

I've never believed in heaven. For that matter, I have also never believed in hell. Most Jews are like that, planning vacations to Patagonia and Prague, but never making long-term celestial plans. But if I *had* imagined heaven, I'd have pictured it like an enormous Guggenheim Museum, with stairs that circle up and up and up into the wild blue yonder. Wherever it is that I've landed now, however, looks and feels more like an upscale fitness resort. It could be any day of the year in San Diego—neither warm nor cold. We are in a sunny solarium. Leaded glass windows overlook a lush green park webbed with cobblestone paths where people of all ages are walking briskly as if they have places to go.

"Now, some of our newcomers," Bob says, "get a little overwhelmed by the ability they discover they have to, hmm, flit about."

"Like yesterday?" One minute I was in Annabel's room, and the next I was staring down at Barry. This was before I moved on to Brie

and Isadora's. I was like the cursor on my computer before I learned how to control the mouse.

"Exactly," Bob says. "You were the proverbial cheap suit."

"Could you use a different metaphor, please? How about wallpaper?"

"Fine. Now, Molly, did you ever practice yoga?"

"Occasionally. Badly."

"Ah," he says. "Then what I would encourage is for you to simply count up to your age—thirty-five, right?—before you allow yourself to relocate. That's the term we prefer, *relocate*. This will help you reserve your powers for where they're needed most."

"But how will I know where they are 'needed' at all?" I sound shrill, but Bob is kind enough not to roll his eyes.

"You will know," he says, articulating each word slowly, clearly, and—I have to admit—as if he has a warm, beating heart. "For example, you have no need to know whether or not the president and First Lady have intercourse, so stop thinking how 'interesting' it would be to see if they share a bedroom and, if so, what they do there."

Damn.

"This leads me to another point. You have discovered that you now possess the ability to hear what people think."

"Incredible."

"You must promise to listen to only one person at a time. If you abuse this privilege, it will end. Do you hear me? Kaput, over. This will mean that while you are monitoring one person, you will miss the thoughts of another, but so be it. Those, dear Molly, are the rules. I cannot emphasize this too strongly. Do you know the term *cacophony*?" Bob asks.

I nod.

"Exercise your eavesdropping talent selectively, or you will feel as if you're living through a Stones concert in the Times Square subway station during rush hour."

"Bob, you look grave," I say. He is a Ken doll that has just lost his job.

"Good one, Molly," he says, chuckling. "I will like working with you. But let's stay on point. If you don't choose to listen to just one voice

or inner thought at a time, I warn you, you will suddenly become . . ." He pauses for emphasis. "Stone deaf."

Got it.

"Now, to the power that you ever so delicately referred to as a bull-shit detector."

Am I blushing?

He waves his hand. "As good a name as any. I'll let you in on a little secret. You always had that ability. You just never bothered to activate it. Not many people who have that gift do."

I try to take it in, but I am distracted by how earnest Bob is. I picture him in a short-sleeved plaid shirt, shopping at Sears, going to the barber for his biweekly trim, never forgetting to floss or remember his grandmother's birthday. I wonder if he showed a calf at the Iowa State Fair.

"Not a calf," he says. "A blue-ribbon sow, as gorgeous as Miss Piggy. And not Iowa. Northern California." He smiles. "And no, I did not eat a deep-fried Twinkie at the fair, but yes, I was an Eagle Scout, played football and French horn, and graduated from med school. Pediatric resident. Engaged. I had a pretty sweet life until the accident. Drunk driver with a big pot belly filled with beer. Splat. Hit and run."

I don't know what to say.

"There's nothing to say," Bob says, and looks at me so kindly his eyes are like sunlamps. "Except that, of course, you can ask me anything you wish, either now or later. Anything, do you hear? In the Duration, I'm your Sherpa, remember?"

But it's all too much. I feel as if I'm at a job interview where I've been quizzed for two hours and now can't manufacture one intelligent question in response. "These powers I have, Bob," I say finally. "How long will they last?"

There isn't a harp in sight, but someone has cued Elvis, who's singing, "I can't help falling in love with you." The taste of raspberries is on my lips. In the distance, a Milky Way of dewy white roses catches the morning light and, faintly, their fragrance wafts our way. It is a fragrance far more pleasing to my nose than Eternity.

"Molly, that I can't tell you, because I don't know. None of us knows. But you are lucky—for most people, these powers are over before they even get here. For a few, of course, they last forever." Bob

touches my arm. "I believe," he says, "and this is purely private speculation, that our powers last only as long as they need to last. I am not a religious man, though neither am I a cynic."

I blink.

Bob is gone. Nearby, a plump robin lands on a branch. I could swear I see it wink.

Seven

A FOOTNOTE IN BRIDAL HISTORY

*B*arry and I were married in my parents' backyard beneath a canopy of willow branches twinkling with—may the God of Abraham, Isaac, and Jacob forgive me—tiny white Christmas lights. Rain misted us halfway through the seven benedictions, so by the time I heard "makest the bridegroom to rejoice in his bride," I was fully engrossed in whether my hair would frizz and thought only for an instant about Barry.

Several months before the wedding, at a restaurant in the Village where Barry and I went for my birthday lunch—I was turning twenty-seven—I found a Burberry box on my chair. Attached to an umbrella inside was a poem Barry had written about protecting me from life's storms. There was also a hunky emerald-cut diamond ring.

I stared at it as if it might explode. We hadn't even talked about living together. I was hoping Barry might be extravagant, and had visions of an Art Deco bracelet or a pair of expensive gold hoop earrings I'd been stalking at Saks. Instead, after only six months of dating, he was asking me to marry him.

"Molly Divine, you are the woman for me," he said. "I knew that the moment I met you."

After Barry and I had briefly dated in college, I'd had three serious relationships: Trevor, who dumped me for Sarah; Jeff, whom I dumped when I began falling asleep during sex; and Christian, whom I broke up with not because he was Christian but because if your idea of hors d'oeuvres is deviled eggs made with Miracle Whip, you can't grow old beside me.

I considered Barry's good qualities. There was his playful manner with friends' small children, and his ability to navigate life without maps—the man was a living, breathing GPS who from memory or by scent, for all I know, could retrace his steps five years later to a remote address he'd visited once, while I have the uncanny ability to consistently turn left for every right. I considered the breadth of his shoulders, the taper of his waist, the length and steadiness of his immaculate surgeon's fingers. I noted the fact that he seemed to know exactly the life he wanted, whereas I couldn't tell you if I'd rather eat a Cobb salad or tuna for lunch.

I liked that he liked me. Wanted me. Loved me, apparently.

I decided on the spot that twenty-seven was the perfect age at which to get engaged: you're young enough not to be too cynical or wrinkled for a long white dress, and old enough—presumably—to know what you're getting into. You also have a fair shot at conceiving before life becomes hot-and-cold running infertility specialists.

The day he popped the question, Barry Marx had all the right words. "I will marry my soul to yours," he said. I cried, spilling tears on the tablecloth. I actually thanked him for proposing.

He must have assumed I'd say yes, because from the restaurant we drove immediately to his mother's apartment, where at least a dozen relatives and family intimates had gathered to toast our future happiness. "To Dr. and Mrs. Marx," Kitty said, raising a glass of Veuve Clicquot. Until that point, it never occurred to me that I'd ever not be Divine. My name was as good as it gets, even if I had to share it with an obese drag queen. But Barry echoed Kitty with "To Mrs. Marx," and I was smothered by well-wishers. Only late that evening, when Barry dropped me at home on Jane Street, did I call my parents.

"Larry who?" my father asked.

"Barry," I said. "Barry Marx. The doctor."

"The plastic surgeon?" my mother asked.

"He prefers *cosmetic.*"

The silence between New York and Chicago stood between us like ice. "Are you sure, sweetie?" my mom continued. "You just ended things with Christopher."

"Christian," I said. "And it's been nine months." Our breakup had been a load off for my mother, who offered me a subscription to J-Date within hours of hearing the news. "Marriage is hard enough without Jesus coming between you," she'd said.

"When will we meet this Barry?" my parents asked more or less in unison; then and there I saw myself as an ungrateful brat because I'd impulsively agreed to marry a man my parents had never laid eyes on. My mother and father, I always felt, had been nothing less than perfect— two people I genuinely respected, who were generous and just interfering enough for me to know they cared.

"We'll work it out," I said quietly.

"Has Lucy met him?" my father asked. If Lucy approved of Barry, it would be good enough for him. Divine family lore classified my father and Lucy as the sensible ones, while I was considered to be a good-hearted and dizzy blonde like my mother.

"Not yet," I said. This wasn't going the way I'd hoped. I wanted my parents to be bouncing with happiness, not shooting questions as if our conversation were a press conference. "Aren't you pleased?" I finally asked. If I whined, I note in my defense that it was late and my face hurt from smiling.

"Molly darling, if you want to marry this man, he must be extremely special," my mother said. Not only was she always a steel beam of support, she knows when to end a conversation. "But don't rush. Have a long engagement."

The next day, Barry and I set a date for only four months later and I kicked into action. Calligraphy or my mother's distinctive penmanship? DJ or band? Cornish hens or Chilean sea bass? Tent or no tent? Peonies or hydrangeas? Noon or twilight? Vintage Bentley or a Cadillac in Mary Kay pink? Hair up or hanging loose? No detail was too small to be deconstructed as if it were a line from the Talmud.

Except for the Bentley and band, Barry didn't voice strong opinions. "You're only going to do this once, Molly—I'll go with whatever you want," he said, and made me feel as loved as I ever had by a man.

"I never took you for a psycho bride," Brie said as we gown-shopped in New York three months before the wedding.

Brie was right. I fulfilled every cliché, obsessing over decisions as if the lives of babies depended on them. A pink wedding? Too cupcake. Yellow? Unflattering on 80 percent of skin types, claims *Allure*. Blue would do, but "nothing too Cozumel," I lectured as I whipped out a paint chip to show the wedding coordinator, whom I'd forced my parents to hire at considerable expense. "It's got to be barely blue, like a duck's egg." Terms like "too matchy-matchy" infected my vocabulary. I am sure people were mocking me, but ensconced as I was in my bride bubble, how could I hear or see?

When it came to the gown, however, Brie talked me down to earth. After I considered no fewer than five hundred possibilities culled from every bridal magazine—even *Las Vegas Wedding*—and we had the ooh-la-la shopping experience, tea and all, I spent one-fifth the cost of a Vera Wang when Brie dragged me to a garment-center hole in the wall. "I'm the last person in the world to ever say no to designer clothes," she said, standing tall and tailored as I tried on fourteen gowns in thirty minutes. "But don't throw money at a dress. You could look good in a dry cleaner's bag, and honestly, strapless is strapless."

In the world of fashion, I'm a foot soldier, not a commanding officer, and so I did whatever Brie suggested. She guided me to a slim column of satin with just a spritz of blue-gray crystals. "To pick up the blue of your eyes," she said, but I suspect she was thinking a sheath made me look thinner. We sewed a pirated Carolina Herrera label into the lining and Kitty not only never knew of the counterfeit, she bragged about the gown to her friends at the engagement party she threw a month later. This is when my parents met Barry. Between his surgery schedule and my bridal dementia, we'd never made it to Chicago.

At the party, held at the country club Kitty made her second home even as a widow, Barry danced with my mother and Lucy and invited my dad to play golf. I assumed the evening had gone splendidly. "So?" I said in my parents' rented car on our drive back to the city, the first moment when we were alone together. "What do you think?"

"He's handsome, Molly," my mother said. "His nose isn't as big as you said. It fits his face."

"Uh-huh," I said, waiting for more.

"Great food tonight, but the mom's a piece of work," my father said. He hates when a woman other than my mother tries to make him samba.

"Yeah, well, what about Barry?"

He paused. "If you love him, we'll love him," he said finally.

"Great dancer," my mother added. I could tell she was stretching.

I turned to my sister.

"He complimented my tits," Lucy said.

"He did not," I shrieked, while I heard my mother sigh. Lucy is the most cleavage-focused woman I've ever met. She thinks every man is staring at her boobs, trying to decide if they're real. They are.

"Did."

"Did not."

"You two . . . ," my mother said.

"Molly, give me three reasons why you want to marry this guy, and that headlight of a ring doesn't count," Lucy said.

I stared at Lucy. I couldn't say "You're just jealous," not so much because the remark crossed a line I didn't want to pass, but because some unplumbed nook of my psyche considered that she might be on to something. I looked out the window, but there were no answers in the passing cars.

"He'll make a good father," I offered.

"That's crucial," my mother quickly responded. She didn't ask me how I could tell, and I wouldn't have been able to explain. Just intuition.

"He worries about me," I said. "I like a man who doesn't want me riding the subway alone past ten." As if I couldn't make that decision for myself.

He may love me more than I love him was something I didn't think I should list. I still thought it was wildly desirable for that to be the working dynamic in a successful relationship, and in our case, the only reason I believed it to be true was that he'd asked me to marry him with record-shattering speed. *Because I'm attracted to him?* I can tell my mother anything, but talking about sex with my dad? Nope. *I trust Barry?* I wasn't sure I did.

"Lame," Lucy snickered.

"Do you want me to screw up by marrying Barry?" I asked her.

"You hardly know the guy." I noticed that this failed to answer my question.

"My fiancé has a name—Barry—and we've been spending every minute together," I said, though it was a lie. His work always seemed to get in the way. "Mom and Dad had an even shorter engagement." After knowing each other for two months, they eloped.

"Point taken," Lucy said.

The four of us remained mute for the rest of the ride.

August arrived. The day of the wedding, Lucy showed more décol-letage than a random Hollywood starlet. It was a small price to pay to have her drop the subject of my making a mistake. "You can still get out of it," she'd said sotto voce at my bridal shower the month before, which she threw at a Chicago lingerie shop that specializes in X-rated undies with toys to match. I got enough thongs to outfit a brothel and the thirty-one guests each received a vibrator disguised as a lipstick.

Three weeks later, I was a comely footnote in bridal history, not a radiant headline. Wearing my hair up was definitely the wrong move—I looked like a hostess at Howard Johnson's—but it wasn't that or the fact that Rabbi S.S. had double-booked and had to send his twitchy sidekick. When I looked at my pictures later, I saw a frightened bride.

I walked down the aisle on my father's arm. Under the chuppa, six feet away from me, a stranger was waiting. It took a moment to realize he was Barry Marx, who in ten minutes would become my husband. Forever. I broke a sweat and, worrying that perspiration stains would show, stumbled on the white carpet that had been unfurled down the middle of our lawn, dividing the Divines from the Marxes. My dad, pale as milk, steadied my arm. We exchanged a glance and in his face I saw the fear I felt.

I don't remember the vows. I don't remember anything about the actual ceremony except Barry's lengthy, theatrical tongue kiss. What was the romantic ballad I had obsessed over that accompanied our first walk as husband and wife? My ears echoed with silence.

But then the reception began—loud, long, throbbing. In summer, the Chicago twilight comes late, and at ten, along with a fistful of stars, lights hidden in the oak trees lit up like pavé diamonds. On account of

the heat, everyone drank not just the pomegranate martinis circulated after the ceremony but cases and cases of crisply cold pinot grigio and, later, Champagne.

There's nothing I find less appealing than a drunken woman, but I definitely had a buzz on. Loose-limbed and smoking, Lucy and I did our Molly and Moosey number, alone in a circle of clapping girlfriends, a performance saved from lewdness only because it was performed in bridal frou-frou. Soon Brie, my other Northwestern friends, and the New York crowd joined in, watched on the sidelines by Isadora, too soignée for such a display.

"This must be what happy feels like," I said to Brie as we twirled in the middle of the dance floor, our booties bouncing to the beat.

When the band took a break, I went in the back door and upstairs to powder myself with scented talc and keep the dainty bride thing going. As I walked out of my bathroom door, I heard Barry's laugh. He owns the kind of guffaw that makes people turn around in movie theaters; aspiring stand-up comics should pay to have that appreciative noise in their audience. The sound stopped abruptly, but it had come from downstairs, and I moved toward it.

I got to the foyer as Barry walked out of the guest bathroom and continued in the other direction, toward the hallway that led outside. I was ready to call his name when the door opened again. One of his guests from New York—Remy, Romy, Ronnie?—exited the bathroom and sashayed in the other direction. Which made us collide.

"Molly," she said, nonplussed. Her Toffee Frost lipstick was smeared, her long red hair disheveled. I couldn't tell if the hairdo was intentional or if a neo-beehive had collapsed due to avid fondling. "Beautiful wedding!" she gushed, and flew away, innocent as a butterfly.

I staggered outside, searching for the nearest chair.

"I've been looking all over for you," Barry said, running toward me. "C'mon, sweetheart—the cake."

"I need a moment," I said, but a waiter was rolling in three towering layers of chocolate pastry, heavy on the whipped cream, studded with enormous strawberries, topped with blazing sparklers. Barry and I completed our drill—his hand on top of mine, the new gold band gleaming against his tan—as the knife sliced through the layers and the shock sliced through my heart. We smiled for the camera.

"Is Mrs. Marx ready for her life to begin?" Barry whispered as he drew me toward him. His breath was minty, his smile confident, his teeth unnaturally white.

Mrs. Marx has another idea about where to stick this knife, I thought as he kissed me and the photographer snapped.

Eight

OLD SOULS

If anyone imagines that during shiva a moratorium is declared on discussing the widower's social life, they would be dead wrong.

"Whenever you're ready, let me know, because my wife's sister—you remember Stacey?"

"Stacey with the chest?" Barry asks.

"Precisely. Stacey and her husband? *Finito.*"

I overhear at least six proposed hook-ups, including one from our accountant, who wants Barry to meet his daughter. She's a senior at Stanford but, he promises, "an old soul."

"I thought you could use some dinner," a divorced mom from Annabel's school class says as she presents an armful of vegetarian lasagna. "For you and Andrea."

I hear Barry think, *Not my type,* as he sizes up her double-wide hips, but the only words out of his mouth are "Thanks. Annabel and I appreciate it." He hands off the Pyrex to Delfina, who crams it into the freezer next to a pot roast, turkey chili, and a tragic casserole of Velveeta and canned pinto beans that's made from a recipe I passed by last month on the AOL home page.

"Should have gone for the bigger Sub-Zero," he says to Delfina as he returns to the living room.

"A lot of things you shoulda done," she says to herself after he leaves the room.

While many Reform Jews do a token shiva for a day or two, my family goes the whole nine yards: seven days, with time off for good behavior on the Sabbath, when Barry shows up at temple, both Friday night and Saturday morning. Throughout the week, I carefully monitor my husband. Has Model Mourner researched funeral customs? Although he dresses carefully, in a black cashmere turtleneck and gray flannel pants, he doesn't shave, which leaves him looking just this side of seedy. On at least a dozen occasions he gets teary when someone mentions my name.

It took me two days to notice, however, that Dr. Barry Marx has varied his meticulous routine. Before dinner, were it not for shiva, he'd have gone for his usual after-work run followed by a shower that would last five to fifteen minutes, depending on whether or not he jerks off. After dinner, he'd log time at his laptop to look at e-mail (he has three accounts: barrymmd@aol.com and bmarx8@earthlink.net, plus the one he doesn't know I know about, bigbare@hotmail.com). He'd then check out the *Wall Street Journal*'s take on medical developments, followed by a spot of porn while he'd blare the TV—always a marital sore point. Because of shiva, he's taken a break from these pursuits, but the rest of his evening remains intact. At eleven-ten, Barry does two hundred sit-ups and fifty push-ups, kisses Annabel's forehead, and spends eight minutes on WaterPik maneuvers. Letterman's opening monologue follows, then exactly one chapter of a book—mystery, history, or athlete's biography—before his midnight curfew.

But he's added an intriguing detail. Barry has taken to wearing his wedding ring, which every night he now deposits in the Cartier box in which it arrived, the one he keeps in his second-from-the-top drawer. The box is in pristine condition, since the ring has seen little action. This never bothered me—my father doesn't wear a wedding band and plenty of cheaters I know do. Nonetheless, the ring—engraved with our wedding date and the word *forever*—has started appearing on his finger.

Tonight he looks at the shiny band as if he'd never seen it before, turning it over in his hand as the phone rings.

"Hideous," he says after picking it up. "I'll be glad when this ordeal is over."

The slightly nasal voice on the other end is the same person who has called around eleven every night for the last week.

"Thank God it's the last day," Barry says.

I study Barry's face. His eyes look puffy, and I see wrinkles, newly engraved.

"How do I feel? Like dog shit."

This does not make me unhappy.

"I think she's doing okay, but it's hard to tell—she's been practically mute."

Wrong. Annabel's been quite a little chatterbox when Barry's not around, especially when she's alone.

"Everyone's all over her—Delfina, my mother-in-law, and that loudmouth Lucy. Oh, and Molly's friends. "

Who've come, one by one and in small groups, every night of shiva.

"Yeah, especially the lipstick lesbians."

My gang has really been here.

"Tomorrow? Impossible. I'm back in surgery."

That poor nose.

"No, my feelings haven't changed."

Does he care about this woman? I can't tell. After the wedding, I never could tell if he cared about me.

"I'm hanging up now."

The voice sounds even more nasal.

"Have a little decency," he says.

He looks at the clock.

"I mean it. I'm beat. Another time, Stephanie."

Stephanie.

Barry crawls into bed. He avoids my side as if rolling there would mean that he, too, will land in a grave, and falls asleep in less than two minutes.

———

It's true that he has surgery in the morning, but not until ten. A detective named Hicks arrives at seven forty-five. He is African American, no older than his early thirties, one earring, a discreet gold stud. I can't resist watching him, a man who is far more handsome than he guesses.

"Mr. Marx," he begins, taking inventory of our living room.

"It's Dr.," Barry answers reflexively. *Putz,* he thinks, *why did I say that?*

"Excuse me," Hicks says. "*Dr.* Marx. I'm sorry for your loss and intruding at this time, sir, but as I told you on the phone, this is standard. Just a few questions."

"I'm all yours," Barry says.

We'll see about that, I hear Hicks think. "The evening that Mrs. Marx went out biking—the night before she was found dead, that is. Where were you?"

Barry answers immediately. "I was running. In Central Park. Training for the marathon."

"Same here," Hicks offers, in a friendlier tone than I would have predicted.

"Well, then you know how much time you have to put in," Barry says. "At least an old guy like me does." He laughs as he attempts to grease his way with charm. He guesses that he isn't actually too many years older than Hicks, but the detective isn't going to reward him with personal workout details.

"Did anyone see you that night?"

Barry takes a minute to answer, but he has already decided what to say. "The doorman."

Alphonso, our evening doorman, can't remember if you had a colony of bats delivered twenty minutes ago, and he loves Barry, who gives him a few Yankee tickets every season.

"And where did you run in the park?" Hicks says.

"Entered across the street, ran south, up to the north end of the park, then back out on Eighty-first," Barry says. "The usual loop."

"How long did it take you?"

Barry shifts in his chair and twists the wedding band. "That run usually takes me about forty-five minutes."

Barry looks as if he is waiting to be congratulated on his seven-minute miles, but instead Hicks asks, "Did anyone see you running?"

What the fuck, Barry thinks. "Sure, a lot of people, I guess, but we don't all stop and introduce ourselves." *It's not speed-dating, for Christ's sake,* he thinks.

"Was there anyone you can think of who would have wanted to harm your wife?" Hicks asks.

After a long, considered pause Barry says, "Everyone loved Molly. She wasn't a threat to anyone." Not exactly the highest praise, but I imagine he thinks he is complimenting me to, well, the heavens.

"Was Mrs. Marx upset about anything?"

Besides me? Barry says to himself. "Nothing out of the ordinary. She led a very fortunate life." Cushy. Pampered. Privileged. True, true, true.

This is really his point, and Hicks gets it.

"So I appreciate your visit, Detective, and I hope"—*and expect,* he thinks—"that all the muscle of the New York Police Department will get behind finding the fucking monster who did this to my wife."

Whoa, Detective Hicks thinks, *this hothead's getting way ahead of himself, considering that his wife's death might be a simple, stupid accident or even a suicide.* "That's all for now—we'll be in touch, Dr. Marx," he says, and gets up from the chair. "Sorry to intrude." He shakes Barry's hand and gives him his card. I notice his hands, large, strong, as meticulously groomed as my husband's.

"No problem," Barry says, slipping the card in his pocket. After the detective leaves, Barry sighs. It sounds like the wheeze of an elderly man. In two minutes he, too, is out the door. It's raining, but he forgets his umbrella.

I check on Annabel. She's been playing rabbi all week long, sitting shiva with her American Girl dolls. I am the pretty blonde, Elizabeth, who serves tea and is presumed to have good penmanship. I, Elizabeth, have been spending the week asleep. I keep wondering if Annabel will let me wake up.

"I miss you, Mommy," she says. "I love you." She tenderly tucks her tattered blankie around Elizabeth. Around me. "Are you warm enough, Mommy?" In her pink flannel nightie and bare feet she pads across the room to the toy baskets and, one by one, dumps them on the floor until she finds a minuscule plastic plate with a tiny brown muffin attached.

She places it next to Elizabeth. "You must be hungry, Mommy," she says. "Got to eat." I recognize the musical tone as my own.

On the dot of eight-fifteen, Delfina quietly raps on the door as she opens it, singing, "Good morning, sunshine." She takes in the mess—toys and books everywhere—and the dolls tidily lined up for prayers.

"You've been busy, haven't you, miss?" she says, love in her voice. "Don't worry—I'll watch over your friends here, but we gotta get dressed—time to go back to school."

Annabel doesn't budge.

"What do you want to wear?" Delfina asks. "Pick anything."

My daughter rummages through her drawer and finds the velour sweats that almost match mine, last Mother's Day's gift from Kitty. I wore my set only once, because they made me feel as if I should be heading out for the early-bird special in Boca. Annabel hasn't worn hers since last summer. Her skinny arms and legs stick out by inches.

"Perfect," Delfina says. "Now hop to it, miss. Waffles!"

After Delfina leaves the room, Annabel takes one last long look at Elizabeth. "You take a long sleep now," she says.

Nine

MISSIONARY'S DOWNFALL

From where I lie now, it's easy to ask myself why I didn't confront Barry at our wedding when I saw that witch wiggle her tush out of my parents' powder room. But what was I supposed to do, yell "rewind" with 250 wedding guests panting for cake? As they say in life, timing is everything. In death, not so much.

Hawaii won the honeymoon sweepstakes, and the morning after our wedding, Barry and I flew west. For the first day, I wanted to strangle him with an orchid lei, but my fury started to mute as I soaked in a hot tub and sipped innumerable pineapple cocktails—not that I could tell a Missionary's Downfall from a Tropical Itch. When we weren't getting hammered we were having sex, on the bed, in the hammock, and on the fine white sand, this way, that way, and yes, once *that* way. By the end of the trip, I'd convinced myself that maybe I'd imagined the debacle of the powder room. I returned to New York with a grass skirt, five new pounds, and a urinary tract infection. In the honeymoon afterglow, I made a secret vow to become a forgive-and-forget kinda wife worthy of a Country Music Award and my husband's everlasting affection.

Three weeks after the wedding, I had lunch with Brie, who hadn't yet started law school and was still the centerpiece of faraway photo shoots—she'd just returned from Kenya—although at almost twenty-eight she'd stopped getting top American bookings. Her last job had been for the second-best women's weekly in Johannesburg.

When she asked me about married life I reported that I'd been dragging myself out of bed every day to kiss Barry goodbye before he left for the hospital. "I'm buying fresh flowers twice a week, and every night I play a bunch of jazz CDs recommended by that guy we like at Tower Records, the one with the dreads."

I didn't tell Brie the half of it, and I don't mean that I also played Lyle Lovett and Michael Bublé. Every day, I made mental notes on wry observations and worthy conversational themes, often stolen from the blogosphere, which, along with three proper courses, I'd serve at dinner to stimulate—make that simulate—amusing repartee. I ordered napkins embossed with "Barry and Molly" and took Barry's shirts to the dry cleaner for laundering. How could I have known he preferred them on hangers, rather than three to a box like a weekly birthday present?

Brie stopped flipping through pictures she'd taken on a safari tacked onto her shoot. "Excuse me," she said, "but have you seen my friend Molly?"

"Your point being?"

"You shouldn't be sweating it like this." Brie leaned forward and nailed me with her eyes, smoky as graphite but not as soft. My bridal sell-by date, which had veiled me from criticism, had apparently expired. It was the first time since I got married that anyone—even Lucy—was talking turkey to me. "You're borderline pathetic," she added, in case I hadn't gotten the message.

I turned my wineglass in a circle on the bare wood table. My wedding band caught the light, its channel-set diamonds marching in a circle promising eternity.

"I hear you," I said.

"I'm not sure you do," she said, putting her hand on mine to stop the twisting. "Look at me."

Reluctantly, I did.

"If anyone belongs on a pedestal, it's you, Molly. Not him. Ever since you met Barry Marx you're acting all 'I'm the bottom, you're the top.' " For extra emphasis, she sang the Cole Porter song.

"Okay, that's enough," I whispered. Brie's singing had captured the attention of two women at the next table. Her vocal stylings leave something to be desired. "Thanks for the big vote of confidence, but I want to make my marriage work."

"Yeah?" she said. "And this is it?"

"Nobody teaches you how to be married," I said, in what even I recognized as a tone better left to a motivational speaker. "I can't very well imitate my parents— they've set the bar so high it's a damn curse." Perhaps I used a different adjective. Anyway, it's not like Dan and Claire Divine coo to the point where you gag, but they still crack each other up, and sometimes I catch my dad staring at my mom—even when she's come in from tennis, sweat dripping down her back and curling the hair around her delicately lined face—with a look that says, *How did a dumb putz like me ever win Mega Millions?* For her part, Mom respects the power of lingerie. I always assumed I could tell a lot about my parents' private life by her boudoir wardrobe, which is heavy on silk charmeuse in styles skimpy enough to show off her cellulite-free legs, each wisp of a gown coordinated with robes—sheer cottons, embroidered kimonos, and velvets in Elizabethan hues. Lucy calls her the Geisha.

"Besides," I added, "you don't even know Barry all that well. I think you're being a little arrogant."

"You're right, Molly," Brie said, leaning back in her chair. "I'm single. What do I know?" Her words were apologetic; her voice was not. "It's just that I don't want you to forget you."

"I love that you worry about me," I said after about a minute. "I worry about you, too. Mostly that you'll elope." Brie was then five boyfriends away from declaring herself a daughter of Sappho. "I'm selfish. I'm afraid I'll lose you to someone who'll make you live without blow-dryers and Crest Whitestrips on the dark side of the moon."

Brie laughed, a deep, throaty gurgle I wish I could hear this very minute. "Tell me again about the photographer you met," I said. She described her latest conquest, Luke whatever, in head-to-toe detail. Black hair, blue eyes, long legs.

My mind was stuck in the Molly-forgetting-Molly groove. Still, I

must have subliminally absorbed something, because a year later, when I met Luke Delaney, wires connected deep in my brain, and I approached this particular man with my version of candor. To begin with, I made a point of looking him in the eye, something Barry repeatedly told me I neglected to do, a deficiency among many that, in the second year of our marriage, he was only too happy to draw to my attention so that I could become a more perfect person and mate.

I was at Kennedy Airport when I met Luke. "Excuse me, but aren't you Molly, Brie's friend?" a black-haired man asked right after I was told my flight to London had been overbooked and I'd need to take the next plane out hours later.

"Yes, I'm Molly," I said. "Molly Marx." I tried to smile but, aggravated as I was about the delay, the best I could do was not frown.

"Luke Delaney," he said. He shook my hand and smiled for both of us. "I got bumped, too."

"Are you as pissed as I am?" I asked. "If there hadn't been so much traffic on the LIE . . ."

"You at least have an excuse," Luke said. "Got a late start. No one to blame but myself." As he spoke, I noticed his eyes were the exact shade I'd wanted for my wedding, blue as a sunny sky over Nantucket. I shifted from his eyes to his mouth. His lips were full, his nose rather long, and his bottom teeth endearingly crooked.

It was going to be a slog waiting for the next flight. Barry'd made no particular fuss about my going away for a week on a business trip, my first since our wedding. In fact, this morning he seemed determined to pick a fight, castigating me for forgetting to take care of paying the cable bill before my departure. He made most of the money, but writing checks was my domain.

My smile arrived.

"What do you say I buy us both a drink?" he asked. "Once we're in London, we'll be working such ridiculous hours I'll be too damn exhausted to hit a pub."

"*We?*"

He grabbed my tote—which overflowed with files, a liter bottle of water, and a pashmina big enough to upholster a couch—and guided me

toward the first-class lounge. "Samuel Wong cancelled this morning. I got booked at noon." That explained why the name Luke Delaney hadn't shown up on my memos.

The lounge was crowded, but photographers have eagle eyes—he spotted two armchairs on the far side of the room. "Grab 'em," he said, "and I'll get us something. You drink . . . ?"

"Thanks. Pinot noir."

As I reached the empty chairs a mom with a toddler catapulted into them. I walked back to Luke, who was balancing wineglasses on a tray along with nuts and a weapon-sized Toblerone bar.

"We lost our spot to a mommy," I said.

"But here's another." He charmed a love seat into vacancy.

After fifteen minutes of unremarkable chat, he asked, "Can I make a confession?"

He's still in love with Brie, I thought. He wouldn't be the first man my best friend had turned into mush after she'd moved on. Knowing he was most likely under her spell made me relax. Or maybe it was the wine, which I'd already finished. "Confess away," I said.

"I'm scared shitless about this shoot."

"Really?" I asked, genuinely surprised. "Why?" To me the assignment was routine. In those days, I ran a magazine's decorating department staffed by four slaves who bushwhacked ahead of me to set up. The magazine was photographing Mayfair district houses, each chicer than the next. It was the kind of job I could do in my sleep, assuming the owners didn't freak about the photographer's aides-de-camp dropping cigarette ashes on Mummy's threadbare rugs. Oh, there'd be dogs to corral—the Brits always had dogs. But as long as I kept them happy with biscuits and picked up the nightly bar tab for the owners and our gang, I expected peace in the kingdom. We'd already made reservations at numerous restaurants deemed "bloody brilliant" by *Time Out London.*

"I'm a fashion guy," Luke said. "But I don't think I can stand one more model tantrum. From now on I want to be all about inanimate objects."

"I don't blame you. Anything I can do—" I started to say, but the loudspeaker interrupted to announce that our flight would be delayed—by how long the plummy voice didn't say.

After Luke returned to gather a second round of drinks, I reported in to Barry, as a wife is supposed to do, even when she's begun to realize she's in a continual state of low-grade anger iced with disappointment. I doubted he'd be home, but I planned to leave a message.

He answered on the first ring. "Really, Molly?" Barry said, and seemed to listen attentively to my tale of transportation inconvenience. "How about I pick you up and take you to dinner?"

Suddenly Barry was acting like an ideal husband while I was guzzling wine with a guy who was looking better by the sip, someone I'd be working with across an ocean for six days. Into what alternate reality had the airport limo deposited me? "You would do that?" I asked, incredulous.

"Why not?" he said. "I'll hop in the car—get there in, say, forty minutes? Tomorrow's my day off. I can afford to get to bed late."

I felt like a horse's ass. Who was this spouse so concerned for my well-being? I wondered as Luke returned with more wine. "Barry, I love you for offering, but they aren't saying when my plane will leave. You could drive all the way out here and I'd take off before you even parked."

He waited a few seconds before responding. "Got it," he said.

"It just seems better this way," I said. That sounded feeble. "But it would have been . . . fun." Feebler still.

"Well, good luck," he said. "Love you."

"Love you, too." I said it loudly, as much to remind myself I was married as to alert Luke in case he'd missed my rings.

Eventually, the two of us boarded and were seated side by side. I debated whether to proceed with dabbing Neosporin in my ears and above my lip, my preferred retaliation against the germ warfare that is airplane air.

The Neosporin stayed in the bag. Luke and I continued to chat, and somewhere above Greenland I discovered that he, too, was a twin, an identical twin. His brother, Micah, taught English at Dartmouth.

"Maybe we should fix up your brother with my sister," I said.

"I think not," he said. "My brother's married. But why not me? That is," he added, "if your sister's anything like you." The fourth glass of wine—or maybe it was the fifth—had erased the shy guy I thought I'd met earlier in the evening.

It's not as if the Virgin Mary appeared in my window to announce that this companion would ever be anyone important in my life, but at that moment I realized that even though I didn't know what to do with Luke, I didn't want to regift him, to my sister or to anyone else.

"Why not, indeed?" I said. "I'll get on it as soon as I'm back."

My first lie.

Luke was dovetailing far too perfectly with my doubts. I needed to shut down, despite the fact that I would have happily jabbered all the way to England. "Better get some sleep," I said. "Supposed to meet my staff tomorrow at eleven to go over two hundred shoot details."

"I'm a babbling idiot," he said. "Sorry." Still, he pulled out an eye mask and put it on. "Do I look like Zorro or just a pathetic perv?" he asked, turning toward me and speaking in a low Jeremy Irons growl. "Are you scared?"

In my wine-addled haze, he looked cuter than a panda with an extra helping of testosterone. "Terrified," I admitted as I burrowed beneath my pashmina tent.

When I woke at dawn, I discovered Luke's legs under the shawl, his feet—in red socks—touching mine. I faked sleep until the flight attendant rocked my shoulder to make sure I was alive.

Those were the days.

Ten

DOO-DAH, DOO-DAH

My mother, my father, and Lucy are gathered around the pine farm table in the kitchen, sipping their second cups of black coffee. Light snow stencils the patio and yard, and whatever sun shines over Illinois cowers under menacing clouds.

Since my death, no one in the family has slept past dawn, even after Ambien—which, unfortunately, Costco does not sell over the counter in jars the size of buckets. Lucy took the commuter train north last night and slept in our childhood bedroom—a circa 1985 homage, lilac for me, aqua for her, Madonna posters, now faded, for both of us. She's made this trip for the last two weekends and believes she's here to console my parents, but it's more the other way around. Lucy is alone; my parents have each other. They speak their grief wordlessly—in the car, while my mother massages my father's neck; as he brings the morning newspaper to their bed; when they spoon through cold, fitful nights.

"Don't pick the crumbs off the crumb cake," my mother says.

"Don't treat me like I'm ten."

"Don't start, you two."

Don't, don't, don't, you two, you two. The Divine family anthem. *Doo-dah, doo-dah.*

"So, should I call Barry?" Lucy asks. She asked the same question last night at dinner. "I want to know if anything's happened with the case that he hasn't told us."

"No, honey," my mother says. "Dad should do it." I hear her worry that if Lucy asks, Barry will get his back up. Lucy can turn a chat about seasoning hamburger patties into a military engagement.

"It's too early to call New York," my dad says, eyes on the sports pages. He dreads speaking to Barry. *Putz,* he's thinking. My father, I have learned, is not quite the gentleman he presents to the world, but he tries hard to see Barry's side. "Poor guy may be full of himself, but he's still just lost his wife and has to raise a daughter alone," he says to the women in his family, though I suspect it's to convince himself to treat Barry with decency.

The Divines are determined to have Annabel visit for Passover. For the last three years, Barry, Annabel, and I spent Thanksgiving with Kitty and Passover with my parents, so my parents and Lucy feel they own that holiday. Since shiva ended, they call Annabel every night on the dot of seven, but the conversations are as unsatisfying as tickling an insect bite.

"Annabel would be up now," my mother points out. "She'd be watching cartoons."

"But Barry might have gone back to sleep," my father counters. "It's Saturday. Give the guy a break."

"A break?" Lucy shrieks. "What about my sister?"

My mother groans. "We can live without the melodrama, Lucy," she says, looking down at her newspaper and pretending to read. Fatigue mutes her voice. "Dan, call at eight our time."

With deep affection, he salutes her. "Yes, Sarge," he booms.

My family returns to their breakfast, but after a minute Lucy pours her coffee down the drain. "I'm going for a run," she announces, and bolts upstairs. From her small duffel, she plucks out sneakers and several layers of winter-ready sports clothes. While I left behind a wardrobe of girly gear—lace, chiffon, clingy cashmere, low-rise thongs, numerous garments constructed of fabrics better suited to gift wrap, and an unworn pink wool jacket trimmed in lace—Lucy believes in

fibers built to withstand a trek from Kathmandu to Everest. If our father were president, her Secret Service code name would be Patagonia.

Lucy pulls her curly hair, the color of dark maple syrup, into a ponytail that bobs beneath a snug knit cap. Its string ties dangle over her ears like the *payes* on a Hasidic rabbi. In a flash of black and purple, without saying goodbye, she's out the door.

Lucy's completed several marathons, which is probably why my equally competitive husband has started training for one. Barry doesn't especially like to run, but what he likes less is my sister outdoing him, and Luce loves to run—in any weather, at any time of day, her gait long and lithe. At a distance, under her gear, a casual observer wouldn't know if she is male or female but would admire her grace.

Sadly, the effect ends as soon as she stops, not so much because her walk is a sturdy clomp but because Lucy is the only person I know for whom exercise becomes foreplay to aggression. After a workout, when most people seem ready to nap, Lucy appears ripe for a fight. The more she runs, the less mellow she becomes.

At least we can dismiss suicide, she thinks. *No one would ever think my sister would or could kill herself.* As she hits her stride, she synchronizes every thought with a footfall. *Loved her Annie-bell too much.* She repeats my daughter's nickname in exactly the too-sweet voice I said it in. *A lot to live for.* She starts up a hill. *But Barry could have driven her to it.* She pushes harder. *He'd drive me nuts—he could make any woman ride her bike into the water.* She turns. *Or off a cliff.* She reaches the top. *All marriages are like that.* Picks up the pace. *Men . . . morons.* She's going strong. *Douche bags. Cretins. Fuckers.*

Wind whistles through bare trees as Lucy runs six miles, her mind circling in and out of possibilities. She whips past the diner where our parents treated us to blueberry pancakes every week after Sunday school. Two former high school friends wave—they're continuing the Country Kitchen tradition with their own kids. Lucy looks through them.

"We sent a hundred-dollar fruit basket," one of the young matrons says. "She could at least stop to say hello."

"Run your butt off, Moosey," the other one hisses softly. "If her sister hadn't just died, I'd shout it," she says to her friend.

Lucy is in her own head and wouldn't have heard. *Pills, maybe.* She

starts to pant a bit as she begins her last mile. *Or carbon monoxide.* She catches her breath on the home stretch. *But not this way.*

Lucy charges back into the kitchen.

"Where were you?" my mother asks. "You were gone almost an hour."

My sister ignores her as she unlaces her shoes and strips, layer by sweaty layer.

"You'll never guess who called," my father says.

Molly? Lucy thinks.

"Barry's mom," my mother says. "Inviting us all to New York for the seder."

Lucy skewers our mother with a stare. "You declined, obviously."

"I thanked her. Said we'd let her know."

"Mom," Lucy snaps. When her face contorts like a gargoyle's, my sister must give her tiny students nightmares. "Why are you such a sucker? It's manipulation. Can't you see that? If Annabel doesn't visit now, a precedent will be set and—"

"Lucy, apologize," my father interrupts, wishing he could be playing poker or listening to his vinyl LPs—Odetta, Buddy Holly, early Bob Dylan—or getting a massage at his golf club, and curses the fact that it's closed through March. He'd like to be anywhere but here, with the difficult daughter, the daughter who rips and rumbles through life, no matter how much she means well, which she usually does.

"Dan, calm down," my mother says. "Lucy has a point. But Kitty claims the trip would upset Annabel. She thinks it's too soon for her to travel, that it will disrupt her schedule. I want what's best for our granddaughter."

"Barry!" Lucy bleats my husband's name as if it's profanity. She's down to her silk long johns and the sports bra that compresses her DDs. My dad looks the other way. "What a wuss. Has his mommy call."

Lucy can't get a rise out of my parents, who've seen it all before. My mother walks to her only living daughter and begins to stroke her matted hair. Lucy shakes off her hand. "I'm calling him myself," she says.

Eleven

REARVIEW MIRROR

*I*n London, I loved that Luke was far more attentive than your usual photographer. He wasn't afraid to ask my opinion, courtship more subtle and effective than roses or the occasional deep, meaningful gaze. "How do you want the shot set up?" "Here or there?" "Think we got it, or do we shoot another roll?" As he picked my brain he would casually touch my arm, the electric whisper of flesh brushing flesh ending almost before it began. He had to notice that I never pulled away.

True to his word, Luke wasn't a partier. Every night he bowed out early. Whether he took dinner in his room or got together with friends—or a woman—he'd never say, and only on the last night did Luke join our posse. "To Molly!" he toasted as the evening began. "Who allowed me to pass through this firing squad barely bruised."

"To Luke," I said, raising my wineglass across the table and admiring his appeal, which was soft enough around the edges for me to believe that he was deep and sensitive. "And beautiful results."

They were. The next week, when my magazine's editor scrutinized our pictures, her praise was like a bath full of bubbles. "I don't know why this Luke Delaney's been wasting his time shooting fashion," she declared. "Put him under contract before someone else does."

By the end of the month she'd signed him. From then on, Luke and I weren't just thrown together on shoots—we began speaking almost every day when we didn't have an actual meeting. There was always a detail over which to obsess: South Beach or Belize? The fussy food stylist or the lazy one who plied us with charm and homemade pumpkin muffins? Brocade love seat or creamy Italian chaise?

This happened just as Brie abandoned modeling—and me, temporarily—for Columbia Law School. While she chewed through contracts and torts, our daily calls dwindled and Luke began standing in as my best friend. At least that's what I told myself. He gave excellent text message and the two of us could soon be mistaken for juniors exchanging gossip in trigonometry class.

Through my rearview mirror, I see that as far as my marriage went, Barry and I were as close to bliss as we were ever going to come—if only I'd recognized it. He didn't worship me, but then again, I didn't see myself as worthy of adoration. He didn't seek my opinions, and that offered a certain relief, since on many topics I'm not sure I would have been confident enough to voice any. He continued to point out flaws I never knew I had—my legs could have been longer from the knee to the ankle or my answers to people's questions shorter. I usually could see his point. Barry and I settled into a routine that may have been a few hallelujahs short of ecstasy but riffed on movies, Sunday night Chinese at Kitty's, and four-course dinners in the company of couples just like us, who owned ten place settings of barely used bone china and dreams to match. Only now do I realize that Barry and I spent virtually no time alone, face-to-face. Not counting bed.

I didn't think of myself as unhappy. I thought of myself as adjusting, and on that I scored an A for effort. If Barry called to say that something had come up, that he'd need to miss dinner, for instance, I wouldn't settle in with a soup bowl full of Raisinets and a large box of tissues. Instead, I'd read an intelligent novel while I ate lean grilled protein, a leafy green vegetable, and a complex carbohydrate. My life felt balanced and whole.

Then Luke got a girlfriend. She wasn't just any girlfriend. Luke started seeing Treena, my assistant, a recent present the publisher wouldn't let me exchange because she was his stepdaughter.

Treena was as fuckable as she was tall, with a jingly laugh you could hear down the hall. She had the kind of innate confidence that beauty breeds and money shines. Her wardrobe, which bore no relationship to her salary, was so ahead of the curve that the week after she broke out something new, which was often, all the other assistants copied her, generally with profoundly painful results. A rumor floated that Treena had a boyfriend, a hedge fund manager. This explains why I paid no heed to the giggly chitchat on her end of the phone whenever Luke called my office.

One night Barry and I were having dinner in the Village with another doctor and his doctor wife. It was a Friday in late June, when outdoor tables fill up first and New Yorkers try to pretend they aren't living in the middle of a malodorous communal steam bath. After dinner, the four of us strolled by Da Silvano, and there was Luke, wound around Treena like a bandage.

"Molly!" Treena called, putting down her glass of prosecco so she could wave an artfully sculpted arm. On her wrist, at least twenty skinny Indian bracelets jangled and didn't even look cheap. "Barry! Hello!" She may as well have been a hunter with a duck call and Barry a brain-damaged mallard. He walked straight toward her, while I lagged behind. Luke froze, or maybe he was simply comatose on account of being skunk drunk. I'll never know, since my first impulse was to feel silly, as if everyone at a party had allowed me to walk around with a price tag hanging off my shirt.

"C'mon—have a drink!" Treena trilled. Luke didn't say a word. I could see that Barry was ready to accept, although there was obviously no room for all of us around their table for two, under which I noticed Luke and Treena's knees touching. But fortunately, our dinner companions had a babysitter at home who was charging more per hour than a plumber, and they weren't eager to drag out the evening. After an exchange of glances with them—not me—Barry shrugged and said, "Another time." There was then so much cheek kissing you'd have thought someone had won a Grammy.

After the goodnights, Barry and I walked to our car. "You never mentioned that your photographer buddy had hooked up with your assistant," he said as we were driving home. His tone drifted in my direction with an edge of condescension overshadowed by curiosity.

"News to me," I admitted. I tried to sound neutral, not furious, which I was slowly realizing I was.

"Lucky schmuck," he said. "Could have sworn he was a *fagele*, though—what do you suppose she sees in him?"

While I tried to parse which part of Barry's question was most offensive, I was asking it in reverse. I didn't have to think hard. Treenas rule the earth.

In the middle of the night I woke from a dream, my teeth clenched so hard my jaw ached. I reached for Barry, and we made love with uncharacteristic roughness and abandon. I stared into his eyes. The face I was seeing was Luke's.

"More, Molly, more!" Barry grunted with each thrust. "Yes, yes!"

No! I was thinking as I arched my back and rotated my hips. *No!*

The next morning Barry brought me breakfast in bed—iced coffee and a chocolate croissant on our wedding china, its blue border perfectly matching a hyacinth in a bud vase.

I didn't respond to Luke's calls, text messages, or IMs on Monday, Tuesday, or Wednesday. But on Thursday we had a meeting, where I acted so excruciatingly polite you'd have thought I was having tea with the First Lady. Afterward, Luke pointed this out. "Do you want to talk?" he asked.

"What's there to say? You're going out with my pea-brained assistant and, speaking of peas, didn't have the balls to tell me." I'd like to admit I only thought the second half of the speech, but I actually did say it.

"It just happened," he said.

"Da Silvano takes planning," I said. "Reservations are involved."

"She asked me."

"You didn't say no," I pointed out.

"I'm not sure why we are having this conversation."

Because I want you all to myself, although I am married and you and I are just friends. Because. Because. Because. Luke had given me an opening, but this was not a door I was ready to walk through. The only thing I was sure about was my own discomfort.

"No good reason, Luke," I said, and forced a laugh, trying to pretend that I had recovered my sense of humor. "I'm being a possessive

bitch. But I wish you'd told me you were seeing Treena. Not that you don't have every right to. But she is my own damn assistant."

"Thank you, Molly Marx, for giving my social life your seal of approval." He spoke this with a particularly corrosive brand of sarcasm.

"Luke, that's enough," I said. "Let's agree I was a baby. A self-centered idiot. I'm sorry."

"Unless you have something else in mind." The expression on his face read, *I double-dog-dare you.*

"Such as?"

"The thing about you, Molly, is that you don't know what you want or who you want it with." He shrugged and walked away. Two days later, he sent a friendly enough text message, as if everything were back to normal. I knew, of course, it wasn't. Everything had changed.

Twelve

KISS, KISS

There's Snuffleupagus, Mommy." Whenever we passed the sprawling granite outcropping crouched over Central Park, Annabel pointed it out. But today, as she holds Delfina's strong, slim hand, the beast who rules my daughter's imagination doesn't get as much as a glance. She soldiers ahead, silent and grim.

Delfina and Annabel enter the elevator at our synagogue, and the nursery school director swoops down to four-year-old level. "We're so happy to have you back, Annabel," she says. "We've missed you."

Though Annabel used to greet this woman with a giddy grin, she bites her lip and says nothing. When she and Delfina reach the threshold of the classroom on the sixth floor, Annabel turns to Delfina. "Do I have to?" she asks.

"Your friends want to play with you," Delfina says. "And school's your job. We all have our jobs."

Annabel's face carries the worry of an old crone. I wait for tears.

"Your dolls?" Delfina asks. "You're thinking about your dolls?"

Annabel nods.

Delfina bends to whisper. "Can you keep a secret? If you go to

school, when I pick you up we'll eat with your friend Ella. It was going to be a surprise."

Annabel allows a small smile to creep across her face and turns to search the classroom. She catches the eye of her best friend, who's already in the playhouse. Ella sees Annabel and runs across the room on her chunky legs. "Annabel!" she shouts. "I'm making pizza. C'mon." Ella towers over my daughter and, in the tradition of anatomy as destiny, considers herself older, wiser, and now responsible for looking after her friend whose mommy died by the river like a character in a goose-pimply Grimm's fairy tale, the ones she won't let her dad read to her anymore.

"See you later, alligator," Delfina says to Annabel, and bends to give her a hug.

"After a while, crocodile," Annabel says. One of her purple mittens is missing, but she hangs her red jacket with the furry trim in her cubby, which features a family picture—Barry, me, Annabel as a toothless baby. Every move is fluid and concise. I hope Barry remembers that I had planned to enroll her in ballet. I am positive she is on the Clara track for *The Nutcracker*.

"I'll be the mommy," Ella says, "and you'll be the girl." They play until the teacher asks all eighteen students to gather in their morning circle. Annabel walks with the rest to the center of the classroom.

"Good morning, class," the teacher says.

"Good morning, Miss Rose," the children sing out.

"Let's talk about what we did this weekend," she says. "Did anything interesting happen to anyone?" A girl raises her hand. "Emily?"

"I saw *Shrek*," she says.

"Me too," a few others yell.

"Class, we wait until we're called on, remember?" A boy waves his hand as if he's conducting an orchestra; with his wild curls he looks like a vest-pocket-size Simon Rattle. Miss Rose points in his direction.

"My gerbil died," he says.

"Last month we had to put our dog to sleep," another boy says. "He had bad cancer inside him."

I beam down on Annabel, trying to absorb her pain. But Annabel does . . . nothing. She looks at the window and fixates on dust floating

in the brilliant morning sun. A few children turn in her direction, but soon Miss Rose calls on Ella. "My babysitter, Narcissa, let me stay up until eleven o'clock," she says.

In the hallway, there's a racket. A mother and child are late for school. "Kiss, kiss, Jordan," the woman says to her son. He is a thin child with sad, deep-set blue eyes and wiry red hair cropped short. He pecks her cheek. The mother is a heavily highlighted brunette whose distinguishing characteristics are very large teeth, very long nails, and very high heels. "Kiss Mommy goodbye." I listen closely. I know that nasal voice.

Stephanie.

I take another lingering peek at Annabel, and while I long to stay and watch her, I cannot resist getting a closer look at this woman who each evening is verbally tucking my husband into bed. I look closely to see if Stephanie was among the unknown bereaved rubbing away their mascara streaks at my funeral, but she looks only vaguely familiar, one of many faces I may have seen milling around the school, waiting to collect a child. Her son enters his classroom and she returns to the elevator.

Downstairs, Stephanie meets another woman, one who has apparently seen *Vertigo* one too many times. The companion has pulled her hair, bleached to platinum, into a French twist, and her sharply tailored gray wool gabardine skirt and jacket recall 1958. She is fiercely attractive, with porcelain skin and carefully reddened lips. Although the weather is brisk, the pair leave their coats open as they walk down the tree-lined street. The height of their heels doesn't prevent them from quickly reaching a coffee shop four blocks away. As they settle into a table near the window, the light betrays Kim Novak. I can see that she is older than I'd estimated, probably early forties. Maybe ten years beyond Stephanie.

"Aren't guys lucky?" Stephanie says. "They can be in the world's worst marriages, but when they lose their wives, the universe genuflects at their doorstep."

"At least you are," the companion says. "What's going on? Did he actually say his marriage sucked?"

Stephanie pauses, sits back in her chair, and looks her friend straight in the eye. "Not exactly, but how good could it have been if he's

showing this much interest?" she says, and smiles as she stirs sweetener into her paper cup.

Is this the circulating myth, that Molly Marx's marriage was as dead as she is now?

"He's been showing interest for some time now, actually," Stephanie adds.

I feel as if I've turned into Lucy; I'd like to tear out this Stephanie's eyeballs after I pull off each long eyelash one by one, pee in her vente latte, rage like Tinker Bell on crystal meth. What marriage is a perfectly made bed, never creased or spotted, without its secrets and disappointments? Like a criminal defense lawyer, I long to defend my relationship with Barry, flawed as it may have been, despite what he might have let dribble out in a chance occurrence with a woman, this woman, any woman.

The blonde puts down her coffee, leaving a kiss of MAC Russian Red on its rim. "Steph, you think you might be getting a little ahead of yourself?" she asks. "And why this guy? He's not the only single man in New York, and you're not exactly staying home every night plucking your eyebrows."

"Some women ask why. I ask, why the fuck not?" She shrugs and sips her latte. Her teeth are as white as its foam.

"Has he even asked you out?"

My bullshit meter is going off so loudly I'm surprised they can't hear it.

"He's saying he wants to wait a few weeks, even a few months," Stephanie says. " 'What will people think?' You know me—Ms. Patience." She pauses, examines her nails, and looks up. "I give it two weeks."

"I've been single for three years and had one boyfriend who was sixty-two and dumped me for a salesgirl from Circuit City," the blonde says with what I am fairly sure is affection. "You're single for a year and have—I can't count that high." This surprises me. The blonde wins the beauty bake-off, but I was always an innocent, thinking that perfection had anything to do with lust or, for that matter, love. "You should be teaching a course at the Learning Annex." She looks at her watch, an Ebel I used to covet because four dozen diamonds don't stop it from masquerading as sporty. "Keep me in the loop on this."

"See you at the gym," Stephanie says as her friend collects her shopping bags and walks out the door. "Kiss, kiss."

Stephanie opens her *Times*. She scans the Thursday Styles section, turns to the movie listings, then reaches for her phone and speed-dials Barry's cell phone.

"I know you're probably in surgery," she says, leaving a message. "But I just wanted to tell you I'm thinking about you." She lowers her voice. "All the time. I'm ready whenever you are."

Wolves, I recall, are highly social animals.

Thirteen

PLAYDATE IN PARADISE

What kind of old lady goes to bed at seven-thirty?" Luke said, standing in the door of my room.

"The kind who's exhausted." *The kind who's trying to behave.*

"Want to join me?" He had changed into flip-flops, linen pants, and a faded Hawaiian shirt. I was always a sucker for a shirt that says aloha.

It was two months past Treena, who'd become engaged to her Wall Street wizard. Luke and I were on location, this time in a warm, sunny place. On the plane, we chatted like two bubbes at bridge, and I was cheerful as a baboon—until we landed. That's when I discovered that the eight enormous suitcases of borrowed objets d'art I'd schlepped from New York—in case I needed to pull an alabaster statue or two out of my ass to accessorize the house we were photographing—were missing. The bags would be arriving on the same once-daily flight the next afternoon, or so Air Banana promised.

Always one to careen toward a worst-case scenario, I was convinced the bags had been delivered to the Bermuda Triangle. Even if they did show up, we'd be getting a late start the next day. Suddenly, I was so tired I couldn't remember my phone number. Luke had to help

complete the claim form. I thanked him, but sulked as we drove to the resort where we'd be staying for the next five days, and as soon as we checked in, I escaped to my room. After a call home and a long shower, I emerged smelling like a smoothie—the management had cornered the market on papaya-infused products—but in a vastly improved state. I was looking forward to room service and an early night. That's when I heard a knock on the wall. *Bump-bump-de-bump-bump. Bump. Bump.*

I knocked back, but this time the return knock was at my door. Through the chain lock, I could see Luke wearing a smirk as silly as a party hat.

"Sorry, Molly Marx is closed for the night," I said.

"I know you're young, but you're not eight," he said. "C'mon."

"Nope, I have a rule against drinking anything that pink," I said, pointing to the half-empty glass in his hand.

"House specialty," he said. "A lot more potent than it looks."

Was it bitchy of me to abandon Luke? The rest of our team had arrived the day before yesterday, and they'd left us a note saying they were off to the other end of the island for roast suckling pig. Luke and I were on our own for the evening, and I'd left him stranded. I stood there, barefoot, trying to decide what to do, when he decided for me.

"I love a woman in pajamas," he said, eyeing me up and down.

I was wearing chaste white cotton PJs—it was my mother's tradition to give Lucy and me a matched set every year for our birthday. The cuffs were embroidered with purple pansies. My hair was wet. I laughed and blushed.

"And I love a woman who blushes."

I didn't say what I was thinking: *You've had a few of those drinks already, haven't you, Luke?* But he looked lonely. Or maybe that was my justification machine talking. "Meet you in the bar in fifteen minutes" slipped out instead.

I towel-dried my hair, put on a minute's worth of makeup, and changed into a white eyelet sundress. My vestal virgin image intact, I walked to the resort's outdoor bar. Next to Luke, a drink the color of a lawn flamingo was waiting, its umbrella angled as if it were an index finger pointing at me. *Get with the program, Molly,* it seemed to say.

"Isn't this better than hibernation?" Luke said as I hopped up onto a tall bamboo stool next to him.

"It depends on whether or not this drink comes with food," I said.

Luke got the attention of our server, and a bowl of chilled jumbo shrimp arrived along with a tangy sauce and a basket of crisp fried plantain chips. We nibbled and drank while the sun faded into the horizon over the quietly lapping sea. Steel band music played in the background, its rhythm easing us into the evening. Soon enough, we could count stars in the navy blue sky, and at the outdoor restaurant next to the bar every table glowed with a fat candle. I had one of those moments when I thought I should pay the magazine for allowing me to be their decorating editor. Tonight was a playdate in paradise.

The maître d' led us to a table close to the sand. As I began sipping Champagne—compliments of the house, as thanks for renting six rooms in what was the shoulder of the off-season—I realized I hadn't been this relaxed in weeks. No, longer, much longer.

Luke and I reviewed minutiae, making plans for far more setups than we'd ever be able to squeeze into one day. "This is all assuming the bags show," I said.

"Why do you worry so much?" he asked. In case I missed the point, in his best West Indian accent, he sang "Don't Worry, Be Happy."

"Worrying is my job," I said.

"You do it well," he said. "The job. Not just the first-class fussing."

"As do you." We clinked our crystal flutes.

Luke and I had quickly become, everyone in the industry agreed, a formidable team. He was hot fudge to my vanilla ice cream, and together we became better than each of us alone. We'd already had an offer from another magazine to buy us out of our contracts at the end of the year.

Since we'd been collaborating I'd become more excited about my work than ever. People who haven't tried to explode their creativity might not understand the high that comes through stretching your imagination, but all of this was very important to me. Where a few months earlier I'd basically checked out, now I woke in the middle of the night to scribble and sketch ideas I dreamt. Half of them weren't bad. After a bike ride, when my mind inevitably wandered, I'd usually get on the phone to tell Luke I knew *exactly* what we needed for the next

job, right down to the vintage gilt napkin rings, the color of the parrot tulips, and the number of almond-stuffed olives in a bowl.

As we were finishing our dinner—pompano for both of us—and sharing coconut sorbet in a frosty aqua dish, the music gave way to a singer performing the kind of tunes my parents play in the car. What the soloist lacked in talent, he made up in enthusiasm. "Dis next song is for de lovers," he said, his gold tooth flashing. Luke and I, who'd finished our Champagne, wore the kind of dopey smiles common to people who flunk Breathalyzer tests.

"Do you wanna dance under de moonlight?" the singer crooned. His rendition crossed the Beach Boys with John Lennon, but the slow calypso beat was all his own. "Hug and kiss all through de night, now. Oh baby, do ya wanna dance?" As he repeated choruses of "wanna wanna wanna" he boogied over to us and motioned for Luke and me to get up on the tiny, empty dance floor. Luke stood.

I hesitated. I didn't trust myself in Luke's embrace. But his look beguiled. I got up to join him, stumbling in my most stratospheric sandals. He grabbed me and held me close. I could feel his heart beating, and within a few minutes, I realized our hearts were beating together. He felt pleasantly warm and smelled of citrusy aftershave, his own sweet sweat, and papaya body scrub. As I swayed in his arms—I was more than a little dizzy—I nestled my head in his neck and tried to name the other fragrance I was picking up. What was that bottom note? I knew that smell, that perfect smell. As the song ended, I figured it out. Desire.

"Do you wanna?" he whispered.

I did.

"I know I do," he continued. The three-piece orchestra had struck up a quicker beat, but we were still moving in slow motion. I, for one, didn't want anything about that night to move fast.

He locked his fingers in mine and rubbed them gently. The gesture was both tender and erotic. "I'm waiting for an answer," he whispered.

"I'm too tired."

My second lie.

"Then just come to my room and sleep."

"Sleep?"

"I'd like to know how that would feel." I'm not sure if Luke spoke

those words or if I just thought them, if he was reading my mind or if I was reading his.

Conventional wisdom suggests that infidelity is about punishing the husband or the wife. I beg to differ, and always did, starting that night. It's too late now to sort this out with Dr. Stafford, my marriage counselor. More's the pity, since last month our health insurance certified Barry and me for ten more sessions. In our therapy, which we went to for several months, I always claimed that I never got involved with another man to get back at him. Well, it's past my dying day, and that's my story and I'm sticking with it. Luke was never, ever the not-Barry. He was always Luke, with his own magnetic field. I can't explain why I was drawn to Luke Delaney. Why does someone love the color orange or a Mozart sonata? I just was.

People who contemplate an affair imagine or pretend that they are on their own little islands, encapsulated in a romantic snow globe, safe from reality. The fact was, Luke and I had indeed landed in Margaritaville. We were literally on an island, fifteen hundred miles away from home, good common sense, and, on that evening, sobriety.

Did Barry have not-Mollys? It's my guess that throughout our engagement and marriage he felt intercourse was compulsory with at least a half dozen women who weren't me. I never tried to prove this in a court of law—only once did I snoop through receipts—yet at some level I always knew he was a cheater and I looked away from it. But this wasn't what was on my mind that night. At the moment when Luke took my hand to walk me to his room, I was thinking only about Luke. Well, condoms and Luke. Carefree I am not.

At his door, he fumbled with his keys. The maid had turned down the quilt, set the rattan ceiling fan to a lazy whirl, and put two chocolates on the pillow. He unwrapped one chocolate and put it in my mouth. I did the same for him. The evening was cool now—it was past midnight—and he lit a candle. The flame danced in the room like a trailer for a romantic French movie.

I kicked off my sandals as he slipped off his shirt and pants. He had a long torso and, even though he was thin, small love handles that only seemed to make him more real and, thus, more appealing. As I closed my eyes, the patch of dark hair on his chest made me think once again of the Bermuda Triangle. Was I getting lost or being found?

Fourteen

MAYBE, BABY

*M*olly, I've been thinking it over," Barry said. We'd decided to start with cocktails at the Four Seasons and follow with dinner at Tao. "But first . . ." He signaled for a server. "Two martinis, please," he said. "Grey Goose."

For a woman whose idea of drinking used to center on scouting wine stores for the most ironically labeled under-$15 pinot grigio, I was relieved that courage was on its way in a stemmed glass. Had Barry actually picked that night to say he didn't think things were working out? It was, after all, our first anniversary.

On a scale of 1 to 10, I gave our wedded life a 5. Straight down the middle, Jack and Jill Doe average. I'd recently read on a tarot card website that only 8 percent of married couples believe their partner is a true soul mate. I'm no math whiz, as my SATs verified, but factoring in today's divorce rates, this means that it's the rare bride who connects with a groom who instinctively puts his hand *there* and stars in the X-rated fantasies that top her playlist.

Barry and I seemed on par with every other married couple we knew. In our three sessions of required premarital counseling, the rabbi singled out sex and money as the sinkholes that swallow most re-

lationships. As far as I could see, we had no terminal problem with either. In fact, since we didn't go in for smarmy public displays of affection, I thought we could definitely expect a longer shelf life than the husband and wife with whom we socialized who practically copulated on the table every time they invited us to dinner. In their shiny condo with its gleaming bamboo floor, I always suspected we'd been summoned to bear witness to their libido as much as to the panoramic city view from the floor-to-ceiling windows on the thirty-third floor.

While I busily categorized myself as garden-variety married, someone might wonder if I conveniently overlooked what had happened with Luke six weeks earlier. Not exactly. After that business trip, I shelved my memory of *l'affaire Luc* in the contemporary women's fiction aisle of my brain. Our fling, I told myself, was meaningless and it was over. I told no one, not even Brie.

Maybe I was wise beyond my years and understood that every union is like a mixed-breed puppy adopted from a shelter: you have no idea how it will turn out until it grows up. That night, in a hotel lounge, Barry was looking as if he had a lot of sleek Labrador retriever in him, with maybe some Tibetan terrier and giant schnauzer. No pit bull in sight. He was wearing all black—well-tailored jacket, fine cotton shirt, lizard belt, jeans—and, fortunately, the effect was more European art snob than Johnny Cash. His nose kept him from being pretty-boy handsome, but with his wavy black hair and dark brown eyes fringed by lashes that rightly should have belonged to me, the overall effect of Dr. Barry Marx was striking. His bravado finished the package.

"To us," he said, raising his glass.

"Us," I echoed as we clinked. "You and me."

"First, I want you to have this," he said, handing me a Bergdorf's bag, always a promising receptacle, especially if small. I carefully opened the box, where a velvet pouch revealed a sterling silver cuff incandescent with quartz stones big as pistachios. Had I been auditioning for the part of goomar, the bracelet would have been a fine accessory. My first thought, however, was that Kitty had selected it.

"Wow," was all I could say. "This is really unexpected." I'd been hoping for a gift, of course, and had done my best to hint about a two-foot shell-encrusted obelisk I'd been ogling in a dusty Village antique shop. But what I imagined would add considerable panache to our cof-

fee table, perhaps Barry saw as competitively phallic. I admired the bracelet, tried to glisten with appreciation, and castigated myself for being ungrateful. Chances were Barry was going to hate the blue enameled cuff links I'd bought for him. Now that I thought about it, I wasn't even sure he liked French-cuffed shirts.

"You deserve it, baby," he said, slipping the present on my wrist. Was he trying to see his reflection in its luster? "And speaking of babies," he added, "it's time, Molly."

In a screenplay, the look on Barry's face would read "long, meaningful gaze." For me, it'd be "sheer, frozen panic."

Some couples chew over the baby question endlessly before they even get engaged. These must be the same people who organize their shoes in transparent boxes, rush their annotated tax prep to an accountant by January 31, and get around to ordering their wedding album. There are also men and women who understand exactly where they stand on parenthood, even if they've only discussed it with their shrinks, as well as husbands and wives who haven't figured out the answer but welcome bright-eyed, bushy-tailed dialogue on the subject. Barry and I fit into none of these categories.

"I'm not sure I feel adult enough to be anyone's mother," I admitted.

"Oh, c'mon," he said. "You'll be a great mommy." His tone was jocular.

In our family, it was Lucy who'd majored in kids—bossing younger children in the neighborhood, working every summer as a camp counselor, teaching nursery school. She loved every child, and they returned the affection.

"Whenever anyone asked me to babysit, I always pleaded term paper," I said. "I'm not maternal."

Barry let loose such a loud, incredulous "Ha!" that people at the next table turned to see if someone required the Heimlich maneuver. "Molly, listen. It's an open secret that most parents only appreciate their own flesh and blood and think other people's kids are sniveling rugrats."

"That's a penetrating observation, Barry," I said, fairly sure he might be right. But what if I didn't like my own child? What if my child didn't like me?

The previous year, I'd volunteered as a reading tutor. My first-grade charge insisted on *Hairy Scary Spiders*. I can still hear his creepy falsetto lip-synching: "My net catches an insect. I kill it with a simple bite. I crash and grind the insect's body with my steel jaws and pulverize it into juice. Dinner is served." An innocent bug in a tarantula's net. I was feeling that way at the moment.

"But I don't know how to be a mom." What if I couldn't understand or slept through my baby's ear-piercing patois? Got revolted by spit-up? I especially didn't want to think about the effect of forty-five extra pounds on my stomach, which wasn't concave even now, or how a nine-pound infant was going to pop out of my nether regions. "May I have another martini, please?" I asked the server.

"Molly, you're being ridiculous—do you think my mother knew how to be a mother?" The answer to that question did not bolster Barry's argument. He gamely switched tactics. "You'll be like your mother," he said.

"I could never be as good a mother as my mother," I snapped back. Who could? Claire Divine is warm and patient. I am the definition of impatience, and although I could be kind enough to deserving parties, Barry liked to point out that people often took me for aloof. When I suggested that these hypersensitive types were sadly unable to discern shyness in a grown woman, I saw his skepticism.

As I finished my second drink, overcome by insecurities I never knew I had, I began to feel claustrophobic, despite the bar's towering ceiling. I was pleased when Barry called for the tab and we moved on. As we entered Tao, a sixteen-foot-tall Buddha gazed down on us. I implored him to tell me what to do, but all Buddha-boy seemed to say was, *Order the Peking duck for two.* We did, and switched to our usual dinner talk, Barry's tales from the operating room, which kept us going through a calorie blitz called a Zen Parfait. I passed on the giant fortune cookie. What fortune had in store for me I would gladly wait to discover.

"How about a Chai Kiss?" Barry said, looking at the menu of after-dinner drinks.

"How about home to Jane Street?" I said. In the taxi, I closed my eyes and leaned against Barry's well-muscled body. With the help of a good romp in bed, perhaps I could talk my husband into postponing

baby making for a few years—maybe a decade—and during that time grow up and figure out what I wanted.

At our apartment, still blurry from all I'd had to drink, I slipped into a blue silk teddy. Barry pulled me toward him tightly. He was in the locked and loaded position. "Happy anniversary, sweetheart," he whispered hotly into my ear. "Molly Divine Marx, you will be a wonderful mother."

I looked at him, sleepily and skeptically.

"I don't know very much," he said, "but I know that."

There was something about the way he said those words that felt utterly tender and authentic. I deeply wanted to believe him, to live up to them, to feel sure about this step that for most women isn't even a choice. "Really?" I asked, a prayer as much as a question. In that moment, I felt that marrying Barry Marx was the smartest and best move I had ever made.

As he blew out the candle I kept by the bed, and the scent of lily of the valley filled our small room, he said, "Let's make a baby, baby."

Months later, we did.

Fifteen

PIECE OF WORK

Detective Hicks stretches his long legs and scans the room. Sitting on a black leather Eames chair, he might be taken for another sleek minimalist object in Brie and Isadora's loft. "Ms. Lawson, was that reading of yours at Mrs. Marx's funeral by Elizabeth Barrett Browning?" he asks, as if he honestly cares about Victorian poetry.

"Emily Dickinson," Brie says. She's wearing her Jessica Rabbit–goes-to-court suit, bought to scare the nuts off opposing counsel. It has a tight jacket, strategically unbuttoned to show a peek of cleavage. The pencil skirt, which hugs her butt, ends just below her knees. Her hair is pulled back into a severe chignon. Isadora sits beside her on the couch, a wrinkle that I've never noticed etching a delicate valley between her slightly hooded hazel eyes.

"I knew it was one of those depressed women," the detective says, helping himself to chocolate biscotti that Isadora has set out on a square white china plate. "Now, I gather from Mrs. Marx's funeral that you two were close," he says. "Can you tell me a little about the . . . relationship?" The question is directed to Brie, but he glances toward Isadora as he drops a crumb, which disappears into the thick charcoal

rug. Isadora's wrinkle deepens as she sees the biscotti bit vanish, but Brie looks straight at Hicks.

"Molly and I were randomly assigned as freshman roommates," she says. "It was one of those fortunate matches. We hit it off and became inseparable. The next year we got an apartment together and kept it until we graduated."

"Can you elaborate?" Hicks' eyes wear an amused expression, in which Brie is reading a taunting, sub rosa suggestion. Which is his intention, to tick her off. *Don't fall for it.* I beam this message with the futile hope that Brie can hear it.

"We did what college friends do," she says. "Study, shop, party."

In reverse order, as I recall.

"Anything else?" he asks.

"Sure," Brie says, "eat pizza, gain ten pounds, diet, meet guys, root for the home team, take vacations in skimpy bikinis, and try not to think about what we'd do when we grew up. Should I go on?" As she reels off this list, the speed of her speech picks up, as does the pitch of her voice. I am surprised that Brie is allowing frustration to show. Don't they teach keeping cool in law school?

"Ms. Vega, would you mind if I had a few moments alone with Ms. Lawson, please?" asks Hicks. Isadora stands and smooths away nonexistent creases on her sleeveless black dress, in which she manages to appear as dignified as a head of state despite the fact that it clings to her tiny waist and curvy hips. Isadora possesses the kind of beauty that generally requires a passport. We were the same height, but she looks a head taller than I ever felt. On the middle finger of her right hand, a ring featuring a large, lemony stone—I have no idea if it's a rare diamond or a hunk of glass—reflects the afternoon light.

"As you wish," she says, and walks into the bedroom and closes the door. Hicks and I both know that through the wall Isadora can hear much of what's said.

"So, Ms. Lawson, what's that phrase people use nowadays? Friends with benefits? Did that apply to you and Mrs. Marx?" I'm getting the feeling that he is going out of his way to offend.

Brie scowls ever so slightly. "No, Molly and I were always friends," she says. "No 'benefits.' " She signals quotation marks with her fingers, her manicure a flawless taupe.

Hicks says . . . nothing.

"In those days I had boyfriends," she adds, although he hasn't asked.

"Thank you for the clarification, Ms. Lawson," he says. "Now, let's see. How would you describe the state of Mrs. Marx's marriage?"

Brie shifts from left to right and back again. "You never really know what's going on in another relationship."

It sounds reasonable to me, but all Hicks says is, "Ms. Lawson, the question, please?"

"They weren't exactly one of those couples with a joint mission statement tucked away in a drawer, but in their own way Barry and Molly were devoted and well matched. He was very caught up with work, has a difficult mother, and could be a flirt, but I always thought Molly took it all in stride. He's a loving, doting daddy, and I know that meant a lot to her. She and Annabel were his home port. His heart. She knew that."

Tell me something I don't know, Hicks thinks. *Did Barry kill his wife? Was she cheating on him? Was he cheating on her and did he want Molly out of the picture? Did this lawyer lady do it, or maybe the jealous señorita in the next room?*

"Barry criticized Molly, but I always read it as affectionate teasing, and assumed Molly did, too," Brie added. "He'd never hurt Molly, if that's what you're wondering."

"Because he loved her?" Hicks asks.

"Well, that," Brie says, "yes, of course—that's a given—and . . ." Brie hesitates.

"Go on," Hicks say.

"Because I imagine that any kind of brutality would effectively terminate his career." She makes an odd noise. It's her nervous laugh, a dry, low gurgle.

"How so?"

"Detective, women are pretty damn scared to go under the knife—can you imagine using a cosmetic surgeon rumored to be a butcher?" *A goddamn butcher* is what Brie thinks.

"Interesting," Hicks says. He gets up from the Eames chair and moves to the far end of the low burnt orange sofa across from its twin, where Brie is sitting. From this spot, the view of her legs is even better.

"And Mrs. Marx—did she love her husband?" he says, picking up a book, a biography of Maxwell Perkins, which he absentmindedly pages through and puts down while he waits for Brie's answer. "Didn't that guy always wear a hat to work? Maybe I should start that."

"Without a doubt, yes," Brie shoots back, and I'm not sure if she means the hat or is answering Hicks' question. "Barry could get to her, but he was also her flotation device." *Where in the hell did I come up with that term?* Brie is asking herself. And why is she so sure about this? I wonder.

"Her what?" the detective asks. Now he's interested.

"I always thought Molly pretended her marriage was worse than it was. Some sort of self-deprecating shtick."

But Brie has it wrong. I think she wanted my marriage to be better than I presented it. Brie was the kind of friend sure enough about herself that she didn't need my happiness to be less so she could convince herself that hers was more.

"Can you elaborate?" Hicks asks.

I wish I could, Brie thinks. *I wish I had evidence.* "Just a sense I had."

Did Brie take me for a big, empty complainer?

"Tell us about the last time you saw Mrs. Marx," Hicks says.

"It was a bike ride. Remember when we had that string of sixty-degree days in February?"

Global warming. I wonder if I'll be around to see how that plays out.

Hicks removes a black leather notebook from his jacket pocket and scribbles in it. "You mention that the husband's family was . . . what was your word, 'difficult'?"

"Molly got along with them fine," she says, although she knows that Kitty only tolerated me, sometimes politely. "The same with her parents and sister."

"The sister," Hicks says. "What's up with her?"

"Excuse me?" Brie asks.

"At the service . . . you don't think she was a little intense?"

"It was her twin sister's funeral," Brie says, icy. "How was she supposed to act?"

"Okay," he says. "Sorry if I'm outta line. But what about the sisters? Were they close?"

"Do you have a brother or sister, Detective?" Brie asks. "You know how it goes. Sometimes you love them, and sometimes you wish your mother had drowned them at birth." As soon as the words fly out of her mouth, Brie regrets them. "The thing with Molly and Lucy is they knew how to press each other's buttons, but they were very tight." *They loved each other,* Brie thinks. *Lucy worshipped Molly. Molly was in awe of Lucy.*

"Were you and Lucy tight, too?" he asks.

Brie pauses. She always found Lucy smug and provincial, probably because she knew Lucy found her smug and pretentious. "Mutually respectful," she says.

Hicks chuckles ever so slightly.

Isadora walks out of the bedroom carrying a large handbag. I can't take my eyes off it—black leather embossed with swirling flowers, possibly even a canary. She walks to Brie, puts her arm around her shoulder, and grazes her lips with a kiss.

Hicks seems to be enjoying the show. He grins. "Well, we'll be winding things up soon here, Ms. Lawson," he says. "Just a few more questions. Where were you the night that your friend died?"

Brie squeezes her eyes shut, trying to stop the onset of tears. "I was working," she said. "In Brazil."

When I was bowling in the Bronx, Hicks thinks. "Anything else you'd like to tell me?"

Brie looks pale and tired. A lock of dark hair falls out of her chignon, and she brushes it away from her face. "Nothing I can think of."

"Okay, then," Hicks says. "Just one more thing. Do you know a Luke?" He pulls out the notebook again. "Luke Delaney?"

"Luke Delaney," she says. "Yes—yes, I do. We met years ago, when I was a model."

A model, Hicks thinks, not surprised. "And what was Mr. Delaney's relationship to Mrs. Marx?" he asks.

"Work associates. He's a photographer."

"That's all you want to tell me?" he asks.

Brie finds her courtroom game face. "That's all I know."

Hicks gets up and shakes Brie's hand. I am fairly certain he holds her palm for a moment longer than necessary, but I can't be held accountable for my observations, because the mention of Luke, whom I have refused to think about, has my mind in orbit.

"If there's anything else that you remember, here's my card," the detective says. He's switched his tone to neutral pointing toward cordial, presses the card into Brie's hand, and walks out the door. His rear view is possibly his best angle.

After he leaves, she steps to a desk and puts the card in the skinny, empty drawer on the right. *Hiawatha Hicks,* it reads. She says the name out loud. "Hiawatha?" The laugh that fills the loft is the laugh I remember, and from where I am, we laugh together.

Sixteen

BAD BANANA

*B*arry?" Lucy said. "I hope I didn't wake you." The truth is that Lucy wishes she could haunt his dreams as a blood-sucking, scythe-wielding vampire. Furthermore, it's Sunday morning, and if he's not up now, at nine o'clock, my sister will surely mark it in the ledger she keeps of Dr. Barry Marx's scurviest sins.

"Who's calling, please?" Barry says. He sounds winded, which doesn't surprise me, because although it's raining heavily, he has just come in from a run. Standing in a baseball cap and poncho, he drips water on our kitchen floor. Barry knows the caller is Lucy: our voices were the only thing about us that was virtually identical, and I doubt he thinks I've rung him up from the grave to tell him he forgot to buy the right kind of milk (organic, 2 percent)—something he's done.

"Your favorite sister-in-law," Lucy announces.

Barry takes a moment to think, *Big-tit bitch.* "Good morning, Lucy," he says. "To what do I owe the pleasure?" He sounds even, pleasant, as behooves a well-paid surgeon. Shortly after we were married, he worked for a few months with a speech consultant in order to soften the New York in his vowels. My idea.

You don't like me and I don't like you—let's not pretend, Lucy thinks. "I

want to make arrangements for Passover," she spits out. "I'll fly into New York, pick up Annabel, and bring her to Chicago for the beginning of her vacation. I'm off myself, so it's easy for me to swing, and I can spend the whole week with her."

"Continue."

"My parents will fly her back," Lucy says, encouraged. "We have a lot of plans—the Field Museum, American Girl Place, the two seders, of course. And matzo brei on the first morning of Passover—Divine tradition."

"Uh-huh."

"Do I take that as a yes?" She is working to keep the exchange breezy but on a pad of paper is drawing circles, heavy and black with her worry.

"Lucy, it's not going to happen," Barry says. "Your dad mentioned something about this, but Annabel's therapist thinks it's too much for her to travel so soon."

Lucy says, "Annabel's therapist?" at the same time as I think it. She has a pediatrician and a dentist. Since when does my daughter have a therapist?

"I've had several consultations with a highly credentialed colleague who specializes in childhood grief," Barry says.

"Oh, really?" Lucy says. "Who might that be?"

"Joseph," Barry says.

"Joseph who?" Lucy asks. She is sitting in front of the computer that my parents keep on the kitchen counter and has already called up Google.

"Joseph is the last name."

"What's his first name?" Lucy asks briskly.

"Why is this important?"

"I asked you a fair question."

"Okay," he says. "Stephanie."

Unfortunately, Lucy can't hear me snort.

"Well, the Divine family has consulted a therapist as well," Lucy lies. "And our highly credentialed expert from the University of Chicago who specializes in early-childhood trauma says that to deprive Annabel of contact with her maternal family right now will be . . ." Lucy

takes a second to think. "Would have long-term, reverberating negative consequences."

"Reverberating, huh?" Barry says. "So, Luce, should we have our
therapists meet in Central Park for a duel? Plenty of room to reverberate there."

Annabel walks into the kitchen in her nightgown. Her toenails
sparkle, the handiwork of Delfina, who left for church this morning as
soon as Barry walked through the door after his run. He's been paying
her extra to sleep in the apartment every night.

My daughter puts her half-empty bowl of Cheerios in the sink and
wanders over to her father. "Daddy?" she says. "Daddy?" The word
flutters from her mouth. "I can't find my Dora DVD. *Fairy Tale Adventure*. I need it. Where is it?"

Barry would have a better chance of finding God. "Lucy," he says,
"Annabel's here. Gotta go."

"Is that Aunt Moosey?" Annabel asks. When she smiles, her dimple shows. "Can I talk to her?"

"Barry, put Annabel on," Lucy says. The breezy tone has blown
away; she's defaulted to shrill with a 70 percent chance of shit storm.
The circles she's doodling have grown as thick as snakes and fill a page
of legal pad.

"Not a good time," Barry says. "Annabel and I are heading out in
five minutes." His eyes settle on a wall calendar decorated with a
lioness and her cubs. "We're going to the zoo."

"I didn't know we were going to the zoo." Annabel examines the
rain pounding the windows in almost horizontal freefall. Even a three-
year-old can look dubious. "And I want to talk to Aunt Moosey."

"Just put her on for a minute," Lucy says. Google has coughed up a
few Stephanie Josephs—two attorneys, a hipper-than-thou teenage
blogger, and an Atlanta podiatrist.

"Hang on," he tells her. "There's a call." Barry puts Lucy on hold.
"Are your ears burning?" Barry asks.

"Not my ears," Stephanie says. She sounds sultrier on a rumpled
Sunday morning than I ever did on my most torrid Saturday night.

"You're a therapist, right?" he asks.

"Was," she says. "Two careers ago. Social worker at a geriatric cen-

ter. Dentures, Depends—not my thing," she laughs. "May I ask where this conversation is going?"

"Not important," he says. "You were saying?"

"I took one look at this storm and had a vision for this afternoon," she says. "Jordan and Annabel could watch cartoons, and we could do . . . whatever."

"Whatever, huh?" he says, talking quietly. "I lettered in whatever in college. How did you know?"

Annabel tugs his hand. "The zoo, Daddy?" she says. "When are we going?"

"Honey, can't you see it's raining?" he says. "And that I'm on the phone?"

"I want to talk to Aunt Moosey! I want to find Dora!" Her face is getting red.

My eyes dart back and forth between Chicago and New York. Left on hold, Lucy sticks out her lower lip and glowers.

My father walks into the kitchen just as she slams down the phone. "Take it easy, partner," he says. "What's wrong?"

Lucy runs upstairs and when she gets to the hallway outside our former bedroom door shouts, "That sleazoid thinks he can have things any way he fucking wants. Well, he better think again." My father stares at his grown daughter with the look men get when they're stuck in an estrogen choke hold.

"Boyfriend trouble again, sweetie?" he shouts back.

My sister slams the bedroom door.

In my New York kitchen, Barry is savoring every detail of the description Stephanie offers up of the afternoon's prix fixe. "Think about it, Dr. Marx," she says, her mind bouncing between the equal appeals of Barry's big dick and big bucks. "Raindrops on the windowpanes, jazz or opera—your pick—and a side trip to the bedroom for as long as you want. Should I go on?"

"Oh yeah, baby—do," Barry says while he idly plays with the curls on Annabel's head. She tugs on his sleeve. He bends over to give her a kiss.

"Daddy," she says loudly, "the zoo! When are we going? And you need to find my Dora DVD, 'member?"

"You're not seriously thinking of going to the zoo, are you?" Stephanie asks.

"*Fairy Tale Adventure*'s my best favorite." Annabel is hanging on Barry's leg. "I want to watch it before we go."

"No, not now," Barry says.

"Are you talking to me, Bear?" Stephanie says. Kitty calls Barry "Bear." Which is why I never did.

"Daddy! I want to see the part where the mean witch puts Boots to sleep."

"Bear, you there?"

Annabel begins to stamp her feet. "Stephanie, actually, maybe this isn't a good time," Barry says. "Call you later?"

She laughs. "Certainly. Promise?"

"Promise," he says as he clicks off, measured seduction replaced by exasperation.

"Dora needs to turn into a True Princess to wake Boots up," Annabel says, dissolving into tears. "He *has* to wake up. He's Dora's best friend. He has to."

"What happened to her friend, honey?" He pulls our daughter onto his lap.

"Daddy—you know!" she wails. "He ate a bad banana. Very, very bad." As a new torrent of tears bursts, Annabel's nose drips on her nightgown, a ribbon of mucus catching on one ear of Alfred the bunny. "We're not going to the zoo, are we?"

"No, kitten, I don't think that's such a great idea," Barry says, trying unsuccessfully to use his nylon poncho to wipe her nose. "Not today."

"You lied!" Annabel says. "You always lie!" As she flies out the door, letting it slam behind her, I am seeing Lucy, circa four years old: my sister a powerhouse, especially next to me, as passive as a sugar cookie. I watch helplessly, in awe of Annabel's will. How will Barry ever manage her alone?

"God damn it, Molly—what the fuck do I do now?" Barry says, clenching his fists. He puts his head down on the kitchen table and softly bangs his forehead several times. I see tears, though whether they are from grief or frustration I cannot say. "Molly, you weren't supposed to die. You weren't supposed to die."

I forgot that someone could yell and cry simultaneously.

I hurt for my Annie-belle, who has lost her mommy. I hurt for my sister, Lucy, for how hard it must be to be her. I hurt for my parents, who have been forced to surrender half their heart. I hurt for all of them and I hurt for me, because I miss every one of these tortured people whom I love and whom I've left behind, broken and bleeding. I hurt for how much I miss my life. I would gladly go to the zoo in the rain and muck; I would stand in shit and sleep in wet straw and smell terrible smells, just to be alive for another day.

But what surprises me most is that I am feeling something new. The emotion is a foreign spice whose name I don't even know and that I can't decide if I like. I am feeling something for Barry.

I am so fixated, I barely notice Bob standing beside me. "Sometimes," he says, "it's best not to watch. Or listen." But I wave him away. I can't stop doing either.

Seventeen

LEMON TART

B eets?" Barry said. "Again?"

When I was pregnant, I had a fetish for beets, which until then I'd bought only in cans and only on sale. Barry started calling me "the Beet Queen," which I took as a compliment, not so much because a novel by that name was one of my favorites, but because fresh beets suddenly struck me as the ultimate root vegetable, food my Middle European great-grandmother must have grown and cooked. I felt as if all the beets I was consuming were allowing me to reconnect with my ancestors. This, I guess, is what pregnancy does to some women.

"I found a new way to make them," I assured Barry as I tied a starched white chef's apron around my eight-and-a-half-months-pregnant girth. "From Nigella." If I had had a girl crush, it would have been on a woman like Nigella Lawson, who, even though her last name is Brie's, reminds me of Lucy, if my sister had a cultivated BBC accent instead of a Chicago honk. Freud would have a chuckle with that one, so forget the crush. But I'd made Nigella's beet, dill, and mustard seed salad at least eight times.

Barry grabbed three big red onions and started juggling, which along with performing surgery and manual foreplay starred in his skill

set. After a two-minute routine, he parked the onions on the counter, came up behind me, and gave me a long hug, pressing his warm palms on the spot where our baby had, for the moment, stopped doing flip turns. His erection pressed against my behind.

"You're in a good mood," I said, not that such a mood was unusual lately. We were getting along exceedingly well. Throughout my pregnancy, Barry's disposition had rarely dipped below good and occasionally spiked off the charts, and his sex drive seemed to increase as gestation progressed.

"I'm enjoying this new domestic you," he said, scanning the recipe in the opened cookbook. As he started to chop fresh mint, I breathed in the picnicky fragrance and had a sudden yen for a tall glass of lemonade. Had it not been past eight on a Saturday night, I might have begged Barry to run out and buy enough lemons to fill a jug with a homemade brew, but I was hungry. The table was set with rustic pottery, chunky amber goblets just right for his wine and my water, and beeswax candles, waiting to be lit. I still had to finish our pasta, a simple recipe heavily reliant on pecorino Romano.

As peak experiences go, there are some women who find pregnancy overrated. Seeing your butt, once hard and high, swell into a beach ball you know will deflate and sink; finding your nose spread across your face; watching tributaries fan out from bulging varicose veins—I was determined not to notice such things happening to me. I was too distracted by the good stuff, like my brand-new, God-given cleavage, which I showcased at all hours in deep V-neck clothes so clingy they literally stretched the boundaries of good taste and should have been labeled Slut Mommy.

During the winter, as my bump grew, it felt cozy and efficient to be a baby-making machine. I was awed by the knowledge of cells multiplying inside of me like disciplined Marines, and I indulged in cup after cup of steaming cocoa, ignoring the verboten caffeine, reminding myself I required the calcium. Every weekend, I settled on the couch wrapped in cuddly cashmere with grilled cheese sandwiches, spending long afternoons watching Turner Classic Movies and memorizing name books.

Barry wanted a boy. He was sure it was a boy. Kitty analyzed my body—the baby bulge staying relatively narrow—and declared that yes,

it would definitely be another Marx heir, since I looked like she did while pregnant with Barry. I interpreted this to mean that I was one of those rare attractive pregnant ladies, since when Kitty favorably compares your appearance to hers it is the highest form of flattery.

Barry insisted on a strapping name, a manly name, a name like a power drill. He tossed off my suggestions—Dylan, Devin, Jesse, Sebastian, Nicholas, Eliah, Raphael, Oliver, Graham, Kieran—like small, twee doilies in favor of Hank, Jake, Cal, Kurt, Max, Nat, Bart, Tom, Abe, and Zack, stopping just short of Thor. I let him know I thought his choices were the kind of names wit-challenged pet owners bestow on Chihuahuas. We ultimately agreed on Alexander William, but when I suggested that Master Marx could be Sasha for short, Barry made a unilateral decision: if the baby was a boy, we would go with William Alexander. Given the remote possibility that we would produce a girl, Barry, marinating in his testosterone, graciously said I could pick whatever name I wanted for this unlikely female offspring.

William Alexander. It was a solid, multitasking name. William Alexander Marx, spelling bee king, bar mitzvah boy, Phi Beta Kappa, juris doctor, and Supreme Court justice. Will Marx, captain of the squash team, not a pimple in sight. Wild Willy Marx, starting pitcher for the Yankees. Billy Marx, renegade indie film director, winner of the Palme d'Or at Cannes. William A. Marx, Ph.D., curer of AIDS or cancer, possibly both. President William Alexander Marx, the first Jew in the White House.

I sometimes let my mind wander to William Alexander's future sibling: Daniel James.

They'd be the Marx brothers, just as wicked, only gorgeous. But living with a sextet of balls—what would that be like? How do you change a boy's diaper without getting a squirt of pee in the eye? Would a small male and I have anything to chat about? What if he was one of those perpetually moving children who start downing Ritalin before solid food? For a number of weeks I felt uniquely unqualified to be the mother of even one son. I warmed to the idea of having a boy, though, when I considered that he might be as attentive to me as Barry is to Kitty, calling at least once a day.

I never focused much on the reality of there being an actual person inside my body, and I learned to keep visions at bay of future projectile

vomiting. I was shocked when people expected to hear me opine on points I'd never considered, like whether I'd let the baby watch the Wiggles, a quartet whose popularity I learned rivaled that of the Beatles, despite the fact—or maybe because of the fact—that they perform "Hava Nagila" in Bavarian folk costume.

I wasn't in a hurry for my pregnancy to end. It was a contentment zone I'd never before imagined or visited. Tonight I sang "I'm a Woman" as I finished cooking our meal—"W-O-M-A-N"—putting the pasta in a big white bowl, snowing the top with even more cheese. I could picture the calcium going straight to my baby's tiny, precious bones, making them hard as diamonds.

Sure, there had been morning sickness, when I'd catapulted from cabs to lose my breakfast in the gutter while enduring withering stares from fellow New Yorkers. Nighttime leg cramps woke me, and my shrieks scared the bejesus out of Barry, although, as a doctor, he was able to massage away the cramps, for which I was grateful. Nor was I immune to belching, backaches, or cravings for mashed potatoes laden with the caramelized goop that KFC calls gravy. Twice I dreamt that my baby was Satan's child, with translucent skin and beady, marble eyes. I also grew sensitive to odors. Barry's oral hygiene could win a national competition, yet his night breath made me gag. But it was all part of the grand pregnancy experience, along with learning to smile benevolently when strangers patted my stomach and asked me if I knew the sex of the baby.

I did not. Pregnancy's mystery was much of its power.

That Saturday, Barry and I lingered over dinner. The beet salad was tangy; the whole-wheat baguette, crusty; the pasta, sensuous; and the candlelight, flattering.

"Dessert?" I asked Barry. "I bought that lemon tart you like."

"Just a sliver," he said. "You're going to drop thirty pounds, bingo, but mine will still be here." He'd gained a pound for each of my ten, but hearing him, you'd think he was now classified as morbidly obese.

I carried the dishes into the kitchen and loaded the dishwasher before I cut the tart, which I'd transferred to my favorite cake stand, heavy turquoise glass with swirls shaped like sperm. If New Year's Eve were a plate, it would look like this. I was wiping the big wooden salad bowl when I heard Barry answer his cell phone.

It wasn't unusual for him to be phoned at all hours, especially on Saturday, since Friday is popular for surgery. Every patient thinks she'll be the lucky ducky who won't bruise like an overmatched prize-fighter. Such a woman is deluded enough to imagine that if she grabs a Friday slot, she'll be back at work on Monday, her colleagues none the wiser, despite heavy spackling and the fact that Barry has reengineered her nose inside and out.

"Not now," he said to the caller.

My husband wasn't speaking in his soothing, practiced Barry Marx, M.D., demeanor. I wouldn't even have noticed the conversation if he didn't seem perturbed. "I will call you tomorrow," he said, clipping each word. *"Promise."*

It was the whisper of "promise" that gave him away.

The cake knife in my hand hovered above the plate as my insides twirled. I'd convinced myself that Barry had become Old Faithful. Just the day before, when Brie and I were layette-shopping, I'd said, "I think my leopard has changed his spots. I practically want to remind him he's still married to me, Molly Never-Gets-It-Quite-Right."

"Are you suggesting this change includes fidelity?" Brie had asked, putting down a sweet green jammie as soon as she saw the whopping price tag for what amounted to less fabric than a dish towel. Brie forced me, as she so often did, to visit a dark street in the fluorescently lit megalopolis of Denial. I turned over the question in my mind.

"I think I do," I'd said, twice. The second time was out loud.

"Not a moment too soon," she'd said, giving my hand a firm squeeze.

I'd always kept Brie informed of what I suspected were Barry's dalliances. I was long on intuition and short on hard evidence, but every six months or so I'd get a psychic whiff of adultery and report in. Brie would then declare that my suspicions qualified only as paranoia and that if I was going to be this pathetically insecure, I would doom my marriage all by myself. Once she'd ruled, it allowed me to relax and concentrate on my congenial, manageable life: work, home, family, friendships and, lately, Baby Marx.

I had been going through a cycle—every three to six months—when I ruminated, complained, and ultimately put my worries to rest. Never once did I confront Barry. But that night's "promise" ricocheted off the

kitchen walls, and as Barry walked in, carrying the empty bottle of pinot noir, my face must have registered panic.

"Molly, what's wrong?" he said. "Are you feeling something?" His voice sounded no less solicitous than it had three minutes before.

"Oh yeah, I'm feeling something," I said. Fury. Malice. The desire to shoot a gun.

"Tell me what's wrong," he said.

"What's *wrong*?" I repeated. "Doctor, why don't *you* tell *me*?"

"Excuse me?" His facial expression withered into resentment and distrust.

"Who is she?" I snarled. "Or should I say, who is she this time?"

"You really know how to turns things foul, don't you? I have no idea what you're talking about, except you've spoiled a perfectly pleasant evening."

"*I've* spoiled things?" I snorted. Barry can handle me when I'm cranky, petulant, sad, or worried. What he can't take is when I show some grit. Like at that moment. So I kept going. From somewhere, I was feeling an energy surge so powerful you'd think I was getting it through an IV drip. "You have a rap sheet four years long," I said, my voice rising. "How many other women have there been, Barry?" I pronounced his name as if it were a fatal virus carried by fruit bats. "All you doctors think you're God!"

"Go ahead, Molly, slam the whole profession," he said with equal contempt. "For this whole pregnancy I've put up with your mood swings, your anxieties, your goddamn beet addiction. I've come to almost every doctor appointment—"

"Was this all a terrible hardship? Did it take you away from your 'special friends'?" Despite the knife in my hand, I made that asinine gesture that suggests quotation marks, while he was sticking with the best-defense-is-a-good-offense strategy. At least he was being offensive.

"Do you think you've been easy to live with?" he said. "Or that you look so cute? And how about your complete lack of interest in sex?" His voice kept getting louder and his face closer. With the third question, spittle landed on my cheek.

That's when I put down the cake knife, hauled off, and threw the plate. I loved that plate, a wedding gift from my aunt Vicki.

"Shit, you're dangerous!" he said as he ducked. "Get a grip!"

"I don't want to get a grip, you jackass," I said. "I want a normal marriage. I want respect. I want—"

"If you act like this, I guess it's just your plight to have no respect."

"So now I have a *plight*?" I said, parking my hands on my massive belly. I suddenly understood what evolutionary biologists don't: why a female praying mantis tears off the male's head when he approaches her from behind, flapping his wings and strutting in hopes of having doggie-style sex. Obviously, she has just heard Mr. Mantis call his girlfriend. "Barry, last I noticed, we are having a baby. If you—when you—cheated on me before, which I'm fairly sure you have, I was willing to write it off as your version of immaturity. But the rules have changed. If you cheat on me now, I swear to God, you will wake up one morning"—I eyed the knife—"and your penis will be gone." Sweat was dripping off my face. "Do not," I shouted, breathing hard, "underestimate me."

"Holy crap," he shouted back. "You make me *want* to cheat on you. And I can think of a few of your friends who'd be more than willing."

Barry turned his back, which was just as well. At the moment the sight of his contorted, purple face, handsome as it might be in repose, repulsed me. "I've got to get out of here before I do something I regret."

"You don't regret what you've already done?" I bellowed as he left the room. "You don't regret anything?" But he didn't answer. Then, like an exclamation point, our front door slammed.

I stood in the kitchen, surrounded by shattered glass, a fitting tribute to our marriage. As I waddled to the closet to find a broom and dust pan, I caught my reflection in the cabinet glass; it took a second to register that this mess was me. My shoes trampled the yellowish ooze that once was a tart. I carefully swept up the larger pieces of broken glass, dumped them in the trash, and filled a pail with soapy water to wash lemon debris off every surface, including my face. What a waste of a luscious tart. What a waste, period.

It took me a full ten minutes until I began to cry, but when I did, the tears came like grenades. I began heaving so intensely I abandoned my cleaning, stumbled into the bedroom, hoisted my heavy body onto the bed, and pulled the comforter up to my neck. I grabbed a pillow and sobbed until I slipped into a dreamless sleep of uncertainty, anguish, and unadulterated exhaustion.

Around three in the morning I woke, my head throbbing. I instinctively felt for Barry in total darkness, but his side of the bed was empty. As I came to, the full force of our battle repeated itself like a badly written, atonal soundtrack for a movie called *Oh, Shit.* I walked into the bathroom and tried to remember what kind of pain meds my obstetrician allowed me to take. Not aspirin, she'd warned. Only Tylenol. My face was swollen and my hair was like burnt grass. I ran warm water in the tub and dumped in the first bath product I found, an unfortunate potion that smelled more like turbo-strength disinfectant than the spruce for which it was named.

I soaked until every bubble popped and the water grew cold. Shivering, I turned on the shower and quickly washed my hair, then wrapped myself in a none-too-clean towel and got out the blow-dryer. My arm felt too weary to lift it. I aborted the mission and began walking back to the bedroom to find a pair of granny underpants and my faded flower-sprigged flannel nightgown, wondering if Lucy still owned its voluminous red twin.

Dribbles of water followed me as I padded across the room. I made nothing of it. But when I bent down to open a drawer, a persistent trickle leaked on the taupe carpeting. Stupidly trying to deny the source of this pink fluid, I stumbled to the bed, laid the towel on the comforter, and crawled on top of it, hoping what was now a small gush would end.

I closed my eyes and dozed. When I woke, the clock on the nightstand read 4:48 and the towel was soaked. I remained inert. At 5:10, I felt a dull pulse inside both thighs, as if I were getting my period. Nothing operatic. But a half hour later, the pain returned with twice the force.

If I lay very still, would the pain and pressure stop? Whose idea of a bad joke was this? *Not now,* I thought. *Not fucking now.*

A more reasonable part of me laughed aloud and began to hear my mom's voice. *Get yourself together, Molly, my darling,* she trilled. *This is a wonderful day. You are going to be a mother. Find Barry and start timing the contractions. Yes, that's what they are, silly goose. Don't you remember what they taught you?*

I called Barry's cell phone. It wasn't turned on. I left a message. "Call me." To make sure he didn't interpret the words as a preamble to

an apology, I repeated the demand. "Call me immediately, you douche bag."

I considered the suitcase I was supposed to have packed. Typically, I'd not gotten around to it. With surprising calm, I threw some random clothes into a large tote. Later on, I wondered what had made me think that in the hospital I'd need lacy camisoles and matching thongs. White silk, yet.

I kept looking at the clock. Each minute ticked by slowly. Maybe nothing was really happening. I was overdramatizing, as Barry often accused me of doing. Now I was sorry I'd called him.

But then another pain came, burning like a torch. Twenty minutes had passed. I found Dr. Kim's number and left a message with her answering service. Five minutes later my doctor returned the call.

"I think my water broke," I said.

"I'll meet you at the hospital, Molly," she answered, upbeat.

I wanted to be strong. Again, I dialed Barry's number. His cell phone was still off. "I'm going to the hospital," I said, trying not to sound electric with emotion. "Nice if you could join me," I added—a phrase impossible to say without sarcasm.

What, I thought, would Lucy do if she were having a baby? Squat on the floor, punch someone's lights out if they suggested medication, drop a ten-pound infant, and run a half marathon? I had a sudden need to talk to my titanium sister. She answered on the fourth ring. "Molly, do you have any idea what time it is here?" she croaked. In Chicago it would be 5:35 A.M., and she is not one of those people who rise and shine.

"Sorry," I said. "But I think I'm having the baby."

"This is not entirely unexpected." There was a long pause. "And?"

"And I'm all alone," I snorted as I wiped my tears on my sleeve. "Don't ask. What should I do?"

"Man, what did I smoke last night? Please tell me I'm dreaming."

"Honest to God, Luce, I'm having contractions. The doctor wants me to go to the hospital." I started to whimper. "Barry is MIA. It wasn't supposed to happen this way."

"Listen to me, and don't be a twit," she said, now firmly in control. "Get in a taxi. Go to Mt. Sinai. That is, unless you want your doorman to deliver that baby."

"Okay," I said. "You're right." My sister, the good teacher, had spoken. "Okay."

"God damn it, I wish I could be there," she barked. "Where's that scumbag husband of yours? No, don't answer. I don't want to know. Call Brie. Have her meet you."

"Call Brie," I repeated mechanically.

"Have her call me!" Lucy shouted as I clicked off.

I took a deep breath. "Good morning," I said to Brie. I sounded almost sane until a contraction tightened around my stomach like a steel band. "Could you meet me at the hospital?" I whispered.

"What's going on?" she answered, wide awake, no doubt having already devoured the *Wall Street Journal* and her usual orange before she set out for a six o'clock training session.

"Nothing, probably," I said. I hoped it was nothing. But "nothing" was hurting at regular intervals, poking deep, as if someone were trying to locate each of my internal organs and rip them out one by one with a garden hoe. "Barry has an emergency," I lied, "and I just need you to hold my hand, okay? I'm thinking it's a false alarm."

"Got it," Brie said. "See you at Sinai."

I mustered the wherewithal to limp out the door and hail a taxi. Which wasn't hard. The sight of a whale-woman flailing her arms on a street corner at dawn tends to get a driver's attention. And evidently I wasn't the first frightened, frantic pregnant patient the hospital crew had seen stagger in solo. Within minutes, I was certified by insurance, wearing a gown, and declared to be six centimeters dilated. By the time Brie arrived I was surrounded by nurse-angels and hooked up to every kind of beeping *Star Wars* machine. Between contractions, I mentally redecorated the birthing room: sky blue paint and orchids. I refused to let myself think about Barry.

I thought it would make me feel better to have Brie at my side, but every time I felt a contraction, her jaw clenched as if she were having a wisdom tooth extracted without anesthetic. She'd yammer away, shouting, "Oh! Does it hurt? Does it hurt a lot? Christ, that was a big one. Whew, it's over now. We can relax." Which meant she could relax. But she didn't. Brie was hopeless; I could see that by the time I gave birth, she'd need a visit to a sanitarium.

One hour passed. Two. And then I lost count. The pain kept com-

ing, as if the Weather Channel were replaying hurricane footage. I didn't think about Barry. What would he have done, anyway? Make me feel it was my fault that the baby was showing up three weeks early, upsetting his surgery schedule?

I tried to let myself feel proud. *Molly Marx, superwimp, a woman who wouldn't be able to dispose of a mousetrap, is having a baby.* Part of me seemed to hover on the ceiling, watching myself groan and grunt and look hideous but mighty all at once. I was a stick of dynamite ready to blow.

When the contractions were down to five minutes apart, I turned to Brie and said, "You don't have to stay."

"I won't leave you," she answered, mopping my forehead with a cool, damp towel.

An epidural was the next order of business. "It's going to get bloody."

"I can handle it."

"Any word from Barry?"

"I didn't try to call him again," she said, and I'll never know if that was true. "What happened between you two?"

I waved away the thought of him. "Not important," I said, which was true, because I suddenly thought my uterus was going to fall on the floor, to be followed by an elephant calf wandering out to nurse at my breast.

"Okay, liftoff," said the deliriously gleeful nurse. I wanted to slap her. With amazing speed, I was greeted by Dr. Kim, who emerged from the haze wearing a smile and a shmatte over her silky black hair. She is one of the few women I know who looks good in aquarium-green drawstring pants and Crocs.

"Are you ready to have a baby, Molly girl?" she said.

"Hell, no," I yelled.

"I beg to differ," she said. "You! Are! Ready! When I tell you to push, push."

What did she mean, push? A wallop of drugs had kicked in, and I wouldn't have been able to feel an apartment building fall on my head.

"Okay, now, push," she said.

"We have to push," Brie said, in case I hadn't heard. Brie was standing now, wearing a gown over her gym clothes. The glimpse of

face behind her mask looked deathly pale. All I could hear were a sorority of women yelling "Push" and "Good girl" and "Wow" and "Great" and finally "Here it comes—here it comes—here it comes." Were we all having a group orgasm?

I felt a creature slither out of me. Then there were cheers, as if the Giants had hammered the Patriots in the Super Bowl. I felt carbonated with joy. Had my feet not been in stirrups, I might have jitterbugged.

I had made and delivered a *baby*. Me, me, me. I could split an atom, box with a bear, dog-paddle to Hawaii.

I closed my eyes and talked to God. *Let this child be healthy. Let him have all the appropriate body parts. Let him be wise and strong and good. Let him not have Barry's nose.* For minutes on end, I believe, I held my breath in suspense.

When I opened my eyes, my little boy was clean and resting on my chest. William Alexander was screaming. He had the most exquisite, pinched face, bigger than a grapefruit, and a few random hairs flattened into a comb-over. "We're a team now, kiddo," I whispered into his miniature ear. "I'm your mommy and I love you. I will always, always, always love and protect you."

I examined my child carefully. He had wrinkly pink skin, ten fingers, and ten toes. He didn't, however, have a penis. My first thought was that the baby was deformed. Then I realized that I, Molly Divine Marx, had produced a female child. A very small me.

"She's unbelievably gorgeous, Molly." Brie looked at me, crying. "She's one of us. I love you both."

I was the mother of a daughter. A girl! I hoped she would love me half as much as I loved my own mother. My second thought was that Barry would be disappointed. My third thought: what he felt didn't matter.

Soon enough, the baby was whisked away, Brie went home to change, and I was wheeled to a room I had to share with a loud, big woman surrounded by her loud, big family who set the air-conditioning so high I thought I was in a meat locker. After I did some heartfelt begging, a nurse finally appeared with an extra cotton blanket, thin as a sheet. I was doing my best to calm my chattering teeth when Barry walked into the room, carrying an enormous vase of pink peonies and a large white teddy bear.

I tried to read his expression, searching for regret. But Barry acted if it were normal to have missed the birth of his five-and-a-half-pound daughter and to find his wife marooned in a maternity wing. He tried, at least, to win me over with a compliment.

"I saw her," he said. "She's the prettiest one in the nursery."

I hadn't comparison-shopped, but I said, "I'm sure you're right."

"I'm proud of you."

I glared. He stared. I glared some more.

"And I'm sorry, very sorry."

What the apology covered wasn't clear. Barry was too proud to elaborate and I was too exhausted to ask. For better or worse, wherever it would take us, we were parents now, together. We called an unspoken cease-fire blessed by the birth of our child, who was—thank God—healthy, a Perdue Oven Stuffer trussed in a pink cap and gown. I cradled her silently, with Barry perched tentatively on the edge of the narrow bed.

"Do you want to hold her?" I asked after a few soundless minutes.

He looked terrified.

"Try it," I said, as if I were coaxing him into sampling gruel. He took his daughter in his arms and started to sing "Born in the U.S.A."

"Be careful," I said as I shut my eyes. "Your tears are falling on her nightie."

I hadn't intended to sleep. When I woke, it was evening and no fewer than eleven supersized versions of my roommate overflowed into my space, sounding joyful in a guttural language. Barry was not in sight.

"Excuse me, but my daughter-in-law needs her rest," I heard Kitty say. "I believe the rule is no more than two visitors at a time." She was using her freezer-burn voice, which could have run Microsoft, and the sound of it caused most of the large merrymakers to scatter. My mother-in-law—dressed impeccably in a fitted gray jacket, black turtleneck, and trim black pants and looking about as much like a grandma as I did the winner of an MTV music video award—grimaced as she brushed away one of the other patient's neon-orange helium balloons, which had invaded Marx turf. "Mazel tov, darling," she said. "How do you feel?"

"Like I ran the marathon in high heels three sizes too small," I said.

"She looks like Barry did as a baby," Kitty said. I took that to mean she was adorable. Was I supposed to thank her for complimenting my child? I'd been a mother for just hours and already was confused, so I said nothing.

Kitty gazed at her rings. Recently colored honey-blond hair framed her determined face. "I want to ask you a small favor." She sucked in a breath and lifted her face to look at me, pushing her mouth into an expression almost like a smile. "I'd like you to name the baby for my mother."

I nodded. "I see," I said. "You want me to name my little girl Gertrude?"

"It tears me apart that she doesn't have a namesake." In case I didn't get the point, Kitty took out a monogrammed handkerchief and dabbed her eyes. I looked carefully. No tears.

I thought of Granny Gert, four foot ten and two hundred pounds. To her credit, she was said to be an ace canasta player, and based on the stockpile of paper bags found after her death, she'd been a recycler far ahead of her time.

"Gertie Marx," Kitty said hopefully. "Those old-fashioned names are chic again."

Sophia, Sadie, Emma, or Isabella, certainly. Violet, Helen, Hazel, or Lily, of course. Fritzi, maybe. Not Gertrude. Not if I had anything to say about it, which I did.

Kitty took my measure. "Gertrude as a middle name? Or maybe just a G-name? Grace? Gabriella? Greer?"

I thought about it for a second. No, less. Like a butterfly, a different name flew into my brain.

I buzzed for the nurse. "Could you bring me my daughter, please?" I asked.

Ten minutes later, as my infant snoozed in my arms, Barry returned, armed with turkey sandwiches, chocolate cupcakes, Champagne, and plastic cups. I sat up as straight as my bloated, beleaguered body allowed.

"You all need to be formally introduced," I said to my husband and Kitty with a tingle of devilish pride. "Meet Annabel. Annabel Divine Marx."

Eighteen

THE FAMILY DIVINE

*L*inden," Detective Hicks tells the taxi driver. "Highland Park."

Hicks is riding through Chicago's northern suburbs, a green belt of wealth that grows more impressive by the mile. He cranes his head to see the flat, gray splendor that is Lake Michigan. *The shining Big-Sea-Water . . . level spread the lake before him . . .*

In my parents' neighborhood, many of the houses have been bought by young couples who've knocked them down to build at oblique angles and accommodate three-car garages and five-thousand-square-foot turreted, gabled, centrally air-conditioned homes with gyms, disco-balled entertainment centers, and ADD-inducing playrooms. Chez Divine, however, is the beta version and looks more or less as it did in 1928, when a one-car garage wasn't a quality-of-life-compromising issue. The twenties were when my grandparents were born, and should I come across them in the Duration, I plan to ask them a thing or two. Did Grandma Phyllis fret about her cellulite? Did Papa Lou consider work/life balance?

My childhood home is neither Snow White adorable nor men's club macho. It's homey, with gray shingles, glossy black shutters, and—in the summer—blue clematis that climbs a filigreed trellis. A flagstone

walk leads to the door, now all but obscured by an evergreen in need of serious pruning. My parents don't decorate this towering fir for Christmas, which makes Mrs. Swenson next door gnash her teeth.

Just take it slow, Hicks says to himself as he steps out of the car and asks the driver to return in three hours. Mine is the first case he's handled solo. He is nervous but reminds himself, as he digs through my history, that he can simply pretend he is a biographer. It is a little known fact that Detective H. Hicks has an undergraduate degree in English literature from one of the windy upstate branches of SUNY.

I admire Hicks not only for his professional joie de vivre but also because he is one of those lean men who wear clothes well. An unbuttoned, bronze Harris tweed overcoat hangs handsomely from his broad shoulders along with a cashmere scarf in a spicy brown. He carefully walks around spots of brackish ice that refuse to melt in the March gloom and gives my parents' door knocker two confident hits.

> *With a look of joy and triumph,*
> *With a look of exultation,*
> *As of one who in a vision*
> *Sees what is to be, but is not,*
> *Stood and waited Hiawatha.*

Detective Hicks of Manhattan's Twentieth Precinct is twenty minutes late, but now that he's here, my mother is more atwitter than before he arrived. A grin paralyzes her face as if she were a stroke victim, and her eagerness is like a cocker spaniel's.

On a usual Sunday afternoon, I'd expect to see my mother in the kitchen making soup, wearing Levi's, an ancient red turtleneck, and worn velvet slippers, her streaky blond hair twisted up in a clip, but today her hair is freshly blow-dried and she's in a midcalf charcoal wool skirt over flat boots polished to a military gloss. Instead of her usual dangling earrings from a random craft show, she is wearing pearl studs. Her geranium-hued sweater set is so mom-correct I wonder if she speed-ordered it from the Lands' End catalog when this appointment was scheduled four days ago. I hope she's tucked the tags inside and will return it tomorrow.

"Detective Hicks," she says. "Welcome to Chicago."

"Thank you," he answers, carefully wiping his shoes on the doormat. "Sorry—my driver couldn't find his way out of an empty parking lot." He sounds harsh, which is not his intent. "But at least I got to see more than I expected. You have a beautiful city."

Could this be any more uncomfortable? both of them are thinking. My father appears only slightly more relaxed. "Take your coat?" he offers after he shakes Hicks' hand—cool, firm grip meets cool, firm grip—and repeats to himself, *Keep it together, keep it together.*

"Glad you didn't run into that blizzard coming our way," he says out loud. The knowing nose predicts snow before nightfall—special delivery from Canada—and the air feels slightly damp.

For my dad's sixtieth birthday, Lucy, Barry, and I gave him a colossal television set—Barry's idea—which dominates one wall in the den, where my father generally parks himself. He's Chicago bred, suckled on team spirit—da Bulls, da Bears, and of course da Cubs—and only last year quit playing sixteen-inch softball, the indigenous sport of his youth. But this afternoon French doors close off his darkened sanctuary, and my parents guide Hicks through the neglected living room, where a fire has been kindled and lamps softly glow.

"Lucy called," my father reports. "The roads are icing up—she's gotta take it slow. She said to eat without her."

From its bosom leaped the sturgeon . . .

For this occasion, my mother has bought out Once upon a Bagel, and not just the sturgeon but the whitefish, the pickled herring, the nova, the works. It's shiva all over again, minus cardboard boxes on which the immediate family shift their butt cheeks, avoiding another cookie for fear that the precarious seating will collapse. In the absence of a pamphlet to guide a mother on how to entertain an officer of the law investigating the mysterious death of her daughter, Claire Divine is making it up as she goes along. She considers hospitality an art form. A New York detective is visiting—on a Sunday, not Saturday, since she and my father are in the traditional, yearlong mourning for a child, and Saturday is their Sabbath, which includes going to the synagogue. Hence, my mother has produced Sunday brunch, in the tradition of our tribe.

"Your daughter Molly—did you have any reason to think she was unhappy?" Hicks begins gently after he offers condolences and they take their seats.

My parents look at each other to determine who should answer. "From what we could tell, she was over the moon," my mother says. "A child, a marriage, a lovely home, even a part-time job—she had it all." She's already cracking. "What kind of monster would take this away?"

"Can you think of anyone who might have meant Molly harm?" Hicks asks.

"What are you talking about—reckless endangerment?" My father, whose favorite author is Elmore Leonard, jumps in. "Of course not. People adored our daughter."

"So you think that if this was . . . a crime . . . the perpetrator was a stranger?"

"To begin with, of course it was a crime," my father says, careful to not add *fucking*. "As to who did it, there are so many goddamn nut jobs out there, I wouldn't know where to look first."

"So you're thinking it wasn't anyone Molly knew."

"I'm not sure about anything," my father says. "Because people, you know, well, they have their secrets."

My mother glances at him as if to say, *What people would that be?*

"Are you thinking of anyone in particular?" Hicks asks. The detective and I both wait for him to expand on the thought, but my father only shakes his head. So Hicks moves on to "How would you describe your daughter?"

I wouldn't be surprised if a string quartet popped out of the den and played a requiem commissioned by my parents. "Adored; many, many friends; a good wife; a great mother," my father says.

Let's canonize her, Hicks thinks. *What about the woman's faults? How do I ask about those?* "Anything else you can tell me to round out the picture?"

My dad stares blankly out the window at snow powdering the edge of the lawn. "Molly could be impulsive, a little scatterbrained, and unsure of herself, especially with her husband's family." His answers sound as if he is responding in a job interview when you're asked to produce faults and you fish for assets disguised as flaws.

"What did you think of your son-in-law?"

Not as worshipful of Molly as he should have been, my mother thinks. *Spoiled egomaniac* rattles around my father's brain. *Way too attached to that haughty mother of his.* But what they offer, in unison, is "We loved him," and they immediately know from Hicks' face that he isn't buying it.

"Okay, the guy could be a hothead—he wasn't the husband I thought my daughter deserved—but he's not a killer," my father says. "That's preposterous."

"No one said he's a killer."

"Well, Detective, if you're wondering, I'm not thinking it," my father says. "Last time I looked, being selfish isn't against the law." His voice rises. "Doesn't even make you a sociopath." It's only taken my father five minutes to lose it. "So, for Christ's sake, let's not mince words and waste our goddamn time. Who do you think did it?"

"Mr. and Mrs. Divine," Hicks says evenly, glancing first at my father and then at my mother, "we're looking . . . everywhere, and at everything." He feels flop sweat gather in his armpits, and is glad he's wearing a sport coat. "And on that score, what about Molly's . . . mental health?"

I can't imagine that my parents have ever once considered any aspect of my health that wasn't physical. I got braces and every appropriate inoculation, took jars of vitamins, and left for college with birth control and a fact sheet about chlamydia. My mother and father are born midwesterners whose set point is caution and optimism, one foot solidly planted in each camp. If anything, they've always thought that Lucy was their *meshuggener,* their nut job, not me.

"Excellent," my father guesses. "Molly's 'mental health' "—he drags out the words—"was exemplary."

"Molly would never hurt herself," my mother adds, picking the world's most obtuse euphemism, "if that's what you're getting at. Never. Obviously, someone meant ill to my daughter, but if you think she brought it on—blaming the victim? Outrageous." As she tenses, I notice that her carefully applied foundation has settled into delicate vertical lines around her lips. I long to reach out and pat it back in place. "Maybe our daughter was simply in the wrong place at the wrong time, that's what I think. I always told her she shouldn't be riding that bike alone. . . ."

She did. I never listened, just as I ignored her when she'd told me to major in education, stay in Chicago, join Hadassah, wear pastels, and not rush to marry Barry.

My mother stares into the middle distance. I can see that she pictures me as I looked at twelve—scrawny, all legs and arms—and wants to reach out and hold that child and breathe in the scent of her newly washed hair and well-scrubbed skin.

"Claire, honey, what is it?" my father says to her, and covers her hand with his large paw. She only shakes her head, dabs away a tear, and takes a deep breath.

"Detective, I can't go on just now," she says. "Please, let's have lunch." *I'd rather they were talking about my death,* she thinks. *Why couldn't it have been me?*

The conversation dwindles away as the three begin to politely peck at their bagels and all four kinds of fish, picking up speed as the meal progresses. They are ready for apple cake—baked by my mother, to mitigate the excess ethnicity—when Lucy blasts through the front door. She hangs her bulky white fox-trimmed parka in the front hall closet, kicks off her Uggs, and walks in green stocking feet to join them, while she shouts, "Hi, everyone—I'm here." She kisses each parent hello. "I'm Lucy," she says, extending her hand to Hicks and meeting his eye. Her hands are a miniature version of my father's, broad and capable.

"Hiawatha Hicks."

He's got to be kidding, Lucy thinks. She almost succeeds in keeping a straight face as she wonders if he has a sister, Minnehaha. Ha, ha, ha. "Sorry . . . traffic," she says, failing to recover self-control before both of my parents show a pulse of embarrassment. "What did I miss?" Before Hicks can answer, she loads up a bagel, including a substantial slice of Bermuda onion, which the others have politely avoided along with difficult questions.

The detective is young and good-looking, Lucy notes, and no gumshoe. He's wearing decent leather oxfords that have escaped slush stains. She registers that his skin is a rich milk chocolate and his hair short and recently barbered. She can't pin him down as either Puerto Rican or African American. A more exotic cocktail, she decides.

"So, your name—someone liked nineteenth-century American poetry, huh?" As Lucy rips into the bagel, she catches our mother's eye

and shoots a look that says, *What's with the food? This guy probably wants sausage and eggs.*

"Fortunately, Mr. Longfellow's not around to ask for a licensing fee," Hicks answers. Nobody laughs, so he moves on to the shock-and-pity approach. "The truth is I never got to ask about the whole name saga. I was eight when my mother was killed in a car accident. I was raised by my grandmother."

My parents and Lucy are too blue-state to ask about a father. None of them is as riveted by Hicks' sad story as they might usually be, because there's something bigger and grimmer that's crept into the room: death. Hicks' declaration has lifted the black veil, and my mother sucks in her breath so fast she almost pants. Now they can get started. "Shall we have coffee in front of the fireplace?" she suggests.

"Great," my father announces, although the question has been pitched to Hicks. They decamp to the living room, which is overrun by family pictures: twin girls with hair in pigtails, cut short, and grown long; graduation pictures, pre- and post-orthodontia; camp snapshots; bat mitzvah portraits; my parents' vacation photos, my mother's right arm always strategically placed around my father's waist to obscure his love handles. There are at least ten photos of Annabel, including the most recent in a silver frame. My daughter wears one of my old smocked Florence Eiseman dresses. The dress is blue, the Molly color; Lucy always wore red.

My parents huddle, holding hands. Facing them, Hicks and Lucy square off like prizefighters.

The room, paneled in cherry, radiates warmth, and Hicks admires it. "Mr. Divine," he says, "please tell me where you were when you got the news."

"Already at work," he says. "I get there early. Claire—my wife, that is—called that morning the minute she heard from Barry." He squeezes my mother's hand.

"I could hardly make out a word he said," my mother adds. After decades of marriage, they are vinaigrette, no longer simply oil and vinegar, and don't even notice that they finish each other's sentences.

"Claire knew from Barry's voice that it was bad," he says.

"Annabel, I thought—something had happened to our baby girl." My mother's eyes flood, and my father pulls her to his barrel chest. I,

too, wish I could feel the familiar comfort of his slightly sweaty protection.

"So I came home, to be with Claire," he says. His voice started off big but has already shrunk. "We got to New York by eight."

"By then we knew the worst," my mother says. "For a few hours, Barry let us think there was hope, but he called us right before we boarded to tell us the real story." She remembers how she spent the flight, staring blindly at the unresponsive heavens, which quickly faded to black. Was I floating in the cosmos like an errant balloon, an unmoored soul? It was a bad dream then, and far worse now—for all of us.

Hicks patiently listens while my parents account in excruciating, small-print detail the most unimaginable day of their life, when, defying every law of nature, their daughter had died, possibly by someone's hand. That the hand might be her own they cannot imagine. Did a stranger lure a foolish me to a remote spot by the river? Was I meeting someone I knew and thought I could trust? Did I simply lose control of my bike? Was I so momentarily insane that I deliberately rode toward the water, perhaps to try to drown? (This last theory is tossed out by Lucy.) They talk until it seems they must be spent, but suddenly the timbre of my father's voice downshifts and darkens, a thundercloud ready to burst.

"What I need to know, Detective," he says, his face dangerously red, "is that you're going to catch the goddamn sonofabitch who did this."

Lucy winces, but he goes on.

"There's a murderer out there," my dad yells. "My daughter's dead. Gone. Our granddaughter's lost her mother. Our lives are shot to hell. Nothing in this family will ever be the same. There's a fucking monster somewhere, and you, my friend, have got to find him. Am I making myself clear? Do I have your word that my daughter Molly's death won't be just another crappy little unsolved case that gets a week's cursory attention before it's shelved for something bigger and flashier?"

Hicks listens. He does not respond. *This guy isn't done yet,* Hicks knows.

"Are you going to turn yourself inside out to find the scum bucket who did this?" With each short blast, my father's voice gets louder, as if

someone's pressing the volume button on the remote. He doesn't feel better for having made his point.

"I hear you, Mr. Divine," Hicks says, awed by this father's pain. *I want to find the killer,* he says to himself. *If there was one.* "Sir, you have my word." And then he turns to Lucy.

She looks nothing like the pictures of Molly. Bigger, taller, tougher. Her mouth is wide, and the lips are sensual and full—fuller than most white women's—and red-stained, as if she's just sucked on hard candy. Probably prefers Chapstick to lipstick. Bitten nails. Starter crow's feet, not unappealing. Wild hair—the kind that defeats a comb, two shades richer and darker than cider. She's a woman who will improve with age, he predicts, as long as gravity is kind to those breasts, too motherly for his taste.

"Lucy, where were you that day?" he asks.

My sister feels he says this with menace, but she tries not to let her hostility crash in a heap at his feet. "Out of town," she answers. Neutral voice, not giving anything away. Hicks' face suggests that she continue, and Lucy does. "It was Presidents' Day weekend. I wanted to snowboard, and some of the other teachers were going to Wisconsin. I started driving there, but then I got Mom's call, so I reversed directions and came home. I flew to New York the next day—first plane out."

A no-alibi alibi, Hicks thinks.

I have a sudden urge to flee this overheated room and zoom in on Annabel with my afterlife babycam. When I checked on her earlier this morning, she was sniffling. Has Barry tutored her in nose blowing? Encouraged her to drink tea with honey? I used to be able to coax Annabel into taking a few swallows, especially if I used one of my grandmother's flowered teacups and set the tiny table with the blue faux Wedgwood doll dishes. But no, I feel this is where I need to be, planted like the evergreen sentinel out front.

"Mr. Hicks," Lucy says in her voice of natural authority, assuming you are four. "Where are you, for real, with Molly's case? Do you have any suspects?"

Lucy is someone who wants what she wants and doesn't give up, Hicks thinks; a woman for whom a defect can become a strength, and strength a defect. "It's a bit premature for suspects," he says. "That's why I'd be interested in hearing from you on that score."

"The obvious," she says. "The husband, for starters—"

"Lucy!" my mother trumpets, as if her daughter had announced that their guest has farted. "You are talking about our son-in-law."

"Mrs. Divine," Hicks says calmly, "Lucy's right." His brown eyes pin my sister. "What do you know?"

I hear inhales and exhales, and Hicks thinks that she knows nothing but can't get past hating that poor schmuck Barry. She probably would have hated any man her sister married.

"It troubles my parents, Detective," she says finally, "but it was a marriage . . . with problems." My father looks out the window. Sugary snowflakes are continuing to fall.

"Big enough problems for it to get this ugly?" Hicks says. *Ugly?* Talk about understatement. "This violent?"

"Maybe," Lucy says. "My sister put up with a lot of"—she looks at our parents and amends her language—"garbage." Still, our parents glare at her. "But it's not for me to say," she says, sinking into the corner of the couch to make the retreat complete. They are back to silence souring the air.

"What I want to tell all of you," Hicks says, "is that in cases like this, don't expect a red carpet to unroll and lead us back to the cause of death." While he elaborates, his eyes catch a photo of three generations of Divines—aunts, uncles, cousins, us—taken at my grandparents' fiftieth-anniversary party. Lucy and I are fourteen. Everyone is smiling into the camera except my sister, who looks accusingly at me. I had never noticed this before—I'd always been focused on myself, horrified by my dotted dress from the girls' department, while Lucy got to wear a black sheath in a woman's size. Now I'm wondering what I might have said or done to piss her off.

"Detective Hicks," Lucy says as he winds down, "want to take a drive? Check out the 'hood?"

My parents wince at her attempt at humor.

"I wouldn't be putting you out?" he answers, writing off her comment as nervousness, glad to spend time with her.

"C'mon, let's go," she says, dangling car keys and offering the smile she reserves for auto mechanics and her best students.

Hicks postpones his driver's arrival by ninety minutes. Lucy begins the Molly Divine Memorial Tour, swinging past Ravinia, the site of

my first make-out session, followed by the homes of three former boyfriends and finally Highland Park High School. Her voiceover proclaims that I was an A-minus student who was in charge of prom decorations and insisted on an unfortunate *Blue Lagoon* theme. In my defense, I was hoping to capture the azure of a Bahamian sea, but under lights the color of turquoise eye shadow, everyone simply looked late-stage tubercular. As both Hicks and I are beginning to worry that the point of this meandering drive is for Lucy to render me solid-gold average, she says, in a voice as rehearsed as a novice trial lawyer's, "I keep wondering if Barry had a girlfriend who . . ."

"Who what?" he says.

"It's a feeling I have, that someone meant Molly harm," she says. "Maybe that person was Barry, or someone Barry knew." She slows the car and parks on a side street. Night has almost cloaked the town in blackness, and through barren trees snow steadily falls. "My parents would freak if they heard this—they thought Molly was an angel even before she died. Not that I'm judging, but my sister may have had another man in her life." *Besides that schmuck husband,* she thinks. "Maybe you can find him."

In the dusk, her face looks hard. "This guy, did you meet him?"

"Never," she says. "I only heard about someone once, and it was before Annabel was even born. Could have been a big nothing, over years ago. Or maybe she made it up, to make me feel like less of a loser, you know, like shaving your head because your sister's going through chemo." Lucy laughs nervously and alone. "I feel disloyal even mentioning this, like I'm besmirching my dead sister's reputation."

Hicks is all ears.

"She and I weren't the type to write little poems about our every feeling, you know. Like I have to tell you that we are—were—very different."

"Keep going."

"My point is, I can't say I'd have blamed her if she played around."

"Uh-huh," Hicks urges—too obviously, it seems to me. As if Lucy needs encouragement.

"She was too damn trusting. If you ask me, to a fault." *Which no one would accuse me of,* Lucy thinks. "Molly was the big-city girl, but she could be alarmingly dense."

Hey. Rewind. *I* always had to take care of *you*. Did you forget?

"Oh well, I'm talking out of my ass," she admits. "Probably wasting your time." Lucy turns the key in the ignition. "If you haven't figured it out already, I'm not the crown jewel of the Divine tiara," she says. "Molly is my mom's clone, and my dad idolizes my mother. End of story. But, God damn it, I did love my sister. I loved her." I wait for Lucy to cry. Not today. I may as well wait for the Pope to get married.

No one speaks for several blocks. As they turn into the drive, Hicks says, "I'll need the names of the friends you were going to meet that day to snowboard."

Lucy twitches ever so slightly. "Of course," she says. Ten minutes later, after goodbyes all around, she's on the road.

Hicks is not so lucky. His driver, once again, gets lost. By the time the man arrives, the wind is whipping snow into a tango and his return flight has been cancelled along with every other airplane flying east.

"I won't hear of a hotel," my mother says.

Which is how Detective Hiawatha Hicks came to spend the night under a faded lavender duvet in the twin bed that was mine, his head on my down pillow. Drifting into sleep, his last thought is of Lucy. He dreams of his first-grade teacher, who placed him in the slow group and was convinced he might never learn to read.

Nineteen

FUNNY BUNNY

Seven months after Annabel was born, I was four pounds over my pre-pregnancy weight, which had been only five pounds over my lifelong goal, a number I glimpsed once on the scale fifteen years ago after a camping trip where the nightly entrée was—I'm fairly certain—squirrels. When I looked in the mirror, I didn't mind what I saw. My hips were a tad wider, my belly even less flat than before, but my breasts appeared no worse for having nursed—I was glad I'd invested in two hundred dollars' worth of bras engineered by the likes of NASA.

"Guess who's paying me a visit?" I said to Brie one morning when she'd called en route to a trial.

I hated that on the first beat she answered, "Luke," and laughed. "Why?"

"Because he's an old friend," I said as I patted a mask over my face. It smelled of apricots and vanilla and promised to make each pore invisible.

"Right," she said, the way that means "I'm not buying it."

"Luke's sweet. He sent Annabel the most exquisite antique rocking chair." It was two feet tall, with original paint the pale yellow of sweet

butter. It awaited my daughter like a throne. I could picture her when she was older, reading as she quietly rocked, identifying with Cinderella, lusting after glass slippers, and starting to plan her wedding.

"And I assume you wrote a lovely thank-you," Brie said. She knew I believed the ghost of Emily Post would stomp on my head if within a week of receiving a gift a sincere, original acknowledgment was not in the mail.

"Of course."

"You've fulfilled your social obligation. Why are you letting him come over?"

"He wants to see the baby, not me." Even I didn't believe me.

"You know how I feel. It's a mistake to let him near you."

"You're not giving me credit," I said, feigning indignation.

"Call me a realist," Brie said lightly. "Luke's always been crazy about you, and you're a little bit lonely and misunderstood." She hummed something that sounded like a dirge.

"Hey, everything's good here," I protested. Despite the fact that Barry was working exceptionally long hours, she knew I felt we were once again on terra firma. No missile launchings. No "promises" bouncing off walls.

"I'll shut up—you're a grown-up," she said, to my relief. "Give him a big, sloppy kiss for me."

"Highly unlikely," I said with my goodbye.

Luke was due in ten minutes. I washed my face. My pores stared back at me, still good-sized pixels. I dabbed on the tiniest bit of makeup and thanked God for inventing black boot-cut jeans. Annabel, all sixteen pounds of powdery innocence, was sleeping in her cool, darkened room. I'd put her down an hour earlier, and if I knew my daughter, she'd wake up merrily right after Luke and I ate lunch. On the kitchen counter, our meal waited—richly gold curried chicken salad, heirloom tomatoes layered with buffalo mozzarella and basil, a few small sourdough rolls, and one formidable fudge brownie, takeout artfully arranged on my second-best dishes. White wine was chilling along with a pitcher of iced green tea garnished with cucumber slices. I wanted Luke to think I'd made an effort, but not too much.

There's no reason to be nervous, I told myself. *Whatever you once felt for*

Luke is an aberration, buried under layers of life. Good, solid, fortunate life. I thought of my father's credo: *Make mistakes—just don't keep making the same goddamn ones.* There was no reason that philosophy couldn't apply now, except that a more cynical brain worm was wiggling for attention: *If you get to live your life over, make the same mistakes, only sooner.*

I fluffed the living room pillows and rearranged the roses. That still left a few minutes to mindlessly scan the arts section of the *Times* before the doorman called to announce that Mr. Delaney had arrived. On the way to the door I checked my reflection. The woman I saw was trying. I hoped only I noticed this.

"For you," Luke said, offering a large bouquet of deep purple anemones, an ear-to-ear grin, and the graze of lips on my cheek. I liked that he didn't wear cologne. He didn't need it. "And for the other lady . . ." From a large shopping bag he pulled out a package wrapped in pale pink paper, tied with a floppy orange silk bow.

I placed the gift on the coffee table. "The other lady needs to finish her nap or she will make a very bad impression," I said as I hung Luke's size forty-four long Burberry next to Barry's forty regular.

Luke's hair was shaggier than I remembered, and I had an impulse to brush it away from his eyes. Perhaps he'd lost weight—his cheekbones punctuated his face like parentheses. He was wearing a V-neck sweater the color of wisteria, which on most men would have been a questionable choice. On Luke it deepened the blue of his eyes.

"I'm glad to see your home hasn't become a toy showroom," he said in a sly, familiar tone. "My brother and sister-in-law apparently hold a major stake in Fisher-Price."

Since I'd stuffed the rest of her possessions in closets, only one basket of Annabel's most presentable playthings was in sight. "Come back in another year and then you can judge me," I said. Annabel had already acquired an obscene number of gaudy plastic contraptions that did everything but burp, and her drawers overflowed with clothes, half of which she'd outgrown before wearing. I was embarrassed by how the Marx family was single-handedly bolstering the gross national product, but was unable to say "Enough," especially to Kitty, my parents, Lucy, or Brie.

"She looks like you," Luke said, picking up a photograph of Barry and me in our Sunday-cozy robes. We were hugging a freshly scrubbed, two-month-old Annabel.

"Especially if you can picture me buck naked." The minute those words slipped out they seemed 200 percent too intimate.

Luke followed me into the kitchen, where I put the flowers in a vase. A few minutes later we sat down to lunch. He gave me an update on his recent shoots—Santa Fe, Prague, Sydney—and the studio he'd bought in Dumbo with a partner, Simon someone. I waxed proud about what a great sleeper Annabel was, how I'd discovered at least ten new cable television channels, and why I'd decided, after considerable debate, to stop making my own organic baby food.

"This stay-home-mommy stuff—do you love it?" he asked about twenty minutes into lunch. I did an instant replay to search for condescension. You never can predict on which side of the fence men your own age will stand regarding whether a mother belongs at home. Even ardent, high-toned, prochoice, antiwar, carbon-footprint-shrinking recyclers sometimes shock you silly with polemics about why a mother needs to make every peanut butter sandwich until kids become postdocs—especially when the mom in question is his wife. Whatever their own mother did was wrong, you invariably discover, and lots of these guys are the sons of fervent seventies feminists.

Nonetheless, my derision meter failed to buzz.

"You're the first person who's had the nerve to ask me that question," I answered, to stall. In fact, I'd originally planned to return to work, but a month after Annabel arrived, my boss was replaced by a new editor in chief whose reputation preceded her like a rogue tidal wave of entitlement. The two of us had one short meeting as my maternity leave was due to end. With an expression straddling shock and boredom, she quietly flipped through a portfolio featuring my last three years' worth of decorating stories. Two days later, the head of human resources called to say my boss was "going in another direction"—and I wasn't on her map.

Since I was twenty-two years old, I'd always had a job. Isolation terrified me. Even after all these months, I still couldn't picture life at home full-time. At a feverish pace, I'd put out feelers for a new position, but every job I heard about had such an insignificant decorating

department that I'd be spending half my time ordering bubble wrap and the remainder packing and unpacking boxes the size of refrigerators. My ideal job would have been part-time, but when I raised that flag, interviewers all but shouted, "Next!" I suspected that each editor who interviewed me thought that, as a new mom, I'd be taking off every other day for this or that baby-related emergency.

"I love being with Annabel," I finally said with what I hoped was conviction, because it was gut-honest true.

"Something tells me there's more to the story," Luke said as he began to sip his second glass of wine. "My brother's wife tells me she can't figure out how one small body can manufacture so much poop."

"What gets me is the competition," I said tentatively. It wasn't just the running tab of which mommy had slimmed down to thinner than before she was pregnant or which child crawled faster, farther, and earlier. People kept score in ways I never would have imagined. Any mother who owned fewer than three strollers—an umbrella model for zipping in and out of taxis, a three-wheeled jogger for all the running she may or may not do, and, for everyday cruising, a heavy-duty Bugaboo Frog, which costs more than most people's first used car—was treated as if she were on food stamps. "I feel as if the rules for being a mother in this town are written in secret code and no one's given me the manual."

I read the expression on Luke's face as sympathetic and kept going. "All the other moms apparently got up at five one day and stood in line in a sleet storm to grab a spot in a *pre*-preschool swim class at the local Jewish community center. I tried to enroll Annabel the next week, but the class was sold out. When I expressed surprise to the woman at the desk, she looked as me as if I'd just wandered over the Mexican border."

"Ooh, nasty," he said, chuckling. "You don't get this in the e-mails. Let's hear more."

I rose to his challenge. "Okay. Nursery school. Really on-the-ball martyr-mommies are already discussing where to apply, and these are babies who can't even sit yet." Luke might have thought I was exaggerating for comic effect. I was not. "While they're mopping up drool, they're dissecting the schools' differences as if they were Harvard and Yale"—my voice sounded like I'd gulped helium—"which they may as

well be, because I've been assured that if Annabel doesn't go to one of the 'right' schools, she can kiss her Ivy League dreams goodbye." As if fantasies of rowing crew on the Charles were what was making her sleeping eyelids flutter whenever I peered into her crib. "Not that I haven't started to get sucked into stuff myself," I admitted. In a few months, my daughter and I were slated to begin Magic Maestros, where we'd be entertained by live musicians who, for all I knew, might be off-duty violinists from the Philharmonic.

"So go back to work," Luke said after I ranted for ten minutes. "Or does Dr. Marx disapprove?" His tone had crossed into snide.

"Barry's okay with whatever I do," I told Luke, sounding as defensive as I felt. "But where, exactly, would I work?"

He idly ran his fingers around the rim of his wineglass. "How about with me?"

I imagined those fingers on my leg—and elsewhere—and shook my head to erase the image.

"Hey, why are you saying no without hearing more?" he said. I was fairly certain I detected disappointment.

"I'm not saying no. I'm not saying anything, because what exactly are you proposing?"

"Nothing full-time. But the jobs are really coming in now," he said, knocking the wood table twice, "and I could give you a lot of regular styling. I've been using lame freelancer after lame freelancer, and either these girls and boys won't get off their lazy rears or they have zero imagination. When they're good, they get booked up by my competitors or raise their rates to prices I can't afford."

Now it was my turn to offer the occasional "hmm."

"I can't pay you benefits or promise the arrangement will last forever—you know how work comes and goes," he continued. "Editors could get sick of me and not renew my contracts." Neither one of us mentioned that Luke owed part of his good fortune to editors' past fickleness: he'd come along when everyone was hungry for a new face and a new look. "Molly, all I can say is that you know how well we work together—you're the other half of my brain."

I couldn't disagree. I thought Luke's talent was astounding. Two-thirds of the glossy pages in my current portfolio came from our shoots.

"And you'd be doing me a favor—not that you owe me." He looked right into my eyes in a way that was both intimate and alarming.

Was this a come-on? *Don't flatter yourself, Molly,* I decided. *This is business. Nothing more. And not only is it the best offer you've gotten lately, it's the only offer, discounting a position that required commuting to a suburban location whose most attractive feature was the office's proximity to a Dairy Queen.*

"It could be fun," he added.

"Fun, huh?" A quaint concept.

I was trying to digest Luke's offer when I heard Annabel. Usually I didn't rush to grab my child from her crib—I liked to eavesdrop and try to translate her babble—but it was already close to two. I was eager to show off. "Do you hear her?" I said. "You'll have to excuse me for a few minutes."

I returned with my chubby, sweet-smelling daughter. At seven months, Annabel's hair had grown in blond and her skin felt as velvety as petunias. I'd dressed her in a lilac striped dress that matched Luke's sweater. My heart swelled with pride as I presented my baby.

Luke looked at her with his photographer's eyes. I knew him well enough to recognize appreciation. "So happy to meet you, Miss Annabel," he said, shaking one of her fat little fingers. She smiled, revealing three newly cut teeth, and kicked her legs like a baby ninja.

"Could you keep her company while I get her sippy cup?" I asked as I secured Annabel in her high chair. Learning to drink from a cup was a recent accomplishment, and I couldn't have been prouder had she mastered Italian verbs. When I got back to the dining room, Luke was playing peekaboo like a pro and Annabel was squealing with delight. He had that effect on women.

"Don't forget her present," he said, handing me the box. I opened it slowly and methodically, a habit that always drove Lucy—a born ripper—nuts. "It was this or the Brad Pitt action figure."

Inside was a large, squishy white rabbit with floppy ears. Annabel reached for it and promptly sucked its gumdrop-sized nose. "Thanks," I said, smiled, and reached over to kiss his cheek. "I'm glad the funny bunny won. What do you think we should call him?"

"Excuse me, but he already has a name. He's Alfred, just like my father—long legs, big ears, loved carrots."

"It's Alfred the bunny, Annabel," I said, rubbing the velvety plush against her arm. "He's from Uncle Luke."

Luke grimaced.

"Correction. He's from Mr. Delaney."

"Alfred is from *Luke*, Annabel," he said, checking his watch. "Luke, who has to leave now. Sorry. Meeting downtown."

I walked to the closet, pulled out his coat, and gave his cheek another hurried, virginal peck.

"Will you think about my offer?" he said.

"I will."

"Really?"

"Promise."

"Promise, then," he said as the elevator arrived. "I'll hold you to it."

When I checked on Annabel, she was curled around Alfred. She slept with him that night, and for every night thereafter, until love rendered him bald. Lack of fur never, however, diminished his appeal. Alfred the bunny became king among animals. He understood Annabel like no teddy bear or donkey ever could, and whenever I looked at them together, Annabel and Alfred, my mind invariably turned to Luke.

As for me, on Monday I interviewed nannies. Two weeks later, Delfina Adams entered our lives. The next week, I ordered business cards. And the week after that, I flew to Sonoma. Luke and I were scheduled for our first shoot.

Twenty

PICKUP LINE

*W*hy is this night different from all other nights? This night is different from all other nights because this night is Passover and this morning Kitty, as she does every year, is putting the finishing touches on a seder worthy of *Gourmet*. It's my tough luck that when I was alive I didn't tail her like I'm doing today, because I have finally learned how she makes her featherweight matzo balls. The recipe she guards as if it were the formula for Ecstasy is—the hubris!—square on the back of the Manischewitz matzo meal box, although she substitutes seltzer for water. That I can't bust that woman is driving me insane. Whom in the Duration can I report to who will care? Bob? I don't think so.

"Pinky, can you get the phone?" Kitty shouts to her maid, which is how she refers to Pinky Mae Springer, who has worked for Kitty these last thirty-eight years.

"It's Dr. Marx," Pinky yells back. She has known Barry since he wet his bed, but when he graduated from med school Kitty insisted that Pinky call him by this honorific.

"In a minute," Kitty says as she slips a large damask napkin into a sterling silver ring. Every napkin is fanned to exactly the same breadth.

I admire Kitty's perfectionism. Even her mind, I suspect, has hospital corners. She walks to the phone in the kitchen, her stiletto mules tapping on the tile floor like a snare drum. "Darling," she says to Barry in a voice she reserves only for him and which I believe she considers melodic and charming. "Did they arrive?"

They would be my parents, who were due in at eleven. Lucy is boycotting the seder and leaving tomorrow for St. Bart's to join a new boyfriend.

"They're in?" she says, having hoped my parents would cancel at the last minute. "Now I have to figure out where to seat them." Kitty always plots her table as if she were giving a state dinner for the crown prince of Saudi Arabia. With the phone still to her ear, she opens a drawer in the Sheraton buffet and retrieves two thick parchment place cards elegantly lettered in calligraphy. Kitty sets my father's card next to her own seat, while she puzzles over my mother's.

"The Girls are taking bets about what Claire will wear," she tells Barry. Linda, Suzette, Nancy, and Kitty have been steadfast friends for decades, with matching bracelets on their ankles. They're not just the original Mean Girls. They're resourceful. Before Google, there were the Girls. Whether you need a hot stock, a hot tamale, or a hot date, they always know the one. Had any of these ya-yas chosen to work, I have no doubt that they would have blasted the glass ceiling to Mars, but I never realized until now that my mother was of sufficient interest for them to critique her wardrobe, too label-deficient for their taste.

"I'm a *what*? Now don't call your mother that, darling," Kitty says, but she comes off playful, as if Barry has served up the most heartfelt term of endearment. "That isn't becoming." While she chats, she straightens the tall ivory tapers in their towering candlesticks and examines the kiddush cup that belonged to Barry's father. Its sterling silver, embossed with vines and grapes, is marred by a millimeter of tarnish. "Pinky," she shouts. "Can you come in here?"

In her crisp gray uniform, Pinky steps to it and removes the offending cup for a second round of polishing.

You can tell from one glance at this dining room that my mother-in-law is someone who takes herself seriously, and you'd better, too. She set the table yesterday, and I have to agree the woman has, as she herself might say, flair. I adore her china, which she had the foresight

to select and receive—service for twenty-four, no less—when she married her second husband, Seymour Katz, who died three years ago. The dishes are an old Meissen pattern featuring a fierce dragon in a color she calls amethyst but which to me looks like regulation shocking pink, nearly the shade Annabel turned last year when she first laid eyes on them and asked why her grandmother uses "monster plates."

Nevertheless, I love the way these dishes set off spring flowers. For tonight's meal, Kitty has cornered the market on dogwood, freesia, and irises, which she's arranged in bouquets worthy of the entrance to the Metropolitan Museum. Her tablecloth is heavy French linen. I can picture it hidden in the bottom of a steamer trunk as an aristocratic family fled Paris when the Nazis came to call, although I believe the real story is that she inherited it from her mother, who won it playing cards at Lido Beach.

I love Passover. I miss Passover, my favorite holiday, although it wasn't always so. Christmas used to be way out in front until Lucy said, "Molly, can't you see through all the hype?" a word she learned when we were eleven.

Most Jews like me—who barely know Purim from Durham—agree that Passover is mostly about the singing. It's definitely not about the matzo, the bread of affliction that our forefathers ate in the land of Egypt, and which their descendants know as the direct route to constipation.

At Kitty's, Barry always chants the four questions—even though he is not the youngest at the table, as tradition demands. Off-key but with gusto, guests chime in on "Dayenu," "Eliyahu Hanavi," and "Had Gadya." The tunes aren't "Away in a Manger," "God Rest Ye Merry, Gentlemen," and "Deck the Halls," but they'll do.

Tonight, I plan to play the part of the Marx family's own personal stunt double for the prophet Elijah, said to drop in on seders worldwide. I'm hoping I'll run into Elijah in the Duration. Maybe the two of us could chat, spirit to spirit. Get his take on the Palestinian situation. But I've had enough seder prep for now. Kitty is moving on to gefilte fish, never my favorite.

I've been checking on Annabel all morning, but soon the teachers will be letting the children out early in honor of the holiday. Hauling my spectral ass to Central Park West takes, of course, no time. The first

person I see in the lobby isn't Annabel—school hasn't let out yet—or even Delfina, waiting for her. It's Stephanie, who's hard to miss in low-rise jeans and an eye-popping bronze leather jacket. She appears to be talking to herself, though in fact she's carrying on a conversation through her headset. Judging by the volume, she's engaged in a full-contact sport with a travel agent, wrangling over the price of first-class tickets to Barcelona. I don't have to wonder who her seatmate will be.

So intently am I watching Stephanie that it almost fails to register that there's something off about this scene. It's not the security guard who peers halfheartedly into people's bags, the one you'd expect to miss a monogrammed set of assault weapons. It's not the nannies gossiping about their bosses in the corner, divided from the moms like the muggles from the wizards, and it's not the three handsome gay fathers who stand to the side in their own fraternity, where the price of admission is an adopted Chinese daughter or a son grown in a rented uterus. It's *her*.

As she stands still among at least a dozen women her own age, pretending to read *People,* I see her out of the corner of my eye, like the rat in the subway you sense before it scampers along the rails. Fading into the crowd, she's one more woman in a black coat and black boots with a black bag waiting for the elevator door to open and dislodge a group of giggly three- and four-year-olds.

Stephanie's son is in the first group that hits the lobby, and her curly-headed boy runs to her side, tugs her jacket, and shouts, "Mommy." She brings her index finger to her lips and mouths "Jordan, shhh." Part of me would like to Taser my sister and say, *"Her! That's who Barry's seeing!"* But that part of me would be the single once-living cell that isn't wondering what the hell Lucy Divine thinks she's doing here, casually pretending she has permission to pick up Annabel.

Two more groups of children run off the elevator. I am hoping that Delfina, usually prompt, will glide through the door. Then I remember that Barry gave her the day off because tonight she's going to help Pinky serve the seder meal. Annabel is supposed to go home with her buddy Ella and Narcissa, Ella's nanny and Delfina's best friend.

The elevator door opens one last time and both girls escape, waving goodbye to their teacher. Each bears a carefully crayoned matzo

cover. Annabel's is decorated with rabbits and eggs in Easter colors. My girl, all right.

"Annie-belle," Lucy shouts. "Over here. Surprise!"

While her teacher chats up one of the mothers, Annabel spins like a dial and winds up pointed at Lucy. "Aunt Moosey!" she squeals. "Daddy said you weren't coming to New York!" She barrels into her aunt's open arms for a tight, lingering hug.

"What's this pretty thing you've made?" Lucy says, admiring Annabel's handiwork. "You know what? You can tell me about it later. Why don't you let me zip your jacket?" Lucy speaks quickly, releases Annabel, and gently pats her on the back.

Oy, *caramba!* Has Lucy lost every last marble? Where is my sister taking my daughter? It doesn't even matter if her motives are innocent—which I want to believe that they are. I have to. I must.

Annabel looks at her friend standing across the lobby and turns to Lucy. "But I was supposed to go home with Ella."

Hearing her name, Ella, who had been waiting near the door for Narcissa, trots over to Annabel and Lucy. There is no doubt in my mind that Ella will grow up to be a Supreme Court justice—that or a prison matron. She considers Lucy with deep suspicion. By the time this child is twenty, she will have a deep furrow requiring state-of-the-art facial filler. "And you would be?" Ella says, sounding flintier than I did, ever.

"I'm Annabel's aunt," Lucy replies. She glances around to look for Ella's mother or nanny and is relieved to see that the child is alone. "We have to run now, but you have a wonderful holiday. Bye!"

"But where's your yellow slip? Annabel needs permission to leave with you. Where *is* it?" I am expecting Ella to cuff Lucy while she arranges for an AMBER Alert. "It's the rule—you're breaking the rule," she adds loudly, which causes the few mothers left in the lobby to rubberneck toward Lucy. Stephanie is among them, still talking into her Bluetooth.

You little four-foot troll, I hear Lucy think. *I hope you grow up to get acne, cankles, and a nose even Barry can't fix.* She grasps Annabel's hand and tugs. Annabel won't budge.

"Ella's right, Aunt Moosey," my daughter says gravely. "It's the rule."

"Annie-belle," my sister says, crouching down and whispering, "I'm going to tell you a secret. One of the things they don't teach you in school is some rules are made to be broken. Got that? Come on. Trust me. I'm not just your aunt. I'm a nursery school teacher and I know stuff."

This time, when she tugs, Annabel looks at Lucy long and hard, hesitates for only a moment, then waves to Ella and follows her aunt. They are on the street when Narcissa ambles heavily through the door, a bakery box in hand. She bends down to kiss Ella, singing out, "Ready, my darling? Sorry I was late. Now where's your friend?"

Ella drags her nanny back to the door and points down the block. "She went with *her*," she bellows. "That lady. She says she's Annabel's aunt." Lucy and Annabel are still standing in the street, Lucy trying to hail a taxi as one after the next sails by filled with passengers. As Narcissa takes it in, her brow furrows, and I see where Ella has acquired her expression. "Annabel went with that bad lady. We need to do something."

"Stop that woman!" Narcissa belts out. Aretha Franklin has nothing on her. "Kidnapper! Pervert!" Ella echoes every word of the tirade, which Narcissa repeats in a loop, and like a sow and a piglet, the two of them begin to make their way down the block just as Stephanie and Jordan walk out of the building.

"What's going on?" Stephanie shouts.

"That woman," Narcissa turns around and yells. "She be stealing Annabel Marx."

"Annabel Marx? No!" Stephanie says, and thinks, *Un-fucking-believable.* "I'll get the security guard. Watch my son." She turns back into the building, leaving a bewildered Jordan standing alone, wondering whom he should chase after, Narcissa and Ella or his mother. Narcissa, weighing in at 210 pounds, is not fleet of foot, but she and Ella reach Lucy and Annabel just as the door of a taxi slams. Narcissa bangs on the car's side with her enormous vinyl tote. The driver presses down on the brakes so fast his turban tilts.

"You two get out this minute!" Narcissa yells as she continues to beat on the door. "Driver, she be stealing that little girl. Stop her! Kidnapper! Don't go!"

Lucy rolls down the window just enough to yell, "Mind your own business, you bitch. I am this child's next of kin. Driver, take off." But the driver stops the car and leans back, taking it all in. He pulls out his cell phone.

"You! Drop that phone!" Lucy orders. *I know what's best for this child,* I hear her think. *Molly would want me to look out for my own flesh and blood. Barry, that sorry excuse for a husband, he doesn't deserve this beautiful daughter, like he didn't deserve my beautiful pain-in-the-butt sister and made her life hell and—*

"You be stealing that child!" Narcissa says, flapping her arms as she pounds the window. Her bakery box falls, and black-and-white cookies spill into the gutter. Ella begins to whimper—those cookies are her favorite—and turns and points down the street, where Stephanie is running with the security guard at her side. She pokes Narcissa, who takes it in. "The cop, he's on the way," Narcissa shouts to Lucy. "Annabel, now don't you worry."

"Lady," the driver yells to Lucy, "you give that child back."

"Don't you dare talk to me that way."

Annabel's heart-shaped face darts back and forth between Lucy, Narcissa and Ella, and the driver, who has lost his turban. She starts to cry, quietly at first, but the noise builds to a wail. "Let me out, Aunt Lucy," she cries. "I'm scared. I want Delfina."

"Annabel, stop that!" Lucy snaps. The loudness of her voice makes Annabel cry harder. "Everything's okay. You're with me, Aunt Moosey. Driver, take off!"

The man won't budge.

"You ain't going nowhere," the guard, who has reached the taxi, shouts as he raps on the window. "Hell, woman, open that door."

"Or what?" my sister shouts. "You'll find a real cop?"

Stephanie is behind him. "I'm calling Dr. Marx now," she says, taking her phone from her right pocket and rapping the window with her left hand. "Whoever you are in there, you're insane. Let Annabel Marx go!"

"Fuck!" Lucy says. *I'm trapped,* she thinks. *Shit out of luck.* "God damn it."

She opens the door. Annabel tumbles into Narcissa's doughy, wel-

coming embrace. Lucy slams the door shut as the guard gives it a wallop. "Driver, take off," she says. This time he peels away as if he's leading the cavalry.

"Annabel, you poor baby, I'm here, I'm here," Narcissa says as she rocks my daughter's birdlike body. "Narcissa and Ella are here. Everything's okay."

But everything is not okay. My child is shaking. My lunatic sister should have known better than to duel with a tough Jamaican nanny. She should have known better, period.

I get inside Lucy's brain as she speeds away in the cab. I try to understand why she would behave like a crackpot, if I may use the technical term. But the inside of Lucy's mind roars with tumult. She is asking herself why she always makes the wrong choice. For now, at least, my sense of filial loyalty has been plucked away as if it were snatched by a big, black crow. All I can hear are my daughter's sobs. I have never felt more useless, more frustrated, or more dead.

Twenty-one

BORDEAUX WISHES

D on't you love it?" Luke all but wagged a tail as he ran, arms out-stretched, from corner to corner of the house and up an open metal staircase.

"It's great if you've always dreamed of living in a giant sardine can," I said.

The house du jour was in Sonoma County, designed by a big-league architect for a Silicon Valley boy genius who'd cashed out just in time. I felt three feet tall standing under the terrifyingly high ceiling and turned full circle to take in the mottled gray concrete floor with its art-ful random cracks, the gunmetal walls, and the exposed circulatory system of pipes. The front window, a glass waffle with six-foot-square panes, had been manufactured for a car dealership. I squinted into the sun and saw miles of vineyards, green and gold, gold and green, that terraced the northern California hills.

"What's with the attitude?" Luke asked. "It's dazzling."

It was dazzling, all right. I'd read that at night you could see the place from miles away, blazing like a UFO, and the instant the resi-dence was finished, zoning ordinances were voted into place to bar Erector Set knock-offs from pockmarking the countryside.

"C'mon," he said "This light—it's amazing. I would kill for a space like this."

"Mr. Delaney, you're not cool enough to live in a space like this," I shouted up to him. But I knew Luke and I would have no trouble taking jaw-dropping photographs here. I started to get excited, too.

"You're lucky I don't have a water balloon to drop on your head," he said, ripped a sheet out of the notebook he always carried, and sailed a paper airplane through the air from the balcony.

A few hours before, Luke had met me at the Oakland airport. He'd had a job in Big Sur and driven up from Los Angeles on the Pacific Coast Highway. As we made our way north, his voice-over described the view with childlike glee. "Seals playing tag in the water!" "Waves like *Moby Dick*!" We hadn't checked into our hotel yet. Luke was too eager to scope out the house where we'd be shooting, starting the next day. We went there first, slowly driving up a steep hill. The air here felt clean and dry. I forecasted three good hair days.

To say I had overprepared for my first job in more than a year was generous. For the past three weeks I'd noodled about the details day and night, putting in so much time that if I averaged it against the fee I'd be receiving, I might have earned more by cashing in bottles salvaged from the street. But I didn't want to disappoint Luke Delaney, my discriminating new boss. I fiddled and fussed, compensating for the fact that the house was not at all my style. I am, after all, the secret love child of Marie Antoinette and Charles Dickens.

"What did you think of the art?" Luke said after we'd cased the place and gotten into our rented convertible, unfurled the car's top, and started driving down the mountain. If Barry had been the driver, I would have bitched about how my hair was blowing into a Marge Simpson updo, but instead I acted as if I thrilled to the sensation of hot red dust grinding into my scalp. I was also aware of the fact that I might not smell all that clean. It was ninety-four degrees, and the minute you stepped outside you felt as if a Navajo blanket had fallen off a mule and onto your head.

The only contemporary art I knew beans about was hung on museum walls, and most of the last Whitney Biennial left me thinking that each artist had simply tattooed his neurosis onto a canvas. "That big blue one looked like Paul Bunyan's ox."

"You mean the Julian Schnabel?" Luke said.

Time to switch topics. From my straw tote I pulled out a pile of restaurant reviews. "Are you getting hungry? I've been reading up."

"I'm always hungry when it's on the client's dime," he said. "This is why I made a reservation for us two weeks ago." He mentioned wine pairings, foie gras, and basil ice cream.

"Terrific—I'm starving. In New York it's past dinner." Seven thirty-six, to be exact, and I was eager to get to my room and check on Annabel. I knew if I spoke to her in front of Luke, my coo would sound maddeningly precious. "Will Eric and Jasper be here in time to join us?" I asked. They were the assistants booked for the shoot.

Luke checked his watch. "They should've arrived by now." I was relieved. Chaperones, even if they were twenty-three, would set a tone of festive camaraderie.

We pulled into a village built around a leafy square. Healdsburg was a few blocks' worth of wine shops, pricey boutiques, restaurants, and hotels, and ours was supposed to be the hippest among them. While Luke disappeared to make sure every last piece of his equipment had arrived, I registered, and as soon as I got to my room, I phoned home.

"Delfina, it's me again," I said in my seventh call of the day. "How's Annabel?"

"She's fine, ma'am," she said. "Ate tofu for dinner." My baby was a little green dragon. "Loved her bath. Already sound asleep."

Aw. I'd wanted Delfina to put the baby's ear to the phone so we could have one of our one-sided heart-to-hearts and I could at least hear her squeak. "Well, that's good, Delfina," I sighed. "That's great. And don't forget, please call me Molly."

"Molly," she said. "I'll do that, Molly. Now, good night, Mrs. Marx. Speak to you tomorrow."

My room cost hundreds of dollars a night—the hotel was revered for its high-principled design, which meant that I had not one drawer or armoire in which to unpack and only a sliver of a closet half covered by a filmy curtain. Piles of clothes landed on every snazzy, pristine, uncluttered surface, until the place looked as if I were closing down a small boutique. I walked into the vast shower tiled with delicate mosaic in the greens of wasabi and edamame. As the warm water hit my head, sandy trickles rolled into the drain. I lathered my hair with grapefruit

and aloe vera shampoo, conditioned with linden blossom balm, and stood comatose for minutes. Dripping and chilled, I dashed across the stone floor to retrieve the white terry robe hung on the bathroom's sole, ill-placed hook.

But first, I glimpsed myself in the full-length mirror—and froze. Who *was* that small but distinctly pear-shaped woman and what was she doing here? I was three thousand miles, three time zones, and one played-out flirtation away from where I belonged. All the scented body cream and caviar in the world, I suddenly realized, couldn't stop me from being homesick. I missed my child and, to my surprise, my husband. I must be out of my mind to have made this trip.

I should be in New York, snapping digital photographs of Annabel to send out to a list of fifty friends and relatives, some of whom, I was sure, would delete the e-mails without even opening them. I should be shopping for a new batch of children's books, looking into classes that would max out Annabel's potential, soaking up every moment of once-in-a-lifetime motherhood like French toast and maple syrup.

Much to the surprise of the woman who used to be me, back in the city Barry, Annabel, and I had settled into snug domesticity. Barry had become reasonably housebroken, and when the weather cooperated, we'd spend hours each weekend at the playground, steaming cups of coffee in hand, eager to meet others who tottered on this strange new precipice called parenthood. After his morning runs, Barry would often be the one to change Annabel's soggy nighttime diaper and give her breakfast. Sometimes I would catch him dancing around the room, Annabel in his arms, and my heart would be jelly.

Every night, after I put the baby to sleep, I'd fix my version of a low-fat homemade dinner, and while we ate, Barry and I would rattle on about Annabel, obviously the most precocious and charming baby on earth. Each Saturday, we paid Delfina an outrageous sum so she would sleep over, and we'd splurge on an evening out, even if all we did was eat pad thai at a local joint.

It wasn't a glamorous Manhattan life. It wasn't even a glamorous Sioux Falls life. But it was comfortable, which was the last word I'd have used to describe how it felt to be sitting in an over-air-conditioned, overdesigned hotel room, weary from travel, knowing that for the next

four hours I'd be trapped in a flouncy four-star restaurant, trying to verbally joust with Luke and two recent graduates of Wesleyan and Yale.

I picked up the phone. "Hey, Luke," I said, trying to sound like one of the guys. "Please don't think I'm a thankless wretch, but room service is looking pretty sweet right now."

"I totally understand," he said, too quickly. "It was clear you were wiped."

Did I look that bad?

"Get some rest," he said, "and I'll see you tomorrow. Seven-thirty?"

I thanked him, hung up, and expected to feel relieved, but my vanity kicked in. Perhaps the real reason I hadn't wanted to have dinner with Luke was because I was afraid he'd put the moves on me, and I wouldn't know how to react. Since it was clear that wasn't going to happen, I felt like the hound at the pound that no one wants. I circled the room twice, flicked the television on and off, called Barry and discussed whether we should install a garbage disposal, devoured my artisanal vegetable salad in seven bites, and fell asleep while watching Johnny Depp on pay-per-view. I was in the wine capital of North America and hadn't even ordered a glass.

For the next three days, I labored like a migrant worker. Rise at six, quit thirteen hours later. Unpack. Pack up. Push away the ottoman. Move it back. Arrange a tray for imaginary guests. Pick a different tray and do it over, once with gherkins, once without. Lay down the hand-tufted wool rug. Decide it's better suited to an English boardinghouse. Roll it back. Run upstairs, forty-seven times. Make the bed. Sweep the floor. Remove stains from the marble counters. Resist the impulse to allow this loftlike aerie to metastasize into a Parisian flat crammed with flea market frippery.

"Beautiful, beautiful," the good-natured Eric would say after every setup. He was working as hard as I was, and not averse to pushing a sectional couch around the room until I decided where it should park.

"You go, girl," Jasper, the Yalie said to me, again and again. That expression should be banned, especially when repeated with an English accent via Nashville. I longed to stuff a linen pillow sham down his throat.

But the best praise came from Luke. "I think this one's going to be great," he'd say before he took a shot. Every time he finished, he'd turn to me with "Told ya so, Molly. Perfect. Just perfect."

As Jasper snapped Polaroids of each setup, he put them in a book, and by two o'clock on the third day, we could all see that our efforts had yielded a major success. There was nothing left to do. If the editor who'd sent us on this mission had any sense, the minute he saw Luke's film he'd put him under contract in perpetuity.

"How shall we celebrate?" Luke said after we'd packed up and gotten into Eric and Jasper's SUV to drive back to Healdsburg. The question was meant for all of us, but he was looking at me, sitting next to him in the backseat. Luke was wearing a black T-shirt and khaki cargo shorts, and his legs were stretched out, tanned and strong.

"My vote is to pull into that winery right there and drink Sonoma's finest until we're shit-faced," Eric said. "See the sign?"

"You go, girl," Jasper said to Eric. We all knew Eric was gay, but I loathed Jasper all the more for banging on it.

"The driver calls the shots," Luke ruled as he rolled his eyes at the back of Jasper's head. Since Eric was behind the wheel, he chose to turn off Dry Creek Road into the Ferrari-Carano Vineyards.

Some of the wineries we'd passed were little more than tumbledown shacks, but we could see we'd hit pay dirt. At the end of a drive, a vast pink stucco estate house with arched leaded-glass windows stood before us, fronted by classical gardens circling a fountain. The lawn was rolling and lush, the privets manicured. Thinking back to it, the place reminds me of the Duration, especially when Puccini wafts through the air.

"Holy cow," Eric said as he led us into the tasting room off the main lobby. It was all but devoid of other customers, but thousands of wine bottles glinted, there for the buying.

From behind a gleaming wood bar a white-aproned man greeted us. I have no idea if he knew a Barolo from a Chianti, but I liked the look of his shoulder-length salt-and-pepper hair, tied back in a ponytail. "Would you care for a pour of our Syrah?" he wondered.

We would. And the zinfandel, the Tresor, the Eldorados—the Noir as well as the Gold—the fumé blanc, and, what the hell, the cabernet sauvignon. All four of us sipped and critiqued with flowing pretension.

We started with "fruity" and "earthy" and shamelessly worked ourselves up to "herbaceous with hints of anise, berry, and tobacco."

After nearly three hours, Eric and Jasper decided to drive back to
town; they were heading to San Francisco. That I, a full-fledged
mother, allowed these two to get into a moving vehicle now fills me
with shame, but that's how drunk I was. "Don't worry," Luke said to
them. "We'll find our way home." The proprietor was only too happy to
give us a card for a taxi company: the longer our stay, the bigger his sale.

Eventually, Luke and I had sampled nearly every wine from the
vineyard. I decided to ship home a case of the zinfandel. Luke picked
the Syrah. I wandered around in a fog, lubricated as much by the past
week's work as by that day's excellent vintages. Nor did the excellent
company hurt. Whatever fear I'd had about living up to Luke's expectations had been washed down the hatch, and we were laughing and
showing off for each other.

"You go, girl," Luke said in Prince Charles' voice. In the moment, I
thought he was hilarious.

Shaky on my feet, I was ready to call our cab when Luke motioned
me out to the big white-tiled center hall and pointed to some steps.
"Let's explore," he said, mischief in his eyes and voice.

"Are you sure it's okay to go down there?"

"The door's unlocked. I took a peek when I took a leak." Another
line of his I'm now embarrassed to say that I felt deserved a hearty
laugh.

We tiptoed down a short flight of creaky wooden stairs into a low-
ceilinged windowless room the size of a basketball court. From wall to
wall, heavy old oak barrels sat like monks, each presumably filled with
wine. The cellar air felt refreshingly cool. Like Alice in her maze, I
walked in one direction and Luke in the other, in and out of narrow
aisles.

"Molly, come here," Luke stage-whispered from across the room.

"What is it?" I asked. Maybe he'd found a barrel with an open tap
and we could polish off our afternoon with one last, secret swig.

"Come over here," he said. "You're going to love this."

I did.

He grabbed both of my hands and pushed me against the side of the
tall wooden barrel. Then he kissed me, hard. His lips tasted better than

any of Ferrari-Carano's premier selections, although I swear I detected a drop of the zin, with just a hint of boysenberry and licorice. He slid his cool tongue deep into my mouth and cupped my face in his hands while he tenderly and sensuously explored. "I've been dying to do that for days," he whispered.

I said nothing, but I let my hands roam to his back and my mouth stayed with his. "No" and "yes" both came to mind as he unzipped my jeans and slid his fingers inside me. I didn't stop him and answered his lust with my own, each sweet movement calibrated for maximum pleasure, his and mine, together, as my own hands found his flesh, hard and inviting.

By the time we heard footsteps, we were both on the floor, which in my bliss felt as comfortable as an inner-spring mattress. "I don't think I want to spend the night here," I said.

My hand in his, we walked up the steps and outside, into the twilight. The winery was closing and we were its last visitors to leave. I gave Luke the card for the taxi, which he called with his arm draped around my shoulder. He leaned heavily and deliciously against my side.

We walked, melted into one, toward the entrance, and stopped to kiss by a towering bronze statue. The figure was a wild boar said to roam the Sonoma Valley, where he stole away the grapes. A plaque announced him as Bordeaux: those who made a wish while they touched the giant snout were said to see their dream come true.

I looked up. The big boy's nose was rubbed to a coppery gleam. I stretched to reach it.

Let me love the right man, I said to myself. *Let me not ruin my life. Let me figure out what will make me happy.*

I knew I'd made three wishes, not one, and hoped that Bordeaux wouldn't fault me on a technicality.

Twenty-two

THREE GUYS GO INTO A BAR

B arry!" Stephanie says.

It better be important, Barry thinks. He's behind schedule, because surgery ran long today, which he's explained to me can happen when the patient is enormously fat.

As Stephanie begins to speak, his nurse steps into his office. "Sorry to interrupt, but Delfina's on line two," she tells him. "She says it's urgent."

"Later, Stephanie." Barry clicks off. He hopes Delfina isn't calling to make a sudden trip back home to take care of a sick relative. Or ask for a raise. Or resign. He worries about this every day. Delfina is the Swiss Army knife of his life, solving virtually every practical problem.

"Dr. Marx?" Delfina says to Barry. "Mrs. Marx's sister—"

"Lucy?" *What now?*

"Mrs. Marx's sister. She snatched Annabel," Delfina blurts out, her usual Zen-like restraint splintered. The way Narcissa, a Mary Higgins Clark devotee, relayed the incident a minute ago, Lucy had been ready to whisk Annabel away to, Narcissa speculates, a bunker under a chicken coop in some undisclosed location.

"Oh my God," Barry says, gulping air. "That bitch. Where's Annabel? Is she okay?"

"Annabel's fine—she's with Narcissa and Ella. I'm on my way over there. Mrs. Marx's sister"—Delfina no longer thinks it seems Christian to call her Lucy—"took off." After Barry reaches Annabel—"Hi, Daddy. Aunt Moosey came to my school! Yes, it was *very* exciting. No, she didn't say why. Daddy, Narcissa's going to make us milkshakes now. Bye"—he cancels four consultations: a sweet-sixteen chin job, a redo on one of those unfortunate noses from Kitty's generation that look as if they were pointed in a pencil sharpener, a postdivorce nose-jowls combo, and a fiftieth-birthday lift on a woman who loathed the neck rings she'd accumulated each year as if she were a redwood. He bolts from his office, hops in a taxi—Barry has the best cab karma of anyone I know— and rushes home, ignoring Stephanie's repeated calls.

When Barry is nervous, he paces. It is twenty minutes later now, and like a panther at a substandard zoo, he's traversed the long hall, the living room, the dining room, the kitchen, and back, again and again and again. Twice he has started to phone his mother and Detective Hicks—in that order—and thought better of it. Finally, he makes a call. "Stephanie. You aren't going to believe this."

"Jesus, finally! I've been trying to reach you everywhere." *God damn it,* she thinks, *who are you to duck my calls?* "Where are you?"

"Home."

"Then I'm on my way over," she says, seizing this unexpected gift. "I should be there in twenty minutes."

Barry continues his loop-de-loop, then suddenly goes into our bedroom and opens an embossed leather book. No BlackBerry for me. It had been my annual ritual to spend the better part of one Sunday in early January entering the stats of my nearest and dearest into a tasteful address book while I deliberated on who should make the cut. This year, I edited away three college friends and two former coworkers, and when four of these people showed at my funeral, I was shamed, deeply.

Barry reaches Brie at work. "Lucy's gone off the deep end," he says. I admire his restraint. "She made a grab for Annabel."

"Back up. That's impossible," Brie says. "Lucy Divine can be off, but she's not ready for an asylum."

"I assure you, she's both."

Brie's pause is a true seven-second delay, while she processes that Barry expects her to take action. Of what sort, she doesn't know, but she recognizes that only face time will do. "Shall I come over?"

"I would appreciate that."

Barry doesn't dislike Brie. He admires her brains and drive and thinks she's "drop-dead sexy." He's convinced that her current partner preference is temporary, contrived to show the world how progressive she is. But rapport between the two has been tamped down by Barry's intuitive, accurate awareness that his every fumble and flirtation has been deconstructed by Brie and me for years.

Thanks to a waiting company car, it takes exactly ten minutes for Brie to drive up Madison and cross the park. In my building, only two apartments' doors open on every floor. Brie and Stephanie enter the building at the same time, silently share an elevator, and, to their mutual surprise, exit together to walk to the Marx residence. Brie turns to Stephanie. Her first impulse is to extend her hand for a shake, but she checks herself. This stranger in tight jeans, spiky boots, and go-getter perfume could be one of my mommy-pals, Brie decides. The woman might take such a gesture as butch.

Brie fears being typecast and tends to overcorrect. Today she is wearing a snug white sheath and spectator oxfords as pointy as tweezers. Their gold metal heels could double as ice picks, and her quietly shimmering snake bracelet winds around one arm. She'd be pleased if you'd guess her occupation as a rock star's publicist, not corporate litigator.

Brie smiles warmly. Stephanie does not respond. "I'm Brie Lawson, Molly's friend," she says nonetheless.

"Stephanie Joseph," she answers coolly. "Annabel's therapist."

Liar, liar, pants on fire!

Barry opens the door. His thinning hair is tangled from running his hands through it and he's padding around barefoot, although he's still in his rumpled dress shirt and suit pants. "Stephanie, meet Brie. Brie, Stephanie." He leads both women to the living room and collapses on the edge of a suede ottoman. "I tried to call that bitch-maniac, but her cell is off."

"Same thing for me," Brie says. "We should get to Claire and Dan."

Claire and Dan. Who might they be? Stephanie wonders. She longs to be strategic and essential, but how? "What about calling the police?" she suggests in her gravelly, nasal voice.

"The police?" Brie says, looking at this therapist dressed for after-hours clubbing. *And when did Annabel start seeing a therapist? Barry never mentioned her.* "Please, let's not go there—at least not yet."

"I'm thinking restraining order," Stephanie says. "We're talking kidnapping, at the very least." But neither Barry nor Brie gives her the courtesy of a response. "Listen, we could all use a drink. Dr. Marx, is that New Zealand sauvignon blanc you served the other night still in the wine fridge?"

Barry turns to Stephanie. "Good idea," he says. "I finished it, but open another."

Stephanie walks toward the kitchen. *Not only does this therapist know what's in Barry's wine refrigerator, she has a damn good body,* Brie thinks, and I have to agree as I size up her endless legs and high, rounded butt.

"How are you thinking you want to approach this?" Brie asks.

"Hey, lawyer," he says. "I was hoping you'd have a plan."

"Dr. Marx?" Stephanie yells out from the kitchen. "Could you give me a hand in here?"

"Excuse me," Barry says, and disappears. After a minute, Brie looks at her watch. Two more minutes pass before they return, Stephanie minus her burgundy gloss, although artfully applied liner remains around her lips.

"None for me, thanks," Brie says when Stephanie offers her a glass of wine. "We shouldn't waste any more time before we call your in-laws," she says to Barry. "The call's got to be from you."

"I'm dialing them now," he says, and reaches my father, who has just finished unpacking at a small hotel in the East Sixties. My mother has walked to Bloomingdale's to scout for Kitty's hostess gift. Scented candle? Chocolate-covered pretzels? Whatever she buys, my mother feels it will be wrong, and on that point she is right.

"Barry," my dad says heartily, answering on the first ring. *"A ziesen pesach."*

"Same to you, Dan, but it's not such a sweet Passover, I'm afraid."

Dan braces himself for a bad joke. A Catholic priest, a Protestant

minister, and a Hasidic rabbi walk into a bar. "Don't tell me. Your mother decided to serve sushi instead of gefilte fish?" he asks genially.

"Are you sitting down?" Barry says, wanting to handle this right. Like most people on earth, Barry genuinely likes my father.

My dad doesn't just sit. He stretches out his bulky body on the bed and looks at the ceiling, his phone pressed to his ear. "Sit down" is never a preamble to anything you want to hear.

"It's Lucy," Barry says, and I see my father exhale with relief.

"Oh, yeah. I am so sorry she's not joining us for the holiday, Barry. It was extremely generous of your mother to invite all three of us, and I hope she's not offended. But you have to understand, Lucy's not ready—"

"She tried to snatch Annabel this afternoon, Dan. She did. She showed up at the school and almost got away with it. Scared Annabel to death," he adds, which I doubt is true, although I certainly haven't forgiven my sister for her colossal insanity.

These New Yorkers, bunch of drama queens, my dad decides. "What? There must be some mistake." *The ceiling has a brown-ringed water stain as big as my head,* he thinks, *yet they charge almost five hundred bucks a night for this airless shithole.* My father hates virtually everything about New York—the industrial-strength coffee, the warp-speed tempo, and the noise to match, but especially the rip-offs. "Barry, kids that age make things up. Molly used to have this imaginary friend, Pogo." He realizes he is shooting off his mouth, too much and too fast.

"There were witnesses," Barry says. "I don't know what was in your daughter's head," he says, still kindly, and I feel admiration for my husband's self-control as he edits himself. "Lucy's head." Because once there were two daughters. "I'm wondering, do you?"

Did he ever? That my father adored us was enough, at least for me. I never expected to be understood.

My father is sitting up now, and his face has flushed to a fevered red. "No, Barry, I don't know what the hell my daughter could possibly have been thinking. But, damn, you have to give her a pass. Don't get me wrong—if she did this . . . thing, it's contemptible and, Christ, goddamn twisted, and we will get to the bottom of it." *How will I tell Claire? She will dissolve into the floor.* "Obviously, Lucy needs help." *We'll see to it that she's on some shrink's couch so fast her head will fall off,* he thinks. "We'll call her in St. Bart's and demand—"

"Whoa. St. Bart's?"

"That's where she's going."

"She was hoping to take Annabel to St. Bart's?" Barry says. Lucy is an even bigger wack job than he thought.

Maybe St. Bart's was the cover, my father realizes. Man, does he feel thick. "Barry, I haven't even spoken to my daughter"—*my only surviving daughter*—"since yesterday. I better try to call her now. Please, son." He is afraid he will cry. "You'll have to excuse me." He hangs up without saying goodbye.

Barry throws his arms up in an exaggerated shrug and looks at the two women facing him.

"Am I correct to assume that Dan and Claire didn't know a thing?" Brie asks, pushing her snake bracelet up and down her arm. She and I both catch Stephanie watching her. Correction: it.

Barry nods. He feels it's safe to say they may rule out Divine conspiracy theories.

"I still think the police should be notified," Stephanie says, not unreasonably. "Maybe she's going to try this again. Lucy could be—anywhere."

Lucy, however, is not *anywhere.* Her plane is getting ready to touch down at O'Hare, and she is debating whether she should call a twenty-four-hour lunatic hotline. She is sweating remorse, stinking with regret, lonelier than she's ever been. *I've really done it this time,* Lucy has the good grace to think. *Too damn impulsive, didn't think through my plan. Lost sight of the ball. Now I'm good as busted.*

Barry is weighing Stephanie's advice when Brie walks to the piano. At my husband's request, my solo photographs have been packed away—"I can't handle looking at them"—but several happy-family pictures remain. Brie's gaze settles on my face. I feel her missing me, remembering me, loving me, wanting to do the right thing on my behalf. *She's the only real friend I could ever trust,* Brie thinks. *Molly lives inside me now, and I owe her. This crazy thing with Lucy's going to suck up energy and divert from finding the pig that's responsible for Molly's murder. Yes, murder. Had to be a murder.*

Am I in the room with a murderer? The thought rattles inside Brie's mind. She turns to Barry and speaks slowly and softly, one of her canniest courtroom techniques. "Barry, let's think about Molly. You know

she would never want you rushing to implicate her sister, no matter how unforgivable the offense. She'd want you to talk it through with Lucy—eventually—and then figure things out. Privately. Discreetly."

Lucy should get what she deserves, and Molly was a wimp, Barry thinks. I always suspected that he thought that, but it hurts to hear it. Stephanie downgrades me to moron and tacks on spoiled bitch. "Come on," she says. The wine has given her courage and a glow that isn't unattractive. "This is crap, people. The right thing is to call the police. Forgive me for saying this, but we shouldn't let sentimentality cloud good judgment."

Brie, Barry, and I all read the boldface subtext: *What does it matter what this Molly thinks? She's dead.*

"Stephanie," Brie says, her voice an icicle, "you're overreacting. Speaking as a lawyer now, I wouldn't rush to judgment. This is strictly an internal family problem."

You, woman, are not part of the family smacks Stephanie between her carefully made-up brown eyes, which she's narrowed to slits. *Neither are you,* her face volleys back. "Speaking as a friend of the family—and a therapist—calling the police seems to be the only responsible, objective, intelligent response." She lands on each adjective slow and hard. This is not a woman to underestimate.

Under other circumstances, Barry thinks, he might sit back and enjoy—even encourage—an old-fashioned catfight. But not today. He knows whom he should call, the person he should have phoned two hours ago. "Pardon me," he says, and disappears into the bedroom.

"Kitty, you're not going to believe this one." For the next few minutes he fills in his elite one-woman security force on the world news of the week. When he's finished, and effectively ten years old, he takes a deep breath. "So what's your call? Get the police on it?"

I see his face whiten as he listens to her directive, blunt and instinctive. He hangs up the phone and returns to the living room.

"So?" Stephanie says.

"Ladies, Kitty Katz has spoken, and as usual, she is right," he announces. "Police equal publicity, and sensational publicity will fuck my practice. No police." He laughs, but he is not amused. "I'll work something out with the Divines. At least for now."

"You're going to do squat?" As Stephanie stammers, she spits an *s*

that lands on Brie, who flicks it off. Unfazed, Stephanie crosses her arms in front of her in a pose that I am certain she's practiced in order to make the most of her full, high breasts, which, Brie and I are both guessing, have benefited from enhancement, perhaps under the steady hand of Barry Marx, M.D.

"For now, yes," he says, and looks at his watch. "And if you will both excuse me, I'm going to pick up my daughter."

Stephanie's eyes bore into Barry's as she waits for him to ask her to join him in collecting Annabel. Maybe he will even ask her to accompany both of them to his mother's seder, about which he seems to have forgotten. He does neither. "Okay, well, see you later," she says.

Brie hugs Barry and squeezes his hand. "We'll talk," she says, and turns to leave.

A minute later, Brie and Stephanie stand silently side by side waiting for the elevator. When they enter and the door closes, they are still alone. Brie faces Stephanie and asks the question at the top of her mind for the last half hour. "Tell me, was it before or after when you two hooked up?"

Go, Brie, go! Departed minds want to know!

"My relationship with Dr. Marx is strictly professional." Stephanie's voice has bounced back to an almost musical timbre. "Although last time I looked, he was single. And now it's my turn." She smiles at Brie, but only with her mouth. "Does it hurt that your girlfriend Molly picked Barry over you?"

"I wouldn't get too attached to Dr. Marx if I were you," Brie says. "He's got the attention span of a jock strap."

"He seems interested enough."

"You'd never pass his mother's sniff test."

"You are so wrong," Stephanie says, and laughs. "It was Kitty who introduced us." She remembers how after a yoga class Barry swung by to pick up Kitty for one of their regular lunch dates. "The famous son," Stephanie had said as she stood on the sidewalk talking to her new pal Kitty, who'd spoken of him often and hadn't overestimated his appeal.

"If you want to be territorial about Barry, why don't you just pee on him?" Brie asks.

"Excuse me? I can't hear you up there on your cross."

The voices are getting louder, higher, and shriller. When Brie walks out to Central Park West and glides into a waiting town car, I want to cheer her, although I had always mocked her for that particular perk.

Stephanie turns the corner. I pray she steps in dog shit.

I despise that woman, Brie and Stephanie each think. *What a piece of work.*

Twenty-three

CLEOPATRA COMMANDS
HER BARGE

I've got tomorrow all planned," Brie says as she wields her hairbrush in fluid strokes while blasting a blow-dryer in the opposite hand. Her arms are slim and defined, like a fourteen-year-old boy's. I always envied them. "I was hoping you'd join us this time."

Brie is bare-breasted, and the only woman I know who can pull off Brazilian-cut panties, which sit high on your hips to reveal a peek of cheek. Nothing droops, which she attributes to genetic roulette, but I know the elliptical machine gets part of the credit.

"Give me the rundown," Isadora says, and slowly sinks into the froth of a deep, free-standing tub. She rarely hurries, and starts each morning with a ritual bath no less than fifteen minutes long. When she designed the apartment, Isadora insisted on a white marble bathroom as big as the bedroom. It looks like a laboratory and is, a buzzing workshop where beauty is nourished and transformation begins.

Brie has plotted Saturday by internal MapQuest. "We'll start with brunch at Sarabeth's on Central Park South because I know Annabel will love the pumpkin waffles, then the carousel and a stroll up Madison, where I saw the most adorable dress—a pale blue gingham pinafore—then frozen hot chocolate at Serendipity. Oh, and a book-

store—she's ready for *Madeline*," she says. "In the late afternoon, a movie and pizza." She turns the mirrors to assess the back of her hair. It's as smooth as if it were painted. "I wish I could take her to the theater again, but I don't want to miss the shopping."

"That's way too much for a five-year-old," Isadora says as she lifts her left leg out of the bubbles, arches her foot, and gently pumices away nonexistent calluses. Her size fives are a point of pride. There is no dithering over polish shades. She gets a weekly pedicure, always Chanel Vamp. Isadora accepts no substitutes.

"Actually, Annabel's almost four," Brie says.

"Even worse. Are you mental?"

"Who made you queen mother?" Brie asks in a low voice. "Annabel's going to love it." She plans to will it so.

"But all this for a *niña*? We'll have one whiny little princess on our hands." Isadora laughs and thinks, *Just like her mother.* In the last three months I have learned that in Isadora's estimation I wasn't worth getting all lathered up about—its own insult. She didn't despise me, but when her mind floats in my direction, condescension is right there, too. "You, my darling Brie, are wrong," she says calmly. *Tía Sabrina es loca.*

"So, don't join us," Brie says, and shrugs. With that she puts on two coats of black mascara, stiffens her shoulders, and walks out of the room, Cleopatra commanding her barge.

When Brie and Isadora are pissed, it doesn't end in plates sailing across the room. They're alpha show dogs—an Irish wolfhound and a standard poodle. It's been almost a year now and there has never been a bite that drew blood: they express their animus through posture, attitude, and the occasional preemptive bark.

Since my death, this will be Brie and Annabel's third outing. It's possible that my daughter has aroused a latent maternal instinct in my dearest friend, who until now has failed to nurture so much as a pot of chives. But perhaps the time passed together, lovely as it is for both, is mostly Brie's way to stay close to me. Or—drilling down, because she's one of the most instinctively competitive women I ever met, which I say with deep respect—it's about one-upping Lucy and now Stephanie. Not that Stephanie's been all that interested in Annabel.

I would read Brie's mind, if only she herself knew it. But I have

learned that despite substantial evidence to the contrary, her head is a lot cloudier inside than anyone would guess. That Brie is one slightly mixed-up babe makes me love her more.

A driver is waiting downstairs to deliver her to the office. When Brie arrives, she logs onto her computer and pulls up a new file. *Annabel.* She scrolls through case after sordid case of disputes where fathers, a surprising number of whom wear mullets and orange prison jumpsuits, have been denied custody of their daughters. Some dads were years delinquent with child support. Others are in the process of, say, switching genders. Nice to know ya, Duane. Y'all meet Dixie!

Brie bites her lip. She isn't finding the legal precedent of a widower who loses his child not to his wife's family but to his wife's friend. She isn't even coming close, and since she doesn't have time to continue the search, she switches to e-mail. A blitz of messages appears, mostly with headings in cryptic legalese. After she scans her inbox, the one she reads first is from hihicks@gmail.com. *Anything new at your end? Today, the mother-in-law.*

I wish I had leads to feed you, Detective Hicks, Brie's thinking. *I wish I could figure this out on my own, but I'm coming up with nothing. I'm counting on you. Why hasn't this case been solved already? What's taking so damn long? Are we forgetting that a woman died, a young, beautiful woman? My best friend. But I've got to keep my head in the game. Stay cool.*

Hello Kitty—watch out—she hisses, Brie writes back, and waits for a response from Hicks. There is none. This doesn't make her unhappy. It makes her thinks he's working hard. No nonsense. Good.

Brie answers a few more e-mails and is interrupted by a buzz from her assistant. Her first deposition waits.

I leave Brie to fight on behalf of liberty and justice for all and circle back to Kitty's building. Hicks enters. I half expect him to be carrying a bouquet: my mother-in-law attracts gifts the way other women do mosquitoes. She has one whole closet filled with tributes: tall reeds that slip into essential oils, Egyptian cotton dish towels in rainbow hues, pithy advice books she'll never read, Florentine notepaper, enemies' scalps.

"Detective," she says. "At last." Kitty Katz ushers Hicks into the living room.

I see an overdecorated Manhattan co-op, everything inert, just so.

But Hicks sees something else as his eyes sweep the room with the swift look-see he's perfected during his eight years on the force. Hicks sees money. His new condo, which is a big step up from his mother's place in a less cultivated section of uptown Manhattan, would fit into the foyer and living room. He never knew that beige came in so many varietals. Yet the room is far from dull, thanks to a mix of muted tapestry, mohair, silk, tweed, and velvet, especially the velvet, whose silken smoothness on a pillow he can't resist stroking when Kitty turns her back. Afternoon light boomerangs off a few well-chosen pieces of antique Murano in tutti-frutti colors. In another life, this taut, handsomely dressed woman was apparently the contessa of the Venice lagoon.

Hicks also can't help noticing that while he sees pictures of Annabel and many of Barry at different ages, there is only one of Barry, Annabel, and me, on a side table overshadowed by a pungent arrangement of tall peach roses and birds of paradise.

"Coffee? Tea?" Kitty says. Pinky is standing ready, unseen, in the kitchen.

"No, thank you," he says. "I'm aware that you're on a tight schedule, so if you agree, Mrs. Katz, let's dive in." Out comes the small black leather notebook, which isn't as pristine as the first time I saw it. He smiles. "Okay, let's take it from the top. Did your son and daughter-in-law have a happy marriage?"

Has he had orthodontia? is Kitty's first thought. Next she considers what the correct answer to the question might be. "Divinely happy." She laughs. "No pun intended." Although it was. "Devoted. Molly adored my son." *Who wouldn't,* her face says.

"No cracks in the surface, Mrs. Katz? Tensions, worries?"

"Of course. What young marriage doesn't have all that?"

"Just answers, Mrs. Katz. Just answers. And your own relationship with the deceased? With Molly?"

Kitty leans forward and extends her hand—age spots lasered away, sporting one hefty, square-cut diamond solitaire in a platinum setting. "You know, Detective," she says, "my own mother-in-law—that would be Barry's father's mother, may she rest in peace—interfered with my life no end." She has to stop herself from rolling her eyes at the memory of that particular hairy-chinned bat. "I made a point of never doing

that." She pronounces "never" as if italicized. "I gave my son and Molly their space."

The truth: Kitty did give me a wide berth, but rarely a day passes when she and Barry don't speak. If she told Hicks this, he would understand, because in his family, interference equals love. The more meddling, the more love—two-thirds of a triangle completed by food.

The Katz woman had no use for Molly, Hicks jots in his notebook, using cop code only he would understand. "Was Molly the wife you pictured for your son?" he asks.

Ah, the answer? Please! Might Kitty have preferred a member of the right charity committees with, say, a golf handicap in the single digits? Too threatening, perhaps. A mini-Kitty? Yes, if the woman worshipped her as much as both of them worshipped Barry and was on board with advancing his practice, a woman who buried her own identify before the Barry throne.

"I never pictured a wife for my son," she says, in what might be her first honest answer of the day. Indeed, my bullshit meter has fallen silent.

A grin crosses Hicks' face. "Then you're a good sight different from my ma. She's had the girl picked out for me since I was twenty-three." Evian, who cornrows his mother's hair. Sweet kid, Evian. A shapely lady, all heart, just like Ma, who invites her to Sunday dinner at least once every two months. One of these days Ma will catch on to the fact that he is not Evian's type, a hot-shit detective who can't dance to save his life. But he and Ev play along and flirt away those Sunday afternoons. Every Christmas, he sends her the biggest box of chocolates Godiva sells. She gives him the thickest history book on the best-seller list. Once a summer, they take in a Yankee game and afterward, over beers and dogs, bemoan the unfortunate state of romance in America, their own lack thereof, in particular.

"Tell me about Molly, things only you know."

"Well," she says, savoring this tasty question as she lights up. "I don't think she had much confidence—"

This may be true, but I was working on it, and dammit, she didn't help.

"—or that many friends."

Heresy! A blatant lie! Kitty just didn't know many of my friends—

dozens of colleagues, current and former; five or six mommies; my book club; bicycle people; college buddies; even a few doctors' wives. Lucy, sort of. Brie!

"Let me amend that," she says, almost as if she heard me. "She has that lawyer from college who spoke at the funeral and, of course, male friends."

"And might you know their names?"

"Unfortunately, I don't, but I'm sure, with your sources . . ." She looks Hicks straight in the eye as she flicks her ash on a Baccarat plate. "And also, I must tell you she was envious of all the attention my son received. As you know, Dr. Marx has a thriving practice."

Envious of Barry? What a crock. I am outraged, but then I concede that Dr. Kitty might be on to something. Perhaps I was envious of how Barry always triple-lutzed through life, self-doubt as foreign to him as flying a helicopter, not that he wouldn't try to do that, given the chance.

"And her twin sister?" she continues. *Maniac,* Kitty thinks as she grinds her cigarette into extinction. "But I gather you're on to Lucy. My revelations will not be enlightening."

"She's a complicated one," he says. Hicks knows the woman wants to be brought up to speed. *Are we ready to throw her in the slammer?*

"Complicated?" Kitty lets loose with her signature cackle, half whinny, half caw.

"And interesting," he says. "Not to worry, we're on her. It's you I'd like to talk more about today, thanks." He looks again at his notebook and, while he's thinking, admires the portrait of a young dark-haired boy with a fox terrier. Barry, *le petit prince.* "Mrs. Katz, on the day of your daughter-in-law's death, where were you?"

"Now, finally, an easy question," Kitty says gaily as she lights a second cigarette. Or maybe it's her third. "In the afternoon I was shopping on Madison Avenue and afterwards played mah-jongg, like I always do on winter Fridays, with three of my oldest friends, Suzette, Linda, and Nancy." *Bam! Dot! Crack!* As if a confirmation from the mahj girls and boutique receipts corroborate innocence.

"So, getting down to business here," Hicks asks, leaning forward, using his most beseeching timbre—intimate, conspiratorial—"was Molly Marx the victim of some random crazy or was she intentionally murdered?" Slowly he pulls out a colored photo from the crime scene.

She gives a little gasp as she sees my face as filet mignon à la Sweeney Todd. "The latter, possibly," she says, rolling the word in her mouth like a sucking candy. "Yes, I think it's entirely possible that someone took her life on purpose."

"Why, Mrs. Katz?" His voice is rougher than before.

"That's what I can't fathom."

"Mrs. Katz, hazard a guess." It is an order.

"Someone would have had to hate Molly. Who, I can't say." Because she can't imagine me engendering that intense a response in another person.

"Could that person be your son?"

"No!" While Kitty is saying the word, her mind is racing. *Is this possible? Could Molly have done something so heinous the poor boy snapped like a bungee cord?*

"Another woman?" Hicks suggests. He lets the grisly photo of me stay face up on the table.

"My son was a faithful husband." My bullshit meter reactivates with a loud bleep. *And if he wasn't,* she's thinking, *so what? Barry's father was no different, though he learned that diamonds cure suspicion and we both got on with our lives.* "And if he wasn't," Kitty adds, "how would I know? But I can safely say any woman—any other woman—my son would ally himself with would never be so vile as to commit murder. Frankly, Detective, I am deeply offended that you would even suggest this."

It's my fucking job, Hicks thinks, but tries to smile with deep sympathy.

"Which is why I'm thinking she . . ." Kitty pauses and takes a deep drag, which she would like to blow in Hicks' handsome face. "She most likely took her own life."

"Really? Suicide?" *That's a joke,* Hicks thinks. *Where's the motive? According to her internist and gynecologist, both of whom Molly saw at the first of the year, good girl that she was, she was healthy—no secret, gruesome disease, no pregnancy by some inconvenient man. The husband, well, he may be a player and a jerk, but folks say he spent plenty of time at home, and it's a pretty exceptional home at that.* "Your daughter-in-law rode her bike off the road, possibly right into the Hudson River? Did she intend

to drown herself but didn't make it far enough? I don't quite get that. But let's not talk about how, tell me *why.*"

"She was one of those sad, unstable people who looked normal enough on the outside but was really the type no one could make happy." *Suicide,* Kitty thinks, *is going to get this detective with his wheedling ways sniffing elsewhere, away from Barry and away from me.*

This is why Bob has warned me not to trail Hicks in his investigations, because it will make *me* want to commit murder. I would like to crush and mash Kitty's most valuable piece of Murano and stir the shards into her tea, then force her to drink it slowly, to max out the poison and pain—even if Hicks ain't buying what she has to sell.

"No one could make her happy, not even your son?" he asks.

Kitty tilts her head down so Hicks can't see it. I can. She looks nervous, deeply agitated. "Some women just can't be content—the well of misery is that deep."

"Others have implied this." Hicks feels a sharp bang in his gut as he articulates this lie designed to draw out Kitty.

"Really?" Kitty asks. She'd like to believe this were true, but she smells a setup, even if this is the first time she's ever been questioned by a police officer.

"Yes, really, and what I'd like to know is, what could have made Molly Marx angry enough, and so deeply disappointed, that she would abandon her daughter and husband by taking her own life?"

As if she might discover the answer inside, Kitty picks up a green lacquered box that Pinky keeps filled with fresh cigarettes. "I'd like to know that, too, Detective Hicks."

He's being stonewalled, and Hicks feels his work here today is as finished as Kitty's last smoke. "Well, if anything comes to you . . ." He stands, stretches his legs, and shakes Kitty's hand formally. She steps back a step, almost as if she's frightened. *Did I overdo it?* she wonders.

Hicks leaves behind his card as Pinky materializes and hands him his raincoat. He does a double-take. *What the fuck. Does this other woman live in Ma's building? Nah, she just looks like that busybody next door.*

Maybe Molly did kill herself, he thinks as he stands in the richly car-

peted hall, ringing for the elevator. Self-defense against big mean Kitty with her claws out.

Hicks has a craving for gravy and biscuits, for home. "Ma," he says on his cell phone as soon as he walks to Seventy-sixth Street, glad to get her on the first ring. "How do you feel about cooking on Sunday?" He shakes his head. "Sure, Ma, invite Ev."

Twenty-four

NEED MEETS WANT

"You were brilliant," Luke said when the Sonoma pictures came back. "Get out your calendar, Molly Marx, because thanks to your good work, we have a job in Bridgehampton, and after that Nantucket, and then one right in town."

"*Our* good work," I said. I thanked him, put down the phone, and penciled in the dates, my hand trembling.

I'd been back from California for five endless days and four sleep-less nights. Luke was taking up all the space in my head. I'd relived our vineyard romp so many times that I could have acted out both the male and female leads for the most discriminating of directors. This was our first post-Sonoma conversation. If there was a next move, I didn't know it, at least as long as I was stone-cold sober, which I fully intended to stay.

Luke downshifted to a low murmur. "Do you have any regrets?"

Did he? Because if so, I could no more imagine standing next to him at a shoot than I could see myself having Annabel's first-birthday party that weekend at Hooters. If Luke felt regretful, I'd simply cancel the jobs I'd written into my calendar. No looking back.

"Molly, are you there?"

"Regrets?" I said. What the hell. I'd tell the truth, and while I was at it impersonate an eighteenth-century courtesan. "None." I couldn't quite get a word like *darling* out of my mouth. "What about you?"

There was no hesitation, although I suspect Luke was waiting for me to elaborate. "I've never been less regretful in my whole life," he said. "Best day of my decade."

I said nothing.

"So how does lunch sound?"

"Great," I answered, trying to respond like a woman with no more at stake than a Cobb salad. "Thanks."

"At my place," he added, whipping out the E-ZPass to every illicit relationship. "What day can you make it?"

I didn't want to make decisions. I wished Luke could read my mind and know that. What I wanted to hear was *How about lunch tomorrow?* To that I would reply that I couldn't accept because Annabel had a play-date. One more day of longing from afar. Which was a lot simpler, and would absolve me of the guilt I was feeling along with the mightier wallops of sexual longing, full-tilt excitement, and plain old curiosity. But unfortunately, Luke was being entirely too flexible. This led to thinking that there was an *us*, which required me to stick around to see what would happen between the members of this attractive couple. I was not able to shout out, *Oops, I am terribly sorry, but it slipped my mind that I've taken a vow of fidelity in front of hundreds of people, a rabbi representing both thousands of years of Judaism and the sovereign state of Illinois, and the man who might be a cheater but just the same is my husband. No, sir. I can't have lunch. I shouldn't even have a Pepsi.*

So we made a date for the following week.

As I was on the way to Luke's apartment, my stomach lurched, and potholes weren't entirely to blame. The taxi driver stopped at his address, a four-story limestone building on a gritty street. There was a sprinkling of trash littering the sidewalk and no doorman. A woman walked out the front door and I breezed in. The lobby had a speckled terrazzo floor and black marble walls. I could see it in a decorating spread titled "Faded Glory." I stepped into the elevator, which rose in slow motion, a

long, brass arrow pointing to each passing floor. I felt as if the arrow might leap off the wall and land in my heart.

A few months ago, Luke had decamped from the West Village for the East Village. To the remotely hip—a demographic to which I do not belong, now or ever—this hadn't been a pioneer neighborhood for more than a decade. *Rent*-style squatters had moved on. I'd heard about cunning boutiques sandwiched between locksmiths and filthy bodegas and knew the area was loaded with bistros serving fusion cuisine far beyond French/Vietnamese—Japanese/Guatemalan, Israeli/Palestinian? On account of this culinary creativity, four-star restaurants in sadly stuffy midtown and above were now empty night after night, especially on weekends. Yet despite all this, on my mental map of Manhattan, the East Village may as well have been the Balkans.

I stood outside 4B. Should I turn around? I'd gotten this far. I knocked.

"I didn't hear you buzz," Luke said a half minute later after he'd looked through the peephole. "Have you been waiting long?"

Yes, I thought, *I have been waiting thirty-five years to behave this way.* I suppose women do this all the time in Paris, in London, and right here in Manhattan. I, however, am a woman more comfortable deciding between wild- and farm-raised salmon than whether or not to sleep—again—with a man who is not my husband. I wished I'd stepped out of a forties movie where the wasp-waisted vamp wears a belted trench coat over a slinky satin dress with shoulder pads. At least then I could deliver some sparkling dialogue. Instead I said, "No, not long."

"C'mon in," he said, hanging my coat on a peg in an oak-paneled hallway that led to a big, square room. Burnished wainscoting ended above my head, beyond which the walls were an inky blue. The room had a twelve-foot-high ceiling; hanging from it, four dimly lit antique brass chandeliers cast a clinquant glow on this sunless day. There were two groupings of squashy brown couches, and a sensual dark red recamier next to a table piled with books. In the air I detected a faint scent. Green tea? Fresh pears? My nose traveled to a small pile of scented black rocks next to a photograph of a family that must be Luke's. In the far corner of the room a round table was set for two with rough beige linen placemats and sleek white dishes.

He really did mean lunch.

"Did you notice that over the outside door it says New York Free Circulating Library?" Luke said eagerly. Ah, he was nervous, too.

"I missed that," I said. "Should we have a do-over?"

"Shall we?" he said, and reached his arms around my shoulders as he melted against me. I closed my eyes and explored his mouth. There I was again, adrift, surrounded by a moat that kept reality at bay. I was circulating, all right. I felt as if I could feel my own blood rushing through my veins and every hair standing on end.

He took my hand. "Let me show you around." His arm encircling my waist, Luke led me to another hall, on which he'd hung dozens of his black-and-white photographs, not just pictures from work but bridges, many bridges. On one side of the corridor, a French door led to a study lined with bookshelves and covered with wallpaper on which peacocks strutted. "The birds are from the previous owner," he said. "I was planning to rip them out, but I'm beginning to think of them as pets."

"If you rip them out, I will kill you," I said, pointing. "The big fellow here just winked at me."

On the other side was the kitchen. Over an enameled sink—pristine and white—a stuffed deer's head stood watch, its graceful antlers the only curve in the room. The two bathrooms' walls were paneled, and in the larger one, a claw-foot tub faced a window overlooking a roof garden with iron furniture and a leafless tree growing in a large terra-cotta tub. Our tour proceeded slowly, Luke an eager guide. "I was able to salvage it from the original" or "Looks authentic, yes? Big fake" or "You've got to see this."

There was one last door at the end of the hall. As Luke placed his hand on the brass knob, I took a deep breath. To enter might be the most regrettable move of my life.

"I don't know what to do with this room," he said as he crossed the threshold. "Any ideas?"

I stepped inside. The walls were stark white. I turned my back on the black iron bed, plainly made with simple linens, and took in a baroquely carved mantel, also white, its hearth laid with birch logs. Hanging above was a blow-up of a nude couple entwined in sheets. I recognized the shot from Luke's portfolio and remembered the highly

publicized story about the models, busted for snorting coke and hooking up on the job. In the center of the ceiling hung a trio of old ships' lanterns, tranquilly sparkling like magnums of vintage Champagne.

"Aside from the hockey stick in the corner, I'd say don't change one thing."

"Sorry, the stick stays—but one thing's missing," he said, emerging from the shadows.

I was wearing a cashmere V-neck, a pencil skirt, tights, and tall boots, but nonetheless I felt chilled. "I don't think I can do this, Luke," I said. My voice was a whisper.

"I want you," he said hoarsely. "And unless I'm crazy, you feel the same way."

"That's irrelevant." Painful, but irrelevant. "I'm sorry." I wasn't sure why I felt the need to apologize.

"Molly, I would never pressure you," he said, and hugged me close for at least a minute. I wanted both to continue and to stop. Luke steered me back to the hall, his hand on the small of my back. We walked into the kitchen and stared at each other without exchanging a word. The music—was it Diana Krall?—had stopped, or maybe I just couldn't hear it over the beat of my heart. He reached for two bowls on an open shelf and from a tall black stockpot ladled steaming carrot soup, redolent with ginger. Crusty bread and olive oil were already on the table, and a salad of soba noodles, sweetened with mango and spiced with chilies and mint, waited in the glass-fronted refrigerator. Our lunch had turned careful, controlled. As we ate and drank and finished with espresso, we spoke only of work.

I'd made the right decision to keep my skirt on and my guard up, I told myself. I felt church-lady solid, the ne plus ultra of virtue.

Shortly before three o'clock, when the last dish was dried, we kissed goodbye—chastely, sweetly. My pheromones behaving themselves, I walked out the door with a promise to e-mail him ideas for the next job.

The taxi hadn't traveled two blocks when I knew. I pulled my phone out of my bag. "Luke," I said, "I forgot something."

"Really?" he said.

"Yes," I answered. "Dessert."

I needed to feel the roughness of his cheek against mine and move

my mouth down the length of his body until I found an even sweeter spot. I wanted to trace his profile with my fingertips and let them linger below. I needed and wanted more of what I'd tasted on that Caribbean island and while pressed against a floor beneath a cool vat of California chardonnay. Need and want were scrambled and I could no longer decipher, or even cared to decipher, my internal code.

I instructed the driver to return to the spot where he'd picked me up. When we got there, he asked if I wanted him to wait. "No," I said. "I may be a while." I twisted around the stone in my engagement ring so it wasn't glaring at me with reproach and dropped a twenty-dollar bill into his hand. The driver seemed happy, as did I.

This time when I walked into Luke's apartment, I headed straight into the bedroom, which is where I stayed until the afternoon ended, along with what remained of my innocence. In its place, I'd found something else.

Twenty-five

WHAT THE HEART WANTS

I know I was hasty," Lucy insists for the umpteenth time, "but I meant no harm."

"Lucy," Mom says wearily, "hasty hardly explains it."

"Okay, foolhardy, reckless, rash."

"Can you explain yourself, please?"

I thought my mother might end that sentence with "young lady."

"I still don't know what was in my head," Lucy says, "but you believe me, don't you, that I didn't mean to hurt Annabel or upset you and Dad?" Lucy's never been as gifted at talking to my parents as I was; she's never been able to charm them, ever. Every time she attempts to talk about the day she snatched Annabel, she sets her own trap.

All Claire Divine believes is that Lucy is certifiable. For exactly what, she's not sure. They are on the way home from the office of Dr. Solomon, the safety net Lucy now jumps into four times a week at five o'clock in the afternoon. My sister rejected the first four therapists Oxford coughed up. She'd have passed on this one, too, if she hadn't been afraid that if she didn't start treatment, she'd be exiled to Camp Wounded Soul to suffer through seminars on how self-destruction is for dummies. *At least,* Lucy thinks, as she and my mother pull into the

driveway, *Daphne Solomon, M.D., has never once used the word* dysfunc-tional, *at least out loud.*

Lucy despises her current life, although she's come to realize this is as good as it's going to get. She'd had to negotiate with our parents, who acted as mediators with Barry, for permission to continue to teach. If it had been up to my husband, she'd have been exiled straight to Hazelden, a captive in a dungeon. To rehab what? she asked. For loving Annabel too much? Wanting a little quality time with her dead sister's kid? Worrying about a child's well-being? This is, of course, how she explained what has become known in my family as "the incident."

Barry has agreed to let Lucy stay under Divine house arrest. Lucy is an upper-middle-class parent's worst nightmare: a single, never-married, childless adult daughter returned to the nest, back in our old bedroom, as if she's been grounded for smoking a joint. If Target sold GPS ankle bracelets, my parents would buy one and solder it in place. Instead, they chauffeur Lucy to her appointments and to her job in the city as if she were fourteen.

Their life has become more embarrassing, suffocating, and un-comfortable than the most hideous reality TV show. When they all sit down to eat or watch a DVD, there is a firewall between my parents and sister, preventing even the most mundane chatter. Lucy can look nei-ther parent in the eye. Today she helps haul in the seven bags of gro-ceries bought at Sunset Market, puts everything away, and excuses herself to read upstairs. Lucy feels like the world's biggest loser as she stands in front of the bathroom mirror and searches for gray hairs. She plucked out her first one last month, and two more yesterday. By the time this nightmare is over, Lucy is sure, she will be silver-haired or bald.

"Fuck," she says aloud, and goes to her twin bed and pounds a pil-low. "Fuck. Fuck. Fuck."

"Are you okay up there?" Mom shouts.

"Just dandy," she shouts back.

If Lucy wasn't cuckoo before—and she is convinced that she wasn't, just extremely "concerned"—living in this suburban petri dish will take her right there. I haven't worked myself up to sympathy, though I'm trying to travel the high road. I have chosen to pretend that Lucy is simply misunderstood. She doesn't have a screw loose, she loved me

deeply, and her intentions are pure. I won't let myself believe that my
sister's motives were those of a monster. I won't.

I also know that if Lucy realized I was thinking all of the above,
she'd say, *Molly, you are such a goddamn dope.* Which takes me to my real
bottom line: the incident makes me furious. It was and is a phenome-
nal time and energy suck, utterly unfair to my parents and to Annabel,
who is now denied the company of her only aunt. It has only deepened
the rift between the Divine and Marx clans, making it almost impossible for my parents to have even the simplest conversation with their
only grandchild, not to mention resurrect the social life they have put
on hiatus. Mostly, it's been a diversion that makes me worry that Hicks
will go off on some tangent that moves him away from figuring out *why,*
despite the fact that I know from observation that he's working 24/7,
more or less, on the Molly Marx case.

But simmering at a slow boil—where will that get me? In the Duration we call people who do that Hornets. They buzz around, full of
righteous indignation, and even other Hornets avoid them as if they
have stinky feet. I've been talking about Lucy to Bob, my Dr. Solomon.

"Focus on the good memories," he said yesterday, as he always
does, when we took our evening constitutional. This is his one-size-
fits-all wisdom to calm the brain and soothe the soul, his downward-
facing dog of celestial advice.

I thought it was a pile of caca. "How do you find a good memory
when your anger's a riptide?" I asked.

"You're angry about a lot of things," he said. "You'll have plenty of
time to sort it out. Tease out a warm memory with your sister and focus
on it."

"Thank you, Angel of Death," I said. He hates when I call him that.

"Molly," he said, "do it. Dig deep. Find a happy Lucy thought."

For days, it was like looking for my pulse, and then I remembered.
It was two years ago. For our thirty-third birthday my parents had been
wildly generous and blew us to a week's stay at a posh Mexican fitness
resort. They thought the adventure would help us bond.

For six days, we roomed together in a stucco hacienda that looked
to be on loan from a miniature golf course. We rose at dawn, when the
air was dewy and cool, and hiked the wildflower-covered hills, Lucy
apace with the leader and I, naturally, at the tail end. After a breakfast

fit for two longshoremen, we sampled every class. Lucy's favorite was Pilates, where she fell in love with a giant widget modeled after a medieval rack. In the afternoon, we played tennis. She won match after match, but I didn't mind, hypnotized as I became by the *thwank-thwank-thwank* of balls hitting the rusty-red clay court, the quintessential warm-weather percussion.

As each afternoon wound down, we treated ourselves to hot stone massages or had sturdy little Mexican ladies wrap our fried muscles in seaweed. Toxins banished, we napped in hammocks, spent the evenings enthusiastically beading bracelets we knew we'd never wear, and snoozed through lectures like What Does a Woman *Really* Need? Magnesium! By nine-thirty, we collapsed without even opening the beach books we'd lugged on the plane.

Somewhere between kick-boxing and Aerobics with Soul, the pampering and the meditating, we became confidantes. "I got dumped again," Lucy said on our last night. We'd turned off the light and the fragrance of jasmine and honeysuckle blew gently through opened shutters.

"Who was he?" I asked. I was aware she'd been seeing someone, but she hadn't mentioned a name and I knew that if I played *Meet the Press*, I'd be decapitated.

"You can call him dickhead."

"What happened?"

"Married."

"I thought you were too smart for that." She didn't say a word for a few minutes following that remark, and I thought maybe she'd fallen asleep, until she started speaking in a soft, unfamiliar voice.

"At first it was just hot, dirty sex and I got off on being part of a covert operation—when we'd finally get to see each other, we'd rip each other's clothes off. We'd meet at my place and every few months go away for the weekend. Remember my trip to South Beach?"

I did: the Delano Hotel, stone crabs, mojitos, underwater music, poolside bungalows. Lucy described it so vividly I thought I'd been there myself. "That was three years ago."

She sighed. "I'd see other guys, but gradually I let myself get totally into this sonofabitch, waiting by the phone, telling lies to my friends, acting unglued if he cancelled at the last minute, which usually he did."

She sat up in bed and wrapped her arms around her strong, tanned legs. "Christ, it's humiliating to tell you all this."

"Don't stop now."

"He kept saying he was going to leave his wife and move in with me. Can you believe I, Lucy Divine, bought that sack of shit?"

I was holding my breath. "What happened?"

"So two weeks ago, Jessica—she's another teacher—was at the hospital visiting her cousin who had a baby. And guess who was there looking through the glass into the nursery?"

"No!"

"She recognized his face from a picture she'd seen on my desk."

I heard Lucy sniffle. It was too dark to check for tears.

"Jessica took me aside the next day, saying she'd been up all night debating whether to tell me. I drove straight to the hospital." She paused. "David and his wife had had a boy. Looked just like him."

My stomach turned over. "Oh, I'm so, so sorry, Luce," I said. "What a jerk—"

"Molly, shut up," she snapped, back to the real Lucy. "I don't need your pity. Got that?"

In the shadows, I stared at my sister, whom I realized I hardly knew and might never know. "Fuck you, Moosey. I won't shut up," I said, and threw a pillow at her head. "You let yourself care for someone. What's so bad about that? If you did it over, do you honestly think you'd do anything differently? The heart wants what the heart wants."

"Who are you, Woody Allen?"

"I love you, that's all," I said. I don't think I'd ever told her that.

Lucy said nothing. Then I heard her voice, muted and fuzzy, a Xerox of a Xerox. "I always feel judged by you, Mrs. Marx with the perfect life."

"Perfect life?" I said incredulously, in a raspy squeak. I decided not to react to "judged" because she was right—I had judged her for more than thirty years.

"The darling toddler, the successful husband, the perfect part-time job, the huge apartment, the blond hair, the size six hips."

Of course she saw it that way. "I'll grant you Annabel, but Barry . . ."

"Trouble in paradise?" she said. Too quickly.

I'd walked into a Lucy ambush. I didn't want to betray Barry, but the sisterly thing would be to share. "Barry is a great dad, but sometimes

he barely notices I'm around, and when he does, it's to criticize. He questions every decision I make. That is, when he hasn't ruled unilaterally and I get to decide on something."

"What did you expect? Do you actually believe all those drunken speeches grooms make at weddings about how flipped-out in love they are and how their wife is their ideal woman, an angel on earth?" I believe she followed this question with a snort.

"I think he sees other women," I said.

She had the decency to wait a moment before saying, "We all think that."

Mom and Dad, too? "But Lucy, there's more." I hesitated. "The thing is, there's this other guy." I didn't give one detail, certainly not Luke's name. "I never meant for it to happen." Even I realized I was speaking every cheater's native language, cliché. "But for a long time now, I've been meeting him at his apartment." I left out Nantucket, Amsterdam, Santa Fe, Yellowstone, and the Mall of America.

"*You* have a lover?"

"I guess you could call him that."

She laughed. "For midwesterners, we are a fucked-up pair."

I thought that was a fitting note on which to end the conversation. I didn't want to tell Lucy more; the details would, like an oil spill, pollute my real life. But as I had almost given in to sleep she said, "Molly, I think you should stop this thing with the other guy. The heart may want what the heart wants, but you could get hurt." She had flipped off the glib Lucy and become someone reflective and wise. "Like me." She sat on the side of her bed and tapped me on the shoulder. "I say this because I love you." The two of us started to cry—noisy, gulping sobs—and neither of us fell asleep for a good hour.

We slept late and missed not only the hike that morning but the van to the San Diego airport. And this, I told Bob, was the happiest memory I would ever have of my sister.

Twenty-six

LOVE ACTUALLY

A re you and the ladies off to the land of very important paintings?"
Luke asked.

Today I had planned to visit galleries with Brie and Isadora, as they were on the prowl for something large and sublime to hang on their naked living room wall and Brie wanted my advice. She'd called early this morning, however, to say that she needed to work. I couldn't picture an afternoon alone with Isadora, a woman as relaxing as gridlock, so Saturday loomed like an unlined page.

Barry was off to San Francisco, attending a pep rally for plastic surgeons. He'd spent weeks prepping—cruising Gucci for a suit that said wildly hip yet Park Avenue, the location of his office. He'd gotten his hair cut exactly ten days before, so it wouldn't look too freshly pruned. Barry wanted to be prime-time polished, ready to expound on his much-heralded weekend butt lift. ("A cheeky booty with zero squats!" *Vogue* had gushed.) He'd hesitated before accepting the speaking invitation, weighing glory against reality. Did he really want to share secrets with the rest of the profession? I believed the tiebreaker was a patient who'd offered to help him rehearse, numerous times, and curiously, always at night. I also believed she was an actress valued less for

her talent than for her juicy body parts, many of which have been re-habbed by Dr. Marx.

"Brie cancelled," I said to Luke. "Something about a settlement meeting. How goes the drive to New Hampshire?" He was visiting his brother this weekend. I checked my watch. Eleven o'clock. "You must be in Massachusetts by now."

"The trip's not happening," he said. "My nephew is celebrating his fourth birthday with strep."

While I let the news wash over me, I said, "Poor kid," with what I hoped was appropriate concern. Maybe Luke and I could see each other. It had been twenty-two days. Clarification. We'd *seen* each other—at meetings, for coffee, and once for lunch at Le Pain Quotidien—but we hadn't been together in the way I'd grown to adore, more and more, for the past year or so. For the last three weeks, Luke had hosted Irish cousins who were enjoying Manhattan so much it appeared as if they were going to sleep on his couches until their green cards came through. On the second week of the Danny-and-Seamus show, Luke splurged on the St. Regis, a Manhattan convenience I recently learned that you can rent for an afternoon, not unlike a carpet shampooer. We wouldn't be returning there soon, though. Not only did the room cost as much as a small painting, but on the way out I spied one of Kitty's Girls, who may have been on a mission similar to my own. I vowed that never again, un-less I was in the vicinity of a grizzly bear, would I cower terrified behind a tree, indoors or out. Hotels were out.

A few hours earlier, Annabel had been spirited away by Kitty, who wouldn't be returning her until bedtime. They'd never spent a whole day alone together, and like many first dates, theirs began awkwardly when the name of the restaurant was revealed: Annabel had counted on Dunkin' Donuts, not Fred's at Barneys. But my daughter regained com-posure when she learned that her grandmother was also taking her to see the Alice in Wonderland statue in Central Park. As to the rest of the schedule, Kitty was sketchy, although I wouldn't have been surprised if she'd cram in an etiquette seminar for three-year-olds.

I'd already accomplished that day's first order of business, finding piles of Barry's credit card receipts and cell phone bills, which I in-tended to scrutinize later for evidence of philandering. Just then I was taking a break. I'd crawled back into bed, a *W* along with me, and had

finished reading a passionate diatribe, "The Fatted Calf: When You Can't Fit into the Season's Boots," being thankful for a problem I didn't have, when Luke called.

"What are you doing right now?"

"I'm in bed." I did my best to purr.

"Really? What are you wearing?"

I looked at my XL T-shirt, left over from a breast cancer race-walk, hanging over saggy cotton boxers. "Not a thing. How about you?"

"Weekend grunge. I had coffee in Little Italy and I'm heading toward Chinatown."

"What do you say to dim sum?" I said, feeling an energy surge. "Meet at Golden Bridge in an hour?"

"I say I prefer your buns to theirs."

"Don't tell me the blarney brothers finally left?" Either way, I could scurry downtown in less than hour. "Did New York run out of beer?"

"No such luck—they're sleeping off last night," Luke said. "I was thinking of a certain elite uptown address on Central Park West."

Oh, really? I had gotten used to Luke's place. I had, in fact, gotten very used to Luke's place, where I knew the woodsy scent of his sandalwood soap, exactly how he folded and hung his thick gray towels, and where he kept his herbal tea, which I'd brew and take back into bed with us in tall pottery mugs, the steam curling my hair and warming my hands. Every time I stole an hour out of a workday to visit him, I'd play pretend, the R-rated edition. This was all too easy to do at Luke's, where there was no evidence of a husband and child or, for that matter, another woman. We'd simply love and laugh, love and talk, love and snap the occasional photograph, after which I'd grab his digital camera and delete the naked evidence. When the tea grew cold, it was a private mental signal to gather my things, kiss him goodbye, and shut the door on this erotic compartment in my lascivious little mind and return to what I used to refer to as normal life.

The home I shared with my family was, however, a vault within a vault, strictly off-limits. I'd never invited Luke here and didn't intend to start. I looked around. Barry's dry cleaning hung on the back of the bedroom door, ready to be divided by genus and species. The potentially incriminating stacks of receipts and phone bills that I'd set aside

lay in a heap, awaiting review. On my dresser, in its simple sterling sil‐
ver frame, Barry peered from our wedding photo. His dark brown eyes
drilled into me.

"Molly, are you there?" Luke said. "I'd hate to think I'm boring
you."

"Just musing," I said lightly.

"I worry when a woman muses. Are you thinking what I'm think‐
ing?"

"And that would be?" I always liked when he'd recite the daily spe‐
cials.

"Us. That bed you're in must be awfully lonely. And as I recall, the
good doctor is in California and Annabel's gone for the day."

His voice was a challenge as much as a conscience‐numbing anes‐
thetic. I felt my resolve float away, revealing an emotion I could not
name. Excitement? Happiness? Some sicko attraction to danger? I
also briefly considered the state of my apartment, which would require
a good twenty minutes of preening. Then there was the fact that I could
use a shower, a shampoo, and, I dimly noted, a psychiatrist. But I said,
"Be here in forty‐five minutes."

"I'll pick up lunch," he said, almost like a considerate husband.

I was snipping the stems off apricot roses bought in a sprint to the
corner deli when the doorman rang. "Alfred Stieglitz is here to see
you," he said.

"Please send him up."

Luke filled my doorway. The smile on his face—bashful with a
raunchy glint—replaced my anxiety with an intimacy certified by a cool,
coffee‐flavored kiss, the kind that requires no breathing. He'd barely
piled his jacket and scarf by the door when I led him around the corner
to the living room and pulled him down into a wide chair, avoiding the
one where I snuggled and read with Annabel.

Normally, I liked to memorize every caress Luke offered, all the
better to replay later when I biked or walked or showered. My rule
was that I fantasized about him only when I was alone, but I'd al‐
ready broken one rule that day and was on to demolishing a second
commandment—number seven of God's top ten being long gone—as we
moved to the rug and got down to basics.

Today, however, I couldn't enjoy myself. I kept glancing at the

grandfather clock, half expecting to see Barry's face staring back at me. Exactly seventeen minutes later, I looked at Luke with relief. We could get dressed now.

"The bathroom is down the hall," I whispered as I pointed in the direction of Annabel's chaste, sunny chamber with its flotilla of rubber ducks and bubble bath marketed to calm overtired, cranky children. When he disappeared, I ran into my own bathroom, stuffed my hair under a shower cap, and blasted the shower water as hot as it ran.

I was happily wielding my loofah until my skin turned pink when over the rush of water, I heard a noise. The bathroom door, which I'd been careful to close securely behind me, flew open. I shrieked so loudly that the intruder let out a primal scream as well. The glass surrounding the shower was steamed—I couldn't see who'd entered. I did my *Psycho* bit again at an eardrum-shattering decibel.

"Calm down," Luke said as he slipped in beside me. "Jesus, Molly, everything's okay, it's okay." He held me to his chest as he deftly adjusted the water to a temperature below a rolling boil. "Are you trying to give yourself third-degree burns?"

Sort of, I thought.

"And what's that on your head?" Luke pulled off my protective purple plastic, gently pushed me under the nozzle, and started massaging shampoo onto my scalp. He ran his sudsy hands gently down my breasts, circling each nipple, and continued further south. I closed my eyes and tried to swim in the pleasure, but the clank of my colliding worlds was all I could feel. When the phone rang, dimly, in the bedroom, I was grateful.

"I better answer that," I said, squirming, shampoo stinging my eyes.

"Can't you let the machine take it?" he said as he held me close.

"It might be about Annabel." Or Barry.

"Ah," he said as he released his embrace. "Of course."

Leaving soapy footprints behind me, I flew into the bedroom, gently closed the door, and reached for the phone on the fifth ring.

"Good, you're there," Brie said. "I'm so sorry about today and was thinking. I could finish up here by two and we could still meet, at least for a movie. I feel like a bad friend standing you up."

"Gee," I said, "I already decided to meet Annabel and Kitty later."

"Gee?" Brie said. "You're spending your holy me-time with Kitty? And wasn't today all about her having Annabel alone for Kitty boot camp? Gee, pardon me, but I'm confused."

"Well, when you cancelled . . ."

"Never mind. I'll just stay here," Brie said, with her usual good nature. "And let me say, you are very weird."

When I returned to the bathroom, Luke was toweling off. The mood of merry seduction had vanished, and putting my arms around his waist did nothing to restore it.

"Listen, honey, do you want me to leave?" he asked as he pushed away my hands and began to walk toward the living room. "Be honest."

That might have been the best idea of the day. Yet as I followed Luke, who was skirted in a towel, the V of his torso trim and hard, I also considered how often I'd craved time with him in New York measured not in minutes but in hours. Perhaps that day was a grave miscalculation, but I wasn't ready to kiss Luke Delaney goodbye.

"What I'd honestly like now is lunch," I said, and tried to produce my most bewitching smile. "Together. Here." It had to be here, because who knew where Kitty might be lurking, Annabel in tow? "But first I'm going to wash out this shampoo and throw on some clothes. Why don't you look through the Netflix and see if there's anything you'd like to watch? They're near the TV in the living room."

He shot me a skeptical look. "Are you absolutely sure?"

"Please stay," I pleaded. "Please." Before he could answer, I left the room.

With each piece of clothing I put on, a bit of apprehension slipped away. When I walked out of my bedroom I wasn't sure if Luke would be there, but he was, barefoot, in jeans and a sweater.

"*Notting Hill, Love Actually,* and *Sabrina,* the 1954 and 1995 versions—I see a pattern here," he said, studying the movies.

"You were expecting *Smokey and the Bandit? Cannonball Run?* Maybe you'd prefer a cooking show? If we're lucky, a luscious babe will make osso bucco in her negligee."

He shuddered. "Just bring out lunch, woman."

Relieved to hear him laugh, I returned with the sandwiches he'd brought and basked in the mundane as we drank an eight-dollar Trader Joe's merlot and huddled under a moth-eaten afghan knit by my

mother. When the movie rolled, I cried where I always cried. *Seems to me that love is everywhere,* I lip-synched. *If you look for it, I've got a sneaky feeling that love actually is all around.* This minute, for me, it was.

When the movie ended, I leaned against Luke's shoulder as we began to watch the Audrey Hepburn *Sabrina*. Ninety minutes later I opened my eyes. My head was in his lap.

"You snore," he said. That I also drooled was evident, but he was polite enough to ignore it.

"What time is it?"

"Time for me to go," Luke said. "I believe you said Annabel's due in the early evening."

"She won't be here for another hour at least." Kitty had said seven, but to be on the safe side, I'd want Luke out of the apartment by five-forty-five. We had twenty-five minutes. I began to kiss him.

Within minutes, our chemistry had kicked back into gear—we were taking pictures and enjoying the silk of each other's skin—when I heard a key in the lock. Bolting upright, I smoothed my hair, which had air-dried into a halo of frizz. I walked quickly to the foyer as Luke deftly disappeared in the direction of my bedroom and Kitty let herself in with a key Barry had apparently given her.

"Mommy!" Annabel said, running into my arms. "See! I got a manicure." She displayed her nails, each twinkling like a turquoise rhinestone.

"You're a princess," I said.

"Me too," Kitty said, and in an oddly girlish gesture presented her long, French-manicured gel tips.

"Mommy, Mommy." Annabel tugged at my sleeve. "Look what Kitty bought me!" She dumped a bag on the floor and pulled out a red feather boa, which she looped numerous times around her neck. It dragged to the floor. She resembled a very short Las Vegas showgirl.

"A lady needs accessories," Kitty said. "I wanted her to come back with me for dinner, but when I mentioned lamb chops, she said absolutely not. What do you and Delfina feed this child?"

I noticed that she left out Barry.

A civil daughter-in-law would take her mother-in-law's coat and insist that she settle in for coffee or wine and, in Kitty's case, a cigarette, although I hated when she smoked in my apartment. But my first action

was a prayer that Kitty would think the beat-up brown leather jacket prominently piled on the chair, which I saw her eyeball, was Barry's. Fat chance. Not only could she recite a verbal inventory of his wardrobe, half of which she had purchased, but once a piece of clothing became the least bit worn she knew that Barry, like her, immediately abandoned it. By Marx standards, this jacket was ready for a thrift shop.

"Molly, do you have company?" She was a dog on a trail.

"Oh," I said. "Yes, I do. One of my colleagues is here. But she's in the bathroom—she's not feeling well or I'd introduce you. Brie and Isadora cancelled, so I scheduled an impromptu meeting."

As I rattled on, Kitty looked at me as if I was a bad liar, which I was. At least a minute of annotated, implausible explanation commenced.

"I wouldn't dream of interrupting—you go back to your *colleague,*" she said, sweeping down in a cloud of Joy to kiss Annabel goodbye. Without so much as grazing my cheek with her lips, she turned and walked out the door. "Sorry to intrude" was all she said.

As I scooped my daughter into my arms, I could smell Kitty's smoke in her hair. "What do you say to a bath, Annie-belle, and then we'll have dinner, okay? But first, close your eyes tight. Very tight."

"A surprise?" she shrieked.

Only if you don't cheat, seemed like a poor choice of words. "Only if you keep your eyes closed," I said, and carried Annabel to her bedroom, glancing at Luke, who'd emerged from the master bedroom, padding quietly in stocking feet. He shrugged and blew me a kiss as he put on his shoes, grabbed his jacket, and tiptoed out the door, leaving it ajar so Annabel wouldn't hear a click. "Keep those eyes closed, Annabel," I warned twice.

A gift was already waiting on her bed, left there a few hours ago. While Annabel tore open the wrapping, I madly straightened the living room. That was when I discovered that in the rush, Luke had forgotten his digital camera. I ran to my bedroom and shoved it in my underwear drawer.

Only late that night—after Annabel's bath, chicken nuggets, reading her brand-new *Fancy Nancy* three times, and a five-minute chat with Barry—did I retrieve the camera to have a look before my normal deleting. There we were, shot after shot from today, each more compromising than the next. Guilty, guiltier, guiltiest.

Twenty-seven

WITNESS

Sometimes you need a witness to ratify that in fact you do see and feel what you think you see and feel. That's why I begged Bob to join me. We followed Hicks to a mom-and-pop coffee shop near his apartment. Over poached eggs, dry whole-wheat toast, and three cups of coffee (two sugars, plenty of milk—hold the hash browns) he's reviewing his thickening file, scrutinizing stacks of cell phone call lists and credit card receipts—mine (did I really spend all that on leg waxing?) as well as those from Barry, Lucy, Luke, Stephanie, Brie, Isadora, and even my parents. He hasn't labeled the file "suspects," but I gather that's who these other people are. Here and there, he circles a date or a phone number or carefully pens in a question mark.

"Thanks, Louise," Hicks says as he leaves a five-dollar tip.

"Solve that case, Detective," the waitress says. "Get them bad guys."

"I'm sure gonna try." *This may be my first case I'm handling as top dog, but I am not going to fuck it up like the Christina Rivera case. It's not just about respect in the NYPD and my future,* he thinks. *I'm getting to like this Molly. She reminds me of Franny, that white girl from college, the one I was afraid to ask out, the one who only now I realize was flirting with me full tilt, but I was too caught up in being one-down to notice. Franny, who got*

mowed by a truck while driving her decrepit Beetle. Franny, Molly, lovely, lonely . . .

I beam at Bob.

Now Hicks is walking to his car, a Honda Civic so stripped it might as well wear DETECTIVE vanity plates. He drives downtown to the Sixties, curses the fact that when Mr. Trump and his cronies put up all those buildings they made it virtually impossible for visitors to park nearby, and finds a spot on West End Avenue. He begins to walk toward the cookie-cutter towers shadowing the Hudson.

"Your Hicks," Bob says, "gives good aura."

"You can see auras?" I wonder what one looks like. Cloud cover that stops rays that cause premature aging? A classic mist of blue ozone? Maybe Bob is using the term metaphorically and an aura is a Kierkegaard mind-twister, like "Life must be understood backward but lived forward."

"It's all around him," Bob says. "One of these days you may be able to pick up on auras yourself. It's an upgrade some of us get."

"If my powers continue?"

"Do you really have to ask?" *Nothing lasts forever,* Bob finds a way to say or imply every time we meet, as if anyone in the Duration needs to be reminded of this. Fond as I am of Bob, the guy could use irony supplements.

Since I first laid eyes on Hicks, he's grown at least two inches in confidence. He strides through Stephanie's lobby as if he's wearing a virtual tuxedo custom-tailored to his physique. What a pair of shoulders. Today Hicks looks ready to present an Oscar. The concierge treats him accordingly and sends him straight up to the thirty-first floor, where Stephanie Joseph stands in her doorway. Her eyeteeth are as lupine as I remember, although I now know that, unlike her sister wolves, she has more than one mating season per year. Stephanie is dressed in the sweet spot between accountant and trollop. Unbuttoned to create a plunging neckline, her snug cardigan is the peach of a blushing bride. A tweedy knee-length wool skirt shows off her narrow-arrow hips, and red peep-toe stilettos reveal a pedicure in a shade that recalls vampires. A silver and crystal pendant dangles between her breasts.

The audition for Law and Order *was yesterday,* I hear Hicks think as they shake hands.

"Detective," Stephanie says as she cocks her head to the side and motions him into the apartment. With the afternoon sun streaming through the floor-to-ceiling windows, you can squint all the way to New Jersey.

I'm tempted to try to pick out Serenity Haven, my final earthly resting place, but Bob pokes me. "You're a decorating specialist, Molly," he says, scanning the room. "What do you make of this place?"

My eyes do a quick 360. "Early model apartment," I bounce back. "Perfect as a snow globe."

Every piece of furniture is plug-and-play pristine, perhaps selected from a catalog for high-tax-bracket transients. There are stiff leather couches, the kind you see in a boutique hotel lobby people wander through on the way to the cigar bar. I pick up a whirl of glass, right angles, black, white, taupe, a tall vase filled with branches, and another with one lonely calla lily, but notice no magazines or piles of mail, no personal photographs, only the variety numbered in a series. I can't bring myself to venture into Stephanie's bedroom, where I might find a remnant of Barry's last moment in flagrante delicto, so instead, leaving Hicks behind, I check out Jordan's room. There is an orderly abundance of toys, stuffed animals, blocks, and books, to which I am always drawn first. Many appear to be well read. I would find this easier if she had the mothering skills of a mascara wand.

"A drink, Detective?" Stephanie says. "Fiji water? Espresso? Something stronger?"

Does she think this is a date? "I'm okay," he replies.

Stephanie points to a fawn suede couch across from a gas fireplace, which she flicks on. In an instant, flames hop and pop. Hicks sits and she faces him, crossing her excellent legs. "I'm going to ask you a few questions about your relationship with Dr. Marx," he says. "How would you describe it?"

"I'm his support team right now," she replies, glad she chose that response yesterday when this meeting was arranged. "He needs a friend." She answers the question with a practiced laugh that glissandos from high to low, and I imagine mermaids luring sailors to their

death. One more reason to loathe this woman. I turn to Bob but see he's heading for the rocks.

"The Stephanies of the world intrigue me," he says.

"You too?" I sigh. I'd taken Bob for a guy who'd go more for a vet or a dental hygienist, like the fiancée he left behind.

"Please," he says. "Not my type. But I'm perennially fascinated by tenacity and nerve. Stephanie is out for Stephanie." He frowns. "But she's wasting this performance on Hicks."

Stephanie with her unearned air of superiority. "I hate her," I say.

"You should," he says, and his frown deepens.

I have never heard him fling one swear word. "Bob!" I say, delighted.

He shrugs. "I call it as it comes."

"When did your relationship with Dr. Marx begin?" Hicks asks, the slightest of smiles curving the corners of his lower lip. *I already know,* he thinks, *but it's more fun to hear it from you.*

"You mean our professional relationship?" This woman is bulletproof. Flinty. *Hicks is definitely into me,* she decides.

"Mrs. Joseph, let's not mess around."

"Ms.," she says in a practiced, sultry voice. "Mr. Joseph was my ex."

"*Ms.* Joseph, we're both busy people. Let's get on with this." Yesterday morning Hicks had another session with Barry, and last week round two in Chicago plus, one by one over the last month, interviews with two dozen coworkers—mine, Barry's, Lucy's. He doesn't need his chain yanked. He wants a break in the case, and his gut tells him Stephanie's got something he can use. What, he doesn't know. Each morning, his first thought is, *Intuition, call home.* "When did you and Barry Marx hook up?" Hicks takes out his black notebook and his pen.

When indeed? "It began after Dr. Marx's wife died."

My bullshit meter comes alive—*bleep, bleep, bleep!*—but I don't want to miss Hicks' reaction. *This broad is smiling too damn much,* he thinks. "You and Dr. Marx made regular calls beginning last fall," he says. A tickertape of calls. *Why would a smart woman like this think I wouldn't know about them?* he wonders.

"He's my doctor," Stephanie says, and in a practiced swish pushes away her shiny brown hair with its tortoiseshell streaks. "Those were professional conversations."

"Why did they generally take place at night or on the weekend?"

"I don't know about your physicians, Detective, but I'm happy to get a call back from mine anytime he feels like making one."

"What kind of condition required seven or nine phone calls a week?" Hicks says, allowing his impatience to show. "There's no record of his treating you."

"*Treating* her?" I say to Bob.

"Shhh," Bob says. "Listen."

"Okay, we started seeing each other last year," Stephanie admits.

A buzz saw slices through to the place where my heart used to be.

"Very casually," she adds, and sends Hicks a defiant look as she stretches out those words. "After his mother introduced us, I saw Barry in a restaurant, and one thing led to another. It took him months to admit he was married." *Faster than some,* I hear her think.

"Has he asked you to marry him?"

"Absurd." She laughs, although I hear her small-prayer that someday he will.

"So at this point you'd call this primarily a physical relationship?" Hicks decides to switch to not-so-good cop.

"He's single and I'm single. Do you have any idea how hard it is to meet someone decent in New York?"

Tell me about it, Hicks thinks. *I haven't had a real relationship in two years.*

"I saw an opportunity and I took it," Stephanie says. "I'm not especially proud of it, but I'm not going to do a guilt trip, either. Barry and I were attracted to each other. I'm not the first woman to hook up with a married man and I won't be the last. The last time I checked, this was still legal. It started before Mrs. Marx died, but"—she regrets that she gave up smoking, because a cigarette would add a certain vodka-and-caviar drama now—"so what?"

"Now, was that so hard?" Hicks asks.

It was for me. Any woman who suspects her husband is cheating always hopes hubby really did have seven business trips to Long Boat Key. The woman from high school he met for drinks *is* as big as an Aga stove. That copy of *Adultery for Beginners* belongs to his partner. Then the evidence plops on her head like pigeon poop. "I can't take this," I say to Bob.

"Buck up," he whispers. *Nothing pretty about self-pity,* he always says, along with *Coulda, shoulda, woulda—where does that get anyone?* In the Duration you learn that festering with regret changes not one thing. Had I reacted to Barry in life, I would have another story to tell, considering that the evidence of his infidelity was hiding in plain sight. I could go on and on with this line of reasoning, but Hicks has asked a question that's gotten my attention. "Tell me when you first met Mrs. Marx," he says.

"I can't—we never met."

BS!

"C'mon. Your children attend the same school."

"School's a big place," she answers, "where the nanny generally picks up Annabel Marx, who is not in the same class as my Jordan, and I'm not the room-mother type. No, we never met." *Molly Marx and I weren't technically introduced—I'm not lying,* Stephanie thinks while a memory flickers, an ember she stamps out in less time than it takes for her to blink. There was that shivery afternoon, murky as sludge. A day to forget.

"What did Dr. Marx say about his wife?" Hicks asks.

"Not much," she answers.

"Oh, come on, Ms. Joseph. Did he deny that he was married?"

"For a while he let me think he was single, but when I asked him point-blank, he practically boasted about his good marriage." *Which I took as a challenge,* she thinks.

"Did they have an understanding? Did she not get him?" *Poor complicated schmuck,* Hicks thinks.

"Actually," she says, "Dr. Marx said he was very, very attracted to me."

"Uh-huh," Hicks says coolly. "So now that your memory's returned, I'm wondering, where were you when Molly Marx was murdered?" The banter has turned as stiff as roadkill, and I believe his hushed tone is one of respect. Stephanie's holding back. Hicks knows it as well as he knows that she's not going to say any more. Not today. He can read it in the lightest twitch around her eye and the way she twists the silver ring that has replaced her wedding band.

"Who says she was murdered?" Stephanie asks.

"Ms. Joseph, the question," Hicks says. "Answer it."

"I must have been in town," she says, "because I remember hearing about it on the news that weekend."

"Dr. Marx says he saw you that night."

Why would Barry admit that, Stephanie wonders, *when we were both quite sure no one saw us and he paid for dinner in cash?* "We might have seen each other that night," she says.

"*Might have?* You don't remember dinner at Landmarc with Barry Marx the night his wife was left to bleed to death by the side of the road?"

I can't listen to this. But Bob gives me a look that says, *If you stay you might learn something.*

Lock me up for shagging and throw away the key, Stephanie thinks. "Okay, I had a bite with Dr. Marx. Very early in the evening. If we were trying to hide something, would we have gone to such a public place?" *There's a damn Whole Foods in the basement of the building, for God's sake.*

"Like I said, I'll ask the questions. Where did Dr. Marx think his wife was at that point?"

"I didn't ask." *I didn't care,* Stephanie thinks.

My bullshit detector, I've noticed, has stopped blaring.

"I think we're through here," Bob says kindly.

"I have to stay." My voice is barely audible.

"Are you sure that you hadn't met Mrs. Marx, ma'am?"

"Like I said, Detective, no." Stephanie is sounding tired, short-tempered, less sure.

"Where were you when Mrs. Marx was out biking the day of her death?" he asks.

"With my child," Stephanie answers. "At home."

Hicks lets the bad cop hammer away. Stephanie might be telling the truth. He can't prove otherwise.

"Please, Molly, can we leave?" Bob asks.

"Molly Marx has left the building." My mind is back in February, trying to put together the pieces.

Twenty-eight

GIVING AS GOOD AS SHE GETS

Is it possible that Barry and his mom had lunch this week at Bergdorf's?" Brie asked when she called a few days after Barry had returned from San Francisco.

"He didn't mention it," I said. "But yes, probably." Every few weeks, Barry and Kitty met at the tiny café folded as neatly as a pocket square into the third floor of the men's store. In fact, he'd arrived home the other day with a navy duchesse satin tie with small red squares and another in plum and silver stripes. Both had Kitty written all over them. "Why do you ask?"

"You know our office manager, who went to Barry for a consultation?"

"The one who got burnt because he suggested she have not just her nose done but a full lift?"

"That one—and for the record, Barry was right."

"So?"

"Barry didn't seem to recognize her."

"A lot of women go in and out of that office. Anyway, he waits for patients to say hello first. Confidentiality and all that. Your point is?"

"I overheard this woman giving a play-by-play to one of the secretaries all about the conversation Barry and Kitty supposedly had at Bergdorf's."

A wave of nausea rose in my stomach.

"Do you want to hear it?" Brie asked. Her voice had dropped.

No! "Sure, spill."

"You won't shoot the messenger?"

"Talk."

I could hear Brie take a deep breath. "Kitty told Barry she thinks *you* are cheating—something about a man's jacket squatting in your foyer like a dirty dog."

"Go on," I said as my queasiness built. I was afraid I was going to puke.

"Barry said something like, 'News flash—we just had wild, animal sex six hours ago and everything's fine in that department.'" Then this woman started laughing so hard I could hardly understand her, but I think she said Kitty answered, 'Now, there's a snapshot for the family album,' and 'Barry Joshua, love, I'm afraid you're missing the point.' "

"Is that it?" I hoped it was.

"No, she scolded him like he was a little boy. That's what this fly-on-the-wall thought was funniest. Said it was time for him to 'grow up and be part of his marriage'—he had a wife and a child and if he didn't pay attention, he was going to lose them both."

"More?" I asked.

"Just that she said, 'Don't be a fool.' Or something like that."

Brie waited for me to respond. When I did not, she added, "Molly, this woman might have the wrong guy or made it all up. She's the twit who started that rumor that I was dating one of the senior partners."

Brie *had* been dating that senior partner. "You're right. It could be some other Barry Joshua's mom telling him off."

"Does any of this make sense?"

"I'm not saying." My synonym for *Guilty, as charged.*

"Okay," Brie said, drawing out the word as if she were taking a long toke on a thick joint. "If you ever want to talk, you know I'm here. But Barry Joshua's mother was right on one thing. Don't be a fool."

As soon as *The Daily Show* ended that night, I picked up *New York*. For two days, I'd been trying to finish an exposé on moms who anonymously rat out other families' babysitters on isawyournanny.blogspot.com. I'd visited the site. Last time, one item was about a caregiver feeding kids Ho Hos instead of organic crackers, and another was about a nanny burping in restaurants like a twelve-year-old boy and coughing insults at fellow diners. But once in a while the description of a nanny's behavior made me want to run to Annabel's room, scoop her up, and promise that nothing bad would happen to her, ever. No bored, mean, trash-talking, cell-phone-obsessed nanny was going to swat my little girl.

"I pinch myself every day that we found Delfina," I said, turning to Barry, but his eyes stayed married to Letterman. "She's amazing, don't you think?"

Barry ignored me. At midnight he flicked off his light without so much as a mumbled goodnight. I moved on to the magazine's culture pages. After I'd started the same review three times, I put out my light as well, stretched under the freshly ironed white sheets, and rubbed my icy feet against Barry's. He stayed as still as a corpse. Moving closer, I laid my arm around his shoulders. "Sweet dreams," I murmured as I felt him shift away.

That morning married life had seemed copasetic, at least on the surface—a location from which our relationship too rarely experienced liftoff. Barry had arrived home late Sunday from San Francisco, bearing gifts: a gold cable car to start a charm bracelet for Annabel, an Alcatraz mug for Delfina, and a small jade box for me. Late that evening, as we finished a pizza and emptied a bottle of Chianti, he'd admitted that he had been nervous about his speech. I found this endearing; I enjoyed my husband most when his guard was down, especially if his ardor was up. We made love that night, gently, and this morning, passionately. But whatever goodwill had existed between us had apparently washed away like a signature in the sand.

"Anything you want to tell me?" I said mildly, staring into the darkness.

"Or you tell me?" Barry answered a few moments later from the west coast of the bed, his voice low and controlled.

That I'm in a chronic state of being crazy pissed at you and disappointed by you, but I've forfeited my right to bitch by being a complete harlot, and on that count I am oozing—no, make that exploding—with regret for my appalling lack of judgment.

"You might want to know I am fully aware of the fact that you weren't alone in San Francisco" was all I said. I despised myself for having the hubris to accuse Barry, especially since I wasn't 100 percent certain about this.

"Come on! If you're talking about the patient who coached me, she's just a friend," he said, as if he'd been expecting an attack. "She was out on the coast visiting her brother. I thought I should say thank you. I took her to dinner." *Big deal,* his tone said.

I decided to drop my bomb. "One of many meals, I see, based on last year's Amex. I'm especially intrigued about the bar bills on those nights when you told me you were chaperoning at the temple's shelter. Was it Take a Homeless Guy to the Ritz-Carlton Month?"

"I can see where you'd want to steer the conversation away from yourself," he said, drily, "given what went down here this weekend."

"Excuse me?"

"You know what I'm talking about."

Did he have Alphonso the doorman on the payroll? Much as he revered his mother, based on Brie's recycled rumors I couldn't believe that he didn't have doubts.

"You said you wanted to talk," I said, "so let's. That is, unless you'd rather move on to your cell phone bills."

Outside, I heard dogs barking. But in our bedroom there was only silence, not counting the thrum of rage and guilt that pulsed through my brain. Barry. Luke. Luke. Barry. The compartments each tidily lived in had collapsed. After minutes—two or ten, I couldn't say—Barry turned on his lamp, walked to the closet, and from a sport coat hanging toward the back took out a pack of cigarettes. He returned to the bed, lit one, and inhaled, blowing blue smoke into the dim light.

"When did you start smoking again?"

"There are a lot of things you don't know," he said, and laughed. "Like that women throw themselves at me all the time. Patients, strangers, your friends."

"You poor, defenseless guy."

"Sometimes I respond, I admit it. But here's the thing—it means nothing. Less than nothing. Zilch."

"You're telling me that being with other women is just some sort of uncontrollable tic, like cracking your knuckles?" I let indignation flood the room, while I tried to ignore another version of myself that circled above, chanting "hypocrite" at the angry, self-righteous wife sitting up in bed, her nightgown falling off one shoulder. That Luke meant something to me, that I thought I loved him—did any of this make it better or different? Holier, perhaps? As I started to shake, tears fell on the blanket.

Barry put out his cigarette in the silver dish he kept on his nightstand. He got up, walked around to my side, pulled me to his chest, and cleared his throat. "Here's the only thing you need to know. You're everything to me," he said. "Correction. You and Annabel." He started to stroke my hair. "Maybe I haven't been the husband I should be. No, let me rephrase. I haven't been the husband I should be. I've been a schmuck. What I need to know is, will you forgive me?"

I felt as ready for this confession as I might be for a full body search at the dry cleaner. Were his words hollow or sincere, true or false, a stall tactic or a miracle breakthrough?

"I'm not sure what I'd be forgiving you for, exactly," I said, hiccupping.

"Don't ask me to elaborate," he said. "Tell me what you want from me, and I'll come through."

I thought I might be reading genuine anguish on Barry's face. "What I want you to do is talk to me," I pleaded. "To share a little of the real you"—whoever he is. Why didn't all men realize that, at least for every woman I knew, being listened to and revealing a secret truth or two is always the ultimate aphrodisiac? Luke got this. Why didn't my husband? Or did he share his dreams and hopes and fears and zany insights only with other women?

"We talk all the time," he said.

"But we don't," I answered wearily. "I don't know that we've ever had a real conversation that didn't relate to your work or Annabel or if the steak should be medium or medium rare."

"Oh, come on. Now you're being ridiculous. Throw me a bone here."

"It might take time," I said. It was definitely not anguish, I decided, that I was reading on Barry's face, at least not anymore. Could he be scared that I was going to blow his cover?

I'd suddenly become so tired I couldn't say or listen to another word. From a few blocks away, the bell of the church chimed once. I stood and grabbed my pillow. "I'm sleeping in the other room," I announced. Barry didn't stop me.

I woke to the smell of freshly brewed hazelnut coffee. Barry was standing next to the couch with two steaming mugs in hand. "Good morning," he said. He kissed me softly on the cheek. His hair was still wet from the shower, and in his face I could see the college senior I'd met almost seventeen years earlier.

"We need to get ourselves to a therapist." The words tumbled out of me, unexpected. "I heard of someone who's supposed to be good." I'd been carrying Felicia Stafford's name and number in my wallet for more than a year.

"If that's what you want, I'm in," Barry said. "Now get that adorable butt into the kitchen, or you're going to miss my pancakes."

Twenty-nine

KOI OR GIRL?

I've decided," Brie says. "I definitely want a baby."

Isadora's face, reflected in the glass of their kitchen cabinets, remains composed. As she reaches for the plates she keeps her back turned to Brie. "What makes you so sure you'll be a good mama?"

"Absolutely nothing," Brie admits.

I wish Brie knew, as I do, that she would be the finest of mothers. Before I died, Barry and I were still debating whom to pick to be Annabel's legal guardian, and Brie was my first choice. I'd have lobbied harder on her behalf if my decision wouldn't have insulted my parents and Lucy. I can't think of better guardians than my parents, but they live far away. And Lucy? Her advanced degree in early childhood development notwithstanding, after a year with my sister, Annabel might require after-school psychotherapy instead of ballet.

Barry wanted Kitty to be Annabel's guardian—"because Annabel's life could continue as it is." True, except that Kitty would send her to fat camp before she digested her first Oreo, and possibly destroy all proof that I was her mother. So the guardian issue remains unresolved. Like so much.

"What kind of mother do you think you'd be?" Brie asks.

Isadora takes two square black plates from the shelf and places them on the honed stone counter where Brie is sitting. From a metal basket she selects a large tangerine and starts to peel it with a sharp mother-of-pearl-handled knife. The rind, which perfumes the air with its fresh scent, snakes into a ribbon as she does the job with artistic precision. "Frightening," she says. "I'm exacting, self-involved, and impatient. Isn't that what you love about me?"

"Seriously, Isadora. You're not hearing me. I want a baby."

Isadora delicately dissects the denuded fruit and begins to slice segments into bite-sized pieces. An amused smile remains on her ageless, symmetrical face. "Do you plan to jet off to Malawi and claw one out of some impoverished woman's womb?"

"I want to get pregnant. That is, unless you'd rather carry our child."

"Have you totally lost your mind?" I do love Isadora's teeth—small, even, white as china. She laughed for so long I got an excellent view of them.

"You're not too old—you're only thirty-nine."

"That's the least of it. I'd rather have liposuction without anesthesia. The species will have to propagate without my help."

"Then I'll be the pregnant one—with your egg, if you want, implanted in my uterus. Done all the time." Brie never stints on research.

"*Mi amada,*" Isadora says, and leans over to cup Brie's firm, pointed chin, the type that gets called "stubborn." "I love our life. Sleeping late, running away to Paris and Barcelona and Buenos Aires, me spoiling you, you spoiling me. Why give any of it up for a *bebé*? And what if that little egg and sperm grew a penis? Could you honestly see me as the mother of some midget jock? Go back to bed and wake up sane."

Brie stands and washes her plate and coffee cup. Even without my powers I know her well enough to realize she's going to table this topic—for now. "Maybe I'm just premenstrual," she says lightly. "You're right—I must be nuts to ever suggest bringing anything as messy as a third party into our life." The remarkable thing is that Brie is able to speak without a scintilla of sarcasm while the words *sybarite* and *indolent brat* flip through her brain. She knows how to bide her time, something I never learned to do.

So I'm surprised when only two nights later she raises the topic again. The two of them are eating at Koi, where the ceilings are as high as the prices. They're seated in a booth, taut thighs touching, ignoring the crowd. I find this hard to do, since obviously everyone here must pass a rigorous grooming and attractiveness test before they check their coats. At their banquette, Isadora selects a tiny rice block blanketed with very spicy, very fresh tuna—mercury levels be damned—and reaches to put the tiny orange delicacy into Brie's mouth.

Brie pushes it away. "Stop for a minute, please."

"Not hungry?"

"We need to continue our conversation."

"Need?"

"Okay, *want*—about the baby."

"What baby?"

"The one you don't want."

"That baby."

"We could adopt, but I'd rather be pregnant," Brie says. "I have to at least try to be a mother." *Molly wants me to have a baby,* I hear her think. It's crazy, the thoughts that we in the Duration hear attributed to us, but I am flattered and intrigued.

Isadora moves on to eggplant, whose glistening purple-black skin matches her inscrutable eyes. After the eggplant disappears, she lazily alternates between sesame-encrusted lobster tail, sautéed asparagus, and shiitake mushrooms, licking her full lips as she samples each one.

"Aren't you going to talk to me?" Brie asks. Apparently not. Isadora is Barry in drag.

"What is there to talk about?" Isadora finally says, defiant. "You know my position. I'm not going to debate or defend myself. I never deceived you. This is who I am. It's me or this mythical baby. Pick, my darling."

"Won't you even consider it?" Brie says, her voice silky smooth.

Isadora rests her chopsticks and meets Brie's gaze. "I had a baby," she says. "In my marriage to Pedro. Had the child lived, she would now be twenty. The *bebé* tore me apart in every way. I know this bloody experience, and now I have earned the right to be a hedonist. I want my decadent life where every day I wake up and think, *What would make me happy? What would make Sabrina happy?* I would like this life with you,

love, but if not, not." Isadora clips every sentence as if she is pruning a rosebush.

I have always been immune to feeling anything toward Isadora except envy, but as I try to make room for empathy, my bullshit detector blares. What a crock. Not the part about Pedro—Isadora was married once, for fourteen months. But there was never a child, not even in Isadora's imagination or in the head of Pedro, which was filled with coke. I want to rattle Brie by the shoulders. I want to send her a harsh wake-up-toots-and-smell-the-bullshit psychogram, a ranting celestial e-mail.

"Honey," Brie says, all sympathy, "why didn't you ever say anything?"

Isadora casts down her eyes, as if she is exercising enormous self-control to maintain dignity.

"Why did you keep this a secret from me?" Brie asks again, taking Isadora's hand.

Isadora removes her hand.

They finish their meal without talking, without sipping a drop of warm, soothing sake. Brie pays the bill, which is steep. I follow them home. Isadora goes directly to bed, while Brie stays up until three, her mind racing. Why can't I be a dancing moonbeam who points her toward the truth? At the very least I long to haunt Brie's dreams, but Bob reminds me, time and again, that such behavior violates the Duration's bylaws, unwritten but transmitted on faith, and will terminate my powers. I can take no credit, then, for the conversation between Brie and Isadora the following week.

"I've made up my mind," Brie says at midnight on the fourth of a series of rainy days and nights. "I need to be in a relationship where having a baby is at least a possibility." She offers these words with tremendous tenderness, after many days of sleepwalking.

Isadora accepts the news without theatrics, but this time I feel compassion for a woman who has bargained and lost. I have searched her heart and believe she loves Brie. Now Isadora will have to search again for her matching sybarite.

When Brie returns from work the next day, Isadora is gone, along with her considerable library of books about twentieth-century art, early jazz, and contemporary architecture, her exquisite bags and

hand-cobbled shoes, her Fendi furs and four-carat diamond studs, her elegant fruit knives and black bone china. Brie has twice as much storage space and an even larger vacancy in her heart, but she doesn't look back. "Molly," she says out loud now, because there is no one to hear her and tell her she is *loca,* "I can feel you guiding me."

She is wrong. The decision was entirely her own.

A few weeks later, Brie rescues Jones, a year-old chocolate Lab, and her apartment is overrun with squeaky toys, organic dog food, and sloppy kisses.

Thirty

THEIR STORIES AND THEY'RE STICKING TO THEM

et's go over this once more," Hicks says. "Your relationship to Molly Marx was—"

"Professional."

"And?"

"Okay, personal—for a while, off and on—but any . . ."—Luke fishes for a word—"intimacy between us was over well before she died."

Intimidation, intestines, indigestion, intifada, intimacy. Could Luke possibly make what went on between us sound colder and uglier?

"Mr. Delaney, the last call Mrs. Marx got was from you, and as I like to remind folks, half the truth is a big fat lie." *This guy's giving me nothing,* I hear Hicks think. *The husband, he's one more doctor who mistakes himself for God. But Delaney—something doesn't add up.* "What did you two talk about that day?"

"I don't recall."

This isn't a lawyer-coached response. It's true. Just as I can't tell you if I put 1 percent or 2 percent milk into my coffee the day I died, Luke has no recollection of cross-the-t-dot-the-i specifics of what went on that day. "My guess is we discussed work."

Until today I've never mustered the courage to witness conversa-

tions between Hicks and Luke. I've been too raw, too confused, and entirely too chickenshit. As they face each other, Hicks towers over Luke, whom I'd always thought of as tall but who now looks not just shorter but older. He could use a posture lesson from my mother: *Shoulders back, chin up, darling.* The blue-gray shadows under his eyes may as well be tattoos, and he appears gaunt and more in need of a haircut than usual. His apartment is worse. Bathroom towels are funky and askew and his hockey equipment hides under a layer of dust in which I could easily scrawl my name if the Duration allowed such folly. Except for some Major Grey's mango chutney whose sell-by date most likely is older than the Colonial occupation, the refrigerator is empty. Luke's freezer, however, is stocked—with Stolichnaya, Absolut, and three vodkas labeled in Cyrillic, as well as Cherry Garcia and Dulce de Leche, unopened.

Since my body left this world in its lumpy radiance, Luke has accepted every job that's come his way, even the one in Sheboygan. Any escape has been better than New York City. But this explains only some of his home's disarray. He's not just backed up in his domesticity but deeply, profoundly sad—guilty and sad.

One of Hicks' more successful techniques is to say nothing and hope that whoever he's grilling will interrupt the discomfort with a shocking disclosure. He has a 62 percent success rate with this ploy, but not today. "There was a time when I loved Molly deeply and she loved me back," Luke says. "I will not deny that. I treasure the memories." Not that Luke lets himself take out those images, carefully archived deep in his mental hard drive. "But before that time, and after it—and during it—we were also colleagues. That's what we were when she died."

Colleagues who wanted to be something more, Hicks thinks. He focuses on how pitiful Luke sounds, but what I notice is that Luke's brain uses the present tense. *Molly and I love each other deeply.* As my ninth-grade English teacher said, there's power in grammar.

"I once thought, for a few weeks at least, that we should and would be together permanently." Two old people making sure the other takes their Lipitor and Avapro, loving the wrinkles in each other's faces, and finding lost reading glasses. "I hated that because of some cosmic

snafu we didn't meet until after she was already married." *To that schmuck.*

"If only we'd met sooner, everything would be different"—the bumper sticker of every cheating man, Hicks thinks. *But I don't care what an asshole a husband is—only a weak, sniffling sonofabitch goes after another guy's wife. And I know this because I've been that weakling.*

This last musing of Hicks' interests me, almost as much as what Luke is thinking: *Molly was married to a man who didn't appreciate her, a man who never got her at all.*

"Did the two of you plan to be together?" Hicks asks.

"Never," Luke says emphatically, and too reflexively for my liking. "You and I have gone over this so many times. I was pure diversion. Molly would never have left her husband." *At least not for me.* "Although I'd be lying if I didn't admit I had the occasional fantasy about winding up together." *We'd have moved to a brownstone, maybe in Brooklyn, where I could see us cooking decadent pastas and me walking Annabel to the public school down the street, teaching her to take pictures and to sing Christmas carols when we'd visit my parents in New Hampshire. On the weekends when Annabel visited Barry, Molly and I would be all over each other, and barely crawl out of bed.*

Hicks' mind is roaming as well, to what happened to one lovely Lola. *Man, was I out of my league with her,* he remembers. He conjures this woman—more cultured, more educated, and infinitely more married than he. After his nonstarter Franny fantasies, Lola and he were a couple, sporadically and secretly, for four years. But Hicks never felt he had as much to offer her as he believed this goddess deserved, never begged for Lola to leave her chump husband. Then, *poof,* over—for Lola but not for him.

Luke fuckin' Delaney's got Lola stamped all over him. This Hicks knows.

Hicks can have his sashay down memory lane, but I don't want to stroll along with him. I'm weighing the knowledge he's convinced of— that Luke's still in love with me. It's an enormous ego stroke to believe this, but I've decided it's also revisionist history. Luke and I didn't make big plans, and a lot of that had to do with me, because I liked our togetherness with a dreamy patina, not the five o'clock shadow of real-

ity. He never begged me to reinvent my life. Luke toyed with me, not the other way around. This is my story and I'm sticking to it, at least when I'm thinking that I'd be alive today had I not accepted that lethal pink flamingo drink from Luke, if we'd never danced, if we'd only been in Buffalo, not on Expense Account Island.

"Who ended things between you two?"

Luke clears his throat with a sound between a sigh and a groan. "The relationship ran its course. We both got tired of the lying and dis-appointment, the frustration and the subterfuge, the high drama. We moved on."

Except you haven't, Hicks decides. *Molly Marx is gnawing like a ter-mite on that wooden heart of yours.* "And after that?"

"Detective, I spend every minute running away from my regrets. Every time the phone rings, I expect it to be Molly springing some bril-liant idea on me for one of our shoots. I try to trick myself into think-ing that she's just temporarily out of my life."

How's that working for you? Hicks wonders. He leans back on the leather couch and takes stock of the room, which could be comfortable were it clean. He can picture me here, taking a stemless wineglass from the tray on the sideboard, opening a decanter, and sharing a glass of decent Syrah with Luke Delaney, the kind of guy women think of as sensitive. *He's currently such a holy mess, it's not fair to judge him as a world-class lover. And as a killer? Could be. Every damn answer is vague and slippery and he has no good alibi. Zippo.*

Despite this, Hicks hasn't come on with a full frontal attack. With Luke, Hicks is Mr. Softie. Maybe it's a been-there-done-that guy thing.

"I don't believe she's gone," Luke continues. "Sometimes I go up to the park and sit and could swear that she's still there."

I am. A lot. I see him watching, waiting, wasting himself on emo-tions as useless as expired MetroCards.

"I think I'm going to see her walking or on her bike, that this is all a grotesque fuck-up."

Hicks decides on this point Luke might be speaking from the heart, because that's how it was for him until finally the big Lola boom faded to an echo. One day, Hicks realized that Lola was no longer the first thing he thought about each dawn and the last thing each night. He

could listen to Marvin Gaye again, and other women started to look quite fine. But it took forever. He's only gotten there now, this year.

Then Hicks snaps back. "When did Dr. Marx find out about you two?"

"Barry Marx? He didn't." *Shit. Was he on to us?* Luke feels the same sickness in his belly that for the last few weeks has kept him from pouring his good or even his not-so-good vodka or breaking into the ice cream.

"You know that for a fact?" Hicks asks.

"No," Luke admits. *This detective is messing with me. Or maybe not. Could Barry have found out,* he's thinking. *Then what?*

"So how'd she die, Delaney?" Hicks' face is so close I wonder if Luke will turn away. He does not.

"I do a head trip about that day and night, Detective."

"Did she kill herself because she felt so damn guilty about you?"

Luke wonders, *Is this policeman mocking me?* "I doubt everything about what you just said—that she killed herself, to begin with." Luke makes this point with dignity, and I am proud he has found some.

"So it was an accident?"

Luke takes his time. "Not necessarily."

"Then say it," Hicks all but hisses. "Murder? Say it."

Luke can't. "That's my vision, and it haunts me."

"Is Barry Marx in this vision?" Hicks takes out his black notebook and his black pen. I hate to think the detective investigating my case can sit across from the big passion in my life and write only the skeptical, critical things I see him scribble about Luke. I miss Luke so much I feel almost physically capable of crying real tears.

"Oh yeah," Luke says. "He is."

Thirty-one

SECOND OPINION

I wish I'd known her," Brie whispered, as awed as the rest of the crowd in this garnet-walled gallery.

Brie and I were at the Met, headed now toward the curator's prize. There she hung, *Madame X*.

"What do you suppose she's thinking?" Brie asked.

" 'My boobs are better than yours'?" The woman's pearly skin shone against a black gown that would have been scandalous on any catwalk in any century. *Madame* wore a bemused smile, her profile turned away from contemporary admirers. I had rarely seen such an arrogant pose. In her day, this woman was considered to be quite the babe. Now, instead of having a sitting with John Singer Sargent, she'd see Barry about that nose.

"What I'd give to have her tutor me in the womanly arts," Brie said.

"Like you need help," I said.

"Do I have to remind you that the last man in my life was a lot more Norman Bates than Carl Jung?"

Brie's most recent suitor had, indeed, given new meaning to the profession of *psycho*analyst. I'd learned not to get Dr. Demented started on fat people who drove up American health care costs.

"Anyway, I've met someone new," Brie said as we moved to the next painting.

"Tell me," I answered, giving most of my attention to a moody rendering of four exquisitely dressed American girls whose fortunate genetic gene toss allowed them to be raised in Paris, not a midwestern suburb closer to Best Buy than a *boulangerie*. I knew this painting well. It had been covered in the art history course where I met Barry.

"He's a she," Brie said. "A gorgeous she." She brushed the hair off her face and tried to look blasé. I could tell she was anything but.

"Excuse me?" I said, spinning away from the portrait. "When did you switch teams? You haven't been without a man for, what, more than six months of the last sixteen years? I've always thought you should have a catch-and-release policy."

"I say it's high time for another gender."

I deposited myself on a bench. "Who is she?" *A venture capitalist? Titled Englishwoman? Cartoon princess? More importantly, will I like her?* When you're lucky enough to be a grown-up with a very best girlfriend, the idea of sharing her with another woman feels uncomfortably close to cuckoldry.

"She's my architect," she said. "Isadora Vega." The syllables rolled off Brie's tongue as if she were savoring a rich, decadent sauce. "Dark hair, big eyes that are almost purple, bigger brain, *muy Latina.*"

"The type Pedro Almodóvar would cast as the lead in a film?"

"A Velázquez Venus."

In silent agreement, the two of us stopped looking at portraits and began to search for one of the museum's cafés, not even stopping to browse among the minimalls of posters, umbrellas, and too-cute wine corks. We wove in and out of the building's familiar chambers as if led on a leash. "My treat," I said as we arrived at a small cafeteria overlooking Central Park, where in the late afternoon light I could see more leaves on the lawn than on the trees. Waving Brie away as I got out my wallet, I paid for two glasses of wine and followed Brie to a table by the window, thinking how she was always, literally, a step ahead of not just me but every other woman I knew.

"To . . . whatever," I said as we toasted.

"To happy surprises," Brie said, and offered up ten more minutes

of juicy, girl-crush details. Lingerie shopping for the same bra size, double entendres, identical taste in Italian shoes.

As I listened, I debated whether to drop my own bomb. It was an afternoon for shocks, and Brie would be the last person to judge me for seeing a man who wasn't my husband. When my glass was almost empty, I said, "Since we're talking about relationships, I need your advice."

"What's Barry done now?" Brie's face was flushed with excitement and fair-to-middling chardonnay.

"Not Barry."

"Ah, Lucy, then?" Brie, who didn't have a sister, typically took the position that Lucy was guilty until proven innocent.

"Not Luce," I said in a low, conspiratorial voice.

"I give up, but for the record, I've suspected something's not right."

"How so?" For the last few months, I'd felt as if I could have won Best Actress for my convincing portrayal of a contented wife and mother.

"You forgot my birthday."

"No!" I said. But the next day was Thanksgiving, and Brie was born on November 17. Months earlier I'd bought her an antique magnifying glass hanging on a silver chain. I realized it remained stowed and wrapped, ready to present with a blank birthday card on which I had planned to copy a quote appropriate for a thirty-fifth birthday: "Life is really simple, but we insist on making it complicated."

"I had to celebrate with Isadora," Brie said, still playful. "Cocktail after cocktail. That's how things got rolling, so if you don't like it, blame yourself."

After I extravagantly apologized for the birthday gaffe, Brie moved on to a giddy account of the couple's first kiss and how Isadora slept over. And over. Now she was moving in.

"Enough about me—let's get back to you," Brie eventually said. "What's going on?"

I began regretting that I'd opened the door to talking about Luke. Brie was, I decided, too in the thrall of new romance, caught up with herself and herself alone. Not only did I doubt her current judgment, it also didn't seem fair to try to dim her bright light. Besides, continuing to keep our relationship all my own allowed me to believe that Luke and

I existed in an alternate universe with flattering light and an endless loop of mutual admiration. This was a place where I would prefer to stay.

"Molly, what's going on?" she repeated.

"Oh, nothing."

Brie tilted back her sleek head and laughed. "We've established that it's not nothing."

"Just forget it."

"Molly?"

"Okay, I'm seeing another man." As I blurted this out, my eyes fixed on an almost naked tree outside, I could swear that some other woman was speaking. "It started by accident." I was feeling like quite the fool.

Brie whistled softly. "Since when?"

"Since a while ago."

"I get it. You're not going to give me specifics. But play fair—tell me something."

I took a deep breath and exhaled words in a whoosh. "As long as it's lasted, he's made me feel like I am the most desirable woman on earth. When we're together I feel beautiful and impossibly clever, like I'm starring in my own movie."

"What does he look like?"

"An Irish poet." Brie nodded in appreciation. "He takes away all my anxiety, all my depression."

"Other women go shopping for that."

"And did I mention the sex?"

"But no, my friend has to get a little something on the side," Brie interrupted again to say, not unkindly, "Is he anyone I know?"

"No!" I lied. "Don't ask for details. Please. And stop smiling—this isn't as hilarious as you may think."

"Why are you offering up these crumbs now?"

Brie wasn't taking my confession nearly as seriously as I'd hoped and expected. I didn't want to admit that the impulse to blab about Luke must have come straight from some misguided desire to show that I, too, had a reckless anything-for-love stripe.

"You haven't decided to leave Barry?" Brie asked. The unspoken words in that sentence were *I hope.*

"Not at all," I said. "I've never imagined that this man"—the thought of calling Luke my lover seemed beyond pretentious, as if this movie I was starring in were Italian—"and I will wind up together, much as I care about him, which I do." Very much so, something Brie doesn't seem to understand. "He's not just a boy toy."

The afternoon sun was gone, and I could see myself, tense and trembling, reflected in the window glass.

"Please don't tell me this is the guy Kitty heard about," Brie said, wincing. "Please."

I stared at Brie. "Do you think I've completely lost it?" Now I really wanted this conversation to end, even if I'd started it. Talking out loud about what I had with Luke had cheapened it.

Brie didn't speak for what felt like minutes. "You're not asking me what I think, but I presume that's why you've brought this up, so I won't sugar-coat," she said finally. "I believe you care about . . . him . . . and I know that things at home aren't exactly in your target zone for perfection, but listen. An affair is never the answer. I say this from having been on the other side, numerous times."

I reached into my pocket and blotted my eyes with a tissue.

"End it—you've had your fun." Brie's tone was gentle, yet unyielding. "You'll kick yourself later if you make any other choice."

I'd counted on Brie for a warm, chummy response, maybe even a winking congratulation, not this. I felt as if she were adding two and two and insisting the answer was five. Didn't she understand that removing Luke from my life right now would be like switching from color to black and white?

"Get out," Brie said, grasping my hand.

Blinking with skepticism, I just looked outside.

"You've done harder," she said.

I had no idea what she was talking about. Nothing in my life had felt nearly as hard as the idea of never again being with Luke.

"We don't pick the people we fall in love with," Brie continued. "If this other man is the one you want to be with, I'm thrilled for you. Go ahead and blow up your life tomorrow to be with him. I'll be there for you. But if you're not willing to do that, your marriage can't get better if he's taking up all the space in your head."

No wonder Brie became a lawyer. She is painfully logical.

This conversation had ended. The two of us started to weave back through the maze of galleries, down the grand steps toward the coat check. Usually we made an obligatory stop to gasp at the ten-foot urns of two-thousand-dollar seasonal flowers. Not today.

I kissed Brie goodbye, hailed a taxi, and sleepwalked through Annabel's dinner, bath, and bedtime story. While Barry howled at YouTube clips, I set the table for the next day's parade-watching brunch, heaping branches and acorns into a centerpiece notches below my usual standard. The result all but screamed, *Paging Martha Stewart.* I gave thanks for the fact that the food for the brunch was being delivered, all the while trying to sell myself on cutting Luke loose. He would be arriving home that night, and in our last e-mails we'd made a date for Monday. I only had to pull the trigger.

But I needed fortification, and regretted, not for the first time, that I wasn't an alcoholic, a pillhead, or a follower of a calming New Age belief system. When I heard Barry start his shower, I decided to seek another opinion and picked up the phone.

"Free at last?" I said.

"Do you really have to ask that question of a teacher? Turkeys are gobbling in my dreams. Want to know what they're saying?"

"Save it—I only have two minutes and I need some instant advice." I heard water blast in the bathroom and Barry belting out "A Hard Day's Night," but I whispered nonetheless. "Remember that other guy I told you about?"

"The one I said you should stop seeing?"

"I didn't." I told Lucy my guilt had been exploding—I couldn't do this anymore.

"You're asking Lucy to open her psychiatric booth?" my sister said. "I'm honored."

Barry walked into the bedroom, a towel wrapped around his lean torso. "Who you talking to?" he mouthed.

"Lucy."

"Hello, Moosey," he shouted as he pulled on clean boxers and walked out of the room.

"Do you realize how much I despise that husband of yours?" she said.

"We don't have much time. What would you do? Quick."

"I'd call it off," she said. "Not worth it. At least, that's what I would do."

On Thanksgiving afternoon, Isadora left by two and Brie finished helping me clean up after forty-two guests, half of whom were under the age of five and had perched on my windowsills to get eyeball to eyeball with Snoopy. When they saw the monster-sized balloons, only three children had complete meltdowns. Fortunately, this year Annabel was not among them.

"I hope you don't hate me for being frank the other day," Brie said. "Was I a bitch?"

"An honest, sensible bitch." I surveyed my kitchen and tied the last gigantic bag of garbage, put my ceramic turkey-embossed platter on the highest shelf, and turned to hug Brie. "I just hate that you might be right."

Thirty-two

A FINE KETTLE OF FISH

During the past week, Brie started dialing the number four times. Today she lets it ring twice before she once again aborts her mission. The moment she puts down the receiver, the phone trills.

"What's on your mind?" Hicks says when she picks up.

"Detective?"

"I figure that you and your lady either want to ask me to dinner"— *or a threesome*—"or you have something to confess."

"On the first count, my partner moved out two weeks ago," Brie says as Jones stands before her, waiting for one more maniacal toss of his favorite chew toy. Brie flings the slimy hot dog across the room.

Hicks feels a twinge of guilt about the fleeting threesome fantasy. "Sorry to hear that," he says, shifting to strictly polite.

"I'm not," Brie says. She has empty spots in her cupboard and closet, but her heart is healing fast. "And on the second . . ." She looks at the picture of the two of us that she's restored to the bookshelf after its Isadora-enforced hiatus. We were twenty-one, prettier than we realized, clinking Champagne flutes on a *bateau-mouche*. Big hair, big dreams. "There's something that might be something. I was hoping we could meet. Please wait a second, and I'll get my BlackBerry."

"Whoa, you're going to squeeze me in between litigation and a manicure? I've got a case to solve, woman. What's wrong with now?"

Brie hadn't expected *now*. Now, she tells herself, is overbooked. Brie believes she's moved on from Isadora, and I can vouch for the fact that she's willed herself not to think about her, a decision reinforced by staying as busy as possible. Now is when Brie had planned to take Jones to the dog run and also when she hasn't yet washed her hair, since she's just returned from ninety minutes at the gym with the trainer she's booked, after which she visited three specialty grocers. All the ingredients for crawfish étouffée, starring a pound of startlingly pink crawfish she had FedExed from Louisiana, are waiting on the counter, since learning to cook is also on her agenda for now, along with calling her mother and reading last month's issue of the *Economist*.

"I'm waiting, Ms. Lawson," Hicks says.

Jones returns, panting for yet another toss. To make sure she gets the message, he barks, loudly and continuously.

"Dog-sitting?"

"No," Brie says. "Jones is all mine. He's the new love of my life, and he desperately needs to burn some energy."

"Same here," Hicks answers. "I'll meet you."

Hicks must be getting nowhere on Molly's case if he's this eager to see me, I hear Brie think. She almost feels sorry for the guy. Then her eye lands on our picture. Her mind switches to me and it makes her both happy and sad to think of meeting Hicks. "Can you be in Union Square at one?" she says.

Hicks smiles; maybe he'll get a break. He sees the pieces of my case spinning in midair, UFOs smacking him in the head. By default, it's looking more and more to him as if my death was random rotten, an accident of dumb luck or the handiwork of a long-gone lunatic who ran me off the road. He's ruled out suicide, which he doesn't think I had the skill set, or sufficient torment, to implement.

For the last week, at eight or nine o'clock, when Hicks turns off the light in his bare-bones office, he's entertained cutting bait, thinking he'll just have to move on and hope to be anointed supersleuth for some other case in the future. I have heard him apologize to me: "Sorry, Molly, no breakthroughs today."

Then all night I'm in his dreams, begging him to figure out how I

wound up dead. *Go*, Hicks, I plead. Please! I'm counting on the Hiawatha Express. I'm praying for it. Someone has to figure out the whys and how-comes to explain why I now reside in the Duration. Down there, I can only hope that you and perhaps you alone are feeling my anger, which roils inside me along with guilt and pain and longing.

During the night, Hicks wakes several times to read his latest library book—this week's is by Cormac McCarthy—or to simply stare at the ceiling or out the window, toward the bodega where his friend Marco sells lottery tickets. The next day while Hicks shaves, he glances in the mirror and decides he looks like hell. Then he usually talks to me. "Molly Marx, tell me what happened, girl. There's got to be an answer." He'll stop to buy his newspapers from Marco, takes the train to his office, and thinks the same thing while he tries to concentrate on the *Post* and the *Daily News*. When he walks into the precinct, he makes a fresh pot of coffee, chews through his files a few times, picks the brains of Detective Gonzalez and the other big and little kahunas nearby, and makes more calls, more appointments. Every few days he walks again down by the river, hoping to find some crumbs that will lead him to the answer.

Hicks has been investigating my case for five months. He needs a break.

"Deal," he says to Brie. "I'll meet you by Charlie, that cheese dealer from Rensselaer County." Charlie's a redneck who knows his Emmental from his Gruyère.

"See you in forty-five minutes," Brie says.

On Saturday, as you stroll the Greenmarket, you can practically smell the succulent meals that will be prepared that night. I had forgotten how much I loved it here. The Marx family always ate well the day I pedaled to the Greenmarket. I'd fill my basket with round, crusty breads; sugar-sweet baby vegetables; buttery lettuces, good black earth still clinging to their leaves; tomatoes exploding with juice; oatmeal-raisin cookies the size of my hand; and always, a huge bouquet of whatever flowers sang out, *Buy me, baby, buy me.*

Hicks gets there early, as I do. He is off duty, looking even more princely in cords and boots than in his finely tailored workaday clothes, the ones that are more expensive than the other guys on the force realize. He heads to one of the biggest stands, deliberates over

seven kinds of potatoes, and finally buys fingerlings, selecting each slender, pale gold jewel one by one.

"How are you going to cook those?" Brie asks, walking up beside him. Despite her firm hand on Jones' leash, the pup jumps up and leaves a dirty paw print on Hicks' heavy gray zippered sweater. "Oh, I am so sorry," she says, yanking away Jones as she brushes the mud off his sweater.

Hicks feels a spark of . . . something. *My luck that she prefers women,* he says to himself. *Don't think about her that way, fool.*

"This guy definitely needs a crash course at obedience school," Brie says.

Hicks laughs. "Don't most men?" He strokes Jones' warm, smooth back. "You like potatoes, huh, boy?"

"He likes everything. He's going to be a hippo when he grows up."

I doubt that, Hicks thinks. He considers how people choose animals that resemble them. This dog's going to be long and leggy, like Brie Lawson, who he has decided looks a lot less brittle in a pair of faded Levi's and a down vest than she does in her uptown attorney togs. "C'mon," Hicks says. "I need some fresh herbs to roast these."

"Show me," she says. "I know nothing."

"That I can't believe, smart lawyer like you."

"Hey, if it wasn't on the bar exam . . ."

"So, you have something to tell me?" he says, leading Brie and Jones to a small booth for dainty, string-tied bunches of rosemary, oregano, and thyme. He lifts some rosemary to Brie's nose and she breathes in its earthy fragrance.

"I doubt it's anything," she says tentatively, her eyes fixed on the herbs. It's hard for Brie to go on, because she has convinced herself that to share this information violates my precious memory and flawless reputation, especially because she's not even sure if she's right. "But Molly," Brie says, turning to look Hicks in the eye, "had a boyfriend." She, of all people, speaks the word as if I had gonorrhea. Shame on you, Brie, but I know it's your worry talking.

That's the big breakthrough? "Who was he?" he asks. Hicks already knows all about Luke, and hopes Brie will be talking about another guy.

"Molly would never say, and I'm fairly sure she broke things off before she died. At least I told her to." *Okay, I'm arrogant,* she thinks, *but*

Molly usually followed my advice. "When I asked her about him, she'd always give me that don't-go-there look. I'm thinking the person who might know more is Lucy. Have you asked her?"

"Done," Hicks says.

"What does she know?"

"Not much," he says. What she had to say filled less than a page. As he leads Brie to the cheese seller, Hicks does exactly what Brie does as a lawyer—says little and hopes his prey will fill in the blanks. This time it works.

"The only thought I have is that the guy might be the one she works with, Luke Delaney, who I'm sure you've talked to," Brie says. "I've been with them together a few times, and you know how you can feel something about a couple?"

He nods. *I certainly do,* Hicks think. *I might be feeling it now.*

"I know Luke from years ago and thought I sensed it," Brie says, "but when I asked Molly, she flat out denied it." Twice.

"Why didn't you say anything sooner about this?"

"I wasn't sure. I'm still not. If Luke and Molly were involved, I couldn't see why he'd deny it, and also, he's a decent guy who I don't want to get in trouble." As soon as she finishes her sentences, she realizes it sounds ridiculous, as if she cared more about Luke than me, but she knows she'll make it worse if she backtracks and tries to correct what she just said.

Hicks turns his head to look at Brie for a full minute, which makes her extremely uncomfortable. *Does he think I'm lying?* she wonders. But that's not what's in Hicks' head. She is relieved when he turns his attention to the guy behind the table.

"What you got today, Charlie?" he asks. Hicks tells himself that if this job doesn't work out, he's going to move upstate, buy a herd of goats, and learn to make cheese. He's already ordered two used books on the subject from Amazon. Every few weeks he logs on to real estate websites and pictures himself with forty acres, a shiny green John Deere, a manure spreader, a brush hog, and a compost heap. Even one of New York's finest can dream.

"Try this ricotta," the vendor says, offering Brie and Hicks tiny wooden spoons filled with opalescent white cheese. "Heaven?"

That's another thing I miss: really sharp, tangy tastes. Also any-

thing salty, crunchy, or spicy. Dammit—and every other word in the vocabulary of your average Tourette's sufferer—I miss food. Fresh, home-cooked, fancy, not fancy. I especially miss Italian—even the Olive Garden—Indian, French, Thai, Vietnamese, Peruvian, everything but midwestern-bland. I miss McDonald's fries, pastrami on rye, dim sum, dark chocolate bars studded with almonds, the hamburgers at Gramercy Tavern, my own spaghetti and meat sauce, my mother's hokey Thanksgiving sweet potatoes with marshmallows, hamentaschen, butterscotch sundaes, and Kitty's cheesecake. I think especially about the fudge cake covered with shaved chocolate I'd planned to buy that last afternoon. *Life is short—eat dessert first* should have been my religion.

"I'm going to have to bring home some of that, Charlie," Hicks says, pulling out his wallet. I've noticed that he actually weeds out its receipts every night so its fine leather doesn't bend and bulge. "And two of those." He points to the chèvre wrapped in green grape leaves. As they walk away, he gives one to Brie.

"Detective, is this bribery?" she says, lifting the cheese high as Jones sniffs it curiously.

"There'll be more where that's coming from if you know anything else about your friend's case," Hicks says.

"I wish I did," Brie says. "You have no idea."

Every day since Brie got Jones, she's been talking to him about me. "You'd have loved Molly, Jonesy. She was silly, like you. There was the time when we didn't have dates on New Year's Eve and at eleven-thirty we got all dressed up to have martinis at a hotel bar in town. And Molly couldn't sing on-key, but she was always the first to volunteer for karaoke, so no one else would feel like an idiot. Her song was 'Night and Day.' "

Brie carries on like that until I have to leave. I can't take it.

When Brie turns to inspect a row of beribboned pound cakes, each loaf no bigger than a good-sized tropical fish, I see Hicks look at her in admiration and outright surprise. *I feel comfortable with this woman,* I hear him think.

The thought flashes through his mind just as Brie is thinking the same thing. *This Hicks, he's easy. I could use a little easy right now.*

I am wondering if my powers have anything to do with this connection. Could I be willing it to happen? I'm going to have to talk this over

with Bob, who has never mentioned the spontaneous combustion of matchmaker capabilities.

I'm getting very excited.

"Detective, what's your opinion on crawfish étouffée?" she asks.

"In my top ten," he says. "Providing it's swimming in garlic and cayenne like my Grandma Hattie cooks it down in New Orleans."

I have never known my friend Brie not to act fast. Do it, Brie, do it, because there's no way Hicks will. Don't fail me now. Don't fail yourself.

"I'm inviting you to dinner then, that is, if you're available," she says before she remembers that she can't cook. "If you promise not to expect too much."

Why can't I hug her? I truly can't recall if I have ever seen my best friend blush.

"I accept," Hicks says. *Maybe I am getting my break,* he thinks, and then he douses the thought. *No expectations, boy,* he says to himself. *No expectations.*

"Seven?" She has shocked herself but doesn't regret it, and since she's on a roll, hoping tonight is a beginning and not another ending, she continues. "I have another question."

He nods.

"May I please call you Hiawatha?"

Once again, Hicks doesn't hesitate. "Absolutely not," he says, and strolls away. Brie can't see the smile on his face, but I can.

Thirty-three

WRAP PARTY

*H*ow about we meet at the Morgan?"

"We haven't seen each for three weeks and you want to meet at a library?" Luke said.

"I was thinking of the dining room," I said, the spot where I could least imagine a fur-flying scene. Decorum bonded the hush-hush Morgan's brown, shoebox-sized bricks, and its restaurant flew so far under the radar I couldn't imagine anyone younger than eighty lunching there. This safely excluded Kitty and every friend she or I had except my neighbors Sophie and Alf, who I happened to know were in the Galápagos.

"Hey," Luke said, "I admire an original Mozart manuscript as much as the next guy, but I've been dreaming about you." While I was searching for a response he elaborated. "Your lips, your skin on my skin, the way you smell like sunlight and happiness—"

"Stop," I said. Through endless motivational self-lectures—during my shower, my sleep, and my commutes—I'd promised myself that after that day Luke and I would be a wrap. But I wanted to terminate everything in person, to see him one last time and dive Lucy-style to

the bottom of our relationship's murky pool. I told myself that whatever we thought we had between us deserved as much. "I don't have a lot of time today."

"So let's reschedule," Luke said, breathing deeply, clearly puzzled that I had brushed off his poetry. "How's Thursday?"

I'd trained for that day as if it were the bad-girls' marathon. Postponing was not an option. I pulled the phone away from my ear and stared at it as if it might offer an answer. "Molly?" I could hear Luke saying. "Are you there?"

What's one more abbreviated apartment visit? the phone asked. *See him. You'll take a mental picture and carry it with you for the rest of your life. Then it will be over. Skedaddled. Monogamy forever forward.*

"Okay," I said. "I'll be at your place at one."

When I arrived, Luke stood in the doorway wearing his usual welcome-mat grin, shy but sly. He enveloped me in a tender, tight embrace, which as my automatic pilot ignited I found I could not resist. Not that I tried. I circled my arms around his shoulders, leaning into him. *God damn you, Luke,* I thought. *I am going to miss everything about you. Every decadent molecule.*

As the kiss continued, a remote, still-functioning part of my brain noted that there I was again, whizzing down the double-black diamond that always led us to the same place. My thumbs slipped into the back of Luke's jeans, where his warm skin invited me to come closer. No underwear. No self-assurance shortage. He easily led me by the hand to the bedroom.

"Would you like your gift before or after?" Luke asked as he lit the remains of a candle I'd given him early in the fall. A faint scent of ginger enveloped the room as the flame burst and sputtered, casting shadows that pirouetted on the walls.

"After," I said. "After."

"Does that mean you want me as much as I want you?" he said as he pulled my sweater and then my lacy camisole over my head.

I would never know the answer to that question. But what I said was "Allow me," unbuttoning his shirt as if he were the promised present. I knew this much: whoever believed that couples should hurry to become stark naked is missing half the point. I lazily moved my fingers

along Luke's bare chest, tracing his dark, curly hair until I reached his belt, which I unbuckled in one deft, practiced move, and continued on to his jeans. I pushed them to the floor as he did the same with mine.

Stop now, Molly, I told myself. *There's still time. All bets off.*

My flesh ignored my brain. As we went on, I was a photojournalist, out of body, circling and shooting away. Who is this wife—not old, but surely old enough to know better—recklessly playing in sheets that aren't hers, running her hands along a man's well-muscled back, tasting his sweet mouth with her tongue and lips? Who is this man who knows exactly how to love her and acts as if he does?

"Molly, where are you?" Luke said, stopping and finding my eyes, which had not closed. "You're in orbit."

I answered with numerous thoroughly animated body parts. Soon enough the journalist left the room and I alone remained, giving myself to Luke with the urgency of a woman shipping her soldier off to war. I memorized every stroke and sigh, every small scream and low, satisfied groan. They would have to last for a lifetime.

Then it was over. The two of us lay side by side, wordless. I closed my eyes and tried to think of . . . nothing.

Luke stepped out of the bed and disappeared into the hall. Cool air touched my shoulders and back, which were beaded with sweat, his with mine, mingled, Luke-and-Molly No. 5, the now and forever fragrance. I wanted to yank the downy comforter to my forehead and burrow beneath it, to postpone what was to come, but when Luke returned I was sitting up, half dressed, if a chartreuse lace hipster thong counts as clothing.

"It's the last of the Syrah," he said, handing me a glass of wine as he sat on the rumpled linen. "To us," he said, clinking my glass. "I told you I missed you. Tell me how much you missed me. This time in words."

He's playing you an overture, Molly girl, I told myself, twice. *Don't miss your cue.* But I was preempted.

"Wait," Luke said. "Your gift." He put down his glass and walked to the armoire. My inner Annie Leibovitz came to life and captured the small scar on his back from when he was a Cub Scout and fell from a tree and needed seven stitches. When Luke returned, he carried a small box. I eyed the white package with curiosity spiked by guilt.

"Open it," he ordered, a smile lifting his face.

I quickly untied its bow and peeked. Catching the candlelight were lilac-blue gemstones, small and round, framed in warm matte gold and dangling from delicate gold threads. The earrings suited me. I might have chosen them myself.

"With your blue eyes," he said, looking for a sign that he'd picked well. "They're Victorian. I bought them at auction."

Luke, you're making this too hard, I thought. "They're perfect," I said. This was true. "But such an extravagance . . ."

"You deserve them." He pulled me to him and we kissed, once for each earring, and I slowly replaced my prim pearl studs with the antique treasures, which Barry surely would not notice. "Thank you. You shouldn't have." *I wish you hadn't.*

"They're for Christmas," he said. "But you know me—zero impulse control."

Which goes for both of us, I thought. *And do I know you?* I didn't even know myself. *Don't be a wuss. Don't waste time. Whatever the protocol might be for what you plan to do, this isn't it. Start talking.* But first I dressed, taking time to wash carefully, including the streaks of mascara that had migrated beyond my lashes, making me look as if I'd lost a fight. By the time I left the bathroom, Luke was back in his jeans, still shirtless, and had moved into the living room.

"What'll it be?" he asked, combing through CDs. "Django Reinhardt? Josephine Baker?"

"You pick," I said. I wondered if a country and western star had written a twangy ballad about a cosmetic surgeon's wife breaking up with her lovable photographer boyfriend. If nobody has, somebody should. But moments later, Edith Piaf's voice began "Les Amants de Paris."

Luke sank into one of his couches and motioned me toward the space beside him. The opened bottle of wine was on the table next to our glasses, which he'd refilled. "Wouldn't it be great to go to Paris?" he said. "Maybe I can cook up a trip. It's corny, but what do you say to April? I know this place near Montparnasse, twice as romantic and half the price of Shutters." Shutters was the exceedingly charming hotel where we'd stayed in Santa Monica. We'd gotten up early each morning to take long windy walks by the Pacific.

"I think we're getting a little ahead of ourselves," I said as I pulled out the camera.

"Oh, man," he said. "There it is. Thanks—I've been missing that sucker. Want to take some shots now?" he said. "Hand her over and give me a big Molly smile. Too bad you have all your clothes on." I believe he winked.

"Luke, I don't think so."

"Not in the mood?" he said. "You look so good right now I'd like to go right back into the bedroom."

"Luke, I can't."

He put the camera on the table, brushed away a lock of hair from my forehead, and cradled my face in his hands. "What's wrong?" he asked.

I closed my eyes to stanch the tears I knew would come. My effort didn't work.

"Please don't tell me we have a problem. Did Barry find out about us?"

I was sorry I was wearing the new earrings—I never should have opened the box, never should have let myself do a lot of things. But I refused to be one orgasm short of rational thought. I was glad I'd prepared a speech.

"Luke," I started. "I can't do this anymore, and it's not because Barry knows about us, because I don't think he does. It's that every minute of every day I feel as if I'm in an opera that keeps getting louder and louder. I can't hear my own voice anymore. I can't think. This feels wrong. I love you, but—"

He put a finger on my lips. " 'I love you, *but.*' " Luke stood, crossed his arms, and walked a few steps away from me. Tension ironed horizontal lines in his forehead. "But you're going to break my heart?"

"But I do love you. That's not it."

He started talking as if he were slicing off each sentence with a knife. "Excuse me, Mrs. Marx, but weren't you more than happy to be all over me fifteen minutes ago? When did you make up your mind about this? Have you spent the last few weeks planning how to break things off or did the idea just occur to you?"

I was despising myself for being the sort of spineless, duplicitous woman who had chosen to have this conversation after I went to bed with him. I looked at Luke miserably, hopelessly. I wished I could go into the bathroom and start banging my head against the tile floor.

"I thought our feelings were based on love and kindness and respect," he said. "I guess I'm the fool here."

He looked angry but he sounded sad, and that made it worse. I'd come here to unload everything I'd been thinking for the last few weeks, to take each particle of doubt and build it into the Great Wall of China, to separate us, and now it was coming out wrong. "We're not together all the time," I added, as if that needed to be pointed out. "We've never discussed that this would last forever, that you wouldn't—couldn't—be with other people."

"I don't want to 'be with other people.' Don't you get that? You're making me feel like a fool, used and deceived."

"How have I deceived you?" I heard my voice rising. "I've no more deceived you than you've deceived me."

"Look who's on her high horse," Luke said quietly. "The doctor's wife." He stared at me. "And by the way, I don't buy that your marriage is one coast-to-coast crap storm. You're never going to leave him, never, not in my lifetime."

I'd hoped for poignant eloquence and gotten a cheesy daytime drama. *But you and I have never even talked about being together,* I thought, and hissed, "Well, I certainly won't leave Barry now." I snatched my bag and walked toward the front hall. I took the time to remove the earrings and place them on a table, then grabbed my jacket and slammed the door behind me, breathing heavily as I ran down the stairs, not bothering to wait for the elevator.

As I reached the second-floor landing, Luke shouted at me, running down two steps at a time, "Molly, come back. I don't want to fight. You've blown everything out of proportion. This is idiotic."

When I shot out the front door, one of his neighbors was exiting a taxi, which I took as a sign. I mumbled apologies as I bumped the woman and catapulted myself into the cab. It tore away as Luke reached the sidewalk. In the rearview mirror, I saw him, still shirtless, growing smaller and smaller.

"Where to, lady?" the driver said.

Good question, I thought.

Thirty-four

DR. STAFFORD AND DR. SCHTUP

*S*o?"

When did marriage counselors convene and decide this was the word to kick off deep introspection? What did Felicia Stafford, M.D., expect me to say, that Barry and I were here to discover, on a scale of 1 to 10, if our conjugal discord was off the charts or merely and pitifully average?

Never had I felt more cynical. I hadn't entered into matrimony a skeptic, but my own behavior and seventy-two questionable charges to Dr. Barry Schtup's credit cards had turned me into one. If I, Molly Divine Marx, could have morphed into a cheater and believed that my husband was unfailingly unfaithful for—basically—always, then couldn't every other wife be in the same stinking, sinking lifeboat?

Snap out of it, Molly, I told myself. *Grow up. You can make this right. Isn't that the reason we're sitting in this tastefully furnished Fifth Avenue office at three o'clock on a glum Tuesday?* I had parked myself across from Dr. Stafford in the middle of a couch upholstered in the orange of a deer hunter's jacket. I wondered if she'd chosen the fabric for its happiness quotient or to remind patients not to pull out a shotgun. There was ample room next to me, but Barry had chosen a stiff Windsor arm-

chair at a right angle to both of us. On the end table separating us was a large box of tissues.

"So, we hoped you could help us," I said, shifting in place, trying to get comfortable. I'd obsessed about what to wear. My version of a mini? Well-worn three-inch ankle boots? Even a hint of cleavage? Bimbo, bimbo, bimbo. Jeans, a cotton T-shirt, or cargo pants? Juvenile. I settled on flat leather boots, a black cashmere turtleneck, and a long black skirt, although God only knows what Dr. Stafford would read into its schitzy diagonal hem.

"And you, Dr. Marx?" Dr. Stafford said.

Barry's voice was even and soothing, waves at the beach. "Things haven't been right for a while."

Or ever, I thought. I glanced at the doctor's hands. Wedding ring. Check. I looked at my own. Yup, still there. As married as yesterday.

"Why do you think that is?" Dr. Stafford asked.

She wasn't the sturdy Margaret Thatcher I'd expected. I asked myself if I could stand to have a psychiatrist this attractive. The doctor was tall and slim as a bread knife, no more than forty-five, and wore a crisp Katharine Hepburn–esque white shirt and trousers of driftwood gray, which sat on the hips she barely had.

Barry gave the doctor his patient-seducing grin and it brought me back to Fifth Avenue. I knew this smile well. Its subliminal message was, *You can rely on me—I reek of integrity. I'm a heck of a plastic surgeon, and an even nicer guy. I would never screw up—at golf, at work, at anything.*

Dr. Stafford, I decided, was going to like him best.

"We haven't taken our vows seriously enough," Barry said in the earnest tone of the Rhodes Scholar he'd missed becoming, he claimed, by *this* much.

Our vows? Could my husband have heard them at all when his mind was on a mission to meet up with another woman during our wedding reception? Dr. Stafford said . . . nothing, her silence an ellipsis that beckoned Barry or me to jump right in and spout whole paragraphs of well-constructed prose explaining why our marriage stopped short of bliss.

"Molly, do you want to weigh in?" she asked.

The session cost two hundred dollars an hour. I thought I'd better speak. "Barry's right. We probably haven't approached our relation-

ship with enough . . ." I fished. Gusto? Sincerity? "Gravitas." *Gravitas?* What kind of an op-ed word was that? I never remembered saying it, ever.

"Do you want to continue to be married to—may I call you Barry?" Dr. Stafford said, looking quickly at Barry and then again at me. "That's one of the initial questions I like to ask in a first session."

But why did you have to start with me? I wondered, although lately I'd asked myself the identical question at least once a week. "Yes, I do, definitely," I said.

I did not want a divorce. Was my impulse due to the lack of an exit strategy—with or without Luke—or actual, albeit conflicted, love in which Annabel played no small part? More the latter. I did not want my daughter to suffer. That sentence sounded meager, but I hated to think that Annabel might ever be in pain, especially if I was the cause of it, and there was something we—Barry and I, together, her parents—could do to give her the childhood she deserved.

"And?" Dr. Stafford asked.

I assumed "and" meant "why." Two pairs of arched eyebrows faced me.

"Barry's essentially a good person," I began. "He adores Annabel— she's our daughter. Three and a half. He's smart. He's funny. We have a history." As Nana Phyllis would say, he's also a great provider, which I both took for granted and thought it was crass to point out. There were also, of course, Barry's looks, which I'd stopped noticing, but were high in the plus column. "He makes me laugh." Sometimes. "Oh, I already said that."

I decided not to add, *I haven't been the best wife. I've screwed things up grandly all on my own, whether Barry knows it or not.*

"Molly," she said, "you could be describing a friend."

"Actually, Dr. Stafford," I said, focusing on a silky cord around her neck—which was easier than looking into her eyes—"that's the thing Barry isn't. I don't think he even likes me much, and he definitely doesn't get me, and so . . ." I felt I might have to live or die by these words; how to say it? "I don't really trust him. I don't think I ever could or have. In the most basic way, I don't feel protected by him." Which has nothing to do with the handsome income he generates, I realized.

"I don't feel safe around Barry, and that's a bigger problem than any-thing."

The room grew as quiet as Manhattan after a heavy snowfall. Dr. Stafford swiveled her chair to the left. Was she delighted that it hadn't taken us even ten minutes to hit nasty?

"Barry?" she asked. As we both waited, my eyes wandered to an ab-stract oil painting hanging over my husband's head. The scrambled rainbow colors could be a diagram of my emotions.

"I see where Molly would think that," he said at last. "I can get very caught up in my work, with my hobbies."

I tried not to roll my eyes. Hobbies? *I live for visits to small, out-of-the-way hotels and to explore the city's finer cigar bars. You: available on nights when I'm 'working,' and for long walks on white-sand beaches near conferences in sunny locales."*

"And Barry, do you want to be married to Molly?" Dr. Stafford asked.

Barry leaned forward. "Unequivocally," he said, looking only at her. "My wife's beautiful, sensual, talented, a great mom, but none of that's as important as the simple fact that"—he leaned to reach for my hand, a foot away from him—"I love her." I jolted slightly at his touch.

"And only her?" the doctor asked.

Dr. Stafford was smarter than I thought.

"Only her."

Do I know you? I wondered.

"Molly says she can't trust you," the doctor said. Her tone was purely reportorial.

"Yes, I heard her."

"We'll get into why not later, I hope, but for now, Barry, I want to know—can you trust her?"

Is this where I break down in tears, wipe away my snot, and inter-rupt? *Hold on—let me tell you why you shouldn't. Because I'm coloring out-side the lines, too! On the bad-wife scale, I'm an eleven.*

"Yes, I think I can," Barry said. "But Dr. Stafford, if she'd seen the need to . . . have another relationship . . . I could understand where Molly might be coming from."

He was still looking only at our shrink. I could have been in Sri

Lanka. His handsome-doctor grin had been replaced by the serious-ness of a Senate candidate apologizing for the hooker in his hotel room.

"Doctor," Barry continued, his fingers clasped and flexed, almost as if he were praying, "I haven't always been faithful."

Oh, really?

"But that's going to change," he said, without a scintilla of visible shame. "Or I wouldn't be here."

"Barry, go a little deeper with this. That is, if you agree, Molly?"

I nodded. *Sure. Drill deep. Right through my heart. Spit out all the gore. If it helps, refer to notes.* This counseling had been my idea, but I'd begun to feel that everything Barry might get off his chest would sink into mine like darts.

"I'm already trying to change," he said. "Only yesterday this ex-tremely attractive patient invited me to lunch, ostensibly to talk about becoming my publicist, but I've already told my receptionist to cancel her."

Would that be Stephanie, or Sherry, or Shelley someone whose card Delfina had found in Barry's pocket before she brought his coat to the dry cleaner? On the back, he'd scrawled an address and apartment number. Riverside Drive. Now I wished I hadn't told Delfina to throw away the evidence. I also wished I could believe Barry.

Dr. Stafford looked in my direction. The half smile she'd used with Barry had collapsed into a horizontal line. She'd definitely taken his side. "If there were one thing you could change about your husband, what would it be?" she asked.

I'd like him not to stare at my thighs as if he thought they should be Photoshopped to 70 percent of their size. No, I can do better than that. I want Barry to like me as much as he does his mother and give me half as much at-tention. Maybe Dr. Stafford would let me ask for two changes. *In that case, I'd like him to think that one in ten of my idiosyncrasies is endearing, not worthy of the kind of reform you plan every New Year's.* But she did ask for one change. I had to pick.

"During dinner, I'd like him to ask me how my day was," I began, "and listen, actually listen, to my answer."

"Uh-huh," she said. "Barry, how about you?" I thought Dr. Staf-ford's tone implied, *That wouldn't be so hard, would it, man?* I hoped

she'd goose him in that direction, but instead she asked, "What would you change about Molly?"

As if he were spiking a volleyball, Barry bounced back. "I want her not to be so dubious. To believe I want a fresh start."

"Okay," Dr. Stafford said like a pleased parent. "Where do we go from here?"

At these rates, why is she asking us? The three of us sucked in air and waited for something to happen. I turned to glance outside, but the shades were drawn. I felt like a bug who'd walked into a roach motel. Then I decided that dishonesty was a luxury I could not afford.

"Doctor," I said, "can we dial back? Because I haven't been entirely honest. I'm probably being naive about marriage and maybe entirely unrealistic," I began, wishing I could ditch the habit of apologizing. Barry never did, nor Kitty nor Brie nor Lucy. Especially not Lucy. "But I think I just set my expectations a little too low."

Dr. Stafford tilted her chin in my direction. Her skin was the kind of flawless that comes from a power higher than Bobbi Brown. I couldn't find a sunspot or a squiggly red vein, and yet she appeared radiantly Botox-free.

"I want more from my marriage than for Barry to pretend to listen to me yak about my day. I want to come first. We can count off my flaws from here to the Fourth of July, but I want him to find at least some of them endearing." I swallowed a big bubble of air. "I want Barry to look at my face and melt." Like my dad does with my mom, even when she's just come out of the shower. That, especially. "I want him to feel that the happiest accident he ever had was meeting Molly Divine, that I'm in every breath he takes." Was I sounding like a bad greeting card? I didn't care. I had the undivided attention of the other two people in the room and was determined to continue.

"I need to feel my husband is absolutely bonkers about me—that our home isn't the Twilight Zone." *Good job, Molly,* I thought, liking that phrase. "And"—I turned toward Barry—"if I can't have this, then maybe we shouldn't be married, because I think I'm at least as deserving of love as the next wife, and I've obviously sold myself short."

I felt as if I'd delivered a commencement address.

"Is there anything else?" Dr. Stafford asked.

"One more thing," I said, watching Barry size me up with the

undisguised curiosity he usually reserves for comely females at other people's dinner parties. "I want to feel exactly the same way about my husband. About you, Barry." I touched him with my eyes.

What could Dr. Stafford possibly say that would change my mind now that I finally knew it? But she began talking. I saw Barry's mouth move, and then the doctor's. Him, her, him, her, him for a long time. My mind had switched off the sound.

As my phone audibly vibrated, both of them looked at me. I felt their eyeballs, but checked the caller's number nonetheless. It was the fourth time Luke had tried me over the last few days.

"Do you have to take that?" Dr. Stafford said.

"No, it's just a work call. Sorry." Deeply sorry. Luke had already left two messages pleading with me to reconsider the previous week's conversation, to make a date to meet him or at the very least to call back. I hadn't responded, not even when he described a trip to Paris for late January. He couldn't wait for April. We'd be staying in a hotel hidden away in a seventeenth-century building on the Left Bank. Visits to the Musée de l'Orangerie and the Cinémathèque Française. Dinner at a candlelit, Michelin three-star restaurant in the shadow of the Eiffel Tower. Nutella crêpes morning, noon, and night if that's what my wounded heart desired.

"Molly," Dr. Stafford said, "is there more you want to add to our conversation?"

"That I'll try," I said, "if Barry will." I meant it.

"So," Dr. Stafford said, "it's time to stop." She looked first at me, then at Barry. "I'd like to see you after Christmas. Then we can dig in with some real work."

I bet Dr. Stafford couldn't wait for her next appointment of the day, where the couple actually had worries they didn't manufacture— serious, sympathy-worthy anguish brought on by losing a child, a breast, a job, or a Pomeranian. She'd probably already classified our problem in the subbasement of hair and waistline loss.

We all did a dance with our calendars and picked weekly slots. Couples counseling would be the gift that kept on giving twice a week, Tuesday and Thursday, at three. I shook the doctor's hand, which felt smooth and small.

We walked out to Fifth Avenue and began to head south. Barry put

his arm around my waist and pulled me close, leaning in. It was a gesture that I like as well as a kiss, although I don't recall ever having mentioned that to my husband. I could feel the warmth of his compact physique. Neither of us spoke.

Across the street, workers at the Met were hanging a blue banner. All I could see was the flourish of a name. Cézanne. I repeated it to myself, and it buzzed in my ear like catchy French music. This caused my mind to make an unfortunate involuntary leap to strolling hand in hand with Luke along the Seine, stopping at the stalls of several *bouquinistes.* I tried to cancel the image and concentrate on Barry, who I saw glance toward the Met as well.

As we got to Seventy-ninth Street, where he would turn left to return to his office on Park, we stopped. "I have an idea," he said. "What do you say to a second honeymoon? I've always wanted to stay at the George V. April in Paris? I'll call the travel agent tomorrow. Why don't you sign up at Berlitz?"

"I'll get right on it," I said.

Thirty-five

COSMIC LAVENDER

Delfina Adams treats my Annabel as if she were her own blood. She detangles curls, dries tears, sells her on asparagus because of its double wallop of vitamins and fiber. Delfina can make the junk mail disappear, set a table to the standard of the First Lady, and never let the shrunken Marx family run low on apple juice, Fig Newtons, or peanut butter, but cleaning is not her métier, nor is it expected of her. Miracle Maids, a battalion of earth-friendly elves, arrive twice a week with dancing mops and lime green noncarcinogenic potions.

The germs, streaks, and smudges in this apartment are gone. I, however, am still here, surprised to see Delfina tenderly polishing my desk. As if she were massaging its creaky two-hundred-year-old bones, she rotates a supple linen dinner napkin retired from active duty. I inhale the lemon scent, an aphrodisiac designed to seduce women into performing homely household tasks. After ten minutes, Delfina stands back, squares her tall, competent frame, and smiles in appreciation of the result. In the burnished mahogany, I see her oval face reflected with its high cheekbones and eyes as warm as brown sugar.

Delfina opens the double doors on the desk's hutch top. "Oh, Lord," she says out loud. "That missus sure could make a mess."

Tidy on the outside, tumult inside, me to a T. Shelves sag under a pile of unpaid bills and envelopes, many envelopes. Roller ball pens—black and only black—discarded pocket calendars, an expired passport, friends' Christmas photo greetings ("Happy everything! Love and kisses, the Cohens and Mugsy"), and dog-eared business cards crowd the cubbyholes along with thirty-nine-cent stamps, a tape measure (*that's* where it is), and, inexplicably, a plumy purple feather.

Delfina whistles. "Okay, Dr. Barry said to empty the desk." She looks at the clock on the nightstand. Ten-fifteen. "Shouldn't take too long," she says, to offer herself encouragement. She sets aside an overdue library book and begins to pluck out the obvious trash. Into a carton saved from the last Fresh Direct delivery go magazine subscription notices, bunches of faded receipts, and an ad for twenty-dollar opera seats. Damn, why hadn't I bought one? For years I lived twenty-five blocks from Lincoln Center, but I never once saw *Madame Butterfly*.

I am recalling other items on my lengthy to-do list—learn to tango, bake sourdough bread, build a house with Habitat for Humanity, plan a trip to the beaches of Croatia, take pole-dancing lessons—when I spot it, a pale lilac envelope carefully sealed with wax, as if the sender were nineteenth-century European aristocracy. Delfina's slim hand, tastefully manicured, reaches for the envelope and, with efficient dispatch, drops it on the heap. It lands right side up.

To my darling Annabel, the envelope says in my loopy penmanship. Based only on the *p*'s and *b*'s, a graphologist once sized up my self-esteem as alarmingly low, but I took care with this document. Every letter is precise and, I hope, pulsing with ego.

Delfina does a double take. "Lord, what is this?" she says, wrinkling her brow. She lifts the fat, square envelope to the light, as if a seventy-five-watt bulb could reveal its secrets. The heavy paper ain't talking.

Delfina stands utterly still, breaks a sweat, and looks around the room to make sure she is alone. She removes a cell phone from her pocket and calls Narcissa. "Can you talk?" she whispers.

"Of course," Narcissa says. In the background, Delfina and I both

hear the Food Network. I, a charter member of the Rachael Ray Sucks Community, am forced to hear that loudmouth reel off fifteen ingredients, ending with truffle mousse pâté, that her ravenous disciples need for her thirty-minute hamburgers. I hope that anyone who believes that life is fair will be disabused of that notion when they consider that I'm in the Duration and Rachael rules the world. Narcissa snaps off the television mid-"yum-o!"

"There's a letter here, hidden, from the missus."

"My, my, my, my, my," Narcissa says. "Imagine that. After all this time."

"What should I do?" Delfina continues to whisper.

"Mail it?"

"It's the kind of letter you just hand to someone."

"Open it, woman! Read it out loud!"

"I can't do that—it's not right." Delfina lives by her church's principles. I was reminded of this on a regular basis, when she would hit me up to buy raffle tickets. Once I won a free meal at a Caribbean restaurant in Brooklyn. Excellent jerk chicken. Her pastor's son owned the place, and as I recall from his family photo on the wall, Delfina's Reverend Moneybags visited the same barber who coifs the Reverend Al Sharpton.

"Who's the letter for? Dr. Barry? A secret boyfriend?"

Did everyone think I had a boyfriend?

"No, Annabel."

"But that little child, she can't even read. You'd need to read it to her." Ella reads not just letters but whole books, as Narcissa never fails to mention. "So technically—"

Like most West Indian housekeepers in our neighborhood, thanks to her powers of persuasion, Narcissa is paid better than not only every editorial assistant in Manhattan but also 20 percent of the attorneys who've recently been sworn into the New York Bar. But Delfina is unconvinced. "I don't think it's my place to open this letter," she says. *God will punish me,* I hear her think.

"Then what are you going to do about it?"

Delfina peers again at the clock—it's almost eleven—as she moves to plan B. "I'll let you know," she says, and hangs up. She places the envelope next to the Bible she keeps next to her bed. With Baby Moses

now safely in the bulrushes, she returns to sort through the rest of the stuff in the desk very carefully. Who knows what else she might find? A winning lottery ticket, perhaps? She checks the Bible every few minutes.

I stare at the envelope and remember everything.

I'm proud to say there were times in my life when I had a sense of occasion. This was one of them. First, I visited a stationery store, since I didn't want to write this letter on my MacBook and simply hit print. As soon as the saleswoman told me a particular shade of paper was called Cosmic Lavender, I decided it was my destiny and ordered a hundred sheets with a swirling white monogram. I sat at this very desk, opened the lid of the navy blue box, lifted a sheet, and slowly copied the text I'd rewritten endlessly over the course of a week. I only earned B's in English, but I felt I made my point.

Darling Annabel, I'd begun. *When you read this letter, there are things I want to make sure you understand. . . .*

Delfina tries to drift through the day as if it were ordinary. She and Annabel visit the butterflies at the Museum of Natural History and cook colorful wagon-wheel pasta for dinner. During Annabel's bath, she reads her *Madeline* and tucks her into bed. At eight-fifteen, Delfina retreats to her bedroom next to the kitchen, where she moved in after my work with Luke started taking me across the globe. We painted it together in a shade Delfina chose after considerable deliberation, a smoky plum called—inexplicably—Lazy Afternoon. Perhaps Delfina picked it because her life has offered so few of those.

"Did the painter fall into grape jelly?" Kitty asked when she saw the walls. But I always admired Delfina's conviction on the matter of this paint and much more. When Annabel pokes her head into this hidden domain with its white organdy curtains, floaty as bridesmaids' dresses, she thinks she's entered an enchanted kingdom.

A few hours later, Barry walks through the door with *her.* Delfina is still up, watching Lifetime, although usually she's asleep by now. She hears Barry leave Stephanie to hang up her own coat while he heads straight to Annabel's room, where he brushes away her blond hair for a soundless kiss on a plump, damp cheek.

"Good night, angel," he whispers. Annabel opens one eyelid, says, "Your whiskers scratch, Daddy," turns over, and tries to reboot her dream.

In the kitchen, Stephanie pulls a bottle of water out of the refrigerator. *Another woman is at home in my home.* She knows where to find the coffee beans and my favorite café au lait bowls, as well as my thickest, newest bath towels and the Dr. Hauschka lemon body oil I hoarded because it cost thirty dollars for only 3.4 fluid ounces. I want to pour the bottle of water on Stephanie's fluffy, salon-blow-dried head. Let her dehydrate, with lips so scaly Barry will refuse to kiss them. See if I care.

Barry and Stephanie walk, arms wound around each other's waist, toward the bedroom. As she sits on my side of the bed and unzips her tall, spiky boots, Stephanie sees the letter. "Hey, Bear," she shouts to him in the bathroom. "There's an envelope here for Annabel."

Stephanie pulls open the drawer on my bedside table, finds an emery board, and begins to file a ragged edge on one of her long nails. The casual intimacy of the gesture makes me as enraged as the fact that Barry shouts back, "Be there in a minute, baby." I despise that he calls her that as much as I loathe the way she carelessly pushes back my ivory matelassé coverlet. My ritual was to carefully fold it in thirds and lay it on the mohair chaise in the corner. I suddenly feel as attached to this bedcover as if it were from my grandmother's trousseau, not casually ordered on sale from a website I can't remember.

Barry walks into the room as Stephanie lights a candle. It gives off a musky scent. My husband is only two steps from the bed when his eyes fall on the envelope. He freezes. "Where'd that come from?" His tone is accusing, as if Stephanie is playing a practical joke. He scowls, which makes her scowl back.

"What's wrong? You look like it's going to explode." She hands him the letter. "Here."

He doesn't want to touch it. "It's for Annabel," he says.

"Okay," Stephanie says. She stretches out the word and gets up to take her turn in the bathroom. *What's gotten into him?* she wonders. *Why's he gone all serious on me?* When Stephanie emerges, doing justice to an abbreviated black camisole, the letter is out of sight, although Barry has read it. He slumps against the pillows, his muscular legs

stretched in front of him. Stephanie walks to his side and waits for him to move over. When he fails to budge, she begins to knead his shoulders.

"Not now," he says, and removes her hands.

"Want to go to sleep?" I admire her seductive tone.

"Actually, I'm wide awake," he says, although in the taxi riding home from the theater, he'd dozed.

"Well, that's good," she says, "very good," and waits for his embrace. It doesn't happen, not even when she circles her tongue in his ear. "What's going on?"

In the same situation I might have cried, but Stephaniewoman, made of razor blades and gumption, feels anger, which is exactly what I myself am feeling now. My wrath is a bottomless well, an echo of a larger, unnameable emotion. When Barry fails to answer Stephanie, she quickly dresses. *This guy is heavy weather,* she thinks. *Or maybe he just needs more time. I can wait,* she thinks. *The good body, the medical practice, the money. I can learn to be patient.* Before my husband's lover leaves the bedroom, she kisses Barry lightly, hoping her touch will be the rabbit's foot that reverses the evening's direction.

He pulls away. "I'm sorry," he says. "This has nothing to do with you."

"Want me to stay?" *Say yes,* she hopes. *I'm your answer.* When he stares ahead, Stephanie says, "I'll speak to you tomorrow." She walks out of the room as confidently as she entered it. As soon as Barry hears the front door shut, he snuffs the candle and takes the letter from the nightstand drawer to reread its three pages. By the end of the first page, he dabs his eyes with the hem of the sheet, deeply exhales, and reaches for the phone.

"What time is it?" Kitty mumbles after the fourth ring.

"Just past eleven."

When my mother-in-law's sleeping pill begins to wear off enough for her to register that her only child is on the phone, her panic registers. "What now? Is something wrong with Annabel?"

"Kitty, we're fine," he says, although he doesn't believe it. "But I've found a letter. From Molly."

"So?" Kitty says. *Why is this an occasion for waking me?* she wonders. *Has Barry gotten weepy over some old love note? Maybe he drank too*

much tonight, or isn't coping nearly as well as he appears to be. He's working and he's dating, for God's sake, and Stephanie's the kind of woman men like. He's moving on with his life, as he should.

"So? Do you want to hear this letter or not?"

"Okay, read the thing," Kitty says as firmly as she can through a pharmaceutical haze, but all she hears is a low snuffle that sounds as if Barry might be crying. She repeats the words, this time with the kindness of a mother. "Read it, darling."

" *'To my darling Annabel,'* " he begins as I lip-synch " *'When a mother loves a child for eternity, every time that daughter breathes the mother is breathing along with her, hoping that every one of her child's dreams come true. My love for you never stops and never will. It goes around and around like a carousel, a hula hoop of hugs.'* "

Barry stops. He squeezes shut his eyes, hoping to stem his tears.

"Is there more?" Kitty whispers hoarsely over the white-noise machine tuned to "country eve." Falling asleep to crickets wouldn't do it for me, but it works for her.

"Yes, a lot. Molly even gets around to me."

"And me?" Kitty is now awake.

"You, Mother, didn't make the cut."

"Just as well." *No love lost there,* she thinks. "Who else knows about this?"

"No one," Barry says, having decided that Stephanie doesn't count. "Absolutely no one." I'm glad Delfina can't hear this. Who does Barry think found the letter?

"First thing in the morning, you've got to call that detective and show this to him," Kitty says as the wires connect. *The letter is the ticket for the Marx family to get its life back. No more sideways stares from the manicurist or the bitch at the dry cleaner who pretends she can't speak English. No more sudden hushes when I walk into the locker room at my club. Of course, everyone will dish the dirt about Molly's having taken her own life, and maybe I'll have to remind them, with Jackie Kennedy dignity, that my daughter-in-law was a bit—how shall I put it?—on the high-strung side. People will shake their heads, feel sad for Barry, and sadly debate the best way to explain the tragedy to poor little Annabel. People will be full of advice on what Barry should say.*

"I'm not going to Hicks before I call Molly's parents."

Right. The Divines, she thinks. "Darling," Kitty says, "that won't be easy. I'm so sorry for you." *My son shouldn't have to be going through this. But this is the end of the road that has taken me on the worst ride of my life,* she thinks, *worse than when Stan*—that would be Barry's father—*gambled away his business and my brother had to bail him out.* "At least we'll have closure."

" 'Closure'? What are you talking about, Mother?" Barry's voice rises despite his fatigue. "I don't see how this letter proves a thing. Molly could have written it anytime after Annabel was born."

"Come on. Sweetie, you don't want to connect the dots. You're too upset. Totally understandable."

"Suicide? Really, I doubt it," he says, but maybe his mother is right. He needs to sleep on the possibility. He repeats this sour-milk word—*suicide*—several times to himself. "Good night, Kitty. And don't tell anyone about the letter, promise?"

"Would I lie?" she says.

Aren't you the mother who promised my life would always be happy? he remembers as he hangs up the phone.

In two minutes Barry is as dead asleep as he always was as a resident. He wakes at his normal hour, doesn't remember a dream about a vacation when we went to Prague and I got lost, and goes for his run as the sun rises over the park. With every tread, his brain considers what to say to my parents. I am warmed by the thought that he wants to cushion the blow. When he returns home, Annabel is eating breakfast.

"Don't forget to leave those muddy shoes in the hall, Daddy," she says, in little-wife mode.

"Don't forget to give your father a big hug," he calls back as he brings in the *Times* and the *Wall Street Journal.* Barry has cancelled the *Post,* since I'm the only one who read it except Delfina, who misses it. I was never able to start my day without Page Six and a glance at my horoscope. He swoops down to snuggle Annabel, who wiggles in her seat as she kisses her father's cheek.

"Ick, you're sweaty," she says.

"Coffee, Doctor?" Delfina asks.

"Good morning, Delfina," Barry says.

If he would actually look at Delfina, standing at the counter, he'd see her biting her lip and twisting her ring. She can't bring herself to ask about the envelope.

"No coffee just yet, but thanks," he adds, depositing the newspapers on the kitchen table and padding to the bedroom in his stocking feet. He rushes through a scalding shower and dresses in a shirt and trousers before he picks up the phone. I am glad it is my father who answers.

"Dan," Barry says, his hearty effort falling short.

My father reads voices like Gypsies do palms. "Everything okay in New York?"

"Annabel's great," he says, but struggles to support this thesis. "Growing like a weed, starting to recognize letters."

"Well, that's good." In Chicago it's not even seven. "What's up that you're calling so early?"

Barry drums his fingers on the nightstand. "Dan, I came across a letter," he says. "From Molly."

Since I died, my father's gained twelve pounds, mostly in his face. He strokes his brand-new jowls. "That so?"

"I'd like you to hear it," he says.

Do I want to endure this alone? my father thinks. Last night my mother, who's developed insomnia, read a mystery from two until four in the morning, and she's still sleeping. The woman is practically a saint, but when he wakes her she nips like a Jack Russell terrier and doesn't mellow until after she's anesthetized by her second jolt of java.

"Dan, are you there?" Barry says.

"I'll call you back in ten minutes, Barry. Claire should be on the line."

Ten minutes, ten hours. It feels the same to Barry. After thirty-five minutes, the phone rings. "Barry dear," my mother says, "good morning. Read us this letter you've found."

She doesn't disintegrate until he gets to the part about her.

No one teaches you how to be a mother, Annabel. I was lucky, because I had Grammy Claire, the best mother in the whole world, who didn't realize that every day she was showing me how to be a parent someday myself. She has special powers. When I

was little, she could just look at me and know if I had a temperature or wanted a graham cracker or had fibbed to Lucy.

My parents, who are sitting side by side, each with a phone to an ear, grab each other's hand as the letter continues to extol my father's fourteen-carat-gold virtues and moves on to what to me passed for wisdom.

1. Don't marry a man who thinks you talk too much, doesn't make you laugh at least twice a day, or farts in front of you and isn't embarrassed. (Feel free to disregard the last part after six months of dating.)
2. Never wear ankle strap shoes, unless your legs turn out to be a lot longer than mine.
3. Learn to roast a chicken.
4. Even though Mandarin Chinese would be more practical, make French your second language. You'll be at home in Paris, where I hope you will take a junior year abroad. When you do, order the hot chocolate at Angelina's.
5. Print out your pictures and put them in an album. Label! Date!
6. Don't waste time balancing your checkbook.
7. When you're crabby, fake a good mood.
8. Never ask a two-year-old a question to which she can answer, "No!"
9. Make at least one new friend every year.
10. Don't judge people by where they went to college.
11. When in doubt, paint your walls the color of vanilla ice cream.
12. Remember that Big Macs have 24 fat grams.
13. Keep your perfume in the refrigerator.

And so on. The list covers every area of banal daily life—hair, friendship, diet, skin care, and, of course, home decoration—until it finally ends.

50. Most important, Annie-belle: toughen up. God gives everyone her own special bag of breaks, but what makes the difference between happy and sad is whether you waste time being jealous and small. Don't. Learn to recognize good luck when it's waving at you, hoping to get your attention. Sometimes the universe tries

very hard to send you a message. No matter what life hands you, angel-girl, bounce back. Be resilient. Self-pity is a waste, and life is short enough without it. Do not feel sorry for yourself and don't expect everything to be perfect. Work on getting a sense of proportion—you'll know what that means when you're older—so you can handle the disappointments that march along every day like ants. When nothing good happens, stand up straight and think of all the better things ahead. . . .

But there is no ahead for Molly Divine Marx, and my parents are shutting down. "Stop, Barry," my father says. "We've heard enough."

"The thing is," Barry asks impatiently, "this is what's spooking me. Do you think Molly . . . knew she was going to die?"

"Like when you're thinking about someone and then the phone rings," my mother says, "that funny feeling in your bones?"

"Not exactly. I'm looking at this letter, which Molly clearly put a lot of thought into, and wondering about . . . something else."

The silence between Highland Park and Manhattan drops like a shroud. "Do you honestly think our daughter might have taken her own life?" my father says, barely choking out the words, as outraged as if Barry has accused me of molesting a child. I love how my parents rise to my defense. They have never made me prouder.

"That's preposterous," my mother says, trying not to bellow at her son-in-law, who she knows is upset. She can't even think suicide. "You lived with our daughter and she was sunshine, pure gold. Is there something you want to tell us?"

There isn't.

Did you make our daughter miserable? they are both thinking, and Barry gets that as the message oozes through the phone lines.

"Have you called Lucy yet?" my mother asks.

"Maybe you want to tell her yourself?" Barry asks, hoping they'll bite.

"We'll call to warn her, but you're the one with the letter," my father points out. "She should hear it."

Even if she'll laugh at my quotidian wisdom.

Barry says goodbye and puts the letter in the inside left pocket of his sport jacket. The envelope is as alive to him as I am not, throbbing

for attention. Five minutes later he's in a taxi, debating whom to call first, Lucy or Hicks, when his cell phone rings.

"Let's get one thing straight—my sister would never kill herself," Lucy says. She has traded her usual voice for the cool, low tone of a corporate president ready to eat another company alive. "I don't know how you can suggest it, even as a boneheaded theory. She'd never commit suicide. Absolute idiocy."

Please make Barry understand this, Lucy, I think as I watch her drive to work and talk on speakerphone.

"Who's saying she did?" Barry asks.

"Whatever you found I need to see. Immediately." *Molly was a sentimental fool,* Lucy thinks. *This is probably one of those earnest letters a mother writes when a child is born and whips out when the kid graduates from high school. She probably got the idea from a women's magazine.*

Lucy is almost right. I wrote the letter when Annabel turned three and was planning to give it to her at her bat mitzvah or when she got her period, whichever rite of passage arrived first.

"You know, Lucy, this letter doesn't seem like the sort of thing to fax." Is that what she wants, to prove that he hasn't faked it? He tries to stop short of sarcasm, but in any conversation he's ever had with his sister-in-law, it's the rhythm he knows best. "But let me read this one part now. *'I have always hoped that someday you'd have a brother, but I'm going to share a secret. Before you were born, I asked God for a little girl, and that's exactly what I would pray for again, because I've had a sister, and there is nothing more wonderful in the whole wide world.'* "

"Barry!" Lucy screams as she skids to avoid an oncoming car. "Stop! I'm going to get into an accident. That's all my parents need, two dead daughters."

"I'll overnight you and your parents copies of the letter—you'll have them by tomorrow," he says, bordering on kind. "And I should alert Hicks. Agree?" He doesn't care what she thinks, because he's already made up his mind.

Lucy likes being asked. "You should," she says. Tears drip on the front of her jacket. She wishes her eyes had windshield wipers. "So I guess we'll talk later, after the letter arrives?"

"We will," Barry says. His taxi passes a flower shop selling big tubs of blue hydrangeas. I filled our home with these flowers the moment

they were sold each spring. *It's a sign,* he tells himself. *Go ahead. Ask.* He flashes to the incident with Lucy at Annabel's school, about which he's still fuming, no matter that my sister has written her own letter to him, of deep apology. Barry considers that he may be losing all reason and that his mother will be ready to commit him to an institution. "Lucy?" he says. "I need a favor. . . ."

She braces herself for a nasty hit. *No, I will not fuck myself,* she thinks. *Why am I being civil to Barry? This guy is vermin.*

"After the High Holidays, could you please come to New York? It's time that someone goes through Molly's stuff. I can't bear to do it my-self." *And Molly would hate it if I asked my mother.* "I was going to ask Delfina or Brie or . . ." *But now that you've been on house arrest for all these months at your parents', you've done your time, and I can ask you,* Barry thinks.

You need me, Lucy thinks. *But more importantly, my sister needs me.* The moment for a smart-ass retort disappears. "I'll be there."

Thirty-six

TRUE CONFESSIONS

I watch Barry slip into a maroon velvet pew. "What do you think of all this?" I ask Bob, who's never attended a Yom Kippur service. He likes bagels, Billy Crystal, and Sandra Bullock (Jew—not a Jew? Discuss) and says *mazel tov,* but that's as Jewish as he's ever gotten.

"Why isn't the place packed? What's with the empty seats? Those of us raised with Confession couldn't get by baring our souls one measly time a year. We'd be hanging from the rafters and snaking a line around the block, banging to get in, begging to upload our sins."

Why didn't I bring Bob last night, when the confessions were in freefall and eleven people tried to squeeze into rows meant for eight? Almost every soul had stripped to emotional underwear, with varied degrees of contrition and honesty. When the collective sob of the Kol Nidre bounced off the vaulted Moorish ceiling, there was a collective swaying and moaning, well-dressed willows in the wind.

"You'll see—the place will fill up as the day goes by." I turn my attention to Barry, standing bull's-eye in a circle of loneliness, trying to pray. I'd love to know for what, exactly.

"For the sin which we have committed before You under duress or willingly," Rabbi Strauss Sherman says in his express-from-heaven

boom. Worshippers listen carefully to the spiritual boilerplate. "For the sin which we have committed before You by hard-heartedness . . . inadvertently . . . with an utterance of the lips . . . with immorality . . . openly or secretly . . . with knowledge and with deceit . . . for all these, God of pardon, pardon us, forgive us, atone for us." After Rabbi S.S. says this, the invisible but exuberant choir repeats it, should anyone have missed the point.

Pardon me, Barry is praying. *Forgive me.* Like my Papa Louie and every male ancestor before him, he's wrapped inside a silky bluestriped *tallit,* determined to make God, today's star, hear him.

Yesterday, after Kitty's dinner—matzo balls floating in golden chicken soup, tangy gefilte fish, prime rib, baked potatoes the size of Annabel's shoes, and mile-high apple tart—Barry started fasting. For him this is new. Already, his stomach is saying, *Feed me,* and because he didn't wean himself off caffeine a few weeks in advance—my secret weapon—his head throbs. I'm not sure why our forefathers felt this particular physical hardship put a person in the mood for prayer. Maybe there's someone in the Duration who can clue me in on that.

I've never thought of either Barry or myself as religious. Even though he'd recently been appointed a trustee of the congregation and once in a while we'd attend a service, on most Friday nights we'd go to a movie, miles from a sweetly braided challah. Since I died, however, Barry—along with other mourners—has ushered in the Sabbath at temple and made a sizable donation to Annabel's school. As a result, on the fifth floor of this very building there's a well-stocked Molly Divine Marx Art Room whose centerpiece is an aquarium filled with hundreds of mollies in cocktail-hour hues—Gold Dust, Creamsicle, and other shimmers, plus the occasional active-wear Molly in neon green or orange.

"Want to see Big Molly?" I ask Bob, eager to get away from Barry's obvious discomfort—and to lose my own. "She's a Ghost Pearl." I often get lost watching her and like to believe a speck of my soul circulates within this plump female and her hundreds of babies.

"Later," Bob says as he settles in.

"For the sin which we have committed before You by false denial and lying," the rabbi continues.

Bob gives me that look of his that telegraphs, *Get serious.* Maybe he

has some atoning to do—I can't get into his head and he rarely talks about himself—but my better guess is that he feels I could do with some of my own confessing. There's plenty of transgression, wickedness, and moral trespassing to go around. I need to be accountable.

Rabbi S.S. has moved along to the sin of scoffing. I consider it. Nope. Scoffing, not my thing.

"For the sin which we have committed before You by a haughty demeanor." On this count, my mind free-associates to Kitty. Where is that woman? Does she feel she needs no atonement? And what about the also absent Stephanie, who must be a member of this synagogue, since her son attends their nursery school? Does she honestly feel she's sailed through the year sin-free? Come on. Let me count the ways. But I'm running up my own tab thinking about both of them, especially now that Rabbi S.S. is shifting into Molly territory.

My own sins are manifold, bacteria on a sponge. My essence curls inside Barry, so that we might beseech God as a team, as together as we've ever been. He is praying intensely, with the strain on his face I see when he does a pull-up, trying his best to make the Big Guy hear him. *I blew it,* he's saying. *Molly is gone and I'm to blame. To blame. To blame, to blame.*

"And for the sin we have committed before you by a confused heart."

A confused heart? Hey, God, over here. Was this always in the service, or did You slip it in expressly for me? I'm still waiting to meet You in the Duration, but I have not given up. You bet my heart was, and is, confused. It's unhinged, in a spin. Do I have regrets? Does Yankee Stadium sell peanuts? Maybe I shouldn't have married Barry or should have gotten out early, after the wedding or even before. But then Annabel wouldn't be here, and how can I regret my child? I know You wanted Annabel to be. Which leads me to think that Barry and I could have learned to live happily ever after, Your five-year plan. Okay, God, maybe we got a running start in the wrong direction, but thanks to Dr. Stafford we'd reversed course. Some people grow up at twenty, the rest of us by forty if we're lucky. But yes, God, in short, my heart was confused.

Should I have stayed away from Luke? Not my finest hour. But God, You know better than anyone that I never intended to hurt Barry. Can

we both at least agree that while he wasn't the best husband, my point wasn't to be cruel? I know You know that what I felt for Luke was authentic. My passion for him was the most glittering emotion You ever let me experience, second only to the love I felt for my child and my parents. It was the rarest rainbow of sentiment: capital-L love. Can that be bad?

God, let's talk. What was I supposed to do when You threw us together? Luke drew me to Luke. I didn't run in his direction because he was the Other Guy. Why did You do that? Not that I'm blaming anyone but myself. You knew I could never resist a man who listened to me the way Luke did, who manipulated my body as if it were a PlayStation 3, and who happened to look and smell and smile like, well, Luke. Did You put him on earth and let him trip me up just to tease?

Ah, but the moment for silent meditation is over. Rabbi S.S. is at it again.

"On Rosh Hashanah it will be inscribed and on Yom Kippur it will be sealed . . . how many will pass from the earth and how many will be created. Who will live and who will die at his predestined time and who before his time?"

My heart's more than confused—it's riddled with questions that I have the rest of eternity to sort out. Top of the list is why I, Molly Divine Marx, stood in this very synagogue twelve months ago, prayed as ardently as the women next to me and behind me to be inscribed and sealed in the Book of Life for one more year, but wasn't among the chosen. Yes, I'm as hideously culpable as any other commandment violator in this room. I am an emotional felon. But I can't believe that Your thinking is so simplistic in the cause-and-effect department that infidelity is what has landed me in the Duration, especially when Barry and Luke got to stick around. You can't possibly have a double standard, that cheating is worse for women than for men.

"Who by water . . . fire . . . sword . . . beast . . . famine . . . thirst . . . storm . . . plague . . . strangulation . . . stoning. Who will rest and who will wander, who will live in harmony and who will be harried . . . who will enjoy tranquillity and who will suffer . . . who will be impoverished and who will be enriched . . . who will be degraded and who will be exalted?"

That elegant, mustached gentleman with the ebony cane who always sits in front of us—he looks as delicate as the white lilies on the altar. Will he be here next year, or six feet under? That enormous mom from Annabel's school—will it make a rat's ass of difference if she deep-sixes the Häagen-Dazs, joins Curves, and hitches her star to Jenny Craig? Will Kitty make the cut? My mother? Does being sealed in the Book of Life truly depend on how many merits and demerits a person has in her account and whether her atonement is heartfelt, or do You have a short list created by celestial lottery?

Barry is counting on the former. I know this much from listening to him. He's fretting more about the future than the past.

"Do you think he's really sorry?" I ask.

"I do," Bob says. I would like to believe him. I'm working on it. Bob's not a cynic. I am.

"He wishes everything were different," Bob says. "Listen to him."

Diffuse early afternoon light floods through stained glass, highlighting congregants in gilded pools of sun as they offer up silent entreaties. I tune back in to Barry, waiting for him to make a wish on Stephanie's behalf, but his head is wrapped around Annabel, his mother, and "poor sweet Molly." It's a pitiful appeal, and I am relieved when he moves on to a lengthy entreaty on his own behalf. He augments his case with anecdotes. *God, remember the time I waived my surgery fee because a child had a cleft palate and the parents couldn't pay? See what a good father I am to Annabel? Take note of all my charitable contributions—thousands and thousands of dollars. Please recall the unsolicited raise I gave Delfina and the way I forgave Lucy. Don't forget I'm a good son. The best. I call my mother every day.*

"In the blowing of the wind and in the chill of winter, we remember them," the rabbi says.

Do they remember me, really? Can they hear my giggle and picture my eyes? Know which eyebrow was higher than the other? Remember the taste of my chocolate chip cookies? Listen to Chris Botti or Chris Rock and recall, *Molly thought those guys rocked.*

I've had enough. All this remembering can bring a girl down when there's no promise of blintzes smothered in sour cream, stuffed with cottage cheese or syrupy blueberries, to reward her at the end of the

day's fast, especially when the whole point is bargaining with God for one more year of blood, sweat, and tears of joy, for one more dizzying year of life. "In the blueness of the skies and in the warmth of summer, we remember them," Rabbi S.S. intones as Bob and I take off. Before I leave, I glance back once more.

Barry's been here all day long, prayer oozing from every pore, but damn, he still looks guilty.

Thirty-seven

WARDROBE MALFUNCTION

*L*ucy lays a trio of my most beloved garments on the bed. "Did my sister think she was a prima ballerina?" she says out loud to herself. "Why would anyone ever need three lace skirts?"

The answer is obvious, if only to me. One skirt is layers of tulle that looked fetching with flats and a boatneck top whenever I tried to channel Audrey Hepburn. Another grazed my ankles. It's the color of iced cappuccino, matches a filmy camisole that Lucy has yet to discover, and makes me feel tall, like an Italian heiress. The third is a gold pouf that barely hits my knees. I wore it once, to an Academy Awards party where I, Oscar the cross-dresser, won for Best Costume.

I don't expect Lucy to appreciate my finery. To Lucy, clothes are a necessity, end of story.

I watch Lucy and not only do I miss my critical, irascible sister, but I'll admit it, I also miss clothes—buying them, fondling them, and pretending that I'm someone else when I wear them. I miss my clothes, strangers', and even mistakes-in-the-making I scoffed at in magazines. Maybe I am a scoffer after all.

Every few hours, Lucy phones my mother. "What should I do with the outfit Molly wore to Annabel's naming?" Another nursing mommy

might have chosen a flowing tunic and stretchy-waist pants that coordinated with projectile vomit, but I'd honored the occasion in a winter-white bouclé sheath and coat.

"I'd like it," my mother says. "Ship it here." She'll hang it next to my wedding gown and hope it still smells of my perfume. Which makes me wonder, would my fortunes have been different if my scent had been, say, Paris by Yves Saint-Laurent and not Eternity by Calvin Klein?

"The sheared beaver coat you gave her senior year? It's molting."

"Maybe a charity wants it."

"Her cheerleading uniform?"

"Home."

Not the Smithsonian? I'm crushed.

"A boatload of black pants?" Lucy asks, wondering why ten pairs were necessary. I wore them all, cheap, expensive, gabardines, silk, wools, low-rise, cropped, cords, and especially the ones designed by Karl Lagerfeld for H&M. Fifty-nine dollars' worth of unadulterated pleasure.

"Honestly," my mother says, moving along to cranky. "Use your own judgment." She catches herself for snapping.

This is the second day of the purge. Lucy already showered Delfina with piles of handbags and sweaters. Today she came to work with a gaily branded satchel—Coach! Coach! Coach!—instead of her reliable vinyl tote. I hope she looks inside the hidden zippered compartment, where she'll find a twenty-dollar bill.

For Lucy this is a triathlon that requires focus and stamina. She doesn't want Annabel to see her mother's worldly possessions exhibited as if a yard sale were in progress, so she's limiting her efforts to when my daughter's away. My sister hasn't even laid eyes on Barry. She's checked into a small hotel on Madison, where she passed last night watching an American League playoff game along with a Kirin beer and a chaser of unagi rolls. This morning she charged through Central Park, timing her power walk to arrive after Annabel left for school.

But now, even though Annabel won't be home for hours, Lucy's heading out, shifting a duffel from hand to hand. The subway pulls into the station as she races down the steps. Good sign. Whenever the mass transit gods smiled on me, I considered the event to have profound cosmic significance. Unfortunately, I also read meaning into reverse

karma, such as picking the seat next to the guy who'd forsworn deodorant or the teenage girl who shrieked "Motherfucka!" because my leg brushed hers.

Lucy gets off at Columbus Circle. Brie suggested lunch spots all over town—the Little Owl, Pastis, Le Cirque—but Lucy vetoed every one: too far, too French, too phony. She is not impressed by forty-dollar entrées, steaks with a resumé, gawking taxidermy, pickle juice cocktails, or snowy white truffles. The last food trend Lucy got on board with was frozen yogurt. What's really going on is, of course, pride and prejudice. Lucy wants to be on an equal footing with Brie, not faced with her air-kissing a maître d' or whipping out a black Amex card, insisting that Lucy be her guest. She'd rather eat toads than let Brie pay.

Brie and Lucy finally agreed to meet in a small café within a vertical mall that overlooks the park. Lucy arrives early and waits. And waits. She's standing at the café's entrance. Bouchon Bakery is first come, first served, not a place where she'd be graciously seated and offered a drink. I wish I could tell her that she may as well read the first two chapters of a book at the Borders on the floor below: it's going to be a while.

Predictably, Brie is twenty minutes late. By the time she waves from the escalator, my sister's face has crimped into a grimace.

"Sorry," Brie says, airy and smiley. "Couldn't get a taxi." Liar. She found one instantly, eight minutes ago, after she left her office on Madison and Sixty-first. I learned to work around Brie time, but Lucy considers tardiness an offense right up there with coveting your neighbor's ox. Brie hesitates about whether to kiss Lucy's cheek. The opportunity passes. "Good to see you!" Brie says, grinning too brightly.

"You too," Lucy answers as they walk to a long communal table. They hop on the tall chairs, facing each other. Brie and Lucy are nearly the same height, although Brie is a champagne flute, Lucy a sturdy highball. Aside from my funeral and shiva, I can't recall them being alone together. Certainly, they've never shared a meal without me as referee.

Lucy decides to get to the point. "I thought you'd like these things," she says, and slides the bag to Brie's side.

Brie eyes the duffel uncomfortably, as if it might contain my head.

"C'mon, Brie," Lucy says. "Look inside."

Brie opens the bag and carefully unfolds the gold skirt; a pair of kiwi-green silk pajamas; a hand-crocheted gray sweater, delicate as

Charlotte's web; and a scarlet jacket elaborately embroidered with silver flowers and butterflies. I'll say this for Lucy—our tastes may have harmonized like olives and ice cream, but in picking these treasures, she's aced it.

Brie keeps her tears locked up inside. After she wordlessly refolds every piece of clothing, remembering how I looked in each one and adored these particular things, she wonders, should she put her hand on Lucy's arm? Get up, walk around, and hug her? My sister exists in a sentimental no-fly zone that Brie knows better than to try to invade. Instead she says simply, "Lucy, thank you. I'm touched—beyond words—and very grateful for all these ways to remember Molly." The formality of the statement does nothing to mitigate the tension that fortifies the air like humidity.

"You're welcome," Lucy says.

"Are you sure you don't want all of this?"

"Could you honestly see me in a gold skirt that wouldn't cover my ass?" Lucy says. *Doesn't Brie know me at all?* she wonders. "I'm sure Molly would've wanted you to have them. In fact, if there's anything else you'd like, let me know."

There is. Brie would like to get Lucy talking—about Barry, about Annabel, and mostly about why exactly she thinks I am not able to be at the table right now, making sure that the two of them don't end in a hammerlock. But Brie doesn't have the combination to Lucy. While she thinks about what to say next, Lucy selects a new topic. "What's good here?" she asks as she glances at the menu. "I'm thinking about tomato soup with the grilled cheese."

"Never had it," says Brie, who, despite her name, isn't the sort to gobble an inch of cheese oozing between thick slabs of white bread. "I always order the endive and watercress salad."

Which is why you have no thighs, Lucy realizes. *What the fuck am I going to talk to this woman about?* Lucy is losing sight not only of the most obvious theme—how I died, ladies—but also of how smart Brie is, how kind, and how much I got out of having a friend twice as resolute as I would ever be. As if I ever would have gone hang-gliding on my own.

"How does Annabel seem to you?" Brie asks. Letting Lucy clean out closets is one thing, but has Barry actually allowed Lucy to be alone with Annabel, given the kidnapping that almost was?

"I haven't spent enough time with her to tell," Lucy says. "We hung out a little yesterday afternoon"—chaperoned by Delfina, who rode shotgun—"but then I had to head out." *To avoid Barry.*

"Saturday after next I'm taking her to MoMA," Brie said.

Exactly what every kid her age needs, Lucy thinks. *She'll take one look at the Van Goghs and have nightmares for weeks. Enough with this small talk,* she decides. "So, what do you hear from that detective? Anything new?" Hicks hasn't returned her call from a few days ago.

"He's evaluating the suicide theory," Brie says. "Given the letter . . ."

"The letter? What a crock," Lucy says. "I don't know when my sister wrote that sop, but I'm positive it wasn't to announce that she was going to off herself."

"Can you prove this?" What Lucy saw as mawkish, Brie found sweet. Then again, she is now the devoted surrogate mother to a leaping canine who sleeps at the foot of her bed. Every day, maternal muscles she never knew she had begin to twitch.

"Of course I can't *prove* it," Lucy says. The look on her face might be defiant—or defensive. "It's a gut feeling."

"Well, for what it's worth, I agree."

"Really?" Brie's stock has spiked on Lucy's Nasdaq. She is enormously pleased. "And how recently did you speak to the good detective?" *The guy who should have unraveled this mystery by now. How could any other case vie for his precious time?*

"Last night," Brie says as the food arrives.

"Really?" She's already on the warpath about Hicks being more responsive to a mere friend than to flesh and blood. "What does New York's finest have to say?"

Nothing that Brie wants to repeat. She takes a small bite of watercress, holding her knife and fork aloft as if she were raised by the Von Somebodies of Vienna, not outside of Portland, born to Sunshine and Herb, stringy, Birkenstock-wearing potters. Brie's table manners annoy Lucy. "I feel like there's something you're keeping from me," Lucy says, using the voice that always works with her students. *Jackson, get out of the block corner this minute—it's snack time! Emily! Look at me. Now.*

Brie tilts her face and tries to stay composed, but she breaks out in a small grin. "Lucy," she whispers after a moment, "the most amazing thing happened last night. Hicks and I slept together."

Lucy doesn't want for friends—fellow teachers, running buddies, college classmates, neighbors of every stripe, dogs, cats, hamsters, old people at the center where she volunteers, friends' toddlers. But she has no friends like Brie, who bill almost a thousand dollars an hour and take up with a spoiled South American heiress who speaks lisping Castilian Spanish.

"What about Isabella?" she blurts out. *Isn't one lover enough?*

"Isadora?" Brie says. "It didn't work out. We want different things."

I'll say, Lucy thinks. *Can't this woman pick a gender and stick with it? It's fucking unfair. I haven't had a date in eight months, and it's not as if I didn't notice Hicks. I have eyes.*

Brie feels the rumble of Lucy's rage and sees that she'll have to float this conversation. "Detective Hicks"—she hasn't yet been able to call him Hiawatha or even Hi—"is different from every other man I've been with, in a remarkably good way." The kissing was longer and sweeter, until she wanted to moan in boldface type, and he caressed her as if she were close to holy, which Brie has no desire to be in this man's presence and plans to make clear. When she looks in Hicks' eyes, every filthy-fabulous thought she's ever imagined suddenly seems like lyrics to a song her body knew by heart.

Brie looks up from her salad at Lucy, thinking, *Give me something here. Act like a girl! Your sister would have been all over me.* Were I there, I'd say, *How did it happen? Were you both drunk? Who said what first? His best move? I've never been with a black man—is it better? Way better? Okay, forgive me for asking, but is he, I don't know how to put this, huge? Does he make you laugh? Listen to you? Are you in love? And, for extra credit, do you think Hicks is?*

Brie is right. I would be rattling on like one of those regrettable squawking parrots you order on QVC after midnight. I want to reach out and hug Brie. I've been rooting for her and Hicks, the kind of standup guy every woman needs if she decides to give men another shot. I predict that she's finally found her equal. And yes, I'm not being entirely unselfish—maybe the relationship will be the kick in the butt Hicks needs to solve my case.

"So you and the detective," Lucy finally says. "I'm curious. How did it happen?" *What do other women do that I don't?* This is what my sister wants to know. Lucy feels as if every female but her has received anno-

tated, illustrated directions on how to attract and keep a man. Were such instructions the secret prize in their first Tampax box?

"It just happened," Brie answers. Like it always does. One minute you're having an ordinary conversation, complaining about presidential campaigns that last as long as getting a master's; the next, all the atoms around you have realigned. Suddenly there's no one else in the bowling alley or on the plane or at the hardware store. You notice that his eyes are undressing you, and you wonder what it would feel like if your hands were under his shirt.

Brie senses an openness she's never noticed before in Lucy's face and for a few seconds feels as if it's me sitting across from her. There's a connection. Brie wonders, *Could I make this woman my friend? I could use a friend.* There's a canyon in her heart that I used to fill. She turns over the question as she takes her last bite of salad.

"It's going to happen for you, Lucy," Brie says. "I know it." The minute the words tumble out she's sure my sister will take them as condescending. She's forded a river and found a grizzly bear on the other bank.

"Yeah, well, whatever," Lucy grunts.

"Do you have time for coffee?" Brie asks.

"No can do," Lucy answers, and waves to the server. "There's a lot I haven't gone through yet, and I don't have much time before Annabel gets back."

"Could you use some help?" Brie asks. "I could cancel my afternoon appointments."

"I've got it covered." Lucy's face has closed down. You can practically hear the grinding grate.

Brie takes out her wallet. "You're my guest."

"Absolutely not," Lucy says as she lays down five crisp tens, gets up, and slips into her jacket. "This one's on me. But I have a favor to ask."

"Shoot," Brie says.

"Your boyfriend. Tell him to find my sister's killer."

The next day—after dragging seven bags of Molly-abilia to the thrift shop—my sister finally gets down to my drawers. Yesterday, knowing Aunt Lucy was visiting, Annabel refused to go to ballet. Delfina reluc-

tantly watches Oprah in her room, popping out every ten minutes to check on my sister and daughter bonding over Nemo. Lucy gives Annabel her bath, reads her a story, and just as our daughter nods off, Barry arrives.

"You're good to take care of all this for me," he says as he pours them each a glass of amaretto. "How's it going?"

"By tomorrow the dig will be complete," Lucy says.

"Any rare finds?" Barry pokes the fire, and the flames salute him.

"Not really, unless you count a green reptile belt—I assume that means I've reached the Paleozoic era, or at least the eighties." Lucy has decided to keep my Swatch, which matches the one she lost years ago.

She glances at Barry, who seems to be studying the fire. She knows she owes him. "About that crazy thing I did at Annabel's school—I was wacko. I wrote you, but I need to say it out loud. I'm so sorry. But it was done out of love, misguided but—"

"Forget it," he says as he refills his glass. "I have." *Almost.*

He certainly doesn't want to talk about it. All day he's been marinating in estrogen. This afternoon was nonstop consultations, culminating with a fifteen-year-old who fought with her mother over the rhinoplasty Madame Pixie Nose was insisting on so the two of them would look related. Then Stephanie lambasted him for forgetting some dinner date she swore they'd made for tonight. Even his nurse eyed him as if he were Dr. Mengele. Barry wishes he could mainline the liqueur. He offers Lucy another pour, but she declines. He looks hard at his sister-in-law, whose straight-arrow posture accentuates her bountiful chest.

Lucy feels his stare. "Time to go," she says abruptly. "I'll see you tomorrow night." But she won't. She's booked an afternoon flight, and she's not in the mood for a weepy goodbye.

The following morning Lucy faces my highboy, whose drawers are carefully lined with pale purple paper that long ago lost its lilac scent. If you were a Victorian woman who owned a chemise, two pair of drawers, a corset, five ribbons, and a bonnet, this narrow chest would have been practical. In my case it's jammed with black tights, bras, thongs, socks, nightgowns, camisoles, and random sex toys. I loved the highboy's walnut sheen, its deeply carved flowers, and especially its wavy

mirror, which allowed me the luxury of merely estimating my hair on off days.

Lucy starts at the top—bras—and works her way down. She sorts quickly to avoid feeling anything, since wandering through another woman's lingerie is like being in the same bed with her when she's having sex. It takes her less than an hour to get to the bottom drawer, where she spots the flannel nightgown she sent me when I was pregnant. Whenever I wore it, I was Maria in *The Sound of Music.* No whiskers-on-kittens gal herself, Lucy nonetheless gently fingers the dainty eyelet around its yoke. This, she suddenly decides, she will save for herself.

She shakes out the nightgown and holds it up. From its voluminous folds, a black-and-white photograph falls on the rug, facedown.

One day Luke set up a tripod and we posed, again and again. This shot was the one I saved. My eyes are closed and I'm laughing. Not an especially flattering pose. What I loved about the photo was the way Luke is looking at me with a pour of pure honeyed tenderness. Only I might know how blue those eyes are, but any casual observer can see they're filled with love. On the back of the photograph, I've written *November.* Lucy can tell from my haircut that the captured moment happened within the last few years.

She feels chilled. Her breath comes in short bursts. Lucy stares at the picture and with her index finger touches my face as if she is stroking my cheek. "Jesus, Molly," she whispers. "How dumb could a woman be? If you loved this guy, whoever this lug nut is, why didn't you leave your husband? And if it's Barry you love, why would you keep this red flag in your drawer?"

She does have a point.

Lucy tries to read the face of the man in the picture. *This guy loves you,* she thinks. *And you probably felt the same way.*

Lucy wipes away a tear. She quickly slips the picture into her pocket, ties together the last bag, and walks out of the room.

Thirty-eight

KLUTZ, CUTS, GUTS

icks' office is nothing special—twitchy fluorescents, a wooden floor that's never flirted with polyurethane, and a metal desk so dented you wonder if it's been kicked. It has. He sits in an oak swivel chair that, to the irritation of Detective Gonzalez, who shares the cubicle, he mindlessly spins—and squeaks—as he studies his bulletin board. On it is what I like to think of as a growing shrine to me, with photos of Barry, Lucy, Kitty, my parents, Brie, Isadora, and Barry's nurses (including the fawning witch who always sniveled, "Dr. Barry will have to return your call"). I also see a cattle call of interchangeable women who I assume are patients. One is Stephanie; others I recognize from the funeral and shiva, the rest are high-maintenance strangers. The centerpiece of this sacred masterpiece is a map Hicks has drawn— rather well—of the path from my home to my next-to-final resting place. X marks the spot where my life ended, the spot that's got Hicks thinking out loud.

"Did someone off you or did you do it to yourself? Tell me, pretty lady."

I wish I could. So does Gonzalez. She's sick of Hicks tossing questions into the office air, which smells of day-old coffee, mustard, and

air freshener working overtime. "Hi, you talkin' to me?" she mutters. Georgia Gonzalez may demonstrate the subtlety of a hockey player, but she has instincts Hicks trusts as much as—maybe more than—his own.

"Sorry there, G.G. I didn't mean to interrupt your solving a Very Important Crime," he says. "Put any drug lords in the slammer today?"

"You don't honestly think that woman killed herself, do you?" They chew over my case every day. Gonzalez read my letter, which almost made her cry—she's a mother, after all—and announced to Hicks immediately that it was too prim to be a suicide note.

It's taken a few days for him to come to the same conclusion. "Nah, I don't think it was a DIY," he admits. "That'd make my life too easy, and it's also too damn hard to kill yourself by running your bike off the road. Unless she screwed up when she was heading for the river to drown. Nope, today I'm leaning back toward damn nasty accident."

He conjures it. Klutz, cuts, guts. Mud, thud, blood.

"I keep thinking the mother-in-law hired 1-800-Kill-Her." Gonzalez says this with a half smile that makes her tough, round face look almost pretty. "When I taught kindergarten I used to tell kids' parents that learning to share's a lifelong job. Wants her boy all to herself."

"Ya think?" Hicks gets up, coffee cup in hand, to face Detective Gonzalez. "And when were you a nursery school teacher? Scares the nuts off me to think that you were entrusted with impressionable young minds."

Gonzalez looks away. "A lot you don't know. I am a woman of deep mystery."

"How do I prove that Kitty Katz did it?"

"Not my case."

"G.G., did you not just tell me about learning to share?"

Gonzalez finishes her coffee and takes out a lipstick in her signature shade of iridescent tangerine. She applies it without looking in a mirror.

"Don't go all cliché there, G.G. Does *your* daughter-in-law hate you?" Hicks went to the wedding last year of Gonzalez's son, eighteen and a father. The kid was a standup guy when his girlfriend got knocked up.

"Maria worships me."

"Kitty Katz more or less said the same thing about Molly."

I didn't overhear that particular conversation, but I love that we're on a first-name basis, Hicks and I.

"What about the demented sister?" Gonzalez looks Hicks in the eye.

"*Crazy*'s not the word for Lucy Divine," Hicks says, even if Lucy can't prove where she was the day Molly died. "You're jerking me around, G.G., my friend." The notes in Hicks' file on Lucy run along the course of *intense, envious, high-strung, bitter.* "But no, I haven't ruled her out," though as Hicks is getting to know Lucy, he likes her more and more. She's no killer, his gut tells him.

"And the bad boy himself?"

"Dr. Strangelove?" Hicks perches on Gonzalez's desk, tosses his coffee cup into the trash, folds his arms, and leans against the wall.

"I was thinking of the other guy," Gonzalez says as she mimics his posture. When Hicks isn't around, I've seen her stare long and hard at Luke's picture. We have that in common.

"I'm leaning more in the doc's direction myself, but no, he hasn't dropped off my list." As predictable as spam, every day Barry hits Hicks with "What's new, Detective?" But my husband's tenacity hasn't convinced Hicks that he's innocent. He can't account without a doubt for where he was at the time of my death. Neither can Luke. Then again, no random runners or bikers have emerged from the ether to pin a crime on either one.

"Where do you stand with the harem?"

"Ah, the ladies. So many women, so little time. Always someone new to meet." Every day, Hicks' trail leads him to yet another current or former patient who he suspects might provide a clue.

"The friend and her Latin babe?"

Ping. Brie's mention turns Hicks to mush. His stern NYPD shell is screeching, *Unprofessional,* but every other constituency within his body is doing a tap dance to celebrate last Saturday. Brie is going to be his little secret. He doesn't want this newly sowed romance—dare he call it that—trampled by the verbal assaults of his dear but cynical friend G.G., although in the past they've shared details of romantic entanglements. There's been no reason for such discussion, however, in longer than Hicks would care to recall. Still, he's not ready to introduce

and beat to death the baffling case of Sabrina Lawson, Esq., and Detective Hiawatha Hicks.

"The friend has been duly interrogated, I assure you. She can account for being in São Paulo the night of the event, and Molly Marx didn't seem to matter much to Ms. Vega one way or another. I can't see her getting herself in a lather over her."

"You don't know Latin women very well, do you, Hi?"

"No," he says. "I don't. I don't claim to know any kind of women very well, G.G." *Molly, especially.* Hicks looks at the bulletin board. *Maybe I should get myself some darts and wherever one hits, that's who did it,* he thinks.

Thirty-nine

A SMALL WORLD, AFTER ALL

I'll take it." I didn't need the dress, but I wanted it—and not just because it made my hips look narrow. I coveted this wisp of wine-red velvet because it was new, which was the way I wanted Barry to see me.

"Will you be taking the package with you?" the waif at the cash register asked as she twirled a coil of wiry copper hair sprung from her bun.

It hadn't occurred to me to have the dress delivered, but the weather forecast was for rain and, what the hell, I was feeling what—for me—amounted to devil-may-care. "You know what?" I said. "Please send it." I gave the girl my credit card, feeling virtuous that the price was 40 percent off. Was this because Barneys' truly haute shoppers had caucused and agreed to snub this garment? No matter. I could picture the spaghetti straps showing off my shoulders and the skirt swirling around my knees as Barry and I took the floor to swing-dance. The other night, after we tucked Annabel into bed, we'd actually popped in a CD and practiced in the kitchen.

We'd been invited to a Valentine's Day party. For the last few years, I'd felt almost like Lucy, inclined to boycott the love-drug holiday even in her classroom, to the relief of most four-year-old boys and the dis-

may of all the girls, who generally threatened to stage their own St. Valentine's Day Massacre when they learned of this outrage. At the very least, I never knew what kind of cards to buy Barry and thus avoided the primary categories—sex addict and snooky-wookums—in favor of those in the neighborhood of funny (*I'm not interested in a normal relationship. I like ours better*). Three cards were tucked away, waiting for my flourishy inscription, along with a pair of silk boxer briefs.

Last February 14 had presented the additional challenge of the Luke factor. But this year I didn't want to think about him, the fondue we'd fed each other at Artisanal, my favorite next-best-to-Paris bistro, or his persistent calls—at least once a week—which I'd been dodging. Every time Luke's face flashed in my brain I tried to activate my denial button. Once in a while, it functioned, blinking *Luke who?* If I visualized him as an alien life force infecting my heart and soul, I could banish his image and voice for hours at a time. I was determined to make room for Barry and Barry alone, whom I reminded myself to think of as "my husband."

I floated out of the store. So did my umbrella, which in a burst of independence reversed and landed in the gutter. I wasn't going to let my favorable mood be washed away by this annoyance or the fact that I appeared to be invisible to every cruising cab. I walked to the bus shelter. When I opened my wallet I discovered I was a quarter short of exact change. With birthday party manners, I begged twenty-five cents from a senior citizen, boarded the bus, and held tightly to the overhead bar as the vehicle belched up Madison Avenue. On the corner of Seventy-ninth Street I waited patiently for a second bus to carry me through the park. On Amsterdam Avenue, I got out, stepped directly into water, and soaked my suede flats.

"I hate when that happens," said a stranger who, in exiting the bus, had leaped over the puddle with a leggy *brisé*. I took in the raincoat, matching hat, and knee-high boots—one Chanel too many, even if the getup was bona fide. The woman was about my age, maybe younger, the type who appeared to have acquired a water-repellent finish.

"No biggie," I said as dirty slush oozed into my tights. I was determined not to let something this inconsequential ruin my afternoon, not after this morning.

Earlier that day, Barry and I had finished our seventh fifty-minute

hour of Dr. Stafford's psychic sorcery. Through the doctor's judicious questioning, fortified by the odd epiphany, half-remembered dreams, and my unmitigated optimism, I'd become positive that this counseling was steering us toward closeness or even—should I let myself think the word?—intimacy. And the day before, while putting away Barry's shirts, I came across legitimate evidence in the form of a package from Kitty's favorite jeweler. I carefully untied the red silk ribbon to snoop, and was rewarded by the wink of a multifaceted pale pink stone heart pendant glittering within a setting of pavé stones the color of plum jelly. It wasn't what I might have chosen for myself—way more Kitty than Molly—but when I carefully lifted the necklace out of the velvet box, it nestled perfectly in the hollow of my neck. I stared at my reflection and felt the thump of my achy-breaky heart.

My husband was making amends, trying to give us another running start toward happiness. I wouldn't let myself think otherwise. I seriously doubted that it was a gift for Kitty, and not even Barry Marx could be brazen enough to buy a tender—okay, rather gaudy but still notably sweet—gift for another woman and store it in our very own bedroom, a mere six feet from our marriage bed. This meant the things he'd been saying in Dr. Stafford's office must be true. As I sloshed along, thinking about the next weekend's Valentine's Day party, my actual heart beat wildly, a sensation I hadn't felt toward Barry since, well, ever.

Halfway down the block I noticed Madame Chanel keeping pace with me, maybe six feet to my right. "Want to get under here?" she said to me, nodding toward her umbrella, apparently escaped from a golf course. "There's plenty of room."

My feet were cold, slipping inside my ruined shoes, and the rain was landing on my head. "Yes!" I said, and scurried toward my savior, thinking this was exactly the sort of fortuitous, munificent gesture I should attempt to write up, speckled with wit, and send to the "Metropolitan Diary" column of the *New York Times*. "Thanks. I'm heading downtown a few blocks to register my daughter for swimming lessons."

Annabel refused to put so much as a toe in the water, and Barry and I had decided that the situation had to be faced. Still, even if it was true, why do I always blather?

"That's where I'm headed, too," the woman said. Her voice was slightly nasal, not up to Chanel standard.

"No kidding?"

"Really," the woman said. "Apparently, my son's amphibious."

"How old is he?"

"Three and a half."

"My daughter is about that age. She's Annabel. And I'm Molly, by the way."

She turned toward me. "Nice to meet you, Molly." She gave me a lingering, sideways smile and pronounced my utilitarian name slowly, as if she'd never heard it before. I waited for her to volunteer her name and perhaps her son's, but she offered nothing. I tried to take a discreet but closer peek at this stranger, but the rain and the difference in our heights—she was tall—made that difficult. Even under the umbrella and in the downpour, however, her teeth were hard to miss. Were they capped or was she just overzealous with a bleaching kit?

The two of us continued to walk silently for several blocks until we reached our destination and stopped under its awning. Coco Chanel snapped shut her umbrella and easily pushed open the heavy glass door for both of us. We entered the building's lobby, which was thick with mothers, nannies, strollers, and toddlers. The smell of damp wool and chaos was in the air.

"Mrs. Marx?" someone shouted as an elevator discharged an additional supply of noisy women and children.

I turned in the crush. "Narcissa?"

"Yes, ma'am," she said, waddling toward me. "You here for the swimming? I just signed up Ella. Better hurry—it's nearly full up."

"Rats," I said, and thought a stronger word. Once again, had every other mother mastered this drill and arrived hours ago? Why had I wasted time shopping or not sent Delfina to take care of this chore? Because I always underestimated the ballsy competition of New York moms and because I wanted that dress and because Delfina was back at the apartment, supervising Annabel and, for that matter, Ella, which was why Narcissa was here. "Well, good to see you, Narcissa. I'll give it a go." At least if Ella was in the swim class, it would be easier to sell Annabel on the idea that practicing the dead man's float in pee-warmed water was something she should look forward to doing every Wednesday at three.

The next elevator was too full to enter. And the one after that. I fi-

nally mashed myself into the fourth car that came along, and when the door opened on the fifth floor, I saw that my umbrella-toting buddy was there, too, and had already reached the front of the line, with only one woman ahead of her. She must have run up the stairs. *Note to self,* I thought. *Next time, haul ass.*

"I saved you a spot," Coco shouted to me, causing the other mothers and nannies to glare.

"Hey, no way," one of them said. "I got here first. Fair's fair."

The complainer was right. "Thanks, anyway," I said. I walked to the back of the small room and started to search in my bag for the Home section of the *Times* when I heard my phone blare "When the Saints Go Marching In." By the time I found the phone—in my coat pocket, under the crumpled Barneys receipt—I'd missed the call. Luke. His third that day, not that I'd answered any of them.

I put away the phone and opened my newspaper. I found it hard to concentrate. Luke was not just back in my head, whispering, taunting, and warmly blowing into my ear—he was coursing through my body like Wi-Fi.

The phone rang again. Once again I ignored his ring. *I've known saints,* I thought, *and you, my friend, are no saint.* The phone sounded again.

"If you're not going to take your calls, at least turn off your damn phone," the woman ahead of me snarled, attracting the attention of everyone in the small room.

Why hadn't I grabbed that bitch's place in line when I had the chance? "I'm sorry if I'm bothering you," I replied, "but I have to keep my phone on." Delfina might call, or Barry.

"You know, you're not only annoying, you're rude," Squawk Box hissed.

The phone rang again. The room grew silent as the woman's stare dared me to answer it. The phone blared and the saints marched.

I felt trapped and intimidated. "Hello," I said. "No, I really can't talk now." Luke's voice was casting its usual spell. "I'm not kidding, I can't . . ." He went on for a bit, his rhetoric less pleading than calmly, appealingly persuasive. "I disagree—that's a terrible idea." Damn, he was persistent.

I felt a force push me toward him, gentle, invisible like a breeze.

"Okay, okay, You should have been a lawyer. Okay, we'll meet . . . we'll talk. But not today, because . . ." I looked outside. The rain had suddenly stopped. The sun had come out. "Because I'm going . . . biking." As I clicked off, my resolve began to crumble.

I sensed that every eye and ear in the room had been trained on me and my call. They were Argentina, I was Evita. I tried to set my cell to vibrate, but the saints blared again. I did my best to lower my head and whisper. "Of course I have feelings for you." As if that were ever the real problem.

"Molly, I love you," Luke said, to me and the whole room. Apparently I'd hit the mechanism for speakerphone.

"I'm going biking now," I said. "We'll work this out some other time." I couldn't listen. "I'm getting off now." I snapped the lid of my phone shut and shoved it in my pocket, trying to avoid glances and snickers.

Fortunately, the registrar motioned me to step forward. The woman's fingers tap-danced on her computer keyboard. There would be room for Annabel, the last slot. *Keep breathing,* I told myself. *It's still a good day.*

As I began to complete the form, the woman in the Chanel raincoat, who I noticed had been standing off to the side, swished past me without saying so much as goodbye. *She certainly runs hot and cold,* I thought just as this woman also got a call.

"Barry," I was almost positive I heard her say. Her volume wasn't pianissimo, and unless I was being utterly paranoid, I had the feeling that she wanted to be overheard. "Well, that's very interesting, but I can top that. You didn't tell me your wife was attractive. Anyway, news flash. You were right. She is definitely seeing someone."

I looked up. The woman was gone.

Forty

EVERYBODY MUST GET STONED

Run this by me again—*why* do we need an unveiling?" Barry and Kitty are finishing their second cup of triple-filtered coffee one Sunday. My husband sees himself reflected in the new double-wide, glass-doored stainless-steel refrigerator and thinks what I think: what was wrong with the kitchen his mother put in nine years ago—Shaker cabinetry, granite countertops, and a fridge that kept food as cold as required? When you have enough money, however, as well as an architect on speed dial, you can amuse yourself by selecting warming drawers and six-burner professional ranges and still eat out five nights a week.

For someone who spends more time each year in a one-legged king pigeon pose than in prayer, my mother-in-law is, nonetheless, the Wikipedia of Judaic heritage. "That's what's done," she says. "The ceremony has to take place before the one-year anniversary of a death."

"Or else?" Barry says.

"Tradition," Kitty says. She discards the fleeting notion of exhibiting self-control. "Besides, let's say you and Stephanie get engaged. You'd want the unveiling to be out of the way, wouldn't you?"

Barry chokes on a thick slab of Bermuda onion, which crowns his poppy-seed bagel.

"I'm talking hypothetically, of course," Kitty says. "Although that girl's just what you need."

What qualifications is my mother-in-law referring to? A big mouth? I'm going with the big ambition. Kitty sees women as the hard drive behind male success. While I believe she's of the opinion that any daughter-in-law is largely just a biological requirement necessary to produce grandchildren, her pragmatic half dictates that as long as a male offspring has to marry, he'd best trade up to someone a lot like her.

"You're way ahead of yourself," Barry says after he stops coughing.

"Am I?" Kitty turns her back to refill her black-and-white-striped porcelain mugs—hers is lined in shocking pink, his in pistachio green—and predicts an engagement before the summer. Maybe a destination wedding. She's always wanted to see the Seychelles. Dubai, Bhutan, and Bali are also on Kitty's wish list, but certainly Stephanie will have her own ideas. One thing Kitty knows is that there's nothing subtle about a thirty-four-year-old woman who invited her to lunch at Saks and then suggested a stroll to her uncle's teensy-weensy jewelry store on Forty-seventh Street, where she casually pointed out a 1920s Art Deco diamond solitaire almost as big as the shop. Asscher cut, significant baguettes. Another mother might have been appalled, but Kitty admires Stephanie's self-assurance. She believes a woman needs focus as much as state-of-the-art bedroom expertise. "Leave the unveiling to me," she says to Barry. "Order the stone."

Barry did—which is why Rabbi S.S. is warming up his vocal cords to once again be in service to my family tomorrow, why I can practically smell the cinnamon-raisin babkas, yeasty and plump, rising in their silvery loaf pans, and why a marble monument waits under wraps at Serenity Haven. It's pinkish gray, not unlike Kitty's recently installed tinted concrete countertops.

I take a gander under the drape, hoping Barry might have exhibited a trace of originality with the stone's inscription. While I haven't decided if I'm more Bette Davis ("She did it the hard way"), Karen Carpenter ("A star on earth, a star in heaven"), or Dean Martin ("Every-

body loves somebody sometime"), surely Barry could have done better than *Molly Divine Marx, beloved daughter, wife, and mother.* Simple and dignified, yes, but where's my mystery? My élan? My cheeky, noir-ish humor? I might have liked *Molly, biker chick.* Or even something in shockingly bad taste: *My grandparents went through the Holocaust and all I got was this?* I did, after all, die at only thirty-five.

My Divines arrived last night, two days ahead of Sunday's noon service. Annabel will be joining Grammy and Grandpa at the Children's Museum later this morning, but Lucy's begged off. I trail her as she leaves a coffee shop on Broadway and begins to walk north. She appears immune to the December air as she tramps briskly past colossal produce markets, Barnes & Noble, and a bank whose unique selling feature seems to be its handy branches in Auckland and Kuala Lumpur. Never looking up, she trudges by glassy condos piercing the gray sky. She all but race-walks, staring ahead.

Not even the somber majesty of Columbia University makes Lucy blink, but on 120th Street she hangs a left and pauses to admire the Gothic splendor of Riverside Church, which makes Temple Emanuel-El, the snazziest synagogue in North America, look as drab as a drugstore. Lucy doesn't, however, linger. She heads over to Grant's Tomb.

Now *there's* a final resting place. Ever since the Parks Department was shamed into spiffing it up—this happened at the moment when Times Square did a 180 from working girls, porn, and peep shows to tourists, Oreo Overload sundaes, and Disney blockbusters—I used to drop in on my friends Ulysses and Julia, parking my bike at the rack outside. "Who's buried in Grant's Tomb?" was Papa Louie's idea of a riddle, which he delivered with his Groucho brows wiggling. By kindergarten Lucy and I could spit back, "No one!" The general and the missus are *entombed* in twin Beaux Arts sarcophagi.

Lucy skips the inside of the monument, although she glances at the engraving above its entrance: *Let us have peace,* which I always thought was an ironic epitaph for one of American history's most hell-bent hawks. Lucy stuffs her hands deep in the pockets of her purple down coat and turns toward the woods skirting one of the designated nature preserves. FOREVER WILD, the sign says.

When Manhattan people think *park* it's Central, with its showy lakes and gondolas, the kelly green Sheep Meadow, and a zoo that's

home to neurotic polar bears. Even if they live nearby, few locals venture into Riverside, the anorexic four-mile stepchild also designed by the grand master, Frederick Law Olmsted. Despite the fact that Meg Ryan and Tom Hanks met cute by its flowerbeds in *You've Got Mail,* Riverside is low-key, as befits this side of the city. Bikers, runners, and dog walkers take care of business here, but it remains a park for a quick hit, not a holiday.

Lucy winds down an overgrown path to the level above the lonesome Hudson, where the wind whips off the water, chilling her face and reddening her cheeks. It feels fifteen degrees colder than on Broadway. Whoever is around at this hour moves at a quick clip, whether on two feet or four. As she strides forward, the tassels of her knit hat bob like Heidi's braids.

Two golden retrievers zoom past. Their master soon follows and stops to check his watch. It's past nine, the witching hour when dogs must return to the leash, lest their owners get slapped with a fine big enough to buy a decent dinner for two. "Sigmund," the owner shouts, "Hamlet, come here." But the dogs ignore him, perhaps embarrassed by their names. They run to Lucy, who bends down to stroke their furry heads and give them a welcome behind-the-ears scratch.

"There you boys are," the man says, reaching them as the larger of the dogs jumps up to lick Lucy's face and the other tries to bite one of her tassels.

She decides that a pet lover is safe for conversation. "Can you tell me how to get down to the river, please?" She points in the direction of the George Washington Bridge, which dangles in the distance like a strand of gray Majorca pearls.

"Sure," the man says with an open smile. He looks like the kind of guy Lucy might like—shaggy-haired and broad-shouldered, not a label in sight, discounting the Yankees cap. He carries the *Times* sports section under his arm. Columbia professor or shrink, I guess. This neighborhood is well stocked with both. "Let's see. There are a few twists and turns." He strokes his beard as he looks into Lucy's eyes. His eyes are green, his accent Australian, and his tone cheery. "I could lead the way."

I decide that he's divorced. His kids are with Mommy this weekend and he has a day stretching ahead of him in which he's going to braise

short ribs with blood-orange juice and *herbes de Provence* while he drinks a Châteauneuf-du-Pape, listens to the Saturday afternoon opera, and reads a sturdy biography of Winston Churchill. Lucy, buy this lottery ticket. I worry about you being alone, and this dog owner has good guy written all over him.

I wish I knew how to flirt, runs through Lucy's head. *Other women meet men everywhere. Me? Never. And I could do worse. This man's eyes are intelligent. I like his taste in animals and reading material.*

But does my sister let him lead the way? "Oh, that won't be necessary" is her knee-jerk response.

"Chicago," the stranger says, and smiles again, wider this time. There is a small, dear space between his front teeth. He knows he's crazy, but what if this woman would join him for a cup of coffee? He likes her face, devoid of makeup or a visible attitude. They'd get to talk, maybe do a movie, browse a bookstore and then, who knows?

"Chi-caw-go, yes. How can you tell?" Lucy, like every midwesterner, believes everyone has an accent but her.

"Actually, I got my degree at the university there," he says, and waits for Lucy to banter. A man would have to sky-write "I am trying to pick you up" before she might notice that someone found her appealing.

"Great school," she says finally. *Should I tell him I live two miles from Hyde Park?* she thinks. *Nah. Why would he care?* "So, if you could point the way for me?"

He does, and curses himself—why didn't he ask for her number?—as he watches Lucy walk north until she is the size of his fingernail, her purple coat small as a berry.

Finally, my sister reaches the water. She stares at New Jersey as if it will reveal the answer: how did Molly die? Barry, she's convinced, has pushed for tomorrow's unveiling to put a lid on the wrack and ruin of was-she-pushed-or-did-she-jump? The unspoken, preposterous assumption wafting toward Chicago seems to be that I must have engineered my own death. "Molly would never do something so idiotic," she screams at the river. Her eyes follow a barge that makes its sluggish way on the choppy water. "Molly's been goddamn Swift-boated." Lucy shakes her head and makes a sound, a laugh mated with a moan.

Lucy spoke to Hicks yesterday. What does *he* know? Nothing, it

seems, at least nothing he's going to tell Lucy. She's been fishing for weeks, debating. Should she show him the photo? She wishes like hell she'd never found my adulterous ephemera, evidence—but of what?

If Mystery Man was involved in my death, Lucy keeps wondering, wouldn't an NYPD detective have sniffed him out on his own by now and hung him by his thumbs until he confessed? She speculates that Hicks has gotten to this guy and that Hicks doesn't think he did it. In that case, why sully my reputation? The person she wants most to protect is Annabel. Why should her niece ever have to think of her parents as anything less than deliriously happy? Why not keep that fiction going?

From her pocket, Lucy withdraws the photograph of Luke and me. *At least you look happy, sister,* she thinks. *I hope you adored this man—and he adored you back. Wherever and whoever this fool is, I hope he still does.*

Lucy turns back to the park and gazes in both directions. *Molly, this is where you took your last breath—I wish I knew where, exactly.* She walks to the water's edge, presses her lips to the image of my smiling face. She thinks about tearing the picture in two and keeping the half with me. "No, you two should be together," she concludes, and tosses the photograph into the Hudson.

"Let there be peace," she murmurs. "Let there be peace." She bends over, puts her crossed arms on her knees, and hangs her head, weeping.

The picture bobs in the waves and floats rapidly downstream in the murky water. Lucy turns away from the Hudson, but I watch the photo as if it were flesh and blood—Luke terrified, running for his life, a man escaping.

Forty-one

SAM I AM

As the photo sinks in the Hudson, I ring with emptiness that falls short of an emotion, because a feeling would be alive, even if—especially if—it smolders with heartbreak and anger. I am a shadow, a dried leaf, a shriveled stalk, a hollow gourd. I am a lost hope, a broken promise, a memory, an unspoken phrase. Mother Nature has cleared her throat and I am . . . gone.

I can't stay and watch Lucy as she walks away from the river. Why didn't she show some good sense, abort today's mission, and have coffee with Sigmund and Hamlet's owner, then go home with him for sex, short ribs, and the rest of her life? They'd join a food co-op, pop out twins—little brown-haired boys, one named Louie for our grandfather and the other Jake, because it's Lucy's favorite name—and live happily ever after, going off to Australia each winter and Italy in August. Lucy would coach Louie and Jake's soccer team, start her own nursery school, and be a very good and beloved wife and mother.

I turn. Bob is in my face. I gasp, scream, and pound his chest. "Dammit, people are imbeciles, aren't they? Life makes no sense."

"It's time," he says quietly, grabbing my wrists to restrain me.

"Time for what?" Was there an obligation I'd missed?

"Time to move on," Bob whispers.

"What are you talking about?" I plead. Just yesterday I watched Annabel learn to write her first shaky *A*, tilting like a crooked chalet. I was there when Brie and Hicks rented a car to drive to a country inn. They plan to snowshoe—that is, if they get out of bed. I checked on my father after his physical—he has to go on Lipitor, but his blood pressure's fine. Oh, and the doctor wants him to drop twenty pounds. I watched my mother plant a quince branch in potting soil covered with velvety moss—she's coaxing spring into arriving early this year, and hopes to be rewarded soon with delicate white buds. I even sat next to Barry and Stephanie and a thousand other screaming sports maniacs at a Knicks game, until I decided that if I was in the mood for torture, there's C-SPAN.

"You have to ask what good your powers are doing you, Molly," Bob says. "Longing for a life that's over, seeing other people making love and chocolate chip cookies and mistakes . . . Do I have to spell it out for you?"

"But I'm not ready to end this. You told me my powers would last until—until they're terminated. Why should I be the terminator?"

I hear my own fear. My plan was to wait it out and pray that my abilities would continue—not forever (who'd want that?), but at least until the mystery of my death is solved and, far more importantly, until Annabel grows up. But when does that happen these days? After she gets into college or turns twenty-one or graduates or starts to work or lives in her own apartment or is married or has a child? I don't want to go AWOL now.

"Having powers doesn't mean you need to use them," Bob says in the voice of the pediatrician he'd hoped to become.

Perhaps we can negotiate. "Okay, let's say I take a break." Not giving up completely, a hiatus. "Then what?"

"I'd say it's a deal, and that it's time for you to meet someone," he says. "I've been watching you—"

No kidding. Does he think he's invisible? Bob's on every corner, Brother Starbucks of the wild blue yonder. "Who's this someone?"

"Don't be so suspicious. You'll see soon enough." Bob, always preaching patience.

As I wait, the days unroll into a long ribbon of nothing. I skip the

trip to Serenity Haven. Thou shalt unveil without me. Mostly I obsess about Annabel. How did the school carnival go? Has she progressed to *B*? Did Delfina take her for a haircut? Not bangs, I'm hoping. Not with her curls.

My mind drifts. Will Stephanie convince Barry to go to Venice, hoping he'll propose? Will Brie like Hicks' mother's Sunday dinner? Will Mama Hicks like Brie or be appalled that her son is with a white woman? Will Isadora try to get Brie back? The trip to Japan my parents cancelled—will they reschedule? Might Lucy replace her futon with a grown-up couch? Adopt a cat? Will Kitty switch dermatologists?

Who's Luke with now—the blonde he met who resembles me more than my own twin or the skinny, surprisingly smart model with the curly black hair and breathy lisp? Will Hicks solve my case, with or without Detective Gonzalez's intuition? My old life is the world's best soap opera, viewing audience of one.

I try to manufacture some willpower that would prevent me from dropping in below. A deeply embedded vein of superstition helps me not to cheat, and as interesting as Down There is, Bob has not just tantalized my imagination, he's gotten me worried. What if the person he says I'll be meeting is from within my own circle? Let's say Kitty topples during a headstand in yoga class, breaks her neck, and we have to be roommates. Or even worse, what if Lucy or Brie or my parents or— don't go there, Molly—Annabel arrives? I freeze-dry myself so I do not have to consider any of these unspeakable options.

On the fourth day, Bob reappears. He is not alone. A tall man is at his side.

"Sam, this is Molly," he says. "Molly, Sam."

"But—but—but what are you doing here?" I'm jabbering. I'm also being rude.

"I'm asking myself the same question," this Sam says. "Who *are* you people?"

"Molly's going to be your guide," Bob says. He gives Sam the same rigmarole he once spoke to me. Relocation, the Duration, powers, up, down, don't cheat, blah, blah.

"What happened to you, Sam?" I say, because I shouldn't be thinking about myself now. This poor guy is in that first posttraumatic stage

I remember well: shock, disbelief, and trying to figure out why he can't find his pulse. "Try to remember."

Eventually he speaks. "I was thinking about this woman I'd just seen, lost in a long riff about what it would be like if we have coffee and I talked her into spending the day with me. There was something about her—the openness of her face, the kindness of her eyes . . . Then one of my dogs broke off his leash—we'd been walking in the park—and ran across Riverside Drive, and I started to chase him. Next I was under an SUV whose driver was on his cell phone." It spills out in a rush. "That's as much as I know."

"What was your dog's name?"

"Sigmund."

"Are you a professor?" I ask.

"No," he says, looking at me as if I forgot to switch on my brain.

"A shrink?"

Please don't tell me I treated this woman, Sam thinks. *Is there some special hell for Freudians where you have to listen to patients drone on for all of eternity, my mother this, my mother that?* "I'm an analyst," he says. He mentions the New York Psychoanalytic Society and Institute.

I can tell I'm supposed to be impressed.

"Why do you ask?" he adds.

"You look like a shrink, that's all, which might come in handy here."

"Where the hell is *here*?" Sam runs his hand through his full head of chestnut hair, which for a dead guy looks remarkably healthy.

"Oh, I'll explain everything, but first I have a few questions." I check to see if Bob is lurking. He's not, but to be safe I lower my voice. "Sam, the woman you were thinking about when your accident happened—what was she like?"

His smile turns him handsome, gap between his front teeth and all. "Gorgeous," he says, looking away, as if he's seeing her this very minute. "And one thing that struck me was I'd guess she's the kind of female who'd never think of herself that way. Almost my height, brown eyes that drill into you, right past the lies. Magnificent eyes. The minute I looked into them I had this tingly sensation that we were supposed to be together. Fuck, I was dying to follow her." He shifts his gaze

to me and doesn't speak for a few minutes. "You know, if a patient were telling me this story, I'd have told him he should have gone after the woman. When you meet someone and know she's it, don't stand there like a tree. All your happiness can depend on how you react to one fucking impulse. You have to pay attention."

Why did Bob think I'd be the right match for Sam? I have no idea of what to say next. I'd like to ask if his dogs survived, but he probably doesn't know, and the image of Sigmund—or was it Hamlet?—writhing in the street is more than I can bear. "Relax, Sam," is all I can think to say. "You'll have plenty of time to sort this out. As we like to say in the Duration, keep breathing."

He laughs, and I know we'll get along.

"Love your accent, by the way. Australian?"

"South African."

Damn.

"You sound like her," he adds. His voice is dreamy, like he's just woken up, which in a way he has. "Are you from Chicago?"

"We have to talk."

Forty-two

CRAZY IN LOVE

Lucy was the athletic one. She left me in the Illinois dust as she kicked and served and swung like a boy, and she wasn't just chosen first for every team but invariably anointed captain. Best all-around camper, Lucy Divine. Below a sad-eyed elk head, a plaque still hangs in the rec hall at Big Beaver Lake Girls' Camp, which I permanently boycotted once I learned the boys' camp's anthem about the girl Beavers across the lake. The end of camp was no big loss, because while I liked the lanyards and weenie roasts well enough, team sports skinned my knees almost as much as my ego. Riding a bike, though, was different— a ticket to freedom that required swatting fewer mosquitoes, memorizing fewer rules. From the time my father liberated my red-hot Huffy from its training wheels, I made that sucker fly.

"Moosey, wanna ride today?" I'd say every summer morning.

Biking never got old, but my bikes did, and every three years, my parents bought me a shiny replacement, a tradition I kept going. My current model was a yellow hybrid worthy of Hermès, recently purchased in honor of turning thirty-five. I was eager to take it out and see if the bike lived up to the salesman's hyperbole. Annabel was out with

Delfina and Ella, and riding would give me a chance to think through the corner I'd backed myself into with Luke. I brooded best on wheels.

I switched into cotton big-girl panties, because a bike and a thong went together, as Barry liked to say, like a dyke and a schlong, and layered on a jersey and the padded pants that gave me an even bigger bustle-butt. As I found my backpack and gloves, the phone rang.

"Barry?" I said.

"Yes, your irresistible husband. Why so surprised?"

"Because I usually have to leave three messages before you call back," I answered with immediate regret; I could hear Dr. Stafford, in her patrician tone, reminding both of us that few relationships improved with sarcasm, which she—given to food metaphors—likened to a heavy hand with cayenne pepper.

"What's for dinner?" Barry asked.

This dear new Barry, who cares if we'll be eating fish or chicken, home-cooked or takeout, couldn't possibly be connected to Chanel Mommy, I told myself.

"Salmon in parchment paper, with sugar snap peas and those fake french fries I bake with kosher salt." I'd already set the table with orange tulips and candles, and I decided that on the way back from my ride I'd swing over to the Silver Moon Bakery and pick up something decadent for dessert. Maybe I could manage Barry's favorite, the fudge cake with a thatched roof of chocolate shavings.

"Did you get Annabel into swimming?" he asked.

He remembered that was on my day's to-do list. The man was trying. "Yes," I said. "Last spot."

"Score one for supermom. And what are you up to, Molls?"

He's awfully chatty, I noted. I loved it. "I'm going to take out my new bike."

"Now?"

"It's almost spring," I said.

"It's February," he said with a top note of criticism. "Where are you going at this hour?"

Central Park functioned as my front yard, but if I went further west I'd be near the bakery. I decided I wanted dessert to be a sweet surprise. "I haven't decided."

"Be careful."

"When am I not?" I said. "See you later."

Did Barry actually think I'd be reckless? Me? I slipped into a wind-breaker with garish reflective stripes augmented by numerous glow-in-the-dark stickers, courtesy of Annabel. In this getup, a blind person could see me.

As I walked toward the kitchen, my cell phone rang. Luke and the Saints again. I hadn't taken him for a guy who'd work this hard for the last word.

"Yes?"

"Can you talk?" he said.

"Only for a second."

"I really need to see you." He sounded like a man recently arrived in triage. "Now, baby."

Baby? Corny as that word may be, when it fell out of Luke's mouth, I was his hostage. His voice began to seep into my skin like a rich, soothing balm. Still, I said, "When I told you before that I'd see you, I didn't mean today."

"But I'm nearby."

Coincidence? I thought not.

"Name the spot," he said. "The diner? Le Pain Q? Anywhere."

Idiot, I thought, applying that label to myself. *You need to be inoculated against Luke as if he were a deadly protozoon.* The other half of my brain ragged back, *Except, dammit, you love that he's interested. Admit it. You're there.*

"Molly, say something."

"I shouldn't, Luke," I answered slowly. *I am a degenerate alcoholic and you are a kegger. I. Will. Not. Take. A. Sip. There should be a twelve-step program for women like me, and I need to attend a daily meeting.*

"I'm off for a bike ride," I said.

"Where to?"

"Riverside, probably. What does it matter? It's too late. But I'll call you tomorrow. I promise. We'll talk."

"You'll call me on Saturday? Really? You've never called me once on Saturday."

That's how rattled he got me. "Monday, then."

"I cannot wait three days, Molly. We have to get this cleared up now."

"Luke, what we have to do is stop"—stop whatever *this* is.

"Give me one good reason."

"Seeing you is making me crazy," I shouted. "I can't handle the deception. It makes me despise myself. I hate women like me. I've always been highly judgmental about cheaters and—"

"Love trumps cheating. I'm crazy in love with you. Don't you get that?"

My eyes landed on a framed snapshot taken at my wedding. Barry and I were having our first dance. Was that the last sane moment in my life, when the band's sultry soloist sang "It Might Be You," which was a good three hours before I saw Barry walk out of my parents' powder room followed by Ms. Toffee Frost?

I could hear Luke breathing, expecting a response. *I'm crazy in love with you, too,* would not be inaccurate, but I only got to crazy. "Luke, I don't know what to say." Except that I had to get out of here.

"How about 'I love you'? Because I think you do."

At the front door, keys were jangling. I didn't want Delfina and Annabel to see me unhinged, tears falling as though I'd turned on the faucet. "I promise you we'll talk—after the weekend. Hold on. But right now, no."

"Molly—please. See me for ten minutes. Today."

"Luke, goodbye," I said. I clicked off and grabbed a paper towel to mop my face, took my helmet from its hook, and slammed the back door as the front door opened. I wheeled my bike through the basement corridors and around to the front.

"You just missed Dr. Marx," Alphonso, the doorman, said. I registered how odd it was that Barry, whom I was in no shape or mood to see, hadn't mentioned coming home early. We'd spoken less than fifteen minutes before. I couldn't think about that now.

I clipped my bike shoes into the pedals and took off, pushing hard.

Only when I was on the street, two blocks away, did I realize I'd left my phone on the kitchen counter.

Forty-three

PERSONS OF INTEREST

I watch Hicks open his mail. Bill, bill, the *Economist*, postcard from the ophthalmologist ("Any way you see it, it's time for a checkup"), *Cook's Illustrated*, and an invitation to his cousin's wedding, about which he knows to expect an earful from his mother, given that Willy is eleven years younger. But the most interesting piece of mail is a flimsy white envelope with no return address and a computer-generated label. The red stamp features a large Hershey kiss and a heart inscribed with the word *love*. He carefully opens the envelope. Why had someone sent him a clipping featuring a suit from Ascot Chang, an ego-tripping Shanghai custom shop he'd poked his head into once and only once? A polo shirt would set him back a hundred bucks.

"Brie, babes, I sure hope you aren't buying me a present," he says when she walks into the kitchen, wearing one of his Macy's shirts and, he hopes, nothing else. That she outearns him five to one is the hot potato in their relationship. She says it doesn't bother her, so why should it bother him? It's a question Hicks contemplates at least twice a day.

"I thought your birthday wasn't for four months," she says, pop-

ping a grape into her mouth and another into his before she hugs him. "Is this a hint?"

"Is *this*?" Only when he waves the clipping in Brie's face does he see its flip side. On a page titled "In This Issue" is a photograph featuring, among others, Luke Delaney and Molly Marx. With a yellow marker, the sender has circled their hands, which may or may not be touching. Hard to tell. A label has been attached to the picture, with a caption: *Killer?*

Person of interest L. Delaney. He isn't an official suspect, though he phoned Molly, Hicks has noted, numerous times on the day she died, including the last call she received. Hicks knows Luke's hiding something. What he's hiding is the question, for Hicks and for me.

Luke's broken up during the interrogations, but his story's been consistent. As recently as two weeks ago, he called to see how the case was progressing. "Nowhere" would be the appropriate answer.

"What magazine do you think this is from?" Hicks asks.

Brie looks at it closely. *"Town and Country."* Actually, it's *Departures.* The photo was taken on a beach in Santo Domingo, my last location trip with Luke. "But what does this picture prove? Molly and Luke Delaney worked together and possibly slept together. Occupational hazard. Happens all the time." Brie should know, since she did the same thing with the same guy, which she's decided she'll never share with Hicks.

"The more important point is who sent this," he says.

"Is that a statement or a question?"

"It's whatever you want it to be."

Brie sits on the aluminum bar stool next to the granite counter that separates Hicks' compact, immaculate kitchen from his small living room with its black leather love seats and circular steel dining table. He won a real estate lottery to buy this condo, which is less than a mile and yet a giant step away from his ma. *Could I live with this man?* Brie is starting to ask herself. If the only thing that matters is how deeply she cares for him and how anal-retentive they both are, the answer is a resounding yes.

"Who sent it?" she says. "My money's on Barry, good old guilty Barry."

"Guilty of what?"

"Of something, I'm sure."

"That'll get you far in a court of law," he laughs. "You don't suppose it's from big bad Lucy?"

"Lucy wouldn't play games. She'd call and say, 'My moron sister was having an affair and the guy whacked her. Nail him.' " Brie's Lucy impersonation used to make both of us convulse with laughter.

"What about Kitty, trying to point the finger away from the good son?" Hicks asks.

"Or herself," Brie said, although in her heart, Brie doesn't see Kitty as a killer. Brie can't read Hicks' look. "You know I'm kidding, right?" she says.

"How about this?" Hicks says as he draws Brie to him and pulls her hair out of its clip so that it hangs loosely down her back. "Molly's in love with Delaney, but Delaney loves someone else. But Molly won't leave him alone. She goes all *Fatal Attraction,* acting like a bitter, vengeful she-devil. So he suggests they take a bike ride together. At a scenic spot they stop and she thinks he's going to kiss her, but instead he pushes her off her bike into the water and leaves her to drown."

"Never," Brie says. "But what about this? Barry and Molly go for a ride together and get in a fight. He pushes Molly—accidentally or on purpose is the piece I haven't worked out yet—and she falls in the river. He panics, pulls her out, and gives her artificial respiration like the good doctor he is. When he realizes she's massively injured and will most likely die, and he's absolutely 200 percent positive no one's seen what happened, he leaves the scene of the crime."

"What's his motive?"

"She knew he was cheating for the nth time, and she was going to sue for divorce and take him for everything."

"Very interesting, Detective Lawson," Hicks says. "Or maybe they fought and then the putz rode off and never looked back, so he never knew Molly lost control of her bike. Reckless endangerment."

"Oh, so you like Barry. Well, maybe Luke really was at the movie he said he went to but left early and caught up with Molly in time to get rid of her because he's a textbook psycho and if she wouldn't leave her husband for him, then he didn't want Barry to have her. Or—"

"No, I've got it," Hicks says. "What about this?" He slips his hands

under the shirt Brie's wearing, quickly establishes what's underneath—nothing—and ends the discussion. Only after Brie leaves, two hours later, does he look again at the clipping.

Hicks makes four phone calls, to Luke, Barry, Kitty, and Stephanie, and tells them to expect a visit from him tomorrow.

Forty-four

KILLJOY

I rode north on Central Park West, slowing or stopping at almost every corner, turned left on Eighty-sixth Street, and passed the apartment building where Marion Davies was kept by William Randolph Hearst. Hats off to Marion. There's a woman who knew how to handle a lover.

Turning right, I ducked into Riverside Park, where an American flag snapped in the breeze. Damn, it was windier than I'd thought. I continued on past the Hippo Playground. If the fair weather held, I'd surprise Annabel with a visit there tomorrow. I traveled for only a bit on the promenade before I rode through the dank fieldstone tunnel that ran under the parkway and took me to the Hudson.

GO SLOWLY, a sign commanded. RESPECT OTHERS. *Exactly. Luke, don't tempt me. Enough. Respect that I'm trying to turn the page.*

I dismounted to take in the view. To the south, the Hudson widened. I could pick out Jersey City, a place I knew only from weather reports. In the northern distance the George Washington Bridge half hid under the mesh of fine gray mist. Even at this time of year, when dusk came before dinner, it was too early in the afternoon for its lights to cast their glow. Closer by, high on a hill, Riverside Church lorded over the tomb of Ulysses S. Grant.

I climbed back onto my bike and picked up speed. A few yards to my right, separated only by a fence better suited to a prison, cars hurried by in the opposite direction, the drivers' eyes straight ahead, on their mission. *Go, go, go. Beat the other guy.* Man, it was loud. The din of traffic never failed to amaze me, but I could tune it out. I always had. Suburban Illinois might have been my birthplace, but I was a New Yorker and I could activate my inner iPod. I sang out off-key, doing my throatiest Janis Joplin. " 'You know, feeling good was good enough for me, good enough for me and my Bobby McGee.' "

I sped past a small stand of scrubby pines guarding the empty tennis courts, winding left to Cherry Walk, a scraggly string of bike path bordered on the left by low stone embankments. The rocks sloped straight down to the lapping edge of the gloomy river barely a foot or two below.

In lyrics, life is always distilled to quaint, deceptive clarity. But women I knew wouldn't drown their woes in Southern Comfort, nor were they willing to trade all their tomorrows for a single yesterday. Before bed, they did fifty sit-ups, popped a Lexapro, contemplated having a baby or a consultation with a top divorce lawyer, and counted the months until their vacation, when they could liquefy into a beach under a broad-brimmed hat and a creamy slather of SPF 45. Until then, they soldiered on and kept their shoes and optimism shined, responsible, cut, and colored, inside and out.

I was determined to do better than that. I couldn't lead a halfway life in a halfway home.

The intermittent sun had called it a day and rain was starting to fall again. It felt refreshing, washing away the old Molly, cleansing my attitude. I planned to cycle all the way to the bridge, make sure that the little red lighthouse Annabel and I loved had withstood the winter, then turn back and zip over to the bakery. If the sprinkle got worse, I'd shift to plan B and exit by Fairway, where I could buy Barry one of those tiny cherry pies he polished off in two servings—a peace offering, even if he thought it was just dessert.

As adrenaline kicked in, my brain began to drain—comfortably, pleasantly, and reliably. That was as much the point of cycling as any benefit to my hip measurement or cardiovascular system. I took scant note of the skate park, the basketball courts, or even the path's painted

dividing line, blue and steady as a vein, separating north-traveling bikers like me from those heading south. With each revolution, I could feel my tension release, my resolve grow.

On Monday I would call Luke. To avoid him was cruel; the sweetness of our history deserved more than jagged conversations. In plain, sans serif language I'd tell him this would be our last conversation. It would be over.

Except—I squinted—there he was, Bobby McGee Delaney himself, a tall streak in a navy windbreaker and jeans, standing by the side of the road. "Stop so we can talk," he shouted.

I was touched that Luke had gone to this length to find me, but I wasn't prepared, and I felt trapped. "Oh, Luke, not now," I shouted back. "It's too late." I meant that in every way, but I tried to keep it kind and casual. "I don't have the time."

"Molly, I'm here and we need to speak," he yelled.

I begged to differ; my face said as much.

"You don't get how much I love you."

Perhaps, but I didn't want to listen. I wanted to keep it clean and manageable.

"I love you, Molly. I do."

Maybe he did. Maybe I owed him. Maybe this was my *Casablanca*. A whole lot of maybe.

"Okay," I said. "Grant's Tomb is up the road. Walk there and wait for me. I'll see you inside."

He shot me a skeptical look. Did he honestly think I'd ditch him?

"I will," I said. "In ten minutes, fifteen at the most."

"Grant's Tomb," he said. "I'll be there." And he was off.

I'd ride to the bridge as I'd planned, check out the lighthouse, circle back, meet Luke, and we'd talk now instead of Monday. I didn't want to pose, to pretend. I wanted to make right in my life what wasn't. I wanted to change. I *would* change, starting that very day. Even if the wrong man loved me, I told myself, I refused to be one more woman who smiled meekly and tried to make the best of her 5-on-a-scale-of-10 life.

I wouldn't get out my knife sharpener. I'd break things off gently but irrevocably, like snapping a brittle twig, and Luke and I would go our separate ways. I'd face my husband with the first layer of guilt

scrubbed away. I knew I was doing the right thing, which gave me a blast of speed.

Yes, I had feelings for Luke.

No, I wasn't prepared to act on them.

Yes, I might always love him.

No, nothing he could do would change my mind.

With each rotation of my wheels, I became more convinced. I, Molly Divine Marx, could do this. I began rehearsing.

Luke, I will love you forever but . . . Nope. Nobody likes a *but*.

Luke, from the beginning we both always knew . . . Except we didn't.

Luke, you are deeply precious to me and because of that . . .

I got busy editing away clichés, picking them off like lint. I barely noticed that the late afternoon sky had darkened as efficiently as if someone had dimmed the lights. The raindrops had become a steady march, pelting my helmet. I heard a clap of thunder. Bass drums.

As I was deciding whether I should skip the lighthouse and go straight to Grant's Tomb, there was suddenly a second, larger thunderclap. Cymbals.

The sky started exploding. Which is why at first I didn't hear the other sound, which began growing louder. And then it was unmistakable: the grinding of another biker's gears behind me. Closer.

Too close.

I thought I heard someone call my name. Had Barry followed me? I twisted back to look over my shoulder. This tailgater apparently had prepared for the weather by cashing in a hefty gift certificate at L.L.Bean. I'm talking serious, textbook gear, rubbery black from toe to head, ending in a hood that slid over a helmet. I was looking at a Garanimal in mourning, a biker so sleek but loosely tailored that the he within might be a she; I could not see the outlines of the person's body, but I did see sunglasses—large, dark, and heavy.

Excuse me, did I miss the paparazzi or the forecast for the hurricane? I wanted to shout. But the rider shouted first.

What was the voice saying? "On your left"? "Be careful"? Or was this person screaming my name? The words were swallowed by thunder. Platinum lightning ripped the heavens and rain began pounding even harder, unmercifully, horizontally. I was trapped in the monsoon cycle of a car wash, but I kept pedaling, trying to ignore the grand vizier

of foul weather chic behind me, concentrating on keeping my line. Yet as my wheels skidded through runoff from the sudden squall, I could sense the presence hovering close. Way too fucking close. Didn't he realize how dangerous this was, or was he right up my ass because he thought I could shepherd him through the tempest? Darth Vader had picked the wrong Girl Scout.

When he failed to pass, I considered cursing him out in my reliable crazy-lady howl, the one that had worked when a thief with an extra dose of hubris had tried to steal my wallet. In a courthouse. At jury duty. But what if this dick-brain was, say, a deranged bike messenger, out to rob me—or worse? This was, after all, a city with a fairly imaginative crime blotter.

I needed to get away. I decided to edge as far as I could toward the fence that separated the bike path from the traffic, even though puddles there were already deep. Water splashed my pants and, for the second time that day, oozed into my shoes. I could feel the slosh under my socks. Whether that was Barry or not, he was right. Who rides a bicycle in February? Had I, a responsible mother with biking skills that didn't surpass average, mistaken myself for a Tour de France contender? I was officially a moron.

I craned my head. The person was yelling. ". . . talk to you." At closer range the voice sounded shrill, nasal, of a higher pitch. Not Barry. And now there was no mistake. He—or she—knew who I was.

"Molly Marx! Slow down!"

"What are you doing?" I screamed. But it actually looked as if this wheeled deviant was coming at me. Pissed off and scared shitless, I tried to yell, "Back off! Stay the fuck away." The sound refused to leave my throat. I started to gasp and wheeze.

"Pull the fuck over!" the biker screeched while skidding into a puddle, flying at me on the right like a missile.

I had to pedal away from this banshee freak. I could do it.

"Face it, Molly. You and Barry are done! He thinks you're a joke. Ignoring me's not going to change that! He doesn't love you anymore."

"Who *are* you?" I shrieked.

"C'mon, you know exactly who I am!"

Suddenly I did. I understood everything and was fortified with an emotion both strong and pure. I believe it was white-hot hatred. I

twisted to try to get another look—to be completely sure. That's when we collided and I lost my grip. My arms flew above my head like a demented cheerleader, any control surrendered. One foot broke loose. But the other refused to budge from its clip as my bike zigzagged in a dizzying swerve to the left. I watched this as I might a horror movie, until I had to close my eyes. Finally, the bike started to slow.

I thanked God. As Papa Louie liked to say, if a Jew doesn't expect miracles, she isn't a realist.

Then I saw my destination, the sharp, serrated edge of a rock. In slow motion, it met the soft plain of my forehead and gashed my skin, dripping blood into my mouth. My bike landed on top of me in a deafening clatter of entwined spokes and jeering, hideously cheerful yellow metal.

"Christ!" someone said. "Don't you dare do this." I was fairly sure the disembodied voice was not my own.

I heard my bike splash and the spray of the Hudson iced my face, my neck, my shoulders. Then I felt . . . nothing.

The bike-bitch towered above me and freed my foot. Or perhaps I disengaged myself, like a hero-mom who'd hoisted four tons of minivan that had pinned her toddler. I was at the water's edge. All I could see and smell was the brackish river. How demon-fast was that current? When was the last time I'd had a tetanus shot? Would I even remember how to swim?

As the Hudson threatened to suck me into its maw, I snaked myself forward—bouncing and sliding in a desperate break-dance—and stretched to reach for the spike of a protruding green-slimed rock. I forced up my arm, the pain virtually unbearable. In the sudden movement my eye caught a glint stuck to the Velcro that fastened the wrist of my windbreaker. I'd snared a treasure, a glittering pink heart pendant encircled by plum-colored pavé stones, the same heart that had dangled from the necklace Barry was going to give me, that or its evil twin. *Happy Valentine's Day, Molly. Here's another knife in your heart.*

With a frozen hand—my glove shredded—I reached for the taunting bauble. I snatched it, cool, hard, and glossy to the touch. As if I were grasping God, I wrapped my fingers tightly around the heart.

My leg seared. My shoulder pulsed with savage pain. I was soaked, yet sweating profusely. From what I remembered of anatomy, I guessed

I'd cracked my clavicle as easily as if it were a wishbone on a rotisserie chicken, yet my leg and shoulder were half the agony of my insides.

I wanted to shut my eyes again.

Gather my breath.

Take a time-out.

I thought I heard a voice imploring me to stay awake, to not surrender to the slicing ache, to the rush of frigid water. It cried, "Molly," a distant soundtrack coming from the middle of a bell. It was a voice that I'm not sure even existed, a voice both filled and filling me with fear.

"Sorry," it said.

Someone bent low. Was the person going to help me or kill me? But all that happened was that the heart was pried from my hand. I heard a small splash. Footsteps. And then I heard . . . nothing.

I was alone now, drowning in my own silence.

I could see the sky. While I couldn't move my neck or raise my head, I could faintly make out a billboard on the parkway. *Getting home late?* it said. *Tell your TiVo to start without you.*

I tried to laugh, and when I couldn't, I cried out, yelling, "Help . . . help me . . . help me, someone," but the traffic was deafening. Could anyone even hear me where I lay, discarded like a piece of garbage, hid amid the brambles? I screamed, flinched, and screamed once more. Each time I yelled out, it felt as if razor blades were digging into my ribs, yet I would catch my breath and scream again and again and again . . . continuing until all that came out were feeble animal mews and gurgling moans.

Someone would find me. Someone had to find me. Soon.

I told myself, out loud, in a whisper, to stay calm and awake. I counted to one thousand and recited the alphabet—in English, then in French—and played the rhyme game, as Lucy and I had done in grade school, taking turns calling out the first word that came to mind.

Lucy, Moosey, juicy, Gary Busey, Watusi, Cousin Brucie, goosey, Debussy.

Molly, trolley, volley, Bengali, dolly, Ollie, holly, Norma Kamali, collie, Salvador Dalí, jolly, Polly, golly, Mexicali, "Zum Gali Gali," folly.

Pure folly.

Was that Luke I was seeing, standing above me—telling me to hang on, that he was going to get help? Was that him, or just a hope, a prayer, love dressed in blue jeans?

Luke, duke, Dubuque, Baruch, fluke, Herman Wouk, puke, spook.

Had I actually been run off the road by a marauding hag dressed in black, Coco Chanel's worst nightmare, or was this a hallucination, a vision fucking with my mind? Had a woman claimed she loved Barry? Was it that Barry loved her and not me?

What did it matter? The only thing that counted was staying alive.

I tried to concentrate on the top spire of Riverside Church, Annabel's Burger King crown pinned against the charcoal sky. I began to run through Annabel's life, starting with that night that I was fairly sure the sperm had gotten the egg and all the cells were busy growing a new person. Almost nine months of astonishing pregnancy, every flutter kick a promise. William Alexander. Alexander William. Would I ever get to meet him? I skipped to Annabel's delivery. Bringing home my pink, bald, beautiful baby. Nursing in the wee hours, a milky team, the two of us alone together rocking in the green velvet chair. Annabel's first tooth, first laugh, first ice cream cone, first lollipop, first doll, first tantrum, first haircut. Learning to crawl like a crab along the shiny wood floor, to walk, to say "mommy." Starting nursery school, ballet, starting everything.

I tried to remember each birthday party, each party dress, each cake, especially the chocolate teddy bear I'd baked myself for her third birthday, showering it with coconut to hide frosting I'd heaved on in slabs to cover my sloppy work. Blowing out candles. *Are you one? Are you two? Are you three? Are you four?* Not four. Not yet. I had to stay alive for four. I needed to get to four. One, two, three . . .

I will always be Annabel's mother. I will always be Annabel's mother, I repeated over and over again. My last thought before I closed my eyes.

Forty-five

HERE'S TAE US

*E*ternity is an endless comfort, settling like a baby's breath or a sweet dusting of confectioner's sugar. In the Duration, I fly through time like a jet does clouds. Time piles up in snowdrifts, pristine and endless. We do not measure in days or decades. We do not measure time at all.

"Back then"—such bad form to say *alive*—"did you think much about death?" Bob asked once. "Did you have nightmares? Premonitions?"

Sam did. As a shrink, he lived in people's heads, one of the world's most consistently terrifying places, tangled by twisted relationships and moth-eaten regrets. Patients would depart his office and, as surely as they exhaled with the relief he afforded, Sam would repeat the captured anxieties in his sleep, working through the puzzles of their hearts.

Worries? Certainly I had them. Worry was my ring tone; I heard it all day long. But authentic nightmares? Rarely. I ruminated about worst-case scenarios, mostly. Yes, too many of them did come true. Yet when I try to recall these problems burning holes in my happiness, my memory feels thick and lumpy as oatmeal.

Sam and Bob are still part of my expanding circle, which gives new meaning to "it takes a village." Jordan, Stephanie's son, is here now, the fatal victim of a heli-ski accident in the Bugaboos. He was gazing at grand granite spires, and *kaboom*. Gone.

Afterward, Stephanie was never the same, the only good that came from that tragedy. She's become tortured by thoughts of divine retribution, which has made Barry's life tricky. A daughter of Great Neck, Stephanie Lipschitz Joseph Marx has taken a turn toward freakishly *frum*. She now keeps glatt kosher, covers her short gray hair with a wig, and believes this headgear looks like the real McCoy. Stephanie refuses to get in the car on the Sabbath. This makes it hard for Dr. and Mrs. Marx to get to his honeymoon gift to her, a soaring glass and steel weekend retreat on a beach on Long Island. Whenever Stephanie's not looking, Barry smuggles spareribs into the cathedral-sized kitchen.

Still, the two of them are almost 100 percent monogamous. If Barry has schtupped anyone else these past twenty-some years, his wife doesn't know or doesn't care. It helps to have so much money she could use it to wipe her tears. That and the anger management classes, which Dr. Stafford insisted Barry take: he and Stephanie were having a joint session in Dr. Stafford's office and Barry threw a book at Stephanie and shouted, "Shee-it, I wouldn't piss in your mouth if your teeth were on fire."

Barry blames Stephanie for . . . something. He doesn't know the half of it, nor does anyone else.

Narcissa arrived soon after Jordan. Diabetes. Delfina badgered her about how big she'd gotten—for her son's wedding she had to sew two emerald green bugle-beaded dresses together—but Narcissa never listened. I love how Narcissa and Jordan have grown to love each other. She took that loose-limbed, frizzy-haired teenager to her ample bosom, and I often see the two of them laughing and singing, he spanning octaves in his Roy Orbison imitation, Narcissa in a sweet soprano that belies her size. Jordan has followed Narcissa to the Born-Agains. What a friend he has in Jesus!

My father's here now. Choked on a thick, juicy steak, medium rare, the day after he ran a marathon with Lucy. Not the worst way to go, although he was only seventy-four, with silver hair curling over his neck like a movie director. "Daddy," I repeated about a hundred times when

he and I were reunited, holding on to each other for what we used to call dear life. "Daddy, Daddy . . ."

"Molly, sweetheart," he responded. "You were robbed, honey." But I shushed him. In the Duration, we don't question when people fall short of their Biblical three-score and ten. We leave the judging for the living. What was, was.

My father couldn't wait to tell me about the Molly Marx trial, hung jury and all. The hideous mess, I learned, was dissected to the point where anyone with an IQ beyond 95 would happily commit corporate reports to memory rather than be tortured with another nanosecond of breathless tabloid coverage. But because the players were photogenic, worldly, and white, producers and editors ran with the story instead of, say, reports of limbless, brain-injured soldiers returning home from Iraq.

"The trial became a Rorschach," my father said. "One day I logged onto AOL and could have voted for who I believed was guilty. By the way, sixty-eight percent of women polled found your friend Luke innocent."

He always calls Luke my "friend," as if the two of us never shared more than a strawberry soda and a taxi.

"I was offered a cameo in the made-for-television movie," he adds. "To play a crusty old detective. Can you believe the bad taste?"

I can. It's been a long time since I was an invisible looky-loo sticking my nose into life below, but I hear things. I hear a lot. What I wanted my dad to talk about, though, was Annabel. Did she really grow up to be brilliant and beautiful and almost five-nine?

"Oh, yeah. She got Kitty's figure, your mother's face, and Lucy's height."

"Too tall to dance Clara in *The Nutcracker*?"

"Well, that, and she gave up ballet for basketball."

"Didn't she get anything of mine?"

"Yes, darling. Your wonderful hair."

Did he not know that I owed my blondness to chemistry? Then I saw a twinkle.

"Annabel got your smile, that way you lit up every room. You can't not love that girl. She's you all over again."

"Why did she go to college in Scotland?" I had it on good authority

that she'd been accepted to Princeton—the director of admissions arrived here after she was gunned down by an alum whose child she'd rejected.

"To get away," my father said, "from strangers pointing fingers, from the squabbling between Barry and Stephanie. And she took Jordan's death hard. Those two kids would always be standing together off to the side, heads together, like ducks on their own private ice floe." He stopped talking and simply gazed into my eyes. For a moment, I could feel what it was like to be whole and alive.

"But life is funny," he said.

Isn't it?

"If Annabel hadn't gone to Scotland, she'd never have met Ewan. At first your mom and I were upset. We thought your little Annie-belle was searching for some kind of father figure. But Lucy came to her defense. She was right."

She often was.

"When she got married, Annabel might have been a child herself—nineteen, a baby—but Ewan is exactly what she needs."

"Tell me about her wedding. Did you and Mom go?"

"Of course! Your mother found Ewan very dashing in his kilt. There were so many candles I thought that old pile of a castle might melt, but your daughter said she wanted it to look like *The Age of Innocence* because Lucy swore it was your favorite movie."

My first thought is that my sister keeps my flame alive as if I'm Princess Diana. My second: is Martin Scorsese still directing?

"Each toast was better than the next," my father said, and broke into a pretty fair Scots accent. "Here's tae us; who's like us?" he said, answering his question with "Damn few—and they're a' deid." Then he looked around and the two of us roared in laughter as only those in the Duration can.

Forty-six

UNENDING LOVE

I'd stopped going below when I recognized my visits as cruel and unusual punishment, self-flagellation making me sadder, angrier, and lonelier. I learned to simply float within the Duration, and allowed my memory to wash away. If I ever knew exactly how I died, I gradually forgot more than I had ever learned or remembered. I stopped searching for answers and started searching for peace.

I'd fallen into what Sam has diagnosed as a hyperthermia of the soul; I'd crawled into a snow cave of amnesia. "It happens to people whose lives end the way yours did"—violently, recklessly, unforgivably. Young. "Feeling your father's love, though, may unlock some memories." Sam's theory sounded like a mountain of psychocrap, but I began to see the truth in it. This made me want to return one last time, though my powers were like muscles hanging loose after a long illness.

Then it wasn't a choice, really. I begged my father to travel with me, but he said he wasn't ready, that he may never be ready. Dan Divine can't stand to see his Claire with another man.

Two years after he died, my mother married her next-door neighbor, a widower who'd confessed that he'd always been nuts about her, which Lucy and I had guessed years ago from the way his admiring eyes

hung on her like Christmas lights. Claire Divine is one for the books, a woman who's twice found true love, with its purple passion, peachy tenderness, and bright white understanding. I don't think my father begrudges my mother her play-it-again happiness, but he doesn't care to hear it sigh and call her "Clairey babe."

Up until now, my complete British Isles experience has consisted only of London—antiquing, eating too many crumpets, and noting that people seem strangely attached to the word *rubbish*. Now here I am. A greenish sea by this coastal Scottish town is calm as ancient porcelain, and the first crocuses are pushing through rocky soil. If a flock of tiny, black-faced sheep wandered down the lane, herded by Little Bo Peep herself, I would not be surprised. In the distance, for some other occasion, bagpipes wail as if they themselves are grieving. Yet in this plain stone chapel, the mood is pumped with joy. I enter and feel at home here, as if I've taken a beloved book from the shelf and stepped inside an earmarked page. The source of this intimacy I cannot explain, but I have learned that just as life is a long, rolling sum of mysteries, death is no different.

I turn and there she is, Annabel, a nasturtium encircled by hummingbirds, standing radiant and straight as she walks to her seat, turning right and left to acknowledge well-wishers. By her side is Ewan, sheltering a very young boy and girl with ruddy cheeks and hair the color of pralines. "The spitting image of their father," someone whispers of the children. Annabel is their fairy stepmother. She is carrying a bundle wearing the Campbell family's christening gown and bonnet, creamy old lace the color of eggnog, its fabric soft as feathers. The sweetly sleeping newborn, unaware of this dignified hoopla, has the other half of my attention.

The chapel fills, its heavy wooden doors thrown open, the air catching a fresh sea breeze. Love flows round, Annabel gazing with warm disbelief at her child as I once looked at her. I drink in everyone, everything, and my emptiness begins to fill.

A clergyman, bent and kindly, starts the service, giving thanks for this moment of gladness, the birth of a child. "Our God, we turn to Thee with full hearts for these thy children, Ewan and Annabel Campbell." His r's roll gently, water flowing over polished old rocks. "Help them, that they be wise and patient parents, understanding the care

required of a young one's growing body and mind. Give them courage in times of difficulty."

I begin to pray involuntarily, to a God with whom I've had my share of differences. *Spare them from grief,* I ask of God. *Protect Annabel, protect her husband and his children. Protect this baby, this grandchild.* I use that word in true wonder. It is grand that my child has a child, a child whom I do not know but who, too, is grand indeed.

The minister goes on, his voice a melody, and I gaze around the room. There's my mother, her face—to my eyes—young. She is leaning on her brand-new rock, a man not half as handsome as my father, but with a round, sympathetic face. He understands that even today's happiness brings it all back. He strokes my mother's hand, arthritic but soft to the touch. She can blink and it could be the February of my death, the future a shadow blocking her view. But she is wise enough to blink again and return to today, where fulfillment rules.

Hicks and Brie whisper and laugh. Around her neck hangs the silver magnifying glass that I gave her long ago. Faint lines etch the decades. She is a queen, with dark hair twisted into a chignon. Hicks has retired his earring, started wearing glasses, and grown thicker, as befits an attorney of his stature. After my unresolved trial, which he took as a personal failure, he studied the law at night. Brie and he practice together, Lawson and Hicks, the go-to firm if you're crawling with guilt. They are doing well, more together than many couples who have married. Yesterday, after golf, they decided that Scotland is so magnificent perhaps they should buy a home here. But how could they give up the hilly green of Columbia County, and where would Hicks keep his goats? Rich people's problems, good to have.

A late arrival, a tall, well-upholstered woman with a plump, unlined face and one white streak in her dark hair, slides into the row behind Annabel. She leans forward to kiss her cheeks and hold her close. Annabel surrenders herself to the embrace and snuggles next to this mother bear. "Aunt Moosey, you got here," she says.

"We're all here now," Lucy answers. We are.

That includes a young, smiling rabbi who's traveled in a red convertible from Edinburgh. A sunbeam bounces off the brocade of his silky square black yarmulke as he offers a *shalom* and calls Barry to pray over sacramental wine. Barry, who has traveled here without

Stephanie, walks a bit stiffly—last month he had his knees replaced, the price for all that running on unforgiving pavement—but he smiles broadly and is the image of his father's pictures. He is one of those rare men improved by his shaved head. Barry raises the family kiddush cup brought from New York, his surgeon's hands still steady around the silvery stem, entwined with grapevines and memories. I hear the Hebrew words, chanted in his strong, sure voice, and wonder what he is thinking.

I realize I no longer care or need to know. He belongs to another woman now.

The minister calls Annabel and Ewan, who places his hand on his wife's slender back and they walk slowly and carefully, she cradling their sleeping child. The two of them reach the front and kiss. Ewan flicks away a tear from Annabel's eyes. I have nestled within her, and this touch returns my powers with a jolt. The emotion Annabel feels is crazy glee dusted with the slight despair she always tries to chase away when she wishes I were present. Today, I am. *God, if you're in this room, make her know that.*

"Will the godmother please come forward?" the minister asks.

Salagadoola, mechicka boola, bibbidi-bobbidi-boo. We have a godmother. She walks to the front. For this occasion, the proud great-aunt is wearing sensible shoes and flowing sapphire blue clothing. With her white streak and her husband's ring on her finger, she is, finally, Lucy in the sky with diamonds. She stands next to Barry and yes, there is an embrace—nothing showy, but a real, albeit short, connection.

"This child," the minister asks, "does she have a name?"

"She does," Ewan answers. He smiles at Annabel. "Her name will be Molly," he says. "Molly Divine."

Perhaps God *is* in the building.

"Molly Divine Campbell," the rabbi says to the sleeping baby. "For whom are you named, my wee *bubbelah*?"

"For my mother," Annabel says. *Long gone,* she thinks, *but in my heart, never forgotten.*

"For my sister," Lucy says. "And if my sister is in this room, I hope she won't mind if I read a poem she wrote when she was a girl."

Will Lucy never cease to embarrass me? We'll see about that.

" 'Strip from me the dove velvet mantle,' " Lucy begins.

Let the bay-pale corn silk glaze my shoulders
As I sing a duet with God.

Before it all, I did believe in God.

The rivers echo choruses
The stars, a silver descant,
Pebbles garnish the sanctified mud
The shells, the snails, the shadows of the starfish.
Amid the crescendo, a plant grows
Chanting the liturgy of roots veining the loam
Beginning to learn of toadstools and Russian olive trees.

Where did Lucy find this? Was I ever really a moony sixteen, waiting for my life to happen? Lucy's eyes pierce me and press me to the stone wall.

My last dream lingers
Now I wait only for spring's kiss
Go now. Let me fall in love.

My sister removes her reading glasses, puts down the poem, and looks at Annabel and then her grandniece. "That's what I wish for little Molly," she says. "That she will fall in love."

Amen. Let her fall in love, young and for forever, the way it seems that her mother has.

In deference to the mingling of two faiths, there will be no sprinkling of water on the baby's head, though if Jesus were present, I'm sure he would be welcomed. He and I still have yet to meet, but others in the Duration, believers, have sightings all the time.

"The godfather? Will he come forward?" the minister asks.

He does, tall as ever, his eyes more deeply sunken than when they looked into mine. He has watched over Annabel all her life, cultivating the role of the witty, wandering uncle with the good stories and the good presents. He is a man who reveals little, a man nobody knows.

I'd always hoped Lucy and Luke might wind up together, but that was my naiveté on overdrive. Once, when both of them drank far too

much, they had an evening of unabridged, ill-considered passion, but afterward each admitted they felt my presence in the bed—even though I absolutely was not. Lucy and Luke sprang back to friendship before its statute of limitations expired. They stay in touch, largely through postcards annotated with cryptic messages. Lucy married many years ago. Her husband is a sculptor of some note and secretly jealous of the mystery his wife and Luke Delaney share, but this husband is not so envious that he would stop transforming Lucy into breathtaking art. My sister was born to be molded in clay, chiseled in marble, cast in bronze. Every piece he crafts shows her enduring strength and determination.

And Luke? Is he happy? I look at him and know. Not yet.

"Annabel has asked me to read a poem she has always recited on the anniversary of her mother's death. Molly Marx," he says, "was my dearest friend." *There's no way Annabel could read this poem herself and keep a dry eye,* he thinks, and wonders if he can. Annabel smiles, urges him to begin, and Luke and I both see my smile in hers.

"We are loved by an unending love." I know this poem, written by a rabbi.

We are embraced by arms that find us.
Even when we are hidden from ourselves
We are touched by fingers that soothe us.

Luke breathes these words in a half whisper. As if he himself is hiding, he wears a soft, trimmed beard, a charcoal smudge on his craggy face, which is beginning to settle into the softness of sixty, which will be his next birthday. He speaks the poem from memory.

Even when we are too proud for soothing.
We are counseled by voices that guide us.
Even when we are too embittered to hear.
We are loved by an unending love.

Little Molly begins to stir. My daughter pushes back the bonnet to admire her baby's face. She lifts the child so that Ewan can stroke her strands of pale blond hair. There are quiet words between them on

which I do not want to intrude, and I have no need to, because seeing Molly and Annabel is all I want.

Annabel, Ewan, and Molly walk down the middle aisle and through the opened doors, outside, where moss connects the old stones the way we connect with one another, our histories mingled. They chat with my mother and her husband, their friends, with Barry, with Hicks and Brie, with Lucy, with Luke, these people I have loved, brought together once again by, as Nana Phyllis would say, such a *simcha*.

Suddenly, Annabel puts her hand on Ewan's arm and stops. She and Molly turn toward where my essence lingers, alone, back by the chapel, peeking out from beside an ancient oak. She is struggling to see someone. She smiles my smile. Molly opens her sleepy eyelids, delicate as butterflies. All our eyes meet, and love joins us as surely as if it were a live current. I know Annabel knows, and it is enough. It is everything.

Then Annabel blinks and returns to her life.

I, the late, lamented Molly Marx, take one last, long look. I am done. Complete. I am rested now. I can return to the Duration, for whatever is to come.

Can they feel it? I do not know.

Acknowledgments

Lucky me. I have had the privilege of working with a superb editor, Laura Ford, publishing's rising star. I thank her along with Ballantine's outstanding team, especially Susan Corcoran, Libby McGuire, Gina Centrello, Kim Hovey, Christine Cabello, Katie O'Callaghan, Alexandra Rudd, Rachel Kind, Rachel Bernstein, and Brian McLendon. Steve Messina, I am grateful to you and your colleague Sue Warga for the careful copyedit. Mary Wirth, Robbin Schiff, and Susan Turner, I applaud your choices for design.

Much gratitude to Christy Fletcher and Melissa Chinchilla of Fletcher & Parry for their energy and enthusiasm, as well as Howard Saunders and Shana Eddy of United Talent Agency, whose confidence and creativity I value tremendously. A loud shout-out, too, to fellow novelist Elizabeth Ziemska, whose early, rousing reaction kept me going.

Our Monday night writing workshop has been my steady pulse these last few years. Thank you, Charles Salzberg, for your leadership, structural brilliance, and deadlines, a writer's most essential tool. Without them I'd still be staring at my computer in pajamas. I am indebted to Vivian Conan, Patricia Crevits, Sharon Gurwitz, Sally Hoskins, Paul Hundt, Marilyn Goldstein, Judy Gorfein, Erica Keirstadt, Margaret Kennedy, Patty Nasey, Leslie Nipkow, and Betty Wald. Your laughter and generous ideas are the Super Glue that keeps me together. Rabbi Rami Shapiro, thank you as well for your inspiring poetry.

My family is my loving infrastructure. Robert, Jed, and Rory, I adore you and am immensely grateful for your sharp wit and tender support. Betsy and Vicki, sisters both, thanks for taking the time to read rough drafts. Last of all, I am beholden to my parents, Fritzie and Sam Platkin. I'd like to think they are in the Duration, smiling.

About the Author

SALLY KOSLOW is the author of the novel *Little Pink Slips*. Her essays have been published in *More, O: The Oprah Magazine*, and *The New York Observer*, among other publications. She was the editor in chief of both *McCall's* and *Lifetime*, was an editor at *Mademoiselle* and *Woman's Day*, and has taught creative writing at the Writing Institute of Sarah Lawrence College. The mother of two sons, she lives in New York City with her husband.

www.sallykoslow.com

About the Type

The text of this book was set in Filosofia. It was designed in 1996 by Zuzana Licko, who created it for digital typesetting as an interpretation of the sixteenth-century typeface Bodoni. Filosofia, an example of Licko's unusual font designs, has classical proportions with a strong vertical feeling, softened by rounded droplike serifs. She has designed many typefaces and is the cofounder of *Emigre* magazine, where many of them first appeared. Born in Bratislava, Czechoslovakia, Licko came to the United States in 1968. She studied graphic communications at the University of California at Berkeley, graduating in 1984.

Point and as officers, taking copious notes and recording every word. Many of those women had since gotten out of the Army, and were serving as stay-at-home moms or working in the civilian world. They were breathtakingly vulnerable about it all—the good, the bad, the ugly. Some wished to stay anonymous, others were happy to attach their name to their stories. Most had deployed at least once, if not multiple times. All of them had lost a friend, a classmate, or a spouse to the wars in Iraq and Afghanistan. More than once, as they shared their stories over the phone, I found myself in tears.

My hope is that *Beyond the Point* does justice to their stories in a way that is relatable to everyone, not just those "inside" the military community. I know that I've only scratched the surface of their experiences—like skipping a stone across a deep reservoir. But I hope through this book to help them feel a bit more understood. Unfortunately, as it stands, the majority of the stories we hear about women in the military focus on nonfiction accounts of sexual assault or the pioneering women who were "firsts." The first female general. The first female Army rangers. And while those stories are harrowing and inspiring, they also create a sense of distance between the average American woman and the picture of that woman in uniform. Those "first" stories might inadvertently discourage younger women from serving, thinking they aren't intense enough to join the military. But that couldn't be further from the truth. The reality is, the Army is full of women just like you and me. Women that have hopes and dreams and friendships and relationships and chipped nail polish and an addiction to Madewell. The world deserves to see more women in uniform in pop culture.

Writing this book has changed my life. The women who made these pages possible are not just interview subjects; they are my friends. They've taught me what it means to go to battle together—in fact, many of them have gone to battle for me, both in my childhood, and now, in my adulthood. And I am forever grateful. ❧

How This Book Came to Be *(continued)*

Man streaking through cadet area.) When I was eleven years old, Matt Kapinos smeared camouflage on my face and taught me how to march, handing me a broom to use as an M16. Female cadets mentored me through an organization called Young Life. At football games, West Point's cheerleaders, also known as Rabble Rousers, let me on the field and lifted me up in the air. In the summers, my friends and I would sunbathe at Stillwell, watching helicopters fly over with cadets in camouflage hanging out the side.

I tell people that growing up at West Point was like growing up at Hogwarts. I knew that I was witnessing magic. During those years, it was the beautiful, athletic, confident women that gathered in our living room that intrigued me the most. Could I be like them someday? Could I be that brave?

In *East of Eden*, John Steinbeck paints a picture of his hometown of Salinas, California— its landscapes, its smells, its sounds, its people. Once I became a writer, I grew jealous of his muse because my childhood home was never fully mine. I was a bystander, a tagalong—a "dependent" (at least that's how the Army categorized me). Even as I contemplated writing about West Point, I hesitated, fearing that I wouldn't do it justice. How could I write about West Point when most of my experiences were from the outside looking in? How could a girl with no class ring touch the long gray line?

And then, in 2013, a voicemail message landed on my phone that changed everything.

A friend and West Point graduate called out of the blue. She'd read some of my writing and wondered if I would be interested in writing about women at West Point. "We all have so many incredible stories to tell," she said, and I knew she was right. I'd lived at West Point long enough to know there was plenty of material for a book, if not ten. At just the right moment, she invited me to lift the curtain and re-experience those years through the lens of female friendship. She invited me back in. I remember raising my eyes to the roof of my car—my hands too— and saying out loud, "Well then. Here we go."

The next four years (Yes, FOUR YEARS, people!) were a slog, to say the least. It still cracks me up to think that I'd expected to knock this novel out in eighteen months, tops. But writing a novel is nothing like writing an essay for a newspaper or magazine. I started by interviewing dozens of women about their experiences at West

How This Book Came to Be

As an Army brat, it's hard for me to remember all the houses I've lived in because I've lived in so many. But I'll never forget the house on Ruger Road. Like West Point itself, it was built in the 1800s and wasn't afraid to boast about its history. It was four stories, with a kitchen in the basement and a dumbwaiter that lifted things (like the neighbor's cat) to the dining room on the second floor. I think it's condemned now, and probably should have been when we moved in. But I didn't know the difference. I was only ten. My father, a lieutenant colonel in the U.S. Army with a PhD in systems engineering, had joined West Point's faculty. All I knew was that we were going to get to stay in one place for a while.

From 1997 to 2003, our lives focused almost completely on cadets. My father taught them. My mother hosted them. My sisters dated them. And I looked up to them (and, err . . . also dated some). Much like Wendy Bennett, my mom was the perpetual hostess, leading a Fellowship of Christian Athletes huddle, and turning our home into an unofficial bed and breakfast for West Point's busiest events, like R-Day and graduation.

Needless to say, we had cadets over constantly. They filled our living room with the smell of sweat and grass. They ate all of the food. And best of all, they would tell stories. (It's possible I decided I wanted to be a writer listening to Dave Shoemaker tell the one about Naked ▶

Meet Claire Gibson

Lindsey Rome

An Army kid who grew up at the
U.S. Military Academy at West Point,
CLAIRE GIBSON is a writer and avid
reader whose work has been featured
in the *Washington Post* and the *Christian
Science Monitor,* among many other
publications. She lives in Nashville,
Tennessee, with her husband, Patrick,
and their son, Sam. Visit her website
at www.clairegibson.com. ❦

in the future you will understand why mothers are so desirous for little girls to be studious and make the most of the time that is going by so rapidly."[2]

If Abby was, in fact, the daughter in charge, even symbolically, she had quite a ménage to watch over. Ned attended the neighborhood public school, Hope High. Stuart and William, eleven and seven respectively, still took their lessons at home with Miss Asenath, as did Abby herself. Ellen, the Irish nanny, looked after Richard and Winthrop, and Bridget was the cook. Abby came into her own adolescence with a precocious maturity imposed by the needs of such a household, a maturity that was not without satisfaction. She enjoyed the little gang of boisterous, good-looking boys clambering around her. She played baseball with them and became an ardent football fan before she was in her teens.

Nelson and Abby Pearce had excellent instincts for child-rearing. They invested their children with responsibility without burdening them. Also, it was not a Victorian household in the patriarchal, authoritarian mode. Abby Pearce derived her own power from her inheritance and her ancestral credentials. However severe her conflicts, she never became submissive. Nelson Aldrich, while accepting the masculine prerogatives of his generation, was a complex mix of aggression and strong, nurturing instincts. If sibling rivalry is interpreted as competition for the love of the parents, the Aldrich children were refreshingly free of that struggle. The spontaneous affection heaped on them by their father and the steadfast devotion of an often exhausted mother seemed to mitigate such rivalry. Abby Aldrich Rockefeller would write to her brother Ned in 1927, "Our feeling of family solidarity and friendship (I am beginning to think) is quite unusual."[3]

The texture of Abby Greene's daily life in Providence in the 1880s was but marginally different from that of her mother's routine twenty years earlier. In winter and summer alike she wore long stockings and high-button shoes. Underclothes were seasonal —woolen in winter, cotton in summer. Petticoats were red or white flannel or muslin, generally ruffled and hand-embroidered. A handmade cotton or woolen frock would complete the ensemble.

Walking was still the most practical means of transportation, much faster than the clumsy horsecars. Needlework was a shared activity among the women. "Everyone was brought up to use her hands," explained Abby Rockefeller's granddaughter Abby Milton O'Neill. "We all sat around and did it together. My grandmother knitted and did needlepoint and she did it very well. So did my mother."[4] Roast beef and Yorkshire pudding were served every Sunday, and Parcheesi, whist, and anagrams were the favorite parlor games. Letters were often delivered by hand—it was quicker and more elegant than the mails—and important messages flew back and forth over the telegraph wire. Every proper entry hall had an umbrella stand and a silver tray for visiting cards. Abby made her calls faithfully, just as her mother had when she was a girl, recording them in her *Visiting List*, a tiny book with a quotation from George Eliot: " 'Tis grievous parting with good company." Babies were delivered at home, goats were still tethered in the parks, and the organ-grinder's operatic tunes filled the air.

The sense of lingering tradition, of an orderly, placid surface, was more apparent than real, however. Abby's larger world was changing in dramatic and irreversible ways. The telephone was revolutionizing communication, and the incandescent light was transforming the environment. The America of big business and heavy industry was now firmly entrenched in Providence, and Nelson Aldrich was in a pivotal position to exploit this America. He had already joined a syndicate of local businessmen to build the luxurious Narragansett Hotel and would become a millionaire when he lent his considerable influence to the consortium that built the Rhode Island electric street railway.

As the Gilded Age approached its zenith, Providence leaders preferred to view their full-blown prosperity as more golden than gilded. The vulgar extravagance characteristic of certain New York and Chicago tycoons never found full expression in proud New England. Colonial houses were restored to their original purity instead of being demolished to make room for marble mansions. The wives of wealthy Providence industrialists founded the Rhode Island School of Design and established Pembroke Women's College at Brown University. They were crusaders for prison reform and women's rights. Although the city tripled in size while Abby

Greene was growing up, it remained accessible and small compared to New York and Washington. Had she spent most of her youth in Providence, cultured though it was, Abby's horizons would have remained as limited as those of any sheltered daughter of the upper class. But she grew up knowing a wider world. Washington, Nelson Aldrich, and her own indomitable spirit made the difference.

Elsie, the youngest of the Aldrich children, was born on August 20, 1888. Two months later, Abby Burgess, Nelson's mother, died at the age of seventy-eight. His father, Anan, then eighty-one, lived on for a few years. Lucy Aldrich was presented to society, and Benjamin Harrison, Nelson's learned friend, returned the Republicans to the White House.

How close Nelson was to the Machiavellian deals that finally swung the election of Harrison is a moot question. As a member of the Republican Congressional Campaign Committee, he could not have been entirely innocent. He departed for Washington in December 1888, elated by the election of a Republican Senate and House, but his confident mood did not take into account the fact that the Republican majority in the House was perilously small and the combined popular vote of all other parties exceeded the Republican Party's by half a million.

A great new constituency was forming in the West whose passions and needs were only superficially acknowledged by the senator from Rhode Island. In the Congress that convened in 1888, the Fifty-first, Nelson's legislative skills were severely tested over three issues which bitterly divided the country—the question of tariffs, the pressure from the West for the free coinage of silver, and the matter of federal control over national elections in the South. Aldrich hammered out compromises on the silver question and the election issue, but his party would ultimately suffer a humiliating defeat over the tariff. The bill that was finally passed in 1890 was known as the McKinley tariff, but it might as well have been called the Aldrich bill, for Aldrich had honed all its provisions.

Its central feature was a general increase in tariff schedules, with some agricultural products added to the protected list. Aldrich completely misjudged the opposition of the ordinary voters. Furi-

The sisters, Lucy and Abby ca. 1890.
Courtesy of the Rhode Island Historical Society.

ous charges raged across the country. Republican tariff policies seemed nothing more than self-serving ruses to gouge the public and inflate the profits of the manufacturers. The congressional election of 1890 gave the Democrats a landslide majority of 138 in the House of Representatives, and Harrison's domestic program came to a standstill. "His friend Aldrich," Stephenson wrote, "was a ruler with nothing to rule."[5]

The denouement arrived two years later in 1892 when Grover Cleveland returned to the White House. Nelson hung on to his own Senate seat, but narrowly, for the social revolution was on, a middle-class revolution that would engulf the Republican Party with the rise of Theodore Roosevelt. The long-run casualty of this election for Nelson, however, was the permanent hostility of the *New York World*. Years later, when Joseph Pulitzer was asked why his paper became the archenemy of the senator from Rhode Island, he replied that he was against Republican policies, and the real leader of the party was Aldrich. The attack, even if accurate on some counts, had a vicious edge. It was Aldrich, the voice of corrupt wealth, Aldrich, the archvillain. The *World* published a cartoon of Nelson as an auctioneer selling the Rhode Island governorship to the highest bidder.

Nelson, scorning the power of the press lords, refused to defend himself, a serious flaw in a political strategist. Sometimes it seemed as though he deliberately wished to flout the popular will. Even his imperturbable confidence, however, could not insulate his children from the embarrassment of ugly publicity. His daughters rallied around him. His sons held him at arm's length. "My father [William Aldrich] rarely spoke of his father, the senator," Nelson Aldrich III said. "Clearly he was made uncomfortable by the robber baron implications of the attacks and the cartoons that had caricatured him."[6]

In his private life, away from the hue and cry of politics, Nelson was able to realize a long-cherished dream, born when he was a poor bookkeeper. He established his family in a setting of historic winter residences among the most affluent of old Providence families. In 1891, after considering many substantial properties, he leased the Robert S. Burrough house at 110 Benevolent Street, a

The city residence of Senator Nelson Aldrich after 1891. 110 Benevolent Street, Providence, Rhode Island.
Courtesy of the Rockefeller Archive Center.

graceful sixty-year-old mansion designed by John Holden Greene in the 1820s. Modified by Colonial Revival alterations, the three-story structure sat on a high foundation, its center entrance displaying a one-story paired-Tuscan-column portico below a Palladian window, with quoins framing the facade.

The interior rooms were spacious and high-ceilinged, with excellent wood paneling and black marble mantels. True to the house's architectural tradition, the finely carved balustrade in the center hall led upstairs to well-proportioned master suites. The third floor was a rabbit warren of children's rooms and servants' quarters. After he was able to buy the house in 1902, Nelson added a ball-room. The surrounding gardens on the corner site were an imaginative mix of rose beds, annuals, and flowering shrubs. A hand-wrought iron bench circled the largest of the specimen trees to create a romantic scene.

Abby Pearce and Nelson together furnished the house in the eighteenth-century American and English antiques and high Chippendale favored by the leading Providence dealer, Charles Pendleton. (In 1904, Pendleton willed his own outstanding collection of furniture, ceramics, glass, and metalwork to the Rhode Island School of Design.) Abby Greene, Ned, and Lucy now received their first serious education in the art of collecting. Nelson's enthusiasms especially were infectious. The fever burned within them all their lives, often in original and unpredictable ways.

At seventeen Abby was set free from Miss Asenath's tutorial supervision to become a day student at Miss Abbott's School for Young Ladies, 280 Benefit Street. It would be a misnomer to call it a mere finishing school. The principal, Miss Josephine Abbott, who taught literature and philosophy herself, directed a first-rate faculty and offered a rigorous academic curriculum. Her girls prepared for such schools as Wellesley and Bryn Mawr. Abby's classmate Madelaine Goddard took a first prize at Oxford for modern foreign languages, going on to study the violin in Berlin.

Abby's own course of study included physics, English composition and literature, French, German, the history of art, and ancient history, as well as gymnastics, hygiene, and dancing. She was always reading, it seemed, at least according to her diary. She read at the Athenaeum, she read when she didn't feel well, she read when it was too cold to venture out. She walked downtown with her friends, amused her little brothers and sister, helped her mother put up preserves, and made calls on elderly acquaintances. Sunday evenings in Providence seemed reserved for chafing-dish parties, and the Aldrich house became a particular favorite, as groups of young people served up Welsh rarebit. The amusements offered were astonishingly innocent—charades, truth or consequences, musical chairs, and rounds of songs at the piano. Although Abby's "coming out" was more than a year off, the names of many young men turn up in her diary. They accompanied her to church and to and from school; they joined her at the theater; they came around for card games or simply for hours and hours of conversation.

Evidently she was a good listener already, not out of mere courtesy, but because her restless curiosity drove her to find out what her friends were thinking and feeling. She knew how to have fun and how to be amusing. She loved parties. "If I had my way," she wrote one of her sons some years later, "I really think I should like to give a party every day."[7] Her spontaneity was known to cause her mother to say with some irritation, "If only I knew before hand what Abby is likely to say or do, life would be a lot simpler."[8] Such a spirit, however, made her popular with her peers. And finally there was the Aldrich charm, which all the siblings possessed. "They are riddled with it, charm that is," said Winthrop Aldrich's daughter Mary Homans, "the women as well as the men. Even I've been teased about it. If I manage to put a point across, at a meeting or something, a groan will go up and someone will say, 'there's that ghastly Aldrich charm coming out.' "[9]

With the approach of summer, the Aldrich family and their friends headed for Warwick Neck. After several summers in the Duncan Chapin house, Nelson rented a three-story frame farmhouse known as the Hoppin place, after its former owner, a China merchant named Benjamin Hoppin. Situated on fifteen acres of high land some distance back from the shore, it offered a pleasantly unbuttoned, gracefully run-down hospitality. One bathroom served for everyone. The rough grass was adequate for improvised lawn tennis and croquet. Weather-beaten outbuildings sheltered the stock and seasonal crops. The young people sailed their catboats, fished for scuppers, and lolled in hammocks.

Newport, twenty miles downshore, represented the other end of the spectrum. Here was opulence on a grand and glittering scale. Like the bankers and merchants of the Italian Renaissance who retired to their villas for the summer and the English industrialists who built castles in the countryside, American railroad and mining barons, too, had their imperial aspirations. The Breakers with its seventy rooms of alabaster and gold, created for Cornelius Vanderbilt II by Richard Morris Hunt, was more palace than villa. Theresa Fair Oelrich presided over Rosecliff, although, in her case, "presiding" had interesting ramifications. Every morning at eight o'clock she personally supervised the housecleaning of the mansion. The daughter of a Belfast immigrant who struck the Comstock Lode and went to Congress as Senator James Fair, Theresa had commissioned Stanford White to design Rosecliff. He gave her a refined, scaled-down version of the Grand Trianon that included the largest ballroom in Newport, a heart-shaped, regal staircase, and perfumed chandeliers. In such "cottage" settings, Nouveau High Society gathered every summer for three months. On their yachts, at the polo matches, or merely driving the length of Bellevue Avenue in victoria and barouche, they made a gorgeous spectacle of themselves. It was surely the epitome of the Gilded Age.

Even after he became the friendly ally of the most powerful business interests in America, Nelson Aldrich rejected the unabashed splendor celebrated in Newport. The $7 million fortune he amassed by the time of his death was paltry when measured against Vanderbilt and Havemayer and Rockefeller wealth. But more fundamental than money was point of view. Although their childhood experiences were different—Abby Pearce was reared in affluence, Nelson in near-poverty—both felt themselves to be patrician. Both absorbed the lessons of New England, to avoid swagger and show. Where Nelson Aldrich parted company with his New England forebears was in his zest for everything of the senses, an impulse that unquestionably affected his daughter Abby.

There is no evidence that Abby participated in the most extravagant of the Newport social functions. Even in the 1890s, a less glamorous, more informal summer life went on in old fashioned houses that really were cottages, albeit large. But there is no reason, for instance, to assume that she attended Gertrude Vanderbilt's coming-out ball at the Breakers, or that she even knew Miss Vanderbilt. In a broader sense, because of Nelson Aldrich's position in Washington, her life as a young unmarried woman was more emancipated than the hothouse existence of a Vanderbilt. On the purely recreational level, however, her social routine was rather tame.

Finally it was the autumn season of 1893, *her* season. She had graduated from Miss Abbott's in June and spent the summer at Warwick. She wrote: "September 27th, Wednesday—we came up from Warwick yesterday after having spent a delightful summer. This morning I unpacked and got my room settled and in the afternoon read. . . . [On Saturday] Frank Smith came to dinner and stayed all evening." The walking, card-playing, sewing, and calling continued. "At 4:30 Billy Weeden came to call on me. I like him very much," she confided to her diary. Saturday football began. The invitations were addressed for the coming-out party. On October 17 she went to Boston to order her dress—white satin, trimmed with white tulle and white roses. "My hat is black velvet trimmed with black feathers and blue ribbon."[10] From the moment she was old enough to preen in front of a mirror, she wore imaginative, even eccentric hats, a clever way of putting into better proportion her Chapman nose.

On Saturday, November 18, 1893, one month after her nineteenth birthday, Abby was introduced at an afternoon tea to the oldest names in Rhode Island—the Browns, the Goddards, the Hoppins, the Dyers. The young people came to the supper dance that followed. Fifty-two calling cards accompanied fifty-two bouquets. Frank Smith was her dinner partner. Abby was tall and small-waisted, with a lovely bosom and the excellent carriage that the era admired. She was more attractive than beautiful, and her poise belied her youth. Her strong features were softened by an impulsive, welcoming smile. Her eyes were pale amber, "piercing, yet serene and far-seeing," her nieces and nephew recalled, "and she had a tremendously interesting voice, almost nasal and yet like music to accompany her conversation."[11]

Her scrapbooks convey the lightheartedness of the winter months that followed. She carefully pasted up the fifty-two calling cards, the football stubs, and the theater party tickets. She danced the "German" with Fred Hoppin, went to lunch with Wallace Howe, played poker with George Hinckley, Frank Thurston, and Dan George. Harry Spooner took her sleighing and she slipped away for a late supper after the Gym Ball with a Mr. Frank Coates, who kept her out until three in the morning. Frank Smith was her steadiest companion; their daily walks suggested a special relationship. For intellectual stimulus she attended lectures in current events, English literature, and history and enrolled in a drawing class. She moved out into the community via the Young Women's Christian Association, known in the 1890s for its concern for minorities and its efforts in behalf of women. During the congressional season she met President Cleveland and her father's friends in the Senate. She attended receptions for the diplomatic corps, the three services, and the naval cadets at Annapolis.

It had always been Nelson Aldrich's intention to be the first one to introduce his children to the glories of Europe. But then Mrs. Elisha Dyer, whose husband was Nelson's close friend and the future governor of Rhode Island, invited Abby and Lucy to join her and her son on a journey to England and the Continent. The senator, heavily involved in the electric railway negotiations, acquiesced, with the proviso that he could join them later in the summer.

It was June 28, 1894, when the Dyer party boarded Cunard's R.M.S. *Lucania* in New York. Everyone, it seemed, was going to Europe. The State Department issued as many as thirty thousand passports that year alone. There were accommodations for every size pocketbook. Vanderbilts and Astors could reserve five deck cabins and book several suites at the deluxe hotels; students and scholars bought the cheapest fares; middle-class families joined Cook tours. If Mrs. Dyer followed New England protocol she was somewhere beneath the Vanderbilts, but well above middle-class.

Both Abby and Lucy kept careful diaries of their itinerary on this, their first grand tour. They went yachting on the River Clyde, met the Duke of Argyll in Scotland, traveled through Germany, sailed down the Rhine, heard *Lohengrin*, took the baths at Baden-Baden. On September 1 they arrived in Switzerland, crossing Lake Lugano to Bellagio, and on to Milan, Venice, Florence, Pisa, and the French Riviera.

In Nice Abby had her horoscope read:

Well educated. Character half gentle, half sharp. The spirit is subject to contrasts and to contradiction. Likes the picturesque, travel and all that touches on the wonderful.

Likes also comedy, gaiety. Her humor is always lively, changeable, mocking and critical without malice.

Likes her comforts, and while quick to trust and very unreserved when people please her, she has also a dose of independence and changeable tastes.

Headstrong and lightly capricious—very likeable on the whole. Also has a mild liking for the theater.

A little greedy, lightly coquettish. Very warmhearted and with a short memory. Still a little childlike at times.

Her judgment is not very firm and not positive enough. Imagination has a great influence on her mind.[12]

CHAPTER 4

---

*A*bby's first grand tour lasted four months. She returned to America on the U.S. Mail Steamer *New York*, in the company of her parents, her sister, and the Dyer party. Two weeks later she was in Providence. Sometime during November of that year she met John Davison Rockefeller, Jr. The occasion was an evening dance at the home of her friend Madelaine Goddard, whose father was a trustee of Brown University. A sophomore at Brown, John had never in his life attended a dance. His strict Baptist rearing forbade dancing, and it was only after considerable hesitation and worry that he accepted Miss Goddard's invitation. His friend Lefferts Dashiell danced him around their rooms at Slater Hall, "polishing me off," as John later explained it.[1] He remembered the Goddard dance floor as being dreadfully glassy and that the only woman he danced with, a Miss Foster, practically held him up. He did not dance with Abby, but she made such an impression on him that nearly sixty years later he would tell his biographer, Raymond B. Fosdick, that "she treated me as if I had all the savoir-faire in the world and her confidence did me a lot of good. . . . From that time on I began thoroughly to enjoy the social aspects of college life."[2]

The young man who responded with such appreciation that the

memory lingered for six decades did not, in his own words, "make friends easily" and had a tendency to get "lost in the crowd."[3] His physical appearance belied such diffidence. He was stocky and handsome, though not tall. (People later perceived him as shorter than Abby; at the very least they were the same height.) But a close look at photographs reveals a certain questioning, even bewilderment, in his eyes. Whether Abby found something appealing about him at that first encounter or was simply being friendly out of habit is not known. She attended a tea he gave in his rooms on January 16, 1895, but then so did Lucy. What she could not know was that he was intimidated by the jolly young men who hung about her, and that he had vowed never to dance with her until he was much better on his feet.

On January 29, 1895, John turned twenty-one. From his father, John Senior, the founder of the Standard Oil Trust, came a check for twenty-one dollars and a simple message. ". . . we rejoice that you know from experience that good for you is inseparably connected with the good you bring to others. But this is not a lecture, only a kind word from an affectionate father to a much loved and only son. . . ."[4]

There was little that was simple, however, in the exhortations of his mother, Laura Spelman Rockefeller. "You can celebrate your birthday in no better way," she wrote ". . . than by such earnest work as I know you are giving, for God and the saving of souls of your fellow students. You who see so clearly the great need of a power beyond yourself to keep him from the temptations of college life and enable him to help others, can persuade them, as no one else can. God grant, and I know that he will, that you may add many stars to your crown—to Him be all the glory."[5]

While John did not take literally his mother's admonition to celebrate his birthday by saving the souls of his college friends, he did not shrug it off either. He was the triumphant product of her Christian fervor, "home-made and hand-trained" in the words of the senior Rockefeller's trusted adviser, Frederick T. Gates.[6]

Laura Celestia Spelman was the pretty brunette daughter of prosperous New Englanders, strict Congregationalists—as strict as the Baptists—who had carried their Puritan ideals with them when they settled in Cleveland. Her father was a successful businessman who was one of the operators of the Underground Railroad and an active participant in the cultural life of his adopted city. Her mother worked and prayed for the cause of temperance, kneeling in bars to persuade errant drinkers to take the pledge. Laura was an early feminist, startling the audience at her high school graduation in 1855 with her plea on behalf of disenfranchised women. "The reason she has so long remained silent," the young speaker proclaimed, "is she has been regarded incapable of being or doing anything, and consequently all her attempts have been ridiculed." She continued: "The temple of science has hitherto been guarded against her approach. . . . She may not aspire to the position of being [man's] competitor. What wonder then that she has so long remained imbecile and powerless? But give woman culture—let her tread the many paths of science—allow mathematics and exact thought on all subjects to exert their influence on her mind, and conventions need not trouble about her 'proper sphere.' "[7]

Laura continued her education at the Oread Collegiate Institute in Worcester, Massachusetts. She was editor of the college newspaper, listened to the speeches of famous New England abolitionists, and became a lifelong advocate of the rights of blacks in America. Later in her life she would be a major financial contributor to programs that offered instruction in sex hygiene to female students in the normal schools and colleges of the nation.

Believing that her calling was to become a teacher, she returned to Cleveland in 1859 to accept a position in the public school system. Her grave charm and occasional sparkle were misleading. Behind an accommodating facade, she was a woman of uncommon determination, irrevocably committed to living the religious life. By the time she married John D. Rockefeller in the living room of the Spelman residence on September 8, 1864, she was ready to invest her ambition and the discipline of her spiritual beliefs in a new calling—that of wife and mother.

Laura Chasin, Laurance Rockefeller's daughter, who practices family therapy and takes a multigenerational perspective, believes that historically, Rockefeller men tended to "marry upward" and in particular to marry socially established, powerful women.[8] She traces this to the Godfrey Rockefeller who in 1806 married Lucy Avery, who was the steady partner of a weak husband. Their son, William Avery Rockefeller, the father of John Senior, was by no stretch of the imagination weak. But he was an unpredictable, morally ambiguous husband who severely taxed the flinty courage and stoicism of his wife. Eliza Davison was the stubborn, red-haired daughter of a well-to-do farmer in the community of Niles in Cayuga County, New York. She ignored the danger signals to marry the erratic, adventurous Rockefeller, with his dancing blue eyes, his beguiling grin, his deep-chested physique.

William Avery knew how to use his personality to advantage. He was a sharp horse trader, he rafted raw lumber, he went on the road periodically to hawk patent medicine and herbal remedies. He was not known as a drinker and he was a man who paid his debts, but in 1849, a hired girl in his household in Moravia, New York, accused him of rape. He was indicted in the Cayuga County courthouse, but the case never came to trial, because "Big Bill" disappeared until the scandal blew over. It was William Avery's style. After months of absence he would suddenly reappear, unapologetic, full of gusto, leading fresh horses, his pockets full of cash. Eliza was the one who held the family together, maintained discipline, saw that the children were fed and educated. Her character traits, as described by Rockefeller biographers, could easily belong to Laura Spelman—intelligent, austere, devout.

To the extent that the Spelmans had more status than the Rockefellers and Laura herself was better educated and more cultivated than John, Laura Chasin's theory holds up. But John was no William Avery. He learned entrepreneurial matters from his father. Indeed, he credits the older man with teaching him all he needed to know about the sacredness of a contract, the harshness of the business world, and the value of capital. But his personal deportment—neatness, modesty, strict avoidance of waste, loyalty to wife and family—was clearly the result of Eliza's indoctrination. Above all he learned piety. John became a good Baptist because his mother would have it no other way. As clerk of the Erie Street Church, he learned his Bible at the church, formed his friendships there, and found an emotional outlet. In their values and in their goals for their children, John D. Rockefeller and Laura Spelman were entirely compatible. It was a marriage of equals.

Cleveland was a booming city in the 1860s, with great factories and ugly slums mushrooming side by side. Industry had taken over, and the oil industry in particular dominated the environment. It had happened almost overnight. "A commodity that had been a curiosity when Lincoln was nominated [in 1860] had become a necessity of civilization . . . before he was murdered," John D. Rockefeller's biographer, Allan Nevins, wrote.[9] Kerosene was the efficient, inexpensive way to light millions of homes, offices, and shops. Oil products lubricated the machinery of mills, factories, and railroads. Cleveland "was flavored and saturated with oil," said a local historian, and "the river and the lake were smeared with it."[10] During the days of his courtship, young Rockefeller often called on Laura Spelman still wearing the muddy boots in which he had splashed around his refinery yard.

By the time he was twenty-six years old, Rockefeller and his fellow Baptist Samuel Andrews were the owners of the largest oil refinery on the greater Cleveland tax rolls. He brought in his brother, William Rockefeller, to build a second refinery and to cultivate the European market. In 1867, Henry Flagler, son of a poor Presbyterian minister, joined the group with some capital of his own and a sizable contribution (as much as ninety thousand dollars) from his wife's uncle, Stephen Harkness.

The German social scientist Max Weber argued persuasively in 1905 that the modern phenomenon of sober, rational bourgeois capitalism had its source in the religious values of sixteenth-century ascetic Protestantism. Calvinism in particular, applauded by its admirers as the best school for economic virtue, was attacked as the sanctimonious ally of commercial sharp practice. It may not be a coincidence that Rockefeller and his early partners were good Calvinists who regarded the pursuit of wealth as not merely a challenge but a sacred duty. Rockefeller fit Weber's description of America's hero of industrial capitalism: "neither dare-devil . . . [nor] economic adventurer, but [a man] who had grown up in the hard school of life, calculating and daring at the same time, above

John D. Rockefeller, Senior, 1895. Portrait by Eastman Johnson. Photographer, Charles Uht.
Courtesy of the Rockefeller Archive Center.

Laura Spelman, from a daguerreotype owned by her son John.
Courtesy of the Rockefeller Archive Center.

all temperate and reliable, shrewd and completely devoted to . . . business."[11]

On January 10, 1870, five men—the Rockefeller brothers, Henry Flagler, Samuel Andrews, and Stephen Harkness—associated themselves under the laws of Ohio to form a joint-stock corporation to be known as the Standard Oil Company. At this juncture it was the biggest refiner of crude oil in the nation. The stock consisted of 10,000 shares of $100 par value, the total capitalization thus being $1 million. No shares were sold to the general public. John D. Rockefeller was the largest individual stockholder, with 2,667 shares. William Rockefeller, Flagler, and Andrews held 1,333 each; Harkness 1,334; the firm of Rockefeller, Andrews and Flagler 1,000; and O. B. Jennings 1,000.

Before the end of the century, the Standard Trust became the most efficient—and the most fiercely assailed—industrial complex in the world. Rockefeller was its undisputed master. Nevins sorts out the reasons for this mastery. "Chill, clear insight . . . allied with a primal urge of ambition. . . . enigmatic to a disconcerting degree. . . . a front of silence which was like smooth steel."[12] In an arena of implacable warfare, he fought ruthlessly and subtly to organize a chaotic industry into a brilliantly managed monopoly. Monopoly was a concept repugnant to most Americans, but to Rockefeller it was the solution to the cruelty of overcompetition. He never hesitated to employ the most odious techniques—rebates, drawbacks, even industrial espionage—to force the unwilling independents to their knees. Cooperative firms, however, were absorbed on generous terms. And all the while he remained a pious Baptist, a contradiction which infuriated his critics, but was no contradiction at all for him.

By this time, Rockefeller had moved his family—Laura and two-year-old Bessie—into a commodious brick residence on Euclid Avenue, the street known locally as Millionaires' Row. Laura, who cared nothing for the decoration of houses, made no changes in the furnishings, recently installed by the previous owner. John, interested in utility and convenience, not interested in aesthetics, built a stone stable and coach house in the rear of the property that were more impressive by far than the house itself. Two more daughters followed—Alta in 1871 and Edith in 1872—and finally John Junior in 1874, all three delivered in the upstairs bedroom of the Euclid Avenue house by Dr. Myra K. Merrick, a pioneering female physician whom Laura admired. (For purposes of the biography, John D. Rockefeller, Jr., is referred to as John; John D. Rockefeller, Sr., as Senior.)

John was a year old when the family, as a consequence of Standard Oil's move into the Eastern refinery industry, began to spend winters in various New York hotels. He was five when his father converted a bankrupt Cleveland investment into a country estate. In 1875, Rockefeller and some colleagues had built a sanitarium on seventy-nine acres of land in Forest Hill, adjacent to the city. When that failed, he ran it as a hotel, but that idea foundered too, as paying guests expected Laura to act as a hostess.

It was a huge, lumbering white structure, its exterior cluttered with superfluous balconies, unnecessary ornamentation, and widow's walks. Laura, oblivious to the curtainless windows and mismatched furniture, encouraged her husband to do what he most enjoyed around the estate—supervise the construction of roads and outbuildings, buy and sell animals, admire the harvest. For the children, except for the isolation, it seemed an ideal setting, with a lake for water sports, sloping meadows and wooded ravines for hikes and picnics, trails for bicycles, a pony ring, bridle paths. Before long it became the Rockefellers' principal Cleveland residence, with Euclid Avenue serving as a seasonal stopover and a "Sunday" house.

The Sabbath routine never varied. A cold lunch, prepared in the country on Saturday, was carried to the city for the family to partake of following Sunday-morning services at the Euclid Avenue Baptist Church. The afternoons were reserved for letter-writing and quiet reading of religious texts. After a late-afternoon drive back to the country, Laura gathered her children about her for "Home Talks." Each child recited her or his ill-conceived action or mistake of the week, with Laura carefully reminding them that it was God against whom they had sinned. A *besetting sin* caused her as much anxiety as a high fever. It was God's forgiveness they must seek, she explained, as she led them in prayer.

Although John's recollections, as told to Fosdick, centered upon a father who was kindly and solicitous, always ready with a wry joke or a whirl on a frozen pond, the reality was that Senior was away for long periods of time. More often it was Laura who skated with him by moonlight. It was Laura who constructed the environment for her children, putting into careful practice every detail of Calvinist doctrine. The same virtues that had inspired her mother and her husband's mother inspired her—piety, diligence, abhorrence of waste, concern for the poor and the deprived. But to Laura the possibility for spiritual failure must have seemed daunting. As the Rockefeller fortune grew, the temptations for idle luxury, for worldly distractions, pressed in upon her from every direction. She fully supported her husband's drive for wealth and power. Her religion reinforced such ambition. But the fruits of his calling must not be permitted to corrupt the lives of her children.

From such stern convictions a household of extreme vigilance emerged. Laura was explicit in her opposition to the theater, card-playing, and dancing. God and church came first with her. The only safe response to temptation was to avoid it. Since she believed that John, as the son and heir, would inherit the greatest responsibilities and encounter the most seductive temptations, her vigil over him was especially close.

With the dangerous outside world kept at bay, and Baptist ministers the most frequent callers, John's only playmate was the son of the Forest Hill housekeeper. His sisters' friends, though years older than he, also became his friends. In a largely female world he was unself-conscious about so-called women's chores, taking it quite for granted that he would mend his own clothes, hem his own handkerchiefs, and iron his trousers. But the hermetic atmosphere contributed to his palpable shyness and reserve.

Senior, despite his kindliness with his family, was essentially an unemotional, impassive man. A sense of humor is no substitute for unrestrained affection, freely given. Laura, preoccupied with her children's souls, was not an easy source of physical closeness. Artistic impulses, provocative ideas, and informal sociability from the larger world were not encouraged. "Everything was centered around the home and the church," John recalled, and there was nothing else.[13]

Actually there was something else, one art form that John was encouraged to enjoy, and that was music. Laura had studied both piano and voice, and sang in the church choir. She provided instruction in a musical instrument for each of the children—Bessie the violin, Edith the cello, Alta the piano, and John the violin also. John's musical training began when he was seven and continued for eight years with the concertmaster of the New York Philharmonic. But it was never for diversion, rather it must be deadly serious, and only the classical compositions that lent themselves to quartets in chaste surroundings were played.

Unwilling perhaps to accept New York as more than a temporary expedient, Senior waited nine years before moving his family from their apartment in the Hotel Buckingham to a mansion at 4 West 54th Street, the former home of Arabella Worsham. It would be hard to find two women more different in life-style and experience than Arabella Worsham and Laura Spelman to preside over the same house in succeeding decades. Abandoned by her lover, John Worsham, when she followed him to New York and became pregnant, Arabella moved into a building owned by Collis P. Huntington, one of the builders of the Southern Pacific Railroad. Her circumstances improved when she became Huntington's intimate companion.

In 1877, Arabella bought the 54th Street building with its stolid Renaissance decor. A woman of imagination and flair, she ordered extensive alterations. "In a time during which confused Victoriana reigned . . . Arabella exercised surprising restraint," one social historian wrote.[14] In her hands the dull edifice became an exquisite *petit palais*, with black mahogany staircase, trompe l'oeil wallpaper, satinwood inlaid with mother-of-pearl.

Senior had been negotiating for the house for at least two years. Then, on October 5, 1883, Huntington's wife died, and nine months later, in July 1884, Arabella and Collis were married. One of her wedding gifts from the groom was his town house at 65 Park Avenue. On October 24, 1884, Senior and Laura traded nine lots on 72nd Street for Arabella's house on 54th with all its furniture, wall hangings, and rugs, the total appraised at $600,000.

Firmly ignoring the character of the adjacent neighborhood— the greatest concentration of wealth and power in the world— Laura maintained the same austere balance of church and home in New York that she had established in Cleveland. The family prayed at the unfashionable Fifth Avenue Baptist Church, a spire- less brownstone structure on the south side of West 46th Street. The Manhattan house, like its Cleveland counterpart, was the headquarters for various religious projects, including missionary meetings, church socials, and temperance lectures.

John, whose early childhood education consisted of a vague pa- rade of tutors with names he could not remember, entered a regular school when he was nine. First there was the New York School of Languages, and after that a tiny establishment that met above a store for a year. The third one, renowned for its program of classi- cal studies and illustrious student body, was the Cutler School. In his plodding, unrelenting way, he achieved a 98.10 grade point average, but he looked so exhausted that Laura took him to Forest Hill for the winter of 1887.

She had worried about his physical well-being when he was an infant; allusions to his frailty continued throughout his childhood. He looked robust enough, but his shyness, his intense fear of mis- takes, and his brooding uneasiness formed a disconcerting picture that Laura could not ignore. Her exacting control of his every action, a conditioning that had assumed Pavlovian dimensions, was in danger of backfiring.

When asked what he did that winter in Forest Hill, John an- swered "Vegetate."[15] What he actually did was chop wood, burn brush, and rake lawns, following the wisdom of the day that hard physical exercise was good for neurasthenic men.

His diary records that he was back in New York in March 1888 and that perhaps for the first time in his life, felt a stirring of desire for a girl his own age. Her name was Bessie Dashiell. She was the sister of his new friend Lefferts Dashiell. She was quiet and pretty, she liked horses and the outdoors, as John did, and the mere fact that he could sit behind her in church was an experience to be recorded.

"I was not sure that I should call her Bessie or Miss Bessie, so I did not call her anything," he wrote. After an evening in which Bessie and her aunt, Mrs. Colby, called on the Rockefellers, John lay awake most of the night. "I surely think I never new [sic] a girl I like better, because she is so near my own age. [John was fifteen, Bessie sixteen.] She is so simple and natural and really one cannot help liking her though I think I have not tried very hard to not like her. I felt very miserable to think I would not see her till Tuesday anyway and perhaps not then. I woke up after five, a little, and could not go to sleep again."

On the pretext of delivering a note to the Colby house, John caught another glimpse of Bessie. "She was as pretty as possible and had on a light morning dress. I stood in the hall, as it was only about one or two minutes I was there. I said good morning and left." For the rest of the afternoon he walked around the neighborhood, as far as 79th Street, around the reservoir, down to 40th, all in the hope that Bessie might be out for a walk too. In the evening he went to a party at the home of Bessie's cousin Everett Colby. "Had a fine time. Bessie looked to [sic] pretty for anything in a lovely pink dress."[16]

In the fall of 1889, John transferred out of Cutler into the Browning School, a block from his house on 54th. John's evaluation of the gifted John Browning lends some insight into his own self-image. "If a person scolded me, I shut up like a clam," he later told Fosdick. "I wasn't much of a scholar but I always tried hard, I didn't like to be reproached. . . . He [Browning] helped me to study and to concentrate. . . . I owe a great deal to him."[17] Even in the protected intimacy of the small school, however, John could not shake the troubled feelings of anxiety that made him a poor sleeper.

Both Leff Dashiell and Ev Colby were fellow students at Browning. Now John was able more easily to cultivate his friendship with Bessie. On Sundays and holidays they took their horses across the Hudson on the Fort Lee ferry to ride across the Palisades. They exchanged long letters during the summer that Bessie went with her family to Alaska. But then the friendship that had come to mean so much to the lonely boy ended.

On January 23, 1891, at the age of eighteen years and two months, Bessie Dashiell died of "recurrent periosteous sarcoma." Her fatal illness began with a hand injury in Alaska, diagnosed as an infection, but eventually confirmed as cancer and treated, unsuccessfully, at the New York Cancer Hospital. Amputation at her forearm did not arrest the spread of the cancer.

John sat beside her at the hospital, horrified and frustrated by her suffering and the hopelessness of the so-called cures. He attended her funeral and cherished for thirty-five years a small carrying case that Bessie's mother had given him as a memento. Haunted by her tragedy, he returned to the New York Hospital after her death to speak with her attending surgeon, Dr. William Coley, who had some interesting ideas for cancer research. In 1896 he persuaded his father to support Dr. Coley's work. Four years later, Rockefeller money built a laboratory for Dr. Coley on the campus of Cornell Medical Center. Thus began the story of Memorial Hospital, which matured seventy years later into Memorial Sloan-Kettering Cancer Center, the outstanding center for cancer research and treatment in the world. Asked once why he became so interested in the cancer problem, John told Fosdick, "It goes back to Bessie Dashiell."[18]

Less than a year after Bessie died, John dropped out of Browning, the second such break in his education and essentially for the same vague reason, "poor health." Migraine headaches, insomnia, the brooding over Bessie's death, tense anticipation of the university experience that lay ahead of him (he had already taken the entrance examinations for Yale)—such were the pressures that converged. He returned to Forest Hill, this time to take over the production of maple syrup on the estate. Obsessively he made lists of the run of sap, the monies earned, the stones broken, the rails split, as though such lists could steady his frayed nerves.

After the winter hiatus in Cleveland, John dropped back a year to graduate in 1893 with his friends Dashiell and Colby. Instead of Yale he chose Brown. It was a much smaller, less prestigious

The Mandolin Club for Brown University undergraduates. John, far right, second row.
Courtesty of the Rockefeller Archive Center.

institution, it had a Baptist character, and its president, E. Benjamin Andrews, was a powerful personality with great moral force, a natural leader of young men. "He had enormous courage," John later related, "and was of great influence in my life . . . [he] came out for Bryan [William Jennings, the fiery populist]. . . . He was never very popular with the business people, but very popular with the students."[19] Of more immediate comfort was the fact that "Ev" and "Leff" were living in adjoining suites in the dormitory and could help him ease into college life. Coming from a social vacuum, innocent of the commonplace experiences that other students took for granted, John faced a formidable adjustment.

His freshman year was one long, exhaustive effort to overcome his personality defects. He joined the glee club, the mandolin club, and a string quartet organized by Madelaine Goddard. He taught a Bible class at the Central Baptist Church and studied conscientiously. His roommates even gave him a nickname—Johnny Rock. But he had no illusions about his deficiencies. He was stiff and inhibited, had no small talk, and was self-conscious about the name Rockefeller. He endured many lonely moments—the stiffness and formality never diminished. But by the fall of his sophomore year he was determined to stir around. An invitation to Miss Goddard's dance had a reassuring tone, and he took the plunge.

*A*bby's introduction to John at the Goddard house changed nothing in her twenty-year-old life. She continued to keep a careful eye on the brood that was growing up under her feet. "Abby was close to all her brothers," remarked her nephew Richard Aldrich, "but she was most maternal toward Stuart. He had taken a bad fall down the stairs, developed a stutter, never went on to college, but took up farming. She always held a wing over him in some form."[1]

With her debut behind her, she was able to manage her own life with considerable freedom. Nelson Aldrich saw to that. In the parlor of 110 Benevolent, she played bridge and poker late into the night with her friends. She went off to house parties at Ivy League campuses, attended the various local balls, and rarely missed the opening of a new play. Frank Smith and Billy Dorrance seemed to head up the roster of escorts. Her calendar included fund-raising and volunteer efforts on behalf of the Providence Day Nursery, the Rhode Island Exchange for Women's Work, the Dorrance Home for Aged Colored Women, and the Providence Art Club.

After the Christmas season in Providence came the annual migration to Washington. With increasing frequency Nelson's notes to Washington friends apologize for his wife's absence because of illness. Whether the illness was emotional conflict, physical exhaustion, dislike of the scene, or a combination of all three is unclear. But Nelson made all the calls and enjoyed all the parties, usually in the company of Abby or Lucy.

He was now chairman of the powerful Senate Finance Committee. With the likelihood that his friend William McKinley would be elected to the White House in 1896, he could anticipate greater power than ever. As his influence widened, controversy followed. The *New York Times* attacked him for accepting a loan from Havemayer's Sugar Trust to finance his purchase of stock in the old horse-drawn Union Street Railway, of which he was president. Relying on innuendo and hearsay, the *Times* hinted at bribery and worse.

Nelson, in a rare public rebuttal, issued a vigorous denial of all charges in cool, precise terms, and the public reaction was favorable. He had, after all, built his entire career on a philosophy that identified the national interests with the needs of business. He was neither dominated nor "bought" by corporate interests. But the *Times* was close to the mark in the sense that favors did accrue to him as a result of his position. An examination of his archives reveals lengthy correspondence with John E. Searles, Jr., the lobbyist for the Sugar Trust, who was Nelson's partner in the Union Street Railway. Nelson was able to borrow as much as $5,500,000 from Searles and his Sugar Trust associates to buy the stock and then to modernize and electrify the railway that became United Traction and Electric.

Even as their editorial writers were attacking him, however, the reporters on the beat respected Nelson and enjoyed many off-the-record conversations with him. They liked him for his candor, his total lack of self-deception, his absence of malice. They knew they were in the presence of an unusual man. He returned their respect. He was absolutely committed to the First Amendment and made his position clear during the acrimonious climate of '94 when the Senate was inclined to hold in contempt certain reporters who would not divulge their sources. Aldrich opposed the appeal for contempt, and his words hold up today: "The value and character of the information which is sent out from this Capitol, and the information which is collected all over the United States, in which the public is so deeply interested, depends very largely upon a certain relation of confidence between the party who gets the information and the party who imparts it; . . . it is as important to the public interests that the confidence should be at least in some degree respected as it is that the confidence between a lawyer and his client, or a physician and his patient, should be maintained."[2]

If Providence represented complacency and a certain sameness, Washington, with its infinite variety of talented people coming and going, the undeniable brilliance of its state events, and the fact of Nelson Aldrich's pivotal position as adviser to presidents, put Abby in touch with a more complex and more challenging world. Women functioned differently in Washington from other cities. They were not merely social arbiters and "do-gooders," but enjoyed impressive professional careers. An astonishing number of literary women flourished there. The writings of half a dozen women journalists commanded attention and respect. Feminists of the day called the American capital "a special center of women," convinced from hard evidence that women could lead a fuller life in Washington than in almost any other American city of the era.[3]

On June 26, 1895, Abby and Lucy and their parents sailed for Southampton on the S.S. *St. Louis*. After a week in London they spent the summer in Germany, Austria, and Switzerland. On August 31 they boarded the S.S. *New York* for America. John Rockefeller during the same season was on a bicycle trip through England and Wales. In autumn of that year, Abby resumed her routine in Providence and Washington, and John returned to Brown as a junior.

Slowly and with great effort and intensity he was struggling to become a more typical undergraduate. He learned to dance and was elected junior class president. His basic eccentricities still clung to him—trimming his frayed cuffs, soaking two-cent stamps apart, pressing his trousers beneath his mattress. He was not known as a big spender! "On the subject of money he was incredible," one of his classmates recalled, "entering every cent of expenditure in the little book he carried in his pocket. It used to be a great joke."[4] If they laughed at him, however, it was with a certain affection. He was so different from most of them, and so unlike a rich man's son. Eventually he came to be accepted—odd ways and all.

It was not until the spring of 1896, more than a year and a half after their initial introduction at Madelaine Goddard's house, that Abby and John saw each other with any frequency. Abby and Lucy and Ned often had Sunday-afternoon open house for their friends. In April, John began to appear with some regularity. One Sunday he told Senator Aldrich of his plans for a summer voyage through the Norwegian waters of the North Cape with his sister Alta.

Some weeks later, Nelson decided to book passage on the same cruise for his wife, himself, and two of his daughters. To surmise that the father might have been playing the role of matchmaker seems a little wide of the mark. He had never demonstrated any inclination to select his daughters' suitors, but he was always poised to take them on journeys that would expand their horizons. They sailed to Southampton on the S.S. *Paris* on July 4, 1896, and on to Hamburg to board the S.S. *Columbia.* "July 15—Wednesday," John recorded in his trip diary, "Saw the Aldrich's of Prov. at breakfast. Took tender from Hamburg at 12:30. Embarked in 'Columbia' at 4."[5] On July 18 he wrote his mother that Senator Aldrich of Providence with his wife and two daughters sat at his table. "I have known the girls for several years."[6]

To Abby, John was still a shy young man among a covey of eager beaux. As for John, even if he had become a discreet admirer of Miss Aldrich, he had been in no mood to step forward. But once at sea, a spark was struck. The documentation is slight, but not that slight. John's trip diaries, generally laconic and dry, take on an eloquent, even passionate tone. The ship sailed north along the coast of Norway into "glorious" nights. Narrow valleys and fjords become "unspeakably" beautiful, or "wildly magnificent."[7] A full moon rises over a cloudless sky. The midnight horizon is suffused with the burning red glow of the sun. Unable to pour any of his feelings for Abby into the diary (in his entries he still refers to her as Miss Aldrich, when in fact they were on a first-name basis), he reserves them for the scenery.

Little imagination is required to evoke the image of a young man under the spell of a warm, lovable woman. Abby, seized with sudden hunger, reaches into the pocket of his suit jacket for his ready supply of graham crackers. Jokes fly back and forth among Abby, Lucy, and the senator, with the caustic wit of Abby Pearce supplying the bite. For the first time in his life John feels a slight loosening of formal restraint. Even a day-long pouring rain serves its purpose as passengers scurry to lounges and card rooms, while Abby and John find those private corners on cruise ships conducive to intimate moments.

On Wednesday, August 5, 1896, the *Columbia* docked in Hamburg. The Aldrich family continued on another ship for Copenhagen, Stockholm, Helsinki, and St. Petersburg. They traveled overland to Moscow, Warsaw, Berlin, and Amsterdam. On September 5 they returned to the United States on the S.S. *Paris*. John meanwhile had returned to Cleveland. "I remember as though it were yesterday," he would write Abby in 1906, "when I received the first letter you ever wrote me. It was after the Norway trip and came to Forest Hill. Do you know, sweetheart, I thought even then that you cared a wee bit for me."[8]

Abby's letter did not lie. "Cared a wee bit" was the polite understatement of a well-bred man. The first thing she did when she returned for the fall semester was to invite him down to Warwick for the weekend. "Last Saturday afternoon I went down to Warwick," he wrote to Laura, "a charming spot a few miles down the bay, to spend Sunday with the Aldriches. Sunday was a perfect day and I was out of doors from morning 'til night chiefly engaged in walking and sitting by the waterside enjoying the society of Miss Aldrich."[9]

What did they find to talk about, this awesomely reserved man and this open, buoyant, mischievous woman? Apparently a great deal, for they spent much of their courtship in solitary walks— on shipboard, around the shores of Narragansett Bay, on autumn Sundays in Providence. For reasons that were not yet clear to John he could relax with Abby, as he had seldom been able to relax with other women—certainly not with his mother, who was bent on molding him. And not with his sisters, even though he was close

On board the S.S. Columbia, *North Cape Cruise, August 1896. John, wearing goatee, middle of the front row. Abby in dashing leghorn, leg-of-mutton sleeves, and bow tie.*
Courtesy of the Rockefeller Archive Center.

to them in the seclusion of their Forest Hill childhood. Those relationships were one-sided, as they came to lean on him.

What of Abby? The people closest to her, and some of John's good friends as well, were puzzled by his attraction for her. They saw the all too obvious differences—his caution and love of order, her impulsive sense of adventure; his piety, her Aldrich irreverence; his narrow austere training, her continuous exposure to the freewheeling political life. Her brothers, with their wit and dash, thought him a bit of a prig. His sisters, especially Alta, feared her as something of a corrupting influence.

But none of the onlookers considered the first element of the romance, perhaps because of the reticence of the times, and that was the sexual component. "Abby was extremely sensuous," her nieces Helena Franklin and Stephanie Edgell told the author. "The way she moved her mouth and spoke was sensuous, in a most

entrancing way." Their mother, who was Abby's sister Elsie, believed that Abby had a great deal of sex appeal and was open and
responsive to passion. "This would mean a great deal to Uncle
John," both women added, "since he had been so restrained and
held down. She wore soft materials, the kind as a child you would
love to hug. Her movements were never nervous. She was self-
possessed without being cold, feminine and independent all at the
same time. She was manipulative, indeed she was, in the sense that
women always are, in order to survive."[10]

John's sexuality, all the more exciting to Abby because he had
kept it so severely in check, aroused hers. And since she was not
merely a sensuous creature but had an eager, inquiring mind, a
well-developed social conscience, and strong nurturing instincts,
cultivated since her childhood, he could appeal to her on many
levels. When she was working with the YWCA on plans for its
new building, he offered her the services of one of his father's
draftsman. The fact that she had never met anyone quite like him
was in his favor. He held strong convictions. If they did not always
mirror hers, she was secure enough in her own values to be open
to his. Even humor, that prized ingredient among Aldriches, was
not entirely lacking in John. When he let down his guard as he did
with Abby, he could be quite funny. And the probability that one
day he would inherit the greatest fortune in America could not
have been lost on her. Not that the money alone would seduce her.
But such an enormous fortune represented power, and as her father's daughter she understood power.

For the present, the magic of discovery held full sway. Following
his visit to Warwick, John's name begins to appear in Abby's appointment book. At least three times a week, he comes to walk, to
drive, to accompany her to church, to take her to the theater.
But then so do Frank Smith, Billy Greer, Billy Dorrance, Frank
Hinckley, and the others, often in tandem with John himself.
"Sunday, November 1. Walk with JDR, Jr. at 3—Billy Greer
coming to dinner at 6:30." Or "Tuesday, November 17. Ride Tandem with Frank Smith. Take chocolate in JDR's rooms."[11] On
one Sunday she went to morning services with Frank and evening
vespers with John.

"She had plenty of suitors," John told Fosdick, "and I used to be very jealous of them. It disturbed me terribly."[12] It could not have been easy for him to go to New York over his Christmas break and know that Frank Smith would happily fill in for him. His own engagement book notes "Flowers for Abby" at least once a week.[13]

After the New Year, however, most of the names leave the pages of her engagement calendar, as John's moves to the foreground. She danced the Cotillion with him, she went to the Gymnasium Ball with him. He was calling on her daily, and she proposed to her mother that she be his houseguest at 4 West 54th. Abby Pearce was cool to the idea. "I cannot say anything now in relation to a visit to New York," she wrote from Augusta, Georgia. ". . . I do not wish Mamma Rockefeller to think you are chasing her son which she might do if he was in N.Y. at the same time. . . . I hope the public at home do not think you are making a set at him."[14] It is doubtful whether Abby cared at this point what the "public" did or did not think, but she dropped the idea for the moment.

On February 23, John asked his mother and father to sponsor a dance he wished to give following Lent. "I owe some return for the kindness I have received. . . . I think no man in college has been more kindly treated. . . . I am sure that if you knew just how things are here you would appreciate what I have said and agree with me."[15] But Laura did not agree. She considered round dancing "promiscuous."[16] Instead she proposed a concert of fine music and refreshments, thus redeeming the entertainment from its "commonness."[17] John compromised to the extent of having the musicale first, but he insisted on the dance, which took place on April 22 at the Trocadero, where the best public parties in Providence were held.

Laura and Senior traveled to Providence for the occasion. Abby was John's honored guest, and Senior stood in the receiving line. Laura, however, remained in her room. "Mother was prevented from attending by a sick headache," he told Fosdick. "Father attended and took Miss Aldrich out to dinner."[18]

Abby and John, knowing what young lovers have always known, that certain moments in their lives are to be cherished because they will never return in quite the same way again, went everywhere together during the last weeks before commencement. In May, Abby took matters into her own hands and told John she would be in New York on Tuesday the 11th "to do some dressmaking." John immediately arranged to be in the city that day to take her for a drive. "Will you be good enough to write a note to Miss Aldrich asking her to take lunch or dinner," he wrote his mother, ". . . whichever she can most conveniently. I will telegraph you tomorrow where to send it. It ought to be mailed tomorrow [Monday] so as to get there the first thing Tuesday morning. . . . Don't think I have lost my head. I am only disappointed that Miss Aldrich cannot stay with us, and since she will probably not be in New York again this spring, want to do what I can for her pleasure and my own." [19]

Abby's calendar confirms that she went to New York by boat on May 10, visited the tailor and milliners on the 11th, had lunch with the Rockefellers, drove at two-thirty with John and went with him to see *Under the Red Robe* in the evening. On the 12th she took the one-o'clock train home.

Back in Providence they rode tandem bicycles and rooted for Brown at the intercollegiate baseball games. They paddled up the Ten-Mile River with their picnic suppers stowed away. In case John—or Abby—should forget how he had been indoctrinated and what was expected of him, Laura's letters were a constant reminder. "And now," she wrote, "[your] future is glowing with possibilities of service for God and man. May the Holy Spirit take possession of your entire being, and guide you into all truth. . . . 'Put on the whole armor of God, that you may be able to withstand in the evil day and having done all, to stand.' " [20]

Abby, carried away by romance and optimism, probably did not realize the full significance of such severe indoctrination. John, although enjoying full-throated happiness, kept looking over his shoulder for potential trouble. When a telegram arrived on the afternoon of the Class Night Dance, he did not open it until he had seen Abby safely home. It was not some sudden bad news, as he feared, but the good news that his married sister Bessie Strong had given birth to an infant girl and that all was well.

Commencement was June 16, 1897. Abby greeted Laura courteously. "I recall my pleasure when you received your diploma," the older woman wrote John—"also that so many young ladies have earned theirs. . . . I remember Abby at the afternoon game, I only spoke to her at a little distance but I recall the hat she wore—a broad brim with red flowers."[21] Abby and the Rockefellers together attended Governor Dyer's reception for the graduates, the same Dyer family with whom Abby had traveled in Europe. Although he feigned disinterest in politics, it was not lost on Senior that his son's young friend was the daughter of one of the most powerful figures in the government. Laura might be expected to view Abby from a different vantage. An obvious assumption—that Laura saw Abby as competition—does not seem to fit her character. She was controlling, but not jealous. Rather it was a question of suitability. Was Abby's worldliness a possible threat to John's value system?

On Friday, June 18, Abby moved to Warwick for the summer. On Monday, the 21st, John joined her for a four-day visit. According to the protocol of the era, inviting a young man for a country holiday was tantamount to announcing one's engagement. Abby apparently was not bound by such traditions. "I came down here in the afternoon," John wrote Laura. "Mr. Aldrich is at home sick. He was obliged to leave Washington about ten days ago, being quite worn out with his constant and prolonged work on the tariff bill. He, however, hopes to be able to return again in a few days. I wish you could see the beautiful view of the bay," he continued, "and its islands, that is stretched before me as I write. . . . Yesterday afternoon we went for a sail. It reminded me of the sail Father and I took over to Capri; only that I am a better sailor now and quite enjoyed the stiff breeze. Lucy and Abby are very good to me and I am enjoying my stay greatly."[22]

Fourteen years later he would recall such experiences more emotionally. "How many blissful evenings we have spent together out of doors at Warwick," he wrote Abby. "I used sometimes to be quite near you then darling . . . to touch you . . . [how] often I longed to be closer to you."[23]

Suddenly it was over—the blithe, untroubled spring of their romance. John went on another bicycle and riding trip in Europe. Abby stayed at Warwick for the summer, a companion to her father, who was recovering from one of his intermittent bouts of severe intestinal discomfort. (Heart attacks in patients were not diagnosed until 1912. The recurrent indigestion from which Nelson Aldrich suffered could have been cardiac-induced.)

In the fall, John returned to 4 West 54th and his suite of rooms on the fourth floor. Gradually he began to lose confidence in his ability to woo Abby. The 186 miles between Manhattan and Providence came to symbolize the chasm between her cultured, colorful life and his barren one.

Abby continued to see other men, but the likelihood is that she kept the door wide open for John. Perhaps she sensed the depth of his needs—needs that were a powerful stimulus to her love, especially in the light of her warm, positive relationship with her own father. If at times she startled him with her unpredictable behavior, she could see, reflected in his eyes, if not always in his words, his fascination with her differences. "What you might say next, I could never tell," he wrote some years later, "but I always knew that I should probably like it better than what you had said last, however captivating that might have been."[24]

She found excuses to go to New York. He called regularly at 110 Benevolent Street, taking the train directly after work, changing into fresh clothes at the University Club in Providence, and appearing at Abby's door, well groomed and ostensibly calm. But a few hours later, he was on the train again, heading back to the city.

He never forgot how bereft he felt as he rode the midnight train back to Grand Central. "Had I known then years ago," he would write her in 1908, "when I used to come here [Providence] and leave with such sorrow that someday I should be staying here by right of being your husband, how much doubt and uncertainty and heartache I would have been saved."[25] And in another letter written in 1906: "Being away from you makes me feel like the old days when you lived at Warwick and the intervals between my visits to you often seemed so long and unending."[26]

He was not reassured by her letters. "Do you mind my telling you . . ." he would write in 1911, "that you write much better and more satisfactory letters than you used to before we were married? Perhaps it is because you really love me now, while then you were interested in so many people that I was only one of a number."[27] *Only one of a number!* The cry reverberated throughout his life. He longed to possess her, psychologically as well as physically. He would never accept the idea that he might have to share her, yet at this point he remained frozen in a state of indecision. He even rationalized that their differences were irreconcilable, that he dare not risk a mistake since divorce was unthinkable. Abby made no effort to jar him out of his quagmire, which suggests that she, too, was feeling cautious.

*I*n November 1898, Abby and her parents met Lucy and William in Naples. Lucy, who had been traveling in England and on the Continent since August, snapped many pictures of her imposing, white-haired father, her vaguely troubled mother, and her siblings. They posed in front of statues, temples, and fountains—the men in bowler hats, vests, and high stiff collars, the women in wasp-waisted, ankle-length traveling suits and hats of every conceivable shape and trim. Most of the captions are brief—*Donkeys at Paestum, More Donkeys at Paestum, S. John Lateran Cloisters, Galileo's Tower.* One picture of Abby, however, suggests something more. She is standing tall and erect with her back to the camera. Her jacket is nipped in snugly at the waist. Her fur piece is hugging her neck, her straw hat resting on her abundant pompadour. She seems to be gazing out at the rooftops of Florence, and Lucy's caption reads, "Longing for——?"

Abby returned to Providence in May 1899. If she let John know what Lucy had hinted at, that she missed him deeply, the message was either too subtle or he was in no mood to hear it. She did not seem to resent his vacillation. She was beginning to demonstrate a wisdom about people that became one of her most conspicuous traits. She knew that John's conscience would never allow him to be less than honest with her. She was too objective to believe that his anxiety had only to do with her. At least as great a crisis as his ambivalence about marriage was his painful disappointment with his career, or lack of it.

From the emancipation of college life he had gone directly to work for his father in the cramped, shabby family office at 26 Broadway. He worshiped his father and wanted only to serve him, but Senior never told him anything, never gave him any idea what he was supposed to do or what was expected of him. He was ill trained for business and compulsively fearful of making a mistake. All he could do for the first few years was to take on the tasks that no one else would bother with, certainly not Senior—such tasks as assuming responsibility for tombstones on the family cemetery plots, selecting wallpaper for rooms in three houses, selling obsolete buckboards and carriages. Haunted by the specter of failure, he could see only the insurmountable distance between his father's towering abilities and his own inadequacies.

The chasm between his unpreparedness and Senior's hard wisdom came into devastating focus when he began to speculate in the stock market. Here again his father said nothing—no warnings, no instruction—only provided a bank account for him to use. John walked into a trap set by a Wall Street shark and lost over $1 million in capital. The humiliation was more than he had ever endured, and it was compounded by the buzz of gleeful publicity. Abby shared his distress. She understood the meaning of public scorn. Her father was a continuing target. But Nelson Aldrich was surefooted and had the disposition to flick away criticism, especially since he believed it to be largely meretricious. John, self-deprecating and insecure, knew that his conduct had been stupidly naive. He had no defense and suffered in silence.

The autumn of 1899 marked the fifth anniversary of Abby's introduction to John at the home of Madelaine Goddard. For at least three years they had been more than friends, if less than lovers. She knew him to be passionate at one moment, severely detached the next, stubborn and full of self-doubt all at the same time. However inflexible he appeared to others, with her he could be at ease. It was almost as though he was begging her to shake him free of the old rigid framework of his life even as he was consumed with apprehension at the possibility.

He had been engaged in some interesting reading, as he explored such titles as *Sane Sex Life and Sane Sex Living* and *What a Young Husband Ought to Know*, the latter one of a series known as *Self and Sex*. Both manuals emphasized the art of love and the art of wooing a woman. Both authors admonished the young suitor/husband to respect the sexual wishes of his partner, as well as her opinions, and stressed that courtship should continue into the marriage and motherhood must never be forced upon an unwilling wife. Already John had shown himself to be a gallant suitor. Now he was grappling with the serious challenge of an enduring relationship.

In the spring of 1900 Abby moved assertively, with the sureness of a woman who knew she was desirable and would not be rejected. Senator Aldrich invited John to join his party on a cruise to Cuba aboard President McKinley's yacht, the *Dolphin*. The object of the journey was to observe political conditions on the island following the United States' defeat of Spain in 1898 and the subsequent American occupation. Nelson Aldrich had opposed armed intervention. He was suspicious of the jingoism of the Pulitzer and Hearst press, and contemptuous of the war hysteria that swept the country. But he agreed to serve on the congressional committee that would draft legislation pertinent to the future of Cuba.

John explored his feelings about the invitation with his mother. She wrote:

> In regard to the trip to Cuba, I must leave the decision to your judgment of what is best. Senator and Mrs. Aldrich would not invite you did they not feel that it was the right thing for them to do. Just what your "relations are to the family," I do not know. You frankly say that you are "largely attracted to the pleasure of being with Abby" and there could be no better way of becoming more thoroughly acquainted. Of course, all Providence will feel certain that you are engaged, and other friends will say that you probably will be. But this does not matter, so long as you know your own mind, and are determined not to move until you do. The place of travel is certainly most delightful and comfortable and the opportunity of seeing our new possessions in this way is a rare one. The outing will

be good for you, even if you do feel quite well again. Please convey to Mr. and Mrs. Aldrich from Father and me, our appreciation of their very kind invitation to you, and our thanks for it.[1]

Apart from her religious fervor, Laura Spelman was highly intelligent and practical. In a single paragraph she had sorted out John's situation.

On Wednesday, March 14, John joined the official group that boarded a private railroad car in Washington's Union Station for the journey south. The entourage consisted of Nelson and Abby Pearce, the Senators Orville Platt and Henry Teller and their wives, a physician, the secretary to the committee, and the three young people—Abby, Ned Aldrich, and John. It was a lengthy trip through scrub and pine forests. At Miami they took the overnight steamer to Key West. On Saturday, March 17, they boarded the *Dolphin*, the president's dispatch boat with its crew of 115 and ten officers under the command of a Captain Sutherland.

The sea was rough, but the ship's amenities were presidential. In Havana Harbor, General Adna Chaffee, the hero of the Battle of Santiago, headed up the welcoming party. On Monday, March 19, the entire group breakfasted at the palace with Governor-General Wood. On Tuesday evening, the wife of the director-general of posts gave a gala in honor of Abby, and the next day she was honored again at a picnic at Morro Castle. Special trains carried them to military installations and distant plantations, and there were constant briefings. All across the island the weather was hot and humid, but the pace never slackened. Havana with its gambling, easy morality, and tropical indolence presented one kind of experience, the stiff army protocol quite another.

For Abby, who had grown up in the glare of politics and understood all the requirements of officialdom, Cuba was simply another interesting challenge to be met with grace and good humor. The more important element was the personal one, the chance to be with John alone when they stole away for an hour of shopping, or thankfully found themselves omitted from an occasional guest list. Once they even had an entire day to themselves on the *Dolphin*.

For John the trip to Havana was complicated. He had never

before spent so much time in the presence of powerful government figures. He had never before traveled with strangers. And since his real reason for going on the journey was to be with Abby, he was hypersensitive to all the nuances of her behavior. Watching her function so deftly and with such evident relish in a world that was at best intimidating to him had to give him uneasy pause. No formal university curriculum could have taught her the skills she had acquired naturally in the company of her astute, urbane father. Once again John was reminded of the sharp differences between his background and hers. Such feelings could only deepen his ambivalence about their chance for a successful marriage.

And so another interlude ended without the engagement that Laura had warned John the public would expect. John wrote a formal letter of thanks to Abby Pearce and an additional note to Nelson. "I could not have seen Cuba and the South under more agreeable conditions, and feel deeply grateful to you for the pleasure and renewed health which you made possible."[2] Laura in her letters of the winter had alluded to John's poor health, the familiar symptoms of sleeplessness and migraine headaches. He was still cutting and splitting logs as a way of working off his tensions, and then running the several miles from his father's stables to the house on 54th Street.

On June 13, two months after returning from Cuba, the Aldrich clan sailed again for Europe. This time the party included fifteen-year-old Winthrop and twelve-year-old Elsie in addition to Lucy, Abby, the senator, Abby Pearce, and a young bachelor named Rush Sturges. John, too, was in Europe, with Senior, Laura, Aunt Lute, Dick Richardson of Brown, and Alta and her fiancé, Ezra Prentice. John later told Fosdick that all the while he was praying for divine guidance, since he knew no other way to resolve his conflict about Abby.

When Alta married Prentice on January 17, 1901, John selected the property behind Senior's at 5 West 53rd for their home. He furnished it down to the last broom. "To the last broom?" inquired the author. "Yes, that is right," Alta's son Spelman Prentice replied. "Uncle John did furnish that house. My father could not have cared less and my mother did not have the know-how. She had grown up in the same rut as Uncle John and had no one to pull her out of it. She was timid, spiritual like her mother, and besides, she had the idea that her brother always knew best."[3]

In Washington, where Nelson was at the height of his power, Abby attended the second inauguration of William McKinley. She continued to see John, but the relationship was at an impasse. Some action was required, and it came in the form of a test featured in a popular fiction of the day. They decided that they would not see each other for six months, they would write no letters, they would effect a complete separation as the final test of their feelings. Who originated such a plan is not known. John, paralyzed with uncertainty, may have seized upon it as a last, desperate measure. And yet it sounds like Abby, since she was the more intuitive one and, like her father, knew how to maneuver, how to circle a problem obliquely. The last time John's name appears on her appointment diary is Saturday, February 16, 1901. A silence settled over them. Abby went out to Warwick for the summer and John went on a coaching trip to England with Everett Colby.

John's recollection of how it all came to a head is somewhat murky, but a rough sequence can be pieced together from his conversations with Fosdick, his letters to Laura, and later letters to Abby. On returning from England he went directly to Cleveland. Walking with his mother around the lake at Forest Hill, his despair was palpable. Did she think he had no heart, that he still could not bring himself to seize the happiness he so obviously craved? "Suddenly she laughed," he confided to Fosdick, speaking of Laura, "and said, 'Of course you love Miss Aldrich. Why don't you go and get her?' "[4] A few days later he was alone in the 54th Street house, considering his mother's frank words, and at the same time still waiting for guidance from the heavenly Father. Finally it came, "that clear and unmistakable voice in the early morning assuring me that this great joy was open to me. . . ." So he wrote Abby ten years later, trying yet again to reconstruct his mood of that climactic moment. "After many years of doubt and uncertainty, great longing and hoping, there came a supreme peace and calm."[5]

The peace and calm were short-lived, however. The ordeal of asking Senator Aldrich for her hand and the proposal itself lay ahead. On Wednesday, August 21, he wrote Laura. "The die is cast, dear mother. I have this morning written and telegraphed Abby asking if I may see her on Friday evening and from the letter she can draw but one inference as to the purpose of my coming."[6]

Two days later he heard from Abby. She would see him that night—August 23. But first he must see her father. He left immediately for Newport, where Nelson Aldrich was vacationing on his yacht. "I told him I wanted to marry his daughter and said something about my own finances and ability to take care of her," John recalled. "He brushed aside the latter part and said, 'I am only interested in what will make my daughter happy.' "[7] Admirable as such sentiments were, Nelson knew that he was losing a dear companion. Of course he hated to let her go. But he acquiesced in style.

The shores of Narragansett Bay were flooded with moonlight when Abby and John walked across the stone bridge on the estate at Warwick. "Do you really love me, John?" she asked in a soft weary voice as she listened to his proposal.[8] The adjective "weary" was John's adjective, an appropriate one in view of the confusing signals he had been sending out for over four years. Something in Abby's expression, or response, suggested that had he hesitated any longer he would have lost her, and the horror of that possibility sent a shudder up his spine. He never forgot the miracle of that moment on the stone bridge, but evoked its magic again and again in love letters down through the years. "How happy you made me that night, darling," he would write in August 1903, "in the radiance of your young womanhood, so beautiful, so fascinating, so loving and so long the one object of my passionate desires."[9] It hardly seemed possible, he wrote in another letter, that a woman so irresistibly charming and enticing physically was really his.

The Aldriches invited him to stay the night, and he woke up at dawn, barely able to contain his euphoria. "I can't wait to tell you," he wrote Laura before going down to breakfast, "that my fond wish of all these years has at length come true and the only woman whom I have ever cared to make my wife and whom I have loved for so long . . . has given me her love in return. . . . I can't believe that it is really true that all this sacred joy . . . is mine. . . . for so long, long a time it has been the one thing in life above all others that I have yearned for."[10] For the moment at least, the caution, the stiffness, all the reserve dissolved. It was as though he felt safe with pen and paper, safe to pour out the emotions he had kept so severely in check.

Reading Abby's letters, one is struck again by the contrast in their personalities. Relaxed with strangers as well as friends, Abby in love sent off straightforward messages, couched in plain words, that were more effective in their plainness, perhaps, than John's extravagant prose. In rapid succession she wrote to John's mother, to her disappointed suitor Frank Smith, to her cousin Lucy Greene, and to the Tetlow sisters.

"You've probably read of my engagement to John Rockefeller in the papers by this time. I am sorry to have it announced to you in that way," she wrote apologetically to Lucy, "but I didn't have time to write before the reporters found it out. . . . I know that you will not be wholly surprised but pleased, I hope. I am very happy Lucy, there are not many men like John. I could write pages about him, but I will spare your feelings. We shall be married sometime late this fall. We haven't decided just where. I hope that we can have the wedding in the little church here in Warwick. I hate big affairs in town and so does John."[11]

By August 26, she had already heard from Frank. "It was very good of you to write me," he said. "If I have been the means of giving you any pleasure I am content; you have helped me more than you will ever know. You know that I wish you every joy and the very best that one can have in life."[12] Asenath and Fanny, as expected, reminded Abby that John was the one to be congratulated, that if he was half as good as she, they would make an ideal pair, and that her news did not exactly feel like a thunderbolt from the sky. This sentiment was repeated by many others who had been watching with some interest young Rockefeller's procrastination.

With Laura, Abby feigned no religious fervor, but merely struck a note of proper modesty. "I have been longing to write you ever since John told me that he loved me because you can appreciate as no one else the great blessing that has come to me. There never was a man like John, so true, so tender, so manly, I am supremely proud of him."[13]

If the courtship had been overly long, the engagement was mercifully short, with the date set for October 9, 1901. As Abby indicated, the reporters spread the news immediately, for it was news! Society pages, editorial pages, financial pages—all took note of the coming alliance. The young people were treated lightly, even kindly, the fathers less so. "It would have been difficult for many years to say which was the more unpopular with the American masses, the father of the bride or that of the groom," Nevins wrote.[14] Public hostility toward the Standard Trust was mounting. The *New York World*, hot on the heels of its nemesis, the inscrutable Nelson Aldrich, sent reporters to Providence in vain to sniff out his alleged improprieties.

Abby's desire to be married in the tiny church in Warwick did not materialize. The fact that she and John hated big affairs did not inhibit her father from underwriting the most lavish wedding on the eastern seaboard since the Vanderbilt-French nuptials at Newport. She did manage once to slip away with John to Pocantico, the site of Senior's country house, accompanied only by her maid. After half a week there, they went on to Cleveland to visit the elder Rockefellers. But by mid-September, Abby was locked into wedding preparations, with John sending forlorn telegrams— "Missing you sadly and needing you."[15] Laura, to whom luxurious events were anathema, made a brave effort to forgive Nelson's elaborate plans and received John's approval of her and Senior's choice of matched pearls for the bride's wedding present.

Not even the assassination of President McKinley in Buffalo on September 6 stopped the senator. His correspondence of the month included a request, dated September 30, from the new president, Theodore Roosevelt, to meet with him during the next fortnight to go over the speech Roosevelt would shortly deliver. With the marriage nine days off, it is not known whether Aldrich obeyed his president. After October 9, however, he resumed his role as unofficial presidential adviser, with Roosevelt consulting him at least as frequently as had his predecessors in the Executive Mansion.

Less than a week before the wedding, workmen were swarming over the property at Warwick, the scene of the coming festivities. Since 1896, when Nelson had made his first purchase—the Governor Hoppin place—he had increased his holdings with several parcels of land and houses, built important access roads, created a model working farm, and designed a shoreline landscape of surpassing beauty. The family still used the original house for the summer season. Some months before the engagement, the playhouse for the young Aldriches, known in the family as the Teahouse, was completed and in use. It had a fully equipped kitchen, billiard room, lounges, and a great ballroom on the second floor with a Renaissance fireplace and dramatic view of Narragansett Bay. It was here, in the ballroom, that the ceremony would take place, with the reception to be held in an adjacent marquee, erected for the occasion.

Wednesday, October 9, was a soft, warm New England morning. Nelson Aldrich's steam yacht, the *Wild Duck*, left from Fox Point wharf in Providence at 10:15 A.M. carrying the guests who would attend the small private ceremony at the Teahouse. These included Aldriches who had not already gathered at Warwick and the Rockefeller party, who had traveled from New York in a private railroad car chartered by Senior. The group consisted of Senior himself; his brother William and William's wife, Almira Goodsell; and John's cousin Percy Rockefeller and his wife, Isabel Goodrich Stillman, and her father, the New York banker James Stillman. Two of John's sisters, Alta and Bessie, came with their husbands, but Edith Rockefeller McCormick was in Switzerland with her husband, Harold Fowler, who was undergoing treatment for a psychiatric disorder. One of the very few people at the ceremony who was not of the immediate family was the former Speaker of the House of Representatives, Thomas B. Reed.

The most conspicuous missing guest was the bridegroom's mother, who remained behind in her suite at the Narragansett

"Everything . . . was lost for me in the beauty . . . of the bride . . . besides whom I saw no one at the ceremony." John to Aunt Lute, October 14, 1901.
Courtesy of the Rockefeller Archive Center.

Hotel under the care of her personal physician. Writing to John two days later, she described the chills and diarrhea that overcame her during the night. "I was somewhat comforted by the thought that my absence would not at all interfere with the plans and that you would be married just the same, which was the principal thing. My disappointment was inexpressible and yours was extreme and that was the worst of it."[16] From the family and the newspapers she learned all the details of the celebration.

Recalling that Laura had not attended John's dance four years earlier, one asks whether these sudden illnesses were her way of avoiding situations that violated her beliefs. The answer is uncertain. She suffered from serious physical ailments—asthma and colitis, to mention two, and both are exacerbated by stress. There is no evidence that she resented Abby or was opposed to the marriage. What she opposed were the worldly trappings of the event. Unwilling to participate, she withdrew, perhaps in that way registering her disapproval.

In any case, her absence did not seem to affect John's exhilaration. As he wrote his Aunt Lute, "It was beautiful, wasn't it? I can not imagine a more ideal spot or day for a wedding. But everything else was lost for me in the beauty and loveliness of the bride for whom I watched so eagerly and impatiently as she came up the stairs and besides whom I saw no one at the ceremony."[17]

The first member of the bridal party to enter John's anxious field of vision was thirteen-year-old Elsie, the flower girl, in a sheer white organza over pale blue silk, her white satin hat with mob-crown and ostrich plume placed carefully on her young head. The ushers followed—three Aldrich brothers and John's friend Lefferts Dashiell. Everett Colby was best man and Lucy Aldrich maid of honor. Lucy's gown, custom-designed and sewn in New York and minutely described by the society reporters who covered the event, was of pale blue Louisine silk and tucked chiffon en train. All the hats were noble creations. The mother of the bride—Abby Pearce —was distinguished in a variation of Lucy's blue silk, with Point de Venise lace substituting for chiffon.

Finally Abby, on the arm of her father, ascended a staircase flanked with vases of mauve chrysanthemums and mauve orchids.

Whether by accident or design she had achieved an effect of great style without pretension. Her only jewelry was the single choker of pearls around her neck. No excess of lace or other ornamentation distracted from the sweeping lines of her ivory satin gown. Orange blossoms caught the tulle of her veil. Her bouquet was fashioned out of superb white orchids.

The expression playing about her face as she viewed the splendor of the setting was faintly roguish. Catching John's eye, she gave him a wide smile, then took her place beside him under a huge conch shell of moss, sprayed with white orchids and lilies of the valley, suspended over the great mantel of the ballroom. Five thousand lilies and several hundred orchids set off the dense greenery of the bridal wreath beneath the shell. Cornucopias of American Beauty roses and garlands of green vines softened the walls of the imposing room and framed the low windows.

The ceremony, lasting just seven minutes, was performed by the same Reverend James G. Vose who had married Abby Pearce Chapman and Nelson Wilmarth Aldrich exactly thirty-five years before to the day. For an hour Abby and John circulated among the thirty-five guests who had witnessed the marriage. Now they would move on to the reception in the marquee, decorated as brilliantly as the Teahouse. The music was played by the Royal Ligrantes Neapolitan Orchestra, and Louis Sherry catered the wedding breakfast.

Two chartered steamers and forty-five electrics, for those who preferred to go by land, had transported five hundred guests to the senator's private boat dock or to Warwick Station, there to complete the journey in special carriages. Nelson's political friends mingled with old Providence names and Senior's partners from Standard Oil. The great industrial families—Comstock, Gould, Whitney, McCormick, Havemeyer—turned out in force. Plain-clothesmen from the Providence police force and Pinkerton detectives circulated unobtrusively, eyeing the glittering crowd, glittering in a literal sense, as the diamonds sparkled in the noon sun. "It was noticeable," the *Journal* society reporter wrote, "that New York upheld its reputation for correctness in fashion, with Providence not far behind and the Boston guests trailing after."[18]

*The setting for Abby's wedding reception. A marquee as blooming garden
on her father's estate at Warwick.*
Courtesy of the Rockefeller Archive Center.

What the Bostonians lacked in style, however, they made up for in
intellect, with college presidents, jurists, and elder statesmen well
represented.

The wedding gifts included a dozen gold plates from the George
Goulds and a second dozen from the William Rockefellers, a Greek
bronze from Harkness, candelabra from the Stillmans, and a rare
ostrich fan from the Havemeyers. In wholesome contrast to such
riches Professor Charles Strong, John's brother-in-law, sent a complete edition of Robert Browning, and Fanny Tetlow, the *Rubaiyat*.

Nelson Aldrich, unruffled by his son-in-law's stand on alcoholic
beverages, personally selected the most expensive vintage wines.
The abstemious president of Brown is reported to have mistaken
the French champagne for the most delicious ginger ale he had ever
tasted. Abby's brothers and their friends, fearing the worst, had
fortified themselves generously before going to John's bachelor
party the night before the wedding. They were not disappointed.

In lieu of wines, John served six varieties of water, but there is disagreement over his intention. Perhaps it was his stuffy Baptist rectitude that had so dismayed them all the while he was a suitor, or perhaps, as one Aldrich nephew contends, "Uncle John was really pulling their leg."[19]

Theodore Green, who became Democratic governor of Rhode Island and was for many years a senator, sent Abby a copy of the ode he had read to the all-male gathering:

Goodbye!

O, Bride-to-be!—O, Abby A.!
We cannot find the words to say
The grief we feel at this "Goodbye":
Each throat is parched, & moist each eye.

O, Bride-to-become Abby R.!
You've shone here long as morning star.
Though setting here, you soon will rise
To shine as bright in other skies.

As Abby A. we've known you well—
A trusty friend—a reigning belle:
We've found you good and wise and gay!
So here's a toast to Abby A.!

As Abby R. you'll not forget
Old friends, but will remember yet
When Time or Distance stretches far.
So here's another to Abby R!

T.G.
Hope Club Oct 8th—The Eve of the great event.[20]

John wrote his Aunt Lute the post-wedding details. Abby was beautiful in her dark blue going-away suit and hat. A special electric took them the several miles to a little station on the New Haven Road, where the New York train stopped to pick them up. They giggled over the items in the newspapers that reported their buying a castle in England or going around the world on their honeymoon. By evening they were relaxing in the privacy of their suite at the Plaza. On Thursday morning Abby R. wrote Laura that their journey to New York had been comfortable and delightful and that they were both too happy for words.

PART TWO

The Yeast in the Bread: A Different Rockefeller

*T*he reporters who wrote of world tours and castles in Devonshire were satisfying their readers' taste for fairy tales. Reality for Abby and John was something quite different. They spent their honeymoon in seclusion thirty miles north of New York City and the first twelve years of their marriage in a townhouse in the West Fifties.

The month at Senior's farmhouse touched an aspect of Abby's character not always recognized by her friends, a reminder that her sensitive mother, too, had often rejected the tumultuous world in which Nelson Aldrich functioned so effectively. "Much as I love people," Abby had said, "I know it's a dangerous thing to become too dependent upon them. Everyone needs a certain amount of solitude in order to learn to know oneself and to get a grasp on things alone."[1] John was learning, if he did not aleady know, that he had married a woman capable of serious reflection.

It was in the summer of 1893 that Senior bought his first parcel of land above the Tarrytowns on the bluffs overlooking the Hudson, that picturesque countryside that had captured the imaginations of wealthy Manhattan families as far back as the colonial era. William Rockefeller, who ran the overseas Standard empire for his brother, already owned the most sumptuous mansion on the river.

Rockwood was a palatial house when William bought it for $100,000. Not satisfied, he commissioned Carrère & Hastings to redecorate and rebuild the entire interior. The mahogany reception room alone was fit for a king's state chamber. William spent $3 million on the renovations, renamed his 204-room palace Rockwood Hall, and staffed it with powdered footmen and liveried attendants.

Senior, and most emphatically Laura Spelman, rejected such splendor. But the idea of a country place within commuting distance appealed to both of them. The beginning of the estate known as Pocantico was a U-shaped tract of 404 acres. The nearest village was Pocantico Hills. The major dwelling was the Parsons-Wentworth house, a homely wooden structure with the broad verandas that Laura and Senior deemed essential for their comfort. Circled by a carriage road, surrounded by groves of trees, with stable, greenhouse, and kitchen garden, it reminded Abby of the old Hoppin house at Warwick. And the house possessed one feature that not even Rockwood Hall could boast of—a panoramic view of the wide sweep of the great river and the Palisades beyond. The site of the house was Kykuit Hill, the highest point in the county.

From 1893 until the season of Abby's marriage, Senior had paid scant attention to the houses on the property. He continued to buy up parcels of land and buildings as they came on the market, but concentrated on carriage trails and roads. Laura, as was her habit, kept the furniture that Mrs. Wentworth had selected twenty years earlier. The elder Rockefellers used Pocantico in about the same proportion as they did the estate in Cleveland and a third country place that Senior acquired in 1901—an old golf clubhouse situated on seventy-five acres of wooded land at Lakewood, New Jersey.

It was to the Parsons-Wentworth house on Kykuit Hill that John brought Abby on the day after their marriage. They found it filled with flowers—chrysanthemums from Laura, orchids from Providence friends, ferns and jardinieres from Senior's staff and Nelson's crew at Warwick. "Being married is simply perfect," he wrote Laura during the first days of the honeymoon.[2] In 1922, over twenty years after the event, John was still recalling to Abby how it had felt to him, so carefree, so ideal.

It was perfect because he had her all to himself. His need to possess her was never entirely satiated. He felt either abandoned or threatened when she was not with him. "He never seemed entirely comfortable without her," Peggy Rockefeller, married to Abby's son David, has observed, and this was after forty years of married life.[3]

Abby loved John, but she also loved her sisters and brothers, her friends and parents. She loved the early-morning mists in the valleys, the ducks on the ponds, the migrating birds, the children in the village. The range of her enthusiasms promised that life with her would never be dull, but for a man whose psyche demanded order and predictability, the risks were large. For her, however, the risks were perhaps greater, since society decreed that wives do the adjusting. During the years that he had hesitated to marry, John wrote extensively of their differences and his apprehension. Abby left no such record, but even in the grip of an intense love affair, while living the idyll of the honeymoon, she evidently knew that certain conflicts had to be met head-on.

One such concern seemed far-fetched in the light of John's character. As they walked about the estate on a pleasant afternoon, she suddenly warned him that if he ever hit her she would leave him. Such an ultimatum caused him some bewilderment, but he assured her that nothing of the kind would ever happen. Undeterred, she repeated her warning. Even as a protected daughter of the upper class, she understood the hazards of domesticity in post-Victorian America.

In the matter of money, a subject which young wives traditionally avoided, Abby was succinct and to the point. John asked her to keep careful account books according to the dictates of Rockefellers. "I won't," was her reply.[4] When he inquired how she had spent the large check he gave her for a wedding present, she replied, "I gave it away," and that was that.[5] Actually he would have approved. She gave it to the Providence YWCA for the new building.

The matter of religion was more complicated. Aldriches took their religion lightly. Nelson Aldrich made no demands on his children, beyond strict tolerance for the beliefs of others. And yet

Abby's own ancestor Roger Williams took his Baptist commitment seriously. Abby knew her Bible well enough to debate interpretation with John and was a full member of the Beneficent Congregational Church in Providence. She agreed not to accept Sunday invitations. For the time being she seemed ready to give John's piety a chance.

From Pocantico Hills, John took Abby to his rooms in his parents' house at 4 West 54th Street, there to await the renovation of the house he had rented at Number 13, across the street. Thirty-seven years earlier, his father had brought his bride to *his* father's house before taking up permanent residence next door. As eager as Abby was to make new friends, she never moved beyond formal relationships with anyone in John's family, with the possible exception of Senior. Ezra Parmelee Prentice was an imperious figure who, as general counsel for the Illinois Steel Company, had held the unchallenged reputation of being the coldest, hardest lawyer in the entire state. Alta, pretty, efficient, and devout, but extremely unworldly, bowed to her Prussian husband in all matters. John's sister Edith, the only Rockefeller daughter with a rebellious streak, and the one who might have interested Abby, married Harold McCormick, son of the inventor of the reaper, and moved to Chicago, there to live in flamboyant splendor. Bessie spent much of her life abroad with her husband, Professor Charles Strong, and died young.

Laurance Rockefeller dismisses his father's sisters as simply eccentric and does not recall any of them as familiar figures of his childhood. "That's kind of a general statement," he admitted, but there was no question "that we saw my mother's family infinitely more than my father's." He added with a smile, "When you talk about the dominance of Rockefellers, isn't that interesting?"[6] But Senior was always the exception. Everyone in the family spoke affectionately of him. In his private world he was the benign old gentleman who carried no guilt and rejoiced in his impish sense of humor. He used events in his and Laura's personal life as the pretext for making gifts of money to Abby—$1,000 in commemoration of Laura's birthday, another $1,000 for his birthday, $5,000 for his fortieth wedding anniversary. The pattern continued throughout his life, not large amounts by Rockefeller standards, but significant sums for Abby.

In all the obvious ways—taste, style, personality, background—Abby and Laura could not have been more dissimilar. But they were both women of considerable character. To her credit, Laura did not become an interfering figure in Abby's life. It was as though she had exhausted all her resources and ingenuity in molding her only son, and now was satisfied that the time for control was over. As a bride in the sober Rockefeller household, however, Abby perceived firsthand what John's childhood must have been like. There were morning and evening prayers, hymns and organ music, total immersion in matters religious. Completely missing were Aldrich earthiness and high spirits. Her Aldrich family had nourished her and enriched her life in ways she had always taken for granted. John's guarded reserve, the tyranny of his conscience, and his conviction planted so successfully by Laura that unearned joy was a sign of weakness were forewarnings of what lay ahead.

Abby visited her own parents and siblings as often as she could. She and John celebrated their first Thanksgiving in Providence. In January 1902 they were in Washington to enjoy Nelson Aldrich's lavish hospitality and meet the dignitaries of Theodore Roosevelt's new administration. In February the interlude at 4 West 54th Street came to an end. They moved into their own house, the narrow four-story limestone residence built on a standard twenty-five foot lot, with raised entrance, and adequate, if not roomy, children's and servants' rooms. It had pleasant features—bay windows, excellent interior wood paneling—but compared to the surroundings it was conspicuously unpretentious.

The Manhattan neighborhood where Abby and John put down their roots was safe, self-assured, and very rich. The Vanderbilts ruled the social scene, their mansions dominating Fifth Avenue like unfortified castles. Richard Morris Hunt, trained at the École des Beaux-Arts in Paris, was their favorite architect. The Cornelius and Alice Gwynne Vanderbilt residence at 58th and Fifth was a product of his distinguished if conservative Renaissance style. Alice Gwynne's daughter was Gertrude, who married Harry Payne

Whitney and moved to 57th Street. Harry's father was William C., who boasted that he could serve a hundred guests in his baronial ballroom at 871 Fifth on a mere hour's notice. Alva Smith and William Kissam Vanderbilt, parents of Consuelo, occupied another Hunt triumph, this one a French chateau at 52nd Street.

The interiors of such mansions were exuberantly eclectic, reflecting the whole range of historical design and culture, with barely a passing nod at the architectural requirements of the exteriors. Pharaohs' heads rested upon mantels and chair arms; painted friezes enlivened cornices. The distorted and twisted shapes of seventeenth-century baroque cheerfully joined the fanciful scrolls and winged cherubs, the ivory and gilt and chinoiserie of eighteenth-century rococo. Medievalism, however, enjoyed the most triumphant popularity. Few great houses did not boast the leaded windows, wrought-iron oddities, inlaid wood panels, and heavily carved wooden ceilings of the Gothic Revival. Finally there was the exoticism of the Orient. The Oriental room was *de rigueur* for the day, with its porcelains, scroll paintings, lacquered boxes, and lanterns.

Portraits of fine ladies and gentlemen, landscapes, even animals were favored by the wealthy collectors. In an era of explosive technological advances, nostalgia reigned. "One could dance in a royal Rococo ballroom, feast in a robber baron's Gothic dining hall, and sleep in an emperor's Napoleonic chamber," Joseph Byron wrote.[7]

The city that surrounded this millionaires' enclave presented an urban scene of startling contrasts. A photojournalist named Jacob Riis became New York's most effective social reformer when his pictures exposed the hideous conditions of tenement life. Graceful colonial pockets survived amid feverish boomtown construction.

"From the Battery to the Plaza . . ." one essayist wrote, "the buildings are so huge that nothing huger is possible. . . . everybody hurries, because haste is in the air . . . in the hammers of the ceaseless skyscrapers ceaselessly going up . . . in the unending noise, the pervading scramble. . . ."[8] Most astonishing, for its height—twenty stories!—and its odd shape, was the emerging Flatiron Building. Scarcely an hour went by that a crowd did not gawk at the site.

The financial district, intersected by Lower Broadway, flanked by two rivers, disappearing into the sea along with Manhattan Island itself, was a seething center of business and trade. The original Standard Oil partners still ran their worldwide empire from rolltop desks at 26 Broadway. J. P. Morgan & Company was the dominant bank on Wall Street. A wooden statue of Peter "Peg-Leg" Stuyvesant stood in front of the venerable Stuyvesant Insurance Company at 157 Broadway, and Crouch & Fitzgerald, selling luggage for sixty years, was a fixture at 161.

Frenetic though it was, the district gave off a strong whiff of history. From the window of his residence on Wall Street, Alexander Hamilton had viewed the inauguration of George Washington on the balcony of Federal Hall across the way. Washington Irving once practiced law in an office on the east corner of New Street, and Daniel Webster had delivered a major oration from the steps of a mansion on Greenwich Street. At the head of Wall Street, the Trinity Church cemetery was a severe reminder that even the greatest fortunes have but slight significance. Where General Washington and Robert Fulton once strolled, thousands of clerks and customers' men, investors and shoppers now jostled each other on the jammed sidewalks. Hansoms, broughams, gigs, and victorias fought the electric trolleys for command of the street.

Two miles north, at 19th and Broadway, Arnold Constable & Company sold the fine fabrics favored by upper-class women for their custom-made gowns. Middle class and affluent alike flocked to the great department stores on Sixth Avenue, while the enterprising poor found coats for fifty cents, hats for a quarter, and trousers for pennies on the pushcarts in Hester Street. The stylish rich dined at Rector's, Delmonico's, and Sherry's. The beleaguered middle class could buy a roast beef dinner at Child's for thirty-five cents. At Louis Fleischmann's Vienna Model Bakery at Broadway and 10th Street, the homeless and the destitute waited patiently, noiselessly, under the protective cover of darkness for the day-old rolls and mugs of hot coffee that the kindly Mr. Fleischmann handed out after closing time.

Even in such a blatantly inegalitarian era, there seemed to be diversions for everyone. Pimps, pickpockets, and prostitutes gathered at Billy McGlory's, that most disreputable of dance halls, on Hester Street. The recreation piers, two along the East River at 24th and 112th, two more on the Hudson at West 50th and 129th, were open from early morning until late evening during the summer and fall. For the children of the slums, the fresh breezes were what Riis called "a chance for life." Their parents, strolling in the twilight, enjoyed free band concerts and sampled strange ethnic foods.

At 27th and Madison, Stanford White had created his most joyous building, Madison Square Garden, with its endless choice of divertissements. In and out of the amphitheater the circus, the Horse Show, the six-day bike races, the Japanese comic opera followed each other in rapid succession. Rising like Seville's Giralda, the lilting tower housed White's legendary private apartments. White himself was a connoisseur of art and antiquities, a sybarite who loved beautiful women and whose most famous erotic improvisation was the red velvet swing in which a naked Evelyn Nesbit nightly swung for his exclusive pleasure.

Some activities transcended class and pocketbook—bathing at Far Rockaway beach, riding the Ferris wheel at Luna Park, skating and sleighing and punting in Central Park. The soda fountain was a national institution, and all ages flocked to the candy shops.

Although the few first-class paintings that did come to America disappeared into private mansions, the Metropolitan Museum of Art was gradually building a collection. (As a barometer of taste, however, *The Horse Fair* by Rosa Bonheur was still the popular favorite.) Italian opera was the overwhelming choice of society. Fashionable women posed in various stages of elaborate undress at charity tableaux. The Divine Sarah (Bernhardt) continued to make her farewell tours, Ibsen and Shaw shocked the straitlaced with such unmentionable subjects as social disease and divorce, and the French artist's model Trilby was the fictional idol of young readers.

Abby was no stranger to the New York establishment. For twenty years, Aldrich family members checked in and out of the Fifth Avenue Hotel with some frequency. But sharp differences in behavior had already surfaced between New England aristocracy and New York society, and Abby at age twenty-seven embodied the qualities of the former rather than the latter.

"There is no question in my mind," she wrote once, "but that I am very much a New Englander and won't get over it. All my reactions seem to be distinctly New England."[9] Social standing on Fifth Avenue had more to do with unceasing pageantry, titled husbands for American heiresses, and the most glittering balls of the season than with conscience and ancestral distinction. If Abby was attracted to the social game, it was as a passing amusement rather than as an end in itself. John's disposition was to shun it altogether, partly from shyness, partly from the principles laid down by his ascetic mother.

There was another dimension to the careful privacy the young couple maintained. While much sharp criticism swirled about the men who built the great fortunes of the Gilded Age, no one was attacked more vehemently than Senior. By the time the antagonism had swelled to a crescendo he had quietly retired. The real power rested with two of his more ruthless partners, the affable William Rockefeller and the clever H. H. Rogers, both of whom were far more reckless and unscrupulous than the silent, deliberate Rockefeller. But Senior remained the titular head of the trust, his partners insisting that they needed the appearance of his leadership to hold the organization together. John flinched from the publicity generated by the muckrakers. Abby's dislike of the press at this juncture was only slightly less passionate than John's, protective as she was of *her* father's reputation.

The fact of Senior's thrift and religious orientation did nothing to assuage the hatred of Americans who felt themselves to be exploited by the system. They saw only his enormous wealth, made public by various investigating commissions. It was eventually far greater than that of either Astors or Vanderbilts. At the close of 1901, Senior's fortune, according to Allan Nevins, went above $200 million for the first time, and it was growing fast, with the greatest expansion of Standard Oil still ahead. (This is approximately $3.3 billion in 1992 dollars.) Net profit for the current year was $58,564,000. Senior spent only a fraction, $439,100 for household expenses. A catchall category of "donations, expenses and losses" totaled $3,706,000.

Abby was raised to believe that money was something to be used and enjoyed. When she managed her father's household he had been grateful that she relieved him of the burden and had left the details to her. Now, however, she was married to a man whose cardinal principle was that money must never be spent imprudently. It was not out of miserliness or some eccentric impulse that John watched pennies; it was an inescapable obligation drilled into his psyche by his Puritan parents. The account book that Abby so bravely rejected was really but a symbol. The reality was that John gave her an allowance, that personal bills went to the family office to be checked for errors before being paid, and that John, with his obsessive attention to detail, was ever watchful of her expenditures.

"The fact is," Laurance Rockefeller pointed out, "she had limited financial independence. It could be a difficult problem to sway him, to prove the value of what she wanted to do, whatever it was."[10] As a true daughter of New England, Abby was far from prodigal. She knew how curtains could be darned to stretch their usefulness, and how to replenish the linen closets at the January white sales. She believed in philanthropy as ardently as Mr. Gates, the astute Baptist minister who was guiding Senior's charitable contributions. But she had been making independent decisions for years and making them intelligently. To have her every financial decision judged was to experience something new and disquieting.

As Abby was trying to adjust to John's vigilance over money matters, she collided with another of his powerful instincts—the desire to construct a daily life that was almost indistinguishable from that of his parents. He may have been attracted to a woman whose personality and background were different from his, but this did not encourage him to experiment. Perhaps Abby thought that her buoyancy would temper his rigid adherence to old verities. But the move from his parents' house to their own house did not change things.

John continued to lead the Men's Bible Class at the Fifth Avenue

Baptist Church. Three nights a week he prepared his Sunday talk and questions for discussion. Abby saw her household become a center for Baptist ministers and their good works, even as Laura's was. John hated surprises; spontaneous hustle and bustle, so much a part of Abby's former life, disturbed him. Card games were alien to him. Unlike Senior, who had left domestic decisions to Laura, John maintained strict control over household matters. Such resistance to change required Abby to move gingerly.

She avoided confrontation when possible, she maneuvered around messy situations, but on occasion she set her own priorities. Instead of following Laura and Alta meekly into Sunday school teaching, she persuaded the women of the church to invite the immigrant neighbors of the congregation to open meetings. People of all nationalities and different religious preferences—Italian, Irish, Hungarian, and Czech; Protestant and Catholic—discussed their living conditions and their aspirations, brought their music and food.

By playing on John's desire to share his innermost feelings with her, she was able to exert her influence on significant family decisions, gradually, subtly, and with hardly a whisper of intrusion. For at least a year John had been eager to establish a philanthropy to improve education for blacks in those Southern states where not a single high school for blacks existed. On February 27, 1902, ten men met with him at 13 West 54th to make the final plans for the General Education Board, one of the most far-reaching philanthropic enterprises to be organized in the twentieth century. In the name of his father, John pledged $1 million to be used during the next ten years for education without distinction of gender, race, or creed. And that was only the beginning. By 1921, Senior would fund the trust with $129 million. The GEB benefited the entire spectrum of higher education in America.

The day after that original meeting, John wrote to his father that "Abby was the only woman present."[11] Four months after they were married, the precedent was established that would be followed for the rest of his life. Abby was the "only woman present" actually as well as symbolically, in every critical decision he made.

If he was reluctant to hand over minuscule daily household matters to her, he showed no reluctance whatever to exploit her shrewd understanding of large issues.

"I think without question," John wrote his mother from Warwick in June 1902, "the last eight months have been the happiest, the most complete, the broadest, and the best [of my life] and each month, yes each day is happier than the last. . . . [Abby] is the one woman of all I have ever known best fitted to supplement my life, develop it to its fullest extent and make me happiest."[12] He had been the center of all of Laura's ambitions, the favorite child, the only son. It was only logical, according to his experience, that the woman he married would make him the center of her life, supplement it, develop it to its fullest extent, make him happy. Such expectations seemed to call for a woman who was part saint, part earth mother, and part lover. Abby Aldrich never remotely resembled a saint, but her nurturing instincts ran deep, and even when their personalities and interests collided, as lovers they were grandly and openly fulfilled.

During this first summer of her marriage, Abby began to spend time at Pocantico. "Pay attention to the filly," one of the local Tarrytown doctors remarked to a neighbor of the Rockefellers. "She's the one really worth watching."[13] This is a significant observation on several counts. It foreshadows the impact Abby was to have one day, not only on her husband and her children, but on the art world and on all the other worlds she entered. It also makes the point that she was not intimidated by the family into which she had married. If she was deferential to John in public, that was mere good manners and never an indication of subservience in private. As her nephew Richard Aldrich rather neatly phrased it, to survive as a Rockefeller she had to be an independent Aldrich. "She had quite a package on her own back when she married Junior," he said.[14]

And finally, it points up the sharp distinctions between Abby and Laura. Laura was seldom seen by the villagers. Her poor health provided the rationalization for withdrawing from secular activities. Abby, tall and exuberant, her long skirts trailing, took an immediate interest in the workers and their families, the schools, the natural environment. She joined the Women's Club of Pocantico and went on the board of the tiny local school district. "We are getting a model school here at Pocantico. We have medical inspection, a play-ground, gardens and a vacation school for the backward children already. . . . I am a great believer in the possibilities of the public school, aren't you," she wrote Lucy Greene.[15] Abby had such a roving curiosity and such an instinctive empathy for ordinary people that it was as natural as breathing for her to be a participant rather than an observer.

In May, Senior gave Abby and John the use of the Rufus Weeks house on the estate, a Hudson Valley Dutch–style country place with dormer windows and awnings. Before long it came to be known as Abeyton Lodge. While some modest renovation went on during the summer, Abby and John had the use of a suite on the second floor of the Parsons-Wentworth house, as did Alta and Parmelee.

On the night of September 17, 1902, barely two weeks after Abby and John returned from a short trip to Scotland, the Parsons-Wentworth house burned to the ground. Abby and John were sleeping in the city on that Wednesday evening after John's meeting with his Bible class. At one in the morning, Parmelee Prentice woke John with the news of the fire. He quickly assured him that no one was hurt, for it had been a slow fire, if extremely thorough. The critical problem was lack of water pressure. Hundreds of people gathered to watch as estate servants, Ezra himself, and even Alta, who was six months pregnant, worked in the smoke and darkness to rescue furniture and clothes. The Prentice belongings were saved, and most of the first-floor furniture, and someone carried out John's violin. But Abby lost her clothes, everything she had bought in Europe, and all the letters she and John had written each other before they were married.

The next morning at 7:50, John and Abby took the train from Grand Central to Pocantico Hills. Together they took complete charge, supervising the removal of everything that could be salvaged from the lawn of the burned-out house to another dwelling, Kent House, down the hill. The object of their effort was to spare Laura any stress. They went about Tarrytown buying linens, fixtures, and a myriad of other items. They went back and forth to the city to round up furniture for the bedrooms. By September 23, Kent house was well furnished, even to a custom-built refrigerator.

To be certain that everything was in readiness for Laura and Senior's arrival from Cleveland, they slept in Kent House for several nights. They were exhausted from the ordeal. Both had caught heavy colds and were coughing. Abby went to Warwick; John returned to Manhattan.

"If you were only here today," Abby wrote on September 29, "it is like summer and we could sit under the trees and read and talk and be lazy and you could rest. I am sure that it would drive the headaches away for two months at least. . . . I was so lonely last night when I went to bed, I decided then that I couldn't leave you again unless it was quite necessary."[16] But in the morning sun he did not seem quite so far away. If her loneliness in one sense reassured him of her love, the fact that she was also enjoying herself triggered his insecurity. She reported how she was playing bridge with Lucy, laughing at Elsie's adolescent antics, and going about the countryside visiting relatives and friends. She even saw his old rival Frank Smith at a party.

But finally, on October 3, she prepared to leave for New York City. Lucy would accompany her. "Will you have Annie make up a bed for Lucy in the room over ours, please, and to have some breakfast for us. . . . I am glad you miss me but I hate to think of your being all alone and lonely. But tomorrow night sweetheart I shall be where I like best to be."[17]

A heavy snow was falling as Abby and John, accompanied by her maid and his valet, boarded George Jay Gould's private railroad car, *Atalanta*, in the terminal at Jersey City on Monday evening, February 16, 1903. John had leased the *Atalanta* (hooked onto a scheduled carrier) from the railroad magnate for an extended holiday across the continental United States and into Mexico. Rich Americans often toured in such cars, complete with brass beds, excellent kitchen staff, and observation platform. As they proceeded south, the weather turned mild. In Virginia, Abby met the faculty and students of Hampton Institute, the black college that had enjoyed major Rockefeller and Spelman financial support. In Georgia they spent the day at Spelman Seminary, the black women's college named after Laura's mother. At Tuskegee, Booker T. Washington was their official guide.

Abby put the rainy days in New Orleans to good use. She took John antiquing in "old furniture stores," as he called them, and introduced him to the pleasures of Creole cuisine. On Sunday morning, March 1, the elder Rockefeller party arrived in their private car, the *Gascony*—Senior, Laura, Aunt Lute, maid, man, and Dr. H. F. Biggar, the homeopathic physician who looked after them. The two cars then left together on a special train via the

Texas & Pacific and the Missouri Pacific lines for Colorado. At Albuquerque, Senior's party swung west, while the *Atalanta* headed for Mexico.

Abby now knew that traveling with John was rather different from traveling with her family. Sudden changes in the itinerary, however innocent or enticing, could not be countenanced. Impulsive adventures of the kind she enjoyed were out of the question. But there were compensations. John mapped their tour with exhaustive thoroughness.

In Cordoba they rode a narrow-gauge railroad into the tropical countryside. In Guadalajara they listened to the soft music wafting across the town square at twilight, visited the pottery works, the cathedral, and the orphan asylum. On Sunday, March 15, they went to church in the morning and to the bullring in the afternoon. The usual parade of government dignitaries presented themselves, but for Abby it was the landscape, the people, and their art that excited her; it was "the most paintable country that I had ever been in," she wrote.[1] Her knowledge of art had largely been confined to the old masters. Now she was responding to primitive Indian art that had survived the Spanish Conquest and the contemporary folk art of anonymous artisans.

The *Atalanta* reentered the United States at El Paso to join Senior's party at the Grand Canyon. They continued to California and then came back to the Midwest. They visited the campus of the University of Chicago, an institution that by the year 1910 would be the recipient of $35 million from Rockefeller philanthropies. Edith McCormick entertained them at her opulent residence at 155 Rush Street, and their last excursion was a sightseeing trolley ride around Niagara Falls.

For Abby the experience had been exhilarating and at the same time sobering, something of an epiphany—more penetrating and more direct than hostile newspaper headlines, defensive position papers, or even family conferences. She confronted the fact of Rockefeller wealth, the fact of Rockefeller power. She saw it in the institutions that they had visited, in the people who had come around to their hotel suites. She sensed with apprehension that a great burden would fall upon John, with his Spelman conscience and his obsessive desire to vindicate his father's life. In her most contemplative moments, perhaps she also pondered what this fortress of wealth and power would mean for her own children, the next generation of Rockefellers. For Abby was now pregnant.

But there was no next generation, not yet, only the promise of one infant. In August, John went west on a mine-inspection tour. "I would love to be on this tour of inspection with you," Abby wrote, "all that sort of thing interests me tremendously."[2] But her pregnancy kept her at Warwick, sewing with the women and sailing with her brothers.

Politics stirred things up around the estate as Nelson's senatorial colleagues joined him for a boathouse meeting. "We all lunched together," she added, "and I left them having their pictures taken."[3] The next day President Roosevelt arrived. "No more boathouse dinners for me, thank fortune," she concluded. "They are going over to try and 'lick him into shape,' I imagine from their conversation. They talk about him as if he were a spoiled child who needed constant watching."[4] In the perspective of history, it was a shrewd observation. Samuel Gompers, the labor leader, wrote her father that he and two of his colleagues would like to meet quietly at Warwick with John, if the senator could arrange it. "Papa asked me to tell you," she wrote, "that he thought it might be a very good thing, if you cared to do it."[5]

John's letters are an amalgam of Victorian paternalism and poetic hyperbole. "My darling child . . ." he wrote en route. "Perhaps the responsibility of the baby [as yet unborn] is too much for the dear child mother, and she needs her husband. . . . I fear you are getting over tired with so much visiting and so many friends."[6] The trip was finally coming to an end, "I want to fly right into your arms, sweetheart. I want my wife with all her tender love, her sweetness and her exquisite beauty. . . . And yet with all the exquisite joy of coming back to the woman I love and covet is the added joy of returning to my wife . . . the one person in the world indispensable to me—and my love, the mother of my baby. Do you wonder then that the minutes become hours and the hours days as I impatiently wait to be reunited with my love and my life?"[7]

Her reply, the last one of their separation, was, as usual, direct and down-to-earth. Lucy and Elsie and she were enjoying keeping "old maid's hall" and Elsie loved exercising the horses.[8] She noted that he expressed his love for her in much more passionate, unabashed terms than she. "My foolish pride or whatever it is [stands] in the way."[9] Perhaps it was not pride, after all, but the sharp differences in their personalities. John, sealed in his protective armor, could acknowledge the depth and intensity of his emotions only with Abby. Abby, at ease in the larger world, with warmth and affection to spare, was not likely to express her love with the same degree of intensity.

On November 8, 1903, Abby wrote Lucy Greene that although everyone spoke of the baby as a *he*, she secretly felt that "he" would be a *she*. The next day, a week before her due date, in the bedroom of her 54th Street house, she delivered an eight-and-a-half-pound infant girl, christened Abby, but always known as Babs. The tabloid press greeted her arrival with headlines, one of them trumpeting, "Richest of all Babies Is Infant Rockefeller."[10]

Abby Pearce, noting in her journal that she was with her daughter during her "confinement which was severe," went back and forth between Washington and New York.[11] Fighting nerves and stomach disorders, she put up with stalled trains and the heaviest snowfall since 1888, to see the two of them. "Baby and Abby both doing well," she wrote. "Baby growing finely, Nelson joined us to visit galleries, Abby took me in her brougham for shopping."[12] In May 1904, John renewed the lease on 13 West 54th, and in the summer Abby took eight-month-old Babs and her baby nurse to Warwick for a series of visits.

It was during these separations that the tone of John's letters changed. No longer was it a matter of simple loneliness. Dejection seemed to envelop him like an ominous cloud. From Abeyton Lodge, from 26 Broadway, from the University Club, he poured out the same, unrelieved despondency. Meals were solitary, trees were dying all about him. The headaches raged. He dreaded the nights without her. "We were made to live together and not apart," he cried.[13] When he felt her love, the sun was bright and life seemed promising; without her, the world turned dark and cold.

Abby and young Abby "Babs," 1904. Summer at Warwick.
Courtesy of the Rockefeller Archive Center.

Abby tried in every letter to encourage him. "Please go out to dinner tonight," she wrote on August 5. "You don't really think that I am so selfish that I don't want you to have a good time in my absence. . . ."[14] And two days later, "Please, sweetheart . . . I have the baby to comfort me and you need some diversion."[15] She tried to convince him that the separation was hard for her as well, giving vent to her feelings in a dramatic way. "When I die you will find my heart torn in two," she wrote on August 9. "I do so hate to be parted from either you or the baby."[16]

She never denied, however, that life could be pleasant in Warwick. Her brothers and sisters were sailing a newer, larger boat and the weather was cool. She became interested in planning the garden beds around the expanding estate, was reading books on horticulture and talking with the workers. Best of all, the baby knew who was her mother and who was merely the nurse. "This morning she cried when Miss E. took her away."[17] Abby loved babies. Family members still remember the loving squeaks she gave when holding them. She, perhaps more than John, wanted a large family.

John's letters contain all the proper sentiments about the bliss of fatherhood and their precious little Babs, but he could not be blamed if, deep in his unconscious, he perceived the child as serious competition. "I am sure the Lord made me with special needs which you alone can supply," he wrote, "and I know that after living so many years without you He intended that when He gave you to me we should always live constantly together."[18]

As John continued to remind her of his misery, Abby struggled for ways to console him. She tried logic. After all, she wrote, in September he would have her all to himself, when they would make a driving trip through the Berkshires. She repeated how much she missed him. "I am very lonely for want of you dear. If you could be brought here by a wish, I am afraid that you would be here even if you don't like it."[19]

When John assumed the martyr's role once too often, she chided him. "Your letter this morning, dear, amused me very much, one might think from reading it that you were obliged to stay in Tarrytown, lonely and alone while I was staying here from choice having a glorious time and quite neglecting you. Dear I am delighted to have you go where you are happiest and I don't blame you for wanting to be in Tarrytown one bit but you haven't been alone for a minute, and although I know that you miss us I can't but feel that it is my duty to stay with the baby except when you really need me to go with you. I don't mean to imply that I have had such an awful time myself because I haven't, the nights that I spent alone I enjoyed reading and at other times I have had a lovely time with the baby and family. Please don't misunderstand me, I am not complaining, simply stating facts."[20]

But facts have little impact on a psyche that is acutely anxious. As she made her way cautiously with John, she very likely realized that she could not erase the scars of his isolated childhood. Nor could she resolve his acute dilemma about what role to take in his father's corporate empire. But she probably believed—and it was more of a hope than anything else—that if she loved him unreservedly and met all his complex needs in her steadfast way, his good spirits would return. Her nephew Nelson Aldrich suggested that part of John's attraction for Abby was how much he needed her. When her father needed her she had responded unreservedly. Transferring her devotion to John had a certain psychological inevitability about it.

Nothing changed, however, in that fall of 1904, only he became more exhausted, more fearful of small mistakes, more debilitated by the migraine headaches. His feelings of worthlessness in his father's office seemed to extend to his marriage. In this crisis of self-esteem, he could persuade himself that he did not deserve such happiness. And if he saw one small child as stealing his beloved Abby from him, the possibility of more children could very well have added to his insecurity.

On November 15, John wrote one of the members of the Men's Bible Class that he was going abroad with his wife and family, that he felt the need of a long rest. In a letter of December 2, he emphatically denied the rumor that he was in poor health, repeating that he was simply overworked. Nearly fifty years later he was still unwilling to admit to his own biographer that anything more than simple exhaustion had forced him to take a leave of absence from 26 Broadway. Even his own sons never realized until recently, when some old correspondence turned up, that their father's migraine headaches and insomnia were symptoms of deep-seated problems.

There was one exception to the pattern of denial, and that, interestingly enough, was not with any member of his family, but with a close friend of his son David. "I was suffering from a nervous breakdown," George Franklin said to the author, "when Mr. Rockefeller came to visit me. As he listened to my troubles, tears began to stream down his face and he told me that he had gone through a similar experience when he was a young man. I had known him as a man of incredible reserve, very withdrawn. His sensitivity and understanding on that afternoon made a great impression on me."[21]

In fairness to John, the most eminent psychiatrists of his day were neurologists convinced that the neurasthenia he demonstrated could indeed be caused by the excessive strains imposed on the nervous system by modern life. Psychological suffering was considered to be largely a matter of physiology. Treatments leaned toward diet, medication, physiotherapy, electrotherapy, and massage, or as in John's adolescent episode, vigorous outdoor exercise. Psychoanalysis as a form of treatment for emotional disorders was in its earliest phase and was considered eccentric at best, scandalous at worst. Freud's classic text *The Interpretation of Dreams* had been published in 1900 to a "tepid, yawning reception"; it was of interest only to that handful of his Viennese disciples who made up the Wednesday Psychological Society.[22]

Abby and John and Babs, accompanied by nurse, maid, and valet, sailed to the south of France at the end of December. They were greeted by cold and frost instead of sunshine, but they rented an apartment at the Hôtel du Parc in Cannes, and John followed a regimen of moderate exercise and diet. Some slight documentation of the scene comes from a few wise letters of Laura Spelman. "I suppose the two eggs a day are shaken or beaten, and not cooked," she wrote. "Dieting is becoming a great remedy and I always believed in it. Every few days some friend or another speaks of being put upon a course of diet." She thanked John for his "kodak" of Abby sewing in the parlor. "I am impressed," she added, "[that] among the many advantages of your rest cure . . . is the time you can give to your dear baby, and I am happy that you write so much about her. This is an education as great for the father, as for the child, and which is worth all it costs."[23]

After three months of rest, walks by the sea, quiet reading aloud, and frolics with year-old Babs, John was ready for something more diverting. Leaving the baby in the care of nurse and maid, Abby went touring with him; a car and driver had been sent down from Paris. Leaving Monte Carlo on March 28, they drove along the Upper Corniche into the Italian Riviera as far as Spezia, averaging about a hundred kilometers a day—when the car did not break down. In 1905 a motor trip was still an unpredictable experiment. Tires blew out, machinery failed. It was an unusual day that the car was not towed, or that Abby and John did not make the last few miles on foot. In spite of the treachery of the car, they ventured into the Maritime Alps and across Provence as far as Saint-Étienne. John clocked them back into Cannes at 3:15 P.M. on April 7.

A few weeks later, on May 15, Charles E. Heydt, John's personal secretary, was writing letters in his behalf, explaining that his employer had returned to the United States, "upon condition that he do as little business as possible. . . . Therefore will you kindly accept his thanks through me for your letter of May 10th." [24] John confided to a physician friend that for the last six months he had been in Europe undertaking to get rested from a slight attack of nervous prostration. "I am on the road to recovery," he continued, "but find it desirable to spend the entire summer out of doors and shall not resume work until the fall." [25]

Abby's second child, John Davison Rockefeller 3rd—petit John, as his Grandmother Aldrich called him—was born on March 21, 1906, in the same upstairs bedroom where Abby had given birth to Babs three years earlier. He was large and healthy and arrived a week late. The publicity surrounding his arrival was so shrill that Abby asked to have her telephone number changed. "So lie there in your cradle," one of the articles went, "and laugh, and glug, and play, And think of all the rebates that shall be yours some day." [26]

The assault on Senior was mounting in intensity and went as follows. He was the architect of the first powerful trust, a monopoly that scooped up small entrepreneurial enterprises of ordinary people; he was associated with ruthless men who had performed illegal acts; he had built what amounted to the greatest concentration of wealth in history. And he was the perpetrator of especially mean offenses, such as robbing widows of their meager savings. The first three charges, even if exaggerated in certain specifics, were verifiable. It was the last set of accusations that were patent untruths. Even Theodore Roosevelt, who was leading the government's prosecution of the Standard company, urged a halt to inflammatory journalism.

One suit loomed above all others. It was filed in November 1906 in the Federal Circuit Court of Eastern Missouri under the Sherman Antitrust Act, and it formally accused Senior and his six partners of conspiracy to control the oil industry through restraint of trade. "As once in their history the American people had said they were tired of kings, as later they said they were tired of slavery, so now they were tired of flagrant monopolies; they would suffer them no more," Alan Nevins wrote.[27] Nelson Aldrich was also inviting a great deal of unflattering attention at the time. Scarcely a month after John 3rd was born, Hearst's *Cosmopolitan* published an article by David Graham Phillips that found Nelson Aldrich as dangerous as "any invading army," with the kind of power that led the masses toward "serfdom."[28]

Abby, for the most part, retained a certain detachment toward the troubles of both fathers. She recognized that they were well able to look after their own interests and that in their imperturbable way they would survive the attacks. It was for her children that she watched the current outcry with foreboding. And she understood how susceptible John was to ridicule. To the press, his leadership of the Men's Bible Class invited particular irony. The spectacle of a Rockefeller teaching Bible lessons was too inviting a target to ignore. "With his hereditary grip on a nation's pocketbook," said the *Pittsburgh Press*, "his talks on spiritual matters are a tax on piety."[29] He was the butt of stinging cartoons, and sarcastic newspaper articles on his role as Bible teacher became almost weekly occurrences. John with his bulldog conscience refused to resign until Abby spoke her mind.

> Sweetheart, I am writing you on a subject about which I feel most strongly and deeply. I am writing instead of speaking of it because I am afraid it may cause you some pain and I hate to see that dear moth [mouth] look hurt. I am convinced that you should give up the leadership of the Class. Firstly because I think it is a greater nervous strain than you realize or are capable of standing. It seems to me that it consumes much of your time and thought that might be . . . better employed on philanthropic work along broader lines. You know, dear, that for the past five years I have done what I could to help you. . . . I have met most of the men and I am very sorry that I

think very few of them of the kind who justify your great sacrifice.
. . . You would not be retiring under fire just now, you have born
all the criticism and ridicule that is necessary to let the world see
that you are sincere. Probably your mother may not agree with me
but I have a feeling that perhaps your Father may. . . . I love you
too entirely not to want you to do what is best for your future and
the world's good. I feel that there is much for you to do and I don't
want you to lessen your chance of doing the really big things. If my
opinion has seemed harsh or unnecessary, forgive me. . . .
Lovingly, Abby.[30]

John did resign from the leadership of the Men's Bible Class of
the Fifth Avenue Baptist Church the following year.

After two babies in four years and a husband in emotional crisis,
Abby was subjected now to the full force of her mother's agitated
depression. The simplest details of daily living seemed too much
for Abby Pearce. Her letters mournfully listed deaths among her
friends. "I feel as if Providence would soon become depopulated,"
she had written from Paris, "and I must hurry back to see those
that are left."[31] She wondered wistfully if Abby could come to
Warwick in the summer to help her open the house. She was more
and more resentful of the obligations of official Washington. "I
have had grippe & colds, dinner parties, luncheons and company
until life is hardly worth living," she wrote from the capital. "But
I determined . . . to do [only] what my strength would allow, regardless of consequences. Your father," she continued dryly, "does
not like to miss anything. . . ."[32]

At times her mind took strange turns, as when she commented
upon Senior's benefactions. "I cut out of the paper yesterday a list
of the educational bequests [of] Mr. Rockefeller . . . and I am quite
consumed with envy. If I was the proud possessor of one million
dollars for the next five years I would spend all my time in buying
all the things I have always wanted and have never been able to
get. I should give nothing towards education. I am not really insane
but approaching it."[33]

The passing reference to insanity was not altogether a sarcastic
thrust. Other signs pointed to some kind of degenerative neurological disorder. Poor health plagued the Rockefeller women as well.

Laura Spelman was increasingly frail. Edith McCormick was exhibiting great bouts of extravagance and aberrant behavior. And Bessie Strong died in Europe at the age of forty.

John's doctors continued to send him on horseback riding trips into the Berkshires and the White Mountains as a way of combating his insomnia and migraines. "Am feeling splendidly," he wrote Abby on October 13, 1906. "Give a kiss and hug to brother and sister for me," he continued, "for though I am not outspoken and demonstrative about them as you are, and have been called an unnatural parent [the emphasis is his], I love them dearly."[34]

Abby never doubted that he loved them. What concerned her was his tight control over his feelings. In every letter she tried to encourage some kind of openness. "I adore it when you show how much you love them. . . . I know you love [them] very dearly and they will be so fond and proud of you some day."[35] Pointedly she described their charms to him and their small, appealing problems. Little John looked wistfully for his absent father in all the rooms of the house; Babs asked Abby to sleep with her and take care of her all the time. "But who will take care of Papa?" asked Abby. Why, the nurses, of course, answered the child with a joyous smile. "Let Miss Lolemeyer sleep with Papa and take care of him."[36]

During the summer of 1907, Abby and the children were in East Hampton, Long Island, and John commuted from the city. When he arrived, the nannies took over and Abby adjusted her routine to his. They did a lot of napping and lolling about. They had breakfast in their room. There were days when they never got out of their lounging clothes. They retreated because John's spirit was restored in Abby's presence and he wanted her all to himself. Their passion certainly had not cooled. Each wrote of loving the other to distraction. Abby's loneliness in East Hampton came over her most when the fog rolled in and the foghorns blew their melancholy note. John would sit out on the piazza at Abeyton Lodge, sniffing the air, watching the moon rise up, and yearn for Abby.

This was the summer when Abby sat for the first of her many portraits; the only one, she wrote, that anyone in the family would ever like. The artist was Abby's friend Adele Herter. John had doubted whether any artist could capture Abby's "true beauty and loveliness of character." But when he saw the portrait, he was satisfied. "You must love her a little as I do," he wrote Adele, "else you could not have painted her so truly as I see her. . . . Yours is a complete success. . . . Although as Abby truly said yesterday my judgement in matters of art is of little or no value, I feel sure you will accept this honest grateful tribute to your art."[37] Poor John. There were times, apparently, when Abby set aside tact in favor of the blunt truth.

CHAPTER 9

—⋅⋅◀◁∞▷▶⋅⋅—

*L*ess than two months after the nocturnal fire had very nearly destroyed his house at Pocantico in 1902, Senior had begun to experiment with ways to rebuild it. John and Abby, however, had other ideas. John dreaded the thought that his father would build another tasteless residence similar to the one in Cleveland. He was convinced that Senior's accomplishments called for something noble, something impressive. Ida Tarbell's stinging personal criticism of Senior's character, published in *McClure's*, only served to sharpen John's conviction—very nearly an obsession now—that his father must at last become the master of a regal house. Tarbell attacked Senior for his "cult of the unpretentious," for having no appreciation of art and beauty. "Here was parsimony made a virtue," she wrote scornfully.[1] The chief vanity of the richest man in the world seemed to be how little he could spend on his household.

Abby, watching her own father create Aldrich House on his property at Warwick, understood the tradition of power architecture, when a great residence becomes a symbol of achievement. She sensed the depth of John's frustration. She knew that he needed a major project, one which could absorb the energy that was being frittered away filling the family inkwells at 26 Broadway. Not least, she herself was fascinated with the aesthetics of design.

Reckoning without Senior's faint interest in the whole matter, they asked the architect, Chester Aldrich, a distant relative and partner of the distinguished firm of Delano & Aldrich, to make a ground plan and elevation for a new mansion on Kykuit Hill. They were still studying Aldrich's sketches in 1904. "I am sorry Chester Aldrich is going abroad," Abby wrote from Warwick in August. "Did you like Mr. Delano?"[2]

John replied, "He has several new ideas regarding the arrangement of both the first and second floors which are admirable, also about the elevation. I think you will like his work and am quite hopeful that Father will. I shall bring his ground plans with me to Warwick for your inspection."[3]

John's hopes were futile. Senior remained aloof, turning from John to an older executive in his organization for opinions about the wisdom of building on the Kykuit site. Another son would have given up, but John, with his doggedness and utter loyalty, continued to study the subtle nuances of his father's taciturnity, and tried to carry out his wishes, which were impossible to gauge, since Senior himself did not know what he wanted.

Then came John's breakdown in the winter of 1904. When he returned to his desk in the autumn of 1905, Senior authorized him to order some preliminary excavations on the site. A shrewd judge of character, he perhaps now recognized the value to John's emotional recovery of having a stake in a major enterprise. Certainly he was paying serious attention to the anxiety beneath his son's courteous reserve. Even if final approval was still tentative, it was enough to get John moving decisively. He counted on Abby as his silent partner, silent to the world outside, but vocal and creative in private. Together they would mobilize the judgment and the taste to create what they devoutly believed would bring honor to the family.

As John later explained it, their aim was to build a home, not a palace, "so apparently simple that any friends visiting father, coming from however humble homes, would be impressed with the simplicity of the house, while those who were familiar with beautiful things and appreciated fine design would say 'how exquisitely beautiful.' "[4] He signed the contracts in the summer of 1906. Thompson-Starett were the builders, Delano & Aldrich the architects.

"I am crazy to hear about the house," Abby wrote John from Marblehead, Massachusetts, on July 24.[5] But this time the house she referred to was not Kykuit. It was their Manhattan house at 13 West 54th, which John had been renting since 1902. In John's behalf, Senior purchased it for $192,000. Remodeling was about to begin, and Chester Aldrich was to be the architect for it as well.

By the spring of 1907 the fieldstone walls of Kykuit, constructed from weather-stained old stones on the estate itself, were rising above the foundation. John was the project manager, approving the subcontracts, checking bills, managing the myriad addenda to specifications. Abby was his artistic consultant. The architects soon realized that the young couple, not the father, were the clients. Over their objections, John commissioned another architect, Ogden Codman, to design the interior of the house.

Ogden Codman, Jr., came out of Abby's milieu. He was descended from Yankee merchants and diplomats, and he designed interiors for prominent Rhode Island families, many of whom were Abby's friends. He and Edith Wharton published in 1897 *The Decoration of Houses*, which swept aside a whole generation's devotion to Victorian clutter. Abby persuaded John of Codman's genius for adapting French and English designs to his own elegant style.

John in turn converted Senior. "I spoke [to him] of the furniture question . . ." John wrote Abby from Cleveland. "I think he will be pleased to have us do what we think desirable in the matter."[6]

Abby and John met regularly with Codman. They approved his preference for luxurious structural materials, such as marble instead of wood for entrance hall and mantels. Codman believed that modern reproductions were entirely suitable, if they were well crafted, and that such pieces were available only from French craftsmen, whom he visited annually on his trips to the Continent. This method involved considerable delays in communication and made John exceedingly nervous, especially since Codman refused to be prodded and his office was as casual about administrative detail as it was precise about artistry. Abby was the one to smooth over the personality clashes.

When Codman was in Europe they exercised their own taste. Abby consulted with her parents, her sister Lucy, and her brother William, who was studying architecture at the École des Beaux-Arts. She subscribed to design periodicals, which she passed on to John, and built up her own library.

During the summer that she was in East Hampton, John reported daily on the progress at Kykuit. On August 7, 1907, he sent her the names and the estimates of the firms that were bidding on interior construction. "I shall confer with you before deciding," he wrote.[7] The contract later was let to William Baumgarten & Company of Manhattan, with the proviso that Codman's office would oversee the Baumgarten work crews.

At the same time a third architect came on the scene—Welles Bosworth, whose primary responsibility would be the garden landscape. He viewed the hillside site as ideal terrain for a series of terraces in the Italian style, with graceful embellishments in the form of pergolas, sculpture, and cascading water. His design was complex and many-tiered, the idea being to lead down from the hilltop in an entirely natural scheme to the rolling lawns that encompassed the golf course. When finished, the estate would include not only a formal sunken garden, stone teahouse, arbor, and marble temple, but fountains and meandering brooks, all electrically lit at night. "Mr. Bosworth showed me two perspectives of the garden and terrace looking from above," John wrote Abby. "They are enchanting. I shall have prints of them to show you. . . ."[8]

It should be no surprise that Senior periodically balked as the costs escalated. "You know, these little brooks run mighty high!" he was overheard to say in jest with some friends.[9] But John, who could fret interminably over small expenditures, was willing to pay large sums for great projects if they met his particular standards.

During the climactic summer of 1908, when Kykuit was being completed, Abby and the children and staff were in Bar Harbor, Maine, receiving John's exhaustive progress reports. ". . . third floor painting complete . . . [wall]paper partly on . . . third story floors have all been finished. . . . carpets fitted and sockets put in the floor . . . electric fixtures up. . . . servants' furniture . . . on the boat today. . . . basement and sub-basement, exclusive of the golf-room . . . cleaned and vacated. . . . etc. etc."[10]

Codman was a continuing source of irritation. For example, he needed to approve the Savonnerie carpet samples designed in Paris for the drawing room, dining room, alcove, and living room of the first floor. All summer he was in the south of France and the manufacturers were unable to locate him. The moment was fast approaching when Senior and Laura expected to move into the house, and John was jittery. Abby could only try to soothe him from afar.

On Saturday, September 12, 1908, Abby and John moved into Kykuit to test all aspects of the house before Senior and Laura arrived. They slept in various rooms, ate meals in the house, determined what was lacking, organized the staff, and assigned tasks.

John was unhappy that Codman was still in Europe. "[We] feel your absence most seriously. . . . Mr. Baumgarten is also abroad . . . so that we are quite helpless."[11] It was not likely that Abby was helpless, but John, tough as he was in auditing expenses, was quite dependent on Codman's judgment. Codman, although flattered by his client's anxiety, was in no mood to leave Paris, certainly not to move furniture about at Kykuit. What he was willing to do, however, was to shop from the list John sent him for clocks, mantel ornaments, writing sets, cachepots, and objets d'art. Only recently Abby had given John a book to read on Chinese porcelains. He included on his list the suggestion that Codman watch out for some really rare pieces.

Laura's entry into her diary for October 8 reads: "The new house all furnished by John and Abby was ready for us. It is beautiful and convenient within and without."[12] Notwithstanding such a benign comment, she was deeply dissatisfied with some critical elements in the house. Senior's original instructions to John had been that he did not want any responsibility for the building of Kykuit to fall on Laura—this in spite of the fact that she was a woman of strong and set ideas and had been fully involved in all of his business dealings since their marriage. Perhaps her illness was a contributing factor. On September 28, ten days before moving, she wrote John that she required day and night nurses and had been sleepless for many nights. Emphysema was one of her serious problems. The philosophy that dominated John's childhood found expression in the concluding lines of her letter. "Disappointment seems, sometimes, the order of the day, and perfection comes through suffering, but it is always better ahead."[13]

It is not clear that Laura *never* saw the house during construction, nor studied the plans. But certainly she moved in with some rude surprises ahead of her. She found the third-floor guest rooms totally inappropriate—too small and too informal. Codman agreed with her. Upon learning later that the house would be extensively remodeled, he wrote that the family was "going to improve those horrid little rooms" and lamented the fact that "the house had not been done by a real architect."[14]

Senior, who had been in close touch with all three architects and the builder and John since 1903, was displeased with certain operational aspects of the house. The elevator when in operation made an annoying racket that could be heard from the three bedrooms nearest it. When Laura used her bathroom, the plumbing noise traveled to the public rooms below. More serious flaws showed up over the winter. Rainwater ran down the flues into the dining room and library hearths. Only the butler's quick move to close the dampers saved the Savonnerie carpets.

The most serious problem of all, the one that John had gone to extreme lengths to avoid, was an unhappy fact. The chimneys and flues were creating serious trouble. Downdrafts were smoking up most of the rooms. This was something Senior would not tolerate, but he tried to ease John's despair by assuring him that it could be solved. (It apparently had to do with the height of the chimneys.) "I know you have given infinite pains and careful attention . . . to every detail of all the construction," he wrote his son, "and have done much better than I could possibly have done."[15]

What finally troubled Senior the most, however, was not the glaring deficiencies, but rather what aggravates most owners—cost overruns. He had been promised a pleasant country estate for approximately $500,000—house, garden grading, everything. What he now saw was a mansion with many unsolved problems that had cost $726,805.23. Bosworth had already spent an additional

$599,017.05 on the landscape, which was far from finished, and John, entranced with his creativity, was in no mood to restrain him.

So Senior was looking at figures nearly three times the original projection. It did not move him that his brother William had spent $3 million on his landscaping alone, or that his partner Henry Flagler had built his Palm Beach palace, the Whitehall, for $4 million. He was at long last beginning to be sensitive to public opinion. "I should not want the public to know what our expenditure has been," he wrote John.[16] Actually, even the large amount spent was a great deal less than his critics assumed.

Abby, meanwhile, was trying to locate a new housekeeper for Laura, one with the managerial skills to run Kykuit. An Englishwoman applied who had worked for one of the Mrs. Vanderbilts, "whom she is leaving for various reasons which we know of and which are not to her discredit," John reported.[17] Next there was the question of the butler. "Abby and I have taken two or three meals in the new house within the last few days to try the [new] man. I think he is going to do admirably."[18] Their effort continued, to relieve an ailing Laura, in Florida for that winter, of all mundane details.

Abby supervised the planting of Kykuit's terraces. "Mr. Bosworth and Mr. Tonetti [François Tonetti, a sculptor] are coming to lunch tomorrow," she wrote John, who was out in Oklahoma with some Standard executives, "and that doesn't please me very much. If I can't have you, I want just the children. Besides, I think they are both foolish. They think women like flattery and they don't. I meant women don't like to be flattered. I wish you were here, as usual I don't sleep as well without you and life isn't nearly as interesting or charming. There is no fun getting undressed by oneself. . . ." She had a sudden terrible thought. "Are they careful about the rear lights on your car, when you are the last on the train?"[19]

The house continued to be a keen disappointment, for Abby and John perhaps more than for Senior and Laura. It had been their conception from the beginning. However much Senior hid his displeasure, John felt the sting of letting him down. Abby had the capacity to absorb disappointment, but it must have been painful to watch John's hopes dashed. Only her garden plantings seemed to please everyone. They were at their prime in August. The cedar trees in the Maze Garden were covered with new growth. All the roses were in bloom. The petunias, most fragrant, were reminiscent of English gardens. The vines on the wall of the Enclosed Garden next to the Grotto had grown splendidly. The Morning Garden and the Brook Garden were enchanting. Abby had the idea of throwing them open to Pocantico residents. Nearly three hundred came. "It was quite like fairyland," John wrote to Laura, "with the illuminated fountains . . . and the many people all about the gardens."[20]

But finally, after two years of conferences and correspondence, the decision was reached to dismantle the house. A radical plan for alteration was devised. The interior partitions of the third and fourth floors would be extensively changed. The attic floor beneath a new green slate mansard roof would provide more servants' quarters. The east end of the house would be extended, a stone loggia would replace the original wooden veranda, and the entire forecourt would be remodeled. All three architects, Aldrich, Codman, and Bosworth, as well as he and Abby, John wrote his father, were in agreement that the new plan would result in a house far more dignified than the present one.

In February 1914, after being bedridden for a year, Laura Spelman Rockefeller moved into the remodeled Kykuit. Her health was so poor that it was a serious question whether she would be able to make the trip from Cleveland at all. But with Senior preceding her to check out every detail for her comfort, and nurses to accompany her on the train, she made the journey without incident.

The Georgian villa over which she would briefly preside—she died the next year—commanded spectacular views of the Hudson River, two miles away. The music room soared into a cupola extending through the second floor, with organ and organ pipes dominating the room. All the public rooms on this, the first floor, were furnished in Codman's eighteenth-century style of Chippendale, Hepplewhite, and Sheraton. On the floors above were the master bedrooms and guest rooms enlarged to please Laura, with ten ser-

Kykuit, the mansion designed by committee. Pocantico Hills.
Courtesy of the Rockefeller Archive Center.

vants' rooms beyond. Beneath the main floor the hotel-style kitchen was tiled in white ceramic and outfitted with the enormous gas ranges and walk-in iceboxes of the era.

Architectural historians have never viewed Kykuit as an artistic triumph. It was, after all, a house designed by committee. But it achieves an ultimate harmony. For John and Abby it held particular significance. The experience that John acquired in managing the project successfully was crucial to his future as a visionary philanthropist. In working with his much-revered father for ten years, he was able to begin the process of separation and self-definition that was overdue in their relationship.

Abby, ever watchful of John, could only be relieved that he not only handled the stress without breaking down, but in fact emerged with more confidence and poise. As for herself, in working with people such as Codman and Bosworth, she sharpened her skills and learned to trust her own aesthetic judgment. It was a continuation of the education that had begun under her father's tutelage.

CHAPTER 10

⸻ ✦ ⸻

*A*bby had been in and out of bed all winter with a cough and
rheumatism and was now four months pregnant. When she
learned that Dr. Thomas was spending the summer in Bar Harbor,
Maine, she decided to follow him there for her delivery. On June
19, 1908, the entire household began the exodus. "We assemble at
No. 13," John wrote, "where we have supper, and at eight o'clock
the train leaves with the residue, sixteen strong. . . . We arrive at
1:30 P.M. tomorrow.

"Abby is very well and I think will stand the journey nicely.
The children with their new socks, which leaves their knees bare,
will not mind the heat."[1] The immediate family was four, the rest
were staff—including stablemen to look after the horses. The train
was the Bar Harbor Express out of Grand Central, north to Bangor, and then east on the Coastal Line to Hancock. Passengers and
horses boarded the Mount Desert ferry for the eight miles across
Frenchman Bay, to be met on the island side by buckboards and
victorias.

Nowhere along the Atlantic seaboard is there such an island as
Mount Desert. Its haunting beauty is as ever-changing as the sea
itself. Great granite cliffs, pounded by the surf, rise starkly from
the ocean floor. More than a dozen mountain peaks, worn smooth

by centuries of erosion, dominate the landscape. Rich forests of spruce, fir, and pine flourish safely in wilderness areas, and over five hundred species of wildflowers bring a riot of springtime color to the hillsides or hide undisturbed in moist and secret haunts. The climate is by turn intimidating and soothing, as fog and rain, sunlight and gentle winds chase each other endlessly.

John Cabot discovered the island in 1497. Samuel de Champlain named it in 1604. In 1613 the French Jesuits established a mission and a settlement, only to see it destroyed by the English, who claimed the region by virtue of the Cabot explorations. The land remained part of French Acadia, however, until France finally relinquished it in the Treaty of Utrecht in 1713. Under English jurisdiction Mount Desert developed as a fishing and lumbering center. In the middle of the nineteenth century, city folks became attracted to the island's possibilities for recreation—trout fishing, hiking, canoeing, sailing, activities that had been eschewed by the residents of the older summer colonies, where stately rituals of a more elegant order prevailed. Even when Bar Harbor became a playground for millionaires, it never took on quite the lush character of Newport. The fêtes were somewhat quieter, the villas, with their wood-and-shingle style, became known as cottages, and active sports remained an essential diversion.

The family occupied Sears Cottage, a rented waterfront house on Wayman Street, owned by Evelyn Walsh MacLean. On June 28, John left for Tarrytown to check up on Kykuit's progress. In his absence Abby occupied herself with quiet tasks. "Mrs. Barnes and I have been putting the bassinet . . . together," she wrote. "I showed it to the children, little John wanted to get in and try it, and Babbie thought it had better be put in her room, if she was going to take care of the baby."[2]

She was reading Emile Zola's *Rome*—"His views of the R.C. church and socialism and Dogma I found very sympathetic."[3] And she asked John to order two more books for her, *On the Training of Parents* by Lawrence Abbott, and a text on Chinese porcelains by Cosure Maukhouse.

John returned from New York on Sunday, July 5. Three days later, at 12:10 P.M., Nelson Aldrich Rockefeller was born, named after Abby's father. To celebrate his safe and healthy arrival, John presented her with an "alluring" piece of jewelry.[4] Two weeks later he was back at Kykuit to supervise the last details before his parents moved in.

"The rain yesterday kept the children in the house and I could have them with me most of the time . . ." Abby wrote him. "We are getting our share of fog now but I don't mind. . . ."[5] Fog was part of the New England climate that she loved. She often said how thankful she was that the Lord did not place her life inland, that she was not really happy unless she was near water, the ocean was the best, but she would settle for a river. Ending her letter on a note of tenderness, she wrote how much he meant to her; neither the children nor all the luxury with which he surrounded her could make up for his absence.

John was hungry for such words. "I am glad your happiness depends so much upon me," he replied. "I should hate to have you just moderately glad to have me with you; my feelings are so ardent."[6] Nothing could make up for her physical presence, the chance to touch her, to feel her closeness. It was an intensity that for him always bordered on desperation. The question, not yet answered, was how he would deal with competition for that closeness from his own children.

A year later, in 1909, the family returned to Mount Desert. This time they rented in Seal Harbor, like its neighbor, Northeast Harbor, a quiet, low-profile enclave. Charles William Eliot, who had transformed narrow, sectarian Harvard College into a democratic, illustrious university, was one of the first summer visitors to build his house in the area. A colony of distinguished scientists, jurists, and architects gathered around him, some of whom, like Eliot himself, were already known to Abby and John. Christian Herter, who did some of the early work on poliomyelitis, was the brother-in-law of Abby's friend Adele Herter. Simon Flexner, head of research for the Rockefeller Institute, and his wife, Helen, returned every summer.

Rich, patrician families, representing the Protestant elite, were regulars, among them the Clarks of Philadelphia and the Hannas of Cleveland. A deliberate shabbiness, characteristic of a certain

kind of old money, gave the villages their special flavor, their cachet. The golf course was only nine holes and the clubhouse mediocre. Tennis courts were plentiful, if indifferently maintained.
Sailing parties that meandered around the many small islands were
Abby's favorite outdoor recreation, especially if they turned into
all-day picnics. Sunday sermons were delivered by the prominent
clergy of several denominations who took their holidays in Northeast Harbor.

John no longer commuted regularly from New York, but formed
the habit of bringing his work with him. The mass of detail he was
handling, as Senior began to shift projects to him, was endless. His
drive for perfection, his passion for "taking pains," dominated his
thinking. He did not care for sailing, not the way Abby did. He
expected her to reserve her afternoons for him, so that he could
take her driving or hiking with him over the footpaths, pausing at
Jordan Pond House for tea, toast, and jam.

With the end of the season Abby was back in Tarrytown to
enjoy the pageantry of the Hudson-Fulton celebration of the ter-
centenary of the Henry Hudson exploration of the Hudson River
in 1609, and the centenary of the first use of steam navigation on
the river by Robert Fulton. John disposed of all the tickets sent to
him by virtue of Senior's contributions and was satisfied to watch
the illuminated regatta, fireworks, etc. from Kykuit's perch. For
Abby, however, the exhibitions were of much greater interest.
The Metropolitan had rounded up an extraordinary loan exhibition
from New York collectors of Dutch paintings—Rembrandts, Hal-
ses, and Vermeers.

At a time when the Met was overwhelmingly Europe-oriented,
Henry Kent, the greatest museum administrator of his era, decided
to mount an exhibition of American industrial arts from 1625 to
1825. Abby, who had been nudging John into "used furniture
stores" for years, saw her taste vindicated. For the first time since
the Philadelphia Centennial of 1876, "grandmother's old things,"
stored for years in America's attics, received the attention that had
been reserved for the decorative arts of Egypt, Greece, and Western Europe.

In October she paid a visit to Dr. Thomas. He confirmed what she suspected, that she was pregnant for the fourth time and the baby could be expected in May.

Abby's neighborhood, Fifth Avenue in the fifties, was changing. The oil magnates of Standard Oil and the great banking families moved northward to upper Fifth Avenue and the East Sixties and Seventies. Alice Gwynne Vanderbilt's mansion at 58th gave way to Bergdorf-Goodman. The Hotel Plaza, a $12 million American Renaissance palace, opened its doors. Manhattan's explosive growth was encroaching on the protected character of the area. The Sixth Avenue Elevated, recently electrified, carried thousands of working people with ease and speed to their downtown jobs. The result was a proliferation of affordable housing, which in turn invited small shops and saloons into the numbered side streets.

In greater New York, as in other cities, slums were a fact of life, quaint neighborhoods were becoming extinct, and the grandest sight was still the railroad terminal. Stanford White was dead, murdered by the deranged husband of his former mistress, but his inspired plans for the new Pennsylvania Station were taking shape on 34th Street, "its interior reflorescent of the Baths of Caracalla." Two tunnels driven under the Hudson and East Rivers brought an army of commuters into the heart of Manhattan. The newest skyscraper was the forty-seven-story Singer Building at 149 Broadway, and electric signs, advertising everything from "pork to pianos," illuminated the city by night.[7]

Ten thousand people ogled fifty-three different makes of cars at the opening of the National Automobile Show at Madison Square Garden. The cheapest was a Buick runabout for $850; the most expensive, the $7,000 Great Arrow limousine. The horseless carriage that had been a plaything of the rich at the turn of the century was now becoming a general utility of the middle class and would run on Standard Oil gasoline. Senior bought a touring Packard, which Abby and John frequently borrowed.

John was bemused by the success of Mr. Wright's airplane in flying the twenty miles from Governors Island to Grant's Tomb in thirty-three minutes. "I am rather planning to skip automobiles and take to flying machines, they look so comfortable and peaceful," he wrote.[8] (When it came down to it, however, neither John nor Abby ever boarded an airplane, and Abby never even learned to drive a car.)

In the wider world, events presaged dramatic turning points. The Republican William Howard Taft was in the White House, but Woodrow Wilson, a Democrat, was elected governor of New Jersey. Edward VII died. Around the corner from Abby's house, Harriet Stanton Blatch and her small band of followers ignored drizzling skies and curbside lines of hooting men to march up Fifth Avenue in support of woman suffrage. Radical new ideas were colliding with the established order.

Income tax, public housing, old-age insurance, progressive education—all were the subjects of heated arguments. Thorstein Veblen, economist and philosopher, delivered the most powerful message—that in freewheeling, capitalistic America human values had become subordinate to money values. Even the conservative Protestant clergy, who preached to the Rockefellers, began to recognize the need for social welfare. Most people lived barely above the poverty line. Industrial innovation had caused tremendous dislocation. The scramble for money and status and power was as fierce as when Nelson Aldrich walked to Providence in the 1860s. Women still lacked the vote, Southern blacks had no meaningful freedoms. And yet, neither socialism nor Karl Marx changed the mind of most Americans. Individual liberty and economic laissez-faire remained the cherished ideals.

The *Providence Daily Journal* broke the news on Saturday, April 16, 1910, that Nelson Aldrich would not be a candidate for reelection. Two days later, Nelson made it official. He would retire from his senatorial seat at the end of his present term. It was an open secret that the progressive tides in the country were running against him. His remaining public ambition was to revamp the banking system. He looked forward to travel, yachting, and the completion of his Warwick estate. His son William was preparing elevations for what he conceived to be a suitable country seat for the senator —a severely magnificent French Renaissance castle of palatial dimensions, complete with stately salons, ballroom, banquet hall, and a sweeping terrace with panoramic view. In a sense it represented the style of life that Abby and John had tried, with only partial success, to impose on Senior.

Abby understood her father's decision to retire from politics, but it did not affect her personally. What did affect her personally, the decision which changed the fundamental direction of her life, rested in the hands of her husband, not her father. After a lifetime of agonizing, after all the conflicts and questions and hesitation, John decided during this same spring of 1910 that he could no longer serve his father's business interests. He was repelled by the rough, tough tactics of contemporary capitalism. When he made a genuine move toward a humane action, his father's partners callously exploited it for their benefit. When they acted in ways he could not approve of, he bore the brunt of the criticism, simply because of his name. The activity which most excited him was philanthropy, and not merely charity, but expert, innovative social betterment on a worldwide scale. If he wasn't yet the billionaire that his father was, someday he would be, and his single focus from now on would be how that fortune could be used to enhance the public good.

What part did Abby play in the decision? A subjective view is that her influence was pivotal. She was the only person to whom John confided his innermost feelings, from whom he held back nothing, and whom he really trusted. He revered his father, but knew that they viewed life very differently. His relationship with his mother was ambivalent. Religion ruled her life in a way that it could never rule his. He believed that Abby would always desire what was best for him, that she was selfless to a degree which no spirited, independent woman could ever be.

It is a fact, however, that Abby had no interest in John's becoming a captain of industry. She did not see herself as a leader in the Game of Social Pretension. She understood, perhaps better than John, that he could never become financially independent of Senior and it was futile to try. She was beginning to develop a broad vision of what the fortune could do. Her own openness, her willingness to experiment, her instinctive empathy for people's needs, was the leavening in John's orderly, bureaucratic way of thinking. When witnesses say that Abby Aldrich humanized the philanthropy, what they really mean, perhaps, is that she humanized John. As Abby's niece Mary Homans put it, "she was the yeast in the bread."[9]

Laurance Spelman Rockefeller, named after his grandmother, was born on May 26, 1910. "Don't you think I am following Mamma's example well," Abby wrote Lucy Greene, "[though] Mamma says our children are not as good-looking as hers were."[10] She watched over Abby Pearce with fearful trepidation, encouraged when her mind was clear, but painfully aware of the slow deterioration. A nurse, Minnie MacFadden, accompanied Abby Pearce everywhere. "Do you remember," Lucy would write John years later, "when Mamma's mind was failing and she thought every flower she had sent her was from 'John.' That was one thing she was right about—they generally were."[11]

With John and Nelson squirming in Senior's Packard and baby Laurance on her lap, Abby made the annual summer journey to Seal Harbor. Babs, eight years old now, went with John on the train. We "had a very grown-up time," he wrote, although she was a little car- and boat-sick.[12] After children and staff were settled, Abby and John returned to Pocantico for a brief private idyll. They swam in Kykuit's pools, had tea in the newly furnished Japanese teahouse, and imported musicians for their private delight. Even their visit to the city was a tryst of sorts. From the rooftop dining room of the Hotel Astor, fifteen stories above the street, the city that they knew as huge and frenetic was bathed in the mystery and romance of twinkling lights. Abby could forget, if only for a few hours, that she was no longer the irrepressible woman of her youth but a responsible thirty-six-year-old Rockefeller wife and mother of four.

In August, Nelson Aldrich sailed his chartered yacht to Seal Harbor. The Rockefeller children clambered aboard, along with J. Pierpont Morgan, the historian James Ford Rhodes, and various bridge-playing friends of Lucy. In September, while Abby Pearce and Nelson were in Europe, Abby and John had the loan of the yacht. Nelson wrote poignant letters from abroad, letters that revealed an unusual depth of tenderness toward his failing wife. Her

The rooftop play area at 13 West 54th, Manhattan.
Left to right, Babs, John 3rd, Nelson.
Courtesy of the Rockefeller Archive Center.

appeals to him for protection from her nurses, he wrote Abby, were so pathetic that he often felt that he could not stand it. The nurse was trying to follow the doctor's orders in urging her to eat or to rest. Angrily, Abby Pearce lashed out in frustration. The dilemma seemed hopeless. Nelson could only think of trying yet another physician, when none of them had anything new to offer.

Abby was at Abeyton Lodge and John was on a fishing trip in upstate New York when the Supreme Court handed down its landmark decision on the Standard conspiracy. "When I came in," she wrote on May 16, 1911, "Edward told me that Mr. Heydt had telephoned up the Supreme Court's decision. . . . Although I think they have made the Company rather a scapegoat, it doesn't seem as if they could have interpreted the law very differently."[13]

What the justices found was that Standard had violated the Sherman Act. Chief Justice White, in his twenty-thousand-word opinion, asserted that " 'the very genius for commercial development and organization' which created the Trust had soon begotten an intent to set up a monopoly. The object of the Standard had been to 'drive others from the field and exclude them from their right to trade.' "[14] Within six months, declared the Court, the Standard must divest itself of its subsidiaries—in other words, dissolution was ordered. Such a division of empire had broad social consequences. But for Abby and the family, the immediate results were twofold. The market value of the various entities soared, making Senior richer than ever. His personal fortune in 1913 peaked at nearly $1 billion, which translates into approximately $15 billion in 1992 dollars. And for the first time in fifteen years, the Rockefeller name was off the front pages of American newspapers.

Senior continued to control the family finances. He paid for land, buildings, and other capital expenditures, and the maintenance of Pocantico. John's yearly salary was $17,000. He received a personal allowance, as did Parmelee Prentice. Alta Prentice and Abby received their allowances from their respective husbands. All the while that he was overseeing the greatest fortune and the most significant philanthropies in America, Senior was busy allocating the crops from Pocantico like any small farmer. ". . . you are entirely welcome to the vegetables, chickens, eggs, etc.," he wrote John. "I prefer to make no charge for them and there will be no charge until further notice. I hope you will all have good health and increase the consumption of them, and that the supply will be equal to the demand."[15]

In a series of letters between John and Senior during this spring of 1911, John explained that the house at 13 West 54th was becoming too small for their growing family, that he was reluctant to move out of the neighborhood away from Senior and Laura, and that he had located a piece of property at Number 10. "I am negotiating with [the owner] for the purchase. If I am successful Abby and I have in mind to tear down the old house and build a modern, roomy, but simple brick house upon the site."[16] The sale of what was known as the McCook property went through for $200,000.

Senior gave John fifteen feet from his land immediately to the east, thus creating forty feet of frontage at 10 West 54th.

The "very modest but roomy house" that John now commissioned Welles Bosworth to design eventually materialized into something quite different. Nine stories high, with infirmary, gymnasium, squash court, and rooftop playground, it would become one of the largest private residences in the city—so large, in fact, that one story, perhaps apocryphal, has John setting a clay pot of violets out on a windowsill, only to lose track of it forever. There were entire floors for staff, suites for the children and their caretakers, two elevators, one for freight, one for family—and the latest equipment for heating and water circulation.

Welles Bosworth was John's choice, not Abby's. He was not her favorite architect. The house became a reflection of John's taste, not Abby's, although she had a hand in selecting some of the English Chippendale and French Louis XV for the public rooms. John considered antiques to be extravagantly priced and ostentatious. To him, a nine-story mansion was not ostentatious, but antiques were. For most of the house, he ordered contemporary pieces, well made but undistinguished, which never appreciated in value the way antiques did. The dominant tone, however, would be formality, in the great marble reception area on the street floor, in the music room with its requisite organ, in the Persian tapestries lining the stone staircase. Laura Spelman's picture would hang on a dining-room wall, and John's vast collection of three-foot-tall Chinese porcelain urns would gradually come to dominate the corners.

In August, John was at Kykuit trying to speed up the remodeling while Abby was in Seal Harbor making some changes in yet another house. Shortly before the close of the previous season, John had negotiated with Stebbins Realty to buy the Eyrie, a sixty-five-room cottage situated on sixteen acres of granite bluff, at a price of $26,000. He took notice of the house when he and Abby were dinner guests of the Miltons, their neighbors from Pocantico. Admiring its view and its amenities, John inquired of Mrs. Milton whether she was planning to rent it again, or perhaps buy it.

No, she replied, she preferred to travel and could easily take a suite at Asticou Inn with her three children. Her husband was a

New York lawyer. They already had an apartment in the city and the country house at Pocantico and had neither the interest nor the wealth to acquire Maine real estate.

It was in Mount Desert that Abby formed her friendship with the man who did become her favorite architect. "Duncan Candler designed the most interesting houses on the island," Henry Stebbins vouchsafed. "He was the kind of architect who did not care for sailing, but went out in the boats just so that he could see what the houses looked like from the perspective of the sea. He and Abby were the same age. They were kindred spirits."[17] Stebbins assured the author that his parents were very fond of John, loved him dearly, but did not think he had any taste. Abby had all the taste, and she and Candler got along famously. His city office was at 753 Fifth Avenue. He owned the building, with tenants' shops on the first floor, his drafting rooms on the second and third, and his own penthouse above.

Over the period of five years, Abby and Candler worked together on the Eyrie, transforming a mere summer residence into a half-timbered Tudor-style "cottage" of a hundred rooms, tended by a staff of twenty-two. Broad terraces looked southwest over Sutton Island, the Cranberry Islands, and the sea. A glorious rock-strewn landscape of moss and ground cover, succulents and small plants, huge boulders and irregular stones, descended to the sea far below. In furnishing the Eyrie, Abby achieved the effect of a seafaring family gathering treasures from around the globe. Room after room reflected that spontaneous quality of comfort, beauty, and artistic integrity which she aspired to in her favorite houses.

Winthrop Rockefeller was the last of Abby's children to be born at 13 West 54th. "I think perhaps he is going to be the family beauty," she wrote John on May 12, twelve days after he was born. John was at a fishing camp in Woodland. "Don't forget my parting words," she added. "Be sure that you frivol."[18] She was the one who had just come through nine months of pregnancy, but he was the one who required the rest and the change. "It is so good to be carefree," he reported. "I have had no pain in my neck or shoulders since I came."[19] As usual when he was away from her, he mused

Number 10 West 54th, Abby's city house from 1913 to 1937. Torn down and property given to the Museum of Modern Art in 1938.
Courtesy of the Rockefeller Archive Center.

Second-floor drawing room, the scene of Babs's wedding in 1925.
Courtesy of the Rockefeller Archive Center.

Abby's private office/study on the third floor.
Courtesy of the Rockefeller Archive Center.

The Hunt of the Unicorn *tapestries, as they hung in the annex at 12 West 54th.*
The tapestry on the back wall is called The Unicorn Is Brought to the Castle,
the fifth of the six original tapestries.
Courtesy of the Rockefeller Archive Center.

about his own need of her. "[I hope you] are not doing too much or seeing too many people. . . . You must get very well this time. . . . Five little people need you now, besides a man who needs you more than ever, and who wants a great deal more of you than he has been having."[20]

On a Monday in the last week of September 1913, Abby and John slept in their new house at 10 West 54th for the first time. Workmen were still underfoot and 54th Street was a sea of mud in the wake of heavy rains because of an unfinished asphalt pavement, but in most respects the house was habitable. For Abby, it would require an attention and supervision undreamed of in the smaller, less formal house across the street. It was never only a private home for a lively family. The worldwide scope of the Rockefeller Foundation, the Institute for Medical Research, the General Education Board, and the Laura Spelman Rockefeller Memorial required it to be a fulcrum for John's experts. As one observer remarked, "Abby's life was punctuated with groups."[21]

In such a setting, with a husband who valued order, excellence of performance, and religious ritual, Abby brought a kind of blithe humor, even a degree of mischief and loosening of strictures, into the lives of the children. In the third-floor library that became the family living room, she created an atmosphere of warmth and intimacy. Here she took afternoon tea with her children, listened to their triumphs and their grievances, helped them with their homework. Chairs were arranged for easy conversation, books spilled over from their shelves. The slightest chill in the air called for a fire in the fireplace. Unwilling to confront John head-on, she circled about his austerity, gradually chipping away at it. She was the one who printed up the Bible verses on small cards and rehearsed the children in their lines, she was the one who straightened out their account books in preparation for the weekly reckoning. Remember, she would warn, "Papa will want to examine them."[22] She planned amusements with them, often on the spur of the moment, which John would never do, bound up as he was in the necessity for "plans." She taught them simple games, Flinch and Numerica, and auction bridge. John seemed interested in only one game, Laura's favorite, Musical Authors.

It was complicated, being a woman in John's household, which was a generational change from earlier Rockefeller families, when the women had set the standards. Whatever his unresolved doubts about the way he had been reared, John emulated that rearing in some startling ways. Echoing his own childhood, he organized family quartets, with Nelson at the cello, both Johns at the violin, and Babs and Laurance at the piano. Nelson, unfortunately, had a habit of stepping on his cello, often putting it out of commission. He hinted to his father that it was too slow an instrument for his temperament and he should be allowed to switch to the piano. Abby acted as audience and saw to the chocolate cake.

The Sabbath was observed strictly as a day of rest and communion, with Sunday school and church. Hymn-singing and music were the acceptable diversions. Daily mealtimes were punctual. Everyone, except for Abby perhaps, who might appear in her wrapper or not at all, ran down the stairs, breathless, fully dressed, at 7:50 A.M. for the recitation of Bible verses and the Lord's prayer. From there the children were dismissed to the formal dining room for breakfast, the one meal during the day when they were assured of seeing their father.

Waste was looked upon with horror. "From our earliest days," David later wrote, "we were told not to leave food on our plates, not to allow electric lights to remain burning when we were not using them, and not to squander our money thoughtlessly. . . ."[23] To teach habits of frugality, the subject of money—essential in the Rockefeller world—was introduced in the form of allowances. Babs at ten received $1 a week, John 3rd at seven thirty cents. Their father set up the guidelines—one third to spend, one third to save, one third for the church. With the allowance went the account book. Unlike Abby, they did not have the privilege of refusing. Once a week, John looked over their ledgers. All pennies must be accounted for, each expenditure defended.

"Then," David continued, "there was the moral stigma attached to unnecessary and involuntary idleness. . . ."[24] Saving and work went hand in hand. Allowances were inflexible. John, terrified that the fortune would wreck his children, started at the earliest possible moment to give them a little less than they needed, with chores to make up the difference. The economic pressure worked, even on seven-year-olds, as flies were caught on the porches of Abeyton Lodge and the Eyrie at $.10 a hundred, and mice were trapped in the attics at $.05 a mouse.

Christmas brought out a side of John that his children too rarely saw. For a few brief, charming moments, the Puritan perfectionist disappeared in the frolicking joy of the holiday. "A very happy day it was for all of us," he wrote Laura. "The children had their stockings in our room before breakfast. After breakfast we all went to the schoolroom and the three older children sang and played little pieces they had learned for us. Next came the Christmas tree in the nursery, which the children had decorated almost wholly themselves, making many of the decorations. Different places in the room were assigned to the various members of the family, at each of which presents were assembled. You can imagine what a noisy, happy time we had opening the presents there together. A Rhode Island turkey kept us all from starvation in the middle of the day. . . . After lunch the four older children, Abby and I went in the automobile up to Fort Washington Park and walked down to the point by the river. . . . It is now snowing. We are all going to Tarrytown this afternoon for a week."[25]

Senior's estate at Pocantico had now expanded into two thousand acres of woods, cultivated farmland, and rugged natural wilderness. The changing seasons brought their own color to the great trees, the delicate shrubs, the rolling lawns—lush green of summer, rust tones of autumn, blinding white of winter. When Abby and John woke up on a Saturday morning in January, five inches of snow lay on the ground and every twig of every tree and bush was heavy with snow; "the picture from every window was simply like fairyland."[26]

In the spring of 1914, Nelson Aldrich returned from Europe bleak over the prospects for continuing peace. He predicted that a long war was imminent and that the United States would eventually be dragged in. His words were prescient. Less than six months later, Russia, France, and Germany ordered general mobilization. On the night of August 3–4, German troops invaded Belgium. On August 4, Great Britain declared war against Germany. A great mood change among the people of all the nations seemed discernible. Nineteenth-century moderation with its humanitarian aims was giving way to the twentieth century's cult of violence. Influential intellectuals became contemptuous of middle-of-the-road solutions advocated by democratic socialists opposed to the war. Parliamentary democracy was dismissed as hopelessly inept. Groups from the left and the right tried to construct a respectable ideology to justify their call for ruthless authoritarianism. And restless young people from across national boundaries began to idealize war as an endurance test, and to long for combat.

The tragedy that engulfed Europe was at a safe distance from the serenity of Pocantico. But a tragedy of a very different character was slowly taking shape in the coalfields of southern Colorado. It began with a strike of nine thousand miners. It escalated into violence, provoked a national wave of indignation, and thrust Abby and John into a crisis of profound and enduring consequences.

CHAPTER 11

Neither Abby nor John was reared in an environment that would have prepared one to understand the bitterness of workers trapped in a company town, victims of the ugliest form of nineteenth-century paternalism and absentee ownership. Abby's father was a Hamiltonian who distrusted the masses, John's an industrialist who was contemptuous of all union organizers as self-serving agitators intimidating contented workers. And yet in the long run, it was probably Abby's instinctive openness to change and John's personal integrity that enabled them finally to step out of the settled verities of their fathers' world into the uncertainty and challenge of their own.

When the United Mineworkers of America organized the strike against the Colorado Fuel and Iron Company in September 1913, the issues seemed sharply defined. The strikers believed their grievances to be self-evident. In the lonely canyons where the mining camps sprang up, they lived under conditions of feudal autocracy, shopping at company stores, occupying company cottages from which they could be evicted with three days' notice, sending their children to company-run schools, even praying in the company church. Company spies ferreted out union sympathizers, and deputies were posted at company-owned roads to screen all incoming travelers. Such oppressive vigilance was uncommon even among conservative capitalists who were totally antagonistic to the idea of labor-management negotiations. In the present crisis, the officials at Colorado Fuel and Iron saw their responsibility solely as a matter of keeping the mines operating and eventually breaking the strike. In fairness it should be stated that a Department of Labor expert who visited Colorado in the early days of the strike stated that CF&I maintained better working conditions than some of its competitors and its wage scale compared favorably to those of Eastern mines.

Senior and John together owned 40 percent of the company's common and preferred stock as well as 43 percent of the bonds. It was the only company on whose board of directors John continued to serve after he withdrew from the corporate world in 1910, and he continued to vote the family stock. News of the strike reached 26 Broadway primarily through the letters of L. M. Bowers, the stubborn chairman of the board, who conceded nothing to the strikers. On October 6, John wrote Bowers that he supported him in his actions and that the position Bowers had taken was in the interest of the employees of the company.

With both sides armed, the company more heavily than the strikers, violence was inevitable. After one exchange of fire on October 17, several strikers in the tent colony outside one of the mining camps were killed. The governor sent in the militia, but that only quieted the situation temporarily. After a winter of turmoil, the Committee on Mines and Mining of the U.S. House of Representatives began an investigation. John agreed to testify, although he believed that as an absentee director he had little to offer. That was the gist of his testimony—he knew nothing of housing and wages, he could only put his trust in the company officers on the scene, and he professed to believe that the majority of the employees were not sympathetic to the strike. It was a weak position, and most thoughtful observers said so.

Two weeks after John's appearance before the committee, the worst happened. It was the morning of April 20, 1914, and a company of about thirty-five militiamen, some of whom were former mine guards, stationed themselves on a hill overlooking a tent colony in Ludlow. A shot rang out from an unknown location. The militiamen raked the camp with machine gun fire, and the pitched battle began. By nightfall the militia captured the camp and set it on fire. There were dead and wounded on both sides, but the final terrible extent of the tragedy came to light in the morning. The bodies of eleven children and two women were found in a cave beneath one of the tents, where apparently they had taken refuge from the inferno.

Exhausted by a winter of deprivation, having no thought now but vengeance, the strikers declared war on the mines, burning and looting and creating the specter of anarchy. Only the arrival of federal troops a week later quelled the insurrection.

Again the chairman of the House Committee on Mines and Mining called on John, this time pleading with him to persuade management to be more conciliatory. Again John refused, reiterating that only the officials of the mining company were competent to deal with the situation. Now the uproar was heard across the country. That the largest stockholder in a corporation, a Rockefeller with legendary power, should refuse to take responsibility for such a "massacre" seemed outrageous, not only to the radical left, but to the ordinary citizen as well. Upton Sinclair's pickets, wearing black armbands, stood outside 26 Broadway and carried their protest signs to the edge of Pocantico. A homemade time bomb exploded in a tenement building on Lexington Avenue, killing four Wobblies (members of the Industrial Workers of the World) and injuring at least seven innocent occupants. Police investigators believed that the conspirators intended the bomb for the Rockefeller family house on 54th Street.

On June 6, 1914, William Lyon MacKenzie King came to 10 West 54th to meet with Abby and John. A recognized expert in labor problems, King had been minister of labor in the Liberal government of Canada. With his party temporarily out of office, he had accepted the Rockefeller Foundation's offer to chair its new division for economic research. As the Colorado situation began to fester, however, Charles Eliot, a member of the foundation board, suggested that he study the labor question first. King's appearance on the scene was fortuitous. Abby and John were beginning to question the entrenched position on Ludlow and to doubt Bowers's reports. John was drawn to his personality—devout, mystical, devoted to his mother. Abby recognized his political acumen. King in turn recognized how much John depended on Abby, not only for her emotional reinforcement, but for her humanity and her practical insights. From then on he took the responsibility for leading them out of the trap of Ludlow.

In September, John took one of his periodic hunting trips in Nova Scotia. "I miss you sadly," he wrote Abby, ". . . but it seemed wise to take this trip."[1] She used their separation as an opportunity to write some words of advice. "I am writing this to urge that you more and more leave to me the petty details of the houses, places, etc. even though I realize that they will not be as well or as inexpensively done; and throw the full force of your thought and time into the big, vital questions that come before you," she wrote. "Frequently in the past I have felt with deep regret, that others were doing the inspiring part of your work while you poor dear were looking after the details. . . . No one else can do the big things as well as you can. . . . I am ready to do anything to help you be what I know you can be. I feel that the time has come when the vast majority are thinking seriously."[2]

She was referring to an industrial plan, devised by King, which embraced the idea of employee representation. For several months she had joined the two men at dinner, on quiet walks, and on drives in the family car to grapple with the problem. Rockefeller secrecy and caution must give way to openness and a willingness to experiment, King insisted. John must understand that a new social spirit was in the air. Corporate investors like himself were as much responsible for labor conditions as on-site managers. King went to Colorado to investigate the situation. Abby and John struggled to move forward in their thinking. In December the strikers, exhausted in defeat, returned to the mines.

A month later, in January 1915, John appeared before the United States Commission on Industrial Relations meeting in New York City. The chairman, Senator Frank P. Walsh, was determined to find John guilty of leading the strike-breaking effort, but John's conversion had begun. Members of the committee heard some surprising testimony—that he welcomed constructive changes in labor-management relations and believed that absentee directors like himself could no longer remain aloof. Outside the hearing room, King introduced him to Mary Harris "Mother" Jones, the matron who traveled around the nation to support poor people in trouble—child laborers, persecuted Wobblies, jailed union leaders, female garment workers on picket lines. Often she languished in jail. In a later meeting arranged by King, she apologized to John for maligning him and said that she had done him an injustice. A news report had it that he promised her then and there that he would go personally to the camps. Evidently Abby met her as well, for John, without providing any details, later said to Fosdick, "She adored my wife."[3]

But Walsh was not finished with John. After subpoenaing John's correspondence with the company officials in Denver during the early days of the strike, Walsh believed that he now had damaging evidence of John's vehement anti-unionism. He called the hearing in Washington, and on a sweltering day in May, John took the stand again. Abby, eight months pregnant, forbidden by her doctor to travel, waited at home for the results. "Could Mr. Lee [Ivy Lee, the Rockefeller publicist] telephone tonight if you are too tired?" she wired John. "Am so anxious to hear how things are going. . . ."[4]

Things went better than expected. Walsh's badgering of the witness angered even his supporters in the press. Although the subpoenaed letters proved that John had backed Bowers's harsh tactics, they did not support Walsh's accusation that John had masterminded the whole tragic episode.

In September, John kept his promise to Mother Jones to visit the mining camps. Abby pleaded to go with him, but she was overruled. The danger was considered too great. Reporters followed him, and King was his guide. Donning miner's overalls, John descended into the deepest shafts, jawboned with workmen, shared the daily fare of beans and mashed potatoes, and sopped up the gravy with pieces of bread.

"The papers are keeping me very well posted on your doings and sayings," Abby wrote. ". . . If you can help bring about a solution of the labor problem . . . I shall die satisfied. . . . I know . . . that this is only one of the first steps . . . but . . . it is in absolutely the right direction. . . . From the papers I gather that your dancing has been one of your greatest assets. I will never demur again."[5]

Her allusion to his dancing refers to one of those spontaneous gestures, seemingly of little consequence, that galvanizes audiences —in this case the unseen audience across the nation. After delivering a short talk at a social evening set up in his honor at the Cameron camp schoolhouse, John asked that the floor be cleared for a dance. The orchestra broke into a fox-trot, John took the arm of the superintendent's wife, and before the evening was over he had danced—or so the exaggerated report declared—with every woman in the room!

On September 30, John was able to get through to Abby on the phone. And on October 6, King fulfilled his promise to write her a full report. Filling eleven pages of typescript, he sketched in most of the details that had been suggested by the press. The dance at Cameron was John's own idea, as much of a surprise to King himself as to John's friends in New York. "Nothing could have been more successful than the work of the first week," he wrote, likening it to a political tour, full of the incidents that public men experience in campaigning. He described the way John entered every corner of the workers' lives, how he listened with patience and humility. Such a tour could have been a disaster. Instead it was a triumph, as bitterness gave way to trust and enmity to goodwill. He closed his letter with some prophetic words. "I cannot but feel that this visit is epoch-making in his [Mr. Rockefeller's] own life, as it will also prove epoch-making in the industrial history of this continent. From now on he will be able to devote his time to advancing the vast projects . . . [relating] to human well-being, without being thwarted at every step by . . . the voice . . . of popular prejudice."[6]

Three years later Abby would finally persuade John to take her to Colorado. The occasion was a memorial service at Ludlow to remember the people who had died in the camp tragedy. Hundreds of families gathered in an open plain for the service. The fuel manager of CF&I warned John that the crowd could "tear him to pieces" and that Abby, in particular, should say behind.[7] But Abby prevailed. John eloquently describes her experience in a letter to Senior dated June 2, 1918.

> If you could know how much good Abby's presence in the mining camps is doing I am sure you would feel that the expense of this trip was more than worth while, not because of its influence on the officials and employees of the Fuel Company, but also because of the help which I believe it will be in inspiring other women, similarly situated, to give tangible evidence of their interest in workers in industry.
>
> I supposed at the outset that after a couple of days in the mining camps Abby would go to Denver to be with Elsie, her sister. She has become so interested in the trip, however, that she has not been willing to omit a single camp and has gone everywhere that the rest of us have. The officials of the company have valued so highly the influence which her presence is having upon the women and children in the camps that they have been eager that she should not skip a single place. In each camp she has met large groups of the women and has chatted with them about the Red Cross and other matters while she knitted. She has also made it a point to gather together as many of the children as possible and treat them to candy, sodas and ice cream.[8]

The climactic months of the Ludlow crisis had been a season of personal grief for both Abby and John. On March 12, 1915, Laura Spelman Rockefeller died. It was not a surprise; her health had been failing for years. But the ambiguous nature of John's relationship to her—awe, dependence, and perhaps resentment, in equal measure—gave his loss a complicated edge.

A month later, on the morning of April 16, Abby was called to her parents' New York residence at 908 Fifth Avenue. Nelson Aldrich was unconscious. Moments after she arrived, to stand at his bedside with Lucy and her brother Winthrop, he died of a cerebral stroke. The family accompanied the body on the train to

Providence for the funeral service at Grace Church. Burial was at the family plot in Swan's Point Cemetery a few feet from the small headstone of polished red granite that marked the grave of an infant child the dead man himself had once mourned, Nelson Aldrich, Jr., 1867–1871.

Abby's sadness over her father's death was pure and unequivocal. He was the parent with whom she had the special relationship, the one who nurtured her and admired her and the one she admired in return. Her mother's condition was so bad now that the family doctor advised against telling her of her husband's death. "Dr. Peterson feels that it might prove fatal to Mamma if we told her, and so far it has not been difficult to keep it from her," Abby wrote to Lucy Greene. "It has been a great comfort to feel that she is being spared this great sorrow, which I am sure would have been too much to bear."[9] Edith Rockefeller McCormick, writing a condolence letter from Zurich, where she was a disciple of Jung, probably summed up as succinctly as anyone the family's view of Abby. "I fancy by nature you are so adaptable. This is a wonderful thing —it simplifies so much."[10]

Abby's sixth and last child, a boy, was born on June 12, three months after the death of Laura Spelman, two months after the death of her father, scarcely a month after John's Washington appearance before the Walsh Commission. Her health had not been good during this pregnancy. The deaths of family members and unremitting tension over Ludlow was certainly part of the reason. "The new baby is splendid," Abby wrote Lucy Greene in August. "He seems to be an exceedingly bright little chap. . . . It's John's turn to name him."[11] John chose David.

In November, Abby went with John to the Spa at Hot Springs, Arkansas. "Much as I would like to have you home," Florence Scales wrote, "I can only urge you to stay and complete the treatment. I know just how much you miss the children, but I feel that you will be able to do more for them this winter if you are well and strong."[12] To describe Miss Scales as a children's nurse misses the mark. She was Abby's surrogate. No matter what other mademoiselles or nannies or tutors came and went, she was the dependable person in charge. Abby trusted her intelligence and her judgment, and that trust created an environment for the children that was dramatically different from what we know of other rich families.

Homesick for the children, Abby received daily reports from Miss Scales. Nelson was on the way to captivating all his caretakers. "I do believe myself," Scales wrote, "that the child could read if he would put his mind on it. He is just as fascinating as ever. I haven't the heart to scold him when he wiggles and loses his place and asks all sorts of questions in the middle of a sentence. John [3rd] thinks that I should be more severe with him!!"[13] But severity did not work with Nelson. He had to give up dessert after dumping his paint powders on Winthrop's head, but then he cheerfully chewed on a piece of gristle while the others were eating their sweets.

There was continued fretting about John 3rd's pallor and sleeplessness. Aunt Lucy Aldrich was quite upset, reported Scales, with the way he looked, but on the other hand, even when he wasn't doing anything he looked tired, and at the moment of this letter was searching for pebbles and a tiny tree to fix up a miniature Japanese garden for his room. Laurance, age five, was, for the time being at least, neither coughing nor sneezing. His greatest excitement was the walk in Central Park with Miss Kline to watch some big boys play football. David, the baby, was just a dear, but he definitely missed his mother.

During weekends in the country, Babs rehearsed the three older boys in a play to be performed for the staff, "The Honest Woodman." Ellen Milton was the good fairy and Nelson was the "dishonest" woodman. John's horror of publicity and adherence to Baptist values combined with Abby's abundantly affectionate nature and old Providence's rejection of glitter created an environment for Babs that was somewhat different from, say, that of a Peggy Guggenheim or a Flora Vanderbilt Whitney. Guggenheim governesses tended to be harshly Germanic and repressed, and the Whitney-Vanderbilt world was symbolized by the extravagant galas and strings of polo ponies that were rarely out of the headlines. Babs's world, by contrast, conveys both innocence and isolation. She sews curtains for her miniature playhouse at Pocantico, plants potatoes, knits dishtowels for the kitchen at Abeyton Lodge. She walks over to the chicken farm to see 375 baby chicks, drawing their pictures on her letter to her mother. "I am going to begin a flower and fern collection with Mlle. Rose, if you will let me buy a flower book to put them into and a lot of blotting paper and a flower press and a fern book. . . . When are you coming home and how are you? Everyone keeps asking me those two questions."[14]

Her current relationship with her father was as easy as could be expected with a man of John's complex character. She was his first child, the daughter he wished to cherish and protect. Perceiving her shyness as akin to his own, he tried to reach out to her. One winter they traveled together from Seal Harbor to New York, sharing supper in their drawing room and stepping outside at Bangor to stroll along the platform. After breakfast, John wrote Abby, he took her to a ladies' dressing room, where she brushed her teeth with toothbrush and powder stored in his pocket.

"I certainly miss you very much," Babs wrote him during one of their early separations, "specially in the morning when you used to come in and sit on the bed and rub my hands and say nice things to me."[15]

Abby returned from Hot Springs in good enough spirits to consider buying herself some sables. After six pregnancies in twelve years, she was ready to think about clothes again. "If you will let me," John wrote, "I should like to give them to you. I like to think of the soft rich fur snuggled up against your neck and cheek, where I should like my head to be."[16]

In August they went to Maine. In September, John went to Nova Scotia. Abby wrote with news of the children. The Sunday-night hymn-singing was a complete failure without him. "Nelson slept with me for 5 nights [Nelson was now eight] and now John [age ten] is having his turn, Laurance [six] comes next."[17] She capitalized on his absence by hiring a boat for a sailing picnic to Cranberry Island.

John could only reply that he was trying simply to exist and not think about anyone but her, "whom I . . . miss very, very much. I am sure I wasn't meant to live away from you."[18]

During the winter in Manhattan, Abby kept a fearful daily

watch over her mother, for Abby Pearce was dying from what John later described as an incurable malady. Her death, from pneumonia, came on February 16, 1917, at the age of seventy-two, in her New York apartment. The family gathered for a private service and then traveled to Providence for the interment beside her husband at Swan Point Cemetery.

"The pain of such a loss as yours," Helen Flexner wrote Abby, "seems hardly lessened by the slowness of its approach, and the world seems somehow a different place when one no longer has in it a parent. . . . On the one occasion when I had the privilege of seeing Mrs. Aldrich I was greatly impressed by the vigor of her intelligence and the power of her personality. These qualities live on in you and your children and are a kind of sacred trust."[19]

Lucy Greene, too, alluded to the years when Abby Pearce had been an assertive presence in the family. "As time goes by," she wrote, ". . . you will have a much clearer recollection as she was then, than you will of these later pathetic years."[20] But what was more immediate, Lucy cautioned, was for Abby herself to recognize what she had been through and take the absolute rest from anxiety that she needed.

Abby appreciated the good advice but did not heed it. One of her immediate worries was her sister Lucy, who admitted to feeling forlorn and homeless, a jarring experience for a woman who prided herself on her independence. During the years since their father's death, she had been their mother's constant companion. Her deafness made living alone impossible. Something had to be done about the Benevolent Street house and also the estate at Warwick. Abby felt a little easier when Minnie MacFadden, who had nursed Abby Pearce, offered to become a paid companion to Lucy, and Lucy agreed.

For the first few weeks after the funeral, Abby charged ahead, managing households and obligations, husband and children, but then suddenly she stopped sleeping and developed a severe neuritis. "Unfortunately," she admitted to Lucy Greene, "I did not follow [your wise counsel] . . . thinking I could disregard my own feelings. . . . The doctor has sent me off to Virginia [for a rest cure]. . . . I think if I had been quiet or had gone away . . . after

Mamma died, that I would have saved myself and the family all this inconvenience and annoyance."[21] Inconvenient and annoying —that was how Abby viewed any problem with her own health. She assumed that the doctor would be satisfied if she withdrew for a few weeks. To her horror he ordered her to postpone all major responsibilities for six months.

CHAPTER 12

The United States declared war on Germany on the evening of April 2, 1917. A light rain fell on Pennsylvania Avenue as Woodrow Wilson, in the presidential limousine, official flags flying, approached the Capitol to deliver the most eloquent speech of his career. In 1916 he had campaigned on a peace platform, but when the German High Command began to sink American merchant ships on sight, he abandoned the idea of neutrality. From the Allied point of view, America's move was not a moment too soon. Overriding the objections of M.P. Winston Churchill and Prime Minister Lloyd George, General Sir Douglas Haig had launched a disastrous assault on German positions near Passchendaele. For three months Haig kept up the attack. Three hundred thousand men died to gain ten thousand yards of swamp and muck. In Russia, Czar Nicholas II had abdicated, leaving the Allies to wonder whether Russia might collapse altogether or withdraw from the war, as Lenin advocated.

America's rapid mobilization confounded the skeptics both at home and abroad. Wilson swept through the confusion with direct presidential intervention and the creation of emergency agencies. The Selective Service Administration delegated to local draft boards the responsibility for registering 24 million young men, of whom over two million were ultimately inducted into the army. Herbert Hoover and Harry Garfield respectively ran the Food Administration and Fuel Administration, and the combination of consumer restraint and powerful market forces sent food and fuel production soaring.

With the resolution of the Ludlow crisis, the public perception of the name Rockefeller had begun to change. John was moving into the field of industrial relations. Senior, the builder of America's oil empire, was accorded fresh respect. "The Allies," Lord Curzon would later declare, "had floated to victory on a wave of oil."[1] The breadth and depth of Rockefeller Foundation philanthropy, from conservation to public health to historic preservation to education, was gradually seeping into the public consciousness. Freed from the hostility that had dogged most of her married life and aroused by the needs of a nation at war, Abby began to venture out in ways that would have been unthinkable earlier.

On August 30, 1917, Raymond Fosdick, chairman of the War Department's Commission on Training Camp Activities, asked Abby to serve on something called the Committee on Protection of Girls. Abby accepted. She realized that this had to do with the problem of runaway teenagers hanging around military camps. Fosdick was John's friend from the days when together they had investigated venereal disease, drug addiction, and juvenile delinquency in New York.

Abby believed that the time had come to instruct young women in "social morality," a euphemism for sex education. But beyond that, she was most concerned about providing decent housing for the women who were entering the work force in great numbers. Fosdick would be in a strategic position to help her when she was ready to move, so it was wise to cooperate with him as much as possible.

She prepared her ground with him carefully. "I am deeply grateful to you for your assistance," she had written in November. "I feel that your having seen the Secretary of War and the Director of Housing has impressed them more than a delegation of women."[2] Over the winter she continued to query him. "I very much want more information about what England is doing in regard to her enlisted women," she wrote. "I am told this information is in the State Department. Could your office get this for us? . . . Can you have someone get for me the facts about the number of women already employed in war work. . . . I am told that the Department of Labor probably knows their figures, and they would be much more likely to give them to someone in your office than to me."[3]

Her tactics evidently bore fruit, for on January 31, 1918, the *New York Times* reported that Mrs. John D. Rockefeller, Jr., was in Washington, conferring with Secretary of War Newton Baker on plans for improving housing conditions among women employed in government and munitions factories. Upon her return to New York she wrote to Fosdick. "I see by this morning's paper that the housing question had been put back in the Labor Department, to be settled and remain there, I hope. . . . Would you be kind enough, the minute you find out who is head of this newly created department, to let me know? I want very much to lay before him the woman side of the question as soon as possible. . . ."[4]

Believing that the War Work Council of the YWCA National Board was the most effective vehicle for implementing her ideas, Abby became chairman of its housing committee. Now she proposed that her people be permitted to erect demonstration housing for women on government land. At the end of ten years, the government would take over the building at a reasonable price and turn it to any purpose it wished.

"Personally," she wrote Fosdick, "I think if some one would help to solve the problem of giving the women who are working in various government departments a decent, quiet, comfortable place to live in, they would not want to give it up at the end of ten years. We would run the cafeteria in such a big way that many of the girls from the department building could go there to lunch and be served quickly. . . . I realize perfectly what a difficult and I might say impossible thing I am trying to do, but if we could get either through your Commission or through the Housing Commission some sort of an arrangement with the Government to house its employees, I think we can put it through. . . ."[5]

On another, more sensitive issue, Abby reminded him, as gently as possible, that he should put a woman on his staff, "a very strong able, tactful woman. . . . perhaps from the west, such as the Dean of Women at the University of Wisconsin, who has been in no way connected with all the discriminations that have existed in the various organizations. . . . This is very confidential. I would not like anyone to know that I had even made such a suggestion, as it would get us both into trouble."[6]

Fosdick was silent about the women's issue, but referred the housing problems to someone on his staff. "I have taken up your plan . . ." a Mr. L. H. Nichols wrote Abby on February 23, "[and] those interested in the Washington housing problem welcomed your suggestion of the erection of a demonstration building by the Y.W.C.A. . . . [Everyone feels] that your plan is an excellent one, and one which should be pushed through immediately. As construction will probably take three or four months, they are anxious to have you start right away."[7]

Charleston, South Carolina, was the site of the first demonstration structure, built to accommodate a hundred women employed in making uniforms for the navy, many of them from isolated mountain villages. The national wire services picked up the story after several reporters, including Margery Rex of the *Progressive Labor World*, interviewed Abby at 10 West 54th. They gathered in her third-floor office, the only one with any heat, for coal was severely rationed. Abby explained the fine details of her planning —shady verandas, recreation and reading rooms, kitchenette on each floor, and supervision for the younger guests, this being still the day of housemothers and parietal rules, but mature women should not be held to the same restrictions.

Across the country in Seattle, the local paper described Abby in headlines as "Sister to the Munition Worker and Side Partner of the Woman Who Goes to the Camp to Work." The writer told its readers about her father, Nelson Aldrich, the smart, silent leader of the Republican Party, and the "daughter, [who] may rightly be measured by the mental standard of the senator, for she is showing that he did not cut her off in his will when his ability was being distributed for posterity. . . . Where other women might have stopped with argument to a world that was too busy to listen, the daughter of the old senator went straight to Washington, to the secretary of war and to the officials with a concrete plan of action and a demand for performance. . . . Citizeness Abby G. Rockefeller . . . heard the bugle calling to the men, and she knew that its echo was intended, also, for the women of the land."[8]

Abby began to speak in public. She went to Charleston to inspect the new residence hall, appearing on a panel with an official from the Department of Labor. "I managed to speak to them for about five minutes," she wrote Lucy. "I wish that I had had more courage, because I keep thinking of things that I might have said."[9]

Closer to home, she persuaded Senior to put his unoccupied house at 4 West 54th on a virtual war footing. In the basement five hundred workers from the Red Cross Auxiliary of the Fifth Avenue Baptist Church sewed flannel pajamas for military hospitals. In the drawing rooms, dining rooms, and hall, young people, including the Rockefeller children, rolled bandages. "We boys were given white uniforms," Winthrop wrote, "and carried the bandages from the places they were being made to the tables where they were being packed. It gave us a feeling that we were participating and helped us to understand the serious realities behind the parades."[10] The three upper floors were converted to living quarters for women who enrolled in special courses conducted by the War Work Council.

Abby organized a shipment of sweaters, mittens, and socks for the Russian front. "I wondered if . . . you would not tell [the Russian women]," she wrote the liaison person, "that all the women who packed these bags are working women; some of them are school teachers, some stenographers, librarians, trained nurses, clerks, etc. I think the Russian women would be glad to know this."[11]

In France, General Pershing's American divisions were taking the offensive. At home, food rationing, bond drives, and victory gardens were the stuff of everyday life. In the Rockefeller kitchens, long rows of glasses bearing the week's ration of sugar were labeled for each member of the family. One young visitor wrote to his parents during the summer of 1918, "The R's are doing everything that [Herbert] Hoover wishes the people of the U.S. to do. . . .

We have bacon only twice a week and I have not had a bite of beef . . . since I've been here."[12]

At Pocantico the children planted and weeded their gardens. Winthrop sold his pumpkins to his father; the others carted their produce to market in their play wagons to be sold at the local grocery store. Nelson and Laurance expanded their operation to raise rabbits. They bought pairs from the Rockefeller Institute, cleaned and fed them, and then sold the progeny back to the institute. Like their father before them, they went tapping for maple syrup, exasperating the cooks with their boiling and stirring of huge caldrons. Much excitement, especially for the younger boys, came from the stocking of the icehouse—cutting ice from the reservoir in the winter, storing it in the insulated icehouse for use in the summer.

The restrained grandeur that the public has come to associate with Pocantico was not yet in evidence. Abeyton Lodge, in spite of its additions and improvements, was still architecturally nondescript, cheerful with cretonne and chintz, rambling off in unexpected directions, its most inviting radius Abby's second-floor sitting room. The surrounding hills were good for coasting, bullfrogs yammered in the tiny pond, Kykuit pools were used for swimming, one tennis court served Babs and John 3rd for their long-running sets.

"It wasn't exactly poverty," Laurance said with a straight face. "We had bicycles and ponies and later on we had the red bugs [four-wheeled buckboards, powered by a Smith Motor Wheel attached to the rear, perfect vehicles for underage drivers]. But we had no idea of the enormous, *latent* wealth. After all, we had to keep those elaborate account books for father. We were on a pretty tight string, though nothing as tough as our Prentice cousins," he added.[13]

Spelman Prentice just laughed at the notion that his Uncle John was forbidding. "I always thought that was funny," he said. "I told Win, you guys don't know what forbidding is." Ezra Prentice required his children to be dressed in formal clothes at dinner every night, and to converse in Latin. For the slightest infraction their allowances were cut off. They were not permitted to bring friends

Winter scene at Abeyton Lodge, Pocantico Hills.
Courtesy of the Rockefeller Archive Center.

home. "It was Aunt Abby who made the difference for the Rocke-fellers," he ruminated. "She was great, always frank, her feet on the ground, relaxed with people. When we went to her house, which wasn't often enough, we were amazed. There was dancing, there were picnics. She tried to get us to mix more, but it was impossible. We were too intimidated. My father ran us and my mother just accepted."[14]

The Prentice children knew that Abby was their advocate. John Prentice would write her some years later, "As [we] grow older, we begin to realize what [a] constant and good friend . . . you have been to us always. . . ."[15] Abby worried about John's lonely, motherless niece Margaret Strong, whose father shepherded her back and forth across the ocean. It was Margaret who would later marry the Spanish marquis George de Cuevas. "I want to thank you very much," she wrote from on board ship, "and most sin-cerely for having me to stay with you. . . . My only regret is that I could not have been more with <u>you</u>—and I fear that I still have rather a grudge against the Y.W. and other societies for taking so much of your time. . . . I am awfully sorry to leave you . . . and already begin to feel how much I shall miss [you]."[16]

For Abby, as for her children, Pocantico offered some release from the formality of city life. Her favorite mode of transportation was the old black Baker electric auto, vintage 1902. She was interested in the forests and the creatures that inhabited them, taking the trouble one year to order special traps to transport an overpopulation of squirrels to an upstate game preserve. She watched the swans parade in the watery landscape, listened to the sound of horses' hooves reverberating through the woods as they trotted across the wide planks of the wooden bridges.

It was at Pocantico that Abby saw the most of Senior. Imperturbable and unhurried, he played his daily round of golf, watched the stock market, enjoyed a game of hide-and-seek with his grandchildren. Every Sunday the whole family trooped up to Kykuit for the two-hour lunch. For the children their grandfather was more fun than their father. His prayers were shorter. He tolerated their rambunctious ways better. And they were positive that he told better stories than Will Rogers. All the correspondence suggests that Abby and Senior interacted in the easiest possible way. "Grandfather and Mother were like two breezes gently waiting each other," Laurance remarked in a simile that seems to describe the complete absence of confrontation in their relationship.[17] A greater contrast to her own husband would be hard to find. "Let the world wag," Senior would counsel his son.[18]

But it was not as an affable old gentleman with the good sense to stay aloof from their lives that Senior shaped Abby's destiny and the destiny of her family. It was the fortune that he gave to the world and the fortune that he gave to his son. His gifts to the four great Rockefeller philanthropies were rapidly approaching $440 million. He had completed the transfer of funds to trusts for his two daughters, Alta and Edith. But the balance of the fortune, nearly $500 million, had yet to be distributed.

Quietly, without the drama of elaborate instructions and restrictions, Senior began the transfer of his fortune to John—huge blocks of stocks and bonds in the following manner:

"I am giving you 20,000 shares of the stock of the Standard oil company of Indiana, of the capitalization of $30,000,000." (1917)[19]

"I am this day giving you . . . 241,012 shares of Standard of California." (1918)[20]

"I am today giving you $20,688,000 par value in bonds of the State of New York and Corporate Stock of the City of New York." (1920)[21]

"I am this day giving you $65,000,000, par value, of the United States government First Liberty Loan of 3½% bonds." (1920)[22]

"I am this day giving you the following securities: $14,970,500 United States Government bonds, 3½% and 3¾%" (1921), etc., etc.[23]

If Senior was laconic, John was voluble. Only rarely was he at a loss for words. "Alas," he wrote once, "your generosity far outstrips my ability to tell you of my gratitude."[24] In response to the gifts of cash, often in increments of $500,000, he resorted to humor. "What a delightful habit you are forming!"[25] But most of the time he wrote long passages of humility and passion. "Just plain 'Thank You' sounds so insufficient, so heartless and so inexpressive, in comparison with the deep feelings of love and gratitude which I have in my heart for you. . . . My only hope is that in my life and the things which I undertake to do, I can prove to you . . . my profound appreciation of the confidence which you repose in me and of the unbounded love which you have shown me."[26]

The passage of the federal inheritance tax in 1916 certainly affected Senior's decision. But even so, the gift tax he paid was not inconsiderable—25 percent on estates of $10 million or more. He had watched John recover from a nervous breakdown, command the loyalty of a farsighted, generous-spirited woman, and surmount the trauma of Ludlow. He now judged, rightly as it turned out, that his only son would manage the fortune with prudence and originality. Senior lived another twenty years. Had he loved money as much as myth would have it, he would not have left himself with a $25 million pittance when he could have held on to half a billion.

As John's net worth was climbing from $20 million to $500 million (approximately $3.5 billion in 1992 dollars), Abby's imme-

Abby and John strike a pose ca. 1916.
Courtesy of the Rockefeller Archive Center.

diate finances and daily life changed only marginally. Her allowance remained the same, John selected art which seemed to please her as well as him, and he bought her beautiful jewels, which she rarely wore in public, but kept in a household vault she laughingly referred to as Aladdin's Cave. As Senior continued to send her $1,000 checks and occasional gifts of stocks and bonds, she hastened to assure him that her personal financial picture was just fine:

> Dear Mr Rockefeller—I didn't half tell you how much I appreciated your giving me those Con Steel and Iron bonds because I was afraid that something I might have said had made you feel that I didn't have all the money I wanted or needed which is very far from being the case. John gives me a most generous allowance of ten thousand dollars a year for my clothes. From the various magnificent presents that you have given me I have an income of $5000.00 which enables me to give sometimes to any charity or good work that I want to. The income of the trust fund which my father gave me will be in the future $5000.00 With this I can do as I please. Then I shall have an income from the one-hundred thousand dollars recently left by my father. So you can see I am an exceedingly fortunate woman. But nevertheless I do like very much to have you show your confidence in me by trusting me with money. . . .[27]

"The only time I ever felt shy or uncomfortable was at certain society affairs when I didn't know the boys who were from the better prep schools," Nelson Rockefeller once said. "I didn't fit into their group."[28] In spite of that, he thanked his Lincoln School experience for his ability to step out of a car in Harlem or Chinatown and feel perfectly at home.

The Lincoln School was inspired by John Dewey, invented in all its details by Abraham Flexner, and financed by the General Education Board. Flexner had convinced the board that only a demonstration school with the freedom to experiment with curricula and teaching methods could reform America's obsolete educational system. For a decade he had run a small school in Kentucky, whose graduates had impressed President Eliot of Harvard. "It was all very simple," Flexner had said disarmingly to Eliot when he traveled to Cambridge to explain his methods. "I treated these boys as individuals and then I let each go at his own pace." Of course, it proved to be much more complicated than that.[29]

The school opened in September 1917 at 646 Park Avenue under the aegis of Columbia University Teachers College. Later it moved to its own new building at 123rd Street and Amsterdam Avenue. It enrolled 113 boys and girls from diverse backgrounds in grades one through twelve. Some were children of teachers, artists, and professionals, a few were from minority families, a few from the rich Jewish establishment such as the Warburgs, but none were quite like the Rockefellers. Flexner handpicked his twenty-three teachers for their originality and dedication to his goals. The elementary school offered special work in music, in the fine and industrial arts, in the natural sciences, in home economics, and in physical education. The high school had courses in mathematics, English, biology, physics, social studies, and the modern foreign languages. Flexner discarded Latin, convinced that the mastery of it served no purpose. Unusual opportunities were created for travel and field trips, the library was outstanding, and an expert testing and guidance program monitored the students from the day they entered.

A democratic atmosphere prevailed, as the students wrote their own class rules and were in charge, as much as practical, of their own conduct. Contrary to popular fears of the day, a kind of happy anarchy did not take hold. The lack of sexual stereotyping was impressive, with boys studying sewing and cooking and girls taking shop courses. Flexner conceded that spelling and the multiplication tables might be taught by compulsion, but relied for the most part on the Dewey method of skills being derived from need. The third-grade study of boats—their design and construction—became the introduction to history, geography, science, etc.

The richness of the curriculum, especially in the arts and in social studies, and the opportunity to work at what one enjoyed touched Abby's intuitive sense of what was right for young people. Apart from all that, her own emotional makeup, the way she stayed close to her brood, watching over them and hugging them to her, made a day school much more appealing than a boarding school.

For John, the value of Lincoln was more socioeconomic than

aesthetic or emotional. He had large ambitions for his sons, not as builders of yet another great fortune, but as individuals who could make a difference in matters of world health and human welfare, matters with which the Rockefeller philanthropies he now headed up were deeply concerned. It troubled him that his children were born into the rarefied hothouse environment of extraordinary wealth. Perhaps the daily give-and-take of Lincoln, the association with young people different from themselves, could prepare them for the awesome challenges he foresaw in their adulthood.

John 3rd did not transfer to Lincoln. He remained in the tiny (six in a class) Browning School, one block from his house, still the inspiration of its original headmaster, the same John A. Browning who had taught his father twenty-five years earlier. Abby and John were uneasy about plunging the somewhat timid, overly conscientious boy into the highly charged, experimental atmosphere of Lincoln. Perhaps they erred. There were benefits for shy boys in such a free environment.

Babs was already receiving a good education at Brearley, which had been founded to give girls an education equal to that available to boys. An atmosphere of scholarship pervaded the entire school. "Fresh from the parochial atmosphere where women were expected to stay at home except when shopping, associating with their friends or engaged in church work," Nathalie Dana, a former student, wrote, "education at Brearley was breath-taking."[30] Babs transferred briefly to Lincoln, but was miserable; she "detested it," she later stated, without being specific.[31] In a letter to Abby written at the time, however, she was quite specific. "I like the teachers and the lessons better than I did at first but I don't like the girls nearly as much as I did. Those of them who live in better houses and have more maids are constantly making very pointed remarks about how little the others have and they of course don't like it and pretend to have things they haven't. They all squabble about who has the prettiest ring or the most expensive watch etc. . . . If in Brearley one girl talked like they do she would be immediately disliked by the rest of the class."[32] Abby could not quarrel with such insights, since they had been carefully inculcated at home.

Babs was unhappy at summer camp too. The isolation of her childhood combined with an inherent shyness and reserve filled her with a feeling of dread, perhaps, when she was thrust among adolescent girls. In any case she soon left Lincoln for Chapin.

Laurance, in his understated, wry style, thrived. "We loved the Lincoln School," he recalled. "It was a blessing, so normalizing, no status connected to it, nothing at all like a fashionable prep school. There we were in the real outer world. That was where I learned to participate, to make my way with all kinds of people."[33] Abby O'Neill agrees. "It was the greatest thing that ever happened to the Rockefeller boys, that they went to Lincoln, because of the absence of rigid standards."[34]

For Nelson, who was alarming his father even as he charmed his mother, Lincoln was a liberating experience. He could argue freely with his teachers. He could try his hand at any project that intrigued him. Although he was a poor reader, he could learn about the world from the "dramatic play" so integral to the curriculum.

At home, however, he was restless, full of jokes, late for meals, a general disturber of his father's peace. Like his father, he was left-handed. Like other parents of the day, John believed that left-handedness was simply an unfortunate habit that could be broken. First he tried simple persuasion, then a device of putting a rubber band around Nelson's left wrist, attaching a string to the rubber band, and holding the string in his own hand from the head of the table. The idea was to tug gently on the string whenever Nelson used his dominant left hand. That this technique caused only some childish confusion and not more serious problems was a lucky accident. Nelson grew up more or less ambidextrous.

His reading problem was much more stubborn. Nelson was a slow reader all his life, with a striking inability to spell. What neither parent realized, because it was not yet understood, was that Nelson's reading disability was a form of dyslexia, a condition which causes children to have difficulty perceiving the shapes of words. Letters and numbers appear to bob and weave on the page, sometimes dancing off the edge, other times transposing themselves. The fundamental cause of the disorder is still uncertain, though there seems to be a biological component, since it often runs in families. It is unrelated to intelligence, and contrary to previous studies, seems to afflict girls and boys in equal numbers.

Referring to himself as one of the "puzzle children," an adult Nelson Rockefeller reminded a television audience that he had followed the advice of a wise counselor at Lincoln. He worked harder and longer, he learned to concentrate, and he made the best possible use of his competitive spirit.

John's affirmation of Flexner's educational philosophy did not carry over to the rearing of his children. Rationally, perhaps, he could acknowledge the noisy self-expression of Lincoln as having some merit, but psychologically he was bound up in Spelman sobriety, caution, and rigid expectations. If the Rockefeller children were ever to reconcile the opposing environments of home and school, it would be Abby, not John, who could ease them from one world to the other.

As constantly as he hectored them to do their duty, sometimes it seemed as though John were really afraid of the children, afraid of the burden of bringing them safely to maturity. Abby was no less ambitious for them, but hers was an ambition tempered by the knowledge that children usually defy expectations. She tried to explain him to his children—his introversion, his conscience, his compulsions. She rationalized to them that he was her tower of strength and they must appreciate him. "Perhaps there is a little bit too much Aldrich in us," she would remark ruefully, "and not enough Rockefeller."[35] But children are intuitive about parents and the Rockefeller children no less than others. They sensed how carefully their father rationed his emotions, how often he went to bed with migraine headaches. They saw how he valued order and predictability and realized that their own high spirits did not always submit to orderliness.

But more significant than personality quirks or differences in outlook was their unhappy conviction that they were the competition. At the most subliminal level of understanding they perceived Abby as belonging to John and they, the children, as in some primitive sense the interlopers. "We grew up realizing that we had to compete with Father for her time and attention," David said.

Abby with her three young sons ca. 1916. From left to right:
Winthrop, David, Laurance.
Courtesy of the Rockefeller Archive Center.

"We knew how much she enjoyed us and cared for us and that the conflict between his needs and ours caused her much anguish. It was her constant and never-ending struggle, it was the cause of her greatest stress, and she was never able to resolve it. He expected her to be available when he needed her and his needs seemed insatiable."[36] In an effort to be even-handed in his reflections, David added that when one of them was with John alone—not as a group; as a group they could overwhelm him and he would retreat —but alone, he could be warm and attentive, even allowing his sense of humor to break through.

Laura Chasin has theorized that John's all-consuming need for Abby and his power to control her environment so that such needs were met taught the next generation of Rockefeller men to place attachment and loyalty to husband above attachment and loyalty to children. According to Chasin's theory, the sons identified with the aggressor, as they watched their father envelop their mother. It is a provocative thesis, but it does not give sufficient weight to Abby's own strength and determination on behalf of her children. To study her letters to her sons is to meet a woman with deep reservoirs of sensitivity to their needs and desires, and as fully cognizant of her responsibilities as mother as of her responsibilities as wife. If she shortchanged anyone, it was very likely to be herself.

David's testimony may be more to the point. The competing needs of husband and children did not set up winner and loser, but rather placed Abby in the permanent situation of meeting unreasonable expectations. From the earliest days of her marriage, she understood John's psyche and what it would demand of her. If she made any misjudgment, it was to overestimate her own emotional and physical resources.

PART THREE

Public Works, Private Collecting

CHAPTER 13

*T*he war was over and Lucy Aldrich was traveling in the Orient. Her letters—like Lucy herself—were sharp, colorful, and opinionated.

"I think the United States had better encourage the expansion of Japan in Korea and Manchuria," she observed shrewdly. "I shouldn't like to have them coming down on us even if it is a small country." The sanitation was hopeless, the transportation worse. "I get tired being trundled around by somebody's grandfather with the perspiration running off him in streams." But she was intrigued with the religion. "I'd much rather be a Buddhist than a Baptist," she declared. She loved the temples, with their gold and lacquer, the beat of the drums, the smell of the incense. "I think you could get more women to belong to the bible class if you could have a stage set like that. . . ."

As for shopping, she reported, the Japanese prints were almost all gone. Even the Russians who had fled from the Communists were buying; those that were left were probably fakes. "I am having an awful case of shell shock about getting you anything. You have so many people who will tell you just how wrong they are after you get them . . . Mr. Candler . . . who will be kind but sad; the moth eaten Mr. Bosworth . . . and the pussy footed Mr.

Herter—I can't expect to please him if he doesn't approve of Sargent."[1]

With apologies to John for being catty, she dissected the personalities and attire of every person she met. The eighty-four-year-old mother of the consul-general of Korea looked like an uncooked English muffin with a liberal sprinkling of flour, wore a hat trimmed with white ostrich feathers in the midst of which she had pinned a bunch of real sweet peas. At a dance given by the French on July 14, Bastille Day, "you never saw such sights—old ladies dressed in 'simple white muslin'—lots of women too fat and lots too thin. We were right by the water," she added, "and I felt as tho the sea had given up its dead."[2]

"Lucy could be really naughty, the way she provoked people," her Aldrich nieces recalled.[3] There was a time, in her youth, when Abby had the same spice, the same frankness, the same unexpected wit. But then she married John. She changed—she had to. Resiliency, discretion, and tact were critical, if the marriage was to succeed. Lucy, on the other hand, never married. She could give in to exasperation. She could make her own decisions. Now that she was financially independent and free of an ailing mother, she could satisfy her roving curiosity, travel the world over, collect whatever she fancied, and still derive all the affection and family warmth she needed from her adoring nieces and nephews. She even used her deafness to advantage. Miss MacFadden listened for her, and with typical perverseness Lucy refused to wear a hearing aid, putting people in the unwelcome position of having to shout.

She was free in a way that Abby could never be. If Abby envied that freedom, she never said so in anyone's presence. Lucy talked about absolutely everything. She asked outrageous questions each time John lowered his head to say grace. Sitting out on the terrace of the Eyrie, if there was any unusual smell in the air, she would sniff and murmur, "Standard Oil."[4] John seemed more amused than offended. He never perceived Lucy as competition or as a threat. Both Abby and Lucy were smart women. They kept their relationship in discreet balance.

With the winding down of war projects, Abby turned her energies to peacetime housing for working women. Mackenzie King encouraged her to identify her YWCA housing committee with the needs of the industrial woman worker. "How can it [the YWCA] retain the word 'Christian,' " he wrote, "and not be concerned with women who are obliged to work for their living, and with the conditions under which they are obliged to work?"[5] Abby agreed. But as she wrote Fosdick, half the YWCA National Board were very timid and the mere word "industry" frightened them. Unable to bring her board with her into the area of legislation, she continued to push for improved housing. Before long she was speaking to a YWCA rally of over two hundred people.

"I dreaded it very much," she wrote Lucy, "but Babs who was there, and who, you know, is pretty critical, said that it went very well, which encouraged me greatly. Mr. Eliot told me that the only trouble with my paper was that it was too short."[6] It felt none too short to Abby. Her words were direct, fervent, and effective. "Women . . . are . . . unable to find decent rooms [within their means]. . . . It is comparatively easy for a man to find a place in which to live. . . . It is the [working] women . . . on whom the burden of the present condition falls most heavily. . . . women have less money and cannot pay high prices. . . . Every year increasing numbers of young women go into factories, shops or offices, and the situation is . . . acute. . . . What can be done to meet this intolerable condition?"

She answered her own rhetorical question. Already the various YWCA branches across the country were running cafeterias, setting up information banks, and surveying boarding homes. "The dream of the Emergency Housing Committee [which she chaired] is a very much enlarged and perfected rooms registry, more and better boarding homes for young girls in shops and industry, hotels for business women and players houses for the girls of the stage. To do this we need much faith, many more workers, and a great deal more money."[7]

She wanted to move ahead on housing for industrial workers' families, as well as for single working women. Ever since she had seen the dreary housing around the mining camps of Colorado, she had dreamed of building a model worker's house. It must be affordable, it must be attractive, and it must meet the needs of mother and children as well as father. The notion may seem simple enough now, but in 1919 it was still a fresh concept. "I have gotten Miss Budd who was the architect for the hostess houses to help me with the plan and we have worked out what seems to me a really excellent design," she wrote Lucy.[8] She was not too proud to use John's contacts. He introduced her to the president of Jersey Standard, who turned her over to Clarence Hicks, the same Hicks who had worked so creatively to improve labor relations at Ludlow.

After visiting various sites with Hicks, Abby decided on a location near the Bayonne plant in Elizabeth, New Jersey, adjacent to fifty company houses that Standard was constructing for its employees. In December 1919, John gave her $7,000, which, added to her own $4,000, enabled her to buy a lot forty by one hundred feet and build, furnish, and landscape a six-hundred-square-foot house.

Very soon she discarded the idea of limiting Bayway Cottage to the use of one family. Better to become a community house that would serve the needs of many families. Created through Abby's vision and resources, the cottage opened in 1920. Activities rotated constantly—baby clinic, English-language classes (most of the women were Polish), current-events lectures put on by the local high school faculty, meetings of the Women's Auxiliary of the Labor-Management Committee, even opportunities for the European women to demonstrate their ethnic crafts. Abby assumed permanent responsibility for the general overhead costs. Her former housekeeper Annie Davies became resident manager, and Florence Scales was her liaison.

When the Board of Education of Elizabeth, New Jersey, asked her to lay the cornerstone of its new Theodore Roosevelt School, the *New York Times* covered the event and the reception was held at Bayway Cottage across the street. Abby wrote her version of the experience to Babs and John 3rd. "I held about twenty-five naked, squirming, cunning, fat little babies, some of whom took the occasion to drench me. . . . every once in awhile they would all begin to howl at once."[9]

The intimacy of Bayway, the unpretentious, practical way it functioned, touched that core of Abby's character that responded

Bayway Cottage and Community House, 1926. Elizabeth, New Jersey.
Courtesy of the Rockefeller Archive Center.

to the ordinary concerns of ordinary people. It was not a matter of grand lady playing simple dairymaid. When Abby visited Bayway she was visiting mothers whose children caught cold exactly as hers did and quarreled as hers did, mothers whose ambitions for their children were not so different from Abby's for hers. She brought her own children to have lunch there and participate, when possible, in activities. "It was never what she did for us, though that was very much," a Bayway woman said. "It was not even what she taught us, though she taught us many new and good things. There was something inside her that got quick inside us and made us cry and laugh at once."[10]

In the winter of 1920, Abby's physician stepped in, as he occasionally did, to suggest that she go away by herself for a few weeks. She had mild hypertension, and she favored all the wrong foods —oysters, whipped cream, marbled meats, French cheeses—and scorned exercise. But his recommendation for the Homestead with its therapeutic baths and massages seemed to indicate a concern for her emotional state rather than some physiological problem. When taking her history he might learn that she was having insomnia again, or that her highly charged environment was causing her some anxiety. As the professional who had observed her over many years, he could understand that her sanguine temperament was working against her. Driven to counter John's constant anxiety with constant reassurance, she would not grant herself the right to be discouraged, certainly not the right to be depressed or rebellious. She might brood inwardly, but on the surface all must be well. It was April before she acquiesced to her doctor's recommendation.

"For the last three days I have felt very much better," she wrote Lucy. "I am having all my meals here in the sitting room and thoroughly enjoying myself. I am ashamed to say that I don't even feel lonely."[11] She dictated letters to her secretary, Anna Kelly; she hemstitched towels. "It is very soothing to my nerves to sew."[12] Her reading ranged across centuries and disciplines—Greek tragedy, history of the Renaissance, Civil War memoirs, questions of war and peace.

John sent her daily telegrams and Miss Scales reported on the children. John 3rd seemed sad in the morning, bright and cheerful by afternoon. Laurance and Nelson were beginning to badger Winthrop, David being too young yet to torment. Spring had come to Pocantico. The forsythia was blooming, and the lilac buds were swelling fast. Even the smallest children gathered bouquets for the staff—hyacinths and tulips, daffodils and pansies.

While Abby was in Virginia, Babs was in Boston sitting for John Singer Sargent. Lucy wrote her impressions to Abby. "Mr. Sargent was awful nice. He makes me think of a statue of Buddha in his colossal calm (it's really indifference of course) and if I could only kow-tow and retire it would make me much more comfortable. I'm so afraid of boring him—tho I don't think he'd let anyone go too far in that direction. I was dying to ask him when he was going to paint you, but thought it wouldn't be tactful. I have only seen the photograph of the sketch but think it is adorable. Not flattering but just Abby [Babs] at her best."[13] Lucy wrote more on Boston and Sargent after she and Babs returned to New York.

"The weather was dreadful. . . . I don't wonder the Boston people are what they are, the climate is too much for them. . . . Abby [Babs] said [the portrait] was much better looking than she is and [that] Mr. S. liked it. He said she was quite like some of Bottichelli's [sic] . . . subjects."[14]

Babs, at sixteen, did not quite believe the great Sargent. She did not think of herself as beautiful at all, and because of her father's chagrin with her lackluster performance at school, she had serious doubts about her intellectual ability. Her relationship with John was beginning to deteriorate. She deeply resented his supervising stance. She believed that as the oldest child she suffered the most from his rigid standards. For too many years now, she had made the early-morning trek to the library for prayers, "watching the fannies wave," as she irritably phrased it.[15] Even as an angry adolescent she knew rationally that her father loved her, but emotionally she was afraid of him, afraid of his sarcasm when she displeased him. Her fragile confidence was undermined by his unreasonable expectations, and she perceived his love to be more of a burden than a pleasure.

"Babs was the child he wanted to be close to," David said. "It was a bitter disappointment to him that they weren't, but he was stricter with her than with the rest of us."[16]

Abby and John wanted their only daughter to go to college. "Thus far she is genuinely adverse to the idea," John wrote Senior. "We have told her that we would not insist, but that we would expect her to pass her college examinations and . . . spend at least one year at college, after which she would be in a better position to decide whether or not it would be wise to go on with the course."[17] Babs had no intention of following such wishes. She acknowledged much later in her life that her way of rebelling against her father was to do badly in school.

Ironically, many of Babs's interests coincided with John's. She loved music, especially the violin and the piano, often playing one or the other instrument in solitude for two or three hours. She

loved the theater as John did. Though she rejected formal education, she read widely and seriously, keeping Shakespeare's plays
on her night table. She was shy as he was, sensitive and high-
strung as he was, and yet they seemed destined to collide. Abby,
who saw the collision coming, was caught in the middle, between
two strong wills. Babs would not be coerced and John would not
budge. A peacemaker herself, Abby perhaps expected more of her
young daughter than Babs was capable of.

Ellen Milton Harrison, Babs's closest friend during her teens,
her neighbor at Pocantico as well as in Seal Harbor, saw John as a
difficult father in the way he tried to control his children. Babs
went off to Ellen's house for days at a time. There was a tremendous amount of freedom in the Milton house, a gaiety that Babs
hungered for. And Dave Milton (Ellen's good-looking, good-
natured older brother) was often around. "Even Mrs. Rockefeller's
warm heart could not rescue Babs," Ellen remarked. "She would
have had to defy her husband much more openly than she was
willing to do."[18] Laurance agrees. "Mother was not in a position to
play coastguard for Babs."[19] As the younger children grew up,
Abby was able to soften or even abolish some of John's sternest
edicts, but by that time it was too late for Babs and John 3rd.

The relationship between mother and daughter was complicated
as well. Babs's daughter Abby O'Neill has pointed out that in
many ways they were quite different, which is not surprising, since
they came from such different eras and were the daughters of such
contrasting parents—the freewheeling Nelson Aldrich versus the
compulsive John D. Rockefeller, Jr., the depressed Abby Pearce
versus the energetic, gregarious, often tenacious Abby Aldrich.
Babs resisted her mother's advice where her brothers did not, and
she shrank from the family gatherings which Abby adored. She
found the YWCA people who gathered around her mother dull
and obsequious, and she wanted no part of Bayway or Abby's
other public commitments. Babs hated Maine, Abby loved it.

If there was conflict between Babs and John and an emotional
distance between Babs and Abby, with Aunt Lucy she felt totally
at ease. Lucy, in her words, "built her up."[20] She loved Lucy for
her frankness, her refusal to defer to wealth or fame. She realized

that both Lucy and her mother were cultivated women with instinctive artistic judgment, but because she was so relaxed with Lucy, she learned the most from her.

On Saturday, May 29, 1920, Abby and John with the four older children, as well as the usual staff, boarded the private railway car *Pioneer* for the first family holiday across the United States and Canada. John modeled the tour after his own youthful travels, right down to having the boys throw a handball up and down the corridor of the Pullman and along the station platform. There were the ritual visits to Forest Hill and the family cemetery in Cleveland and to the McCormick relatives in Chicago. Measles struck in Denver. "Naturally, we are marooned here . . ." Charles Heydt wrote, "the whole crowd was . . . pretty well tired out. A collapse was bound to come."[21]

By June 20, everyone was healthy again and the hectic schedule resumed, with pack trips into the wilderness and courtesy calls by Standard Oil presidents and directors. Not a glacier, not a mountain peak, not an Indian reservation was missed. Occasionally, under the right circumstances, Abby ventured onto a horse. The family got as far south as Los Angeles and as far west as Vancouver. In Tacoma they called on Mrs. Weyerhauser of the lumber Weyerhausers, and in Montreal they had lunch with Sir Arthur Currie, who had been the general in charge of all Canadian forces in the Great War.

They reached Bangor, Maine, on August 6. A week later, Abby was writing Lucy from the Eyrie about her redecorating schemes.

"Ever since we have made the house over," she wrote, "I have wondered what to do with my little office room. I have just finished hanging my set of fourteen Utomara prints there and . . . it occurs to me that I could make this room very attractive if you would bring me back some Korean things [Lucy was preparing to return to the Far East]. . . . I will make a drawing of the room with measurements, which will be more convenient for you."[22] So convinced was Abby of the importance of this Oriental art form that she invited a hundred people to tea to hear an illustrated lecture on the subject of Japanese prints.

During the years she was working with Duncan Candler on the renovation and reconstruction of the Eyrie, Abby had incorporated several of her father's concepts. There was the Playhouse, with a kitchen where Babs and the boys cooked a weekly supper for their parents and the staff. There was the Rest House, a five-room bungalow in the giant pines to which Abby and John removed themselves for naps and Abby's favorite snack of blueberries and bread.

And there was the ballroom, where John could indulge in his love of social dancing. A big dance craze was sweeping over America, led by Vernon and Irene Castle. Hotels across the country featured ballroom dancing every night of the week. John regularly set up tea dances in the Eyrie ballroom for Babs and her friends and even the younger boys. "Mr. Rockefeller liked to dance with all of us," Ellen Harrison recalled. "He was quite a good dancer except that he was a head shorter than I was and I dreaded it when he asked me."[23] Henry Stebbins remembers Babs from those dances. "She may have looked like a Rockefeller," he said, "but she had the Aldrich spirit. She would do anything and say anything, at least when I knew her."[24]

Abby often went over to friends' houses to play bridge, thereby escaping John's silent disapproval of the game. She ran continuous activities for all the neighborhood children, depending on the weather. One rainy afternoon a sudden squall sent all the boys over to the Eyrie. Henry Stebbins, who was fifteen at the time, suggested an election to be held as follows: "If you didn't have your own mother, which of all the mothers would you choose?" Abby won hands down, said Stebbins; they all loved her.[25]

Becka Stebbins, who came to Northeast Harbor every summer to visit her grandfather, the historian James Ford Rhodes, was reared in a strict Massachusetts household by "awful" Victorian aunts. "Mrs. Rockefeller was the first grown-up to recognize me as a person," Becka said. "She asked me sensible questions. It was nice to be asked."[26] Other people remember Abby the same way. One, a librarian at Rockefeller University, recalls going to the Morgan Library when she was twelve and noticing the gentle, warm friendliness of a woman who stepped out of the shadows to speak to her with perfectly open interest. Someone later identified the woman as Abby Aldrich Rockefeller.

Becka remembers clearly the occasion of her first meeting with Abby. It was a luncheon at the Eyrie, and all the Rockefeller children were present, as well as Abby and John. "Mr. and Mrs. wore bibs and all the children—we were perhaps eight years old—were handed grown-up napkins. No servants were in evidence."[27] She remembers the house, huge as it was, as not forbidding, except on the outside, and that it was the first time she did not feel shy and foolish at a party. That was the day that Winthrop led her to Babs's room at the far end of one of the many corridors and put chicken bones in Babs's bed, and then showed Becka where they could hide.

For Abby, who preferred to have all her children under her roof, the autumn and winter of 1920 felt abnormally quiet and deserted. She returned from the Eyrie to prepare Babs for her departure on October 10 with Lucy for six months in the Far East and Europe. John 3rd and Laurance were enrolled in the Olmstead School, a tiny (ten boys) boarding school in Lakewood, New Jersey. John 3rd was there to be tutored for prep school, Laurance because he was always catching colds and flu. The Olmsteads promoted healthy outdoor activities in a rural setting and a work-study program.

From the moment they left, Abby watched impatiently for her first letter. "There are so many things I want to know," she wrote. "Please tell me everything—where you put your clothes, whether you have the right things, the names of all the boys and every little detail that you can think of."[28] Her questions and advice cascaded over them like gentle rainfall. Why did two boys fall off the horses? Did the horses rear or kick or what? They should write Nelson often. He misses them terribly. Are their Bibles satisfactory, or are they a little too large? Since she was an indifferent speller, perhaps Laurance should correct the mistakes in her letters the same way she corrected his. They would be less apt to catch cold if they put on an extra wrap when they came in from riding, if they were going to stand around. Nelson was having trouble with his multiplication tables. It made her wonder how well they knew theirs.

A different sort of advice concerned nine-year-old Peter Goelet. "I feel very sorry for [him]. . . . I am sure that he has a very sweet disposition," she wrote Laurance. "I hope that you and John will be very nice and kind to him and never make fun of him when he is slow. I think little boys are often cruel to each other without meaning to be."[29]

The matter of how little boys treated each other was very much on her mind. Nelson and Laurance continually badgered Winthrop, who in turn took his frustration out on David. With Laurance away, Winthrop and David seemed to be getting along better, or at least it seemed so to her. "I hope when you and John come home," she wrote Laurance, "you will do nothing to disturb his friendly feelings for Winthrop. It seems so cruel to me that you big boys should make poor little Winthrop the goat all the time. I know that he is often trying but the only way to help Winthrop is by being kind to him. Abuse only makes him angry and worse, while for love and kind treatment he will do anything."[30]

It is not altogether clear why Winthrop became the goat. Suggestions and theories abound. He was overweight and clumsy as a small child. He was the middle child—two years younger than Laurance, three years older than David—and that is never an easy position. Nelson's tireless energy and Laurance's quick wit were too much for him. It was hopeless for him to try to force his way into their world, and beating up on David did not make up for being tormented by the bigger boys. He felt himself abandoned when the family left him behind with David on the trip west. There was little he could do, at age eight, except lash out in frustration or suffer in silence.

The Lincoln School did provide him some outlets. He liked to do things with his hands, and Lincoln respected mechanical and artistic skills. As he advanced through the system he learned what Rockefeller sons learned at Lincoln, to understand and feel at home with people who were different from themselves. But as he himself would write years later to his own son, "I was exposed in my early years to two widely different training methods, which were confusing . . . and hard to reconcile. One was Father's strictness in certain matters and the other was the system at the Lincoln School, where the emphasis was entirely on self-expression."[31]

On November 3, Abby went to the polling booth for the first time in her life. By virtue of the Nineteenth Amendment, American women now had the right to vote. It was a monumental victory, but it followed seventy-five years of grinding battles. Abby had made a point of registering (John evidently did not), and wrote Laurance that she voted the Republican national ticket, but broke ranks to vote for two Democratic judges. She pinned her hopes on Warren Harding and Calvin Coolidge, because she believed that they would steer the United States into the League of Nations and world peace. It was a vain hope

CHAPTER 14

Events moved in the spring of 1921 as they often did in Abby's life, with pell-mell rapidity. She was in Washington to give the keynote speech at the meeting of the YWCA National Board, urging her audience to take more seriously the needs and problems of younger women. "If we fail to catch a glimmer of their vision, then I think we forfeit our right as guide."[1] She took the Congressional Express home to New York, then left at three the next afternoon for Providence and the wedding of her brother Richard.

"I really think it is a good thing for Richard to marry a widow," she wrote Lucy. "He is so quiet and shy and unaggressive that I think he needs some one to manage him."[2] Richard Aldrich already managed his political life quite well. The only one of Senator Aldrich's sons to enter politics, he was presently sitting in the Rhode Island senate and in 1922 would be elected to the U.S. House of Representatives, where he would serve with distinction for ten years. According to Abby, he was so nervous the night before the ceremony that she had to calm him with "rhubarb and soda and bromide and all sorts of things to make him sleep."[3]

On the morning of the event she took some fresh flowers to the graves of her parents. On Saturday evening she rode the train back to New York. By Monday she was on the move again, this time to

Loomis Institute at Windsor, Connecticut, with John 3rd. As opposed as she was to sending any of her children away to boarding school, now and then her husband's arguments for manliness and self-reliance proved too much for her. "I hope that you will try to be very manly and strong . . ." she would write David when he turned twelve, "without having to be away from us much before you go to college."[4] Right now she was worried about introspective, solitary John 3rd, the loneliness that had pervaded his letters from Lakewood, and the stranglehold of his conscience as he felt the brunt of his father's expectations. "I hope very much that I don't have to go to boarding school next year," he had written her in February. "I hope you can arrange it so I live at home with you."[5] But she could not arrange it, and now they traveled to Loomis so that he could take the entrance examinations.

When the question of summer camp came up, he again gave way to his feelings. "Why I should have to go away most of the summer is more than I can make out. . . . I don't see why you want me to go away half the summer besides being away all winter. . . . It makes you feel as if you were not wanted at home. If Nelson wants to go so much, let him go, but I don't see why I have to. He has never been away from home before, and doesn't know what it is like."[6]

Abby tried to comfort him. "Neither Papa nor I would consider for a moment . . . suggesting that you go to camp this year were we expecting to be at home. . . . I wouldn't go to China if I didn't feel that Papa needed the change and rest very badly. And he isn't willing to go alone. I think that he needs me. I try to be with the member of the family that needs me most. Try and forget about camp now. It is a long way ahead."[7]

Abby was preparing for the most ambitious journey of her life, one that would take her halfway around the world for several months. The occasion was the official opening of the Peking Union Medical College, built and endowed by the Rockefeller Foundation under John's direction. Being away from the children was always difficult for her emotionally. And like their own mother, she reminded Lucy, she found it hard to leave home.

But the decision was probably never in doubt. As a substitute for camp, Lucy offered to stay with the boys, and in addition to the usual caretakers there was Zenos Miller, the first of a series of unusual young men who acted as companion-tutors to the Rockefeller brothers. A flying ace during the late war and a fourth-year student at Harvard Medical School, twenty-three-year-old Miller was daring and thoughtful at the same time, with the special appeal of the student-athlete. And he was not so absorbed with his charges that he did not take note of Babs, who at eighteen had burst out of her cocoon of shyness.

Perhaps it was the trip around the world with Lucy, and Lucy's unqualified approval, that hastened the transformation. Babs was beginning to demonstrate a stamina and a decisiveness that had not previously been conspicuous in her personality. She could dance for hours, play tennis tirelessly. She loved speeding cars and was learning to navigate the narrow island roads. Such headlong verve appealed to the young men of the summer colony, who saw it as a provocative counterpoint to her careful Rockefeller breeding and delicate beauty. "Tell Babs," Zenos wrote Abby on August 7, "that Seal Harbor is prostrate with grief over her departure."[8]

The S.S. *Empress of China* sailed out of Vancouver at 5:30 P.M. on August 18, 1921. The mission included, among others, Abby, John, Babs, and their personal staff of four; the chairman of the board of trustees of the University of Chicago; the president-elect of the AMA; the superintendent of Mount Sinai Hospital of New York; and Mary G. Wooley, president of Mount Holyoke, a particular favorite of Abby's.

After one night of brilliant moonlight, the fog set in and the sea grew rough. Abby, who was a good sailor, felt perfectly well as long as she stayed in bed, reading and enjoying herself. John, who at home routinely drove himself to the point of collapse, became a different companion from the father Babs had sparred with. Every night he took her dancing in the ship's lounge. Knowing how vehemently he objected to her smoking, she agreed to stop, and he offered to double her allowance if she succeeded. This was irresistible bait, since she was determined to buy herself a car as soon as possible.

The whole contingent docked in Yokohama on Monday, August

*The family gathers at Seal Harbor, Maine. Summer 1921. From left to right:
Laurance, Babs, John 3rd, Abby, David, Winthrop, John, and Nelson.*
Courtesy of the Rockefeller Archive Center.

29. For the next two and a half months they traveled by motor-car, riverboat, train, ocean liner, and even sedan chair, to Korea, Manchuria and China, Hong Kong, Manila, and Japan. Ceremony and Standard Oil officials followed them everywhere. The dedication of Peking Union Medical College, magnet for the entire pilgrimage, spanned two weeks of celebration. Abby, a seasoned political hostess, plunged ahead with gusto. When she wasn't standing at John's side, nodding and smiling, she was visiting shrines and educating herself in the art and religion of the people.

For his part, John was feasting his eyes upon rare porcelains. The control, the attention to detail, the centuries of tradition represented in the elaborate flower and animal symbols, even the impersonal nature of the pieces—such characteristics pleased and reassured him. He began to concentrate on the most coveted products of the potter's art, those pieces crafted during the reign of the seventeenth-century Manchu emperor K'ang Hsi, of the Ch'ing dynasty. Never again would their configurations and colors be duplicated by any civilization, although forgeries and imitations proliferated. A calm interest became a consuming fascination.

In 1915, before he had a private fortune, John had asked Senior to lend him $2 million so that he could buy the Morgan collection of first-quality pieces. His appeal was eloquent—that he never squandered money on horses or yachts, that a fondness for the porcelains was his only hobby. He added that they could be considered a good investment. Senior did not lend him the money, he gave it to him. John's pleasure in porcelains never faded. They brought him contentment for the rest of his life. They did not, however, prove to be a good financial investment.

Ten sedan chairs, four food carriers, and a small army of donkeys transported the party to the Ming tombs. On Sunday, September 25, they were cruising down the Whangpoo River through Shanghai on two Chinese houseboats, meandering along canals. In Canton on October 11 they had lunch with Dr. and Mrs. Sun Yat-sen. On October 13 they boarded the *Empress of Russia* for Kobe and a month's stay in Japan.

Abby's letters to the boys were a diary of impressions. "Every morning and evening [Chinese owners lead] groups of horses up and down the street like little dogs on a leash." Birds seemed to be pets, too, as serious businessmen with bird cages in their hand took their favorite bird for a walk in the cool of the day. "If they go to a teahouse," she wrote Laurance, "they put the bird beside them to sing while they sip their tea."[9] She admired the Chinese people for their cheerfulness, and patience and diligence, and saw many similarities between their country and her own. "But as yet," she wrote, "they have no real sense of patriotism. Everyone is so busy looking out for himself that he doesn't seem to care what happens to the country as a whole or to his neighbor."[10]

With letters requiring five days to cross the continent and two weeks over the sea, and who knew how many days into China or Japan, it is a logistical wonder that any letters at all reached Abby. But they did. From Florence Scales in Maine she learned whether it was foggy or beautiful, what Winthrop wore to church (black-

and-white linen suit and black shoes and stockings), and that there was scarlet fever in the area. Who had boils, who went to the dentist, what Nelson was up to since returning from camp (eating constantly and never sitting still for a moment). Laurance had spells of looking very "hollow-eyed," but Scales concluded that since he was eating and sleeping well, it must be his natural look.

Zenos Miller, digressing from his report of tennis tournaments and overnight camping trips with John 3rd, had some interesting advice for Mr. Rockefeller couched in the most respectful language, but very much to the point:

> John . . . has reached the age when boys grow up very rapidly. You will notice a big difference in him when you get back from China. I believe that Mr. Rockefeller should try to recall his own youth and as far as his time permits try to be with John as much as he can. . . . If Mr. Rockefeller visits Loomis occasionally and takes an interest in John's activities, extra-curricular in particular, it will be a fine thing for John and he will get in the habit of bringing his questions to his own father.
>
> In my own life I saw practically nothing of Father after I was fifteen [his father was a missionary] and I can tell you I have often felt the lack of his sympathy and advice. If the father . . . takes time to be interested in his son's life there are very few sons, I am sure, who will not respond by taking their paters into their confidence.
>
> I hope Mr. Rockefeller will pardon these remarks, but I write them because I have seen several fathers who let their business life crowd out their interest in their own boy's life at a time when the boys needed their father's interest in them even more than they needed their mother's. If you don't keep up with a boy's development you may find some day that he has . . . grown away from you and beyond the reach of your persuasion and influence.[11]

On Saturday, December 3, 1921, at 5:30 P.M., the *Pioneer* delivered its passengers to Grand Central Station. Less than three weeks later, Lucy was writing Abby from Santa Barbara. "You have sent me so much," she wrote, "that I don't know where to begin to thank you. . . . I am going to put all my first editions in one room some day and hang your pictures on the wall and sit in the middle of it all and think what a kind sister I have. . . . I'm afraid you'll spoil me (but I love to be spoiled)." She was in Santa Barbara to help Elsie, their younger sister, whose husband, Maurice Edgell, had died in the influenza epidemic. "She [is] so tense that I felt as if she might go to pieces any minute. . . . I don't think we should leave her until she is safe in the East. . . . Stephanie . . . really does look like Mamma, beautiful blue eyes and very fair. . . . I am not crazy about Santa Barbara . . . too little to do. I never liked the Riviera you know, or Honolulu or Manila. After I have looked a place like that over and said how lovely! I want to go away. Lots of love from your devoted sister, L. T. Aldrich."[12]

In November 1922, Lucy returned to the Far East, accompanied as always by Minnie MacFadden and her devoted maid, Mathilde Schoneberg. Abby, who returned from the Orient permanently fascinated with the art and the culture and the religion of Asia, was reading up on Buddhism and the entire range of Indian art. "You probably know all about it," she wrote Lucy, "but it is a brand new subject to me and very illuminating because of the influence it has exerted on Chinese art and also because of the influence that the Greeks and the Persians had upon India. When I [imagine] you out there," she continued, "I envy you very much."[13] Actually envy played but a slight part in her relationship with Lucy. "I think of you so constantly that sometimes I feel as if I were in communication with you, which of course does not do you any good."[14]

Lucy, writing from Calcutta, admitted to developing a fondness for Scotch. "Miss MacFadden has taken to betting on the races and if we were here much longer we'd probably end up with dope."[15] In Japan she found a gorgeous priest robe, which she promised to leave Abby in her will. (Lucy was already known in the family as the one who changed her will every few months.) Now she was on her way to Peking.

It was on a quiet Sunday evening in May 1923 that Abby learned that Lucy never reached Peking. Lucy had been kidnapped! Chinese bandits, storming the Shanghai-Peking sleeping cars, forced the passengers into the treacherous countryside at gunpoint, presumably holding them hostage, for what purpose no one seemed to

The Eyrie, Seal Harbor, Maine.
Courtesy of the Rockefeller Archive Center.

know. It must be a hideous mistake, everyone in the Rockefeller household kept telling each other, even as they burned up the telephone wires to Standard Oil officials and State Department functionaries. "You needn't worry about Aunt Lucy," Nelson declared. "She can take care of herself."[16] John 3rd, calling from Loomis, assured his mother that Aunt Lucy would love it.

"We really don't know very much about it yet," Abby wrote Lucy later, "except that you were taken and then released by the bandits. . . . All day Monday," she continued, "I sat by the telephone. By afternoon I could hardly speak. . . . I think it was early Tuesday morning that a cable came from [the] Tsinanfu S.O. man that you were in the Hospital there and that Miss MacF. and Mathilde were with you. . . . All the boys envy you the experience, but I don't. . . . R.G. [a member of John's staff] and I feel that the bandits were probably driven to do this by poverty, per-

Treasures from the Far East. Interior of the Eyrie, photographed by Ezra Stoller, 1960.
Courtesy of the Rockefeller Archive Center.

haps hunger. I am sure that it will not kill your love of China any more than it does ours. . . . Ned and Winthrop [Aldrich] and Elsie think you might want to come right home. They wanted me to cable you that you must, but I told them I thought you had better decide that yourself. W. said that he had always felt that you were taking awful risks when you took to traveling, but I say that travel is not nearly as hazardous for a woman as matrimony. I told him I say this not from experience but observations."[17]

Nelson and John were both right. Aunt Lucy could indeed take care of herself. If she did not exactly "love" the experience—she admitted to being rather jumpy, now that it was behind her—she certainly went through it with her curiosity and humor intact. "For the rest of my life," she wrote Abby, "when I am 'stalled' conversationally, it will be a wonderful thing to fall back on: 'Oh, I must tell you about the time I was captured by Chinese bandits.' That remark, from a fat, domestic-looking old lady in a Worth gown, ought to wake up the dullest dinner party."[18] In the letter to her sister, she started at the beginning. How she was aroused, in the middle of the night, by the sound of gunfire (clear even to her deaf ears), the shattering of glass, and a gang of wild-looking men ripping open her bags and pawing through her purse. When one man snatched Miss MacFadden's precious string of jade and then broke it, Lucy sternly told him to pick up the beads. "Before he realized what he was doing, he did pick up a few of them, then straightened and held a revolver at my head, while I groped for [the rest]."

Moments later, another pistol at her back, she was forced off the train, shoved down a steep embankment, and ordered to mount a kicking, plunging pony. Separated from her maid and her companion, she fixed her attention on one task only—to stay astride the pony. "I bossed my bandit terribly," she wrote, "I made him lead my pony . . . scolded him when we went too fast." The idea that she might be in real danger, that these unruly men would harm her, suddenly seemed ludicrous. "My poor pony, who had lost his first fine careless rapture after carrying nearly one hundred and seventy pounds for miles . . . [collapsed,] his little legs trembling." She continued the climb into the high country on foot, her bandit half-dragging, half-pushing her up the steep walls of shifting rock and stone.

Always the obsessive collector, she became interested in the chains the bandits wore to fasten their tobacco pouches. "One man had a lovely piece of old white jade with a carved flying-fox as a netsuke [a buttonlike fixture hanging on a man's sash]. If they had left me any money, I should have tried to buy it." They did share their food, such as it was, offering her thin flat cakes of what looked and tasted like wrapping paper. "Papa always said I would eat anything . . . so, true to form, I tried . . . it."

But then, in the late afternoon, the situation turned ominous. Behind them the soldiers seemed to close the gap. Ahead, a huge storm was brewing. Already the wildest of the bandits had fired several rounds of ammunition into the body of an exhausted Chinese prisoner, and now turned on Lucy, beating her as she slipped and stumbled. "My coat and cape were so thick I didn't feel it—it only made me angry." But she was completely spent, streaming with perspiration, so thirsty that her lips were covered with a dry, cottonlike substance. Her "kind" bandit stepped in. Speaking perfect English (!), he pointed toward a village. "My wife lives in that village; you go there." Obediently, Lucy trotted down between the paddy fields. By the time she reached the closed gates and the blank mud wall, she realized that she was completely alone. All her captors had vanished.

The rest of her letter brought Abby to the moment of the rescue and beyond. How she slept all night in the rain outside the village wall because no one inside would stir. How the women of the village ushered her into the courtyard at daylight, how they picked the straw out of her hair, offered her tea from a filthy teapot, touched her one gold tooth, fingered raptly the tattered lace of her wrapper. "My heart bled for those kind women. . . . I wish I could go back to carry them—not religion, or even food, but a little beauty, bright color, pictures. . . ." Late in the day, her bandit returned to guide her across many more miles, past other villages, through more paddy fields, changing donkeys, finally pulling her in a wheelbarrow. "I never for an instant suspected that I was being rescued . . . fatigue made me stupid." But then suddenly, there she was, beside a little railroad station, surrounded by excited soldiers and railmen. She asked the one American present how much was paid to get her out. "Not one cent," was the reply. He had been walking around all day with $50,000 in his pocket, but it had not been needed.

In the spring of 1922, Abby and John went to the White House to honor the Speaker of the House. It was an evening full of pomp and nostalgia. "It made me a little sad," Abby wrote Lucy, "because everyone of course spoke of Papa and Mama and it brought up all the past very vividly to me."[19] She was disappointed in President Harding in spite of his geniality and good looks. Even though the entire journey was less than thirty-six hours, she managed to maneuver John over to the Dodge Hotel for tea and a complete tour of the facility. "He was so much pleased with the building and its furniture," so pleased, she boasted to Lucy, that he wanted one of his own construction committees to look it over for ideas.[20]

It had been high on Abby's agenda, since the end of the war, to build a comfortable Washington hotel for business and professional women in government, as well as visitors to the city. Under the auspices of the National Board of the YWCA she went on to chair the Grace Dodge Hotel Committee for fifteen years. No private real estate developer lavished more attention on an investment than she did on her hotel. "Mrs. Rockefeller [was] an outstanding business woman. She had great business ability and the Dodge Hotel gave her a chance to use it," one of the hotel staff members recalled.[21]

Professionals would have given up—there were so many obstacles. But Abby's stubbornness, and that of her committee, had kept the project alive. They located the site, appointed the architect —Duncan Candler—drew and redrew the plans, raised the money, and battled skyrocketing prices. They managed to build 350 rooms at a cost of $1,200,000. They named it after Grace Dodge, who had organized the National Board of the YWCA, was one of the founders of Columbia University Teachers College, and had worked tirelessly for women's causes.

In its attention to the quality of the environment, both interior and exterior, the taste was all Abby's. She demanded, and got, sunny lounges on each floor, specially equipped rooms for mothers traveling with small children, valeting rooms with irons, ironing boards, and tubs, ice water in the corridors, telephones in every room. And in another reflection of her Ludlow experience, she insisted on special consideration for the health and convenience of the employees.

Understanding the value of advertising and publicity, she gave out interviews and distributed brochures when she traveled. "I am glad we are going to get a 'write-up' in the Tribune," she wrote Mary Lindsley, the manager, who became her friend. "Has anything ever come out in Good Housekeeping about us yet?"[22] To a New York Times reporter she stated emphatically that the Grace Dodge Hotel was not a philanthropy. Women were entitled to have hotels that were comfortable and pleasant. They were not eager for charity, but wanted to pay their way. She had set out to demonstrate that an inexpensive hotel for women could succeed financially, and she was opposed to tipping. "Women in all lines of work should be paid an adequate wage. . . . We have women clerks, women to run the elevators and even the 'bellhops' are girls only we call them messengers."[23]

As she traveled up and down the eastern seaboard with John, Abby always managed to stop off at the hotel. No detail escaped her attention. "Do you think that the ice which is used with the oysters might be chopped a little finer," she wrote Lindsley after one of her visits.[24] "I'm getting in touch with the Standard Oil Company of Indiana," she wrote on another occasion, "who, I find are the ones who make candles and I hope that within a few days to be able to send you some sample candles with quotations in wholesale lots. I am afraid if we put black candles in the candlesticks that they will look too spotty in the room."[25] The media were forever bemused that the rich Mrs. Rockefeller stayed at "the unpretentious Y.W.C.A. hotel . . . riding to and from conferences in taxicabs" rather than chauffeur-driven limousines.[26] They would have been more bemused if they had seen David and Winthrop folding napkins and running the mangle in the hotel laundry.

Abby made a conscientious effort to respect John's opinions when she committed her energies and her resources to her philanthropies, both public and private. "I should like very much," she wrote Fosdick, "to make a contribution to the Women's Trade Union League Club House, and the Student Forum and to the fund for the families of the striking coal miners in West Virginia— neither of which objects has the entire approval of Mr. Rockefeller. . . . he has asked me to suggest that you get me further information about the [first two]. Probably it is better that I should not give to the fund for the miners' families."[27]

Ever since Ludlow, John had moved in the direction of labor statesmanship, but his natural caution was bound to give Abby the fits occasionally. When he did speak out she was transported. "I was perfectly delighted," she wrote Fosdick on November 28, 1922, "with Mr. Rockefeller's statement . . . about labor in the oil fields. I don't know when I have been so thrilled . . . by anything as I have by [this] public announcement. [The statement, as published in *Survey Graphic*, was John's forthright denouncement of the wretched living and working conditions in Elk Basin, Wyoming, where Standard of Indiana held property.] If you have any interesting reactions to [the] statement, would you be good enough to share them with me."[28] Fosdick obeyed, sending her favorable comments from across the country.

When Amelia Pinchot, finance chairman of the newly formed National League of Women Voters, first solicited her for support, Abby had replied, rather wistfully, "I seem to have inherited a keen interest in politics and I have an ardent desire that women should accept their new responsibilities of citizenship in the most intelligent . . . way. But, even in spite of this, I feel that it is not wise for me to be connected actively or even nominally with any organizations that are political in any sense of the word. Much as I regret it, I feel it is a wise decision."[29] She apologized for not making an immediate financial pledge, explaining that for the current year her funds were pledged, and she had made it a rule not to ask her husband for contributions. (In later years Abby became a generous financial supporter of the league.)

CHAPTER 15

During the few times that he was separated from Abby, John's letters always rang with the familiar note of desperation. "Miss you . . . so sadly . . . need you so much . . . it seems as though you have been away from home for months," he wrote.[1] (It was only a day.) Abby reached out for fresh language to comfort him. "I am sure that you write the most beautiful love letters of anyone in the world." The violets he sent her were a reminder of her youth in Providence when he didn't yet love her but still sent her beautiful flowers. The fragrance of the orange blossoms that arrived in the morning delivery made her long to be with him, just him. "I wish that I had a new way of sending my love to you so that it would seem more real to you."[2] But for John, her love was never quite real enough. Whether in Florida with his father or in Seal Harbor with all six children, so pervasive was his dependence upon her that life in her absence became "empty and cheerless."[3]

Abby, writing from the Eyrie, nonchalantly summarized her ailments of the season—very bad colds, bronchitis, sprained ankle (from stepping on a small stone on a path near the house), and surgery to remove a sewing needle imbedded in her leg. It was John's health, not her own, that was the overriding concern. The migraine headaches that incapacitated him for days at a time were not getting any better. Finally, on October 17, 1922, accompanied by Charles Heydt, he went to the Battle Creek Sanitarium, hoping that the doctors there could find the cause of the headaches.

"They gave him every imaginable kind of test . . ." Abby reported to Lucy, "[and] found him in extremely good condition. . . . They said that he worked much too hard and that he should be out-of-doors more and take more recreation and they also convinced him that a vegetarian diet would be the best thing in the world for him. . . ."[4] The headaches continued. As far as anyone in the family knows, psychotherapy was not considered.

While John was still at Battle Creek, he received a poignant letter from Babs. "This is going to be the hardest letter I have ever had to write . . ." she confessed. "I've smoked, thereby losing my car. Mama told me to take it up to Tarrytown tomorrow and put it away. . . . I was ten million kinds of a fool to do it but now that it's done there is nothing left for me to do but tell you about it, thus carrying out my part of the bargain."[5] The "bargain" had been struck between John and each of his children—$2,500 at age twenty-one if they refrained from smoking. In Babs's case, it was more than that. He made her a gift of her beloved roadster, in exchange for her taking the nonsmoking vow. "Imagine the crushing moral pressure she was under," Laurance remarked, "that required her to tell her father about that one cigarette."[6] The pressure was heavy enough to fill her with guilt, but never enough to stem her defiance. In the battle of wills, she was the winner, although at times it was an empty triumph. John, for his part, was never as stern as his demeanor might suggest. Within weeks, she had recovered the use of her car and was still smoking.

Abby, aware of Babs's love of speeding cars, breathed a little easier with the roadster temporarily out of circulation. Babs at eighteen had already barely escaped two serious accidents. Winthrop Aldrich, who seemed to know about such things, predicted that she would be a great belle and should come out soon. John was indignant that her young men stayed so late. Abby, who had been one of the popular girls herself, tried to persuade him to let up on Babs. She understood the rules of the game—that you trained for a debut, like a marathon. There was the whirl of attention, the nonstop excitement, the need for balance to prepare for the letdown.

The press expected Babs's debut to be that of the billionaire heiress. In truth it was a quiet affair, a startling contrast to the extravaganzas of the other great New York families. Barbara Vanderbilt Whitney came out at a mammoth event for eight hundred guests in the oak-paneled ballroom of the Whitney mansion at 871 Fifth Avenue, with its gold ornaments and Gobelin tapestries. Abby and John introduced Babs to their friends, much as Abby's parents had years before, at a musicale to hear the violinist Mischa Elman.

"Sherry served the supper," Abby wrote Lucy, "and I think they must have tried rather hard, because it was extremely good. . . . It seemed to be a very simple, nice, friendly affair. . . . [Babs] wore a silver tissue dress covered with a sort of bluish-mauve tulle, and wore some orchids that Lem Page sent her and carried a perfectly beautiful bouquet. . . . She was . . . sweet to everyone and seemed very happy and responsive. . . . We are going to have a dance here at the house for her on the 26th of December—50 for dinner . . . 250 more for dancing. . . . I hope I enjoy [it] as much as I did the musicale. I really had an awfully good time."[7]

John took to his bed with influenza on December 18 and missed the musicale and the dance, but his friend Ev Colby stood in for him. He was still in bed on January 3. "Babby has been going out madly day and night . . . " he wrote. "I presume the chances are that she will pull through without getting sick. . . . There has been such a riot of gaiety in the house as almost makes my hair stand on end."[8]

Abby was proud of Babs. She had returned to Miss Chapin's to study French and American history, and three times a week took a course in political economy at the Commonwealth School. David remembers that she often came home in the morning from her dates just as he was starting off for school. But she still had time for tennis and movies with her brothers. "She seems to have had a wonderful time . . ." Abby wrote Lucy after the winter of parties, "altho instead of spoiling her, it seems rather to have sobered . . . her. . . . She hasn't had time to have any very violent affairs. She has turned down all the ardent ones. They still come to see her but not as frantically."[9] It is not clear how much Babs actually told Abby. Her own recollection is that she said very little.

Nelson brought the family some unwanted publicity when he shot himself in the leg with BB shot that he had glued to a .22 blank and fired in a toy pistol. "Nelson has been the family problem this winter [January 1923] . . . ." Abby wrote, "his father and I have been rather anxious and puzzled about him. . . . He has a desire to seek the toughest gang he can find. . . ."[10]

As a foreshadowing perhaps of what was ahead, he discovered girls and they him. "Nelson [age fourteen] went to six parties Christmas vacation," her letter to Lucy continued. "He seemed to have enjoyed himself hugely. . . . Mrs. Hubble says that he dances beautifully." One of Abby's friends told her "very confidentially that her little girl Harriet . . . is crazy about Nelson. She is very tall, quite pretty. She told [her mother] that every time she danced with Nelson she wanted to kiss his ear."[11]

Reluctantly Abby spoke to the headmaster at Loomis about Nelson's going to boarding school, but then the Lincoln principal advanced him a grade so that he would have to work harder and deal with older boys. "As you know . . ." Abby wrote Mr. Batchelder at Loomis, "[we] much prefer to keep the boys at home, unless it seems absolutely necessary. . . . By the time the spring term is over, we will have a clearer idea of whether school life in New York is no longer practicable for Nelson."[12]

In the American consciousness, the Roaring Twenties forever evoke the image of women dancing the Charleston in rolled stockings, the compelling sound of New Orleans jazz, the forbidden taste of bootleg liquor. But there was an ugly underside to this time of the booming stock market and sudden cornucopia of material goods. Blacks were still being mobbed and shot and beaten. The Ku Klux Klan in the North and South alike was growing more powerful, recruiting as many as four million people by the middle of the decade. Anti-radical hysteria was rampant. The more subtle forms of discrimination, as practiced by the Protestant establishment, flourished against Jews and Catholics.

In this climate of fear and conformity, Abby paid close attention to the emerging values of her own children. On February 8, 1923, from Senior's home in Florida, she wrote the following words to her three older sons:

> For a long time I have had very much on my mind and heart a certain subject. . . . Out of my experience and observation has grown the . . . conviction that one of the greatest causes of evil in the world is race hatred or race prejudice; in other words the feeling of dislike that a person or a nation has against another person or nation without just reason, an unreasoning aversion. The two peoples . . . who suffer most in this country from this kind of treatment are the Jews and the Negroes. In Europe it is different. The French hate the Italians who in turn hate the Austrians, until in the Balkans every country hates every other country and they all hate the Turks, so it goes on in a "vicious circle." You boys are still young. No group of people have done you personal injury. . . . I want to make an appeal to your sense of fair play . . . to begin your lives by giving the other fellow a fair chance and a square deal. It is to the everlasting disgrace of the United States that horrible lynchings and brutal race riots frequently occur in our midst. The social ostracism of the Jews is less barbaric, but . . . causes cruel injustice. . . . I long to have our family stand firmly for what is best and highest in life. . . . If you older boys will do it the younger will follow.[13]

Laurance, at thirteen, was already puzzling over matters of morality and religion. (He was the brother who would major in philosophy.) He wrote his mother that he would always keep the letter she wrote about the injustice of race hatred. (He did.) This led Abby into some introspection of her own about the behavior of the family. "We seem so apt to be critical and fault-finding as a family," she wrote him from Palm Beach, "that I feel as if I had failed to make you children realize the meaning of love and the need of it in the world." Of course they read the Bible, of course they prayed, but was that enough? Were they really kind? Were they really humble? On every side she saw the result of people having too much money. "It makes life too easy; people become self-indulgent and selfish and cruel."[14] Even as she enjoyed to the fullest the beautiful houses she occupied and the beautiful objects she bought, she often stated with great conviction that Senior's fortune was a trust to be sacredly administered.

In mid-January, as a reluctant concession to John's post-influenza neurasthenia, Abby accompanied him to the Casements, Senior's gray-shingled house at Ormond Beach, Florida. "We have settled down to an old people's reunion," she wrote Laurance, "[and] I am having what Papa would call my Sunday illness so that I couldn't go to church."[15] She tried to make the best of the boredom. Meals lasted two and three hours. Numerica and bird-watching were the principal forms of excitement. John, to please his father, took up golf, and Abby, to please John, agreed to take a lesson or two. "I like walking on the grass and looking at the view," she rationalized to Lucy.[16] She learned from Laurance that the great excitement at home was the arrival of a radio set. Apparently the boys were dragging it everywhere, even listening to three sermons on Sunday.

In April, John took Abby away again, this time to Hot Springs, Virginia, to take the "cure." She had hoped that their stay in Florida would restore him to good health. To her it appeared that his nerves were better than they had been since the war. But after one hectic week at 10 West 54th, he persuaded her that they would both benefit from treatment at the spa. Craving her full attention, he could always find some impeccable logic for separating her from his competition. Often it was on the basis of *her* needing a rest that he inveigled her to join him. "But in fact," said David, "he wanted to get her away so he could have her to himself."[17]

In the summer they took Babs and the three older boys to Europe. With John at the helm, all possible mishaps were anticipated, privacy zealously protected. The boys had their French tutor, Babs her Mademoiselle. Dr. Boots of the Rockefeller Institute watched over their health. For Abby it was the first time in Paris after eighteen years. There was a certain innocence in the juxtaposition of fêtes, grand luncheons, and great private collections on the one hand, with John and his boys playing Musical Authors on the other. "I think instead of playing a game that they play so much at home that they should be reading [their] guide books," Abby commented ruefully.[18]

Five years after the war, the French countryside was still haunted by death and destruction—fourteen thousand soldiers buried at the American Cemetery at Romaine, cathedrals crumbling, ruined villages that never recovered. For Abby, who was passionate about world peace and invested her hopes in the faltering League of Nations, it was further depressing evidence of the horror of the war. "We spent 3 days visiting the battle fields," she wrote David. "My heart was very sad all the time that we were there, it is so awful. I had no idea of the extent of the damage. I shall spend the rest of my life trying to prevent war which is so cruel and so stupid. I hope that all of you boys also work for peace; and the best way to do it is to keep hatred out of your hearts." [19]

John, viewing the decaying palace at Versailles and the ravaged Rheims Cathedral, thought in terms of restoration. A reverence for the historical past and an emotional identification with religious inspiration ran deep in him. Over a span of fifteen years he would contribute $2,166,000 to the renovation of Versailles, $570,000 to Rheims, and $114,000 to Fontainebleau. For now, however, he was negotiating with a certain Monsieur Larcade to acquire an extraordinary series of six tapestries and a fragment of a seventh, known as *The Hunt of the Unicorn*. Woven in the Middle Ages to celebrate the marriage of Anne of Brittany to Louis XII, they had belonged to the Rochefoucald family for many generations and had received excellent treatment throughout, except for a brief period during the French Revolution when they were used as a cover to keep potatoes from freezing in a damp cellar. The colors were fresh and brilliant, the story of the hunt for the mythical unicorn told with a vitality and profusion of pictorial detail.

John paid $1,200,000 to the present count, who planned to build a golf course with the money. He hung the tapestries on the walls of a special room set aside for them at 12 West 54th. This was the building adjacent to Number 10 that John bought as an annex and used for various family purposes.

A year later, in the summer of 1924, John took the three older boys on a camping and motor trip to the Rocky Mountain states, while Abby took Babs to Europe. "We are going to spend five weeks in Paris, where she will study French, trying to improve her pronunciation," Abby wrote Charles Eliot, "and two weeks in Germany, where we are going on an art pilgrimage."[20]

Babs, who already had a good grasp of French grammar and literature, plus the benefit of several French-speaking governesses, was hardly in need of further study. The reasons for the trip were more complicated. Over the winter a crisis had occurred, which, while not serious in itself, had set off a chain of unhappy consequences. Babs had continued to drive her car too fast. Twice she was summoned to traffic court to answer charges of speeding on New York streets. Although she pleaded guilty both times, in each instance the case was dismissed. Her friend Dave Milton, a third-year law student, acted as her attorney during the hearings. But then the affair broke in the press.

"Following publication on May 13 of the news of Miss Rockefeller's court experiences," the *New York Times* reported, "several chauffeurs and motorists wrote to Mayor Hylan complaining that the suspension of sentence on Miss Rockefeller made it appear that there was 'one law for the rich and one law for the poor.' "[21] The worst of it for Babs was that she had tried to keep both incidents from John. He issued a statement that he had learned of the matter only from the papers, that he had never tried to interfere in behalf of his daughter, as the press and others were implying, and that he was emphatically opposed to unequal treatment before the law. Mayor Hylan ordered an investigation.

All this only heightened the tension between father and daughter. Babs yearned for independence and a certain hedonism. She saw her brothers as going along with John's system, her mother as an ally of her father, or at best a referee, and herself as the only one with courage to rebel. She still smoked, she drank. "We were lucky we weren't injured," she said, recalling that she had once lit a match to some alcohol to be sure it was drinkable. She often lied about her whereabouts. When her uncle William Rockefeller died in 1922, she had to be located for the funeral; she left a house party on Long Island to attend the services. "Luckily for me, that was one time when I was where I was supposed to be."[22]

When the speeding story broke, almost overnight, her spirit

seemed snuffed out. She was so ashamed, so embarrassed by the uproar, that she could barely face her father. Family members believe that John showed some understanding, but that did not come through to Babs. All she saw was the dull pain and disappointment in his eyes. Abby suffered for her. She watched her turn silent and brooding, eat scarcely at all, smoke heavily, avoid her friends. Finally, despairing of any other remedy, she invited her to Europe. "Babs is beginning to look better . . ." Abby wrote John from Paris. "I think that the Hyland, Hirschfield situation has troubled her greatly. . . . Dave seems to have done well in the case."[23] Hyland was Mayor Hylan; Hirschfield was the investigator assigned to the case.

The unspoken third presence in Europe that summer was David Milton, the older brother of Babs's best friend, Ellen Milton Harrison. Babs and David had known each other as children at Pocantico. David began to fall in love with Babs when he was sixteen and she was thirteen. Even when she was running around with Princeton beaux, he was the man who occupied her thoughts. Letters of the period hint at the relationship. Nurse Albertson reported that Babs invited Dave to lunch. "I offered to have the little folks downstairs," she wrote to Abby, "but she [Babs] wants them to eat with her." Nurse Kline noted that Dave seemed very dependable and she was sure that it was good for Babs to have such a friend. Earlier in the courtship Abby wrote John 3rd that "David came to lunch yesterday. He first went to the Men's Bible Class and staid [sic] to church, then came back. The boys think he must be quite devoted to Babs if he is willing to do that."[24]

They made a handsome couple and they were obviously in love, but their personalities and interests were markedly different. Perhaps the differences made for the excitement. Dave had been raised by a freethinking mother who followed her two sons when they went to Williams College and bought a farm for them to take care of while they were day students. Dave was exuberant and original. Everything he did was highly charged. "Instead of merely riding a horse," Abby O'Neill, his daughter, remarked, "he would want to break a young stallion."[25] Dave loved the country, its smells and its animals. Babs, as she left her rebellious years behind, became the more orderly, the more systematic. She loved the city, its theater and its cinema, its stimulus, its sophistication. Too often she would retreat into her Rockefeller reserve, burying her conflicts behind a cloak of psychosomatic symptoms. Dave burned off his conflicts in frenetic activity. Both families worried about them.

Ellen Harrison thought the love affair a huge mistake, but while acknowledging that they were ill-suited, realized that the attraction between them was too intense to cool off. John probably hoped by this time that if it was to be Dave, his obvious devotion to Babs would disarm her rebellion and help her to grow up. Abby, understanding the depth of her daughter's resentments, even if she could not defuse them, worried that she would marry Dave to escape the strictures of her life as John's daughter.

All the while Abby was having a merry time in Paris with Babs, letters were going back and forth between her and her two sons at home. "I am so glad that you had . . . a beautiful stay in my old home," she wrote David, upon learning that his tutor had taken him to Warwick. "I remember those crabs. They used to bite me."[26] Reading his letters, she could feel the chill of the cold surf off Narragansett Pier, the spin of the carousel at Rocky Point.

At the same time she continued to worry about Winthrop. Events seemed to conspire to keep him home when everyone else was traveling. In 1920 he broke out with the measles. In 1923, he was left behind to be company for David. This year, he had a flare-up of an acute nephritis at the last minute and could not go west with his father and brothers. His letters were sweet and wistful, written in his slanted scrawl, decorated with stick figures, full of such detail as what he was eating—cereal, buttermilk, orange juice, cold soup, etc. (Diet and rest were the only treatment for nephritis.)

Abby and Babs danced at Pré Catelan, heard the Yale band at an all-night café, and went to the Folies-Bergère. "Being thinner," Abby wrote John, "I can dance better and enjoy it more."[27] Old Providence turned up in the guise of her brilliant, bossy friend Madelaine Goddard, now the Marquise d'Andigne. Because John was financing the restoration of Versailles, Abby was invited to state functions. "She [Madelaine] is the same exactly . . . up to all sorts of pranks . . . it amuses me that at all the functions she has to follow <u>after</u> me."[28] She was not amused that so few women were invited to the state luncheons. Even when Madame Herriot, wife of the premier of France, was present, the men outnumbered the women, two to one. "I'm not sure if all the wives are out of town or if they don't ask them."[29] She suspected the latter.

Lately she had become interested in the art of Persia. Illuminated manuscripts had originated in the seventh century with the calligraphy of the Koran. By the fifteenth century the Persian miniaturists had achieved an unparalleled degree of skill. Finally, late in the century, the acknowledged master of Persian painting, Bahsad of Herat, revolted against the dictates of the calligrapher to eliminate the text altogether or permit at most just a few lines of verse. With his rich palette and wonderful color nuance he created a naturalistic landscape and figures of realistic countenance and bearing. In the spring of 1925, Abby was able to purchase an authentic, signed Bahsad miniature, one of the few extant works indisputably by his hand.

During this 1924 trip to Paris, however, she saw few works that satisfied her. Even the collection at the Louvre was a disappointment. But then a dealer named Kelekian brought her some that she could not resist. Her own resources were modest, requiring John to finance these purchases. Knowing how he watched over expenditures, even in an era when his income after taxes was at least $50 million a year, she rationalized in her letter to him that she had bought nothing else on the trip, not even a single inexpensive Japanese print. Perhaps there would come a day when her selections would displease him. But for now she was on safe terrain. Miniatures of theological origin, in flawless condition, encrusted with jewels, could cause him no discomfort.

In July, Lucy came to Paris. The sisters played off each other's enthusiasm for shopping and for gossiping. Abby introduced Lucy to the people at Worth who were assembling her winter wardrobe, and Lucy offered to assume that task in the future. After all, if the couturier had Abby's form, Lucy could make the selections.

The time now arrived for the climactic two weeks of the trip, the art pilgrimage that Abby anticipated with keen impatience.

William R. Valentiner, the director of the Detroit Museum of Art, arrived in Paris to accompany her and Babs and Lucy through the ateliers and galleries of Vienna, Munich, Nuremberg, and Berlin. It promised to be a pivotal experience. Her family, broad political issues, women's problems, society's ills—a whole range of areas engaged Abby's attention and commitment. Art, however, was her obsession. Art was her passion. Art reached deep into her being, offering her excitement and challenge and solace, in a way that nothing else could. There was the utmost significance in the fact that John did not accompany her. Valentiner could instruct and explain, but his opinion as the impersonal art expert was vastly different from the presence of a controlling husband. This time Abby was on her own, free to react, free to accept or reject, free to grow.

CHAPTER 16

ⵥⵥ⸻

On February 17, 1913, four thousand people had come to
the opening of the International Exhibition of Modern Art
of the Association of American Painters and Sculptors. The exhibition came to be known as the Armory Show, because it was
mounted in the 69th Regiment Armory at Lexington Avenue and
26th Street in Manhattan. The "association" was a small breakaway
group of twenty-five artists who were fed up with a stifling academic tradition that elevated historical scenes and allegorical females in flowing robes to the only acceptable standard of taste.
The crowd that wandered through eighteen improvised rooms saw
nothing less than a history of modern art, from Goya, Ingres, and
Delacroix through the Impressionists, Postimpressionists, Fauves,
and cubists.

Calculated from the outset as a "mental jolt to stir America out
of its long aesthetic complacency," in the words of Milton Brown,
historian of the show, it succeeded brilliantly.[1] A rapt, confused,
and often furious audience viewed a collection of over twelve hundred objects gathered with incredible resourcefulness from Europe
and America. European artists dominated the press coverage.
Matisse provoked the most anger among conservatives. How
could a presumably sophisticated artist turn his back on tradi-

tion, his attackers wailed, to willfully distort and try to see like a child!

The New York old guard collectors, committed to the masters of the sixteenth and seventeenth centuries, were in the main antagonistic, though one banker, James Stillman, a Rockefeller in-law, is credited with the classic comment "Something is wrong with the world. These men know."[2] The younger, more adventurous collectors and art-watchers, however, who would enter Abby's life in the 1920s and 1930s, were closely connected to the Armory Show. There were the artists themselves, Arthur B. Davies and Walt Kuhn, especially, who conceived it. There were the lenders, the buyers, the willing workers, the financial backers. Lillie Bliss, Abby's childhood acquaintance from Washington days, gave an anonymous contribution and made some brave purchases under the artistic guidance of Davies. Stephen C. Clark, future chairman of the board of MoMA, bought a Lehmbruck plaster, *Standing Woman*, which later became the model for the bronze cast at the museum. Eliza Radeke of the Rhode Island School of Design Museum in Providence, an institution heavily supported by Aldriches, bought a Matisse drawing for $67.50 (approximately $1,000 in 1992 dollars). Walter Pach, whom Abby would assist in the 1930s, rounded up the best of the European art, and William Valentiner became her adviser and friend.

It was now eleven years later, the summer of 1924, and the travel arrangements for Abby's art tour with Valentiner were pure Rockefeller. "We travelled like princes," he wrote in his diary.[3] But the camaraderie was all Aldrich. Abby, who had spent a lifetime understanding the moods of some very sensitive people, kept everyone relaxed, even Babs, who, according to Valentiner, was "bored stiff in museums" and sulked much of the time.[4] He felt sorry for Abby, wondering if perhaps she was *too* sensitive to Babs's moods. Lucy, announcing that she had no use for modern art, regaled everyone with her running commentary. Valentiner and Abby discovered almost immediately that many of their interests converged. His ideas for workers' housing touched on her project at Bayway. He believed in the museum as a force for public education, a concept that very much intrigued her.

Political terrorism and galloping inflation were the twin battering rams that threatened the fragile Weimar Republic during the 1920s. Ugly factions formed, street fighting broke out, a frightened government turned to the reactionary right to suppress the protests and the marches. The latest crisis had barely subsided when Abby and her companions reached Germany in this summer of 1924. But the creative life of the nation was still free and innovative, if tinged with anxiety and foreboding for the future.

After spending the prewar years as curator of decorative arts at the Metropolitan, William Valentiner had returned to his native Germany to enlist in the German army. But then the horror and disillusionment set in, the outraged call from the intellectuals for peace. In 1919, Valentiner had joined radical artists and writers in Berlin to found the Arbeitsrat für Kunst ("Working Council for Art") and became its chairman. Arbeitsrat members believed that art in all its manifestations could humanize a brutal world. They anticipated the Bauhaus. They spoke of restructuring art schools, of building workers' housing instead of war monuments. Such were the dreams of the Expressionist movement born during the idealistic prewar era.

By the time Valentiner returned to America to take up his post in Detroit, he had formed close friendships with some of the greatest German Expressionists: Schmidt-Rottluff, Nolde, Pechstein, Feininger, Kollwitz, Heckel; the sculptors Kolbe, Lehmbruck, Marck. Abby originally met him in Long Island when he was preparing a catalogue for Clarence Mackay. She grasped immediately that Valentiner's eclectic background could work in her favor. He was an expert in seventeenth-century Dutch art, but at the same time admired the direction of the avant-garde. He was the trusted adviser to major American collectors. His traditional training could reassure John, who was always uneasy with Abby's impetuous embrace of anything unconventional. She laid her plans carefully, confident that with Valentiner her art education would go forward.

The contemporary works that Abby confronted, under Valentiner's tutelage, were so different from the porcelains and medieval tapestries favored by John as to be out of a different universe. Faithful imitation, meticulous craftsmanship, accepted perspective

—all the tests of quality that he lived by—were set aside by the Expressionists in favor of distortion, primary colors, immediacy of feeling. Like their peers across Western Europe, they identified romantically with the exotic works of faraway peoples. (In Germany this often included the inspiration of a medieval heritage.) In addition, however, a violent and tragic vision of the world, as suggested by van Gogh and Edvard Munch, dominated much of their work. Less lyrical than the French Fauves, the German subject matter often became bitter and tormented, an evocation of a defeated and demoralized society.

If such art could be said to embody one overriding, authenticating principle, it was the right of the artist to frank self-expression, the assertion of "the inner wish of the artists."[5] Such art called for a new kind of collector, a collector such as Abby, who could respond viscerally, who did not permit reason to stifle emotion, who was willing to set aside some of the cherished technical values out of respect for the pulse of the creator. An artist who exercised such freedom was not a threat to her, nor did it leave her uncomfortable, as it clearly did her husband.

John's Puritan upbringing was a formidable barrier between him and modern art. The artist's desire for self-expression seemed to him to be irresponsible and self-indulgent, without humility or discipline. The wild experimentation, the distortions, the blobs and swirls that so disturbed the critics disturbed him as well. As Abby tried to move him ever so gently from his stern preconceptions, he frankly acknowledged that he was torn between her way of looking at life, which brought him such fresh excitement, and his mother's, whose influence would always weigh heavily. "My mother would say, 'we have always done this. Why should we do anything else?' But my wife's typical question was: '. . . why not do it another way, or better still, why not do something else?' "[6] When Abby developed an enthusiasm for thirteenth-century Italian primitives and Joseph Duveen sent a Duccio to the house, John tried conscientiously to understand their importance. He even began to buy them. But then her zest for discovery drove her to other periods and other artists, and John was left with some trepidation. What had she in store for him next? When such a quest led her into the most bewildering and controversial area of all, he refused to follow.

Modern art, offering some insight to the creative process itself, touched something creative in Abby. A woman of dynamic energy who did not herself paint or write books or compose music, she was eager to participate directly in the cultural life of her time. There was more adventure—perhaps even more significance—to be found in this raw, unconfirmed art than in the settled canon of old masters. And something deeper, perhaps, was working its way into her consciousness, that broad vision that often accompanied her impulses. It was time to leave behind the old and the cloistered and the safe, time to consider art as it related to the aesthetic needs of society, rather than as a simple extension of her own love of objects. The Museum of Modern Art was five years away, but the possibility of it may already have seized her imagination.

When Conger Goodyear began to write his history of the first ten years of MoMA, he asked Abby how she came to buy contemporary art. "I first started with Japanese prints," she replied, "and early American prints . . . and went on to Buddhistic art and European china and all sorts of very beautiful things . . . in [older] civilizations. Constantly as I did this [I wondered] what . . . things mean to the present and how [would] they affect the art and artists of today? . . . My thought turned to [such art] and those who were developing it."[7]

Abby bought her first piece of contemporary art in the company of Valentiner. It was a signed watercolor, *Landscape*, 18¼ by 23¼ inches, by Erich Heckel. She paid $500. Heckel was a seminal member of the German Expressionist movement, one of the four young architectural students who in 1905 had founded the community known as Die Brücke ("the Bridge"). Frustrated with the suffocating historicism of their profession, they issued a manifesto for cultural freedom and became visual artists, largely self-taught. With extraordinary prescience they anticipated the fundamental tenets that would propel Expressionism through several decades. In 1911, Heckel had published a portfolio of woodcuts that exploited the power of that medium, with its inherent demand for abbreviation, its imposition of pure, flat color, and its decisively drawn line. The images were varied—freely moving nudes in unity with nature, a complex sequence of street life, intended perhaps as a metaphor for tension. Underlying all his work was his intense concern for spiritual, as opposed to material, values—an attitude which was very much a part of the Expressionist movement. After the pain and destruction of the war, he became ardently political, pinning his hopes for a better society on workers' councils such as the Arbeitsrat.

Valentiner was delighted with Abby's interest. What impressed him the most, however, was her desire to come into contact with works of the highest quality, whatever the field might be. "[Her] receptivity," he later wrote, "to diversity is most exceptional and almost as rare as art creation itself."[8] To his satisfaction, Abby wanted to study not only the famous picture galleries, but the architecture and sculpture within and without the buildings. They visited collections "off the main circuit," as he phrased it—Far and Near Eastern and African art, the great manuscripts of the Otto-nian age, the Fouquet and the French Gothic miniaturists. Again and again he was struck by how little the actual feeling of posses-sion consumed her. "She wanted to be surrounded by a few works utterly congenial to her conception of art, works which would provide a criterion for developing a sense of quality . . . [and al-ways] she wanted her collection to be enjoyed by others."[9]

However much John demanded Abby's full attention and devo-tion, even at the risk of alienating his own children, she still man-aged to enjoy the admiration of interesting men. Her need for people was in its way as strong as his need for privacy. The one element that did not seem to be present in John's desire to possess Abby was sexual jealousy. He was a confident lover and she was a fulfilled partner. Infidelity, or at the very least flirtation, did not seem to be of interest to either of them, in the way it serves as a titillating edge in some relationships. Abby's friendships flourished in the exchange of ideas through letters or across the table at dinner parties.

Her correspondence with MacKenzie King and Raymond Fos-dick is well documented. She exchanged reading lists with Henry

Morgenthau, the former ambassador to Turkey, her neighbor on Mount Desert. She recommended that he read E. M. Forster's *A Passage to India*. Knowing of her keen interest in political history, he sent her his copy of Disraeli's biography of Lord George Bentinck, the independent-minded British parliamentarian. "You will find it most instructive and illuminating on the very points that seem to interest you," Morgenthau wrote.[10]

The man whose opinions she valued the most—and that may have included John's—was Charles Eliot. As she wrote to Lucy when they exchanged their views of various individuals, "none of them [is] quite in the class with . . . Mr. Eliot . . . in [his] best days."[11] They both had a keen interest in the cause of world peace. "I think the outstanding event for the winter to me was the Conference on the Cause and Cure of the War," she wrote Eliot in 1925. "I was able to spend four days only there [in Washington, D.C.] but it was most inspiring and worthwhile. I am sending you the findings of the Conference in which you may be interested."[12]

When Eliot received an announcement of the opening of "International House" in Manhattan, he immediately wrote Abby, suspecting that it was one of her projects. John had endowed it, she replied, but she was his representative on the Construction Committee, also chairman of the Furnishings Committee. "I will serve on the Board of Directors," she explained. "As soon as the personnel of the Board . . . is made up, I shall be very glad to send you the list. There are to be about fifteen members, five or six of whom will be women. . . . I [am] deeply interested in the problem of making better international relations. . . . If the future leaders of the world are brought together while they are still young, [perhaps] there will be an understanding that will make world peace."[13]

Eliot had served on the Rockefeller Foundation when John was president. He was the one who brought King down from Canada at the time of Ludlow, and he worked closely with John in the creation of Acadia National Park, on Mount Desert Island. Eliot was not only humane and wise, but a shrewd judge of character, and he recognized the crucial role Abby played in the family, especially in the life of her husband. In 1917 he had been seriously concerned for John's mental health if he continued as chairman of the board of the Rockefeller Foundation.

"As President of Harvard," he had written John, "I have had occasion to observe . . . how rapidly a life of labor and chronic anxiety . . . brings men to grief after they pass middle life. Now that has been your condition for years. You work hard and long, often without enjoyment in your work; and you experience constant anxiety." He cited much else in the letter, and concluded with this statement. "Your best adviser is, of course, Mrs. Rockefeller. If she does not agree with the substance of this letter, I shall feel like withdrawing it."[14]

Abby knew exactly what Eliot meant. As she wrote him subsequently, "Being less humble and less conscientious than John and harboring in my heart a secret conviction that most worldly success, political, professional or commercial is of a fleeting and uncertain value, I take life more lightly."[15]

Valentiner assumed a special place in Abby's life following their European tour. He became art adviser and personal friend, and through her advised John as well. Should John buy a Veneziano and a Botticelli that were at that very moment hanging in the music room, she asked. "I don't know whether they have come to stay or not but my husband very much likes the portrait which is really quite weirdly like Laurance even when you see him standing in front of it. I am sure that he also admires the Botticelli but feels that Duveen wants quite an exorbitant price for it. . . . I am also glad that you approve of the way in which I arranged the Chinese room and my Persian miniatures. . . . We also have a very small Fra Angelico which belongs to Gimpel. . . . It seems to me that it is a fragment of perhaps a larger picture, as it is very small and rather incomplete. It is quite lovely, but there is something about the expression of the angel's face that I do not quite like. Perhaps I am wrong. I should like very much to know what you think of it."

She wrote him the news of Babs's engagement to Dave Milton two days before the public announcement, hoping that he and his wife could come to the wedding. "There is great excitement . . . as it is to appear in the paper this Saturday [February 24, 1925].

. . . I think you will like him very much. He is so kind and gentle and thoughtful. . . . They are to be married the middle of May [actually it was pushed up to April 24] and I fear that the preparation for the wedding is going to drive every other thought out of my mind."[16] John 3rd wrote in his diary that Babs and Dave had been secretly engaged for a year. Babs wrote Senior that of course to her David was the most wonderful person that ever lived and that she had known him since she was six years old.

The Rockefeller veil of privacy was lifted as society reporters from around the country covered the event in the usual careless tabloid prose about the richest girl in the world marrying a penniless law clerk. For the least exaggerated version of the wedding day, the good, gray columns of the *New York Times* are probably the best source, since a *Times* reporter was invited into the house from the press pool across the street. As the *Times* reported, a thousand people lined the sidewalks to watch the private cars and taxicabs approach the entrance to 10 West 54th. Inside, the lower two floors were transformed into a blooming botanical garden of pink and white dogwood, Japanese flowering quince blossoms, palms, azaleas, and much more. Babs wore silver-colored net and Pointe de Paris lace, Abby wore blue-and-gold brocaded satin. Fifty family members and staff from the country house and the city house witnessed the ceremony at four-thirty in the afternoon.

Although there was no dancing at the reception that followed and wine was not served, the ghost of Nelson Aldrich could have presided happily over the twelve hundred invited guests who streamed up the broad staircase—among them politicians, including Governor Alfred Smith himself, educators, financiers, and the socially prominent. After Babs and Dave slipped away and the last guest departed, John strolled out to the sidewalk to visit with people who were still lingering in the twilight. In small groups he ushered them into the house, showed them to the room where the ceremony had taken place, and gathered bouquets of roses for each of the beaming young women. As the very last group assembled he took the arm of an elderly black woman carrying a shopping bag and personally assisted her into the house.

The *Times* reported other anecdotes as well. Babs was quoted as saying that she was experiencing her "first day of freedom," and that she had deleted the words "obey" and "serve" from the service.[17] Abby sent wedding cake to the aging Asenath and Fanny Tetlow, and the bride and groom sailed for Europe. They were still there in October when Abby and John met them in Paris.

However crowded their schedule, however different their special interests, there was always a touch of romance when Abby and John traveled together. Whether it was an evening walk through picturesque, dark and deserted *arrondissements*, when Abby was sure they were lost and John proved otherwise, or a drive along the Seine "when Papa was tired," the magic of Paris for lovers found its way into Abby's letters home.[18] Sometimes she took John to her fittings. Married nearly twenty-five years, she still expected him to admire her clothes. Although he barely tolerated parties, he did not stop her from inviting 125 guests to a festive tea at the Hôtel Crillon on November 4. The guest list included Providence friends, the American ambassador, assorted art experts from the Louvre, her brother William and his wife, Dorothea, and a sprinkling of titled Bourbons.

Abby's interest in illuminated manuscripts extended to the small prayer books commissioned by the aristocratic laity of Western Europe, intended to be held in the hand and admired. Known as a Book of Hours, such a treasure customarily contained the series of short services honoring the Virgin Mary for each of the canonical hours of the day. One of the very greatest monuments of this art is the Hours of Etienne Chevalier, who was the treasurer of France in the fifteenth century; the illumination is by the supreme French medieval painter, Jean Fouquet. During the French Revolution, the surviving pages became the property of the government; they were mounted in frames and eventually displayed as panel paintings at Chantilly, where on October 15, Abby saw them for the first time. John ordered for her a complete set of lantern slides of the forty-seven miniatures.

During the summer of 1925, before she went to Europe, Abby had been studying Duncan Candler's proposal for a playhouse to be constructed adjacent to Abeyton Lodge at Pocantico. In her enthusiasm to build something really grand for her children and their children (with Babs now married, she could indulge in the fantasy of grandchildren), Abby laid aside her New England conservatism to think on the scale of a Rockefeller. This structure dwarfed the Playhouse at the Eyrie in all aspects. It offered a delicious range of wholesome recreation—squash and tennis courts, twenty-by-sixty-foot heated swimming pool, billiard room, gymnasium, basketball court, changing rooms, bowling alleys. She ordered sculpture for the garden from Valentiner, located rustic furniture in Cannes, and found just the right pewter in Paris for the kitchen. "It will be a very nice occupation," she wrote David, "for you and me to polish it." [19]

CHAPTER 17

―――――・・・❦・・・――――――

*J*ohn 3rd entered Princeton in September 1925, after spending
four years at Loomis. His diary of those years confirms what
Abby always suspected and tried with only partial success to
combat. As an adolescent at boarding school he was nervous, diffi-
dent, and self-deprecating. His personality was her own husband's
carried to the farthest reaches of loneliness. And he did not have a
father like Senior, who, whatever his faults, never placed stern
demands or unreasonable expectations on his only son. Babs stated
with some bitterness that all the children suffered from the "primarily correcting supervising stance" that their father took toward
them, but that John 3rd was hurt the most. Only Nelson, according to Babs, had been able to keep John's criticism at "some
kind of distance."[1]

Abby, on the other hand, took particular care not to criticize
him. And while John wrote long, pedantic letters proclaiming the
need for closeness, she tried in a number of ways to draw near
without embarrassing him. When he came home for holidays she
played cards with him, shared her favorite books, shopped with
him, tried to make life easier in small ways. "I am going to order
your suitcase today and am thinking of having it marked just J R
III. I remember your saying that you didn't like the attention that

your baggage received when it was marked J D R III."[2] She never planned parties for him without making sure that he favored them, and in her weekly letters she revealed more about her relationship with his father than even she realized.

"I was dreadfully disappointed not to write you on Sunday. I had planned to do it as soon as I had put the boys in bed," she wrote, "but when I came down to the library about nine o'clock I found that Papa felt dreadfully tired and he wanted to go to bed at once and I knew it would waken him if I staid up later."[3] John 3rd knew how much she enjoyed using the telephone and how much his father disliked it, that she often sneaked into the bathroom when she made her long phone calls to the various children, so as not to upset him. She was also known to ask that her sons call her. "I hope you telephone from the office," she wrote Nelson, "and get it put on the bill there, for I am sure your dear father would be shocked if I started telephoning freely to you, which I have a great desire to do."[4] As David phrased it, "His calls were business and therefore justifiable, hers were personal, and possibly frivolous."[5]

John 3rd was painfully aware of his own difficulties with his father. He showed him elaborate deference even as his anger swelled and he agonized how to confront him. He recognized the subtleties his mother contrived to protect herself. "F. always has own way," he wrote in his diary. "He is . . . broad in business relations, but so narrow in some of his family ideas. . . . M. certainly is wonderful to him on the details. Lets him always have his own way yet makes him think he is giving her her way."[6] Whether he also perceived the stress Abby labored under, to maintain this equilibrium in her marriage, is not clear. He could, after all, marvel at her diplomacy, and still assume that wives were expected to take that role, the role of resilience, of adaptation, of looking out for interests other than their own.

Nelson in his last year at Lincoln was setting his sights on Dartmouth, believing that he had a better chance of admission there because of its lower entrance requirements. There was no guarantee, however, that he would be accepted. He loved Lincoln, with its problem-solving approach, its attention to the "whole person," its exciting field trips, but his grades continued to be terrible; the dyslexia had driven him further and further behind. As a senior he set out to correct—in one year—what had been several years in developing. He stopped seeing girls except on weekends. "To make up, I have been to see her three times on Sunday," he wrote Abby.[7] He locked up his phonograph and radio and studied four and five hours every day. He dropped Spanish, taking special tutoring in mathematics and French instead, and labored all winter, convinced that his program would pay off. His father plied him with a formal agenda and schedules. Abby was cautious with advice and maintained her sense of humor. "[Nelson] is most amusing about his lessons," she had written Laurance over the summer, "and says that now he has gotten past the third grade in spelling and only missed two words."[8]

Abby barely concealed her enjoyment of Nelson, even when he was in trouble. Stocky, handsome, irrepressible, devoid of Rockefeller guilt and reserve, he seemed to trust his instincts the way she did. His very name, Nelson Aldrich, had a certain significance. More than the others, did he remind her of her father? Was it the Aldrich in him that touched her? Laurance believes that it was. "Nelson, and later David, delighted my mother because they were affirmative and outgoing."[9] Perhaps too Nelson reminded Abby of her younger self, the unpredictable girl whose mother could never guess what she would say or do next, before she harnessed her spirit to her sober, cautious, exacting lover. Winthrop, also, would grow up to be handsome and fun-loving, but Winthrop was uncertain about himself, in a way that was inconceivable for Nelson. Winthrop did not always know how to fight back. When Nelson saw himself at a disadvantage, as when he suffered the acute embarrassment and agony of not being able to read, he drew on his indomitable will and pride to become an achiever.

Laurance at sixteen continued to be the member of the family who stepped back as an observer. He was not quite robust enough to satisfy Abby, but she acknowledged that he was perfectly well and had come to appreciate his reflective nature. Winthrop seemed less restless since the older boys had begun to treat him better. He had impressed them with his bravery in the summer of 1924 when his tutor crashed the family Dodge truck into a stone wall, hurling

Winthrop through the windshield. Because of his kidney condition at that time, the doctor took three hours to stitch up ten deep facial gashes without benefit of anesthetic. Apparently he joked and talked as the doctor prepared each stitch. John rewarded him with his very own red bug for driving around Pocantico.

David was excelling in domestic science with a dozen jars of jelly and a good chocolate cake to his credit. He sang in Lincoln's Christmas program and took the part of a pumpkin in an amusing French play. He certainly looked the part, wrote his mother. David was beginning to benefit from being the youngest. It was inevitable that John would finally ease up. Babs pointed out how stern their father had been about Nelson's left-handedness, but that he relented when David favored his left hand. Perhaps John had learned from the futility of trying to rein in Babs's defiance, perhaps Abby's liberality had gradually worn away some of his rigidity, but the beneficiary, without a doubt, was David.

For their spring break in 1926, Laurance, Winthrop, and David went with their parents to visit Hampton Institute and the old plantations along the James River. At some point the itinerary changed to include a detour to Williamsburg, Virginia. Abby was pleased. She knew that John liked historic sites and that two years before he had heard some interesting possibilities for a Williamsburg restoration at a Phi Beta Kappa banquet in New York. The speaker had been one Dr. William A. R. Goodwin, rector of Bruton Parish Church of Williamsburg and professor of sacred and profane literature and social ethics at the College of William and Mary. The eager guide waiting to show them around on this March afternoon was the same Dr. Goodwin.

In its prime, Williamsburg had been the cultural and political capital of the vast colony of Virginia. Now it was a dilapidated, lethargic Southern town with scarcely a trace of its former splendor, although it was still home to some descendants of original colonial families. After traversing the shabby streets, still in their eighteenth-century pattern, after gazing upon the Wren Building, the oldest surviving academic structure in the land, much the worse for neglect, after absorbing Dr. Goodwin's great fund of knowledge, Abby and John left with some understanding of the potential for a restoration of truly national significance. Abby saw John exhilarated and challenged in a way that reminded her of her own excitement at a new art discovery.

For the next weeks and months, as was his habit and his need, he drew her into his intense self-examination and the testing of doubts and possibilities concerning a Williamsburg restoration. He exploited her intuition, her imagination, the judgment that he trusted, the unchallengeable fact that she was *for* him, in a way that no one else could be, that she knew him in a way no one else could, and that she would never betray his interests. She understood his respect for history, his excruciating attention to detail, his experience in construction, his bottomless desire for perfection. It seemed to her that the project and the man were made for each other. Without her as his partner and sounding board, it is doubtful that he would have proceeded, even more doubtful that the Williamsburg restoration would have been the remarkable success that it became. With her, he made the commitment and "underwent all the pleasures and pangs of creation."[10] He authorized Dr. Goodwin to purchase various properties and commission architects to draw up sketches and blueprints as part of the master plan to restore the shabby town to its colonial past. A year after the first tour of the town, Abby and John returned.

They studied the plans carefully, Dr. Goodwin's secretary recalled. "Their grasp of the situation was astonishing."[11] She was observing what everyone connected with Colonial Williamsburg during the restoration would confirm. Edwin Kendrew, the resident architect, recalled incident after incident that went something as follows: "Mr. Rockefeller would come to Williamsburg to listen to all our schemes, very carefully, absorbing everything. Eventually he would smile and say that now he would have to find the money. But then, before excusing himself, he would very politely ask to take the portfolios home with him. A few days later he would return with the candid admission that he had gone over everything with Mrs. Rockefeller and they had walked all over the sites and made notes, and now he had some questions. It might relate to something they could not locate on the site, or some doubt raised by Mrs. Rockefeller. Could I please fill in the missing data or consider her objection? It was obvious to me that he was working very closely with her."[12]

Three months later, following Nelson's graduation from Lincoln and his departure with John 3rd for a bicycle tour of Europe, Abby and John and the younger boys went on another one of the private railway tours of the Western United States. Abby left the logistics and the management of the boys to John. He had set ideas about which one handled the luggage and who tipped the porters. For Abby, a conventional family tour turned into an artistic adventure when they reached New Mexico and she experienced for the first time the true variety and quality of Native American art.

She had the advantage of an expert guide, much as she had had William Valentiner in Germany. Kenneth Chapman was one of the founders of the Indian Arts Fund, which had its own extensive collection of Native American art, and he was also a staff member of the Museum of New Mexico at Santa Fe. At her behest he took the entire party, including the three boys, to view the Indian Arts Fund's holding of Pueblo pottery.

Abby then suggested that they visit the actual pueblos where the artists were working—Santa Clara, San Ildefonso, and Taos. David Rockefeller remembers the visit as the time when he was permitted to buy a small pot for $3. It was at San Ildefonso that Abby raptly watched the great Pueblo potter María Martínez form and fire her famous polychrome pieces. At Chapman's polite insistence, Martínez reluctantly showed Abby her lustrous black-on-black wares, which she kept hidden because she disliked them! (An American archaeologist had persuaded her and her painter husband to reinvent the technique, which had been lost for eight hundred years.) Abby became the first collector of the black pottery, and John agreed with her idea of decorating their Eyrie Rest House with handsome Native American jugs and bowls and baskets.

Chapman next took them to see some of the works of Pueblo painters, and again Abby was stirred by the artistry of an ancient civilization, in much the same way that she had been moved by Japanese prints and Persian miniatures. The delicate drawings and watercolors of Awa Tsireh, nephew-in-law of Martínez, resembled miniatures in their degree of precision and sophistication. Abby eventually acquired works by Tsireh, as well as those of the only woman painter in the San Ildefonso movement, Tonita Pena. Pena painted what and as she liked; she was "the first woman to throw off the shackles of sex-determined art forms and express herself in new . . . ways," according to later critics.[13] In 1932 she was invited to exhibit at the Venice Biennial.

In Taos (the town proper as distinguished from the pueblo to the north and Ranchos de Taos to the south), Chapman introduced Abby and the others to the art colony. American painters, attracted to the grandeur of the New Mexico landscape, its sunbaked Spanish-Indian adobe architecture, and the relative stability and vibrancy of the Pueblo culture, had begun to settle in Taos before the Great War. Writers followed, along with intellectuals of every stripe, people with a little money who wanted to live in a picturesque setting, expatriate bohemians, all of whom gave Taos its exotic flavor.

Joseph Henry Sharp, Eanger Irving Couse, and Bert Geer Phillips were the most significant members of the Taos art colony to commit to canvas their view of the Native Americans of the Southwest. But they were less interested in ethnographic accuracy than in their romantic belief in the Native American as a symbol of spiritual tranquillity, undisturbed by the realities of white domination. In this respect they were in step with an American public, which no longer saw the Indian as a savage threat to the march of civilization, but as a sentimental object of pity, even a tragic hero. Sharp was the most conscientious in respecting the artifacts and costumes that belonged to the individual tribes. Phillips was an early activist for the rights of Native Americans to ancestral lands and holy places. Couse, whose talent was unchallenged, and who enjoyed the greatest critical acclaim, was the most romantic and the most willing to scramble his cultural data.

Abby bought works by all three, the most—eighteen in all— from Couse. Writing from Seal Harbor later in the summer, she thanked him for the gift which he inscribed with her name. "It was such a charming painting of the clouds which I loved so much in your beautiful country. . . . At last Mr. Rockefeller and I have arranged your paintings in our 'Rest House' . . . I think also they will inspire the people who visit our little cottage with a sympathetic interest in the American Indians and their work."[14]

Abby's visit to Taos and the pueblos was but a day in the family's two-month journey, but the exposure to the primitive art of native peoples added to her artistic maturation. The travelers now embarked by train and by motorcar on serious sight-seeing—across Arizona, into California and Oregon, weaving this way and that. On July 13, at the gate to West Yellowstone, Horace Albright, superintendent of Yellowstone National Park, met them with two touring cars and personally escorted them on a four-day swing through the park, the Grand Tetons, and Jackson Hole Valley. This was an area of awesome sawtoothed mountains rising as much as fourteen thousand feet, exquisite piedmont lakes, rolling grassland, and scattered stands of virgin forest. Albright, an energetic young conservationist, was dedicated to preserving the area and protecting it from the developers. He had already met John in 1924 and knew him as the leading patron of wilderness conservation. What he had done and was still doing for Acadia National Park on Mount Desert was already a legend in the Park Service.

On the third day of the expedition, Albright, according to memoirs edited by his daughter, Marian Albright Schenck, drove Abby and John on a new road that led to Jenny Lake. There they encountered all the ugliness permitted by the Forest Service against Albright's vehement objections—ramshackle buildings, gas stations, litter of all kinds, a dance hall and saloon (this was during Prohibition), even a sagging telephone line between the road and the Tetons. Abby became increasingly agitated. Wasn't there something that could be done to prevent such desecration, she asked. Albright, who had been warned not to proselytize, had his opening. Slowly, carefully, he explained the opposition from developers, and that most of the magnificent surroundings were in private hands and if a way was not found to protect the area it would only get worse.

In less than a year John informed Albright that he would support his vision for a Grand Tetons National Park in a most dramatic way. He would acquire all the private land in the valley and then give it to the federal government for the proposed park. What followed, however, was not the smooth execution of an idea, as had happened on Mount Desert, but twenty years of bitter, protracted struggle among bureaucrats, politicians, local residents, timber and cattle interests, and the conservationists themselves. In the final outcome, however, Albright and John were victorious. The area was preserved, the region prospered, and the public has been the ultimate beneficiary.

Abby and John were at the Eyrie for their twenty-fifth wedding anniversary, on October 9. "It will amuse you to hear what we did," she wrote David, and proceeded to describe breakfast in bed, lunch in the boathouse because it was raining, chocolate by the fire, and then two hours of changing the furniture about and reading until dinnertime. "It was pouring when we started back to the house," she continued, "and so dark I had to hold on to Papa and he had to feel his way back with his feet. . . . We put on our best clothes for dinner and had a lovely cake."[15]

She wrote Lucy that she missed Nelson, who had just entered Dartmouth, but it was some comfort to know that she would stop over at Hanover on her way back to the city for the winter. And finally, in the same letter, she mentioned her new garden for the first time. "Mrs. Farrand is helping me and fortunately she likes Chinese sculpture. We are going to put the Korean (Ming tomb sort of) figures along one side making a walk by the garden into the woods beyond."[16]

Beatrix Jones Farrand, who formed a creative collaboration with Abby that lasted twenty years, was one of the great landscape architects of her era, although she always thought of herself as a gardener. In 1899 she was a founding member, at the age of twenty-seven, of the American Institute of Landscape Architects, the only woman among eleven members. Her origins, like Abby's, were eastern seaboard and aristocratic. Her father, Frederick Rhinelander Jones, was born into the safe, well-ordered Manhattan milieu of the mid-nineteenth century, in which everyone of importance seemed to be related. His sister, with whom he had absolutely nothing in common, was Edith Jones Wharton, the novelist, who interpreted the repressive structure of that milieu with piercing insight.

Beatrix's mother, Minnie Jones, had been raised in an entirely different culture, one of artistic and political diversity. She was a woman of uncommon intelligence, originality, and kindness, a Philadelphia Rawle, the first Rawle having been a friend of William Penn. She was beautiful, she was fluent in French, and she had already met Henry James, William Thackeray, and two American presidents when she married Freddy Jones and moved to New York. But the marriage was not a happy one. Minnie divorced Jones when Beatrix was twelve. She supplemented her income by acting as literary agent for her sister-in-law Edith Wharton, and presided over one of the liveliest literary salons in Manhattan.

Beatrix was fortunate in having the influence of two remarkable women, her mother and her aunt Edith, and an unusual man, her uncle John Cadwalader. John Lambert Cadwalader was a distinguished New York lawyer who founded the New York Public Library, and more important for Beatrix, respected women of talent and independence. "Let her be a gardener or, for that matter, anything she wants to be," he said of his niece. "What she wishes to do will be well done." [17]

It was in her mother's drawing room when she was still in her teens that Beatrix Jones met Charles Sprague Sargent, the director of the Arnold Arboretum. She was already fascinated with horticulture. Professor Sargent, recognizing her quick, retentive mind and an eager ambition that set her apart from other young women in her set, invited her to live with him and his wife in Boston and study at the Arboretum. There were no schools of landscape architecture as yet. Harvard's opened eight years later, in 1900, for men only. Beatrix remained with the Sargents for four years. She learned surveying from him. She observed closely how he and Frederick Law Olmsted laid out the grounds of the arboretum. She absorbed his deep love of plants, his respect for nature, his commitment to research. Her entire professional career reflected two of his basic dictums, to "make the plan fit the ground and not twist the ground to fit the plan," and, most significant in her relationship with Abby at the Eyrie, to "carefully study the tastes of the owner."[18]

Sargent's final suggestion to his apprentice was to visit the great gardens and parks of Europe. Beatrix traveled for six months, keeping a careful journal and assembling her impressive reference collection of prints and books on landscape design. She met Gertrude Jekyll, the English gardener, whose principles of color harmony in planting made a profound impression on the young American.

In the fall in 1895, she set up practice on the top floor of Minnie Jones's New York brownstone. Her first clients came from her network of Jones and Cadwalader connections. Soon she was designing estate gardens in Newport, Tuxedo, Long Island, and Bar Harbor. She knew the advantage and disadvantage of every tree, plant, shrub, and flower. But beyond her professional skill, there were personal qualities that, as described by one observer, could just as easily apply to Abby Aldrich Rockefeller. It is not at all surprising that they admired each other. "Skilled at handling people," it was said about Beatrix, "[she] soothed ruffled feathers, and usually managed to persuade people to her way of thinking."[19]

Beatrix married Max Farrand, chairman of the Yale history department, in 1913. When Max Farrand left Yale to take up his position as director of the Huntington Library in San Marino, California, Beatrix closed her New Haven office to open one in California, but kept the other two, in Bar Harbor and New York. She commuted between coasts looking after her clients, which now included Princeton, Yale, the Rockefeller Institute, and Dumbarton Oaks in Washington, D.C.

Abby Rockefeller's seeking out Beatrix Farrand has an air of inevitability, considering how their networks intersected. Beatrix had been spending her summers at Reef Point, her family's estate in Bar Harbor, at least as long as Abby had been coming to the Eyrie. The Bliss family of Dumbarton Oaks were old friends of Abby, reaching back to Nelson Aldrich's time. Abby had been studying gardens since her father built Warwick, and knew exactly who the experts were. In keeping with her intuitive way of making judgments, she decided that Beatrix Farrand would respect her desire to create an authentic Oriental garden, not as a mere ornamental adjunct to the estate but as a spiritual retreat.

Finally there was the fact that Beatrix was a woman. Not just any woman, nor even a woman of indifferent talent who deserved patronage, but a superbly qualified woman whose skills towered over those of many of her male colleagues. Abby liked women. She was proud of accomplished women, as proved by her loyalty to her YWCA associates, and the women who ran Bayway and the Grace Dodge Hotel. She liked to see them get ahead. "I like the looks of the young women I meet," she said to a group at the Cosmopolitan Club. (Abby was one of the founders of the Club in 1911.) "Being naturally frank myself, I am not shocked by the lack of reserve that one notices in their conversation. I am delighted that [they] are having a chance to express themselves; I love to see the old hypocrisies being shattered by scientific blows from the truth-seekers."[20]

"The Abby Aldrich Rockefeller Garden," Patrick Chassé, a specialist in East Asian landscape aesthetics, writes, "holds a significant place in American garden history. . . . The ideas in this garden are a meeting of East and West, imaginatively original in applying an English garden tradition within an Oriental framework, built in a stunning natural setting."[21] Abby, the client, educated Farrand, the professional. Beatrix Farrand had never traveled to the Far East and had scant exposure to Asian aesthetics. Abby, on the other hand, had returned from her three months in the Orient in 1921 with a fresh appreciation of Asian art and philosophy. For five years she had been reading assiduously and discussing her ideas with Lucy, who had become a serious and informed collector of Oriental art. Recently she had acquired the Korean tomb sculpture referred to in her letter.

Abby had a strong affinity for the intrinsic meaning of funerary sculpture, its serenity and the power of its placement. Both the Imperial Palace and the Temple of Heaven in Peking became her models for the garden walls and openings. The circular Moon Gate and the design known as the Bottle Gate were hallmarks of imperial Chinese wall design. News from far-off Peking—the rumor that glazed coping tiles from a demolished section of the Forbidden

Moon Gate. Abby's walled garden at the Eyrie, Seal Harbor, Maine, 1935.
Courtesy of the Rockefeller Archive Center.

City might be for sale—precipitated Abby's decision to enclose the garden in a spiraling wall, "a deliberate, intelligent wall," as one observer phrased it.[22] It would become the climactic decision in the garden's history. Ten thousand salvaged yellow roofing tiles were shipped to Maine to cap the wall, ultimately to be pierced by the South Gate, the East Gate, the Moon Gate, and the Bottle Gate. Farrand was able to simulate in the new stucco-and-brick wall the rose red of its Chinese ancestor.

Abby's vision, Farrand's respect for natural elements and her horticultural competence, and John's attention to detail formed an effective combination. Over a period of several years the basic scale and form of the garden would be developed—drainage system, auxiliary structures, placement and relocation of trees, parameters set for the sunken panel that came to be known as the annual garden and the intimate, naturalistic pool garden. Abby kept control of every aesthetic decision, conferring with Farrand daily when they were in Seal Harbor together, while John continued to check the bills and follow the changes that Abby freely made.

By 1934, the year the garden would reach the peak of its development, it began to receive national attention and appear on the list of gardens to be visited by the Garden Club of America. It was here, in her private sanctuary, that Abby would find her greatest solace, to read, to muse, to lose track of time. John, who was so punctual, tried to understand, but David noticed that whenever his mother retreated into dreamy contemplation, his father's patience, never noteworthy, would evaporate, and he would firmly summon her out of her reverie.

CHAPTER 18

*rohibition was still the law of the land, the stock market was still booming, and the third Republican in a decade—Herbert Hoover—would soon be elected to the White House. In Abby's private world, however, it was a time of change, change both obvious and subtle. She became a grandmother. Laurance went off to Princeton and Winthrop to Loomis. David was the solitary child living in the nine-story house. The skepticism that still clung to the name of Rockefeller continued to fade as John devoted his energy and his fortune to worldwide good works. His exhaustive preoccupation with such projects gave Abby some breathing room. After meeting his complex needs and desires for twenty-seven years, perhaps she felt her own power, not the power to destroy, but power as it related to freedom. Her lifetime of loyalty had earned her a certain immunity. Sensing all this, she began to offer selective support to the people and the causes that were important to her.

If John remained staunchly nonpolitical and noncontroversial, she was somewhat less so. She gave one luncheon for Margaret Bondfield, Labour member of Parliament, and a second to raise money for Bryn Mawr's Labor School. She invited Rabbi Stephen S. Wise of the Free Synagogue to speak before the Women's

Bible Class and William Green, president of the American Federation of Labor, to address the Fellowship Council of the Baptist Church.

Her suspicion of the press and investigative reporting in general had mellowed since the early days of the century when her father was the target of the muckrakers. When she traveled to Washington in February 1928 to address the National Women's Press Club, her remarks were carried over the wire services. "When I was a girl," she said, "I had an ambition to own a newspaper of my own because I thought that then I could have a paper that would always tell the truth. But I have now learned how difficult it is sometimes to find the truth."[1]

After a conversation in Williamsburg with John Steward Bryan, the editor and publisher of the *Richmond News-Leader*, she and Bryan exchanged letters. Abby posed some of the questions that still plague thoughtful people about all media. "One sometimes wonders whether the demand comes from the public 'for the kind of news they get, or whether the press is not cultivating in the public a taste for the kind of news which it gives them."[2]

Bryan replied in part as follows:

Your letter was most suggestive. . . . I think we can agree that newspapers do dramatize crime for the purpose, primarily, of selling papers, and while the aim is not an admirable one, yet I have no doubt that literacy has been greatly increased by making people read.

He went on to tell the story of a newsboy who tossed aside both the *New York Times* and the *New York World* in favor of a tabloid, with the following analysis:

There are very few of us who can, as Matthew Arnold said: "Follow with delighted apprehension the reasoning of Plato," and I sometimes wonder if a . . . truck driver doesn't get something of the same idea of the inexplicable tragedies of life from reading some sordid murder trial that the educated Athenian got from the great tragedies of Aeschylus or Sophocles.[3]

When John embarked on a low-cost housing development, the Avenue A apartments opposite the laboratories of the Rockefeller Institute, the *New York Times* called upon Abby for a statement. "Nothing that Mr. Rockefeller has done recently pleased me more than his building of the Avenue A garden homes and his part in the construction of the Bayonne garden apartments, because I know that homes with sunshine and fresh air and beauty are essential for all of us, and especially for children."[4]

Abby went to Providence to participate in the final disposition of her parents' personal property, ten years after their deaths. "The division . . . went off most happily," she wrote Lucy. "I am delighted with my share. I have portraits of Aunt Abby and Uncle Duty Greene. . . . Every time I go by them they recall to my mind our life at 110 Benevolent Street. . . . I also have practically all the contents of [Papa's] library [except for the texts on economics that were given to Harvard]."[5] The siblings agreed to turn over the Benevolent Street house to Lucy and the Warwick estate to Ned.

As if to bring the remote past more poignantly into focus, Abby received a long letter from the Tetlow sisters. Asenath was bedridden from a stroke and Fanny was battling blindness. Lucy and Abby and Mathilde and Miss MacFadden watched over the two women. Always the pedagogue, Fanny wrote what a pity it was that Lucy was not poor! "[If she had been] obliged to work she would have written books . . . and published them. She always did write interesting letters and she hasn't lost the art now."[6]

Nor had she lost the art of good taste in clothes. Abby had concluded long ago that were it not for Lucy she would look like a frump. Writing from Paris, Lucy reported on her progress. "I got most of the things at Worth, the models there were much prettier and decidedly smarter. Your vendeuse . . . is a wonder. . . . After we had chosen the models we put them all down in a row in one of the fitting rooms and we four chose the colors and decided how they should be changed to be becoming to you. . . . We took the samples to Reboux and Mme. Caroline chose the hats. They were then all six made on my head. I don't look much like you but they have to be made on somebody and they thought I was the nearest.

. . . Your evening coat is just like the Queen of the Belgians new one (she has Mme. Jaune your vendeuse) only hers is white and gold trimmed with sable; and I didn't quite dare do that. . . . I'm afraid you would be horrified at the price of your things but if you had come over you would have had to pay your passage, your hotel . . . and your automobile . . . and think of the time saved too."[7]

Lucy's knowledge of Parisian sources was encyclopedic— blouses, buckles, bootmakers; corsets, lingerie, coats, suits, jewelry. And twenty-one expert hat makers, since hats were one of Abby's most dependable indulgences. "I have a new hat with lilies of the valley on it. It is very silly but it does cheer me up." On another occasion she noted that everyone at the board meeting liked her hat, "though I think they were a bit startled at first by the odd fruit on it. I told them it was meant to suggest a Harvest Home Supper." She thought better of a college president who was intrigued with her hat. "I have a new hope for education, when the president of a woman's college is not blind to hats. As a matter of fact she had on an encouraging one herself." And once, when she was dreading a conference, she sent a hurried note to a friend. "Have you a really wild hat that I might borrow. . . . Mine are all too tame and I want something to amuse those worried women."[8]

On April 27, 1928, Abby became a grandmother when Babs gave birth to Abby Milton, eight pounds four ounces, born in the infirmary at 10 West 54th and delivered by the same Dr. Thomas who had delivered Babs. "She is really a beautiful baby," Grandmother Abby enthused to Great-Aunt Lucy. "She has a lovely head and her little body is perfect in every way. Her nose at the moment [May 7] turns up but may come down later. . . . She . . . is not a bit red but just a nice pink and white. . . . The nurse and I both feel that she has a great deal of charm and personality." Abby conceded that such talk might be the imagination of a proud grandmother, but even Dr. Thomas raved about her. "I am delighted to say that she [Babs] is nursing the baby. She has lots of milk which is splendid I think. I tell her that I quite envy her as I was never able to nurse any of our children."[9]

The press, still taken with the idea that the Rockefeller heiress had married a man of modest means, liked to remind readers that

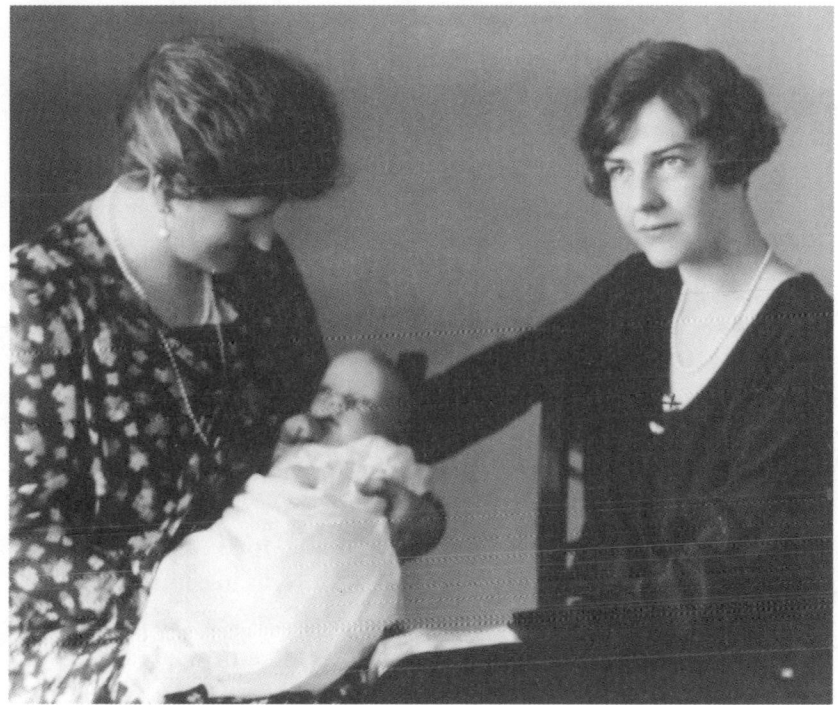

Three generations: Abby, infant Abby Milton, and Babs Rockefeller Milton, 1928.
Courtesy of the Rockefeller Archive Center.

according to various third parties, the young couple were determined to live within David's income as a junior lawyer. How Dave and Babs actually handled the huge disparity in their finances is much more complicated than any rumor would have it. Both Abby and John were well aware of the delicate problems involved. Dave, ambitious and proud, was uncertain how to compete with Rockefeller money. John, in one letter to Abby, referred to having a long talk with his daughter on her financial situation. "She is very wise and diplomatic," he wrote.[10] So far as is known, John did not turn great blocks of assets over to Babs. But a month before the baby was born, he authorized his office to advance her whatever sum might be necessary up to $50,000 to renovate an East Side apartment.

Babs replied on April 12. "I don't know when I've gotten more of a thrill than that message gave me. The fact that you didn't even ask any questions but put that large sum of money at my immediate disposal was more than generous. . . ."[11] Earlier she had tried to communicate to him what all his children felt as they observed him from their perspective. "You have so many important problems on your mind and so little time for pleasure, that to give up some of those precious minutes means even more . . . than the writing of a check."[12]

Abby, who should have known better, fell into the same trap as John did with Babs, and that was to offer unsolicited advice. Babs had written Abby in great excitement that she was going to visit Lucy in Paris, at which point Abby said that Babs should go to Maine or Long Island instead, and she said many other things that were perhaps none of her business. Abby was wrong, Babs insisted, about Maine or Long Island as places for Babs to spend the summer. Abby was wrong about Babs only living in the past and in the future. Abby was wrong about challenging Babs's decision to leave Dave for two weeks to go to Europe, and Babs pointed out that Abby was contradicting herself. "A great many people feel that every so often a <u>short</u> separation is just the thing that is needed to freshen one's viewpoint . . ." she wrote.[13]

In the fall of 1928, David became the only child at home when Winthrop and Laurance went away to school. As much as Abby resisted sending her children to boarding school, she did apparently agree with the decision to transfer Winthrop out of Lincoln and wrote the following letter to the administration:

> After much deliberation and anxious thought, Mr. Rockefeller and I have very reluctantly come to the conclusion that it will be better for Winthrop to go to boarding school for the next two years.
>
> We have reached this decision because Winthrop finds it extremely difficult to study at home. He allows the slightest distraction to interfere with his studying, and it has not been possible for us in the past to correct this fault.
>
> Another reason, which we feel is important, is the fact of his size. He is now 6 feet 1 inch in his stocking feet, and weighs, after losing

13 pounds, 185 lbs. His height and general appearance give the impression that he is much older than he really is [Winthrop was sixteen], and therefore he is quite often treated with a deference which is beyond his years and which is not good for him. . . .

We feel very sorry to take him away from the Lincoln School. . . . We have just reached this decision and Loomis Institute has very kindly offered to take him in. . . .[14]

Winthrop himself, in writing to his own son years later, evaluated the experience at each of the schools. "At Lincoln the emphasis was on the development of personality, of individual qualities, more than on the three R's. I wasn't prepared to meet the stiffer scholastic standards of Loomis. But that . . . was not entirely the fault of . . . Lincoln. I was always much more interested in things I could do with my hands than I was in textbooks. . . . there were many things about [Loomis] that I liked. . . . All the boys shared the chores, without reference to money or family background. There weren't any chambermaids or housecleaners in the dormitories. Each boy made his own bed and cleaned his room, and we took turns cleaning the halls. The job of waiting on tables was rotated too. . . . Since neither money nor family brought any great advantages, nobody paid much attention to them. . . . Loomis gave its boys a much more genuine feeling of democracy than many other schools . . . and only confirmed and supplemented the principles I had learned from mother and father."[15] He reiterated, however, that on the academic side Loomis *was* tough.

Abby, as she watched the boys apply to college, was uneasy about their lack of preparation. "Winthrop has never studied much," she acknowledged, "and he has gotten lots of managerial skills out of the L. School, but I don't like the feeling that our children can't go anywhere to college because we have sent them to a school that has failed to train them. Life is certainly full of problems."[16]

Lucy had a different idea about Winthrop. "I think [he] is a wonder," she wrote, "and don't think it makes one bit of difference whether he goes to college or not. If he doesn't go he wont miss it in the least. He will always be the centre of the stage some where and when he is with the other boys they wont talk about their college experiences they will be trying to keep up with him. He is so alive and eager."[17]

Perhaps Lucy was right. Some of the sweetness that ran through his letters was a legacy from Abby. She wrote him frequently, sent him Indian pictures for his walls, new curtains according to the measurements and diagram he sent her, a box of fresh pears, chocolate bars, extra blankets, a new typewriter, and a warm woolen muffler. "There is one thing that I would like you to send me," he wrote, "and that is a picture of yourselves and a picture of John that I can put in my frame and one of Sis and the baby."[18] His letters were tinged with homesickness, but he assured her that everything was going well with him—except for marks. "I suppose by this time you have heard the worst about my last marks and are just about as disappointed as I am, and rightly should be, for they certainly were about as poor as they could be."[19]

He did manage to pull up some of his grades from F's to C's and D's, but it was a constant struggle, as his interests always seemed to veer away to girls and projects. All the dances were huge successes, all the girls were "peaches," couldn't be nicer, including one Eleanor Hoyt who came to Hartford in the family amphibian plane, piloted by a British aviator. At the Loomis Agricultural Show he was able to raise some much-needed money for an Indian artist friend by raffling some of his pictures. A perfect weekend at Pocantico was followed by an F in English.

Laurance invited all his classmates at Lincoln to Pocantico for a weekend houseparty to celebrate their graduation. "They certainly have bright children there," Abby reported to Lucy, "especially the girls. They seemed to have read everything and knew all about the latest plays and pictures, in fact about everything that is going on in the world today. I was quite impressed by them."[20]

Laurance entered Princeton in mid-September. One of the very few freshmen who came from a progressive, nonsectarian day school, Laurance had his share of adjustments, too. "There is an art to taking exams," he said later, "and I didn't have it. In terms of study habits, I paid a price, but on balance I think I gained vastly more at Lincoln than if I had gone to a fashionable prep school, a wholeness, an adaptive sense of living wherever I was."[21]

He seemed to have an easier time with girls than his brother John, and when the inevitable crunch over grades came in November, he expressed himself in that pragmatic, faintly ironic tone which was now part of his personality. He did not waste his energy on guilt or self-recrimination, but rather offered a cool analysis of the situation and its remedy. "Having rather tired of discussing why I fail exams," he wrote his parents, "I shall merely state here what plans I am making for the future. Tomorrow I shall go to see Dean Hermance and my advisor Mr. Scoon. In view of the results of the exams I didn't go to the Prom as planned. . . . As far as weekends are concerned I shall arrange to stay in Princeton . . . until after the next exam. At Thanksgiving I will not return to New York after coming back here Thursday night. . . . This will so arrange my schedule that outside of regular exercise all my time can be given to study. . . . I hope that you won't feel that I have failed to meet my obligation entered into in coming here and that you will leave all the worrying to be done about it to me."[22]

His last letter written before his Christmas break dealt with lighter matters, but couched in the same droll, mildly caustic way.

Altho my opinion is not necessary to matters pertaining to cars, may I nevertheless say that I see good reasons to agree with your suggestions about our use of cars. However, in regards to the use of the Buick by no one except Nelson, I feel that a little further consideration of this point would at least do no harm. . . . If anyone is still interested, it has occurred to me that I would like new hairbrushes and a comb for Christmas. . . . I am in serious need of a financial settlement as I have spent about $200.00 since I've been here which I am going to make an effort to recover from you. Judging by the number of things we have coming up for discussion, it looks as tho most of the vacation is to be spent in conference.[23]

John and Laurance together drew up a petition to the "management of No. 10; and that is that the radio be returned from the seventh floor to the little room off the library, or a new one be purchased to take its place. [We] hope that the management will give the question due consideration in the near future. . . ."[24]

———··◦◦◦◦··———

*D*ear Mrs. Rockefeller, Jr. I wish to thank you most sincerely for the kindly interest of showing my pictures in your home. I feel it to be the most important event of my whole career. I think I am the happiest man in the world. Will be most delighted to come and thank you in person Dec. 17. Sincerely yours, Pop Hart."[1]

George Overbury "Pop" Hart was a vagabond American artist, self-taught, who wandered the world over, from Iceland to Tahiti to Mexico, recording the scenes that intrigued his whimsical eye. Although admired in certain circles, he was not a major figure. Abby, who was taking chances now with artists who had not yet made their mark, decided to collect his works. In eleven months she bought over a hundred lithographs and many of his fluent watercolors, with titles such as *Landscape in Morocco* and *Orchestra at Cockfight*—some from Keppel & Company, but a much greater number from a young dealer named Edith Gregor Halpert who had opened her Downtown Gallery in Greenwich Village in 1926 to promote contemporary American artists.

It was a rainy, blustery Monday on December 17, 1928, when artists, critics, and interested friends gathered to meet the itinerant Hart, an unusual guest in the conservative Rockefeller household. "Indoors, all was snug," Edward Jewell wrote in the *New York*

Times, "and before an open fire in the room where tea was served one found the artist himself."[2] Halpert had already made him the subject of her first monograph with its twenty-four plates and twenty-six-page text. Abby, whose forays into the world of modern art had begun quietly, was now perceived, to the surprise of a public who had assumed her to have a conventional outlook, as an adventurous collector of unpredictable and original opinions. As a result of Abby's support, Hart enjoyed a good press and sales of his works increased dramatically. His long-term reputation, however, did not keep pace with the temporary success. Abby's aesthetic intuition, which would be vindicated so many times in the years ahead, fell short.

To John, the art that Abby now proposed to hang on the walls of their home seemed too strange and irresponsible. "I showed Papa the [Hart] pictures," she wrote Nelson, ". . . and he thinks they are terrible beyond words."[3] That art should be self-expression flowing from within, rather than discipline and order imposed from without, defied John's deepest convictions. Abby, familiar with such convictions, and understanding their emotional component, made her compromise. She would segregate her new art on the seventh floor, a little-used floor, where he would be safe from it and not have to confront it daily.

Abby's financial situation as it affected her purchases of art had changed in 1927. In April of that year John informed her by letter that in addition to her allowance of $50,000 for charitable gifts, she could now begin to draw an amount up to a total of $25,000 for "such art purchases as you might care to make during the year 1927. . . . These credits are available in the office . . . without reference to me. Hoping that this will facilitate the carrying out of your desires, I am affectionately, John."[4] Such a personal fund did not preclude their buying art objects together. Only a few months earlier she had located a sixth-century Bodhisattva of the T'ang period. The life-size marble figure of a young Buddha acolyte—slender, delicately sculptured—was to be placed in the reception hall at 10 West 54th. Bernard Berenson himself congratulated her on having made such an unchallengeable purchase, for there were not more than three or four in existence.

In 1928, John doubled her art purchase fund. While such sums might seem large in some quarters, they were modest for a husband who controlled a personal fortune of $1 billion as well as participating indirectly in foundations capitalized at another $500 million. In her letter of thanks, Abby expressed her appreciation and immediately set out on her shopping expeditions.

"I [heard] that you had gotten the large pictures in the Quinn Collection and I am very much pleased . . ." she wrote Valentiner on May 24, 1927, referring to the John Quinn estate auction of his superb collection of Postimpressionist and twentieth-century art. "I got three small pictures myself—an oil painting by Prendergast for which I paid $1,200, a small water-color by a Frenchman named Henri Gross, for which I paid only $30, and a delightful Derain water-color in blue and red and white for which I paid $140. I have bought a few more water-colors since you were here: [including] a lovely Winslow Homer of two men in an open boat pulling in a large shark, about which I am most enthusiastic. . . . I have also bought a number of Davies' lithographs and an etching by John Sloan. I am very eager to show them all to you. . . ."[5]

Abby's decision to pass up the "large pictures" had a practical element. "She did not have a lot of money to spend," David recalled, "and so missed a lot of opportunities. . . . But certainly she bought astutely and well. A small Manet flower painting, a Seurat drawing—modest purchases in their day—are now enormously valuable. The expensive things my parents bought, they bought together."[6] Then too, art acquisition for Abby was less a matter of ego than of the emotional satisfaction derived from the experience. "To me," she wrote Nelson, "art is one of the great resources of my life. I feel that it enriches the spiritual life and makes one more sane and sympathetic, more observant and understanding, as well as being good for one's nerves."[7]

She wanted her children to understand art and share her enthusiasm. "I am greatly touched that you should have sent me the photographs of the Daumier pictures from the *Literary Digest*," she had written Laurance. "I will feel that I have not lived in vain if I have introduced Daumier to the family and his work is appreciated by them. . . . [He] is one of the founders of modern painting."[8] She bought prints for the walls of their college rooms and took with her whoever was willing to gallery-hop (mainly Nelson). On a more fundamental level, it was not only an eagerness for new experience and knowledge that drove her to buy contemporary art, but a keen desire to support the art that would be her gift to future generations.

Abby made some key purchases in 1928. She paid Halpert $3,000 for the oil *Dorothy and Flapper* by Walt Kuhn and $2,550 for the pastel *Silence-Memory-Reverie* by Odilon Redon. She located an Edward Hopper watercolor, *Back Street, Gloucester*, at Rehn Gallery ($600); a Matisse ink drawing, *Girl in Feathered Hat*, at Kraushaar ($250); and a Picasso pen-and-ink drawing of nude figures at Kelekian ($600). At least twenty-five other artists came into her collection beginning in 1926, including Max Weber, John Marin, and Guy Pène du Bois. It is impossible to group them according to school or subject. She seemed to favor Americans over French. But that may have been because the American works were cheaper, or because Edith Halpert was promoting them.

Abby took an immense liking to the twenty-eight-year-old Halpert, a young woman who combined entrepreneurial shrewdness with an intimate knowledge of the art world learned from her artist husband, Samuel Halpert. She was the child of Russian-Jewish immigrants who brought her to the United States when she was five. Diane Tepfer, Halpert's biographer, has suggested that Edith preached a form of cultural nationalism in devoting her life to the cause of the American artists. Such a passion—i.e., support of American art—would appeal to Abby, who believed deeply in American creativity. The fact that Edith was a woman making her way in the man's world of art dealers would also appeal to her; "very interesting and able," Abby wrote of Edith.[9]

And Edith was the age of Abby's own daughter, the daughter who resisted all of Abby's efforts to make her a partner in her various quiet crusades—whether it was Bayway or the YWCA or art education. Abby and Edith could form a spontaneous friendship built on something more than the dealer-and-client relationship and free of the tensions that too often impinge on a relationship between mother and daughter.

Having set aside about half of her 1928 purchase fund for oils, drawings, and watercolors, Abby spent the balance on prints— etchings, lithographs, woodcuts, signed proofs, aquatints, etc. Examining the evolution of a talent had meaning for her, and she understood the educational value of an exhaustive print collection. She had prepared her ground well, learning as much as possible from her own excellent library, then consulting with her advisers —Valentiner; the artist Arthur B. Davies; Holger Cahill, an early champion of American modernism and American folk art; the dealers Halpert, Keppel, and Kraushaar; her French friend Eustache de Lorey. But finally the decision came back to her.

Among the Americans, where prices averaged about $20 per image, she roamed widely, buying obscure names as well as recognized ones. Unlike her commitment to Hart, who ultimately fell into the second tier, her investment in John Sloan, $2,244 for 101 etchings, was fully justified. Sloan was the outstanding member of the Ashcan School, a politically conscious social critic who caught the infinite variety of city life in "all its splendor and squalor," as John Gross wrote in the Sunday *New York Times* in 1988. "The spectacle Sloan recorded, in his prime, was overwhelmingly urban. Women parading down Fifth Avenue in their fashionable plumes, young women clustering round a nickelodeon, the back room of McSorley's saloon, the overhead tracks of the 'El' disappearing into the drizzle, tenement roofs on a summer night, the startling orange glare of a bonfire that children have built up in the snow; such were [the] scenes that touched [Sloan] to the quick."[10]

Abby loved New York. Her letters repeatedly communicate this. "If you should ask me what I thought was the most perfect place in the world to be in I should say New York without a doubt. In New York, which is so tremendously interesting and stimulating, the weather doesn't count."[11] So she wrote David from Arizona, where the weather evidently did count (but not for much!). In the instance of Sloan, she was drawn to an artist who understood her beloved New York and could express that understanding with solid humor and warmth. His work descended from a long tradition of European graphic art represented by Abby's perennial favorite, the great French caricaturist of human behavior

Honoré Daumier. In Sloan's activist Socialist days, he drew a cover for *The Masses* showing John D. Rockefeller, Sr., with his hands steeped in blood, actually a rather tame political cartoon for those angry times. Perhaps Abby did not know about that cartoon, or perhaps she did know and chose to forgive.

When it came to making selections among the French prints where the average price was $500–$600, Abby favored names of proven quality such as Degas, Pisarro, Gauguin, and Fantin-Latour. Yet here too, her most original purchase, the one which suggests the greatest degree of sophistication, was none of these, but another in the tradition of Daumier. She paid $2,440 for three extremely rare etchings by the French draftsman Jean Louis Forain.

As 1929 approached, Abby prepared to go on a lengthy journey. "How are your plans for the Christmas holidays going?" she wrote Laurance. "I have just talked with Nelson and he says that you certainly should go to all the parties." Laurance had already told her that he might go away for part of the vacation. She thought about that. "[Perhaps] it would be easier for me to leave home without your being here. As the time approaches I am getting very shaky about going so far away." [12]

"Very shaky about going so far away." There it was again, the persistent, unresolved conflict of a woman whose spirit was at war with her psyche. She was so zestful, so full of enthusiasm, so curious about the world out there, its problems and its people and its culture. And yet if the opportunity for firsthand experience meant that she had to travel far from home, she fought an inexplicable anxiety. It was no longer a matter of worrying about the children she was leaving behind. Babs was married, and all the boys except for David were independent young men. It was not lack of maturity or sophistication or accomplishment.

It seemed to be entirely irrational. It reached deep into her past, to the depressed, nervous mother who had constantly to shuttle back and forth between home and the capital, separated from a preoccupied husband; or to the sudden premature deaths of her tiny siblings; or perhaps to that which we understand least, something genetic. A diagnosis known as panic attack has even entered the medical literature. People who suffer from panic disorder are capable and conscientious; the symptoms often appear without warning and are very possibly inherited. Both psychiatry and drug therapy can be effective; neither was utilized by Abby. The surprise is not that she struggled against such fears when a journey was imminent, but that she acknowledged them and then got on with her life.

On January 3, Abby and John and their party sailed out of New York Harbor on the S.S. *Augustus* bound for the Middle East. Not since she went to China and Japan in 1921 had an adventure promised so much in the way of insights into an ancient civilization, interpreted by a scholar of such impeccable credentials. Dr. James H. Breasted, director of the Oriental Institute of the University of Chicago, was the scholar. John, and various Rockefeller-funded foundations, had already supported his archaeological research and his various ideas for great edifices, including the Palestine Museum, with over $11 million. He had set up permanent Egyptian headquarters at Luxor, and field expeditions were established in every important cultural region of the ancient Near East.

In addition to Dr. Breasted and his adult son Charles, there were the usual staff people and a tutor for David, who at age fourteen was excused from classes to make the journey. The most unexpected member of the party was Mary Todhunter Clark, age twenty-one. It is not clear whose idea it was for her to join the party, but she was the one whom Abby enjoyed the most. "Tod," as family and friends referred to her, was a Philadelphia Clark, which meant that she was a member of one of the oldest, wealthiest, and most socially prominent clans in Pennsylvania. Every summer she and her siblings and her parents and various aunts, uncles, and cousins went to Northeast Harbor for the summer. Since their childhood Tod and Nelson had been friends. Lately the friendship had ripened into a romance.

Although nothing was yet declared, Tod was known as Nelson's girl. In some ways she was emphatically different from Nelson. Henry Stebbins thought of her as an intellectual. "I do not think you could accuse Nelson of being an intellectual," he had remarked dryly.[13] She was tall and slender with perfect carriage, "ramrod straight" according to Laurance.[14] Not pretty, perhaps even rather plain, but witty, amusing, always interesting to talk to, said Stebbins, who was one of the young people in the Northeast crowd. Not at all the wide-open, exuberant person that Nelson was, again from Stebbins. More reserved people, such as John, however, thought her quite open and uninhibited. And she was totally self-possessed, which observers believe attracted Nelson.

"First of all," Abby wrote Laurance (the emphasis is hers), "Mary is a great success! She is so natural & simple and sincere that everyone likes her. It is much pleasanter for me having another woman in the party and she is sweet about David, who likes her tremendously. I had much rather have her than an older woman whom I should have to pay more attention to. Then it's very nice that she can play bridge. . . . We are learning contract."[15] She wrote much the same to Lucy. John agreed. "Mary is the life of the party," he explained to the family back home. "She is running true to form in every way. She is always ready to do whatever is suggested, never is the slightest bit of trouble. . . ."[16] Tongues wagged, of course. The Rockefeller party ran into Philadelphia people in Cairo who insisted that Mary must be engaged to one of the brothers, and wanted to know which one. Nelson's cable suggested that he was not entirely at ease with Mary so far away and in the bosom of his family. "Nobody sick yet," he wired, "all still in college. How is Mary behaving?"[17]

The crossing on the Atlantic was stormy. Abby attributed the "fearful" pain in her stomach to nerves, which the doctor confirmed, but a sore throat and cold kept her in the hotel while the healthy members of the group toured the Neapolitan coast, Pompeii, and Herculaneum. The weather cleared as they boarded the S.S. *Ausonia* for the cruise across the Mediterranean to the port of Alexandria. Abby had recovered sufficiently to bask in the bright warm sunlight on the bridge where the captain had steamer chairs placed for her.

In Alexandria it rained again. The noise, as they disembarked, was deafening. Egyptians, Abby decided, could make more racket than any people she had ever heard. Passengers and porters, Arabs in red fezzes, guides in flowing robes—all swarmed on the dock. A private railroad car transported them to Cairo, half of it fitted up with dining area and galley, the other half with parlor-car seats. In the distance were the pyramids. Along the tracks were water buffalo, donkeys, and camels plodding ahead of the farmers who poked and prodded them through the rich black soil of the delta.

Abby compared the experience to going to the most extraordinary movie. "I am afraid that I shall never want to do anything useful again in my life," she wrote. "David studies. Papa and Mr. Gumbel have a little correspondence that they look after, but . . . I just sleep, eat and watch the [amazing] scenery go by."[18]

John's letters were models of detail, filling many single-spaced typewritten pages. Abby's were scrawled in her own hand—homely advice alternating with quick, graphic information. "I heard that the flu was raging in N.Y., so I cabled first the office to ask how the family was," she wrote Laurance, "and got an answer from Nelson. As I didn't think that he would know about the rest of you I cabled Miss Kelly."[19] They dined with Lord Allenby. "He used to be the High Commissioner of Egypt and was the general who took Jerusalem from the Turks in the war."[20] She reminded him—Laurance, that is—not to forget his cod-liver pills and liver extract. "Tomorrow I am going to be received by the queen [of Egypt]. . . . I am eager to see her palace and garden."[21] The queen proved to be more interested in movie stars than anything else.

On February 4 the entire group boarded the *Dahabeah Serapis* for the month-long journey up the Nile. "Great joy on the 'Serapis,' " Abby exclaimed in her February 10 letter to Laurance, "when letters were received at Assuit. . . . still greater joy when cable came saying that you had passed your mid-years."[22]

The *Dahabeah* tied up at Luxor for four days, along with so many cook's boats that Abby's group never knew which dinner gong was for them and which was for other parties. Across the river were the ruins of the Temple of Luxor, two miles out of the village the great temple enclosure of Karnak. They visited the tomb of Tutankhamen, had picnics by moonlight in the shadows of great temples, and watched the sun set from the top of a temple gate. On February 20 they were in Wadi Halfa, "as far south as one can go on the Nile by boat," she wrote. "It is here that one meets the impassable barrier of the 2nd Cataract. It is also the first town in the Sudan. The Nubians and Sudanese people are wonderful looking. They are very black, extremely tall and handsome." From descriptions of spectacular scenery she switched to the important question of Laurance's and John's weight. "I am overcome with pleasure to know that you [both] are still gaining in spite of the hard studying." The reality of infection in an era before antibiotics was justification enough for a mother to believe in extra pounds as extra protection. Only five weeks more, she wrote, it made her homesick when she thought of it. "Robert G. says that there is no use in our sending letters after we leave Cairo. . . . We have been coming down the Nile which makes me feel that we are on the way home—when in reality we go to Palestine before we start on the homeward journey."[23]

By June 1929, when the family gathered at Princeton for John 3rd's commencement, summer plans were in place. David would go to a sailing camp on Cape Cod, and Winthrop, bowing to the inevitable, would be enrolled in a tutoring camp in Maine. Nelson and Laurance, after some hesitation, decided to sign on as seamen aboard Sir Wilfred Grenfell's small hospital ship, *Maravan*, that sailed every summer to Labrador to bring medical aid and Christian evangelism to the local population. John 3rd opted for one of those highly serious, Rockefeller-type fact-finding trips around the world before entering his father's office at 26 Broadway, as John himself had done thirty-two years earlier.

Seal Harbor beckoned. But first there was a motor trip to Philadelphia, Washington, Richmond, Charlottesville, and Williamsburg. Two cars set out from Pocantico, a chauffeur-driven Lincoln touring car and the family Nash. John, unsure of Winthrop's driving ability, suggested that Abby go in the Lincoln with Thomas rather than in the Nash with Winnie. She acquiesced, but when she saw Thomas drive up the road to Abeyton Lodge her heart sank. "I was much surer of [Winnie]." Her instinct was sound. Later Thomas careened over a bump on the highway, sending her straight up to the steel rib that held up the top of the car.

"Ever since," she reported, "I have looked as if I had been in a prizefight. I suppose I should be thankful my nose wasn't broken."[24]

The rest of the journey proceeded without mishap. They enjoyed the hospitality of the governor of Virginia, Harry F. Byrd. Abby decided that one of the young guests at the Byrd party, who had been president of her class at Smith and was quite "splendid . . . very good-looking and able," was just right for John 3rd. "J. [3rd] did not seem greatly impressed," she conceded.[25] Their last stopover was Williamsburg, where the restoration was underway, and where Abby finally gave in and went to bed while everyone else went sight-seeing.

Her doctor in Seal Harbor recommended that she continue to rest. "You know how my 'hart' is," she wrote David. "I think it will be better just as soon as it has had time to rest a bit! There is really nothing serious the matter with it except that it is tired, the doctor says. . . . I really believe the trouble is that since last January I haven't stayed in one place for more than five minutes."[26]

Cardiac diagnosis was primitive in 1929, but there is no evidence for believing that Abby at age fifty-five had organic heart disease. Physicians often used the expression "tired heart" as a tactful evasion for emotional stress. Some still do, with patients who might be troubled by the idea that emotional conflicts lead to physical symptoms. Abby was not such a patient. She wrote frankly to Lucy about her nerves and her fatigue. But since there was little in the way of psychotherapy—people were still traveling to Europe for psychoanalysis—doctors felt justified in simply prescribing bed rest, particularly for their female patients. Women received notoriously poor medical care; for instance, iron-deficiency anemia was routinely missed. Gynecologists in particular blamed fainting spells, caused by severe anemia, on hysterics.

Abby was not one to take to her bed. She fought through most of her conflicts by sublimating them. But with John nodding vigorous agreement to the doctor's insistence that she rest, she acquiesced gracefully. Perhaps she welcomed the solitude.

The new garden gave her a great sense of peace. She finished

Countess Tolstoy's *Letters*, also Haldane's *Autobiography*, and was struggling with *The Nature of the Physical World* by Eddington, "hard going," she wrote. All this in her letters to the four sons who were not with her. She went sailing on the *Jack Tar* to watch the boat races, with only the captain for company. This was the one summer in Maine when she did not welcome the fog and the rain, worrying that Laurance and Nelson might be out in it someplace. She studied the map of Labrador, feeling strange that she did not really know where they were. And then there was the nightly experimenting with the new radio, trying to establish contact with New York, but hearing static most of the time.

Besides her preoccupation with absent children and the daily activities at the Eyrie, something else was on her mind. During the months between her return from North Africa and her departure for the Eyrie, she had reached a momentous decision, one with far-reaching, even historic consequences. Late in August she summarized it all in the form of a letter to her friend Eustache de Lorey. Monsieur de Lorey, charming, modest, and distinguished, held the title of Conseiller du Haut-Commissariat pour les Arts, Directeur de l'Institut Français d'Archéologie et d'art Musulmans.

> Dear Monsieur de Lorey: . . . I took the liberty of suggesting to Mr. Conger Goodyear that he look you up when he is in Paris. During the spring a small group of New York people got together and took the first step toward a museum of modern art in New York. Mr. Goodyear is the Chairman of the Committee and is in Europe hoping to enlist the interest and sympathy of European collectors, as we shall be obliged to borrow pictures for our exhibitions the first two years.
>
> I told Mr. Goodyear that you were deeply interested in Modern painting and that I knew you would be glad to give him advice as to where he might find some of the best pictures. My husband is not at all interested in modern painting so that I have to go into it myself in a very modest way and unfortunately I only have one small painting and one drawing by Matisse and a number of his prints. Please tell him [Matisse] the only reason I have not more is my inability to acquire them.
>
> If it would not be too much trouble to you, I would be very glad

if you would give me the names of some of the younger French painters who have not arrived yet, but who you think have great ability. In this Museum we are eager to show the pictures of the younger men. Perhaps it will be possible for me to buy pictures of some of the young men when I cannot buy the masters.[27]

PART FOUR

MoMA: A Far More Ambitious Agenda

CHAPTER 20

The "small group of New York people" who had gotten together in the spring were three women—Abby, Lillie Bliss, and Mary Sullivan.[1] It was late in May. They met for luncheon at Abby's Manhattan residence. Their invited guest was Mr. A. Conger Goodyear. After some amenities Abby asked him if he would accept the chairmanship of a committee to organize a new gallery or museum in New York that would exhibit works of art of the modern school. Goodyear was thunderstruck and intrigued. He asked for a week to think it over, but actually needed only one night. He accepted the very next day.

Everyone who watched the museum during its first ten years—curators, journalists, historians, trustees—carefully refers to "three ladies." But close observers believe that in fact there was one lady, and that lady was Abby. "There is no doubt that the moving spirit was Abby Aldrich Rockefeller." Philip Johnson, who mounted MoMA's first exhibition of modern architecture in 1932, said as much to the author. "She had the foresight and the wisdom. Lillie Bliss had the collection and Mary Sullivan had a wonderful spirit, but Abby was the leader. Had she been a man she could have commanded an army. The museum was her full-time occupation, as compelling and demanding as any high-powered position in the larger world."[2] Stephen Clark, a millionaire collector of unshakable opinions and an early trustee, agreed. "The Museum of Modern Art was essentially her creation. Many people have contributed to its development but it was her interest and her imagination that carried it through to success."[3] Eliza Cobb, whose aunt was Lillie Bliss, and who became a trustee herself, believes along with the others that without Abby the museum would not have come into existence and that it would not have survived without her continued involvement.

Abby had met Mary Quinn Sullivan when both were interested in psychotherapy for the returning soldiers of World War I. They became friends because of their interest in art. Mary was an amateur artist, art teacher, and social dealer, married to a successful lawyer, Cornelius Sullivan, who was a collector of rare books and paintings. Abby saw to it that Mary received a commission to redecorate the Cosmopolitan Club, she introduced her to Babs, and she bought prints that Mary located for her. She responded appreciatively to Mary's gaiety and charm and her luminous beauty. Friends described her as "pure Irish mystic." Young people at MoMA later considered it a great treat to be invited to her informal country house with its lawns and trees and picket fence, "nestling under the Astoria end of the Hell Gate Bridge."[4]

Abby and Lillie Bliss had been friends since their youth. The Bliss fortune came out of the textile mills of Fall River, Massachusetts. Lillie's father, Cornelius Bliss, and Nelson Aldrich were political allies, both Republican high-tariff men and both in Washington during the McKinley administration. Bliss twice refused to be his party's candidate for governor of New York and only with great reluctance agreed to serve in McKinley's cabinet as secretary of the interior. Although Lillie and Abby went on to lead opposite lives in many respects, each had acted as her father's Washington hostess—Abby for reasons already examined, Lillie because her mother emphatically refused to join her husband in the capital. As adults in New York the women saw each other.

"My aunt was conspicuously different from Abby. She had lived a life that no woman would contemplate living today," Eliza told the author. "It was the nineteenth-century Victorian life. She never married. She took care of a mother who claimed to be an invalid. [Eliza was not sure that she actually was.] After her father died, Lillie moved into her mother's bedroom so that she could watch over her. She was a beautiful musician, a pianist, proficient enough to play privately with the Kneisel Quartet. She practiced every morning for two hours, then played for her mother every evening."

Eliza continued, "Aunt Lillie told me that she became terribly depressed when she was in her early forties. [This would be in the decade before World War I.] Perhaps she knew that she was in an impossible trap, that her youth was ebbing. One day she walked into the shop of a famous Oriental rug dealer. 'Please just show me some rugs and tell me about them.' The dealer, being very kind, told her a great deal, and sensing her desperation directed her to the MacBeth Art Gallery, where she first saw the paintings of Arthur B. Davies. She returned again and again to view them, finally asking Mr. MacBeth to introduce her to the artist."[5]

It was Davies who had been the driving force behind the Armory Show of 1913. As an artist, however, the consensus is that he does not fall in the first rank, although he enjoyed considerable recognition in his lifetime. He had a profound appreciation of the new movements in France, and he never compromised his artistic independence. He experimented with skill in many media—oils, printmaking, sculpture, glass, weaving, and in the last years of his life some delicate watercolor landscapes. But Brooks Wright, his biographer, has suggested that the extreme dislocation of his sexual life determined the course of his work, inhibiting it and confusing it. "[The work] . . . is saturated with . . . an eroticism that is veiled by cryptic symbolism or muted by the dreamlike atmosphere and depersonalized quality of the figures. It is futile to speculate what he would have become had he achieved wholeness . . . in his personal life . . . though whether he would have become a better painter no one can say."[6]

The dislocation of his sexual life, as suggested by Wright, involved his simultaneous relationships with two women. He was married to Lucy Meriwether, a dedicated country doctor, ahead of her time in the compassionate way she cared for her patients. She was the mother of his two sons and she managed the thirty-six-acre

Davies family farm in Rockland County, New York. Davies had pursued her ardently. When they married, the plan was for her to practice medicine and for him to paint. But there were problems growing out of her very competence, as well as his restlessness with country life. He took a studio on Fifth Avenue, returning to the farm on the weekends only, while Lucy stayed behind, rooted to her practice and the security of the rural environment.

By the time Lillie met him, he was involved with the second woman, a young dancer and model, Edna Potter, intuitive and imaginative, an able artist herself. The affair was a secret, carefully guarded from Lucy. One wonders why she did not grow suspicious. Perhaps she did. There was deception all around. Davies lied to Lucy, but he also lied to Edna, telling her that Lucy would never divorce him, that she would kill the children if he asserted his independence, and Edna chose to believe him. Finally, when Edna became pregnant and bore Davies an infant daughter, he divided his life into three separate worlds, the world of Lucy and the farm, the world of Edna and Ronnie his daughter, whom he set up under an assumed name in a household on 52nd Street, and the professional world of his studio. Each area was rigidly defined, with absolutely no encroachment.

Lillie Bliss may very well have been the only person to whom Davies was not an enigma, and the only woman of the three in his life who was not damaged by his duplicity. She became his trusted confidante, perhaps the most loyal he would ever have. She never judged him, she simply became his friend and his patron, possibly his lover. She knew about Edna and later about Ronnie, but being a deeply private person herself, she respected the privacy of others. When her mother protested that it was not suitable for her to be in the studio alone with Arthur B. Davies, Lillie defied her, one of the very few occasions she did so. She moved a piano into the studio, played for him, taught him about music, and learned from him about art.

The conspicuous legacy of this close friendship that spanned more than twenty years was the Lillie Bliss collection. Alfred Barr placed it in clear perspective. "[It] was largely because of [Arthur B.] Davies' inspiration and guiding enthusiasm that before the [Armory Exhibition closed in 1913] five important paintings had passed into Miss Bliss' possession. The Renoir landscape, the oil and pastel by Degas, and the two Redons were the foundation upon which Miss Bliss began to build her collection." Under Davies's informed tutelage, Lillie assembled an extraordinary group of Cézannes, some of them masterpieces. Daumier, Picasso, Matisse, Pissarro—all are represented in her collection, and in a climactic move she acquired nine drawings by Seurat. "Seurat's painstaking methods of work, the scant ten years of his active career," Barr continued, "and the importance of his art make this group of drawings unrivaled in America and one of Miss Bliss' most remarkable achievements as a collector."[7]

Davies advised Lillie to acquire the Americans as well, believing that someday the United States would be the center of modern art. But none of her treasures could be displayed. "Her mother did not like her pictures, she did not approve of them," Eliza explained. "They were kept out of sight, in a storeroom, to be brought out briefly when Europeans who knew about them asked for the privilege. In that event a man from the MacBeth Gallery would come over, dust them off, place them on easels, and later return them to their hiding place."[8] Lillie took her quiet revenge after Mrs. Bliss died in 1922. She sold the house, bought an apartment on Park Avenue, created a gallery three floors high, and hung all her pictures.

When the opportunity presented itself, Lillie could be an eloquent spokesperson for the modernists, writing the following to a self-important academician: "The truth is you older men seem intolerant and supercilious, a state of mind incomprehensible to a philosopher who looks on and enjoys watching for and finding the new men in music, painting and literature who have something to say worth saying and claim for themselves only the freedom to express it in their own way, a claim which you have always maintained as your inalienable right."[9]

Arthur B. Davies died in Florence of a heart attack on October 23, 1928. He had been spending six months a year traveling in Europe, always accompanied by Edna and Ronnie. According to

Eliza Cobb, Edna, who was traveling with a separate passport and could not get his body out of Italy, returned to New York to seek Lillie's counsel. "Lillie told her she would have to confront Lucy at the farm. So she did. She banged on the door and when the wife appeared, said in effect, 'I am your husband's mistress and have been for twenty years. And he is dead.' To everyone's surprise, Lucy went to Europe with Edna, claimed the body, and in subsequent years treated Ronnie generously." [10]

Abby learned of Davies's death from the newspapers on December 18, two weeks before she left for the Middle East. She wrote immediately to one of his sons:

> I have just read with very deep sorrow in the morning paper of the death of your father. I had for him the deepest admiration, and altho I had known him only for a few years, I felt a very real affection for him. I feel that I owe to him a very great deal, because he inspired and encouraged me to acquire modern paintings, and without the confidence which his approval gave me I should never have dared venture into the field of modern art.
>
> The last time I saw your father in his studio, he showed me a small sketch which he said was for one of the two additional decorations that he was planning to make for International House. . . . [Abby, who was chairperson for the furnishings committee, had sent the commission his way.]
>
> I should like your mother to know that the very last time that I saw your father, he said to me 'I want you to meet Mrs. Davies [that is, Lucy], for I feel sure that you and she would have very much in common. . . .' [11]

Here Abby confirms what has long been assumed—that she met Davies around 1925 or 1926 and that he was one of the people who encouraged her to buy modern art. After he died she paid his widow $8,000 for one of his tapestries, *A Thousand Flowers*, so perhaps she did meet Lucy after all. Other assumptions—never confirmed—are that Lillie introduced Davies to Abby and that their shared dream, discussed in his studio with their friend Mary Sullivan, was to found a modern art museum in New York.

Lillie had begun to buy Davies's work as soon as they met—in such great quantity that she was able to bequeath two Davies paintings apiece to one museum in every state of the union. Abby became a major patron also—she gave nearly a hundred of his prints to the Museum of Modern Art in 1940, and kept many watercolors for her family. But there is the sense that it was not so much an infatuation with the work itself that drew her to Davies as a thirst for knowledge—for intellectual and artistic stimulus. The qualities that impressed the art community at large impressed Abby as well. "This shy, reticent and coolly formal person," Brown wrote in sizing up Davies's accomplishments with the Armory Show, "turned out to be a creature of driving energy, incisive command, organizational ability. . . . Once in the seat, he drove with unswerving directness and amazing control."[12]

It was a series of shipboard coincidences that led, in the final months, to the luncheon at 10 West 54th and the surprising invitation extended to Conger Goodyear. Eliza Cobb was traveling with her father and her Aunt Lillie in the Middle East when the Bliss party encountered the Rockefeller party. "We were coming off a steamer at Haifa," Eliza recalled, "and the Rockefellers were traveling from Cairo to Jerusalem."[13] Evidently Lillie and Abby took up their favorite subject—how to push ahead with a gallery or museum that would foster contemporary art.

Upon leaving Haifa, Abby continued on to Paris and the return voyage aboard the *Île de France*. It was on that sailing that she ran into the third of the conspirators, Mary Quinn Sullivan, and once again the conversation quickly turned to modern art and what Lillie had said and what the possibilities were.

The Metropolitan in its august wisdom was clearly neglecting modern art. The Hearn Fund, established in 1906 to enable the Metropolitan to support the avant-garde, was languishing. "So far as one can judge from the Hearn collection," a disgruntled architect wrote in the *Herald Tribune* in 1927, "American art might have ceased in 1913."[14] Gertrude Vanderbilt Whitney, whose Studio Club was managed by her assistant Juliana Force, tried to repair that situation by accumulating a huge collection of new American art. But Gertrude, although she never articulated it, seemed to

view her patronage as a "sort of social service agency to help dis-
advantaged people, the disadvantaged being artists."[15] This from
Thomas Armstrong, former director of the Whitney Museum.
Such a philosophy obviously led to an uneven collection. And
Gertrude, an aspiring sculptor herself, threw up an unbreachable
wall between her life as an artist and patron and her life as a
Whitney socialite. She had no interest in reaching beyond Juliana
Force to build a broad base of support.

Abby, with a far more ambitious agenda, made use of every
opportunity at her disposal, including her personal network. She
had learned political skills from Nelson Aldrich. She had been
negotiating for years in a demanding family setting. And she had
acquired the Rockefeller penchant for building a broad base, bringing other people into her venture. She read the art criticism of Lee
Simonson, editor of *Creative Art*, and Forbes Watson, who made
The Arts one of the leading art journals of the 1920s. She listened
to some wise heads. "I talked with a number of people about the
idea," she later wrote Conger Goodyear, "and received great
encouragement from Mr. Martin A. Ryerson, himself a great
collector, Mr. Howard Mansfield, a Trustee of the Metropolitan Museum of Art and a connoisseur and collector, Mr.
Valentiner, Director of the Detroit Museum . . . and a number
of others."[16]

One of the pivotal "others," as has already been noted, was
Arthur B. Davies, because he, more perhaps than anyone, even
Valentiner, instructed Abby in the accomplishments of the European modernists. It is perhaps not an exaggeration to suggest, as
Thomas Armstrong has, that Abby founded the Museum of Modern Art so that American artists could learn about modern art from
the French and the Germans. This conviction of Davies had led
him to weigh the Armory Show heavily with Europeans, much to
the chagrin of the Americans. It was a calculated, carefully
thought-out vision, and fundamental decisions reached in the earliest days of MoMA would enforce it.

And finally there was Abby's young friend Edith Halpert, who
cherished her own dreams. At Abby's request, she put her ideas
in the form of a proposal. She suggested housing a collection of

LIVING AMERICAN ARTISTS (the capitals are Halpert's) within the walls of the Metropolitan, at the same time acknowledging that the Met might frown at first. Her proposal was interesting for its suggestions about women as organizing forces. "To me," Halpert wrote, "it seems fitting that women should foster this new plan. Tradition points to greater courage in women toward reform and new ideas. Women are privileged to 'change their minds' and therefore have that advantage in making experiments."[17]

They were an impressive team, Mrs. Rockefeller, Miss Bliss, and Mrs. Sullivan—much more intimate in friendship and outlook than the formal way in which they always addressed each other would suggest. "It was the perfect combination . . ." Nelson Rockefeller wrote years later. "[They] had the resources, the tact, and the knowledge. . . . More to the point, they had the courage to advocate the cause of the modern movement in the face of widespread division, ignorance, and a dark suspicion that the whole business was some sort of Bolshevik plot."[18]

Conger Goodyear, a Yale graduate of military bearing, with a private fortune and a collection that included works by Cézanne, Gauguin, and van Gogh, had come to New York from Buffalo to flee an unhappy love affair. The women heard about his vigorous defense of modern art as a trustee of the Albright Gallery in Buffalo. When he spent $5,000 of the gallery's funds for Picasso's *La Toilette*, he was voted off the Albright board. To the three founders, he seemed just the man for the job. Apparently the fact of his being a *man* suited their strategy. They assumed that the museum establishment would not rally behind a woman in an experiment of such magnitude.

Nothing in Abby's personal life paused merely because she wanted to found a museum. Preparations went ahead for John 3rd's graduation. Nelson, Laurance, Winthrop, and David hopped around her with their summer plans. Husband John expected her to be at his side as usual. While she went back and forth between Princeton, Pocantico, Manhattan, and Williamsburg, Goodyear made the initial moves, using the telephone and the U.S. mail to keep her informed.

"I . . . will hope to have the papers of incorporation and other legal matters attended to," he wrote on June 23, "so that at the next meeting of the committee we may be prepared to go ahead. I have written to Mr. Sachs, asking him to suggest someone for director. . . . It seems to me that it is important that we shall hold the opening exhibition in November at the latest. . . . I have asked Mr. Sachs if he can attend a meeting the first week in July. . . . as soon as I hear from him, will write you again. I am sending a copy of this letter to the other members of the committee."[19]

The legal matters were handled by Cornelius Sullivan, including the incorporation of the name—Museum of Modern Art. Mr. Sachs was Professor Paul J. Sachs of the Fogg Museum of Harvard University, a rigorous scholar who gave the course at Harvard known as "the museum course," and in the process trained an entire generation of directors and chief curators. The other members of Abby's original committee, in addition to Lillie Bliss and Mary Sullivan, were Frank Crowninshield, the editor of *Vanity Fair*, and Abby's personal friend the generous Josephine Boardman Crane. Abby agreed to be treasurer, at least temporarily.

The meeting for the first week of July went off as scheduled, and Paul Sachs introduced his candidate for the job of director. His name was Alfred Barr. He was twenty-seven years old, the son of a Presbyterian clergyman, educated in the fine arts at Princeton and Harvard, already a self-assured collector within his own stringent budget. "[Not only does he have a] mind stored with facts," Sachs had written of his former student to a colleague at Princeton, ". . . one gets the impression that he [has] thought deeply and ranged widely over the whole field. I predict . . . he is going to be a scholar of distinction."[20]

Although thoroughly trained in the past, Barr aligned himself with the modernists. As an associate professor of art history at Wellesley College, he designed and taught the first course in contemporary art on any American campus. It included all of the arts, not just painting and sculpture, but photography, cinema, architecture, and machine-made objects. This course became the outline for his plans for the Museum of Modern Art. In the spring of 1929 he was awarded a Carnegie Resident Fellowship to continue his research at the Institute of Fine Arts at New York University. "My thesis," he had proposed, "would probably concern some aspect of the influence of primitive and erotic forms upon modern European painting."[21]

Then came Sachs's invitation. Barr responded on July 1 by suggesting other qualified candidates. Having satisfied the law of modesty, however, he admitted that he was thrilled. "The fact that you are even considering me as a possible participant in this great scheme has set my mind teeming with ideas and plans. This is something I could give my life to—unstintedly."[22]

Abby met Barr at the morning meeting, but could not stay through the afternoon for the private discussions. The annual migration to Seal Harbor was about to begin. "I liked Mr. Barr," she wrote Goodyear from the Eyrie on July 12, "and felt that his youth, enthusiasm and knowledge would make up for his not having a more impressive appearance." (Alfred was tall and almost skinny, with stooped shoulders, sunken cheeks, and austere wire-rimmed spectacles—the very epitome of an aesthetic intellectual. But appearances, as Abby very well knew, could be misleading.) She continued, "In regard to the exhibits . . . we must show only the best, even if we have to go to great trouble and expense to acquire it. . . . Are you going to be in New York this summer? I should like very much to be able to keep in communication with you. . . ."[23]

Goodyear wrote frequently and at length for the next three months. Abby and her secretary Anna Kelly began the arduous task of raising money. On July 6 she wired Lord Duveen for $10,000 a year for two years, and asked him to put in a good word for her with his client Jules Bache the banker. She was successful with both men, as well as obtaining pledges from such names as Harriman, Harkness, and Chester Dale. She and Goodyear each pledged $5,000. The committee wanted $75,000 in firm commitments before officially hiring Alfred and renting gallery space. On July 15, Abby was able to authorize Goodyear to do both, the space already having been located on the twelfth floor of the Heckscher Building at Fifth Avenue and 57th Street.

On July 27, Abby invited Alfred to visit her in Seal Harbor.

"During that week [of August 5th]," she wrote, "my sister, Miss Lucy Aldrich, will be here for a few days and Mr. and Mrs. William Zorach [the husband-and-wife artists] will also be here. They all have very stimulating ideas on the subject, altho they may not entirely agree with us."[24]

Marguarite Zorach was identified in the Weyhe Gallery catalogue of September 1928 as "wife of William Zorach . . . well-known for her paintings and embroideries." Dahlov Zorach Ipcar, daughter of Marguarite and William, and herself an artist, describes her mother in somewhat more colorful language. "She was independent and outspoken, a feminist ahead of her time. She was anti-establishment, anti-religious, pro-art, pro-creative. Such feelings were in the air, even if unspoken, when Edith [Halpert], Mrs. Rockefeller, and my mother were together."[25]

As a nineteen-year-old Quaker from California, Marguarite Thompson went to Paris in 1907 to study art. In 1909 at La Palette (an art school) she met another American, William Zorach, the twenty-two-year-old son of Russian-Jewish immigrants in Cleveland. Zorach's father was a peddler, his mother ran a boarding-house. Together the two students came under the influence of all the art ferment of Paris, especially the Fauves and the cubists. They were married in 1912 in the City Hall of New York City and lived and worked for the next twenty years in a four-room apartment on 10th Street that rented for $30 a month. Marguarite, insisting that they support themselves as artists, cooked the meals and sewed the family's clothes. She experimented with lithography and watercolor. She designed, in a handsome abstract pattern, the concrete floor for Edith Halpert's new exhibition space behind the Downtown Gallery. When William turned from painting to sculpture in 1922, she worked closely with him. "A collaboration," Dahlov suggested, "although she never asked for credit."[26]

William understood the pressures under which she struggled; he wrote in his memoir *Art Is My Life* that "uninterrupted time was a necessity for the kind of painting she did in oil. . . . To be . . . torn away at a crucial moment was very destructive to her. There was no uninterrupted time with caring for two small children, cooking and running a house; and running a house came hard for her. I helped but it didn't come easy to me either."

He went on to explain how she came to make tapestries. "When we began to use brilliant color, Marguarite had been fascinated by the brilliancy and range of color in woolen yarns—beyond anything in paint. . . . [When] she was unhappy over a picture . . . [she] redid it in wool—with all the pinks and reds and cerises, the blues and greens and yellows. . . . She varied her stitches amazingly. . . . Her embroideries looked like tapestries and that is what they were, embroidered tapestries. At that time they seemed to be like nothing else done in this world . . . the art critics devoted columns to them. For many years they were really our main source of income and brought us unexpected security and gave us money to carry on our painting and sculpture."[27] For William it meant working in the medium he loved, achieving recognition, and attracting major commissions.

Abby, who already knew of Marguarite as the mother of Tessim Zorach, David's friend at the Lincoln School, saw her work at the Downtown Gallery and bought a signed drawing, six watercolors, and six lithographs. Edith Halpert, who represented Marguarite, arranged for artist and client to meet. At that point Abby, who stitched and sewed herself, and was conversant with the art of medieval tapestries, commissioned Marguarite to create a modern one. She wrote Laurance and Nelson in Newfoundland about her scheme.

Dearest boys. I am sitting at my desk and I have just been making out a list of the chief interests and characteristics of each of you children. Mrs. Zorach is going to make an embroidered picture of our life here at Seal Harbor and I am going to hang it in the playhouse at Tarrytown. Mrs. Z is coming up here next week to make sketches of the place and the boats etc. If either of you have any special hobby of yours that you want in it, just write it to me. The picture will be about 6 by 10 feet and will be correct with small figures, flowers, water, boats, horses, buildings etc., something like a 13th century tapestry, only very modern. . . . I haven't told Papa

about it. I am paying for it myself until he sees it, then he <u>may</u> love
it and want to have it where he can see it.[28]

Both William and Dahlov have reminisced about their week at
the Eyrie. Dahlov remembers the overwhelming scale of everything, the uniformed maids, etc., but that she played happily
around the estate (she was eleven) and that Abby took her shopping. William recalls that Abby's driver, with Abby as guide, took
them all over the island in a horse and buggy and that she also took
them sailing. Understanding the excruciating attention to detail
that the tapestry required, Abby insisted upon paying for the work
by the month.

Marguarite spent a year planning it and another two years for
the execution. "Each month," William wrote, "the check would
come, Edith would deduct her commission (25%) and send Marguarite her share. . . . I have always loved this tapestry. The creative vision, the interweaving and juxtaposition of colors and forms;
in the sea, the clouds, in the details of woods and rocks and plants
. . . the incorporation of the members of the family in the landscape." There is no documentation of John's reaction—whether he
liked it or whether he didn't. It was William's impression that he
did not. "It was too modern for his taste."[29]

Alfred Barr visited Abby at the Eyrie for two days. Whatever
contrary ideas the others may have expressed, they found themselves in total accord. Alfred, never one to be effusive, and certainly not given to hyperbole, expressed his feelings to her in a tone
of astonished pleasure:

> . . . It wasn't at all to be expected that we should agree so spontane-
> ously and completely on almost every question concerning our great
> enterprise. I feel now a certain <u>entente</u> between us which gives me
> greater confidence in suggesting to the committee a German exhibi-
> tion, for instance, or the small periodical library, or the need for a
> uniform and artificial lighting.
>
> Jere Abbott [Alfred's friend and colleague who became the first
> associate director of MoMA in November 1929] whom I visited for
> a few hours was also overjoyed to learn of your remarkably uncon-
> ventional and youthful tastes in art.[30]

Two major issues remained to be resolved before Abby returned to New York in the fall. The first had to do with her being treasurer. Goodyear was about to sail for Europe to borrow works for the first exhibition when Abby wrote him of her dilemma. "My husband seems very much opposed to my being treasurer. He feels that it would be much better to have a man in this position."[31] What John really felt is uncertain. Was it merely the question of man vs. woman, or was it perhaps something deeper, that as treasurer she would call too much attention to herself, or that her energies would be drawn away from him to an unbearable degree?

Goodyear settled it in his letter of August 7. "We are all very strongly of the opinion, if it is possible for you to do so, it would be most desirable to have you continue as treasurer. This is not only because you are far the best person for the position, but for the further reason that to make a change might perhaps be unfavorably interpreted by some people whose support we hoped to have. . . . I am sailing this evening and hope that it will be possible to get some of the European artists, collectors and dealers interested in our plans."[32]

The second issue was the question of the opening exhibition. Abby was giving it serious thought. Sachs, Barr, and Crowninshield wanted to open in October with a small American show, consisting of Ryder, Homer, and Eakins, but Abby was opposed to that. "I thoroughly agree with Mr. Sachs that you are the one to thrash out this matter," she wrote Alfred, but then went on to make a strong case for her own preference. ". . . a stunning exhibition of the French artists—Cézanne, Seurat, Gauguin, Daumier, Van Gogh—would still be my first choice. I feel this because I believe the modern movement was started by these men and I believe it is chronologically appropriate. . . . It would seem to me to be a little bit flat to start with a purely American exhibition of the older men. . . . Another thought rather disturbs me; if we select for instance ten living American artists for our first exhibition, we are going to antagonize at the very beginning the friends and admirers of all the others, whereas if we start out with a French exhibition we may have a chance to establish ourselves before we have to plunge into the obvious difficulties of an American exhibition."[33]

On September 4, 1929, Crowninshield cabled Goodyear that they had capitulated. "How soon can we get the French pictures to New York from Paris stop Barr Sachs and I willing to join the adamantine ladies Cheerio Regards from us all."[34] That settled it. The First Loan Exhibition was scheduled for November and the walls would be graced with the four great ancestors of modern art —Paul Cézanne, Paul Gauguin, Georges Seurat, and Vincent van Gogh.

CHAPTER 21

———————··⟨∞⟩··———————

S ome months after the opening of the museum, Alfred Barr returned to the Eyrie to visit Abby. "What I remember with most satisfaction," he wrote her from his parents' summer home in Vermont, "is the feeling of your continued enthusiasm for our great undertaking. I foresee periods of discouragement but in your courage and endurance I have implicit trust." But then he continued, "Remember me most cordially to Mr. Rockefeller (who I find hard to forgive his granite indifference to what interests you so much)."[1]

Both David and Laurance confirm Alfred's impression. Their father's "granite indifference" to their mother's vision for the museum was demonstrated over and over. Even as they tried to be fair to him, they found his stubborn rejection troubling. Laurance explains it in terms of the art. "These were strange, irresponsible objects that she was bringing into his home. He did not approve of them. And now she wanted to start a museum to house them. He could not support that. She wanted a building for it, he would not oblige. Like the rest of us, she was on a tight string financially. So she did not have the money and she did not have the moral support."[2]

David, who was still a day student at the Lincoln School, often came home for lunch during MoMA's founding years. Mary Sullivan, or Lillie Bliss, or even Alfred himself, might be in the dining room with Abby. David was aware of his mother's hopefulness and her excitement. A tender, loving boy, really an only child now, with all his siblings away, he was quietly angry at his father's behavior. "She had always devoted an enormous amount of time to his needs," he said. "Always. I suppose he never accepted her being taken away from him, whether it was for us, or for the museum."[3] He knew that his father's feelings and demands determined the amount of time Abby rationed for MoMA.

Outside the family, impressions were quickly formed, because Abby was entirely frank. "I won't be able to give you any large sums of money or any important pictures," she told Lillie Bliss, "because John does not like modern art."[4] When Edith Halpert wrote her from Berlin that she had seen two wonderful Cézannes for sale and she was sending Abby the photographs, Abby wrote Goodyear that of course they were much too expensive for her to think of buying. Philip Johnson concluded that it must have been awful for her to be Mrs. John D. Rockefeller, Jr., and not be able to make major acquisitions for her own institution. "He was a bulldog," said Johnson of John, "a very strong man, one who would say, 'As my wife you can do this and not that.' The museum was her revolt all right. She had to do it."[5] Blanchette Hooker Rockefeller, who married John 3rd, rarely saw John at MoMA. "Perhaps he came to the opening," she recalled, "but it must have been with a great deal of horror."[6]

Whatever the toll, Abby plowed ahead, compromising here, staking out her position there, digging in her heels if the cause was important enough. Nelson always believed that his mother loved a good fight. John declared that she argued like a grasshopper. If she saw herself losing ground in one area she blithely moved to another one. Perhaps that was her way of circling his stringent convictions. Younger family members were well aware of her powers of cajolery, which could entertain and irritate, but before which they confessed themselves to be helpless. When John complained about her attending too many trustees' meetings, she resorted to the telephone more than usual to keep abreast of the problems. If the art she was buying bewildered him, she moved it out of his sight. If he remained obdurate in spite of her untiring efforts to convert him, she transferred her instruction to her children.

Anyone who believed in modern art as fervently as Abby did, Conger Goodyear wrote, must be a believer in discovery, in the future. Stephen Clark, a strange and difficult man but with a razor-sharp mind, believed that Abby's concept of the museum went far beyond her personal aesthetic preferences. It was more nearly her conviction that art deserved to be brought into the lives of ordinary citizens, and more significant, that even the most extreme and un-popular art had the right to be seen.

John's unyielding resentment is puzzling. In public arenas of controversy he had shown a surprising ability to reverse course, to make rational judgments that defied old, dearly held ideas. He had been a pioneer in industrial relations; he aligned himself with liberal Christianity; he would soon abandon his support of Prohibition. It is conceivable that in another setting he might encourage the kind of statesmanship in the art world that Abby practiced. But his implacable hostility to "Mother's museum," as her sons would come to call it, defied all reason. It went to the heart of his emotional state, the fear of abandonment perhaps, the fear of losing everything, a condition that he could neither articulate nor control. Abby had brought into his lonely young manhood a degree of affection and attention and reassurance that became as crucial to him as air. If these were diluted even in the slightest, as when she gave too much of herself to his children or to the museum, he could think only of his own safety and survival.

Russell Lynes, the historian of the Museum of Modern Art, declared in his recapitulation of the frenetic days before the opening that Abby and Lillie Bliss stayed away out of courtesy to the harried volunteers and professional staff. Courtesy may have explained Lillie's absence, but not Abby's. Nothing would have pleased her more than to absorb the excitement, discreetly watch the beige monk's cloth being hung, view the installation of the great borrowed paintings hung at eye level, perhaps read Alfred's final catalogue copy, which he would rewrite again and again, even after it had been set in galleys. But she was in Seal Harbor with John, who preferred to remain there through the Indian summer, when most of the summer people had departed.

"We are going to leave here next Thursday . . . and go directly to Pocantico," she wrote Laurance on October 27. "Then on the 6th we are planning to move to New York for the winter. Our new Museum opens on the 7th. I shall enjoy being in town, there is much that I am eager to do."[7] She planned to register for a class in music appreciation at Columbia and a correspondence course in modern poetry, also offered by Columbia.

Goodyear's last letter to Abby before the private preview reception scheduled for Thursday afternoon was dated October 30, 1929, twenty-four hours after the most devastating day in the history of the New York stock market. The letter was about fundraising. "The stock market break, of course, will make it much more difficult to get in additional subscriptions," he wrote. "I think there are many people not yet approached, however, who might possibly feel like giving."[8] The *New York Times* in its lead story was not so sanguine. "From point of view, in the extent of losses sustained, in total turnover, in the number of speculators wiped out, the day was the most disastrous in Wall Street's history."[9]

The several thousand people who rode the elevator to the twelfth floor of the Heckscher Building on November 8, the day of the public opening, did not seem to have stocks on their mind. Admission was free. The exhibition ran for a month. In four weeks some 47,000 people visited it. Alfred's catalogue was a model of scholarship and accessibility. Abby's strong preference for the French "ancestors" was vindicated. Edward Jewell in the *New York Times* wrote: "So superb is the initial offering that those of us who were prepared, perhaps, again to deplore the decision to start off with a French art show face palpable embarrassment. Quality disarms. And in view of the rewards so lavishly spread before a visitor's eye, it will be well to dissolve all carping in a more generous fluid of welcome."[10] Goodyear paid Abby his own tribute: "I believe that you are more responsible than any one other person for our beginning and I think that you can and do count that among your happy experiences."[11]

The second exhibition, Nineteen Living Americans, which

opened on December 12, was not a "happy experience," although both Alfred and the board had agreed to salute domestic talent. But the attendance was poor. Abby was apparently still the exception, a collector in the vanguard who valued American artists and bought them. The critics complained. Why this one and not that one? Who was Feininger? Why the Japanese-born Kuniyoshi?

But then the third exhibition, Painting in Paris, opened on January 18, 1930, and MoMA's reputation shot up again. Alfred in his foreword to the catalogue explained Fauvism and cubism and surrealism to the uninitiated. "Bonnard, Matisse, Rouault, Derain, Picasso, Segonzac and Giorgio de Chirico—surely Paris in the early twentieth century need bow to no other period of painting."[12] The crowds came in renewed force. The critics were back on the bandwagon. "Even more important than the Armory Show," Henry McBride wrote. "That was promise, this is fulfillment."[13] Louis Sherwin, the Roving Reporter of the *New York Post*, noticed something else about this new museum, an ambience that was different from that of other buildings where paintings were hung. "Modern Art Museum Glows with Life Even on Dull Days" was the headline that introduced his column. It was not only the show that had vitality, he wrote, the whole atmosphere hummed.[14]

This vitality, so visible to Sherwin and others, was no accident, nor was it a temporary aberration. It became inseparable from Abby's dream of an institution that would be free to experiment, to abandon old prejudices, to be curious about life. "Anything to which man applied his eyes and which might be given the dignity of an artist's or an artisan's or a designer's concern, was in Barr's concept, a proper study and province of the Museum," Lynes wrote.[15] It was the essence of his museum course at Wellesley, and it became the foundation of the philosophy for MoMA. It made possible the unusual understanding that sprang up between Alfred and Abby.

Abby was, after all, the same woman whose unself-conscious joy in the new and untried so attracted young John Rockefeller at the same time that it alarmed him. Perhaps it is an overstatement to call the museum her revolt, as Johnson did. In current nomenclature it might be considered her midlife career. Did she secretly think of it as a revolt? We will never know. It is no disparagement of her motivations in founding the museum to believe that to participate in an event that was so different from her orderly, restrained Rockefeller life must have brought her mischievous satisfaction.

To Stephen Clark it was a constant source of astonishment that she instinctively understood those (to him) strange and emotional people whose background and experience in life had been so different from her own. "Somebody had to quiet their emotions," he wrote, "soothe their wounded feelings and disengage them from violent controversies. In this field Mrs. Rockefeller had no equal." [16] The intuitive good sense, the empathy, the enthusiasm that had humanized the monolith of Rockefeller wealth and Rockefeller Baptist righteousness were the same qualities that Alfred Barr relied upon as he dealt with a prickly population of trustees, artists, and staff.

Early in January 1930, Goodyear met with Abby in her private office to discuss current MoMA problems. August Heckscher was threatening the museum with dispossession because of tenant complaints about noise and crowds. What help could she offer in locating a permanent building? What was the current news on money and membership? And how could the museum acquire the painting *Parade* by Peter Blume? Alfred considered it a work of great importance that should not be allowed to slip into the hands of someone outside New York.

By the time Abby left for Ormond Beach in March she was able to report that subscriptions of $150,000 were already on the books, and that she would buy *Parade*, along with *Study for Parade*, and give both to the museum at some future date. As for her investigations of various parcels of property, she had no luck.

Abby was in Florida when the fourth exhibition opened on March 12. "Please go in and see the new Weber, Klee, Maillot, Lehmbruck exhibition at the Modern Gallery," she wrote David. "I want to know how you like it and I am also anxious to have a catalogue. I have two Webers and two Lehmbrucks in it. I wonder if you will recognize them. I fear that I may miss the exhibition." [17] She was disgusted with the Florida weather. Ormond Beach was not her favorite place, and two weeks of hot, damp air, day and night, was doing nothing for her cough. She rationalized that the change was good for John and, as often when she was idling in an unstimulating setting, she thought about her children.

Although John was perceived as the parent with the high expectations, Abby was no less ambitious, sometimes giving in to lofty flights of inspirational prose. "I expect you to be five of the leading citizens of New York," she wrote them, "each with characters above reproach, and I really don't believe it need be simply a doting mother's fond dream. There are great opportunities awaiting you, why let other people take them. Of course I know that there will be great temptations and great difficulties, you must train yourself to overcome them. . . . Being shut up so long has given me much time in which to think, hence these few words of advice."[18]

Words of advice evidently had made little impression on twenty-one-year-old Nelson, who had announced in the fall of 1929 that he was going to marry Mary Todhunter Clark. Since he had first discovered girls and they him he had been in and out of love more times than anyone could count. European sailings were made much more interesting by the various young women who turned up. One was a "peach" and had a "great deal of savoir faire." A second "sort of broadened me out a little more as far as girls are concerned."[19] By the time of his junior year at Dartmouth, however, he was returning to Mary Clark with some regularity.

Then came the loneliness and tedium aboard the missionary ship, and a sudden sharpening of his feelings. "You know," he wrote Abby at that time, "I'm beginning to think that I really am in love with Tod, whatever being in love means. I can shake it off for awhile now and then, but it always comes back and I've never been able to develop a real affection and an admiration that is all inclusive for anyone else. She is the only girl I know who measures up anywhere nearly to the standards set by you, Mum. But don't get worried. I'm not going to run into anything in a headstrong way."[20]

But of course he did essentially that, writing from Dartmouth that he was truly, desperately in love and was absolutely going to marry Tod. Such a declaration could only anger his father, who declared that even if Mary Clark was a splendid young woman, he was too young, and dead wrong not to consult his parents first. Abby, whatever her misgivings, defended Nelson and soothed John's concerns. When John finally relented, he did it in style, personally selecting the matched pearls for the bride as his mother had done for Abby in 1901. Nelson always knew who had taken up his cause. "I still am thrilling over Pa's wonderful letter," he wrote on November 23, "but, Mum, I shall always feel that if it wasn't for you things wouldn't be the way they are now."[21]

Members of the family, as well as thoughtful observers, have long ruminated over the special relationship between Abby and Nelson. The curiosity continued into recent years because of Nelson's all-consuming passion for art. Blanchette Hooker Rockefeller, who knew Nelson before she met John 3rd, watched him in action. "He was bursting with energy and enthusiasm," she told the author, "one of those men who is full of power and excitement and who could not get along without women. In many ways he was the jewel of the family, in other ways always remained a naughty boy. He was just a little out of hand all the time."[22] Eliza Cobb suggests that his unqualified approval and support of the museum compensated Abby for John's discomfort. Abby had a personality that cried out for sharing—sharing experience, sharing enthusiasms, sharing ideas. Nelson gave back in unrestrained measure.

On vacations from college he was the one to accompany her to the galleries and studios. "Dear Ma," he had written in January 1928. "You don't know how much I enjoyed our two trips to Mr. Davies and the visit to the Downtown Galleries, I feel as if I had been introduced to a new world of beauty, and for the first time I think I have really been able to appreciate and understand pictures, even though only a little bit. I hope to continue this when I am in New York and maybe do a tiny bit of collecting myself."[23] Abby wrote him later in the spring that her mind was full of ideas for a new museum of modern art for New York. "I have great hopes for it. Wouldn't it be splendid if it would be ready for you to be interested in when you get back to New York to live."[24]

To suggest that Abby "trained" Nelson is going too far. His natural preference was for the visual arts. He was highly tactile and sensuous, always excited by shapes and colors, objects of all kinds. Perhaps it had something to do with his dyslexia; perhaps images communicated to him in a way words could not. In his junior year at Dartmouth he took a test on distinguishing original masterpieces from copies that had been mutilated in some way—a tree moved or an arm changed. He ranked in the exceptional group of all those who competed throughout the country. When he was named a senior fellow and freed from routine classroom work, he took up painting and sketching and landscape design and explored the possibility of becoming an architect. He was editor in chief of the *Dartmouth Pictorial*, a photographic magazine that recorded campus life (he took many of the photographs himself), and edited a campus journal, *The Five Lively Arts*, that featured the works of poets, musicians, and painters. In his final year he was elected president of The Arts, the club that imported gifted speakers.

It was Nelson who kept Abby current on the exhibitions of the Harvard Society for Contemporary Art, often cited as the precursor of the Museum of Modern Art. An undergraduate gallery for the visual arts, it was founded by three students, Lincoln Kirstein, John Walker III, and Edward Warburg, who had gathered in Paul Sachs's living room in the winter of 1928–1929 to make their final plans. They borrowed works by Miró and Lachaise, among many others. Alexander Calder rode up on the train from New York with a reel of bailing wire and some clippers to create his first "circus." Alfred reviewed the first exhibition. There has been much conjecture that Abby herself visited the gallery, but Lincoln Kirstein doubts it. Nelson, however, went to Boston often. On one day he swept through two museums and two libraries. "And finally," he wrote Abby, "we went to visit the exhibition of Modern Mexican painters shown by the Harvard Modern Art Society. I met the fellows who were running it and enjoyed both the exhibition and the sponsors."[25]

Nelson majored in economics, but many times in his life he was frustrated with that decision, regretting that he had not become an architect. He apparently never considered majoring in art history and becoming a museum professional, such as someone like Barr or Paul Sachs. He did not have the scholarship for it. Art remained his obsession, however, if not his career. Barr wrote about Nelson and art. "Nelson needs art more than any man I know. Works of art give him a deep, almost therapeutic delight. . . . As art was a necessity to him, he felt that it was a necessity for all people, and he made it his task to provide it—with courage, persuasiveness, and generosity."[26] Like Abby, Nelson hung and rehung his pictures for relaxation.

It was Abby, as much as anyone, who discouraged him from becoming an architect, one instance where her larger ambition may have preempted her sensitivity. When Nelson confided his dream to her, she reminded him of greater obligations. "I am terribly eager that the high standard of citizenship set by your father shall be maintained by you boys. It seems as if all of you would have to join in the battle for righteousness in all walks of life, business, church, professions and private life, no small or easy job. This has always been the dream of my life, but of course each of you will have to work out your own salvation."[27]

Was it also the dream of her life that he go into politics, as her father had done, though politics had been off-limits to Rockefellers? Even aspire to the presidency? Perhaps she was clear-eyed about Nelson after all. With his power base and independent fortune, his Rockefeller training in community service combined with the zest and the charm, he came to personify, to a great degree, the consummate American public man.

Nelson and Tod were married in the fashionable Philadelphia suburb of Bala-Cynwyd on June 23, 1930, within a day or two of his commencement. Henry Stebbins, their friend from Maine, learning of the marriage from the wedding invitation that reached him in Germany, was amazed. "I was absolutely nonplussed," he said. "They seemed so different."[28] Laurance, who was the closest of all the brothers to Nelson, was puzzled too, although he admired Tod tremendously. "Maybe it was the difference that appealed to him," he theorized. "Remember, they had grown up together. She was Main Line, imperious, hard to get perhaps. Philadelphia looked down on Rockefellers. That would be a challenge for Nelson. She was not gregarious, like Nelson, but she was totally honest and courageous and had that sly wit. Always stood straight up and spoke out, never mumbled."[29]

The differences were dramatized by Nelson's last-minute arrival at the church. He bounded from the limousine, tossed his hat into the hands of the surprised sexton, and slapped him on the shoulder. "The bride's lean patrician face had a radiance approaching beauty . . ." Joseph E. Persico wrote. "Beneath her gown she wore flat slippers out of consideration for her shorter husband."[30] After the reception they boarded a ship for an around-the-world honeymoon that lasted nine months.

CHAPTER 22

*M*argaret Scolari (Marga) married Alfred Barr in New York on May 8, 1930, followed by a church wedding in Paris. "I believe our German show next winter should be a sensation," Alfred wrote Abby from Berlin while on his honeymoon. "Visited Erich Heckel this morning—a most charming man. Daumiers are most exceedingly hard to borrow and the woods are full of fakes."[1]

In September the young couple visited the Eyrie. "She was tall," Marga said of Abby, "with incredibly beautiful posture, extremely gracious, very gentle. Very gentle," she repeated to the author, "with beautiful manners." Marga, a trained art historian who prided herself on telling the blunt truth, at least as it appeared to her, described their visit. "We were given a vast corner bedroom with five or six or seven corners and at least thirteen vases of orchids all about. It seemed excessive to me. After dinner she asked us, in that same gracious way, if we would like our breakfast in bed or if we would prefer to come down. We learned later that she rarely came down. Alfred and I had never had breakfast in bed. If we did come down, then we had to arrive at seven-thirty, fully dressed obviously. It was a seated breakfast and I was on Mr. Rockefeller's left. The butler came by with a silver tray and there was a Bible on it and you helped yourself as if you were taking a

Alfred H. Barr, Jr., Philip Johnson, and Margaret Scolari Barr, Cortona, Italy, 1932.
Courtesy of the Museum of Modern Art Archives, New York. Alfred H. Barr, Jr., Papers.

roll. 'Now we will read the thirteenth chapter of Corinthians,' he said. 'I will start reading a verse and then clockwise you will all read a verse,' which we did. Only when this was all over did we get orange juice and coffee." Marga thought for a moment and then continued. "I think it must have been unbearable to be his wife."[2]

After her houseguests departed, Abby dictated a long letter to William Valentiner:

I have delayed writing you thinking every day that Duveen would send me the prints that you have gotten for me in Germany. I am most deeply grateful to you for taking so much trouble. . . . I can hardly wait to have them come, I am so eager to see them all.

I am particularly glad to have some things by Nolde. He seems to have made more impression on me than anyone else whose pictures I saw in Germany. I hope some day to have a very good painting of his.

It was awfully good of you to think of letting me have the water-color by Gross [Grosz]. May I let you know later whether I am taking it or not. At this time of year I am in the same state as probably your Museum is in—I am entirely out of funds, but per-haps I can manage it somehow. . . .

I appreciate more than I can tell you your willingness to help me with my collection of German prints. I should really like to have a very complete collection of German prints, either to pass on to Nel-son—if he is interested—or to give to the Modern Museum. In a way it is very difficult for me to make this collection because it is practically never possible for me to buy modern prints in Europe. When we are over there I do not like to desert Mr. Rockefeller and prowl about, and over here I can only buy what the dealers have seen fit to import. . . .

I found my seventh floor gallery finished; now it only remains to be furnished. I am very reluctant to buy what is entirely known as modern furniture for it; I have seen so little that I really like. I am now thinking of putting simple comfortable chairs and sofas in it and perhaps nice old tables and not attempting anything in the way of modern furniture. What do you think of this plan? Very confiden-tially I feel that Miss Bliss' gallery, which has lots of lovely pictures, is also full of small elephants in the way of furniture. It all looks so big and clumsy to me.[3]

Abby's concept of a gallery that would be the correct setting for contemporary art moved from merely so-so to innovative when she discovered the machine-age designer Donald Deskey. "I had returned from Paris," he told the author, "and was doing window displays for Saks Fifth Avenue. Mrs. Rockefeller saw them, asked Edith Halpert to bring us together, which she did, and that led to my commission to design the gallery."[4] During this same period Halpert was negotiating with him to design the interior of an annex to her Downtown Gallery, another commission that became semi-nal to his career.

The Donald Deskey that Abby had met in that winter of 1929 was a study in sophistication. He wore a pencil-thin mustache, and always had a cigarette dangling from his lips. His dark blue suit was severely and impeccably tailored. A white handkerchief peeped out from the breast pocket. Gray spats completed the image of suave elegance, but his easy, hearty, deep-throated laugh and his rural origins belied such an image.

He was born in Blue Earth, Minnesota, in 1894. He studied architecture at UC Berkeley and painting in Paris. After visiting the Bauhaus and lingering long over the Exposition Internationale des Arts, he joined the world of interior and industrial design. He drew his inspiration from the Art Deco return to historical forms of furniture and the use of luxurious materials such as fine wood. At the same time he made use of industrial materials such as steel, glass, and plastics in mass-produced geometric forms, preferred by proponents of Art Moderne.

After he returned to the United States, the Newark Museum organized an exhibition, Modern American Design in Metal, that featured Deskey's metal furnishings and accessories, as well as others by William Zorach and Lee Simonson. Deskey's choice of materials—standard cork flooring, corrugated gray asbestos Transite (asbestos and cement)—created striking abstract backgrounds for the new designer clothes featured at the chic department stores. He was one of the first to construct interior glass-brick walls, lit from behind. Eventually he built his own company to execute his own designs—screens, furniture, lamps, light fixtures, tables, even rugs of cubist patterns and bold colors.

The design of Abby's gallery became a joint venture, with Duncan Candler and Deskey working as partners. On January 14, 1930, Candler had submitted the final bid for all alterations to the seventh floor, the estimated cost of $33,290 to include woodwork and metalwork, lighting reflectors and fixtures, terrazzo, carpets, plasterwork, etc. Candler projected three months to do the job. It took about a year. "Quietly and without fanfare or publicity, one of the most personal and, therefore, one of the most interesting collections of contemporary art has been forming during the last four years," a correspondent for *Vogue* wrote. "This is the Mrs. John D. Rockefeller, Junior, collection, which has recently been installed in modern galleries designed by Donald Deskey. . . . Her collection has

Abby's seventh-floor gallery at 10 West 54th. From left to right on fireplace wall: Child with Dog, *artist unidentified, probably 1770–1790.* The Palette, *Henri Rousseau.* The True Cross, *artist unidentified, probably 1880–1900.* Flowers in a Green Vase, *Odilon Redon.* Baby in Red Chair, *artist unidentified, ca. 1810–1830. On right wall: second from left,* Portrait of Gala *(wife of artist), Salvador Dali. Large picture to the right,* The Residence of David Twining, *attributed to Edward Hicks, 1846–1847.*
Courtesy of the Rockefeller Archive Center.

Abby's print room. Works on the wall by German expressionists. The Matisse sculpture of 1909 on the window sill was the first sculpture by the artist to enter an American museum collection, a gift by Abby to MoMA in 1939.
Courtesy of the Rockefeller Archive Center.

the validity of a strongly felt personal predilection and a spirit of adventure resulting from exploring uncharted aesthetic territory."[5]

The print room, with its neutral gray Bakelite walls and an ingenious arrangement of channeled aluminum strips, enabled the art to be hung and changed with ease. Deskey designed the contemporary lighting, which threw uniform light over the room, and placed warm gray carpet on the floor. For the walls of the larger gallery, where the drawings and watercolors and the few paintings hung, he selected pale gray hardwood panels. Abby's curator worked out of a small adjacent office where most of the prints were stored. A ceramics room and a great glass cabinet displayed her collection of eighteenth-century porcelains from England and Germany and the Orient.

Dorothy Miller, who became curator of painting at MoMA, wrote that Abby was probably the first American collector of contemporary art to build in her home a gallery of modern design. "Here she arranged continually changing exhibitions of the works in her collection in order that she might study the various phases of contemporary expression. . . . Here many of her friends saw modern American art for the first time." By hanging the small pieces—drawings, watercolors, and sketches for larger works—she could study them carefully before proceeding to the purchase of the oils. "The richness and variety of her collection of watercolors and drawings are in part the result of this procedure," Miller wrote.[6]

To Philip Johnson the seventh-floor gallery was Abby's world. She invited prospective donors and friends to hear interesting lectures. Henry Russell Hitchcock, Jr., the architectural historian, spoke there, as did Johnson himself. She served sherry to her guests. Her daughters-in-law learned about modern art in her gallery, as she drew them into support groups for the museum. Alfred conferred with her, as did Philip and Monroe Wheeler, who became director of publications. "Once in a great while, me," Marga explained, "but rarely. Mostly it was Alfred. But she adored him, all the women did."[7]

All of them remember the conversations during lunches at her house, her sharp questions, her analysis of museum problems, her enormous warmth with its edge of caustic sharpness. "She was a quick study," Johnson added, "the best I've ever known, and the quality of her gaze, the way she fastened you with those eyes, at the same time that she bucked you up. Her presence was so commanding, it made you want to do whatever it was she wanted. She was brilliant at picking people who had great eyes for art. She was incredible with Alfred. They made such a team as you wouldn't believe."[8]

William Lieberman of the Metropolitan elaborated on that. "Their relationship was often tense, not emotionally, for they were close friends, but he knew what he thought and she knew what she thought. She knew that he knew much more, but she still had strong opinions."[9] Blanchette remembers going to the gallery and listening to Alfred lecture on the art that surrounded them. "She [Abby] and Alfred were choosing some modest works by contemporary artists for her to acquire and hang in the gallery for an informal exhibition," Blanchette said. "Alfred was a born teacher, among many other attributes. . . . We were fascinated by his slow, meditative analysis of each work. After considerable discussion . . . Mrs. R. made her own independent choice. I remember that some beautiful Demuth watercolors as well as some Ben Shahns were in our conversation that day."[10]

It was this world that John refused to enter. "On Monday I got the pictures hung in my gallery," she wrote him later in the spring when he was in Arizona and she was in New York. "I hate to say 'my gallery' but I know you object to my saying 'our gallery.' Mrs. Halpert and I got out all my pictures painted by Americans of America, commonly known as The American Scene and we both feel quite proud of the result."[11] John's reply is revealing. "I can imagine how much you are enjoying playing with your picture gallery again and only wish I could really share with you sincerely the interest which you take in it."[12] If John could conceive of Abby's commitment as "play," then it really was beyond his comprehension.

Abby returned from Maine on September 19, 1930. Goodyear scheduled a trustees' meeting during the one week that she would be in Manhattan before she sailed to Europe with John on October 4. "It is my feeling," he wrote in preparation for that meeting, "that we will have this year the real test of the value of the Museum. Last year, thanks to a certain novelty and the very striking exhibitions we were able to have in at least two cases we made a beginning which by its very success makes it more difficult to maintain interest during the coming season. The Daumier and Corot exhibition should attract a great deal of interest, and the German exhibition will also undoubtedly command attention, as very few important examples of German art have been seen here." [13] The finances of the museum were very much on his mind—how could they possibly raise $2,500,000 for a new building and endowment in the worsening Depression?

In France the government had fallen and the franc was 24.68 to the dollar. While in Paris, Abby took steps to acquire a van Gogh drawing, *Street at Saintes-Maries*, from a German owner. "The price quoted as I told you," the dealer wrote, "was 16,000 marks ($3,800.00) net to me, but I shall do my best to secure it for less. Van Gogh drawings, not as important as this one, have been sold for prices ranging from five to eight thousand dollars." [14]

From Fontainebleau, Abby and John, Jean the chauffeur, and John's valet departed for a three-week tour of Spain, via Biarritz, San Sebastián, Burgos, Madrid, the Escorial, Segovia, and back to Paris. "If we were not staying in a Ritz Hotel and riding about in an Hispana-suiza car, I should think that we were back in the middle ages," she wrote Laurance. "We go into a gorgeous 13th or 14th century church full of priceless treasures and come out to find it surrounded by poverty. . . . I have fallen in love with the paintings of El Greco, the father of modern painting. Jean confided in me that he thought that within ten years there would be a republic here. . . . We start for Paris on Tuesday . . . which means that we are turning our faces toward home. . . . I hope that Princeton wins from Yale." [15]

Abby did not see the Daumier and Corot exhibition, which closed on November 23. Winter storms on the North Atlantic delayed her arrival in New York just long enough to make her miss it. She had to be satisfied with Goodyear's description and Alfred's introduction to the catalogue. According to Goodyear, this was the first time in their history that the Louvre and the National Gallery in Berlin had lent pictures to an American museum, surely a tribute to Alfred's persistence and powers of persuasion. Other lenders of Daumier's work included the Folkwang Museum at Essen (*Ecce Homo!*), Lillie Bliss (*Laundress*), and Sam Lewisohn (*Drinkers*). And as a reminder that the more things change the more they remain the same, there was a theft! The picture, one of Daumier's finest small canvases, called *The Print Collector*, belonged to Joseph Stransky. As of 1943, according to Goodyear, it had not been recovered.

Of Corot, Alfred wrote, "The girl in the plaid dress is so perfect that one can only think of Holbein's early paintings . . . or Vermeer of Delft. . . ." And his remarks about Daumier serve to remind the reader of Abby's prescience in regards to this giant of the nineteenth century. "The extraordinary neglect and even ignorance of his painting . . . in America, is almost unbelievable. . . . Only one of his oils, a small study, has ever been purchased by an American museum . . . and so far as New York is concerned the present exhibition is almost certainly the first occasion upon which more than four of his paintings have ever been seen together."[16] Imagine the masterpieces that might have found their way into the same American museums had Abby Aldrich had access to John's Rockefeller fortune.

Immediately after Thanksgiving, Abby turned her attention to an important social event. Henri Matisse was coming to dinner on December 18. Alfred wrote the following advice on December 5th:

> I have been thinking over some of the people for your Matisse dinner. I still feel that Mr. Crowninshield could perhaps give you the best advice. Gay, young people who speak French would probably please Matisse.
>
> [Several] names occur, not all gay, not all young; Henry McBride [the critic] who, of course knows Matisse; Jere Abbott [associate director of the museum] . . . who [speaks] adequate and occasionally voluble French and [is] interested in Matisse. . . . You will perhaps consult Mr. Goodyear about the advisability of having the Dales [Chester Dale was a trustee]. I do not remember exactly what relations exist between you and that redoubtable pair.

I hope these suggestions are of some use. I will send all further names when they occur to me. I regret to say that Mrs. Barr and myself will be unable to come since the 18th is in the midst of a week which we had hoped to spend with Philip Johnson at his house in Pinehurst. Mrs. Barr hopes to have her tonsils out at that time so that I am sure you will pardon our absence.[17]

Monroe Wheeler further refined Alfred's suggestions. "Matisse would most enjoy tall, beautiful blonde girls, he said."[18] And so Abby wrote the following to Laurance. "You can suggest anyone you like as long as she is good-looking, as I am told that Matisse very much likes pretty girls."[19] She had already invited Mary French, Betsy Clark, and Eliza Bliss. Eliza remembers the event well. "Yes, I was invited to the Matisse dinner. I was seated next to him, ostensibly because I spoke French. I was not told about the other criteria, although I found out later."[20]

Beyond their shared appreciation of contemporary art, both Abby and Matisse were fascinated by Persian miniatures. These small manuscript illustrations, so intelligently collected by Abby, offered Matisse an alternative to Western perspective. After viewing an exhibition of Islamic art in 1910, he began to adapt the decorative universe of the miniatures to his interiors of 1911.

Matisse was bewildered that a man of John's many interests, a man who played the violin, danced extremely well, spoke French fluently, and was even embarking on a great experiment in architecture (Rockefeller Center), could shut his eyes to the wonders of Cézanne, Seurat, van Gogh, Picasso, and the other French modernists. After coffee was served, Matisse turned to John and half seriously began to plead his cause, to explain, according to Frank Crowninshield, that "the men who had created the incredibly beautiful green, yellow, red and black porcelains that were all about us, were really in pursuit of exactly the same aesthetic goals as those to which Matisse had personally dedicated himself.

"He tried, too, to convince him that Braque, Juan Gris, and Picasso (in his more abstract canvases) had merely followed the decorative designs and emotive experiences of the Persians who had woven what Matisse called Mr. Rockefeller's 'modern' (though seventeenth century) Polonaise rugs; that, in short, there was no such thing as modern art, or ancient art, or art of the Middle Ages; that the youngest and liveliest art, today, was that of Egypt, China, and Greece; whereas, the deadest art imaginable was that of the hack painters who now flourish in so many of our academies of art.

"But the philanthropist," continued Crowninshield, "who had listened very politely, regretted quite as politely, and in the most polished French, that he must still appear adamant. Then, with an engaging burst of confidence, he added that Mr. Matisse must not altogether despair, because, though he might still seem to be stone, he suspected that Mrs. Rockefeller, thanks to her very special gifts of persuasion, would eventually wear him down to the consistency of jelly."[21]

For at least two years Abby had been writing members of the immediate family that John was sleeping poorly and was more exhausted than usual. On February 21, 1931, she wrote Lucy that they were leaving shortly for Tucson. "After we came back from Europe John went to the Institute and was looked over by Dr. Cohn. About a month ago Dr. Flexner announced the result of their examination was that altho they felt John was perfectly all right he was very much overtired and had very little resistance, and they practically insisted that he should get away for two months. . . . We are leaving on Tuesday for the Arizona Inn. . . . They say it is an extremely good climate for the nerves."[22]

The anxiety and insomnia that had afflicted John in the past were rarely precipitated by external events. This time it was different. It had to do with money, huge sums of capital, huge even for Rockefellers, and a project of enormous complexity and risk—the building of Rockefeller Center.

In September 1928, John had agreed to lease from Columbia University most of the land between 48th and 51st Streets and Fifth and Sixth Avenues, and buy up what Columbia did not own. The impetus for the development was the relocation of the Metropolitan Opera House to this new parklike setting flanked by leaseholds to various corporations that would then develop and construct their own giant buildings. "Two events in 1929 threw a long shadow over these ambitious plans," Fosdick wrote.[23] The

Metropolitan Opera board withdrew because of financial and legal difficulties, and the Depression brought the investment and industrial plans of an entire nation to a virtual halt. Now there was no possibility of subletting unimproved land.

It was a bleak prospect. Already he had spent nearly $10 million for fees, licenses, rent, salaries, etc. From a high of nearly $1 billion in 1928, his net worth had already shrunk by several hundred million, and in 1930 no one knew what the end would be. There were two choices open—to cut his losses and abandon the project, which would encompass fourteen massive commercial buildings, or to go forward alone—to build, finance, and lease it alone. "I chose the latter course," he told Fosdick, knowing all the while that the cost would be somewhere between $120 million and $160 million, and the lending agencies would insist that he be personally liable. When later asked whether it did not take considerable courage to go ahead with the development in such unpropitious times, he replied: "I don't know whether it is courage or not. Often a man gets into a situation where there is just one thing to do. There is no alternative. He wants to run, but there is no place to run to. So he goes ahead on the only course that is open, and people call it courage."[24]

By the time his doctors ordered John to Arizona in the spring of 1931, considerable progress had been made. Three leading architectural firms were developing the plans. An experienced group of builders, headed by John R. Todd, was running the huge development. And most critical of all, a major tenant had signed on for the flagship building, to be known ultimately as 30 Rockefeller Plaza. The Radio Corporation of America negotiated leases for its corporate headquarters, for the NBC Studio, and for Radio City Music Hall.

Arizona was much more to Abby's liking than Florida. Anna Kelly helped John with his correspondence, and Abby started to ride again. A local doctor put her on a salt-free diet, to help her lose weight, but it also had the effect of lowering her blood pressure. The daughter of her friends the Douglas family was an artist. "She and I had a wonderful modern art talk last night," she wrote Laurance. "She said there was no one in her family she could talk with about modern art. I said I was very much in the same boat, so we had a good time together."[25]

She wrote Lucy that everyone connected with the museum was working hard, "or I hope is working hard on getting ready to make an appeal for a permanent organization. Perhaps you will remember we only asked for money to last two years and a half and now if it isn't going to be a failure, we must raise the money for the endowment as well as for permanent quarters."[26]

Money continued to be the pressing problem for the museum, and it grew worse with each passing day. The most stringent economies could not drive the expenses below $90,000 a year, and it was not at all certain that enough pledges would be fulfilled to meet those expenses. Even so rich a man as Stephen Clark was complaining, and people without private fortunes were severely curtailed in what they could provide to public institutions. Abby, frustrated by the limits on her own purse strings, stretched her resources whenever possible. She subsidized the salary of an important member of Alfred's staff. She increased her own pledge from $5,000 to $10,000 and agreed that the $10,000 she had given to the building fund could be used for current remodeling if the museum moved its quarters. She was still the trustee who had the most success in raising money.

Goodyear reached all over for ideas. "I noticed in the paper this morning," he wrote Abby, "that the Payne Whitney Estate has some thirty million left for the trustees to contribute. . . . Perhaps through Jock Whitney we might be able to get some."[27] After the Carnegie Foundation agreed to give $5,000 a year to defray expenses (it would not do a major funding), he raised the possibility of going to the Rockefeller Foundation. Abby did not discourage him—she knew Max Mason, the current chairman—but she was not hopeful. MoMA was not yet the educational institution that might fit the foundation's profile of a worthy recipient. (MoMA was subsequently turned down.)

"I still feel just as strongly as I ever did," she wrote Alfred, "that we cannot ask other people to give to the Museum in large amounts without the Trustees themselves having expressed their confidence in it by making substantial pledges for its future. . . . I think it is perfectly possible and also feasible to work the Museum on the Russian five-year or ten-year plan. . . . It seems to me the educational side of the work is much the easiest and simplest to work out. The part that distresses me most is how we are going to remain modern and at the same time satisfy donors that the pictures they give will not be disposed of in a manner that would be objectionable to them."

This was the first letter in which Abby addressed Alfred by his first name. "I am calling you 'Alfred' this morning. Sometimes I call you 'Mr. Barr' as you may notice. I think that I am so much of an old fashioned New Englander that it comes a little hard for me to get out of the habit of calling people by their titles rather than the informal and nicer way of calling them by their first name."[28]

On March 14 she received a sad telegram from Conger Goodyear. Lillie Bliss was dead. "You can imagine what a great shock it was for me to learn of Miss Bliss' death," Abby wrote Goodyear, "and how deeply grieved I am. I had the greatest admiration and respect as well as deep affection for her and I feel that her loss to the museum is almost irreparable."[29] A week later she wrote to Alfred. "Of course Miss Bliss has been very much in my heart and on my mind during the last few days, as I am sure she must have been upon yours. I wish that we might have some lovely exhibition that would be in the nature of a memorial for her or do something that would express our appreciation of what she has done for and meant to the Museum. One thing has occurred to me. Do you suppose it would be possible for us to have a loan exhibition of her pictures? I can think of nothing that would reveal her more to the public and nothing that would show them better how remarkable was her taste and prove the real contribution she made to the Museum. . . . I shall reach home almost as soon as this letter, but I thought you might be thinking about it."[30]

———————————·⟋∞⟍·———————————

*T*he funeral service for Lillie Bliss was held in the gallery of her three-story Park Avenue apartment. Walter Hampden, the actor, delivered the eulogy. The museum honored her with a memorial exhibition of her collection, as Abby had suggested. At the preview opening on May 17, 1931, music was the keynote, performed by the young musicians who had received Lillie's largess. Eleanor Belmont's words were still remembered fifty years later by Marga Barr: "God gave us memory so that we might have roses in December."[1]

The disposition of the collection had been very much on Lillie's mind. She had discussed the question with her brother Cornelius, with Goodyear, with Abby herself. When the terms of the will became known, it was evident that Lillie was practical as well as idealistic about the future of the museum. She stipulated that the cream of the collection would go to MoMA, but only on the condition that, in the view of her executors, it be sufficiently endowed, on a firm financial basis, and in the hands of a competent board of trustees. The executors decided that an endowment fund of $1 million could provide such a basis. Abby and her compatriots understood the assignment and set out to raise the money. But this was 1931, and the task was formidable.

Early in June, Marga and Alfred left for a summer in Europe to prepare for the Matisse exhibition planned for November at MoMA. "Matisse has recently returned from Tahiti," Marga wrote in her chronicle of events published in 1987. "When A. inquires what had prompted such a long journey, Matisse replies that he had wanted to see the light of the Marquesas Islands, so vividly rendered by Gauguin."[2] While in Paris, Alfred and Marga set out to buy French prints and lithographs that would fill in some missing names for Abby's collection. Already she had an impressive inventory—Daumier, Rouault, Picasso, Delacroix, Fantin-Latour, Gauguin, Laurencin, Degas, Redon, and Toulouse-Lautrec. The Barrs made careful purchases—Fernand Léger, Jean Lurcat, Louis Marcoussis, four more Picassos, Maurice de Vlaminck, Juan Gris, Giorgio de Chirico, Juan Miró.

When Abby wrote Lucy that in spite of every precaution she still got tonsillitis, Lucy tried to straighten her out about a few things. "I do wish you would take some care of yourself, tonsillitis doesn't come from bad weather; it comes from being run down, and I am sure you do too much. By that I don't mean the things you want to do—they never really tire anyone, and if they do, it isn't the kind of being tired that knocks you out. . . . I wish you could drop everything and come abroad for awhile but I suppose it is too much to expect you to be as sensible as that. I wish I could dig up some of our ancestors and insult them for leaving us . . . their . . . conscientiousness. I think it is a terrible drag on all New Englanders and does more harm (to everybody) than good."[3]

Carefully ignoring such counseling, Abby wrote instead the news of the family, Rockefellers as well as Aldriches, with some scraps of old Providence gossip. Babs had a new baby girl, Marilyn Ellen, named after Marilyn Miller, the Ziegfeld star, and Dave's mother. Nelson had joined John 3rd in the family offices at 26 Broadway and together with Tod was haunting the back roads of New England for bargain-priced antiques to use in their small house at Pocantico. Congressman Richard Aldrich had joined the liberals in Congress to vote for the Bonus Bill to provide veterans with some ready cash. "Winthrop [Aldrich] and everybody else I have seen greatly disapprove."[4] Abby preferred to listen to Richard's reasoning before criticizing him.

Then there was the matter of Frank Smith, her old beau, who met a very attractive widow (Frank was by this time a widower) on a ship that was passing through the Panama Canal. By the time they reached California they were already engaged! The question of Abby's wardrobe took up much discussion between the sisters, as Lucy and Minnie MacFadden marched back and forth from Lanvin to Patou to Worth. As for Lucy herself, "I personally have spent my last cent. I think I may as well spend it as leave it, but you and John may have to bury me."[5]

Winthrop, "thank fortune," had at last graduated from Loomis. "I am now hoping . . ." Abby wrote, "that he can pass his examinations for Yale."[6] Poor Winthrop. There seemed no end to his academic troubles. Trigonometry remained a mystery, history and English teetered on the brink; he went to tutoring camps, and seemed at times to be camping out with his headmaster. Through it all he remained stubbornly optimistic that it would all work out, and he still had something of a childlike wonder that his siblings really liked him. He planted pansies in his window box at Loomis, unself-consciously expressed his love for Abby, and had an egalitarian streak that made him the most popular boy at the school. When some of his classmates didn't have enough money for haircuts he cut the hair of forty boys before the headmaster stopped him.

Even the fact that he won the highest prize in the class for industry and loyalty was no guarantee of acceptance at Yale. Abby disagreed with Lucy that college was not important. She believed that the world worked differently and it was important. "I think President Angell is very anxious to have him come there," she wrote. "He likes Winthrop and also I think would like to have a member of the family go to Yale. Not that we would like to ask for any special favors or concessions on his behalf, because we wouldn't."[7] In August, Winthrop learned that he had passed the entrance examination and was admitted.

As a veteran campaigner who knew how to modify John's stiff regulations without causing an uproar, Abby was able to effect some modest changes on behalf of the children. "I shall be delighted to get a radio for your room for your birthday present [his twenty-fifth]," she wrote John 3rd. Like his father before him he had moved back to the family house after his graduation from Princeton. "When Papa heard about it [her buying one for John 3rd], he was a little disturbed to have another radio right over his head, but I assured him he wouldn't be able to hear it through the thick floors of Number Ten, and that you would probably not be running it when he is in his room. I cannot imagine your sitting up very late nights listening to the radio."[8]

The question of Sundays at Pocantico had to be attacked. Abby worked out a compromise. "Having in mind the churchgoing habits . . . of the family," she wrote, "it seems best that the sport and game facilities of the playhouse and the place, including horses, golf, croquet and tennis, should be availed of on Sundays at hours other then between 10:30 and 12:30 in the morning."[9]

Neither family responsibilities nor her involvement with MoMA distracted Abby from the social programs that looked to her for support. Whether it was the New England conscience that Lucy deplored, or habits that reached back to her girlish idealism, or a refusal to be insulated by great wealth, she sent her charitable dollars of $50,000 per year in all directions.

In some years she provided as much as a third of the operating budget of the National Women's Trade Union League. Organized labor, despite its lip service, paid scant attention to women in the workplace. The league, organized in the years before World War I, was active in the union movement, advocated equal pay for equal work regardless of sex or race, and campaigned for laws that would improve working conditions for women.

Rose Schneiderman, the president of the league, was a Jewish immigrant child from Poland with a sixth-grade education. While working ten hours a day in a factory, she helped organize a branch of the United Cloth Hat and Cap Makers of North America. She was nineteen years old. By 1920 she was a candidate for the U.S. Senate on the Farmer-Labor Party ticket. Mary Elizabeth Drier, the league's vice president, came from the opposite end of the social spectrum. She was born in New York City, was a member of the

German Evangelical Church, and was educated in private schools and with tutors. First she went into philanthropy, then into industrial relations. She served on many commissions and worked steadily for minimum-wage legislation. Abby, whose life was so different from that of either woman, shared their basic goals—world peace, women's rights, and programs that made a difference for children.

Women and children came in for the largest share of her charitable donations in 1931—$4,798.32 to Bayway, $10,352 to the YWCA, $5,850 to the Harlem Sewing Room. But the size of the check was not the only consideration, for even a small amount from Abby sent a message of approval. Among the recipients were the settlement houses on the East Side, the Art Workers Club for Women, Bethune-Cookman College, and the American Birth Control League.

Margaret Sanger, the pioneer advocate of birth control, expressed her gratitude to Abby and at the same time described the problems still to be overcome. "I was so encouraged with the progress that the movement has made in Germany and England. . . . It was a blow to return here and find our financial situation in such desperate plight," she wrote. "This has, of course, come about because of unemployment which makes it impossible for the mothers to pay for their supplies, and then owing to the fact that we are having hundreds and hundreds of the very poorest of the poor women. . . . We want to encourage them to come here and yet the strain on our finances is terrific. We are already two weeks behind in our schedule with so many mothers clamoring to come here. . . . I wish you could come down and visit us some morning or afternoon in the near future. I know how you may hesitate to do this thinking of publicity, etc., but I wish to assure you that nothing of the kind would happen and if I could have the pleasure of taking you through the Clinic it would be unnecessary to have even a member of the staff know of your identity. . . . The object of this letter, however, was not to tell you my woes, but to thank you for your help and your fine interest, and to tell you how much I appreciate it at this particular time."[10]

Whenever possible, however, Abby did take public positions.

The *New York Times* put her name in headlines when she joined the "Block-Aiders." "Mrs. John D. Rockefeller Jr. and John D. Rockefeller 3rd joined the ranks yesterday of 'block-aiders' under the command of the Block Community organization, which is organizing an army of 100,000 volunteers throughout the city to seek 'adoption' of families suffering under distress of unemployment. The campaign is to be waged in more than 10,000 city blocks, each of which will be asked to 'adopt' one or more unemployed heads of families or their bread-winners. The 'adoption' will assume the form of a contribution of $15 a week to the fund of the Emergency Unemployment Relief Committee, which will provide emergency jobs for those 'adopted.' "[11]

Grim statistics can in some measure dramatize the scope of the economic collapse. A million people were without jobs in New York City alone. (One of the considerations that influenced John to go ahead with Rockefeller Center, while not the determining factor, of course, was the employment of thousands of workers, reliably estimated to be 225,000, directly or indirectly.) The auto industry was operating at one-fifth of its 1929 capacity. For farmers the Depression was cataclysmic. The price of a bushel of wheat dropped 50 percent; subsidies were unheard of. There was no unemployment insurance, no social security, no farm credit, no Aid to Dependent Children. The poorest and the weakest were the most vulnerable—tenant farmers, migratory workers, women, blacks. There was no clear idea why it all had happened, which is, perhaps, why President Hoover was unable to find measures that worked.

During this unhappy period when the president was summoning national leaders to the White House, Abby and John went twice. No longer was it inappropriate for presidents to confer with Rockefellers. Abby was a Republican, but she listened respectfully to her Democratic friends. At a luncheon in Bar Harbor she was seated next to Henry Morgenthau, "whom I enjoyed talking with," she later wrote John 3rd. "[He] told me quite a little about the Democratic hopes and possibilities. He thinks Franklin Roosevelt is going to be the next president and he tells me that Mr. R. is most eager to be president and that he feels it is his destiny."[12]

The year ended with Lucy writing a cranky letter from Providence upon hearing that Abby was sick again. "I am so sorry you have the flu and have such a hard time getting over it. Why don't you cut out church for a while," she suggested archly. "I don't think it agrees with the Aldrich family. As far as I can understand Elsie put a bone out in her spine kneeling in prayer. I think it is better for us to pray on our feet." She then reported on the death of their brother's wife. "Ned looks dreadfully and his hands shook . . . but he seems much less nervous and more cheerful than he did when his wife was alive. Matrimony is beyond me! . . ." Finally she took up the question of her will and who should get what. "It makes my blood run cold to think of 'in-laws' chipping my old china, letting my rugs get moth-eaten and banging up my old furniture. . . . Providence is just about as cheerful as ever, everybody sick or dead or away."[13]

At Christmas, Abby's friends gave her a silk-covered book with messages of affection. Her housekeeper, Bella Orton, wrote that "only we who work with her understand the demands made upon her patience." A friend named Saunders thanked her for encouraging recently emancipated women and races to grow. And Edith Halpert wrote as one who clearly benefited from Abby's purchases, but who also understood perhaps more than anyone what American artists owed her. "Some have vision, some have courage, but it is rare to find someone who has both vision and courage. . . . American art, American artists, and the American public . . . acknowledge a great debt to you."[14]

The Matisse retrospective opened on November 3 to critical and popular acclaim. Marga translated Matisse's *Notes d'un Peintre*, originally published in Paris in 1908, which Alfred then incorporated in the catalogue. "I cannot copy nature in a servile way," the artist had written. "I must interpret nature and submit it to the spirit of the picture. . . . The chief aim of color should be to serve expression as well as possible. . . . I discover the quality of colors in a purely instinctive way. . . . What interests me most is neither still life nor landscape but the human figure. . . . The role of the artist, like that of the scholar, consists in penetrating truths as well-known to him as to others, but will take on for him a new aspect and so enable him to master them in their deepest significance."[15]

On December 22, 150 works by Diego Rivera, including seven frescoes painted for the occasion, were on exhibit. The show broke all daily records with a five-week attendance of 56,575. Philip Johnson was the inspiration for the first exhibition on architecture, which opened on February 9, 1932. The show—The International Style—became synonymous with the discipline itself. It was the first traveling exhibition ever mounted by a museum, and as a result of its success, the trustees established a Department of Architecture.

The search for new quarters had continued throughout the year. At one point Goodyear had written Abby that John's property at 11 West 53rd Street, a five-story house with sixty feet of frontage, was empty and could be rented for $12,000 a year. Goodyear had a scheme whereby John could sell the house to the museum on a conditional purchase plan, saving the museum substantial taxes, but John was not interested. He did, however, instruct his agent to revise the rental downward, since the property was not earning any income. A figure of $10,000 a year was agreed upon. On December 12, 1931, the trustees authorized the leasing of the house for five years and allocated $20,000 for renovation. John subsequently reduced the rent to $8,000.

The renovation of 11 West 53rd and the move from the Heckscher Building was accomplished in four months. On May 2, the *New York Herald Tribune* announced the opening. "More than 5,000 persons, including art collectors, artists, architects, museum directors and educators, have been invited to attend the formal opening tomorrow of the Museum of Modern Art's new home at 11 West Fifty-third Street. . . . A special exhibition of murals by forty-nine painters and photographers will be a feature in the opening exhibition."[16] The remodeling was entirely successful. At last it would be possible to plan for a permanent collection, as yet more of a dream than a reality. There was room to carry on educational programs (still largely on the drawing board), and there were a small library, auditorium (also small), and executive offices on the top floor, which had once been occupied by family servants and which was reached by a tiny elevator, just big enough, as one of the staff put it, "for one fat man and me."[17] Abby had converted President Hoover to her cause, for he wrote a letter which Alfred read on the air on Station WJZ a few days after the opening. "The establishment of the Museum of Modern Art opens wide opportunities for the appreciation by the public of the trends of the times in the fine arts. . . ."[18]

The one person who could not be at the opening was Abby herself. "Papa and I are leaving for the Hot Springs at 5:30 on Friday PM," she wrote Laurance on April 10. ". . . I fear that I shall not be here . . . for the opening of the new building of the Modern Museum. But Papa needs the rest."[19]

If the new building was generally applauded, the mural show, Murals by American Painters and Photographers, which ushered in the event was not. It became the catalyst for the biggest uproar the museum had yet generated. It was the brainchild of the junior advisory committee, engineered by Lincoln Kirstein, and caused much anguish among trustees before it was finally placed before the public.

The junior advisory committee had been formed in 1930, not many months after the museum itself. The trustees realized that it was important to gather around the museum a body of younger people who would feel an involvement in it, and if possible share some of its responsibilities. It included Elizabeth Bliss (Eliza Cobb), John Nicholas Brown, Philip Johnson, Lincoln Kirstein, James Johnson Sweeney, Edward M. M. Warburg, and other amateurs and potential collectors. When Nelson returned from his honeymoon he plunged into the affairs of the committee and the museum at large with his customary zeal.

Eliza Cobb gives an informal view of how the committee operated. "We were told that our opinions would be valued because we were young. The middle-aged members of the board of trustees wanted to know how young people felt, and we were to criticize them, which of course we loved doing. We would have meetings all day long, usually in Mrs. Rockefeller's gallery, sitting on the floor, screaming at each other, interrupting. We loved it. We were angry because they were only showing European art, and since it was the Depression we wanted the American artists to get some attention.

"We thought that if we had an American artists' mural show, all those rich people would have murals done for their homes and the artists would make some money. Finally the trustees said to go ahead and we appointed Lincoln, the only one who was a professional by then and knew what he was doing, to organize a show."[20] Lincoln selected thirty-five painters and commissioned from each a small study for a triptych and one of the three panels in full size. Julien Levy, whose upstairs gallery on Madison Avenue near 57th Street was one of the very few galleries that took photography seriously, was in charge of selecting the photographers.

The trouble began when it came time to show pictures of the works to the board. Two were attacks on the establishment and hewed closely to the current Communist line. Hugh Gellart had J. P. Morgan, John D. Rockefeller, Sr., Herbert Hoover, and Henry Ford sitting behind their money bags, with Al Capone in front of them aiming a machine gun. William Gropper did an odious picture of Morgan, this time with Andrew Mellon. The third that generated some emotion was Ben Shahn's depiction of Sacco and Vanzetti in their coffins.

"All hell broke loose," according to Eliza. "Sam Lewisohn, who often dozed during meetings but generally knew when to open his eyes, said, 'I thought this museum needed money.'" Some of the young people wanted to placate the board and remove the offensive murals, but Lincoln said that if the museum didn't hang all of them, he would have an independent show and make it quite clear that the museum had backed out. "Nelson stood up for Lincoln," Eliza said. "He told us we had to support him, and he went to Mr. Morgan to explain and Mr. Morgan was quite nice about it. Some of our committee resigned and those who stayed were loyal to Lincoln and we were a better group afterwards."[21]

Telegrams flew back and forth. On April 18, Alfred had wired Abby in Hot Springs that the situation was more complicated than when she had left, that Goodyear was still determined to throw the controversial ones out, that Lewisohn on second thought was inclined to leave all of them in, that Clark was for taking them out, even after he (Alfred) explained that she (Abby) was willing to leave them in. "Will keep you informed," he wrote. "Problem has been extremely difficult."[22]

On April 28, Alfred made his final plea in the form of a telegram to Goodyear. "We have had ten days of Hell over these pictures—the decision of Lewisohn, Clark and Nelson was made after the most careful consideration and after Mrs. Rock, before she left, had agreed to leave them in—DeBevoise and Lee are with them and they are acting principally on behalf of the persons caricatured stop they knew that you doubt strongly and had threatened to resign but they believe you would have been with them had you been here. I implore you not to make a hasty decision but to talk with Mrs. Rock as well as Clark and Lewisohn stop please keep this confidential."[23]

After all the hoopla the exhibition opened as originally conceived. The popular press ran such headlines as "Insurgent Art Stirs Up Storm." Nelson was singled out as the one who stood up for the artists. Abby was described as neutral, which was not the case, of course. The critics were skeptical at first, using such words as "childish, uninspired, the saddest event of a none too cheerful winter."[24] By the end of the month, however, opinion had shifted. The *New York Times* editorialized: "The Museum enters upon its larger program of activity securely entrenched and well equipped to serve. . . . Its spirit is further revealed in the present exhibition, devoted to American mural art. Our artists, most of them, have much to learn about mural painting. But it is only by practice that vision and skill can come, and the Museum of Modern Art, by providing a laboratory of this kind, gives an impetus that may yield telling results in the future."[25] Even Stephen Clark conceded that there was a good deal to be said for some of the best of them.

After the mural show closed, Nelson was elected to the board of trustees of MoMA and to the much more venerable board of the Metropolitan Museum of Art. He was then twenty-four years old. John had opposed the idea of his serving on the Metropolitan. Abby explained to George Blumenthal of the Met that her husband was concerned that Nelson might spread himself too thin. But

Abby was strongly in favor of Nelson's taking the position, and she prevailed. Perhaps she felt that Nelson at the Metropolitan could effect a useful rapprochement between the two institutions. There were several flirtations over the years, but no alliance was ever forged.

All the men and women who worked around the museum in the early years have stories to tell about Abby. Lincoln Kirstein, who never claimed to know her well, although he became a close friend of Nelson's, remembers exactly how she treated him during the mural show imbroglio. "She was a wonderful woman," he said. "She never blamed me for the silly mistakes I made. She never let me feel uncomfortable." With a smile to the author he called himself the Red Jew in their midst. "She was just very decent during the whole affair," he continued. "She was beautiful. I had tea with her. She was so wise, so sensible. Only a few women in America were like her, she understood so much."[26]

Then there were Eliza's anecdotes, recalled with affection. "There really wasn't much of a staff. Perhaps Alfred had a secretary, but most of us were volunteers. When it came time to have the opening party for the new building, someone asked me to put it together. So I just went to Tiffany's and ordered the stationery and went to the Colony Club and hired a secretary, and decided on lovely flowers and all of that. But then later I learned that there was no money at the museum to pay for such extravagances. I sent my own check from my clothes allowance to cover the bills. Three days later, Mrs. Rockefeller wrote me a note with my check returned. 'I see no reason why you should know how to give a cheap party.' That's the way she was. She had her eye on everything."

One afternoon Tod and Nelson invited Eliza to Pocantico and everyone went swimming at the Playhouse. Abby was wearing the kind of bathing suit that came to the knees and had a white lace collar, and she wore stockings. "I always dressed in the latest fashion," Eliza explained, "and I was wearing a one-piece bathing suit, very scanty. I was so embarrassed I wanted the pool to open up and drown me! Everyone thought they could make me feel at home by talking about it, and of course that only made it worse. Then Mrs. R. suddenly announced, 'You know, I think I'll take off my stockings.' Which she did and then she said, 'There, that feels so much nicer.' "[27]

Philip Johnson has a particular reason to appreciate Abby's magnanimity. Following a series of triumphant exhibitions in which he demonstrated his talent for display and design, he abruptly went off to confer with Huey Long in Louisiana. "I'm leaving in three weeks to be Huey's . . . Minister of Fine Arts," he is supposed to have announced to the startled trustees of MoMA. Huey paid scant attention to him, but he continued along a somewhat disreputable political path, uncomfortably close to a brand of neofascism. Eventually he sobered up and returned to the museum. Other trustees may not have been forgiving, but Abby said at the time, "Every young man is entitled to one bad mistake."[28]

When Alfred told Abby that he could afford to pay his assistant, Dorothy Miller, a mere $20 a week, she was horrified. "She immediately suggested that I could earn some extra money by cataloguing her collection of art books on Saturdays when she was in the country," Dorothy recalled. "She had a huge wall of them. She told me to look around the house as much as I wished. I saw the Renaissance paintings in the main rooms, and over in the annex [12 West 54th] I sat and stared and stared at the unicorn tapestries. It was staggering to see them hanging on the wall, dominating the room. Mrs. R. was gorgeous—tall, imposing, and her clothes were just unbelievable."[29] Dorothy would know. According to Eliza Cobb, she herself was a beautiful woman and one of the best-dressed of her day, even though she bought her clothes at second-hand shops and thrift stores.

Monroe Wheeler added his reminiscences. "She thought about the museum every moment of her life. Whenever she had an idea, she would not wait until she saw you, but would call you up immediately—what might be done, how soon. How everyone on the staff was getting along, if they liked each other, or if they didn't, what could be done about that? She was always hyperconscious of her large nose, which wasn't all that large. She liked to wear hats that would astonish her friends. She didn't come to the museum as often as she would have liked, because of Mr. Rockefeller, but she watched over everything. She handled Mr. Clark [Stephen] with velvet gloves. His mind and his eye were not as elastic as hers, and he took some handling. She was always opening new windows, especially fascinated with things she had not seen before."[30]

Wheeler was right about her fascination with the new and untried. Thinking about the Metropolitan versus the Modern, she wrote to Alfred, "It [MoMA] is running so smoothly it rather frightens me. It would be terrible if we descended into being a second Metropolitan not but what I admire the Metropolitan very much."[31] Feeling obliged to qualify, she went on, "I simply [mean] it might be easy for the Trustees and even for the Junior Advisory Council, to get into the way of doing the safest and easiest thing rather than undertaking a program that might cause controversy and be a challenge."[32]

Wheeler continued, "I lived just around the corner from her. Sometimes she and her driver would take me home after meetings. 'What do all those jockeys mean on that building?' she asked me one afternoon. I explained that that was '21.' Had she never been to '21'? Perhaps she would permit me to take her and Mr. Rockefeller to dinner there. She demurred, explaining that Mr. R. preferred to eat at home." In 1944 an American army officer did take her and John to "21." It fulfilled all her expectations except for one. The maître d' was so solicitous of John that he placed them upstairs, too far away from the other diners for Abby to see all the action.

Finally Wheeler remembered one of Alfred's favorite stories. When Abby walked him through her folk art collection for the first time, in order to convince him of its aesthetic value, they paused in front of her giant carving of an American eagle. "Don't you think that beak is a little like mine?" she asked, giving Alfred a sly smile.[33]

*T*he exhibition American Folk Art—The Art of the Common Man in America, 1750–1900, opened at MoMA on November 30, 1932. Holger Cahill, the foremost authority on folk art, organized it, and, except for a carved horse lent by Cahill, the entire exhibition was an anonymous showcase for Abby's collection—174 pieces. After its New York debut, the show traveled to six cities. It established American folk art as a force in art history that would never again be taken lightly. Cahill's catalogue is still being quoted, sixty years later, by curators and collectors. "The work of these men [and women] is folk art because it is the expression of the common people, made by them and intended for their use and enjoyment. It is not the expression of professional artists made for a small cultured class, and it has little to do with the fashionable art of its period. It does not come out of an academic tradition passed on by schools, but out of craft tradition plus the personal quality of the rare craftsman who is an artist."[1]

Abby's interest in folk art had a strong aesthetic component. Like the modernists whose works she was already acquiring, she brought a sophisticated understanding to the primitive quality of the nineteenth-century pieces. Valentiner had already introduced her to Der Blau Reiter and Die Brücke in Germany, whose members were attracted to the art of peasants and children. She had studied Italian primitives and early Japanese prints, buying examples of each. She saw the relationship between contemporary art and the simplified shapes, arbitrary perspective, and bold colors of folk art. From the modern artist's viewpoint, this was a decided departure from the highly "realistic" coloration of representational art of previous years. For those artists adventurous enough to break from the academic tradition, these "American Ancestors" (the phrase was coined by Halpert) could legitimize their own experimentation.

Both Halpert and Cahill were introduced to the genre in 1926 and 1927 at Robert Laurent's art colony in Perkins Cove, Ogunquit, Maine. Laurent and his patron, Hamilton Easter Field, had long furnished the studios on the property with carvings and paintings that had languished in the junk shops and attics of the area. Halpert began to buy an occasional weathervane or portrait for her Downtown Gallery, believing that they would lend dignity to the contemporary works she was promoting. Abby, a steady customer of the gallery, made her first purchase of American folk art in 1929. When Halpert realized how eager she was for pieces of real quality, she and Cahill went out on collecting trips through New England and Pennsylvania.

Abby's art account of 1931 reflects her financial commitment to folk art. On July 17, the Rockefeller office sent Halpert a check for $7,000, on July 21, $2,465, and on August 10, $1,312, all earmarked for the subheading, Primitive account. Between September 30 and October 3, $11,195 was mailed to the American Folk Art Gallery, Halpert's newest addition to 113 West 11th Street. The official announcement of her opening on September 22 appeared in *Art Digest* under the headline "Folk Art of America Now Has a Gallery of Its Own." Halpert, the source for the article, made it clear that the paintings and sculpture were selected, not because of antiquity or historical association, but because of their relationship to vital elements in contemporary American art, which Halpert would continue to champion.

If Edith Halpert was the salesperson who made folk art accessible and popular and Holger Cahill was the sleuth who located it and wrote about it, Abby was the collector who bought it. But Abby did not simply buy what a dealer recommended. She knew everything about each item in her collection. Tessim Zorach gained the impression from his father that Abby had a very, very good eye. But this does not detract from Halpert and Cahill—Abby learned from both of them.

Carolyn J. Weekley, the present director of the Abby Aldrich Rockefeller Folk Art Center at Williamsburg, agrees that Abby's capabilities in determining great art were extraordinary. As she walked the author through the center, pointing out which pieces had come to the center from Abby herself in 1939, Weekley communicated a kind of fresh amazement at the quality of some of the works that hung on the walls in 1986. "Her decisions were *very* discriminating," she said. "A lot of material that was on the market in her day was of inferior quality. It was a serious assessment on her part. She managed to get some very key things that no one realized at the time *were* key."[2] Because of her judgment, the center has the greatest known collection of Edward Hicks paintings, a fact which draws scholars from all over the world. Fernand Léger believed, or at least he so stated when he saw one of the "Peaceable Kingdom" series, that Hicks was a more important artist than Rousseau. Abby bought kingdoms representing each phase of Hicks's career. She also bought other Hicks works, including *The Residence of David Twining*, a carefully worked-out memory picture reflecting the quiet farm where Hicks's earliest religious ideas had been formulated.

Baby in Red Chair is immensely valuable, so valuable that the center could never go out and acquire it today. "Nothing is known of the origin of this picture," Nina Fletcher Little, the folk art expert, writes, "yet it captures the hearts of all who see it. . . . By his naive and unabashed expression of homely sentiment, the folk painter has unconsciously created a masterpiece which—in its small and unassuming way—approaches the realm of fine art."[3] So much of Abby's collection is one-of-a-kind: portraits by Erastus Salisbury Field, Ammi Phillips, the Beardsley Limner. In 1935, recognizing that her collection was dominated geographically by the Northeast, Abby sent Cahill into the South on a search for additional works. He made two stunning discoveries. *The Old Plantation*, a watercolor on paper, by an unknown artist, is one of the earliest depictions of blacks in the United States. African-American scholars continue to debate the meaning of the ceremonial dance being performed in the picture. *The Portrait of a Merchant*, by an innovative itinerant artist, R. B. Crafft, demonstrates why the artists at Ogunquit, who were experimenting with multiple perspectives, were attracted to folk paintings. Crafft's work seems to parallel the distortions and spatial experiments that the Ogunquit artists were pursuing, as well as European painters such as Picasso.

Abby roamed across the landscape of folk art, buying not only oils on canvas but theorem paintings on textiles, mourning pictures, needlework, fraktur, sculptures, weathervanes. She chose arguably the best theorem painting made in nineteenth-century America, *Basket of Fruit*, executed by Mary Bradley, circa 1830. The word "theorem" refers to the systematic process by which these paintings were created. Paper stencils, cut out in appropriate shapes, were used as aids to form major elements. Created mainly by young women, the smaller details were often added by pens or small brushes. Among many mediocre examples of Pennsylvania-Dutch fraktur pieces ("fraktur" refers to the broken Gothic lettering found on many German-American drawings and written documents) Abby selected several rare examples.

Folk sculpture, like its counterpart in painting, embodies some of the characteristics that fascinated the modernists—a linear quality, often very direct and flat, and distortion of shapes and spatial relationships among elements within the pictures. In 1931, Abby bought a carving from Edith Halpert that reflects these qualities. Entitled *The Preacher*, it is a small dynamic figure with a primitive power and dignity that seem to recall peasant art admired by the early German Expressionists. Originally it was thought to represent Henry Ward Beecher, but is now believed to have been inspired by a metal replica of Ernst Rietschel's enormous bronze monument to Martin Luther erected in Worms in 1868.

The impulse that drove Abby to build such a distinctive and wide-ranging collection of American folk art over a period of twenty years was not exclusively aesthetic, however. Just as she founded the Museum of Modern Art for reasons that extended far beyond her obsession with contemporary art—a recognition of the public stake in art, a desire to shorten the lag between creation and appreciation—so too a whole set of emotions and beliefs fed into her folk art acquisitions.

She was a child of the Colonial Revival in New England. No Americans were more eager to collect old furniture and bric-a-brac than the educated elite of Boston and Providence at the turn of the century. Abby was not the only collector of folk art to come out of Rhode Island. Eliza Greene Radeke, a Vassar graduate who worked at the Rhode Island Pavilion at the 1876 Centennial Exhibition, preceded her. Maxim Karolik and his wife, Martha Codman, were Abby's contemporaries, and like Abby were admirers of Elie Nadelman and his vast collection. Daphne Farago succeeded them both. All three were benefactors of the Museum of Art of the Rhode Island School of Design, a facility designed by Abby's brother William.

Abby also championed folk art as a valuable record of middle-class American life in the same way that Edith Halpert did. Edith, while deploring Yankee chauvinism, was as proud as any native-born American of the nation's early founders, and although she never used the term, went so far as to preach a form of cultural nationalism. Abby's other public involvements contributed to her interest in folk art. Bayway epitomized her respect for ethnic crafts, and for the works of unknown amateurs motivated by a desire for artistic expression. In 1928 the League of Nations created an American chapter of the International Commission on Folk Arts, with headquarters in Brooklyn. The purpose of the commission was to document and preserve traditional folk arts and crafts and, through exhibitions, demonstrations, and articles, to use folk art to foster better understanding among peoples of all nations. Abby was an active supporter of the League, and such an activity reinforced her interest in preserving the efforts of American folk artists.

And finally, there was Williamsburg. As John devoted more and more of his time and money to the restoration, Abby began to direct his attention to this other aspect of American cultural life that was worth preserving. Folk art with its historical context could

Mary "Tod" Rockefeller and Grandmother Abby with a very small
Rodman Rockefeller, 1932.
Courtesy of the Rockefeller Archive Center.

appeal to him in a way that modern art did not. The fact that he underwrote Abby's purchases in a rather sudden, dramatic way seems to suggest his approval, or at the very least, his acquiescence. It does not depreciate her aesthetic interest in the art to suggest that collecting it served some additional purpose in their complex relationship.

Abby was in Hot Springs, Virginia, when Nelson's first child, Rodman, was born. "Much as I am dying to go to New York . . . and see my new grandson," she wrote Lucy on April 30, "I am not even mentioning it. . . . John has had a terrible headache for the past two days. I feel that it would be a . . . mistake for him to leave just now." The next day, Sunday, she continued the letter. "Today is Winthrop R's birthday, he is 20. So I called up Tarry-town and had a nice talk with him, and also with Babs, Nelson, Laurance, David—much to John's horror. You know how he feels about telephoning, especially when I am doing it."[4]

In June, Laurance graduated from Princeton and David from Lincoln; Laurance would enter Harvard Law School in the fall, and David would enter Harvard College as a freshman. Summer plans were in place. David would go to Europe, Laurance to the Canadian Rockies, and Winthrop to a boys' camp as a counselor. Abby and John settled in at the Eyrie. The rest of the family came and went. In Chicago, Edith Rockefeller McCormick was dying of cancer at the age of sixty while Senior, who was ninety-three, continued to enjoy life in Ormond or Lakewood or Pocantico with benign acceptance.

Babs set aside her dislike of Maine to spend some time with her parents at Seal Harbor. "She comes to lunch every day or dinner, one or the other," Abby wrote David. "It is so nice if she happens to come in the evening because she sits quietly with Papa and me while we knit and talk and it seems quite like the old days to have her back again. Dave Milton seems very busy about something and only spends his weekends up here."[5] The Depression was hard on Dave. Determined to establish his financial independence from Babs's family, he gave up the practice of law to race from one deal to another. And since there was no way that he could even re-motely create a Rockefeller-like fortune, the frustrations were in-tractable. Laurance and David agree that there was a dramatic change in Babs after the first few years of her marriage. "It was not a happy marriage," David suggested. "They were so very different. Dave was so anxious to make a lot of money on his own so that he would not be dependent on her, he was like a squirrel in a cage. The family liked him, he was a charming, decent man, but nothing seemed to go right for her in those years."[6]

For most of the season, John was confined to the house with a wretched case of shingles. His doctors blamed it on nervous ex-haustion. For Laurance, Abby was trying to "get some light" on

*Blanchette Ferry Hooker, August 1932. She married John D. Rockefeller 3rd
on November 11, 1932.*
Courtesy of the Rockefeller Archive Center.

the question of his law school rooms. That meant asking her friend
Mrs. Smyth, whose husband was professor of Greek at Harvard
and knew everybody, to gather opinions. John told Abby that she
was spoiling Laurance by doing such things, but she stood her
ground. In her opinion it was important for him to have a comfortable room and have as little nervous strain as possible his first year.
She wrote him out in Alberta that "a room had just been given up
in Walter Hastings Hall, which is the best Law School dormitory.
I have looked it up on the plans and it is a delightful room on the
third floor with a sitting room facing south. . . . The price of the
room (which is No. 53) is \$350. . . . I am perfectly delighted be-
cause you will now be with all the other law students, which your
Uncle Winthrop tells me is a great advantage because they are
constantly discussing the cases that are brought up and one gets
lots of information that way."[7]

Things picked up a bit at the Eyrie when Blanchette Hooker arrived. She was the houseguest of John 3rd and had driven in with Nelson, who was joining Tod and the baby. She remembered the five brothers from the early years when their small heads bobbed up and down in front of her at the Fifth Avenue Baptist Church. She had met Nelson first, since he was the dashing brother who got around. It was not until John 3rd turned up at a dance in Greenwich, Connecticut, in the fall of 1931 and asked her to dance that they did more than exchange perfunctory nods. They danced once around the floor, then sat down to an earnest discussion about welfare. "We had a wonderful time," she recalled with a smile. "We talked a lot and were deadly serious."[8] John wrote a few lines on a Christmas card, inviting her to go riding on New Year's Day. Blanchette accepted promptly, and slept with the card tucked under her pillow for days.

Both Hooker parents were descended from seventeenth-century settlers. Elon Huntington Hooker was an engineer, exuberant and entrepreneurial, who had served in the administration of Theodore Roosevelt before founding the Hooker Electrochemical Company; he was much like Nelson Aldrich in his eager enjoyment of the good life. Blanche Ferry Hooker was an heiress and a feminist, a graduate of Vassar, who raised four daughters while being involved in good causes. Two of the daughters were liberated young women who traveled to the Soviet Union in 1930, wrote about it, and later married unusual men. Blanchette was the easy child. She had a cool beauty that contrasted with her unaffected manner. She had common sense and an excellent Vassar education.

Recognizing that this was not a Nelson-type flirtation, but attention from a man who did not know how to be frivolous, Blanchette responded warmly to John's hesitant overtures. They began to exchange long, introspective confidences, more about each other than about welfare. Blanchette met Abby and John informally at Pocantico, formally at 10 West 54th. During the few weeks in July that John 3rd was at the Eyrie without her, daily letters—lengthy and intense—went back and forth between Greenwich and Seal Harbor, although John's diary, terse and businesslike as usual, reveals nothing of his feelings.

Blanchette recalled the trip up to Maine with amusement, although she was not at all amused at the time. "I was supposed to take the train, but at the last minute Nelson called to say that he was driving and I should go with him. I knew Nelson, and I should have known he simply liked having girls around, but I said yes, without realizing that the trip involved an overnight boat trip with the car aboard. Of course we had separate rooms, but when we went into the dining room, there sitting next to us was a whole table of Aldrich relatives.

"The next day was even worse. The roads from Boston to Mount Desert were under repair, we were an hour and a half late for dinner, and John [3rd] was furious. There was always a lot of rivalry between him and Nelson, and Nelson always won. The frost did not last long," she added, "but it was hard for the moment."[9] The rest of the week, however, was something of an idyll, as they explored romantic trails and for moments of privacy disappeared into Abby and John's Rest House. On the last day of Blanchette's visit they decided to become engaged.

In September they returned to the Eyrie together to discuss the details of their wedding plans with Abby and John. It was on this visit that Blanchette formed her first bond with Abby. "We sat together in her garden, just the two of us, on several occasions. She knew that it was exciting for me, and yet at the same time strange. She spoke frankly about all her children, but especially, of course, about John. His shyness, his self-doubts, how difficult it had been for him, as the oldest son. How difficult it might be for me, since I was the more outgoing." Abby was careful not to alarm the young woman, but rather to prepare her. "It was a tremendous help to me, those conversations," Blanchette said.[10]

Her son, Senator Jay Rockefeller, agrees. "My mother was very close to my grandmother. She was the one my mother could talk to. I knew my grandmother only through my mother. Evidently she helped her enter the family, which has always been perceived as a difficult thing to do."[11] Blanchette came to see the startling similarities in the two Johns. So did Jay. But they both saw a gentleness and later an openness in John 3rd which came straight from Abby.

Blanchette continued, "When I came to know Mr. Rockefeller better and we would ride together, with his teaching me how to hold a pair of horses, I realized how intense he was, that he was really scared to death about so many things, and Mrs. Rockefeller did bring him out of himself. The family would have been quite different, enormously different, had it not been for her. She saved the whole thing."[12]

Abby's daughters-in-law idolized her, each for different reasons. Tod, who was raised within the narrow bounds of the Main Line, looked to Abby to open up the larger world for her. She admired Abby's personal sparkle, her sense of humor. She noticed immediately that nothing, not even constant stress, cramped her style. As Tod followed Nelson into the art world, she saw how deeply pained her father-in-law was over Abby's commitment to MoMA, and yet how Abby hung on to the museum as her domain. Abby, for her part, loved Tod. Understanding Nelson without condoning some of his actions, she was a steady bulwark for Tod in highly charged situations.

Mary French, who married Laurance, was the daughter of a very powerful woman, "distant and unavailable," Laura Chasin, Mary's daughter, pointed out. "Naturally my mother would love Abby, who was so warm and approachable, so much heart, so good-humored. Maybe in a way, Abby was part of the package in that she offset some of the problems they encountered as Rockefeller wives." Laura repeated what others outside the family theorized, that there was an implicit contract in the marriages. Abby had accepted it, Mary French accepted it, and the other Rockefeller wives did, too. "The wives were supposed to give up certain things and take on certain things and not want certain things," Laura added.[13] Harriet Aldrich Bering, Winthrop Aldrich's daughter, agrees. "We seemed to feel that we had to wait quietly to be recognized."[14]

Russell Lynes explained at the time Blanchette was elected president of the museum that "she is not the sort of woman who could be manipulated against her will, but when she became a Rockefeller she was quite aware that she was assuming a role with very stringent demands, a public aspect that was inescapable, a private aspect that was clannish."[15] Abby, more perhaps even than the younger women, could identify with Lynes's remarks, which, phrased in another way, said that you preserved your integrity at the same time that you played by the ground rules. From the day of her marriage in 1901, Abby had to come to terms with the power that belonged to the name. She knew that it could be constricting on the women as well as the men.

Jay Rockefeller agrees. It is still spoken of as a fact in his generation. He doubts that it even breaks along gender lines. "One carries with one the notion and conviction that ours is a difficult family to marry into, for men as well as for women. There is something discomforting about the very phrase 'you marry into the Rockefeller family.' "[16] But it was the men in Abby's generation and in her sons' generation who wielded the power. It behooved the wives to circumvent it if they wished to have an identity of their own.

It was not a coincidence that Abby drew Blanchette into MoMA. "She had an important influence on my life," Blanchette said proudly. "She carried on at MoMA as long as she could, but after I was married and had three children she suggested that I get involved. I became more and more interested. It was such an exciting institution, and the people who worked there were so fascinating." Blanchette, like Abby, had to hang her own modern art in a location where it would not upset John 3rd, in her case a tiny town house designed by Philip Johnson. "I wasn't up on modern art." She had majored in music at Vassar. "But I learned."[17] She learned so well that she was president of MoMA for thirteen years. Never mind that her husband, like his father, disliked contemporary art, even seemed to fear it, and was rigid in his belief that she should give up her own interests in deference to his. Everyone knew, to quote Henry Allen Moe, that her husband "didn't have a damn bit of interest in the museum. Blanchette was following in the footsteps of her mother-in-law and doing it awfully well."[18]

CHAPTER 25

Three years after he became director, the trustees of MoMA voted to give Alfred a sabbatical. Marga wrote in her chronicle that "Mrs. Rockefeller [Abby] who sees A. very often, notices his exhaustion and knows about his constantly stinging eyes and persistent insomnia; a doctor of her choosing recommends a year's leave of absence."[1] Abby understood Alfred's temperament, and she appreciated his obsession with the museum and what his genius had accomplished. She knew that the trustees would be guided by her recommendations and those of her personal physician. And she was the one to suggest Holger Cahill, whom Alfred trusted, for his temporary replacement.

Throughout Alfred's year in Europe, Abby monitored his problems. When Goodyear placed an unexpected demand on him—it had to do with a possible MoMA exhibition at the Louvre—and Alfred's sleeplessness returned, Abby reassured him. "I personally was very sorry that Mr. Goodyear asked you to hang the exhibition that was supposed to go to Paris because I knew you were . . . not ready to do this sort of thing. . . . If one has been a long time in running down, he must realize that it takes a long time to pull up again. Nature is very slow and exacting. It takes longer and is harder to run up hill than down. . . . I think you are very wise to interest yourself in some new phase of art. [Alfred was studying Italian baroque painting.] To me it is very refreshing to meditate upon the pictures of many divergent periods and schools."[2]

Alfred replied, "You are quite right about its taking 'a long time to pull up again.' I'm not satisfied about my sleeping and shall probably go to a specialist in Vienna. European acquaintances feel that psychoanalysis is a natural step in curing insomnia if there is no apparent physiological cause. What I really want now is advice on how to rest so that I may use the remaining months to most advantage."[3] Abby cabled him to hold off on psychoanalysis until he had a chance to read a book that she was sending him. He, in the meantime, heard about a Dr. Otto Garthe of Stuttgart—not an analyst—who could help him. He and Marga set out for that city, and wrote Abby accordingly.

"I was very pleased and quite relieved to receive your last letter [about Dr. Garthe]," she replied on March 4, 1933. "After I cabled you not to see the psychoanalyst until you had read the book I was sending, I thought you might feel it was none of my affair what you did. I have gotten a very strong impression that often psycho-analysis adds a new complication rather than removes the old ones. . . . I do hope that the book on 'Progressive Relaxation' has reached you and that you may be able to master it. I confess that as yet I am not very expert in relaxing, but it does help me when I cannot sleep. I am beginning to think that perhaps I don't need as much sleep as I thought I did. If one lies perfectly quietly and relaxed in bed, is it necessary that one should be asleep? Perhaps one's body and nerves can rest if they are properly controlled when awake."

As he read on in the letter, Alfred discovered that Abby's advice was not proffered from ignorance or mere good intentions. "In regard to the Sterne show," she wrote, "I have been able to see it only once. Unfortunately I have not been at all well for the last six weeks and have seen practically nothing and nobody, the doctor having put me on a rest cure."[4] Abby's doctor apparently shared the view of his colleagues that when women complained of nervous exhaustion it was because they were overstimulated. They should go to bed at once and see no one. For Abby such a regimen simply separated her from the activities she most enjoyed. It was the opposite for men, who were advised to embark on a program of vigorous exercise.

"I am still in bed," she wrote Laurance, "and as yet I haven't been able to persuade the doctor to say when I can get up. . . . I am debarred from having any of the nice tea-parties that you had when you were recovering. . . . I am sorry that I have no news to tell you; as I see no one, I hear nothing. John [3rd] is coming in to see me this afternoon, and I am hoping that the doctor will soon lift the ban on company."[5] The most fun she had all spring was going to the Sterne show with Philip Johnson. "[Philip] came back to lunch with me and we had a most amusing and delightful time," she had written Alfred, "and I thoroughly enjoyed it."[6] Johnson reported back to Alfred that Mrs. R. did not seem at all unwell.

The whole question of Abby's "nervous breakdown," as John persisted in calling it, remains a mystery. He wrote Mackenzie King that "Mrs. Rockefeller has been suffering for some months from a nervous breakdown which has been coming on for years and which you will understand will take a long time to get over. . . . Aside from seeing the children in installments and briefly, Mrs. Rockefeller is seeing almost no one else; not that she is not frequently quite able to do so but because these cycles of nervous depression come on every few days, quite without warning, and when they come, it is of the utmost importance that there be no plans made in advance that prevent complete quiet and rest."[7]

Abby, who had spent thirty years coping with John's exhaustion, his headaches, his insomnia, seemed chagrined and rather embarrassed to admit that she might have some problems of her own. She acknowledged that, in her words, she might not always be up to the mark. But she used aromatic spirits of ammonia to give her a temporary lift, an accepted remedy in an era when there were neither antidepressants nor tranquilizers. She used luminal occasionally for insomnia, never regularly, because she knew it was addicting. Massage helped the painful tension across her neck and shoulders. Her "doctors," in addition to the one M.D., were John and Thomas DeBevoise. It is difficult to imagine a husband and his legal adviser (DeBevoise) to be the best therapists for a woman in conflict. At one point, DeBevoise even recommended that she do nothing at all except play solitaire or do puzzles, or drive or walk with John, a routine that seemed singularly counterproductive for Abby. John, knowing how often other people, including his own children, wore him out, apparently assumed that they must wear Abby out as well, however much she protested that such was not the case.

John brought passion and loyalty to their relationship, and she responded eagerly to both gifts. Their private moments seemed touched with humor and deep affection. But his needs were so complex and unyielding, his control so pervasive, that the wonder is not that Abby finally internalized her anger in the form of depression, but that she had sublimated such feelings for so long. As she wrote Alfred Barr, she was skeptical of psychoanalysis, having watched Edith McCormick work with Jung for ten years without visible improvement. Other forms of psychological counseling available today were not in the mainstream.

Neither David nor Laurance remembers a nervous breakdown in their mother's life. They both support the hypothesis that their father, deeply pained over her stubborn commitment to MoMA and modern art, viewed such independence as a kind of illness. "In the name of preserving your health," as Laurance phrased it, "you can no longer do what I do not wish you to do."[8] Laurance also recalled a tendency in the Rockefeller family to turn the women into neurasthenics, mentioning that Laura Spelman became a semi-invalid early in her marriage, having to be carried up and down the stairs and so on. Actually, neurasthenia was a common diagnosis to pin on troubled women who were trapped in situations beyond their control.

What does seem evident is that Abby never had a classic breakdown, but fought her way out of the invalidism that John and DeBevoise and her doctor seemed eager to impose upon her. To read her correspondence during this period and to follow her activities—the alacrity with which she sprang out of bed at every opportunity—is to watch resiliency and energy in action, even if her nerves, as she put it to Lucy, were slightly out of order.

In May she visited Lucy in Providence for ten days. Everyone in the family knew what Lucy's steadfast love and sharp tongue meant to her. "When things got too rough, Mrs. Rockefeller could visit Lucy," Blanchette observed.[9] John did not view Lucy as a threat. She was not in competition. She could tease him at the same time that she appreciated his generosity, and after all, he caused her no difficulty.

When she reminded Abby that doing too much of the things you really want to do never caused the kind of exhaustion that knocked you out, she was right. When she would urge Abby to come away with her and Minnie MacFadden, she was pinpointing what everyone else was too circumspect to suggest, that Abby needed an occasional respite from John, implying that John, at the very least, might be part of the problem.

John's barrage of telegrams and letters speaks loudly of the yawning emptiness he felt in her absence. An ineffable sadness permeates even his relief that she might be feeling better. "While I cannot understand your sudden and complete change of plans and you will be sadly missed at home, I will cheerfully fall in with any program that gives you greatest pleasure." Evidently Abby was enjoying life in Providence so much that she had decided to extend her visit. "I fear . . . that Lucy's enthusiasm and your own eagerness to see people and do things may lead you into a social and sight-seeing program that will be trying. . . . It seems like years since you left home and like a graveyard in the house without you. . . . I am trying to make myself believe that your stay in Providence is the best thing . . . for your health . . . and so am seeking to forget how drab life seems without you. . . . I fancy it may be some time before you have . . . regained your strength and equilibrium."[10]

Nelson did not seem to doubt his mother's "strength and equilibrium" when he proposed that she become president of MoMA. "After considering the matter carefully, he [Alan Blackburn] said candidly that he thought it was an inspiration," Nelson wrote her on April 22, during the period when she was supposed to be having the breakdown. "He said further that if it had not been for you . . . he thought Alfred would have gone to pieces long before he did and he has been very much worried about the coming year because he does not feel that Alfred, under Mr. Goodyear's leadership, will last much longer. . . . Knowing Alfred's fondness for you personally, and the wonderful way in which you handle him, he felt Alfred would have no recurrence of his troubles. . . . Alan said he thought Mr. Clark would be glad to be vice-president if you were president. I'll have you in the chair before you come back [from the Homestead]."[11]

Nelson must be joking to propose such a thing, she replied, but then she realized he was serious. "I feel like saying," she wrote, "as the young woman did when she received a proposal 'This is so sudden!' . . . Do you think it is proper for a son to go around campaigning for his mother's promotion in office. It seems to me it might be thought a little strange. . . . If you have not already talked to Mr. Goodyear, whom I personally think adores being president of the Museum, I advise you not to do so before my return. . . . My main desire is to cease being treasurer and Mr. Goodyear's main desire is to keep me as treasurer because he feels that with me as treasurer it gives a sort of financial backing to the Museum that it might not have otherwise."[12]

Abby continued to act as the indispensable buffer between Alfred and Conger Goodyear. She was wise in the ways of powerful men of money. Barr and Goodyear were arguing about everything —museum policy, matters of taste, future exhibitions, Alfred's salary, when he would or would not resume his responsibilities. To a self-important man of conviction like Goodyear, Barr appeared fragile, which was quite off the mark. Alfred could be immovable and inscrutable when he felt he was protecting his artistic goals for the museum. The fact that in the long run Goodyear and Barr fought "if not exactly happily, at least productively," Lynes wrote, had a lot to do with Abby.[13]

She managed to see Alfred privately before each crucial confrontation with Goodyear. When he summoned Barr to New York in June 1933, before the end of his leave of absence, against the advice of Dr. Garthe, Alfred wrote her for help. "Now if you really feel up to it, I would like very much to talk with you after—or before (if you think it better) I see Mr. Goodyear on the 22nd. In any case I do not intend to come to any agreement [about exhibitions] without consulting you. It may be that a crisis will be averted at this time, but if it comes up I wish to go through with it with your complete knowledge."[14] On June 22, Abby and Alfred spent the day together, and many other conferences followed. She kept after Goodyear, persuading him that Alfred would do much better work now that he had the year off. "It seems only fair to leave things quite open for him. . . . He will come back with his mind filled with interesting and important things for us to do."[15]

This relationship between Abby and Alfred was far from the simple one of older woman counseling younger man, although she did see something of the son in him, and was pleased that at least two of her own sons, Nelson and David, learned from him. Largely self-educated herself, and having experienced life from the vantage of a rich, if enlightened, conservative, she was informed and challenged as much by the range of his interests and the acuity of his mind as by his expertise in aesthetics. Here is the reading list he proposed for her summer in Seal Harbor:

For light and entertaining reading, I suggest two books by Vollard, one on Cézanne and the other on Renoir. They are mostly conversations and are very amusing. You have them, I think. . . . three books by Lewis Mumford; *The Golden Day*, on American Literature before the Civil War; *Sticks and Stones*, a very interesting study of American Architecture and backgrounds, and the *Brown Decades*, on the period since the Civil War, principally literature and architecture. I should read the second and third before reading the first.

I think you will find Calverton's *"Liberation of American Literature"* very worthwhile. It was published in December 1932 and is a discussion on American Art in relation to American social and economic life. Calverton's attitude is Marxian but by no means orthodox. I think he places good literature above any social theory.

There is one fundamental book which I think every person interested in modern culture ought to read. That is Thorstein Veblen's *"The Theory of the Leisure Class."* It is not very easy reading but is an exciting, witty and clarifying discussion. Its iconoclasm is perhaps carried a bit too far, but I think you will enjoy it even tho it may prove at times exasperating. . . . Probably you will disagree with many of their conclusions, but the act of disagreement will, I think, prove valuable.

Another extraordinary book which would serve as an ideal balance to Veblen and Calverton is Jacques Maritain's *Art et Scholastique*. . . . This is a rich and profound study of the nature of art and by a man who knew St. Thomas Aquinas and Aristotle as well as Cocteau & Valéry and Picasso. Try it anyway.[16]

Six months in Germany left both Marga and Alfred shocked and disturbed by the extremism, the fanatic racism, the attack on all modern and innovative art. Alfred wrote a long piece warning the public that this virulent brand of fascism threatened all of Western culture, not only the visual arts, but music, history, and literature. Then he discovered that neither the daily press nor even the liberal periodicals would publish it. "Is it indifference or disbelief?" Marga asked in her chronicle.[17] Only *The Hound & Horn*, edited by Lincoln Kirstein, responded.

If Alfred's association with Goodyear was strained at times, nothing seemed to get in the way of the trust and empathy between him and Abby. He brought her all his ideas and not a few of his fears. They spoke of the need to build up a permanent collection, the quality and size and frequency of exhibitions, their mutual hopes for a film department and a good library. "I keep hammering on the library question," he wrote, "but it seems to make no impression upon the gentlemen of the Executive Committee. . . . I fail to impress upon [them] what you so clearly see, that a library is not merely a collection of books or slides but is a collection plus catalogue plus supervision."[18]

She responded to a bewildering number of cries for help, including last-minute requests for loans of her own works. "I wish to thank you on behalf of the Trustees for your generous loan of two watercolors by Edward Hopper," Alfred wrote on November 10. "Both the painter and those who assembled the exhibition are very grateful to you for your share in it. I think it will interest you to know that Hopper pointed out *Box Factory, Gloucester* as one of his best watercolors. I fully agree with him. I do hope that before the exhibition is over you will be able to get in to see it. We would be glad to open the Museum at a special time so that you might see it without interruption."[19] Several of her wedding gifts from 1901—

table silver, a jewel box, Tiffany glass finger bowls—turned up in Philip Johnson's exhibition Objects 1900 and Today. By 1934 she was lending two and three times as much as any other trustee, including significant works by Rouault, Rivera, Beckmann, Sheeler, Ben Shahn, and van Gogh.

But neither her hand-holding of Alfred, nor her diplomacy with the staff, nor her willingness to lend pictures, nor her stalwart support for every innovative scheme was as critical to the museum's future as the fact of her being treasurer. Goodyear knew exactly what he was up to when he wanted her to continue in that office. And she knew, uneasily perhaps and with some degree of resignation, that she could not pass it off to someone else. It was chancy enough trying to raise the modest yearly budget, with the nation sinking deeper into the Depression, and Roosevelt and his cabinet inventing new programs almost daily to rescue a paralyzed nation. But the museum was now in danger of losing the Bliss collection. It was two years since Lillie's death. Her brother Cornelius, a MoMA trustee who did not care for modern art but was devoted to Lillie, doubted whether the museum could qualify for her collection before the expiration date specified in her will.

Alfred wrote Abby passionately of the importance of the collection to the future of the museum, a legacy that included twenty-four works by Cézanne, nine by Seurat, eight by Degas, plus examples of Daumier, Picasso, and Matisse, among many others. "I have a feeling that you are being preserved incommunicado and that I oughtn't to disturb you in any way, but the situation . . . is of the utmost seriousness." He laid out for her why they must meet the terms of the Bliss will. Failure to do so would put into serious doubt the stability and permanence of the institution. Failure would involve a loss of bargaining power with the Metropolitan. It would damage efforts to persuade other collectors to give the Museum their works. Finally, he pleaded that "Miss Bliss expected us to have her collection!"[20]

None of Goodyear's ideas for raising the necessary endowment had yet materialized. Even if Mr. Bliss lowered the amount from $1 million, which under the present economic climate he showed some willingness to do, it still looked bleak. Then, on May 15,

1933, one sentence in one of Goodyear's letters to Abby jumps out. "You have told me recently that you felt that Mr. Rockefeller was becoming more interested in the Museum."[21] On August 15, Alan Blackburn wrote Alfred that "Mrs. R. came to town. . . . I am seeing her today." Later in the same letter, "P.S. I have seen Mrs. R. . . . <u>She is ready to get that money and that collection</u> [the emphasis was his]. I am tremendously encouraged."[22]

During two days in September with both partners living in the same hundred-room house, an exchange of notes took place as follows:

Mr. R. September 14, 1933
The Eyrie, Seal Harbor, Maine.
to Mrs. R. The Eyrie, Seal Harbor Maine

Dear Abby:
   Any time between now and July 1, 1934 that a gift of up to $200,000 to the Modern Museum will enable the Museum to qualify under the terms of Miss Bliss' will to receive as a gift Miss Bliss' collection of modern paintings, I will give to it the amount mentioned above or as much thereof as may be necessary.
                    Affectionately, John D. Rockefeller, Jr.

A second note from John followed on the heels of the first.

Dear Abby:
   . . . This is to say that the pledge to the Modern Museum . . . is entirely separate from and in addition to any other financial arrangement between us either now or that may be made another year.
                    Affectionately, John D. Rockefeller, Jr.

At two in the afternoon on the same day, Abby replied:

Dear J.
   I am so sorry that I spoke to you this morning about giving to the Modern Museum, it was very stupid of me and quite unnecessary of me to pain you. . . . I am terribly, terribly sorry, please forgive me and let us never mention it again. Very lovingly, Abby.
   Many, many thanks for your generous offer.[23]

The next day, September 15th, John responded:

Dear Abby:

   Thank you for your sweet note, which I greatly appreciate. Nothing would distress me as much as not to have you carry out the arrangement which we made yesterday and which my letter covers. I could not think for a moment of cancelling the pledge. It will stand to be availed of any time up to July first, 1934.

Affectionately, John. [24]

At the time of these formal declarations, John wrote his side of the story to Nelson. Abby had told him that she was going to pledge $10,000 a year to the museum for ten years. John made a strong case, on technical grounds, against such a move and moreover insisted that it was a serious mistake for her and MoMA to undertake major fund-raising in such bad economic times. Why not simply allow the Bliss collection to go to the Metropolitan, where it would be equally available to the public? If, in John's words, the money were being sought to care for the sick, feed the hungry, provide homes and clothing for the destitute, that would be a different matter.

   "All these things I have said to Mama," he wrote. "She does not see the situation as I do." [25] One may imagine that behind such laconic words stood an aroused Abby, heels dug in, marshaling every argument to prove him wrong.

   Twenty-four hours later, Alfred wired Abby. "Magnificent good news received through Nelson. We are much encouraged but worried about your health. Bless you and thank you. And get well soon." [26] The campaign was officially underway. Four months later, on January 24, 1934, Blackburn wrote Paul Sachs: "To date, we have raised $400,000: $100,000 from Carnegie [the Carnegie Foundation], $200,000 from Mrs. Rockefeller, and $100,000 anonymously." [27] When the rest of the trustees together pledged $200,000, Bliss persuaded the executors to reduce their initial demand to $600,000, with the stipulation that the fund committee raise $150,000 from smaller donations. On March 12, the board officially established ownership by the museum of the Lillie P. Bliss Collection, and received the endowment fund.

   Nelson solved the mystery of the anonymous $100,000 in his

344

letter to his mother. "If it were not for you, the Museum of Modern Art would be a thing of the past today and I am not exaggerating when I say that you did a job which any of the so-called 'big executives' would have been proud to have maneuvered! It is your personality projected into the Museum which has made it what it is today. To show you that I mean what I have just written, and how strongly I feel, and have felt, about the whole situation, I am going to tell you now what I have not wanted to before for many reasons, that is that the anonymous gift of $100,000 was made by your son in grateful appreciation of all the many, many things you have done for him."[28] This was a major contribution for Nelson, who had not yet received substantial capital gifts from his father.

On March 30, Abby wrote Goodyear that she would shortly be sailing for Italy, but would be back in New York again around June 10. "Mr. Rockefeller read me the letter that you wrote him and was very much pleased to receive it. I am very glad that you wrote it because really without his cooperation we could not have succeeded and I feel that it was very broad-minded of him to reverse his decision of not contributing to the Modern Museum."[29]

Why *did* he reverse his decision? Not because Abby had converted him to her taste in art. Not because he was expanding his philanthropy. On the contrary, he was contracting it. Some observers have wondered if perhaps she struck a bargain with him, that she would beat a gradual retreat from MoMA, transferring her power to Nelson, in return for John's rescue. But the next years in the history of the museum confound that theory. Nelson did move to the center, but Abby continued to monitor everything from the wings, just as she always had.

Perhaps it was simply the right moment in their relationship for him to step up to her side, loving her as he did, needing her with something akin to desperation, and having a conscience that went straight back to Laura Spelman. Such a grand gesture was entirely in character. Abby had no financial card to play. But she had an emotional one. It is entirely plausible that she would use it.

On November 6, 1933, less than two months after he gave MoMA the $200,000, he wrote Mackenzie King that "Mrs. Rockefeller is doing splendidly and is making real progress."[30]

*D*iego Rivera and his *oeuvre* became known to Abby through Frances Flynn Paine, one of the many unusual women who intersected her life in crucial ways. Professor Charles Richards, director of the Division of Industrial Arts of the General Education Board, described her as "a woman of . . . quiet power and resolution, with a fine mind . . . a perfect knowledge of Spanish, [and] unusual insight into the Mexican crafts and into the character of the Mexican Indian."[1]

Born in Laredo, Texas, Frances had spent most of her early days in Mexico, where her father was superintendent of railways and for a time, acted as American consul. As he traveled to remote parts of the country, his daughter accompanied him, acquiring a deep knowledge and appreciation of Indian arts.

In recommending her to Thomas Appleget for a Rockefeller Foundation grant, Richards wrote in 1928: "The Indians are distrustful not only of the American government but of American business methods. They consider Mrs. Paine one of their own. It is believed that in a few years Mexican and American industry will both make increasing use not only of the materials but of the art forms. As far as friendship between America and Mexico is concerned, the project is small but undoubtedly sound as a factor in strengthening the mutual appreciation and helpfulness which underlie any lasting international relations."[2]

Appleget, a vice president of the Rockefeller Foundation, brought the grant proposal to John's attention. "In view of the fact . . . that you have been greatly interested in Indian Art, and in further view of the fact that Mrs. Rockefeller herself made considerable purchases at the last Mexican exhibit at the Art Center, we feel obliged to refer this request to you."[3] Two weeks later, Appleget informed Ms. Paine that Mr. Rockefeller was authorizing the foundation to pay her $15,000 over a period of three years to be used for her traveling expenses and other contingent costs.

Frances now set out to solve some of the pressing needs of the artisans: the formation of a craft guild in Mexico to which the Indians could belong and from which they could obtain small advances for raw materials; people from the guild who spoke their language to assist them with packing, shipping, etc.; and an expert on ceramics to test the clays and suggest a process for making the pottery durable. (Abby ordered from the guild pottery and other items for the Playhouse.) In one of the shipments an Indian ceramist, Pedro Padierna, sent two plates for Senior with a bust of his image on them. Frances explained that the Indians of Mexico respected two Americans—Dwight Morrow, the enlightened ambassador, and John D. Rockefeller, Sr., because of the good work of the foundation.

In 1929, at the same time that she was founding MoMA, Abby had joined Frances in organizing a nonprofit corporation to promote friendship between the people of Mexico and the United States by encouraging cultural relations and the interchange of fine and applied arts. Elizabeth Morrow, wife of the ambassador, served with Abby on the board of directors, along with Frederick P. Keppel of the Carnegie Foundation, Appleget of the Rockefeller Foundation, Winthrop Aldrich as president, Frank Crowinshield from MoMA, and others. Abby was becoming increasingly admiring of Frances Paine. "[She] seems to be doing an enormous amount of work with very little backing, thru her own sheer ability," she wrote her brother.[4]

Alfred, Jere Abbott, and Frances Paine planned the details for the Diego Rivera Exhibition, which opened at MoMA on December 23, 1931. Frances tried to convey to Abby something of the political climate of Mexico as it related to artists such as Rivera. "In 1928 I told Dr. Richards that I felt sure that most Mexican artists, though 'Reds' would cease to be 'Reds' if we could get them artistic recognition. [At that time] Diego was the most powerful 'Red' in Latin America. . . . In 1929, with Dr. Richards' help, the American Institute of Architects became aware of his painting and awarded him their highest honor. In 1930 he was expelled from the Red Ranks, and a few months later accepted a commission from Mr. Morrow for a mural in Cuernavaca. Yet he still is, sincerely and intensely for 'the peopla' but one can now reason with him and from that viewpoint much can be hoped."[5]

Such a notion was overly sanguine, perhaps—the idea that reason would prevail with someone as flamboyant and controversial, as fond of distortion, as Rivera, an unpredictable giant of a man. Most of what was written about him seemed to have originated in his own fertile imagination, "an endless labyrinth of tales," in the words of his biographer Bertram Wolfe.[6] But a few facts are incontrovertible. A champion of the worker, he was born into an upper-middle-class family with a trace of aristocracy. Although he idealized Mexico's Aztec heritage, he was himself only one-quarter Indian, the other three-quarters being Russian, Spanish, and Portuguese-Jewish. As Paine suggested, he was in and out of favor with the Communist Party of Mexico throughout his life. One year it might expel him, the next year embrace him. Neither stern ideology nor the objective evidence of history had any appeal for him. He was an exuberant and tireless artist, a lover and user of women, a prankster, a propagandist. "To be in the midst of some uproarious disturbance is Rivera's idea of heaven," Geoffrey Hellman wrote in the *New Yorker* in 1933 when commotion raged all about him.[7]

By the 1930s, Rivera was considered the great muralist of the Western world, but he had arrived at that exalted position only after thirty years of artistic experimentation and many detours. He had been a child prodigy; thanks to his father he had received a sound art training with plenty of freedom. He studied in Spain, in

England, and in France, becoming a feverish worshiper of Cézanne's paintings, then a disciple of Picasso, devouring his cubist phase. The detours away from art were political; he was a Marxist, a Communist, a Trotskyite, a homegrown Mexican rebel.

The revolutionary spirit that erupted in the wake of the World War of 1914–1918 inspired Rivera, not only politically, but also in his art. Cubism seemed too intellectual, too sophisticated. He began to see murals as a way of nourishing the spirit of the masses. He went to Italy in 1920, saw the frescoes of Giotto, and made over four hundred sketches. Between 1921 and 1927 he painted 184 frescoes in the patios of the Ministry of Education Building in Mexico City, portraying common people and their labors, showing agriculture enslaved by clericalism, militarism, and capitalism. This was the series that made his name famous and the Mexican art movement famous as well. In 1927, at the urging of his Communist friends, he went to Moscow to attend the tenth anniversary of the inauguration of the Russian Revolution.

"From his place on the reviewing stand against the old Kremlin wall, he watched the Red Army file through the historic Red Square. . . . With greedy eyes he watched, notebook in hand, sketching as well on the tablets of his tenacious brain," Wolfe wrote, "saw the surging seas of crimson banners, spirited horses rearing . . . caught the rattle of wheel and streak of moving line as horse-drawn artillery flashed by at full gallop, the cubic pattern of trucks loaded with riflemen, solid squares of marching infantry, then the vast banner-plumed, float-bearing serpentine line of the masses of men and women marching until nightfall through the square. All this he noted in forty-five watercolor sketches and innumerable penciled notes, out of which he hoped to build murals for Russian walls."[8]

But the walls never materialized. A year of Soviet bureaucratic bickering held up the necessary go-ahead. Diego's artistic integrity was offended by the banality of Russian socialist realism and the unhappy knowledge that some of the most talented Russians were fleeing Soviet censorship. He returned to Mexico to be attacked as bourgeois and expelled from the party under circumstances that were both wounding and bitter. Wolfe, who was Diego's friend and a former Communist himself, wished that after expelling him they had at least left him alone to paint. Instead they carried on a noisy campaign against him.

On July 14, 1931, Frances Paine wired Abby from Mexico City that Rivera was offering a set of forty-five watercolors, the artistic product of his May Day experience, for $3,000, though in her opinion he would accept $2,500, provided the set was not broken up. On July 28, Abby wired $2,500 to the Bank of Montreal in Mexico City earmarked for Paine, who now was acting as Rivera's agent. By the end of the year, according to her art account, Abby had paid Rivera a total of $9,002.50. This would include payment for the watercolors, as well as nine oils and drawings and several mural studies. Such a sum was critical for Diego; it financed the expenses he incurred when he agreed to come to New York to create seven new frescoes, constructed on movable steel frames, for the exhibition at MoMA. And it established Abby as a major Rivera collector.

Abby responded positively to the distinctive radiance of Rivera's mature easel works, notable for their absence of political propaganda. Even his May Day sketches evoke a people's mood and a dramatic scene as much as partisan ideology. Her appreciation of folk art, with its artlessness and simplicity, may very well have prepared her for Rivera. The directness of his images, the warm, glowing colors, the strong plastic sense, the ease that cubism had brought him in his arbitrary use of form—all these characteristics permitted her to forgive the propaganda.

Abby was not the only patron of Rivera among major American families. His network was beginning to stretch across the nation. After the American Institute of Architects awarded him the Fine Arts Gold Medal, Diego was invited to San Francisco to paint a fresco at the California School of Fine Arts. The sculptor Ralph Stackpole arranged a commission for him to do a wall in the luncheon club of the local stock exchange. He was lionized and fêted by artists, politicians, socialites, and financiers. His twenty-year-old third wife (Diego was then forty-four), the self-dramatizing, intense Frida Kahlo, striking in her embroidered Mexican blouses and ruffled skirts with the ribbons and jewels woven into her braids, charmed everyone. (In 1937, Frida dropped the Nordic "e" in her name as a protest against the Nazis.) Several wealthy, prominent Bay Area collectors bought his works and commissioned him to decorate their private residences.

In December 1930, William Valentiner was in San Francisco. He wrote in his autobiography that he met Rivera through Helen Wills, the famous tennis player. "Her little green Cadillac was overflowing when it stopped for me, jammed in the rumble seat I saw a strange-looking, heavy-set man, wearing a black serape and a large Mexican hat. . . . Rivera's wife . . . wore a large reboso [rebozo shawl], a white veil over her forehead, a red rose in her hair. . . . She was natural and direct, and her unfailing artistic intuition was very helpful to Diego. She did small paintings on silver . . . that showed a curious imagination."[9]

Valentiner persuaded his friend and patron Edsel Ford to commission two large Rivera frescoes for the courtyard of the Detroit Museum. But first Diego and Frida went to New York to prepare the MoMA exhibition.

During the months that Rivera was working at MoMA, Abby became something of a friend to him as well as a major patron. She saw another side to him—the unexpected gentleness in the midst of explosive talent, the wit and the charm. David remembers both Diego and Frida coming to the house. "The whole family liked him," David said. "He was a likable fellow."[10] Nelson and Tod became friends as well. Abby commissioned him to make a drawing of Babs and arranged for him to store his movable frescoes in her garage after his show was dismantled.

She watched over Frida in the way that a warmhearted mature woman would watch over a young person of unusual courage. As a bold, streetwise teenager, Frida had been badly injured in a bus accident. She suffered spinal injuries, a triple fracture of the pelvis, and a crushed foot. After a year encased in plaster, strapped to a board, able to move nothing but her hands, she then endured a series of fruitless surgical procedures. Scorning sympathy, she ignored her disability, invited danger, and found an outlet in her self-revelatory paintings. Abby had other reasons for feeling protective of Frida. Diego was a well-known philanderer, and Frida, in spite of the long insults to her poor body, was trying to become pregnant.

On January 22, 1932, Frida wrote Abby from her hotel room at the Barbizon-Plaza, thanking her for the book and the flowers. Her doctor had ordered her to bed. "After this eight days indoors," she wrote, "I am very ugly and thin. . . . Diego sends his love to you. Many kisses from Frieda Rivera. Pleaze excuse my terrible English."[11] A few days later she wrote again. "[Diego] misses very much your daughter's baby [little Abby Milton] and he told me he loves her more than me. . . . He is very glad that you and Mr. Rockefeller liked his drawing of Mrs. Milton and he thanks you."[12]

Nothing relaxed Abby more than good, lively art talk, which Diego supplied in abundance when he showed up. She described such an occasion in a letter to Laurance. "Thursday I had Nelson, 4 architects, Rivera & Babs & Mrs. Paine for lunch. We had an amusing and I hope worthwhile discussion. My plea was for the life we are living in the wall painting of today. We even talked of Peter Arno [the cartoonist]."[13]

The catalyst for such a discussion was the possibility of a Rivera mural at Rockefeller Center. Abby had been involved in decisions about Rockefeller Center from the beginning, in the same way that she had been involved in the resolution of the Ludlow tragedy, the cleanup of Yellowstone, the restoration of Colonial Williamsburg, and John's other major projects and problems.

In the words of Paul Goldberger, writing in the *New York Times* in 1988, Rockefeller Center is "not just a cluster of buildings in New York City; it is a national symbol of distinguished corporate design, far and away the finest groupings of skyscrapers ever built, the model for dozens of complexes around the world . . . [no one of which] has come up to its quality."[14] That aspect of Rockefeller Center which concerned Abby the most—its art and architecture —has been, in other words, what distinguished it from other commercial projects. If the court of last resort, to quote Fosdick, was John—his final approval was required for all matters relating to exteriors, elevations, the relations of masses, foyers, sculpture, and murals—John's "last resort" was Abby.

The feeling on the part of family members and outside observers alike is that Abby had an effect on everything she touched. One nephew, Richard Aldrich, called it giving direction to the Rockefeller projects. Alexander Aldrich, a great-nephew, feels that a major portion of the creative and public-spirited drive found in the Rockefellers of his generation is traceable to her. Wallace Harrison, the architect who worked with the Rockefeller Center team and later was the principal architect of both the United Nations complex and Lincoln Center, believed Abby to be one of the most creative women he had ever known. William Valentiner, regarded by John as an honest, trustworthy adviser, has stated unequivocally that "the influence she exerted on the architecture and decoration of Rockefeller Center in the encouragement of artists, collectors and museum workers is equal in importance to the accomplishments in the sixteenth century of women like Margarita of Austria, the great patroness of arts and letters, and Isabella d'Este, the friend and supporter of the chief artists of her period."[15]

When John asked George Vincent, the urbane former president of the Rockefeller Foundation and a man known for a strong measure of common sense, to reflect upon the various schemes for the decoration of Rockefeller Center, he was "plunged into futility. . . . The more I ponder the subject," he wrote, "the more I find myself in agreement with Mrs. J.D.R., Jr." What exactly they were in agreement on is not known. All that seems clear is that Abby was a principal in the discussions.[16]

In June 1932, Donald Deskey received the commission to design the interior of Radio City Music Hall—thirty lobby areas, smoking rooms, retiring rooms, foyers, and lounges. In less than six months he created an Art Deco masterpiece, valued even today as a high point in such design. Deskey was Abby's designer of choice; John had had an opportunity to observe him when he was working on her seventh-floor gallery.

Deskey believed that sculpture and wall paintings by major artists should be integrated with the space. For that he turned to another member of Abby's network—Edith Halpert. Halpert did a brilliant job of persuading her artists—Robert Laurent, William Zorach, Stuart Davis, Yasuo Kuniyoshi—as well as some women whom she did not personally represent to offer their talent for meager rewards. The budget for art in the Music Hall was so stringent that for a while it looked as though it might be eliminated altogether. According to Deskey's biographer, the Rockefellers and the architects intervened, but only to the limit of $1,500 per installation.

Money was not the only problem. Two weeks before the formal opening, in December 1932, a quarrel erupted over William Zorach's *Dancing Girl* and Gwen Lux's *Eye*, both nude sculpture. The matter was resolved, however, and the integrated interior to which they belong enjoys universal praise. Rockefeller Center's patronage of art projects was a reality.

The selection of American artists to decorate Deskey's Music Hall interiors, despite a few such touchy incidents, proved to be a fairly straightforward process. But the negotiations with Diego Rivera to execute a mural at the most conspicuous interior site in the whole center—the huge interior wall facing the plaza entrance of the RCA Building—were protracted and often precarious. They began in the winter at MoMA, continued over such luncheons as had taken place with Abby and Nelson, and were building momentum as the Riveras prepared to leave for Detroit, where Diego would commence work on the murals commissioned by Edsel Ford. The architects first proposed a competition among Picasso, Matisse, and Rivera himself, which proved unworkable for obvious reasons. International superstars are not interested in competitions. Diego explained his position in French to Raymond Hood, the most creative of the architects. "I thank you," he wrote on May 9. "Ten years ago I would have accepted your kind invitation with pleasure. . . . but since then . . . I am known enough to ask of each one who wants my work that he ask for it on my value. One can always have me make a sketch and take it or leave it, naturally, but no 'competition'—I am no more at that point."[17]

Hood was ready to drop Rivera, but Nelson, an executive vice president for Rockefeller Center, intervened, and Abby backed him up. It now seemed assumed that Rivera would do the mural, even though arguments dragged on during the summer between architect and artist over Rivera's demands. Such demands were entirely sensible, according to his experience—that he be permitted to use color (only black, gray, and white had been specified) and that he do fresco in place of a canvas mural. Always it was Nelson who defended Diego, Nelson, with his diplomacy and charm and passionate love of art.

In Detroit, Rivera began to work on a Rockefeller sketch. In Paris, Hood was trying to see Picasso and Matisse about doing murals along the side walls that would flank a Rivera. Picasso was nowhere to be found. Letters and telegrams had been sent ahead, and his dealers were, of course, very anxious to locate him, but everywhere it was the same story. "He is a whimsical fellow," Hood wrote, "who often goes away from time to time leaving no trace of himself."[18]

The hope that Matisse might be interested sprang from the fact of his friendship with Abby. But he declined, very graciously and respectfully. He was already committed to the Barnes Foundation in Philadelphia and had reservations about his work being suitable for such a large, bustling public environment. Later he wrote to Abby, "For a long time I wished to express my regrets at not accepting the offer made to me by Mr. Hood. . . . As you know, my method of work is not rapid, and the harmony of line and color which are personal to me, as well as the heaviness of my work, caused my feelings to develop slowly. Mr. Hood has made known to me the special interest which you have in my painting. . . . I was happy . . . to assure him that it would give me the greatest pleasure to execute the work you have requested if the architects assign me a place in sympathy with my painting, and accord the time necessary for the execution of a work which would fully satisfy me."[19]

Hood went on to complete arrangements with the Spaniard José María Sert and the Englishman Frank Brangwyn for the side murals. Rivera made a fuss about that too, having only contempt for the work of both. But Nelson seemed to pacify him there as well. And on October 13, 1932, he wrote Rivera that Hood and Harrison now agreed that he could use some color in his mural. "May I take this opportunity," he added, "to again tell you how much my mother and I appreciate your spirit in doing this mural under the existing circumstances. Please let me know when your frescoes in Detroit are finished so that we can arrange to come up and see them. Everybody is terribly anxious to see how you have interpreted the industrial life of Detroit."[20]

Diego was having a glorious time interpreting the industrial life of Detroit. His fascination with technology was eclipsed only by his emotional identification with the workers who could be exploited by it. As his fears and his hopes collided, in the end he gave the city an entire history of scientific progress, contrasting the benefits with the evils—preventive medicine versus poison gas, passenger planes versus bombs. The usual controversies swirled about him. Church functionaries attacked him for a so-called Nativity scene in which a child is being vaccinated with serum made from the blood of cows and horses shown in the foreground. Local artists resented a foreigner being given the commission. Competing auto tycoons were angry that the Ford plant was enjoying the publicity.

Standing by Rivera's side throughout the controversy was Edsel Ford himself. Abby and Ford had become friends as neighbors on Mount Desert. They shared a passion for modern art. One day he would become a trustee at MoMA. A modest, sensitive man, he protected Rivera against his antagonists, gave him extra funds as he needed them, and in the process preserved a splendid legacy for his city.

For the Riveras personally, however, it was a sad time. Frida, finally pregnant, grew pale and nauseated in the Detroit heat. On the night of July 4, she began to hemorrhage badly and by the next day had lost the baby. According to Wolfe, Diego temporarily abandoned his negligent ways to treat her with great tenderness. Frida battled her depression by going back to painting now and then, "strange, witty . . . fantastic" things totally unlike anything that Rivera was doing.[21] She wrote Abby something of it over the winter. "I am painting a little bit too. Not because I consider myself an artist . . . but simply because I have nothing else to do here, and because working I can forget a little all the troubles I had last year. I am doing oils on small plates of aluminum. . . . I made two lithographs which are absolutely rotten. If I do some others and they are better I will show them to you in New York."[22] In 1984, in recognition of her preeminence, the Mexican government declared Kahlo's art to be a national patrimony.

On November 5, Diego sent Abby a penciled composition study (the sketch), on brown paper, for the Rockefeller Center mural painting, with a separate copy for Nelson. He inscribed Abby's copy as follows: "Avec mes hommages très respectueux et affectueux à Madame Abby Aldrich de Rockefeller." (In 1935, Abby gave it anonymously to MoMA.) In his accompanying letter he made another fervent plea for fresco instead of canvas (the plea was granted), his argument resting on the premise that since it would occupy such a prominent place in the complex, it must be of monumental character. "I assure you that in any case," he wrote Abby, "I shall try to do for Rockefeller Center, and especially for you Madame, the best of all the work I have done to this time. Permit me to thank you now for this wonderful opportunity which you have given me and this, added to all the good things for which I owe you already in aiding my work."[23]

Two days later Diego received a telegram from Hood indicating Nelson's approval of a written synopsis or text. In January 1933, Hood traveled to Detroit to sign off on the drawing without, according to three Rivera assistants, doing more than glancing at it. Diego then signed his contract with Rockefeller Center Inc. The fee was $21,500 to cover a space of 1,071 square feet. "You better have your lawyer see it," said Hood. Diego replied, "You signed my sketch without looking it over. You trust me. I trust you!"[24]

If Nelson had paid close attention to Rivera's synopsis, if he had had some experience with Marxist ideology, perhaps he might not have been quite so surprised by ensuing events. The language was long-winded and only slightly less pompous than the theme suggested to Diego by Rockefeller officialdom—Man at the Crossroads Looking with Hope and High Vision to the Choosing of a New and Better Future. But Diego's vision of a "new and better future" was a Communist heaven, and read as follows: ". . . my panel will show the Workers arriving at a true understanding of their rights regarding the means of production which has resulted in the planning of the liquidation of Tyranny. . . . It will also show the Workers of the cities and the country inheriting the Earth."[25]

The sketch, on the other hand, gave no hint of political iconography, but then it had none of the imagination and excitement associated with a Rivera mural. What Hood approved was a rather static rendering of figures engaged in various states of activities—sports, science, agriculture, industry, maternity. Abby, who understood that art was a process, not a rational hypothesis, was confident that however verbose his synopsis or however sterile his drawing, when Rivera mounted the scaffold he would create something magnificent. She was right about his artistry. What she did not understand was his character. And what she could not anticipate—no one could—was that outside forces would overtake the event itself.

Over the winter, Frida continued to write Abby from Detroit. "We were very sorry to hear that you were sick, but your letter brought good news and we are so glad that you are feeling better."[26] This was the period when Abby's doctor first sent her to bed because of the so-called nervous breakdown. Diego and Frida returned to New York in March 1933. Franklin Roosevelt had just been inaugurated. The banks were closed—the famous "bank holiday" devised by the president to restore some kind of public confidence. Long lines of the unemployed stood in breadlines, and Rockefeller Center was the only significant urban development being built in the entire nation.

On April 4, Diego's crew of assistants finally was able to prepare his wall for him. The only firsthand account of the actual creation of the mural comes from the diary of Lucienne Bloch, the twenty-two-year-old daughter of Ernest Bloch, the composer, and an artist herself. When Lucienne met Diego at a MoMA party she offered to grind his colors for him. He accepted, and she became a permanent member of his crew, both in Detroit and in New York. She recalled the first night at 30 Rockefeller Plaza when the layers of plaster were being applied for the section that Diego had marked to paint. He painted an average of thirty square feet at a time, and if the next day he did not like what he saw, the crew scraped it off and the process was repeated.

Here are two entries from Lucienne's diary:

April 5. Like schoolboys the union workmen arrive, streaming in lazily, staring at the wall, some of them very angry that a non-union man is doing this . . . and all night too! [The Center had struck a deal with the Plasterers Union that Diego's workers could plaster if one union man was hired to stand by.] . . . At twilight . . . Diego was still painting. It represents war and fascism—airplanes, gas masks, death rays, men in green-gray, masked contraptions looking futuristic. . . .

April 8. . . . today he sure loosened up! He's on the right side of the wall painting communism, with women in kerchiefs singing, and red flags all over—and they're RED. . . . Diego had been expelled from the Communist party three years earlier for refusing to toe the line. He wanted desperately to return to the fold, but on his own terms, so it is to prove to them that he is not afraid of any capitalists that he paints the Moscow May Day with gusto and with plenty of Venetian red.[27]

By April 10 he was back on the fascist side. Weird tones of red and orange represented the germs of syphilis, gonorrhea, and other such evils of capitalism. With the end of Prohibition, Lucienne's sister was able to bring beer to the scaffold. The pace picked up as the crew worked twenty-four hours without rest. When it was time to paint in the decadent ladies playing bridge, Diego called for live models.

Abby in Hot Springs wrote Anna Kelly on April 24 that Babs might be able to find a young blond woman to model for Mr. Rivera. "I'm sure I don't know of anyone," she added.[28] Frida told Lucienne that Abby visited the lobby and climbed the scaffold and was delighted with what she saw. Frida was mistaken. It was Tod who visited the scaffold; Frida referred to the wrong Rockefeller. Frida also told Lucienne that Abby wanted Diego to paint a copy of his fresco from Mexico showing the millionaires, John D. (Senior), Morgan, and Ford, sitting at a table, looking at the ticker tape, holding champagne glasses, except John D. with his glass of milk. Geoffrey Hellman in the *New Yorker* gave a variation of the same bit of apocrypha.

On April 21, Rivera painted the scene of police on their horses ready to club desperate workers. On April 24, a reporter for the *World-Telegram*, Joseph Lilly, broke a story that described the mural in some detail under a provocative headline: "Rivera Perpetrates Scenes of Communist Activity for R.C.A. Walls—and Rockefeller Foots the Bill." Three days later another article appeared, this one an interview with Communist artists and journalists denouncing Rivera. Now Diego painted Lenin into the mural, lifelike and dominant, the strongest face in the fresco. The mural, in all its power, was revealed to a public that crowded around to gawk.

"It was breathtaking: a vortex of color vibrating," Lucienne wrote. "The disk of television, the electric generator swirling in a dark center, rays of poison spray at the left facing a chorus of singing people, the violent fresh-red ellipse of microbes swinging boldly across balanced by the ellipse of stars and nebulae."[29]

Twenty-five-year-old Nelson Rockefeller, with his ingrained optimism and confidence that he could resolve any disagreement, was the family member who had tried to represent Diego's interest to the project managers and theirs to him. In the respectful tone of a well-brought-up scion, Nelson wrote Diego on May 4 about the sticky question of Lenin. "The piece is beautifully painted," he readily conceded, "but it seems to me that his portrait appearing in this mural might very easily seriously offend a great many people. If it were in a private house it would be one thing, but this mural is in a public building and the situation is therefore quite different. As much as I dislike to do so, I am afraid we must ask you to substitute the face of some unknown man where Lenin's face now appears."[30]

He reminded Rivera that no one had hitherto restricted his subject nor his treatment. The family was not challenging the celebration of Soviet-style Communism in Venetian red, nor war as a distinct product of capitalism, nor venereal disease as related to an American civilization that revolved around nightclubs and card games. Apparently both Abby and Nelson (and John, too, who had to deal most closely with the hard-nosed builders) were willing to live with broad strokes of ideology. But tenants could not be expected to ignore so defiant an icon as the portrait of Vladimir Ilyich Lenin.

In one of the murkier subplots, Clifford Wight, an English sculptor who signed on as an assistant, wrote a letter in December 1932 to Ralph Stackpole. It seems that Diego told Wight that it was Abby who asked him to include a portrait of Lenin, saying that he hadn't given Communism enough importance. Considering the individual involved—an artist of wildly fluctuating moods who was also a Communist trying to zigzag successfully according to party discipline—any such evidence that relates Abby to the portrait of Lenin is less than convincing.

On May 6, Rivera replied to Nelson. He protested that he had merely given a specific face to a generalized figure. As far as he was concerned, Lenin was not negotiable, but he might consider substituting some great American, such as Abraham Lincoln, for the women playing cards. On the morning of May 9, Hugh Robertson of the management company took over in place of Nelson. One of Nelson's biographers, Joe Alex Morris, wrote that he had been "conveniently sent out of town on another mission." Abby, according to her letter to Lucy, planned to reach New York from Virginia on May 7, with only a week in town before leaving for Boston and Providence.

Frances Paine delivered Robertson's letter in person to Diego. "There was not the slightest intimation," Robertson stated, "either in the description or in the sketch that you would include in the mural any portrait or any subject matter of a controversial nature."[31] He was right about the sketch, wrong about the description (synopsis), but that point was never raised. After a year of wrangling, neither he nor his partners was in any mood to bend to Diego's will. They were heavily involved in a $125 million sparsely rented piece of real estate. There was too much controversy already. In the evening they called him into the on-site office, paid him in full, and dismissed him from the project. Workmen nailed canvas across the fresco and then boarded it up. Diego seemed unfazed. "Maintenant c'est bataille," he shouted, as he tried to comfort his distraught young crew.[32]

•

The outcry was immediate and intense. Demonstrators, carrying picket signs, swarmed outside Radio City demanding the unveiling of the mural. Messages of protest poured into the Rockefeller offices from artists and intellectuals and even apolitical art lovers. The Communist Party, according to Wolfe, was caught in "no man's land." "A revolutionary painter for millionaires," he wrote, "a millionaire patron of revolutionary painting, and a Communist Party silent on the fight between them, constituted a triple absurdity."[33]

Not everyone who deplored the dismissal defended Rivera. To Holger Cahill, who had supported him in the Detroit imbroglio, Diego was an incorrigible publicity hunter. "He would do anything for publicity," Cahill said, "and the Communists certainly muddied things up."[34] To William Valentiner, his staunch friend among museum people, it was simply incongruous that he should paint a portrait of Lenin opposite the entrance to a building bearing the name of Rockefeller. Thoughtful people reached around for some compromise. Walter Pach, the critic, wrote Abby on May 11 that perhaps Rivera should be allowed at least to finish the work, then a committee would be selected to view it, in that way silencing professional troublemakers (presumably referring to the Communists). Pach even suggested that perhaps John could override the objections of the business agents and deflate the whole episode.

Abby never replied personally to Pach's letter. So far as is known she maintained a strict silence. A formal statement was devised for all queries and sent in the form of a telegram to Pach: "Your letters May tenth and eleventh to Mrs. Rockefeller have been referred to the Managing Directors of the Rockefeller Center." Signed, Anna Kelly, Secretary.[35]

Summer came on, the crowds' attention wavered, Abby and John left the city for Maine. In September, Walter Pach tried again. "I cannot tell whether it's right to write you again about the Rivera fresco at Rockefeller Center. It may be only an annoyance, if the matter is one that you want to leave in other hands; it may not be fair to suggest your taking it in hand if it could make complications with the managing directors, to whom your telegram referred me in May. But I did see them after that and have twice asked since for their decision—being told on all three occasions that none had been arrived at."[36]

This time he received a personal letter, though still signed by Anna Kelly. "Mrs. Rockefeller wishes me to thank you for your letter and also for your article on 'Modern Art in Perspective' which she greatly enjoyed reading. Mrs. Rockefeller has been not at all well for some time and I am taking care of her mail for her. Mr. Rockefeller is most anxious that she should not become involved in any way in the controversial question mentioned in your letter, particularly as the whole matter is in the hands of Todd, Robertson, Todd Engineering Corporation, Managing Directors of Rockefeller Center, who have full data on the subject. Mrs. Rockefeller hopes to be very much better by the latter part of the winter, when she trusts she can see you and Mrs. Pach."[37]

It is unlikely that Abby's silence was due to her illness. It may have slowed her down for a week or two at a time, but she had a way of popping up again rather quickly. This was the season that she was consulting closely with Goodyear and Alfred about the Bliss collection and the endowment for MoMA. She was working with Beatrix Farrand in the garden. She was entertaining college presidents and high government officials. And the assumption, if the recent past was any indication, is that Nelson was reporting all intrigues to her as they occurred.

One can only imagine how she felt about Rivera. She had trusted him, offered him and Frida her friendship, supported him as an artist. His was an act of betrayal. He had a different agenda and he pursued it recklessly, some would say ruthlessly. But then there was the art, the fresco, which had legitimate qualities of greatness, propaganda notwithstanding, and it deserved to be seen and preserved. She was known to support unpopular art. Considering Diego's insolent behavior, she could hardly be blamed if she retreated into an injured silence. But if Nelson and others were right about her—that she loved a good fight—perhaps her silence was not an entirely voluntary retreat. Since she was the one who had foisted the crazy Mexican on management in the first place, and now they were well rid of him, there was a rough logic in management muzzling her.

But what if she had not moved to the sidelines? What if she, and not Robertson, had faced down Diego? Had he not made his original commitment to her? It is possible that she could have shamed him into keeping his end of the bargain. Not likely, but anything is possible. Her tact and negotiating skills had been honed over a lifetime. It would have been an interesting confrontation.

A comparison between the Detroit situation and the Rockefeller Center dispute has often been drawn to the credit of Edsel Ford and the discredit of the Rockefellers. But such a comparison is deceiving. Edsel Ford was defending a mural, not in a commercial complex, but in a museum, where controversies over art are inevitable facts of life. Ford, when asked how he, as president of the Arts Commission, could allow such blasphemy on the sacred walls of the museum, simply replied that he liked the murals. Abby and Nelson, while they may have liked the Rivera frescoes, were backed into quite a different corner.

During the fall and winter, Nelson and Abby and people from MoMA were trying to find a way for the fresco to be removed intact and transported to the museum. On December 16, Nelson wrote a detailed letter to Alan Blackburn, MoMA's executive secretary, that seemed to represent a significant breakthrough:

> This morning I received a note from Mr. John R. Todd that he had discussed the mural situation with the managers and that they are all favorably inclined towards the idea. In his letter he suggests the following method of handling the situation.
>
> The Museum of Modern Art should write a letter to Rockefeller Center requesting them to give the three murals to the Museum, stating that if Rockefeller Center will be willing to do so, they will be glad to remove the mural from the building at their own expense. (I am sure Rockefeller Center will be willing to advance the money to the Museum for this work.) Rockefeller Center will then apply to the latter accepting the Museum's proposition and covering all the details of the situation very carefully. These two letters can be given to the press and will form the basis of whatever publicity there is concerning the matter. Mr. Todd suggests further that it might be well for the Museum to arrange with Rivera to touch up and finish

the work before they ask Rockefeller Center for it. However, this is a point which I am not quite sure about myself. . . .

The less said the better about this situation for the time being. I certainly wouldn't get in touch with Rivera until we have had further talks.[38]

The idea was noble, but no technique for removing the fresco safely proved to be workable. At midnight on Saturday, February 9, 1934, the mural was destroyed and the chunks of plaster loaded into fifty-gallon oil drums. There were fresh howls of rage. It was one thing to cover up the mural, another to smash it to bits. In less than two weeks the first Municipal Arts Exhibition was scheduled to open in the same building at Rockefeller Center. Nelson had persuaded management to construct thirty-one galleries at a cost of $50,000. Many artists threatened to withdraw from the show. But Edith Halpert, who mounted the exhibition, persuaded most of them, after heated arguments, to remain. Diego probably made her task easier by stating to the United Press that as far as he was concerned the issue was purely political. There was the belief, in the art community, that Abby was not culpable. "I cannot believe," John Sloan wrote in the *New York Times*, "that either Mr. or Mrs. John D. Rockefeller, Jr., was consulted about this deplorable act [destruction of the frescoes]. . . . I think the matter must have got ten out of their hands."[39] William Valentiner quotes Abby as having told him that the frescoes would not have been destroyed if the architects had not insisted on it. Forty years later, Nelson was still lamenting that both he and his mother "lost ground" on the Rivera mural.[40]

Diego, in Mexico City, made certain that the whole world could see what had been destroyed. On a wall in the Palace of Fine Arts he painted a modified version of the RCA Building fresco, adding a few additional figures, among them Trotsky and Marx. Peering down at the card game, directly under the germs of venereal disease, holding a martini glass, is John D. Rockefeller, Jr.

CHAPTER 27

*A*bby gave a large sigh of relief when Winthrop got into Yale, taking the conventional view that he belonged in college. But she was wrong. "I realized from the first," he explained to his own son years later, ". . . that I wasn't suited for the academic life. . . . I wanted to get out in the world, to work, to prove my own worth."[1] At Yale he fell in with a card-playing, drinking crowd. He was on probation most of the time. Only two courses interested him, art appreciation and sociology, the former because he could build on what he had learned from Abby, the latter because he was curious about relationships among people and groups. In the summer of 1933 he spent some time as a trainee in industrial relations for Jersey Standard. He lived at the local YMCA and spent his leisure time at the Bayway Community Center, where as a boy he had tagged along with his mother.

He finished off that summer vacation in the Texas fields of the Humble Oil and Refining Company. "That was what I had been looking for!" he recalled exultantly. ". . . men working with their hands, producing something real. . . . I was fascinated by everything I saw—I wanted to become a part of it, to do what they were doing, to prove to myself that I was as good a man as any of them."[2]

Six months later he left Yale and formal education. Like the child of the Lincoln School that he was, he wanted to "learn by doing." He returned to Texas to work for Humble, the first Rockefeller since Senior to go on the payroll of an oil company. He stayed for three years, learning everything about oil production, from cleanup work in the blistering heat as a roustabout, to handling twenty-five-pound wrenches as an apprentice driller, to exploring for oil with the geophysicists.

With his sorry history of never being able to balance his account books to the satisfaction of his father, piling up debts so forbidding that once he even thought of stealing to avoid a reprimand, now he vowed to live on his earnings. "I have only used my earnings for everything that I want or do, and it . . . makes me wonder how these boys with big families ever make ends meet. We are now, however, much encouraged by the report that we are to get a 3¢ hourly raise starting next week."[3] The greatest satisfaction came from being accepted by the other men on the crew, invited to their tiny shacks for a meal, praised for his stamina and strength.

Winthrop, perhaps because of childish hurts, loved Abby with a deep humility and sensitivity, taking nothing for granted. He understood, perhaps better than anyone except Lucy, the foolishness of forcing her to rest. "I think that for Mother to be completely away from everything will not eliminate the nervous tension of not being able to do the things that she so enjoyed. . . . I also think that this [enforced idleness] has been a rather important element in keeping her from complete recovery—I know that it would work that way with me."[4]

More than any of her other children, more even than Nelson, with all his political charm and shrewdness, Winthrop had Abby's egalitarian outlook. He was at ease with men of totally opposite experience and social status in the same way that Abby valued the friendship of the immigrant women at Bayway and the working families of Pocantico. It was not a matter of guilt or rejection of luxury. It seemed more a question of personality, of being modest and affable without rejecting one's own accidental place in the scheme of things. Winnie could spend his weekends with the president of the oil company, gracefully circulating in the country clubs

Mary French in the season of her marriage to Laurance Rockefeller, 1934.
Courtesy of the Rockefeller Archive Center.

and mansions of Houston, and then on Monday slip back into the job of "roughneck" without missing a step.

In August 1934 he traveled by train and plane to be a groomsman at Laurance's wedding in Woodstock, Vermont. In June, Laurance, petitioning his father in a formal letter, had announced his desire to marry Mary French. "[We] are thoroughly convinced that we are deeply and permanently in love. Our greatest desire is to make the best possible use of the creative forces of our affection [written like a true philosophy major]. . . . Until I have had the opportunity . . . to win your <u>approval</u> and <u>support,</u> I am in no position to ask her to marry me."[5]

Of approval there was no question. Mary's mother was Abby's longtime friend from the World Council of the YWCA. Her brother had been Nelson's roommate at Dartmouth. Her maternal grandfather, Frederick Billings, had reorganized and headed up the

Northern Pacific Railroad, settling in Vermont in 1869. Mary was sensitive and artistic and lovely to look at. She was a gifted sculptor, working in Cambridge when Laurance entered Harvard Law. She later studied with William Zorach.

Support was another matter. For a graduate student that meant money. All the brothers, and Babs as well, were still receiving allowances. Monetary decisions flowed from their father. In an effort to persuade him of their changing circumstances—some of them were already married, two had children of their own—they presented him with a cautiously crafted proposal. Instead of tedious, painstaking family conferences taken up with how various sums of money were to be used, could he not simply turn over an annual sum, tailored to individual needs? The tone of the letter suggested that something more fundamental than economic independence was at stake. "We want and need your advice and guidance more than ever, now that our problems are larger and our responsibilities greater. . . . You do not realize how much pleasure we get from being with you and discussing informally your many interests. . . . It is this intimate relationship, which we all value so highly, in regard to which we are particularly concerned. . . . Our regret is . . . that . . . business matters . . . occupy such a large proportion of our very limited time with you."[6]

In the presence of his children, en masse, John drew a protective shell about him, handing down his decisions with great solemnity. Abby alone seemed to know the private John. The young people wanted to believe that under the remote figure that was their father, there was an approachable, relaxed person. Sadly, this seldom was to be. Some years later, at Nelson's urging, the brothers met as a group with the hope and the expectation that their father would join them. But he refused, David recalled. "He felt uncomfortable and threatened. He would meet with us as individuals but felt ganged up on by a group. My mother on the other hand would have loved it."[7]

It was Fosdick's opinion, formed during his lengthy interviews with John, that the 1933 letter from the children resulted in his setting up trusts for them. At the very least their message had an impact in a financial climate that was changing rapidly, changes that would finally transform the way John's fortune was distributed. Major new tax laws had already been passed during the last days of the Hoover administration, and tax rates on income, on estates, and on gifts were raised sharply. The New Deal Congress continued the redistribution of wealth to finance government expenditures on behalf of the farmers, the middle class, the elderly, and the unemployed. By the time John completed the entities known in the family as the "1934 trusts" he had paid approximately $35,700,000 in gift taxes on a capital transfer of $105 million.

It is David's impression that Abby was not included in the original estate-planning that led to the creation of the trusts. "But when it became obvious that there was great disparity between what we were being given and what she was being given," he recalled, "it must have rankled. She did not express her irritation to me of course, but there must have been many private discussions."[8]

What John finally did was to make Abby's trust the largest—$18,300,000 in oil stocks, with the possibility, depending upon the economic recovery, of $1 million in pretax income per year, the annual income tax being approximately 50 percent. The children's trusts were funded with approximately $14 million to $16 million each. John, unlike his father, gave meticulous and far-reaching thought to restrictions. His temperament was entirely different, the times different, and his children were much younger. The trusts were generation-skipping and irrevocable. The income would be doled out gradually. John would receive no income from the trusts and retain no control over them, the management vested in his most reliable advisers and the Chase Bank.

His sons could draw on the capital with the approval of the trustees; his wife and his daughter could not. And he went one step further with Abby. He named the beneficiaries of her trust—John 3rd, Nelson, and Laurance. Eventually Abby was granted access to the corpus, but the discriminations were obvious. She could not have been surprised by John's behavior. She knew all about the psychological factors at work in money as control. She saw how Senior had handled his estate—giving a disproportionate share to his only son. But at the very least she was free of Rockefeller accounting and she was at last in a position to support MoMA in a major way.

The Fifth Anniversary Exhibition opened at MoMA on November 19, 1934. Abby attended the preview reception. "I am very glad indeed that you will be able to be present at the opening of the Anniversary Exhibition," Goodyear wrote her. "To mark the occasion, several of the Trustees and Friends of the Museum are making gifts to the Permanent Collection, which will be announced on that evening. . . . I am sure that you understand that this is merely for your information and not intended as a solicitation."[9]

Whether intended as a solicitation or not, in consultation with Alfred, Abby selected Charles Sheeler's *American Landscape: Ford Factory at River Rouge, Michigan* as her anniversary gift. Sheeler was a painter of the first rank as well as a photographer and artisan who designed on fabric, silver, and glass. He brought exceptional clarity and admirable precision to his rendering of American exteriors and interiors, championing the beauty of everyday objects. Through Edith Halpert, Abby learned about the economic struggle of this greatly respected artist. As she began to consider what pieces in her collection to offer to her children, she wrote John 3rd and Blanchette: "You will notice that I have not included . . . the Sheeler among the list of pictures that I am happy to give you I still feel very strongly that as Mr. Sheeler is in very difficult circumstances it would be much better for you to buy some of his pictures. He is not very old and will probably paint lots of pictures better than this. . . . Mr. Sheeler's paintings can be bought at the Downtown Gallery."[10]

The Fifth Anniversary Exhibition was a birthday celebration for MoMA, and the birthday child had a right to be proud. Many of the works came from Abby's personal holdings. "Any words of thanks to you for your generous loans would be an understatement. The Toulouse-Lautrec, the Kopman, the Blume, the Van Gogh, the McFee, were especially important items in the exhibition . . . ," Alfred wrote. "In view of your plan to give so many things to the Museum in the near future I am afraid this may be the last letter of thanks for loans that I may write you, at least involving so many works."[11]

Alfred was right. There would be fewer loans from Abby's seventh-floor gallery, because she was transferring a major portion of her holdings to the museum. It was the most significant event in the life of MoMA since the Lillie Bliss bequest. And it would begin to satisfy Abby's lofty dream of what the museum could stand for in the world of modern art.

MoMA announced the gift—181 paintings, drawings, and watercolors—in its May 1935 bulletin. Goodyear released the news to the press on May 23. The *New York Times*, the *Herald Tribune*, and *Literary Digest*, as well as numerous syndicates and wire services, covered the event. It was the first time that the country at large was informed that Abby had been a founder of the museum.

One anecdote was repeated in every article. Even if apocryphal, it captures the personalities of both Abby and Edith Halpert. Duncan Candler had persuaded Abby to lend her Winslow Homer *Shark Fishing* to the Downtown Gallery for its exhibition American Landscape, mounted by Edith in February 1928. It was hung between a Marin and a Zorach. "When visitors to the show asked about buying the Homer," so the tale went, "the dealer replied that it was not for sale—and neither, she added indignantly, were the Marin and the Zorach, except 'to the idiot who owns the Homer and doesn't have the descendants to go with it.' Just before the show closed, a friendly woman with a sharp, prominent nose, alert eyes and an elaborate hat came in. She asked the price of the two modern seascapes (they were $750 and $250 respectively), said, 'I am the idiot,' and bought both paintings."[12]

The official inventory of Abby's gift had a fair market value of $107,270 on June 20. There were oils by Alexander Brook, John Kane, Georgia O'Keeffe, Walt Kuhn, Charles Sheeler, and Max Weber; watercolors by Charles Demuth, Preston Dickenson, John Marin, Maurice Prendergast; and Diego Rivera's May Day sketches. Some of the works purchased for modest sums have since attained great stature. Alfred called attention in the *New York Times* especially to the watercolors by Demuth, the still life drawings by Sheeler, the oil by Brook, and Blume's *Parade*.

All talk had ceased about Abby being nervous or depressed. In March 1935, she sailed with John for Sicily. "I am sitting on our balcony . . ." she wrote David on April 1 from Palermo. "The sea is marvelous today, near the shore it is a heavenly greenish blue, out on the horizon it is dark blue and the cloud shadows are purple. The mountains are hazy and soft, a grayish blue. If you were only here it would be perfect." Mussolini was preparing his attack on Ethiopia. In Naples, Abby saw the young soldiers lining up to go to war. "I hated to see them. No one here even pretends that there is any just cause for their going into Africa, it is simply a question of getting rid of the unemployed, having more raw materials and a new colony!!! . . . Mankind seems to learn nothing from the past. . . . I have just read that Abyssinia has one b and two s's. Lots and lots of love from your mother."[13]

From Sorrento she wrote Lucy that she was *very well* and eager to get some new clothes. "A good sign, don't you think."[14] She promised to telephone Lucy from wherever she was. "I am not at all sure how it is done, but I don't imagine Europe is so far behind the United States that we cannot do long distance telephoning. . . . Probably Mussolini will listen in, but I will be discreet."[15]

Three members of the Dyer family from Providence were joining her for lunch. "How many years ago was it that we were here with Anthony and Mrs. Dyer. I believe it was 40!!!"[16] They motored from Sorrento to Rome. "A beautiful ride in a fertile valley. . . . the women work in the fields with the men," she wrote David. "But there are thousands of soldiers and priests who do not appear to be very busy. I like the look of the peasants best. . . . In spite of Huey Long and Father C. [Coughlin] and everything else awful that is going on 'chez nous' I shall be glad when I am in the United States again."[17]

With fresh energy and a significant income of her own, Abby resumed her leadership of MoMA. She had sent Nelson a progress report on February 18, 1935. "John Hay Whitney . . . has just accepted the chairmanship of the Motion Picture Committee. . . . Walter Chrysler . . . is raising $25,000 for the library. . . . It was decided at [Alfred's suggestion] that we have a very large, compre-

hensive exhibition of the paintings and drawings of Van Gogh.
. . . For the large spring exhibition we are planning a retrospective exhibition of abstract art. All the younger people connected
with the Museum have been pressing for this for the last two
years. . . ." She concluded her letter, as usual, with the problem
of the budget. "This fiscal year ends on October 1st 1935 and . . .
the funds of the Museum are running rather low."[18]

One of Alfred's cherished goals was a Department of Film,
which would collect and preserve classic films that could be lent to
other museums and colleges, and from time to time show films
from all countries to the community at large. As early as 1932 he
had proclaimed that such a department was being organized (more
hope than reality). Abby liked the idea and often discussed the
possibility with him over lunch. The outlook brightened with the
arrival at the museum of an experienced film critic, Iris Barry, who
signed on as a librarian when there was actually no library and
Philip Johnson paid her salary. In 1934 the MoMA bulletin reported some progress, and in 1935 the Rockefeller Foundation gave
$100,000 to the museum for the establishment of the Film Library.
The bulletin made it official in November. A Department of Film
was in place. Iris Barry was in charge. In January 1936, Nelson
reported to Abby, who was in Boston, that the first showing of
films was a great success.

Alfred sailed to Europe on May 28, 1935, with his first purchase
money ever—$1,000 from Abby to buy art for the museum. It had
been an embarrassment to him that the museum had only been
borrowing, never buying. Even this modest amount was critical.
"Things are very cheap, both sculpture and paintings," he wrote
Abby on July 20. "For instance one can get a fine terracotta a foot
high by Laurens, one of the best French sculptors of the middle
generations, for $35. A Picasso gouache for which Rosenberg was
asking $1,000 last year in New York for $350. . . . A Léger oil 2x3
feet for $140. These are not bargains but ordinary prices."[19] What
he finally selected reinforces the sorry state of the art market at that
time: two Giorgio de Chirico oils for $500; sculpture, oils, and
wood reliefs by Hans Arp, most of them less than $30 each; an oil
by Joan Miró for $164; and an Yves Tanguy for $100.

Abby gave him an additional $500 to spend on American artists who were, in Alfred's words, "hard up," and an occasional museum fellowship of $350 which he administered. When she made selective purchases on her own, it was always with the museum in mind. Hearing that she had bought a Dalí, Alfred wrote from Paris in great excitement. "I had no idea that it was the portrait of Gala Dalí, the painter's wife. It has just been reproduced in *Minotaurs* and Dalí speaks of it as his finest painting!"[20]

Most of the time Alfred was the messenger with the suggestions. "Mr. Brummer [a gallery owner] is considering giving Loren MacIver a one-man exhibition," he wrote. "I think a very slight nudge would help him make up his mind. Miss MacIver's work is . . . very exceptional in quality and in imaginative invention. I believe that even the slightest indication that you would like to see an exhibition of her work would persuade Mr. Brummer to go ahead with it. I bought two of her things last year out of the $500 which you gave me to spend for American paintings by hard-up artists."[21]

After exhibiting Reuben Nakian's *Young Calf*, a sculpture in marble, twice at the museum, he wrote Abby that Edith Halpert could obtain it for $500. "The *Young Calf* is, I think, a distinguished piece of sculpture by an American and one that I should like to have in the museum. As I shall be sailing, perhaps Miss Kelly could write or phone Mrs. Halpert, if you are interested."[22] (She was.) Later in the year he told Abby about a Tchelitchew pastel, "one of the finest . . . I have ever seen. . . . I think it could be had for less than $250, the asking price. . . . I thought you would like to look at it over the weekend. I would certainly be most happy to see it in the Museum's collection. If we don't get it Mr. Austin will get it for Hartford."[23] Mr. Austin did not get it. Abby penciled "YES" in the margin of Alfred's letter.

On May 29, Conger Goodyear sent a letter to Alfred care of the American Express Co., The Hague, Holland, which was Alfred and Marga's first stop in their quest for the van Goghs that would travel to America in time for the fall retrospective. "I spoke to Mrs. Rockefeller about the desirability of having a new building for the Museum and I explained the necessity of getting a site. I think that there is some real prospect that Mr. Rockefeller might be willing to donate a site if we could get the money from the Government for the erection of a building. He has a large amount of surplus real estate, of course, and I judge from what Mrs. Rockefeller said that he is somewhat less prejudiced against the Museum than he has been. . . . The less we say about it, for the time being, the better, however." [24]

The government did not come up with the money, and John, whatever his feelings about the museum, was not about to hand over real estate. But after a year of private and unrecorded negotiations, he and Abby evidently reached an accord. He would sell to the museum for $250,000 his lots at Numbers 15, 17, and 19 on West 53rd. Abby contributed to the museum $250,000 from her personal funds to defray the cost. Although the money was routed through MoMA, in effect she was reimbursing John. [25] The cost of the building, estimated at $1 million, would be raised by subscription among trustees and friends of the museum.

The Vincent van Gogh Exhibition opened on November 4, 1935. "Lines to Fifth Avenue," Marga wrote in her chronicle. "Mrs. Roosevelt visits twice. No one, A. least of all, expected such crowds." [26] Alfred had gathered sixty-six oils and fifty drawings, most of them from the Netherlands. For the catalogue he selected poignant excerpts from the artist's letters. The response was overwhelming, a precursor of the hold van Gogh has to this day on the contemporary imagination.

Abby and John were in Boston when the exhibition of Abby's pictures was put on view at MoMA in January 1936. "I wouldn't . . . be sorry if they were never exhibited as a whole," she had written Alfred. [27] She didn't object to publicity if it served some function, but splashy events had no appeal for her, if she was at the center. The exhibition opened on January 14. "I wish you were here for the opening," Alfred wrote, "but I think you are coming back before the show closes. [She did, just barely.] I can't tell you how delighted I am, especially with the American watercolors. I think we have the finest group of Demuth, Hart and Burchfield of any museum in the country." [28]

The attention that Abby had not courted reached a climax when

Time placed her on the cover of its January 27 issue. "Abby Greene Aldrich Rockefeller . . . has a nose for new talent."

> Any exhibit opening in the wake of the enormously popular van Gogh show at Manhattan's Museum of Modern Art was bound to begin with an initial handicap. . . . The Museum's principal bene-factor happens to have a great name and a great modesty. . . . Only those long of wind and strong of purpose who clumped up to the third and fourth floors were rewarded with the sight of 127 paint-ings, water colors and drawings by most of the best known names in modern painting, collected during the past ten years by Mrs. John D. Rockefeller, Jr. Because the name of Rockefeller had been suc-cessfully minimized in the papers, comment on the exhibition was limited to a few desultory paragraphs. It deserved more, since Mrs. Rockefeller's gift . . . has made the Museum of Modern Art one of the greatest collections of modern painting in the world. Probably no person of great wealth has done more for living U.S. artists than Gertrude Vanderbilt Whitney. But her purchases are now all regulated by Manhattan's Whitney Museum. Mrs. Rockefeller is not yet incorporated as an impersonal buying agency. The prizes she offers, the pictures she acquires and the gifts she makes are all done with such skillful reticence that few recognize her for what she is: the outstanding individual patron of living artists in the U.S.[30]

The Whitney Museum of American Art, an outgrowth of the Whitney Studio Club, had opened on November 18, 1931. Four town houses on West 8th Street were joined together and renovated to create a handsome classical facade. The interior preserved the ambience of a private home, with galleries, offices, and the personal apartment of Juliana Force flowing cleverly, one to another. Ger-trude Whitney paid for everything—the land, the buildings, the art, the salaries. Juliana was the sole executive. There was no board of trustees, only Gertrude, who detached herself almost completely from the administration, and Juliana, and the handful of associates to carry out the intentions of the two women.

Gertrude's intention was as it had been for at least twenty years —to support American artists, preferably realists, whatever their merits, by buying their art. (Abby readily acknowledged that she too was moved to help out an artist by buying the work, but it was an occasional act rather than a guiding principle.) Gertrude was the very rich woman as creative artist who suffered the rejection of a philandering husband, but remained loyal to her tight web of social obligations. Juliana had moved from obscurity to a position of power in the art world because of her professional relationship with Gertrude. She carried Gertrude's philosophy to the marketplace, where she used the Vanderbilt money to buy the works of artists who had earned her loyalty—a passionate, often ferocious, loyalty. She was unwilling, perhaps even unable, to lay aside such loyalty in favor of objective aesthetic judgment. This question of personal sympathy versus aesthetic judgment was one that would haunt the Whitney Museum from the moment of its inception. "Sentiment," Avis Berman, historian of the Whitney and biographer of Juliana, wrote, "was their pride and their albatross."[30] Gertrude's philanthropic impulse and Juliana's emotional identification with certain artists and not with others tarnished the Whitney with mediocrity.

Again Berman:

> . . . in arriving at any fair reckoning of the Whitney's stature in its early years, it must be measured against the one institution that consistently surpassed it—the Museum of Modern Art. Indeed because they were inaugurated at about the same time, the Whitney from its advent was doomed to debilitating comparisons with the Museum of Modern Art and Barr's unmatchable legacy of connoisseurship and erudition.[31]

In the eyes of the public, Gertrude *was* the Whitney. Her persona overpowered everything to do with the museum. In sharp contrast, if any one individual was identified with MoMA it was Alfred Barr. Abby would have it no other way.

As dominant a role as Alfred played in shaping the museum, he could not always control events. Power was shifting on the board of trustees. Abby had moved down from first vice president to a simple member of the board to make room for Nelson, who stepped into her former office. Samuel Lewisohn was treasurer. Stephen

Clark, irritable with MoMA in the past, was moving to the foreground again. Mary Sullivan and Frank Crowninshield had resigned. Both had felt the ravages of the Depression. Abby's friend Edsel Ford did agree to go on the board. "He really seemed very much pleased," Abby had written Goodyear, "to have been asked to become a trustee of the Museum, and I think he is anxious to do it, but poor man, he looks overtired and driven. . . . I feel quite sure that you would like to write him too and assure him that we would do everything we could to make his membership on the board a pleasure rather than a burden."[32]

Now that the site was in hand for the new building and the fundraising had begun, there was the question of the architect. "I think very wisely," Abby wrote Lucy on March 16, 1936, "we have decided to employ Philip Goodwin, one of our own [meaning he too was a trustee], as architect, and have asked him to associate with himself a young, very modern architect. Between them we feel that we can get something that is not too extreme and that will be a credit to ourselves and the city."[33] On March 30 she wrote Alfred that she wanted very much to discuss with him some of her ideas for the new building before he sailed for France.

Alfred had firm ideas about the architecture. His was a museum that stood for the adventurous and the progressive in all art forms, the museum that had introduced the International Style to Americans, had named it, in fact. He envisaged one of the great architects of the world for the new building, someone not merely distinguished, but brilliant. He did not mean to criticize Goodwin, who was a man of impeccable taste, wise, generous (he was contributing his architect's fee to the building fund), and never one to compromise with excellence. It was as a fastidious collector of contemporary art that he became associated with the museum. But his roots were in the neoclassicism of the Paris École des Beaux-Arts. Not even the members of the building committee—Nelson, Goodyear, and Clark—expected him to design the modern structure that the museum's reputation demanded. As Abby explained to Lucy, a young modern architect should be associated with him.

Alfred and Marga left for Europe on May 12 to begin work on the winter exhibition, Fantastic Art, Dada and Surrealism. Alfred

"Souvenir de la Visite." Abby at Versailles, summer 1936.
Courtesy of the Rockefeller Archive Center.

had permission from the building committee to consult with Jacobus Oud, Walter Gropius, and Mies van der Rohe as possible collaborators. (Frank Lloyd Wright and Le Corbusier were set aside as being too difficult to work with.) Gropius and Oud demurred, but Mies was interested. Alfred was elated. Mies van der Rohe was one of the great innovators of modern architecture. His reputation rested on many major projects, including the Tugendhat House in Czechoslovakia, and the ultimate realization of his "open plane" concept, the German Pavilion in Barcelona in 1929. As his biographers have noted, it was his declared choice to accept the nature of industrial society and to express it in his architecture.

On June 20, David, recently graduated from Harvard, went with his parents to Europe. The occasion was the Versailles Fête, ceremonies which would publicly acknowledge John's gift of $3 million to a nearly bankrupt French government for the restoration of three national treasures—Versailles, Fontainebleau, and Rheims. Abby, always reluctant to be photographed, flinched at the sight of forty cameramen following the dignitaries. "Mamma . . . made up her mind to accept whatever came, and therefore she did not allow herself to be annoyed by the cameramen and as a result the pictures of her were extraordinarily good," John wrote. The street facing the entrance of the palace was renamed Avenue Rockefeller and a tablet set up on an interior wall commemorating the relation of John Davison Rockefeller, Jr., to the work of the restoration. The young minister of education, M. Jean Zay, was seated next to Abby at the palace luncheon. After that elegant affair, the entire party repaired to the little Marie Antoinette theater near the Petit Trianon, also restored in every exquisite detail. "Mamma sat in the chair which Marie Antoinette had occupied, and the Minister of Education and I sat beside her."[34] Later in the day the president of France awarded the Grand Cross of the Legion of Honor to John in another ceremony at the Palais de l'Élysée.

Alfred, still in Europe when the Rockefeller party reached Paris, called on Abby at the Hôtel Crillon on the afternoon of July 3 to press his case for Mies. Rona Roob, an art historian as well as the archivist of MOMA, and the individual most conversant with the Alfred Barr papers, published in 1983 her careful documentation of all the events that surrounded the question of architects. Letters and telegrams evidently went back and forth across the Atlantic. Decisions seemed to stumble over each other in a confusing fashion. Alfred was shocked to learn from Tom Mabry that the building committee had engaged a young unknown, Edward Durell Stone, to work with Goodwin. Mabry, whose job it was to take care of administrative details for the museum—his title was executive director and secretary—admired and respected Alfred, but he also saw that his behavior could be counterproductive. "I'm afraid," he wrote Barr, "your technique of letting everybody fry until the last minute will not work so well in this case, unfortunately because how can you undraw plans? And Goodwin is working away like a beaver. He wants the job."[35]

Edward D. Stone was young and he was not well known, but he had already worked under Raymond Hood and Wallace Harrison as the principal designer of the Radio City Music Hall. Donald Deskey respected his talent. He was a disciple of Wright, and he had trained at several superb institutions, although he was quoted as saying that he had never graduated from anywhere since junior high school. During two years on a traveling fellowship he had studied Le Corbusier's published designs and doctrine, and he admired the same architects as Alfred did. He would mature to become a renowned figure who valued the romantic and the formal, blending it effectively with classic modern. But he was no Mies van der Rohe and would not claim to be.

To prepare for his meeting with Abby, Alfred wrote her a lengthy memorandum on July 2. "To rest content," he pleaded, "with a mediocre building . . . would be to betray the very purposes for which the Museum was founded. . . . [Nelson] agreed that the Museum should secure the collaboration of the best possible architect and spoke of Mies van der Rohe [Alfred did not know that it was Nelson and his brother-in-law Wallace Harrison who had brought Stone into the picture]. . . . Mr. Goodyear . . . has shown no interest in the quality of the architecture. Just after the appointment of Mr. Goodwin he even proposed to eliminate entirely a modern collaborator in order to save money."[36] (To be fair to Goodyear, money *was* a large problem.)

Marga, who accompanied Alfred to the Crillon, recalls that Abby listened attentively, that David sitting beside her "discreetly seems to agree with A., but Mrs. Rockefeller feels that the architect should be American and in any case she is unwilling to tip the balance without the endorsement of the other trustees. However, she has not vetoed all consideration of the foreign architects."[37]

The conversation lasted well over an hour. Abby, moved by Alfred's arguments, immediately cabled Nelson to delay action on the collaborating architect until after she and Alfred were back in New York—*if* he had not actually been engaged. "Everyone agrees he [Mies] is the best possible man," she wired.[38] But Stone *had* been engaged, although there seems to be some disagreement about that, too. Alfred continued to write long, eloquent, and, as it turned out, futile letters to Nelson, to Goodyear, to Goodwin himself. His dream of having a building by Mies in midtown Manhattan was not realized until the 1950s when the Seagram Building was designed and constructed.

Abby, as chairman of the exhibitions committee, paid close attention to Alfred's plans for the two major shows of 1936. Whatever her private opinion of some of the more peculiar works, she never interfered with his choices. Cubism and Abstract Art opened on March 2, 1936. The next day Edward Jewell in the *Times* called it "complex . . . a monumental undertaking . . . a journey through strange worlds."[39] Barr made the journey easier by first introducing the by now familiar Gauguin and van Gogh, then easing the viewer into the more radical works of Matisse, Picasso, Franz Marc, Lyonel Feininger, and Kandinsky. Conservative critics were still in an uproar over sculpture that did not imitate the human form. Twenty-three years after the Armory Show, abstract art was still a threat.

The next major exhibition, Fantastic Art, Dada and Surrealism, opening on December 7, caused more commotion and was even more controversial, in spite of the cogent words that Barr himself wrote as an introduction to the Georges Hugnet essay on Dada and surrealism published in the catalogue:

Much . . . may seem wantonly outrageous and iconoclastic; in fact, these movements in advocating anti-rational values seem almost to have declared war on conventions and standards of established Society. But it may be remembered that the Dadaists and Surrealists hold society responsible for the Great War, the variety of social, political and economic follies which have made the realities of Christendom in their eyes a spectacle of madness just as shocking as their most outrageous super-realities may be to the outside world.[40]

Such thoughtful analysis notwithstanding, the popular critics derided many of the seven hundred objects in the show. Alfred had set out to educate the public in the history of art. There were works by Dürer and Holbein, by Tanguy, Dalí, and Breton, Marcel Duchamp and Max Ernst. But the most widely publicized piece, the one that most irritated Conger Goodyear and other trustees, was Meret Oppenheim's *The Fur-lined Teacup*, which was precisely what its title said it was.

While Goodyear was complaining to Abby about what seemed to him to be irrelevant nonsense in the exhibition, she was reflecting soberly on the broad question of the administration of the museum. It troubled her that the exhibitions committee had met only once in two years and that the executive committee did not have a more active chairman. "It worries me," she wrote Goodyear on December 16, 1936, "that money should have been promised to the Museum and no one followed up on verbal pledges into signed pledges. . . . It does not seem wise to me that Nelson should be Chairman of all the important committees of the Museum. At present he is Chairman of the Finance Committee, the Building Committee, and the World Fair Committee. I protest that this is unwise, unfortunate, and inappropriate. It may be convenient for the President [Goodyear himself] and the First Vice President [Nelson] to center all the authority of the Museum in their hands, but personally—as you well know—from my point of view, it does not seem to me it is conducive to a happy or successful future for the Museum."

Then, for the first time, at least so far as it is known, Abby aired her concerns about Alfred's future role at the museum. "As you know, I greatly admire and respect and trust Alfred Barr. I have often said that he is the Museum, because through the catalogs he has made the greatest possible contribution to the study of modern art in America, but I feel that he is neither physically nor temperamentally fitted to cope with the intricate problems of the management of the Museum or the management of the Trustees, if I may use that expression.

"Perhaps you will be sorry that you wrote me, but I have had these things very much on my heart and my mind and I should like to talk them over with you alone at first and later with any group that you would like to suggest."[41]

Since Alfred came to the museum seven years earlier, Abby had been his buffer with the trustees, especially the curmudgeons Goodyear and Clark. When Goodyear argued with him during the year of his sabbatical, Abby took up his defense. When Stephen Clark was irritable with some of his artistic moves, Abby, acting through Nelson, brought the two men together over dinner and peace was declared. But now she saw the museum facing a different set of challenges, with the expansion and new trustees and new departments. Mabry put it in plain language. "As things are now," he wrote Nelson, "Alfred's perfectionist neurosis frustrates all activity. It's absolutely impossible for him to begin work until the other fellow has finished—then he tears down what the other fellow has done and laboriously starts all over again. Such a method is all right in the artist where a single mind creates the whole work, but you can't run an organization that way. I think I understand Alfred and I most certainly like and admire him—but he has got to be saved from himself for the Museum."[42]

Goodyear made no move to reduce the centralization of authority on the board (his and Nelson's) to which Abby objected, but he began immediately to think about how to trim Alfred's burdens— not that Alfred thought of them as burdens. Goodyear discussed the situation with Paul Sachs and then reported back to Abby. "It seems to me," he wrote on June 18, 1937, "that it might be well if you could have a talk with Alfred sometime this summer . . . with the possibility in mind . . . of his accepting the place of Curator of painting and sculpture or possibly Curator in Chief with direct charge of the Department of Painting and Sculpture and thereby, be entirely relieved of any of the functions of a Director."[43]

Whatever Abby did or did not say to Alfred, when Goodyear spoke to him on July 6, Alfred was not offended but appeared to support the whole idea. Again Goodyear reported back to Abby. "The matter is shaping up very well. . . . [I believe] we will each work out of a troublesome situation quite satisfactorily."[44] But such encouraging words did nothing to move the "troublesome situation" forward. Abby watched for signs of change, but saw none. Goodyear had promised to appoint a committee for the reorganization but had done nothing about it. The new building had raised excitement to such a pitch that no one around MoMA was focusing on such mundane matters as organization.

The MoMA bulletin of July 1937 made it official. "Through the generosity of its trustees, friends and patrons, the Museum of Modern Art has already raised more than three-fourths of the million dollars necessary for the erection of its new building. The site includes 130 feet on 53rd between 5th and 6th Avenues, New York, and extends north through that block to a 70-foot frontage on West 54th Street."[45] Ten West 54th, to be specific! Abby and John had decided to move to an apartment on Park Avenue. The nine-story mansion would be torn down. The land, which John gave to the museum in several increments, would eventually become the setting for the Abby Aldrich Rockefeller Sculpture Garden. "The value of that gift is incalculable," David said. "My father did not give great amounts of capital to the museum. But he did give land."[46]

CHAPTER 28

*I*n the summer and fall of 1937, Abby had four houses open, all of which "more or less" needed her attention. "Here at No. 10," she wrote Lucy, "we are . . . sorting out, giving away, putting into storage, and repairing things for the new apartment [at 740 Park Avenue]. . . . We are all . . . peacefully moved into Mr. Rockefeller, Sr's house [Kykuit]. . . . Babs . . . is living at Abeyton Lodge . . . and the house at Seal Harbor has been opened. . . . I forgot to mention Bassett Hall, as that makes the fifth house."[1] There was no need for Lucy in London to shop for furniture, she added, as they had more than enough furniture everywhere.

Such was not the case with pictures. Most of what hung in her seventh-floor gallery had been given to the museum. She placed Rivera's *Rivals* over the mantle in David's sitting room in the Park Avenue apartment. "It really is stunning there," she wrote him.[2] "I have decided I shall buy a few really good pictures. This house [Kykuit] needs them. . . . I saw a Reynolds of a young man in red that I . . . love and a small Hogarth."[3] She must be very careful about rearranging the rest of the mansion, but she was having fun with her own sitting room. "I got together 18 small pictures that I really didn't have any very good places for and I have turned them in for what I paid for them, which will help me greatly on the price. I do wish you were here to help me [David was studying at the London School of Economics]. . . . I have seen a truly beautiful Cézanne for my sitting room in N.Y., but the price is terrible. If you see any lovely pictures in London let me know. I have more to trade off."[4]

Senior had died in his sleep at Ormond Beach on May 23, 1937, only six weeks before his ninety-eighth birthday. The funeral was at Pocantico. Abby, aided by a Mr. Smythe, who as a boy had watered the flowers at 4 West 54th, took charge of the flower arrangements. The mourners included all of Senior's grandchildren and descendants of his original employees from the estate. Nelson and Tod chartered a Pan American plane from Panama, picking up Winthrop in Dallas. "It nearly killed me to have them do it," Abby wrote Lucy, referring to the panic that overtook her when her children flew, "but it came out perfectly all right."[5]

After Laura's death in 1915, Senior had spent more time at Lakewood and Ormond Beach than he had at Pocantico. But the golf was convenient, and Sunday dinner was the ritual for gathering the family. After his father died, John wanted to move into Kykuit immediately. The 250 acres that formed the core of the estate had assumed the character of an exquisitely landscaped park. The fairways and greens meandered gracefully around the big house. Twenty miles of macadam and dirt roads intersected the property. There were greenhouses, orangerie, coach house and ninety or so cottages rented to two hundred full-time workers, including painters, carpenters, plumbers, etc.

Laurance referred to Kykuit as "the Winter Palace."[6] Most of the family liked it, even as they missed the faint shabbiness of Abeyton Lodge. "I am still fussing about," Abby wrote David, "trying to make it look better and more homelike. . . . But as a matter of fact I love living up here [meaning, perhaps, the spectacular view]. Last night we had a wet, clinging snow and this morning when the sun came out it was too beautiful, the trees were a grey brown, the river and sky were bright blue, with lovely white clouds making blue shadows and the ground covered with untrodden snow."[7]

She was not to enjoy such stillness for long. When the premature

October snow melted, John ordered the workmen back to renovate the golf course and regrade the lawns. In the city it was worse. "Living here in Number Ten," she wrote, "is rather like living in the infernal regions. They are beginning to drill out the basement of the Modern Museum [directly behind her] most energetically and they are still tearing down all the houses around us so that there are blasts and crashes and drilling that sound like machine guns going off about one all the time. . . . I cannot help having rather a longing for Williamsburg, where we will have peace and quiet and no improvements being made."[8]

It was now ten years since John had decided to restore Colonial Williamsburg according to the best research minds of the day. John's goal, according to Fosdick, was to rediscover an atmosphere, not to create one, but as early as the 1940s, Edward Kendrew, the resident architect, gently reminded John that not everything should be "spic and span" all the time; after all, eighteenth-century owners did not paint and refurbish every season. "But Mr. Rockefeller did not like that at all," Kendrew recalled. "He wanted everything to be perfect."[9] Today the officials at Williamsburg are making an effort to portray the realities of eighteenth-century life, not only from the vantage of the cultural and intellectual leaders, but as experienced by the mentally ill, the African slaves (in 1775 Williamsburg was 52 percent black), the working poor, both women and men. The idea, according to the director of Colonial Williamsburg's research, is to temper elegance with realism.

John, however, envisioned Colonial Williamsburg as an architectural restoration, not social history. His investment, modest in the beginning, would ultimately grow to $66 million, buying the skill and imagination of the most gifted architects, engineers, archaeologists, and scholars. The historic boundary was finally established at 173 acres, including ninety acres of gardens and greens. Original eighteenth-century sites were acquired and their buildings carefully returned to their colonial appearance. For the descendants of colonial families who still occupied their historic homes, a life-tenure plan was devised, whereby the houses would be sold to the Colonial Williamsburg Foundation and restored, but the occupants would be offered life tenure without rent, taxes, or insurance.

By the year 1937 the Wren Building had been restored, the Raleigh Tavern rebuilt, and the two most ambitious undertakings —the rebuilding of the Capitol and the Governor's Palace—completed. Merchant and craft shops had been resurrected. The Ludwell-Paradise House, one of the town's largest, housed a loan exhibit of Abby's folk art, and the Public Gaol was completed. John gave his personal attention to every problem, as Williamsburg continued to bring him deep and sustained satisfaction.

No one knew this better than Abby. She was his daily consultant, the only one, not excluding his closest advisers, who knew what his concerns were and how to sort them out. But such loyalty did not preclude her own imagination being fired. There were many elements in the Williamsburg world to challenge her creative impulse and touch her humanitarian instinct. And this during the decade of the 1930s when she was founding and guiding the museum, overseeing the operation of the Dodge Hotel, building her collection of modern and folk art, and welcoming her children's newly formed families. A period when she had not only John's traditional anxiety and exhaustion to deal with, but her own personal conflicts as well.

As the technicians swarmed over old Williamsburg, as buildings that had long ago turned to dust slowly reappeared, as shabby landmarks were restored to eighteenth-century dignity, the question of furnishings had to be raised. It was not enough to reconstruct *exteriors*, interiors had to be brought to life. It was at that point that Abby stepped out from behind the scenes. Since the earliest days of Kykuit she had been intimately involved in the decoration of houses. She had the taste, the ingenuity, the instinct for achieving artistry without resorting to pretension. John's letters of the period confirm their partnership. Regarding the Governor's Palace, he wrote to Kenneth Chorley, his chief deputy in the restoration, that "as to Item I, the pair of Van Dyck Portraits, $1,800, both Mrs. Rockefeller and I would like to see them and where they could be hung to advantage before reaching a conclusion."[10]

To the presiding architect, William Perry: "In regard to the furniture in Boston most of which Mrs. Rockefeller and I saw on

Saturday last . . . Mrs. Rockefeller heartily concurs. . . . The two mirrors, one red lacquer, the other walnut . . . Mrs. Rockefeller and I did not feel interested to inquire."[11] And to Perry again, "In my father's house there [is] . . . a four-poster rosewood bed which it has occurred to Mrs. Rockefeller and me might be useful in one of the bedrooms of the Governor's Palace."[12]

There was no mystery where talent for interior decoration resided. Ed Kendrew tells how during World War II, John shipped some furniture down from various Rockefeller attics to furnish one of the cottages as a guest house. Abby was appalled. She knew how outmoded all the stuff was. John smiled sheepishly. "I don't think you and I will get any prizes for this," he confessed to Kendrew.[13]

On June 22, 1931, Abby had written Frances Paine some of her ideas. "Just a word further about the things that you will look for on your trip to Mexico. As I explained to you, I am very much interested in getting early American things for Williamsburg, and particularly things that may have come from the West Indies or Mexico, otherwise colonial. I would be glad if you could find any mirrors or water colors, portraits or tinsel pictures or paintings on velvet or any little porcelain or pottery figures, or Lowestoft, or furniture if it is unusual. I am quite intrigued with the idea of bringing back to Williamsburg the same sort of thing that was originally carried there by ships."[14] Paine did locate a superb antique table, but the Mexican government would not give permission for its exportation, believing it to be a museum piece and wishing to retain it.

Three weeks later she wrote to Edith Halpert to explain how the restoration operated and what the future possibilities were for her and Edith's involvement. The person most interested in what she and Edith cared about would be the consulting decorator, Susan Higginson Nash:

> I am especially glad to know that you are going to Williamsburg. If we do have a house there, we will have a place called Bassett Hall. It was partly burned last year and certain modern restoration has been made. . . . The main part of the building . . . would remain

the same. There are two lovely downstairs rooms and two very fine large bedrooms upstairs. Then we would add a dining room, etc. It would be a large undertaking to tell you where I think things would go, as you will see when you get there, but the next thing to be opened and used is the Raleigh Tavern. . . .

In regard to furniture, of course there is a committee of all the great experts of early American furniture in charge of the purchasing of furniture for the Palace and the old House of Burgesses which are to be made into museums. If you come across anything extraordinarily fine, I could . . . bring it to the attention of the committee unless it is something that it would be attractive for us to put into Bassett Hall, which, if we take we will furnish ourselves. But as for myself, I am interested only in furniture that has beauty and charm. The historical side of it doesn't appeal to me as much. If I have got to live with a thing, I would like to have it good-looking.[15]

It was Dr. Goodwin who proposed that Abby and John have a house of their own from which they could comfortably watch the progress of the restoration. The idea to acquire Bassett Hall was first mentioned in Rockefeller office correspondence in 1927. Soon thereafter, John bought the house and the 585 acres of surrounding woodland for $30,000, although they had not yet decided to make it their home. For the present, life tenure was offered to the aging sisters who owned it, the Misses Alice and Edith Smith. After the fire struck in May 1930, consuming the roof and part of the second floor, the Smith ladies moved to an adjacent bungalow renovated for them. Now John acquiesced in Abby's wishes. Abby, who always could laugh at herself, told one of the hostesses that John said she could have Bassett Hall if she promised not to take in tourists.

Bassett Hall has a romantic history. It owes its name to Burwell Bassett, a nephew of Martha Washington, descended from five generations of Virginia leaders, himself a congressman. He acquired the property about 1800. After forty-five years, it came into the ownership of a Colonel Goodrich Durfey, whose family lived there during the Civil War. A wounded Confederate officer fell in love with Colonel Durfey's daughter; they were married at Bassett Hall in August 1862. Colonel George Armstrong Custer, serving with the Union occupying force at Williamsburg, took part in the wedding as the officer's best man. In 1869, Bassett Hall was purchased by the Smith family, who lived there until the fire.

By the summer of 1936 the renovation as proposed by Abby in her 1931 letter to Halpert was finished. The enlarged projecting wing now had a new dining room and service area. Additional bedrooms were added on the corresponding floor above. The original interior woodwork on the first floor, paneling, mantels, yellow pine flooring, and even the banister (carried out during the fire by Kenneth Chorley) were preserved. A three-car garage was built with chauffeur's quarters, as well as a boat house and a cozy teahouse. But Bassett Hall never became an imposing mansion; it was deliberately not meant to be one. Soon it became Abby's favorite house, intimate, relaxed, with the same ambience as her sitting rooms in the big houses, full of an astonishing array of objects —Turkish prayer rugs, Chinese glass paintings, American folk art. The chairs were comfortable, the colors pleasing. It was an eighteenth-century house, but she introduced nineteenth- and twentieth-century pieces, shipping furniture down from various dismantled family dwellings and arranging it in a charming, even coherent fashion.

"At last we have gotten around to the point of furnishing [Bassett Hall]. . . . I have decided to take down there the beautiful chest that you made for me and gave me as a wedding present," she wrote her brother, Stuart Aldrich. "It fits in perfectly with the Georgian and early American furniture and I shall be very proud to show it to my friends as having not only been given by you but carved by you."[16]

She consulted with Lucy regularly. "I cabled you some time ago," she wrote her on May 28, 1937, "that if you did happen to find an 18th century or early 19th century embroidered carpet for the drawing room in Williamsburg I should be delighted as the one I have down there is a little too dull for the room. . . . I am sure you can carry the color of the room in your eye, and you will remember that the curtains are to be a pale green."[17] A month later she wrote again, this time for a little rug for the front door and if possible two little square rugs for the stair landing. "I am counting

on you to supply these since you have all the measurements. . . .
I have finished all my needlework squares except one. . . . I am
wondering how Miss MacFadden has gotten along with hers."[18]
Lucy filled Abby's order at the Royal School of Needlework. And
so it was that the area rugs at Bassett Hall are as eclectic as everything else—French Aubusson, superior English handcraft, and
Abby's and Minnie MacFadden's colorful hooked squares.

Several contemporary watercolors are hung in Bassett Hall, and
Charles Sheeler is represented by two paintings that hang on the
north wall of the dining room. In 1935, Abby commissioned
Sheeler to photograph, as a kind of documentation, the Williamsburg restoration. Sheeler was as great a photographer as
painter, with each medium playing off the other for him. Abby
believed in photography as an art form, having supported Alfred
Barr's longtime desire to mount an exhibition of photographs at
MoMA on the scale of the large painting exhibitions. (In 1937
under the leadership of Beaumont Newhall, the first such exhibition was held, followed the next year by a one-man show of Walker
Evans, and finally in 1940 by a Department of Photography.)

Edith Halpert, however, who was Sheeler's dealer and close
friend, had only slight respect for photography, going so far as to
stifle his creative photographic output for a decade. It was Dorothy
Miller who suggested that Abby invite him to Williamsburg.
Edith, hearing of the commission, urged Abby to let him paint
Bassett Hall and the Governor's Palace. Sheeler spent three months
shivering in the cold, hampered in his photography by the pouring
rain. But eventually he produced 130 photographs and the two
paintings, and, as a creative artist will often do, he put the experience to work a year later in one of his major works, *Kitchen at
Williamsburg*.

For the visitors who currently walk through Bassett Hall (it is
now a house museum), the most striking feature is the quality and
variety of the folk art. It reflects Abby's refined taste as a mature
collector and includes weathervanes, chalkware, needlework pictures patiently embroidered and painted on silk by unknown
schoolgirls. The most interesting porcelain figurine, barely six
inches tall, is based on a portrait of Hannah More, the great pam-

Spring at Bassett Hall, Williamsburg, Virginia.
Courtesy of the Colonial Williamsburg Foundation.

phleteer, a "bluestocking" English reformer of the early nineteenth century. The most endearing portrait is *Child Posing with Cat*, attributed to Beardsley Limner.

Abby's landmark folk art collection—that collection which was exhibited at MoMA in 1932 and then traveled to six other museums —was first lent (1935) and then given to Colonial Williamsburg in 1939 for exhibition at the Ludwell-Paradise House. Accompanied by James Cogar, the curator of furnishings, Abby went about placing several (less than ten) undistinguished folk paintings and numerous English prints and other decorative accessories in some of the small, restored guest houses operated by the Williamsburg Inn.

"They would simply go around and decide what looked nice where," Eleanor Robinson Bradshaw recalled. "They never told anyone what they were doing or where anything was being hung."[19] When Abby decided to loan some of her collection for exhibit at the Ludwell-Paradise House in 1935, Eleanor, Abby's art secretary, assisted Holger Cahill in hunting down and locating folk art that had been dispersed around Rockefeller family houses or stored at 10 West 54th. Some things had been lent to Rockefeller family members who did not want to return them. Eleanor, who was a trained curator, participated in preparing the Ludwell-Paradise House exhibition along with Edith Halpert and an expert from the Detroit Museum, courtesy of Valentiner.

Although some art historians and critics were beginning to re-spect folk art, it was still a matter of amusement to connoisseurs. "The public was still joking about it," Eleanor recalled, "and cer-tain experts seemed to find it embarrassing."[20] With all the finicky attention to authenticity, they grumbled, how could one justify placing nineteenth-century American primitives in an eighteenth-century restoration?

One of the archivists, Helen Duprey Bullock, a specialist trained in historic preservation, expressed her indignation quite forcefully in an oral history given in 1956. "Mrs. Rockefeller had collected folk art through the influence of Holger Cahill, I think his name was. . . . a sort of left-of-center kind of character who dramatized the folk artist as the person who didn't need bourgeois education in order to be an artist; he wasn't trained and just expressed art spontaneously from his soul." Her accusation has the ring of the outraged dilettante who sees standards deteriorating. To her, "they" were transplanting a New England folk art to a Virginia setting where it did not belong; the exhibition at Ludwell-Paradise was simply a "mess, a complete uncomprehension, a lack of direc-tion, a lack of real thinking."[21]

Susan Nash, although she conceded that the Ludwell-Paradise House might not be the most appropriate setting for the collection, had empathy for Abby, sensing that she found it particularly agree-able. "I was with her quite a little when she was hanging it or directing its hanging," Ms. Nash recalled, "so I was sort of discon-certed, truthfully, when it was decided recently [in the 1950s] to take the collection out of the building. . . . I remember Mrs.

Rockefeller's great interest in hanging it herself. She loved that early folk art!"[22]

With curious travelers beginning to visit the Historic Area in greater numbers, John's experts realized that the small hostelries were inadequate for visitors who wished to linger for a night or two. One of the many feasibility studies recommended that a first-class hotel be built. By this time Abby had found a niche for her friend Mary Lindsley, the manager of the Dodge Hotel, in the Williamsburg hierarchy. Lindsley had become consultant on inns and taverns. As John turned to Abby for advice, so Abby turned to Mary.

"Mr. Rockefeller has given me the plans for the new Williamsburg Hotel to study," she had written Lindsley in 1933. "On the whole I am extremely pleased with it but the basement rather worries me because without enforced ventilation it would be a very uncomfortable place in hot weather. At the moment I am trying to find a better place for the chauffeur's dining room. I always feel that if people like chauffeurs are made comfortable, they prove to be very good advertising mediums. So far I have discovered no place that I consider better for the dining room. I will let you know if I do. . . . Mr. Rockefeller and I may go to Williamsburg . . . after the first of November. If we do, please join us there and we can go over lots of the questions on the ground that you would like to talk to me about. . . . I am so glad that we are on the same job again, although I am not officially recognized."[23]

John was loath to go into the hotel business, but Abby convinced him that it was necessary. She and Lindsley watched over every detail, with John carrying their ideas and criticisms back to the architects. "I cannot tell you how pleased I am to be associated with you once more in business," Abby wrote Mary, "although I must say that . . . it is a very one-sided affair; I seem to be getting all the benefit and you doing all the work."[24] Even after the Inn opened with sixty-one guest rooms in 1937, Abby was trying to improve the decor. "I have worked very hard over the hotel lobby and dining room," she wrote David, "which have never been quite as attractive as they should have been. I feel as if Mr. Cogar & I had really helped a little and we are planning to do more to cheer the dining room by changing the paint and by adding murals (perhaps)."[25]

Williamsburg in the 1930s was a segregated city of the old South. John, although descended from abolitionists and committed to improving the educational opportunities of blacks, was not moved to challenge the community's mores. On the contrary, one of the strictest dictums of the restoration was to respect the majority culture, and the majority culture was white. To be as unobtrusive as possible was not an easy task when you were tearing up a village, moving owners in and out of their dwellings, recreating a historical environment where a dozing, if largely contented, citizenry had resided.

Abby, whatever she personally thought of the antebellum behavior, obeyed the rules, but in her pragmatic way watched for an opening. "[On] Wednesday," she wrote David from Bassett Hall, "the Judge, the Mayor, the Doctor, and the Red Cross nurse & two other women came to dinner with Mr. Chorley and myself to discuss the Negro problem in Wmsburg. [John was still in New York.] It was most interesting. . . . They were inclined to feel that the only need of the Negroes was a new hospital. . . . I didn't . . . agree but didn't say so."[26] She had already noticed that what the Negroes needed as much as anything was a new school to replace a dilapidated one.

John, who paid attention when Abby spoke up, put his people to work. They located and paid for the site, the city council appropriated some money, and the General Education Board underwrote certain equipment. Secretary of the Interior Harold Ickes arranged a federal grant. But they were still $50,000 short. At that point Abby stepped in with her own money to complete Bruton Heights School. For the first time in the history of Williamsburg, black children had access to modern facilities.

No one phrased it more succinctly than Clara Byrd Baker, a retired teacher: "When boys and girls of minority groups have a decent high school, our commonwealth is a safer place for all the other boys and girls."[27] With the same economy of language she summed up Abby as having the courage for the great tasks of life and the patience for small ones. It wasn't only the money, she explained when she gave her oral history in 1978 at the age of ninety-two, it was the personal contact they had with her. "When she had us teachers to her house one evening for dinner, seven of us, we had a lovely dinner. When she passed, I was the one who had the eulogy for her. We really missed her because—I don't mean she was always at the school but she remembered you, not always by giving you money, though she did that too in the way of scholarships, but she'd come and encourage the children. . . . The first scholarship that went from her for our children was given to a fellow who is now a doctor in Salt Lake City. He went to Bruton Heights and got that scholarship. That helped him to go to med school."[28]

Abby visited Williamsburg often, sometimes going ahead of John, sometimes staying for a few days after he left. "Thank you for your birthday wishes," she wrote David in October. "I spent the day happily in Williamsburg. My stay there did me lots of good & Papa too altho he doesn't like to admit it for fear I want to go back too soon."[29] In another letter, "I have been delighted that during our stay here Papa has felt sufficiently rested and well for us to see something of our neighbors who are such nice people. . . . I am always glad when he does feel up to having them here at Bassett Hall."[30]

It was obvious to officials and town folk alike that John was the reserved, formal Rockefeller who coveted his privacy, Abby the one who needed people and welcomed them into her life. Perhaps that was the meaning behind her comment to David; John's fear that she would go back too soon was really the old fear that he would not have her all to himself. Williamsburg offered her an informality that evoked old Providence. Bassett Hall was not so grand that it might intimidate visitors, certainly not as grand as the surrounding plantations, nothing like the Eyrie with its hundred rooms, or Kykuit set in pristine splendor, or the new three-story Park Avenue apartment.

Abby discussed her love of needlework with the women who acted as hostesses in the various sites—many of them crocheted between tours. She arranged a handcraft exhibition in 1935 as a way for the women to earn extra money. She purchased for one of her own guest rooms at Bassett Hall a pair of handmade crocheted bedspreads. She enjoyed bridge games with Jim Cogar and some of the younger secretaries. Her closest neighbors, life tenants living in a tiny house, were the Misses Pinkie and Kitty Morecock, unmarried sisters, witty and charming and intelligent, who visited frequently. She had a freedom of movement in the village that could not be duplicated elsewhere. John, in his circumspect way, tasted a little of it. It was said that he was curious about the people who lived in the historic houses. With Abby he could stroll about the narrow streets on mild evenings, glancing surreptitiously in the windows. "I think we may get arrested as peeping Toms," he confessed shyly to Ed Kendrew.[31]

But it was Abby who knew how to make people feel at ease, people who were living so differently from her. Mildred Layne, Kenneth Chorley's associate, who often helped Abby with her correspondence, called it her "largeness of heart. She was so full of vitality, so compassionate. She needed us around her. She never took any pleasures for granted, appreciating every blossom in the garden."[32] Jean Chorley, Melinda Kendrew, Mildred—they all remembered lunch with her as such fun, when she reported the gossip from New York and they told her the news of Williamsburg.

In 1937 she lost weight—eighteen pounds, she boasted to Lucy —the year that she took long walks, danced at parties, wore her gray-white hair in a sculpted bob. Her good looks still rested with the piercing amber eyes and welcoming smile, the commanding Chapman nose and proud carriage. If she was egalitarian with people and watchful of her bank account, beautiful clothes were still her indulgence, and she was more elegant at sixty-three than she had been at twenty-five.

To read Abby's letters during this period is to follow the daily headlines and what she made of them. There was the matter of John L. Lewis and his drive to unionize the oil companies. "Thirty [twenty] years ago," she wrote, "Papa took the right road [toward industrial peace after Ludlow]. . . . I . . . pray that we may have the vision and the wisdom to stand for what is right."[1] There was the matter of Hugo Black, whose nomination to the Supreme Court in 1937 was in jeopardy because he had once belonged to the Klan. "The present excitement here is Mr. Justice Black is going to speak in his own defense over the radio tonight. I am sending you [David] an editorial from the New York Times, which seems to me most timely and appropriate."[2] Justice Black matured into one of the most progressive jurists on the Court.

George VI was crowned king of England. "I am really very glad indeed, now that it is all over, that you [Lucy] went to the Coronation. It must have been very thrilling."[3] She was not as keen on the Duke and Duchess of Windsor, having declined an invitation to dine with them at Williamsburg and at the British embassy. "One of the Vice Presidents of the S.O. of N.J. said that the W's wanted to visit Bayway," she wrote, "and could they eat in the Clubhouse or the Cottages? I was much amused by it all because I felt that they were trying so hard to be respectable & meet only the most conservative people and now in the morning paper I read that the trip has been called off which seems very wise to me. Many resented their going to Germany and no one felt that they were in a position to be very useful. . . . Their visit would only have embarrassed everyone in this country. . . . Perhaps you had better not mention our having declined those invitations. The English may still think an invitation of even ex-royalty is a command."[4]

The strident New Deal attacks on the business community offended her, but the pejorative phrase "economic royalist" brought back with unpleasant force the muckrakers' hostility toward her father and Senior. She often said that as a daughter of Nelson Aldrich she held conservative views of money and banking. And she disapproved of Roosevelt's scheme to pack the court.

But she had only quiet scorn for the ugly personal invective leveled against the president by the Republican old guard. Her friends in the administration included Harold Ickes, secretary of the interior, and his young wife, Jane. "I want to tell you how very much Harold and I enjoyed our all too brief evening with you and Mr. Rockefeller," Jane Dahlman Ickes wrote after one of their visits. "Speaking more particularly for myself, last evening shall be one of my most glowing memories. Since my early youth your name has been familiar to me. To talk with you was a great privilege. Harold joins me in the very earnest hope that we shall meet again before too long."[5]

They met again at Williamsburg. "Mrs. Rockefeller and I are delighted to know that at last you have found it possible to visit us in our little colonial house . . . and are looking forward with the greatest pleasure to welcoming you and Mrs. Ickes there for the weekend," John wrote in November.[6] Abby and Jane toured the craft houses and together selected a wedding present for the newly married Ickeses of six finger bowls. John, learning later of the decision, objected. "When I told Mr. Rockefeller," Abby wrote, "that you had finally decided on finger bowls from the Williamsburg Craft House . . . and that I had . . . sent you only six . . . he took me very severely to task and insisted that the present was a most inadequate one and that it should have been at least a dozen. To appease him and because, frankly, I myself agreed that 'his wrath was righteous' . . . I have asked the Craft House to adjust the matter."[7]

Abby supported much of the social legislation of the New Deal and watched with pride when women stepped into the limelight. "Wherever I go and wherever I see . . . young women today," she wrote the president of Wheaton College, "they give me a feeling of confidence for the future."[8] She placed herself comfortably in the moderate wing of her party (Republican), open to opinions more liberal than her own. As an example she thought Dorothy Thompson, the journalist, did extremely well as the first woman to speak at a Chamber of Commerce dinner.

As a longtime supporter of the League of Nations, she followed events in Europe with great trepidation. "I went . . . to a luncheon of the Foreign Policy Association to hear Lord Robert Cecil," she wrote. "I gathered that Lord R.C. feels that the democratic nations may have to fight to exist since the League of Nations no longer functions."[9]

Abby expressed her own views on Germany quite firmly. "I wonder if Germany ever understood the world or had a sense of proportion. . . . How tragically mistaken they seem to be. In fact most of the world is putting its strength and resources into mistaken objectives. I wonder if you [David] have read Ambassador Bullitt's speech in Paris? It had a great deal of common sense in the part I read of it."[10] William Bullitt had been a member of the peace delegation at the end of the Great War, but resigned from service when his report favoring recognition of the Soviet Union was disregarded. Under Roosevelt he had served as first ambassador to the USSR and was now ambassador to France, articulating an internationalist rather than isolationist point of view. Like most Americans, safe on their continent, however, Abby could not believe that "any man or men would risk . . . the destruction of Europe. I don't know just what Hitler is up to, altho I feel sure that whatever it is, he has the backing of Mussolini."[11]

She was outraged over the persecution of German Jews. Politically both she and John stood with minorities. Nowhere in her private correspondence is there evidence of the social anti-Semitism that pervaded the upper reaches of the Christian establishment. John did acquiesce in the discrimination against Jews at the Harbor Club in Seal Harbor, but that seemed more a matter of not wishing to "make waves" than active prejudice. Enrolling their children in the Lincoln School was in itself an avowal of racial and ethnic tolerance. Abby's pride in her ancestry reflected her affinity for Roger Williams and his belief in religious freedom rather than the snobbism of being a First Family.

Within the family circle, Abby was watchful, though from a polite distance. The lively brood she had nurtured were forming clusters of their own. Winthrop returned from the oilfields to move into his own apartment in Manhattan. The four married couples had homes both in the city and in the country, and the spouses had families to whom *they* were obligated. The grandchildren were important to her. "I do not believe that she cared more for the boys than for the girls, although this has been claimed," Eleanor Bradshaw recalled.[12] There is no denying that Abby was at home with boys. With five brothers and five sons, it was not surprising. "I love my eight little granddaughters," she wrote Lucy in 1938, "but I have to admit that a few more grandsons would be welcome." She now had four.[13]

During their childhood and into their adolescence, Babs's daughters, Abby and Marilyn, spent most weekends with Abby and John, first at Abeyton Lodge, later at Kykuit. Babs did not like the country. Dave was usually off somewhere working on a deal. So Abby invited them into her life in the most natural and loving way. As a result they learned much about her. They knew, for instance, that she always had her breakfast on a tray and they could sit on the edge of the bed beside her, while John ate in the adjoining room with his newspaper. Their rooms at Kykuit were on the fourth floor and had been decorated by Abby especially for them, with a Victorian sitting room that years later became Happy Rockefeller's study. In the evening she would invite them into her dressing room and encourage them to choose a dress for her to wear—a long tea gown perhaps—and the proper shoes and the jewelry. "It was interesting, looking back" Abby O'Neill said. "I think Grandmother was teaching us what went together. Margaret [her personal maid] would help her dress, sometimes what we chose was wrong, it was kind of a game we played. And then Grandfather would come in and approve or whatnot. She was very interested in his opinion."[14] On Sundays they drove to church in the electric car, and there was always afternoon tea, just as there had been for her own children.

Abby missed David with an intensity that was palpable. ". . . I don't allow myself to think how much I am going to miss David. At times it seems as if I couldn't bear it," she had confided to Lucy.[15] At the same time that she knew it was the right thing for him, that it would do him a great deal of good being in London, she still dreaded his being so far away that she could not snatch little visits now and again, as she had when he was in Cambridge. The reasons for their closeness are not hard to fathom. David's own personality and place in the family had something to do with it—his poise, his competence; the fact that his father eased up on him, as the youngest; the fact that Abby did not have to worry about him; the fact that they both loved good food and sailing and were together in the house after the others had grown up and left; the fact that he openly adored her and was not afraid to show it. And not least, the fact that he wasn't John, her husband. He was not easily exhausted, he did not suffer from migraines, he was not rigid and compulsive, he did not continuously test her resiliency and capacity to please.

As the beneficiary of her unqualified love and joyous approval, he became the most sensitive of the brothers to the importance of equality in a marriage. As a witness to his father's tangle of dominance and dependence and the pressures it exerted on his mother, he learned a valuable lesson—how to accommodate the needs of an independent wife who would insist upon equality.

Abby, in her periodic pulse-taking of the rest of the family, sent only the most sanguine news in a joint letter to David and Aunt Lucy in London. Nelson was a wonderful father. Tod showed an enormous amount of courage to follow him in his journeys to South America. "I have the greatest admiration for her spirit."[16] Winthrop, when he put his mind to it, had remarkably good taste. He made a most delightful and comfortable apartment for himself.

"I am beginning to feel much better about [him]. . . . He spoke extremely well at the Bayway dinner. . . . [He] has left the bank . . . to work . . . as vice-chairman of a big drive to raise money jointly for the Protestant, Jewish & Catholic charities of New York City . . . and is doing extraordinarily well."[17]

This was the year, 1938, that the *Saturday Evening Post* published a major feature entitled "The Rockefeller Boys." Fifteen lines were assigned to Babs's 1922 debut and her marriage to David Milton. Hundreds of lines examined all the details of the childhood, youth, and burgeoning careers of the five boys, details which formed the basis for many subsequent biographies. As for Babs, Abby wrote David that she had had several fine visits with her, that she found her "more and more satisfactory. She is so sensible and wise in her point of view. Devoted to Dave and the children and really intelligent. Also very good-looking, also she has good taste."[18]

This is not to suggest that Abby was oblivious to the strains in Babs's marriage and in Nelson's. It was discretion, not ignorance, that forbade her putting in letters what she strongly suspected— that the difference in temperament between Babs and Dave threatened to overwhelm their passion and that Nelson, exuberant and self-willed, relishing the power of his magnetic personality, might not find Tod's quick intelligence and loyalty a permanent substitute for sexual excitement outside their marriage. "Very little passed her by," David remarked. "It troubled her greatly, his behavior. Certainly she talked to him about it, but never to the rest of us."[19]

She did, however, make one indirect reference to the problems John 3rd was having. "[He] has been going through rather trying conferences with his father," she wrote David, "but I had rather tell you about these. I feel sorry for dear Johnny."[20] John 3rd was the conscientious oldest son who tried in every way to satisfy his father. Periods of high tension were inevitable when they worked together on projects that were not of John's choosing. The other siblings had pulled back or fought it through. Babs rebelled. Winthrop, the inept student, caused sighs of relief if he simply stayed out of trouble. Nelson had the manipulative skills to get what he wanted. And Laurance, perhaps the most complex and detached, was ruled by a sharp intellect and a droll wit. His business acumen reminded people of Senior's. His decision to drop out of Harvard Law in his third year left him free to pursue his own interests—conservation, cancer research, and aeronautics. But John 3rd bore the brunt of his father's autocratic style and had not yet learned how to deal with it.

Abby had formed her own strong bonds with her children. To the degree that their personalities allowed it, they absorbed some of her openness, her buoyancy, her ability to adapt. As the only one to penetrate their father's formidable guard, she tried to explain him to his children. But she resisted the impulse to act as referee. In the long run, they had to confront him on their own. The risk was collision, but the possible reward was genuine understanding.

Abby and John spent their first night in the new apartment at 740 Park Avenue on February 10, 1938, eighteen months after deciding to give up 10 West 54th. They solved the problem of exposed balconies by putting in an elaborate security system, installed an elevator, used the new Wendall lighting for the art, and introduced an occasional piece of new furniture. Abby's greatest challenge, as she explained to Lucy, was to find room for John's porcelains. Three-foot-tall beakers are not exactly inconspicuous. "None of us were allowed even to catalogue them," Eleanor Bradshaw explained. "Only Mr. Williams, Mr. John's valet."[21] With much tact Abby finally persuaded him that "enough is as good as a feast."[22]

"I am . . . tired of being an interior decorator," she admitted to David. (With her other children living close by, Abby wrote most often to David.) " . . . I should like to return to some of the interesting things I want to accomplish before I die. And . . . I do want to travel with Papa before we are too old to enjoy it."[23]

The "interesting things" she wanted to accomplish had mostly to do with MoMA. Bayway House, so close to her heart, was prospering. In February 1938 she deeded the property over to the recently incorporated Bayway Community Center. Winthrop pleased her by becoming a trustee, and her financial commitment continued. She had imported an eighteenth-century pine-paneled room from a dismantled manor house in Surrey to provide a museum setting for Lucy's collection of European porcelain figures. Abby's old friend Theodore Green, now a U.S. senator, wrote her in 1937 of his appreciation for the gift, housed in the museum of the Rhode Island School of Design. "It was exceedingly kind of you," Abby replied, "to write me about my small contribution. . . . As you probably know, I love Providence . . . and I am so proud of Lucy. . . . The longer I live, the more impressed I am by her taste and judgment and perception. Perhaps one should not speak with such enthusiasm of one's own family, but I have a feeling that you may share my affection and admiration for her."[24] Her folk art collection was formally accepted by Colonial Williamsburg, and James Bryant Conant, president of Harvard, acknowledged with gratitude her gift of $7,500 toward a staff salary at the Fogg Museum.

As for traveling with John, events in Europe were so ominous that he could be forgiven for hesitating. Abby, on the other hand, would not give up the idea of seeing David. When she announced that she would make a quick trip by herself, he capitulated. "We have to be home during the first week in May for the opening of the Cloister Museum," she wrote David, " . . . but we have actually taken passage for London on the 18th [of May]. . . . Papa asked me when I thought we should come home and I very boldly suggested the middle of July and he accepted the idea very calmly."[25]

Not even the Williamsburg restoration, which was evolving simultaneously, brought John quite the feeling of elemental joy as did the Cloisters. "Entranced" is not too strong a word to describe his response. Ruminating with Fosdick years later, he credited Abby as the one who in the earliest days of their courtship had opened up to him the possibility of art as a spiritual resource. Although suspicious of the modern art she championed, he had only the most profound respect for the craftsmanship of his porcelains, the anonymity of Gothic and Renaissance sculpture, and the vibrancy of his unicorn tapestries.

In 1925 he gave the Metropolitan Museum $1 million to purchase George Grey Bernard's exotic collection of architectural fragments from medieval abbeys that had been scattered for centuries across the French countryside. In 1930 the city of New York accepted his gift of fifty-six acres of wooded land that came to be known as Fort Tryon Park, agreeing to his proviso that four acres be set aside for a new museum of medieval art. And he put up $2,500,000 to pay for the entire cost of the project as well as its maintenance.

For the next eight years, as was his custom, he watched over every detail of the design, sharing the vision of James Rorimer, the inspired twenty-nine-year-old curator of the Metropolitan's Medieval Department, and the architect, Charles Collens. What finally rose on the bluffs of the Hudson was the most distinguished branch museum in America, no empty imitation of some Gothic edifice, but a frankly modern building incorporating the Barnard fragments and in perfect harmony with the medieval cloisters. In a final magnanimous gesture, John parted with his beloved unicorn tapestries in time for the opening.

Abby's network had played its part. Rorimer had been trained at Harvard by her friend Paul Sachs. Early on, John consulted William Valentiner, who wrote a cogent analysis of problems and possibilities that became part of the working papers. But in the larger sense, Abby did not really participate in the creation of the Cloisters. She and John were moving on parallel tracks (she with MoMA), and there was little intersection. At the end of the decade, both museums were flourishing. And each could be construed as reflecting the personality and character and resources of its founder-patron. The Museum of Modern Art, adventurous and unpredictable, prone to mistakes and controversy, always fighting for money, pointed to the exciting if unknown future. The Cloisters Museum, austere, impeccable, profoundly religious, was a stranger to tight budgets (in 1952 John would give $10 million for further enrichment and development) and was a comforting window on the remote past.

Abby and John sailed for England on the North German Lloyd Line S.S. *Europa* on May 18, 1938, two months after Adolf Hitler decreed Austria to be a territory of the German Reich. The German march for *Lebensraum* had begun. Sir Neville Henderson, the British ambassador, was still assuring Hitler that his majesty's government would not intervene forcefully to prevent territorial changes in Central and Eastern Europe. France under Daladier proclaimed along with Neville Chamberlain that the Czechs should prepare to make territorial concessions to the Germans.

In London, David was completing his year of study. Various noble families had invited him to their balls and great houses and introduced him to their daughters. This was the set who wished to placate Hitler at all costs, believing that if they just cosseted him he would behave. Abby did not care for their politics, but she used them to further her ambitions for MoMA. Alfred was eager to "pry loose" three important American paintings from the National Gallery for the upcoming New York World's Fair: Sargent's *Asher Wertheimer* and two works by Whistler, *Battersea Bridge* and *Miss Alexander*. "Mr.Goodyear and I do not think that there is much chance of securing these paintings by simply asking for them through the routine channels," he wrote from Paris, describing the exasperating, one-sided English rules, and suggesting that she might appeal to Ambassador Joseph Kennedy and various titled heads of museum boards. "If you could sound out any of these gentlemen it would, I am sure, influence their attitude."[26]

"My dear Alfred," she replied, "I have . . . been busy trying to help you out in regard to the two Whistlers and the Sargent. . . . I happened to sit next to Sir Godfrey Thomas at lunch and found that he was very much interested in painting, so I consulted him. He suggested that I get in touch with Lord Crawford, who was Trustee of the National Gallery and is the Chairman of the Royal Fine Arts Commission. So I got Sir William Beveridge to give me a letter of introduction to him, and wrote to him. This morning I received his reply saying that he was no longer Trustee of the National Gallery, but that he had passed my letter on to his son, Lord Balniel, who is now trustee, and from whom I might expect to hear. I have also written to Sir Ronald Lindsey, the British Ambassador in Washington, who happens to be a brother of Lord Crawford. I hope we may get some result."[27]

Her letter to Sir Ronald, excerpted in part, is a model of charm and persuasion:

I am told over here that Lord Crawford is the person who will be most able to help us . . . But I cannot help feeling that a kind word from you about the importance and respectability of the Museum would be of great assistance. As Lady Lindsay and I have often spoken of the Museum of Modern Art, I am sure that she will be able to tell you still more about its standing in the United States.

I have just spent four delightful weeks in London and I am even more impressed than I have ever been before of the importance of doing everything we can on both sides of the Atlantic to encourage the good feeling that already exists between our two countries. You may remember how very touched the people were all over the United States when the Louvre loaned Whistler's portrait of his Mother to the Modern Museum. It even so impressed our Government that they used a very bad reproduction of the portrait on one of our stamps! I believe it was the first time a woman had ever appeared on an American stamp. Of course this does not mean that Asher Wertheimer may appear on an American stamp, but it does mean that the American people would be very much pleased if the National Gallery could see its way to loan us these pictures by American artists. Please give my love to Lady Lindsay.[28]

Abby did not need to spend every moment with David to satisfy her longing to see him. "We don't want to be a nuisance," she had written.[29] And so in a hired Daimler with driver, she and John ventured out into the countryside, visiting the villages of Shrewtham, Basingstoke, Yoevil, Chovelly, and others. On June 29, after the school year, David joined them for the balance of the trip. They visited Lucy and Minnie MacFadden in Holland, where Lucy had rented a house. On July 10 they checked into the Hôtel Crillon in Paris for eight days.

After six years of futile negotiations with patronizing French bureaucrats, Conger Goodyear had succeeded in arranging for MoMA to present the exhibition Trois Siècles d'art aux États-Unis at the Musée du Jeu de Paume, an adjunct of the Louvre. The exhibition opened on May 24 with much pomp and a series of formal luncheons, but mostly dismissive glances from the French critics. According to Marga Barr's chronicle, the attendance was meager, with the chief attractions being the films and the architectural galleries. The picture that met with the most favor was Grant Wood's *Daughters of Revolution*, because, according to Marga, the middle-aged schoolteachers in the painting were recognizable as tourist types to the French. Marga had nothing but admiration for Goodyear's perseverance. "[He] should have been awarded the Légion d'Honneur."[30] In a footnote to her chronicle she later wrote that only those who went through the humiliation of that event could appreciate Alfred's joy when, some twenty years later, the New York School began to gain recognition in Europe. Goodyear, however, managed to enjoy himself thoroughly, strolling through the galleries in tweeds with his two Sealyhams on a leash.

Abby went to the exhibition with Alfred, who was still in Paris when she arrived. She wrote her reactions to her friend Eustache de Lorey from shipboard on July 23. She was "heart-broken" that she had missed seeing the Persian Exhibitions with him. "The next time I am in Paris," she wrote, "I am going to first see the people and the galleries that I like and secondly the dressmakers. . . . I wanted very much indeed to talk over the American Show with you. Lucy said that you had much to tell me about it. I trust that you were not too much disappointed in it. You worked so hard to bring it about, we are all very grateful to you. I was well-satisfied with everything except the pictures. I feel that the choice was not entirely happy. When you come to New York next winter may we talk it all over? I feel that we have all learned from this experience. When I say 'we' I mean we of the Museum of Modern Art."[31]

———••⋙≈⋘••———

*A*bby formed a committee of five to organize the celebration of the opening of MoMA's new building. During the next year, letters followed her to Europe, to Maine, to Williamsburg, and to Sea Island, Georgia. Tom Mabry, Alfred, Conger Goodyear, Nelson—they all solicited her opinion on every aspect of the momentous event. In her effort to stay behind the scenes, she contacted few people directly. But her sure hand was everywhere. Right up until opening night, hurried consultations took place. She soothed hurt feelings, she untangled knotty arguments. "Since you left," Mabry wrote her in Sea Island, "the other members of the Opening Committee and several other trustees have been reconsidering the advisability of having two opening evenings. . . . The majority . . . believe it would be a mistake. . . . Will you please wire me if you see any reason why this new, and I hope final, plan cannot be carried out."[1] On March 22, 1939, he wrote to her friend Robert Hutchins, president of the University of Chicago. "Mrs. Rockefeller has asked me to write you further about the broadcast on the evening of May 10 when the Museum of Modern Art will open its new building. . . . She has asked me to apologize for not writing herself, but thinks I can give you a more detailed description of our plan."[2]

Conger Goodyear was unsettled at the prospect of giving up the presidency after ten years, especially when his successor was the very young Nelson Rockefeller. He hinted at his discomfort in a handwritten letter to Abby at Bassett Hall. "Sometimes of late I have felt that in little things a certain tension [presumably between him and Nelson] had appeared where none had been before—but yesterday Nelson came in to see me and my slight gloom is no more." He emphasized—perhaps too insistently—that future prospects were good, but concluded with emotional words that did not come easily to him. "Someday I hope to be able to say what I feel about you." The emphasis is his.[3]

Alfred, too, was uneasy about Nelson, much as he liked him. They were friends and thoroughly enjoyed each other. There came a time, later, when Alfred believed Nelson to be one of the best presidents the museum ever had, but that was *much* later. Only three days before the opening he wrote a confidential letter to Paul Sachs, who would be one of the speakers at the trustees' dinner. "It is perhaps unwise and unfair to anticipate difficulties before they arise, but I am afraid that our incoming president may be under the influence of high-pressure publicity and radio people who are more concerned with pleasing him than with understanding the ultimate welfare of the Museum. . . . Do not think that I am over-worried or unmindful of the extremely good luck we have run into in having our new building completed. . . . our Board is just about the most enlightened and understanding group of Museum trustees in the country, but we must watch carefully to guard them and ourselves against both the subtle and obvious pressures which I hinted above [mediocrity and the danger of timidity]."[4]

Abby returned from Bassett Hall just in time to cohost, with Goodyear, the trustees' dinner on the sixth floor of the new building. She wore a deep red chiffon gown by Lanvin. "You know," Marga wrote, "he cuts everything on the bias. She [Abby] looked magnificent." Alexander Calder designed the silver table candelabras that looped their way among the greenery and the lilies. Goodyear, forgetting his pique for the moment, reminisced with affection and humor, praising trustees and staff, recalling with rare impishness the dignified gray suit, "my Rockefeller suit," that he had originally worn when the adamantine ladies invited him to lunch. He tipped his hat to one spouse. "In the early days of ten years ago," he said, "I sometimes felt almost furtive when I went to 10 West 54th Street. Modern art was strictly confined to the top floor. But while Mr. Rockefeller came to scoff, I think in some degree at least he has remained to praise. Without his cooperation and generosity certainly this building could not be." But he reserved his moving tributes for the two people who deserved it the most—Alfred Barr and Abby. "It is useless for me to attempt to tell you what Alfred has done for us. I need only say, look about you." As for Abby, it was her "influence and example, her counsel and guidance, her determination and courage" that was the constant inspiration.[5]

Nelson Rockefeller followed. Explaining with a straight face that his mother opposed any more speeches, he read a telegram from Stephen Clark, who would become the first chairman of the board, containing special thanks to Conger Goodyear for his tenure. Then Nelson presented Conger with a trompe l'oeil painting by William M. Harnett, *Playbill and Dollar Bill*, after which the guests adjourned to view the building and the exhibition, Art in Our Time. There was some unease about the appropriateness of the gift. Nelson had bought it from Edith Halpert, who, on April 29 at the Downtown Gallery, had mounted a one-man Harnett show, "A is nervous about Goodyear's reactions: perhaps he would like to have been begged to stay on," Marga wrote. "As a man of considerable museum experience, he surely must not like passing on the torch to a young man of thirty. But the worst of it is the gift. How appropriate is it to pay off such a distinguished collector with a trompe l'oeil dollar bill. The expression 'dollar-a-year man' is current, but still, the choice of this gift as compensation for ten years of intense work and dedication is not wise, especially in view of Goodyear's touchiness."[6]

Abby, never one to fret about wearing a gown twice, made her appearance at the official opening on May 10 in the same Lanvin dress, which was "marvelous," according to Dorothy Miller, who still remembered it thirty-seven years later.[7] It was a brief appearance. John hated crowds. Forty dinner parties preceded the formalities. Abby's guest list, recorded by Cholly Knickerbocker, the society scribe, in the "Mr. and Mrs." style of the era, was a nice mixture of family (Harriet and Winthrop Aldrich, Tod and Nelson), New York politics (Mr. and Mrs. Grover Whelan), foundations (Fosdick of the Rockefeller and Keppel of the Carnegie), and banking (Thomas Lamont, the J. P. Morgan partner, and Mrs. Lamont). Finally, the loyal supporters of MoMA: Mr. and Mrs. Edsel Ford and the Ernest Kanslers (Josephine Kansler was Mrs. Ford's sister), and the Guggenheims. Simon Guggenheim of American Smelting and Refining had sat in the U.S. Senate with Nelson Aldrich. His wife, Olga Hirsch Guggenheim, was a particular favorite of Abby's; "seems quite shy," she wrote David, "has a great deal of ability . . . and is wise and intelligent."[8] Olga Guggenheim had provided Alfred with the funds to acquire Picasso's *Girl Before a Mirror*.

Abby's committee, Monroe Wheeler's committee, and the indefatigable staff parceled out the celebrities so that every party glittered. Nearly seven thousand fashionable and influential people from around the nation and from across foreign borders made their appearance, including Sir Kenneth Clark, Anne Morrow Lindbergh, Lillian Gish, Salvador Dalí, Ruth Vanderbilt Twombley, Katherine Anne Porter, and the historian of MoMA himself, Russell Lynes. "Nobody, of course, could see anything," Lynes wrote, "but that was not the point of a vernissage; it wasn't even to see other people that most of them came, it was to be seen."[9]

When not gazing at each other, they rode up and down the elevators, strolled through the floodlit embryonic garden, where Abby's house had once stood, and commented upon the building, a severely functional expression of the new International Style. It was constructed of reinforced steel and concrete, its facades a graceful design in plate glass, aluminum, and a new translucent material known as Thermolux, a substitute for the Georgia white marble originally specified. Whatever the merits of the architecture—it was scorned by some, lauded by others—the needs of the young institution were admirably served. Encompassing over a million cubic feet, built at a cost of a dollar a foot, it provided three floors of gallery space, auditorium, staff offices, shipping rooms, projection

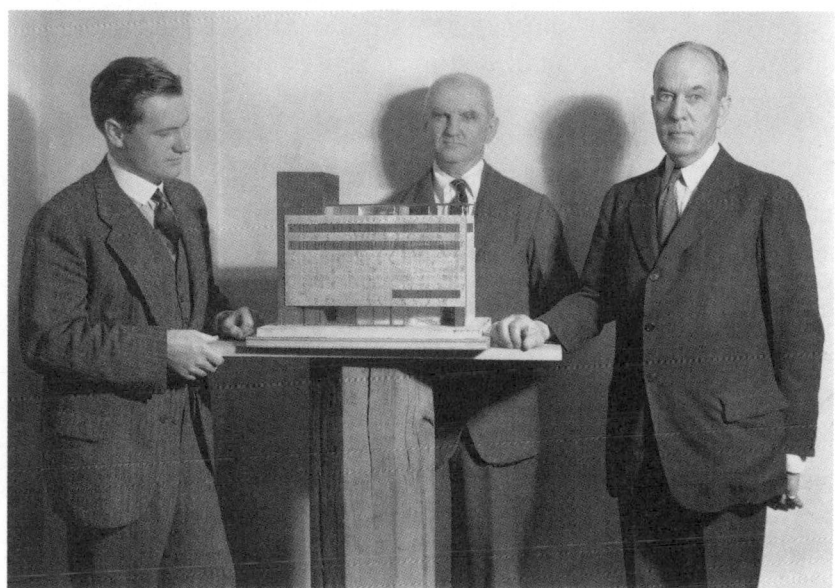

The Museum of Modern Art Building Committee: Nelson A. Rockefeller, A. Conger Goodyear, and Stephen C. Clark, with model of proposed museum building (1939).
Courtesy the Photographic Archives of the Museum of Modern Art, New York.

rooms and storage for the film library, and private lounge and meeting areas for members.

But it was impossible, in such a crowd, to do justice to such an awesome exhibition. Art in Our Time was conceived by Alfred, the educator, as not simply another view of modern art, but an outline of the museum's entire curriculum—oil paintings, water-colors, prints, sculpture, industrial art, photography, architecture, and films. Stephen Clark lent his Winslow Homer, Jock Whitney a Renoir, and Calder's brand-new mobile hung on the stair landing.

The radio broadcast went off exactly as planned. Edsel Ford spoke, also Walt Disney and Robert Hutchins, and at 10:45 P.M. from the White House, Franklin Roosevelt came on the air with eloquent words on how the standards of American taste were being raised by the traveling exhibitions of MoMA. Marga's fears about Conger Goodyear's sensitivities, however, were unhappily correct. When the broadcast did not pay tribute to his considerable accomplishments, his feelings were quite simply hurt. Nelson tried to placate him, but his interest in the museum gradually declined. His great collection found its permanent home, not at MoMA as Barr had a right to hope, but in the Albright-Knox Gallery in Buffalo, whose trustees had once rejected both it and its owner.

Abby understood better than anyone, even Alfred himself, how hard the young people had worked to make the great event a success. She identified with them in the same way that she did with her own domestic staff. "I have talked to no one who worked with her or for her," Lynes wrote, "and I have talked to a great many, who does not speak of her with delight. . . ."[10] Only days after the opening each member received a letter which thanked him or her for the lighting, the arrangement of the galleries, the decorations, the perfection of the workmanship. Tucked into each envelope was a check from MoMA for a month's salary. "Like a shot in the arm," recalled one of the staff people. "We couldn't believe it." But everyone knew whose idea it was. In the ten years of the museum's life thus far, only Abby regularly opened her purse for the staff. Wheeler confirms that in this instance she personally solicited Stephen Clark to contribute, too. "He looked sour," Wheeler said, "but he had to agree."[11]

Six months after the opening celebration, the second of the museum's founders, Mary Sullivan, died at the age of sixty. When her personal collection was auctioned at the Parke-Bernet Gallery, Abby bought *Window at Vers* by André Derain and a limestone *Head* by Amadeo Modigliani. She presented both works to the museum in memory of her friend.

Within the museum's inner circle it was apparent that Abby was easing out of a leadership role. Nelson was her man, and she was prepared to give him all the space he needed. "Mrs. R. consciously diminishes her involvement so as not to interfere with her son's newly acquired position. A. sees her less often," Marga wrote.[12] What they could not know for certain, although they had their suspicions, was how eager John was for her to give up MoMA altogether. "My father deeply resented her involvement," David declared. "The reason she backed off in 1939 was because of his pressure. It was a world that was uncongenial to him and different from his. She was able to shield him from the art she bought that was offensive to him. With the museum itself, however, her organizing responsibilities were major, she had to see a lot of people, spend a lot of time on the telephone and at meetings, all of which took her attention away from him. We children, who had been his competition, were on our own now—presumably our needs were no longer a threat to him. But here was the museum, more complex than ever, demanding her energy, and it rankled."[13]

Peggy McGrath Rockefeller, who tried to be even-handed, saw John as "terribly shy, terribly anxious, terribly insecure. I would not wish to be critical of him," she cautioned, "for he was a remarkable person. Think of all the magnificent things he did all over America and Europe, the breadth of his thinking. But his need for her seemed almost primitive and uncontrollable. The museum was alien to him and he resented the time she put into it, but he could not say so, not in so many words, because he knew it was wrong to feel that way. After all, she had a right to do what she wished." She paused to select her words carefully. Then she continued, "She loved him, in spite of all the restraints placed upon her. She understood him very well. She really was extraordinary. We all —her daughters-in-law—adored her. Any one of us would have dropped everything if she called up and asked us to visit with her."[14]

David, in musing over conditions at the museum after Abby backed away, believes that it would have been much better if his father had permitted her to continue to exert leadership. "Turning it over to Nelson in 1939 did not work. Mother was strong; intellectually she saw what Alfred's problems were, but she had the tact and the sensitivity that Nelson lacked. And Nelson went off to Washington a year later, leaving Stephen Clark as chairman of the board, in full charge. [The office of president was dropped from the masthead.] There is no doubt that she got on with the young, temperamental staff people better than Nelson, and certainly better than Clark, who admitted as much."[15]

While the situation did not exactly "fester" during Nelson's watch, a mini-squall erupted in July, while Alfred and Marga were in Europe assembling the great Picasso show, Forty Years of His

Art, scheduled to open in November. Alfred had been working on it since 1931; it was only when his friend Daniel Catton Rich, of the Art Institute of Chicago, persuaded his trustees to cofinance the exhibition that it moved ahead.

Nelson, as Alfred fearfully predicted, had called in his efficiency experts to see what could be done about putting the museum on a businesslike basis. Considering that the yearly deficit was $300,000 out of a budget of $500,000, Nelson cannot be blamed for trying to do something. Apparently, however, what his experts recommended was a more efficient use of personnel. Frances Collins, a friend of Alfred's since Vassar, who had produced some of MoMA's most admired catalogues, was summarily discharged. Her outraged friends on the staff should not have been surprised. She had circulated a mock invitation to the Opening that spoofed the trustees ("oil that glitters is not gold"—"Museum of Standard Oil" —"Better dresses—5th floor"). "You've got to remember," she later acknowledged, "that I was extremely young and terribly snooty. . . . I wrote this abominably impudent invitation! . . . Nelson [upon seeing it] suggested to Mr. Mabry that my services should be dispensed with. . . ."16 Monroe Wheeler stepped into her position as director of publications. He was a good choice. He was a designer of originality and style and, perhaps as important for the future of the museum, he had the diplomatic skills to navigate safely between staff and trustees.

Tom Mabry's dismissal was another matter entirely. Mabry had been brought into the museum four years before by Lincoln Kirstein expressly to relieve Alfred of administrative duties. It seemed to make sense. Alfred trusted him, and Tom saw the problems clearly. As far back as 1937, he had analyzed Alfred's way of operating, what needed to be changed, etc. "I am confident," he had written, "that I can straighten this out with him if the cards are once put on the table."17

What happened to the "cards" is not clear. Abby had agreed with Mabry that Alfred should become curator of painting and sculpture, and Alfred seemed interested. (By 1950 something similar would come to pass, to the benefit of MoMA, but not before a decade of dissension.) Months went by, everyone was preoccupied with urgent matters, and Mabry never got anyone's attention long enough to move ahead.

It was frightening to Alfred's loyalists that such firings could take place in his absence. They cabled him the news. Marga wrote that "Nelson Rockefeller has bypassed A's authority and has played havoc with its central nervous system . . . the loss of two essential members of the staff leaves A. breathless."[18] Alfred cabled Abby in Seal Harbor:

> Profoundly shocked by purge. Staff moral [sic] seriously under-mined during past month by insecurity and even more by loss of faith in capacity to maintain standards and ideals. No word from Nelson. Do you want me to stay. Need your personal advice and support.[19]

Abby replied:

> Executive Committee unanimously voted drastic reduction of budget which necessitates reorganization of museum work. This was done after much study and serious consideration. Personally feel that you have no reason for anxiety. Think first step has been taken towards smoothly running, efficient, harmonious institution in every way better for you. Affectionate greetings.[20]

Abby acknowledged privately that Alfred had good reason to feel anxious. She hinted to both Clark and Nelson that for him to learn of the events while in Europe with no forewarning was a clear violation of his position. Clark conceded as much, though he blamed the misunderstanding on malicious staff people. Nelson, who engineered the coup, tried to finesse the situation by assuring Alfred that it was really to protect him that the disagreeable steps were taken in his absence. "We are counting on you as before," he wrote. "No one appreciates more than I what your integrity, taste and leadership mean to the Museum."[21]

In removing herself from the center of the museum's administra-tive life, Abby effectively met John's most vehement objections.

She ended the schedule of luncheons and late-afternoon meetings that had regularly taken place in her seventh-floor gallery, which of course no longer existed. With the move to Park Avenue it had been dismantled along with the entire building, removing the unwelcome reminder that what had meant so much to her was anathema to John. She and Anna Kelly cut back on the number of letters that went forth to the various players, who in turn wrote less frequently to her. How much of the daily intrigue reached her is not clear. Nelson moved to Washington, Goodyear drifted away, and Alfred was not predisposed to gossip, at least not with Abby. With Clark clearly in the leadership role, Abby in 1941 accepted the position of first vice-chairman, becoming a discreet major consultant, as it were.

Giving up close supervision of the institution in no way reduced her long-range financial and artistic commitment. In December 1937, Nelson, with her approval, had given two thousand shares of the capital stock of the Pantepec Oil Company of Venezuela (fair market value of $20,000) to establish the Mrs. John D. Rockefeller, Jr., Purchase Fund. Abby herself gave $20,000 in 1938 and $30,000 in 1939. For MoMA's future this was an event of great significance. Alfred wrote to Nelson:

> We have so long been handicapped by inadequate purchasing money that this gift is doubly welcome. . . . It is not merely a matter of adding to the permanent collection, which of course we should do, but also a matter . . . of our borrowing credit. . . . We ordinarily pay no rental fees to artists or dealers, who often lend works to us for a very long time. We like to believe that this adds to the artists' reputation, but the artist has to live on more than a reputation, so it is really essential that we buy from time to time so that we may continue to borrow. Already in the past we have suffered several important disappointments in borrowing because, as the dealers put it, they had far greater chance of selling if they did _not_ lend to Museum.
>
> I am particularly pleased that you should give the fund in your mother's name.[22]

On October 25, 1938, the museum exhibited the first nine pieces Alfred selected from Abby's fund—paintings by Blumenschein,

Cikovsky, Gallatin, Kuniyoshi, MacIver, and Sterne; sculpture by Flannagan, Harkavy, and Nakian. Abby placed no restrictions on his flexibility, and he invited her into the process, carefully explaining the logic behind each of his choices. When he solicited her ideas for the $30,000, she suggested that $10,000 be spent on American art where it would do the most good for the artists and for the reputation of the museum, and the balance spent for works of primary importance. "I can't tell you how happy I am about this fund," Alfred wrote, "for we seem to be faced with a national artists' emergency somewhat similar to the dark days of 1933."[23] Holger Cahill, now director of the Federal Art Project, offered to locate paintings by first-rate artists who had been laid off from federal subsidy.

Other benefactions followed as a direct result of Abby's move. Samuel Lewisohn sent a check to Nelson for $1,000 and a second one for $1,500, "as a contribution towards the Purchase Fund which you and your mother started for providing new acquisitions for the Museum of Modern Art."[24] Olga Guggenheim's long and happy association with MoMA continued with the $25,000 check she sent, unsolicited, at this juncture. ". . . I can't tell you how much your generous check to the Purchasing Fund means to all of us," Abby wrote Mrs. Guggenheim, "and what a tremendous help it is at this particular time . . . You already know from Mr. Barr of the use which has been made of these funds. This great masterpiece by Rousseau [*Sleeping Gypsy*] will stand in the Museum of Modern Art as a living testimony of your generosity."[25]

The sums that Nelson's efficiency experts managed to shave off administrative costs were paltry compared to the larger money troubles that confronted the trustees. Unlike New York museums on city property such as the Metropolitan, MoMA could expect no local government subsidy. With no endowment fund to speak of, the trustees had to reach into their pockets each year to make up the deficit. "You can figure out what it costs to be a trustee!" David McAlpin, a Rockefeller cousin, had written when he was elected to the board.[26] Abby seemed to have the deepest pockets after John set up her "1934 trust." The fact that she directed most of her income to an institution which gave him many unhappy moments did not preclude him from continuing to bear the cost of their personal expenses. His own philanthropic instincts ran too deep for such revenge. In addition to her original contribution of $250,000 to the building fund, she continued to support the Film Library, the scholarship fund, and a catchall category called Miscellaneous, and was faithful to her original 1929 annual membership fee of $10,000.

But the building still carried a mortgage of $500,000. One July afternoon in 1941, Abby invited Stephen Clark for tea to discuss with him how she might provide for the museum in her will. "Since I had tea with you the other afternoon," Clark wrote, "I have been giving further thought to the matter of your proposed gift. . . . It seems to me that it would be better to pay off the mortgage on the building than to leave a similar amount . . . in your will. My principal reason for feeling that way is that notwithstanding prevailing New Deal ideas of economics, I have a horror of being in debt. Moreover, I am inclined to think that such a gift from you might . . . stimulate one or two of the other trustees to emulate your generosity."[27]

In less than a month Abby made her proposal. She would pay off half the debt, provided the balance was raised from other sources before September 1, 1942. With such a signed pledge in hand, Clark was able to secure the balance from John Hay Whitney, his sister Joan Whitney Payson, Cornelius Bliss, and others, himself included. One and a half years later, on January 14, 1943, he would write the following to Abby:

> A formal note of thanks from me, as Chairman of the Board of the Museum, to you, its most interested and generous supporter, can never express the Museum's gratitude for all that you have done. I am writing, however, to let you know that the condition under which you agreed to pay the balance due on your pledge of October 30, 1941, has been met, and subscriptions and pledges totaling $255,000 have been received from other contributing sources towards the retirement of the indebtedness of the building of the Museum of Modern Art. . . . You understand, I know, that I simply haven't the words to tell you what your interest and help means.[28]

(Abby's accounts confirm that she fulfilled her pledge in two installments—$127,500 in 1942 and $127,500 in 1943.)

The trustees were dazzled by Abby's financial largess. Alfred, while he never undervalued the cash, could be forgiven if he became most eloquent when thanking her for her gifts of art, the latest being her sculpture collection. "I wonder if you or the other trustees realize that with this gift our collection of modern sculpture is probably the finest and most complete in the world. [Fair market value in 1940, at time of gift, $33,528.] I am going to try to find a way to make this known."[29] He did just that, placing Abby's sculptures on public view in the third-floor galleries. Among the thirty-six pieces, he singled out *Torso* in cast stone by Wilhelm Lehmbruch, *Head* by Modigliani, and *Seated Youth* in bronze by Charles Despiau as the most important. Three months later, in the spring of 1940, she wrote him that she was now ready to offer most of the drawings and watercolors still in her private collection. (Fair market value $14,927.) These included the works of Sheeler, Blume, Orozco, Picasso, Modigliani, and Matisse. Finally, she communicated her intention to turn over her entire print collection (fair market value $52,209)—approximately 1,630 pieces—which would immediately establish MoMA as the repository of the greatest collection of twentieth-century prints, both European and American, in the world.

During the years that she was buying prints, Abby was doubtful whether Alfred valued them to the degree that she did. He tried to reassure her. "We have often spoken about the Print Department, and at times I have felt that you did not quite understand my feeling, which may have seemed to you unenthusiastic," he wrote on August 23, 1938. "Actually I am very much interested in building up the Print Department of the Museum, especially after our experience of two years ago with the Metropolitan, at which time . . . Mr. Ivins refused to lend a group of prints which I understood he had promised to let us have. The Metropolitan Print Room is run as a kind of sacrosanct reference library, where an obscure print will be kept on the chance that a student may wish to look at it. . . . I want to use our Print Room not as a reference library but as a source for exhibitions both here and in other museums so that the maximum use can be made of the prints, which will stand traveling far better than oil paintings."[30]

He was now ready to take such steps as were necessary to create a print department—proper storage, cataloguing, the appointment of a curator. But the year was 1940, and except for storage, nothing could be done. The world was at war.

PART FIVE

War and Peace, Celebration and Sorrow

CHAPTER 31

S hortly before five in the morning on September 1, 1939, the German Luftwaffe launched its deadly air attack on Poland. An hour later the swift armored columns of the Wehrmacht crossed the Polish frontier. Great Britain and France, with their sorry record of slaking Hitler's thirst for conquest, reluctantly declared war on Germany. The Führer gambled that the French, whose formidable army was the only force capable of relieving the pressure on the Poles, would elect to sit out the campaign behind their Maginot Line. His gamble paid off. "Peering through the battlements of our fortifications," a weary Charles de Gaulle had predicted in 1936, "we shall watch the enslavement of Europe."[1] The Poles, who fought valiantly, were doomed.

Joseph Stalin, having signed a nonaggression pact with Germany only weeks before, was now free to move. Two Soviet armies were ordered into Poland from the east. In three weeks the country was partitioned, the Poles "victims of a squalid deal worked by two despots . . . and betrayed by two allies whose leaders had been regarded as honorable men," in the words of William Manchester.[2] Polish intellectuals, professional figures, all those who might challenge Nazi authority, were executed. Time had run out for all

Eastern European Jews. Hitler's Final Solution—*Endlösung*—marked them for extermination.

During the winter and the spring both dictators maneuvered to seal the fate of the small nations in their own neighborhood. Hitler occupied Norway and Denmark. Stalin obtained strategic control of Finland and the three Baltic states. A strange quietude had settled over the western front. To Americans it came to be known as the Phony War, to Britons the Bore War—as in boring. The Allies were leaving it to Hitler to take the offensive. Finally, on May 10, 1940, he mounted a blitzkrieg of awesome mobility and power. German paratroopers landed in Belgium. Units of the Panzer Korps drove through Luxembourg into the wooded ravines of the Ardennes. Rotterdam airfield was in Nazi hands. The British Expeditionary Force marched toward Belgium, to be trapped there in a gigantic pincer movement by Rundstedt's Army Group A. All of this before nightfall.

Neville Chamberlain, more responsible than any leader in Europe for the rearming of Germany, now requested an audience with his king. In his last act as prime minister he offered his resignation. George VI knew there was only one person who could form a new government of national character—a coalition that would include the Liberal and Labour parties as well as the majority Tories: Winston Churchill. Churchill had been warning for years of Hitler's obscene ambitions. While the Tory leaders of Britain—Chamberlain and Baldwin—sought accommodation with a criminal regime, believing and hoping that it would be a buffer against Bolshevism, Churchill, who despised the Communist dictatorship as much as any conservative, called year after year for collective security, even collective security with Stalin, if that would stop Hitler.

Now, in this desperate moment in the history of Western civilization, Churchill took the reins of power. In his short statement before the House of Commons, he delivered the words that still reverberate. "I would say to the House, as I have said to those who have joined this Government: 'I have nothing to offer but blood, toil, tears, and sweat.' "[3]

In seventeen days, Luxembourg, the Netherlands, and Belgium capitulated. Between May 26 and June 3, 198,000 British troops and 140,000 Allied troops, mainly French, were evacuated by sea from Dunkirk. The German drive into France began on June 5. Paris was occupied on June 14, and on June 16, Marshal Henri Pétain, the aged hero of Verdun, sued for peace. On June 22 at Rethondes, scene of the signing of the Armistice of 1918, the new Franco-German Armistice was signed. France was divided into two zones, the northern zone under German military occupation, the southeastern zone left to French sovereignty. Göring's "Eagle Day" directive, laying the plan for a massive air attack over England, was drafted on August 2, 1940, less than three months after the invasion of the Low Countries.

In the United States, where isolationist sentiment ran high, Franklin Roosevelt had been adroit in his management of dissent. Shrewd politician that he was, he gave more attention to domestic economic problems than to foreign policy during his first administration. But like Churchill, he had long believed that Hitler was a mortal threat. After the events of 1937–1939 confirmed this, he was able to nudge the electorate into a belated recognition of creeping dangers. When Hitler invaded Poland, he called Congress into special session to repeal the Neutrality Act. In June 1940 he declared that the United States would extend to the opponents of force the material resources of this nation. The Burke-Wadsworth Act established the first peacetime draft in America's history. In September he authorized by executive order the transfer of fifty old destroyers to the British in exchange for Atlantic bases. And finally, after safely being elected to a third term, he called for legislation to make such lend-lease official. This was the bill, signed on March 11, 1941, that laid the foundation for the United States as an arsenal of democracy.

"We personally," Abby wrote a friend directly after the signing, "are among those who are thankful for the passing of the 'lend-lease' bill, and glad that we are able now to give full aid to Great Britain. I hope that very soon our country will fully realize the seriousness of the situation in Europe, and that we may have total production to offset Hitler's total destruction."[4] All during the pacifist 1920s and early 1930s, Abby's revulsion of war had led her to support efforts for world peace, such as the League of Nations and the Conferences on the Cause and Cure of War. But finally Hitler's vicious anti-Semitism, his demagoguery, his dangerous strutting, and above all his ruthless conquest of small nations persuaded her that even the risk of war was preferable to fascist domination. She was repelled by the shrill cries of the America Firsters, and withheld support from Republicans who proclaimed their isolationism. John represented her point of view when he wrote in a letter to the *New York Times* of April 28, 1941, that he would "rather die fighting the brutal, barbarous, inhuman force represented by Hitlerism than live in a world which is dominated by that force."[5]

During the months before Pearl Harbor the aura of war, if not the actuality, seeped into daily life. The women in the family were knitting—Tod, Mary French, Babs, and Abby herself. "Your knitting bag was a perfect godsend," she wrote Mrs. Evans in Daytona. "The only bag I seemed to have for knitting was the one I used in the last war, and it doesn't look very well anymore." She bought hundreds of pounds of wool wholesale, which she distributed to various friends for socks, helmets, sweaters, and blankets. She herself preferred squares. "I am starting on some grey and blue nine inch squares which I shall make into an . . . afghan to be used, I hope, by the R.A.F. when they are in the hospital."[6]

This was the winter of the Blitz—the air bombardment that would test the resolve of Great Britain. All of Roosevelt's moves were made with an eye to saving England. Churchill himself was the son of an American mother. Abby, even if she played no favorites among ethnic peoples, was herself the descendant of original settlers—English settlers—and it was family, in the metaphorical sense, who were in terrible trouble. Lucy brought over Jill and John Watson, children of friends from Scotland, to live with her for the duration. Everybody had a hand in watching over them. They visited the Milton children in Tarrytown and Elsie Aldrich Campbell in Cambridge, and spent the summer of 1941 at the Eyrie. "They have riding lessons three mornings a week," Minnie MacFadden reported to their parents in England. "Then two mornings a week they have swimming lessons. . . . On the estate there is what is called a playhouse which has tennis courts, bowling alleys, a kitchen and a recreation hall, all of which the children have the freedom of. Miss Aldrich rented a piano so that Jill could continue her practicing. . . . Also they are helping wait on table. . . . Both children have a list of books to read. . . . Mrs. Rockefeller is right next door, and . . . the Nelson Rockefellers, whom the children see constantly."[7]

Abby was liberal with hardheaded advice. "Please don't forget that you are going to have Jill and John with you for a long time," she wrote Lucy. "Children are very adaptable and soon get over homesickness. . . . Of course, you know all this as well as I do but you are so kindhearted that you let your sympathies get the better of your judgment."[8] She gave liberally to war-related organizations, such as the USO, but did not forget favorite causes that were still not popular with mainstream upper-crust philanthropists—Planned Parenthood, the Women's Trade Union League, the United Jewish Appeal, the World Center for Women's Archives, the Art Workers Club for Women, Bennington College. She sent money to families overseas as well, and the letters that came back told her more about the reality of the war than anything she could read in the newspaper or hear over the radio.

"Dear Abby," her friend Helen Connal-Rowan wrote from Stirling, in Scotland. "I feel that you will be interested to know what I am doing with your wonderful check." Changes of clothing for people bombed out of their homes, particularly elderly women and very young children, she explained, and subsidies for desperately ill incurable patients, for whom a few shillings a week make all the difference. "I always say from 'an American friend' and this helps to cement even more the wonderful bond which I feel is growing up between these two great nations."

We are well; George is in London, but sleeping out of town for these summer months I'm thankful to say, although of course he has to take his turn for nights of fire-watching in London. He gets home occasionally "on leave." I have the house very full; rather like the "old woman's shoe"! Still have the group of Glasgow children & many relatives & friends with & without children all ages and sizes! Life is so extraordinary & yet so ordinary; the daily routine & the tremendous & tragic daily events. Mercifully we are busy from morning till night; time has no meaning & we live from day to day! . . . The Watsons are grateful beyond words for all that Lucy is doing for Jill and John. . . .

I know how much you and John will be feeling "the agony" of this war! I see Nelson's name occasionally in the papers; he seems to be playing a valuable & important part in South America. Also Winthrop's photograph "in uniform" has appeared over here.[9]

Winthrop had not waited for Pearl Harbor to go to war. Restless with New York banking and fund-raising, he enlisted in the army in January 1941 as a buck private, to become an instant celebrity. His comrades at Fort Dix did not hold that against him. He was strong and uncomplaining. The years in the oilfields had toughened him up. He seemed to welcome military discipline. On the weekends he introduced his army buddies to his friends at the Stork Club and El Morocco. As a private he was selected for noncommissioned officers' training school where he excelled as a machine gunner. Soon after he was made a sergeant, he applied and was accepted for officers' candidate school.

"There is a rumor that Nelson Rockefeller has learned to speak Spanish," Marga wrote in her chronicle in the summer of 1940. "No one quite knows why."[10] Nelson's Spanish lessons went back to his first trip to Venezuela in 1937. Having made a substantial investment in Creole Petroleum, a subsidiary of Standard Oil of New Jersey, he had traveled to the site of his investment. He was immediately fascinated by the culture and traditions of Latin America, angry that the Spanish aristocrats dismissed the Indian culture as inferior. He made friends with local intellectuals and politicians, sought the advice of President Betancourt of Venezuela and President Cárdenas of Mexico. Gradually, Standard executives began to listen to the young Rockefeller when he lectured to them on accepting some responsibility for an exploited, poverty-stricken local population.

All the while he was the tireless collector, like his mother, with his enthusiasms bounding in all directions. His collection of Mexican folk art, acquired during the many trips to Mexico, is the finest single collection in the United States, now housed in two museums —the San Antonio Museum of Art and the Mexican Museum, San Francisco.

In June 1940, Harry Hopkins, intimate adviser to the president, summoned Nelson to the White House to hear his ideas for economic aid to Latin America to counteract Nazi infiltration. In July, Nelson returned to meet Roosevelt. The fact that Rockefellers were traditional Republicans and behind-the-scenes contributors to the Republican Party at least since the turn of the century did not faze the aristocratic Democratic president. Nor did a lifetime of firm family conditioning not to meddle in politics give Nelson pause. The country at large may not have fully comprehended an America at war, but Nelson and his family did. When he mentioned his connection to Latin American oil as a possible problem, Roosevelt merely grinned his famous grin, waved his cigarette holder, and assured the thirty-two-year-old political novice that he was not worried.

On August 16, the president established by executive order the Office for Coordination of Commercial and Cultural Relations Between American Republics (later shortened to CIAA—Coordinator of Inter-American Affairs). Nelson was in charge. At first he commuted to Washington. In January, however, he resigned as president of MoMA and brought Tod and the five children to a house on Foxhall Road. What he lacked in experience Nelson made up for in energy and ideas. "He was ever ready to reach out for any . . . projects that might be lying around unattended for the moment on the theory that practically anything could be coordinated into the CIAA," Joe Alex Morris wrote, "an attitude that appalled and frequently irritated the capital's established bureaucrats."[11]

Abby, ever the watchful mother, reminded him in an early letter not to be careless with his personal belongings. "From now on I imagine that you will have many confidential papers. Probably it will be better if you do not leave them about [in your room]."[12] Gently she suggested that perhaps one of his aides could let her know the condition of his cold, and as usual wistfully wished that she could phone him more often.

Everything changed after December 7, 1941. The Japanese bombed Pearl Harbor, and the United States declared war on Japan. Three days later, Germany and Italy declared war on the United States, and Congress reciprocated unanimously. Germany and the Soviet Union were already at war, Hitler having invaded Russia in June. The battle lines now stretched across two mighty oceans, the islands of the Pacific, and the Asian mainland. The Japanese secured their eastern flank with the capture of the Philippines, Wake, Guam, and Tarawa in the Gilberts. In Southeast Asia they routed the British, Dutch, and Australian defenders, occupying Hong Kong, Thailand, Burma, Malaya, Singapore, and the oil-rich East Indies. It was a year of military disasters. The German army had reached the gates of Stalingrad, and in the deserts of North Africa Marshal Erwin Rommel's Afrika Korps was scoring dramatic victories over the British.

Immediately following the outbreak of war, John 3rd and Laurance joined Nelson at desk jobs in Washington for the duration. John, commissioned as a lieutenant in the Naval Reserve, was assigned to the Bureau of Personnel. Laurance, also a naval lieutenant, spent most of the time traveling to aircraft plants around the country to expedite production.

David had married Margaret McGrath on September 7, 1940. They were each twenty-five at the time of their marriage, and they had known each other for seven years. Peggy, the daughter of an attorney, grew up in the relaxed informality of suburban Mount Kisco. She rode and jumped horses, was an excellent sailor, and had the kind of agile curiosity that drove her to learn new skills— everything from interior design to pig farming. Her independent spirit and indomitable will made her a challenging partner for David. Her good looks added to the excitement of the relationship.

Abby, writing to them after the wedding, analyzed the bridesmaids' hats, as usual. "I loved . . . them . . . they really fitted their heads. Usually bridesmaids' hats are unbecoming to most of the bridesmaids. . . . Of course I thoroughly enjoyed the reception as I always do parties, and was very much pleased when several of the ushers kissed me as well as Peggy."[13] Winthrop stationed himself opposite her to intercede when she was tempted into too much

Margaret McGrath at the time of her engagement to
David Rockefeller, 1940.
Courtesy of the Rockefeller Archive Center.

conversation with people passing through the receiving line. He was ready with water and sherry when she needed it.

David, like Winthrop, enlisted in the army as a raw recruit, going to basic training in May 1942. Eventually he was posted to OCS (officers' candidate school) at Fort Belvoir, Virginia, and received further training in military intelligence at Camp Ritchie, Maryland.

With four sons in uniform and a fifth manning a complicated bureau in Washington, Abby followed political maneuvers and military campaigns with equal attention. She hoped that Congress would enact some kind of pay-as-you-go tax plan to finance the war. She was anxious to hear what David thought of the meetings in Casablanca between Roosevelt and Churchill. "I was deeply disappointed that Giraud and De Gaulle had not gotten together and that we have not appointed a Commander-in-Chief."[14] When Churchill addressed a joint session of Congress she asked that a copy of the speech be sent to her. "It was extremely kind of you," she wrote a friend, "to send me a copy. . . . I told Dr. Cohn, when I was in the hospital, how extraordinarily tactful and wise I thought Mr. Churchill had been. . . . I am particularly glad to be able to reread this one because it seems to me that [he] had helped to steady and unite us after the tragedy of Pearl Harbor."[15] Abby was in the hospital for investigation of a possible gall bladder problem, and chest pain.

She studied maps, ordered books on military strategy, and through the family network of officialdom managed to find out how her sons were faring. Winthrop's commanding officer wrote about the extremely good job he was doing. Nelson may have been having his troubles with Sumner Welles, under secretary of state, but while sharing a taxi one day with John in Washington, Welles had some nice things to say about Nelson, and a State Department official assured her that Nelson was acquitting himself creditably. If she was resourceful in watching over her own sons, she did not forget that other mothers worried about their sons. ". . . officers who have no way of meeting people outside the Service must be lonely,"[16] she wrote David, who was enjoying the hospitality of Standard officials. "Perhaps you can help them."

She airily dismissed all questions about her own health. Her correspondence, however, points to some problems. Her ankles had a tendency to swell, which suggests that her hypertension was not under control. The doctors wanted her to stay inside, safe from the cold New York winter. Their caution brings up the question of angina, since such chest discomfort is exacerbated by cold temperatures. ". . . I am trying to become reconciled to spending most, if not all of this [season] in the house," she wrote in February.[17] But of course she was not at all reconciled. She assured David that her hospitalization for a suspicious gall bladder attack did not show anything. Here too the picture is muddy, for stomach discomfort often masks cardiac symptoms.

•

David, an intelligence officer, received his overseas orders in September 1943. He was assigned to the Allied headquarters in Algiers. Abby with her maid, Margaret, took the train down to Washington to see him off. Her feelings and actions were quite in character. She moved unobtrusively out of the way to give Peggy and David plenty of privacy. She relished the look of her son in his uniform, and had this to say in her first letter: "I started to feel very lonely [until] Peggy returned [to tell] me how thrilling it was to see your beautiful plane start off. . . . and that you would have such interesting and pleasant companionship on the plane [he traveled with the commanding general of the unit]. . . . It made me wish more than ever that I was going with you because I am perfectly sure you are going to have a most tremendously interesting experience and that you are going to do your job very well. I wish I could be where I could see you doing it."[18]

Peggy, who had left their two small children behind in Manhattan, returned to New York with Abby. The motor trip, emotional for both women, strengthened Abby's admiration for her daughter-in-law—for her courage, her intelligence, her self-control. The relationship between them became a special one. "She really was extraordinary," Peggy said. "I came to love her more than my own mother, I think. At least in a better way, for I was less dependent on her."[19] David was happy for Peggy, but he was aware that the friendship between the two women caused tension between his parents. "I was out of the country for two and a half years, saw Peggy only once in all that time," he said. "She already had two babies—our third was born while I was overseas. The time she had with Mother meant so much to her. But my father made it quite obvious that he did not want Peggy taking up her time, at least not to the degree that she did. I don't believe it was that much, but it evidently seemed too much for him. His need for her ran that deep."[20]

Lucy, who was occupying Nelson's New York apartment in his absence, took strenuous exception to a Matisse that hung over the fireplace. "She thinks there must be something wrong with my character that I bought it," Abby wrote David.[21] Nothing would satisfy Lucy but to remove it from the wall and hang something conventional from the eighteenth century in its place. With considerable pride, Abby showed her their—her and John's—lovely new cemetery lot in Sleepy Hollow. "I think she would like to have suggested that she be buried there too." Abby acknowledged that it seemed to upset the children when they mentioned that they were designing their gravestones. "Nelson left the room when we showed him the drawing, and Peggy won't let me say a word about it, but as far as I am concerned, it interests me very much."[22]

Perhaps in an effort to save her marriage, Babs agreed to build a country house at this time that would also include a working farm, Hudson Pines, just outside the boundary of Pocantico. She enjoyed the planning and the construction and the decorating, but the farm less so, especially when the pigs got into the swimming pool, the goats ate the azaleas, and the bees swarmed through the garage and flew into the car. It was not all that popular with Abby and John either, especially John, who objected to the noise, but the Milton girls thought it was marvelous to make honey and cider and pitch hay. "My father loved farming," Abby Milton O'Neill recalled. "He knew a lot about it, even if his exuberance sometimes got him into trouble, as when he put so many heaters in the chicken house that the chickens burned to death. Independence was very important to him, and he wanted us to be independent as well. He was the one who woke us at five A.M. and we would saddle our own horses and ride off to his little cottage in the woods, where we had to cook and make beds. He really taught us how to keep house. There is very little I can't do, from plucking a chicken to milking a cow to making yogurt."[23]

She was grateful to her mother for different decisions, for making it clear to her and Marilyn that they were Miltons, not Rockefellers, and should grow up paying their own bills and balancing their own checkbooks. "She knew when it was time to move us to Long Island, where we would be less isolated than at Pocantico, even though she did not care for the Island. It was a very smart move. She really only liked the city. She may not have been good on the little things, but she was great on the big things."[24]

Babs filed suit for divorce in the summer of 1943. She arrived in Reno at three in the morning to be met at the train station by reporters eager for a story. "I'm very glad that you think I did alright with the publicity," she wrote her father. "I really felt remarkably calm and the reporters were very nice. . . . They thanked me for letting them take pictures & that's all there was to it. . . . Every day I get several crank letters. . . . most of them have been very friendly & nice, not asking for anything, just wishing me luck. . . . Winthrop telephoned yesterday from Phoenix. He thinks he will get a three day leave next week & if he does he will come to see me."[25]

"Win and my mother were very close," Abby O'Neill said. "He was very handsome—he liked women and they liked him. He introduced her to Mary Martin and other people in the theater, and she loved that. They used to sit up for hours, talking together."[26]

Winthrop did get the three-day leave and drove all night to see her and stand by her. They reminisced over old times and the demands and expectations of being who they were—Rockefellers. Babs said she personally was happy not to be carrying the name. All she ever wanted was a good home life and her own friends, and while she was happy to be generous, she was not eager to save the world. Then she described the strains in her marriage, repeating to Winnie what others in the family already realized: that Dave was sweet and kind, but addicted, not to other women—"It has nothing to do with other women," Babs said—but to gambling in investments.[27] He was addicted to traveling, always trying to put a deal together, but never staying with anything long enough to make it work. There were times when she would not see him for weeks, not knowing when he would turn up.

Abby O'Neill was fifteen at the time of the divorce. "I was totally shocked," she recalled. "I was away at boarding school. It's amazing how naive I was about their life together. My sister, who was twelve, seemed to understand more than I did, perhaps because she was still living at home. I think I was imbued with a lot of family spirit, and the idea was almost incomprehensible." She paused. "Nelson was a great help to me during that period. He was in Washington, of course, which was close to Foxcroft, where I was."

How did her grandmother react to this, the first divorce in the family? Did Babs confide in her? Did Abby offer advice? Was she surprised, worried? "I do not believe she confided in her. My mother was so very private. Of course Grandmother gave advice. She gave everyone advice. But Mother would not welcome a lot of comments. Mainly, though, Grandmother worried about us as children, what it would mean for us."[28]

John, for whom divorce was a sin, came around, once the decision was made. Again, according to Abby O'Neill, he actually became a wise counselor to Dave, saying, in effect, "You have no father; please come to me for help."[29] Keeping Dave in the family circle was more comfortable for the children than some kind of estrangement, but it could not have been easy for Babs. Her relationship with her father was still unresolved, with her craving for approval always colliding with her struggle for independence. John's embrace of her former husband left her with the sense that somehow she was at fault for not making the marriage work.

After the divorce was granted, Babs's spirits soared. She was free and happy in a way that she had not been for years. Abby wrote repeatedly how well she looked, how often she came for lunch, that she showed new interest in everything. The name of Irving Pardee came up in Babs's letters. "Last Sunday," she wrote her father on October 23, 1943, "I unthinkingly said something that while literally true I now realize must have given a false impression & I want to correct it. When you spoke of Dr. Pardee I said I hadn't been to his office since March. That is true as I am no longer his patient, but I have seen him since as a friend."[30]

Irving Hotchkiss Pardee was clinical professor of neurology at Columbia University College of Physicians and Surgeons, president of the New York Neurological Society, and a practicing neurologist. He was eleven years older than Babs, his home was in Long Island, and his own divorce would not become final until 1945. Apparently Babs met him as his patient, and as she explained to John, they were now friends. John assured her that her wanting to be so completely frank with him and to leave no chance for a misinterpretation touched him deeply. A few months later, in a note thanking him for flowers, she offered to introduce them— both Abby and John—to Irving. "In spite of the unfortunate way he has been brought to your attention, I think you would like him."[31] What could have been unfortunate? Unwelcome publicity, perhaps? Abby did meet him and wrote to a close friend that the more she saw of him the more attractive she found him.

Babs was in love. "She adored him," Abby O'Neill said.[32] They were married on October 10, 1946, and spent their honeymoon at Babs's Bermuda house. "Dear Mama and Papa," she would write from Tuckerstown. "It doesn't seem possible that we have been here almost a week, the time has passed so fast. . . . I do want to thank you both for being so perfectly wonderful about the wedding. . . . I can't begin to tell you how much it meant to Irving & me and how much we appreciate it. . . . No one could have been more considerate, thoughtful & affectionate, nor a more pleasant & happy companion than he has. It's a beginning & we both are going to try very hard to profit from our past mistakes. . . . I must stop now as there is a full moon & we are going to sit out on the porch and enjoy it."[33]

Irving Pardee died of leukemia on March 10, 1949, less than three years after Babs married him.

CHAPTER 32

We are just off for Williamsburg," Abby wrote David less than a month after he shipped out. (The documentation for these years continues to be her letters to David, who kept all of them. Winthrop's seem to have been lost. The other siblings were close by.) ". . . I can't tell you what pleasure [it will give me] to be back at Bassett Hall. I really love that place."[1] She loved the house and the town in equal measure—the house for its New England character in the middle of Virginia stateliness, for its folk art, for its gardens, and the town for its intimacy, for the spinsters and widows who were her friends, including hundred-year-old Mrs. Hankins, who called her Mrs. Roosevelt, and for the village movie theater with its changing bill of fare.

"They used to come several times a week," the manager recalled, "to practically all the mystery [films], and that used to bother me. Mrs. Rockefeller had a rope of pearls—and it was a rope, tremendous pearls—and it would hang way down . . . in her lap. She would twist those pearls during the exciting parts, and it nearly drove me mad because I could see them breaking and running down the slope of the theater, all over the audience. Each one of them was as big as a marble—worth a fortune I guess."[2] Finally he asked her what would happen if she broke them. No problem, she replied, they were strung on unbreakable wire.

Her imagination was fired by the historic setting. "With Williamsburg full of soldiers and sailors, surrounded by camps and the activities of war," she wrote a friend, "I constantly feel myself carried back in my mind to the days of the American Revolution. Particularly at night, when we walk along the streets, I feel as if I might hear swords clanking. There is so much going on here that I am not sure but what John feels it less restful but it is certainly tremendously interesting." She went on to thank the friend for the gift of a new biography of Jefferson. "Having lived for the last ten years or more very much in the same atmosphere that Thomas Jefferson lived in, I am enormously interested to read anything about him."[3]

The present, however, consumed her attention in a way that the past never could. With restoration work halted for the duration, the resources of the staff turned to the care, both physical and intellectual, of servicemen and servicewomen stationed at the nearby military installations. Abby shared with John the cost of what became known as the Soldier-Sailor Training Program, in which enlisted personnel were bused into Colonial Williamsburg to learn their American history, on site, as it were. Then there was the matter of looking after the tremendous influx of families following their draftees. First Abby paid for the operation of a two-room service center. When that proved inadequate she funded the renovation and furnishing of an entire USO building.

In her whimsical yet pragmatic way, she kept her eye fixed as well on needs, which if not exactly ignored, were likely to be passed over. Upon noticing that young soldiers had no place to sit when they ogled the female students from the College of William and Mary, she provided benches for them. She insisted that her driver give rides to uniformed men. ". . . we picked up an awfully nice young sailor whose ship was being loaded at the Navy Mine Depot. . . . in speaking of his ship it was a pretty poor one, he said, and he would not wonder if it would sink on the way out." On another occasion it was a young marine officer and a sailor. "I turned round and looked them over carefully and told them how glad we were to have them with us, but they never said a word. I am sure I don't know what frightened them. . . . Maybe before the war is over these boys may be heroes."[4] She fed as many as she could, relying on produce and beef shipped from Pocantico, coupons scrupulously hoarded, and limiting all dinners to three courses, amazed that one could actually subsist on fish.

Her letters to David are a testimony to their shared love of food, and she good-naturedly chided herself. "It amuses me very much the amount of writing I do . . . about food. I am always telling you what we have had, or going to have, or hope to have."[5] There was the political dinner at Carters Grove Plantation, when the hostess imported a government official to do the mint juleps. ". . . when we arrived the mint juleps had just arrived. . . . Mrs. McCrea gave us a marvelous, what she called 'high tea.' The first course was crab meat. . . . Then we had shad roe, tomatoes stuffed with mayonnaise, delicious Virginia ham . . . biscuits & coffee. Then we had a most delicious dessert which was angel cake covered with heavy whipped cream surrounded by strawberries." Two days later they were invited to the naval base. ". . . we had the most delicious food . . . tongue and chicken in aspic and then squab and . . . asparagus from their garden and ending with a very rich but good meringue filled with whipped cream. As Winthrop says, the navy has good food."[6] Her own menus, she hastened to add, were no competition for such extravagances, merely prosaic grapefruit and good beefsteak with various vegetables and fried potatoes and ice cream with butterscotch sauce.

She wanted to send him a cookbook in her package of chocolate bars and pralines. When the package proved to be too large, she sent it on later, a classic New Orleans collection to amuse his French friends in North Africa. "Then when you are unable to get anything very good to eat . . . you can read it all over to yourself."[7]

Her admiration for Southern women as hostesses did not extend to their philosophy of race relations. "As I tell your father, I think the women of the South might as well make up their minds now to organize their households on a different basis. In the future . . . Negro servants should be given wages that are commensurate with their services . . . they should be given regular times off and on, just as we do in the North, and . . . they should be treated with not only kindness, but with consideration for their ability. . . . Probably none of these ladies would like to have me say this to them."[8] Quietly she went about her task of improving life for the black citizens of Williamsburg. (She had already contributed to a new elementary and high school.) When the city published a survey laying out the need for job training, recreational facilities, and a health clinic for the black community, she responded promptly. "I am informed," she wrote the school board, "that the program calls for the erection of a plant at an approximate cost of $254,000, including equipment. In order to assist the city in the attainment of the splendid purposes this outlined . . . it will give me great pleasure to contribute to this project the sum of $50,000."[9]

Winthrop was now stationed at Fredericksburg and taking amphibious training at Norfolk, and Abby wanted to spend as much of the winter as possible in Virginia. "She held him close to her heart," Melinda Kendrew recalled. "She worried about him and felt very tender toward him."[10] Ed Kendrew added that in the 1950s when Winthrop became chairman of Colonial Williamsburg, he did a splendid job; he was a wonderful host and supported the new projects. "He justified her faith in him, for she had fought his battles all the way."[11]

Winthrop in turn was dedicated to Bayway because of what it meant to Abby. Even in the army he looked out for it. "As you know," she wrote David, "Winthrop and I are enormously interested in the work of Bayway, which is being reorganized and [he] brought me up to date as he had just had quite important meetings with several of the Esso men."[12] Abby was concerned lest the Standard Company withdraw its support as hers diminished. Winthrop evidently was persuasive, for the president of the company assured her that Standard would continue the program and looked forward to years of its continued usefulness. "They have [finally] accepted all the recommendations . . . I have been trying to get them to consider for the past twenty-five years," she wrote.[13]

Over New Year's they met Winthrop's adjutant, a new friend named Frank Newell from Arkansas. "Winthrop says he is . . . a great politician," Abby wrote, ". . . and very clever . . . he has read everything in the world. I liked him because he was interested in Russian Literature. . . . We sat up until half past twelve talking."[14] Newell became Winthrop's closest friend and adviser when Winthrop eventually took up residency in Arkansas and became governor of the state.

The next night Abby met the colonels, less impressive by far than the younger officers. "[They] looked dissipated and soft to me. Fortunately I can't remember their names or I might have been tempted to tell the General what I thought of them!"[15] On the last night of his weekend leave, Winthrop brought twenty of his sergeants to Bassett Hall for dinner. "I really think it was the most successful party we had. . . . They were such fine men and they all seemed to adore Winthrop. . . . When he came into the room [he was a little late] they all jumped to their feet and saluted and I jumped up with them and I am afraid I saluted too!"[16]

Two months later, Winthrop returned to Bassett Hall alone. "He didn't bring anyone with him and he didn't get here until after eight o'clock," she wrote David. "I had told Nelson that as far as we knew Winthrop would not get another leave so he and Mary hurriedly got reservations on the one o'clock train from Washington. . . . I can't tell you how much I appreciated their thoughtfulness. . . . I think it meant a great deal to Winthrop. . . . he looked more . . . refreshed than I had seen him in a long time. . . . I think he has worked terribly hard getting ready for his trip into the unknown. Papa and I had such a lovely visit with him until . . . he had to go back to camp late Sunday afternoon. After he left we went out for a long walk in the woods. It was a beautiful afternoon."[17]

On March 15 they received Winthrop's APO card and address:

> Service Co.
> 305th Infantry
> APO 77
> c/o Postmaster
> San Francisco, CA.

•

Business as usual—art business, that is—was not possible at MoMA after Pearl Harbor. Major retrospectives of European artists could no longer be mounted. The last one, Picasso: Forty Years of His Art, a culmination of Alfred's eight years of preparation, had opened on November 15, 1939. *Guernica*, the artist's rendition of German bombing of a Basque town, would hang in the museum at Picasso's request for the next forty years, until democracy was restored in Spain. The rescue of Jewish and antifascist artists had been an urgent matter for Alfred and Abby and Marga since 1937. Often it was a question of buying significant high-quality works from refugees in dire need. Abby responded, as in the case of Franz Marc and Oskar Kokoschka, by pressuring MoMA trustees to make purchases, or for Lyonel Feininger, by buying something herself.

Actually getting the works or the artists themselves out of Europe was much more difficult and expensive. "I thought you would be interested in seeing the enclosed pamphlet, which reports the work of the Emergency Rescue Committee," Alfred wrote her in September 1941. "You will remember that we raised money for the work of this committee through the purchase of a bronze by Jo Davidson who gave the entire proceeds [of $10,000] to the Committee. You have generously contributed to this purchase fund. . . . several of the artists about whom we were most concerned are now safely in this country, including André Masson, Marc Chagall, Jacques Lipchitz, Max Ernst. Three others: Kandinsky, Pierre Roy, and Hans Arp, are still in Europe, though hope for them has not yet been abandoned. I want to thank you again for your help."[18]

One of Alfred's most dramatic moves was to rescue *The Blue Window (La fenêtre bleue)* by Henri Matisse from the cellar of Hermann Göring, the Nazi air minister, in a secret private sale.

James Thrall Soby, a collector and art critic, accepted the position of director of MoMA's armed services committee early in 1942. He was not new to MoMA, having pledged his "allegiance, his intelligence, his bank account, and his perceptive and adventurous critical eye twelve years earlier," according to Russell Lynes.[19] He and Alfred were good friends, and each admired the other. His easy manner was a valuable asset in the highly charged atmosphere.

Soby's committee supervised war-related exhibitions, got art materials into the camps, ran hemisphere poster contests, and analyzed enemy propaganda films. The Sculpture Garden became the site of parties for uniformed personnel. Originally the happy improvisation of John McAndrew and Alfred, the garden was slowly evolving into an integrated design. At Abby's urging, inviting benches were introduced and some ailing trees were replaced. A garden canteen was manned by the Salvation Army. Abby sent over money and staff; other family members subsidized events. Even John made an appearance. His acute unease with modern art did not get in the way of his patriotism.

On a Thursday in September 1944, Abby met with a committee at MoMA to organize a program that came to mean more to her than any other war-related philanthropy—the War Veterans Art Center, to be set up on two floors of a nearby Fifth Avenue building. The call went out to men who had served in any branch of the service to join classes in drawing, painting, sculpture and ceramics, woodwork, metalwork, and weaving. Stephen Clark and Abby underwrote the project. Victor d'Amico, whom Abby already knew as the head of the museum's Department of Education, supervised the program. "I asked one fellow why he had taken up art," d'Amico recalled, "and he said, 'Well, I just came back from destroying everything. I made up my mind that if I ever got out of the army and out of the war I was never going to destroy another thing in my life, and I decided that art was the thing I would do.' "[20] Even officials from the Veterans Administration studied its operation. Clark, a man not easily moved, described the center as very close to Abby's heart.

The climactic event that came to be known in the history of the museum as the "firing of Alfred Barr" was played out in Abby's absence. She was spending the winter in Williamsburg. But the entire cast of characters—principals, supporting players, and chorus—have had their say, many of them in Russell Lynes's *Good Old Modern*, a few as recently as 1986 and 1987 in interviews with the author.

Marga Barr recalled that October 16, 1943, was a gray Saturday, that Alfred seemed listless, that she prevailed upon him to go to an

During gas rationing, Abby and John drove about Tarrytown in a
1908 electric car. July 4, 1943.
Courtesy of the Rockefeller Archive Center.

afternoon movie. On the way home he told her that in the morning mail he had received a letter from Stephen Clark asking him to resign as director. "It was a three-page single-spaced letter," said Marga, "accusing him of being perfectly useless to the museum, that the only thing he was good at was writing, that a salary of six thousand dollars [half his current salary] was more than sufficient. Alfred was infuriated, then despondent, not so much over the humiliation of being fired, but that Mr. Clark had no notion of what the museum's mission was. His emotions were anger and contempt. Mine was fear. I began to look at tenement apartments." According to her chronicle, she asked a friend how one lives cheaply. The friend replied that she could switch from the Fifth Avenue bus, which was ten cents, to the Madison Avenue one, which was five. "In November," Marga continued, "Mrs. Rockefeller sent him a typewritten note saying that it was all for the best, all for Alfred's good. Of course she had no notion of what it meant to live on six thousand dollars a year [thirty thousand in 1992 dollars]."[21]

Eliza Cobb, a trustee at that time, agrees that the so-called firing (it was in fact a major demotion) was done very badly. "It hurt his feelings terribly, and it hurt the people around him. And there is no question that he built up the collection, no question at all. So of course, he wouldn't go away. It was his museum. He stayed in the little cubicle, reserved for him in a corner of the library, and wrote his book, while a committee ran the museum."[22] Dorothy Miller spoke for his admirers on the staff. "There was a sort of path worn in the floor toward the little alcove . . . because everyone had to ask his advice about everything."[23]

Abby had warned Conger Goodyear seven years earlier that the management of the museum had grown too complicated for someone of Alfred's temperament, that even if he continued to be the artistic conscience, he should no longer be the administrator. Close friends of Alfred—Tom Mabry, Philip Johnson, Edward Warburg —echoed her appraisal. Marga herself conceded that Alfred found it hard to make decisions because he saw multiple aspects of each question. But when Abby had raised her worries, everyone was preoccupied with the new building; Nelson made a few clumsy attempts to shift things about and then went off to Washington. The war came and Stephen Clark's tenure began.

Lynes charts the tensions between Clark and Alfred and between Alfred and disgruntled members of his staff, and on the opposite pole, describes the fierce loyalty and devotion of Alfred's partisans. Stephen Clark's inherited fortune was derived from the Singer Sewing Machine Company. He was perceived by people around him as a distant, lonely figure, but he was one of the very few trustees whom Abby could depend on for financial support. To quote Monroe Wheeler, "She had to handle him with velvet gloves, and believe me, he took some handling. He was a strange man; his mind was not as elastic as hers."[24] Clark wanted MoMA to operate as a business and he wanted harmony among the staff, and both were impossible. He kept a close watch on the museum's budget, and he had the stubborn conviction of a connoisseur whose eye was entirely his own. He was an orderly man who woke early, walked from his vast house on 70th Street to the museum and then on to his office. He did not understand people who showed up at their offices at noon, took coffee breaks and tea breaks, but then worked far into the night.

Clark's letter to Alfred of October 15—the one Marga summed up so bitterly—was uncompromising and etched with exasperation. He reminded Barr that competent people had been brought in to lighten his load, that for at least several years he—Clark—and Abby had been urging him to change his ways, and that as recently as ten months before he had told Barr frankly that unless he resumed his literary activities his usefulness to the museum would be ended. "You have great talents and a great reputation in the world of art," he concluded, "but for several years past you have done little to justify that reputation."[25] A harsh indictment indeed!

The people who had found Alfred uncommunicative or moody, who felt cut loose from his concerns and were in effect left to fight their own battles, had carried their frustrations to Clark. Clark had delegated such problems to John Abbott, who had been appointed executive director when Tom Mabry was discharged. Abbott proved to be an unhappy choice. He was a Wall Street broker who was in over his head intellectually, and he was perceived by several observers as a slippery character. Eliza Cobb recalls him as not so much devious as dull. "Abbott just wasn't very bright. . . and you had to be bright in that company."[26] Yet Clark had anointed him as his right-hand man, and it wasn't until he became embroiled in a divorce, was racked with tuberculosis, and began to drink too much that Clark eased him out.

The correspondence between Abby and Clark confirms what seems obvious already—that Abby backed the idea that Alfred should be relieved of his administration of the museum. It is possible that the transition would have been smoother if she had managed it. Her reputation for tact and understanding when controversy erupted is well documented. "Even when she had a disagreeable task to perform, she left no scars behind," Clark said.[27] And certainly he left near-fatal scars behind. But Abby could be tough, too. She clearly believed that the museum was in crisis, and in a different context, that Alfred was in crisis, as well. No soothing words from her would make the situation easier for him to accept. Perhaps her vaunted patience was exhausted. What is more significant is that Alfred came to agree with her. In an important footnote to her published chronicle, Marga writes: "By 1948 he had forgiven her. . . . One has the impression that he had come to feel that in the long run she was right in saying that it was better for him not to be the director of the museum."[28]

Abby wrote David a matter-of-fact summary of the events of October. After years of uncertainty, she explained, Stephen Clark had decided that it was time to change directors, that Alfred would become advisory director. "I do not know what happened to poor Alfred. He seemed to have gotten to the point where it was impossible for him to do anything creative. I am quite sure that the shock he has received is going to be one of the best things that ever happened to him. . . . I feel very sorry for him. . . . Mr. Soby is going to be curator of paintings and sculpture. . . . We are going to employ René d'Harnoncourt to be in charge of all the work we are doing in South America. We have taken him over from Nelson's organization. . . . Mr. Clark says that the Museum will benefit very much by this shake-up and he is much encouraged . . . by the future."[29]

Clark's optimism was premature. The rifts were deep and painful. Alfred Barr's value had not dwindled to that of scribe. Members of the coordination committee that was supposed to make decisions during the interregnum quarreled among themselves. It was not until René d'Harnoncourt became director in 1949 that permanent peace was declared. René, a sensitive, superbly qualified executive, a master diplomat, agreed to the appointment only if Alfred became director of the museum's collection. "You should know," said Edward Warburg, a trustee, "that René was the luckiest thing that ever happened to the museum. He made the setting for what Alfred had to do."[30]

Like Conger Goodyear before him, Stephen Clark drifted away in the early 1950s, finally leaving the museum precisely nothing. His taste was subject to change. When he decided that Matisse was "out" he sold his entire collection. He couldn't take Pollock, Rothko floored him, and he found Giacometti repugnant. "Imagine," Dorothy Miller remarked, "he just couldn't stand Giacometti."[31] He left his pictures to the Yale Art Gallery and the Metropolitan Museum.

With Abby it was quite another story. Her personal taste did not interfere with her support of the institution, which is not to suggest that she liked everything Alfred selected. When he asked her for $1,000 to buy Picasso's formidable print *Minotauromachy*, she grimaced and then acquiesced, saying, "Let's label this: 'Purchased with a Fund for prints which Mrs. Rockefeller doesn't like.' "[32] She was disturbed by the inclusion of *Figure of Erotic Torture* by Ben Culwell in the 1947 exhibition Fourteen Americans. She informed both René and Alfred of her objections, which rested on her concern about the threat of censorship from groups that would welcome an opportunity to attack the museum. "There could not have been a less fortunate time to force this question upon the notice of the public."[33] But she was careful to keep her concerns within the museum family. Both men explained the artistic considerations that brought the painting into the exhibition and assured her that they would discuss her criticism. That ended the correspondence.

In the spring of 1944, Abby made a critical decision regarding the museum's financial future. ". . . about ten days ago," she wrote David on April 17, "I decided that instead of waiting until I died, I would give the Museum now the money I had planned to give it some day—which was really practically all the money I happened to have over which I have any control. . . . I sent word to the office that I was going to do it and poor Mr. Keebler nearly had a fit because I almost gave away more money than I really had! In other words I did not leave enough to pay my extra income tax. I almost left myself bankrupt, but Mr. Keebler rescued me and I now have enough to pay my taxes. Of course I have always wanted to do this and I felt that the time had come because I could not help feeling that the other trustees of the Museum would not act until they were quite sure what I was going to do. Now they know—the worst or the best, whichever it may be."[34]

The fair market value of the securities on the date of the gift—April 12, 1944—was $598,087, approximately 3 million in 1992 dollars.

CHAPTER 33

⸻⸻⸻ ⟨∞⟩ ⸺

I have had a most extraordinarily strange feeling the past week of
leading a double life," Abby wrote David. "My mind seemed
completely divided between the achievements of the 77th Division
on Leyte and the tragic news from the Western Front."[1] Winthrop,
a major and the senior supply officer of the 305th Infantry Regiment, had fought with the 77th in the recapture of Guam, and now
in the winter of 1944 was behind enemy lines on the island of
Leyte. In newspaper reports Abby read of desperate jungle warfare
in torrential rain. "Of course I think of it as Winthrop's battle."[2]
The horror of it did not escape her—hundreds of thousands of men
on a tiny island trying to destroy one another. Yet she had to
believe that they must fight on. The tragic news from the western
front was the German counteroffensive, launched just before dawn
on December 16, 1944, in the country of the Ardennes. Six months
earlier, during the night of June 6, 1944, Abby had lain sleepless,
resisting the impulse to turn on the radio for fear of waking John.
Finally at dawn she had listened to the announcement of the Allied
invasion of Normandy. It was D-day. "The news had been coming
over the wire all night," she wrote, "and I am perfectly convinced
the reason I was so on edge all day and night was a subconscious
knowledge that something was happening in the world and that I

wanted to know what it was."[3] All summer the news had been of stunning Allied advances across France. Even so, Abby was apprehensive, believing that there was serious fighting ahead. The December offensive proved her right.

In the autumn of 1944, David had traveled with an intelligence unit of the Seventh Army to an area of southern France—the mission to find out what was happening in the region under the control of the Vichy government. As he moved west and north, he described the battlefields in Alsace, how entire towns had been destroyed by German soldiers tossing hand grenades into houses, whose residents were burned alive. "Sometimes . . ." Abby wrote, "I just can't bear the destruction that is going on in the world. . . . Many people . . . feel the answer is economic, but . . . I feel that more fundamentally the great trouble is lack of moral values. . . . I am becoming more and more of an advocate of . . . my favorite quotation from the Old Testament 'What doth the Lord require of thee but to do justice, love kindness and walk humbly before Thy God.' "[4]

She took up the results of the 1944 election, which saw Thomas Dewey lose to Roosevelt. Always dubious about Vice President Henry Wallace ("honest but no judgement"), she rejoiced when Harry Truman came on the ticket. "The poor socialists seem to be rather out of the picture. I have always had a good deal of respect for Norman Thomas. I believe he is a sincere, honest and upright person and even if I do not agree with his point of view I can respect him. As a matter of fact, I have a good deal of sympathy for Mr. Roosevelt . . . [for having the] courage to face four years of . . . the most difficult this country has ever seen without great physical strength. . . . I [hope] that the Republicans will forget their differences and will back the country up."[5]

The question of Germany troubled her, the cruelty of its people —vices and deceit combined with great cleverness and ability. David had harsh words for Germany's future in the family of nations. His hope was that Americans at home would not insist upon soft peace terms. "I say all of this," he added, "while still feeling that Germans are often delightful people to meet and that Germany is a most pleasant country to visit. It is simply as a nation they cannot be trusted or tolerated."[6]

The success of the German counteroffensive was short-lived, and the flawed operation ended any chance of maintaining prolonged resistance to a renewed Allied drive. The Soviets were advancing on the east, and bombing attacks on Germany were lethal. Hitler was issuing scorched-earth instructions to his ministers. His maniacal illusions continued to grow. He even professed to believe that the death of Franklin Roosevelt on April 12 was the miracle that would rescue him. But by April 25, Berlin was isolated. The Soviet and American forces met at the Elbe River. Adolf Hitler committed suicide in the ruins of the Chancellery, and the war in Europe came officially to an end on May 8, 1945.

David was now stationed in Paris, assigned to the American embassy as a military attaché. Of the president's death, Abby wrote how tragic it was that he should die just when the goal appeared in sight. "On the other hand, he has been frail for so long and I suspect that a more vigorous government is what we will need in the future. I was much impressed by the restraint and wisdom of President Truman's address to the Congress. . . . I was relieved that he did not promise very much to anyone."[7]

As for the German surrender, she wrote on May 7, "I turned on the radio . . . and heard many references suddenly to this being V. E. Day . . . but so far no official proclamation has been issued. . . . I have been quite overcome by the realization that this day has come at last, so I shall not write more now."[8]

It was a moment for somber reflection, but not yet a time for joy. Winthrop, who had already suffered a bout of pneumonia and jaundice and had rejoined his regiment for the battle of Okinawa, was playing poker in the officers' wardroom of the command ship *Henrico* when a Japanese kamikaze crashed into the ship's bridge. All the senior officers were killed, except for Winthrop, who survived with flash burns of the hands and face. Seventy-five men in all were killed, 150 wounded. Abby learned the early details from the former head of the Rockefeller Institute, Dr. John Rivers, who directed the army hospital on Guam where Winthrop was recovering. Through the doctor, Winthrop sent word that his face had recovered sufficiently to be shaved, but that his hands resembled catcher's mitts. "I think we must prepare ourselves," Abby wrote David, "for the fact that as soon as he is well he will go back into action. . . . I am only grateful that he escaped without greater harm."[9]

Abby was right about Winthrop and the army. By May 15 he was back on Okinawa, in spite of the history of pneumonia, jaundice, burns, and a loss of forty-five pounds. His friends who came to New York on leave brought Abby stories of his bravery, his modesty, the devotion of his men, and indirectly, the terrible ordeal of the fighting. "You spoke of the vacant, haunted look in the men still left alive at Dachau," she wrote David late in June. "I couldn't help thinking of the look on Winthrop's face in his photographs after his experience on the ship . . . and the look on the faces of the Marines whom I met after they returned from fighting in the Pacific. They not only had a look of unbearable fatigue, but also a haunted look from the terrible things they had seen happen. . . . Major Kriendler said to me that we must be very understanding and sympathetic of Winthrop when he comes home."[10]

For a month she heard nothing at all. Finally a letter came that filled her with both relief and apprehension. He was back in the hospital somewhere in the Philippines, jaundiced and weak. The army, however, finally acknowledging that they had a seriously ill soldier who might never recover in the blinding heat of Leyte, ordered him home, first to Halloran Hospital on Staten Island and then to the Rockefeller Institute for further study. Winthrop qualified for the latter not because of his name, but because he was the only patient with a history of two jaundice infections.

Abby and John were in Maine when the news broke that the atomic bomb had been dropped on Hiroshima. "I have so many conflicting emotions and ideas about it all, what it may mean to the war, both good and evil . . . that I do not know where I am at—to use vulgar speech," she wrote David on August 9.[11] For five days she waited breathlessly for the announcement of peace. Perhaps she could then admit how much she missed him and how much she wanted him home safely.

At seven o'clock on Tuesday, the 14th, she and John were sitting very quietly in her garden enjoying the cool of the day when there was the sound of bells carried by the prevailing wind from the direction of Seal Harbor. "At last it has come," she said. "At last it has come. That means the president has declared peace." Clinging to each other for a moment, they rushed to turn on the radio, in time to hear the proclamation. "For once your father, I think, was thankful for the radio," Abby wrote David, "for he stood with me in the middle of the room, where it seemed to give the best reception, for almost an hour while we listened to what was happening all over the world."[12]

The war was over, the sons returned to civilian life, and Babs would marry Irving Pardee in three days. Abby, on October 7, 1946, celebrated forty-five years of her own marriage. It *was* a celebration of sorts, even if no letters record it. "It always surprises me," she had written, "coming back to New York, how quickly I forget Williamsburg and adjust my life to living in New York and Pocantico. As a matter of fact I know I am happy and contented wherever your father happens to be. He means home to me. I really feel sorry for the unhappy people who cannot find companionship in their married lives. I do not believe that it is something that happens, I think it is something that is achieved."[13]

This conviction—shared by John—that marriage and family deserved maximum attention was a fundamental tenet of her philosophy. But it was left to her to mobilize the energy and intelligence required to meet the needs of everyone around her. She seemed to welcome the role as pivotal and primary. What she finally achieved in her relationship with a lover whose personality was as complex and repressed as John's was a kind of negotiated peace. If not always fair to both partners, at least it offered her a settlement that supported her self-esteem. It was a relationship that rode to success on the passion that ignited their emotions, on a core of stubbornness that drove her to demand, with a certain grace, what she felt was her due, and a mischievous sense of whimsy that could puncture even the most pompous attitudes.

When the Stephen Clarks invited them to dinner, John gave her a long lecture previous to their departure about the dangers of spending the entire evening talking to Mr. Clark about the museum. Abby listened politely and then tucked into her elegant evening bag the list of items she needed to discuss with him. At the Arizona Inn she delighted in going down to the pool with the guests who congregated for swimming and lunch. "Your father feels that it is not a safe place for me," she wrote Laurance. "He thinks if I once go there I will become intimate with all sorts of people and will want to talk to them, so generally we eat in what I call the old people's dining room; where he feels I am safer."[14] It was not a question of her safety, of course, but John's.

Her letters to Lucy attest to her skill in circumventing John's resistance to the social scene. Whether in Williamsburg, Seal Harbor, or Tucson, she managed to nudge him into the occasional luncheon, tea, or, most infrequently, an evening party. Sometimes his own sense of humor rescued him. "During one summer in Maine I was her personal secretary," Eleanor Robinson Bradshaw recalled. "She sent me over to Mr. Rockefeller's study to show him their social calendar. 'My wife is like a piano roll,' he said, 'she can't bear to see any spaces left.' "[15]

Some Providence women in Tucson were living cooperatively. "[They] do absolutely all their own work, even to the washing. Between times they paint and study and have more intellectual occupations," she wrote Laurance and Mary. "I am hoping I may persuade your father to have all of them here for lunch."[16] There is no evidence that she succeeded. Sooner or later, he dug in his heels. "I think [he] is beginning to show an enormous amount of resistance to any social activities," she wrote to her friend Olivia Cutting, as though that were something new. ". . . I am sure that 'au fond' he thoroughly enjoys parties, but seems to feel that there is a limit."[17]

But the truth is John did not enjoy parties, not the way Abby did. He much preferred to go to the theater, to a concert, to a film in Radio City. He liked to drive his team of horses with her beside him, to take dancing lessons with her alone, in the apartment, to read aloud from *Jane Eyre* or *Barchester Towers*. He was a solitary romantic, and Abby loved him for it. She picked her battles carefully, knowing when to stand firm and when to give in.

His last stronghold was Pocantico. There, in stately isolation, he attempted to separate her from all the wonderful activity that she relished but which gave him migraines. As much as possible, she cooperated, for she, too, appreciated the natural setting. "Your father went to Church and I sat in the sun for two hours," she wrote David, "and watched the battle that was going on between the squirrels and the Junkos. There was so much snow on the ground that the squirrels wanted to eat all the bird food. I try to like squirrels, but I don't really. Crows and squirrels are my betes noirs and we have lots of them up in Pocantico now. On our way down to New York in the afternoon, I persuaded Papa to drive me by the lake where I could see the swan and the ducks keeping an open place in the water where they could enjoy swimming about."[18]

Even in the country, however, he had to compete for her attention, or so it seemed to him, not with the museum or with the distractions of the larger world, but with his own grandchildren, seventeen of them as of 1946, from Mitzi, age eighteen, down to Laurance's Larry, age two. "He expected her to go driving with him every afternoon," Peggy recalled. "It was his favorite relaxation. Every morning she would ask him what his plans were. He might not know in the morning, but he expected her to be available for the afternoon drive. He really did not want her to be doing anything else, except to be with him or to wait for him. Her conflict was that she yearned to be with the little ones. Only once do I recall her admitting that it bothered her. 'I really think I should be free to see my grandchildren while I can, don't you?' "[19]

Abby felt the tug of conflicting loyalties, hinting at it to Olivia Cutting. "I find our very large family of children and grandchildren so absorbing and even so exciting that since I returned from Maine . . . [I] spend a great deal of my time trying to get acquainted [with them]. As I think you know, I love little children, to me it is one of the things that give me the greatest comfort and pleasure in life. Perhaps I should put my husband before the grandchildren, where he really belongs."[20]

Such ambivalence could not be resolved, and she knew it. When it looked as though David and Peggy would have to go abroad, she carefully analyzed little David's place in the family and how she might help. "He is in rather a difficult position in life with those two adorable little sisters, who are of an age to charm, that immediately attracts the attention of everyone who sees them and pushes David out into the cold. . . . all that is happening to him is that he is trying to hold his own in the competition," she wrote his parents, "and if he could be separated from them for a few weeks, I imagine that it would be a good thing. I would adore having him with me. Of course, this brings up that very difficult question of what your father thinks about it . . . but I am sure you both realize it would be a great pleasure to me. . . . Having said all this I am still in a quandary, for I never like to do, if I can possibly help it, what your father doesn't want me to do."[21] The upshot was that all the children, including young David, stayed with Peggy's mother.

The comfort and pleasure of being an affectionate grandmother was only part of the story. Abby had a keen interest in how children grew up, what made them good citizens, how best they could fulfill their potential, to dip into modern jargon, and best of all, she became the Boswell of the third generation. When Blanchette and John's three came to lunch at 740 Park, she had this to say:

> Sandra used to be a rather repressed, shy little girl whom you couldn't see beyond her great big glasses, but now she has blossomed into a most amusing, quite witty child. Little Jay seems almost like a man he is so grown-up. Of course, he is perfectly enormous and has always seemed much older than his years. Hope is, as always, diverting. I attribute their charm to the fact that John and Blanchette devote a very large part of their time to those children, so that they feel very free, happy and confident. I wonder how many parents realize that it is from them that children gather their feelings of security and happiness.[22]

What other grandmother could compare a dripping-wet, shivering little girl just out of the swimming pool to a child in a portrait from Picasso's blue period? As for food, she seemed to be establishing quite a reputation among her grandchildren for giving them good food. She was beginning to wonder what they got at home.

Abby's doctor, concerned about the frequency of her upper respiratory infections as well as the effect of the cold winter on her heart, suggested she consider spending part of the season in a warm, dry climate. "I wish you [knew] him," she wrote Olivia, referring to her physician, "he really gives me a great feeling of confidence, because he pays no attention to me at all, which makes me think I am very well. And when I do need him he is always frightfully busy, doing research work on Welfare Island, and having taken on the direction of the Lenox Hill Hospital, temporarily, I hope. . . . He has only a few private patients, I imagine he takes us on as a sort of discipline."[23]

Left to herself, she later wrote, she would risk another winter in New York rather than be so far away from the family, but prudence prevailed and she and John spent the months of February and March 1947 in Tucson. Only weeks before their departure, John had made one of his most historic public gifts—$8,500,000 to purchase six Manhattan blocks along the East River for the permanent site of the United Nations. On December 21, Margaret Carnegie, daughter of Andrew Carnegie, wrote Abby how stirred she was by John's decision. "Dear Margaret," Abby replied. "I entirely agree with you that it could have not been more opportune, in fact I think it saved the whole situation. . . ."[24]

Lucy and Minnie MacFadden moved into 740 Park while Abby and John were in Arizona. Letters resumed between the sisters. "I miss you very much," Lucy wrote. "I told Nelson last night it was like Hamlet with Hamlet left out." It was Lucy who first called attention to the presence of Barbara "Bobo" Sears in Winthrop's bachelor life.

"Winthrop Rockefeller [as distinct from Winthrop Aldrich] telephoned in the morning and asked Miss MacFadden and me to come to tea so we went. He had a strange girl there, a married girl. Her name was Sears and she knew Alice and George. I wanted to ask her where her husband was but didn't quite dare to. She seemed nice and quiet. I don't know whether she was asked to chaperon us or we to chaperon them. No maids were evident and Winthrop asked Mrs. Sears to make some cinnamon toast and she said she had to confess that she didn't know how to make it. But Winthrop and she disappeared into the pantry and they finally produced some cinnamon toast. . . . I told him I hope to have him come here anytime he wanted to and bring anyone he wanted to. He didn't look enthusiastic about it. I think he has a horror of being tied down by family."[25]

Sunshine and pleasant people notwithstanding, when the time came to leave Arizona, Abby was ready for New York and its excitement. John's eagerness to return to Pocantico, however, called for the usual compromise. "Unfortunately," she wrote Nelson on April 7, "we cannot accept the kind invitation of the Museum for dinner on April 25th, for from now on we expect to spend our weekends in the country."[26] The dinner would be honoring twenty of Abby's favorite artists, those whom she collected as well as those she had personally supported—Edward Hopper, Peter Blume, Stuart Davis, William Zorach, and Pavel Tchelitchew among others. MoMA was rarely out of her thoughts. "I think it was most generous and thoughtful of you," she wrote David, "to make up the deficit of the Modern Museum as a gesture of appreciation to me. Of course, I am always rather anxious about the Modern Museum because Nelson is so frightfully busy that he probably doesn't give as much time to it as he should and Mr. Clark does not seem temperamentally fitted to raising money and there is always a deficit. But it is such a wonderful institution and doing such splendid work that I know it should be continued. I have given just as much as I possibly can or should give to it."[27]

In July they returned to the Eyrie. "I feel rather conscious of there being so many empty rooms," Abby wrote Olivia. "I am threatening to push part of it off a cliff." She was daydreaming about a small New England cottage, white with green blinds, with room just for her and John. But she had lost none of her love for her walled garden. Nature and five years of war had not been kind to it. Many of the beautiful birch trees had been lost to blight. Seeds and bulbs were still in short supply. Once more she had looked to Beatrix Farrand for help, although there were still areas which she wished might be more expressive of her and less of the experts. At last, this summer, it was beautifully green. One dose of sunshine would wake up the blossoms.

Abby returned with John to Arizona on February 1, 1948. The first week was peaceful; the second week brought a series of shocks. During a quiet Saturday lunch, John was called to the phone, with Abby following him. It was Laurance, breaking the news as gently as possible that an Eastern Airlines Constellation, Flight 611 from Boston to Miami, had crash-landed at an abandoned Florida airfield. Winthrop, who had boarded the plane at La Guardia, was safe. Another passenger described the event to the author. "A weakened propeller broke off, slicing into the cabin, decapitating the stewardess. We were ordered to put on life belts as the aircraft lost two engines. Another passenger, Dick Merrill, who had flown mails with Eddie Rickenbacker, took over the manual controls. Unsure whether the Connie could stay up in water, he was able to keep it in the air, finally landing it safely in the fog in Bonell, Florida."[28]

As usual, Abby wrote Lucy, when terrible things happened to the family she took it calmly at first, but then began to buckle. On Sunday she was able to speak to Winthrop himself. He assured her that he was all right and that what the newspapers reported was accurate—Dick Merrill's skill had saved them.

Two days later he called to tell them that he and Barbara Sears would be married on Friday, February 14, in Palm Beach at the home of Winston Guest. Laurance and Nelson were flying down, and Laurance would be best man.

"I can't say that we were entirely surprised," she wrote Peggy and David in Venezuela.

> . . . both your father and I had felt that probably Winthrop's recent, harrowing experience and miraculous escape would bring things to a head. In a way we were right and in a way we were wrong, because Winthrop told your father that he had an engagement ring in his pocket when they had to make the crash landing, but the date of the wedding was certainly a surprise. We are both very glad that this happiness has come to Winthrop and Barbara (I refuse to call her

Bobo). . . . I asked if I couldn't speak to Barbara. . . . She . . . told me that although she has been married once before she was so moved that both she and Winthrop were very far from calm.[29]

Barbara Sears was thirty-two years old and beautiful, the beauty of natural blond hair, fine complexion, radiant health. Her friends found her to be warm and amusing and unaffected, with a charming, guileless personality. She had been introduced to Winthrop by her friend Mary Elizabeth Whitney, the former wife of Jock Whitney. Winthrop, handsome, sweet-natured, and very rich, moved in a conspicuous café-society set, but the reporters who followed that scene did not know about Barbara. The friendship was carried on out of the limelight, in her walk-up apartment, at the homes of friends, and in obscure restaurants. When a local Florida newspaper saw the posting of the marriage license, however, the news raced across the wire services. Huge attention was fixed on a Cinderella marriage.

Barbara had been born Jievute Paulekiute of Lithuanian immigrant parents in a coal patch near Noblestown, Pennsylvania. She was raised in a humble Chicago neighborhood. At age seventeen she was crowned Miss Lithuania at the Chicago World's Fair. She had been a model and a minor actress, and had married a proper Bostonian, Richard Sears, who was in the diplomatic service. In December 1947, she obtained her divorce in Reno from Sears. Less than two months later she married Winthrop.

If Abby was apprehensive about the future of a young couple from such wildly different backgrounds, she gave no such sign in her correspondence of the following weeks. Letters went back and forth among family members and friends. Everyone closed ranks around Barbara. As Lucy wrote, "I think everybody has resented the publicity for that poor girl's sake and yours too; but in a way I think it has been a very good thing, because everybody is so furious and thinks it is so overdone that they have reacted in her favor. I have told everyone that I had met her twice and thought she was such a nice girl; and I quote . . . Harriet; and I think everybody is prepared to welcome her with open arms. I don't think it is any least bit of importance who people are; it is what they are."[30]

"Harriet" was Harriet Crocker Aldrich, married to Winthrop Aldrich. The Aldriches were staying with the Harold Vanderbilts in Lake Worth on the day of the wedding. Abby and John did not attend. "We went into Palm Beach yesterday," Harriet wrote Abby, "& called on him and met 'Bobo'. . . . We both liked the girl <u>very</u> much. She was genuinely upset by all the publicity & seemed very sweet and simple and natural. They seem very much in love and I think the future looks rosy for them. She spoke so nicely about her own mother and about you & John and that she minded the publicity more for all of you than for herself. I liked her attitude enormously. . . . I must say he has waited long enough to know his own mind . . . so I think their chances of happiness in this uncertain world are better than average."[31]

On March 11, Abby wrote Barbara's mother, who had divorced her husband when Barbara was a child, but who had since remarried:

Dear Mrs. Neveckas: . . . I have been wanting, ever since Barbara and Winthrop were married, to have an opportunity of telling you how happy Mr. Rockefeller and I are about the marriage. Barbara has such a sweet, charming disposition and such a friendly spirit that she has already made a very warm place for herself in the hearts of all the Rockefeller family. I notice that our numerous grandchildren are especially drawn toward her. As we rejoice for Winthrop we hope that he will be able to make Barbara happy. He has such a friendly, kindly disposition that I know it will be his desire to do so. . . .[32]

To John 3rd she wrote that she liked the idea of Barbara being a Lithuanian very much; it was good for the family to have a little Slavic blood. "I have always, for some reason, been interested in the Lithuanian people from reading about them, and have great sympathy for them as a nation. They were just beginning to have a very successful republic when Russia swooped down on them. I have a feeling that if any of those satellite nations are able to pull out from under the Russian orbit it will be the Lithuanians."[33]

Writing him again a month later she thanked him for including her in the letters he wrote his father. "As all of you children must realize . . . what you do and think and feel touches me deeply. But, as Nelson once said to me, there is nothing more that I can do for you all except be a good example. However," she added ruefully, "I can't help feeling that it is a little difficult to be a good example way out here in Arizona." She tried to keep up with national politics by reading the New York papers and searching out stimulating guests. "The news last night cheered [me] greatly," she wrote. "And to have Mr. Truman take a firm stand on the question of the Marshall Plan . . . and the selective service, was most encouraging. . . . Mr. and Mrs. Ellery Sedgwick [editor of the *Atlantic Monthly*], Mr. and Mrs. Mathews—he is editor of the Arizona Star, and Lord Astor came here for tea. . . . I don't know when I have listened to more intelligent and interesting conversation. . . . Your father and I were . . . glad that Lady Astor was not here. . . . she . . . does not make for peaceful conversation."[34]

As she was preparing to leave for the East Coast, she received one last letter from Lucy, giving her the same advice she had been offering for years. "I really felt quite indignant to think you didn't go to the two parties. I find that doing anything that amuses me and interests me doesn't tire me, and being bored puts me to bed. So if you would just do what you feel like doing, I think it would do you a lot of good." She included the gossip of Providence and the complaint that since it was Holy Week "almost everybody [herself excluded] spends the entire week on their knees."[35]

CHAPTER 34

———— ·•·⟨∞⟩·•· ————

*A*bby and John reached Manhattan on Friday, April 2, 1948. Early Saturday morning the whole family gathered in Pocantico for a reunion. Nelson drove Abby in his car and on the way up gave her the news of the museum. (He had returned to the presidency after the war in 1946.) She declared that she was ready to take an active role again and that she was scheduling meetings with Alfred, d'Harnoncourt, and others. She wanted to know who the young artists were, and promised to buy their best works for MoMA.

It was a joyful two days, with all her favorite ingredients; the gardens in early springtime color, grandchildren romping about, no shortage of friendly arguments. In an earlier letter to David, she caught the tone of family dialogue. "Papa hates arguing, Laurance is so amusing that he puts me off and always gets the better of me, and of course John wouldn't think of arguing with me. But Nelson and I have a marvelous time frankly expressing our opinions to each other and it is a great comfort to me—but of course we both remained unconvinced!"[1]

On the way back to town on Sunday she rode with David. Her newest grandchild, Peggy Dulany, age six months, sat on her lap. Abby was wearing a new dress and new hat, because "I've never

471

been so happy in all my life."[2] Before returning to 740 Park she stopped off to visit with Barbara Sears Rockefeller, the first opportunity to greet her since the wedding. Barbara, four months pregnant, had not felt well enough to drive to the country. Before going to sleep, Abby called Lucy in Providence to give her all the news.

Early the next morning, April 4, she woke up feeling ill. Again it seemed to be a stomach upset, similar to incidents she had had before. Apparently she did not identify the pain as cardiac, but after an hour the doctor was called. While he was taking a history and listening to her symptoms, her head fell back against the pillow. She was dead of a heart attack at age seventy-three.

". . . The doctor, listening to her heart, had said it was all over," John 3rd wrote in his diary. ". . . Father was terribly hard hit, the end coming so suddenly and so completely out of the blue. . . . Nelson and I stayed for the night."[3]

Abby's children and their spouses watched helplessly as John reeled from the shock. "He was totally devastated by her death," Peggy Rockefeller recalled. "He wanted to have her cremated immediately, it was as though he could not deal with the mourning period, but rushed it through. 'Take this blow away,' he was crying."[4] She was in fact cremated on the day of her death, but then virtually by demand, as two thousand letters and telegrams reached him, John arranged for a memorial service to be held on May 23 at Riverside Church.

Nellie Romon, her hairdresser, wrote: "I always felt like she was the First Lady of this country."[5] Robert Moses, commissioner of New York City parks, suggested that the general public might not realize how greatly she had contributed to her husband's remarkable achievements, "but those of us who had the privilege of knowing her have a dim idea of it."[6] Margaret Sanger was one of the last of her friends in Arizona to see her. "It was such a joy to me to have had a nice laughing talk with Mrs. Rockefeller the morning you left for New York," she wrote. "I felt then how fortunate you and your children were to have had good rich years of her . . . care and companionship. . . . her silent backing of our cause gave me great confidence through the years of darkest night."[7]

And then there was a letter that would perhaps have delighted her the most, for it reached back into her irrepressible youth. "In 1897 I was Ev Colby's country cousin at Yale; you invited me to go to your senior party in Providence," Arthur Walworth wrote to John. "I went with some trepidation. Ev introduced me to Miss Abby Aldrich, the queen of the evening. Since I didn't know how to dance I was duly miserable. However, the happy lasting memory was that of the vibrant personality of Abby Aldrich."[8]

On Sunday morning, June 20—a sunny morning when dew still sparkled on the ground—Abby's ashes were mingled with the earth in the private burial place at Pocantico that she and John had selected only a few years earlier, beside the headstones that they had together designed. Late in the summer, John returned to the Eyrie to work with Beatrix Farrand on Abby's garden. "We are fellow travellers along a lonely road," he wrote Farrand.[9] Abby O'Neill visited him for three weeks. "It was a time when he was terribly lonely, hopelessly lonely. Somehow, because of his reserved relationship with his own children, I filled a need that they could not," she recalled.[10]

Abby's daughters-in-law, who loved her so dearly, comforted his as well. Tod and Blanchette had alternated staying with him at Bassett Hall when he visited Williamsburg in the spring and in the fall. Dana Creel used the analogy that a set of wheels had gone out of his life. But John turned to work as a kind of compensation and antidote, and Fosdick believes that he grew in gentleness and understanding after Abby's death. In 1951 he married Martha Baird Allen, who was herself the widow of a Brown classmate.

Alfred Barr heard the news of Abby's death while he was in Europe. He wrote to Nelson from on board ship. "Fever kept me from writing you as soon as I heard of your mother's passing but now . . . I have a clearer head—and some perspective on what she meant to the Museum—and to me. During the first years of the Museum—up to 1939—I used to see your mother constantly. I think the Museum interested her more than anything else, excepting her family. She thought about it continually and worried about it and planned for it. . . . perhaps because I was very young at the beginning (even younger than my age) we used to talk together with great candor, even intimacy, so that often I used to feel almost as if she were a second mother—she was so thoughtful and kind." He continued to write from his heart. And then, as an acute observer of the cultural scene, he reminded Nelson that though the outside world assumed she could do almost anything with her wealth and power, "few realize what positive acts of courage her interest in modern art required. Not only is modern art artistically radical but it is often assumed to be radical morally and politically, and sometimes indeed it is. But these factors which might have given pause to a more circumspect or conventional spirit did not deter your mother. Although on a few occasions, they caused her anxiety, as they did us all."[11]

Abby's will was filed for probate on April 22, 1948. The gross estate, including art, was appraised at $1,156,269. Although she had already given most of her art collection and the bulk of her assets to MoMA, she bequeathed four major works. Two were drawings by Georges Seurat—*Lady with a Parasol* and *Seated Woman*, both ca. 1885. The third was a drawing by van Gogh, *Street at Saintes-Maries* (1888), and the fourth, a gouache and watercolor, also by van Gogh, *Corridor at Saint-Remy* (1889). According to the terms of the will, all four would reside at MoMA for fifty years, after which the Seurats would go to the Art Institute of Chicago and the van Goghs to the Metropolitan. However, the intermuseum agreement was terminated in 1953, when MoMA decided to have its own masterworks collection. She left her Oriental miniatures to the Fogg Museum, with John enjoying a life interest. Her entire residuary estate of $850,848, minus estate taxes of approximately $250,000, went to the Museum of Modern Art.

During the years that John was mourning Abby, he continued to wrestle with his ambivalence about modern art and the museum. How could he justify his intense disapproval of that which had been so fundamental to her happiness? He knew that she had supported him in everything he set out to do. Had he let her down in some way? It was an old wound, and it continued to fester. In 1949, when Mary Ellen Chase, a professor from Smith College, was preparing her memoir of Abby, John found himself trying to sort out some uncomfortable feelings:

Dear Miss Chase: In spite of my, to put it mildly, lack of enthusiasm about modern art and the Modern Museum, simply as a cold fact it is worth noting that the lands and buildings which I have given to the Museum had an appraised value at the time of the gift of over $1,100,000, while further gifts have brought the total to over $1,250,000. Thus, I have been the largest, single contributor to the Museum.

This I mention only to show that although I did not share Mrs. Rockefeller's interest in modern art, I did support that interest.

Please do not think that this letter is written from a boasting point of view. It is written simply from a historical point of view.[12]

If it was not exactly boasting, it was surely not mere history.

On November 6, 1952, still grappling with his conscience, John wrote to Nelson as president of MoMA that although modern art had never greatly appealed to him he wished to make a gift. "In memory of Mama's devotion to the Museum and the realization of its objectives, it gives me pleasure to enclose herewith certificates in the name of the Museum for 40,000 shares of IBEC as a gift to the Museum's Endowment Fund."[13] The fair market value at that time was $4 million.

The Abby Aldrich Rockefeller Print Room at MoMA opened on May 15, 1949, nine years after the museum accepted Abby's gift of sixteen hundred prints. William S. Lieberman, with the title of associate curator, was placed in charge. A custodian of prints would be responsible for their care and cataloguing. For the benefit of the trustees and friends of the museum, Alfred wrote a short history of the evolution of the idea for a room. "As the depression 'thirties drew to a close, the Trustees began to plan the new Museum building. Mrs. Rockefeller, with gentle insistence, argued for the inclusion of a print room, reminding her colleagues that prints, because they were low priced enough to be available on a democratic scale, should hold a place of special importance in a museum concerned with encouraging the widespread collecting of original works by living artists."

Alfred continued, "In 1945 . . . at her expense . . . the collection was catalogued. . . . [She] began again to buy prints for the collection, particularly works by Bonnard, Signac and others of the period about 1900. . . . [In] 1946 she gave the Museum her very valuable group of sixty Lautrec lithographs. Then she turned her attention, which had lapsed during the war, to more recent prints. . . . in the last week of her life she was eagerly looking forward to exploring the achievements of the younger American printmakers. [She] died . . . just as final plans for opening the print room were being prepared."[14]

On December 15, 1953, John formally presented Colonial Williamsburg with securities valued at $1 million to construct a building outside the historic boundaries to maintain and exhibit Abby's folk art collection. He personally selected the site, adjacent to the Williamsburg Inn, and conferred closely with Ed Kendrew and others about the design details and the gardens. The Abby Aldrich Rockefeller Folk Art Center opened in 1957. The present collection numbers more than two thousand objects, and in addition to research on American folk art the museum supports a year-round program of changing exhibitions, lectures, and publications. As the center's capacity was pushed to its limits, a 19,000-square-foot addition was dedicated on April 25, 1992.

However much the experts may have argued over the presence of nineteenth-century folk art in an eighteenth-century restoration, the Folk Art Center remains the most beloved of all the Williamsburg installations.

An ailing Henri Matisse, eighty-four years old, confined to a bed in his studio in Vence, received a letter from Alfred Barr, representing the Rockefeller family, in the spring of 1954. Would the great man design a stained-glass window for the Union Church of Pocantico as a memorial to Abby Aldrich Rockefeller? Matisse had already created his masterpiece—the windows of the Chapel of the Rosary of the Dominican nuns in Vence. Those windows were first designed in paper cutouts—gouache color on cut-and-pasted paper—in a technique invented by Matisse making it possible for him to work on large compositions, although bedridden.

On May 11, 1954, Matisse declined the commission, explaining that as his health did not permit him to travel, he would be deprived of the opportunity to study the setting. "I regret, especially, that my decision prevents an expression of my feelings towards

Mrs. Rockefeller of whom I have such a warm and vivid memory."[15]

Alfred did not let the matter rest, however. He sent an enlargement of an architect's drawing of the east window of the church, mounted on muslin, ninety by ninety inches, to Matisse. There followed black-and-white and color photographs of the Union Church, interior and exterior. On August 23, Matisse wrote Alfred that he had changed his mind. "I have installed the [blueprints] on the wall of my studio," he wrote, "and have lived with them. . . . Fatigued at the beginning of the summer, I have spent some weeks resting but now I want to tell you that I feel my spirit caught by this project."[16]

The artist insisted on perfection. More drawings, photographs, questions, answers—all concerning the window—brought the church closer to the artist. On October 28, Matisse wrote a progress report. The glass would be made in Paris by the master glazier who was accustomed to working with his designs. On November 1, he wrote again. "I have been able to complete, I think happily, the work which I had undertaken."[17] Two days later he died.

On an editorial page known for discussions of weighty national issues, the *New York Times* published an intimate tribute to Abby. "The world is lesser today by the passing of Mrs. John D. Rockefeller, Jr. . . . Hers was the spirit that held them [the family] together. . . . When she was away from her sons she was accustomed to call them on the telephone periodically, to talk to them for hours. Their most vivid and lasting recollections of their early years are the long talks they had with their mother. . . . Possibly never again, and at least not in our times, will an immense fortune such as that of the Rockefeller family be built up. . . . In the handling of that wealth the character, the integrity, the uncompromising principles and beliefs of Mrs. Rockefeller played an important part. This has been a fortunate thing for society, for this country and for the world."[18]

NOTES

Letters and manuscripts used in the text may be located in the following library holdings, either as originals or accurate copies:

Colonial Williamsburg Foundation Archives, Williamsburg, Va.: Oral History Collection (CWFA; OHC).

Library of Congress, Washington, D.C.: Manuscript Division. Nelson W. Aldrich Papers (L. of C.; NWA)

Museum of Modern Art Archives, New York (MoMA Arch.): The Archives Pamphlet File; Alfred H. Barr, Jr., Papers (selective availability on microfilm through the Archives of American Art) (AHB Jr. Papers); A. Conger Goodyear Papers (ACG Papers); Public Information Scrapbooks; Abby Aldrich Rockefeller Correspondence; Abby Aldrich Rockefeller Scrapbooks.

Rhode Island Historical Society, Providence, R.I. (RIHS): Lucy Aldrich Collection (LAC).

Rockefeller Archive Center (RAC), Pocantico Hills, North Tarrytown, N.Y. Rockefeller Family Archives (RFA) Record Group 1 (1): John D. Rockefeller Papers (JDR). Record Group 2 (2), Office of the Messrs. Rockefeller (OMR): Abby Aldrich Rockefeller Series (AAR Se.), unprocessed, meaning folder numbers not yet assigned (unpr.); Business Interests Series (B.I. Se.); Cultural Interests Series (C.I. Se.); Educational Interests Series (E.I. Se.); Friends and Services Series (F. & S. Se.); Homes Series (H. Se.); John D. Rockefeller, Junior, Personal Series (JDR

Jr. P. Se.); John D. Rockefeller, Senior Series (JDR, Sr. P. Se.); Rockefeller Boards Series (R.B. Se.); Welfare Interests Series (W.I. Se.).

Rockefeller Archive Center, Pocantico Hills, North Tarrytown, N.Y. By special permission the author examined selected correspondence to and from David Rockefeller and Laurance Rockefeller.

Due to unique circumstances special permission was granted to the author to examine correspondence between Abby Aldrich Rockefeller and Nelson A. Rockefeller (spec. perm.).

Winthrop Rockefeller Collection (WRC), University of Arkansas Library at Little Rock (U. of A.).

Initials of Individuals

AGA	Abby Greene Aldrich
APA	Abby Pearce Aldrich
LA	Lucy Aldrich
NWA	Nelson Wilmarth Aldrich
AHB	Alfred H. Barr
MSB—I	Margaret Scolari Barr—Interview
ERB—I	Eleanor Robinson Bradshaw—Interview
APC	Abby Pearce Chapman
LC—I	Laura Chasin—Interview
SC	Stephen Clark
EC—I	Eliza Cobb—Interview
EdeL	Eustache de Lorey
SE—I	Stephanie Edgell—Interview
RBF	Raymond B. Fosdick
HF—I	Helena Franklin—Interview
ACG	A. Conger Goodyear
LG	Lucy Greene
EMH—I	Ellen Milton Harrison—Interview
EK—I	Edwin Kendrew—Interview
BK	Bernice Kert
WLMK	William Lyon MacKenzie King
ML	Mary Lindsley
AM	Abby Mauze
ARM	Abby Rockefeller Milton
AO—I	Abby O'Neill—Interview
FKR	Frida Kahlo Rivera

AAR	Abby Aldrich Rockefeller
BR	Babs Rockefeller
BlR—I	Blanchette Rockefeller—Interview
DR	David Rockefeller
DR—I	David Rockefeller—Interview
JDR Jr.	John D. Rockefeller, Jr.
JDR Sr.	John D. Rockefeller, Sr.
JDR 3rd	John D. Rockefeller 3rd
LR	Laurance Rockefeller
LR—I	Laurance Rockefeller—Interview
LR—(Pr. Coll.)	Laurance Rockefeller—Private Collection
LSR	Laura Spelman Rockefeller
NR	Nelson Rockefeller
PR—I	Peggy Rockefeller—Interview
WR	Winthrop Rockefeller
HS—I	Henry Stebbins—Interview
MW—I	Monroe Wheeler—Interview

Chapter 1

1. Paul R. Campbell and Patrick Conley, *Providence: A Pictorial History*, p. 101.
2. Mary Ellen Chase, *Abby Aldrich Rockefeller*, p. 27.
3. Nathaniel Wright Stephenson, *Nelson W. Aldrich: A Leader in American Politics*, p. 20.
4. NWA to APC, 15 February 1865, L. of C., NWA Papers.
5. James MacGregor Burns, *The Workshop of Democracy*, p. 78.
6. Ibid.
7. NWA to APC, September 1865, L. of C., NWA Papers.
8. Stephenson, p. 32.
9. NWA to APC, 4 September 1865, L. of C., NWA Papers.
10. NWA to APC, 28 October 1865, L. of C., NWA Papers.
11. NWA to APC, 10 February 1866 and undated, ca. 1866, L. of C., NWA Papers.
12. NWA to APC, August 1866, L. of C., NWA Papers.
13. Stephenson, p. 20.
14. NWA to APC, ca. 1866, L. of C., NWA Papers.
15. "Obituary," *Providence Journal*, 11 July 1871.
16. NWA to APC, 18 December 1872, L. of C., NWA Papers.

17. NWA to APC, 2 January 1873, L. of C., NWA Papers.
18. NWA to APC, 26 December 1872, L. of C., NWA Papers.
19. NWA to APC, 15 February 1873, L. of C., NWA Papers.
20. Ibid.

Chapter 2

1. Stephenson, p. 20.
2. NWA to AGA, 5 May 1881, RFA 2, AAR Se. B9 (unpr).
3. AAR Speech to YWCA, 28 April 1921, RFA 2, AAR Se. B28 (unpr).
4. Ellen Maury Slayden, *Washington Wife, 1879–1919*, p. 7.
5. NWA to AGA, ca. 1885, RFA 2, AAR Se. B9 (unpr).
6. Stephenson, p. 372.
7. AGA to NWA, 8 June 1884, L. of C., NWA Papers.
8. Attorney General Colt to NWA, June 1884, L. of C., NWA Papers.
9. NWA to APA, 14 June 1884 and 16 June 1884, L. of C., NWA Papers.
10. NWA to APA, 16 June 1884, L. of C., NWA Papers.
11. NWA to APA, 14 June 1884, L. of C., NWA Papers.
12. LR—I to BK, 20 March 1986.
13. Chase, p. 73.
14. APA to NPA, Series of Telegrams, Summer 1884, L. of C., NWA Papers.
15. NWA to APA, undated 1884, L. of C., NWA Papers.
16. APA to NWA, Series of Telegrams, Summer 1884, L. of C., NWA Papers.
17. LA to NWA, 15 February 1886, L. of C., NWA Papers.
18. APA to NWA, 15 February 1886, L. of C., NWA Papers.
19. S.A. Nightingale to NWA, 31 July 1885, L. of C., NWA Papers.
20. A. M. Keily to NWA, 9 June 1886, L. of C., NWA Papers.

Chapter 3

1. NWA to AGA, 20 May 1887, RFA 2, AAR Se. B9 (unpr).
2. APA to AGA, 31 January 1887 and 4 February 1887, RFA 2, AAR Se. B9 (unpr).
3. AAR to Ned Aldrich, 29 March 1927, RFA 2, AAR Se. B9 (unpr).
4. AO to BK, 11 June 1986. I
5. Stephenson, p. 91.
6. Nelson Aldrich III to BK, 20 May 1986. I

7. Chase, p. 9.
8. Chase, p. 10.
9. Mary Homans to BK, 19 March 1986. I
10. AGA Daily Diary 1893, RFA 2, AAR Se. B38 (unpr).
11. HR and SE to BK, 9 June 1986, I; Nelson Aldrich III to BK, 20 May 1986. I.
12. AGA Horoscope, RFA 2, AAR Se. B36 (unpr).

Chapter 4

1. Raymond B. Fosdick, *John D. Rockefeller Jr.: A Portrait*, p. 56.
2. Ibid.
3. Ibid., p. 46.
4. Ibid., p. 58.
5. Ibid.
6. Ibid., p. 42.
7. LSR Valedictory Essay 1855, RFA 2, JDR Jr. P. Se. LB I.
8. LC to BK, 19 May 1986. I.
9. Alan Nevins, *Study in Power: John D. Rockefeller—Industrialist and Philanthropist*, 1:326.
10. Fosdick, *JDR Portrait*, p.2.
11. Max Weber, *The Protestant Ethic and the Spirit of Capitalism*, p. 69.
12. Nevins, 2:427 and 1:326.
13. Fosdick, *JDR Portrait*, p. 35.
14. James T. Maher, *The Twilight of Splendor*, p. 270
15. Fosdick, *JDR Portrait*, p. 39.
16. JDR Jr. Diary, 16 November 1888, RFA 2, JDR Jr. P. Se. B3.
17. Fosdick, *JDR Portrait*, p. 41.
18. Ibid., p. 383, and "The Legacy of Bessie Dashiell."
19. Fosdick, *JDR Portrait*, p. 79.

Chapter 5

1. Richard Aldrich to BK, 27 May 1986. I.
2. Stephenson, p. 118.
3. Constance McLaughlin Green, *Washington: Capital City 1879–1950*, p. 96.
4. Fosdick, *JDR Portrait*, p. 60.
5. JDR Jr. Trip Diary 1896, RFA 2, JDR Jr. P. Se. B37.
6. Fosdick, *JDR Portrait*, p. 66.

7. JDR Jr. Trip Diary 1896, RFA 2, JDR Jr. P. Se. B37.
8. JDR Jr. to AAR, 18 August 1906, RFA 2, JDR Jr. P. Se. B55.
9. Fosdick, *JDR Portrait*, p. 67.
10. HF and SE to BK, 8 June 1986. I.
11. AAR Engagement Calendar 1896, RFA 2, AAR Se. B38 (unpr).
12. JDR Jr. to RBF, 19 May 1953, RFA 2, JDR Jr. P. Se. Fosdick Notes, B50.
13. Fosdick, *JDR Portrait*, p. 67.
14. APA to AGA, 6 March 1897, RFA 2, AAR Se. B9 (unpr).
15. JDR Jr. to LSR, 23 February 1897, RFA 2, JDR Jr. P. Se. B20.
16. JDR Jr. to RBF, 9 June 1952, RFA 2, JDR Jr. P. Se. Fosdick Notes B44.
17. LSR to JDR Sr., 1 March 1897, RFA 2, JDR Jr. P. Se. B20.
18. JDR Jr. to RBF, 9 June 1952, RFA 2, JDR Jr. P. Se. Fosdick Notes B44.
19. JDR Jr. to LSR, 9 May 1897, RFA 2, JDR Jr. P. Se. B20.
20. LSR to JDR Jr., 28 June 1897, RFA 2, JDR Jr. P. Se. B20.
21. LSR to JDR Jr., 22 June 1902, RFA 2, JDR Jr. P. Se. B20.
22. JDR Jr. to LSR, 24 June 1897, RFA 2, JDR Jr. P. Se. B20.
23. JDR Jr. to AAR, 21 May 1911, RFA 2, JDR Jr. P. Se. B55.
24. Chase, p. 26.
25. JDR Jr. to AAR, 25 February 1908, RFA 2, JDR Jr. P. Se. B55.
26. JDR Jr. to AAR, 26 July 1906, RFA 2, JDR Jr. P. Se. B55.
27. JDR Jr. to AAR, 11 August 1911, RFA 2, JDR Jr. P. Se. B55.

Chapter 6

1. LSR to JDR Jr., 3 March 1900, RFA 2, JDR Jr. P. Se. B20.
2. NWA to JDR Jr., 10 April 1900, L. of C., NWA Papers.
3. Spelman Prentice to BK, 12 March 1988. I.
4. RFA 2, JDR Jr. P. Se. Fosdick Notes B50.
5. JDR Jr. to AAR, 13 August 1911, RFA 2, JDR Jr. P. Se. B55.
6. JDR Jr. to LSR, 21 August 1901, RFA 2, JDR Jr. P. Se. B20.
7. RFA 2, JDR Jr. P. Se. Fosdick Notes B50.
8. JDR Jr. to AAR, 23 August 1903, RFA 2, JDR Jr. P. Se. B55.
9. Ibid.
10. JDR Jr. to LSR, 24 August 1901, RFA 2, JDR Jr. P. Se. B20.
11. AGA to LG, undated 1901, RFA 2, AAR Se. B9 (unpr).
12. Frank Smith to AGA, 26 August 1901, RFA 2, AAR Se. B9 (unpr).
13. AGA to LSR, undated 1901, RFA 2, JDR Jr. P. Se. B20.

14. Nevins, 2:297.
15. JDR Jr. to AGA, 20 September 1901, RFA 2, JDR Jr. P. Se. B55.
16. LSR to JDR Jr., 12 October 1901, RFA 2, JDR Jr. P. Se. B20.
17. JDR Jr. to Aunt Lute, 14 October 1901, RFA 2, JDR Jr. P. Se. B20.
18. *Providence Journal*, 10 October 1901.
19. Richard Aldrich to BK, 27 May 1986. I.
20. Theodore Green to AGA, 8 October 1901, RFA 2, AAR Se. B9 (unpr).

Chapter 7

1. Chase, p. 60.
2. JDR Jr. to LRS, 16 October 1901, RFA 2, JDR Jr. P. Se. B20.
3. PR to BK, 25 October 1986. I.
4. Chase, p. 28.
5. Ibid., p. 26.
6. LR—I to BK, 13 June 1986.
7. Joseph Byron, *Photographs of New York Interiors at the Turn of the Century*, p. XVIII.
8. Grace Mayer, *Once upon a City*, pp. 1, 3, 4.
9. AAR to DR, 31 August 1944, RFA 2, AAR Se. B12 (unpr).
10. LR—I to BK, 1 June 1987.
11. Fosdick, *JDR Portrait*, p. 118.
12. JDR Jr. to LSR, 15 June 1902, RFA 2, JDR Jr. P. Se. B20.
13. EMH to BK, 5 August 1987. I.
14. Richard Aldrich to BK, 27 May 1986. I.
15. AAR to LG, April 1910, RFA 2, AAR Se. B9 (unpr).
16. AAR to JDR Jr., 29 September 1902 and 1 October 1902, RFA 2, JDR Jr. P. Se. B55.
17. AAR to JDR Jr., 2 October 1902, RFA 2, JDR Jr. P. Se. B55.

Chapter 8

1. AAR to DR, 29 January 1946, RFA 2, AAR Se. B12 (unpr).
2. AAR to JDR Jr., 19 August 1903, RFA 2, JDR Jr. P. Se. B55.
3. AAR to JDR Jr., 11 August 1903, RFA 2, JDR Jr. P. Se. B55.
4. AAR to JDR Jr., 12 August 1903, RFA 2, JDR Jr. P. Se. B55.
5. AAR to JDR Jr., 27 August 1903, RFA 2, JDR Jr. P. Se. B55.
6. JDR Jr. to AAR, 21 August 1903, RFA 2, JDR Jr. P. Se. B55.
7. JDR Jr. to AAR, 27 August 1903, RFA 2, JDR Jr. P. Se. B55.

8. AAR to JDR Jr., 27 August 1903, RFA 2, JDR Jr. P. Se. B55.
9. AAR to JDR Jr., October 1903, RFA 2, JDR Jr. P. Se. B55.
10. Reprint, undated, RFA 2, AAR Se. B29 (unpr).
11. APA Diary, 26 November 1903, L. of C., NWA papers.
12. APA Diary, undated 1903, L. of C., NWA papers.
13. JDR Jr. to AAR, 25 July 1904, RFA 2, JDR Jr. P. Se. B55.
14. AAR to JDR Jr., 5 August 1904, RFA 2, JDR Jr. P. Se. B55.
15. AAR to JDR Jr., 7 August 1904, RFA 2, JDR Jr. P. Se. B55.
16. AAR to JDR Jr., 9 August 1904, RFA 2, JDR Jr. P. Se. B55.
17. Ibid.
18. JDR Jr. to AAR, 9 August 1904, RFA 2, JDR Jr. P. Se. B55.
19. AAR to JDR Jr., 27 August 1904, RFA 2, JDR Jr. P. Se. B55.
20. AAR to JDR Jr., 29 August 1904, RFA 2, JDR Jr. P. Se. B55.
21. George Franklin to BK, 9 June 1986. I.
22. Peter Gay, *Freud: A Life for Our Times*, p. 3.
23. LSR to JDR Jr., 24 January 1905, RFA 2, JDR Jr. P. Se. B20.
24. Chas Heydt to B.W. Foote, 15 May 1905, RFA 1, JDR Papers, LB 269, p. 383.
25. JDR Jr. to E. L. Trudeau, 22 May 1905, RFA 1, JDR Papers. LB 269, p. 443.
26. John Ensor Harr and Peter J. Johnson, *The Rockefeller Century: Three Generations of America's Greatest Family*, p. 91.
27. Nevins, 2:363.
28. Harr and Johnson, p. 91.
29. Fosdick, *JDR Portrait*, p. 126.
30. AAR to JDR Jr., 14 August 1907, RFA 2, JDR Jr. P. Se. B55.
31. APA to AAR, 8 May 1906, RFA 2, AAR Se. B9 (unpr).
32. APA to AAR, 8 March 1909, RFA 2, AAR Se. B9 (unpr).
33. APA to AAR, 12 July 1909, RFA 2, AAR Se. B9 (unpr).
34. JDR Jr. to AAR, 13 October 1906, RFA 2, JDR Jr. P. Se. B55.
35. AAR to JDR Jr., 16 October 1906, RFA 2, JDR Jr. P. Se. B55.
36. AAR to JDR Jr., 15 July 1907, RFA 2, JDR Jr. P. Se. B55.
37. JDR Jr. to Adele Herter, undated 1907, RFA 2, AAR Se. B10 (unpr).

Chapter 9

1. Albert I. Berger, "My Father's House at Pocantico Hills," p. 134.
2. AAR to JDR Jr., 23 August 1904, RFA 2, JDR Jr. P. Se. B55.
3. JDR Jr. to AAR, 29 August 1904, RFA 2, JDR Jr. P. Se. B55.
4. Berger, p. 408.

5. AAR to JDR Jr., 24 July 1906, RFA 2, JDR Jr. P. Se. B55.
6. AAR to JDR Jr., 20 August 1906, RFA 2, JDR Jr. P. Se. B55.
7. AAR to JDR Jr., 7 August 1907, RFA 2, JDR Jr. P. Se. B55.
8. AAR to JDR Jr., 12 July 1907, RFA 2, JDR Jr. P. Se. B55.
9. Berger, p. 203.
10. JDR Jr. to AAR, 24 July 1908, RFA 2, JDR Jr. P. Se. B55.
11. Berger, pp. 263–64.
12. LSR Diary, 8 October 1908, RFA 1, JDR Papers, Spelman Family Se. LSR file, B2 F10.
13. LSR to JDR Jr, 28 September 1908, RFA 2, JDR Jr. P. Se. B20.
14. Berger, p. 279.
15. Ibid., p. 280.
16. Ibid., p. 293.
17. JDR Jr. to LSR, 17 March 1909, RFA 2, JDR Jr. P. Se. B20.
18. JDR Jr. to LSR, 6 April 1909, RFA 2, JDR Jr. P. Se. B20.
19. AAR to JDR Jr., 25 May 1909, RFA 2, JDR Jr. P. Se. B55.
20. JDR Jr. to LSR, 8 August 1910, RFA 2, JDR Jr. P. Se. B20.

Chapter 10

1. JDR Jr. to LSR, 22 June 1908, RFA 2, JDR Jr. P. Se. B20.
2. AAR to JDR Jr., 29 June 1908, RFA 2, JDR Jr. P. Se. B55.
3. AAR to JDR Jr., 1 July 1908, RFA 2, JDR Jr. P. Se. B55.
4. JDR Jr. to AAR, 21 July 1908, RFA 2, JDR Jr. P. Se. B55.
5. AAR to JDR Jr., 24 July 1908, RFA 2, JDR Jr. P. Se. B55.
6. JDR Jr. to AAR, 3 July 1908, RFA 2, JDR Jr. P. Se. B55.
7. Mayer, pp. 13–14.
8. JDR Jr. to LSR, 5 October 1909, RFA 2, JDR Jr. P. Se. B20.
9. Mary Homans to BK, 19 March 1986. I.
10. AAR to LG, Spring 1910, AAR Se. B9 (unpr).
11. LA to JDR Jr., undated 1940, RFA 2, JDR Jr. P. Se. B23.
12. JDR Jr. to LSR, ca. 1910, RFA 2, JDR Jr. P. Se. B20.
13. AAR to JDR Jr., 16 May 1911, RFA 2, JDR Jr. P. Se. B55.
14. Nevins, 2:379.
15. JDR Sr. to JDR Jr., 3 November 1909, RFA 2, JDR Jr. P. Se. B2.
16. JDR Jr. to JDR Sr., 6 February 1911, RFA 2, JDR Sr. Se. B34 F.264.
17. HS to BK, 5 August 1987. I.
18. AAR to JDR Jr., 12 May 1912, RFA 2, JDR Jr. P. Se. B55.
19. JDR Jr. to AAR, 13 May 1912, RFA 2, JDR Jr. P. Se. B55.

20. JDR Jr. to AAR, 15 May 1912, RFA 2, JDR Jr. P. Se. B55.
21. Fred Smith, "A Time to Remember."
22. Chase, p. 40.
23. DR, *Unused Resources and Economic Waste* (Chicago: U. of C. Press, 1941).
24. Ibid.
25. JDR Jr. to LSR, 13 December 1913, RFA 2, JDR Jr. P. Se. B20.
26. JDR Jr. to LSR, 19 January 1914, RFA 2, JDR Jr. P. Se. B20.

Chapter 11

1. JDR Jr. to AAR, 28 September 1914, RFA 2, JDR Jr. P. Se. B55.
2. AAR to JDR Jr., 4 October 1914, RFA 2, JDR Jr. P. Se. B55.
3. Fosdick Notes. RFA 2, JDR Jr. P. Se. B50.
4. AAR to JDR Jr., 10 May 1915, RFA 2, JDR Jr. P. Se. B55.
5. AAR to JDR Jr., 27 September 1915, RFA 2, JDR Jr. P. Se. B55.
6. WLMK to AAR, 6 October 1915, RFA 2, AAR Se. B11 (unpr).
7. Fosdick Notes. RFA 2, JDR Jr. P. Se. B50.
8. JDR Jr. to JDR Sr., 2 June 1918, RFA 2, JDR Sr. P. Se. B35 F271.
9. AAR to LG, 22 April 1915, RFA 2, AAR Se. B9 (unpr).
10. Edith McCormick to AAR, 22 September 1915, RFA 2, AAR Se. B10 (unpr).
11. AAR to LG, 11 August 1915, RFA 2, AAR Se. B9 (unpr).
12. Florence Scales to AAR, 17 November 1915, RFA 2, AAR Se. B15 (unpr).
13. Florence Scales to AAR, 16 November 1915, RFA 2, AAR Se. B15 (unpr).
14. BR to AAR, 12 May 1917, RFA 2, AAR Se. B12 (unpr).
15. BR to JDR Jr., 12 April 1919, RFA 2, AAR Se. B15 (unpr).
16. JDR Jr. to AAR, 28 April 1916, RFA 2, JDR Jr. P. Se. B55.
17. AAR to JDR Jr., Summer 1916, RFA 2, JDR Jr. P. Se. B55.
18. JDR Jr. to AAR, 23 September 1916, RFA 2, JDR Jr. P. Se. B55.
19. Helen Flexner to AAR, 17 February 1917, RFA 2, AAR Se. B1 (unpr).
20. LG to AAR, 19 February 1917, RFA 2, AAR Se. B1 (unpr).
21. AAR to LG, 8 August 1917, RFA 2, AAR Se. B9 (unpr).

Chapter 12

1. Peter Collier and David Horowitz, *The Rockefellers: An American Dynasty*, p. 131.

2. AAR to RBF, 27 November 1917, RFA 2, AAR Se. B4 (unpr).
3. AAR to RBF, 19 January 1918, RFA 2, AAR Se. B4 (unpr).
4. AAR to RBF, 8 February 1918, RFA 2, AAR Se. B4 (unpr).
5. Ibid.
6. AAR to RBF, 20 February 1918, RFA 2, AAR Se. B4 (unpr).
7. RH Nichols to AAR, 23 February 1918, RFA 2, AAR Se. B4 (unpr).
8. *Seattle Washington Times*, 17 February 1918, RFA 2, AAR Se. B29 (unpr).
9. *AAR Letters*, 30 April 1919, p. 6.
10. WR, "Letter to My Son," p. 2.
11. AAR to A. C. Harte, 21 November 1917, RFA 2, AAR Se. B10 (unpr).
12. Alvin Moscow, *The Rockefeller Inheritance*, p. 43.
13. LR to BK, 13 June 1988. I.
14. Spelman Prentice to BK, 12 March 1988. I.
15. John R. Prentice to AAR, 30 December 1940, RFA 2, JDR Jr. P. Se., Spec. Lett. P–Q B24.
16. Margaret Strong to AAR, 30 December 1919, RFA 2, JDR Sr. P. Se. B35 F.273.
17. LR—I to BK, 1 October 1988.
18. Fosdick, *JDR Portrait*, p. 415.
19. JDR Sr. to JDR Jr., 13 March 1917, RFA 2, JDR Sr. P. Se. B35.
20. JDR Sr. to JDR Jr., 29 April 1918, RFA 2, JDR Sr. P. Se. B36.
21. JDR Sr. to JDR Jr., 15 December 1920, RFA 2, JDR Sr. P. Se. B36.
22. JDR Sr. to JDR Jr., 17 February 1921, RFA 2, JDR Sr. P. Se. B35.
23. JDR Sr. to JDR Jr., 12 December 1921, RFA 2, JDR Sr. P. Se. B36 F277.
24. JDR Jr. to JDR Sr., 16 November 1920, RFA 2, JDR Sr. P. Se. B36 F275.
25. JDR Jr. to JDR Sr., 28 October 1920, RFA 2, JDR Sr. P. Se. B36 F275.
26. JDR Jr. to JDR Sr., 29 October 1915, RFA 2, JDR Sr. P. Se. B35 F267.
27. AAR to JDR Sr., 29 April 1915, RFA 2, JDR Sr. P. Se. B34 F266.
28. Joseph E. Persico, *The Imperial Rockefeller: A Biography of Nelson Rockefeller*, p. 18.
29. Fosdick, *JDR Portrait*, p. 213.
30. Nathalie Dana, *Young in New York: A Memoir of a Victorian Girlhood*, p. 84.
31. AM to LC, 10 November 1973. I.

32. BR to AAR, 7 March 1918, RFA 2, AAR Se. B12 (unpr).
33. LR—I to BK, 20 March 1986; 13 June 1986 and 1 October 1988.
34. AO to BK, 11 June 1986. I.
35. Chase, p. 44.
36. DR—I to BK, 25 October 1986 and 7 August 1987.

Chapter 13

1. LA to AAR, 12 May 1919, RFA 2, AAR Se. B7 (unpr).
2. LA to AAR, 18 July 1919, RFA 2, AAR Se. B7 (unpr).
3. SE and HF to BK, 9 June 1986. I.
4. EMH to BK, 5 August 1987. I.
5. WLMK to AAR, 27 December 1919, RFA 2, AAR Se. B11 (unpr).
6. *AAR Letters*, 16 August 1920, p. 32.
7. "Housing for Employed Girls and Women," 15 August 1920, RFA 2, AAR Se. B28 (unpr).
8. *AAR Letters*, 6 June 1919, p. 11.
9. AAR to JDR 3rd, 14 October 1920, and AAR to BR, 19 October 1920, RFA 2, AAR Se. B12 (unpr).
10. Chase, p. 124
11. *AAR Letters*, 10 April 1920, p. 27.
12. *AAR Letters*, 16 April 1920, p. 28.
13. LA to AAR, ca. 1920, RFA 2, AAR Se. B7 (unpr).
14. LA to AAR, 14 April 1920, RFA 2, AAR Se. B7 (unpr).
15. AM to LC, 10 November 1973. I.
16. DR—I to BK, 7 August 1987.
17. JDR Jr. to JDR Sr., 28 April 1920, RFA 2, JDR Jr. P. Se. B22.
18. EMH to BK, 5 August 1987. I.
19. LR—I to BK, 20 March 1986.
20. AM to LC, 10 November 1973. I.
21. Chas Heydt to Houston, 11 June 1920, RFA 2, JDR Jr. P. Se. B41.
22. *AAR Letters*, 14 August 1920, p. 31.
23. EMH to BK, 5 August 1987. I.
24. HS to BK, 5 August 1987. I.
25. Ibid.
26. Becka Stebbins to BK, 7 August 1987. I.
27. Ibid.
28. AAR to JDR 3rd, 6 October 1920, RFA 2, AAR Se. B12 (unpr).
29. AAR to LR, 5 November 1920 (pr. coll.).

30. AAR to LR, 6 December 1920, RFA 2, AAR Se. B12 (unpr).
31. WR, "Letter to My Son," p. 27.

Chapter 14

1. AAR speech to YWCA, 28 April 1921, RFA 2, AAR Se. B28 (unpr).
2. *AAR Letters*, 18 February 1921, p. 47.
3. Ibid., 9 May 1921, p. 54.
4. AAR to DR, 20 March 1927, RFA 2, AAR Se. B12 (unpr).
5. JDR 3rd to AAR, 28 February 1921, RFA 2, AAR Se. B12 (unpr).
6. JDR 3rd to AAR, 11 May 1921 and 18 May 1921, RFA 2, AAR Se. B12 (unpr).
7. AAR to JDR 3rd, ca. May 1921, RFA 2, AAR Se. B12 (unpr).
8. Zenos Miller to AAR, 7 August 1921, RFA 2, AAR Se. B15 (unpr).
9. AAR to LR, 29 September 1921 (pr. coll.).
10. AAR to LR, ca. 1921 (pr. coll.).
11. Zenos Miller to AAR, 11 September 1921, RFA 2, AAR Se. B15 (unpr).
12. LA to AAR, 31 December 1921, RFA 2, AAR Se. B7 (unpr).
13. *AAR Letters*, 14 September 1922, p. 77.
14. Ibid., 29 November 1922, p. 84.
15. LA to AAR, 11 January 1923, RFA 2, AAR Se. B7 (unpr).
16. *AAR Letters*, May 1923, p. 103.
17. Ibid., 24 May 1923, p. 103.
18. Ibid., 20 May 1923, pp. 308–28.
19. Ibid., 23 February 1922, p. 69.
20. Ibid., p. 68.
21. Frances A. Burns, "The Reminiscences of Frances A. Burns," transcript of interview, 22 and 25 January 1957, CWFA; OHC.
22. AAR to ML, 15 February 1923, RFA 2, AAR Se. B28 (unpr).
23. *New York Times*, 19 March 1922.
24. AAR to ML, 13 January 1922, RFA 2, AAR Se. B28 (unpr).
25. AAR to ML, 17 March 1922, RFA 2, AAR Se. B28 (unpr).
26. *New York Evening World*, 22 January 1925, RFA 2, AAR Se. B29 (unpr).
27. AAR to RBF, 28 July 1922, RFA 2, AAR Se. B4 (unpr).
28. AAR to RBF, 10 October 1922, RFA 2, AAR Se. B10 (unpr).
29. AAR to Mrs. G. Pinchot, 27 April 1921, RFA 2, AAR Se. B10 (unpr).

Chapter 15

1. JDR Jr. to AAR, 6 July 1922 and 8 July 1922, RFA 2, JDR Jr. P. Se. B55.
2. AAR to JDR Jr., 23 March 1922. RFA 2, JDR Jr. P. Se. B55.
3. JDR Jr. to AAR, 6 July 1922, RFA 2, JDR Jr. P. Se. B55.
4. *AAR Letters*, 29 November 1922, p. 85.
5. BR to JDR Jr., 30 October 1922, RFA 2, JDR Jr. P. Se. B12.
6. LR—I to BK, 11 June 1987.
7. *AAR Letters*, 29 November 1922, pp. 86, 87.
8. JDR Jr. to LA, 23 January 1923, RFA 2, JDR Jr. P. Se. B55.
9. *AAR Letters*, 28 January 1923, p. 90.
10. Ibid., pp. 90–91.
11. Ibid., 14 September 1922, pp. 77–78.
12. AAR to N. H. Batchelder, 29 December 1922, RFA 2, AAR Se. B10 (unpr).
13. AAR to JDR 3rd, NR, LR, 8 February 1923 (pr. coll.).
14. AAR to LR, 8 March 1923 (pr. coll.).
15. AAR to LR, ca. 1923 (pr. coll.).
16. *AAR Letters*, 12 April 1923, p. 101.
17. DR—I to BK, 9 September 1989.
18. AAR to DR, 3 July 1923, RFA 2, AAR Se. B12 (unpr).
19. AAR to DR, 12 July 1923, RFA 2, AAR Se. B12 (unpr).
20. AAR to Chas. Eliot, 27 May 1924, RFA 2, AAR Se. B29 (unpr).
21. *New York Times*, 29 May 1924, Reprint, RFA 2, AAR Se. B29 (unpr).
22. AM to LC, 10 October 1973. I.
23. AAR to JDR Jr., 15 July 1924, RFA 2, JDR Jr. P. Se. B55.
24. Albertson to AAR, 23 April 1923, RFA 2, AAR Se. B15 (unpr); AAR to JDR 3rd, 6 March 1922, RFA 2, AAR Se. B12 (unpr).
25. AO to BK, 11 June 1986. I.
26. AAR to DR, 8 July 1924, RFA 2, AAR Se. B12 (unpr).
27. AAR to JDR Jr., 15 July 1924, RFA 2, JDR Jr. P. Se. B55.
28. AAR to JDR Jr., 21 July 1924, RFA 2, JDR, Jr. P. Se. B55.
29. Ibid.

Chapter 16

1. Milton W. Brown, *The Story of the Armory Show*, p. 43.
2. Ibid., p. 144.

3. Margaret Sterne, *The Passionate Eye: The Life of William R. Valentiner*, p. 152.
4. Ibid.
5. Peter Guenther, "An Introduction to the Expressionist Movement," p. 7.
6. Chase, p. 130.
7. AAR to ACG, 23 March 1936, RFA 2, AAR Se. MoMA B25 (unpr).
8. WV to Chase, 24 June 1949, RFA 2, C.I. Se. MoMA B19.
9. Ibid.
10. Henry Morgenthau to AAR, September 1925, RFA 2, AAR Se. B6 (unpr).
11. *AAR Letters*, 8 August 1925, p. 133.
12. AAR to Chas. Eliot, 11 February 1925, RFA 2, AAR Se. B10 (unpr).
13. AAR to Eliot, 5 May 1924, RFA 2, AAR Se. B10 (unpr).
14. Eliot to JDR Jr., 10 February 1917, RFA 2, F. & S. Se. B59.
15. AAR to Eliot, 9 May 1921, RFA 2, AAR Se. B10 (unpr).
16. AAR to WV, 2 April 1925 and 24 February 1925, RFA 2, AAR Se. B11 (unpr).
17. Harr and Johnson, p. 254.
18. AAR to DR, 24 October 1925, RFA 2, AAR Se. B12 (unpr).
19. Ibid.

Chapter 17

1. AM to LC, 10 November 1973. I.
2. AAR to JDR 3rd, 15 March 1926, RFA 2, AAR Se. B12 (unpr).
3. AAR to JDR 3rd, 9 March 1926, RFA 2, AAR Se. B12 (unpr).
4. Joe Alex Morris, *Nelson Rockefeller: A Biography*, p. 72.
5. DR—I to BK, 7 August 1987.
6. Harr and Johnson, p. 268.
7. Morris, *NR Bio*, p. 72.
8. AAR to LR, 16 July 1925, RFA 2, AAR Se. B12 (unpr).
9. LR—I to BK, June 11, 1987.
10. Fosdick, *JDR Portrait*, p. 300.
11. Ibid., p. 285.
12. EK to BK, 3 June 1986. I.
13. Peter T. Furst, *American Indian Art and Painting by Taos Artists: The David and Peggy Rockefeller Collection*, p. 344.

14. AAR to Irving Couse, 14 August 1926, RFA 2, JDR Jr. P. Se. Trips B42.
15. AAR to DR, 10 October 1926, RFA 2, AAR Se. B12 (unpr).
16. *AAR Letters*, 12 October 1926, p. 145.
17. Diana Balmori, Diana Kostial, and Eleanor McPeck, *Beatrix Farrand's American Landscapes: Her Gardens and Campuses*, p. 14.
18. Patrick Chassé, *The Abby Aldrich Rockefeller Garden: A Visitor's Guide*, p. 11.
19. *Princeton Alumni Weekly*, 86:9 (15 January 1986).
20. "Cosmopolitan Club," 8 May 1927, RFA 2, AAR Se. B28 (unpr).
21. Chassé, p. 5.
22. MSB to BK, 6 June 1987. I.

Chapter 18

1. *San Francisco Bulletin*, 17 February 1928, RFA 2, AAR Se. B29 (unpr).
2. AAR to John Stewart Bryan, 6 July 1929, RFA 2, AAR Se. B10 (unpr).
3. Bryan to AAR, 16 July 1929, RFA 2, AAR Se. B10 (unpr).
4. *New York Times*, 2 October 1925, p. 25.
5. *AAR Letters*, 26 May 1927, p. 148.
6. Asenath and Fanny Tetlow to AAR, 1 March 1927, RFA 2, AAR Se. B10 (unpr).
7. LA to AAR, 19 November 1926, RFA 2, AAR Se. B7 (unpr).
8. Chase, pp. 47–48.
9. *AAR Letters*, 7 May 1928, p. 152.
10. JDR Jr. to AAR, 13 August 1928, RFA 2, JDR Jr. P. Se. B55.
11. ARM to JDR Jr., 12 April 1928, RFA 2, AAR Se. B12 (unpr).
12. ARM to JDR Jr., 4 January 1927, RFA 2, AAR Se. B12 (unpr).
13. ARM to AAR, 23 March 1927, RFA 2, AAR Se. B12 (unpr).
14. AAR to Jesse Newlon, 12 September 1928, RFA 2, AAR Se. B10 (unpr).
15. WR, "Letter to My Son," p. 24.
16. AAR to boys, ca. 1928 (pr. coll.).
17. LA to AAR, July 1931, RFA 2, AAR Se. B7 (unpr).
18. WR to AAR, 23 September 1928, WRC (U. of A.).
19. WR to AAR, 11 November 1928, WRC (U. of A.).
20. *AAR Letters*, 7 May 1928, p. 153.
21. LR—I to BK, 20 March 1986.

22. LR to AAR and JDR Jr., 3 November 1928, RFA 2, AAR Se. B12 (unpr).
23. LR to AAR and JDR Jr., 16 December 1928, RFA 2, AAR Se. B12 (unpr).
24. JDR 3rd to AAR and JDR Jr., 18 November 1928, RFA 2, AAR Se. B12 (unpr).

Chapter 19

1. George Hart to AAR, 11 December 1928, RFA 2, AAR Se. B10 (unpr).
2. *New York Times*, 23 September 1928.
3. Diane Tepfer, *Edith Gregor Halpert and the Downtown Gallery: 1926–1940*, p. 138.
4. JDR Jr. to AAR, 14 April 1927, RFA 2, JDR Jr. P. Se. B55.
5. AAR to WV, 24 May 1927, RFA 2, AAR Se. B11 (unpr).
6. DR—I to BK, 8 June 1986.
7. *Bassett Hall Guide Book*, CWF, 1984, p. 42.
8. AAR to LR, 18 October 1927, RFA 2, AAR Se. B12 (unpr).
9. AAR to ML, 28 July 1931, RFA 2, AAR Se. B28 (unpr).
10. *New York Times*, 8 May 1988, NR H 35.
11. AAR to DR, undated, RFA 2, AAR Se. B12 (unpr).
12. AAR to LR, 9 December 1928, RFA 2, AAR Se. B12 (unpr).
13. HS to BK, 5 August 1987. I.
14. LR—I to BK, 29 March 1989.
15. AAR to LR, 12 January 1929, RFA 2, AAR Se. B12 (unpr).
16. JDR Jr. to children, 19 January 1929, RFA 2, JDR Jr. P. Se. B40 Trips 1929.
17. AAR to LR, undated 1929 (pr. coll.).
18. AAR to LR, 10 February 1929 (pr. coll.).
19. AAR to LR, undated 1929 (pr. coll.).
20. Ibid.
21. AAR to LR, 31 January 1929 (pr. coll.).
22. AAR to LR, 10 February 1929 (pr. coll.).
23. AAR to LR, 18, 20, 23, and 25 February 1929 (pr. coll.).
24. AAR to boys, 30 June 1929 (pr. coll.).
25. AAR to boys, 30 June 1929 (pr. coll.).
26. AAR to DR, 13 July 1929, RFA 2, AAR Se. B12 (unpr).
27. AAR to EdeL, 26 August 1929, RFA 2, AAR Se. B11 (unpr).

Chapter 20

1. AAR to EdeL, 26 August 1929, RFA 2, AAR Se. B11 (unpr).
2. Philip Johnson to BK, 27 October 1986. I.
3. SC memo, July 1949, RFA 2, AAR Se. MoMA B26 (unpr).
4. Russell Lynes, *Good Old Modern*, pp. 7, 8.
5. EC to BK, 5 June 1987. I.
6. Brooks Wright, *The Artist and the Unicorn: The Lives of Arthur B. Davies*, p. 123.
7. A. Conger Goodyear, *The Museum of Modern Art: The First Ten Years*, p. 5.
8. EC to BK, 5 June 1987. I.
9. Goodyear, p. 3.
10. EC to BK, 5 June 1987. I.
11. AAR to Arthur David Davies, 18 December 1928, RFA 2, AAR Se. B10 (unpr).
12. Milton W. Brown, *The Story of the Armory Show*, pp. 57–58.
13. EC to BK, 5 June 1987. I.
14. Calvin Tompkins, *Merchants and Masterpieces*, p. 296.
15. Thomas Armstrong to BK, 2 June 1987. I.
16. AAR to ACG, 23 March 1936, RFA 2, AAR Se. MoMA B25 (unpr).
17. Tepfer, p. 147.
18. *Museum of Modern Art, New York: The History and the Collection*, p. 10.
19. ACG to AAR, 23 June 1929, RFA 2, AAR Se. MoMA B25 (unpr).
20. Rona Roob, "Alfred H. Barr, Jr.: A Chronicle of the Years 1902–1929," p. 7.
21. Ibid., p. 17.
22. Lynes, p. 33.
23. AAR to ACG, 12 July 1929, RFA 2, AAR Se. MoMA B25 (unpr).
24. AAR to AHB, 27 July 1929, MoMA Arch., AHB Jr. Papers (AAA 3264; 1278).
25. Dahlov Ipcar to BK, 10 January 1988. I.
26. Ibid.
27. William Zorach, *Art Is My Life*, pp. 56, 58.
28. AAR to LR, 28 July 1929 (pr. coll.).
29. Zorach, p. 96.
30. AHB to AAR, 12 August 1929, MoMA Arch., AHB Jr. Papers (AAA: 3264; 1272).
31. AHB to AAR, 2 August 1929, MoMA Arch., AHB Jr. Papers (AAA: 3264; 1273).

32. ACG to AAR, 7 August 1929, RFA 2, AAR Se. MoMA B25 (unpr).
33. AAR to ACG, 23 August 1929, RFA 2, AAR Se. MoMA B25 (unpr).
34. Crowninshield to ACG, 4 September 1929, RFA, 2 AAR Se. MoMA B25 (unpr).

Chapter 21

1. AHB to AAR, 8 September 1930, MoMA Arch., AHB Jr. Papers (AAA: 3264; 1242–48).
2. LR—I to BK, 11 June 1987.
3. DR—I to BK, 16 August 1987.
4. EC to BK, 5 June 1987. I.
5. Philip Johnson to BK, 11 June 1987. I.
6. BlR to BK, 10 June 1987. I.
7. AAR to LR, 27 October 1929 (pr. coll.).
8. ACG to AAR, 30 October 1929, RFA 2, AAR Se. MoMA B25 (unpr).
9. Burns, p. 542.
10. Lynes, p. 64.
11. ACG to AAR, 13 November 1929, RFA 2, AAR Se. MoMA B25 (unpr).
12. AHB, Foreword to 3rd Loan Exhibition, *Painting in Paris 1930*, p. 16, MoMA Arch., ACG Papers.
13. Lynes, p 72
14. *New York Evening Post*, 29 January 1930, MoMA Arch., ACG Papers.
15. Lynes, p. 72.
16. SC Memo, July 1949, RFA 2, AAR Se. MoMA B26 (unpr).
17. AAR to DR, March 1930, RFA 2, AAR Se. B12 (unpr).
18. AAR to LR, March 1930 (pr. coll.).
19. Morris, *NR Bio*, p. 78.
20. Ibid., p. 81.
21. Ibid., p. 82.
22. BlR to BK, 19 March 1986. I.
23. Morris, *NR Bio*, p. 73.
24. Ibid., p. 24.
25. Ibid., p. 75.
26. Dorothy C. Miller, *The Nelson Rockefeller Collection: Masterpieces of Modern Art*, p. 20.
27. Morris, *NR Bio*, pp. 74–75.
28. HS to BK, 5 August, 1987. I.

29. LR—I to BK, 1 October 1988.
30. Persico, p. 18.

Chapter 22

1. AHB to AAR, Summer 1930, MoMA Arch., AHB Jr. Papers (AAA: 3264; 1249).
2. MSB to BK, 5 June 1987. I.
3. AAR to WV, 23 August 1930, RFA 2, AAR Se. B11 (unpr).
4. Donald Deskey to BK, August 1987. I.
5. Helen Appleton Read, "Modern Art: The Collection of Mrs. John D. Rockefeller, Jr.," *Vogue*, April 1939.
6. Miller, "Contemporary American Paintings in the Collection of Mrs. John D. Rockefeller, Jr.," *Art News*, 1938, p. 183.
7. MSB to BK, 5 June 1987. I.
8. Philip Johnson to BK, 27 October 1986. I.
9. William Lieberman to BK, 4 June 1987. I.
10. BlR to BK, 19 March 1986. I.
11. AAR to JDR Jr., 3 April 1931, RFA 2, JDR Jr. P. Se. B55.
12. AAR to JDR Jr., 6 April 1931, RFA 2, JDR Jr. P. Se. B55.
13. ACG to AAR, 26 September 1930, RFA 2, AAR Se. MoMA B25 (unpr).
14. M. Burnbaum to AAR, 18 October 1930, RFA 2, AAR Se. Servants B28 (unpr).
15. AAR to LR, 1 November 1930, (pr. coll.).
16. AHB Foreword to 3rd Loan Exhibition, *Painting in Paris 1930*, pp. 11–12, MoMA Arch., ACG Papers.
17. AHB to AAR, 5 December 1930, MoMA Arch., AHB Jr. Papers (AAA: 3264; 1238).
18. MW to BK, 5 June 1987. I
19. AAR to LR, 9 December 1930, RFA 2, AAR Se. B12 (unpr).
20. EC to BK, 5 June 1987. I
21. Fosdick, *JDR Portrait*, p. 329.
22. *AAR Letters*, 21 February 1931, pp. 162–63.
23. Fosdick, *JDR Portrait*, p. 264.
24. Ibid., pp. 264, 266.
25. AAR to LR, 2 March 1931 (pr. coll.).
26. *AAR Letters*, 21 February 1931, p. 165.
27. ACG to AAR, 1 September 1931, RFA 2, AAR Se. MoMA B25 (unpr).

28. AAR to AHB, 14 March 1931, MoMA Arch., AHB Jr. Papers (AAA: 3264; 1230).

29. AAR to ACG, 14 March 1931, RFA 2, AAR Se. MoMA B25 (unpr).

30. AAR to AHB, 21 March 1931, RFA 2, AAR Se. MoMA B25 (unpr).

Chapter 23

1. Margaret Scolari Barr, "Our Campaigns," p. 26

2. Ibid., p. 27.

3. LA to AAR, July 1931, RFA 2, AAR Se. B7 (unpr).

4. *AAR Letters*, 21 March 1931, p. 168.

5. LA to AAR, July 1931, RFA 2, AAR Se. B7 (unpr).

6. *AAR Letters*, 10 June 1931, p. 169.

7. AAR to Mrs. Batchelder, 18 March 1931, RFA 2, AAR Se. B10 (unpr).

8. AAR to JDR 3rd, 17 March 1931, RFA 2, AAR Se. B12 (unpr).

9. AAR to family, 8 May 1930, RFA 2, AAR Se. B12 (unpr).

10. AAR to Margaret Sanger, 29 September 1930, RFA 2, AAR Se. B11 (unpr).

11. *New York Times*, 9 March 1932.

12. AAR to JDR 3rd, 21 July 1931, RFA 2, AAR Se. B12 (unpr).

13. LA to AAR, December 1931, RFA 2, AAR Se. B7 (unpr).

14. Book of Tributes, RFA 2, AAR Se. B30 (unpr).

15. "Notes of a Painter 1908," pp. 29–36, MoMA Arch., ACG Papers.

16. *New York Herald Tribune*, 2 May 1932, MoMA Arch., ACG Papers.

17. Lynes, p. 96.

18. Ibid., p. 97.

19. AAR to LR, 10 April 1932 (pr. coll.).

20. EC to BK, 5 June 1987. I.

21. Ibid.

22. AHB to AAR, 18 April 1932, MoMA Arch., AHB Jr. Papers (AAA: 3264; 1214).

23. AHB to ACG, 28 April 1932, MoMA Arch., ACG Papers.

24. Lynes, p. 101.

25. NR to AAR, 31 May 1932 (spec. perm.).

26. Lincoln Kirstein to BK, 12 June 1987. I.

27. EC to BK, 5 June 1987. I.

28. Lynes, pp. 92–93.

29. Dorothy Miller to BK, 10 June 1986. I.

30. MW to BK, 27 October 1986. I.

31. AAR to AHB, 7 March 1933, MoMA Arch., AHB Jr. Papers (AAA: 3264; 1181).
32. AAR to AHB, 24 April 1933, MoMA Arch., AHB Jr. Papers (AAA: 3264; 1177).
33. MW to BK, 27 October 1986. I.

Chapter 24

1. Beatrix Rumford, "Uncommon Art of the Common People: A Review of Trends in the Collecting and Exhibiting of American Folk Art," p. 36.
2. Carolyn Weekley to BK, 3 June 1986. I
3. Nina Fletcher Little, *American Folk Art from the Abby Aldrich Rockefeller Folk Art Collection*, p. 25.
4. *AAR Letters*, 30 April 1932, p. 177.
5. AAR to DR, 5 August 1932, RFA 2, AAR Se. B12 (unpr).
6. DR—I to BK, 25 October 1986.
7. AAR to LR, 29 July 1932 (pr. coll.).
8. BlR to BK, 19 March 1986. I.
9. Ibid.
10. Ibid.
11. Jay Rockefeller to BK, 28 June 1989. I.
12. BlR to BK, 19 March 1986. I.
13. LC to BK, 19 May 1986. I.
14. Harriet Bering to BK, 24 August 1987. I.
15. Lynes, p. 379.
16. Jay Rockefeller to BK, 28 June 1989. I.
17. BlR to BK, 19 March 1986. I.
18. Lynes, p. 379.

Chapter 25

1. Barr, M.S., p. 28.
2. AAR to AHB, 9 January 1933, RFA 2, AAR Se. MoMA B25 (unpr).
3. AHB to AAR, 4 February 1933, MoMA Arch., AHB Jr. Papers (AAA: 3264; 1183).
4. AAR to AHB, 7 March 1933, MoMA Arch., AHB Jr. Papers (AAA: 3264; 1183).
5. AAR to LR, 8 February 1933, RFA 2, AAR Se. B12 (unpr).

6. AAR to AHB, 7 March 1933, MoMA Arch., AHB Jr. Papers (AAA: 3264; 1181).
7. JDR Jr. to WLMK, 23 October 1933, RFA 2, F. & S. Se. B72.
8. LR—I to BK, 29 March 1989.
9. BlR to BK, 10 June 1987. I.
10. JDR Jr. to AAR, 18 May 1933; 19 May 1933; 23 May 1933, RFA 2, JDR Jr. P. Se. B55.
11. NR to AAR, 22 April 1933 (spec. perm.).
12. AAR to NR, 26 April 1933 (spec. perm.).
13. Lynes, p. 106.
14. AHB to AAR, 7 June 1933, MoMA Arch., AHB Jr. Papers (AAA: 3264; 1174).
15. AAR to ACG, 28 April 1933, MoMA Arch., AHB Jr. Papers (AAA: 3264; 1172).
16. AHB to AAR, 29 June 1933. MoMA Arch., AHB Jr. Papers (AAA: 3264; 1167).
17. Barr, M.S., p. 32.
18. AHB to AAR, 28 June 1932, MoMA Arch., AHB Jr. Papers (AAA: 3264; 1174).
19. AHB to AAR, 10 November 1933, MoMA Arch., AIIB Jr. Papers (AAA: 3264; 1160).
20. AHB to AAR, 6 November 1933, MoMA Arch., AHB Jr. Papers (AAA: 3264; 1102).
21. ACG to AAR, 15 May 1933, RFA 2, AAR Se. MoMA B25 (unpr).
22. A. Blackburn to AB, 15 August 1933, MoMA Arch., AHB Jr. Papers (AAA: 2165; 1014).
23. JDR Jr. to AAR; AAR to JDR Jr., 14 September 1933, RFA 2, JDR Jr. P. Se. B55.
24. JDR Jr. to AAR, 15 September 1933, RFA 2, JDR Jr., P. Se. B55.
25. JDR Jr. to NR, 14 September 1933, RFA 2, C.I. Se. B22.
26. AHB to AAR, 16 September 1933, MoMA Arch., AHB Jr. Papers (AAA: 3264; 1163).
27. Lynes, p. 80.
28. NR to AAR, May 1934 (spec. perm.).
29. AAR to ACG, 30 March 1934, RFA 2, AAR Se. MoMA B25 (unpr).
30. JDR Jr. to WLMK, 6 November 1933, RFA 2, F. & S. Se. B72.

Chapter 26

1. Chas. R. Richards to Thomas B. Appleget, 23 May 1928, RFA 2, AAR Se. B11 (unpr).
2. Chas. R. Richards to Thomas B. Appleget, 31 May 1928, RFA 2, AAR Se. B11 (unpr).
3. Thomas B. Appleget to JDR Jr., 1 June 1928, RFA 2, AAR Se. B11 (unpr).
4. AAR to Winthrop Aldrich, 17 February 1931, RFA 2, AAR Se. B11 (unpr).
5. Frances Flynn Paine to AAR, 13 August 1930, RFA 2, AAR Se. B11 (unpr).
6. Bertram D. Wolfe, *The Fabulous Life of Diego Rivera*, p. 6.
7. Geoffrey T. Hellman, "Profiles, Enfant Terrible," *New Yorker*, 20 May 1933, p. 22.
8. Wolfe, p. 216.
9. Sterne, p. 189.
10. DR—I to BK, 23 September 1988.
11. FKR to AAR, 22 January 1932, RFA 2, B.I. Se. Rock Center B95 Rivera.
12. FKR to AAR, 27 January 1932, RFA 2, B.I. Se. Rock Center B95 Rivera.
13. AAR to LR, January 1932 (pr. coll.).
14. Paul Goldberger, "A Gesture to the 'Good' Rockefeller Center," *New York Times*, 21 May 1989, H32.
15. WV to Chase, 24 June 1949, RFA 2, C.I. Se. Museums B19.
16. George Vincent to Arthur Woods, 23 March 1932, RFA 2, B.I. Se. Rock Center B142 Themes.
17. Wolfe, p. 318.
18. Raymond Hood to JDR Jr., 7 October 1932, RFA 2, B.I. Se. Rock Center B94.
19. Henri Matisse to AAR, 6 January 1933, AAR Se. B10 (unpr).
20. NR to Rivera, 13 October 1932, RFA 2, B.I. Se. Rock Center B95 Rivera.
21. Wolfe, p. 310.
22. FKR to AAR, 24 January 1933, RFA 2, B.I. Se. Rock Center B95 Rivera.
23. Rivera to AAR, 5 November 1932, RFA 2, B.I. Se. Rock Center B95 Rivera.

24. Lucienne Bloch, "The Making of Rivera's Rockefeller Center," p. 108.
25. Wolfe, pp. 320–21.
26. FKR to AAR, 6 March 1933, RFA 2, B.I. Se. Rock Center B95 Rivera.
27. Bloch, p. 113.
28. AAR to Anna Kelly, 24 May 1933, RFA 2, AAR Se. B10 (unpr).
29. Bloch, p. 116.
30. NR to Rivera, 4 May 1933, RFA 2, B.I. Se. Rock Center B95 Rivera.
31. Hugh S. Robertson to Rivera, 9 May 1933, RFA 2, B.I. Se. Rock Center B95 Rivera.
32. Bloch, p. 118.
33. Wolfe, p. 329.
34. *The Reminiscences of Holger Cahill*, Columbia Oral History, p. 280 (unpub).
35. Anna Kelly to Walter Pach, 12 May 1933, RFA 2, B.I. Se. Rock Center B95 Rivera.
36. Walter Pach to AAR, 11 September 1933, RFA 2, B.I. Se. Rock Center B95 Rivera.
37. Anna Kelly to Pach, 18 September 1933, RFA 2, B.I. Se. Rock Center B95 Rivera.
38. NR to Alan Blackburn, 16 December 1933, RFA 2, B.I. Se. Rock Center B95 Rivera.
39. Tepfer, p. 203.
40. Marion Oettinger, Jr., *Folk Treasures of Mexico: The Nelson A. Rockefeller Collection*, p. 42.

Chapter 27

1. WR, "Letter to My Son," p. 30.
2. Ibid., pp. 32–33.
3. WR to AAR and JDR Jr., 14 July 1934, WRC (U. of A.)
4. WR to JDR Jr., 26 March 1934, WRC (U. of A.)
5. LR to AAR, 5 June 1934, RFA 2, AAR Se. B12 (unpr).
6. Rockefeller siblings to JDR Jr., 1 May 1933, RFA 2, JDR Jr. P. Se. Fosdick Notes B49.
7. DR—I to BK, 7 August 1987.
8. Ibid.

9. ACG to AAR, 14 November 1934, RFA 2, AAR Se. MoMA B25 (unpr).

10. AAR to JDR 3rd, 16 February 1935, RFA 2, AAR Se. MoMA B25.

11. AHB to AAR, 5 February 1935, MoMA Arch., AHB Jr. Papers (AAA: 3264; 1066).

12. Saarinen, *The Proud Possessors*, p. 359.

13. AAR to DR, 1 April 1935, RFA 2, AAR Se. B12 (unpr).

14. *AAR Letters*, 17 April 1935, pp. 218–19.

15. Ibid., 23 March 1934, pp. 215–16.

16. Ibid., 17 April 1935, pp. 218–19.

17. AAR to DR, 26 April 1935, RFA 2, AAR Se. B12 (unpr).

18. NR to AAR, 18 February 1935 (spec. perm.).

19. AHB to AAR, 20 July 1935, MoMA Arch., AHB Jr. Papers (AAA: 3264; 1057)

20. Ibid.

21. AHB to AAR, 24 December 1935, MoMA Arch., AHB Jr. Papers (AAA: 3264; 1050).

22. AHB to AAR, 7 May 1936, RFA 2, AAR Se. MoMA B25 (unpr).

23. AHB to AAR, 28 December 1935, RFA 2, AAR Se. MoMA B25 (unpr).

24. ACG to AHB, 29 May 1935, MoMA Arch., AHB Jr. Papers (AAA: 2165; 1014).

25. Closing Statement, 2 July 1937, RFA 2, C.I. Se. MoMA B23 F235; AAR to MoMA, 20 June 1936, RFA 2, C.I. Se. MoMA B23 F236.

26. Barr, M.S., p. 43.

27. AAR to AHB, 23 August 1935, MoMA Arch., AHB Jr. Papers (AAA: 3264).

28. AHB to AAR, 14 January 1936, MoMA Arch., AHB Jr. Papers (AAA: 3264; 1047)

29. *Time*, 27:4 (27 January 1936), p. 28.

30. Avis Berman, *Rebels on Eighth Street*, p. 228.

31. Ibid., p. 287.

32. AAR to ACG, 12 August 1935, RFA 2, AAR Se. MoMA B25 (unpr).

33. *AAR Letters*, 16 March 1936, pp. 230–31.

34. JDR Jr. to boys, 11 August 1936, RFA 2, JDR Jr. P. Se. Trips B37.

35. Tom Mabry to AHB, 18 June 1936, MoMA Arch., AHB Jr. Papers (AAA: 2165; 1014).

36. AHB to AAR, 2 July 1936, MoMA Arch., AHB Jr. Papers (AAA: 2164; 1134).

37. Barr, M.S., p. 46.

38. AAR to NR, July 1936, MoMA Arch., AHB Jr. Papers (AAA: 3264; 1122).
39. Lynes, pp. 137–38.
40. Lynes, p. 145.
41. AAR to ACG, 16 December 1936, MoMA Arch., AHB Jr. Papers (AAA: 3264; 1119).
42. Tom Mabry to NR, 31 December 1937, RFA 2, AAR Se. MoMA B25 (unpr).
43. ACG to AAR, 18 June 1937, RFA 2, AAR Se. MoMA B25 (unpr).
44. ACG to AAR, 6 July 1937, RFA 2, AAR Se. MoMA B25 (unpr).
45. MoMA Bulletin, 6:7 p. 2, RFA 2, RFA AAR Se. MoMA B25 (unpr).
46. DR—I to BK, 7 August 1987.

Chapter 28

1. *AAR Letters*, 25 June 1937, p. 243.
2. AAR to DR, 12 December 1937, RFA 2, AAR Se. B12 (unpr).
3. AAR to DR, 11 and 28 November 1937, RFA 2, AAR Sc. B12 (unpr).
4. AAR to DR, 28 November 1937, RFA 2, AAR Se. B12 (unpr).
5. *AAR Letters*, 28 May 1937, p. 240.
6. AAR to DR, 10 October 1937, RFA 2, AAR Se. B12 (unpr).
7. AAR to DR, 6 November and 22 October 1937, RFA 2, AAR Se. B12 (unpr).
8. AAR to DR, 1 October 1937, RFA 2, AAR Se. B12 (unpr).
9. EK to BK, 3 June 1986. I.
10. JDR Jr. to Kenneth Chorley, 11 December 1936, RFA 2, C.I. Se. Folk Art B154 F1344.
11. JDR Jr. to W. G. Perry, 4 September 1935, RFA 2, C.I. Se. Folk Art B154 F1344.
12. JDR Jr. to W. G. Perry, 11 June 1935, RFA 2, C.I. Se. Folk Art B154 F1344.
13. EK to BK, 3 June 1986. I.
14. AAR to Frances Flynn Paine, 22 June 1931, RFA 2, AAR Se. B11 (unpr).
15. AAR to Edith Halpert, 18 July 1931, RFA 2, AAR Se. B11 (unpr).
16. *Bassett Hall*, CWF 1984, p. 33.
17. *AAR Letters*, 28 May 1937, p. 241.
18. Ibid., 25 June 1937, p. 244.
19. ERB to BK, 10 June 1987. I.

20. Ibid.
21. Helen Duprey Bullock, "The Reminiscences of Helen Duprey Bullock," transcript of interview, 1956, CWFA; OHC.
22. Susan Higginson Nash, "The Reminiscences of Susan Higginson Nash," transcript of interview, 1956, CWFA; OHC.
23. AAR to ML, 11 September 1933; 26 October 1936, RFA 2, AAR Se. B28 (unpr).
24. AAR to ML, 16 January 1937, RFA 2, AAR Se. B28 (unpr).
25. AAR to DR, 19 December 1937, RFA 2, AAR Se. B12 (unpr).
26. AAR to DR, 24 October 1937, RFA 2, AAR Se. B12 (unpr).
27. Clara Byrd Baker, "Dedicational Address to the Memory of Mrs. John D. Rockefeller, Jr.," 2 March 1950, RFA 2, AAR Se. B11 (unpr).
28. Clara Byrd Baker, "The Reminiscences of Clara Byrd Baker," transcript of interview, 1978, CWFA; IHC.
29. AAR to DR, 6 November 1937, RFA 2, AAR Se. B12 (unpr).
30. AAR to DR, 22 April 1938, RFA 2, AAR Se. B12 (unpr).
31. EK to BK, 3 June 1986. I.
32. Mildred Layne to BK, 2 June 1986. I.

Chapter 29

1. AAR to DR, ca. 1937, RFA 2, AAR Se. B12 (unpr).
2. AAR to DR, 1 October 1937, RFA 2, AAR Se. B12 (unpr).
3. *AAR Letters*, 25 June 1937, p. 243.
4. AAR to DR, 6 November 1937, RFA 2, AAR Se. B12 (unpr).
5. Jane Ickes to AAR, 2 June 1938, RFA 2, AAR Se. B10 (unpr).
6. JDR Jr. to Harold L. Ickes, 7 November 1938, RFA 2, C.I. Se. Wil. B146 F1286.
7. AAR to Jane Ickes, 22 December 1938, RFA 2, C.I. Se. Wil. B146 F1286.
8. AAR to President of Wheaton College, 26 April 1938, RFA 2, AAR Se. B11 (unpr).
9. AAR to DR, 22 October 1937, RFA 2, AAR Se. B12 (unpr).
10. AAR to DR, 6 November 1937, 22 January 1938, RFA 2, AAR Se. B12 (unpr).
11. AAR to DR, 5 November 1938, RFA 2, AAR Se. B12 (unpr).
12. ERB to BK, 10 June 1987. I.
13. *AAR Letters*, 18 September 1938, p. 255.
14. AO to BK, 11 June 1986. I.

15. *AAR Letters*, September 1937, p. 250.

16. Ibid., 28 May 1937, p. 240.

17. AAR to DR, 6 November 1937; 20 February 1938, RFA 2, AAR Se. B12 (unpr).

18. Ibid.

19. DR—I to BK, 7 August 1987.

20. AAR to DR, 20 February 1938, RFA 2, AAR Se. B12 (unpr).

21. ERB to BK, 10 June 1987. I.

22. AAR to DR, 6 March 1938, RFA 2, AAR Se. B12 (unpr).

23. AAR to DR, 2 January 1938, RFA 2, AAR Se. B12 (unpr).

24. AAR to Theodore Green, 13 May 1937, RFA 2, AAR Se. B10 (unpr).

25. AAR to DR, 2 January 1938; 27 March 1938, RFA 2, AAR Se. B12 (unpr).

26. AHB to AAR, 4 June 1938, RFA 2, AAR Se. B25 (unpr).

27. AAR to AHB, 29 June 1938, RFA 2, AAR Se. B25 (unpr).

28. AAR to Sir Ronald Lindsay, 28 June 1938, RFA 2, AAR Se. B10 (unpr).

29. AAR to DR, 22 April 1938, RFA 2, AAR Se. B12 (unpr).

30. Barr, M.S., p. 52.

31. AAR to EdeL, 23 July 1938, RFA 2, AAR Se. B11 (unpr).

Chapter 30

1. Tom Mabry to AAR, 2 March 1939, RFA 2, AAR Se. MoMA B26 (unpr).

2. Mabry to Robert Hutchins, 22 March 1939, RFA 2, AAR Se. MoMA B26 (unpr).

3. ACG to AAR, 21 April 1939, RFA 2, AAR Se. MoMA B26 (unpr).

4. AHB to Paul Sachs, 5 May 1939, MoMA Arch., AHB Jr. Papers (AAA: 3265; 1330).

5. MoMA Bulletin, 3-4:6 (May–June 1939), pp. 9, 7, 12.

6. Barr, M.S., p. 55.

7. Dorothy Miller to BK, 10 June 1986. I.

8. AAR to DR, 25 January 1944, RFA 2, AAR Se. B12 (unpr).

9. Lynes, p. 205.

10. Ibid., p. 153.

11. MW to BK, 27 October 1986. I.

12. Barr, M.S., p. 59.

13. DR—I to BK, 16 August 1987; 25 September 1988.

14. PR to BK, 25 October 1986. I.
15. DR—I to BK, 16 August 1987.
16. Lynes, pp. 207–208.
17. Tom Mabry to NR, 31 December 1937, RFA 2, AAR Se. MoMA B25 (unpr).
18. Barr, M.S., p. 56.
19. AHB to AAR, 15 July 1939, RFA 2, AAR Se. MoMA B26 (unpr).
20. AAR to AHB, 17 July 1939, RFA 2, AAR Se. MoMA B26 (unpr).
21. NR to AHB, 27 July 1939, MoMA Arch., AHB Jr. Papers (AAA: 3265; 1325).
22. AHB to NR, 28 December 1937, RFA 2, C.I. Se. MoMA B22 F. 220.
23. AHB to AAR, 8 August 1939, RFA 2, C.I. Se. MoMA B22 F. 220.
24. Sam A. Lewisohn to NR, 29 November 1938, 11 January 1939, RFA 2, C.I. Se. MoMA B22 F220.
25. AAR to Olga Guggenheim, 26 December 1939, RFA 2, C.I. Se. MoMA B22 F220.
26. Lynes, p. 213.
27. SC to AAR, 12 July 1941, RFA 2, AAR Se. MoMA B26 (unpr).
28. SC to AAR, 14 January 1943, RFA 2, AAR Se. MoMA B26 (unpr).
29. AHB to AAR, 5 April 1940, RFA 2, AAR Se. MoMA B26 (unpr).
30. AHB to AAR, 23 August 1938, MoMA Arch., AHB Jr. Papers (AAA: 3264; 1113).

Chapter 31

1. William Manchester, *The Last Lion: Winston Spencer Churchill—Alone 1932–1940*, p. 592.
2. Ibid., p. 590.
3. Ibid., p. 682.
4. AAR to Mrs. Alan Gardiner, March 1941, RFA 2, AAR Se. B10 (unpr).
5. Harr and Johnson, p. 409.
6. AAR to Fannie Evans, 14 October 1940, RFA 2, AAR Se. B10 (unpr).
7. Minnie MacFadden to Mrs. Watson, 17 July 1941, RIHS, LAC.
8. *AAR Letters*, 1 May 1941, p. 259.
9. Helen Connal Rowan to AAR, 14 June 1941, RIHS, LAC.
10. Barr, M.S., p. 60.
11. Morris, *NR Bio*, p. 139.

12. Ibid., p. 143.
13. AAR to PR and DR, 14 September 1940, RFA 2, AAR Se. B12 (unpr).
14. AAR to DR, 27 January 1943, RFA 2, AAR Se. B12 (unpr).
15. AAR to Frank Altschul, 17 February 1942, RFA 2, AAR Se. B10 (unpr).
16. AAR to DR, 1 November 1943, RFA 2, AAR Se. B12 (unpr).
17. AAR to DR, 16 February 1943, RFA 2, AAR Se. B12 (unpr).
18. AAR to DR, 27 September 1943, RFA 2, AAR Se. B12 (unpr).
19. PR to BK, 25 October 1986, RFA 2, AAR Se. B12 (unpr).
20. DR—I to BK, 7 August 1987.
21. AAR to DR, 13 October 1943, RFA 2, AAR Se. B12 (unpr).
22. AAR to DR, 7 February 1944, RFA 2, AAR Se. B12 (unpr).
23. AO to BK, 11 June 1986. I.
24. Ibid.
25. ARM to JDR Jr., 26 July 1943, RFA 2, AAR Se. B12 (unpr).
26. AO to BK, 11 June 1986. I.
27. Moscow, p. 202.
28. AO to BK, 11 June 1986. I.
29. Ibid.
30. ARM to JDR Jr., 10 October 1943, RFA 2, AAR Se. B12 (unpr).
31. ARM to JDR Jr., 9 January 1944, RFA 2, AAR Se. B12 (unpr).
32. AO to BK, 11 June 1986. I.
33. Abby R. Pardee to AAR and JDR Jr., 11 October 1946, RFA 2, AAR Se. B12 (unpr).

Chapter 32

1. AAR to DR, 22 October 1943; 10 January 1944, RFA 2, AAR Se. B12 (unpr).
2. Thomas G. McCaskey, "The Reminiscences of Thomas G. McCaskey," transcript of interview, 1957, CWFA; OHC.
3. AAR to Alice Griswold, 30 April 1943, RFA 2, AAR Se. B10 (unpr).
4. AAR to DR, 11 November 1943, RFA 2, AAR Se. B12 (unpr).
5. AAR to DR, 14 February 1945, RFA 2, AAR Se. B12 (unpr).
6. AAR to DR, 1 May 1944, RFA 2, AAR Se. B12 (unpr).
7. AAR to DR, 8 November 1943, RFA 2, AAR Se. B12 (unpr).
8. AAR to DR, 17 November 1944, RFA 2, AAR Se. B12 (unpr).
9. AAR to School Board of the City of Williamsburg, 15 December 1942, RFA 2, AAR Se. B11 (unpr).

10. Melissa Kendrew to BK, 3 June 1986. I.
11. EK to BK, 3 June 1986. I.
12. AAR to DR, 29 November 1943, RFA 2, AAR Se. B12 (unpr).
13. AAR to DR, 13 December 1944, RFA 2, AAR Se. B12 (unpr).
14. AAR to DR, 10 January and 16 February 1944, RFA 2, AAR Se. B12 (unpr).
15. AAR to DR, 10 January 1944, RFA 2, AAR Se. B12 (unpr).
16. Ibid.
17. AAR to DR, 6 March 1944, RFA 2, AAR Se. B12 (unpr).
18. AHB to AAR, 22 September 1941, RFA 2, AAR Se. B26 (unpr).
19. Lynes, p. 235.
20. Ibid, p. 237.
21. MB to BK, 5 June 1987. I.
22. EC to BK, 5 June 1987. I.
23. Lynes, p. 263.
24. MW to BK, 27 October 1987. I.
25. SC to AB, 15 October 1943, RFA 2, AAR Se. MoMA B26 (unpr).
26. EC to BK, 5 June 1987. I.
27. SC Memo, July 1949, RFA 2, AAR Se. MoMA B26 (unpr).
28. Barr, M.S., p. 69.
29. AAR to DR, 1 November 1943, RFA 2, AAR Se. B12 (unpr).
30. Lynes, p. 278.
31. Ibid., p. 244.
32. Chase, p. 142.
33. AAR to Barr, D'Harnoncourt, et al., 21 February 1947, RFA 2, AAR Se. MoMA B26 (unpr).
34. AAR to DR, 17 April 1944, RFA 2, AAR Se. B12 (unpr).

Chapter 33

1. AAR to DR, 28 December 1944, RFA 2, AAR Se. B12 (unpr).
2. AAR to DR, 13 December 1944, RFA 2, AAR Se. B12 (unpr).
3. AAR to DR, 6 June 1944, RFA 2, AAR Se. B12 (unpr).
4. AAR to DR, 8 March 1945, RFA 2, AAR Se. B12 (unpr). Paraphrase is from Prophets, Micah 6:8.
5. AAR to DR, 26 October 1943; 10 November 1944, RFA 2, AAR Se. B12 (unpr).
6. DR to AAR and JDR Jr., 25 February 1945, RFA 2, AAR Se. B12 (unpr).
7. AAR to DR, 17 April 1945, RFA 2, AAR Se. B12 (unpr).

8. AAR to DR, 7 May 1945, RFA 2, AAR Se. B12 (unpr).
9. AAR to DR, 17 April 1945, RFA 2, AAR Se. B12 (unpr).
10. AAR to DR, 26 June 1945, RFA 2, AAR Se. B12 (unpr).
11. AAR to DR, 9 August 1945, RFA 2, AAR Se. B12 (unpr).
12. AAR to DR, 22 August 1945, RFA 2, AAR Se. B12 (unpr).
13. AAR to DR, 14 May 1945, RFA 2, AAR Se. B12 (unpr).
14. AAR to LR, 10 March 1947, RFA 2, AAR Se. B12 (unpr).
15. ERB to BK, 10 June 1987. I.
16. AAR to LR, 10 March 1947, RFA 2, AAR Se. B12 (unpr).
17. AAR to Olivia Cutting, 30 July 1947, RFA 2, AAR Se. B10 (unpr).
18. AAR to DR, 1 March 1945, RFA 2, AAR Se. B12 (unpr).
19. PR to BK, 25 October 1986. I.
20. AAR to Olivia C., 29 October 1946, RFA 2, AAR Se. B10 (unpr).
21. AAR to PR and DR, 4 March 1947, RFA 2, AAR Se. B12 (unpr).
22. AAR to DR, 3 April 1945, RFA 2, AAR Se. B12 (unpr).
23. AAR to Olivia C., 31 July 1946, RFA 2, AAR Se. B10 (unpr).
24. AAR to Margaret Carnegie Miller, 21 December 1946, RFA 2, AAR Se. B10 (unpr).
25. LA to AAR, 5 March 1947, RFA 2, AAR Se. B6 (unpr).
26. AAR to DR, 18 November 1947, RFA 2, AAR Se. B12 (unpr).
27. AAR to Olivia C., 31 July 1946, RFA 2, AAR Se. B10 (unpr).
28. Maurice Gross to BK, December 1985.
29. AAR to PR and DR, 12 February 1948, RFA 2, AAR Se. B12 (unpr).
30. LA to AAR, 21 February 1948, RFA 2, AAR Se. B7 (unpr).
31. Harriet Aldrich to AAR, 14 February 1948, RFA 2, AAR Se. B9 (unpr).
32. AAR to Mrs. Peter Neveckas, 11 March 1948, RFA 2, AAR Se. B10 (unpr).
33. AAR to JDR 3rd, 18 February 1948, RFA 2, AAR Se. B12 (unpr).
34. AAR to JDR 3rd, 20 March 1948, RFA 2, AAR Se. B12 (unpr).
35. LA to AAR, 22 March 1948, RFA 2, AAR Se. B7 (unpr).

Chapter 34

1. AAR to DR, 12 December 1943, RFA 2, AAR Se. B12 (unpr).
2. Chase, p. 158.
3. Harr and Johnson, p. 468.
4. PR to BK, 25 October 1986.
5. Nelly Romon to JDR Jr., 19 April 1948, RFA 2, AAR Se. B4 (unpr).
6. Robert Moses to JDR Jr., 21 April 1948, RFA 2, AAR Se. B4 (unpr).

7. Margaret Sanger to JDR Jr., 20 April 1948, RFA 2, AAR Se. B4 (unpr).
8. Arthur C. Walworth to JDR Jr., 9 April 1948, RFA 2, AAR Se. B4 (unpr).
9. Paul Deitz, "The Abby Aldrich Rockefeller Garden," *House and Garden*, 28 February 1985, p. 184.
10. AO to BK, 11 June 1986. I.
11. AB to NR, 1 June 1948, RFA 2, AAR Se. B4 (unpr).
12. JDR Jr. to Mary Ellen Chase, RFA 2, C.I. Se. MoMA B23 F233.
13. JDR Jr. to NR, 6 November 1952, RFA 2, C.I. Se. MoMA B23 F233.
14. AHB, Modern Prints and the Museum, RFA 2, AAR Se. MoMA B26 (unpr).
15. The Abby Aldrich Rockefeller Memorial Window, RFA 2, AAR Se. Mem. Win. B16 (unpr).
16. Ibid.
17. Ibid.
18. *New York Times*, 7 April 1948, p. 24.

BIBLIOGRAPHY

Abby Aldrich Rockefeller's Letters to Her Sister Lucy. New York: John D. Rockefeller, Jr., 1957. *(AAR Letters)*

Aldrich, Nelson W., Jr. *Old Money.* New York: Knopf, 1988.

Amory, Cleveland. *Who Killed Society?* New York: Harper, 1960.

Balmori, Diana; McGuire, Diana Kostial; and McPeck, Eleanor M. *Beatrix Farrand's American Landscapes: Her Gardens and Campuses.* Sagaponack, N.Y.: Saga Press, 1985.

Baltzell, E. Digby. *The Protestant Establishment.* New York: Random House, 1964.

Barr, Margaret Scolari. "Our Campaigns." *New Criterion,* Summer 1987.

Berger, Albert I. "My Father's House at Pocantico Hills: Kykuit and the Business Education of JDR Jr." Unpublished manuscript.

Berman, Avis. *Rebels on Eighth Street: Juliana Force and the Whitney Museum of American Art.* New York: Atheneum, 1990.

Bloch, Lucienne. "The Making of Rivera's Rockefeller Center Mural: A Memoir." *Art in America,* February 1986, pp. 103–23.

Brigham, Herbert Olin, and Brigham, Mary Halton. *Ancestry of Nelson Wilmarta Aldrich and Abby Pearce Truman Chapman.* Providence, 1938. Courtesy of Rockefeller Archive Center.

Brown, Henry Collins. *Valentines City of New York: A Guide Book.* New York: Chauncey Holt, 1920.

Brown, Milton. *American Painting from the Armory Show to the Depression.* Princeton, N.J.: Princeton University Press, 1955.

Brown, Milton W. *The Story of the Armory Show*. New York: Abbeville Press, 1988.

The Bulletin of the Museum of Modern Art. 1933–1940, vol. 1. New York: MoMA Arno, 1967.

Burns, James MacGregor. *The Workshop of Democracy*. New York: Knopf, 1985.

Byron, Joseph. *Photographs of New York Interiors at the Turn of the Century*. Text by Clay Lancaster. New York: Dover in cooperation with the Museum of the City of New York, 1976.

Campbell, Paul R., and Conley, Patrick. *Providence: A Pictorial History*. Norfolk, Va.: Donning, 1982.

Chase, Mary Ellen. *Abby Aldrich Rockefeller*. New York: Macmillan, 1950.

Chassé, Patrick. *The Abby Aldrich Rockefeller Garden: A Visitor's Guide*. David and Peggy Rockefeller, 1990.

Cheek, Richard, and Gannon, Thomas. *Newport Mansions: The Gilded Age*. Foremost Publishers, 1982.

Collier, Peter, and Horowitz, David. *The Rockefellers: An American Dynasty*. New York: Holt, Rinehart & Winston/Signet, 1976.

Dana, Nathalie. *Young in New York: A Memoir of a Victorian Girlhood*. Garden City, N.Y.: Doubleday, 1963.

Day, Paula, and Pyle, Tom. *Pocantico: Fifty Years on the Rockefeller Domain*. New York: Sloan & Pearce, 1964.

Fosdick, Raymond B. *Adventure in Giving: The Story of the GEB*. New York: Harper & Row, 1962.

Fosdick, Raymond B. *John D. Rockefeller Jr.: A Portrait*. New York: Harper, 1956. *(JDR Portrait)*

Friedman, B.H. *Gertrude Vanderbilt Whitney*. Garden City, N.Y.: Doubleday, 1978.

Furst, Peter T. *American Indian Art and Painting by Taos Artists: The David and Peggy Rockefeller Collection*. Preface by David Rockefeller. New York: Published privately, 1988.

Gay, Peter: *Freud: A Life for Our Time*. New York: Norton, 1988.

Goldstein, Judith S. *Histories of Jews and Gentiles in Three Communities*. New York: Morrow, 1992.

Goodyear, A. Conger. *The Museum of Modern Art: The First Ten Years*. New York: A. Conger Goodyear, 1943.

Green, Constance McLaughlin. *Washington: Capital City 1879–1950*. Princeton, N.J.: Princeton University Press, 1963.

Guenther, Peter. "An Introduction to the Expressionist Movement." *Ger-*

man *Expressionist Prints and Drawings*. Munich, Germany: Los Angeles County Museum of Art and Prestel-Verlag, 1989.

Harr, John Ensor, and Johnson, Peter J. *The Rockefeller Century: Three Generations of America's Greatest Family*. New York: Scribner's, 1988.

Hawks, David A., and Toher, Jennifer. *Donald Deskey: Decorative Designs and Interiors*. New York: Dutton, 1987.

Heilbrun, Carolyn. *Writing a Woman's Life*. New York: Norton, 1988.

Hochschild, Adam. *Half the Way Home: A Memoir of Father and Son*. New York: Viking, 1986.

Jones, Caroline A. *Modern Art at Harvard*. New York: Abbeville Press, 1985.

"The Legacy of Bessie Dashiell." Woodstock Foundation, 1978.

The Lillie P. Bliss Collection. New York: MoMA, 1934.

Little, Nina Fletcher. "Introduction," *American Folk Art from the Abby Aldrich Rockefeller Folk Art Collection*. Colonial Williamsburg, 1959.

Lynes, Russell. *Good Old Modern*. New York: Atheneum, 1973.

MacDonald, Dwight. "Profile of Alfred Barr." *New Yorker*, December 12, 1953.

Maher, James T. *The Twilight of Splendor*. Boston: Little, Brown, 1975

Manchester, William. *The Last Lion: Winston Spencer Churchill— Alone 1932–1940*. Boston: Little, Brown, 1988.

Mayer, Grace. *Once upon a City*. New York: Macmillan, 1958.

Miller, Dorothy C. "Contemporary American Painting in the Collection of Mrs. John D. Rockefeller, Jr." *Art News*, March 16, 1938.

Miller, Dorothy Canning, ed. *The Nelson Rockefeller Collection: Masterpieces of Modern Art*. New York: Hudson Hills Press, 1981.

Morris, Joe Alex. *Nelson Rockefeller: A Biography*. New York: Harper, 1960. (NR Bio)

Morris, Joe Alex. *Those Rockefeller Brothers*. New York: Harper, 1953.

Moscow, Alvin. *The Rockefeller Inheritance*. Garden City, N.Y.: Doubleday, 1977.

Mount, Charles Merrill. *John Singer Sargent*. New York: Norton, 1955.

Museum of Modern Art, New York: The History and the Collection. Introduction by Sam Hunter. New York: Abrams in association with MoMA, 1984.

Nevins, Alan. *Study in Power: John D. Rockefeller—Industrialist and Philanthropist*. Vols. 1 and 2. New York: Scribner's, 1953.

Oettinger, Marion, Jr. *Folk Treasures of Mexico: The Nelson A. Rockefeller Collection*. New York: Abrams, 1990.

The Peggy and David Rockefeller Collection. Vol. 1. Published privately.

Persico, Joseph E. *The Imperial Rockefeller: A Biography of Nelson Rockefeller.* New York: Washington Square Press, 1982.

Read, Helen Appleton. "Modern Art: The Collection of Mrs. John D. Rockefeller, Jr." *Vogue*, April 1, 1931.

The Reminiscences of Holger Cahill. New York: Columbia University Oral History Research Office, 1957.

Rockefeller, Winthrop. "Letter to My Son." Unpublished manuscript, RAC Library.

Roob, Rona. "Alfred H. Barr, Jr.: A Chronicle of the Years 1902–1929." *New Criterion*, Summer 1987.

Roob, Rona. "The Museum Selects an Architect." *Archives of American Art*, vol. 23, no. 1 (1983).

Rumford, Beatrix T. "Uncommon Art of the Common People: A Review of Trends in the Collecting and Exhibiting of American Folk Art." In *Perspectives on American Folk Art.* Ed. Ian M. G. Quimby and Scott T. Swank. New York: Norton, 1980.

Saarinen, Aline. *The Proud Possessors.* New York: Random House, 1958.

Simon, Kate. *Fifth Avenue: A Very Social History.* New York: Harcourt Brace Jovanovich, 1978.

Slayden, Mary Ellen. *Washington Wife 1897–1919.* New York: Harper & Row, 1962.

Smith, Fred. "A Time to Remember." Unpublished monograph.

Stephenson, Nathaniel Wright. *Nelson W. Aldrich: A Leader in American Politics.* New York: Scribner's, 1930.

Sterne, Margaret. *The Passionate Eye: The Life of William R. Valentiner.* Detroit: Wayne State University, 1980.

Sternstein, Jerome L. "Corruption in the Gilded Age Senate: Nelson W. Aldrich and the Sugar Trust." In *Capitol Studies*, vol. 6. Ed. William M. Maury. Washington, D.C.: U.S. Capitol Historical Society, 1978.

Tarbell, Ida M. *The History of the Standard Oil Company.* New York: Peter Smith, 1950.

Tepfer, Diane. *Edith Gregor Halpert and the Downtown Gallery: 1926–1940. A Study in American Art Patronage.* Vols. 1 and 2. Ann Arbor, Mich.: UMI Dissertation Information Services, 1990.

Tompkins, Calvin. *Merchants and Masterpieces.* New York: Dutton, 1970.

Veblen, Thorstein. *The Theory of the Leisure Class.* New York: Modern Library, 1934.

Weber, Max. *The Protestant Ethic and the Spirit of Capitalism*. New York: Scribner's, 1976.

Wecter, Dixon. *The Saga of American Society*. New York: Scribner's, 1937.

Wolfe, Bertram D. *The Fabulous Life of Diego Rivera*. New York: Stein & Day, 1963.

Wright, Brooks. *The Artist and The Unicorn: The Lives of Arthur B. Davies*. New City, N.Y.: Historical Society of Rockland County, 1978.

Zorach, William. *Art Is My Life: The Autobiography of William Zorach*. Cleveland, Ohio: World, 1967.

INDEX

Rich, Daniel Catton, 420
Richards, Charles, 346, 348
Richardson, Dick, 76
Rietschel, Ernst, 325
Riis, Jacob, 96, 98
Rivals (Rivera), 387
Rivera, Diego, 315, 346–52, 354–65, 387
Rivers, John, 459–60
Robertson, Hugh, 361, 364
Rockefeller, Abby (Babs), *see* Pardee,
  Abby Rockefeller Milton (Babs)
Rockefeller, Abby Aldrich:
  artistic taste and judgment of, 4, 18, 39,
    106, 139, 196, 214–15, 217–21, 238–
    240, 252–56, 324, 325
  art purchase fund of, 252, 253, 255, 371,
    374, 375
  Asian travels of, 191–95
  bridge playing of, 26, 186, 258, 400
  as business woman, 201
  car injury of, 260–61
  childhood and adolescence of, 17–43,
    19, 36
  coal-mine strike and, 145–52
  on Cuba cruise, 74–76
  death of, 399, 471–77
  as debutante, *iv*, 41–42
  depression of, 336–37
  detachment of, 114
  diary of, 39, 41–44
  domestic and foreign policy as viewed
    by, 401–4, 431–32
  education of, 23–24, 25, 39, 42, 340
  enthusiasm and optimism of, 28, 68, 93,
    256
  European travels of, 43–45, 62, 63–64,
    65, 72, 76, 112–13, 209–15, 225, 301,
    373, *380*, 381–83, 408–12
  family background of, 4–16
  folk art collection of, 321–27, 394–97, 408
  as grandmother, 226, 244, 327, *327*,
    404–5, 463–65
  health problems of, 153, 156–57, 181–
    182, 204, 309, 314, 335–37, 358, 438,
    465
  horoscope of, 43–44
  imagination of, 4, 44
  independence of, 44, 66, 93, 100, 102
  interviews of, 161, 202
  Kykuit and, 118–27
  loneliness of, 104, 116
  magnanimity of, 319–20
  male friendships of, 221–24
  manipulativeness of, 66, 101
  marriage of, *see* Rockefeller, John
    Davison, Jr.
  Middle East travels of, 257–60, 273

money as viewed by, 93, 100, 402
as mother vs. wife, 174, 191, 228, 405
nonprejudicial nature of, 208, 403–4
office study of, *141*
openness and adaptability of, 146, 153,
  180–81, 407
panic attack of, 256–57
physical appearance of, 42, 46, *167,
  173, 193, 245*, 294, 320, 372, 400
Pocantico fire and, 103–4
political activities of, 241–42
political skills of, 4, 75, 76, 193, 274
portraits of, 116–17
pregnancies and childbirths of, 107,
  108, 113, 128–32, 135, 139, 150, 153
public image of, 161–62, 313, 377
public speaking of, 162, 179, 190, 242
reading of, 39, 129, 182, 262, 335, 340–
  341
religious background of, 93–94
sense of fun and amusement of, 25, 33,
  39–40
sensuousness of, 65–66
seventh-floor gallery of, 296–97, *298,
  299*, 353, 372, 387
social conscience of, 42–43, 66, 101,
  102–3, 159–62, 178–81, 398, 432–34
solitude of, 91
spontaneity of, 40
stress and anxiety of, 153, 156–57, 174,
  182, 228, 261
suitors of, 41–42, 60, 66–67, 71, 79
trust of, 370–71, 423–24
U.S. and Mexican travels of, 105–6,
  185, 232–34
at Versailles, *380*, 381
voting of, 189
at Warwick Neck, 31, 40, 41, 64, 69–
  70, 77, 80–86, 107–10, *109*
war work of, 159–62, 431–34, 445–46,
  450
will of, 424, 474
wisdom of, 72–73
wit of, 4, 178
Abby Aldrich Rockefeller Folk Art
  Center, 476
Abby Aldrich Rockefeller Sculpture
  Garden, 386
Rockefeller, Almira Goodsell, 81
Rockefeller, Alta, *see* Prentice, Alta
  Rockefeller
Rockefeller, Barbara Sears (Bobo), 465–
  469, 472
Rockefeller, Bessie, *see* Strong, Bessie
  Rockefeller
Rockefeller, Blanchette Hooker, 284, 290,
  329, 330–33, 338, 464

Bassett Hall in, 387, 391–97, *395*, 399–400, 444, 448
Williamsburg Inn, 395, 397
Wills, Helen, 351
Wilson, Woodrow, 133, 158
Windsor, Duchess of, 401–2
Windsor, Duke of, 401–2
Wise, Stephen S., 241–42
Wolfe, Bertram, 348, 349–50, 356, 362
women:
  Abby's liking for, 238, 254, 403
  hotel for, 201–2
  housing for, 159–62, 178–80
  Nelson Aldrich's veneration of, 27, 30–31
  neurasthenia and, 337
  Southern, 446–47
  voting rights of, 189, 203
  in Washington, 62, 201–2
  working, 159–62, 178–80
  World War I and, 159–62
Wood, Grant, 412
Wooley, Mary G., 192

World War I, 144–45, 158–62
World War II, 429–39, 445–50, 457–61
Worsham, Arabella, 54–55
Worsham, John, 54
Wright, Brooks, 269
Wright, Frank Lloyd, 381

Yellowstone National Park, 234
Young Calf (Nakian), 375
Young Women's Christian Association (YWCA), 42–43, 66, 93, 179, 312
  Dodge Hotel and, 201–2
  National Board of, 160, 179, 190, 201
  War Work Council of, 160–62

Zay, M. Jean, 381
Zorach, Dahlov, 278, 280
Zorach, Marguarite Thompson, 278–79
Zorach, Tessim, 279, 324
Zorach, William, 278–79, 280, 297, 353–354, 369, 372, 466

BERNICE KERT is the author of *The Hemingway Women*, the major study of Hemingway's wives, his mother, Grace, and four other women who influenced his work. She received a John Simon Guggenheim Memorial Foundation Fellowship in 1988 to support her Rockefeller research. Born in St. Louis, she was educated at the University of Michigan, where she was an Avery Hopwood finalist and a teaching fellow in the Department of English. At present she resides in Beverly Hills, California.

ABOUT THE TYPE

The text of this book was set in Janson, a misnamed typeface designed in about 1690 by Nicholas Kis, a Hungarian in Amsterdam. In 1919 the matrices became the property of the Stempel Foundry in Frankfurt. It is an old-style book face of excellent clarity and sharpness. Janson serifs are concave and splayed; the contrast between thick and thin strokes is marked.